THE WORKS OF
G. K. CHESTERTON

THE WORKS OF
G. K. Chesterton

Wordsworth Editions

In loving memory of
MICHAEL TRAYLER
the founder of Wordsworth Editions

2

Readers who are interested in other titles from Wordsworth Editions are invited to visit our website at www.wordsworth-editions.com

For our latest list and a full mail-order service, contact Bibliophile Books, 5 Datapoint, South Crescent, London E16 4TL
TEL: +44 (0)20 7474 2474 FAX: +44 (0)20 7474 8589
ORDERS: orders@bibliophilebooks.com
WEBSITE: www.@bibliophilebooks.com

This edition published in 2008 by Wordsworth Editions Limited
8B East Street, Ware, Hertfordshire SG12 9HJ

ISBN 978 1 84022 081 0

Typeset by Antony Gray
Printed and bound by Clays Ltd, St Ives plc

CONTENTS

THE NAPOLEON OF NOTTING HILL

The Napoleon of Notting Hill

To Hilaire Belloc

For every tiny town or place
God made the stars especially;
Babies look up with owlish face
And see them tangled in a tree:
You saw a moon from Sussex Downs,
A Sussex moon, untravelled still,
I saw a moon that was the town's,
The largest lamp on Campden Hill.

Yea; Heaven is everywhere at home,
The big blue cap that always fits,
And so it is (be calm; they come
To goal at last, my wandering wits),
So is it with the heroic thing;
This shall not end for the world's end,
And though the sullen engines swing,
Be you not much afraid, my friend.

This did not end by Nelson's urn
Where an immortal England sits –
Nor where your tall young men in turn
Drank death like wine at Austerlitz.
And when the pedants bade us mark
What cold mechanic happenings
Must come; our souls said in the dark,
'Belike; but there are likelier things.'

Likelier across these flats afar
These sulky levels smooth and free
The drums shall crash a waltz of war
And Death shall dance with Liberty;
Likelier the barricades shall blare
Slaughter below and smoke above,
And death and hate and hell declare
That men have found a thing to love.

Far from your sunny uplands set
I saw the dream; the streets I trod,
The lit straight streets shot out and met
The starry streets that point to God.
This legend of an epic hour
A child I dreamed, and dream it still,
Under the great grey water-tower
That strikes the stars on Campden Hill.

G. K. C.

Contents

BOOK ONE

CHAPTER I

Introductory Remarks on the Art of Prophecy

The human race, to which so many of my readers belong, has been playing at children's games from the beginning, and will probably do it till the end, which is a nuisance for the few people who grow up. And one of the games to which it is most attached is called 'Keep tomorrow dark', and which is also named (by the rustics in Shropshire, I have no doubt) 'Cheat the Prophet'. The players listen very carefully and respectfully to all that the clever men have to say about what is to happen in the next generation. The players then wait until all the clever men are dead, and bury them nicely. They then go and do something else. That is all. For a race of simple tastes, however, it is great fun.

For human beings, being children, have the childish wilfulness and the childish secrecy. And they never have from the beginning of the world done what the wise men have seen to be inevitable. They stoned the false prophets, it is said; but they could have stoned true prophets with a greater and juster enjoyment. Individually, men may present a more or less rational appearance, eating, sleeping, and scheming. But humanity as a whole is changeful, mystical, fickle, delightful. Men are men, but Man is a woman.

But in the beginning of the twentieth century the game of Cheat the Prophet was made far more difficult than it had ever been before. The reason was, that there were so many prophets and so many prophecies, that it was difficult to elude all their ingenuities. When a man did something free and frantic and entirely his own, a horrible thought struck him afterwards; it might have been predicted. Whenever a duke climbed a lamp post, when a dean got drunk, he could not be really happy, he could not be certain that he was not fulfilling some prophecy. In the beginning of the twentieth century you could not see the ground for clever men. They were so common that a stupid man was quite exceptional, and when they found him, they followed him in crowds down the street and treasured him up and gave him some high post in the State. And all these clever men were at work giving accounts of what would happen in the next age, all quite clear, all quite keen-sighted and ruthless, and all quite different. And it seemed that the good old game of hoodwinking your ancestors could not really be managed this time, because the ancestors neglected meat and sleep and practical politics, so that they might meditate day and night on what their descendants would be likely to do.

But the way the prophets of the twentieth century went to work was this. They took something or other that was certainly going on in their time, and then said that it would go on more and more until something extraordinary happened. And very often they added that in some odd place that extraordinary thing had happened, and that it showed the signs of the times.

Thus, for instance, there were Mr H. G. Wells and others, who thought that science would take charge of the future; and just as the motor car was quicker than the coach, so some lovely thing would be quicker than the motor car; and so on for ever. And there arose from their ashes Dr Quilp, who said that a man could be sent on his machine so fast round the world that he could keep up a long, chatty conversation in some old-world village by saying a word of a sentence each time he came round. And it was said that the experiment had been tried on an apoplectic old major, who was sent round the world so fast that there seemed to be (to the inhabitants of some other star) a continuous band round the earth of white whiskers, red complexion and tweeds – a thing like the ring of Saturn.

Then there was the opposite school. There was Mr Edward Carpenter, who thought we should in a very short time return to Nature, and live simply and slowly as the animals do. And Edward Carpenter was followed by James Pickie, D.D. (of Pocohontas College), who said that men were immensely improved by grazing, or taking their food slowly and continuously, after the manner of cows. And he said that he had, with the most encouraging results, turned city men out on all fours in a field covered with veal cutlets. Then Tolstoy and the Humanitarians said that the world was growing more merciful, and therefore no one would ever desire to kill. And Mr Mick not only became a vegetarian, but at length declared vegetarianism doomed ('shedding', as he called it finely, 'the green blood of the silent animals'), and predicted that men in a better age would live on nothing but salt. And then came the pamphlet from Oregon (where the thing was tried), the pamphlet called 'Why should Salt suffer?' and there was more trouble.

And on the other hand, some people were predicting that the lines of kinship would become narrower and sterner. There was Mr Cecil Rhodes, who thought that the one thing of the future was the British Empire, and that there would be a gulf between those who were of the Empire and those who were not, between the Chinaman in Hong Kong and the Chinaman outside, between the Spaniard on the Rock of Gibraltar and the Spaniard off it, similar to the gulf between man and the lower animals. And in the same way his impetuous friend, Dr Zoppi ('the Paul of Anglo-Saxonism'), carried it yet further, and held that, as a result of this view, cannibalism should be held to mean eating a member of the Empire, not eating one of the subject peoples, who should, he said, be killed without needless pain. His horror at the idea of eating a man in British Guiana showed how they misunderstood his stoicism who thought him devoid of feeling. He was, however, in a hard position; as it was said that he had attempted the experiment, and, living in London, had to subsist entirely on Italian organ-grinders. And his end was terrible, for just when he had begun, Sir Paul Swiller read his great paper at the Royal Society, proving that the savages were not only quite right in eating their enemies, but right on moral and hygienic grounds, since it was true that the qualities of the enemy, when eaten, passed into the eater. The notion that the nature of an Italian organ-man was irrevocably growing and burgeoning inside him was almost more than the kindly old professor could bear.

There was Mr Benjamin Kidd, who said that the growing note of our race would be the care for and knowledge of the future. His idea was developed more powerfully by William Borker, who wrote that passage which every schoolboy knows by heart, about men in future ages weeping by the graves of their descendants, and tourists being shown over the scene of the historic battle which was to take place some centuries afterwards.

And Mr Stead, too, was prominent, who thought that England would in the twentieth century be united to America; and his young lieutenant, Graham Podge, who included the states of France, Germany, and Russia in the American Union, the State of Russia being abbreviated to Ra.

There was Mr Sidney Webb, also, who said that the future would see a continuously increasing order and neatness in the life of the people, and his poor friend Fipps, who went mad and ran about the country with an axe, hacking branches off the trees whenever there were not the same number on both sides.

All these clever men were prophesying with every variety of ingenuity what would happen soon, and they all did it in the same way, by taking something they saw 'going strong', as the saying is, and carrying it as far as ever their imagination could stretch. This, they said, was the true and simple way of anticipating the future. 'Just as', said Dr Pellkins, in a fine passage – 'just as when we see a pig in a litter larger than the other pigs, we know that by an unalterable law of the Inscrutable it will someday be larger than an elephant – just as we know, when we see weeds and dandelions growing more and more thickly in a garden, that they must, in spite of all our efforts, grow taller than the chimney-pots and swallow the house from sight, so we know and reverently acknowledge, that when any power in human politics has shown for any period of time any considerable activity, it will go on until it reaches to the sky.'

And it did certainly appear that the prophets had put the people (engaged in the old game of Cheat the Prophet) in a quite unprecedented difficulty. It seemed really hard to do anything without fulfilling some of their prophecies.

But there was, nevertheless, in the eyes of labourers in the streets, of peasants in the fields, of sailors and children, and especially women, a strange look that kept the wise men in a perfect fever of doubt. They could not fathom the motionless mirth in their eyes. They still had something up their sleeve; they were still playing the game of Cheat the Prophet.

Then the wise men grew like wild things, and swayed hither and thither, crying, 'What can it be? What can it be? What will London be like a century hence? Is there anything we have not thought of? Houses upside down – more hygienic, perhaps? Men walking on hands – make feet flexible, don't you know? Moon . . . motorcars . . . no heads . . . ' And so they swayed and wondered until they died and were buried nicely.

Then the people went and did what they liked. Let me no longer conceal the painful truth. The people had cheated the prophets of the twentieth century. When the curtain goes up on this story, eighty years after the present date, London is almost exactly like what it is now.

CHAPTER 2

The Man in Green

Very few words are needed to explain why London, a hundred years hence, will be very like it is now, or rather, since I must slip into a prophetic past, why London, when my story opens, was very like it was in those enviable days when I was still alive.

The reason can be stated in one sentence. The people had absolutely lost faith in revolutions. All revolutions are doctrinal – such as the French one, or the one that introduced Christianity. For it stands to common sense that you cannot upset all existing things, customs, and compromises, unless you believe in something outside them, something positive and divine. Now, England, during this century, lost all belief in this. It believed in a thing called Evolution. And it said, 'All theoretic changes have ended in blood and ennui. If we change, we must change slowly and safely, as the animals do. Nature's revolutions are the only successful ones. There has been no conservative reaction in favour of tails.'

And some things did change. Things that were not much thought of dropped out of sight. Things that had not often happened did not happen at all. Thus, for instance, the actual physical force ruling the country, the soldiers and police, grew smaller and smaller, and at last vanished almost to a point. The people combined could have swept the few policemen away in ten minutes: they did not, because they did not believe it would do them the least good. They had lost faith in revolutions.

Democracy was dead; for no one minded the governing class governing. England was now practically a despotism, but not an hereditary one. Someone in the official class was made King. No one cared how: no one cared who. He was merely a universal secretary.

In this manner it happened that everything in London was very quiet. That vague and somewhat depressed reliance upon things happening as they have always happened, which is with all Londoners a mood, had become an assumed condition. There was really no reason for any man doing anything but the thing he had done the day before.

There was therefore no reason whatever why the three young men who had always walked up to their Government office together should not walk up to it together on this particular wintry and cloudy morning. Everything in that age had become mechanical, and Government clerks especially. All those clerks assembled regularly at their posts. Three of those clerks always walked into town together. All the neighbourhood knew them: two of them were tall and one short. And on this particular morning the short clerk was only a few seconds late to join the other two as they passed his gate: he could have overtaken them in three strides; he could have called after them easily. But he did not.

For some reason that will never be understood until all souls are judged (if they are ever judged; the idea was at this time classed with fetish worship) he did not join his two companions, but walked steadily behind them. The day was dull, their dress was dull, everything was dull; but in some odd impulse he walked through street after street, through district after district, looking at the backs of the two men, who would have swung round at the sound of his voice. Now, there is a law written in the darkest of the Books of Life, and it is this: If you look at a thing nine hundred and ninety-nine times, you are perfectly safe; if you look at it the thousandth time, you are in frightful danger of seeing it for the first time.

So the short Government official looked at the coat-tails of the tall Government officials, and through street after street, and round corner after corner, saw only coat-tails, coat-tails, and again coat-tails – when, he did not in the least know why, something happened to his eyes.

Two black dragons were walking backwards in front of him. Two black dragons were looking at him with evil eyes. The dragons were walking backwards, it was true, but they kept their eyes fixed on him none the less. The eyes which he saw were, in truth, only the two buttons at the back of a frock-coat: perhaps some traditional memory of their meaningless character gave this half-witted prominence to their gaze. The slit between the tails was the nose-line of the monster: whenever the tails flapped in the winter wind the dragons licked their lips. It was only a momentary fancy, but the small clerk found it embedded in his soul ever afterwards. He never could again think of men in frock-coats except as dragons walking backwards. He explained afterwards, quite tactfully and nicely, to his two official friends, that (while feeling an inexpressible regard for each of them) he could not seriously regard the face of either of them as anything but a kind of tail. It was, he admitted, a handsome tail – a tail elevated in the air. But if, he said, any true friend of theirs wished to see their faces, to look into the eyes of their soul, that friend must be allowed to walk reverently round behind them, so as to see them from the rear. There he would see the two black dragons with the blind eyes.

But when first the two black dragons sprang out of the fog upon the small clerk, they had merely the effect of all miracles – they changed the universe. He discovered the fact that all romantics know – that adventures happen on dull days, and not on sunny ones. When the chord of monotony is stretched most tight, then it breaks with a sound like song. He had scarcely noticed the weather before, but with the four dead eyes glaring at him he looked round and realised the strange dead day.

The morning was wintry and dim, not misty, but darkened with that shadow of cloud or snow which steeps everything in a green or copper twilight. The light there is on such a day seems not so much to come from the clear heavens as to be a phosphorescence clinging to the shapes themselves. The load of heaven and the clouds is like a load of waters, and the men move like fishes, feeling that they are on the floor of a sea. Everything in a London street completes the fantasy; the carriages and cabs themselves resemble deep-sea creatures with eyes of flame. He had been startled at first to meet two dragons. Now he found he was among deep-sea dragons possessing the deep sea.

The two young men in front were like the small young man himself, well-dressed. The lines of their frock-coats and silk hats had that luxuriant severity which makes the modern fop, hideous as he is, a favourite exercise of the modern draughtsman; that element which Mr Max Beerbohm has admirably expressed in speaking of 'certain congruities of dark cloth and the rigid perfection of linen'.

They walked with the gait of an affected snail, and they spoke at the longest intervals, dropping a sentence at about every sixth lamp post.

They crawled on past the lamp posts; their mien was so immovable that a fanciful description might almost say, that the lamp posts crawled past the men, as in a dream. Then the small man suddenly ran after them and said: 'I want to get my hair cut. I say, do you know a little shop anywhere where they cut your hair properly? I keep on having my hair cut, but it keeps on growing again.'

One of the tall men looked at him with the air of a pained naturalist.

'Why, here is a little place,' cried the small man, with a sort of imbecile cheerfulness, as the bright bulging window of a fashionable toilet-saloon glowed abruptly out of the foggy twilight. 'Do you know, I often find hairdressers when I walk about London. I'll lunch with you at Cicconani's. You know, I'm awfully fond of hairdressers' shops. They're miles better than those nasty butchers'.' And he disappeared into the doorway.

The man called James continued to gaze after him, a monocle screwed into his eye.

'What the devil do you make of that fellow?' he asked his companion, a pale young man with a high nose.

The pale young man reflected conscientiously for some minutes, and then said: 'Had a knock on his head when he was a kid, I should think.'

'No, I don't think it's that,' replied the Honourable James Barker. 'I've sometimes fancied he was a sort of artist, Lambert.'

'Bosh!' cried Mr Lambert, briefly.

'I admit I can't make him out,' resumed Barker, abstractedly; 'he never opens his mouth without saying something so indescribably half-witted that to call him a fool seems the very feeblest attempt at characterisation. But there's another thing about him that's rather funny. Do you know that he has the one collection of Japanese lacquer in Europe? Have you ever seen his books? All Greek poets and mediaeval French and that sort of thing. Have you ever been in his rooms? It's like being inside an amethyst. And he moves about in all that and talks like – like a turnip.'

'Well, damn all books. Your blue books as well,' said the ingenuous Mr Lambert, with a friendly simplicity. 'You ought to understand such things. What do you make of him?'

'He's beyond me,' returned Barker. 'But if you asked me for my opinion, I should say he was a man with a taste for nonsense, as they call it – artistic fooling, and all that kind of thing. And I seriously believe that he has talked nonsense so much that he has half bewildered his own mind and doesn't know the difference between sanity and insanity. He has gone round the mental world, so to speak, and found the place where the East and the West are one, and extreme idiocy is as good as sense. But I can't explain these psychological games.'

'You can't explain them to me,' replied Mr Wilfrid Lambert, with candour.

As they passed up the long streets towards their restaurant the copper twilight cleared slowly to a pale yellow, and by the time they reached it they stood discernible in a tolerable winter daylight. The Honourable James Barker, one of the most powerful officials in the English Government (by this time a rigidly official one), was a lean and elegant young man, with a blank handsome face and bleak blue eyes. He had a great amount of intellectual capacity, of that peculiar kind which raises a man from throne to throne and lets him die loaded with honours without having either amused or enlightened the mind of a single man. Wilfrid Lambert, the youth with the nose which appeared to impoverish the rest of his face, had also contributed little to the enlargement of the human spirit, but he had the honourable excuse of being a fool.

Lambert would have been called a silly man; Barker, with all his cleverness, might have been called a stupid man. But mere silliness and stupidity sank into insignificance in the presence of the awful and mysterious treasures of foolishness apparently stored up in the small figure that stood waiting for them outside Cicconani's. The little man, whose name was Auberon Quin, had an appearance compounded of a baby and an owl. His round head, round eyes, seemed to have been designed by nature playfully with a pair of compasses. His flat dark hair and preposterously long frock-coat gave him something of the look of a child's 'Noah'. When he entered a room of strangers, they mistook him for a small boy, and wanted to take him on their knees, until he spoke, when they perceived that a boy would have been more intelligent.

'I have been waiting quite a long time,' said Quin, mildly. 'It's awfully funny I should see you coming up the street at last.'

'Why?' asked Lambert, staring. 'You told us to come here yourself.'

'My mother used to tell people to come to places,' said the sage.

They were about to turn into the restaurant with a resigned air, when their eyes were caught by something in the street. The weather, though cold and blank, was now quite clear, and across the dull brown of the wood pavement and between the dull grey terraces was moving something not to be seen for miles round – not to be seen perhaps at that time in England – a man dressed in bright colours. A small crowd hung on the man's heels.

He was a tall stately man, clad in a military uniform of brilliant green, splashed with great silver facings. From the shoulder swung a short green furred cloak, somewhat like that of a Hussar, the lining of which gleamed every now and then with a kind of tawny crimson. His breast glittered with medals; round his neck was the red ribbon and star of some foreign order; and a long straight sword, with a blazing hilt, trailed and clattered along the pavement. At this time the pacific and utilitarian development of Europe had relegated all such customs to the Museums. The only remaining force, the small but well-organised police, were attired in a sombre and hygienic manner. But even those who remembered the last Life Guards and Lancers who disappeared in 1912 must have known at a glance that this was not, and never had been, an English uniform; and this conviction would have been heightened by the yellow aquiline face, like Dante carved in bronze, which rose, crowned with white hair, out of the green military collar, a keen and distinguished, but not an English face.

The magnificence with which the green-clad gentleman walked down the centre of the road would be something difficult to express in human language. For it was an ingrained simplicity and arrogance, something in the mere carriage of the head and body, which made ordinary moderns in the street stare after him; but it had comparatively little to do with actual conscious gestures or expression. In the matter of these merely temporary movements, the man appeared to be rather worried and inquisitive, but he was inquisitive with the inquisitiveness of a despot and worried as with the responsibilities of a god. The men who lounged and wondered behind him followed partly with an astonishment at his brilliant uniform, that is to say, partly because of that instinct which makes us all follow one who looks like a madman, but far more because of that instinct which makes all men follow (and worship) anyone who chooses to behave like a king. He had to so sublime an extent that great quality of royalty – an almost imbecile unconsciousness of everybody, that people went after him as they do after kings – to see what would be the first thing or person he would take notice of. And all the time, as we have said, in spite of his quiet splendour, there was an air about him as if he were looking for somebody; an expression of enquiry.

Suddenly that expression of enquiry vanished, none could tell why, and was replaced by an expression of contentment. Amid the rapt attention of the mob of idlers, the magnificent green gentleman deflected himself from his direct course down the centre of the road and walked to one side of it. He came to a halt opposite to a large poster of Colman's Mustard erected on a wooden hoarding. His spectators almost held their breath.

He took from a small pocket in his uniform a little penknife; with this he made a slash at the stretched paper. Completing the rest of the operation with his fingers, he tore off a strip or rag of paper, yellow in colour and wholly irregular in outline. Then for the first time the great being addressed his adoring onlookers: 'Can anyone,' he said, with a pleasing foreign accent, 'lend me a pin?'

Mr Lambert, who happened to be nearest, and who carried innumerable pins for the purpose of attaching innumerable buttonholes, lent him one, which was received with extravagant but dignified bows, and hyperboles of thanks.

The gentleman in green, then, with every appearance of being gratified, and even puffed up, pinned the piece of yellow paper to the green silk and silver-lace adornments of his breast. Then he turned his eyes round again, searching and unsatisfied.

'Anything else I can do, sir?' asked Lambert, with the absurd politeness of the Englishman when once embarrassed.

'Red,' said the stranger, vaguely, 'red.'

'I beg your pardon?'

'I beg yours also, Señor,' said the stranger, bowing. 'I was wondering whether any of you had any red about you.'

'Any red about us? – well really – no, I don't think I have – I used to carry a red bandanna once, but – '

'Barker,' asked Auberon Quin, suddenly, 'where's your red cockatoo? Where's your red cockatoo?'

'What do you mean?' asked Barker, desperately. 'What cockatoo? You've never seen me with any cockatoo!'

'I know,' said Auberon, vaguely mollified. 'Where's it been all the time?'

Barker swung round, not without resentment.

'I am sorry, sir,' he said, shortly but civilly, 'none of us seem to have anything red to lend you. But why, if one may ask – '

'I thank you, Señor, it is nothing. I can, since there is nothing else, fulfil my own requirements.'

And standing for a second of thought with the penknife in his hand, he stabbed his left palm. The blood fell with so full a stream that it struck the stones without dripping. The foreigner pulled out his handkerchief and tore a piece from it with his teeth. The rag was immediately soaked in scarlet.

'Since you are so generous, Señor,' he said, 'another pin, perhaps.'

Lambert held one out, with eyes protruding like a frog's.

The red linen was pinned beside the yellow paper, and the foreigner took off his hat.

'I have to thank you all, gentlemen,' he said; and wrapping the remainder of the handkerchief round his bleeding hand, he resumed his walk with an overwhelming stateliness.

While all the rest paused, in some disorder, little Mr Auberon Quin ran after the stranger and stopped him, with hat in hand. Considerably to everybody's astonishment, he addressed him in the purest Spanish: 'Señor,' he said in that language, 'pardon a hospitality, perhaps indiscreet, towards one who appears to be a distinguished, but a solitary guest in London. Will you do me and my friends, with whom you have held some conversation, the honour of lunching with us at the adjoining restaurant?'

The man in the green uniform had turned a fiery colour of pleasure at the mere sound of his own language, and he accepted the invitation with that profusion of bows which so often shows, in the case of the Southern races, the falsehood of the notion that ceremony has nothing to do with feeling.

'Señor,' he said, 'your language is my own; but all my love for my people shall not lead me to deny to yours the possession of so chivalrous an entertainer. Let me say that the tongue is Spanish but the heart English.' And he passed with the rest into Cicconani's.

'Now, perhaps,' said Barker, over the fish and sherry, intensely polite, but burning with curiosity, 'perhaps it would be rude of me to ask why you did that?'

'Did what, Señor?' asked the guest, who spoke English quite well, though in a manner indefinably American.

'Well,' said the Englishman, in some confusion, 'I mean tore a strip off a hoarding and . . . er . . . cut yourself . . . and . . . '

'To tell you that, Señor,' answered the other, with a certain sad pride, 'involves merely telling you who I am. I am Juan del Fuego, President of Nicaragua.'

The manner with which the President of Nicaragua leant back and drank his sherry showed that to him this explanation covered all the facts observed and a great deal more. Barker's brow, however, was still a little clouded.

'And the yellow paper,' he began, with anxious friendliness, 'and the red rag . . . '

'The yellow paper and the red rag,' said Fuego, with indescribable grandeur, 'are the colours of Nicaragua.'

'But Nicaragua . . . ' began Barker, with great hesitation, 'Nicaragua is no longer a . . . '

'Nicaragua has been conquered like Athens. Nicaragua has been annexed like Jerusalem,' cried the old man, with amazing fire. 'The Yankee and the German and the brute powers of modernity have trampled it with the hoofs of oxen. But Nicaragua is not dead. Nicaragua is an idea.'

Auberon Quin suggested timidly, 'A brilliant idea.'

'Yes,' said the foreigner, snatching at the word. 'You are right, generous Englishman. An idea *brilliant*, a burning thought. Señor, you asked me why, in my desire to see the colours of my country, I snatched at paper and blood. Can you not understand the ancient sanctity of colours? The Church has her symbolic colours. And think of what colours mean to us – think of the position of one like myself, who can see nothing but those two colours, nothing but the red and the yellow. To me all shapes are equal, all common and noble things are in a democracy of combination. Wherever there is a field of marigolds and the red cloak of an old woman, there is Nicaragua. Wherever there is a field of poppies and a yellow patch of sand, there is Nicaragua. Wherever there is a lemon and a red sunset, there is my country. Wherever I see a red pillar-box and a yellow sunset, there my heart beats. Blood and a splash of mustard can be my heraldry. If there be yellow mud and red mud in the same ditch, it is better to me than white stars.'

'And if,' said Quin, with equal enthusiasm, 'there should happen to be yellow wine and red wine at the same lunch, you could not confine yourself to sherry. Let me order some Burgundy, and complete, as it were, a sort of Nicaraguan heraldry in your inside.'

Barker was fiddling with his knife, and was evidently making up his mind to say something, with the intense nervousness of the amiable Englishman.

'I am to understand, then,' he said at last, with a cough, 'that you, ahem, were the President of Nicaragua when it made its – er – one must, of course, agree – its quite heroic resistance to – er – '

The ex-President of Nicaragua waved his hand.

'You need not hesitate in speaking to me,' he said. 'I'm quite fully aware that the whole tendency of the world of today is against Nicaragua and against me. I shall not consider it any diminution of your evident courtesy if you say what you think of the misfortunes that have laid my republic in ruins.'

Barker looked immeasurably relieved and gratified.

'You are most generous, President,' he said, with some hesitation over the title, 'and I will take advantage of your generosity to express the doubts which, I must confess, we moderns have about such things as – er – the Nicaraguan independence.'

'So your sympathies are,' said Del Fuego, quite calmly, 'with the big nation which – '

'Pardon me, pardon me, President,' said Barker, warmly; 'my sympathies are with no nation. You misunderstand, I think, the modern intellect. We do not disapprove of the fire and extravagance of such commonwealths as yours only to become more extravagant on a larger scale. We do not condemn Nicaragua because we think Britain ought to be more Nicaraguan. We do not discourage small nationalities because we wish large nationalities to have all their smallness, all their uniformity of outlook, all their exaggeration of spirit. If I differ with the greatest respect from your Nicaraguan enthusiasm, it is not because a nation or ten nations were against you; it is because civilisation was against you. We moderns believe in a great cosmopolitan civilisation, one which shall include all the talents of all the absorbed peoples – '

'The Señor will forgive me,' said the President. 'May I ask the Señor how, under ordinary circumstances, he catches a wild horse?'

'I never catch a wild horse,' replied Barker, with dignity.

'Precisely,' said the other; 'and there ends your absorption of the talents. That is what I complain of your cosmopolitanism. When you say you want all peoples to unite, you really mean that you want all peoples to unite to learn the tricks of your people. If the Bedouin Arab does not know how to read, some English missionary or schoolmaster must be sent to teach him to read, but no one ever says, "This schoolmaster does not know how to ride on a camel; let us pay a Bedouin to teach him." You say your civilisation will include all talents. Will it? Do you really mean to say that at the moment when the Esquimaux has learnt to vote for a County Council, you will have learnt to spear a walrus? I recur to the example I gave. In Nicaragua we had a way of catching wild horses – by lassooing the fore feet – which was supposed to be the best in South America. If you are going to include all the talents, go and do it. If not, permit me to say what I have always said, that something went from the world when Nicaragua was civilised.'

'Something, perhaps,' replied Barker, 'but that something a mere barbarian dexterity. I do not know that I could chip flints as well as a primeval man, but I know that civilisation can make these knives which are better, and I trust to civilisation.'

'You have good authority,' answered the Nicaraguan. 'Many clever men like you have trusted to civilisation. Many clever Babylonians, many clever Egyptians, many clever men at the end of Rome. Can you tell me, in a world that is flagrant with the failures of civilisation, what there is particularly immortal about yours?'

'I think you do not quite understand, President, what ours is,' answered Barker. 'You judge it rather as if England was still a poor and pugnacious island; you have been long out of Europe. Many things have happened.'

'And what,' asked the other, 'would you call the summary of those things?'

'The summary of those things,' answered Barker, with great animation, 'is that we are rid of the superstitions, and in becoming so we have not merely become rid of the superstitions which have been most frequently and most enthusiastically so described. The superstition of big nationalities is bad, but the superstition of small nationalities is worse. The superstition of reverencing our own country is bad, but the superstition of reverencing other people's countries is worse. It is so everywhere, and in a hundred ways. The superstition of monarchy is bad, and the superstition of aristocracy is bad, but the superstition of democracy is the worst of all.'

The old gentleman opened his eyes with some surprise.

'Are you, then,' he said, 'no longer a democracy in England?'

Barker laughed.

'The situation invites paradox,' he said. 'We are, in a sense, the purest democracy. We have become a despotism. Have you not noticed how continually in history democracy becomes despotism? People call it the decay of democracy. It is simply its fulfilment. Why take the trouble to number and register and enfranchise all the innumerable John Robinsons, when you can take one John Robinson with the same intellect or lack of intellect as all the rest, and have done with it? The old idealistic republicans used to found democracy on the idea that all men were equally intelligent. Believe me, the sane and enduring democracy is founded on the fact that all men are equally idiotic. Why should we not choose out of them one as much as another? All that we want for Government is a man not criminal and insane, who can rapidly look over some petitions and sign some proclamations. To think what time was wasted in arguing about the House of Lords, Tories saying it ought to be preserved because it was clever, and Radicals saying it ought to be destroyed because it was stupid, and all the time no one saw that it was right because it was stupid, because that chance mob of ordinary men thrown there by accident of blood, were a great democratic protest against the Lower House, against the eternal insolence of the aristocracy of talents. We have established now in England, the thing towards which all systems have dimly groped, the dull popular despotism without illusions. We want one man at the head of our State, not because he is brilliant or virtuous, but because he is one man and not a chattering crowd. To avoid the possible chance of hereditary diseases or such things, we have abandoned hereditary monarchy. The King of England is chosen like a juryman upon an official rotation list. Beyond that the whole system is quietly despotic, and we have not found it raise a murmur.'

'Do you really mean,' asked the President, incredulously, 'that you choose any ordinary man that comes to hand and make him despot – that you trust to the chance of some alphabetical list . . .'

'And why not?' cried Barker. 'Did not half the historical nations trust to the chance of the eldest sons of eldest sons, and did not half of them get on tolerably well? To have a perfect system is impossible; to have a system is indispensable. All hereditary monarchies were a matter of luck: so are alphabetical monarchies. Can you find a deep philosophical meaning in the difference between the Stuarts and the Hanoverians? Believe me, I will undertake to find a deep philosophical meaning in the contrast between the dark tragedy of the A's, and the solid success of the B's.'

'And you risk it?' asked the other. 'Though the man may be a tyrant or a cynic or a criminal?'

'We risk it,' answered Barker, with a perfect placidity. 'Suppose he is a tyrant – he is still a check on a hundred tyrants. Suppose he is a cynic, it is to his interest to govern well. Suppose he is a criminal – by removing poverty and substituting power, we put a check on his criminality. In short, by substituting despotism we have put a total check on one criminal and a partial check on all the rest.'

The Nicaraguan old gentleman leaned over with a queer expression in his eyes.

'My church, sir,' he said, 'has taught me to respect faith. I do not wish to speak with any disrespect of yours, however fantastic. But do you really mean that you will trust to the ordinary man, the man who may happen to come next, as a good despot?'

'I do,' said Barker, simply. 'He may not be a good man. But he will be a good despot. For when he comes to a mere business routine of government he will endeavour to do ordinary justice. Do we not assume the same thing in a jury?'

The old President smiled.

'I don't know,' he said, 'that I have any particular objection in detail to your excellent scheme of Government. My only objection is a quite personal one. It is, that if I were asked whether I would belong to it, I should ask first of all, if I was not permitted, as an alternative, to be a toad in a ditch. That is all. You cannot argue with the choice of the soul.'

'Of the soul,' said Barker, knitting his brows, 'I cannot pretend to say anything, but speaking in the interests of the public – '

Mr Auberon Quin rose suddenly to his feet.

'If you'll excuse me, gentlemen,' he said, 'I will step out for a moment into the air.'

'I'm so sorry, Auberon,' said Lambert, good-naturedly; 'do you feel bad?'

'Not bad exactly,' said Auberon, with self-restraint; 'rather good, if anything. Strangely and richly good. The fact is, I want to reflect a little on those beautiful words that have just been uttered. "Speaking," yes, that was the phrase, "speaking in the interests of the public." One cannot get the honey from such things without being alone for a little.'

'Is he really off his chump, do you think?' asked Lambert.

The old President looked after him with queerly vigilant eyes.

'He is a man, I think,' he said, 'who cares for nothing but a joke. He is a dangerous man.'

Lambert laughed in the act of lifting some macaroni to his mouth.

'Dangerous!' he said. 'You don't know little Quin, sir!'

'Every man is dangerous,' said the old man without moving, 'who cares only for one thing. I was once dangerous myself.'

And with a pleasant smile he finished his coffee and rose, bowing profoundly, passed out into the fog, which had again grown dense and sombre. Three days afterwards they heard that he had died quietly in lodgings in Soho.

* * *

Drowned somewhere else in the dark sea of fog was a little figure shaking and quaking, with what might at first sight have seemed terror or ague: but which was really that strange malady, a lonely laughter. He was repeating over and over to himself with a rich accent – 'But speaking in the interests of the public . . . '

CHAPTER 3

The Hill of Humour

'In a little square garden of yellow roses, beside the sea,' said Auberon Quin, 'there was a Nonconformist minister who had never been to Wimbledon. His family did not understand his sorrow or the strange look in his eyes. But one day they repented their neglect, for they heard that a body had been found on the shore, battered, but wearing patent-leather boots. As it happened, it turned out not to be the minister at all. But in the dead man's pocket there was a return ticket to Maidstone.'

There was a short pause as Quin and his friends Barker and Lambert went swinging on through the slushy grass of Kensington Gardens. Then Auberon resumed.

'That story,' he said reverently, 'is the test of humour.'

They walked on further and faster, wading through higher grass as they began to climb a slope.

'I perceive,' continued Auberon, 'that you have passed the test, and consider the anecdote excruciatingly funny; since you say nothing. Only coarse humour is received with pot-house applause. The great anecdote is received in silence, like a benediction. You felt pretty benedicted, didn't you, Barker?'

'I saw the point,' said Barker, somewhat loftily.

'Do you know,' said Quin, with a sort of idiot gaiety, 'I have lots of stories as good as that. Listen to this one.'

And he slightly cleared his throat.

'Dr Polycarp was, as you all know, an unusually sallow bimetallist. "There," people of wide experience would say, "there goes the sallowest bimetallist in Cheshire." Once this was said so that he overheard it: it was said by an actuary, under a sunset of mauve and grey. Polycarp turned upon him. "Sallow!" he cried fiercely, "sallow! *Quis tulerit Gracchos de seditione querentes.*" It was said that no actuary ever made game of Dr Polycarp again.'

Barker nodded with a simple sagacity. Lambert only grunted.

'Here is another,' continued the insatiable Quin. 'In a hollow of the grey-green hills of rainy Ireland, lived an old, old woman, whose uncle was always Cambridge at the Boat Race. But in her grey-green hollows, she knew nothing of this: she didn't know that there was a Boat Race. Also she did not know that she had an uncle. She had heard of nobody at all, except of George the First, of whom she had heard (I know not why), and in whose historical memory she put her simple trust. And by and by in God's good time, it was discovered that this uncle of hers was not really her uncle, and they came and told her so. She smiled through her tears, and said only, "Virtue is its own reward." '

Again there was a silence, and then Lambert said: 'It seems a bit mysterious.'

'Mysterious!' cried the other. 'The true humour is mysterious. Do you not realise the chief incident of the nineteenth and twentieth centuries?'

'And what's that?' asked Lambert, shortly.

'It is very simple,' replied the other. 'Hitherto it was the ruin of a joke that people did not see it. Now it is the sublime victory of a joke that people do not see it. Humour, my friends, is the one sanctity remaining to mankind. It is the one thing you are thoroughly afraid of. Look at that tree.'

His interlocutors looked vaguely towards a beech that leant out towards them from the ridge of the hill.

'If,' said Mr Quin, 'I were to say that you did not see the great truths of science exhibited by that tree, though they stared any man of intellect in the face, what would you think or say? You would merely regard me as a pedant with some unimportant theory about vegetable cells. If I were to say that you did not see in that tree the vile mismanagement of local politics, you would dismiss me as a Socialist crank with some particular fad about public parks. If I were to say that you were guilty of the supreme blasphemy of looking at that tree and not seeing in it a new religion, a special revelation of God, you would simply say I was a mystic, and think no more about me. But if' – and he lifted a pontifical hand – 'if I say that you cannot see the humour of that tree, and that I see the humour of it – my God! you will roll about at my feet.'

He paused a moment, and then resumed.

'Yes; a sense of humour, a weird and delicate sense of humour, is the new religion of mankind! It is towards that men will strain themselves with the asceticism of saints. Exercises, spiritual exercises, will be set in it. It will be asked, "Can you see the humour of this iron railing?" or "Can you see the humour of this field of corn? Can you see the humour of the stars? Can you see the humour of the sunsets?" How often I have laughed myself to sleep over a violet sunset.'

'Quite so,' said Mr Barker, with an intelligent embarrassment.

'Let me tell you another story. How often it happens that the MPs for Essex are less punctual than one would suppose. The least punctual Essex MP, perhaps, was James Wilson, who said, in the very act of plucking a poppy – '

Lambert suddenly faced round and struck his stick into the ground in a defiant attitude.

'Auberon,' he said, 'chuck it. I won't stand it. It's all bosh.'

Both men stared at him, for there was something very explosive about the words, as if they had been corked up painfully for a long time.

'You have,' began Quin, 'no – '

'I don't care a curse,' said Lambert, violently, 'whether I have "a delicate sense of humour" or not. I won't stand it. It's all a confounded fraud. There's no joke in those infernal tales at all. You know there isn't as well as I do.'

'Well,' replied Quin, slowly, 'it is true that I, with my rather gradual mental processes, did not see any joke in them. But the finer sense of Barker perceived it.'

Barker turned a fierce red, but continued to stare at the horizon.

'You ass,' said Lambert; 'why can't you be like other people? Why can't you say something really funny, or hold your tongue? The man who sits on his hat in a pantomime is a long sight funnier than you are.'

Quin regarded him steadily. They had reached the top of the ridge and the wind struck their faces.

'Lambert,' said Auberon, 'you are a great and good man, though I'm hanged if you look it. You are more. You are a great revolutionist or deliverer of the world, and I look forward to seeing you carved in marble between Luther and Danton, if possible in your present attitude, the hat slightly on one side. I said as I came up the hill that the new humour was the last of the religions. You have made it the last of the superstitions. But let me give you a very serious warning. Be careful how you ask me to do anything *outré*, to imitate the man in the pantomime, and to sit on my hat. Because I am a man whose soul has been emptied of all pleasures but folly. And for twopence I'd do it.'

'Do it, then,' said Lambert, swinging his stick impatiently. 'It would be funnier than the bosh you and Barker talk.'

Quin, standing on the top of the hill, stretched his hand out towards the main avenue of Kensington Gardens.

'Two hundred yards away,' he said, 'are all your fashionable acquaintances with nothing on earth to do but to stare at each other and at us. We are standing upon an elevation under the open sky, a peak as it were of fantasy, a Sinai of humour. We are in a great pulpit or platform, lit up with sunlight, and half London can see us. Be careful how you suggest things to me. For there is in me a madness which goes beyond martyrdom, the madness of an utterly idle man.'

'I don't know what you are talking about,' said Lambert, contemptuously. 'I only know I'd rather you stood on your silly head, than talked so much.'

'Auberon! for goodness' sake . . . ' cried Barker, springing forward; but he was too late. Faces from all the benches and avenues were turned in their direction. Groups stopped and small crowds collected; and the sharp sunlight picked out the whole scene in blue, green and black, like a picture in a child's toy-book. And on the top of the small hill Mr Auberon Quin stood with considerable athletic neatness upon his head, and waved his patent-leather boots in the air.

'For God's sake, Quin, get up, and don't be an idiot,' cried Barker, wringing his hands; 'we shall have the whole town here.'

'Yes, get up, get up, man,' said Lambert, amused and annoyed. 'I was only fooling; get up.'

Auberon did so with a bound, and flinging his hat higher than the trees, proceeded to hop about on one leg with a serious expression. Barker stamped wildly.

'Oh, let's get home, Barker, and leave him,' said Lambert; 'some of your proper and correct police will look after him. Here they come!'

Two grave-looking men in quiet uniforms came up the hill towards them. One held a paper in his hand.

'There he is, officer,' said Lambert, cheerfully; 'we ain't responsible for him.'

The officer looked at the capering Mr Quin with a quiet eye.

'We have not come, gentlemen,' he said, 'about what I think you are alluding to. We have come from headquarters to announce the selection of His Majesty the King. It is the rule, inherited from the old *régime*, that the news should be brought to the new Sovereign immediately, wherever he is; so we have followed you across Kensington Gardens.'

Barker's eyes were blazing in his pale face. He was consumed with ambition throughout his life. With a certain dull magnanimity of the intellect he had really believed in the chance method of selecting despots. But this sudden suggestion, that the selection might have fallen upon him, unnerved him with pleasure.

'Which of us,' he began, and the respectful official interrupted him.

'Not you, sir, I am sorry to say. If I may be permitted to say so, we know your services to the Government, and should be very thankful if it were. The choice has fallen . . . '

'God bless my soul!' said Lambert, jumping back two paces. 'Not me. Don't say I'm autocrat of all the Russias.'

'No, sir,' said the officer, with a slight cough and a glance towards Auberon, who was at that moment putting his head between his legs and making a noise like a cow; 'the gentleman whom we have to congratulate seems at the moment – er – er – occupied.'

'Not Quin!' shrieked Barker, rushing up to him; 'it can't be. Auberon, for God's sake pull yourself together. You've been made King!'

With his head still upside down between his legs, Mr Quin answered modestly: 'I am not worthy. I cannot reasonably claim to equal the great men who have previously swayed the sceptre of Britain. Perhaps the only peculiarity that I can claim is that I am probably the first monarch that ever spoke out his soul to the people of England with his head and body in this position. This may in some sense give me, to quote a poem that I wrote in my youth:

A nobler office on the earth
Than valour, power of brain, or birth
Could give the warrior kings of old.

The intellect clarified by this posture – '

Lambert and Barker made a kind of rush at him.

'Don't you understand?' cried Lambert. 'It's not a joke. They've really made you King. By gosh! they must have rum taste.'

'The great Bishops of the Middle Ages,' said Quin, kicking his legs in the air, as he was dragged up more or less upside down, 'were in the habit of refusing the honour of election three times and then accepting it. A mere matter of detail separates me from those great men. I will accept the post three times and refuse it afterwards. Oh! I will toil for you, my faithful people! You shall have a banquet of humour.'

By this time he had been landed the right way up, and the two men were still trying in vain to impress him with the gravity of the situation.

'Did you not tell me, Wilfrid Lambert,' he said, 'that I should be of more public value if I adopted a more popular form of humour? And when should a popular form of humour be more firmly riveted upon me than now, when I am the darling of the people? Officer,' he continued, addressing the startled messenger, 'are there no ceremonies to celebrate my entry into the city?'

'Ceremonies,' began the official, with embarrassment, 'have been more or less neglected for some little time, and – '

Auberon Quin began gradually to take off his coat.

'All ceremony,' he said, 'consists in the reversal of the obvious. Thus men, when they wish to be priests or judges, dress up like women. Kindly help me on with this coat.' And he held it out.

'But, your Majesty,' said the officer, after a moment's bewilderment and manipulation, 'you're putting it on with the tails in front.'

'The reversal of the obvious,' said the King, calmly, 'is as near as we can come to ritual with our imperfect apparatus. Lead on.'

The rest of that afternoon and evening was to Barker and Lambert a nightmare, which they could not properly realise or recall. The King, with his coat on the wrong way, went towards the streets that were awaiting him, and the old Kensington Palace which was the Royal residence. As he passed small groups of men, the groups turned into crowds, and gave forth sounds which seemed strange in welcoming an autocrat. Barker walked behind, his brain reeling, and, as the crowds grew thicker and thicker, the sounds became more and more unusual. And when he had reached the great marketplace opposite the church, Barker knew that he had reached it, though he was roods behind, because a cry went up such as had never before greeted any of the kings of the earth.

BOOK TWO

CHAPTER I

The Charter of the Cities

Lambert was standing bewildered outside the door of the King's apartments amid the scurry of astonishment and ridicule. He was just passing out into the street, in a dazed manner, when James Barker dashed by him.

'Where are you going?' he asked.

'To stop all this foolery, of course,' replied Barker; and he disappeared into the room.

He entered it headlong, slamming the door, and slapping his incomparable silk hat on the table. His mouth opened, but before he could speak, the King said: 'Your hat, if you please.'

Fidgeting with his fingers, and scarcely knowing what he was doing, the young politician held it out.

The King placed it on his own chair, and sat on it.

'A quaint old custom,' he explained, smiling above the ruins. 'When the King receives the representatives of the House of Barker, the hat of the latter is immediately destroyed in this manner. It represents the absolute finality of the act of homage expressed in the removal of it. It declares that never until that hat shall once more appear upon your head (a contingency which I firmly believe to be remote) shall the House of Barker rebel against the Crown of England.'

Barker stood with clenched fist, and shaking lip.

'Your jokes,' he began, 'and my property – ' and then exploded with an oath, and stopped again.

'Continue, continue,' said the King, waving his hands.

'What does it all mean?' cried the other, with a gesture of passionate rationality. 'Are you mad?'

'Not in the least,' replied the King, pleasantly. 'Madmen are always serious; they go mad from lack of humour. You are looking serious yourself, James.'

'Why can't you keep it to your own private life?' expostulated the other. 'You've got plenty of money, and plenty of houses now to play the fool in, but in the interests of the public – '

'Epigrammatic,' said the King, shaking his finger sadly at him. 'None of your daring scintillations here. As to why I don't do it in private, I rather fail to understand your question. The answer is of comparative limpidity. I don't do it in private, because it is funnier to do it in public. You appear to think that it would be amusing to be dignified in the banquet hall and in the street, and at my own fireside (I could procure a fireside) to keep the company in a roar. But that is what everyone does. Everyone is grave in public, and funny in private. My sense of humour suggests the reversal of this; it suggests that one should be funny in public, and solemn in private. I desire to make the State functions, parliaments, coronations, and so on, one roaring old-fashioned pantomime. But, on the other hand, I shut myself up alone in a small storeroom for two hours a day, where I am so dignified that I come out quite ill.'

By this time Barker was walking up and down the room, his frock-coat flapping like the black wings of a bird.

'Well, you will ruin the country, that's all,' he said shortly.

'It seems to me,' said Auberon, 'that the tradition of ten centuries is being broken, and the House of Barker is rebelling against the Crown of England. It would be with regret (for I admire your appearance) that I should be obliged forcibly to decorate your head with the remains of this hat, but – '

'What I can't understand,' said Barker, flinging up his fingers with a feverish American movement, 'is why you don't care about anything else but your games.'

The King stopped sharply in the act of lifting the silken remnants, dropped them, and walked up to Barker, looking at him steadily.

'I made a kind of vow,' he said, 'that I would not talk seriously, which always means answering silly questions. But the strong man will always be gentle with politicians.

> The shape my scornful looks deride
> Required a God to form;

if I may so theologically express myself. And for some reason I cannot in the least understand, I feel impelled to answer that question of yours, and to answer it as if there were really such a thing in the world as a serious subject. You ask me why I don't care for anything else. Can you tell me, in the name of all the gods you don't believe in, why I should care for anything else?'

'Don't you realise common public necessities?' cried Barker. 'Is it possible that a man of your intelligence does not know that it is everyone's interest – '

'Don't you believe in Zoroaster? Is it possible that you neglect Mumbo-Jumbo?' returned the King, with startling animation. 'Does a man of your intelligence come to me with these damned early Victorian ethics? If, on studying my features and manner, you detect any particular resemblance to the Prince Consort, I assure you you are mistaken. Did Herbert Spencer ever convince you – did he ever convince anybody – did he ever for one mad moment convince himself – that it must be to the interest of the individual to feel a public spirit? Do you believe that, if you rule your department badly, you stand any more chance, or one half of the chance, of being guillotined, than an angler stands of being pulled into the river by a strong pike? Herbert Spencer refrained from theft for the same reason that he refrained from wearing feathers in his hair, because he was an English gentleman with different tastes. I am an English gentleman with different tastes. He liked philosophy. I like art. He liked writing ten books on the nature of human society. I like to see the Lord Chamberlain walking in front of me with a piece of paper pinned to his coat-tails. It is my humour. Are you answered? At any rate, I have said my last serious word today, and my last serious word I trust for the remainder of my life in this Paradise of Fools. The remainder of my conversation with you today, which I trust will be long and stimulating, I propose to conduct in a new language of my own by means of rapid and symbolic movements of the left leg.' And he began to pirouette slowly round the room with a preoccupied expression.

Barker ran round the room after him, bombarding him with demands and entreaties. But he received no response except in the new language. He came out banging the door again, and sick like a man coming on shore. As he strode along the streets he found himself suddenly opposite Cicconani's restaurant, and for some reason there rose up before him the green fantastic figure of the Spanish General, standing, as he had seen him last, at the door, with the words on his lips, 'You cannot argue with the choice of the soul.'

The King came out from his dancing with the air of a man of business legitimately tired. He put on an overcoat, lit a cigar, and went out into the purple night.

'I will go,' he said, 'and mingle with the people.'

He passed swiftly up a street in the neighbourhood of Notting Hill, when suddenly he felt a hard object driven into his waistcoat. He paused, put up his single eyeglass, and beheld a boy with a wooden sword and a paper cocked hat, wearing that expression of awed satisfaction with which a child contemplates his work when he has hit someone very hard. The King gazed thoughtfully for some time at his assailant, and slowly took a notebook from his breast-pocket.

'I have a few notes,' he said, 'for my dying speech'; and he turned over the leaves. 'Dying speech for political assassination; ditto, if by former friend – h'm, h'm. Dying speech for death at hands of injured husband (repentant). Dying speech for same (cynical). I am not quite sure which meets the present . . .'

'I'm the King of the Castle,' said the boy, truculently, and very pleased with nothing in particular.

The King was a kind-hearted man, and very fond of children, like all people who are fond of the ridiculous.

'Infant,' he said, 'I'm glad you are so stalwart a defender of your old inviolate Notting Hill. Look up nightly to that peak, my child, where it lifts itself among the stars so ancient, so lonely, so unutterably Notting. So long as you are ready to die for the sacred mountain, even if it were ringed with all the armies of Bayswater – '

The King stopped suddenly, and his eyes shone.

'Perhaps,' he said, 'perhaps the noblest of all my conceptions. A revival of the arrogance of the old mediaeval cities applied to our glorious suburbs. Clapham with a city guard. Wimbledon with a city wall. Surbiton tolling a bell to raise its citizens. West Hampstead going into battle with its own banner. It shall be done. I, the King, have said it.' And, hastily presenting the boy with half a crown, remarking, 'For the war-chest of Notting Hill,' he ran violently home at such a rate of speed that crowds followed him for miles. On reaching his study, he ordered a cup of coffee, and plunged into profound meditation upon the project. At length he called his favourite Equerry, Captain Bowler, for whom he had a deep affection, founded principally upon the shape of his whiskers.

'Bowler,' he said, 'isn't there some society of historical research, or something of which I am an honorary member?'

'Yes, sir,' said Captain Bowler, rubbing his nose, 'you are a member of "The Encouragers of Egyptian Renaissance", and "The Teutonic Tombs Club", and "The Society for the Recovery of London Antiquities", and – '

'That is admirable,' said the King. 'The London Antiquities does my trick. Go to the Society for the Recovery of London Antiquities and speak to their secretary, and their sub-secretary, and their president, and their vice-president, saying, "The King of England is proud, but the honorary member of the Society for the Recovery of London Antiquities is prouder than kings. I should like to tell you of certain discoveries I have made touching the neglected traditions of the London boroughs. The revelations may cause some excitement, stirring burning memories and touching old wounds in Shepherd's Bush and Bayswater, in Pimlico and South Kensington. The King hesitates, but the honorary member is firm. I approach you invoking the vows of my initiation, the Sacred Seven Cats, the Poker of Perfection, and the Ordeal of the Indescribable Instant (forgive me if I mix you up with the Clan-na-Gael or some other club I belong to), and ask you to permit me to read a paper at your next meeting on the 'Wars of the London Boroughs'." Say all this to the Society, Bowler. Remember it very carefully, for it is most important, and I have forgotten it altogether, and send me another cup of coffee and some of the cigars that we keep for vulgar and successful people. I am going to write my paper.'

The Society for the Recovery of London Antiquities met a month after in a corrugated-iron hall on the outskirts of one of the southern suburbs of London. A large number of people had collected there under the coarse and flaring gas-jets when the King arrived, perspiring and genial. On taking off his greatcoat, he was perceived to be in evening dress, wearing the Garter. His appearance at the small table, adorned only with a glass of water, was received with respectful cheering.

The chairman (Mr Huggins) said that he was sure that they had all been pleased to listen to such distinguished lecturers as they had heard for some time past (hear, hear). Mr Burton (hear, hear), Mr Cambridge, Professor King (loud and continued cheers), our old friend Peter Jessop, Sir William White (loud laughter), and other eminent men, had done honour to their little venture (cheers). But there were other circumstances which lent a certain unique quality to the present occasion (hear, hear). So far as his recollection went, and in connection with the Society for the Recovery of London Antiquities it went very far (loud cheers), he did not remember that any of their lecturers had borne the title of King. He would therefore call upon King Auberon briefly to address the meeting.

The King began by saying that this speech might be regarded as the first declaration of his new policy for the nation. 'At this supreme hour of my life I feel that to no one but the members of the Society for the Recovery of London Antiquities can I open my heart (cheers). If the world turns upon my policy, and the storms of popular hostility begin to rise (no, no), I feel that it is here, with my brave Recoverers around me, that I can best meet them, sword in hand' (loud cheers).

His Majesty then went on to explain that, now old age was creeping upon him, he proposed to devote his remaining strength to bringing about a keener sense of local patriotism in the various municipalities of London. How few of them knew the legends of their own boroughs! How many there were who had never heard of the true origin of the Wink of Wandsworth! What a large proportion of the younger generation in Chelsea neglected to perform the old Chelsea Chuff! Pimlico no longer pumped the Pimlies. Battersea had forgotten the name of Blick.

There was a short silence, and then a voice said 'Shame!'

The King continued: 'Being called, however unworthily, to this high estate, I have resolved that, so far as possible, this neglect shall cease. I desire no military glory. I lay claim to no constitutional equality with Justinian or Alfred. If I can go down to history as the man who saved from extinction a few old English customs, if our descendants can say it was through this man, humble as he was, that the Ten Turnips are still eaten in Fulham, and the

Putney parish councillor still shaves one half of his head, I shall look my great fathers reverently but not fearfully in the face when I go down to the last house of Kings.'

The King paused, visibly affected, but collecting himself, resumed once more.

'I trust that to very few of you, at least, I need dwell on the sublime origins of these legends. The very names of your boroughs bear witness to them. So long as Hammersmith is called Hammersmith, its people will live in the shadow of that primal hero, the Blacksmith, who led the democracy of the Broadway into battle till he drove the chivalry of Kensington before him and overthrew them at that place which in honour of the best blood of the defeated aristocracy is still called Kensington Gore. Men of Hammersmith will not fail to remember that the very name of Kensington originated from the lips of their hero. For at the great banquet of reconciliation held after the war, when the disdainful oligarchs declined to join in the songs of the men of the Broadway (which are to this day of a rude and popular character), the great Republican leader, with his rough humour, said the words which are written in gold upon his monument, "Little birds that can sing and won't sing, must be made to sing." So that the Eastern Knights were called Cansings or Kensings ever afterwards. But you also have great memories, O men of Kensington! You showed that you could sing, and sing great war-songs. Even after the dark day of Kensington Gore, history will not forget those three Knights who guarded your disordered retreat from Hyde Park (so called from your hiding there), those three Knights after whom Knightsbridge is named. Nor will it forget the day of your re-emergence, purged in the fire of calamity, cleansed of your oligarchic corruptions, when, sword in hand, you drove the Empire of Hammersmith back mile by mile, swept it past its own Broadway, and broke it at last in a battle so long and bloody that the birds of prey have left their name upon it. Men have called it, with austere irony, the Ravenscourt. I shall not, I trust, wound the patriotism of Bayswater, or the lonelier pride of Brompton, or that of any other historic township, by taking these two special examples. I select them, not because they are more glorious than the rest, but partly from personal association (I am myself descended from one of the three heroes of Knightsbridge), and partly from the consciousness that I am an amateur antiquarian, and cannot presume to deal with times and places more remote and more mysterious. It is not for me to settle the question between two such men as Professor Hugg and Sir William Whisky as to whether Notting Hill means Nutting Hill (in allusion to the rich woods which no longer cover it), or whether it is a corruption of Nothing-ill, referring to its reputation among the ancients as an Earthly Paradise. When a Podkins and a Jossy confess themselves doubtful about the boundaries of West Kensington (said to have been traced in the blood of Oxen), I need not be ashamed to confess a similar doubt. I will ask you to excuse me from further history, and to assist me with your encouragement in dealing with the problem which faces us today. Is this ancient spirit of the London townships to die out? Are our omnibus conductors and policemen to lose altogether that light which we see so often in their eyes, the dreamy light of

> "Old unhappy far-off things
> And battles long ago"

– to quote the words of a little-known poet who was a friend of my youth? I have resolved, as I have said, so far as possible, to preserve the eyes of policemen and omnibus conductors in their present dreamy state. For what is a state without dreams? And the remedy I propose is as follows:

'Tomorrow morning at twenty-five minutes past ten, if Heaven spares my life, I purpose to issue a Proclamation. It has been the work of my life, and is about half finished. With the assistance of a whisky and soda, I shall conclude the other half tonight, and my people will receive it tomorrow. All these boroughs where you were born, and hope to lay your bones, shall be reinstated in their ancient magnificence – Hammersmith, Kensington, Bayswater, Chelsea, Battersea, Clapham, Balham, and a hundred others. Each shall immediately build a city wall with gates to be closed at sunset. Each shall have a city guard, armed to the teeth. Each shall have a banner, a coat-of-arms, and, if convenient, a gathering cry. I will not enter into the details now, my heart is too full. They will be found in the proclamation itself. You will all, however, be subject to enrolment in the local city guards, to be summoned together by a thing called the Tocsin, the meaning of which I am studying in my researches into history. Personally, I believe a tocsin to be some kind of highly paid official. If, therefore, any of you happen to have such a thing as a halberd in the house, I should advise you to practise with it in the garden.'

Here the King buried his face in his handkerchief and hurriedly left the platform, overcome by emotion.

The members of the Society for the Recovery of London Antiquities rose in an indescribable state of vagueness. Some were purple with indignation; an intellectual few were purple with laughter; the great majority found their minds a blank. There remains a tradition that one pale face with burning blue eyes remained fixed upon the lecturer, and after the lecture a red-haired boy ran out of the room.

CHAPTER 2

The Council of the Provosts

The King got up early next morning and came down three steps at a time like a schoolboy. Having eaten his breakfast hurriedly, but with an appetite, he summoned one of the highest officials of the Palace, and presented him with a shilling. 'Go and buy me,' he said, 'a shilling paintbox, which you will get, unless the mists of time mislead me, in a shop at the corner of the second and dirtier street that leads out of Rochester Row. I have already requested the Master of the Buckhounds to provide me with cardboard. It seemed to me (I know not why) that it fell within his department.'

The King was happy all that morning with his cardboard and his paintbox. He was engaged in designing the uniforms and coats-of-arms for the various municipalities of London. They gave him deep and no inconsiderable thought. He felt the responsibility.

'I cannot think,' he said, 'why people should think the names of places in the country more poetical than those in London. Shallow romanticists go away in trains and stop in places called Hugmy-in-the-Hole, or Bumps-on-the-Puddle. And all the time they could, if they liked, go and live at a place with the dim, divine name of St John's Wood. I have never been to St John's Wood. I dare not. I should be afraid of the innumerable night of fir trees, afraid to come upon a blood-red cup and the beating of the wings of the Eagle. But all these things can be imagined by remaining reverently in the Harrow train.'

And he thoughtfully retouched his design for the headdress of the halberdier of St John's Wood, a design in black and red, compounded of a pine tree and the plumage of an eagle. Then he turned to another card. 'Let us think of milder matters,' he said. 'Lavender Hill! Could any of your glebes and combes and all the rest of it produce so fragrant an idea? Think of a mountain of lavender lifting itself in purple poignancy into the silver skies and filling men's nostrils with a new breath of life – a purple hill of incense. It is true that upon my few excursions of discovery on a halfpenny tram I have failed to hit the precise spot. But it must be there; some poet called it by its name. There is at least warrant enough for the solemn purple plumes (following the botanical formation of lavender) which I have required people to wear in the neighbourhood of Clapham Junction. It is so everywhere, after all. I have never been actually to Southfields, but I suppose a scheme of lemons and olives represent their austral instincts. I have never visited

Parson's Green, or seen either the Green or the Parson, but surely the pale-green shovel-hats I have designed must be more or less in the spirit. I must work in the dark and let my instincts guide me. The great love I bear to my people will certainly save me from distressing their noble spirit or violating their great traditions.'

As he was reflecting in this vein, the door was flung open, and an official announced Mr Barker and Mr Lambert.

Mr Barker and Mr Lambert were not particularly surprised to find the King sitting on the floor amid a litter of watercolour sketches. They were not particularly surprised because the last time they had called on him they had found him sitting on the floor, surrounded by a litter of children's bricks, and the time before surrounded by a litter of wholly unsuccessful attempts to make paper darts. But the trend of the royal infant's remarks, uttered from amid this infantile chaos, was not quite the same affair. For some time they let him babble on, conscious that his remarks meant nothing. And then a horrible thought began to steal over the mind of James Barker. He began to think that the King's remarks did not mean nothing.

'In God's name, Auberon,' he suddenly volleyed out, startling the quiet hall, 'you don't mean that you are really going to have these city guards and city walls and things?'

'I am, indeed,' said the infant, in a quiet voice. 'Why shouldn't I have them? I have modelled them precisely on your political principles. Do you know what I've done, Barker? I've behaved like a true Barkerian. I've . . . but perhaps it won't interest you, the account of my Barkerian conduct.'

'Oh, go on, go on,' cried Barker.

'The account of my Barkerian conduct,' said Auberon, calmly, 'seems not only to interest, but to alarm you. Yet it is very simple. It merely consists in choosing all the provosts under any new scheme by the same principle by which you have caused the central despot to be appointed. Each provost, of each city, under my charter, is to be appointed by rotation. Sleep, therefore, my Barker, a rosy sleep.'

Barker's wild eyes flared.

'But, in God's name, don't you see, Quin, that the thing is quite different? In the centre it doesn't matter so much, just because the whole object of despotism is to get some sort of unity. But if any damned parish can go to any damned man – '

'I see your difficulty,' said King Auberon, calmly. 'You feel that your talents may be neglected. Listen!' And he rose with immense magnificence. 'I solemnly give to my liege subject, James Barker, my special and splendid favour, the right to override the obvious text of the Charter of the Cities, and to be, in his own right, Lord High Provost of South Kensington. And now, my dear James, you are all right. Good-day.'

'But – ' began Barker.

'The audience is at an end, Provost,' said the King, smiling.

How far his confidence was justified, it would require a somewhat complicated description to explain. 'The Great Proclamation of the Charter of the Free Cities' appeared in due course that morning, and was posted by bill-stickers all over the front of the Palace, the King assisting them with animated directions, and standing in the middle of the road, with his head on one side, contemplating the result. It was also carried up and down the main thoroughfares by sandwichmen, and the King was, with difficulty, restrained from going out in that capacity himself, being, in fact, found by the Groom of the Stole and Captain Bowler, struggling between two boards. His excitement had positively to be quieted like that of a child.

The reception which the Charter of the Cities met at the hands of the public may mildly be described as mixed. In one sense it was popular enough. In many happy homes that remarkable legal document was read aloud on winter evenings amid uproarious appreciation, when everything had been learnt by heart from that quaint but immortal old classic, Mr W. W. Jacobs. But when it was discovered that the King had every intention of seriously requiring the provisions to be carried out, of insisting that the grotesque cities, with their tocsins and city guards, should really come into existence, things were thrown into a far angrier confusion. Londoners had no particular objection to the King making a fool of himself, but they became indignant when it became evident that he wished to make fools of them; and protests began to come in.

The Lord High Provost of the Good and Valiant City of West Kensington wrote a respectful letter to the King, explaining that upon State occasions it would, of course, be his duty to observe what formalities the King thought proper, but that it was really awkward for a decent householder not to be allowed to go out and put a postcard in a pillar-box without being escorted by five heralds, who announced, with formal cries and blasts of a trumpet, that the Lord High Provost desired to catch the post.

The Lord High Provost of North Kensington, who was a prosperous draper, wrote a curt business note, like a man complaining of a railway company, stating that definite inconvenience had been caused him by the presence of the halberdiers, whom he had to take with him everywhere. When attempting to catch an omnibus to the City, he had found that while room could have been found for himself, the halberdiers had a difficulty in getting in to the vehicle – believe him, theirs faithfully.

The Lord High Provost of Shepherd's Bush said his wife did not like men hanging round the kitchen.

The King was always delighted to listen to these grievances, delivering lenient and kingly answers, but as he always insisted, as the absolute *sine qua non*, that verbal complaints should be presented to him with the fullest pomp of trumpets, plumes, and halberds, only a few resolute spirits were prepared to run the gauntlet of the little boys in the street.

Among these, however, was prominent the abrupt and businesslike gentleman who ruled North Kensington. And he had, before long, occasion to interview the King about a matter wider and even more urgent than the problem of the halberdiers and the omnibus. This was the great question which then and for long afterwards brought a stir to the blood and a flush to the cheek of all the speculative builders and house agents from Shepherd's Bush to the Marble Arch, and from Westbourne Grove to High Street, Kensington. I refer to the great affair of the improvements in Notting Hill. The scheme was conducted chiefly by Mr Buck, the abrupt North Kensington magnate, and by Mr Wilson, the Provost of Bayswater. A great thoroughfare was to be driven through three boroughs, through West Kensington, North Kensington and Notting Hill, opening at one end into Hammersmith Broadway, and at the other into Westbourne Grove. The negotiations, buyings, sellings, bullying and bribing took ten years, and by the end of it Buck, who had conducted them almost single-handed, had proved himself a man of the strongest type of material energy and material diplomacy. And just as his splendid patience and more splendid impatience had finally brought him victory, when workmen were already demolishing houses and walls along the great line from Hammersmith, a sudden obstacle appeared that had neither been reckoned with nor dreamed of, a small and strange obstacle, which, like a speck of grit in a great machine, jarred the whole vast scheme and brought it to a standstill, and Mr Buck, the draper, getting with great impatience into his robes of office and summoning with indescribable disgust his halberdiers, hurried over to speak to the King.

Ten years had not tired the King of his joke. There were still new faces to be seen looking out from the symbolic head gear he had designed, gazing at him from amid the pastoral ribbons of Shepherd's Bush or from under the sombre hoods of the Blackfriars Road. And the interview which was promised him with the Provost of North Kensington he anticipated with a particular pleasure, for 'he never really enjoyed', he said, 'the full richness of the mediaeval garments unless the people compelled to wear them were very angry and businesslike'.

Mr Buck was both. At the King's command the door of the audience-chamber was thrown open and a herald appeared in the purple colours of Mr Buck's commonwealth emblazoned with the Great Eagle which the King had attributed to North Kensington, in vague reminiscence of Russia, for he always insisted on regarding North Kensington as some kind of semi-arctic neighbourhood. The herald announced that the Provost of that city desired audience of the King.

'From North Kensington?' said the King, rising graciously. 'What news does he bring from that land of high hills and fair women? He is welcome.'

The herald advanced into the room, and was immediately followed by twelve guards clad in purple, who were followed by an attendant bearing the banner of the Eagle, who was followed by another attendant bearing the keys of the city upon a cushion, who was followed by Mr Buck in a great hurry. When the King saw his strong animal face and steady eyes, he knew that he was in the presence of a great man of business, and consciously braced himself.

'Well, well,' he said, cheerily coming down two or three steps from a dais, and striking his hands lightly together, 'I am glad to see you. Never mind, never mind. Ceremony is not everything.'

'I don't understand your Majesty,' said the Provost, stolidly.

'Never mind, never mind,' said the King, gaily. 'A knowledge of Courts is by no means an unmixed merit; you will do it next time, no doubt.'

The man of business looked at him sulkily from under his black brows and said again without show of civility: 'I don't follow you.'

'Well, well,' replied the King, good-naturedly, 'if you ask me I don't mind telling you, not because I myself attach any importance to these forms in comparison with the Honest Heart. But it is usual – it is usual – that is all, for a man when entering the presence of Royalty to lie down on his back on the floor and elevating his feet towards heaven (as the source of Royal power) to say three times "Monarchical institutions improve the manners." But there, there – such pomp is far less truly dignified than your simple kindliness.'

The Provost's face was red with anger, and he maintained silence.

'And now,' said the King, lightly, and with the exasperating air of a man softening a snub; 'what delightful weather we are having! You must find your official robes warm, my Lord. I designed them for your own snow-bound land.'

'They're as hot as hell,' said Buck, briefly. 'I came here on business.'

'Right,' said the King, nodding a great number of times with quite unmeaning solemnity; 'right, right, right. Business, as the sad glad old Persian said, is business. Be punctual. Rise early. Point the pen to the shoulder. Point the pen to the shoulder, for you know not whence you come nor why. Point the pen to the shoulder, for you know not when you go nor where.'

The Provost pulled a number of papers from his pocket and savagely flapped them open.

'Your Majesty may have heard,' he began, sarcastically, 'of Hammersmith and a thing called a road. We have been at work ten years buying property and getting compulsory powers and fixing compensation and squaring vested interests, and now at the very end, the thing is stopped by a fool. Old Prout, who was Provost of Notting Hill, was a business man, and we dealt with him quite satisfactorily. But he's dead, and the cursed lot has fallen on a young man named Wayne, who's up to some game that's perfectly incomprehensible to me. We offer him a better price than anyone ever dreamt of, but he won't let the road go through. And his Council seems to be backing him up. It's midsummer madness.'

The King, who was rather inattentively engaged in drawing the Provost's nose with his finger on the window-pane, heard the last two words.

'What a perfect phrase that is!' he said. ' "Midsummer madness"!'

'The chief point is,' continued Buck, doggedly, 'that the only part that is really in question is one dirty little street – Pump Street – a street with nothing in it but a public-house and a penny toy-shop, and that sort of thing. All the respectable people of Notting Hill have accepted our compensation. But the ineffable Wayne sticks out over Pump Street. Says he's Provost of Notting Hill. He's only Provost of Pump Street.'

'A good thought,' replied Auberon. 'I like the idea of a Provost of Pump Street. Why not let him alone?'

'And drop the whole scheme!' cried out Buck, with a burst of brutal spirit. 'I'll be damned if we do. No. I'm for sending in workmen to pull down without more ado.'

'Strike for the purple Eagle!' cried the King, hot with historical associations.

'I'll tell you what it is,' said Buck, losing his temper altogether. 'If your Majesty would spend less time in insulting respectable people with your silly coats-of-arms, and more time over the business of the nation – '

The King's brow wrinkled thoughtfully.

'The situation is not bad,' he said; 'the haughty burgher defying the King in his own Palace. The burgher's head should be thrown back and the right arm extended; the left may be lifted towards Heaven, but that I leave to your private religious sentiment. I have sunk back in this chair, stricken with baffled fury. Now again, please.'

Buck's mouth opened like a dog's, but before he could speak another herald appeared at the door.

'The Lord High Provost of Bayswater,' he said, 'desires an audience.'

'Admit him,' said Auberon. 'This *is* a jolly day.'

The halberdiers of Bayswater wore a prevailing uniform of green, and the banner which was borne after them was emblazoned with a green bay-wreath on a silver ground, which the King, in the course of his researches into a bottle of champagne, had discovered to be the quaint old punning cognisance of the city of Bayswater.

'It is a fit symbol,' said the King, 'your immortal bay-wreath. Fulham may seek for wealth, and Kensington for art, but when did the men of Bayswater care for anything but glory?'

Immediately behind the banner, and almost completely hidden by it, came the Provost of the city, clad in splendid robes of green and silver with white fur and crowned with bay. He was an anxious little man with red whiskers, originally the owner of a small sweet-stuff shop.

'Our cousin of Bayswater,' said the King, with delight; 'what can we get for you?' The King was heard also distinctly to mutter, 'Cold beef, cold 'am, cold chicken,' his voice dying into silence.

'I came to see your Majesty,' said the Provost of Bayswater, whose name was Wilson, 'about that Pump Street affair.'

'I have just been explaining the situation to his Majesty,' said Buck, curtly, but recovering his civility. 'I am not sure, however, whether his Majesty knows how much the matter affects you also.'

'It affects both of us, yer see, yer Majesty, as this scheme was started for the benefit of the 'ole neighbourhood. So Mr Buck and me we put our 'eads together – '

The King clasped his hands.

'Perfect!' he cried in ecstasy. 'Your heads together! I can see it! Can't you do it now? Oh, do do it now!'

A smothered sound of amusement appeared to come from the halberdiers, but Mr Wilson looked merely bewildered, and Mr Buck merely diabolical.

'I suppose,' he began bitterly, but the King stopped him with a gesture of listening.

'Hush,' he said, 'I think I hear someone else coming. I seem to hear another herald, a herald whose boots creak.'

As he spoke another voice cried from the doorway: 'The Lord High Provost of South Kensington desires an audience.'

'The Lord High Provost of South Kensington!' cried the King. 'Why, that is my old friend James Barker! What does he want, I wonder? If the tender memories of friendship have not grown misty, I fancy he wants something for himself, probably money. How are you, James?'

Mr James Barker, whose guard was attired in a splendid blue, and whose blue banner bore three gold birds singing, rushed, in his blue and gold robes, into the room. Despite the absurdity of all the dresses, it was worth noticing that he carried his better than the rest, though he loathed it as much as any of them. He was a gentleman, and a very handsome man, and could not help unconsciously wearing even his preposterous robe as it should be worn. He spoke quickly, but with the slight initial hesitation he always showed in addressing the King, due to suppressing an impulse to address his old acquaintance in the old way.

'Your Majesty – pray forgive my intrusion. It is about this man in Pump Street. I see you have Buck here, so you have probably heard what is necessary. I – '

The King swept his eyes anxiously round the room, which now blazed with the trappings of three cities.

'There is one thing necessary,' he said.

'Yes, your Majesty,' said Mr Wilson of Bayswater, a little eagerly. 'What does yer Majesty think necessary?'

'A little yellow,' said the King, firmly. 'Send for the Provost of West Kensington.'

Amid some materialistic protests he was sent for, and arrived with his yellow halberdiers in his saffron robes, wiping his forehead with a handkerchief. After all, placed as he was, he had a good deal to say on the matter.

'Welcome, West Kensington,' said the King. 'I have long wished to see you touching that matter of the Hammersmith land to the south of the Rowton House. Will you hold it feudally from the Provost of Hammersmith? You have only to do him homage by putting his left arm in his overcoat and then marching home in state.'

'No, your Majesty; I'd rather not,' said the Provost of West Kensington, who was a pale young man with a fair moustache and whiskers, who kept a successful dairy.

The King struck him heartily on the shoulder.

'The fierce old West Kensington blood,' he said; 'they are not wise who ask it to do homage.'

Then he glanced again round the room. It was full of a roaring sunset of colour, and he enjoyed the sight, possible to so few artists – the sight of his own dreams moving and blazing before him. In the foreground the yellow of the West Kensington liveries outlined itself against the dark blue draperies of South Kensington. The crests of these again brightened suddenly into green as the almost woodland colours of Bayswater rose behind them. And over and behind all, the great purple plumes of North Kensington showed almost funereal and black.

'There is something lacking,' said the King – 'something lacking. What can – Ah, there it is! there it is!'

In the doorway had appeared a new figure, a herald in flaming red. He cried in a loud but unemotional voice: 'The Lord High Provost of Notting Hill desires an audience.'

CHAPTER 3

Enter a Lunatic

The King of the Fairies, who was, it is to be presumed, the godfather of King Auberon, must have been very favourable on this particular day to his fantastic godchild, for with the entrance of the guard of the Provost of Notting Hill there was a certain more or less inexplicable addition to his delight. The wretched navvies and sandwich-men who carried the colours of Bayswater or South Kensington, engaged merely for the day to satisfy the Royal hobby, slouched into the room with a comparatively hangdog air, and a great part of the King's intellectual pleasure consisted in the contrast between the arrogance of their swords and feathers and the meek misery of their faces. But these Notting Hill halberdiers in their red tunics belted with gold had the air rather of an absurd gravity. They seemed, so to speak, to be taking part in the joke. They marched and wheeled into position with an almost startling dignity and discipline.

They carried a yellow banner with a great red lion, named by the King as the Notting Hill emblem, after a small public-house in the neighbourhood, which he once frequented.

Between the two lines of his followers there advanced towards the King a tall, red-haired young man, with high features and bold blue eyes. He would have been called handsome, but that a certain indefinable air of his nose being too big for his face, and his feet for his legs, gave him a look of awkwardness and extreme youth. His robes were red, according to the King's heraldry, and, alone among the Provosts, he was girt with a great sword. This was Adam Wayne, the intractable Provost of Notting Hill.

The King flung himself back in his chair, and rubbed his hands.

'What a day, what a day!' he said to himself. 'Now there'll be a row. I'd no idea it would be such fun as it is. These Provosts are so very indignant, so very reasonable, so very right. This fellow, by the look in his eyes, is even more indignant than the rest. No sign in those large blue eyes, at any rate, of ever having heard of a joke. He'll remonstrate with the others, and they'll remonstrate with him, and they'll all make themselves sumptuously happy remonstrating with me.'

'Welcome, my Lord,' he said aloud. 'What news from the Hill of a Hundred Legends? What have you for the ear of your King? I know that troubles have arisen between you and these others, our cousins, but these troubles it shall be our pride to compose. And I doubt not, and cannot doubt, that your love for me is not less tender, no less ardent, than theirs.'

Mr Buck made a bitter face, and James Barker's nostrils curled; Wilson began to giggle faintly, and the Provost of West Kensington followed in a smothered way. But the big blue eyes of Adam Wayne never changed, and he called out in an odd, boyish voice down the hall: 'I bring homage to my King. I bring him the only thing I have – my sword.'

And with a great gesture he flung it down on the ground, and knelt on one knee behind it.

There was a dead silence.

'I beg your pardon,' said the King, blankly.

'You speak well, sire,' said Adam Wayne, 'as you ever speak, when you say that my love is not less than the love of these. Small would it be if it were not more. For I am the heir of your scheme – the child of the great Charter. I stand here for the rights the Charter gave me, and I swear, by your sacred crown, that where I stand, I stand fast.'

The eyes of all five men stood out of their heads.

Then Buck said, in his jolly, jarring voice: 'Is the whole world mad?'

The King sprang to his feet, and his eyes blazed.

'Yes,' he cried, in a voice of exultation, 'the whole world is mad, but Adam Wayne and me. It is true as death what I told you long ago, James Barker, seriousness sends men mad. You are mad, because you care for politics, as mad as a man who collects tram tickets. Buck is mad, because he cares for money, as mad as a man who lives on opium. Wilson is mad, because he thinks himself right, as mad as a man who thinks himself God Almighty. The Provost of West Kensington is mad, because he thinks he is respectable, as mad as a man who thinks he is a chicken. All men are mad but the humorist, who cares for nothing and possesses everything. I thought that there was only one humorist in England. Fools! – dolts! – open your cows' eyes; there are two! In Notting Hill – in that unpromising elevation – there has been born an artist! You thought to spoil my joke, and bully me out of it, by becoming more and more modern, more and more practical, more and more bustling and rational. Oh, what a feast it was to answer you by becoming more and more august, more and more gracious, more and more ancient and mellow! But this lad has seen how to bowl me out. He has answered me back, vaunt for vaunt, rhetoric for rhetoric. He has lifted the only shield I cannot break, the shield of an impenetrable pomposity. Listen to him. You have come, my Lord, about Pump Street?'

'About the city of Notting Hill,' answered Wayne, proudly, 'of which Pump Street is a living and rejoicing part.'

'Not a very large part,' said Barker, contemptuously.

'That which is large enough for the rich to covet,' said Wayne, drawing up his head, 'is large enough for the poor to defend.'

The King slapped both his legs, and waved his feet for a second in the air.

'Every respectable person in Notting Hill,' cut in Buck, with his cold, coarse voice, 'is for us and against you. I have plenty of friends in Notting Hill.'

'Your friends are those who have taken your gold for other men's hearthstones, my Lord Buck,' said Provost Wayne. 'I can well believe they are your friends.'

'They've never sold dirty toys, anyhow,' said Buck, laughing shortly.

'They've sold dirtier things,' said Wayne, calmly: 'they have sold themselves.'

'It's no good, my Buckling,' said the King, rolling about on his chair. 'You can't cope with this chivalrous eloquence. You can't cope with an artist. You can't cope with the humorist of Notting Hill. Oh, *Nunc dimittis* – that I have lived to see this day! Provost Wayne, you stand firm?'

'Let them wait and see,' said Wayne. 'If I stood firm before, do you think I shall weaken now that I have seen the face of the King? For I fight for something greater, if greater there can be, than the hearthstones of my people and the Lordship of the Lion. I fight for your royal vision, for the great dream you dreamt of the League of the Free Cities. You have given me this liberty. If I had been a beggar and you had flung me a coin, if I had been a peasant in a dance and you had flung me a favour, do you think I would have let it be taken by any ruffians on the road? This leadership and liberty of Notting Hill is a gift from your Majesty, and if it is taken from me, by God! it shall be taken in battle, and the noise of that battle shall be heard in the flats of Chelsea and in the studios of St John's Wood.'

'It is too much – it is too much,' said the King. 'Nature is weak. I must speak to you, brother artist, without further disguise. Let me ask you a solemn question. Adam Wayne, Lord High Provost of Notting Hill, don't you think it splendid?'

'Splendid!' cried Adam Wayne. 'It has the splendour of God.'

'Bowled out again,' said the King. 'You will keep up the pose. Funnily, of course, it is serious. But seriously, isn't it funny?'

'What?' asked Wayne, with the eyes of a baby.

'Hang it all, don't play any more. The whole business – the Charter of the Cities. Isn't it immense?'

'Immense is no unworthy word for that glorious design.'

'Oh, hang you! But, of course, I see. You want me to clear the room of these reasonable sows. You want the two humorists alone together. Leave us, gentlemen.'

Buck threw a sour look at Barker, and at a sullen signal the whole pageant of blue and green, of red, gold, and purple, rolled out of the room, leaving only two in the great hall, the King sitting in his seat on the dais, and the red-clad figure still kneeling on the floor before his fallen sword.

The King bounded down the steps and smacked Provost Wayne on the back.

'Before the stars were made,' he cried, 'we were made for each other. It is too beautiful. Think of the valiant independence of Pump Street. That is the real thing. It is the deification of the ludicrous.'

The kneeling figure sprang to his feet with a fierce stagger.

'Ludicrous!' he cried, with a fiery face.

'Oh, come, come,' said the King, impatiently, 'you needn't keep it up with me. The augurs must wink sometimes from sheer fatigue of the eyelids. Let us enjoy this for half an hour, not as actors, but as dramatic critics. Isn't it a joke?'

Adam Wayne looked down like a boy, and answered in a constrained voice: 'I do not understand your Majesty. I cannot believe that while I fight for your royal charter your Majesty deserts me for these dogs of the gold hunt.'

'Oh, damn your – But what's this? What the devil's this?'

The King stared into the young Provost's face, and in the twilight of the room began to see that his face was quite white and his lip shaking.

'What in God's name is the matter?' cried Auberon, holding his wrist.

Wayne flung back his face, and the tears were shining on it.

'I am only a boy,' he said, 'but it's true. I would paint the Red Lion on my shield if I had only my blood.'

King Auberon dropped the hand and stood without stirring, thunderstruck.

'My God in Heaven!' he said; 'is it possible that there is within the four seas of Britain a man who takes Notting Hill seriously?'

'And my God in Heaven!' said Wayne passionately; 'is it possible that there is within the four seas of Britain a man who does not take it seriously?'

The King said nothing, but merely went back up the steps of the dais, like a man dazed. He fell back in his chair again and kicked his heels.

'If this sort of thing is to go on,' he said weakly, 'I shall begin to doubt the superiority of art to life. In Heaven's name, do not play with me. Do you really mean that you are – God help me! – a Notting Hill patriot; that you are – ?'

Wayne made a violent gesture, and the King soothed him wildly.

'All right – all right – I see you are; but let me take it in. You do really propose to fight these modern improvers with their boards and inspectors and surveyors and all the rest of it?'

'Are they so terrible?' asked Wayne, scornfully.

The King continued to stare at him as if he were a human curiosity.

'And I suppose,' he said, 'that you think that the dentists and small tradesmen and maiden ladies who inhabit Notting Hill, will rally with war-hymns to your standard?'

'If they have blood they will,' said the Provost.

'And I suppose,' said the King, with his head back among the cushions, 'that it never crossed your mind that' – his voice seemed to lose itself luxuriantly – 'never crossed your mind that anyone ever thought that the idea of a Notting Hill idealism was – er – slightly – slightly ridiculous?'

'Of course they think so,' said Wayne. 'What was the meaning of mocking the prophets?'

'Where,' asked the King, leaning forward – 'where in Heaven's name did you get this miraculously inane idea?'

'You have been my tutor, Sire,' said the Provost, 'in all that is high and honourable.'

'Eh?' said the King.

'It was your Majesty who first stirred my dim patriotism into flame. Ten years ago, when I was a boy (I am only nineteen), I was playing on the slope of Pump Street, with a wooden sword and a paper helmet, dreaming of great wars. In an angry trance I struck out with my sword, and stood petrified, for I saw that I had struck you, Sire, my King, as you wandered in a noble secrecy, watching over your people's welfare. But I need have had no fear. Then was I taught to understand Kingliness. You neither shrank nor frowned. You summoned no guards. You invoked no punishments. But in august and burning words, which are written in my soul, never to be erased, you told me ever to turn my sword against the enemies of my inviolate city. Like a priest pointing to the altar, you pointed to the hill of Notting. "So long," you said, "as you are ready to die for the sacred mountain, even if it were ringed with all the armies of Bayswater." I have not forgotten the words, and I have reason now to remember them, for the hour is come and the crown of your prophecy. The sacred hill is ringed with the armies of Bayswater, and I am ready to die.'

The King was lying back in his chair, a kind of wreck.

'Oh, Lord, Lord, Lord,' he murmured, 'what a life! what a life! All my work! I seem to have done it all. So you're the red-haired boy that hit me in the waistcoat. What have I done? God, what have I done? I thought I would have a joke, and I have created a passion. I tried to compose a burlesque, and it seems to be turning halfway through into an epic. What is to be done with such a world? In the Lord's name, wasn't the joke broad and bold enough? I abandoned my subtle humour to amuse you, and I seem to have brought tears to your eyes. What's to be done with people when you write a pantomime for them – call the sausages classic festoons, and the policeman cut in two a tragedy of public duty? But why am I talking? Why am I asking questions of a nice young gentleman who is totally mad? What is the good of it? What is the good of anything? Oh, Lord! Oh, Lord!'

Suddenly he pulled himself upright.

'Don't you really think the sacred Notting Hill at all absurd?'

'Absurd?' asked Wayne, blankly. 'Why should I?'

The King stared back equally blankly.

'I beg your pardon?' he said.

'Notting Hill,' said the Provost, simply, 'is a rise or high ground of the common earth, on which men have built houses to live, in which they are born, fall in love, pray, marry, and die. Why should I think it absurd?'

The King smiled.

'Because, my Leonidas – ' he began, then suddenly, he knew not how, found his mind was a total blank. After all, why was it absurd? Why was it absurd? He felt as if the floor of his mind had given way. He felt as all men feel when their first principles are hit hard with a question. Barker always felt so when the King said, 'Why trouble about politics?'

The King's thoughts were in a kind of rout; he could not collect them.

'It is generally felt to be a little funny,' he said vaguely.

'I suppose,' said Adam, turning on him with a fierce suddenness – 'I suppose you fancy crucifixion was a serious affair?'

'Well, I – ' began Auberon – 'I admit I have generally thought it had its graver side.'

'Then you are wrong,' said Wayne, with incredible violence. 'Crucifixion is comic. It is exquisitely diverting. It was an absurd and obscene kind of impaling reserved for people who were made to be laughed at – for slaves and provincials, for dentists and small tradesmen, as you would say. I have seen the grotesque gallows-shape, which the little Roman gutter-boys scribbled on walls as a vulgar joke, blazing on the pinnacles of the temples of the world. And shall I turn back?'

The King made no answer.

Adam went on, his voice ringing in the roof.

'This laughter with which men tyrannise is not the great power you think it. Peter was crucified, and crucified head downwards. What could be funnier than the idea of a respectable old Apostle upside down? What could be more in the style of your modern humour? But what was the good of it? Upside down or right side up, Peter was Peter to mankind. Upside down he still hangs over Europe, and millions move and breathe only in the life of his Church.'

King Auberon got up absently.

'There is something in what you say,' he said. 'You seem to have been thinking, young man.'

'Only feeling, sire,' answered the Provost. 'I was born, like other men, in a spot of the earth which I loved because I had played boys' games there, and fallen in love, and talked with my friends through nights that were nights of the gods. And I feel the riddle. These little gardens where we told our loves.

These streets where we brought out our dead. Why should they be commonplace? Why should they be absurd? Why should it be grotesque to say that a pillar-box is poetic when for a year I could not see a red pillar-box against the yellow evening in a certain street without being wracked with something of which God keeps the secret, but which is stronger than sorrow or joy? Why should anyone be able to raise a laugh by saying "the Cause of Notting Hill"? – Notting Hill where thousands of immortal spirits blaze with alternate hope and fear.'

Auberon was flicking dust off his sleeve with quite a new seriousness on his face, distinct from the owlish solemnity which was the pose of his humour.

'It is very difficult,' he said at last. 'It is a damned difficult thing. I see what you mean; I agree with you even up to a point – or I should like to agree with you, if I were young enough to be a prophet and poet. I feel a truth in everything you say until you come to the words "Notting Hill". And then I regret to say that the old Adam awakes roaring with laughter and makes short work of the new Adam, whose name is Wayne.'

For the first time Provost Wayne was silent, and stood gazing dreamily at the floor. Evening was closing in, and the room had grown darker.

'I know,' he said, in a strange, almost sleepy voice, 'there is truth in what you say, too. It is hard not to laugh at the common names – I only say we should not. I have thought of a remedy; but such thoughts are rather terrible.'

'What thoughts?' asked Auberon.

The Provost of Notting Hill seemed to have fallen into a kind of trance; in his eyes was an elvish light.

'I know of a magic wand, but it is a wand that only one or two may rightly use, and only seldom. It is a fairy wand of great fear, stronger than those who use it – often frightful, often wicked to use. But whatever is touched with it is never again wholly common; whatever is touched with it takes a magic from outside the world. If I touch, with this fairy wand, the railways and the roads of Notting Hill, men will love them, and be afraid of them for ever.'

'What the devil are you talking about?' asked the King.

'It has made mean landscapes magnificent, and hovels outlast cathedrals,' went on the madman. 'Why should it not make lamp posts fairer than Greek lamps; and an omnibus-ride like a painted ship? The touch of it is the finger of a strange perfection.'

'What is your wand?' cried the King, impatiently.

'There it is,' said Wayne; and pointed to the floor, where his sword lay flat and shining.

'The sword!' cried the King; and sprang up straight on the dais.

'Yes, yes,' cried Wayne, hoarsely. 'The things touched by that are not vulgar; the things touched by that – '

King Auberon made a gesture of horror.

'You will shed blood for that!' he cried. 'For a cursed point of view – '

'Oh, you kings, you kings!' cried out Adam, in a burst of scorn. 'How humane you are, how tender, how considerate! You will make war for a frontier, or the imports of a foreign harbour; you will shed blood for the precise duty on lace, or the salute to an admiral. But for the things that make life itself worthy or miserable – how humane you are! I say here, and I know well what I speak of, there were never any necessary wars but the religious wars. There were never any just wars but the religious wars. There were never any humane wars but the religious wars. For these men were fighting for something that claimed, at least, to be the happiness of a man, the virtue of a man. A Crusader thought, at least, that Islam hurt the soul of every man, king or tinker, that it could really capture. I think Buck and Barker and these rich vultures hurt the soul of every man, hurt every inch of the ground, hurt every brick of the houses, that they can really capture. Do you think I have no right to fight for Notting Hill, you whose English Government has so often fought for tomfooleries? If, as your rich friends say, there are no gods, and the skies are dark above us, what should a man fight for, but the place where he had the Eden of childhood and the short heaven of first love? If no temples and no scriptures are sacred, what is sacred if a man's own youth is not sacred?'

The King walked a little restlessly up and down the dais.

'It is hard,' he said, biting his lips, 'to assent to a view so desperate – so responsible . . . '

As he spoke, the door of the audience chamber fell ajar, and through the aperture came, like the sudden chatter of a bird, the high, nasal, but well-bred voice of Barker.

'I said to him quite plainly – the public interests – '

Auberon turned on Wayne with violence.

'What the devil is all this? What am I saying? What are you saying? Have you hypnotised me? Curse your uncanny blue eyes! Let me go. Give me back my sense of humour. Give it me back – give it me back, I say!'

'I solemnly assure you,' said Wayne, uneasily, with a gesture, as if feeling all over himself, 'that I haven't got it.'

The King fell back in his chair, and went into a roar of Rabelaisian laughter.

'I don't think you have,' he cried.

BOOK THREE

CHAPTER I

The Mental Condition of Adam Wayne

A little while after the King's accession a small book of poems appeared, called 'Hymns on the Hill'. They were not good poems, nor was the book successful, but it attracted a certain amount of attention from one particular school of critics. The King himself, who was a member of the school, reviewed it in his capacity of literary critic to 'Straight from the Stables', a sporting journal. They were known as the Hammock School, because it had been calculated malignantly by an enemy that no less than thirteen of their delicate criticisms had begun with the words, 'I read this book in a hammock: half asleep in the sleepy sunlight, I . . . '; after that there were important differences. Under these conditions they liked everything, but especially everything silly. 'Next to authentic goodness in a book,' they said – 'next to authentic goodness in a book (and that, alas! we never find) we desire a rich badness.' Thus it happened that their praise (as indicating the presence of a rich badness) was not universally sought after, and authors became a little disquieted when they found the eye of the Hammock School fixed upon them with peculiar favour.

The peculiarity of 'Hymns on the Hill' was the celebration of the poetry of London as distinct from the poetry of the country. This sentiment or affectation was, of course, not uncommon in the twentieth century, nor was it, although sometimes exaggerated, and sometimes artificial, by any means without a great truth at its root, for there is one respect in which a town must be more poetical than the country, since it is closer to the spirit of man; for London, if it be not one of the masterpieces of man, is at least one of his sins. A street is really more poetical than a meadow, because a street has a secret. A street is going somewhere, and a meadow nowhere. But, in the case of the book called 'Hymns on the Hill', there was another peculiarity, which the King pointed out with great acumen in his review. He was naturally interested in the matter, for he had himself published a volume of lyrics about London under his pseudonym of 'Daisy Daydream'.

This difference, as the King pointed out, consisted in the fact that, while mere artificers like 'Daisy Daydream' (on whose elaborate style the King, over his signature of 'Thunderbolt', was perhaps somewhat too severe) thought to praise London by comparing it to the country – using nature, that is, as a background from which all poetical images had to be drawn – the more robust author of 'Hymns on the Hill' praised the country, or nature, by comparing it to the town, and used the town itself as a background. 'Take,' said the critic, 'the typically feminine lines, "To the Inventor of the Hansom Cab":

> "Poet, whose cunning carved this amorous shell,
> Where twain may dwell."

'Surely,' wrote the King, 'no one but a woman could have written those lines. A woman has always a weakness for nature; with her art is only beautiful as an echo or shadow of it. She is praising the hansom cab by theme and theory, but her soul is still a child by the sea, picking up shells. She can never be utterly of the town, as a man can; indeed, do we not speak (with sacred propriety) of "a man about town"? Who ever spoke of a woman about town? However much, physically, "about town" a woman may be, she still models herself on nature; she tries to carry nature with her; she bids grasses to grow on her head, and furry beasts to bite her about the throat. In the heart of a dim city, she models her hat on a flaring cottage garden of flowers. We, with our nobler civic sentiment, model ours on a chimney pot; the ensign of civilisation. And rather than be without birds, she will commit massacre, that she may turn her head into a tree, with dead birds to sing on it.'

This kind of thing went on for several pages, and then the critic remembered his subject, and returned to it.

> 'Poet, whose cunning carved this amorous shell,
> Where twain may dwell.'

'The peculiarity of these fine though feminine lines,' continued 'Thunderbolt', 'is, as we have said, that they praise the hansom cab by comparing it to the shell, to a natural thing. Now, hear the author of "Hymns on the Hill", and how he deals with the same subject. In his fine nocturne, entitled "The Last Omnibus" he relieves the rich and poignant melancholy of the theme by a sudden sense of rushing at the end:

> "The wind round the old street corner
> Swung sudden and quick as a cab."

'Here the distinction is obvious. "Daisy Daydream" thinks it a great compliment to a hansom cab to be compared to one of the spiral chambers of the sea. And the author of "Hymns on the Hill" thinks it a great compliment to the immortal whirlwind to be compared to a hackney coach. He surely is the real admirer of London. We have no space to speak of all his perfect applications of the idea; of the poem in which, for instance, a lady's eyes are compared, not to stars, but to two perfect street lamps guiding the wanderer. We have no space to speak of the fine lyric, recalling the Elizabethan spirit, in which the poet, instead of saying that the rose and the lily contend in her complexion, says, with a purer modernism, that the red omnibus of Hammersmith and the white omnibus of Fulham fight there for the mastery. How perfect the image of two contending omnibuses!'

Here, somewhat abruptly, the review concluded, probably because the King had to send off his copy at that moment, as he was in some want of money. But the King was a very good critic, whatever he may have been as King, and he had, to a considerable extent, hit the right nail on the head. 'Hymns on the Hill' was not at all like the poems originally published in praise of the poetry of London. And the reason was that it was really written by a man who had seen nothing else but London, and who regarded it, therefore, as the universe. It was written by a raw, red-headed lad of seventeen, named Adam Wayne, who had been born in Notting Hill. An accident in his seventh year prevented his being taken away to the seaside, and thus his whole life had been passed in his own Pump Street, and in its neighbourhood. And the consequence was, that he saw the street lamps as things quite as eternal as the stars; the two fires were mingled. He saw the houses as things enduring, like the mountains, and so he wrote about them as one would write about mountains. Nature puts on a disguise when she speaks to every man; to this man she put on the disguise of Notting Hill. Nature would mean to a poet born in the Cumberland hills, a stormy skyline and sudden rocks. Nature would mean to a poet born in the Essex flats, a waste of splendid waters and splendid sunsets. So nature meant to this man Wayne a line of violet roofs and lemon lamps, the chiaroscuro of the town. He did not think it clever or funny to praise the shadows and colours of the town; he had seen no other shadows or colours, and so he praised them – because they were shadows and colours. He saw all this because he was a poet, though in practice a bad poet. It is too often forgotten that just as a bad man is nevertheless a man, so a bad poet is nevertheless a poet.

Mr Wayne's little volume of verse was a complete failure; and he submitted to the decision of fate with a quite rational humility, went back to his work, which was that of a draper's assistant, and wrote no more. He still retained his feeling about the town of Notting Hill, because he could not possibly have any other feeling, because it was the back and base of his brain. But he does not seem to have made any particular attempt to express it or insist upon it.

He was a genuine natural mystic, one of those who live on the border of fairyland. But he was perhaps the first to realise how often the boundary of fairyland runs through a crowded city. Twenty feet from him (for he was very short-sighted) the red and white and yellow suns of the gaslights thronged and melted into each other like an orchard of fiery trees, the beginning of the woods of elf-land.

But, oddly enough, it was because he was a small poet that he came to his strange and isolated triumph. It was because he was a failure in literature that he became a portent in English history. He was one of those to whom nature has given the desire without the power of artistic expression. He had been a dumb poet from his cradle. He might have been so to his grave, and carried unuttered into the darkness a treasure of new and sensational song. But he was born under the lucky star of a single coincidence. He happened to be at the head of his dingy municipality at the time of the King's jest, at the time when all municipalities were suddenly commanded to break out into banners and flowers. Out of the long procession of the silent poets, who have been passing since the beginning of the world, this one man found himself in the midst of an heraldic vision, in which he could act and speak and live lyrically. While the author and the victims alike treated the whole matter as a silly public charade, this one man, by taking it seriously, sprang suddenly into a throne of artistic omnipotence. Armour, music, standards, watch-fires, the noise of drums, all the theatrical properties were thrown before him. This one poor rhymster, having burnt his own rhymes, began to live that life of open air and acted poetry of which all the poets of the earth have dreamed in vain; the life for which the Iliad is only a cheap substitute.

Upwards from his abstracted childhood, Adam Wayne had grown strongly and silently in a certain quality or capacity which is in modern cities almost entirely artificial, but which can be natural, and was primarily almost brutally natural in him, the quality or capacity of patriotism. It exists, like other virtues and vices, in a certain undiluted reality. It is not confused with all kinds of other things. A child speaking of his country or his village may make every mistake in Mandeville or tell every lie in Munchausen, but in his statement there will be no psychological lies any more than there can be in a good song. Adam Wayne, as a boy, had for his dull streets in Notting Hill the ultimate and ancient sentiment that went out to Athens or Jerusalem. He knew the secret of the passion, those secrets which make real old national songs sound so strange to our civilisation. He knew that real patriotism tends to sing about sorrows and forlorn hopes much more than about victory. He knew that in proper names themselves is half the poetry of all national poems. Above all, he knew the supreme psychological fact about patriotism, as certain in connection with it as that a fine shame comes to all lovers, the fact that the patriot never under any circumstances boasts of the largeness of his country, but always, and of necessity, boasts of the smallness of it.

All this he knew, not because he was a philosopher or a genius, but because he was a child. Anyone who cares to walk up a side slum like Pump Street, can see a little Adam claiming to be king of a paving-stone. And he will always be proudest if the stone is almost too narrow for him to keep his feet inside it.

It was while he was in such a dream of defensive battle, marking out some strip of street or fortress of steps as the limit of his haughty claim, that the King had met him, and, with a few words flung in mockery, ratified for ever the strange boundaries of his soul. Thenceforward the fanciful idea of the defence of Notting Hill in war became to him a thing as solid as eating or drinking or lighting a pipe. He disposed his meals for it, altered his plans for it, lay awake in the night and went over it again. Two or three shops were to him an arsenal; an area was to him a moat; corners of balconies and turns of stone steps were points for the location of a culverin or an archer. It is almost impossible to convey to any ordinary imagination the degree to which he had transmitted the leaden London landscape to a romantic gold. The process began almost in babyhood, and became habitual like a literal madness. It was felt most keenly at night, when London is really herself, when her lights shine in the dark like the eyes of innumerable cats, and the outline of the dark houses has the bold simplicity of blue hills. But for him the night revealed instead of concealing, and he read all the blank hours of morning and afternoon, by a contradictory phrase, in the light of that darkness. To this man, at any rate, the inconceivable had happened. The artificial city had become to him nature, and he felt the kerbstones and gas-lamps as things as ancient as the sky.

One instance may suffice. Walking along Pump Street with a friend, he said, as he gazed dreamily at the iron fence of a little front garden, 'How those railings stir one's blood!'

His friend, who was also a great intellectual admirer, looked at them painfully, but without any particular emotion. He was so troubled about it that he went back quite a large number of times on quiet evenings and stared at the railings, waiting for something to happen to his blood, but without success. At last he took refuge in asking Wayne himself. He discovered that the ecstasy lay in the one point he had never noticed about the railings even after his six visits – the fact that they were, like the great majority of others – in London, shaped at the top after the manner of a spear. As a child, Wayne had half unconsciously compared them with the spears in pictures of Lancelot and St George, and had grown up under the shadow of the graphic association. Now, whenever he looked at them, they were simply the serried weapons that made a hedge of steel round the sacred homes of Notting Hill. He could not have cleansed his mind of that meaning even if he tried. It was not a fanciful comparison, or anything like it. It would not have been true to say that the familiar railings reminded him of spears; it would have been far truer to say that the familiar spears occasionally reminded him of railings.

A couple of days after his interview with the King, Adam Wayne was pacing like a caged lion in front of five shops that occupied the upper end of the disputed street. They were a grocer's, a chemist's, a barber's, an old curiosity shop and a toy-shop that sold also newspapers. It was these five shops which his childish fastidiousness had first selected as the essentials of the Notting Hill campaign, the citadel of the city. If Notting Hill was the heart of the universe, and Pump Street was the heart of Notting Hill, this was the heart of Pump Street. The fact that they were all small and side by side realised that feeling for a formidable comfort and compactness which, as we have said, was the heart of his patriotism, and of all patriotism. The grocer (who had a wine and spirit licence) was included because he could provision the garrison; the old curiosity shop because it contained enough swords, pistols, partisans, crossbows, and blunderbusses to arm a whole irregular regiment; the toy and paper shop because Wayne thought a free press an essential centre for the soul of Pump Street; the chemist's to cope with outbreaks of disease among the besieged; and the barber's because it was in the middle of all the rest, and the barber's son was an intimate friend and spiritual affinity.

It was a cloudless October evening settling down through purple into pure silver around the roofs and chimneys of the steep little street, which looked black and sharp and dramatic. In the deep shadows the gas-lit shop fronts gleamed like five fires in a row, and before them, darkly outlined like a ghost against some purgatorial furnaces, passed to and fro the tall birdlike figure and eagle nose of Adam Wayne.

He swung his stick restlessly, and seemed fitfully talking to himself.

'There are, after all, enigmas,' he said, 'even to the man who has faith. There are doubts that remain even after the true philosophy is completed in every rung and rivet. And here is one of them. Is the normal human need, the normal human condition, higher or lower than those special states of the soul which call out a doubtful and dangerous glory? Those special powers of knowledge or sacrifice which are made possible only by the existence of evil? Which should come first to our affections, the enduring sanities of peace or the half-maniacal virtues of battle? Which should come first, the man great in the daily round or the man great in emergency? Which should come first, to return to the enigma before me, the grocer or the chemist? Which is more certainly the stay of the city, the swift chivalrous chemist or the benignant all-providing grocer? In such ultimate spiritual doubts it is only possible to choose a side by the higher instincts, and to abide the issue. In any case, I have made my choice. May I be pardoned if I choose wrongly, but I choose the grocer.'

'Good-morning, sir,' said the grocer, who was a middle-aged man, partially bald, with harsh red whiskers and beard, and forehead lined with all the cares of the small tradesman. 'What can I do for you, sir?'

Wayne removed his hat on entering the shop, with a ceremonious gesture, which, slight as it was, made the tradesman eye him with the beginnings of wonder.

'I come, sir,' he said soberly, 'to appeal to your patriotism.'

'Why, sir,' said the grocer, 'that sounds like the times when I was a boy and we used to have elections.'

'You will have them again,' said Wayne, firmly, 'and far greater things. Listen, Mr Mead. I know the temptations which a grocer has to a too cosmopolitan philosophy. I can imagine what it must be to sit all day as you do surrounded with wares from all the ends of the earth, from strange seas that we have never sailed and strange forests that we could not even picture. No Eastern king ever had such argosies or such cargoes coming from the sunrise and the sunset, and Solomon in all his glory was not enriched like one of you. India is at your elbow,' he cried, lifting his voice and pointing his stick at a drawer of rice, the grocer making a movement of some alarm, 'China is before you, Demerara is behind you, America is above your head, and at this very moment, like some old Spanish admiral, you hold Tunis in your hands.'

Mr Mead dropped the box of dates which he was just lifting, and then picked it up again vaguely.

Wayne went on with a heightened colour, but a lowered voice, 'I know, I say, the temptations of so international, so universal a vision of wealth. I know that it must be your danger not to fall like many tradesmen into too dusty and mechanical a narrowness, but rather to be too broad, to be too general, too liberal. If a narrow nationalism be the danger of the pastry-cook, who makes his own wares under his own heavens, no less is cosmopolitanism the danger of the grocer. But I come to you in the name of that patriotism which no wanderings or enlightenments should ever wholly extinguish, and I ask you to remember Notting Hill. For, after all, in this cosmopolitan magnificence, she has played no small part. Your dates may come from the tall palms of Barbary, your sugar from the strange islands of the tropics, your tea from the secret villages of the Empire of the Dragon. That this room might be furnished, forests may have been spoiled under the Southern Cross, and leviathans speared under the Polar Star. But you yourself – surely no inconsiderable treasure – you yourself, the brain that wields these vast interests – you yourself, at least, have grown to strength and wisdom between these grey houses and under this rainy sky. This city which made you, and thus made your fortunes, is threatened with war. Come forth and tell to the ends of the earth this lesson. Oil is from the North and fruits from the South; rices are from India and spices from Ceylon; sheep are from New Zealand and men from Notting Hill.'

The grocer sat for some little while, with dim eyes and his mouth open, looking rather like a fish. Then he scratched the back of his head, and said nothing. Then he said: 'Anything out of the shop, sir?'

Wayne looked round in a dazed way. Seeing a pile of tins of pineapple chunks, he waved his stick generally towards them.

'Yes,' he said; 'I'll take those.'

'All those, sir?' said the grocer, with greatly increased interest.

'Yes, yes; all those,' replied Wayne, still a little bewildered, like a man splashed with cold water.

'Very good, sir; thank you, sir,' said the grocer with animation. 'You may count upon my patriotism, sir.'

'I count upon it already,' said Wayne, and passed out into the gathering night.

The grocer put the box of dates back in its place.

'What a nice fellow he is!' he said. 'It's odd how often they are nice. Much nicer than those as are all right.'

Meanwhile Adam Wayne stood outside the glowing chemist's shop, unmistakably wavering.

'What a weakness it is!' he muttered. 'I have never got rid of it from childhood – the fear of this magic shop. The grocer is rich, he is romantic, he is poetical in the truest sense, but he is not – no, he is not supernatural. But the chemist! All the other shops stand in Notting Hill, but this stands in Elf-land. Look at those great burning bowls of colour. It must be from them that God paints the sunsets. It is superhuman, and the superhuman is all the more uncanny when it is beneficent. That is the root of the fear of God. I am afraid. But I must be a man and enter.'

He was a man, and entered. A short, dark young man was behind the counter with spectacles, and greeted him with a bright but entirely business-like smile.

'A fine evening, sir,' he said.

'Fine indeed, strange Father,' said Adam, stretching his hands somewhat forward. 'It is on such clear and mellow nights that your shop is most itself. Then they appear most perfect, those moons of green and gold and crimson, which from afar oft guide the pilgrim of pain and sickness to this house of merciful witchcraft.'

'Can I get you anything?' asked the chemist.

'Let me see,' said Wayne, in a friendly but vague manner. 'Let me have some sal volatile.'

'Eightpence, tenpence, or one and sixpence a bottle?' said the young man, genially.

'One and six – one and six,' replied Wayne, with a wild submissiveness. 'I come to ask you, Mr Bowles, a terrible question.'

He paused and collected himself.

'It is necessary,' he muttered – 'it is necessary to be tactful, and to suit the appeal to each profession in turn.'

'I come,' he resumed aloud, 'to ask you a question which goes to the roots of your miraculous toils. Mr Bowles, shall all this witchery cease?' And he waved his stick around the shop.

Meeting with no answer, he continued with animation: 'In Notting Hill we have felt to its core the elfish mystery of your profession. And now Notting Hill itself is threatened.'

'Anything more, sir?' asked the chemist.

'Oh,' said Wayne, somewhat disturbed – 'oh, what is it chemists sell? Quinine, I think. Thank you. Shall it be destroyed? I have met these men of Bayswater and North Kensington – Mr Bowles, they are materialists. They see no witchery in your work, even when it is wrought within their own borders. They think the chemist is commonplace. They think him human.'

The chemist appeared to pause, only a moment, to take in the insult, and immediately said: 'And the next article, please?'

'Alum,' said the Provost, wildly. 'I resume. It is in this sacred town alone that your priesthood is reverenced. Therefore, when you fight for us you fight not only for yourself, but for everything you typify. You fight not only for Notting Hill, but for Fairyland, for as surely as Buck and Barker and such men hold sway, the sense of Fairyland in some strange manner diminishes.'

'Anything more, sir?' asked Mr Bowles, with unbroken cheerfulness.

'Oh yes, jujubes – Gregory powder – magnesia. The danger is imminent. In all this matter I have felt that I fought not merely for my own city (though to that I owe all my blood), but for all places in which these great ideas could prevail. I am fighting not merely for Notting Hill, but for Bayswater itself; for North Kensington itself. For if the gold-hunters prevail, these also will lose all their ancient sentiments and all the mystery of their national soul. I know I can count upon you.'

'Oh yes, sir,' said the chemist, with great animation; 'we are always glad to oblige a good customer.'

Adam Wayne went out of the shop with a deep sense of fulfilment of soul.

'It is so fortunate,' he said, 'to have tact, to be able to play upon the peculiar talents and specialities, the cosmopolitanism of the grocer and the world-old necromancy of the chemist. Where should I be without tact?'

CHAPTER 2

The Remarkable Mr Turnbull

After two more interviews with shopmen, however, the patriot's confidence in his own psychological diplomacy began vaguely to wane. Despite the care with which he considered the peculiar rationale and the peculiar glory of each separate shop, there seemed to be something unresponsive about the shopmen. Whether it was a dark resentment against the uninitiate for peeping into their masonic magnificence, he could not quite conjecture.

His conversation with the man who kept the shop of curiosities had begun encouragingly. The man who kept the shop of curiosities had, indeed, enchanted him with a phrase. He was standing drearily at the door of his shop, a wrinkled man with a grey pointed beard, evidently a gentleman who had come down in the world.

'And how does your commerce go, you strange guardian of the past?' said Wayne, affably.

'Well, sir, not very well,' replied the man, with that patient voice of his class which is one of the most heart-breaking things in the world. 'Things are terribly quiet.'

Wayne's eyes shone suddenly.

'A great saying,' he said, 'worthy of a man whose merchandise is human history. Terribly quiet; that is in two words the spirit of this age, as I have felt it from my cradle. I sometimes wondered how many other people felt the oppression of this union between quietude and terror. I see blank well-ordered streets and men in black moving about inoffensively, sullenly. It goes on day after day, day after day, and nothing happens; but to me it is like a dream from which I might wake screaming. To me the straightness of our life is the straightness of a thin cord stretched tight. Its stillness is terrible. It might snap with a noise like thunder. And you who sit, amid the debris of the great wars, you who sit, as it were, upon a battlefield, you know that war was less terrible than this evil peace; you know that the idle lads who carried those swords under Francis or Elizabeth, the rude Squire or Baron who swung that mace about in Picardy or Northumberland battles, may have been terribly noisy, but were not like us, terribly quiet.'

Whether it was a faint embarrassment of conscience as to the original source and date of the weapons referred to, or merely an engrained depression, the guardian of the past looked, if anything, a little more worried.

'But I do not think,' continued Wayne, 'that this horrible silence of modernity will last, though I think for the present it will increase. What a farce is this modern liberality! Freedom of speech means practically, in our modern civilisation, that we must only talk about unimportant things. We must not talk about religion, for that is illiberal; we must not talk about bread and cheese, for that is talking shop; we must not talk about death, for that is depressing; we must not talk about birth, for that is indelicate. It cannot last. Something must break this strange indifference, this strange dreamy egoism, this strange loneliness of millions in a crowd. Something must break it. Why should it not be you and I? Can you do nothing else but guard relics?'

The shopman wore a gradually clearing expression, which would have led those unsympathetic with the cause of the Red Lion to think that the last sentence was the only one to which he had attached any meaning.

'I am rather old to go into a new business,' he said, 'and I don't quite know what to be, either.'

'Why not,' said Wayne, gently having reached the crisis of his delicate persuasion – 'why not be a colonel?'

It was at this point, in all probability, that the interview began to yield more disappointing results. The man appeared inclined at first to regard the suggestion of becoming a colonel as outside the sphere of immediate and relevant discussion. A long exposition of the inevitable war of independence, coupled with the purchase of a doubtful sixteenth-century sword for an exaggerated price, seemed to resettle matters. Wayne left the shop, however, somewhat infected with the melancholy of its owner.

That melancholy was completed at the barber's.

'Shaving, sir?' enquired that artist from inside his shop.

'War!' replied Wayne, standing on the threshold.

'I beg your pardon,' said the other, sharply.

'War!' said Wayne, warmly. 'But not for anything inconsistent with the beautiful and the civilised arts. War for beauty. War for society. War for peace. A great chance is offered you of repelling that slander which, in defiance of the lives of so many artists, attributes poltroonery to those who beautify and polish the surface of our lives. Why should not hairdressers be heroes? Why should not – '

'Now, you get out,' said the barber, irascibly. 'We don't want any of your sort here. You get out.'

And he came forward with the desperate annoyance of a mild person when enraged.

Adam Wayne laid his hand for a moment on the sword, then dropped it.

'Notting Hill,' he said, 'will need her bolder sons'; and he turned gloomily to the toy-shop.

It was one of those queer little shops so constantly seen in the side streets of London, which must be called toy-shops only because toys upon the whole predominate; for the remainder of goods seem to consist of almost everything else in the world – tobacco, exercise-books, sweet-stuff, novelettes, halfpenny paper clips, halfpenny pencil sharpeners, bootlaces, and cheap fireworks. It also sold newspapers, and a row of dirty-looking posters hung along the front of it.

'I am afraid,' said Wayne, as he entered, 'that I am not getting on with these tradesmen as I should. Is it that I have neglected to rise to the full meaning of their work? Is there some secret buried in each of these shops which no mere poet can discover?'

He stepped to the counter with a depression which he rapidly conquered as he addressed the man on the other side of it – a man of short stature, and hair prematurely white, and the look of a large baby.

'Sir,' said Wayne, 'I am going from house to house in this street of ours, seeking to stir up some sense of the danger which now threatens our city. Nowhere have I felt my duty so difficult as here. For the toy-shop keeper has to do with all that remains to us of Eden before the first wars began. You sit here meditating continually upon the wants of that wonderful time when every staircase leads to the stars, and every garden-path to the other end of nowhere. Is it thoughtlessly, do you think, that I strike the dark old drum of peril in the paradise of children? But consider a moment; do not condemn me hastily. Even that paradise itself contains the rumour or beginning of that danger, just as the Eden that was made for perfection contained the terrible tree. For judge childhood, even by your own arsenal of its pleasures. You keep bricks; you make yourself thus, doubtless, the witness of the constructive instinct older than the destructive. You keep dolls; you make yourself the priest of that divine idolatry. You keep Noah's Arks; you perpetuate the memory of the salvation of all life as a precious, an irreplaceable thing. But do you keep only, sir, the symbols of this prehistoric sanity, this childish rationality of the earth? Do you not keep more terrible things? What are those boxes, seemingly of lead soldiers, that I see in that glass case? Are they not witnesses to that terror and beauty, that desire for a lovely death, which could not be excluded even from the immortality of Eden? Do not despise the lead soldiers, Mr Turnbull.'

'I don't,' said Mr Turnbull, of the toy-shop, shortly, but with great emphasis.

'I am glad to hear it,' replied Wayne. 'I confess that I feared for my military schemes the awful innocence of your profession. How, I thought to myself, will this man, used only to the wooden swords that give pleasure, think of the steel swords that give pain? But I am at least partly reassured. Your tone suggests to me that I have at least the entry of a gate of your fairyland – the gate through which the soldiers enter, for it cannot be denied – I ought, sir, no longer to deny, that it is of soldiers that I come to speak. Let your gentle employment make you merciful towards the troubles of the world. Let your own silvery experience tone down our sanguine sorrows. For there is war in Notting Hill.'

The little toy-shop keeper sprang up suddenly, slapping his fat hands like two fans on the counter.

'War?' he cried. 'Not really, sir? Is it true? Oh, what a joke! Oh, what a sight for sore eyes!'

Wayne was almost taken aback by this outburst.

'I am delighted,' he stammered. 'I had no notion –'

He sprang out of the way just in time to avoid Mr Turnbull, who took a flying leap over the counter and dashed to the front of the shop.

'You look here, sir,' he said; 'you just look here.'

He came back with two of the torn posters in his hand which were flapping outside his shop.

'Look at those, sir,' he said, and flung them down on the counter.

Wayne bent over them, and read on one:

LAST FIGHTING. REDUCTION OF THE
CENTRAL DERVISH CITY.
REMARKABLE ETC.

On the other he read –

LAST SMALL REPUBLIC ANNEXED.
NICARAGUAN CAPITAL SURRENDERS AFTER
A MONTH'S FIGHTING. GREAT SLAUGHTER.

Wayne bent over them again, evidently puzzled; then he looked at the dates. They were both dated in August fifteen years before.

'Why do you keep these old things?' he said, startled entirely out of his absurd tact of mysticism. 'Why do you hang them outside your shop?'

'Because,' said the other, simply, 'they are the records of the last war. You mentioned war just now. It happens to be my hobby.'

Wayne lifted his large blue eyes with an infantile wonder.

'Come with me,' said Turnbull, shortly, and led him into a parlour at the back of the shop.

In the centre of the parlour stood a large deal table. On it were set rows and rows of the tin and lead soldiers which were part of the shopkeeper's stock. The visitor would have thought nothing of it if it had not been for a certain odd grouping of them, which did not seem either entirely commercial or entirely haphazard.

'You are acquainted, no doubt,' said Turnbull, turning his big eyes upon Wayne – 'you are acquainted, no doubt, with the arrangement of the

American and Nicaraguan troops in the last battle.' And he waved his hand towards the table.

'I am afraid not,' said Wayne. 'I – '

'Ah! you were at that time occupied too much, perhaps, with the Dervish affair. You will find it in this corner.' And he pointed to a part of the floor where there was another arrangement of children's soldiers grouped here and there.

'You seem,' said Wayne, 'to be interested in military matters.'

'I am interested in nothing else,' answered the toy-shop keeper, simply.

Wayne appeared convulsed with a singular, suppressed excitement.

'In that case,' he said, 'I may approach you with an unusual degree of confidence. Touching the matter of the defence of Notting Hill, I – '

'Defence of Notting Hill? Yes, sir. This way, sir,' said Turnbull, with great perturbation. 'Just step into this side room'; and he led Wayne into another apartment, in which the table was entirely covered with an arrangement of children's bricks. A second glance at it told Wayne that the bricks were arranged in the form of a precise and perfect plan of Notting Hill. 'Sir,' said Turnbull, impressively, 'you have, by a kind of accident, hit upon the whole secret of my life. As a boy, I grew up among the last wars of the world, when Nicaragua was taken and the dervishes wiped out. And I adopted it as a hobby, sir, as you might adopt astronomy or bird-stuffing. I had no ill-will to anyone, but I was interested in war as a science, as a game. And suddenly I was bowled out. The big Powers of the world, having swallowed up all the small ones, came to that confounded agreement, and there was no more war. There was nothing more for me to do but to do what I do now – to read the old campaigns in dirty old newspapers, and to work them out with tin soldiers. One other thing had occurred to me. I thought it an amusing fancy to make a plan of how this district of ours ought to be defended if it were ever attacked. It seems to interest you too.'

'If it were ever attacked,' repeated Wayne, awed into an almost mechanical enunciation. 'Mr Turnbull, it is attacked. Thank Heaven, I am bringing to at least one human being the news that is at bottom the only good news to any son of Adam. Your life has not been useless. Your work has not been play. Now, when the hair is already grey on your head, Turnbull, you shall have your youth. God has not destroyed it, He has only deferred it. Let us sit down here, and you shall explain to me this military map of Notting Hill. For you and I have to defend Notting Hill together.'

Mr Turnbull looked at the other for a moment, then hesitated, and then sat down beside the bricks and the stranger. He did not rise again for seven hours, when the dawn broke.

* * *

The headquarters of Provost Adam Wayne and his Commander-in-Chief consisted of a small and somewhat unsuccessful milk-shop at the corner of Pump Street. The blank white morning had only just begun to break over the blank London buildings when Wayne and Turnbull were to be found seated in the cheerless and unswept shop. Wayne had something feminine in his character; he belonged to that class of persons who forget their meals when anything interesting is in hand. He had had nothing for sixteen hours but hurried glasses of milk, and, with a glass standing empty beside him, he was writing and sketching and dotting and crossing out with inconceivable rapidity with a pencil and a piece of paper. Turnbull was of that more masculine type in which a sense of responsibility increases the appetite, and with his sketch-map beside him he was dealing strenuously with a pile of sandwiches in a paper packet, and a tankard of ale from the tavern opposite, whose shutters had just been taken down. Neither of them spoke, and there was no sound in the living stillness except the scratching of Wayne's pencil and the squealing of an aimless-looking cat. At length Wayne broke the silence by saying: 'Seventeen pounds, eight shillings and ninepence.'

Turnbull nodded and put his head in the tankard.

'That,' said Wayne, 'is not counting the five pounds you took yesterday. What did you do with it?'

'Ah, that is rather interesting!' replied Turnbull, with his mouth full. 'I used that five pounds in a kindly and philanthropic act.'

Wayne was gazing with mystification in his queer and innocent eyes.

'I used that five pounds,' continued the other, 'in giving no less than forty little London boys rides in hansom cabs.'

'Are you insane?' asked the Provost.

'It is only my light touch,' returned Turnbull. 'These hansom-cab rides will raise the tone – raise the tone, my dear fellow – of our London youths, widen their horizon, brace their nervous system, make them acquainted with the various public monuments of our great city. Education, Wayne, education. How many excellent thinkers have pointed out that political reform is useless until we produce a cultured populace. So that twenty years hence, when these boys are grown up – '

'Mad!' said Wayne, laying down his pencil; 'and five pounds gone!'

'You are in error,' explained Turnbull. 'You grave creatures can never be brought to understand how much quicker work really goes with the assistance of nonsense and good meals. Stripped of its decorative beauties, my statement was strictly accurate. Last night I gave forty half-crowns to forty little boys, and sent them all over London to take hansom cabs. I told them in every case to tell the cabman to bring them to this spot. In half an hour from now the declaration of war will be posted up. At the same time the cabs will have begun to come in, you will have ordered out the guard, the little boys will drive up in state, we shall commandeer the horses for cavalry, use the cabs for barricade, and give the men the choice between serving in our ranks and detention in our basements and cellars. The little boys we can use as scouts. The main thing is that we start the war with an advantage unknown in all the other armies – horses. And now,' he said, finishing his beer, 'I will go and drill the troops.'

And he walked out of the milk-shop, leaving the Provost staring.

A minute or two afterwards, the Provost laughed. He only laughed once or twice in his life, and then he did it in a queer way as if it were an art he had not mastered. Even he saw something funny in the preposterous coup of the half-crowns and the little boys. He did not see the monstrous absurdity of the whole policy and the whole war. He enjoyed it seriously as a crusade, that is, he enjoyed it far more than any joke can be enjoyed. Turnbull enjoyed it partly as a joke, even more perhaps as a reversion from the things he hated – modernity and monotony and civilisation. To break up the vast machinery of modern life and use the fragments as engines of war, to make the barricade of omnibuses and points of vantage of chimney-pots, was to him a game worth infinite risk and trouble. He had that rational and deliberate preference which will always to the end trouble the peace of the world, the rational and deliberate preference for a short life and a merry one.

CHAPTER 3

The Experiment of Mr Buck

An earnest and eloquent petition was sent up to the King signed with the names of Wilson, Barker, Buck, Swindon, and others. It urged that at the forthcoming conference to be held in his Majesty's presence touching the final disposition of the property in Pump Street, it might be held not inconsistent with political decorum and with the unutterable respect they entertained for his Majesty if they appeared in ordinary morning dress, without the costume decreed for them as Provosts. So it happened that the company appeared at that council in frock-coats and that the King himself limited his love of ceremony to appearing (after his not unusual manner), in evening dress with one order – in this case not the Garter, but the button of the Club of Old Clipper's Best Pals, a decoration obtained (with difficulty) from a halfpenny boys' paper. Thus also it happened that the only spot of colour in the room was Adam Wayne, who entered in great dignity with the great red robes and the great sword.

'We have met,' said Auberon, 'to decide the most arduous of modern problems. May we be successful.' And he sat down gravely.

Buck turned his chair a little, and flung one leg over the other.

'Your Majesty,' he said, quite good-humouredly, 'there is only one thing I can't understand, and that is why this affair is not settled in five minutes. Here's a small property which is worth a thousand to us and is not worth a hundred to anyone else. We offer the thousand. It's not businesslike, I know, for we ought to get it for less, and it's not reasonable and it's not fair on us, but I'm damned if I can see why it's difficult.'

'The difficulty may be very simply stated,' said Wayne. 'You may offer a million and it will be very difficult for you to get Pump Street.'

'But look here, Mr Wayne,' cried Barker, striking in with a kind of cold excitement. 'Just look here. You've no right to take up a position like that. You've a right to stand out for a bigger price, but you aren't doing that. You're refusing what you and every sane man knows to be a splendid offer simply from malice or spite – it must be malice or spite. And that kind of thing is really criminal; it's against the public good. The King's Government would be justified in forcing you.'

With his lean fingers spread on the table, he stared anxiously at Wayne's face, which did not move.

'In forcing you . . . it would,' he repeated.

'It shall,' said Buck, shortly, turning to the table with a jerk. 'We have done our best to be decent.'

Wayne lifted his large eyes slowly.

'Was it my Lord Buck,' he enquired, 'who said that the King of England "shall" do something?'

Buck flushed and said testily: 'I mean it must – it ought to. As I say, we've done our best to be generous; I defy anyone to deny it. As it is, Mr Wayne, I don't want to say a word that's uncivil. I hope it's not uncivil to say that you can be, and ought to be, in gaol. It is criminal to stop public works for a whim. A man might as well burn ten thousand onions in his front garden or bring up his children to run naked in the street, as do what you say you have a right to do. People have been compelled to sell before now. The King could compel you, and I hope he will.'

'Until he does,' said Wayne, calmly, 'the power and government of this great nation is on my side and not yours, and I defy you to defy it.'

'In what sense,' cried Barker, with his feverish eyes and hands, 'is the Government on your side?'

With one ringing movement Wayne unrolled a great parchment on the table. It was decorated down the sides with wild watercolour sketches of vestrymen in crowns and wreaths.

'The Charter of the Cities,' he began.

Buck exploded in a brutal oath and laughed.

'That tomfool's joke. Haven't we had enough –'

'And there you sit,' cried Wayne, springing erect and with a voice like a trumpet, 'with no argument but to insult the King before his face.'

Buck rose also with blazing eyes.

'I am hard to bully,' he began – and the slow tones of the King struck in with incomparable gravity: 'My Lord Buck, I must ask you to remember that your King is present. It is not often that he needs to protect himself among his subjects.'

Barker turned to him with frantic gestures.

'For God's sake don't back up the madman now,' he implored. 'Have your joke another time. Oh, for Heaven's sake – '

'My Lord Provost of South Kensington,' said King Auberon, steadily, 'I do not follow your remarks, which are uttered with a rapidity unusual at Court. Nor do your well-meant efforts to convey the rest with your fingers materially assist me. I say that my Lord Provost of North Kensington, to whom I spoke, ought not in the presence of his Sovereign to speak disrespectfully of his Sovereign's ordinances. Do you disagree?'

Barker turned restlessly in his chair, and Buck cursed without speaking. The King went on in a comfortable voice: 'My Lord Provost of Notting Hill, proceed.'

Wayne turned his blue eyes on the King, and to everyone's surprise there was a look in them not of triumph, but of a certain childish distress.

'I am sorry, your Majesty,' he said; 'I fear I was more than equally to blame with the Lord Provost of North Kensington. We were debating somewhat eagerly, and we both rose to our feet. I did so first, I am ashamed to say. The Provost of North Kensington is, therefore, comparatively innocent. I beseech your Majesty to address your rebuke chiefly, at least, to me. Mr Buck is not innocent, for he did no doubt, in the heat of the moment, speak disrespectfully. But the rest of the discussion he seems to me to have conducted with great good temper.'

Buck looked genuinely pleased, for business men are all simple-minded, and have therefore that degree of communion with fanatics. The King, for some reason, looked, for the first time in his life, ashamed.

'This very kind speech of the Provost of Notting Hill,' began Buck, pleasantly, 'seems to me to show that we have at least got on to a friendly footing. Now come, Mr Wayne. Five hundred pounds have been offered to you for a property you admit not to be worth a hundred. Well, I am a rich man and I won't be outdone in generosity. Let us say fifteen hundred pounds, and have done with it. And let us shake hands.' And he rose, glowing and laughing.

'Fifteen hundred pounds,' whispered Mr Wilson of Bayswater; 'can we do fifteen hundred pounds?'

'I'll stand the racket,' said Buck, heartily. 'Mr Wayne is a gentleman and has spoken up for me. So I suppose the negotiations are at an end.'

Wayne bowed.

'They are indeed at an end. I am sorry I cannot sell you the property.'

'What?' cried Mr Barker, starting to his feet.

'Mr Buck has spoken correctly,' said the King.

'I have, I have,' cried Buck, springing up also; 'I said – '

'Mr Buck has spoken correctly,' said the King; 'the negotiations are at an end.'

All the men at the table rose to their feet; Wayne alone rose without excitement.

'Have I, then,' he said, 'your Majesty's permission to depart? I have given my last answer.'

'You have it,' said Auberon, smiling, but not lifting his eyes from the table. And amid a dead silence the Provost of Notting Hill passed out of the room.

'Well?' said Wilson, turning round to Barker. 'Well?'

Barker shook his head desperately.

'The man ought to be in an asylum,' he said. 'But one thing is clear – we need not bother further about him. The man can be treated as mad.'

'Of course,' said Buck, turning to him with sombre decisiveness. 'You're perfectly right, Barker. He is a good enough fellow, but he can be treated as mad. Let's put it in simple form. Go and tell any twelve men in any town, go and tell any doctor in any town, that there is a man offered fifteen hundred pounds for a thing he could sell commonly for four hundred, and that when asked for a reason for not accepting it he pleads the inviolate sanctity of Notting Hill and calls it the Holy Mountain. What would they say? What more can we have on our side than the common sense of everybody? On what else do all laws rest? I'll tell you, Barker, what's better than any further discussion. Let's send in workmen on the spot to pull down Pump Street. And if old Wayne says a word, arrest him as a lunatic. That's all.'

Barker's eyes kindled.

'I always regarded you, Buck, if you don't mind my saying so, as a very strong man. I'll follow you.'

'So, of course, will I,' said Wilson.

Buck rose again impulsively.

'Your Majesty,' he said, glowing with popularity, 'I beseech your Majesty to consider favourably the proposal to which we have committed ourselves. Your Majesty's leniency, our own offers, have fallen in vain on that extraordinary man. He may be right. He may be God. He may be the devil. But we think it, for practical purposes, more probable that he is off his head. Unless that assumption were acted on, all human affairs would go to pieces. We act on it, and we propose to start operations in Notting Hill at once.'

The King leaned back in his chair.

'The Charter of the Cities . . . ' he said with a rich intonation.

But Buck, being finally serious, was also cautious, and did not again make the mistake of disrespect.

'Your Majesty,' he said, bowing, 'I am not here to say a word against anything your Majesty has said or done. You are a far better educated man than I, and no doubt there were reasons, upon intellectual grounds, for those proceedings. But may I ask you and appeal to your common good-nature for a sincere answer? When you drew up the Charter of the Cities, did you contemplate the rise of a man like Adam Wayne? Did you expect that the Charter – whether it was an experiment, or a scheme of decoration, or a joke – could ever really come to this – to stopping a vast scheme of ordinary business, to shutting up a road, to spoiling the chances of cabs, omnibuses, railway stations, to disorganising half a city, to risking a kind of civil war? Whatever were your objects, were they that?'

Barker and Wilson looked at him admiringly; the King more admiringly still.

'Provost Buck,' said Auberon, 'you speak in public uncommonly well. I give you your point with the magnanimity of an artist. My scheme did not include the appearance of Mr Wayne. Alas! would that my poetic power had been great enough.'

'I thank your Majesty,' said Buck, courteously, but quickly. 'Your Majesty's statements are always clear and studied; therefore I may draw a deduction. As the scheme, whatever it was, on which you set your heart did not include the appearance of Mr Wayne, it will survive his removal. Why not let us clear away this particular Pump Street, which does interfere with our plans, and which does not, by your Majesty's own statement, interfere with yours.'

'Caught out!' said the King, enthusiastically and quite impersonally, as if he were watching a cricket match.

'This man Wayne,' continued Buck, 'would be shut up by any doctors in England. But we only ask to have it put before them. Meanwhile no one's interests, not even in all probability his own, can be really damaged by going on with the improvements in Notting Hill. Not our interests, of course, for it has been the hard and quiet work of ten years. Not the interests of Notting Hill, for nearly all its educated inhabitants desire the change. Not the interests of your Majesty, for you say, with characteristic sense, that you never contemplated the rise of the lunatic at all. Not, as I say, his own interests, for the man has a kind heart and many talents, and a couple of good doctors would probably put him righter than all the free cities and sacred mountains in creation. I therefore assume, if I may use so bold a word, that your Majesty will not offer any obstacle to our proceeding with the improvements.'

And Mr Buck sat down amid subdued but excited applause among the allies.

'Mr Buck,' said the King, 'I beg your pardon, for a number of beautiful and sacred thoughts, in which you were generally classified as a fool. But there is another thing to be considered. Suppose you send in your workmen, and Mr Wayne does a thing regrettable indeed, but of which, I am sorry to say, I think him quite capable – knocks their teeth out?'

'I have thought of that, your Majesty,' said Mr Buck, easily, 'and I think it can simply be guarded against. Let us send in a strong guard of, say, a hundred men – a hundred of the North Kensington Halberdiers' (he smiled grimly), 'of whom your Majesty is so fond. Or say a hundred and fifty. The whole population of Pump Street, I fancy, is only about a hundred.'

'Still they might stand together and lick you,' said the King, dubiously.

'Then say two hundred,' said Buck, gaily.

'It might happen,' said the King, restlessly, 'that one Notting Hiller fought better than two North Kensingtons.'

'It might,' said Buck, coolly; 'then say two hundred and fifty.'

The King bit his lip.

'And if they are beaten too?' he said viciously.

'Your Majesty,' said Buck, and leaned back easily in his chair, 'suppose they are. If anything be clear, it is clear that all fighting matters are mere matters of arithmetic. Here we have a hundred and fifty, say, of Notting Hill soldiers. Or say two hundred. If one of them can fight two of us – we can send in, not four hundred, but six hundred, and smash him. That is all. It is out of all immediate probability that one of them could fight four of us. So what I say is this. Run no risks. Finish it at once. Send in eight hundred men and smash him – smash him almost without seeing him. And go on with the improvements.'

And Mr Buck pulled out a bandanna and blew his nose.

'Do you know, Mr Buck,' said the King, staring gloomily at the table, 'the admirable clearness of your reason produces in my mind a sentiment which I trust I shall not offend you by describing as an aspiration to punch your head. You irritate me sublimely. What can it be in me? Is it the relic of a moral sense?'

'But your Majesty,' said Barker, eagerly and suavely, 'does not refuse our proposals?'

'My dear Barker, your proposals are as damnable as your manners. I want to have nothing to do with them. Suppose I stopped them altogether. What would happen?'

Barker answered in a very low voice: 'Revolution.'

The King glanced quickly at the men round the table. They were all looking down silently: their brows were red.

He rose with a startling suddenness, and an unusual pallor.

'Gentlemen,' he said, 'you have overruled me. Therefore I can speak plainly. I think Adam Wayne, who is as mad as a hatter, worth more than a million of you. But you have the force, and, I admit, the common sense, and he is lost. Take your eight hundred halberdiers and smash him. It would be more sportsmanlike to take two hundred.'

'More sportsmanlike,' said Buck, grimly, 'but a great deal less humane. We are not artists, and streets purple with gore do not catch our eye in the right way.'

'It is pitiful,' said Auberon. 'With five or six times their number, there will be no fight at all.'

'I hope not,' said Buck, rising and adjusting his gloves. 'We desire no fight, your Majesty. We are peaceable business men.'

'Well,' said the King, wearily, 'the conference is at an end at last.'

And he went out of the room before anyone else could stir.

* * *

Forty workmen, a hundred Bayswater Halberdiers, two hundred from South, and three from North Kensington, assembled at the foot of Holland Walk and marched up it, under the general direction of Barker, who looked flushed and happy in full dress. At the end of the procession a small and sulky figure lingered like an urchin. It was the King.

'Barker,' he said at length, appealingly, 'you are an old friend of mine – you understand my hobbies as I understand yours. Why can't you let it alone? I hoped that such fun might come out of this Wayne business. Why can't you let it alone? It doesn't really so much matter to you – what's a road or so? For me it's the one joke that may save me from pessimism. Take fewer men and give me an hour's fun. Really and truly, James, if you collected coins or humming-birds, and I could buy one with the price of your road, I would buy it. I collect incidents – those rare, those precious things. Let me have one. Pay a few pounds for it. Give these Notting Hillers a chance. Let them alone.'

'Auberon,' said Barker, kindly, forgetting all royal titles in a rare moment of sincerity, 'I do feel what you mean. I have had moments when these hobbies have hit me. I have had moments when I have sympathised with your humours. I have had moments, though you may not easily believe it, when I have sympathised with the madness of Adam Wayne. But the world, Auberon, the real world, is not run on these hobbies. It goes on great brutal wheels of facts – wheels on which you are the butterfly; and Wayne is the fly on the wheel.'

Auberon's eyes looked frankly at the other's.

'Thank you, James; what you say is true. It is only a parenthetical consolation to me to compare the intelligence of flies somewhat favourably with the intelligence of wheels. But it is the nature of flies to die soon, and the nature of wheels to go on for ever. Go on with the wheel. Goodbye, old man.'

And James Barker went on, laughing, with a high colour, slapping his bamboo on his leg.

The King watched the tail of the retreating regiment with a look of genuine depression, which made him seem more like a baby than ever. Then he swung round and struck his hands together.

'In a world without humour,' he said, 'the only thing to do is to eat. And how perfect an exception! How can these people strike dignified attitudes, and pretend that things matter, when the total ludicrousness of life is proved by the very method by which it is supported? A man strikes the lyre, and says, "Life is real, life is earnest," and then goes into a room and stuffs alien substances into a hole in his head. I think Nature was indeed a little broad in her humour in these matters. But we all fall back on the pantomime, as I have in this municipal affair. Nature has her farces, like the act of eating or the shape of the kangaroo, for the more brutal appetite. She keeps her stars and mountains for those who can appreciate something more subtly ridiculous.' He turned to his equerry. 'But, as I said "eating", let us have a picnic like two nice little children. Just run and bring me a table and a dozen courses or so, and plenty of champagne, and under these swinging boughs, Bowler, we will return to Nature.'

It took about an hour to erect in Holland Lane the monarch's simple repast, during which time he walked up and down and whistled, but still with an unaffected air of gloom. He had really been done out of a pleasure he had promised himself, and had that empty and sickened feeling which a child has when disappointed of a pantomime. When he and the equerry had sat down, however, and consumed a fair amount of dry champagne, his spirits began mildly to revive.

'Things take too long in this world,' he said. 'I detest all this Barkerian business about evolution and the gradual modification of things. I wish the world had been made in six days, and knocked to pieces again in six more. And I wish I had done it. The joke's good enough in a broad way, sun and moon and the image of God, and all that, but they keep it up so damnably long. Did you ever long for a miracle, Bowler?'

'No, sir,' said Bowler, who was an evolutionist, and had been carefully brought up.

'Then I have,' answered the King. 'I have walked along a street with the best cigar in the cosmos in my mouth, and more Burgundy inside me than you ever saw in your life, and longed that the lamp post would turn into an elephant to save me from the hell of blank existence. Take my word for it, my evolutionary Bowler, don't you believe people when they tell you that people sought for a sign, and believed in miracles because they were ignorant. They did it because they were wise, filthily, vilely wise – too wise to eat or sleep or put on their boots with patience. This seems delightfully like a new theory of the origin of Christianity, which would itself be a thing of no mean absurdity. Take some more wine.'

The wind blew round them as they sat at their little table, with its white cloth and bright wine-cups, and flung the treetops of Holland Park against each other, but the sun was in that strong temper which turns green into gold. The King pushed away his plate, lit a cigar slowly, and went on: 'Yesterday I thought that something next door to a really entertaining miracle might happen to me before I went to amuse the worms. To see that red-haired maniac waving a great sword, and making speeches to his incomparable followers, would have been a glimpse of that Land of Youth from which the Fates shut us out. I had planned some quite delightful things. A Congress of Knightsbridge with a treaty, and myself in the chair, and perhaps a Roman triumph, with jolly old Barker led in chains. And now these wretched prigs have gone and stamped out the exquisite Mr Wayne altogether, and I suppose they will put him in a private asylum somewhere in their damned humane way. Think of the treasures daily poured out to his unappreciative keeper! I wonder whether they would let me be his keeper. But life is a vale. Never forget at any moment of your existence to regard it in the light of a vale. This graceful habit, if not acquired in youth – '

The King stopped, with his cigar lifted, for there had slid into his eyes the startled look of a man listening. He did not move for a few moments; then he turned his head sharply towards the high, thin, and lath-like paling which fenced certain long gardens and similar spaces from the lane. From behind it there was coming a curious scrambling and scraping noise, as of a desperate thing imprisoned in this box of thin wood. The King threw away his cigar, and jumped on to the table. From this position he saw a pair of hands hanging with a hungry clutch on the top of the fence. Then the hands quivered with a convulsive effort, and a head shot up between them – the head of one of the Bayswater Town Council, his eyes and whiskers wild with fear. He swung himself over, and fell on the other side on his face, and groaned openly and without ceasing. The next moment the thin, taut wood of the fence was struck as by a bullet, so that it reverberated like a drum, and over it came tearing and cursing, with torn clothes and broken nails and bleeding faces, twenty men at one rush. The King sprang five feet clear off the table on to the ground. The moment after the table was flung over, sending bottles and glasses flying, and the debris was literally swept along the ground by that stream of men pouring past, and Bowler was borne along with them, as the King said in his famous newspaper article, 'like a captured bride'. The great fence swung and split under the load of climbers that still scaled and cleared it. Tremendous gaps were torn in it by this living artillery; and through them the King could see more and more frantic faces, as in a dream, and more and more men running. They were as miscellaneous as if someone had taken the lid off a human dustbin. Some were untouched, some were slashed and battered and bloody, some were splendidly dressed, some tattered and half naked, some were in the fantastic garb of the burlesque cities, some in the dullest modern dress. The King stared at all of them, but none of them looked at the King. Suddenly he stepped forward.

'Barker,' he said, 'what is all this?'

'Beaten,' said the politician – 'beaten all to hell!' And he plunged past with nostrils shaking like a horse's, and more and more men plunged after him.

Almost as he spoke, the last standing strip of fence bowed and snapped, flinging, as from a catapult, a new figure upon the road. He wore the flaming red of the halberdiers of Notting Hill, and on his weapon there was blood, and in his face victory. In another moment masses of red glowed through the gaps of the fence, and the pursuers, with their halberds, came pouring down the lane. Pursued and pursuers alike swept by the little figure with the owlish eyes, who had not taken his hands out of his pockets.

The King had still little beyond the confused sense of a man caught in a torrent – the feeling of men eddying by. Then something happened which he was never able afterwards to describe, and which we cannot describe for him. Suddenly in the dark entrance, between the broken gates of a garden, there appeared framed a flaming figure.

Adam Wayne, the conqueror, with his face flung back, and his mane like a lion's, stood with his great sword point upwards, the red raiment of his office flapping round him like the red wings of an archangel. And the King saw, he knew not how, something new and overwhelming. The great green trees and the great red robes swung together in the wind. The sword seemed made for the sunlight. The preposterous masquerade, born of his own mockery, towered over him and embraced the world. This was the normal, this was sanity, this was nature; and he himself, with his rationality and his detachment and his black frock-coat, he was the exception and the accident – a blot of black upon a world of crimson and gold.

BOOK FOUR

CHAPTER I

The Battle of the Lamps

Mr Buck, who, though retired, frequently went down to his big drapery stores in Kensington High Street, was locking up those premises, being the last to leave. It was a wonderful evening of green and gold, but that did not trouble him very much. If you had pointed it out, he would have agreed seriously, for the rich always desire to be artistic.

He stepped out into the cool air, buttoning up his light yellow coat, and blowing great clouds from his cigar, when a figure dashed up to him in another yellow overcoat, but unbuttoned and flying behind him.

'Hullo, Barker!' said the draper. 'Any of our summer articles? You're too late. Factory Acts, Barker. Humanity and progress, my boy.'

'Oh, don't chatter,' cried Barker, stamping. 'We've been beaten.'

'Beaten – by what?' asked Buck, mystified.

'By Wayne.'

Buck looked at Barker's fierce white face for the first time, as it gleamed in the lamplight.

'Come and have a drink,' he said.

They adjourned to a cushioned and glaring buffet, and Buck established himself slowly and lazily in a seat, and pulled out his cigar-case.

'Have a smoke,' he said.

Barker was still standing, and on the fret, but after a moment's hesitation, he sat down as if he might spring up again the next minute. They ordered drinks in silence.

'How did it happen?' asked Buck, turning his big bold eyes on him.

'How the devil do I know?' cried Barker. 'It happened like – like a dream. How can two hundred men beat six hundred? How can they?'

'Well,' said Buck, coolly, 'how did they? You ought to know.'

'I don't know; I can't describe,' said the other, drumming on the table. 'It seemed like this. We were six hundred, and marched with those damned poleaxes of Auberon's – the only weapons we've got. We marched two abreast. We went up Holland Walk, between the high palings which seemed to me to go straight as an arrow for Pump Street. I was near the tail of the line, and it was a long one. When the end of it was still between the high palings, the head of the line was already crossing Holland Park Avenue. Then the head plunged into the network of narrow streets on the other side, and the tail and myself came out on the great crossing. When we also had reached the northern side and turned up a small street that points, crookedly as it were, towards Pump Street, the whole thing felt different. The streets dodged and bent so much that the head of our line seemed lost altogether: it might as well have been in North America. And all this time we hadn't seen a soul.'

Buck, who was idly dabbing the ash of his cigar on the ashtray, began to move it deliberately over the table, making feathery grey lines, a kind of map.

'But though the little streets were all deserted (which got a trifle on my nerves), as we got deeper and deeper into them, a thing began to happen that I couldn't understand. Sometimes a long way ahead – three turns or corners ahead, as it were – there broke suddenly a sort of noise, clattering, and confused cries, and then stopped. Then, when it happened, something, I can't describe it – a kind of shake or stagger went down the line, as if the line were a live thing, whose head had been struck, or had been an electric cord. None of us knew why we were moving, but we moved and jostled. Then we recovered, and went on through the little dirty streets, round corners, and up twisted ways. The little crooked streets began to give me a feeling I can't explain – as if it were a dream. I felt as if things had lost their reason, and we should never get out of the maze. Odd to hear me talk like that, isn't it? The streets were quite well-known streets, all down on the map. But the fact remains. I wasn't afraid of something happening. I was afraid of nothing ever happening – nothing ever happening for all God's eternity.'

He drained his glass and called for more whisky. He drank it, and went on.

'And then something did happen. Buck, it's the solemn truth, that nothing has ever happened to you in your life. Nothing had ever happened to me in my life.'

'Nothing ever happened!' said Buck, staring. 'What do you mean?'

'Nothing has ever happened,' repeated Barker, with a morbid obstinacy. 'You don't know what a thing happening means? You sit in your office expecting customers, and customers come; you walk in the street expecting friends, and friends meet you; you want a drink, and get it; you feel inclined for a bet, and make it. You expect either to win or lose, and you do either one or the other. But things happening!' and he shuddered ungovernably.

'Go on,' said Buck, shortly. 'Get on.'

'As we walked wearily round the corners, something happened. When something happens, it happens first, and you see it afterwards. It happens of itself, and you have nothing to do with it. It proves a dreadful thing – that there are other things besides one's self. I can only put it in this way. We went round one turning, two turnings, three turnings, four turnings, five. Then I lifted myself slowly up from the gutter where I had been shot half senseless, and was beaten down again by living men crashing on top of me, and the world was full of roaring, and big men rolling about like ninepins.'

Buck looked at his map with knitted brows.

'Was that Portobello Road?' he asked.

'Yes,' said Barker. 'Yes; Portobello Road. I saw it afterwards; but, my God, what a place it was! Buck, have you ever stood and let a six foot of a man lash and lash at your head with six feet of pole with six pounds of steel at the end? Because, when you have had that experience, as Walt Whitman says, "you re-examine philosophies and religions".'

'I have no doubt,' said Buck. 'If that was Portobello Road, don't you see what happened?'

'I know what happened exceedingly well. I was knocked down four times; an experience which, as I say, has an effect on the mental attitude. And another thing happened, too. I knocked down two men. After the fourth fall (there was not much bloodshed – more brutal rushing and throwing – for nobody could use their weapons), after the fourth fall, I say, I got up like a devil, and I tore a poleaxe out of a man's hand and struck where I saw the scarlet of Wayne's fellows, struck again and again. Two of them went over, bleeding on the stones, thank God; and I laughed and found myself sprawling in the gutter again, and got up again, and struck again, and broke my halberd to pieces. I hurt a man's head, though.'

Buck set down his glass with a bang, and spat out curses through his thick moustache.

'What is the matter?' asked Barker, stopping, for the man had been calm up to now, and now his agitation was far more violent than his own.

'The matter?' said Buck, bitterly; 'don't you see how these maniacs have got us? Why should two idiots, one a clown and the other a screaming lunatic, make sane men so different from themselves? Look here, Barker; I will give you a picture. A very well-bred young man of this century is dancing about in a frock-coat. He has in his hands a nonsensical seventeenth-century halberd, with which he is trying to kill men in a street in Notting Hill. Damn it! don't you see how they've got us? Never mind how you felt – that is how you looked. The King would put his cursed head on one side and call it exquisite. The Provost of Notting Hill would put his cursed nose in the air and call it heroic. But in Heaven's name what would you have called it – two days before?'

Barker bit his lip.

'You haven't been through it, Buck,' he said. 'You don't understand fighting – the atmosphere.'

'I don't deny the atmosphere,' said Buck, striking the table. 'I only say it's their atmosphere. It's Adam Wayne's atmosphere. It's the atmosphere which you and I thought had vanished from an educated world for ever.'

'Well, it hasn't,' said Barker; 'and if you have any lingering doubts, lend me a poleaxe, and I'll show you.'

There was a long silence, and then Buck turned to his neighbour and spoke in that good-tempered tone that comes of a power of looking facts in the face – the tone in which he concluded great bargains.

'Barker,' he said, 'you are right. This old thing – this fighting, has come back. It has come back suddenly and taken us by surprise. So it is first blood to Adam Wayne. But, unless reason and arithmetic and everything else have gone crazy, it must be next and last blood to us. But when an issue has really arisen, there is only one thing to do – to study that issue as such and win in it. Barker, since it is fighting, we must understand fighting. I must understand fighting as coolly and completely as I understand drapery; you must understand fighting as coolly and completely as you understand politics. Now, look at the facts. I stick without hesitation to my original formula. Fighting, when we have the stronger force, is only a matter of arithmetic. It must be. You asked me just now how two hundred men could defeat six hundred. I can tell you. Two hundred men can defeat six hundred when the six hundred behave like fools. When they forget the very conditions they are fighting in; when they fight in a swamp as if it were a mountain; when they fight in a forest as if it were a plain; when they fight in streets without remembering the object of streets.'

'What is the object of streets?' asked Barker.

'What is the object of supper?' cried Buck, furiously. 'Isn't it obvious? This military science is mere common sense. The object of a street is to lead from one place to another; therefore all streets join; therefore street fighting is quite a peculiar thing. You advanced into that hive of streets as if you were advancing into an open plain where you could see everything. Instead of that, you were advancing into the bowels of a fortress, with streets pointing at you, streets turning on you, streets jumping out at you, and all in the hands of the enemy. Do you know what Portobello Road is? It is the only point on your journey where two side streets run up opposite each other. Wayne massed his men on the two sides, and when he had let enough of your line go past, cut it in two like a worm. Don't you see what would have saved you?'

Barker shook his head.

'Can't your "atmosphere" help you?' asked Buck, bitterly. 'Must I attempt explanations in the romantic manner? Suppose that, as you were fighting blindly with the red Notting Hillers who imprisoned you on both sides, you had heard a shout from behind them. Suppose, oh, romantic Barker! that behind the red tunics you had seen the blue and gold of South Kensington taking them in the rear, surrounding them in their turn and hurling them on to your halberds.'

'If the thing had been possible,' began Barker, cursing.

'The thing would have been as possible,' said Buck, simply, 'as simple as arithmetic. There are a certain number of street entries that lead to Pump Street. There are not nine hundred; there are not nine million. They do not grow in the night. They do not increase like mushrooms. It must be possible, with such an overwhelming force as we have, to advance by all of them at once. In every one of the arteries, or approaches, we can put almost as many men as Wayne can put into the field altogether. Once do that, and we have him to demonstration. It is like a proposition in Euclid.'

'You think that is certain?' said Barker, anxious, but dominated delightfully.

'I'll tell you what I think,' said Buck, getting up jovially. 'I think Adam Wayne made an uncommonly spirited little fight; and I think I am confoundedly sorry for him.'

'Buck, you are a great man!' cried Barker, rising also. 'You've knocked me sensible again. I am ashamed to say it, but I was getting romantic. Of course, what you say is adamantine sense. Fighting, being physical, must be mathematical. We were beaten because we were neither mathematical nor physical nor anything else – because we deserved to be beaten. Hold all the approaches, and with our force we must have him. When shall we open the next campaign?'

'Now,' said Buck, and walked out of the bar.

'Now!' cried Barker, following him eagerly. 'Do you mean now? It is so late.'

Buck turned on him, stamping.

'Do you think fighting is under the Factory Acts?' he said; and he called a cab. 'Notting Hill Gate Station,' he said; and the two drove off.

* * *

A genuine reputation can sometimes be made in an hour. Buck, in the next sixty or eighty minutes, showed himself a really great man of action. His cab carried him like a thunderbolt from the King to Wilson, from Wilson to Swindon, from Swindon to Barker again; if his course was jagged, it had the jaggedness of the lightning. Only two things he carried with him – his inevitable cigar and the map of North Kensington and Notting Hill. There were, as he again and again pointed out, with every variety of persuasion and violence, only nine possible ways of approaching Pump Street within a quarter of a mile round it; three out of Westbourne Grove, two out of Ladbroke Grove, and four out of Notting Hill High Street. And he had detachments of two hundred each, stationed at every one of the entrances before the last green of that strange sunset had sunk out of the black sky.

The sky was particularly black, and on this alone was one false protest raised against the triumphant optimism of the Provost of North Kensington. He overruled it with his infectious common sense.

'There is no such thing,' he said, 'as night in London. You have only to follow the line of street lamps. Look, here is the map. Two hundred purple North Kensington soldiers under myself march up Ossington Street, two hundred more under Captain Bruce, of the North Kensington Guard, up Clanricarde Gardens.* Two hundred yellow West Kensingtons under Provost Swindon attack from Pembridge Road. Two hundred more of my men from the eastern streets, leading away from Queen's Road. Two detachments of yellows enter by two roads from Westbourne Grove. Lastly, two hundred green Bayswaters come down from the North through Chepstow Place, and two hundred more under Provost Wilson himself, through the upper part of Pembridge Road. Gentlemen, it is mate in two moves. The enemy must either mass in Pump Street and be cut to pieces; or they must retreat past the Gaslight & Coke Co., and rush on my four hundred; or they must retreat past St Luke's Church, and rush on the six hundred from the West. Unless we are all mad, it's plain. Come on. To your quarters and await Captain Bruce's signal to advance. Then you have only to walk up a line of gas-lamps and smash this nonsense by pure mathematics. Tomorrow we shall all be civilians again.'

His optimism glowed like a great fire in the night, and ran round the terrible ring in which Wayne was now held helpless. The fight was already over. One man's energy for one hour had saved the city from war.

For the next ten minutes Buck walked up and down silently beside the motionless clump of his two hundred. He had not changed his appearance in any way, except to sling across his yellow overcoat a case with a revolver in it. So that his light-clad modern figure showed up oddly beside the pompous purple uniforms of his halberdiers, which darkly but richly coloured the black night.

At length a shrill trumpet rang from some way up the street; it was the signal of advance. Buck briefly gave the word, and the whole purple line, with its dimly shining steel, moved up the side alley. Before it was a slope of street, long, straight, and shining in the dark. It was a sword pointed at Pump Street, the heart at which nine other swords were pointed that night.

A quarter of an hour's silent marching brought them almost within earshot of any tumult in the doomed citadel. But still there was no sound and no sign of the enemy. This time, at any rate, they knew that they were closing in on it mechanically, and they marched on under the lamplight and the dark

* Clanricarde Gardens at this time was no longer a *cul-de-sac*, but was connected by Pump Street to Pembridge Square.

without any of that eerie sense of ignorance which Barker had felt when entering the hostile country by one avenue alone.

'Halt – point arms!' cried Buck, suddenly, and as he spoke there came a clatter of feet tumbling along the stones. But the halberds were levelled in vain. The figure that rushed up was a messenger from the contingent of the North.

'Victory, Mr Buck!' he cried, panting; 'they are ousted. Provost Wilson of Bayswater has taken Pump Street.'

Buck ran forward in his excitement.

'Then, which way are they retreating? It must be either by St Luke's to meet Swindon, or by the Gas Company to meet us. Run like mad to Swindon, and see that the yellows are holding the St Luke's Road. We will hold this, never fear. We have them in an iron trap. Run!'

As the messenger dashed away into the darkness, the great guard of North Kensington swung on with the certainty of a machine. Yet scarcely a hundred yards further their halberd-points again fell in line gleaming in the gaslight; for again a clatter of feet was heard on the stones, and again it proved to be only the messenger.

'Mr Provost,' he said, 'the yellow West Kensingtons have been holding the road by St Luke's for twenty minutes since the capture of Pump Street. Pump Street is not two hundred yards away; they cannot be retreating down that road.'

'Then they are retreating down this,' said Provost Buck, with a final cheerfulness, 'and by good fortune down a well-lighted road, though it twists about. Forward!'

As they moved along the last three hundred yards of their journey, Buck fell, for the first time in his life, perhaps, into a kind of philosophical reverie, for men of his type are always made kindly, and as it were melancholy, by success.

'I am sorry for poor old Wayne, I really am,' he thought. 'He spoke up splendidly for me at that Council. And he blacked old Barker's eye with considerable spirit. But I don't see what a man can expect when he fights against arithmetic, to say nothing of civilisation. And what a wonderful hoax all this military genius is! I suspect I've just discovered what Cromwell discovered, that a sensible tradesman is the best general, and that a man who can buy men and sell men can lead and kill them. The thing's simply like adding up a column in a ledger. If Wayne has two hundred men, he can't put two hundred men in nine places at once. If they're ousted from Pump Street they're flying somewhere. If they're not flying past the church they're flying past the Works. And so we have them. We business men should have no chance at all except that cleverer people than we get bees in their bonnets that prevent them from reasoning properly – so we reason alone. And so I, who am comparatively stupid, see things as God sees them, as a vast machine. My God, what's this?' And he clapped his hands to his eyes and staggered back.

Then through the darkness he cried in a dreadful voice: 'Did I blaspheme God? I am struck blind.'

'What?' wailed another voice behind him, the voice of a certain Wilfred Jarvis of North Kensington.

'Blind!' cried Buck; 'blind!'

'I'm blind too!' cried Jarvis, in an agony.

'Fools, all of you,' said a gross voice behind them; 'we're all blind. The lamps have gone out.'

'The lamps! But why? where?' cried Buck, turning furiously in the darkness. 'How are we to get on? How are we to chase the enemy? Where have they gone?'

'The enemy went – ' said the rough voice behind, and then stopped doubtfully.

'Where?' shouted Buck, stamping like a madman.

'They went,' said the gruff voice, 'past the Gas Works, and they've used their chance.'

'Great God!' thundered Buck, and snatched at his revolver; 'do you mean they've turned out – '

But almost before he had spoken the words, he was hurled like a stone from a catapult into the midst of his own men.

'Notting Hill! Notting Hill!' cried frightful voices out of the darkness, and they seemed to come from all sides, for the men of North Kensington, unacquainted with the road, had lost all their bearings in the black world of blindness.

'Notting Hill! Notting Hill!' cried the invisible people, and the invaders were hewn down horribly with black steel, with steel that gave no glint against any light.

* * *

Buck, though badly maimed with the blow of a halberd, kept an angry but splendid sanity. He groped madly for the wall and found it. Struggling with crawling fingers along it, he found a side opening and retreated into it with the remnants of his men. Their adventures during that prodigious night are not to be described. They did not know whether they were going towards or away from the enemy. Not knowing where they themselves were, or where their opponents were, it was mere irony to ask where was the rest of their army. For a thing had descended upon them which London does not know – darkness, which was before the stars were made, and they were as much lost in it as if they had been made before the stars. Every now and then, as those frightful hours wore on, they buffeted in the darkness against living men, who struck at them and at whom they struck, with an idiot fury. When at last the grey dawn came, they found they had wandered back to the edge of the Uxbridge Road. They found that in those horrible eyeless encounters, the North Kensingtons and the Bayswaters and the West Kensingtons had again and again met and butchered each other, and they heard that Adam Wayne was barricaded in Pump Street.

CHAPTER 2

The Correspondent of the Court Journal

Journalism had become, like most other such things in England under the cautious government and philosophy represented by James Barker, somewhat sleepy and much diminished in importance. This was partly due to the disappearance of party government and public speaking, partly to the compromise or deadlock which had made foreign wars impossible, but mostly, of course, to the temper of the whole nation which was that of a people in a kind of backwater. Perhaps the most well known of the remaining newspapers was the *Court Journal*, which was published in a dusty but genteel-looking office just out of Kensington High Street. For when all the papers of a people have been for years growing more and more dim and decorous and optimistic, the dimmest and most decorous and most optimistic is very likely to win. In the journalistic competition which was still going on at the beginning of the twentieth century, the final victor was the *Court Journal*.

For some mysterious reason the King had a great affection for hanging about in the *Court Journal* office, smoking a morning cigarette and looking over files. Like all ingrainedly idle men, he was very fond of lounging and chatting in places where other people were doing work. But one would have thought that, even in the prosaic England of his day, he might have found a more bustling centre.

On this particular morning, however, he came out of Kensington Palace with a more alert step and a busier air than usual. He wore an extravagantly long frock-coat, a pale-green waistcoat, a very full and *dégagé* black tie, and curious yellow gloves. This was his uniform as Colonel of a regiment of his own creation, the 1st Decadents Green. It was a beautiful sight to see him drilling them. He walked quickly across the Park and the High Street, lighting his cigarette as he went, and flung open the door of the *Court Journal* office.

'You've heard the news, Pally – you've heard the news?' he said.

The Editor's name was Hoskins, but the King called him Pally, which was an abbreviation of Palladium of our Liberties.

'Well, your Majesty,' said Hoskins, slowly (he was a worried, gentlemanly-looking person, with a wandering brown beard) – 'well, your Majesty, I have heard rather curious things, but I – '

'You'll hear more of them,' said the King, dancing a few steps of a kind of negro shuffle. 'You'll hear more of them, my blood-and-thunder tribune. Do you know what I am going to do for you?'

'No, your Majesty,' replied the Palladium, vaguely.

'I'm going to put your paper on strong, dashing, enterprising lines,' said the King. 'Now, where are your posters of last night's defeat?'

'I did not propose, your Majesty,' said the Editor, 'to have any posters exactly – '

'Paper, paper!' cried the King, wildly; 'bring me paper as big as a house. I'll do you posters. Stop, I must take my coat off.' He began removing that garment with an air of set intensity, flung it playfully at Mr Hoskins' head, entirely enveloping him, and looked at himself in the glass. 'The coat off,' he said, 'and the hat on. That looks like a subeditor. It is indeed the very essence of subediting. Well,' he continued, turning round abruptly, 'come along with that paper.'

The Palladium had only just extricated himself reverently from the folds of the King's frock-coat, and said bewildered: 'I am afraid, your Majesty – '

'Oh, you've got no enterprise,' said Auberon. 'What's that roll in the corner? Wallpaper? Decorations for your private residence? Art in the home, Pally? Fling it over here, and I'll paint such posters on the back of it that when you put it up in your drawing-room you'll paste the original pattern against the wall.' And the King unrolled the wallpaper, spreading it over the whole floor. 'Now give me the scissors,' he cried, and took them himself before the other could stir.

He slit the paper into about five pieces, each nearly as big as a door. Then he took a big blue pencil, and went down on his knees on the dusty oilcloth and began to write on them, in huge letters:

FROM THE FRONT.
GENERAL BUCK DEFEATED.
DARKNESS, DANGER AND DEATH.
WAYNE SAID TO BE IN PUMP STREET.
FEELING IN THE CITY.

He contemplated it for some time, with his head on one side, and got up, with a sigh.

'Not quite intense enough,' he said – 'not alarming. I want the *Court*

Journal to be feared as well as loved. Let's try something more hard-hitting.' And he went down on his knees again. After sucking the blue pencil for some time, he began writing again busily. 'How will this do?' he said:

WAYNE'S WONDERFUL VICTORY.

'I suppose,' he said, looking up appealingly, and sucking the pencil – 'I suppose we couldn't say "wictory" – "Wayne's wonderful wictory"? No, no. Refinement, Pally, refinement. I have it.'

WAYNE WINS.
ASTOUNDING FIGHT IN THE DARK
The gas-lamps in their courses fought against Buck.

'(Nothing like our fine old English translation.) What else can we say? Well, anything to annoy old Buck'; and he added, thoughtfully, in smaller letters:

RUMOURED COURT-MARTIAL ON GENERAL BUCK.

'Those will do for the present,' he said, and turned them both face downwards. 'Paste, please.'

The Palladium, with an air of great terror, brought the paste out of an inner room.

The King slabbed it on with the enjoyment of a child messing with treacle. Then taking one of his huge compositions fluttering in each hand, he ran outside, and began pasting them up in prominent positions over the front of the office.

'And now,' said Auberon, entering again with undiminished vivacity – 'now for the leading article.'

He picked up another of the large strips of wallpaper, and, laying it across a desk, pulled out a fountain-pen and began writing with feverish intensity, reading clauses and fragments aloud to himself, and rolling them on his tongue like wine, to see if they had the pure journalistic flavour.

'The news of the disaster to our forces in Notting Hill, awful as it is – awful as it is – (no, distressing as it is), may do some good if it draws attention to the what's-his-name inefficiency (scandalous inefficiency, of course) of the Government's preparations. In our present state of information, it would be premature (what a jolly word!) – it would be premature to cast any reflections upon the conduct of General Buck, whose services upon so many stricken fields (ha, ha!), and whose honourable scars and laurels, give him a right to have judgement upon him at least suspended. But there is one matter on which we must speak plainly. We have been silent on it too long, from feelings, perhaps of mistaken caution, perhaps of mistaken loyalty. This situation would never have arisen but for what we can only call the indefensible conduct of the King. It pains us to say such things, but, speaking as we do in the public interests (I plagiarise from Barker's famous epigram), we shall not shrink because of the distress we may cause to any individual, even the most exalted. At this crucial moment of our country, the voice of the People demands with a single tongue, "Where is the King?" What is he doing while his subjects tear each other in pieces in the streets of a great city? Are his amusements and his dissipations (of which we cannot pretend to be ignorant) so engrossing that he can spare no thought for a perishing nation? It is with a deep sense of our responsibility that we warn that exalted person that neither his great position nor his incomparable talents will save him in the hour of delirium from the fate of all those who, in the madness of luxury or tyranny, have met the English people in the rare day of its wrath.'

'I am now,' said the King, 'going to write an account of the battle by an eyewitness.' And he picked up a fourth sheet of wallpaper. Almost at the same moment Buck strode quickly into the office. He had a bandage round his head.

'I was told,' he said, with his usual gruff civility, 'that your Majesty was here.'

'And of all things on earth,' cried the King, with delight, 'here is an eyewitness! An eyewitness who, I regret to observe, has at present only one eye to witness with. Can you write us the special article, Buck? Have you a rich style?'

Buck, with a self-restraint which almost approached politeness, took no notice whatever of the King's maddening geniality.

'I took the liberty, your Majesty,' he said shortly, 'of asking Mr Barker to come here also.'

As he spoke, indeed, Barker came swinging into the office, with his usual air of hurry.

'What is happening now?' asked Buck, turning to him with a kind of relief.

'Fighting still going on,' said Barker. 'The four hundred from West Kensington were hardly touched last night. They hardly got near the place. Poor Wilson's Bayswater men got cut about, though. They fought confoundedly well. They took Pump Street once. What mad things do happen in the world. To think that of all of us it should be little Wilson with the red whiskers who came out best.'

The King made a note on his paper: '*Romantic Conduct of Mr Wilson.*'

'Yes,' said Buck; 'it makes one a bit less proud of one's h's.'

The King suddenly folded or crumpled up the paper, and put it in his pocket.

'I have an idea,' he said. 'I will be an eyewitness. I will write you such letters from the Front as will be more gorgeous than the real thing. Give me my coat, Palladium. I entered this room a mere King of England. I leave it,

Special War Correspondent of the *Court Journal*. It is useless to stop me, Pally; it is vain to cling to my knees, Buck; it is hopeless, Barker, to weep upon my neck. "When duty calls" – the remainder of the sentiment escapes me. You will receive my first article this evening by the eight-o'clock post.'

And, running out of the office, he jumped upon a blue Bayswater omnibus that went swinging by.

'Well,' said Barker, gloomily, 'well.'

'Barker,' said Buck, 'business may be lower than politics, but war is, as I discovered last night, a long sight more like business. You politicians are such ingrained demagogues that even when you have a despotism you think of nothing but public opinion. So you learn to tack and run, and are afraid of the first breeze. Now we stick to a thing and get it. And our mistakes help us. Look here! at this moment we've beaten Wayne.'

'Beaten Wayne,' repeated Barker.

'Why the dickens not?' cried the other, flinging out his hands. 'Look here. I said last night that we had them by holding the nine entrances. Well, I was wrong. We should have had them but for a singular event – the lamps went out. But for that it was certain. Has it occurred to you, my brilliant Barker, that another singular event has happened since that singular event of the lamps going out?'

'What event?' asked Barker.

'By an astounding coincidence, the sun has risen,' cried out Buck, with a savage air of patience. 'Why the hell aren't we holding all those approaches now, and passing in on them again? It should have been done at sunrise. The confounded doctor wouldn't let me go out. You were in command.'

Barker smiled grimly.

'It is a gratification to me, my dear Buck, to be able to say that we anticipated your suggestions precisely. We went as early as possible to reconnoitre the nine entrances. Unfortunately, while we were fighting each other in the dark, like a lot of drunken navvies, Mr Wayne's friends were working very hard indeed. Three hundred yards from Pump Street, at every one of those entrances, there is a barricade nearly as high as the houses. They were finishing the last, in Pembridge Road, when we arrived. Our mistakes,' he cried bitterly, and flung his cigarette on the ground. 'It is not we who learn from them.'

There was a silence for a few moments, and Barker lay back wearily in a chair. The office clock ticked exactly in the stillness.

At length Barker said suddenly: 'Buck, does it ever cross your mind what this is all about? The Hammersmith to Maida Vale thoroughfare was an uncommonly good speculation. You and I hoped a great deal from it. But is it worth it? It will cost us thousands to crush this ridiculous riot. Suppose we let it alone?'

'And be thrashed in public by a red-haired madman whom any two doctors would lock up?' cried out Buck, starting to his feet. 'What do you propose to do, Mr Barker? To apologise to the admirable Mr Wayne? To kneel to the Charter of the Cities? To clasp to your bosom the flag of the Red Lion? To kiss in succession every sacred lamp post that saved Notting Hill? No, by God! My men fought jolly well – they were beaten by a trick. And they'll fight again.'

'Buck,' said Barker, 'I always admired you. And you were quite right in what you said the other day.'

'In what?'

'In saying,' said Barker, rising quietly, 'that we had all got into Adam Wayne's atmosphere and out of our own. My friend, the whole territorial kingdom of Adam Wayne extends to about nine streets, with barricades at the end of them. But the spiritual kingdom of Adam Wayne extends, God knows where – it extends to this office, at any rate. The red-haired madman whom any two doctors would lock up is filling this room with his roaring, unreasonable soul. And it was the red-haired madman who said the last word you spoke.'

Buck walked to the window without replying. 'You understand, of course,' he said at last, 'I do not dream of giving in.'

* * *

The King, meanwhile, was rattling along on the top of his blue omnibus. The traffic of London as a whole had not, of course, been greatly disturbed by these events, for the affair was treated as a Notting Hill riot, and that area was marked off as if it had been in the hands of a gang of recognised rioters. The blue omnibuses simply went round as they would have done if a road were being mended, and the omnibus on which the correspondent of the *Court Journal* was sitting swept round the corner of Queen's Road, Bayswater.

The King was alone on the top of the vehicle, and was enjoying the speed at which it was going.

'Forward, my beauty, my Arab,' he said, patting the omnibus encouragingly, 'fleetest of all thy bounding tribe. Are thy relations with thy driver, I wonder, those of the Bedouin and his steed? Does he sleep side by side with thee – '

His meditations were broken by a sudden and jarring stoppage. Looking over the edge, he saw that the heads of the horses were being held by men in the uniform of Wayne's army, and heard the voice of an officer calling out orders.

King Auberon descended from the omnibus with dignity. The guard or picket of red halberdiers who had stopped the vehicle did not number more than twenty, and they were under the command of a short, dark, clever-looking young man, conspicuous among the rest as being clad in an ordinary frock-coat, but girt round the waist with a red sash and a long seventeenth-century sword. A shiny silk hat and spectacles completed the outfit in a pleasing manner.

'To whom have I the honour of speaking?' said the King, endeavouring to look like Charles I, in spite of personal difficulties.

The dark man in spectacles lifted his hat with equal gravity.

'My name is Bowles,' he said. 'I am a chemist. I am also a captain of O company of the army of Notting Hill. I am distressed at having to incommode you by stopping the omnibus, but this area is covered by our proclamation, and we intercept all traffic. May I ask to whom I have the honour – Why, good gracious, I beg your Majesty's pardon. I am quite overwhelmed at finding myself concerned with the King.'

Auberon put up his hand with indescribable grandeur.

'Not with the King,' he said; 'with the special war correspondent of the *Court Journal*.'

'I beg your Majesty's pardon,' began Mr Bowles, doubtfully.

'Do you call me Majesty? I repeat,' said Auberon, firmly, 'I am a representative of the press. I have chosen, with a deep sense of responsibility, the name of Pinker. I should desire a veil to be drawn over the past.'

'Very well, sir,' said Mr Bowles, with an air of submission, 'in our eyes the sanctity of the press is at least as great as that of the throne. We desire nothing better than that our wrongs and our glories should be widely known. May I ask, Mr Pinker, if you have any objection to being presented to the Provost and to General Turnbull?'

'The Provost I have had the honour of meeting,' said Auberon, easily. 'We old journalists, you know, meet everybody. I should be most delighted to have the same honour again. General Turnbull, also, it would be a gratification to know. The younger men are so interesting. We of the old Fleet Street gang lose touch with them.'

'Will you be so good as to step this way?' said the leader of O company.

'I am always good,' said Mr Pinker. 'Lead on.'

CHAPTER 3

The Great Army of South Kensington

The article from the special correspondent of the *Court Journal* arrived in due course, written on very coarse copy-paper in the King's arabesque of handwriting, in which three words filled a page, and yet were illegible. Moreover, the contribution was the more perplexing at first, as it opened with a succession of erased paragraphs. The writer appeared to have attempted the article once or twice in several journalistic styles. At the side of one experiment was written, 'Try American style,' and the fragment began: 'The King must go. We want gritty men. Flapdoodle is all very . . . ' and then broke off, followed by the note, 'Good sound journalism safer. Try it.'

The experiment in good sound journalism appeared to begin: 'The greatest of English poets has said that a rose by any . . . '

This also stopped abruptly. The next annotation at the side was almost undecipherable, but seemed to be something like: 'How about old Steevens and the *mot juste*? E.g. . . . '

'Morning winked a little wearily at me over the curt edge of Campden Hill and its houses with their sharp shadows. Under the abrupt black cardboard of the outline, it took some little time to detect colours; but at length I saw a brownish yellow shifting in the obscurity, and I knew that it was the guard of Swindon's West Kensington army. They are being held as a reserve, and lining the whole ridge above the Bayswater Road. Their camp and their main force is under the great Waterworks Tower on Campden Hill. I forgot to say that the Waterworks Tower looked swart.

'As I passed them and came over the curve of Silver Street, I saw the blue cloudy masses of Barker's men blocking the entrance to the highroad like a sapphire smoke (good). The disposition of the allied troops, under the general management of Mr Wilson, appears to be as follows: The Yellow army (if I may so describe the West Kensingtonians) lies, as I have said, in a strip along the ridge, its furthest point westward being the west side of Campden Hill Road, its furthest point eastward the beginning of Kensington Gardens. The Green army of Wilson lines the Notting Hill High Road itself from Queen's Road to the corner of Pembridge Road, curving round the latter, and extending some three hundred yards up towards Westbourne Grove. Westbourne Grove itself is occupied by Barker of South Kensington. The fourth side of this rough square, the Queen's Road side, is held by some of Buck's Purple warriors.

'The whole resembles some ancient and dainty Dutch flower-bed. Along the crest of Campden Hill lie the golden crocuses of West Kensington. They are, as it were, the first fiery fringe of the whole. Northward lies our hyacinth Barker, with all his blue hyacinths. Round to the south-west run the green rushes of Wilson of Bayswater, and a line of violet irises (aptly symbolised by Mr Buck) complete the whole. The argent exterior . . . (I am losing the style. I should have said "Curving with a whisk" instead of merely "Curving". Also I should have called the hyacinths "sudden". I cannot keep this up. War is too rapid for this style of writing. Please ask office-boy to insert *mots justes*.)

'The truth is that there is nothing to report. That commonplace element which is always ready to devour all beautiful things (as the Black Pig in the Irish Mythology will finally devour the stars and gods); that commonplace element, as I say, has in its Black Piggish way devoured finally the chances of any romance in this affair; that which once consisted of absurd but thrilling combats in the streets, has degenerated into something which is the very prose of warfare – it has degenerated into a siege. A siege may be defined as a peace plus the inconvenience of war. Of course Wayne cannot hold out. There is no more chance of help from anywhere else than of ships from the moon. And if old Wayne had stocked his street with tinned meats till all his garrison had to sit on them, he couldn't hold out for more than a month or two. As a matter of melancholy fact, he has done something rather like this. He has stocked his street with food until there must be uncommonly little room to turn round. But what is the good? To hold out for all that time and then to give in of necessity, what does it mean? It means waiting until your victories are forgotten, and then taking the trouble to be defeated. I cannot understand how Wayne can be so inartistic.

'And how odd it is that one views a thing quite differently when one knows it is defeated! I always thought Wayne was rather fine. But now, when I know that he is done for, there seems to be nothing else but Wayne. All the streets seem to point at him, all the chimneys seem to lean towards him. I suppose it is a morbid feeling; but Pump Street seems to be the only part of London that I feel physically. I suppose, I say, that it is morbid. I suppose it is exactly how a man feels about his heart when his heart is weak. "Pump Street" – the heart is a pump. And I am drivelling.

'Our finest leader at the front is, beyond all question, General Wilson. He has adopted alone among the other Provosts the uniform of his own halberdiers, although that fine old sixteenth-century garb was not originally intended to go with red side-whiskers. It was he who, against a most admirable and desperate defence, broke last night into Pump Street and held it for at least half an hour. He was afterwards expelled from it by General Turnbull, of Notting Hill, but only after desperate fighting and the sudden descent of that terrible darkness which proved so much more fatal to the forces of General Buck and General Swindon.

'Provost Wayne himself, with whom I had, with great good fortune, a most interesting interview, bore the most eloquent testimony to the conduct of General Wilson and his men. His precise words are as follows: "I have bought sweets at his funny little shop when I was four years old, and ever since. I never noticed anything, I am ashamed to say, except that he talked through his nose, and didn't wash himself particularly. And he came over our barricade like a devil from hell." I repeated this speech to General Wilson himself, with some delicate improvements, and he seemed pleased with it. He does not, however, seem pleased with anything so much just now as he is with the wearing of a sword. I have it from the front on the best authority that General Wilson was not completely shaved yesterday. It is believed in military circles that he is growing a moustache . . .

'As I have said, there is nothing to report. I walk wearily to the pillar-box at the corner of Pembridge Road to post my copy. Nothing whatever has happened, except the preparations for a particularly long and feeble siege, during which I trust I shall not be required to be at the Front. As I glance up Pembridge Road in the growing dusk, the aspect of that road reminds me that there is one note worth adding. General Buck has suggested, with characteristic acumen, to General Wilson that, in order to obviate the possibility of such a catastrophe as overwhelmed the allied forces in the last advance on Notting Hill (the catastrophe, I mean, of the extinguished lamps), each soldier should have a lighted lantern round his neck. This is one of the things which I really admire about General Buck. He possesses what people used to mean by "the humility of the man of science", that is, he learns steadily from his mistakes. Wayne may score off him in some other way, but not in that way. The lanterns look like fairy lights as they curve round the end of Pembridge Road.

* * *

'*Later* – I write with some difficulty, because the blood will run down my face and make patterns on the paper. Blood is a very beautiful thing; that is why it is concealed. If you ask why blood runs down my face, I can only reply that I was kicked by a horse. If you ask me what horse, I can reply with some pride that it was a warhorse. If you ask me how a warhorse came on the scene in our simple pedestrian warfare, I am reduced to the necessity, so painful to a special correspondent, of recounting my experiences.

'I was, as I have said, in the very act of posting my copy at the pillar-box, and of glancing as I did so up the glittering curve of Pembridge Road, studded with the lights of Wilson's men. I don't know what made me pause to examine the matter, but I had a fancy that the line of lights, where it melted into the indistinct brown twilight, was more indistinct than usual. I was almost certain that in a certain stretch of the road where there had been five lights there were now only four. I strained my eyes; I counted them again, and there were only three. A moment after there were only two; an instant after only one; and an instant after that the lanterns near to me swung like jangled bells, as if struck suddenly. They flared and fell; and for the moment the fall of them was like the fall of the sun and stars out of heaven. It left everything in a primal blindness. As a matter of fact, the road was not yet legitimately dark. There were still red rays of a sunset in the sky, and the brown gloaming was still warmed, as it were, with a feeling as of firelight. But for three seconds after the lanterns swung and sank, I saw in front of me a blackness blocking the sky. And with the fourth second I knew that this blackness which blocked the sky was a man on a great horse; and I was trampled and tossed aside as a swirl of horsemen swept round the corner. As they turned I saw that they were not black, but scarlet; they were a sortie of the besieged, Wayne riding ahead.

'I lifted myself from the gutter, blinded with blood from a very slight skin-wound, and, queerly enough, not caring either for the blindness or for the slightness of the wound. For one mortal minute after that amazing cavalcade had spun past, there was dead stillness on the empty road. And then came Barker and all his halberdiers running like devils in the track of them. It had been their business to guard the gate by which the sortie had broken out; but they had not reckoned, and small blame to them, on cavalry. As it was, Barker and his men made a perfectly splendid run after them, almost catching Wayne's horses by the tails.

'Nobody can understand the sortie. It consists only of a small number of Wayne's garrison. Turnbull himself, with the vast mass of it, is undoubtedly still barricaded in Pump Street. Sorties of this kind are natural enough in the majority of historical sieges, such as the siege of Paris in 1870, because in such cases the besieged are certain of some support outside. But what can be the object of it in this case? Wayne knows (or if he is too mad to know anything, at least Turnbull knows) that there is not, and never has been, the smallest chance of support for him outside; that the mass of the sane modern inhabitants of London regard his farcical patriotism with as much contempt as they do the original idiocy that gave it birth – the folly of our miserable King. What Wayne and his horsemen are doing nobody can even conjecture. The general theory round here is that he is simply a traitor, and has abandoned the besieged. But all such larger but yet more soluble riddles are as nothing compared to the one small but unanswerable riddle: Where did they get the horses?

* * *

'*Later* – I have heard a most extraordinary account of the origin of the appearance of the horses. It appears that that amazing person, General Turnbull, who is now ruling Pump Street in the absence of Wayne, sent out, on the morning of the declaration of war, a vast number of little boys (or cherubs of the gutter, as we pressmen say), with half-crowns in their pockets, to take cabs all over London. No less than a hundred and sixty cabs met at Pump Street; were commandeered by the garrison. The men were set free, the cabs used to make barricades, and the horses kept in Pump Street, where they were fed and exercised for several days, until they were sufficiently rapid and efficient to be used for this wild ride out of the town. If this is so, and I have it on the best possible authority, the method of the sortie is explained. But we have no explanation of its object. Just as Barker's Blues were swinging round the corner after them, they were stopped, but not by an enemy; only by the voice of one man, and he a friend. Red Wilson of Bayswater ran alone along the main road like a madman, waving them back with a halberd snatched from a sentinel. He was in supreme command, and Barker stopped at the corner, staring and bewildered. We could hear Wilson's voice loud and distinct out of the dusk, so that it seemed strange that the great voice should come out of the little body. "Halt, South Kensington! Guard this entry, and prevent them returning. I will pursue. Forward, the Green Guards!"

'A wall of dark blue uniforms and a wood of poleaxes was between me and Wilson, for Barker's men blocked the mouth of the road in two rigid lines. But through them and through the dusk I could hear the clear orders and the clank of arms, and see the green army of Wilson marching by towards the west. They were our great fighting-men. Wilson had filled them with his own fire; in a few days they had become veterans. Each of them wore a silver medal of a pump, to boast that they alone of all the allied armies had stood victorious in Pump Street.

'I managed to slip past the detachment of Barker's Blues, who are guarding the end of Pembridge Road, and a sharp spell of running brought me to the tail of Wilson's green army as it swung down the road in pursuit of the flying Wayne. The dusk had deepened into almost total darkness; for some time I only heard the throb of the marching pace. Then suddenly there was a cry, and the tall fighting men were flung back on me, almost crushing me, and again the lanterns swung and jingled, and the cold nozzles of great horses pushed into the press of us. They had turned and charged us.

' "You fools!" came the voice of Wilson, cleaving our panic with a splendid cold anger. "Don't you see? the horses have no riders!"

'It was true. We were being plunged at by a stampede of horses with empty saddles. What could it mean? Had Wayne met some of our men and been defeated? Or had he flung these horses at us as some kind of ruse or mad new mode of warfare, such as he seemed bent on inventing? Or did he and his men want to get away in disguise? Or did they want to hide in houses somewhere?

'Never did I admire any man's intellect (even my own) so much as I did Wilson's at that moment. Without a word, he simply pointed the halberd (which he still grasped) to the southern side of the road. As you know, the streets running up to the ridge of Campden Hill from the main road are peculiarly steep, they are more like sudden flights of stairs. We were just opposite Aubrey Road, the steepest of all; up that it would have been far more difficult to urge half-trained horses than to run up on one's feet.

' "Left wheel!" hallooed Wilson. "They have gone up here," he added to me, who happened to be at his elbow.

' "Why?" I ventured to ask.

' "Can't say for certain," replied the Bayswater general. "They've gone up here in a great hurry, anyhow. They've simply turned their horses loose, because they couldn't take them up. I fancy I know. I fancy they're trying to get over the ridge to Kensingston or Hammersmith, or somewhere, and are striking up here because it's just beyond the end of our line. Damned fools, not to have gone further along the road, though. They've only just shaved our last outpost. Lambert is hardly four hundred yards from here. And I've sent him word."

' "Lambert!'" I said. "Not young Wilfrid Lambert – my old friend."

' "Wilfrid Lambert's his name," said the general; "used to be a 'man about town'; silly fellow with a big nose. That kind of man always volunteers for some war or other; and what's funnier, he generally isn't half bad at it. Lambert is distinctly good. The yellow West Kensingtons I always reckoned the weakest part of the army; but he has pulled them together uncommonly well, though he's subordinate to Swindon, who's a donkey. In the attack from Pembridge Road the other night he showed great pluck."

' "He has shown greater pluck than that," I said. "He has criticised my sense of humour. That was his first engagement."

'This remark was, I am sorry to say, lost on the admirable commander of the allied forces. We were in the act of climbing the last half of Aubrey Road, which is so abrupt a slope that it looks like an old-fashioned map leaning up against the wall. There are lines of little trees, one above the other, as in the old-fashioned map.

'We reached the top of it, panting somewhat, and were just about to turn the corner by a place called (in chivalrous anticipation of our wars of sword and axe) Tower Crecy, when we were suddenly knocked in the stomach (I can use no other term) by a horde of men hurled back upon us. They wore the red uniform of Wayne; their halberds were broken; their foreheads bleeding; but the mere impetus of their retreat staggered us as we stood at the last ridge of the slope.

' "Good old Lambert!" yelled out suddenly the stolid Mr Wilson of Bayswater, in an uncontrollable excitement. "Damned jolly old Lambert! He's got there already! He's driving them back on us! Hurrah! hurrah! Forward, the Green Guards!"

'We swung round the corner eastwards, Wilson running first, brandishing the halberd:

'Will you pardon a little egotism? Everyone likes a little egotism, when it takes the form, as mine does in this case, of a disgraceful confession. The thing is really a little interesting, because it shows how the merely artistic habit has bitten into men like me. It was the most intensely exciting occurrence that had ever come to me in my life; and I was really intensely excited about it. And yet, as we turned that corner, the first impression I had was of something that had nothing to do with the fight at all. I was stricken from the sky as by a thunderbolt, by the height of the Waterworks Tower on Campden Hill. I don't know whether Londoners generally realise how high it looks when one comes out, in this way, almost immediately under it. For the second it seemed to me that at the foot of it even human war was a triviality. For the second I felt as if I had been drunk with some trivial orgy, and that I had been sobered by the shock of that shadow. A moment afterwards, I realised that under it was going on something more enduring than stone, and something wilder than the dizziest height – the agony of man. And I knew that, compared to that, this overwhelming tower was itself a triviality; it was a mere stalk of stone which humanity could snap like a stick.

'I don't know why I have talked so much about this silly old Waterworks Tower, which at the very best was only a tremendous background. It was that, certainly, a sombre and awful landscape, against which our figures were relieved. But I think the real reason was, that there was in my own mind so sharp a transition from the tower of stone to the man of flesh. For what I saw first when I had shaken off, as it were, the shadow of the tower, was a man, and a man I knew.

'Lambert stood at the further corner of the street that curved round the tower, his figure outlined in some degree by the beginning of moonrise. He looked magnificent, a hero; but he looked something much more interesting than that. He was, as it happened, in almost precisely the same swaggering attitude in which he had stood nearly fifteen years ago, when he swung his walking-stick and struck it into the ground, and told me that all my subtlety was drivel. And, upon my soul, I think he required more courage to say that than to fight as he does now. For then he was fighting against something that was in the ascendant, fashionable, and victorious. And now he is fighting (at the risk of his life, no doubt) merely against something which is already dead, which is impossible, futile; of which nothing has been more impossible and futile than this very sortie which has brought him into contact with it.

People nowadays allow infinitely too little for the psychological sense of victory as a factor in affairs. Then he was attacking the degraded but undoubtedly victorious Quin; now he is attacking the interesting but totally extinguished Wayne.

'His name recalls me to the details of the scene. The facts were these. A line of red halberdiers, headed by Wayne, were marching up the street, close under the northern wall, which is, in fact, the bottom of a sort of dyke or fortification of the Waterworks. Lambert and his yellow West Kensingtons had that instant swept round the corner and had shaken the Waynites heavily, hurling back a few of the more timid, as I have just described, into our very arms. When our force struck the tail of Wayne's, everyone knew that all was up with him. His favourite military barber was struck down. His grocer was stunned. He himself was hurt in the thigh, and reeled back against the wall. We had him in a trap with two jaws. "Is that you?" shouted Lambert, genially, to Wilson, across the hemmed-in host of Notting Hill. "That's about the ticket," replied General Wilson; "keep them under the wall."

'The men of Notting Hill were falling fast. Adam Wayne threw up his long arms to the wall above him, and with a spring stood upon it; a gigantic figure against the moon. He tore the banner out of the hands of the standard-bearer below him, and shook it out suddenly above our heads, so that it was like thunder in the heavens.

' "Round the Red Lion!" he cried. "Swords round the Red Lion! Halberds round the Red Lion! They are the thorns round the rose."

'His voice and the crack of the banner made a momentary rally, and Lambert, whose idiotic face was almost beautiful with battle, felt it as by an instinct, and cried: "Drop your public-house flag, you footler! Drop it!"

' "The banner of the Red Lion seldom stoops," said Wayne, proudly, letting it out luxuriantly on the night wind.

'The next moment I knew that poor Adam's sentimental theatricality had cost him much. Lambert was on the wall at a bound, his sword in his teeth, and had slashed at Wayne's head before he had time to draw his sword, his hands being busy with the enormous flag. He stepped back only just in time to avoid the first cut, and let the flagstaff fall, so that the spear-blade at the end of it pointed to Lambert.

' "The banner stoops," cried Wayne, in a voice that must have startled streets. "The banner of Notting Hill stoops to a hero." And with the words he drove the spear-point and half the flagstaff through Lambert's body and dropped him dead upon the road below, a stone upon the stones of the street.

' "Notting Hill! Notting Hill!" cried Wayne, in a sort of divine rage. "Her banner is all the holier for the blood of a brave enemy! Up on the wall, patriots! Up on the wall! Notting Hill!"

'With his long strong arm he actually dragged a man up on to the wall to be silhouetted against the moon, and more and more men climbed up there, pulled themselves and were pulled, till clusters and crowds of the half-massacred men of Pump Street massed upon the wall above us.

' "Notting Hill! Notting Hill!" cried Wayne, unceasingly.

' "Well, what about Bayswater?" said a worthy working-man in Wilson's army, irritably. "Bayswater for ever!"

' "We have won!" cried Wayne, striking his flagstaff in the ground. "Bayswater for ever! We have taught our enemies patriotism!"

' "Oh, cut these fellows up and have done with it!" cried one of Lambert's lieutenants, who was reduced to something bordering on madness by the responsibility of succeeding to the command.

' "Let us by all means try," said Wilson, grimly; and the two armies closed round the third.

* * *

'I simply cannot describe what followed. I am sorry, but there is such a thing as physical fatigue, as physical nausea, and, I may add, as physical terror. Suffice it to say that the above paragraph was written about 11 p.m., and that it is now about 2 a.m., and that the battle is not finished, and is not likely to be. Suffice it further to say that down the steep streets which lead from the Waterworks Tower to the Notting Hill High Road, blood has been running, and is running, in great red serpents, that curl out into the main thoroughfare and shine in the moon.

* * *

'*Later* – The final touch has been given to all this terrible futility. Hours have passed; morning has broken; men are still swaying and fighting at the foot of the tower and round the corner of Aubrey Road; the fight has not finished. But I know it is a farce.

'News has just come to show that Wayne's amazing sortie, followed by the amazing resistance through a whole night on the wall of the Waterworks, is as if it had not been. What was the object of that strange exodus we shall probably never know, for the simple reason that everyone who knew will probably be cut to pieces in the course of the next two or three hours.

'I have heard, about three minutes ago, that Buck and Buck's methods have won after all. He was perfectly right, of course, when one comes to think of it, in holding that it was physically impossible for a street to defeat a city. While we thought he was patrolling the eastern gates with his Purple army; while we were rushing about the streets and waving halberds and lanterns; while poor old Wilson was scheming like Moltke and fighting like Achilles to entrap the wild Provost of Notting Hill – Mr Buck, retired draper, has simply driven down in a hansom cab and done something about as plain as butter and about as useful and nasty. He has gone down to South Kensington, Brompton, and Fulham, and by spending about four thousand pounds of his private means, has raised an army of nearly as many men; that is to say, an army big enough to beat, not only Wayne, but Wayne and all his present enemies put together. The army, I understand, is encamped along High Street, Kensington, and fills it from the church to Addison Road Bridge. It is to advance by ten different roads uphill to the north.

'I cannot endure to remain here. Everything makes it worse than it need be. The dawn, for instance, has broken round Campden Hill; splendid spaces of silver, edged with gold, are torn out of the sky. Worse still, Wayne and his men feel the dawn; their faces, though bloody and pale, are strangely hopeful . . . insupportably pathetic. Worst of all, for the moment they are winning. If it were not for Buck and the new army they might just, and only just, win.

'I repeat, I cannot stand it. It is like watching that wonderful play of old Maeterlinck's (you know my partiality for the healthy, jolly old authors of the nineteenth century), in which one has to watch the quiet conduct of people inside a parlour, while knowing that the very men are outside the door whose word can blast it all with tragedy. And this is worse, for the men are not talking, but writhing and bleeding and dropping dead for a thing that is already settled – and settled against them. The great grey masses of men still toil and tug and sway hither and thither around the great grey tower; and the tower is still motionless, as it will always be motionless. These men will be crushed before the sun is set; and new men will arise and be crushed, and new wrongs done, and tyranny will always rise again like the sun, and injustice will always be as fresh as the flowers of spring. And the stone tower will always look down on it. Matter, in its brutal beauty, will always look down on those who are mad enough to consent to die, and yet more mad, since they consent to live.'

* * *

Thus ended abruptly the first and last contribution of the special correspondent of the *Court Journal* to that valued periodical.

The correspondent himself, as has been said, was simply sick and gloomy at the last news of the triumph of Buck. He slouched sadly down the steep Aubrey Road, up which he had the night before run in so unusual an excitement, and strolled out into the empty dawn-lit main road, looking vaguely for a cab. He saw nothing in the vacant space except a blue-and-gold glittering thing, running very fast, which looked at first like a very tall beetle, but turned out, to his great astonishment, to be Barker.

'Have you heard the good news?' asked that gentleman.

'Yes,' said Quin, with a measured voice. 'I have heard the glad tidings of great joy. Shall we take a hansom down to Kensington? I see one over there.'

They took the cab, and were, in four minutes, fronting the ranks of the multitudinous and invincible army. Quin had not spoken a word all the way, and something about him had prevented the essentially impressionable Barker from speaking either.

The great army, as it moved up Kensington High Street, calling many heads to the numberless windows, for it was long indeed – longer than the lives of most of the tolerably young – since such an army had been seen in London. Compared with the vast organisation which was now swallowing up the miles, with Buck at its head as leader, and the King hanging at its tail as journalist, the whole story of our problem was insignificant. In the presence of that army the red Notting Hills and the green Bayswaters were alike tiny and straggling groups. In its presence the whole struggle round Pump Street was like an ant-hill under the hoof of an ox. Every man who felt or looked at that infinity of men knew that it was the triumph of Buck's brutal arithmetic. Whether Wayne was right or wrong, wise or foolish, was quite a fair matter for discussion. But it was a matter of history. At the foot of Church Street, opposite Kensington Church, they paused in their glowing good humour.

'Let us send some kind of messenger or herald up to them,' said Buck, turning to Barker and the King. 'Let us send and ask them to cave in without more muddle.'

'What shall we say to them?' said Barker, doubtfully.

'The facts of the case are quite sufficient,' rejoined Buck. 'It is the facts of the case that make an army surrender. Let us simply say that our army that is fighting their army, and their army that is fighting our army, amount altogether to about a thousand men. Say that we have four thousand. It is very simple. Of the thousand fighting, they have at the very most, three hundred, so that, with those three hundred, they have now to fight four thousand seven hundred men. Let them do it if it amuses them.'

And the Provost of North Kensington laughed.

The herald who was despatched up Church Street in all the pomp of the South Kensington blue and gold, with the Three Birds on his tabard, was attended by two trumpeters.

'What will they do when they consent?' asked Barker, for the sake of saying something in the sudden stillness of that immense army.

'I know my Wayne very well,' said Buck, laughing. 'When he submits he will send a red herald flaming with the Lion of Notting Hill. Even defeat will be delightful to him, since it is formal and romantic.'

The King, who had strolled up to the head of the line, broke silence for the first time.

'I shouldn't wonder,' he said, 'if he defied you, and didn't send the herald after all. I don't think you do know your Wayne quite so well as you think.'

'All right, your Majesty,' said Buck, easily; 'if it isn't disrespectful, I'll put my political calculations in a very simple form. I'll lay you ten pounds to a shilling the herald comes with the surrender.'

'All right,' said Auberon. 'I may be wrong, but it's my notion of Adam Wayne that he'll die in his city, and that, till he is dead, it will not be a safe property.'

'The bet's made, your Majesty,' said Buck.

Another long silence ensued, in the course of which Barker alone, amid the motionless army, strolled and stamped in his restless way.

Then Buck suddenly leant forward.

'It's taking your money, your Majesty,' he said. 'I knew it was. There comes the herald from Adam Wayne.'

'It's not,' cried the King, peering forward also. 'You brute, it's a red omnibus.'

'It's not,' said Buck, calmly; and the King did not answer, for down the centre of the spacious and silent Church Street was walking, beyond question, the herald of the Red Lion, with two trumpeters.

Buck had something in him which taught him how to be magnanimous. In his hour of success he felt magnanimous towards Wayne, whom he really admired; magnanimous towards the King, off whom he had scored so publicly; and, above all, magnanimous towards Barker, who was the titular leader of this vast South Kensington army, which his own talent had evoked.

'General Barker,' he said, bowing, 'do you propose now to receive the message from the besieged?'

Barker bowed also, and advanced towards the herald.

'Has your master, Mr Adam Wayne, received our request for surrender?' he asked.

The herald conveyed a solemn and respectful affirmative.

Barker resumed, coughing slightly, but encouraged.

'What answer does your master send?'

The herald again inclined himself submissively, and answered in a kind of monotone.

'My message is this. Adam Wayne, Lord High Provost of Notting Hill, under the charter of King Auberon and the laws of God and all mankind, free and of a free city, greets James Barker, Lord High Provost of South Kensington, by the same rights free and honourable, leader of the army of the South. With all friendly reverence, and with all constitutional consideration, he desires James Barker to lay down his arms, and the whole army under his command to lay down their arms also.'

Before the words were ended the King had run forward into the open space with shining eyes. The rest of the staff and the forefront of the army were literally struck breathless. When they recovered they began to laugh beyond restraint; the revulsion was too sudden.

'The Lord High Provost of Notting Hill,' continued the herald, 'does not propose, in the event of your surrender, to use his victory for any of those repressive purposes which others have entertained against him. He will leave you your free laws and your free cities, your flags and your governments. He will not destroy the religion of South Kensington, or crush the old customs of Bayswater.'

An irrepressible explosion of laughter went up from the forefront of the great army.

'The King must have had something to do with this humour,' said Buck, slapping his thigh. 'It's too deliciously insolent. Barker, have a glass of wine.'

And in his conviviality he actually sent a soldier across to the restaurant opposite the church and brought out two glasses for a toast.

When the laughter had died down, the herald continued quite monotonously: 'In the event of your surrendering your arms and dispersing under the superintendence of our forces, these local rights of yours shall be carefully observed. In the event of your not doing so, the Lord High Provost of Notting Hill desires to announce that he has just captured the Waterworks Tower, just above you, on Campden Hill, and that within ten minutes from now, that is, on the reception through me of your refusal, he will open the great reservoir and flood the whole valley where you stand in thirty feet of water. God save King Auberon!'

Buck had dropped his glass and sent a great splash of wine over the road.

'But – but – ' he said; and then by a last and splendid effort of his great sanity, looked the facts in the face.

'We must surrender,' he said. 'You could do nothing against fifty thousand tons of water coming down a steep hill, ten minutes hence. We must surrender. Our four thousand men might as well be four. *Vicisti Galilae!* Perkins, you may as well get me another glass of wine.'

In this way the vast army of South Kensington surrendered and the Empire of Notting Hill began. One further fact in this connection is perhaps worth mentioning – the fact that, after his victory, Adam Wayne caused the great tower on Campden Hill to be plated with gold and inscribed with a great epitaph, saying that it was the monument of Wilfrid Lambert, the heroic defender of the place, and surmounted with a statue, in which his large nose was done something less than justice to.

BOOK FIVE

CHAPTER I

The Empire of Notting Hill

On the evening of the third of October, twenty years after the great victory of Notting Hill, which gave it the dominion of London, King Auberon came, as of old, out of Kensington Palace.

He had changed little, save for a streak or two of grey in his hair, for his face had always been old, and his step slow, and, as it were, decrepit.

If he looked old, it was not because of anything physical or mental. It was because he still wore, with a quaint conservatism, the frock-coat and high hat of the days before the great war. 'I have survived the Deluge,' he said. 'I am a pyramid, and must behave as such.'

As he passed up the street the Kensingtonians, in their picturesque blue smocks, saluted him as a King, and then looked after him as a curiosity. It seemed odd to them that men had once worn so elvish an attire.

The King, cultivating the walk attributed to the oldest inhabitant ('Gaffer Auberon' his friends were now confidentially desired to call him), went toddling northward. He paused, with reminiscence in his eye, at the Southern Gate of Notting Hill, one of those nine great gates of bronze and steel, wrought with reliefs of the old battles, by the hand of Chiffy himself.

'Ah!' he said, shaking his head and assuming an unnecessary air of age, and a provincialism of accent. 'Ah! I mind when there warn't none of this here.'

He passed through the Ossington Gate, surmounted by a great lion, wrought in red copper on yellow brass, with the motto, 'Nothing Ill.' The guard in red and gold saluted him with his halberd.

It was about sunset, and the lamps were being lit. Auberon paused to look at them, for they were Chiffy's finest work, and his artistic eye never failed to feast on them. In memory of the Great Battle of the Lamps, each great iron lamp was surmounted by a veiled figure, sword in hand, holding over the flame an iron hood or extinguisher, as if ready to let it fall if the armies of the South and West should again show their flags in the city. Thus no child in Notting Hill could play about the streets without the very lamp posts reminding him of the salvation of his country in the dreadful year.

'Old Wayne was right in a way,' commented the King. 'The sword does make things beautiful. It has made the whole world romantic by now. And to think people once thought me a buffoon for suggesting a romantic Notting Hill. Deary me, deary me! (I think that is the expression) – it seems like a previous existence.'

Turning a corner, he found himself in Pump Street, opposite the four shops which Adam Wayne had studied twenty years before. He entered idly the shop of Mr Mead, the grocer. Mr Mead was somewhat older, like the rest of the world, and his red beard, which he now wore with a moustache, and long and full, was partly blanched and discoloured. He was dressed in a long and richly embroidered robe of blue, brown, and crimson, interwoven with an Eastern complexity of pattern, and covered with obscure symbols and pictures, representing his wares passing from hand to hand and from nation to nation. Round his neck was the chain with the Blue Argosy cut in turquoise, which he wore as Grand Master of the Grocers. The whole shop had the sombre and sumptuous look of its owner. The wares were displayed as prominently as in the old days, but they were now blended and arranged with a sense of tint and grouping, too often neglected by the dim grocers of those forgotten days. The wares were shown plainly, but shown not so much as an old grocer would have shown his stock, but rather as an educated virtuoso would have shown his treasures. The tea was stored in great blue and green vases, inscribed with the nine indispensable sayings of the wise men of China. Other vases of a confused orange and purple, less rigid and dominant, more humble and dreamy, stored symbolically the tea of India. A row of caskets of a simple silvery metal contained tinned meats. Each was wrought with some rude but rhythmic form, as a shell, a horn, a fish, or an apple, to indicate what material had been canned in it.

'Your Majesty,' said Mr Mead, sweeping an Oriental reverence. 'This is an honour to me, but yet more an honour to the city.'

Auberon took off his hat.

'Mr Mead,' he said, 'Notting Hill, whether in giving or taking, can deal in nothing but honour. Do you happen to sell liquorice?'

'Liquorice, sire,' said Mr Mead, 'is not the least important of our benefits out of the dark heart of Arabia.'

And going reverently towards a green and silver canister, made in the form of an Arabian mosque, he proceeded to serve his customer.

'I was just thinking, Mr Mead,' said the King, reflectively, 'I don't know why I should think about it just now, but I was just thinking of twenty years ago. Do you remember the times before the war?'

The grocer, having wrapped up the liquorice sticks in a piece of paper (inscribed with some appropriate sentiment), lifted his large grey eyes dreamily, and looked at the darkening sky outside.

'Oh yes, your Majesty,' he said. 'I remember these streets before the Lord Provost began to rule us. I can't remember how we felt very well. All the great songs and the fighting change one so; and I don't think we can really estimate all we owe to the Provost; but I can remember his coming into this very shop twenty-two years ago, and I remember the things he said. The singular thing is that, as far as I remember, I thought the things he said odd at that time. Now it's the things that I said, as far as I can recall them, that seem to me odd – as odd as a madman's antics.'

'Ah!' said the King; and looked at him with an unfathomable quietness.

'I thought nothing of being a grocer then,' he said. 'Isn't that odd enough for anybody? I thought nothing of all the wonderful places that my goods come from, and wonderful ways that they are made. I did not know that I was for all practical purposes a king with slaves spearing fishes near the secret pool, and gathering fruits in the islands under the world. My mind was a blank on the thing. I was as mad as a hatter.'

The King turned also, and stared out into the dark, where the great lamps that commemorated the battle were already flaming.

'And is this the end of poor old Wayne?' he said, half to himself. 'To inflame everyone so much that he is lost himself in the blaze. Is this his victory that he, my incomparable Wayne, is now only one in a world of Waynes? Has he conquered and become by conquest commonplace? Must Mr Mead, the grocer, talk as high as he? Lord! what a strange world in which a man cannot remain unique even by taking the trouble to go mad!'

And he went dreamily out of the shop.

He paused outside the next one almost precisely as the Provost had done two decades before.

'How uncommonly creepy this shop looks!' he said. 'But yet somehow encouragingly creepy, invitingly creepy. It looks like something in a jolly old nursery story in which you are frightened out of your skin, and yet know that things always end well. The way those low sharp gables are carved like great black bat's wings folded down, and the way those queer-coloured bowls underneath are made to shine like giant's eyeballs. It looks like a benevolent warlock's hut. It is apparently a chemist's.'

Almost as he spoke, Mr Bowles, the chemist, came to his shop door in a long black velvet gown and hood, monastic as it were, but yet with a touch of the diabolic. His hair was still quite black, and his face even paler than of old. The only spot of colour he carried was a red star cut in some precious stone of strong tint, hung on his breast. He belonged to the Society of the Red Star of Charity, founded on the lamps displayed by doctors and chemists.

'A fine evening, sir,' said the chemist. 'Why, I can scarcely be mistaken in supposing it to be your Majesty. Pray step inside and share a bottle of sal volatile, or anything that may take your fancy. As it happens, there is an old acquaintance of your Majesty's in my shop carousing (if I may be permitted the term) upon that beverage at this moment.'

The King entered the shop, which was an Aladdin's garden of shades and hues, for as the chemist's scheme of colour was more brilliant than the grocer's scheme, so it was arranged with even more delicacy and fancy. Never, if the phrase may be employed, had such a nosegay of medicines been presented to the artistic eye.

But even the solemn rainbow of that evening interior was rivalled or even eclipsed by the figure standing in the centre of the shop. His form, which was a large and stately one, was clad in a brilliant blue velvet, cut in the richest Renaissance fashion, and slashed so as to show gleams and gaps of a wonderful lemon or pale yellow. He had several chains round his neck, and his plumes, which were of several tints of bronze and gold, hung down to the great gold hilt of his long sword. He was drinking a dose of sal volatile, and admiring its opal tint. The King advanced with a slight mystification towards the tall figure, whose face was in shadow; then he said: 'By the Great Lord of Luck, Barker!'

The figure removed his plumed cap, showing the same dark head and long, almost equine face which the King had so often seen rising out of the high collar of Bond Street. Except for a grey patch on each temple, it was totally unchanged.

'Your Majesty,' said Barker, 'this is a meeting nobly retrospective, a meeting that has about it a certain October gold. I drink to old days'; and he finished his sal volatile with simple feeling.

'I am delighted to see you again, Barker,' said the King. 'It is indeed long since we met. What with my travels in Asia Minor, and my book having to be written (you have read my "Life of Prince Albert for Children", of course?), we have scarcely met twice since the Great War. That is twenty years ago.'

'I wonder,' said Barker, thoughtfully, 'if I might speak freely to your Majesty?'

'Well,' said Auberon, 'it's rather late in the day to start speaking respectfully. Flap away, my bird of freedom.'

'Well, your Majesty,' replied Barker, lowering his voice, 'I don't think it will be so long to the next war.'

'What do you mean?' asked Auberon.

'We will stand this insolence no longer,' burst out Barker, fiercely. 'We are not slaves because Adam Wayne twenty years ago cheated us with a water-pipe. Notting Hill is Notting Hill; it is not the world. We in South Kensington, we also have memories – ay, and hopes. If they fought for these trumpery shops and a few lamp posts, shall we not fight for the great High Street and the sacred Natural History Museum?'

'Great Heavens!' said the astounded Auberon. 'Will wonders never cease? Have the two greatest marvels been achieved? Have you turned altruistic, and has Wayne turned selfish? Are you the patriot, and he the tyrant?'

'It is not from Wayne himself altogether that the evil comes,' answered Barker. 'He, indeed, is now mostly wrapped in dreams, and sits with his old sword beside the fire. But Notting Hill is the tyrant, your Majesty. Its Council and its crowds have been so intoxicated by the spreading over the whole city of Wayne's old ways and visions, that they try to meddle with everyone, and rule everyone, and civilise everyone, and tell everyone what is good for him. I do not deny the great impulse which his old war, wild as it seemed, gave to the civic life of our time. It came when I was still a young man, and I admit it enlarged my career. But we are not going to see our own cities flouted and thwarted from day to day because of something Wayne did for us all nearly a quarter of a century ago. I am just waiting here for news upon this very matter. It is rumoured that Notting Hill has vetoed the statue of General Wilson they are putting up opposite Chepstow Place. If that is so, it is a black and white shameless breach of the terms on which we surrendered to Turnbull after the battle of the Tower. We were to keep our own customs and self-government. If that is so – '

'It is so,' said a deep voice; and both men turned round.

A burly figure in purple robes, with a silver eagle hung round his neck and moustaches almost as florid as his plumes, stood in the doorway.

'Yes,' he said, acknowledging the King's start, 'I am Provost Buck, and the news is true. These men of the Hill have forgotten that we fought round the Tower as well as they, and that it is sometimes foolish, as well as base, to despise the conquered.'

'Let us step outside,' said Barker, with a grim composure.

Buck did so, and stood rolling his eyes up and down the lamp-lit street.

'I would like to have a go at smashing all this,' he muttered, 'though I am over sixty. I would like – '

His voice ended in a cry, and he reeled back a step, with his hands to his eyes, as he had done in those streets twenty years before.

'Darkness!' he cried – 'darkness again! What does it mean?'

For in truth every lamp in the street had gone out, so that they could not see even each other's outline, except faintly. The voice of the chemist came with startling cheerfulness out of the density.

'Oh, don't you know?' he said. 'Did they never tell you this is the Feast of the Lamps, the anniversary of the great battle that almost lost and just saved Notting Hill? Don't you know, your Majesty, that on this night twenty-one years ago we saw Wilson's green uniforms charging down this street, and driving Wayne and Turnbull back upon the gasworks, fighting with their handful like fiends from hell? And that then, in that great hour, Wayne sprang through a window of the gasworks, with one blow of his hand brought darkness on the whole city, and then with a cry like a lion's, that was heard through four streets, flew at Wilson's men, sword in hand, and swept them, bewildered as they were, and ignorant of the map, clear out of the sacred street again? And don't you know that upon that night every year all lights are turned out for half an hour while we sing the Notting Hill anthem in the darkness? Hark! there it begins.'

Through the night came a crash of drums, and then a strong swell of human voices:

> 'When the world was in the balance, there was night on Notting Hill,
> (There was night on Notting Hill): it was nobler than the day;
> On the cities where the lights are and the firesides glow,
> From the seas and from the deserts came the thing we did not know,
> Came the darkness, came the darkness, came the darkness on the foe,
> And the old guard of God turned to bay.
>
> For the old guard of God turns to bay, turns to bay,
> And the stars fall down before it ere its banners fall today.
> For when armies were around us as a howling and a horde,
> When falling was the citadel and broken was the sword,
> The darkness came upon them like the Dragon of the Lord,
> When the old guard of God turned to bay.'

The voices were just uplifting themselves in a second verse when they were stopped by a scurry and a yell. Barker had bounded into the street with a cry of 'South Kensington!' and a drawn dagger. In less time than a man could blink, the whole packed street was full of curses and struggling. Barker was flung back against the shop front, but used the second only to draw his sword as well as his dagger, and calling out, 'This is not the first time I've come through the thick of you,' flung himself again into the press. It was evident that he had drawn blood at last, for a more violent outcry arose, and many other knives and swords were discernible in the faint light. Barker, after having wounded more than one man, seemed on the point of being flung back again, when Buck suddenly stepped out into the street. He had no weapon, for he affected rather the peaceful magnificence of the great burgher, than the pugnacious dandyism which had replaced the old sombre dandyism in Barker. But with a blow of his clenched fist he broke the pane of the next shop, which was the old curiosity shop, and, plunging in his hand, snatched a kind of Japanese scimitar, and calling out, 'Kensington! Kensington!' rushed to Barker's assistance.

Barker's sword was broken, but he was laying about him with his dagger. Just as Buck ran up, a man of Notting Hill struck Barker down, but Buck struck the man down on top of him, and Barker sprang up again, the blood running down his face.

Suddenly all these cries were cloven by a great voice, that seemed to fall out of heaven. It was terrible to Buck and Barker and the King, from its seeming to come out the empty skies; but it was more terrible because it was a familiar voice, and one which at the same time they had not heard for so long.

'Turn up the lights,' said the voice from above them, and for a moment there was no reply, but only a tumult.

'In the name of Notting Hill and of the great Council of the City, turn up the lights.'

There was again a tumult and a vagueness for a moment, then the whole street and every object in it sprang suddenly out of the darkness, as every lamp sprang into life. And looking up they saw, standing upon a balcony near the roof of one of the highest houses, the figure and the face of Adam Wayne, his red hair blowing behind him, a little streaked with grey.

'What is this, my people?' he said. 'Is it altogether impossible to make a thing good without it immediately insisting on being wicked? The glory of Notting Hill in having achieved its independence, has been enough for me to dream of for many years, as I sat beside the fire. Is it really not enough for you, who have had so many other affairs to excite and distract you? Notting Hill is a nation. Why should it condescend to be a mere Empire? You wish to pull down the statue of General Wilson, which the men of Bayswater have so rightly erected in Westbourne Grove. Fools! Who erected that statue? Did Bayswater erect it? No. Notting Hill erected it. Do you not see that it is the glory of our achievement that we have infected the other cities with the idealism of Notting Hill? It is we who have created not only our own side, but both sides of this controversy. O too humble fools, why should you wish to destroy your enemies? You have done something more to them. You have created your enemies. You wish to pull down that gigantic silver hammer, which stands, like an obelisk, in the centre of the Broadway of Hammersmith. Fools! Before Notting Hill arose, did any person passing through Hammersmith Broadway expect to see there a gigantic silver hammer? You wish to abolish the great bronze figure of a knight standing upon the artificial bridge at Knightsbridge. Fools! Who would have thought of it before Notting Hill arose? I have even heard, and with deep pain I have heard it, that the evil eye of our imperial envy has been cast towards the remote horizon of the west, and that we have objected to the great black monument of a crowned raven, which commemorates the skirmish of Ravenscourt Park. Who created all these things? Were they there before we came? Cannot you be content with that destiny which was enough for Athens, which was enough for Nazareth, the destiny, the humble purpose, of creating a new world? Is Athens angry because Romans and Florentines have adopted her phraseology for expressing their own patriotism? Is Nazareth angry because as a little village it has become the type of all little villages out of which, as the Snobs say, no good can come? Has Athens asked everyone to wear the chlamys? Are all followers of the Nazarene compelled to wear turbans? No! but the soul of Athens went forth and made men drink hemlock, and the soul of Nazareth went forth and made men consent to be crucified. So has the soul of Notting Hill gone forth and made men realise what it is to live in a city. Just as we inaugurated our symbols and ceremonies, so they have inaugurated theirs; and are you so mad as to contend against them? Notting Hill is right; it has always been right. It has moulded itself on its own necessities, its own *sine qua non*; it has accepted its own ultimatum. Because it is a nation it has created itself; and because it is a nation it can destroy itself. Notting Hill shall always be the judge. If it is your will because of this matter of General Wilson's statue to make war upon Bayswater – '

A roar of cheers broke in upon his words, and further speech was impossible. Pale to the lips, the great patriot tried again and again to speak; but even his authority could not keep down the dark and roaring masses in the street below him. He said something further, but it was not audible. He descended at last sadly from the garret in which he lived, and mingled with the crowd at the foot of the houses. Finding General Turnbull, he put his hand on his shoulder with a queer affection and gravity, and said: 'Tomorrow, old man, we shall have a new experience, as fresh as the flowers of spring. We shall be defeated. You and I have been through three battles together, and have somehow or other missed this peculiar delight. It is unfortunate that we shall not probably be able to exchange our experiences, because, as it most annoyingly happens, we shall probably both be dead.'

Turnbull looked dimly surprised.

'I don't mind so much about being dead,' he said, 'but why should you say that we shall be defeated?'

'The answer is very simple,' replied Wayne, calmly. 'It is because we ought to be defeated. We have been in the most horrible holes before now; but in all those I was perfectly certain that the stars were on our side, and that we ought to get out. Now I know that we ought not to get out; and that takes away from me everything with which I won.'

As Wayne spoke he started a little, for both men became aware that a third figure was listening to them – a small figure with wondering eyes.

'Is it really true, my dear Wayne,' said the King, interrupting, 'that you think you will be beaten tomorrow?'

'There can be no doubt about it whatever,' replied Adam Wayne; 'the real reason is the one of which I have just spoken. But as a concession to your materialism, I will add that they have an organised army of a hundred allied cities against our one. That in itself, however, would be unimportant.'

Quin, with his round eyes, seemed strangely insistent.

'You are quite sure,' he said, 'that you must be beaten?'

'I am afraid,' said Turnbull, gloomily, 'that there can be no doubt about it.'

'Then,' cried the King, flinging out his arms, 'give me a halberd! Give me a halberd, somebody! I desire all men to witness that I, Auberon, King of England, do here and now abdicate, and implore the Provost of Notting Hill to permit me to enlist in his army. Give me a halberd!'

He seized one from some passing guard, and, shouldering it, stamped solemnly after the shouting columns of halberdiers which were, by this time, parading the streets. He had, however, nothing to do with the wrecking of the statue of General Wilson, which took place before morning.

CHAPTER 2

The Last Battle

The day was cloudy when Wayne went down to die with all his army in Kensington Gardens; it was cloudy again when that army had been swallowed up by the vast armies of a new world. There had been an almost uncanny interval of sunshine, in which the Provost of Notting Hill, with all the placidity of an onlooker, had gazed across to the hostile armies on the great spaces of verdure opposite; the long strips of green and blue and gold lay across the park in squares and oblongs like a proposition in Euclid wrought in a rich embroidery. But the sunlight was a weak and, as it were, a wet sunlight, and was soon swallowed up. Wayne spoke to the King, with a queer sort of coldness and languor, as to the military operations. It was as he had said the night before – that being deprived of his sense of an impracticable rectitude, he was, in effect, being deprived of everything. He was out of date, and at sea in a mere world of compromise and competition, of Empire against Empire, of the tolerably right and the tolerably wrong. When his eye fell on the King, however, who was marching very gravely with a top-hat and a halberd, it brightened slightly.

'Well, your Majesty,' he said, 'you at least ought to be proud today. If your children are fighting each other, at least those who win are your children. Other kings have distributed justice, you have distributed life. Other kings have ruled a nation, you have created nations. Others have made kingdoms, you have begotten them. Look at your children, father!' And he stretched his hand out towards the enemy.

Auberon did not raise his eyes.

'See how splendidly,' cried Wayne, 'the new cities come on – the new cities from across the river. See where Battersea advances over there – under the flag of the Lost Dog; and Putney – don't you see the Man on the White Boar shining on their standard as the sun catches it? It is the coming of a new age, your Majesty. Notting Hill is not a common empire; it is a thing like Athens, the mother of a mode of life, of a manner of living, which shall renew the youth of the world – a thing like Nazareth. When I was young I remember, in the old dreary days, wiseacres used to write books about how trains would get faster, and all the world be one empire, and tramcars go to the moon. And even as a child I used to say to myself, "Far more likely that we shall go on the crusades again, or worship the gods of the city." And so it has been. And I am glad, though this is my last battle.'

Even as he spoke there came a crash of steel from the left, and he turned his head.

'Wilson!' he cried, with a kind of joy. 'Red Wilson has charged our left. No one can hold him in; he eats swords. He is as keen a soldier as Turnbull, but less patient – less really great. Ha! and Barker is moving. How Barker has improved; how handsome he looks! It is not all having plumes; it is also having a soul in one's daily life. Ha!'

And another crash of steel on the right showed that Barker had closed with Notting Hill on the other side.

'Turnbull is there!' cried Wayne. 'See him hurl them back! Barker is checked! Turnbull charges – wins! But our left is broken. Wilson has smashed Bowles and Mead, and may turn our flank. Forward, the Provost's Guard!'

And the whole centre moved forward, Wayne's face and hair and sword flaming in the van.

The King ran suddenly forward.

The next instant a great jar that went through it told that it had met the enemy. And right over against them through the wood of their own weapons Auberon saw the Purple Eagle of Buck of North Kensington.

On the left Red Wilson was storming the broken ranks, his little green figure conspicuous even in the tangle of men and weapons, with the flaming red moustaches and the crown of laurel. Bowles slashed at his head and tore away some of the wreath, leaving the rest bloody, and, with a roar like a bull's, Wilson sprang at him, and, after a rattle of fencing, plunged his point into the chemist, who fell, crying, 'Notting Hill!' Then the Notting Hillers wavered, and Bayswater swept them back in confusion. Wilson had carried everything before him.

On the right, however, Turnbull had carried the Red Lion banner with a rush against Barker's men, and the banner of the Golden Birds bore up with difficulty against it. Barker's men fell fast. In the centre Wayne and Buck were engaged, stubborn and confused. So far as the fighting went, it was precisely equal. But the fighting was a farce. For behind the three small armies with which Wayne's small army was engaged lay the great sea of the allied armies, which looked on as yet as scornful spectators, but could have broken all four armies by moving a finger.

Suddenly they did move. Some of the front contingents, the pastoral chiefs from Shepherd's Bush, with their spears and fleeces, were seen advancing, and the rude clans from Paddington Green. They were advancing for a very good reason. Buck, of North Kensington, was signalling wildly; he was surrounded, and totally cut off. His regiments were a struggling mass of people, islanded in a red sea of Notting Hill.

The allies had been too careless and confident. They had allowed Barker's force to be broken to pieces by Turnbull, and the moment that was done, the astute old leader of Notting Hill swung his men round and attacked Buck behind and on both sides. At the same moment Wayne cried, 'Charge!' and struck him in front like a thunderbolt.

Two-thirds of Buck's men were cut to pieces before their allies could reach them. Then the sea of cities came on with their banners like breakers, and swallowed Notting Hill for ever. The battle was not over, for not one of Wayne's men would surrender, and it lasted till sundown, and long after. But it was decided; the story of Notting Hill was ended.

When Turnbull saw it, he ceased a moment from fighting, and looked round him. The evening sunlight struck his face; it looked like a child's.

'I have had my youth,' he said. Then, snatching an axe from a man, he dashed into the thick of the spears of Shepherd's Bush, and died somewhere far in the depths of their reeling ranks. Then the battle roared on; every man of Notting Hill was slain before night.

Wayne was standing by a tree alone after the battle. Several men approached him with axes. One struck at him. His foot seemed partly to slip; but he flung his hand out, and steadied himself against the tree.

Barker sprang after him, sword in hand, and shaking with excitement.

'How large now, my lord,' he cried, 'is the Empire of Notting Hill?'

Wayne smiled in the gathering dark.

'Always as large as this,' he said, and swept his sword round in a semicircle of silver.

Barker dropped, wounded in the neck; and Wilson sprang over his body like a tiger-cat, rushing at Wayne. At the same moment there came behind the Lord of the Red Lion a cry and a flare of yellow, and a mass of the West Kensington halberdiers ploughed up the slope, knee-deep in grass, bearing the yellow banner of the city before them, and shouting aloud.

At the same second Wilson went down under Wayne's sword, seemingly smashed like a fly. The great sword rose again like a bird, but Wilson seemed to rise with it, and, his sword being broken, sprang at Wayne's throat like a dog. The foremost of the yellow halberdiers had reached the tree and swung his axe above the struggling Wayne. With a curse the King whirled up his own halberd, and dashed the blade in the man's face. He reeled and rolled down the slope, just as the furious Wilson was flung on his back again. And again he was on his feet, and again at Wayne's throat. Then he was flung again, but this time laughing triumphantly. Grasped in his hand was the red and yellow favour that Wayne wore as Provost of Notting Hill. He had torn it from the place where it had been carried for twenty-five years.

With a shout the West Kensington men closed round Wayne, the great yellow banner flapping over his head.

'Where is your favour now, Provost?' cried the West Kensington leader.

And a laugh went up.

Adam struck at the standard-bearer and brought him reeling forward. As the banner stooped, he grasped the yellow folds and tore off a shred. A halberdier struck him on the shoulder, wounding bloodily.

'Here is one colour!' he cried, pushing the yellow into his belt; 'and here!' he cried, pointing to his own blood – 'here is the other.'

At the same instant the shock of a sudden and heavy halberd laid the King stunned or dead. In the wild visions of vanishing consciousness, he saw again something that belonged to an utterly forgotten time, something that he had seen somewhere long ago in a restaurant. He saw, with his swimming eyes, red and yellow, the colours of Nicaragua.

Quin did not see the end. Wilson, wild with joy, sprang again at Adam Wayne, and the great sword of Notting Hill was whirled above once more. Then men ducked instinctively at the rushing noise of the sword coming down out of the sky, and Wilson of Bayswater was smashed and wiped down upon the floor like a fly. Nothing was left of him but a wreck; but the blade that had broken him was broken. In dying he had snapped the great sword and the spell of it; the sword of Wayne was broken at the hilt. One rush of the enemy carried Wayne by force against the tree. They were too close to use halberd or even sword; they were breast to breast, even nostrils to nostrils. But Buck got his dagger free.

'Kill him!' he cried, in a strange stifled voice. 'Kill him! Good or bad, he is none of us! Do not be blinded by the face! . . . God! have we not been blinded all along!' and he drew his arm back for a stab, and seemed to close his eyes.

Wayne did not drop the hand that hung on to the tree-branch. But a mighty heave went over his breast and his whole huge figure, like an earthquake over great hills. And with that convulsion of effort he rent the branch out of the tree, with tongues of torn wood; and, swaying it once only, he let the splintered club fall on Buck, breaking his neck. The planner of the Great Road fell face foremost dead, with his dagger in a grip of steel.

'For you and me, and for all brave men, my brother,' said Wayne, in his strange chant, 'there is good wine poured in the inn at the end of the world.'

The packed men made another lurch or heave towards him; it was almost too dark to fight clearly. He caught hold of the oak again, this time getting his hand into a wide crevice and grasping, as it were, the bowels of the tree. The whole crowd, numbering some thirty men, made a rush to tear him away from it; they hung on with all their weight and numbers, and nothing stirred. A solitude could not have been stiller than that group of straining men. Then there was a faint sound.

'His hand is slipping,' cried two men in exultation.

'You don't know much of him,' said another, grimly (a man of the old war). 'More likely his bone cracks.'

'It is neither – by God, it is neither!' said one of the first two.

'What is it, then?' asked the second.

'The tree is falling,' he replied.

'As the tree falleth, so shall it lie,' said Wayne's voice out of the darkness, and it had the same sweet and yet horrible air that it had had throughout, of coming from a great distance, from before or after the event. Even when he was struggling like an eel or battering like a madman, he spoke like a spectator. 'As the tree falleth, so shall it lie,' he said. 'Men have called that a gloomy text. It is the essence of all exultation. I am doing now what I have done all my life, what is the only happiness, what is the only universality. I am clinging to something. Let it fall, and there let it lie. Fools, you go about and see the kingdoms of the earth, and are liberal and wise and cosmopolitan, which is all that the devil can give you – all that he could offer to Christ, only to be spurned away. I am doing what the truly wise do. When a child goes out into the garden and takes hold of a tree, saying, "Let this tree be all I have," that moment its roots take hold on hell and its branches on the stars. The joy I have is what the lover knows when a woman is everything. It is what a savage knows when his idol is everything. It is what I know when Notting Hill is everything. I have a city. Let it stand or fall.'

As he spoke, the turf lifted itself like a living thing, and out of it rose slowly, like crested serpents, the roots of the oak. Then the great head of the tree, that seemed a green cloud among grey ones, swept the sky suddenly like a broom, and the whole tree heeled over like a ship, smashing everyone in its fall.

CHAPTER 3

Two Voices

In a place in which there was total darkness for hours, there was also for hours total silence. Then a voice spoke out of the darkness, no one could have told from where, and said aloud: 'So ends the Empire of Notting Hill. As it began in blood, so it ended in blood, and all things are always the same.'

And there was silence again, and then again there was a voice, but it had not the same tone; it seemed that it was not the same voice.

'If all things are always the same, it is because they are always heroic. If all things are always the same, it is because they are always new. To each man one soul only is given; to each soul only is given a little power – the power at some moments to outgrow and swallow up the stars. If age after age that power comes upon men, whatever gives it to them is great. Whatever makes men feel old is mean – an empire or a skinflint shop. Whatever makes men feel young is great – a great war or a love-story. And in the darkest of the books of God there is written a truth that is also a riddle. It is of the new things that men tire – of fashions and proposals and improvements and change. It is the old things that startle and intoxicate. It is the old things that are young. There is no sceptic who does not feel that many have doubted before. There is no rich and fickle man who does not feel that all his novelties are ancient. There is no worshipper of change who does not feel upon his neck the vast weight of the weariness of the universe. But we who do the old things are fed by nature with a perpetual infancy. No man who is in love thinks that anyone has been in love before. No woman who has a child thinks that there have been such things as children. No people that fight for their own city are haunted with the burden of the broken empires. Yes, O dark voice, the world is always the same, for it is always unexpected.'

A little gust of wind blew through the night, and then the first voice answered: 'But in this world there are some, be they wise or foolish, whom nothing intoxicates. There are some who see all your disturbances like a cloud of flies. They know that while men will laugh at your Notting Hill, and will study and rehearse and sing of Athens and Jerusalem, Athens and Jerusalem were silly suburbs like your Notting Hill. They know that the earth itself is a suburb, and can feel only drearily and respectably amused as they move upon it.'

'They are philosophers or they are fools,' said the other voice. 'They are not men. Men live, as I say, rejoicing from age to age in something fresher than progress – in the fact that with every baby a new sun and a new moon are made. If our ancient humanity were a single man, it might perhaps be that he would break down under the memory of so many loyalties, under the burden of so many diverse heroisms, under the load and terror of all the goodness of men. But it has pleased God so to isolate the individual soul that it can only learn of all other souls by hearsay, and to each one goodness and happiness come with the youth and violence of lightning, as momentary and as pure. And the doom of failure that lies on all human systems does not in real fact affect them any more than the worms of the inevitable grave affect a children's game in a meadow. Notting Hill has fallen; Notting Hill has died. But that is not the tremendous issue. Notting Hill has lived.'

'But if,' answered the other voice, 'if what is achieved by all these efforts be only the common contentment of humanity, why do men so extravagantly toil and die in them? Has nothing been done by Notting Hill that any chance clump of farmers or clan of savages would not have done without it? What might have been done to Notting Hill if the world had been different may be a deep question; but there is a deeper. What could have happened to the world if Notting Hill had never been?'

The other voice replied: 'The same that would have happened to the world and all the starry systems if an apple tree grew six apples instead of seven; something would have been eternally lost. There has never been anything in the world absolutely like Notting Hill. There will never be anything quite like it to the crack of doom. I cannot believe anything but that God loved it as He must surely love anything that is itself and unreplaceable. But even for that I do not care. If God, with all His thunders, hated it, I loved it.'

And with the voice a tall, strange figure lifted itself out of the debris in the half-darkness.

The other voice came after a long pause, and as it were hoarsely.

'But suppose the whole matter were really a hocus-pocus. Suppose that whatever meaning you may choose in your fancy to give to it, the real meaning of the whole was mockery. Suppose it was all folly. Suppose – '

'I have been in it,' answered the voice from the tall and strange figure, 'and I know it was not.'

A smaller figure seemed half to rise in the dark.

'Suppose I am God,' said the voice, 'and suppose I made the world in idleness. Suppose the stars, that you think eternal, are only the idiot fireworks of an everlasting schoolboy. Suppose the sun and the moon, to which you sing alternately, are only the two eyes of one vast and sneering giant, opened alternately in a never-ending wink. Suppose the trees, in my eyes, are as foolish as enormous toadstools. Suppose Socrates and Charlemagne are to me only beasts, made funnier by walking on their hind legs. Suppose I am God, and having made things, laugh at them.'

'And suppose I am man,' answered the other. 'And suppose that I give the answer that shatters even a laugh. Suppose I do not laugh back at you, do not blaspheme you, do not curse you. But suppose, standing up straight under the sky, with every power of my being, I thank you for the fools' paradise you have made. Suppose I praise you, with a literal pain of ecstasy, for the jest that has brought me so terrible a joy. If we have taken the child's games, and given them the seriousness of a Crusade, if we have drenched your grotesque Dutch garden with the blood of martyrs, we have turned a nursery into a temple. I ask you, in the name of Heaven, who wins?'

The sky close about the crests of the hills and trees was beginning to turn from black to grey, with a random suggestion of the morning. The slight figure seemed to crawl towards the larger one, and the voice was more human.

'But suppose, friend,' it said, 'suppose that, in a bitterer and more real sense, it was all a mockery. Suppose that there had been, from the beginning of these great wars, one who watched them with a sense that is beyond expression, a sense of detachment, of responsibility, of irony, of agony. Suppose that there were one who knew it was all a joke.'

The tall figure answered: 'He could not know it. For it was not all a joke.'

And a gust of wind blew away some clouds that sealed the skyline, and showed a strip of silver behind his great dark legs. Then the other voice came, having crept nearer still.

'Adam Wayne,' it said, 'there are men who confess only in *articulo mortis*; there are people who blame themselves only when they can no longer help others. I am one of them. Here, upon the field of the bloody end of it all, I come to tell you plainly what you would never understand before. Do you know who I am?'

'I know you, Auberon Quin,' answered the tall figure, 'and I shall be glad to unburden your spirit of anything that lies upon it.'

'Adam Wayne,' said the other voice, 'of what I have to say you cannot in common reason be glad to unburden me. Wayne, it was all a joke. When I made these cities, I cared no more for them than I care for a centaur, or a merman, or a fish with legs, or a pig with feathers, or any other absurdity. When I spoke to you solemnly and encouragingly about the flag of your freedom and the peace of your city, I was playing a vulgar practical joke on an honest gentleman, a vulgar practical joke that has lasted for twenty years. Though no one could believe it of me, perhaps, it is the truth that I am a man both timid and tender-hearted. I never dared in the early days of your hope, or the central days of your supremacy, to tell you this; I never dared to break the colossal calm of your face. God knows why I should do it now, when my farce has ended in tragedy and the ruin of all your people! But I say it now. Wayne, it was done as a joke.'

There was silence, and the freshening breeze blew the sky clearer and clearer, leaving great spaces of the white dawn.

At last Wayne said, very slowly: 'You did it all only as a joke?'

'Yes,' said Quin, briefly.

'When you conceived the idea,' went on Wayne, dreamily, 'of an army for Bayswater and a flag for Notting Hill, there was no gleam, no suggestion in your mind that such things might be real and passionate?'

'No,' answered Auberon, turning his round white face to the morning with a dull and splendid sincerity; 'I had none at all.'

Wayne sprang down from the height above him and held out his hand.

'I will not stop to thank you,' he said, with a curious joy in his voice, 'for the great good for the world you have actually wrought. All that I think of that I have said to you a moment ago, even when I thought that your voice was the voice of a derisive omnipotence, its laughter older than the winds of heaven. But let me say what is immediate and true. You and I, Auberon Quin, have both of us throughout our lives been again and again called mad. And we are mad. We are mad, because we are not two men, but one man. We are mad, because we are two lobes of the same brain, and that brain has been cloven in two. And if you ask for the proof of it, it is not hard to find. It is not merely that you, the humorist, have been in these dark days stripped of the joy of gravity. It is not merely that I, the fanatic, have had to grope without humour. It is that, though we seem to be opposite in everything, we have been opposite like man and woman, aiming at the same moment at the same practical thing. We are the father and the mother of the Charter of the Cities.'

Quin looked down at the debris of leaves and timber, the relics of the battle and stampede, now glistening in the growing daylight, and finally said: 'Yet nothing can alter the antagonism – the fact that I laughed at these things and you adored them.'

Wayne's wild face flamed with something godlike, as he turned it to be struck by the sunrise.

'I know of something that will alter that antagonism, something that is outside us, something that you and I have all our lives perhaps taken too little account of. The equal and eternal human being will alter that antagonism, for the human being sees no real antagonism between laughter and respect, the human being, the common man, whom mere geniuses like you and me can only worship like a god. When dark and dreary days come, you and I are necessary, the pure fanatic, the pure satirist. We have between us remedied a great wrong. We have lifted the modern cities into that poetry which everyone who knows mankind knows to be immeasurably more common than the commonplace. But in healthy people there is no war between us. We are but the two lobes of the brain of a ploughman. Laughter and love are everywhere. The cathedrals, built in the ages that loved God, are full of blasphemous grotesques. The mother laughs continually at the child, the lover laughs continually at the lover, the wife at the husband, the friend at the friend. Auberon Quin, we have been too long separated; let us go out together. You have a halberd and I a sword, let us start our wanderings over the world. For we are its two essentials. Come, it is already day.'

In the blank white light Auberon hesitated a moment. Then he made the formal salute with his halberd, and they went away together into the unknown world.

THE CLUB OF QUEER TRADES

The Club of Queer Trades

Contents

I

The Tremendous Adventures of Major Brown

Rabelais, or his wild illustrator Gustave Doré, must have had something to do with the designing of the things called flats in England and America. There is something entirely Gargantuan in the idea of economising space by piling houses on top of each other, front doors and all. And in the chaos and complexity of those perpendicular streets anything may dwell or happen, and it is in one of them, I believe, that the enquirer may find the offices of the Club of Queer Trades. It may be thought at the first glance that the name would attract and startle the passer-by, but nothing attracts or startles in these dim immense hives. The passer-by is only looking for his own melancholy destination, the Montenegro Shipping Agency or the London office of the *Rutland Sentinel*, and passes through the twilight passages as one passes through the twilight corridors of a dream. If the Thugs set up a Strangers' Assassination Company in one of the great buildings in Norfolk Street, and sent in a mild man in spectacles to answer enquiries, no enquiries would be made. And the Club of Queer Trades reigns in a great edifice hidden like a fossil in a mighty cliff of fossils.

The nature of this society, such as we afterwards discovered it to be, is soon and simply told. It is an eccentric and Bohemian Club, of which the absolute condition of membership lies in this, that the candidate must have invented the method by which he earns his living. It must be an entirely new trade. The exact definition of this requirement is given in the two principal rules. First, it must not be a mere application or variation of an existing trade. Thus, for instance, the Club would not admit an insurance agent simply because instead of insuring men's furniture against being burnt in a fire, he insured, let us say, their trousers against being torn by a mad dog. The principle (as Sir Bradcock Burnaby-Bradcock, in the extraordinarily eloquent and soaring speech to the club on the occasion of the question being raised in the Stormby Smith affair, said wittily and keenly) is the same. Secondly, the trade must be a genuine commercial source of income, the support of its inventor. Thus the Club would not receive a man simply because he chose to pass his days collecting broken sardine tins, unless he could drive a roaring trade in them. Professor Chick made that quite clear. And when one remembers what Professor Chick's own new trade was, one doesn't know whether to laugh or cry.

The discovery of this strange society was a curiously refreshing thing; to realise that there were ten new trades in the world was like looking at the first ship or the first plough. It made a man feel what he should feel, that he was still in the childhood of the world. That I should have come at last upon so singular a body was, I may say without vanity, not altogether singular, for I have a mania for belonging to as many societies as possible: I may be said to collect clubs, and I have accumulated a vast and fantastic variety of specimens ever since, in my audacious youth, I collected the Athenaeum. At some future day, perhaps, I may tell tales of some of the other bodies to which I have belonged. I will recount the doings of the Dead Man's Shoes Society (that superficially immoral, but darkly justifiable communion); I will explain the curious origin of the Cat and Christian, the name of which has been so shamefully misinterpreted; and the world shall know at last why the Institute of Typewriters coalesced with the Red Tulip League. Of the Ten Teacups, of course I dare not say a word. The first of my revelations, at any rate, shall be concerned with the Club of Queer Trades, which, as I have said, was one of this class, one which I was almost bound to come across sooner or later, because of my singular hobby. The wild youth of the metropolis call me facetiously 'The King of Clubs'. They also call me 'The Cherub', in allusion to the roseate and youthful appearance I have presented in my declining years. I only hope the spirits in the better world have as good dinners as I have. But the finding of the Club of Queer Trades has one very curious thing about it. The most curious thing about it is that it was not discovered by me; it was discovered by my friend Basil Grant, a stargazer, a mystic, and a man who scarcely stirred out of his attic.

Very few people knew anything of Basil; not because he was in the least unsociable, for if a man out of the street had walked into his rooms he would have kept him talking till morning. Few people knew him, because, like all poets, he could do without them; he welcomed a human face as he might welcome a sudden blend of colour in a sunset; but he no more felt the need of going out to parties than he felt the need of altering the sunset clouds. He lived in a queer and comfortable garret in the roofs of Lambeth. He was surrounded by a chaos of things that were in odd contrast to the slums around him; old fantastic books, swords, armour – the whole dust-hole of romanticism. But his face, amid all these quixotic relics, appeared curiously keen and modern – a powerful, legal face. And no one but I knew who he was.

Long ago as it is, everyone remembers the terrible and grotesque scene that occurred in ——, when one of the most acute and forcible of the English judges suddenly went mad on the bench. I had my own view of that occurrence; but about the facts themselves there is no question at all. For some months, indeed for some years, people had detected something curious in the judge's conduct. He seemed to have lost interest in the law, in which he had been beyond expression brilliant and terrible as a K.C., and to be occupied in giving personal and moral advice to the people concerned. He talked more like a priest or a doctor, and a very outspoken one at that. The first thrill was probably given when he said to a man who had attempted a crime of passion: 'I sentence you to three years imprisonment, under the firm, and solemn, and God-given conviction, that what you require is three months at the seaside.' He accused criminals from the bench, not so much of their obvious legal crimes, but of things that had never been heard of in a court of justice, monstrous egoism, lack of humour, and morbidity deliberately encouraged. Things came to a head in that celebrated diamond case in which the Prime Minister himself, that brilliant patrician, had to come forward, gracefully and reluctantly, to give evidence against his valet. After the detailed life of the household had been thoroughly exhibited, the judge requested the Premier again to step forward, which he did with quiet dignity. The judge then said, in a sudden, grating voice: 'Get a new soul. That thing's not fit for a dog. Get a new soul.' All this, of course, in the eyes of the sagacious, was premonitory of that melancholy and farcical day when his wits actually deserted him in open court. It was a libel case between two very eminent and powerful financiers, against both of whom charges of considerable defalcation were brought. The case was long and complex; the advocates were long and eloquent; but at last, after weeks of work and rhetoric, the time came for the great judge to give a summing-up; and one of his celebrated masterpieces of lucidity and pulverising logic was eagerly looked for. He had spoken very little during the prolonged affair, and he looked sad and lowering at the end of it. He was silent for a few moments, and then burst into a stentorian song. His remarks (as reported) were as follows:

> O Rowty-owty tiddly-owty
> Tiddly-owty tiddly-owty
> Highty-ighty tiddly-ighty
> Tiddly-ighty ow.

He then retired from public life and took the garret in Lambeth.

I was sitting there one evening, about six o'clock, over a glass of that gorgeous Burgundy which he kept behind a pile of black-letter folios; he was striding about the room, fingering, after a habit of his, one of the great swords in his collection; the red glare of the strong fire struck his square features and his fierce grey hair; his blue eyes were even unusually full of dreams, and he had opened his mouth to speak dreamily, when the door was flung open, and a pale, fiery man, with red hair and a huge furred overcoat, swung himself panting into the room.

'Sorry to bother you, Basil,' he gasped. 'I took a liberty – made an appointment here with a man – a client – in five minutes – I beg your pardon, sir,' and he gave me a bow of apology.

Basil smiled at me. 'You didn't know,' he said, 'that I had a practical brother. This is Rupert Grant, Esquire, who can and does all there is to be done. Just as I was a failure at one thing, he is a success at everything. I remember him as a journalist, a house-agent, a naturalist, an inventor, a publisher, a schoolmaster, a – what are you now, Rupert?'

'I am and have been for some time,' said Rupert, with some dignity, 'a private detective, and there's my client.'

A loud rap at the door had cut him short, and, on permission being given, the door was thrown sharply open and a stout, dapper man walked swiftly into the room, set his silk hat with a clap on the table, and said, 'Good-evening, gentlemen,' with a stress on the last syllable that somehow marked him out as a martinet, military, literary and social. He had a large head streaked with black and grey, and an abrupt black moustache, which gave him a look of fierceness which was contradicted by his sad sea-blue eyes.

Basil immediately said to me, 'Let us come into the next room, Gully,' and was moving towards the door, but the stranger said: 'Not at all. Friends remain. Assistance possibly.'

The moment I heard him speak I remembered who he was, a certain Major Brown I had met years before in Basil's society. I had forgotten altogether the black dandified figure and the large solemn head, but I remembered the peculiar speech, which consisted of only saying about a quarter of each sentence, and that sharply, like the crack of a gun. I do not know, it may have come from giving orders to troops.

Major Brown was a V.C., and an able and distinguished soldier, but he was anything but a warlike person. Like many among the iron men who recovered British India, he was a man with the natural beliefs and tastes of an old maid. In his dress he was dapper and yet demure; in his habits he was precise to the point of the exact adjustment of a teacup. One enthusiasm he had, which was of the nature of a religion – the cultivation of pansies. And when he talked about his collection, his blue eyes glittered like a child's at a new toy, the eyes that had remained untroubled when the troops were roaring victory round Roberts at Candahar.

'Well, Major,' said Rupert Grant, with a lordly heartiness, flinging himself into a chair, 'what is the matter with you?'

'Yellow pansies. Coal cellar. P. G. Northover,' said the Major, with righteous indignation.

We glanced at each other with inquisitiveness. Basil, who had his eyes shut in his abstracted way, said simply: 'I beg your pardon.'

'Fact is. Street, you know, man, pansies. On wall. Death to me. Something. Preposterous.'

We shook our heads gently. Bit by bit, and mainly by the seemingly sleepy assistance of Basil Grant, we pieced together the Major's fragmentary, but excited narration. It would be infamous to submit the reader to what we endured; therefore I will tell the story of Major Brown in my own words. But the reader must imagine the scene. The eyes of Basil closed as in a trance, after his habit, and the eyes of Rupert and myself getting rounder and rounder as we listened to one of the most astounding stories in the world, from the lips of the little man in black, sitting bolt upright in his chair and talking like a telegram.

Major Brown was, I have said, a successful soldier, but by no means an enthusiastic one. So far from regretting his retirement on half-pay, it was with delight that he took a small neat villa, very like a doll's house, and devoted the rest of his life to pansies and weak tea. The thought that battles were over when he had once hung up his sword in the little front hall (along with two patent stew-pots and a bad watercolour), and betaken himself instead to wielding the rake in his little sunlit garden, was to him like having come into a harbour in heaven. He was Dutch-like and precise in his taste in gardening, and had, perhaps, some tendency to drill his flowers like soldiers. He was one of those men who are capable of putting four umbrellas in the stand rather than three, so that two may lean one way and two another; he saw life like a pattern in a freehand drawing-book. And assuredly he would not have believed, or even understood, anyone who had told him that within a few yards of his brick paradise he was destined to be caught in a whirlpool of incredible adventure, such as he had never seen or dreamed of in the horrible jungle, or the heat of battle.

One certain bright and windy afternoon, the Major, attired in his usual faultless manner, had set out for his usual constitutional. In crossing from one great residential thoroughfare to another, he happened to pass along one of those aimless-looking lanes which lie along the back-garden walls of a row of mansions, and which in their empty and discoloured appearance give one an odd sensation as of being behind the scenes of a theatre. But mean and sulky as the scene might be in the eyes of most of us, it was not altogether so in the Major's, for along the coarse gravel footway was coming a thing which was to him what the passing of a religious procession is to a devout person. A large, heavy man, with fish-blue eyes and a ring of irradiating red beard, was pushing before him a barrow, which was ablaze with incomparable flowers. There were splendid specimens of almost every order, but the Major's own favourite pansies predominated. The Major stopped and fell into conversation, and then into bargaining. He treated the man after the manner of collectors and other mad men, that is to say, he carefully and with a sort of anguish selected the best roots from the less excellent, praised some, disparaged others, made a subtle scale ranging from a thrilling worth and rarity to a degraded insignificance, and then bought them all. The man was just pushing off his barrow when he stopped and came close to the Major.

'I'll tell you what, sir,' he said. 'If you're interested in them things, you just get on to that wall.'

'On the wall!' cried the scandalised Major, whose conventional soul quailed within him at the thought of such fantastic trespass.

'Finest show of yellow pansies in England in that there garden, sir,' hissed the tempter. 'I'll help you up, sir.'

How it happened no one will ever know, but that positive enthusiasm of the Major's life triumphed over all its negative traditions, and with an easy leap and swing that showed that he was in no need of physical assistance, he stood on the wall at the end of the strange garden. The second after, the flapping of the frock-coat at his knees made him feel inexpressibly a fool. But the next instant all such trifling sentiments were swallowed up by the most appalling shock of surprise the old soldier had ever felt in all his bold and wandering existence. His eyes fell upon the garden, and there across a large bed in the centre of the lawn was a vast pattern of pansies; they were splendid flowers, but for once it was not their horticultural aspects that Major Brown beheld, for the pansies were arranged in gigantic capital letters so as to form the sentence:

DEATH TO MAJOR BROWN

A kindly looking old man, with white whiskers, was watering them.

Brown looked sharply back at the road behind him; the man with the barrow had suddenly vanished. Then he looked again at the lawn with its incredible inscription. Another man might have thought he had gone mad, but Brown did not. When romantic ladies gushed over his V.C. and his military exploits, he sometimes felt himself to be a painfully prosaic person, but by the same token he knew he was incurably sane. Another man, again, might have thought himself a victim of a passing practical joke, but Brown could not easily believe this. He knew from his own quaint learning that the garden arrangement was an elaborate and expensive one; he thought it extravagantly improbable that anyone would pour out money like water for a joke against him. Having no explanation whatever to offer, he admitted the fact to himself, like a clear-headed man, and waited as he would have done in the presence of a man with six legs.

At this moment the stout old man with white whiskers looked up, and the watering can fell from his hand, shooting a swirl of water down the gravel path.

'Who on earth are you?' he gasped, trembling violently.

'I am Major Brown,' said that individual, who was always cool in the hour of action.

The old man gaped helplessly like some monstrous fish. At last he stammered wildly, 'Come down – come down here!'

'At your service,' said the Major, and alighted at a bound on the grass beside him, without disarranging his silk hat.

The old man turned his broad back and set off at a sort of waddling run towards the house, followed with swift steps by the Major. His guide led him through the back passages of a gloomy, but gorgeously appointed house, until they reached the door of the front room. Then the old man turned with a face of apoplectic terror dimly showing in the twilight.

'For heaven's sake,' he said, 'don't mention jackals.'

Then he threw open the door, releasing a burst of red lamplight, and ran downstairs with a clatter.

The Major stepped into a rich, glowing room, full of red copper, and peacock and purple hangings, hat in hand. He had the finest manners in the world, and, though mystified, was not in the least embarrassed to see that the only occupant was a lady, sitting by the window, looking out.

'Madam,' he said, bowing simply, 'I am Major Brown.'

'Sit down,' said the lady; but she did not turn her head.

She was a graceful, green-clad figure, with fiery red hair and a flavour of Bedford Park. 'You have come, I suppose,' she said mournfully, 'to tax me about the hateful title-deeds.'

'I have come, madam,' he said, 'to know what is the matter. To know why my name is written across your garden. Not amicably either.'

He spoke grimly, for the thing had hit him. It is impossible to describe the effect produced on the mind by that quiet and sunny garden scene, the frame for a stunning and brutal personality. The evening air was still, and the grass was golden in the place where the little flowers he studied cried to heaven for his blood.

'You know I must not turn round,' said the lady; 'every afternoon till the stroke of six I must keep my face turned to the street.'

Some queer and unusual inspiration made the prosaic soldier resolute to accept these outrageous riddles without surprise.

'It is almost six,' he said; and even as he spoke the barbaric copper clock upon the wall clanged the first stroke of the hour. At the sixth the lady sprang up and turned on the Major one of the queerest and yet most attractive faces he had ever seen in his life; open, and yet tantalising, the face of an elf.

'That makes the third year I have waited,' she cried. 'This is an anniversary. The waiting almost makes one wish the frightful thing would happen once and for all.'

And even as she spoke, a sudden rending cry broke the stillness. From low down on the pavement of the dim street (it was already twilight) a voice cried out with a raucous and merciless distinctness: 'Major Brown, Major Brown, where does the jackal dwell?'

Brown was decisive and silent in action. He strode to the front door and looked out. There was no sign of life in the blue gloaming of the street, where one or two lamps were beginning to light their lemon sparks. On returning, he found the lady in green trembling.

'It is the end,' she cried, with shaking lips; 'it may be death for both of us. Whenever – '

But even as she spoke her speech was cloven by another hoarse proclamation from the dark street, again horribly articulate.

'Major Brown, Major Brown, how did the jackal die?'

Brown dashed out of the door and down the steps, but again he was frustrated; there was no figure in sight, and the street was far too long and empty for the shouter to have run away. Even the rational Major was a little shaken as he returned in a certain time to the drawing-room. Scarcely had he done so than the terrific voice came: 'Major Brown, Major Brown, where did – '

Brown was in the street almost at a bound, and he was in time – in time to see something which at first glance froze the blood. The cries appeared to come from a decapitated head resting on the pavement.

The next moment the pale Major understood. It was the head of a man thrust through the coal-hole in the street. The next moment, again, it had vanished, and Major Brown turned to the lady. 'Where's your coal-cellar?' he said, and stepped out into the passage.

She looked at him with wild grey eyes. 'You will not go down,' she cried, 'alone, into the dark hole, with that beast?'

'Is this the way?' replied Brown, and descended the kitchen stairs three at a time. He flung open the door of a black cavity and stepped in, feeling in his pocket for matches. As his right hand was thus occupied, a pair of great slimy hands came out of the darkness, hands clearly belonging to a man of gigantic stature, and seized him by the back of the head. They forced him down, down in the suffocating darkness, a brutal image of destiny. But the Major's head, though upside down, was perfectly clear and intellectual. He gave quietly under the pressure until he had slid down almost to his hands and knees. Then finding the knees of the invisible monster within a foot of him, he simply put out one of his long, bony, and skilful hands, and gripping the leg by a muscle pulled it off the ground and laid the huge living man, with a crash, along the floor. He strove to rise, but Brown was on top like a cat. They rolled over and over. Big as the man was, he had evidently now no desire but to escape; he made sprawls hither and thither to get past the Major to the door, but that tenacious person had him hard by the coat collar and hung with the other hand to a beam. At length there came a strain in holding back this human bull, a strain under which Brown expected his hand to rend and part from the arm. But something else rent and parted; and the dim fat figure of the giant vanished out of the cellar, leaving the torn coat in the Major's hand; the only fruit of his adventure and the only clue to the mystery. For when he went up and out at the front door, the lady, the rich hangings, and the whole equipment of the house had disappeared. It had only bare boards and whitewashed walls.

'The lady was in the conspiracy, of course,' said Rupert, nodding. Major Brown turned brick red. 'I beg your pardon,' he said, 'I think not.'

Rupert raised his eyebrows and looked at him for a moment, but said nothing. When next he spoke he asked: 'Was there anything in the pockets of the coat?'

'There was sevenpence halfpenny in coppers and a threepenny-bit,' said the Major carefully; 'there was a cigarette-holder, a piece of string, and this letter,' and he laid it on the table. It ran as follows:

> Dear Mr Plover – I am annoyed to hear that some delay has occurred in the arrangements re Major Brown. Please see that he is attacked as per arrangement tomorrow. The coal-cellar, of course.
>
> Yours faithfully,
>
> P. G. Northover

Rupert Grant was leaning forward listening with hawklike eyes. He cut in: 'Is it dated from anywhere?'

'No – oh, yes!' replied Brown, glancing upon the paper; '14 Tanner's Court, North – '

Rupert sprang up and struck his hands together.

'Then why are we hanging here? Let's get along. Basil, lend me your revolver.'

Basil was staring into the embers like a man in a trance; and it was some time before he answered: 'I don't think you'll need it.'

'Perhaps not,' said Rupert, getting into his fur coat. 'One never knows. But going down a dark court to see criminals – '

'Do you think they are criminals?' asked his brother.

Rupert laughed stoutly. 'Giving orders to a subordinate to strangle a harmless stranger in a coal-cellar may strike you as a very blameless experiment, but – '

'Do you think they wanted to strangle the Major?' asked Basil, in the same distant and monotonous voice.

'My dear fellow, you've been asleep. Look at the letter.'

'I am looking at the letter,' said the mad judge calmly; though, as a matter of fact, he was looking at the fire. 'I don't think it's the sort of letter one criminal would write to another.'

'My dear boy, you are glorious,' cried Rupert, turning round, with laughter in his blue bright eyes. 'Your methods amaze me. Why, there *is* the letter. It *is* written, and it does give orders for a crime. You might as well say that the Nelson Column was not at all the sort of thing that was likely to be set up in Trafalgar Square.'

Basil Grant shook all over with a sort of silent laughter, but did not otherwise move.

'That's rather good,' he said; 'but, of course, logic like that's not what is really wanted. It's a question of spiritual atmosphere. It's not a criminal letter.'

'It is. It's a matter of fact,' cried the other in an agony of reasonableness.

'Facts,' murmured Basil, like one mentioning some strange, far-off animals, 'how facts obscure the truth. I may be silly – in fact, I'm off my head – but I never could believe in that man – what's his name, in those capital stories? – Sherlock Holmes. Every detail points to something, certainly; but generally to the wrong thing. Facts point in all directions, it seems to me, like the thousands of twigs on a tree. It's only the life of the tree that has unity and goes up – only the green blood that springs, like a fountain, at the stars.'

'But what the deuce else can the letter be but criminal?'

'We have eternity to stretch our legs in,' replied the mystic. 'It can be an infinity of things. I haven't seen any of them – I've only seen the letter. I look at that, and say it's not criminal.'

'Then what's the origin of it?'

'I haven't the vaguest idea.'

'Then why don't you accept the ordinary explanation?'

Basil continued for a little to glare at the coals, and seemed collecting his thoughts in a humble and even painful way. Then he said: 'Suppose you went out into the moonlight. Suppose you passed through silent, silvery streets and squares until you came into an open and deserted space, set with a few monuments, and you beheld one dressed as a ballet girl dancing in the argent glimmer. And suppose you looked, and saw it was a man disguised. And suppose you looked again, and saw it was Lord Kitchener. What would you think?'

He paused a moment, and went on: 'You could not adopt the ordinary explanation. The ordinary explanation of putting on singular clothes is that you look nice in them; you would not think that Lord Kitchener dressed up like a ballet girl out of ordinary personal vanity. You would think it much more likely that he inherited a dancing madness from a great grandmother; or had been hypnotised at a séance; or threatened by a secret society with death if he refused the ordeal. With Baden-Powell, say, it might be a bet – but not with Kitchener. I should know all that, because in my public days I knew him quite well. So I know that letter quite well, and criminals quite well. It's not a criminal's letter. It's all atmospheres.' And he closed his eyes and passed his hand over his forehead.

Rupert and the Major were regarding him with a mixture of respect and pity. The former said: 'Well, I'm going, anyhow, and shall continue to think – until your spiritual mystery turns up – that a man who sends a note recommending a crime, that is, actually a crime that is actually carried out, at least tentatively, is, in all probability, a little casual in his moral tastes. Can I have that revolver?'

'Certainly,' said Basil, getting up. 'But I am coming with you.' And he flung an old cape or cloak round him, and took a sword-stick from the corner.

'You!' said Rupert, with some surprise, 'you scarcely ever leave your hole to look at anything on the face of the earth.'

Basil fitted on a formidable old white hat.

'I scarcely ever,' he said, with an unconscious and colossal arrogance, 'hear of anything on the face of the earth that I do not understand at once, without going to see it.'

And he led the way out into the purple night.

We four swung along the flaring Lambeth streets, across Westminster Bridge, and along the Embankment in the direction of that part of Fleet Street which contained Tanner's Court. The erect, black figure of Major Brown, seen from behind, was a quaint contrast to the hound-like stoop and flapping mantle of young Rupert Grant, who adopted, with childlike delight, all the dramatic poses of the detective of fiction. The finest among his many fine qualities was his boyish appetite for the colour and poetry of London. Basil, who walked behind, with his face turned blindly to the stars, had the look of a somnambulist.

Rupert paused at the corner of Tanner's Court, with a quiver of delight at danger, and gripped Basil's revolver in his greatcoat pocket.

'Shall we go in now?' he asked.

'Not get police?' asked Major Brown, glancing sharply up and down the street.

'I am not sure,' answered Rupert, knitting his brows. 'Of course, it's quite clear, the thing's all crooked. But there are three of us, and – '

'I shouldn't get the police,' said Basil in a queer voice. Rupert glanced at him and stared hard.

'Basil,' he cried, 'you're trembling. What's the matter – are you afraid?'

'Cold, perhaps,' said the Major, eyeing him. There was no doubt that he was shaking.

At last, after a few moments' scrutiny, Rupert broke into a curse.

'You're laughing,' he cried. 'I know that confounded, silent, shaky laugh of yours. What the deuce is the amusement, Basil? Here we are, all three of us, within a yard of a den of ruffians – '

'But I shouldn't call the police,' said Basil. 'We four heroes are quite equal to a host,' and he continued to quake with his mysterious mirth.

Rupert turned with impatience and strode swiftly down the court, the rest of us following. When he reached the door of No. 14 he turned abruptly, the revolver glittering in his hand.

'Stand close,' he said in the voice of a commander. 'The scoundrel may be attempting an escape at this moment. We must fling open the door and rush in.'

The four of us cowered instantly under the archway, rigid, except for the old judge and his convulsion of merriment.

'Now,' hissed Rupert Grant, turning his pale face and burning eyes suddenly over his shoulder, 'when I say "Four", follow me with a rush. If I say "Hold him", pin the fellows down, whoever they are. If I say "Stop", stop. I shall say that if there are more than three. If they attack us I shall empty my revolver on them. Basil, have your sword-stick ready. Now – one, two, three, four!'

With the sound of the word the door burst open, and we fell into the room like an invasion, only to stop dead.

The room, which was an ordinary and neatly appointed office, appeared, at the first glance, to be empty. But on a second and more careful glance, we saw seated behind a very large desk with pigeonholes and drawers of bewildering multiplicity, a small man with a black waxed moustache, and the air of a very average clerk, writing hard. He looked up as we came to a standstill.

'Did you knock?' he asked pleasantly. 'I am sorry if I did not hear. What can I do for you?'

There was a doubtful pause, and then, by general consent, the Major himself, the victim of the outrage, stepped forward.

The letter was in his hand, and he looked unusually grim.

'Is your name P. G. Northover?' he asked.

'That is my name,' replied the other, smiling.

'I think,' said Major Brown, with an increase in the dark glow of his face, 'that this letter was written by you.' And with a loud clap he struck open the letter on the desk with his clenched fist. The man called Northover looked at it with unaffected interest and merely nodded.

'Well, sir,' said the Major, breathing hard, 'what about that?'

'What about it, precisely,' said the man with the moustache.

'I am Major Brown,' said that gentleman sternly.

Northover bowed. 'Pleased to meet you, sir. What have you to say to me?'

'Say!' cried the Major, loosing a sudden tempest; 'why, I want this confounded thing settled. I want –'

'Certainly, sir,' said Northover, jumping up with a slight elevation of the eyebrows. 'Will you take a chair for a moment.' And he pressed an electric bell just above him, which thrilled and tinkled in a room beyond. The Major put his hand on the back of the chair offered him, but stood chafing and beating the floor with his polished boot.

The next moment an inner glass door was opened, and a fair, weedy, young man, in a frock-coat, entered from within.

'Mr Hopson,' said Northover, 'this is Major Brown. Will you please finish that thing for him I gave you this morning and bring it in?'

'Yes, sir,' said Mr Hopson, and vanished like lightning.

'You will excuse me, gentlemen,' said the egregious Northover, with his radiant smile, 'if I continue to work until Mr Hopson is ready. I have some books that must be cleared up before I get away on my holiday tomorrow. And we all like a whiff of the country, don't we? Ha! ha!'

The criminal took up his pen with a childlike laugh, and a silence ensued; a placid and busy silence on the part of Mr P. G. Northover; a raging silence on the part of everybody else.

At length the scratching of Northover's pen in the stillness was mingled with a knock at the door, almost simultaneous with the turning of the handle, and Mr Hopson came in again with the same silent rapidity, placed a paper before his principal, and disappeared again.

The man at the desk pulled and twisted his spiky moustache for a few moments as he ran his eye up and down the paper presented to him. He took up his pen, with a slight, instantaneous frown, and altered something, muttering – 'Careless.' Then he read it again with the same impenetrable reflectiveness, and finally handed it to the frantic Brown, whose hand was beating the devil's tattoo on the back of the chair.

'I think you will find that all right, Major,' he said briefly.

The Major looked at it; whether he found it all right or not will appear later, but he found it like this:

Major Brown to P. G. Northover	£	*s.*	*d.*
January 1, to account rendered	5	6	0
May 9, to potting and embedding of 200 pansies	2	0	0
To cost of trolley with flowers		15	0
To hiring of man with trolley		5	0
To hire of house and garden for one day	1	0	0
To furnishing of room in peacock curtains, copper ornaments, etc.	3	0	0
To salary of Miss Jameson	1	0	0
To salary of Mr Plover	1	0	0
Total	£14	6	0

A Remittance will oblige.

'What,' said Brown, after a dead pause, and with eyes that seemed slowly rising out of his head, 'what in heaven's name is this?'

'What is it?' repeated Northover, cocking his eyebrow with amusement. 'It's your account, of course.'

'My account!' The Major's ideas appeared to be in a vague stampede. 'My account! And what have I got to do with it?'

'Well,' said Northover, laughing outright, 'naturally I prefer you to pay it.'

The Major's hand was still resting on the back of the chair as the words came. He scarcely stirred otherwise, but he lifted the chair bodily into the air with one hand and hurled it at Northover's head.

The legs crashed against the desk, so that Northover only got a blow on the elbow as he sprang up with clenched fists, only to be seized by the united rush of the rest of us. The chair had fallen clattering on the empty floor.

'Let me go, you scamps,' he shouted. 'Let me – '

'Stand still,' cried Rupert authoritatively. 'Major Brown's action is excusable. The abominable crime you have attempted – '

'A customer has a perfect right,' said Northover hotly, 'to question an alleged overcharge, but, confound it all, not to throw furniture.'

'What, in God's name, do you mean by your customers and overcharges?' shrieked Major Brown, whose keen feminine nature, steady in pain or danger, became almost hysterical in the presence of a long and exasperating mystery. 'Who are you? I've never seen you or your insolent tomfool bills. I know one of your cursed brutes tried to choke me – '

'Mad,' said Northover, gazing blankly round; 'all of them mad. I didn't know they travelled in quartettes.'

'Enough of this prevarication,' said Rupert; 'your crimes are discovered. A policeman is stationed at the corner of the court. Though only a private detective myself, I will take the responsibility of telling you that anything you say – '

'Mad,' repeated Northover, with a weary air.

And at this moment, for the first time, there struck in among them the strange, sleepy voice of Basil Grant.

'Major Brown,' he said, 'may I ask you a question?'

The Major turned his head with an increased bewilderment.

'You?' he cried; 'certainly, Mr Grant.'

'Can you tell me,' said the mystic, with sunken head and lowering brow, as he traced a pattern in the dust with his sword-stick, 'can you tell me what was the name of the man who lived in your house before you?'

The unhappy Major was only faintly more disturbed by this last and futile irrelevancy, and he answered vaguely: 'Yes, I think so; a man named Gurney something – a name with a hyphen – Gurney-Brown; that was it.'

'And when did the house change hands?' said Basil, looking up sharply.

His strange eyes were burning brilliantly.

'I came in last month,' said the Major.

And at the mere word the criminal Northover suddenly fell into his great office chair and shouted with a volleying laughter.

'Oh! it's too perfect – it's too exquisite,' he gasped, beating the arms with his fists. He was laughing deafeningly; Basil Grant was laughing voicelessly; and the rest of us only felt that our heads were like weathercocks in a whirlwind.

'Confound it, Basil,' said Rupert, stamping. 'If you don't want me to go mad and blow your metaphysical brains out, tell me what all this means.'

Northover rose.

'Permit me, sir, to explain,' he said. 'And, first of all, permit me to apologise to you, Major Brown, for a most abominable and unpardonable blunder, which has caused you menace and inconvenience, in which, if you will allow me to say so, you have behaved with astonishing courage and dignity. Of course you need not trouble about the bill. We will stand the loss.' And, tearing the paper across, he flung the halves into the wastepaper basket and bowed.

Poor Brown's face was still a picture of distraction. 'But I don't even begin to understand,' he cried. 'What bill? what blunder? what loss?'

Mr P. G. Northover advanced in the centre of the room, thoughtfully, and with a great deal of unconscious dignity. On closer consideration, there were apparent about him other things beside a screwed moustache, especially a lean, sallow face, hawklike, and not without a careworn intelligence. Then he looked up abruptly.

'Do you know where you are, Major?' he said.

'God knows I don't,' said the warrior, with fervour.

'You are standing,' replied Northover, 'in the office of the Adventure and Romance Agency, Limited.'

'And what's that?' blankly enquired Brown.

The man of business leaned over the back of the chair, and fixed his dark eyes on the other's face.

'Major,' said he, 'did you ever, as you walked along the empty street upon some idle afternoon, feel the utter hunger for something to happen – something, in the splendid words of Walt Whitman: "Something pernicious and dread; something far removed from a puny and pious life; something unproved; something in a trance; something loosed from its anchorage, and driving free." Did you ever feel that?'

'Certainly not,' said the Major shortly.

'Then I must explain with more elaboration,' said Mr Northover, with a sigh. 'The Adventure and Romance Agency has been started to meet a great modern desire. On every side, in conversation and in literature, we hear of the desire for a larger theatre of events for something to waylay us and lead us splendidly astray. Now the man who feels this desire for a varied life pays a yearly or a quarterly sum to the Adventure and Romance Agency; in return, the Adventure and Romance Agency undertakes to surround him with startling and weird events. As a man is leaving his front door, an excited sweep approaches him and assures him of a plot against his life; he gets into a cab, and is driven to an opium den; he receives a mysterious telegram or a dramatic visit, and is immediately in a vortex of incidents. A very picturesque and moving story is first written by one of the staff of distinguished novelists who are at present hard at work in the adjoining room. Yours, Major Brown (designed by our Mr Grigsby), I consider peculiarly forcible and pointed; it is almost a pity you did not see the end of it. I need scarcely explain further the monstrous mistake. Your predecessor in your present house, Mr Gurney-Brown, was a subscriber to our agency, and our foolish clerks, ignoring alike the dignity of the hyphen and the glory of military rank, positively imagined that Major Brown and Mr Gurney-Brown were the same person. Thus you were suddenly hurled into the middle of another man's story.'

'How on earth does the thing work?' asked Rupert Grant, with bright and fascinated eyes.

'We believe that we are doing a noble work,' said Northover warmly. 'It has continually struck us that there is no element in modern life that is more lamentable than the fact that the modern man has to seek all artistic existence in a sedentary state. If he wishes to float into fairyland, he reads a book; if he wishes to dash into the thick of battle, he reads a book; if he wishes to soar into heaven, he reads a book; if he wishes to slide down the banisters, he reads a book. We give him these visions, but we give him exercise at the same time, the necessity of leaping from wall to wall, of fighting strange gentlemen, of running down long streets from pursuers – all healthy and pleasant exercises. We give him a glimpse of that great morning world of Robin Hood or the Knights Errant, when one great game was played under the splendid sky. We give him back his childhood, that godlike time when we can act stories, be our own heroes, and at the same instant dance and dream.'

Basil gazed at him curiously. The most singular psychological discovery had been reserved to the end, for as the little business man ceased speaking he had the blazing eyes of a fanatic.

Major Brown received the explanation with complete simplicity and good humour.

'Of course; awfully dense, sir,' he said. 'No doubt at all, the scheme excellent. But I don't think – ' He paused a moment, and looked dreamily out of the window. 'I don't think you will find me in it. Somehow, when one's seen – seen the thing itself, you know – blood and men screaming, one feels about having a little house and a little hobby; in the Bible, you know, "There remaineth a rest".'

Northover bowed. Then after a pause he said: 'Gentlemen, may I offer you my card. If any of the rest of you desire, at any time, to communicate with me, despite Major Brown's view of the matter – '

'I should be obliged for your card, sir,' said the Major, in his abrupt but courteous voice. 'Pay for chair.'

The agent of Romance and Adventure handed his card, laughing.

It ran, 'P. G. Northover, B.A., C.Q.T., Adventure and Romance Agency, 14 Tanner's Court, Fleet Street.'

'What on earth is "C.QT."?' asked Rupert Grant, looking over the Major's shoulder.

'Don't you know?' returned Northover. 'Haven't you ever heard of the Club of Queer Trades?'

'There seems to be a confounded lot of funny things we haven't heard of,' said the little Major reflectively. 'What's this one?'

'The Club of Queer Trades is a society consisting exclusively of people who have invented some new and curious way of making money. I was one of the earliest members.'

'You deserve to be,' said Basil, taking up his great white hat, with a smile, and speaking for the last time that evening.

When they had passed out the Adventure and Romance agent wore a queer smile, as he trod down the fire and locked up his desk. 'A fine chap, that Major; when one hasn't a touch of the poet one stands some chance of being a poem. But to think of such a clockwork little creature of all people getting into the nets of one of Grigsby's tales,' and he laughed out aloud in the silence.

Just as the laugh echoed away, there came a sharp knock at the door. An owlish head, with dark moustaches, was thrust in, with deprecating and somewhat absurd enquiry.

'What! back again, Major?' cried Northover in surprise. 'What can I do for you?'

The Major shuffled feverishly into the room.

'It's horribly absurd,' he said. 'Something must have got started in me that I never knew before. But upon my soul I feel the most desperate desire to know the end of it all.'

'The end of it all?'

'Yes,' said the Major. ' "Jackals", and the title-deeds, and "Death to Major Brown".'

The agent's face grew grave, but his eyes were amused.

'I am terribly sorry, Major,' said he, 'but what you ask is impossible. I don't know anyone I would sooner oblige than you; but the rules of the agency are strict. The Adventures are confidential; you are an outsider; I am not allowed to let you know an inch more than I can help. I do hope you understand – '

'There is no one,' said Brown, 'who understands discipline better than I do. Thank you very much. Good-night.'

And the little man withdrew for the last time.

* * *

He married Miss Jameson, the lady with the red hair and the green garments. She was an actress, employed (with many others) by the Romance Agency; and her marriage with the prim old veteran caused some stir in her languid and intellectualised set. She always replied very quietly that she had met scores of men who acted splendidly in the charades provided for them by Northover, but that she had only met one man who went down into a coal-cellar when he really thought it contained a murderer.

The Major and she are living as happily as birds, in an absurd villa, and the former has taken to smoking. Otherwise he is unchanged – except, perhaps, there are moments when, alert and full of feminine unselfishness as the Major is by nature, he falls into a trance of abstraction. Then his wife recognises with a concealed smile, by the blind look in his blue eyes, that he is wondering what were the title-deeds, and why he was not allowed to mention jackals. But, like so many old soldiers, Brown is religious, and believes that he will realise the rest of those purple adventures in a better world.

2

The Painful Fall of a Great Reputation

Basil Grant and I were talking one day in what is perhaps the most perfect place for talking on earth – the top of a tolerably deserted tramcar. To talk on the top of a hill is superb, but to talk on the top of a flying hill is a fairy tale.

The vast blank space of North London was flying by; the very pace gave us a sense of its immensity and its meanness. It was, as it were, a base infinitude, a squalid eternity, and we felt the real horror of the poor parts of London, the horror that is so totally missed and misrepresented by the sensational novelists who depict it as being a matter of narrow streets, filthy houses, criminals and maniacs, and dens of vice. In a narrow street, in a den of vice, you do not expect civilisation, you do not expect order. But the horror of this was the fact that there was civilisation, that there was order, but that civilisation only showed its morbidity, and order only its monotony. No one would say, in going through a criminal slum, 'I see no statues. I notice no cathedrals.' But here there were public buildings; only they were mostly lunatic asylums. Here there were statues; only they were mostly statues of railway engineers and philanthropists – two dingy classes of men united by their common contempt for the people. Here there were churches; only they were the churches of dim and erratic sects, Agapemonites or Irvingites. Here, above all, there were broad roads and vast crossings and tramway lines and hospitals and all the real marks of civilisation. But though one never knew, in one sense, what one would see next, there was one thing we knew we should not see – anything really great, central, of the first class, anything that humanity had adored. And with revulsion indescribable our emotions returned, I think, to those really close and crooked entries, to those really mean streets, to those genuine slums which lie round the Thames and the City, in which nevertheless a real possibility remains that at any chance corner the great cross of the great cathedral of Wren may strike down the street like a thunderbolt.

'But you must always remember also,' said Grant to me, in his heavy abstracted way, when I had urged this view, 'that the very vileness of the life of these ordered plebeian places bears witness to the victory of the human soul. I agree with you. I agree that they have to live in something worse than barbarism. They have to live in a fourth-rate civilisation. But yet I am practically certain that the majority of people here are good people. And being good is an adventure far more violent and daring than sailing round the world. Besides – '

'Go on,' I said.

No answer came.

'Go on,' I said, looking up.

The big blue eyes of Basil Grant were standing out of his head and he was paying no attention to me. He was staring over the side of the tram.

'What is the matter?' I asked, peering over also.

'It is very odd,' said Grant at last, grimly, 'that I should have been caught out like this at the very moment of my optimism. I said all these people were good, and there is the wickedest man in England.'

'Where?' I asked, leaning over further, 'where?'

'Oh, I was right enough,' he went on, in that strange continuous and sleepy tone which always angered his hearers at acute moments, 'I was right enough when I said all these people were good. They are heroes; they are saints. Now and then they may perhaps steal a spoon or two; they may beat a wife or two with the poker. But they are saints all the same; they are angels; they are robed in white; they are clad with wings and haloes – at any rate compared to that man.'

'Which man?' I cried again, and then my eye caught the figure at which Basil's bull's eyes were glaring.

He was a slim, smooth person, passing very quickly among the quickly passing crowd, but though there was nothing about him sufficient to attract a startled notice, there was quite enough to demand a curious consideration when once that notice was attracted. He wore a black top-hat, but there was enough in it of those strange curves whereby the decadent artist of the eighties tried to turn the top-hat into something as rhythmic as an Etruscan vase. His hair, which was largely grey, was curled with the instinct of one who appreciated the gradual beauty of grey and silver. The rest of his face was oval and, I thought, rather Oriental; he had two black tufts of moustache.

'What has he done?' I asked.

'I am not sure of the details,' said Grant, 'but his besetting sin is a desire to intrigue to the disadvantage of others. Probably he has adopted some imposture or other to effect his plan.'

'What plan?' I asked. 'If you know all about him, why don't you tell me why he is the wickedest man in England? What is his name?'

Basil Grant stared at me for some moments.

'I think you've made a mistake in my meaning,' he said. 'I don't know his name. I never saw him before in my life.'

'Never saw him before!' I cried, with a kind of anger; 'then what in heaven's name do you mean by saying that he is the wickedest man in England?'

'I meant what I said,' said Basil Grant calmly. 'The moment I saw that man, I saw all these people stricken with a sudden and splendid innocence. I saw that while all ordinary poor men in the streets were being themselves, he was not being himself. I saw that all the men in these slums, cadgers, pickpockets, hooligans, are all, in the deepest sense, trying to be good. And I saw that that man was trying to be evil.'

'But if you never saw him before – ' I began.

'In God's name, look at his face,' cried out Basil in a voice that startled the driver. 'Look at the eyebrows. They mean that infernal pride which made Satan so proud that he sneered even at heaven when he was one of the first angels in it. Look at his moustaches, they are so grown as to insult humanity. In the name of the sacred heavens look at his hair. In the name of God and the stars, look at his hat.'

I stirred uncomfortably.

'But, after all,' I said, 'this is very fanciful – perfectly absurd. Look at the mere facts. You have never seen the man before, you – '

'Oh, the mere facts,' he cried out in a kind of despair. 'The mere facts! Do you really admit – are you still so sunk in superstitions, so clinging to dim and prehistoric altars, that you believe in facts? Do you not trust an immediate impression?'

'Well, an immediate impression may be,' I said, 'a little less practical than facts.'

'Bosh,' he said. 'On what else is the whole world run but immediate impressions? What is more practical? My friend, the philosophy of this world may be founded on facts, its business is run on spiritual impressions and atmospheres. Why do you refuse or accept a clerk? Do you measure his skull? Do you read up his physiological state in a handbook? Do you go upon facts at all? Not a scrap. You accept a clerk who may save your business – you refuse a clerk that may rob your till, entirely upon those immediate mystical impressions under the pressure of which I pronounce, with a perfect sense of certainty and sincerity, that that man walking in that street beside us is a humbug and a villain of some kind.'

'You always put things well,' I said, 'but, of course, such things cannot immediately be put to the test.'

Basil sprang up straight and swayed with the swaying car.

'Let us get off and follow him,' he said. 'I bet you five pounds it will turn out as I say.'

And with a scuttle, a jump, and a run, we were off the car.

The man with the curved silver hair and the curved Eastern face walked along for some time, his long splendid frock-coat flying behind him. Then he swung sharply out of the great glaring road and disappeared down an ill-lit alley. We swung silently after him.

'This is an odd turning for a man of that kind to take,' I said.

'A man of what kind?' asked my friend.

'Well,' I said, 'a man with that kind of expression and those boots. I thought it rather odd, to tell the truth, that he should be in this part of the world at all.'

'Ah, yes,' said Basil, and said no more.

We tramped on, looking steadily in front of us. The elegant figure, like the figure of a black swan, was silhouetted suddenly against the glare of intermittent gaslight and then swallowed again in night. The intervals between the lights were long, and a fog was thickening the whole city. Our pace, therefore, had become swift and mechanical between the lampposts; but Basil came to a standstill suddenly like a reined horse; I stopped also. We had almost run into the man. A great part of the solid darkness in front of us was the darkness of his body.

At first I thought he had turned to face us. But though we were hardly a yard off he did not realise that we were there. He tapped four times on a very low and dirty door in the dark, crabbed street. A gleam of gas cut the darkness as it opened slowly. We listened intently, but the interview was short and simple and inexplicable as an interview could be. Our exquisite friend handed in what looked like a paper or a card and said: 'At once. Take a cab.'

A heavy, deep voice from inside said: 'Right you are.'

And with a click we were in the blackness again, and striding after the striding stranger through a labyrinth of London lanes, the lights just helping us. It was only five o'clock, but winter and the fog had made it like midnight.

'This is really an extraordinary walk for the patent-leather boots,' I repeated.

'I don't know,' said Basil humbly. 'It leads to Berkeley Square.'

As I tramped on I strained my eyes through the dusky atmosphere and tried to make out the direction described. For some ten minutes I wondered and doubted; at the end of that I saw that my friend was right. We were coming to the great dreary spaces of fashionable London – more dreary, one must admit, even than the dreary plebeian spaces.

'This is very extraordinary!' said Basil Grant, as we turned into Berkeley Square.

'What is extraordinary?' I asked. 'I thought you said it was quite natural.'

'I do not wonder,' answered Basil, 'at his walking through nasty streets; I do not wonder at his going to Berkeley Square. But I do wonder at his going to the house of a very good man.'

'What very good man?' I asked with exasperation.

'The operation of time is a singular one,' he said with his imperturbable irrelevancy. 'It is not a true statement of the case to say that I have forgotten my career when I was a judge and a public man. I remember it all vividly, but it is like remembering some novel. But fifteen years ago I knew this square as well as Lord Rosebery does, and a confounded long sight better than that man who is going up the steps of old Beaumont's house.'

'Who is old Beaumont?' I asked irritably.

'A perfectly good fellow. Lord Beaumont of Foxwood – don't you know his name? He is a man of transparent sincerity, a nobleman who does more work than a navvy, a socialist, an anarchist, I don't know what; anyhow, he's a philosopher and philanthropist. I admit he has the slight disadvantage of being, beyond all question, off his head. He has that real disadvantage which has arisen out of the modern worship of progress and novelty; and he thinks anything odd and new must be an advance. If you went to him and proposed to eat your grandmother, he would agree with you, so long as you put it on hygienic and public grounds, as a cheap alternative to cremation. So long as you progress fast enough it seems a matter of indifference to him whether you are progressing to the stars or the devil. So his house is filled with an endless succession of literary and political fashions; men who wear long hair because it is romantic; men who wear short hair because it is medical; men who walk on their feet only to exercise their hands; and men who walk on their hands for fear of tiring their feet. But though the inhabitants of his salons are generally fools, like himself, they are almost always, like himself, good men. I am really surprised to see a criminal enter there.'

'My good fellow,' I said firmly, striking my foot on the pavement, 'the truth of this affair is very simple. To use your own eloquent language, you have the "slight disadvantage" of being off your head. You see a total stranger in a public street; you choose to start certain theories about his eyebrows. You then treat him as a burglar because he enters an honest man's door. The thing is too monstrous. Admit that it is, Basil, and come home with me. Though these people are still having tea, yet with the distance we have to go, we shall be late for dinner.'

Basil's eyes were shining in the twilight like lamps.

'I thought,' he said, 'that I had outlived vanity.'

'What do you want now?' I cried.

'I want,' he cried out, 'what a girl wants when she wears her new frock; I want what a boy wants when he goes in for a slanging match with a monitor – I want to show somebody what a fine fellow I am. I am as right about that man as I am about your having a hat on your head. You say it cannot be tested. I say it can. I will take you to see my old friend Beaumont. He is a delightful man to know.'

'Do you really mean – ?' I began.

'I will apologise,' he said calmly, 'for our not being dressed for a call,' and walking across the vast misty square, he walked up the dark stone steps and rang at the bell.

A severe servant in black and white opened the door to us: on receiving my friend's name his manner passed in a flash from astonishment to respect. We were ushered into the house very quickly, but not so quickly but that our host, a white-haired man with a fiery face, came out quickly to meet us.

'My dear fellow,' he cried, shaking Basil's hand again and again, 'I have not seen you for years. Have you been – er – ' he said, rather wildly, 'have you been in the country?'

'Not for all that time,' answered Basil, smiling. 'I have long given up my official position, my dear Philip, and have been living in a deliberate retirement. I hope I do not come at an inopportune moment.'

'An inopportune moment,' cried the ardent gentleman. 'You come at the most opportune moment I could imagine. Do you know who is here?'

'I do not,' answered Grant, with gravity. Even as he spoke a roar of laughter came from the inner room.

'Basil,' said Lord Beaumont solemnly, 'I have Wimpole here.'

'And who is Wimpole?'

'Basil,' cried the other, 'you must have been in the country. You must have been in the antipodes. You must have been in the moon. Who is Wimpole? Who was Shakespeare?'

'As to who Shakespeare was,' answered my friend placidly, 'my views go no further than thinking that he was not Bacon. More probably he was Mary Queen of Scots. But as to who Wimpole is – ' and his speech also was cloven with a roar of laughter from within.

'Wimpole!' cried Lord Beaumont, in a sort of ecstasy. 'Haven't you heard of the great modern wit? My dear fellow, he has turned conversation, I do not say into an art – for that, perhaps, it always was – but into a great art, like the statuary of Michael Angelo – an art of masterpieces. His repartees, my good friend, startle one like a man shot dead. They are final; they are – '

Again there came the hilarious roar from the room, and almost with the very noise of it, a big, panting apoplectic old gentleman came out of the inner house into the hall where we were standing.

'Now, my dear chap,' began Lord Beaumont hastily.

'I tell you, Beaumont, I won't stand it,' exploded the large old gentleman. 'I won't be made game of by a twopenny literary adventurer like that. I won't be made a guy. I won't – '

'Come, come,' said Beaumont feverishly. 'Let me introduce you. This is Mr Justice Grant – that is, Mr Grant. Basil, I am sure you have heard of Sir Walter Cholmondeliegh.'

'Who has not?' asked Grant, and bowed to the worthy old baronet, eyeing him with some curiosity. He was hot and heavy in his momentary anger, but even that could not conceal the noble though opulent outline of his face and body, the florid white hair, the Roman nose, the body stalwart though corpulent, the chin aristocratic though double. He was a magnificent courtly gentleman; so much of a gentleman that he could show an unquestionable weakness of anger without altogether losing dignity; so much of a gentleman that even his *faux pas* were well-bred.

'I am distressed beyond expression, Beaumont,' he said gruffly, 'to fail in respect to these gentlemen, and even more especially to fail in it in your house. But it is not you or they that are in any way concerned, but that flashy half-caste jackanapes – '

At this moment a young man with a twist of red moustache and a sombre air came out of the inner room. He also did not seem to be greatly enjoying the intellectual banquet within.

'I think you remember my friend and secretary, Mr Drummond,' said Lord Beaumont, turning to Grant, 'even if you only remember him as a schoolboy.'

'Perfectly,' said the other. Mr Drummond shook hands pleasantly and respectfully, but the cloud was still on his brow. Turning to Sir Walter Cholmondeliegh, he said: 'I was sent by Lady Beaumont to express her hope that you were not going yet, Sir Walter. She says she has scarcely seen anything of you.'

The old gentleman, still red in the face, had a temporary internal struggle; then his good manners triumphed, and with a gesture of obeisance and a vague utterance of, 'If Lady Beaumont . . . a lady, of course,' he followed the young man back into the *salon*. He had scarcely been deposited there half a minute before another peal of laughter told that he had (in all probability) been scored off again.

'Of course, I can excuse dear old Cholmondeliegh,' said Beaumont, as he helped us off with our coats. 'He has not the modern mind.'

'What is the modern mind?' asked Grant.

'Oh, it's enlightened, you know, and progressive – and faces the facts of life seriously.' At this moment another roar of laughter came from within.

'I only ask,' said Basil, 'because of the last two friends of yours who had the modern mind; one thought it wrong to eat fishes and the other thought it right to eat men. I beg your pardon – this way, if I remember right.'

'Do you know,' said Lord Beaumont, with a sort of feverish entertainment, as he trotted after us towards the interior, 'I can never quite make out which side you are on. Sometimes you seem so liberal and sometimes so reactionary. *Are* you a modern, Basil?'

'No,' said Basil, loudly and cheerfully, as he entered the crowded drawing-room.

This caused a slight diversion, and some eyes were turned away from our slim friend with the Oriental face for the first time that afternoon. Two people, however, still looked at him. One was the daughter of the house,

Muriel Beaumont, who gazed at him with great violet eyes and with the intense and awful thirst of the female upper class for verbal amusement and stimulus. The other was Sir Walter Cholmondeliegh, who looked at him with a still and sullen but unmistakable desire to throw him out of the window.

He sat there, coiled rather than seated on the easy chair; everything from the curves of his smooth limbs to the coils of his silvered hair suggesting the circles of a serpent more than the straight limbs of a man – the unmistakable, splendid serpentine gentleman we had seen walking in North London, his eyes shining with repeated victory.

'What I can't understand, Mr Wimpole,' said Muriel Beaumont eagerly, 'is how you contrive to treat all this so easily. You say things quite philosophical and yet so wildly funny. If I thought of such things, I'm sure I should laugh outright when the thought first came.'

'I agree with Miss Beaumont,' said Sir Walter, suddenly exploding with indignation. 'If I had thought of anything so futile, I should find it difficult to keep my countenance.'

'Difficult to keep your countenance,' cried Mr Wimpole, with an air of alarm; 'oh, do keep your countenance! Keep it in the British Museum.'

Everyone laughed uproariously, as they always do at an already admitted readiness, and Sir Walter, turning suddenly purple, shouted out: 'Do you know who you are talking to, with your confounded tomfooleries?'

'I never talk tomfooleries,' said the other, 'without first knowing my audience.'

Grant walked across the room and tapped the red-moustached secretary on the shoulder. That gentleman was leaning against the wall regarding the whole scene with a great deal of gloom; but, I fancied, with very particular gloom when his eyes fell on the young lady of the house rapturously listening to Wimpole.

'May I have a word with you outside, Drummond?' asked Grant. 'It is about business. Lady Beaumont will excuse us.'

I followed my friend, at his own request, greatly wondering, to this strange external interview. We passed abruptly into a kind of side room out of the hall.

'Drummond,' said Basil sharply, 'there are a great many good people, and a great many sane people here this afternoon. Unfortunately, by a kind of coincidence, all the good people are mad, and all the sane people are wicked. You are the only person I know of here who is honest and has also some common sense. What do you make of Wimpole?'

Mr Secretary Drummond had a pale face and red hair; but at this his face became suddenly as red as his moustache.

'I am not a fair judge of him,' he said.

'Why not?' asked Grant.

'Because I hate him like hell,' said the other, after a long pause and violently.

Neither Grant nor I needed to ask the reason; his glances towards Miss Beaumont and the stranger were sufficiently illuminating. Grant said quietly: 'But before – before you came to hate him, what did you really think of him?'

'I am in a terrible difficulty,' said the young man, and his voice told us, like a clear bell, that he was an honest man. 'If I spoke about him as I feel about him now, I could not trust myself. And I should like to be able to say that when I first saw him I thought he was charming. But again, the fact is I didn't. I hate him, that is my private affair. But I also disapprove of him – really I do believe I disapprove of him quite apart from my private feelings. When first he came, I admit he was much quieter, but I did not like, so to speak, the moral swell of him. Then that jolly old Sir Walter Cholmondeliegh got introduced to us, and this fellow, with his cheap-jack wit, began to score off the old man in the way he does now. Then I felt that he must be a bad lot; it must be bad to fight the old and the kindly. And he fights the poor old chap savagely, unceasingly, as if he hated old age and kindliness. Take, if you want it, the evidence of a prejudiced witness. I admit that I hate the man because a certain person admires him. But I believe that apart from that I should hate the man because old Sir Walter hates him.'

This speech affected me with a genuine sense of esteem and pity for the young man; that is, of pity for him because of his obviously hopeless worship of Miss Beaumont, and of esteem for him because of the direct realistic account of the history of Wimpole which he had given. Still, I was sorry that he seemed so steadily set against the man, and could not help referring it to an instinct of his personal relations, however nobly disguised from himself.

In the middle of these meditations, Grant whispered in my ear what was perhaps the most startling of all interruptions.

'In the name of God, let's get away.'

I have never known exactly in how odd a way this odd old man affected me. I only know that for some reason or other he so affected me that I was, within a few minutes, in the street outside.

'This,' he said, 'is a beastly but amusing affair.'

'What is?' I asked, baldly enough.

'This affair. Listen to me, my old friend. Lord and Lady Beaumont have just invited you and me to a grand dinner-party this very night, at which Mr Wimpole will be in all his glory. Well, there is nothing very extraordinary about that. The extraordinary thing is that we are not going.'

'Well, really,' I said, 'it is already six o'clock and I doubt if we could get home and dress. I see nothing extraordinary in the fact that we are not going.'

'Don't you?' said Grant. 'I'll bet you'll see something extraordinary in what we're doing instead.'

I looked at him blankly.

'Doing instead?' I asked. 'What are we doing instead?'

'Why,' said he, 'we are waiting for one or two hours outside this house on a winter evening. You must forgive me; it is all my vanity. It is only to show you that I am right. Can you, with the assistance of this cigar, wait until both Sir Walter Cholmondeliegh and the mystic Wimpole have left this house?'

'Certainly,' I said. 'But I do not know which is likely to leave first. Have you any notion?'

'No,' he said. 'Sir Walter may leave first in a glow of rage. Or again, Mr Wimpole may leave first, feeling that his last epigram is a thing to be flung behind him like a firework. And Sir Walter may remain some time to analyse Mr Wimpole's character. But they will both have to leave within reasonable time, for they will both have to get dressed and come back to dinner here tonight.'

As he spoke the shrill double whistle from the porch of the great house drew a dark cab to the dark portal. And then a thing happened that we really had not expected. Mr Wimpole and Sir Walter Cholmondeliegh came out at the same moment.

They paused for a second or two opposite each other in a natural doubt; then a certain geniality, fundamental perhaps in both of them, made Sir Walter smile and say: 'The night is foggy. Pray take my cab.'

Before I could count twenty the cab had gone rattling up the street with both of them. And before I could count twenty-three Grant had hissed in my ear: 'Run after the cab; run as if you were running from a mad dog – run.'

We pelted on steadily, keeping the cab in sight, through dark mazy streets. God only, I thought, knows why we are running at all, but we are running hard. Fortunately we did not run far. The cab pulled up at the fork of two streets and Sir Walter paid the cabman, who drove away rejoicing, having just come in contact with the more generous among the rich. Then the two men talked together as men do talk together after giving and receiving great insults, the talk which leads either to forgiveness or a duel – at least so it seemed as we watched it from ten yards off. Then the two men shook hands heartily, and one went down one fork of the road and one down another.

Basil, with one of his rare gestures, flung his arms forward.

'Run after that scoundrel,' he cried; 'let us catch him now.'

We dashed across the open space and reached the juncture of two paths.

'Stop!' I shouted wildly to Grant. 'That's the wrong turning.'

He ran on.

'Idiot!' I howled. 'Sir Walter's gone down there. Wimpole has slipped us. He's half a mile down the other road. You're wrong . . . Are you deaf? You're wrong!'

'I don't think I am,' he panted, and ran on.

'But I saw him!' I cried. 'Look in front of you. Is that Wimpole? It's the old man . . . What are you doing? What are we to do?'

'Keep running,' said Grant.

Running soon brought us up to the broad back of the pompous old baronet, whose white whiskers shone silver in the fitful lamplight. My brain was utterly bewildered. I grasped nothing.

'Charlie,' said Basil hoarsely, 'can you believe in my common sense for four minutes?'

'Of course,' I said, panting.

'Then help me to catch that man in front and hold him down. Do it at once when I say "Now". Now!'

We sprang on Sir Walter Cholmondeliegh, and rolled that portly old gentleman on his back. He fought with a commendable valour, but we got him tight. I had not the remotest notion why. He had a splendid and full-blooded vigour; when he could not box he kicked, and we bound him; when he could not kick he shouted, and we gagged him. Then, by Basil's arrangement, we dragged him into a small court by the street side and waited. As I say, I had no notion why.

'I am sorry to incommode you,' said Basil calmly out of the darkness; 'but I have made an appointment here.'

'An appointment!' I said blankly.

'Yes,' he said, glancing calmly at the apoplectic old aristocrat gagged on the ground, whose eyes were starting impotently from his head. 'I have made an appointment here with a thoroughly nice young fellow. An old friend. Jasper Drummond his name is – you may have met him this afternoon at the Beaumonts. He can scarcely come though till the Beaumonts' dinner is over.'

For I do not know how many hours we stood there calmly in the darkness. By the time those hours were over I had thoroughly made up my mind that the same thing had happened which had happened long ago on the bench of a British Court of Justice. Basil Grant had gone mad. I could imagine no other explanation of the facts, with the portly, purple-faced old country gentleman flung there strangled on the floor like a bundle of wood.

After about four hours a lean figure in evening dress rushed into the court. A glimpse of gaslight showed the red moustache and white face of Jasper Drummond.

'Mr Grant,' he said blankly, 'the thing is incredible. You were right; but what did you mean? All through this dinner-party, where dukes and duchesses and editors of Quarterlies had come especially to hear him, that extraordinary Wimpole kept perfectly silent. He didn't say a funny thing. He didn't say anything at all. What does it mean?'

Grant pointed to the portly old gentleman on the ground.

'That is what it means,' he said.

Drummond, on observing a fat gentleman lying so calmly about the place, jumped back, as from a mouse.

'What?' he said weakly, '. . . what?'

Basil bent suddenly down and tore a paper out of Sir Walter's breast pocket, a paper which the baronet, even in his hampered state, seemed to make some effort to retain.

It was a large loose piece of white wrapping paper, which Mr Jasper Drummond read with a vacant eye and undisguised astonishment. As far as he could make out, it consisted of a series of questions and answers, or at least of remarks and replies, arranged in the manner of a catechism. The greater part of the document had been torn and obliterated in the struggle, but the termination remained. It ran as follows:

C. Says . . . Keep countenance.
W. Keep . . . British Museum.
C. Know whom talk . . . absurdities.
W. Never talk absurdities without . . .

'What is it?' cried Drummond, flinging the paper down in a sort of final fury.

'What is it?' replied Grant, his voice rising into a kind of splendid chant. 'What is it? It is a great new profession. A great new trade. A trifle immoral, I admit, but still great, like piracy.'

'A new profession!' said the young man with the red moustache vaguely; 'a new trade!'

'A new trade,' repeated Grant, with a strange exultation, 'a new profession! What a pity it is immoral.'

'But what the deuce is it?' cried Drummond and I in a breath of blasphemy.

'It is,' said Grant calmly, 'the great new trade of the Organiser of Repartee. This fat old gentleman lying on the ground strikes you, as I have no doubt, as very stupid and very rich. Let me clear his character. He is, like ourselves, very clever and very poor. He is also not really at all fat; all that is stuffing. He is not particularly old, and his name is not Cholmondeliegh. He is a swindler, and a swindler of a perfectly delightful and novel kind. He hires himself out at dinner-parties to lead up to other people's repartees. According to a preconcerted scheme (which you may find on that piece of paper), he says the stupid things he has arranged for himself, and his client says the clever things arranged for him. In short, he allows himself to be scored off for a guinea a night.'

'And this fellow Wimpole – ' began Drummond with indignation.

'This fellow Wimpole,' said Basil Grant, smiling, 'will not be an intellectual rival in the future. He had some fine things, elegance and silvered hair, and so on. But the intellect is with our friend on the floor.'

'That fellow,' cried Drummond furiously, 'that fellow ought to be in gaol.'

'Not at all,' said Basil indulgently; 'he ought to be in the Club of Queer Trades.'

3

The Awful Reason of the Vicar's Visit

The revolt of Matter against Man (which I believe to exist) has now been reduced to a singular condition. It is the small things rather than the large things which make war against us and, I may add, beat us. The bones of the last mammoth have long ago decayed, a mighty wreck; the tempests no longer devour our navies, nor the mountains with hearts of fire heap hell over our cities. But we are engaged in a bitter and eternal war with small things; chiefly with microbes and with collar studs. The stud with which I was engaged (on fierce and equal terms) as I made the above reflections, was one which I was trying to introduce into my shirt collar when a loud knock came at the door.

My first thought was as to whether Basil Grant had called to fetch me. He and I were to turn up at the same dinner-party (for which I was in the act of dressing), and it might be that he had taken it into his head to come my way, though we had arranged to go separately. It was a small and confidential affair at the table of a good but unconventional political lady, an old friend of his. She had asked us both to meet a third guest, a Captain Fraser, who had made something of a name and was an authority on chimpanzees. As Basil was an old friend of the hostess and I had never seen her, I felt that it was quite possible that he (with his usual social sagacity) might have decided to take me along in order to break the ice. The theory, like all my theories, was complete; but as a fact it was not Basil.

I was handed a visiting card inscribed: 'Revd Ellis Shorter', and underneath was written in pencil, but in a hand in which even hurry could not conceal a depressing and gentlemanly excellence, 'Asking the favour of a few moments' conversation on a most urgent matter.'

I had already subdued the stud, thereby proclaiming that the image of God has supremacy over all matters (a valuable truth), and throwing on my dress-coat and waistcoat, hurried into the drawing-room. He rose at my entrance, flapping like a seal; I can use no other description. He flapped a plaid shawl over his right arm; he flapped a pair of pathetic black gloves; he flapped his clothes; I may say, without exaggeration, that he flapped his eyelids, as he rose. He was a bald-browed, white-haired, white-whiskered old clergyman, of a flappy and floppy type. He said: 'I am so sorry. I am so very sorry. I am so extremely sorry. I come – I can only say – I can only say in my defence, that I come – upon an important matter. Pray forgive me.'

I told him I forgave perfectly and waited.

'What I have to say,' he said brokenly, 'is so dreadful – it is so dreadful – I have lived a quiet life.'

I was burning to get away, for it was already doubtful if I should be in time for dinner. But there was something about the old man's honest air of bitterness that seemed to open to me the possibilities of life larger and more tragic than my own.

I said gently: 'Pray go on.'

Nevertheless the old gentleman, being a gentleman as well as old, noticed my secret impatience and seemed still more unmanned.

'I'm so sorry,' he said meekly; 'I wouldn't have come – but for – your friend Major Brown recommended me to come here.'

'Major Brown!' I said, with some interest.

'Yes,' said the Reverend Mr Shorter, feverishly flapping his plaid shawl about. 'He told me you helped him in a great difficulty – and my difficulty! Oh, my dear sir, it's a matter of life and death.'

I rose abruptly, in an acute perplexity. 'Will it take long, Mr Shorter?' I asked. 'I have to go out to dinner almost at once.'

He rose also, trembling from head to foot, and yet somehow, with all his moral palsy, he rose to the dignity of his age and his office.

'I have no right, Mr Swinburne – I have no right at all,' he said. 'If you have to go out to dinner, you have of course – a perfect right – of course a perfect right. But when you come back – a man will be dead.'

And he sat down, quaking like a jelly.

The triviality of the dinner had been in those two minutes dwarfed and drowned in my mind. I did not want to go and see a political widow, and a captain who collected apes; I wanted to hear what had brought this dear, doddering old vicar into relation with immediate perils.

'Will you have a cigar?' I said.

'No, thank you,' he said, with indescribable embarrassment, as if not smoking cigars was a social disgrace.

'A glass of wine?' I said.

'No, thank you, no, thank you; not just now,' he repeated with that hysterical eagerness with which people who do not drink at all often try to convey that on any other night of the week they would sit up all night drinking rum-punch. 'Not just now, thank you.'

'Nothing else I can get for you?' I said, feeling genuinely sorry for the well-mannered old donkey. 'A cup of tea?'

I saw a struggle in his eye and I conquered. When the cup of tea came he drank it like a dipsomaniac gulping brandy. Then he fell back and said: 'I have had such a time, Mr Swinburne. I am not used to these excitements. As Vicar of Chuntsey, in Essex' – he threw this in with an indescribable airiness of vanity – 'I have never known such things happen.'

'What things happen?' I asked.

He straightened himself with sudden dignity.

'As Vicar of Chuntsey, in Essex,' he said, 'I have never been forcibly dressed up as an old woman and made to take part in a crime in the character of an old woman. Never once. My experience may be small. It may be insufficient. But it has never occurred to me before.'

'I have never heard of it,' I said, 'as among the duties of a clergyman. But I am not well up in church matters. Excuse me if perhaps I failed to follow you correctly. Dressed up – as what?'

'As an old woman,' said the vicar solemnly, 'as an old woman.'

I thought in my heart that it required no great transformation to make an old woman of him, but the thing was evidently more tragic than comic, and I said respectfully: 'May I ask how it occurred?'

'I will begin at the beginning,' said Mr Shorter, 'and I will tell my story with the utmost possible precision. At seventeen minutes past eleven this morning I left the vicarage to keep certain appointments and pay certain visits in the village. My first visit was to Mr Jervis, the treasurer of our League of Christian Amusements, with whom I concluded some business touching the claim made by Parkes the gardener in the matter of the rolling of our tennis lawn. I then visited Mrs Arnett, a very earnest churchwoman, but permanently bedridden. She is the author of several small works of devotion, and of a book of verse, entitled (unless my memory misleads me) *Eglantine*.'

He uttered all this not only with deliberation, but with something that can only be called, by a contradictory phrase, eager deliberation. He had, I think, a vague memory in his head of the detectives in the detective stories, who always sternly require that nothing should be kept back.

'I then proceeded,' he went on, with the same maddening conscientiousness of manner, 'to Mr Carr (not Mr James Carr, of course; Mr Robert Carr) who is temporarily assisting our organist, and having consulted with him (on the subject of a choir boy who is accused, I cannot as yet say whether justly or not, of cutting holes in the organ pipes), I finally dropped in upon a Dorcas meeting at the house of Miss Brett. The Dorcas meetings are usually held at the vicarage, but my wife being unwell, Miss Brett, a newcomer in our village, but very active in church work, had very kindly consented to hold them. The Dorcas society is entirely under my wife's management as a rule, and except for Miss Brett, who, as I say, is very active, I scarcely know any members of it. I had, however, promised to drop in on them, and I did so.

'When I arrived there were only four other maiden ladies with Miss Brett, but they were sewing very busily. It is very difficult, of course, for any person, however strongly impressed with the necessity in these matters of full and exact exposition of the facts, to remember and repeat the actual details of a conversation, particularly a conversation which (though inspired with a most worthy and admirable zeal for good work) was one which did not greatly impress the hearer's mind at the time and was in fact – er – mostly about socks. I can, however, remember distinctly that one of the spinster ladies (she was a thin person with a woollen shawl, who appeared to feel the cold, and I am almost sure she was introduced to me as Miss James) remarked that the weather was very changeable. Miss Brett then offered me a cup of tea, which I accepted, I cannot recall in what words. Miss Brett is a short and stout lady with white hair. The only other figure in the group that caught my attention was a Miss Mowbray, a small and neat lady of aristocratic manners, silver hair, and a high voice and colour. She was the most emphatic member of the party; and her views on the subject of pinafores, though expressed with a natural deference to myself, were in themselves strong and advanced. Beside her (although all five ladies were dressed simply in black) it could not be denied that the others looked in some way what you men of the world would call dowdy.

'After about ten minutes' conversation I rose to go, and as I did so I heard something which – I cannot describe it – something which seemed to – but I really cannot describe it.'

'What did you hear?' I asked, with some impatience.

'I heard,' said the vicar solemnly, 'I heard Miss Mowbray (the lady with the silver hair) say to Miss James (the lady with the woollen shawl), the following extraordinary words. I committed them to memory on the spot, and as soon as circumstances set me free to do so, I noted them down on a piece of paper. I believe I have it here.' He fumbled in his breast-pocket, bringing out mild things, notebooks, circulars and programmes of village concerts. 'I heard Miss Mowbray say to Miss James, the following words: "Now's your time, Bill." '

He gazed at me for a few moments after making this announcement, gravely and unflinchingly, as if conscious that here he was unshaken about his facts. Then he resumed, turning his bald head more towards the fire.

'This appeared to me remarkable. I could not by any means understand it. It seemed to me first of all peculiar that one maiden lady should address another maiden lady as "Bill". My experience, as I have said, may be incomplete; maiden ladies may have among themselves and in exclusively spinster circles wilder customs than I am aware of. But it seemed to me odd, and I could almost have sworn (if you will not misunderstand the phrase), I should have been strongly impelled to maintain at the time that the words, "Now's your time, Bill," were by no means pronounced with that upper-class intonation which, as I have already said, had up to now characterised Miss Mowbray's conversation. In fact, the words, "Now's your time, Bill," would have been, I fancy, unsuitable if pronounced with that upper-class intonation.

'I was surprised, I repeat, then, at the remark. But I was still more surprised when, looking round me in bewilderment, my hat and umbrella in hand, I saw the lean lady with the woollen shawl leaning upright against the door out of which I was just about to make my exit. She was still knitting, and I supposed that this erect posture against the door was only an eccentricity of spinsterhood and an oblivion of my intended departure.

'I said genially, "I am so sorry to disturb you, Miss James, but I must really be going. I have – er – " I stopped here, for the words she had uttered in reply, though singularly brief and in tone extremely businesslike, were such as to render that arrest of my remarks, I think, natural and excusable. I have these words also noted down. I have not the least idea of their meaning; so I have only been able to render them phonetically. But she said,' and Mr Shorter peered short-sightedly at his papers, 'she said: "Chuck it, fat 'ead," and she added something that sounded like "It's a kop," or (possibly) "a kopt". And then the last cord, either of my sanity or the sanity of the universe, snapped suddenly. My esteemed friend and helper, Miss Brett, standing by the mantelpiece, said: "Put 'is old 'ead in a bag, Sam, and tie 'im up before you start jawin'. You'll be kopt yourselves some o' these days with this way of doin' things, har lar theatre."

'My head went round and round. Was it really true, as I had suddenly fancied a moment before, that unmarried ladies had some dreadful riotous society of their own from which all others were excluded? I remembered dimly in my classical days (I was a scholar in a small way once, but now, alas! rusty), I remembered the mysteries of the Bona Dea and their strange female freemasonry. I remembered the witches' Sabbaths. I was just, in my absurd light-headedness, trying to remember a line of verse about Diana's nymphs, when Miss Mowbray threw her arm round me from behind. The moment it held me I knew it was not a woman's arm.

'Miss Brett – or what I had called Miss Brett – was standing in front of me with a big revolver in her hand and a broad grin on her face. Miss James was still leaning against the door, but had fallen into an attitude so totally new, and so totally unfeminine, that it gave one a shock. She was kicking her heels, with her hands in her pockets and her cap on one side. She was a man. I mean he was a wo – no, that is I saw that instead of being a woman she – he, I mean – that is, it was a man.'

Mr Shorter became indescribably flurried and flapping in endeavouring to arrange these genders and his plaid shawl at the same time. He resumed with a higher fever of nervousness: 'As for Miss Mowbray, she – he, held me in a ring of iron. He had her arm – that is she had his arm – round her neck – my neck I mean – and I could not cry out. Miss Brett – that is, Mr Brett, at least Mr something who was not Miss Brett – had the revolver pointed at me. The other two ladies – or er – gentlemen, were rummaging in some bag in the background. It was all clear at last: they were criminals dressed up as women, to kidnap me! To kidnap the Vicar of Chuntsey, in Essex. But why? Was it to be Nonconformists?

'The brute leaning against the door called out carelessly, " 'Urry up, 'Arry. Show the old bloke what the game is, and let's get off."

' "Curse 'is eyes," said Miss Brett – I mean the man with the revolver – "why should we show 'im the game?"

' "If you take my advice you bloomin' well will," said the man at the door, whom they called Bill. "A man wot knows wot 'e's doin' is worth ten wot don't, even if 'e's a potty old parson."

' "Bill's right enough," said the coarse voice of the man who held me (it had been Miss Mowbray's). "Bring out the picture, 'Arry."

'The man with the revolver walked across the room to where the other two women – I mean men – were turning over baggage, and asked them for something which they gave him. He came back with it across the room and held it out in front of me. And compared to the surprise of that display, all the previous surprises of this awful day shrank suddenly.

'It was a portrait of myself. That such a picture should be in the hands of these scoundrels might in any case have caused a mild surprise; but no more. It was no mild surprise that I felt. The likeness was an extremely good one, worked up with all the accessories of the conventional photographic studio. I was leaning my head on my hand and was relieved against a painted landscape of woodland. It was obvious that it was no snapshot; it was clear that I had sat for this photograph. And the truth was that I had never sat for such a photograph. It was a photograph that I had never had taken.

'I stared at it again and again. It seemed to me to be touched up a good deal; it was glazed as well as framed, and the glass blurred some of the details. But there unmistakably was my face, my eyes, my nose and mouth, my head and hand, posed for a professional photographer. And I had never posed so for any photographer.

' "Be'old the bloomin' miracle," said the man with the revolver, with ill-timed facetiousness. "Parson, prepare to meet your God." And with this he slid the glass out of the frame. As the glass moved, I saw that part of the picture was painted on it in Chinese white, notably a pair of white whiskers and a clerical collar. And underneath was a portrait of an old lady in a quiet black dress, leaning her head on her hand against the woodland landscape. The old lady was as like me as one pin is like another. It had required only the whiskers and the collar to make it me in every hair.

' "Entertainin', ain't it?" said the man described as 'Arry, as he shot the glass back again. "Remarkable resemblance, parson. Gratifyin' to the lady. Gratifyin' to you. And hi may hadd, particlery gratifyin' to us, as bein' the probable source of a very tolerable haul. You know Colonel Hawker, the man who's come to live in these parts, don't you?"

'I nodded.

' "Well," said the man 'Arry, pointing to the picture, "that's 'is mother. 'Oo ran to catch 'im when 'e fell? She did," and he flung his fingers in a general gesture towards the photograph of the old lady who was exactly like me.

' "Tell the old gent wot 'e's got to do and be done with it," broke out Bill from the door. "Look 'ere, Reverend Shorter, we ain't goin' to do you no 'arm. We'll give you a sov. for your trouble if you like. And as for the old woman's clothes – why, you'll look lovely in 'em."

' "You ain't much of a 'and at a description, Bill," said the man behind me. "Mr Shorter, it's like this. We've got to see this man Hawker tonight. Maybe 'e'll kiss us all and 'ave up the champagne when 'e sees us. Maybe on the other 'and – 'e won't. Maybe 'e'll be dead when we goes away. Maybe not. But we've got to see 'im. Now as you know, 'e shuts 'isself up and never opens the door to a soul; only you don't know why and we does. The only one as can ever get at 'im is 'is mother. Well, it's a confounded funny coincidence," he said, accenting the penultimate, "it's a very unusual piece of good luck, but you're 'is mother."

' "When first I saw 'er picture," said the man Bill, shaking his head in a ruminant manner, "when I first saw it I said – old Shorter. Those were my exact words – old Shorter."

' "What do you mean, you wild creatures?" I gasped. "What am I to do?"

' "That's easy said, your 'oliness," said the man with the revolver, good-humouredly; "you've got to put on those clothes," and he pointed to a poke-bonnet and a heap of female clothes in the corner of the room.

'I will not dwell, Mr Swinburne, upon the details of what followed. I had no choice. I could not fight five men, to say nothing of a loaded pistol. In five minutes, sir, the Vicar of Chuntsey was dressed as an old woman – as somebody else's mother, if you please – and was dragged out of the house to take part in a crime.

'It was already late in the afternoon, and the nights of winter were closing in fast. On a dark road, in a blowing wind, we set out towards the lonely house of Colonel Hawker, perhaps the queerest cortège that ever straggled up that or any other road. To every human eye, in every external, we were six very respectable old ladies of small means, in black dresses and refined but antiquated bonnets; and we were really five criminals and a clergyman.

'I will cut a long story short. My brain was whirling like a windmill as I walked, trying to think of some manner of escape. To cry out, so long as we were far from houses, would be suicidal, for it would be easy for the ruffians to knife me or to gag me and fling me into a ditch. On the other hand, to attempt to stop strangers and explain the situation was impossible, because of the frantic folly of the situation itself. Long before I had persuaded the chance postman or carrier of so absurd a story, my companions would certainly have got off themselves, and in all probability would have carried me off, as a friend of theirs who had the misfortune to be mad or drunk. The last thought, however, was an inspiration; though a very terrible one. Had it come to this, that the Vicar of Chuntsey must pretend to be mad or drunk? It had come to this.

'I walked along with the rest up the deserted road, imitating and keeping pace, as far as I could, with their rapid and yet ladylike step, until at length I saw a lamppost and a policeman standing under it. I had made up my mind. Until we reached them we were all equally demure and silent and swift. When we reached them I suddenly flung myself against the railings and roared out: "Hooray! Hooray! Hooray! Rule Britannia! Get your 'air cut. Hoop-la! Boo!" It was a condition of no little novelty for a man in my position.

'The constable instantly flashed his lantern on me, or the draggled, drunken old woman that was my travesty. "Now then, mum," he began gruffly.

' "Come along quiet, or I'll eat your heart," cried Sam in my ear hoarsely. "Stop, or I'll flay you." It was frightful to hear the words and see the neatly shawled old spinster who whispered them.

'I yelled, and yelled – I was in for it now. I screamed comic refrains that vulgar young men had sung, to my regret, at our village concerts; I rolled to and fro like a ninepin about to fall.

' "If you can't get your friend on quiet, ladies," said the policeman, "I shall have to take 'er up. Drunk and disorderly she is right enough."

'I redoubled my efforts. I had not been brought up to this sort of thing; but I believe I eclipsed myself. Words that I did not know I had ever heard of seemed to come pouring out of my open mouth.

' "When we get you past," whispered Bill, "you'll howl louder; you'll howl louder when we're burning your feet off."

'I screamed in my terror those awful songs of joy. In all the nightmares that men have ever dreamed, there has never been anything so blighting and horrible as the faces of those five men, looking out of their poke-bonnets; the figures of district visitors with the faces of devils. I cannot think there is anything so heart-breaking in hell.

'For a sickening instant I thought that the bustle of my companions and the perfect respectability of all our dresses would overcome the policeman and induce him to let us pass. He wavered, so far as one can describe anything so solid as a policeman as wavering. I lurched suddenly forward and ran my head into his chest, calling out (if I remember correctly), "Oh, crikey, blimey, Bill." It was at that moment that I remembered most dearly that I was the Vicar of Chuntsey, in Essex.

'My desperate coup saved me. The policeman had me hard by the back of the neck.

' "You come along with me," he began, but Bill cut in with his perfect imitation of a lady's finnicking voice.

' "Oh, pray, constable, don't make a disturbance with our poor friend. We will get her quietly home. She does drink too much, but she is quite a lady – only eccentric."

' "She butted me in the stomach," said the policeman briefly.

' "Eccentricities of genius," said Sam earnestly.

' "Pray let me take her home,'" reiterated Bill, in the resumed character of Miss James, "she wants looking after." '

' "She does," said the policeman, "but I'll look after her."

' "That's no good," cried Bill feverishly. "She wants her friends. She wants a particular medicine we've got."

' "Yes,'" assented Miss Mowbray, with excitement, "no other medicine any good, constable. Complaint quite unique."

' "I'm all righ'. Cutchy, cutchy, coo!" remarked, to his eternal shame, the Vicar of Chuntsey.

' "Look here, ladies," said the constable sternly, "I don't like the eccentricity of your friend, and I don't like 'er songs, or 'er 'ead in my stomach. And now I come to think of it, I don't like the looks of you. I've seen many as quiet dressed as you as was wrong 'uns. Who are you?"

' "We've not our cards with us," said Miss Mowbray, with indescribable dignity. "Nor do we see why we should be insulted by any Jack-in-office who chooses to be rude to ladies, when he is paid to protect them. If you choose to take advantage of the weakness of our unfortunate friend, no doubt you are legally entitled to take her. But if you fancy you have any legal right to bully us, you will find yourself in the wrong box."

'The truth and dignity of this staggered the policeman for a moment. Under cover of their advantage my five persecutors turned for an instant on me faces like faces of the damned and then swished off into the darkness. When the constable first turned his lantern and his suspicions on to them, I had seen the telegraphic look flash from face to face saying that only retreat was possible now.

'By this time I was sinking slowly to the pavement, in a state of acute reflection. So long as the ruffians were with me, I dared not quit the role of drunkard. For if I had begun to talk reasonably and explain the real case, the officer would merely have thought that I was slightly recovered and would have put me in charge of my friends. Now, however, if I liked I might safely undeceive him.

'But I confess I did not like. The chances of life are many, and it may doubtless sometimes lie in the narrow path of duty for a clergyman of the Church of England to pretend to be a drunken old woman; but such necessities are, I imagine, sufficiently rare to appear to many improbable. Suppose the story got about that I had pretended to be drunk. Suppose people did not all think it was pretence!

'I lurched up, the policeman half-lifting me. I went along weakly and quietly for about a hundred yards. The officer evidently thought that I was too sleepy and feeble to effect an escape, and so held me lightly and easily enough. Past one turning, two turnings, three turnings, four turnings, he trailed me with him, a limp and slow and reluctant figure. At the fourth turning, I suddenly broke from his hand and tore down the street like a maddened stag. He was unprepared, he was heavy, and it was dark. I ran and ran and ran, and in five minutes' running, found I was gaining. In half an hour I was out in the fields under the holy and blessed stars, where I tore off my accursed shawl and bonnet and buried them in clean earth.'

The old gentleman had finished his story and leant back in his chair. Both the matter and the manner of his narration had, as time went on, impressed me favourably. He was an old duffer and pedant, but behind these things he was a country-bred man and gentleman, and had showed courage and a sporting instinct in the hour of desperation. He had told his story with many quaint formalities of diction, but also with a very convincing realism.

'And now – ' I began.

'And now,' said Shorter, leaning forward again with something like servile energy, 'and now, Mr Swinburne, what about that unhappy man Hawker. I cannot tell what those men meant, or how far what they said was real. But surely there is danger. I cannot go to the police, for reasons that you perceive. Among other things, they wouldn't believe me. What is to be done?'

I took out my watch. It was already half-past twelve.

'My friend Basil Grant,' I said, 'is the best man we can go to. He and I were to have gone to the same dinner tonight; but he will just have come back by now. Have you any objection to taking a cab?'

'Not at all,' he replied, rising politely, and gathering up his absurd plaid shawl.

A rattle in a hansom brought us underneath the sombre pile of workmen's flats in Lambeth which Grant inhabited; a climb up a wearisome wooden staircase brought us to his garret. When I entered that wooden and scrappy interior, the white gleam of Basil's shirt-front and the lustre of his fur coat flung on the wooden settle, struck me as a contrast. He was drinking a glass of wine before retiring. I was right; he had come back from the dinner-party.

He listened to the repetition of the story of the Revd Ellis Shorter with the genuine simplicity and respect which he never failed to exhibit in dealing with any human being. When it was over he said simply: 'Do you know a man named Captain Fraser?'

I was so startled at this totally irrelevant reference to the worthy collector of chimpanzees with whom I ought to have dined that evening, that I glanced sharply at Grant. The result was that I did not look at Mr Shorter. I only heard him answer, in his most nervous tone, 'No.'

Basil, however, seemed to find something very curious about his answer or his demeanour generally, for he kept his big blue eyes fixed on the old clergyman, and though the eyes were quite quiet they stood out more and more from his head.

'You are quite sure, Mr Shorter,' he repeated, 'that you don't know Captain Fraser?'

'Quite,' answered the vicar, and I was certainly puzzled to find him returning so much to the timidity, not to say the demoralisation, of his tone when he first entered my presence.

Basil sprang smartly to his feet.

'Then our course is clear,' he said. 'You have not even begun your investigation, my dear Mr Shorter; the first thing for us to do is to go together to see Captain Fraser.'

'When?' asked the clergyman, stammering.

'Now,' said Basil, putting one arm in his fur coat.

The old clergyman rose to his feet, quaking all over.

'I really do not think that it is necessary,' he said.

Basil took his arm out of the fur coat, threw it over the chair again, and put his hands in his pockets.

'Oh,' he said, with emphasis. 'Oh – you don't think it necessary; then,' and he added the words with great clearness and deliberation, 'then, Mr Ellis Shorter, I can only say that I would like to see you without your whiskers.'

And at these words I also rose to my feet, for the great tragedy of my life had come. Splendid and exciting as life was in continual contact with an intellect like Basil's, I had always the feeling that that splendour and excitement were on the borderland of sanity. He lived perpetually near the vision of the reason of things which makes men lose their reason. And I felt of his insanity as men feel of the death of friends with heart disease. It might come anywhere, in a field, in a hansom cab, looking at a sunset, smoking a cigarette. It had come now. At the very moment of delivering a judgement for the salvation of a fellow creature, Basil Grant had gone mad.

'Your whiskers,' he cried, advancing with blazing eyes. 'Give me your whiskers. And your bald head.'

The old vicar naturally retreated a step or two. I stepped between.

'Sit down, Basil,' I implored, 'you're a little excited. Finish your wine.'

'Whiskers,' he answered sternly, 'whiskers.'

And with that he made a dash at the old gentleman, who made a dash for the door, but was intercepted. And then, before I knew where I was the quiet room was turned into something between a pantomime and a pandemonium by those two. Chairs were flung over with a crash, tables were vaulted with a noise like thunder, screens were smashed, crockery scattered in smithereens, and still Basil Grant bounded and bellowed after the Revd Ellis Shorter.

And now I began to perceive something else, which added the last half-witted touch to my mystification. The Revd Ellis Shorter, of Chuntsey, in Essex, was by no means behaving as I had previously noticed him to behave, or as, considering his age and station, I should have expected him to behave. His power of dodging, leaping, and fighting would have been amazing in a lad of seventeen, and in this doddering old vicar looked like a sort of farcical fairytale. Moreover, he did not seem to be so much astonished as I had thought. There was even a look of something like enjoyment in his eyes; so there was in the eye of Basil. In fact, the unintelligible truth must be told. They were both laughing.

At length Shorter was cornered.

'Come, come, Mr Grant,' he panted, 'you can't do anything to me. It's quite legal. And it doesn't do anyone the least harm. It's only a social fiction. A result of our complex society, Mr Grant.'

'I don't blame you, my man,' said Basil coolly. 'But I want your whiskers. And your bald head. Do they belong to Captain Fraser?'

'No, no,' said Mr Shorter, laughing, 'we provide them ourselves. They don't belong to Captain Fraser.'

'What the deuce does all this mean?' I almost screamed. 'Are you all in an infernal nightmare? Why should Mr Shorter's bald head belong to Captain Fraser? How could it? What the deuce has Captain Fraser to do with the affair? What is the matter with him? You dined with him, Basil.'

'No,' said Grant, 'I didn't.'

'Didn't you go to Mrs Thornton's dinner-party?' I asked, staring. 'Why not?'

'Well,' said Basil, with a slow and singular smile, 'the fact is I was detained by a visitor. I have him, as a point of fact, in my bedroom.'

'In your bedroom?' I repeated; but my imagination had reached that point when he might have said in his coal scuttle or his waistcoat pocket.

Grant stepped to the door of an inner room, flung it open and walked in. Then he came out again with the last of the bodily wonders of that wild night. He introduced into the sitting-room, in an apologetic manner, and by the nape of the neck, a limp clergyman with a bald head, white whiskers and a plaid shawl.

'Sit down, gentlemen,' cried Grant, striking his hands heartily. 'Sit down all of you and have a glass of wine. As you say, there is no harm in it, and if Captain Fraser had simply dropped me a hint I could have saved him from dropping a good sum of money. Not that you would have liked that, eh?'

The two duplicate clergymen, who were sipping their Burgundy with two duplicate grins, laughed heartily at this, and one of them carelessly pulled off his whiskers and laid them on the table.

'Basil,' I said, 'if you are my friend, save me. What is all this?'

He laughed again.

'Only another addition, Cherub, to your collection of Queer Trades. These two gentlemen (whose health I have now the pleasure of drinking) are Professional Detainers.'

'And what on earth's that?' I asked.

'It's really very simple, Mr Swinburne,' began he who had once been the Revd Ellis Shorter, of Chuntsey, in Essex; and it gave me a shock indescribable to hear out of that pompous and familiar form come no longer its own pompous and familiar voice, but the brisk sharp tones of a young city man. 'It is really nothing very important. We are paid by our clients to detain in conversation, on some harmless pretext, people whom they want out of the way for a few hours. And Captain Fraser – ' and with that he hesitated and smiled.

Basil smiled also. He intervened.

'The fact is that Captain Fraser, who is one of my best friends, wanted us both out of the way very much. He is sailing tonight for East Africa, and the lady with whom we were all to have dined is – er – what is I believe described as "the romance of his life". He wanted that two hours with her, and employed these two reverend gentlemen to detain us at our houses so as to let him have the field to himself.'

'And of course,' said the late Mr Shorter apologetically to me, 'as I had to keep a gentleman at home from keeping an appointment with a lady, I had to come with something rather hot and strong – rather urgent. It wouldn't have done to be tame.'

'Oh,' I said, 'I acquit you of tameness.'

'Thank you, sir,' said the man respectfully, 'always very grateful for any recommendation, sir.'

The other man idly pushed back his artificial bald head, revealing close red hair, and spoke dreamily, perhaps under the influence of Basil's admirable Burgundy.

'It's wonderful how common it's getting, gentlemen. Our office is busy from morning till night. I've no doubt you've often knocked up against us before. You just take notice. When an old bachelor goes on boring you with hunting stories, when you're burning to be introduced to somebody, he's from our bureau. When a lady calls on parish work and stops hours, just when you wanted to go to the Robinsons', she's from our bureau. The Robinson hand, sir, may be darkly seen.'

'There is one thing I don't understand,' I said. 'Why you are both vicars.'

A shade crossed the brow of the temporary incumbent of Chuntsey, in Essex.

'That may have been a mistake, sir,' he said. 'But it was not our fault. It was all the munificence of Captain Fraser. He requested that the highest price and talent on our tariff should be employed to detain you gentlemen. Now the highest payment in our office goes to those who impersonate vicars, as being the most respectable and more of a strain. We are paid five guineas a visit. We have had the good fortune to satisfy the firm with our work; and we are now permanently vicars. Before that we had two years as colonels, the next in our scale. Colonels are four guineas.'

4

The Singular Speculation of the House-Agent

Lieutenant Drummond Keith was a man about whom conversation always burst like a thunderstorm the moment he left the room. This arose from many separate touches about him. He was a light, loose person, who wore light, loose clothes, generally white, as if he were in the tropics; he was lean and graceful, like a panther, and he had restless black eyes.

He was very impecunious. He had one of the habits of the poor, in a degree so exaggerated as immeasurably to eclipse the most miserable of the unemployed; I mean the habit of continual change of lodgings. There are inland tracts of London where, in the very heart of artificial civilisation, humanity has almost become nomadic once more. But in that restless interior there was no ragged tramp so restless as the elegant officer in the loose white clothes. He had shot a great many things in his time, to judge from his conversation, from partridges to elephants, but his slangier acquaintances were of opinion that 'the moon' had been not unfrequently amid the victims of his victorious rifle. The phrase is a fine one, and suggests a mystic, elvish, nocturnal hunting.

He carried from house to house and from parish to parish a kit which consisted practically of five articles. Two odd-looking, large-bladed spears, tied together, the weapons, I suppose, of some savage tribe, a green umbrella, a huge and tattered copy of the *Pickwick Papers*, a big game rifle, and a large sealed jar of some unholy Oriental wine. These always went into every new lodging, even for one night; and they went in quite undisguised, tied up in wisps of string or straw, to the delight of the poetic gutter boys in the little grey streets.

I had forgotten to mention that he always carried also his old regimental sword. But this raised another odd question about him. Slim and active as he was, he was no longer very young. His hair, indeed, was quite grey, though his rather wild almost Italian moustache retained its blackness, and his face was careworn under its almost Italian gaiety. To find a middle-aged man who has left the Army at the primitive rank of Lieutenant is unusual and not necessarily encouraging. With the more cautious and solid this fact, like his endless flitting, did the mysterious gentleman no good.

Lastly, he was a man who told the kind of adventures which win a man admiration, but not respect. They came out of queer places, where a good man would scarcely find himself, out of opium dens and gambling hells; they had the heat of the thieves' kitchens or smelled of a strange smoke from cannibal incantations. These are the kind of stories which discredit a person almost equally whether they are believed or no. If Keith's tales were false he was a liar; if they were true he had had, at any rate, every opportunity of being a scamp.

He had just left the room in which I sat with Basil Grant and his brother Rupert, the voluble amateur detective. And as I say was invariably the case, we were all talking about him. Rupert Grant was a clever young fellow, but he had that tendency which youth and cleverness, when sharply combined, so often produce, a somewhat extravagant scepticism. He saw doubt and guilt everywhere, and it was meat and drink to him. I had often got irritated with this boyish incredulity of his, but on this particular occasion I am bound to say that I thought him so obviously right that I was astounded at Basil's opposing him, however banteringly.

I could swallow a good deal, being naturally of a simple turn, but I could not swallow Lieutenant Keith's autobiography.

'You don't seriously mean, Basil,' I said, 'that you think that that fellow really did go as a stowaway with Nansen and pretend to be the Mad Mullah and –'

'He has one fault,' said Basil thoughtfully, 'or virtue, as you may happen to regard it. He tells the truth in too exact and bald a style; he is too veracious.'

'Oh! if you are going to be paradoxical,' said Rupert contemptuously, 'be a bit funnier than that. Say, for instance, that he has lived all his life in one ancestral manor.'

'No, he's extremely fond of change of scene,' replied Basil dispassionately, 'and of living in odd places. That doesn't prevent his chief trait being verbal exactitude. What you people don't understand is that telling a thing crudely and coarsely as it happened makes it sound frightfully strange. The sort of things Keith recounts are not the sort of things that a man would make up to cover himself with honour; they are too absurd. But they are the sort of things that a man would do if he were sufficiently filled with the soul of skylarking.'

'So far from paradox,' said his brother, with something rather like a sneer, 'you seem to be going in for journalese proverbs. Do you believe that truth is stranger than fiction?'

'Truth must of necessity be stranger than fiction,' said Basil placidly. 'For fiction is the creation of the human mind, and therefore is congenial to it.'

'Well, your lieutenant's truth is stranger, if it is truth, than anything I ever heard of,' said Rupert, relapsing into flippancy. 'Do you, on your soul, believe in all that about the shark and the camera?'

'I believe Keith's words,' answered the other. 'He is an honest man.'

'I should like to question a regiment of his landladies,' said Rupert cynically.

'I must say, I think you can hardly regard him as unimpeachable merely in himself,' I said mildly; 'his mode of life – '

Before I could complete the sentence the door was flung open and Drummond Keith appeared again on the threshold, his white Panama on his head.

'I say, Grant,' he said, knocking off his cigarette ash against the door, 'I've got no money in the world till next April. Could you lend me a hundred pounds? There's a good chap.'

Rupert and I looked at each other in an ironical silence. Basil, who was sitting by his desk, swung the chair round idly on its screw and picked up a quill-pen.

'Shall I cross it?' he asked, opening a chequebook.

'Really,' began Rupert, with a rather nervous loudness, 'since Lieutenant Keith has seen fit to make this suggestion to Basil before his family, I – '

'Here you are, Ugly,' said Basil, fluttering a cheque in the direction of the quite nonchalant officer. 'Are you in a hurry?'

'Yes,' replied Keith, in a rather abrupt way. 'As a matter of fact I want it now. I want to see my – er – business man.'

Rupert was eyeing him sarcastically, and I could see that it was on the tip of his tongue to say, enquiringly, 'Receiver of stolen goods, perhaps.' What he did say was: 'A business man? That's rather a general description, Lieutenant Keith.'

Keith looked at him sharply, and then said, with something rather like ill-temper: 'He's a thingamy-bob, a house-agent, say. I'm going to see him.'

'Oh, you're going to see a house-agent, are you?' said Rupert Grant grimly. 'Do you know, Mr Keith, I think I should very much like to go with you?'

Basil shook with his soundless laughter. Lieutenant Keith started a little; his brow blackened sharply.

'I beg your pardon,' he said. 'What did you say?'

Rupert's face had been growing from stage to stage of ferocious irony, and he answered: 'I was saying that I wondered whether you would mind our strolling along with you to this house-agent's.'

The visitor swung his stick with a sudden whirling violence.

'Oh, in God's name, come to my house-agent's! Come to my bedroom. Look under my bed. Examine my dustbin. Come along!' And with a furious energy which took away our breath he banged his way out of the room.

Rupert Grant, his restless blue eyes dancing with his detective excitement, soon shouldered alongside him, talking to him with that transparent camaraderie which he imagined to be appropriate from the disguised policeman to the disguised criminal. His interpretation was certainly corroborated by one particular detail, the unmistakable unrest, annoyance, and nervousness of the man with whom he walked. Basil and I tramped behind, and it was not necessary for us to tell each other that we had both noticed this.

Lieutenant Drummond Keith led us through very extraordinary and unpromising neighbourhoods in the search for his remarkable house-agent. Neither of the brothers Grant failed to notice this fact. As the streets grew closer and more crooked and the roofs lower and the gutters grosser with mud, a darker curiosity deepened on the brows of Basil, and the figure of Rupert seen from behind seemed to fill the street with a gigantic swagger of success. At length, at the end of the fourth or fifth lean grey street in that sterile district, we came suddenly to a halt, the mysterious lieutenant looking once more about him with a sort of sulky desperation. Above a row of shutters and a door, all indescribably dingy in appearance and in size scarce sufficient even for a penny toy-shop, ran the inscription: 'P. Montmorency, House-Agent'.

'This is the office of which I spoke,' said Keith, in a cutting voice. 'Will you wait here a moment, or does your astonishing tenderness about my welfare lead you to wish to overhear everything I have to say to my business adviser?'

Rupert's face was white and shaking with excitement; nothing on earth would have induced him now to have abandoned his prey.

'If you will excuse me,' he said, clenching his hands behind his back, 'I think I should feel myself justified in – '

'Oh! Come along in,' exploded the lieutenant. He made the same gesture of savage surrender. And he slammed into the office, the rest of us at his heels.

P. Montmorency, House-Agent, was a solitary old gentleman sitting behind a bare brown counter. He had an egglike head, froglike jaws, and a grey hairy fringe of aureole round the lower part of his face; the whole combined with a reddish, aquiline nose. He wore a shabby black frock-coat, a sort of semi-clerical tie worn at a very unclerical angle, and looked, generally speaking, about as unlike a house-agent as anything could look, short of something like a sandwich man or a Scotch Highlander.

We stood inside the room for fully forty seconds, and the odd old gentleman did not look at us. Neither, to tell the truth, odd as he was, did we look at him. Our eyes were fixed, where his were fixed, upon something that was crawling about on the counter in front of him. It was a ferret.

The silence was broken by Rupert Grant. He spoke in that sweet and steely voice which he reserved for great occasions and practised for hours together in his bedroom. He said: 'Mr Montmorency, I think?'

The old gentleman started, lifted his eyes with a bland bewilderment, picked up the ferret by the neck, stuffed it alive into his trousers pocket, smiled apologetically, and said: 'Sir.'

'You are a house-agent, are you not?' asked Rupert.

To the delight of that criminal investigator, Mr Montmorency's eyes wandered unquietly towards Lieutenant Keith, the only man present that he knew.

'A house-agent,' cried Rupert again, bringing out the word as if it were 'burglar'.

'Yes . . . oh, yes,' said the man, with a quavering and almost coquettish smile. 'I am a house-agent . . . oh, yes.'

'Well, I think,' said Rupert, with a sardonic sleekness, 'that Lieutenant Keith wants to speak to you. We have come in by his request.'

Lieutenant Keith was lowering gloomily, and now he spoke.

'I have come, Mr Montmorency, about that house of mine.'

'Yes, sir,' said Montmorency, spreading his fingers on the flat counter. 'It's all ready, sir. I've attended to all your suggestions – er – about the br –'

'Right,' cried Keith, cutting the word short with the startling neatness of a gunshot. 'We needn't bother about all that. If you've done what I told you, all right.'

And he turned sharply towards the door.

Mr Montmorency, House-Agent, presented a picture of pathos. After stammering a moment he said: 'Excuse me . . . Mr Keith . . . there was another matter . . . about which I wasn't quite sure. I tried to get all the heating apparatus possible under the circumstances . . . but in winter . . . at that elevation . . .'

'Can't expect much, eh?' said the lieutenant, cutting in with the same sudden skill. 'No, of course not. That's all right, Montmorency. There can't be any more difficulties,' and he put his hand on the handle of the door.

'I think,' said Rupert Grant, with a satanic suavity, 'that Mr Montmorency has something further to say to you, lieutenant.'

'Only,' said the house-agent, in desperation, 'what about the birds?'

'I beg your pardon,' said Rupert, in a general blank.

'What about the birds?' said the house-agent doggedly.

Basil, who had remained throughout the proceedings in a state of Napoleonic calm, which might be more accurately described as a state of Napoleonic stupidity, suddenly lifted his leonine head.

'Before you go, Lieutenant Keith,' he said. 'Come now. Really, what about the birds?'

'I'll take care of them,' said Lieutenant Keith, still with his long back turned to us; 'they shan't suffer.'

'Thank you, sir, thank you,' cried the incomprehensible house-agent, with an air of ecstasy. 'You'll excuse my concern, sir. You know I'm wild on wild animals. I'm as wild as any of them on that. Thank you, sir. But there's another thing . . .'

The lieutenant, with his back turned to us, exploded with an indescribable laugh and swung round to face us. It was a laugh, the purport of which was direct and essential, and yet which one cannot exactly express. As near as it said anything, verbally speaking, it said: 'Well, if you must spoil it, you must. But you don't know what you're spoiling.'

'There is another thing,' continued Mr Montmorency weakly. 'Of course, if you don't want to be visited you'll paint the house green, but – '

'Green!' shouted Keith. 'Green! Let it be green or nothing. I won't have a house of another colour. Green!' and before we could realise anything the door had banged between us and the street.

Rupert Grant seemed to take a little time to collect himself; but he spoke before the echoes of the door died away.

'Your client, Lieutenant Keith, appears somewhat excited,' he said. 'What is the matter with him? Is he unwell?'

'Oh, I should think not,' said Mr Montmorency, in some confusion. 'The negotiations have been somewhat difficult – the house is rather – '

'Green,' said Rupert calmly. 'That appears to be a very important point. It must be rather green. May I ask you, Mr Montmorency, before I rejoin my companion outside, whether, in your business, it is usual to ask for houses by their colour? Do clients write to a house-agent asking for a pink house or a blue house? Or, to take another instance, for a green house?'

'Only,' said Montmorency, trembling, 'only to be inconspicuous.'

Rupert had his ruthless smile. 'Can you tell me any place on earth in which a green house would be inconspicuous?'

The house-agent was fidgeting nervously in his pocket. Slowly drawing out a couple of lizards and leaving them to run on the counter, he said: 'No; I can't.'

'You can't suggest an explanation?'

'No,' said Mr Montmorency, rising slowly and yet in such a way as to suggest a sudden situation, 'I can't. And may I, as a busy man, be excused if I ask you, gentlemen, if you have any demand to make of me in connection with my business. What kind of house would you desire me to get for you, sir?'

He opened his blank blue eyes on Rupert, who seemed for the second staggered. Then he recovered himself with perfect common sense and answered: 'I am sorry, Mr Montmorency. The fascination of your remarks has unduly delayed us from joining our friend outside. Pray excuse my apparent impertinence.'

'Not at all, sir,' said the house-agent, taking a South American spider idly from his waistcoat pocket and letting it climb up the slope of his desk. 'Not at all, sir. I hope you will favour me again.'

Rupert Grant dashed out of the office in a gust of anger, anxious to face Lieutenant Keith. He was gone. The dull, starlit street was deserted.

'What do you say now?' cried Rupert to his brother. His brother said nothing now.

We all three strode down the street in silence, Rupert feverish, myself dazed, Basil, to all appearance, merely dull. We walked through grey street after grey street, turning corners, traversing squares, scarcely meeting anyone, except occasional drunken knots of two or three.

In one small street, however, the knots of two or three began abruptly to thicken into knots of five or six and then into great groups and then into a crowd. The crowd was stirring very slightly. But anyone with a knowledge of the eternal populace knows that if the outside rim of a crowd stirs ever so slightly it means that there is madness in the heart and core of the mob. It soon became evident that something really important had happened in the centre of this excitement. We wormed our way to the front, with the cunning which is known only to cockneys, and once there we soon learned the nature of the difficulty. There had been a brawl concerned with some six men, and one of them lay almost dead on the stones of the street. Of the other four, all interesting matters were, as far as we were concerned, swallowed up in one stupendous fact. One of the four survivors of the brutal and perhaps fatal scuffle was the immaculate Lieutenant Keith, his clothes torn to ribbons, his eyes blazing, blood on his knuckles. One other thing, however, pointed at him in a worse manner. A short sword, or very long knife, had been drawn out of his elegant walking-stick, and lay in front of him upon the stones. It did not, however, appear to be bloody.

The police had already pushed into the centre with their ponderous omnipotence, and even as they did so, Rupert Grant sprang forward with his incontrollable and intolerable secret.

'That is the man, constable,' he shouted, pointing at the battered lieutenant. 'He is a suspicious character. He did the murder.'

'There's been no murder done, sir,' said the policeman, with his automatic civility. 'The poor man's only hurt. I shall only be able to take the names and addresses of the men in the scuffle and have a good eye kept on them.'

'Have a good eye kept on that one,' said Rupert, pale to the lips, and pointing to the ragged Keith.

'All right, sir,' said the policeman unemotionally, and went the round of the people present, collecting the addresses. When he had completed his task the dusk had fallen and most of the people not immediately connected with the examination had gone away. He still found, however, one eager-faced stranger lingering on the outskirts of the affair. It was Rupert Grant.

'Constable,' he said, 'I have a very particular reason for asking you a question. Would you mind telling me whether that military fellow who dropped his sword-stick in the row gave you an address or not?'

'Yes, sir,' said the policeman, after a reflective pause; 'yes, he gave me his address.'

'My name is Rupert Grant,' said that individual, with some pomp. 'I have assisted the police on more than one occasion. I wonder whether you would tell me, as a special favour, what address?'

The constable looked at him.

'Yes,' he said slowly, 'if you like. His address is The Elms, Buxton Common, near Purley, Surrey.'

'Thank you,' said Rupert, and ran home through the gathering night as fast as his legs could carry him, repeating the address to himself.

* * *

Rupert Grant generally came down late in a rather lordly way to breakfast; he contrived, I don't know how, to achieve always the attitude of the indulged younger brother. Next morning, however, when Basil and I came down we found him ready and restless.

'Well,' he said sharply to his brother almost before we sat down to the meal. 'What do you think of your Drummond Keith now?'

'What do I think of him?' enquired Basil slowly. 'I don't think anything of him.'

'I'm glad to hear it,' said Rupert, buttering his toast with an energy that was somewhat exultant. 'I thought you'd come round to my view, but I own I was startled at your not seeing it from the beginning. The man is a translucent liar and knave.'

'I think,' said Basil, in the same heavy monotone as before, 'that I did not make myself clear. When I said that I thought nothing of him I meant grammatically what I said. I meant that I did not think about him; that he did not occupy my mind. You, however, seem to me to think a lot of him, since you think him a knave. I should say he was glaringly good myself.'

'I sometimes think you talk paradox for its own sake,' said Rupert, breaking an egg with unnecessary sharpness. 'What the deuce is the sense of it? Here's a man whose original position was, by our common agreement, dubious. He's a wanderer, a teller of tall tales, a man who doesn't conceal his acquaintance with all the blackest and bloodiest scenes on earth. We take the trouble to follow him to one of his appointments, and if ever two human beings were plotting together and lying to everyone else, he and that impossible house-agent were doing it. We followed him home, and the very same night he is in the thick of a fatal, or nearly fatal, brawl, in which he is the only man armed. Really, if this is being glaringly good, I must confess that the glare does not dazzle me.'

Basil was quite unmoved. 'I admit his moral goodness is of a certain kind, a quaint, perhaps a casual kind. He is very fond of change and experiment. But all the points you so ingeniously make against him are mere coincidence or special pleading. It's true he didn't want to talk about his house business in front of us. No man would. It's true that he carries a sword-stick. Any man might. It's true he drew it in the shock of a street fight. Any man would. But there's nothing really dubious in all this. There's nothing to confirm – '

As he spoke a knock came at the door.

'If you please, sir,' said the landlady, with an alarmed air, 'there's a policeman wants to see you.'

'Show him in,' said Basil, amid the blank silence.

The heavy, handsome constable who appeared at the door spoke almost as soon as he appeared there.

'I think one of you gentlemen,' he said, curtly but respectfully, 'was present at the affair in Copper Street last night, and drew my attention very strongly to a particular man.'

Rupert half rose from his chair, with eyes like diamonds, but the constable went on calmly, referring to a paper.

'A young man with grey hair. Had light grey clothes, very good, but torn in the struggle. Gave his name as Drummond Keith.'

'This is amusing,' said Basil, laughing. 'I was in the very act of clearing that poor officer's character of rather fanciful aspersions. What about him?'

'Well, sir,' said the constable, 'I took all the men's addresses and had them all watched. It wasn't serious enough to do more than that. All the other addresses are all right. But this man Keith gave a false address. The place doesn't exist.'

The breakfast table was nearly flung over as Rupert sprang up, slapping both his thighs.

'Well, by all that's good,' he cried. 'This is a sign from heaven.'

'It's certainly very extraordinary,' said Basil quietly, with knitted brows. 'It's odd the fellow should have given a false address, considering he was perfectly innocent in the – '

'Oh, you jolly old early Christian duffer,' cried Rupert, in a sort of rapture, 'I don't wonder you couldn't be a judge. You think everyone as good as yourself. Isn't the thing plain enough now? A doubtful acquaintance; rowdy stories, a most suspicious conversation, mean streets, a concealed knife, a man nearly killed, and, finally, a false address. That's what we call glaring goodness.'

'It's certainly very extraordinary,' repeated Basil. And he strolled moodily about the room. Then he said: 'You are quite sure, constable, that there's no mistake? You got the address right, and the police have really gone to it and found it was a fraud?'

'It was very simple, sir,' said the policeman, chuckling. 'The place he named was a well-known common quite near London, and our people were down there this morning before any of you were awake. And there's no such house. In fact, there are hardly any houses at all. Though it is so near London, it's a blank moor with hardly five trees on it, to say nothing of Christians. Oh, no, sir, the address was a fraud right enough. He was a clever rascal, and chose one of those scraps of lost England that people know nothing about. Nobody could say off-hand that there was not a particular house dropped somewhere about the heath. But as a fact, there isn't.'

Basil's face during this sensible speech had been growing darker and darker with a sort of desperate sagacity. He was cornered almost for the first time since I had known him; and to tell the truth I rather wondered at the almost childish obstinacy which kept him so close to his original prejudice in favour of the wildly questionable lieutenant. At length he said: 'You really searched the common? And the address was really not known in the district – by the way, what was the address?'

The constable selected one of his slips of paper and consulted it, but before he could speak Rupert Grant, who was leaning in the window in a perfect posture of the quiet and triumphant detective, struck in with the sharp and suave voice he loved so much to use.

'Why, I can tell you that, Basil,' he said graciously as he idly plucked leaves from a plant in the window. 'I took the precaution to get this man's address from the constable last night.'

'And what was it?' asked his brother gruffly.

'The constable will correct me if I am wrong,' said Rupert, looking sweetly at the ceiling. 'It was: The Elms, Buxton Common, near Purley, Surrey.'

'Right, sir,' said the policeman, laughing and folding up his papers.

There was a silence, and the blue eyes of Basil looked blindly for a few seconds into the void. Then his head fell back in his chair so suddenly that I started up, thinking him ill. But before I could move further his lips had flown apart (I can use no other phrase) and a peal of gigantic laughter struck and shook the ceiling – laughter that shook the laughter, laughter redoubled, laughter incurable, laughter that could not stop.

Two whole minutes afterwards it was still unended; Basil was ill with laughter; but still he laughed. The rest of us were by this time ill almost with terror.

'Excuse me,' said the insane creature, getting at last to his feet. 'I am awfully sorry. It is horribly rude. And stupid, too. And also unpractical, because we have not much time to lose if we're to get down to that place. The train service is confoundedly bad, as I happen to know. It's quite out of proportion to the comparatively small distance.'

'Get down to that place?' I repeated blankly. 'Get down to what place?'

'I have forgotten its name,' said Basil vaguely, putting his hands in his pockets as he rose. 'Something Common near Purley. Has anyone got a timetable?'

'You don't seriously mean,' cried Rupert, who had been staring in a sort of confusion of emotions. 'You don't mean that you want to go to Buxton Common, do you? You can't mean that!'

'Why shouldn't I go to Buxton Common?' asked Basil, smiling.

'Why should you?' said his brother, catching hold again restlessly of the plant in the window and staring at the speaker.

'To find our friend, the lieutenant, of course,' said Basil Grant. 'I thought you wanted to find him?'

Rupert broke a branch brutally from the plant and flung it impatiently on the floor. 'And in order to find him,' he said, 'you suggest the admirable expedient of going to the only place on the habitable earth where we know he can't be.'

The constable and I could not avoid breaking into a kind of assenting laugh, and Rupert, who had family eloquence, was encouraged to go on with a reiterated gesture: 'He may be in Buckingham Palace; he may be sitting astride the cross of St Paul's; he may be in gaol (which I think most likely); he may be in the Great Wheel; he may be in my pantry; he may be in your store cupboard; but out of all the innumerable points of space, there is only one where he has just been systematically looked for and where we know that he is not to be found – and that, if I understand you rightly, is where you want us to go.'

'Exactly,' said Basil calmly, getting into his greatcoat; 'I thought you might care to accompany me. If not, of course, make yourselves jolly here till I come back.'

It is our nature always to follow vanishing things and value them if they really show a resolution to depart. We all followed Basil, and I cannot say why, except that he was a vanishing thing, that he vanished decisively with his greatcoat and his stick. Rupert ran after him with a considerable flurry of rationality.

'My dear chap,' he cried, 'do you really mean that you see any good in going down to this ridiculous scrub, where there is nothing but beaten tracks and a few twisted trees, simply because it was the first place that came into a rowdy lieutenant's head when he wanted to give a lying reference in a scrape?'

'Yes,' said Basil, taking out his watch, 'and, what's worse, we've lost the train.'

He paused a moment and then added: 'As a matter of fact, I think we may just as well go down later in the day. I have some writing to do, and I think you told me, Rupert, that you thought of going to the Dulwich Gallery. I was rather too impetuous. Very likely he wouldn't be in. But if we get down by the 5.15, which gets to Purley about 6, I expect we shall just catch him.'

'Catch him!' cried his brother, in a kind of final anger. 'I wish we could. Where the deuce shall we catch him now?'

'I keep forgetting the name of the common,' said Basil, as he buttoned up his coat. 'The Elms – what is it? Buxton Common, near Purley. That's where we shall find him.'

'But there is no such place,' groaned Rupert; but he followed his brother downstairs.

We all followed him. We snatched our hats from the hat-stand and our sticks from the umbrella-stand; and why we followed him we did not and do not know. But we always followed him, whatever was the meaning of the fact, whatever was the nature of his mastery. And the strange thing was that we followed him the more completely the more nonsensical appeared the thing which he said. At bottom, I believe, if he had risen from our breakfast table and said: 'I am going to find the Holy Pig with Ten Tails,' we should have followed him to the end of the world.

I don't know whether this mystical feeling of mine about Basil on this occasion has got any of the dark and cloudy colour, so to speak, of the strange journey that we made the same evening. It was already very dense twilight when we struck southward from Purley. Suburbs and things on the London border may be, in most cases, commonplace and comfortable. But if ever by any chance they really are empty solitudes they are to the human spirit more desolate and dehumanised than any Yorkshire moors or Highland hills, because the suddenness with which the traveller drops into that silence has something about it as of evil elf-land. It seems to be one of the ragged suburbs of the cosmos half-forgotten by God – such a place was Buxton Common, near Purley.

There was certainly a sort of grey futility in the landscape itself. But it was enormously increased by the sense of grey futility in our expedition. The tracts of grey turf looked useless, the occasional wind-stricken trees looked useless, but we, the human beings, more useless than the hopeless turf or the idle trees. We were maniacs akin to the foolish landscape, for we were come to chase the wild goose which has led men and left men in bogs from the beginning. We were three dazed men under the captaincy of a madman going to look for a man whom we knew was not there in a house that had no existence. A livid sunset seemed to look at us with a sort of sickly smile before it died.

Basil went on in front with his coat collar turned up, looking in the gloom rather like a grotesque Napoleon. We crossed swell after swell of the windy common in increasing darkness and entire silence. Suddenly Basil stopped and turned to us, his hands in his pockets. Through the dusk I could just detect that he wore a broad grin as of comfortable success.

'Well,' he cried, taking his heavily gloved hands out of his pockets and slapping them together, 'here we are at last.'

The wind swirled sadly over the homeless heath; two desolate elms rocked above us in the sky like shapeless clouds of grey. There was not a sign of man or beast to the sullen circle of the horizon, and in the midst of that wilderness Basil Grant stood rubbing his hands with the air of an innkeeper standing at an open door.

'How jolly it is,' he cried, 'to get back to civilisation. That notion that civilisation isn't poetical is a civilised delusion. Wait till you've really lost yourself in nature, among the devilish woodlands and the cruel flowers. Then you'll know that there's no star like the red star of man that he lights on his hearthstone; no river like the red river of man, the good red wine, which you, Mr Rupert Grant, if I have any knowledge of you, will be drinking in two or three minutes in enormous quantities.'

Rupert and I exchanged glances of fear. Basil went on heartily, as the wind died in the dreary trees.

'You'll find our host a much more simple kind of fellow in his own house. I did when I visited him when he lived in the cabin at Yarmouth, and again in the loft at the city warehouse. He's really a very good fellow. But his greatest virtue remains what I said originally.'

'What do you mean?' I asked, finding his speech straying towards a sort of sanity. 'What is his greatest virtue?'

'His greatest virtue,' replied Basil, 'is that he always tells the literal truth.'

'Well, really,' cried Rupert, stamping about between cold and anger, and slapping himself like a cabman, 'he doesn't seem to have been very literal or truthful in this case, nor you either. Why the deuce, may I ask, have you brought us out to this infernal place?'

'He was too truthful, I confess,' said Basil, leaning against the tree; 'too hardly veracious, too severely accurate. He should have indulged in a little more suggestiveness and legitimate romance. But come, it's time we went in. We shall be late for dinner.'

Rupert whispered to me with a white face: 'Is it a hallucination, do you think? Does he really fancy he sees a house?'

'I suppose so,' I said. Then I added aloud, in what was meant to be a cheery and sensible voice, but which sounded in my ears almost as strange as the wind: 'Come, come, Basil, my dear fellow. Where do you want us to go?'

'Why, up here,' cried Basil, and with a bound and a swing he was above our heads, swarming up the grey column of the colossal tree.

'Come up, all of you,' he shouted out of the darkness, with the voice of a schoolboy. 'Come up. You'll be late for dinner.'

The two great elms stood so close together that there was scarcely a yard anywhere, and in some places not more than a foot, between them. Thus occasional branches and even bosses and boles formed a series of footholds that almost amounted to a rude natural ladder. They must, I supposed, have been some sport of growth, Siamese twins of vegetation.

Why we did it I cannot think; perhaps, as I have said, the mystery of the waste and dark had brought out and made primary something wholly mystical in Basil's supremacy. But we only felt that there was a giant's staircase going somewhere, perhaps to the stars; and the victorious voice above called to us out of heaven. We hoisted ourselves up after him.

Halfway up some cold tongue of the night air struck and sobered me suddenly. The hypnotism of the madman above fell from me, and I saw the whole map of our silly actions as clearly as if it were printed. I saw three modern men in black coats who had begun with a perfectly sensible suspicion of a doubtful adventurer and who had ended, God knows how, halfway up a naked tree on a naked moorland, far from that adventurer and all his works, that adventurer who was at that moment, in all probability, laughing at us in some dirty Soho restaurant. He had plenty to laugh at us about, and no doubt he was laughing his loudest; but when I thought what his laughter would be if he knew where we were at that moment, I nearly let go of the tree and fell.

'Swinburne,' said Rupert suddenly, from above, 'what are we doing? Let's get down again,' and by the mere sound of his voice I knew that he too felt the shock of wakening to reality.

'We can't leave poor Basil,' I said. 'Can't you call to him or get hold of him by the leg?'

'He's too far ahead,' answered Rupert; 'he's nearly at the top of the beastly thing. Looking for Lieutenant Keith in the rooks' nests, I suppose.'

We were ourselves by this time far on our frantic vertical journey. The mighty trunks were beginning to sway and shake slightly in the wind. Then I looked down and saw something which made me feel that we were far from the world in a sense and to a degree that I cannot easily describe. I saw that the almost straight lines of the tall elm trees diminished a little in perspective as they fell. I was used to seeing parallel lines taper towards the sky. But to see them taper towards the earth made me feel lost in space, like a falling star.

'Can nothing be done to stop Basil?' I called out.

'No,' answered my fellow climber. 'He's too far up. He must get to the top, and when he finds nothing but wind and leaves he may go sane again. Hark at him above there; you can just hear him talking to himself.'

'Perhaps he's talking to us,' I said.

'No,' said Rupert, 'he'd shout if he was. I've never known him to talk to himself before; I'm afraid he really is bad tonight; it's a known sign of the brain going.'

'Yes,' I said sadly, and listened. Basil's voice certainly was sounding above us, and not by any means in the rich and riotous tones in which he had hailed us before. He was speaking quietly, and laughing every now and then, up there among the leaves and stars.

After a silence mingled with this murmur, Rupert Grant suddenly said, 'My God!' with a violent voice.

'What's the matter – are you hurt?' I cried, alarmed.

'No. Listen to Basil,' said the other in a very strange voice. 'He's not talking to himself.'

'Then he is talking to us,' I cried.

'No,' said Rupert simply, 'he's talking to somebody else.'

Great branches of the elm loaded with leaves swung about us in a sudden burst of wind, but when it died down I could still hear the conversational voice above. I could hear two voices.

Suddenly from aloft came Basil's boisterous hailing voice as before: 'Come up, you fellows. Here's Lieutenant Keith.'

And a second afterwards came the half-American voice we had heard in our chambers more than once. It called out: 'Happy to see you, gentlemen; pray come in.'

Out of a hole in an enormous dark egg-shaped thing, pendent in the branches like a wasps' nest, was protruding the pale face and fierce moustache of the lieutenant, his teeth shining with that slightly Southern air that belonged to him.

Somehow or other, stunned and speechless, we lifted ourselves heavily into the opening. We fell into the full glow of a lamp-lit, cushioned, tiny room, with a circular wall lined with books, a circular table, and a circular seat around it. At this table sat three people. One was Basil, who, in the instant after alighting there, had fallen into an attitude of marmoreal ease as if he had been there from boyhood; he was smoking a cigar with a slow pleasure. The second was Lieutenant Drummond Keith, who looked happy also, but feverish and doubtful compared with his granite guest. The third was the little bald-headed house-agent with the wild whiskers, who called himself Montmorency. The spears, the green umbrella, and the cavalry sword hung in parallels on the wall. The sealed jar of strange wine was on the mantelpiece, the enormous rifle in the corner. In the middle of the table was a magnum of champagne. Glasses were already set for us.

The wind of the night roared far below us, like an ocean at the foot of a lighthouse. The room stirred slightly, as a cabin might in a mild sea.

Our glasses were filled, and we still sat there dazed and dumb. Then Basil spoke.

'You seem still a little doubtful, Rupert. Surely there is no further question about the cold veracity of our injured host.'

'I don't quite grasp it all,' said Rupert, blinking still in the sudden glare. 'Lieutenant Keith said his address was – '

'It's really quite right, sir,' said Keith, with an open smile. 'The bobby asked me where I lived. And I said, quite truthfully, that I lived in The Elms on Buxton Common, near Purley. So I do. This gentleman, Mr Montmorency, whom I think you have met before, is an agent for houses of this kind. He has a special line in arboreal villas. It's being kept rather quiet at present, because the people who want these houses don't want them to get too common. But it's just the sort of thing a fellow like myself, racketing about in all sorts of queer corners of London, naturally knocks up against.'

'Are you really an agent for arboreal villas?' asked Rupert eagerly, recovering his ease with the romance of reality.

Mr Montmorency, in his embarrassment, fingered one of his pockets and nervously pulled out a snake, which crawled about the table.

'W–well, yes, sir,' he said. 'The fact was – er – my people wanted me very much to go into the house-agency business. But I never cared myself for anything but natural history and botany and things like that. My poor parents have been dead some years now, but – naturally I like to respect their wishes. And I thought somehow that an arboreal villa agency was a sort of – of compromise between being a botanist and being a house-agent.'

Rupert could not help laughing. 'Do you have much custom?' he asked.

'N–not much,' replied Mr Montmorency, and then he glanced at Keith, who was (I am convinced) his only client. 'But what there is – very select.'

'My dear friends,' said Basil, puffing his cigar, 'always remember two facts. The first is that though when you are guessing about anyone who is sane, the sanest thing is the most likely; when you are guessing about anyone who is, like our host, insane, the maddest thing is the most likely. The second is to remember that very plain literal fact always seems fantastic. If Keith had taken a little brick box of a house in Clapham with nothing but railings in front of it and had written "The Elms" over it, you wouldn't have thought there was anything fantastic about that. Simply because it was a great blaring, swaggering lie you would have believed it.'

'Drink your wine, gentlemen,' said Keith, laughing, 'for this confounded wind will upset it.'

We drank, and as we did so, although the hanging house, by a cunning mechanism, swung only slightly, we knew that the great head of the elm tree swayed in the sky like a stricken thistle.

5

The Noticeable Conduct of Professor Chadd

Basil Grant had comparatively few friends besides myself; yet he was the reverse of an unsociable man. He would talk to anyone anywhere, and talk not only well but with perfectly genuine concern and enthusiasm for that person's affairs. He went through the world, as it were, as if he were always on the top of an omnibus or waiting for a train. Most of these chance acquaintances, of course, vanished into darkness out of his life. A few here and there got hooked on to him, so to speak, and became his lifelong intimates, but there was an accidental look about all of them as if they were windfalls, samples taken at random, goods fallen from a goods train or presents fished out of a bran-pie. One would be, let us say, a veterinary surgeon with the appearance of a jockey; another, a mild prebendary with a white beard and vague views; another, a young captain in the Lancers, seemingly exactly like other captains in the Lancers; another, a small dentist from Fulham, in all reasonable certainty precisely like every other dentist from Fulham. Major Brown, small, dry, and dapper, was one of these; Basil had made his acquaintance over a discussion in a hotel cloakroom about the right hat, a discussion which reduced the little major almost to a kind of masculine hysterics, the compound of the selfishness of an old bachelor and the scrupulosity of an old maid. They had gone home in a cab together and then dined with each other twice a week until they died. I myself was another. I had met Grant while he was still a judge, on the balcony of the National Liberal Club, and exchanged a few words about the weather. Then we had talked for about an hour about politics and God; for men always talk about the most important things to total strangers. It is because in the total stranger we perceive man himself; the image of God is not disguised by resemblances to an uncle or doubts of the wisdom of a moustache.

One of the most interesting of Basil's motley group of acquaintances was Professor Chadd. He was known to the ethnological world (which is a very interesting world, but a long way off this one) as the second greatest, if not the greatest, authority on the relations of savages to language. He was known to the neighbourhood of Hart Street, Bloomsbury, as a bearded man with a bald head, spectacles, and a patient face, the face of an unaccountable Nonconformist who had forgotten how to be angry. He went to and fro between the British Museum and a selection of blameless tea-shops, with an armful of books and a poor but honest umbrella. He was never seen without the books and the umbrella, and was supposed (by the lighter wits of the Persian manuscript room) to go to bed with them in his little brick villa in the neighbourhood of Shepherd's Bush. There he lived with three sisters, ladies of solid goodness, but sinister demeanour. His life was happy, as are almost all the lives of methodical students, but one would not have called it exhilarating. His only hours of exhilaration occurred when his friend, Basil Grant, came into the house, late at night, a tornado of conversation.

Basil, though close on sixty, had moods of boisterous babyishness, and these seemed for some reason or other to descend upon him particularly in the house of his studious and almost dingy friend. I can remember vividly (for I was acquainted with both parties and often dined with them) the gaiety of Grant on that particular evening when the strange calamity fell upon the professor. Professor Chadd was, like most of his particular class and type (the class that is at once academic and middle-class), a Radical of a solemn and old-fashioned type. Grant was a Radical himself, but he was that more discriminating and not uncommon type of Radical who passes most of his time in abusing the Radical party. Chadd had just contributed to a magazine an article called 'Zulu Interests and the New Makango Frontier', in which a precise scientific report of his study of the customs of the people of T'Chaka was reinforced by a severe protest against certain interferences with these customs both by the British and the Germans. He was sitting with the magazine in front of him, the lamplight shining on his spectacles, a wrinkle in his forehead, not of anger, but of perplexity, as Basil Grant strode up and down the room, shaking it with his voice, with his high spirits and his heavy tread.

'It's not your opinions that I object to, my esteemed Chadd,' he was saying, 'it's you. You are quite right to champion the Zulus, but for all that you do not sympathise with them. No doubt you know the Zulu way of cooking tomatoes and the Zulu prayer before blowing one's nose; but for all that you don't understand them as well as I do, who don't know an assegai from an alligator. You are more learned, Chadd, but I am more Zulu. Why is it that the jolly old barbarians of this earth are always championed by people who are their antithesis? Why is it? You are sagacious, you are benevolent, you are well informed, but, Chadd, you are not savage. Live no longer under that rosy illusion. Look in the glass. Ask your sisters. Consult the librarian of the British Museum. Look at this umbrella.' And he held up that sad but still respectable article. 'Look at it. For ten mortal years to my certain knowledge you have carried that object under your arm, and I have no sort of doubt that you carried it at the age of eight months, and it never occurred to you to give one wild yell and hurl it like a javelin – thus – '

And he sent the umbrella whizzing past the professor's bald head, so that it knocked over a pile of books with a crash and left a vase rocking.

Professor Chadd appeared totally unmoved, with his face still lifted to the lamp and the wrinkle cut in his forehead.

'Your mental processes,' he said, 'always go a little too fast. And they are stated without method. There is no kind of inconsistency' – and no words can convey the time he took to get to the end of the word – 'between valuing the right of the aborigines to adhere to their stage in the evolutionary process, so long as they find it congenial and requisite to do so. There is, I say, no inconsistency between this concession which I have just described to you and the view that the evolutionary stage in question is, nevertheless, so far as we can form any estimate of values in the variety of cosmic processes, definable in some degree as an inferior evolutionary stage.'

Nothing but his lips had moved as he spoke, and his glasses still shone like two pallid moons.

Grant was shaking with laughter as he watched him.

'True,' he said, 'there is no inconsistency, my son of the red spear. But there is a great deal of incompatibility of temper. I am very far from being certain that the Zulu is on an inferior evolutionary stage, whatever the blazes that may mean. I do not think there is anything stupid or ignorant about howling at the moon or being afraid of devils in the dark. It seems to me perfectly philosophical. Why should a man be thought a sort of idiot because he feels the mystery and peril of existence itself? Suppose, my dear Chadd, suppose it is we who are the idiots because we are not afraid of devils in the dark?'

Professor Chadd slit open a page of the magazine with a bone paperknife and the intent reverence of the bibliophile.

'Beyond all question,' he said, 'it is a tenable hypothesis. I allude to the hypothesis which I understand you to entertain, that our civilisation is not or may not be an advance upon, and indeed (if I apprehend you), is or may be a retrogression from states identical with or analogous to the state of the Zulus. Moreover, I shall be inclined to concede that such a proposition is of the nature, in some degree at least, of a primary proposition, and cannot adequately be argued, in the same sense, I mean, that the primary proposition of pessimism, or the primary proposition of the non-existence of matter, cannot adequately be argued. But I do not conceive you to be under the impression that you have demonstrated anything more concerning this proposition than that it is tenable, which, after all, amounts to little more than the statement that it is not a contradiction in terms.'

Basil threw a book at his head and took out a cigar.

'You don't understand,' he said, 'but, on the other hand, as a compensation, you don't mind smoking. Why you don't object to that disgustingly barbaric rite I can't think. I can only say that I began it when I began to be a Zulu, about the age of ten. What I maintained was that although you knew more about Zulus in the sense that you are a scientist, I know more about them in the sense that I am a savage. For instance, your theory of the origin of language, something about its having come from the formulated secret language of some individual creature, though you knocked me silly with facts and scholarship in its favour, still does not convince me, because I have a feeling that that is not the way that things happen. If you ask me why I think so I can only answer that I am a Zulu; and if you ask me (as you most certainly will) what is my definition of a Zulu, I can answer that also. He is one who has climbed a Sussex apple tree at seven and been afraid of a ghost in an English lane.'

'Your process of thought – ' began the immovable Chadd, but his speech was interrupted. His sister, with that masculinity which always in such families concentrates in sisters, flung open the door with a rigid arm and said: 'James, Mr Bingham of the British Museum wants to see you again.'

The philosopher rose with a dazed look, which always indicates in such men the fact that they regard philosophy as a familiar thing, but practical life as a weird and unnerving vision, and walked dubiously out of the room.

'I hope you do not mind my being aware of it, Miss Chadd,' said Basil Grant, 'but I hear that the British Museum has recognised one of the men who have deserved well of their commonwealth. It is true, is it not, that Professor Chadd is likely to be made keeper of Asiatic manuscripts?'

The grim face of the spinster betrayed a great deal of pleasure and a great deal of pathos also. 'I believe it's true,' she said. 'If it is, it will not only be great glory which women, I assure you, feel a great deal, but great relief, which they feel more; relief from worry from a lot of things. James' health has never been good, and while we are as poor as we are he had to do journalism and coaching, in addition to his own dreadful grinding notions and discoveries, which he loves more than man, woman, or child. I have often been afraid that unless something of this kind occurred we should really have to be careful of his brain. But I believe it is practically settled.'

'I am delighted,' began Basil, but with a worried face, 'but these red-tape negotiations are so terribly chancy that I really can't advise you to build on hope, only to be hurled down into bitterness. I've known men, and good men like your brother, come nearer than this and be disappointed. Of course, if it is true – '

'If it is true,' said the woman fiercely, 'it means that people who have never lived may make an attempt at living.'

Even as she spoke the professor came into the room still with the dazed look in his eyes.

'Is it true?' asked Basil, with burning eyes.

'Not a bit true,' answered Chadd after a moment's bewilderment. 'Your argument was in three points fallacious.'

'What do you mean?' demanded Grant.

'Well,' said the professor slowly, 'in saying that you could possess a knowledge of the essence of Zulu life distinct from –'

'Oh! confound Zulu life,' cried Grant, with a burst of laughter. 'I mean, have you got the post?'

'You mean the post of keeper of the Asiatic manuscripts,' he said, opening his eye with childlike wonder. 'Oh, yes, I got that. But the real objection to your argument, which has only, I admit, occurred to me since I have been out of the room, is that it does not merely presuppose a Zulu truth apart from the facts, but infers that the discovery of it is absolutely impeded by the facts.'

'I am crushed,' said Basil, and sat down to laugh, while the professor's sister retired to her room, possibly to laugh, possibly not.

* * *

It was extremely late when we left the Chadds, and it is an extremely long and tiresome journey from Shepherd's Bush to Lambeth. This may be our excuse for the fact that we (for I was stopping the night with Grant) got down to breakfast next day at a time inexpressibly criminal, a time, in point of fact, close upon noon. Even to that belated meal we came in a very lounging and leisurely fashion. Grant, in particular, seemed so dreamy at table that he scarcely saw the pile of letters by his plate, and I doubt if he would have opened any of them if there had not lain on the top that one thing which has succeeded amid modern carelessness in being really urgent and coercive – a telegram. This he opened with the same heavy distraction with which he broke his egg and drank his tea. When he read it he did not stir a hair or say a word, but something, I know not what, made me feel that the motionless figure had been pulled together suddenly as strings are tightened on a slack guitar. Though he said nothing and did not move, I knew that he had been for an instant cleared and sharpened with a shock of cold water. It was scarcely any surprise to me when a man who had drifted sullenly to his seat and fallen into it, kicked it away like a cur from under him and came round to me in two strides.

'What do you make of that?' he said, and flattened out the wire in front of me.

It ran: 'Please come at once. James' mental state dangerous. Chadd.'

'What does the woman mean?' I said after a pause, irritably. 'Those women have been saying that the poor old professor was mad ever since he was born.'

'You are mistaken,' said Grant composedly. 'It is true that all sensible women think all studious men mad. It is true, for the matter of that, all women of any kind think all men of any kind mad. But they don't put it in telegrams, any more than they wire to you that grass is green or God all-merciful. These things are truisms, and often private ones at that. If Miss Chadd has written down under the eye of a strange woman in a post-office that her brother is off his head you may be perfectly certain that she did it because it was a matter of life and death, and she can think of no other way of forcing us to come promptly.'

'It will force us of course,' I said, smiling.

'Oh, yes,' he replied; 'there is a cab-rank near.'

Basil scarcely said a word as we drove across Westminster Bridge, through Trafalgar Square, along Piccadilly, and up the Uxbridge Road. Only as he was opening the gate he spoke.

'I think you will take my word for it, my friend,' he said; 'this is one of the most queer and complicated and astounding incidents that ever happened in London or, for that matter, in any high civilisation.'

'I confess with the greatest sympathy and reverence that I don't quite see it,' I said. 'Is it so very extraordinary or complicated that a dreamy somnambulant old invalid who has always walked on the borders of the inconceivable should go mad under the shock of great joy? Is it so very extraordinary that a man with a head like a turnip and a soul like a spider's web should not find his strength equal to a confounding change of fortunes? Is it, in short, so very extraordinary that James Chadd should lose his wits from excitement?'

'It would not be extraordinary in the least,' answered Basil, with placidity. 'It would not be extraordinary in the least,' he repeated, 'if the professor had gone mad. That was not the extraordinary circumstance to which I referred.'

'What,' I asked, stamping my foot, 'was the extraordinary thing?'

'The extraordinary thing,' said Basil, ringing the bell, 'is that he has not gone mad from excitement.'

The tall and angular figure of the eldest Miss Chadd blocked the doorway as the door opened. Two other Miss Chadds seemed in the same way to be blocking the narrow passage and the little parlour. There was a general sense of their keeping something from view. They seemed like three black-clad ladies in some strange play of Maeterlinck, veiling the catastrophe from the audience in the manner of the Greek chorus.

'Sit down, won't you?' said one of them, in a voice that was somewhat rigid with pain. 'I think you had better be told first what has happened.'

Then, with her bleak face looking unmeaningly out of the window, she continued, in an even and mechanical voice: 'I had better state everything that occurred just as it occurred. This morning I was clearing away the breakfast things, my sisters were both somewhat unwell, and had not come down. My brother had just gone out of the room, I believe, to fetch a book. He came back again, however, without it, and stood for some time staring at the empty grate. I said, "Were you looking for anything I could get?" He did not answer, but this constantly happens, as he is often very abstracted. I repeated my question, and still he did not answer. Sometimes he is so wrapped up in his studies that nothing but a touch on the shoulder would make him aware of one's presence, so I came round the table towards him. I really do not know how to describe the sensation which I then had. It seems simply silly, but at the moment it seemed something enormous, upsetting one's brain. The fact is, James was standing on one leg.'

Grant smiled slowly and rubbed his hands with a kind of care.

'Standing on one leg?' I repeated.

'Yes,' replied the dead voice of the woman without an inflection to suggest that she felt the fantasticality of her statement. 'He was standing on the left leg and the right drawn up at a sharp angle, the toe pointing downwards. I asked him if his leg hurt him. His only answer was to shoot the leg straight at right angles to the other, as if pointing to the other with his toe to the wall. He was still looking quite gravely at the fireplace.

' "James, what is the matter?" I cried, for I was thoroughly frightened. James gave three kicks in the air with the right leg, flung up the other, gave three kicks in the air with it also and spun round like a teetotum the other way. "Are you mad?" I cried. "Why don't you answer me?" He had come to a standstill facing me, and was looking at me as he always does, with his lifted eyebrows and great spectacled eyes. When I had spoken he remained a second or two motionless, and then his only reply was to lift his left foot slowly from the floor and describe circles with it in the air. I rushed to the door and shouted for Christina. I will not dwell on the dreadful hours that followed. All three of us talked to him, implored him to speak to us with appeals that might have brought back the dead, but he has done nothing but hop and dance and kick with a solemn silent face. It looks as if his legs belonged to someone else or were possessed by devils. He has never spoken to us from that time to this.'

'Where is he now?' I said, getting up in some agitation. 'We ought not to leave him alone.'

'Dr Colman is with him,' said Miss Chadd calmly. 'They are in the garden. Dr Colman thought the air would do him good. And he can scarcely go into the street.'

Basil and I walked rapidly to the window which looked out on the garden. It was a small and somewhat smug suburban garden; the flower beds a little too neat and like the pattern of a coloured carpet; but on this shining and opulent summer day even they had the exuberance of something natural, I had almost said tropical. In the middle of a bright and verdant but painfully circular lawn stood two figures. One of them was a small, sharp-looking man with black whiskers and a very polished hat (I presume Dr Colman), who was talking very quietly and clearly, yet with a nervous twitch, as it were, in his face. The other was our old friend, listening with his old forbearing expression and owlish eyes, the strong sunlight gleaming on his glasses as the lamplight had gleamed the night before, when the boisterous Basil had rallied him on his studious decorum. But for one thing the figure of this morning might have been the identical figure of last night. That one thing was that while the face listened reposefully the legs were industriously dancing like the legs of a marionette. The neat flowers and the sunny glitter of the garden lent an indescribable sharpness and incredibility to the prodigy – the prodigy of the head of a hermit and the legs of a harlequin. For miracles should always happen in broad daylight. The night makes them credible and therefore commonplace.

The second sister had by this time entered the room and came somewhat drearily to the window.

'You know, Adelaide,' she said, 'that Mr Bingham from the Museum is coming again at three.'

'I know,' said Adelaide Chadd bitterly. 'I suppose we shall have to tell him about this. I thought that no good fortune would ever come easily to us.'

Grant suddenly turned round. 'What do you mean?' he said. 'What will you have to tell Mr Bingham?'

'You know what I shall have to tell him,' said the professor's sister, almost fiercely. 'I don't know that we need give it its wretched name. Do you think that the keeper of Asiatic manuscripts will be allowed to go on like that?' And she pointed for an instant at the figure in the garden, the shining, listening face and the unresting feet.

Basil Grant took out his watch with an abrupt movement. 'When did you say the British Museum man was coming?' he said.

'Three o'clock,' said Miss Chadd briefly.

'Then I have an hour before me,' said Grant, and without another word threw up the window and jumped out into the garden. He did not walk straight up to the doctor and lunatic, but strolling round the garden path drew near them cautiously and yet apparently carelessly. He stood a couple of feet off them, seemingly counting halfpence out of his trousers pocket, but, as I could see, looking up steadily under the broad brim of his hat.

Suddenly he stepped up to Professor Chadd's elbow, and said, in a loud familiar voice, 'Well, my boy, do you still think the Zulus our inferiors?'

The doctor knitted his brows and looked anxious, seeming to be about to speak. The professor turned his bald and placid head towards Grant in a friendly manner, but made no answer, idly flinging his left leg about.

'Have you converted Dr Colman to your views?' Basil continued, still in the same loud and lucid tone.

Chadd only shuffled his feet and kicked a little with the other leg, his expression still benevolent and enquiring. The doctor cut in rather sharply. 'Shall we go inside, professor?' he said. 'Now you have shown me the garden.

A beautiful garden. A most beautiful garden. Let us go in,' and he tried to draw the kicking ethnologist by the elbow, at the same time whispering to Grant: 'I must ask you not to trouble him with questions. Most risky. He must be soothed.'

Basil answered in the same tone, with great coolness: 'Of course your directions must be followed out, doctor. I will endeavour to do so, but I hope it will not be inconsistent with them if you will leave me alone with my poor friend in this garden for an hour. I want to watch him. I assure you, Dr Colman, that I shall say very little to him, and that little shall be as soothing as – as syrup.'

The doctor wiped his eyeglass thoughtfully.

'It is rather dangerous for him,' he said, 'to be long in the strong sun without his hat. With his bald head, too.'

'That is soon settled,' said Basil composedly, and took off his own big hat and clapped it on the egglike skull of the professor. The latter did not turn round but danced away with his eyes on the horizon.

The doctor put on his glasses again, looked severely at the two for some seconds, with his head on one side like a bird's, and then saying, shortly, 'All right,' strutted away into the house, where the three Misses Chadd were all looking out from the parlour window on to the garden. They looked out on it with hungry eyes for a full hour without moving, and they saw a sight which was more extraordinary than madness itself.

Basil Grant addressed a few questions to the madman, without succeeding in making him do anything but continue to caper, and when he had done this slowly took a red notebook out of one pocket and a large pencil out of another.

He began hurriedly to scribble notes. When the lunatic skipped away from him he would walk a few yards in pursuit, stop, and make notes again. Thus they followed each other round and round the foolish circle of turf, the one writing in pencil with the face of a man working out a problem, the other leaping and playing like a child.

After about three-quarters of an hour of this imbecile scene, Grant put the pencil in his pocket, but kept the notebook open in his hand, and walking round the mad professor, planted himself directly in front of him.

Then occurred something that even those already used to that wild morning had not anticipated or dreamed. The professor, on finding Basil in front of him, stared with a blank benignity for a few seconds, and then drew up his left leg and hung it bent in the attitude that his sister had described as being the first of all his antics. And the moment he had done it Basil Grant lifted his own leg and held it out rigid before him, confronting Chadd with the flat sole of his boot. The professor dropped his bent leg, and swinging his weight on to it kicked out the other behind, like a man swimming. Basil crossed his feet like a saltire cross, and then flung them apart again, giving a leap into the air. Then before any of the spectators could say a word or even entertain a thought about the matter, both of them were dancing a sort of jig or hornpipe opposite each other; and the sun shone down on two madmen instead of one.

They were so stricken with the deafness and blindness of monomania that they did not see the eldest Miss Chadd come out feverishly into the garden with gestures of entreaty, a gentleman following her. Professor Chadd was in the wildest posture of a *pas-de-quatre*, Basil Grant seemed about to turn a cartwheel, when they were frozen in their follies by the steely voice of Adelaide Chadd saying, 'Mr Bingham of the British Museum.'

Mr Bingham was a slim, well-clad gentleman with a pointed and slightly effeminate grey beard, unimpeachable gloves, and formal but agreeable manners. He was the type of the over-civilised, as Professor Chadd was of the uncivilised pedant. His formality and agreeableness did him some credit under the circumstances. He had a vast experience of books and a considerable experience of the more dilettante fashionable salons. But neither branch of knowledge had accustomed him to the spectacle of two grey-haired middle-class gentlemen in modern costume throwing themselves about like acrobats as a substitute for an after-dinner nap.

The professor continued his antics with perfect placidity, but Grant stopped abruptly. The doctor had reappeared on the scene, and his shiny black eyes, under his shiny black hat, moved restlessly from one of them to the other.

'Dr Colman,' said Basil, turning to him, 'will you entertain Professor Chadd again for a little while? I am sure that he needs you. Mr Bingham, might I have the pleasure of a few moments' private conversation? My name is Grant.'

Mr Bingham, of the British Museum, bowed in a manner that was respectful but a trifle bewildered.

'Miss Chadd will excuse me,' continued Basil easily, 'if I know my way about the house.' And he led the dazed librarian rapidly through the back door into the parlour.

'Mr Bingham,' said Basil, setting a chair for him, 'I imagine that Miss Chadd has told you of this distressing occurrence.'

'She has, Mr Grant,' said Bingham, looking at the table with a sort of compassionate nervousness. 'I am more pained than I can say by this dreadful calamity. It seems quite heart-rending that the thing should have happened just as we have decided to give your eminent friend a position which falls far short of his merits. As it is, of course – really, I don't know what to say. Professor Chadd may, of course, retain – I sincerely trust he will – his extraordinarily valuable intellect. But I am afraid – I am really afraid – that it would not do to have the curator of the Asiatic manuscripts – er – dancing about.'

'I have a suggestion to make,' said Basil, and sat down abruptly in his chair, drawing it up to the table.

'I am delighted, of course,' said the gentleman from the British Museum, coughing and drawing up his chair also.

The clock on the mantelpiece ticked for just the moments required for Basil to clear his throat and collect his words, and then he said: 'My proposal is this. I do not know that in the strict use of words you could altogether call it a compromise, still it has something of that character. My proposal is that the Government (acting, as I presume, through your Museum) should pay Professor Chadd £800 a year until he stops dancing.'

'Eight hundred a year!' said Mr Bingham, and for the first time lifted his mild blue eyes to those of his interlocutor – and he raised them with a mild blue stare. 'I think I have not quite understood you. Did I understand you to say that Professor Chadd ought to be employed, in his present state, in the Asiatic manuscript department at eight hundred a year?'

Grant shook his head resolutely.

'No,' he said firmly. 'No. Chadd is a friend of mine, and I would say anything for him I could. But I do not say, I cannot say, that he ought to take on the Asiatic manuscripts. I do not go so far as that. I merely say that until he stops dancing you ought to pay him £800. Surely you have some general fund for the endowment of research.'

Mr Bingham looked bewildered.

'I really don't know,' he said, blinking his eyes, 'what you are talking about. Do you ask us to give this obvious lunatic nearly a thousand a year for life?'

'Not at all,' cried Basil, keenly and triumphantly. 'I never said for life. Not at all.'

'What for, then?' asked the meek Bingham, suppressing an instinct meekly to tear his hair. 'How long is this endowment to run? Not till his death? Till the Judgement day?'

'No,' said Basil, beaming, 'but just what I said. Till he has stopped dancing.' And he lay back with satisfaction and his hands in his pockets.

Bingham had by this time fastened his eyes keenly on Basil Grant and kept them there.

'Come, Mr Grant,' he said. 'Do I seriously understand you to suggest that the Government pay Professor Chadd an extraordinarily high salary simply on the ground that he has (pardon the phrase) gone mad? That he should be paid more than four good clerks solely on the ground that he is flinging his boots about in the back yard?'

'Precisely,' said Grant composedly.

'That this absurd payment is not only to run on with the absurd dancing, but actually to stop with the absurd dancing?'

'One must stop somewhere,' said Grant. 'Of course.'

Bingham rose and took up his perfect stick and gloves.

'There is really nothing more to be said, Mr Grant,' he said coldly. 'What you are trying to explain to me may be a joke – a slightly unfeeling joke. It may be your sincere view, in which case I ask your pardon for the former suggestion. But, in any case, it appears quite irrelevant to my duties. The mental morbidity, the mental downfall, of Professor Chadd, is a thing so painful to me that I cannot easily endure to speak of it. But it is clear there is a limit to everything. And if the Archangel Gabriel went mad it would sever his connection, I am sorry to say, with the British Museum Library.'

He was stepping towards the door, but Grant's hand, flung out in dramatic warning, arrested him.

'Stop!' said Basil sternly. 'Stop while there is yet time. Do you want to take part in a great work, Mr Bingham? Do you want to help in the glory of Europe – in the glory of science? Do you want to carry your head in the air when it is bald or white because of the part that you bore in a great discovery? Do you want –'

Bingham cut in sharply: 'And if I do want this, Mr Grant – '

'Then,' said Basil lightly, 'your task is easy. Get Chadd £800 a year till he stops dancing.'

With a fierce flap of his swinging gloves Bingham turned impatiently to the door, but in passing out of it found it blocked. Dr Colman was coming in.

'Forgive me, gentlemen,' he said, in a nervous, confidential voice, 'the fact is, Mr Grant, I – er – have made a most disturbing discovery about Mr Chadd.'

Bingham looked at him with grave eyes.

'I was afraid so,' he said. 'Drink, I imagine.'

'Drink!' echoed Colman, as if that were a much milder affair. 'Oh, no, it's not drink.'

Mr Bingham became somewhat agitated, and his voice grew hurried and vague. 'Homicidal mania – ' he began.

'No, no,' said the medical man impatiently.

'Thinks he's made of glass,' said Bingham feverishly, 'or says he's God – or – '

'No,' said Dr Colman sharply; 'the fact is, Mr Grant, my discovery is of a different character. The awful thing about him is – '

'Oh, go on, sir,' cried Bingham, in agony.

'The awful thing about him is,' repeated Colman, with deliberation, 'that he isn't mad.'

'Not mad!'

'There are quite well-known physical tests of lunacy,' said the doctor shortly; 'he hasn't got any of them.'

'But why does he dance?' cried the despairing Bingham. 'Why doesn't he answer us? Why hasn't he spoken to his family?'

'The devil knows,' said Dr Colman coolly. 'I'm paid to judge of lunatics, but not of fools. The man's not mad.'

'What on earth can it mean? Can't we make him listen?' said Mr Bingham. 'Can none get into any kind of communication with him?'

Grant's voice struck in sudden and clear, like a steel bell: 'I shall be very happy,' he said, 'to give him any message you like to send.'

Both men stared at him.

'Give him a message?' they cried simultaneously. 'How will you give him a message?'

Basil smiled in his slow way.

'If you really want to know how I shall give him your message,' he began, but Bingham cried: 'Of course, of course,' with a sort of frenzy.

'Well,' said Basil, 'like this.' And he suddenly sprang a foot into the air, coming down with crashing boots, and then stood on one leg.

His face was stern, though this effect was slightly spoiled by the fact that one of his feet was making wild circles in the air.

'You drive me to it,' he said. 'You drive me to betray my friend. And I will, for his own sake, betray him.'

The sensitive face of Bingham took on an extra expression of distress as of one anticipating some disgraceful disclosure. 'Anything painful, of course –' he began.

Basil let his loose foot fall on the carpet with a crash that struck them all rigid in their feeble attitudes.

'Idiots!' he cried. 'Have you seen the man? Have you looked at James Chadd going dismally to and fro from his dingy house to your miserable library, with his futile books and his confounded umbrella, and never seen that he has the eyes of a fanatic? Have you never noticed, stuck casually behind his spectacles and above his seedy old collar, the face of a man who might have burned heretics, or died for the philosopher's stone? It is all my fault, in a way: I lit the dynamite of his deadly faith. I argued against him on the score of his famous theory about language – the theory that language was complete in certain individuals and was picked up by others simply by watching them. I also chaffed him about not understanding things in rough and ready practice. What has this glorious bigot done? He has answered me. He has worked out a system of language of his own (it would take too long to explain); he has made up, I say, a language of his own. And he has sworn that till people understand it, till he can speak to us in this language, he will not speak in any other. And he shall not. I have understood, by taking careful notice; and, by heaven, so shall the others. This shall not be blown upon. He shall finish his experiment. He shall have £800 a year from somewhere till he has stopped dancing. To stop him now is an infamous war on a great idea. It is religious persecution.'

Mr Bingham held out his hand cordially.

'I thank you, Mr Grant,' he said. 'I hope I shall be able to answer for the source of the £800 and I fancy that I shall. Will you come in my cab?'

'No, thank you very much, Mr Bingham,' said Grant heartily. 'I think I will go and have a chat with the professor in the garden.'

The conversation between Chadd and Grant appeared to be personal and friendly. They were still dancing when I left.

6

The Eccentric Seclusion of the Old Lady

The conversation of Rupert Grant had two great elements of interest – first, the long fantasias of detective deduction in which he was engaged, and, second, his genuine romantic interest in the life of London. His brother Basil said of him: 'His reasoning is particularly cold and clear, and invariably leads him wrong. But his poetry comes in abruptly and leads him right.' Whether this was true of Rupert as a whole, or no, it was certainly curiously supported by one story about him which I think worth telling.

We were walking along a lonely terrace in Brompton together. The street was full of that bright blue twilight which comes about half-past eight in summer, and which seems for the moment to be not so much a coming of darkness as the turning on of a new azure illuminator, as if the earth were lit suddenly by a sapphire sun. In the cool blue the lemon tint of the lamps had already begun to flame, and as Rupert and I passed them, Rupert talking excitedly, one after another the pale sparks sprang out of the dusk. Rupert was talking excitedly because he was trying to prove to me the nine hundred and ninety-ninth of his amateur detective theories. He would go about London, with this mad logic in his brain, seeing a conspiracy in a cab accident, and a special providence in a falling fusee. His suspicions at the moment were fixed upon an unhappy milkman who walked in front of us. So arresting were the incidents which afterwards overtook us that I am really afraid that I have forgotten what were the main outlines of the milkman's crime. I think it had something to do with the fact that he had only one small can of milk to carry, and that of that he had left the lid loose and walked so quickly that he spilled milk on the pavement. This showed that he was not thinking of his small burden, and this again showed that he anticipated some other than lacteal business at the end of his walk, and this (taken in conjunction with something about muddy boots) showed something else that I have entirely forgotten. I am afraid that I derided this detailed revelation unmercifully; and I am afraid that Rupert Grant, who, though the best of fellows, had a good deal of the sensitiveness of the artistic temperament, slightly resented my derision. He endeavoured to take a whiff of his cigar, with the placidity which he associated with his profession, but the cigar, I think, was nearly bitten through.

'My dear fellow,' he said acidly, 'I'll bet you half a crown that wherever that milkman comes to a real stop I'll find out something curious.'

'My resources are equal to that risk,' I said, laughing. 'Done.'

We walked on for about a quarter of an hour in silence in the trail of the mysterious milkman. He walked quicker and quicker, and we had some ado to keep up with him; and every now and then he left a splash of milk, silver in the lamplight. Suddenly, almost before we could note it, he disappeared down the area steps of a house. I believe Rupert really believed that the milkman was a fairy; for a second he seemed to accept him as having vanished. Then calling something to me which somehow took no hold on my mind, he darted after the mystic milkman, and disappeared himself into the area.

I waited for at least five minutes, leaning against a lamppost in the lonely street. Then the milkman came swinging up the steps without his can and hurried off clattering down the road. Two or three minutes more elapsed, and then Rupert came bounding up also, his face pale but yet laughing; a not uncommon contradiction in him, denoting excitement.

'My friend,' he said, rubbing his hands, 'so much for all your scepticism. So much for your philistine ignorance of the possibilities of a romantic city. Two and sixpence, my boy, is the form in which your prosaic good nature will have to express itself.'

'What?' I said incredulously, 'do you mean to say that you really did find anything the matter with the poor milkman?'

His face fell.

'Oh, the milkman,' he said, with a miserable affectation at having misunderstood me. 'No, I – I – didn't exactly bring anything home to the milkman himself, I – '

'What did the milkman say and do?' I said, with inexorable sternness.

'Well, to tell the truth,' said Rupert, shifting restlessly from one foot to another, 'the milkman himself, as far as merely physical appearances went, just said, "Milk, Miss," and handed in the can. That is not to say, of course, that he did not make some secret sign or some – '

I broke into a violent laugh. 'You idiot,' I said, 'why don't you own yourself wrong and have done with it? Why should he have made a secret sign any more than anyone else? You own he said nothing and did nothing worth mentioning. You own that, don't you?'

His face grew grave.

'Well, since you ask me, I must admit that I do. It is possible that the milkman did not betray himself. It is even possible that I was wrong about him.'

'Then come along with you,' I said, with a certain amicable anger, 'and remember that you owe me half a crown.'

'As to that, I differ from you,' said Rupert coolly. 'The milkman's remarks may have been quite innocent. Even the milkman may have been. But I do not owe you half a crown. For the terms of the bet were, I think, as follows, as I propounded them, that wherever that milkman came to a real stop I should find out something curious.'

'Well?' I said.

'Well,' he answered, 'I jolly well have. You just come with me,' and before I could speak he had turned tail once more and whisked through the blue dark into the moat or basement of the house. I followed almost before I made any decision.

When we got down into the area I felt indescribably foolish – literally, as the saying is, in a hole. There was nothing but a closed door, shuttered windows, the steps down which we had come, the ridiculous well in which I found myself, and the ridiculous man who had brought me there, and who stood there with dancing eyes. I was just about to turn back when Rupert caught me by the elbow.

'Just listen to that,' he said, and keeping my coat gripped in his right hand, he rapped with the knuckles of his left on the shutters of the basement window. His air was so definite that I paused and even inclined my head for a moment towards it. From inside was coming the murmur of an unmistakable human voice.

'Have you been talking to somebody inside?' I asked suddenly, turning to Rupert.

'No, I haven't,' he replied, with a grim smile, 'but I should very much like to. Do you know what somebody is saying in there?'

'No, of course not,' I replied.

'Then I recommend you to listen,' said Rupert sharply.

In the dead silence of the aristocratic street at evening, I stood a moment and listened. From behind the wooden partition, in which there was a long lean crack, was coming a continuous and moaning sound which took the form of the words: 'When shall I get out? When shall I get out? Will they ever let me out?' or words to that effect.

'Do you know anything about this?' I said, turning upon Rupert very abruptly.

'Perhaps you think I am the criminal,' he said sardonically, 'instead of being in some small sense the detective. I came into this area two or three minutes ago, having told you that I knew there was something funny going on, and this woman behind the shutters (for it evidently is a woman) was moaning like mad. No, my dear friend, beyond that I do not know anything about her. She is not, startling as it may seem, my disinherited daughter, or a member of my secret seraglio. But when I hear a human being wailing that she can't get out, and talking to herself like a mad woman and beating on the shutters with her fists, as she was doing two or three minutes ago, I think it worth mentioning, that is all.'

'My dear fellow,' I said, 'I apologise; this is no time for arguing. What is to be done?'

Rupert Grant had a long clasp-knife naked and brilliant in his hand.

'First of all,' he said, 'house-breaking.' And he forced the blade into the crevice of the wood and broke away a huge splinter, leaving a gap and glimpse of the dark window-pane inside. The room within was entirely unlighted, so that for the first few seconds the window seemed a dead and opaque surface, as dark as a strip of slate. Then came a realisation which, though in a sense gradual, made us step back and catch our breath. Two large dim human eyes were so close to us that the window itself seemed suddenly to be a mask. A pale human face was pressed against the glass within, and with increased distinctness, with the increase of the opening came the words: 'When shall I get out?'

'What can all this be?' I said.

Rupert made no answer, but lifting his walking-stick and pointing the ferrule like a fencing sword at the glass, punched a hole in it, smaller and more accurate than I should have supposed possible. The moment he had done so the voice spouted out of the hole, so to speak, piercing and querulous and clear, making the same demand for liberty.

'Can't you get out, madam?' I said, drawing near the hole in some perturbation.

'Get out? Of course I can't,' moaned the unknown female bitterly. 'They won't let me. I told them I would be let out. I told them I'd call the police. But it's no good. Nobody knows, nobody comes. They could keep me as long as they liked only – '

I was in the very act of breaking the window finally with my stick, incensed with this very sinister mystery, when Rupert held my arm hard, held it with a curious, still, and secret rigidity as if he desired to stop me, but did not desire to be observed to do so. I paused a moment, and in the act swung slightly round, so that I was facing the supporting wall of the front door steps. The act froze me into a sudden stillness like that of Rupert, for a figure almost as motionless as the pillars of the portico, but unmistakably human, had put his head out from between the doorposts and was gazing down into the area. One of the lighted lamps of the street was just behind his head, throwing it into abrupt darkness. Consequently, nothing whatever could be seen of his face beyond one fact, that he was unquestionably staring at us. I must say I thought Rupert's calmness magnificent. He rang the area bell quite idly, and went on talking to me with the easy end of a conversation which had never had any beginning. The black glaring figure in the portico did not stir. I almost thought it was really a statue. In another moment the grey area was golden with gaslight as the basement door was opened suddenly and a small and decorous housemaid stood in it.

'Pray excuse me,' said Rupert, in a voice which he contrived to make somehow or other at once affable and underbred, 'but we thought perhaps that you might do something for the Waifs and Strays. We don't expect – '

'Not here,' said the small servant, with the incomparable severity of the menial of the non-philanthropic, and slammed the door in our faces.

'Very sad, very sad – the indifference of these people,' said the philanthropist with gravity, as we went together up the steps. As we did so the motionless figure in the portico suddenly disappeared.

'Well, what do you make of that?' asked Rupert, slapping his gloves together when we got into the street.

I do not mind admitting that I was seriously upset. Under such conditions I had but one thought.

'Don't you think,' I said a trifle timidly, 'that we had better tell your brother?'

'Oh, if you like,' said Rupert, in a lordly way. 'He is quite near, as I promised to meet him at Gloucester Road Station. Shall we take a cab? Perhaps, as you say, it might amuse him.'

Gloucester Road Station had, as if by accident, a somewhat deserted look. After a little looking about we discovered Basil Grant with his great head and his great white hat blocking the ticket-office window. I thought at first that he was taking a ticket for somewhere and being an astonishingly long time about it. As a matter of fact, he was discussing religion with the booking-office clerk, and had almost got his head through the hole in his excitement. When we dragged him away it was some time before he would talk of anything but the growth of an Oriental fatalism in modern thought, which had been well typified by some of the official's ingenious but perverse fallacies. At last we managed to get him to understand that we had made an astounding discovery. When he did listen, he listened attentively, walking between us up and down the lamp-lit street, while we told him in a rather feverish duet of the great house in South Kensington, of the equivocal milkman, of the lady imprisoned in the basement, and the man staring from the porch. At length he said: 'If you're thinking of going back to look the thing up, you must be careful what you do. It's no good you two going there. To go twice on the same pretext would look dubious. To go on a different pretext would look worse. You may be quite certain that the inquisitive gentleman who looked at you looked thoroughly, and will wear, so to speak, your portraits next to his heart. If you want to find out if there is anything in this without a police raid I fancy you had better wait outside. I'll go in and see them.'

His slow and reflective walk brought us at length within sight of the house. It stood up ponderous and purple against the last pallor of twilight. It looked like an ogre's castle. And so apparently it was.

'Do you think it's safe, Basil,' said his brother, pausing, a little pale, under the lamp, 'to go into that place alone? Of course we shall be near enough to hear if you yell, but these devils might do something – something sudden – or odd. I can't feel it's safe.'

'I know of nothing that is safe,' said Basil composedly, 'except, possibly – death,' and he went up the steps and rang at the bell. When the massive respectable door opened for an instant, cutting a square of gaslight in the gathering dark, and then closed with a bang, burying our friend inside, we could not repress a shudder. It had been like the heavy gaping and closing of the dim lips of some evil leviathan. A freshening night breeze began to blow up the street, and we turned up the collars of our coats. At the end of twenty minutes, in which we had scarcely moved or spoken, we were as cold as icebergs, but more, I think, from apprehension than the atmosphere. Suddenly Rupert made an abrupt movement towards the house.

'I can't stand this,' he began, but almost as he spoke sprang back into the shadow, for the panel of gold was again cut out of the black house front, and the burly figure of Basil was silhouetted against it coming out. He was roaring with laughter and talking so loudly that you could have heard every syllable across the street. Another voice, or, possibly, two voices, were laughing and talking back at him from within.

'No, no, no,' Basil was calling out, with a sort of hilarious hostility. 'That's quite wrong. That's the most ghastly heresy of all. It's the soul, my dear chap, the soul that's the arbiter of cosmic forces. When you see a cosmic force you don't like, trick it, my boy. But I must really be off.'

'Come and pitch into us again,' came the laughing voice from out of the house. 'We still have some bones unbroken.'

'Thanks very much, I will – good-night,' shouted Grant, who had by this time reached the street.

'Good-night,' came the friendly call in reply, before the door closed.

'Basil,' said Rupert Grant, in a hoarse whisper, 'what are we to do?'

The elder brother looked thoughtfully from one of us to the other.

'What is to be done, Basil?' I repeated in uncontrollable excitement.

'I'm not sure,' said Basil doubtfully. 'What do you say to getting some dinner somewhere and going to the Court Theatre tonight? I tried to get those fellows to come, but they couldn't.'

We stared blankly.

'Go to the Court Theatre?' repeated Rupert. 'What would be the good of that?'

'Good? What do you mean?' answered Basil, staring also. 'Have you turned Puritan or Passive Resister, or something? For fun, of course.'

'But, great God in Heaven! What are we going to do, I mean!' cried Rupert. 'What about the poor woman locked up in that house? Shall I go for the police?'

Basil's face cleared with immediate comprehension, and he laughed.

'Oh, that,' he said. 'I'd forgotten that. That's all right. Some mistake, possibly. Or some quite trifling private affair. But I'm sorry those fellows couldn't come with us. Shall we take one of these green omnibuses? There is a restaurant in Sloane Square.'

'I sometimes think you play the fool to frighten us,' I said irritably. 'How can we leave that woman locked up? How can it be a mere private affair? How can crime and kidnapping and murder, for all I know, be private affairs? If you found a corpse in a man's drawing-room, would you think it bad taste to talk about it just as if it was a confounded dado or an infernal etching?'

Basil laughed heartily.

'That's very forcible,' he said. 'As a matter of fact, though, I know it's all right in this case. And there comes the green omnibus.'

'How do you know it's all right in this case?' persisted his brother angrily.

'My dear chap, the thing's obvious,' answered Basil, holding a return ticket between his teeth while he fumbled in his waistcoat pocket. 'Those two fellows never committed a crime in their lives. They're not the kind. Have either of you chaps got a halfpenny? I want to get a paper before the omnibus comes.'

'Oh, curse the paper!' cried Rupert, in a fury. 'Do you mean to tell me, Basil Grant, that you are going to leave a fellow creature in pitch darkness in a private dungeon, because you've had ten minutes' talk with the keepers of it and thought them rather good men?'

'Good men do commit crimes sometimes,' said Basil, taking the ticket out of his mouth. 'But this kind of good man doesn't commit that kind of crime. Well, shall we get on this omnibus?'

The great green vehicle was indeed plunging and lumbering along the dim wide street towards us. Basil had stepped from the kerb, and for an instant it was touch and go whether we should all have leaped on to it and been borne away to the restaurant and the theatre.

'Basil,' I said, taking him firmly by the shoulder, 'I simply won't leave this street and this house.'

'Nor will I,' said Rupert, glaring at it and biting his fingers. 'There's some black work going on there. If I left it I should never sleep again.'

Basil Grant looked at us both seriously.

'Of course if you feel like that,' he said, 'we'll investigate further. You'll find it's all right, though. They're only two young Oxford fellows. Extremely nice, too, though rather infected with this pseudo-Darwinian business. Ethics of evolution and all that.'

'I think,' said Rupert darkly, ringing the bell, 'that we shall enlighten you further about their ethics.'

'And may I ask,' said Basil gloomily, 'what it is that you propose to do?'

'I propose, first of all,' said Rupert, 'to get into this house; secondly, to have a look at these nice young Oxford men; thirdly, to knock them down, bind them, gag them, and search the house.'

Basil stared indignantly for a few minutes. Then he was shaken for an instant with one of his sudden laughs.

'Poor little boys,' he said. 'But it almost serves them right for holding such silly views, after all,' and he quaked again with amusement; 'there's something confoundedly Darwinian about it.'

'I suppose you mean to help us?' said Rupert.

'Oh, yes, I'll be in it,' answered Basil, 'if it's only to prevent your doing the poor chaps any harm.'

He was standing in the rear of our little procession, looking indifferent and sometimes even sulky, but somehow the instant the door opened he stepped first into the hall, glowing with urbanity.

'So sorry to haunt you like this,' he said. 'I met two friends outside who very much want to know you. May I bring them in?'

'Delighted, of course,' said a young voice, the unmistakable voice of the Isis, and I realised that the door had been opened, not by the decorous little servant girl, but by one of our hosts in person. He was a short, but shapely young gentleman, with curly dark hair and a square, snub-nosed face. He wore slippers and a sort of blazer of some incredible college purple.

'This way,' he said; 'mind the steps by the staircase. This house is more crooked and old-fashioned than you would think from its snobbish exterior. There are quite a lot of odd corners in the place really.'

'That,' said Rupert, with a savage smile, 'I can quite believe.'

We were by this time in the study or back parlour, used by the young inhabitants as a sitting-room, an apartment littered with magazines and books ranging from Dante to detective stories. The other youth, who stood with his back to the fire smoking a corncob, was big and burly, with dead brown hair brushed forward and a Norfolk jacket. He was that particular type of man whose every feature and action is heavy and clumsy, and yet who is, you would say, rather exceptionally a gentleman.

'Any more arguments?' he said, when introductions had been effected. 'I must say, Mr Grant, you were rather severe upon eminent men of science such as we. I've half a mind to chuck my D.Sc. and turn minor poet.'

'Bosh,' answered Grant. 'I never said a word against eminent men of science. What I complain of is a vague popular philosophy which supposes itself to be scientific when it is really nothing but a sort of new religion and an uncommonly nasty one. When people talked about the fall of man they knew they were talking about a mystery, a thing they didn't understand. Now that they talk about the survival of the fittest they think they do understand it, whereas they have not merely no notion, they have an elaborately false notion of what the words mean. The Darwinian movement has made no difference to mankind, except that, instead of talking unphilosophically about philosophy, they now talk unscientifically about science.'

'That is all very well,' said the big young man, whose name appeared to be Burrows. 'Of course, in a sense, science, like mathematics or the violin, can only be perfectly understood by specialists. Still, the rudiments may be of public use. Greenwood here,' indicating the little man in the blazer, 'doesn't know one note of music from another. Still, he knows something. He knows enough to take off his hat when they play "God save the King". He doesn't take it off by mistake when they play "Oh, dem Golden Slippers". Just in the same way science – '

Here Mr Burrows stopped abruptly. He was interrupted by an argument uncommon in philosophical controversy and perhaps not wholly legitimate. Rupert Grant had bounded on him from behind, flung an arm round his throat, and bent the giant backwards.

'Knock the other fellow down, Swinburne,' he called out, and before I knew where I was I was locked in a grapple with the man in the purple blazer. He was a wiry fighter, who bent and sprang like a whalebone, but I was heavier and had taken him utterly by surprise. I twitched one of his feet from under him; he swung for a moment on the single foot, and then we fell with a crash amid the litter of newspapers, myself on top.

My attention for a moment released by victory, I could hear Basil's voice finishing some long sentence of which I had not heard the beginning.

' . . . wholly, I must confess, unintelligible to me, my dear sir, and I need not say unpleasant. Still one must side with one's old friends against the most fascinating new ones. Permit me, therefore, in tying you up in this antimacassar, to make it as commodious as handcuffs can reasonably be while . . . '

I had staggered to my feet. The gigantic Burrows was toiling in the garotte of Rupert, while Basil was striving to master his mighty hands. Rupert and Basil were both particularly strong, but so was Mr Burrows; how strong, we knew a second afterwards. His head was held back by Rupert's arm, but a convulsive heave went over his whole frame. An instant after his head plunged forward like a bull's, and Rupert Grant was slung head over heels, a catherine wheel of legs, on the floor in front of him. Simultaneously the bull's head butted Basil in the chest, bringing him also to the ground with a crash, and the monster, with a Berserker roar, leaped at me and knocked me into the corner of the room, smashing the wastepaper basket. The bewildered Greenwood sprang furiously to his feet. Basil did the same. But they had the best of it now.

Greenwood dashed to the bell and pulled it violently, sending peals through the great house. Before I could get panting to my feet, and before Rupert, who had been literally stunned for a few moments, could even lift his head from the floor, two footmen were in the room. Defeated even when we were in a majority, we were now outnumbered. Greenwood and one of the footmen flung themselves upon me, crushing me back into the corner upon the wreck of the paper basket. The other two flew at Basil, and pinned him against the wall. Rupert lifted himself on his elbow, but he was still dazed.

In the strained silence of our helplessness I heard the voice of Basil come with a loud incongruous cheerfulness.

'Now this,' he said, 'is what I call enjoying oneself.'

I caught a glimpse of his face, flushed and forced against the bookcase, from between the swaying limbs of my captors and his. To my astonishment his eyes were really brilliant with pleasure, like those of a child heated by a favourite game.

I made several apoplectic efforts to rise, but the servant was on top of me so heavily that Greenwood could afford to leave me to him. He turned quickly to come to reinforce the two who were mastering Basil. The latter's head was already sinking lower and lower, like a leaking ship, as his enemies pressed him down. He flung up one hand just as I thought him falling and hung on to a huge tome in the bookcase, a volume, I afterwards discovered, of St Chrysostom's theology. Just as Greenwood bounded across the room towards the group, Basil plucked the ponderous tome bodily out of the shelf, swung it, and sent it spinning through the air, so that it struck Greenwood flat in the face and knocked him over like a rolling ninepin. At the same instant Basil's stiffness broke, and he sank, his enemies closing over him.

Rupert's head was clear, but his body shaken; he was hanging as best he could on to the half-prostrate Greenwood. They were rolling over each other on the floor, both somewhat enfeebled by their falls, but Rupert certainly the more so. I was still successfully held down. The floor was a sea of torn and trampled papers and magazines, like an immense wastepaper basket. Burrows and his companion were almost up to the knees in them, as in a drift of dead leaves. And Greenwood had his leg stuck right through a sheet of the *Pall Mall Gazette*, which clung to it ludicrously, like some fantastic trouser frill.

Basil, shut from me in a human prison, a prison of powerful bodies, might be dead for all I knew. I fancied, however, that the broad back of Mr Burrows, which was turned towards me, had a certain bend of effort in it as if my friend still needed some holding down. Suddenly that broad back swayed hither and thither. It was swaying on one leg; Basil, somehow, had hold of the other. Burrows' huge fists and those of the footman were battering Basil's sunken head like an anvil, but nothing could get the giant's ankle out of his sudden and savage grip. While his own head was forced slowly down in darkness and great pain, the right leg of his captor was being forced in the air. Burrows swung to and fro with a purple face. Then suddenly the floor and the walls and the ceiling shook together, as the colossus fell, all his length seeming to fill the floor. Basil sprang up with dancing eyes, and with three blows like battering-rams knocked the footman into a cocked hat. Then he sprang on top of Burrows, with one antimacassar in his hand and another in his teeth, and bound him hand and foot almost before he knew clearly that his head had struck the floor. Then Basil sprang at Greenwood, whom Rupert was struggling to hold down, and between them they secured him easily. The man who had hold of me let go and turned to his rescue, but I leaped up like a spring released, and, to my infinite satisfaction, knocked the fellow down. The other footman, bleeding at the mouth and quite demoralised, was stumbling out of the room. My late captor, without a word, slunk after him, seeing that the battle was won. Rupert was sitting astride the pinioned Mr Greenwood, Basil astride the pinioned Mr Burrows.

To my surprise the latter gentleman, lying bound on his back, spoke in a perfectly calm voice to the man who sat on top of him.

'And now, gentlemen,' he said, 'since you have got your own way, perhaps you wouldn't mind telling us what the deuce all this is?'

'This,' said Basil, with a radiant face, looking down at his captive, 'this is what we call the survival of the fittest.'

Rupert, who had been steadily collecting himself throughout the latter phases of the fight, was intellectually altogether himself again at the end of it. Springing up from the prostrate Greenwood, and knotting a handkerchief round his left hand, which was bleeding from a blow, he sang out quite coolly: 'Basil, will you mount guard over the captive of your bow and spear and antimacassar? Swinburne and I will clear out the prison downstairs.'

'All right,' said Basil, rising also and seating himself in a leisured way in an armchair. 'Don't hurry for us,' he said, glancing round at the litter of the room, 'we have all the illustrated papers.'

Rupert lurched thoughtfully out of the room, and I followed him even more slowly; in fact, I lingered long enough to hear, as I passed through the room, the passages and the kitchen stairs, Basil's voice continuing conversationally: 'And now, Mr Burrows,' he said, settling himself sociably in the chair, 'there's no reason why we shouldn't go on with that amusing argument. I'm sorry that you have to express yourself lying on your back on the floor, and, as I told you before, I've no more notion why you are there than the man in the moon. A conversationalist like yourself, however, can scarcely be seriously handicapped by any bodily posture. You were saying, if I remember right, when this incidental fracas occurred, that the rudiments of science might with advantage be made public.'

'Precisely,' said the large man on the floor in an easy tone. 'I hold that nothing more than a rough sketch of the universe as seen by science can be . . . '

And here the voices died away as we descended into the basement. I noticed that Mr Greenwood did not join in the amicable controversy. Strange as it may appear, I think he looked back upon our proceedings with a slight degree of resentment. Mr Burrows, however, was all philosophy and chattiness. We left them, as I say, together, and sank deeper and deeper into the underworld of that mysterious house, which, perhaps, appeared to us somewhat more Tartarean than it really was, owing to our knowledge of its semi-criminal mystery and of the human secret locked below.

The basement floor had several doors, as is usual in such a house; doors that would naturally lead to the kitchen, the scullery, the pantry, the servants' hall, and so on. Rupert flung open all the doors with indescribable rapidity. Four out of the five opened on entirely empty apartments. The fifth was locked. Rupert broke the door in like a bandbox, and we fell into the sudden blackness of the sealed, unlighted room.

Rupert stood on the threshold, and called out like a man calling into an abyss: 'Whoever you are, come out. You are free. The people who held you captive are captives themselves. We heard you crying and we came to deliver you. We have bound your enemies upstairs hand and foot. You are free.'

For some seconds after he had spoken into the darkness there was a dead silence in it. Then there came a kind of muttering and moaning. We might easily have taken it for the wind or rats if we had not happened to have heard it before. It was unmistakably the voice of the imprisoned woman, drearily demanding liberty, just as we had heard her demand it.

'Has anybody got a match?' said Rupert grimly. 'I fancy we have come pretty near the end of this business.'

I struck a match and held it up. It revealed a large, bare, yellow-papered apartment with a dark-clad figure at the other end of it near the window. An instant after it burned my fingers and dropped, leaving darkness. It had, however, revealed something more practical – an iron gas bracket just above my head. I struck another match and lit the gas. And we found ourselves suddenly and seriously in the presence of the captive.

At a sort of work box in the window of this subterranean breakfast-room sat an elderly lady with a singularly high colour and almost startling silver hair. She had, as if designedly to relieve these effects, a pair of Mephistophelian black eyebrows and a very neat black dress. The glare of the gas lit up her piquant hair and face perfectly against the brown background of the shutters. The background was blue and not brown in one place; at the place where Rupert's knife had torn a great opening in the wood about an hour before.

'Madam,' said he, advancing with a gesture of the hat, 'permit me to have the pleasure of announcing to you that you are free. Your complaints happened to strike our ears as we passed down the street, and we have therefore ventured to come to your rescue.'

The old lady with the red face and the black eyebrows looked at us for a moment with something of the apoplectic stare of a parrot. Then she said, with a sudden gust or breathing of relief: 'Rescue? Where is Mr Greenwood? Where is Mr Burrows? Did you say you had rescued me?'

'Yes, madam,' said Rupert, with a beaming condescension. 'We have very satisfactorily dealt with Mr Greenwood and Mr Burrows. We have settled affairs with them very satisfactorily.'

The old lady rose from her chair and came very quickly towards us.

'What did you say to them? How did you persuade them?' she cried.

'We persuaded them, my dear madam,' said Rupert, laughing, 'by knocking them down and tying them up. But what is the matter?'

To the surprise of everyone the old lady walked slowly back to her seat by the window.

'Do I understand,' she said, with the air of a person about to begin knitting, 'that you have knocked down Mr Burrows and tied him up?'

'We have,' said Rupert proudly; 'we have resisted their oppression and conquered it.'

'Oh, thanks,' answered the old lady, and sat down by the window.

A considerable pause followed.

'The road is quite clear for you, madam,' said Rupert pleasantly.

The old lady rose, cocking her black eyebrows and her silver crest at us for an instant.

'But what about Greenwood and Burrows?' she said. 'What did I understand you to say had become of them?'

'They are lying on the floor upstairs,' said Rupert, chuckling. 'Tied hand and foot.'

'Well, that settles it,' said the old lady, coming with a kind of bang into her seat again, 'I must stop where I am.'

Rupert looked bewildered.

'Stop where you are?' he said. 'Why should you stop any longer where you are? What power can force you now to stop in this miserable cell?'

'The question rather is,' said the old lady, with composure, 'what power can force me to go anywhere else?'

We both stared wildly at her and she stared tranquilly at us both.

At last I said, 'Do you really mean to say that we are to leave you here?'

'I suppose you don't intend to tie me up,' she said, 'and carry me off? I certainly shall not go otherwise.'

'But, my dear madam,' cried out Rupert, in a radiant exasperation, 'we heard you with our own ears crying because you could not get out.'

'Eavesdroppers often hear rather misleading things,' replied the captive grimly. 'I suppose I did break down a bit and lose my temper and talk to myself. But I have some sense of honour for all that.'

'Some sense of honour?' repeated Rupert, and the last light of intelligence died out of his face, leaving it the face of an idiot with rolling eyes.

He moved vaguely towards the door and I followed. But I turned yet once more in the toils of my conscience and curiosity. 'Can we do nothing for you, madam?' I said forlornly.

'Why,' said the lady, 'if you are particularly anxious to do me a little favour you might untie the gentlemen upstairs.'

Rupert plunged heavily up the kitchen staircase, shaking it with his vague violence. With mouth open to speak he stumbled to the door of the sitting-room and scene of battle.

'Theoretically speaking, that is no doubt true,' Mr Burrows was saying, lying on his back and arguing easily with Basil; 'but we must consider the matter as it appears to our sense. The origin of morality . . .'

'Basil,' cried Rupert, gasping, 'she won't come out.'

'Who won't come out?' asked Basil, a little cross at being interrupted in an argument.

'The lady downstairs,' replied Rupert. 'The lady who was locked up. She won't come out. And she says that all she wants is for us to let these fellows loose.'

'And a jolly sensible suggestion,' cried Basil, and with a bound he was on top of the prostrate Burrows once more and was unknotting his bonds with hands and teeth.

'A brilliant idea. Swinburne, just undo Mr Greenwood.'

In a dazed and automatic way I released the little gentleman in the purple jacket, who did not seem to regard any of the proceedings as particularly sensible or brilliant. The gigantic Burrows, on the other hand, was heaving with herculean laughter.

'Well,' said Basil, in his cheeriest way, 'I think we must be getting away. We've so much enjoyed our evening. Far too much regard for you to stand on ceremony. If I may so express myself, we've made ourselves at home. Good-night. Thanks so much. Come along, Rupert.'

'Basil,' said Rupert desperately, 'for God's sake come and see what you can make of the woman downstairs. I can't get the discomfort out of my mind. I admit that things look as if we had made a mistake. But these gentlemen won't mind perhaps . . . '

'No, no,' cried Burrows, with a sort of Rabelaisian uproariousness. 'No, no, look in the pantry, gentlemen. Examine the coal-hole. Make a tour of the chimneys. There are corpses all over the house, I assure you.'

This adventure of ours was destined to differ in one respect from others which I have narrated. I had been through many wild days with Basil Grant, days for the first half of which the sun and the moon seemed to have gone mad. But it had almost invariably happened that towards the end of the day and its adventure things had cleared themselves like the sky after rain, and a luminous and quiet meaning had gradually dawned upon me. But this day's work was destined to end in confusion worse confounded. Before we left that house, ten minutes afterwards, one half-witted touch was added which rolled all our minds in cloud. If Rupert's head had suddenly fallen off on the floor, if wings had begun to sprout out of Greenwood's shoulders, we could scarcely have been more suddenly stricken. And yet of this we had no explanation. We had to go to bed that night with the prodigy and get up next morning with it and let it stand in our memories for weeks and months. As will be seen, it was not until months afterwards that by another accident and in another way it was explained. For the present I only state what happened.

When all five of us went down the kitchen stairs again, Rupert leading, the two hosts bringing up the rear, we found the door of the prison again closed. Throwing it open we found the place again as black as pitch. The old lady, if she was still there, had turned out the gas: she seemed to have a weird preference for sitting in the dark.

Without another word Rupert lit the gas again. The little old lady turned her birdlike head as we all stumbled forward in the strong gaslight. Then, with a quickness that almost made me jump, she sprang up and swept a sort of old-fashioned curtsey or reverence. I looked quickly at Greenwood and Burrows, to whom it was natural to suppose this subservience had been offered. I felt irritated at what was implied in this subservience, and desired to see the faces of the tyrants as they received it. To my surprise they did not seem to have seen it at all: Burrows was paring his nails with a small penknife. Greenwood was at the back of the group and had hardly entered the room. And then an amazing fact became apparent. It was Basil Grant who stood foremost of the group, the golden gaslight lighting up his strong face and figure. His face wore an expression indescribably conscious, with the suspicion of a very grave smile. His head was slightly bent with a restrained bow. It was he who had acknowledged the lady's obeisance. And it was he, beyond any shadow of reasonable doubt, to whom it had really been directed.

'So I hear,' he said, in a kindly yet somehow formal voice, 'I hear, madam, that my friends have been trying to rescue you. But without success.'

'No one, naturally, knows my faults better than you,' answered the lady with a high colour. 'But you have not found me guilty of treachery.'

'I willingly attest it, madam,' replied Basil, in the same level tones, 'and the fact is that I am so much gratified with your exhibition of loyalty that I permit myself the pleasure of exercising some very large discretionary powers. You would not leave this room at the request of these gentlemen. But you know that you can safely leave it at mine.'

The captive made another reverence. 'I have never complained of your injustice,' she said. 'I need scarcely say what I think of your generosity.'

And before our staring eyes could blink she had passed out of the room, Basil holding the door open for her.

He turned to Greenwood with a relapse into joviality. 'This will be a relief to you,' he said.

'Yes, it will,' replied that immovable young gentleman with a face like a sphinx.

We found ourselves outside in the dark blue night, shaken and dazed as if we had fallen into it from some high tower.

'Basil,' said Rupert at last, in a weak voice, 'I always thought you were my brother. But are you a man? I mean – are you only a man?'

'At present,' replied Basil, 'my mere humanity is proved by one of the most unmistakable symbols – hunger. We are too late for the theatre in Sloane Square. But we are not too late for the restaurant. Here comes the green omnibus!' and he had leaped on it before we could speak.

* * *

As I said, it was months after that Rupert Grant suddenly entered my room, swinging a satchel in his hand and with a general air of having jumped over the garden wall, and implored me to go with him upon the latest and wildest of his expeditions. He proposed to himself no less a thing than the discovery of the actual origin, whereabouts, and headquarters of the source of all our joys and sorrows – the Club of Queer Trades. I should expand this story for ever if I explained how ultimately we ran this strange entity to its lair. The process meant a hundred interesting things. The tracking of a member, the bribing of a cabman, the fighting of roughs, the lifting of a paving stone, the finding of a cellar, the finding of a cellar below the cellar, the finding of the subterranean passage, the finding of the Club of Queer Trades.

I have had many strange experiences in my life, but never a stranger one than that I felt when I came out of those rambling, sightless, and seemingly hopeless passages into the sudden splendour of a sumptuous and hospitable dining-room, surrounded upon almost every side by faces that I knew. There was Mr Montmorency, the Arboreal House-Agent, seated between the two brisk young men who were occasionally vicars, and always Professional Detainers. There was Mr P. G. Northover, founder of the Adventure and Romance Agency. There was Professor Chadd, who invented the dancing Language.

As we entered, all the members seemed to sink suddenly into their chairs, and with the very action the vacancy of the presidential seat gaped at us like a missing tooth.

'The president's not here,' said Mr P. G. Northover, turning suddenly to Professor Chadd.

'N – no,' said the philosopher, with more than his ordinary vagueness. 'I can't imagine where he is.'

'Good heavens,' said Mr Montmorency, jumping up, 'I really feel a little nervous. I'll go and see.' And he ran out of the room.

An instant after he ran back again, twittering with a timid ecstasy.

'He's there, gentlemen – he's there all right – he's coming in now,' he cried, and sat down. Rupert and I could hardly help feeling the beginnings of a sort of wonder as to who this person might be who was the first member of this insane brotherhood. Who, we thought indistinctly, could be maddest in this world of madmen: what fantastic was it whose shadow filled all these fantastics with so loyal an expectation?

Suddenly we were answered. The door flew open and the room was filled and shaken with a shout, in the midst of which Basil Grant, smiling and in evening dress, took his seat at the head of the table.

How we ate that dinner I have no idea. In the common way I am a person particularly prone to enjoy the long luxuriance of the club dinner. But on this occasion it seemed a hopeless and endless string of courses. *Hors-d'oeuvre* sardines seemed as big as herrings, soup seemed a sort of ocean, larks were ducks, ducks were ostriches until that dinner was over. The cheese course was maddening. I had often heard of the moon being made of green cheese. That night I thought the green cheese was made of the moon. And all the time Basil Grant went on laughing and eating and drinking, and never threw one glance at us to tell us why he was there, the king of these capering idiots.

At last came the moment which I knew must in some way enlighten us, the time of the club speeches and the club toasts. Basil Grant rose to his feet amid a surge of songs and cheers.

'Gentlemen,' he said, 'it is a custom in this society that the president for the year opens the proceedings not by any general toast of sentiment, but by calling upon each member to give a brief account of his trade. We then drink to that calling and to all who follow it. It is my business, as the senior member, to open by stating my claim to membership of this club. Years ago, gentlemen, I was a judge; I did my best in that capacity to do justice and to administer the law. But it gradually dawned on me that in my work, as it was, I was not touching even the fringe of justice. I was seated in the seat of the mighty, I was robed in scarlet and ermine; nevertheless, I held a small and lowly and futile post. I had to go by a mean rule as much as a postman, and my red and gold was worth no more than his. Daily there passed before me taut and passionate problems, the stringency of which I had to pretend to relieve by silly imprisonments or silly damages, while I knew all the time, by the light of my living common sense, that they would have been far better relieved by a kiss or a thrashing, or a few words of explanation, or a duel, or a tour in the West Highlands. Then, as this grew on me, there grew on me continuously the sense of a mountainous frivolity. Every word said in the court, a whisper or an oath, seemed more connected with life than the words I had to say. Then came the time when I publicly blasphemed the whole bosh, was classed as a madman and melted from public life.'

Something in the atmosphere told me that it was not only Rupert and I who were listening with intensity to this statement.

'Well, I discovered that I could be of no real use. I offered myself privately as a purely moral judge to settle purely moral differences. Before very long these unofficial courts of honour (kept strictly secret) had spread over the whole of society. People were tried before me not for the practical trifles for which nobody cares, such as committing a murder, or keeping a dog without a licence. My criminals were tried for the faults which really make social life impossible. They were tried before me for selfishness, or for an impossible vanity, or for scandalmongering, or for stinginess to guests or dependents. Of course these courts had no sort of real coercive powers. The fulfilment of their punishments rested entirely on the honour of the ladies and gentlemen involved, including the honour of the culprits. But you would be amazed to know how completely our orders were always obeyed. Only lately I had a most pleasing example. A maiden lady in South Kensington whom I had condemned to solitary confinement for being the means of breaking off an engagement through backbiting, absolutely refused to leave her prison, although some well-meaning persons had been inopportune enough to rescue her.'

Rupert Grant was staring at his brother, his mouth fallen agape. So, for the matter of that, I expect, was I. This, then, was the explanation of the old lady's strange discontent and her still stranger content with her lot. She was one of the culprits of his Voluntary Criminal Court. She was one of the clients of his Queer Trade.

We were still dazed when we drank, amid a crash of glasses, the health of Basil's new judiciary. We had only a confused sense of everything having been put right, the sense men will have when they come into the presence of God. We dimly heard Basil say: 'Mr P. G. Northover will now explain the Adventure and Romance Agency.'

And we heard equally dimly Northover beginning the statement he had made long ago to Major Brown. Thus our epic ended where it had begun, like a true cycle.

[illegible] and personal problems, the [illegible], of which Ebert [illegible] by silly [illegible] or silly [illegible]. What I knew at the time [illegible] the [illegible] of my [illegible] common sense, that they would have been far better [illegible] a few words of [illegible] in the [illegible]. Then, as the [illegible], there [illegible] the [illegible] of [illegible] whispers or [illegible] with the [illegible] the words [illegible]. Then came the [illegible] and [illegible] the whole [illegible] and [illegible] from [illegible].

Something in the [illegible] told me that [illegible] and I [illegible] listening [illegible] to the [illegible].

With, I discovered that I [illegible] of [illegible] in a purely moral [illegible] moral differences [illegible] of honour [illegible] the whole [illegible]. [illegible] the [illegible] a murder, or [illegible] without [illegible]. [illegible] were [illegible] and [illegible] make [illegible]. They were [illegible] before me [illegible] for an impossible [illegible] or for [illegible] orders [illegible] of [illegible] the [illegible] of their [illegible] the honour of the [illegible] and [illegible] including the [illegible] would [illegible] to a [illegible]. [illegible] in some [illegible] when I [illegible] of being the [illegible] through the [illegible] had [illegible] enough [illegible].

Rupert [illegible] his mouth [illegible] the [illegible] I [illegible] the [illegible] the [illegible] of the [illegible] Criminal Court. She was one of the [illegible] Queen's Trade.

We [illegible] when [illegible] the [illegible] of Basil [illegible]. We had [illegible] of [illegible] the [illegible] will have [illegible] they [illegible] into the [illegible] of [illegible] Adventure and Romance [illegible].

[illegible] had [illegible] what [illegible] had begun.

THE MAN WHO WAS THURSDAY

The Man Who Was Thursday

A Nightmare

Contents

TO EDMUND CLERIHEW BENTLEY

A cloud was on the mind of men, and wailing went the weather,
Yea, a sick cloud upon the soul when we were boys together.
Science announced nonentity and art admired decay;
The world was old and ended: but you and I were gay;
Round us in antic order crippled vices came –
Lust that had lost its laughter, fear that had lost its shame.
Like the white lock of Whistler, that lit our aimless gloom,
Men showed their own white feather as proudly as a plume.
Life was a fly that faded, and death a drone that stung;
The world was very old indeed when you and I were young.
They twisted even decent sin to shapes not to be named:
Men were ashamed of honour; but we were not ashamed.
Weak if we were and foolish, not thus we failed, not thus;
When that black Baal blocked the heavens he had no hymns from us.
Children we were – our forts of sand were even as weak as we,
High as they went we piled them up to break that bitter sea.
Fools as we were in motley, all jangling and absurd,
When all church bells were silent our cap and bells were heard.

Not all unhelped we held the fort, our tiny flags unfurled;
Some giants laboured in that cloud to lift it from the world.
I find again the book we found, I feel the hour that flings
Far out of fish-shaped Paumanok some cry of cleaner things;
And the Green Carnation withered, as in forest fires that pass,
Roared in the wind of all the world ten million leaves of grass;
Or sane and sweet and sudden as a bird sings in the rain –
Truth out of Tusitala spoke and pleasure out of pain.
Yes, cool and clear and sudden as a bird sings in the grey,
Dunedin to Samoa spoke, and darkness unto day.
But we were young; we lived to see God break their bitter charms.
God and the good Republic come riding back in arms:
We have seen the City of Mansoul, even as it rocked, relieved –
Blessed are they who did not see, but being blind, believed.

This is a tale of those old fears, even of those emptied hells,
And none but you shall understand the true thing that it tells –
Of what colossal gods of shame could cow men and yet crash,
Of what huge devils hid the stars, yet fell at a pistol flash.
The doubts that were so plain to chase, so dreadful to withstand –
Oh, who shall understand but you; yes, who shall understand?
The doubts that drove us through the night as we two talked amain,
And day had broken on the streets ere it broke upon the brain.
Between us, by the peace of God, such truth can now be told;
Yes, there is strength in striking root, and good in growing old.
We have found common things at last, and marriage and a creed,
And I may safely write it now, and you may safely read.

G. K. C.

CHAPTER I

The Two Poets of Saffron Park

The suburb of Saffron Park lay on the sunset side of London, as red and ragged as a cloud of sunset. It was built of a bright brick throughout; its skyline was fantastic, and even its ground plan was wild. It had been the outburst of a speculative builder, faintly tinged with art, who called its architecture sometimes Elizabethan and sometimes Queen Anne, apparently under the impression that the two sovereigns were identical. It was described with some justice as an artistic colony, though it never in any definable way produced any art. But although its pretensions to be an intellectual centre were a little vague, its pretensions to be a pleasant place were quite indisputable. The stranger who looked for the first time at the quaint red houses could only think how very oddly shaped the people must be who could fit in to them. Nor when he met the people was he disappointed in this respect. The place was not only pleasant, but perfect, if once he could regard it not as a deception but rather as a dream. Even if the people were not 'artists', the whole was nevertheless artistic. That young man with the long, auburn hair and the impudent face – that young man was not really a poet; but surely he was a poem. That old gentleman with the wild, white beard and the wild, white hat – that venerable humbug was not really a philosopher; but at least he was the cause of philosophy in others. That scientific gentleman with the bald, egglike head and the bare, birdlike neck had no real right to the airs of science that he assumed. He had not discovered anything new in biology; but what biological creature could he have discovered more singular than himself? Thus, and thus only, the whole place had properly to be regarded; it had to be considered not so much as a workshop for artists, but as a frail but finished work of art. A man who stepped into its social atmosphere felt as if he had stepped into a written comedy.

More especially this attractive unreality fell upon it about nightfall, when the extravagant roofs were dark against the afterglow and the whole insane village seemed as separate as a drifting cloud. This again was more strongly true of the many nights of local festivity, when the little gardens were often illuminated, and the big Chinese lanterns glowed in the dwarfish trees like some fierce and monstrous fruit. And this was strongest of all on one particular evening, still vaguely remembered in the locality, of which the auburn-haired poet was the hero. It was not by any means the only evening of which he was the hero. On many nights those passing by his little back garden might hear his high, didactic voice laying down the law to men and particularly to women. The attitude of women in such cases was indeed one of the paradoxes of the place. Most of the women were of the kind vaguely called emancipated, and professed some protest against male supremacy. Yet these new women would always pay to a man the extravagant compliment which no ordinary woman ever pays to him, that of listening while he is talking. And Mr Lucian Gregory, the red-haired poet, was really (in some sense) a man worth listening to, even if one only laughed at the end of it. He put the old cant of the lawlessness of art and the art of lawlessness with a certain impudent freshness which gave at least a momentary pleasure. He was helped in some degree by the arresting oddity of his appearance, which he worked, as the phrase goes, for all it was worth. His dark red hair parted in the middle was literally like a woman's, and curved into the slow curls of a virgin in a pre-Raphaelite picture. From within this almost saintly oval, however, his face projected suddenly broad and brutal, the chin carried forward with a look of cockney contempt. This combination at once tickled and terrified the nerves of a neurotic population. He seemed like a walking blasphemy, a blend of the angel and the ape.

This particular evening, if it is remembered for nothing else, will be remembered in that place for its strange sunset. It looked like the end of the world. All the heaven seemed covered with a quite vivid and palpable plumage; you could only say that the sky was full of feathers, and of feathers that almost brushed the face. Across the great part of the dome they were grey, with the strangest tints of violet and mauve and an unnatural pink or pale green; but towards the west the whole grew past description, transparent and passionate, and the last red-hot plumes of it covered up the sun like something too good to be seen. The whole was so close about the earth, as to express nothing but a violent secrecy. The very empyrean seemed to be a secret. It expressed that splendid smallness which is the soul of local patriotism. The very sky seemed small.

I say that there are some inhabitants who may remember the evening if only by that oppressive sky. There are others who may remember it because it marked the first appearance in the place of the second poet of Saffron Park. For a long time the red-haired revolutionary had reigned without a rival; it was upon the night of the sunset that his solitude suddenly ended. The new poet, who introduced himself by the name of Gabriel Syme, was a very mild-looking mortal, with a fair, pointed beard and faint, yellow hair. But an impression grew that he was less meek than he looked. He signalised his entrance by differing with the established poet, Gregory, upon the whole nature of poetry. He said that he (Syme) was poet of law, a poet of order; nay, he said he was a poet of respectability. So all the Saffron Parkers looked at him as if he had that moment fallen out of that impossible sky.

In fact, Mr Lucian Gregory, the anarchic poet, connected the two events. 'It may well be,' he said, in his sudden lyrical manner, 'it may well be on such a night of clouds and cruel colours that there is brought forth upon the earth such a portent as a respectable poet. You say you are a poet of law; I say you are a contradiction in terms. I only wonder there were not comets and earthquakes on the night you appeared in this garden.'

The man with the meek blue eyes and the pale, pointed beard endured these thunders with a certain submissive solemnity. The third party of the group, Gregory's sister Rosamond, who had her brother's braids of red hair, but a kindlier face underneath them, laughed with such mixture of admiration and disapproval as she gave commonly to the family oracle.

Gregory resumed in high oratorical good humour.

'An artist is identical with an anarchist,' he cried. 'You might transpose the words anywhere. An anarchist is an artist. The man who throws a bomb is an artist, because he prefers a great moment to everything. He sees how much more valuable is one burst of blazing light, one peal of perfect thunder, than the mere common bodies of a few shapeless policemen. An artist disregards all governments, abolishes all conventions. The poet delights in disorder only. If it were not so, the most poetical thing in the world would be the Underground Railway.'

'So it is,' said Mr Syme.

'Nonsense!' said Gregory, who was very rational when anyone else attempted paradox. 'Why do all the clerks and navvies in the railway trains look so sad and tired, so very sad and tired? I will tell you. It is because they know that the train is going right. It is because they know that whatever place they have taken a ticket for that place they will reach. It is because after they have passed Sloane Square they know that the next station must be Victoria, and nothing but Victoria. Oh, their wild rapture! oh, their eyes like stars and their souls again in Eden, if the next station were unaccountably Baker Street!'

'It is you who are unpoetical,' replied the poet Syme. 'If what you say of clerks is true, they can only be as prosaic as your poetry. The rare, strange thing is to hit the mark; the gross, obvious thing is to miss it. We feel it is epical when man with one wild arrow strikes a distant bird. Is it not also epical when man with one wild engine strikes a distant station? Chaos is dull; because in chaos the train might indeed go anywhere, to Baker Street or to Baghdad. But man is a magician, and his whole magic is in this, that he does say Victoria, and lo! it is Victoria. No, take your books of mere poetry and prose; let me read a time table, with tears of pride. Take your Byron, who commemorates the defeats of man; give me Bradshaw, who commemorates his victories. Give me Bradshaw, I say!'

'Must you go?' enquired Gregory sarcastically.

'I tell you,' went on Syme with passion, 'that every time a train comes in I feel that it has broken past batteries of besiegers, and that man has won a battle against chaos. You say contemptuously that when one has left Sloane Square one must come to Victoria. I say that one might do a thousand things instead, and that whenever I really come there I have the sense of hair-breadth escape. And when I hear the guard shout out the word "Victoria", it is not an unmeaning word. It is to me the cry of a herald announcing conquest. It is to me indeed "Victoria"; it is the victory of Adam.'

Gregory wagged his heavy, red head with a slow and sad smile.

'And even then,' he said, 'we poets always ask the question, "And what is Victoria now that you have got there?" You think Victoria is like the New Jerusalem. We know that the New Jerusalem will only be like Victoria. Yes, the poet will be discontented even in the streets of heaven. The poet is always in revolt.'

'There again,' said Syme irritably, 'what is there poetical about being in revolt? You might as well say that it is poetical to be seasick. Being sick is a revolt. Both being sick and being rebellious may be the wholesome thing on certain desperate occasions; but I'm hanged if I can see why they are poetical. Revolt in the abstract is – revolting. It's mere vomiting.'

The girl winced for a flash at the unpleasant word, but Syme was too hot to heed her.

'It is things going right,' he cried, 'that is poetical! Our digestions, for instance, going sacredly and silently right, that is the foundation of all poetry. Yes, the most poetical thing, more poetical than the flowers, more poetical than the stars – the most poetical thing in the world is not being sick.'

'Really,' said Gregory superciliously, 'the examples you choose – '

'I beg your pardon,' said Syme grimly, 'I thought we had abolished all conventions.'

For the first time a red patch appeared on Gregory's forehead.

'You don't expect me,' he said, 'to revolutionise society on this lawn?'

Syme looked straight into his eyes and smiled sweetly.

'No, I don't,' he said; 'but I suppose that if you were serious about your anarchism, that is exactly what you would do.'

Gregory's big bull's eyes blinked suddenly like those of an angry lion, and one could almost fancy that his red mane rose.

'Don't you think, then,' he said in a dangerous voice, 'that I am serious about my anarchism?'

'I beg your pardon?' said Syme.

'Am I not serious about my anarchism?' cried Gregory, with knotted fists.

'My dear fellow!' said Syme, and strolled away.

With surprise, but with a curious pleasure, he found Rosamond Gregory still in his company.

'Mr Syme,' she said, 'do the people who talk like you and my brother often mean what they say? Do you mean what you say now?'

Syme smiled.

'Do you?' he asked.

'What do you mean?' asked the girl, with grave eyes.

'My dear Miss Gregory,' said Syme gently, 'there are many kinds of sincerity and insincerity. When you say "thank you" for the salt, do you mean what you say? No. When you say "the world is round", do you mean what you say? No. It is true, but you don't mean it. Now, sometimes a man like your brother really finds a thing he does mean. It may be only a half-truth, quarter-truth, tenth-truth; but then he says more than he means – from sheer force of meaning it.'

She was looking at him from under level brows; her face was grave and open, and there had fallen upon it the shadow of that unreasoning responsibility which is at the bottom of the most frivolous woman, the maternal watch which is as old as the world.

'Is he really an anarchist, then?' she asked.

'Only in that sense I speak of,' replied Syme; 'or if you prefer it, in that nonsense.'

She drew her broad brows together and said abruptly: 'He wouldn't really use – bombs or that sort of thing?'

Syme broke into a great laugh that seemed too large for his slight and somewhat dandified figure.

'Good Lord, no!' he said. 'That has to be done anonymously.'

And at that the corners of her own mouth broke into a smile, and she thought with a simultaneous pleasure of Gregory's absurdity and of his safety.

Syme strolled with her to a seat in the corner of the garden, and continued to pour out his opinions. For he was a sincere man, and in spite of his superficial airs and graces, at root a humble one. And it is always the humble man who talks too much; the proud man watches himself too closely. He defended respectability with violence and exaggeration. He grew passionate in his praise of tidiness and propriety. All the time there was a smell of lilac all round him. Once he heard very faintly in some distant street a barrel-organ begin to play, and it seemed to him that his heroic words were moving to a tiny tune from under or beyond the world.

He stared and talked at the girl's red hair and amused face for what seemed to be a few minutes; and then, feeling that the groups in such a place should mix, rose to his feet. To his astonishment, he discovered the whole garden empty. Everyone had gone long ago, and he went himself with a rather hurried apology. He left with a sense of champagne in his head, which he could not afterwards explain. In the wild events which were to follow, this girl had no part at all; he never saw her again until all his tale was over. And yet, in some indescribable way, she kept recurring like a motive in music through all his mad adventures afterwards, and the glory of her strange hair ran like a red thread through those dark and ill-drawn tapestries of the night. For what followed was so improbable, that it might well have been a dream.

When Syme went out into the starlit street, he found it for the moment empty. Then he realised (in some odd way) that the silence was rather a living silence than a dead one. Directly outside the door stood a street lamp, whose gleam gilded the leaves of the tree that bent out over the fence behind him. About a foot from the lamppost stood a figure almost as rigid and motionless as the lamppost itself. The tall hat and long frock-coat were black; the face, in an abrupt shadow, was almost as dark. Only a fringe of fiery hair against the light, and also something aggressive in the attitude, proclaimed that it was the poet Gregory. He had something of the look of a masked bravo waiting sword in hand for his foe.

He made a sort of doubtful salute, which Syme somewhat more formally returned.

'I was waiting for you,' said Gregory. 'Might I have a moment's conversation?'

'Certainly. About what?' asked Syme in a sort of weak wonder.

Gregory struck out with his stick at the lamppost, and then at the tree.

'About *this* and *this*,' he cried; 'about order and anarchy. There is your precious order, that lean, iron lamp, ugly and barren; and there is anarchy, rich, living, reproducing itself – there is anarchy, splendid in green and gold.'

'All the same,' replied Syme patiently, 'just at present you only see the tree by the light of the lamp. I wonder when you would ever see the lamp by the light of the tree.' Then after a pause he said, 'But may I ask if you have been standing out here in the dark only to resume our little argument?'

'No,' cried Gregory, in a voice that rang down the street, 'I did not stand here to resume our argument, but to end it for ever.'

The silence fell again, and Syme, though he understood nothing, listened instinctively for something serious. Gregory began in a smooth voice and with a rather bewildering smile.

'Mr Syme,' he said, 'this evening you succeeded in doing something rather remarkable. You did something to me that no man born of woman has ever succeeded in doing before.'

'Indeed!'

'Now I remember,' resumed Gregory reflectively, 'one other person succeeded in doing it. The captain of a penny steamer (if I remember correctly) at Southend. You have irritated me.'

'I am very sorry,' replied Syme with gravity.

'I am afraid my fury and your insult are too shocking to be wiped out even with an apology,' said Gregory very calmly. 'No duel could wipe it out. If I struck you dead I could not wipe it out. There is only one way by which that insult can be erased, and that way I choose. I am going, at the possible sacrifice of my life and honour, to prove to you that you were wrong in what you said.'

'In what I said?'

'You said I was not serious about being an anarchist.'

'There are degrees of seriousness,' replied Syme. 'I have never doubted that you were perfectly sincere in this sense, that you thought what you said well worth saying, that you thought a paradox might wake men up to a neglected truth.'

Gregory stared at him steadily and painfully.

'And in no other sense,' he asked, 'you think me serious? You think me a *flâneur* who lets fall occasional truths. You do not think that in a deeper, a more deadly sense, I am serious.'

Syme struck his stick violently on the stones of the road.

'Serious!' he cried. 'Good Lord! is this street serious? Are these damned Chinese lanterns serious? Is the whole caboodle serious? One comes here and talks a pack of bosh, and perhaps some sense as well, but I should think very little of a man who didn't keep something in the background of his life that was more serious than all this talking – something more serious, whether it was religion or only drink.'

'Very well,' said Gregory, his face darkening, 'you shall see something more serious than either drink or religion.'

Syme stood waiting with his usual air of mildness until Gregory again opened his lips.

'You spoke just now of having a religion. Is it really true that you have one?'

'Oh,' said Syme with a beaming smile, 'we are all Catholics now.'

'Then may I ask you to swear by whatever gods or saints your religion involves that you will not reveal what I am now going to tell you to any son of Adam, and especially not to the police? Will you swear that! If you will take upon yourself this awful abnegation, if you will consent to burden your soul with a vow that you should never make and a knowledge you should never dream about, I will promise you in return – '

'You will promise me in return?' enquired Syme, as the other paused.

'I will promise you a very entertaining evening.'

Syme suddenly took off his hat.

'Your offer,' he said, 'is far too idiotic to be declined. You say that a poet is always an anarchist. I disagree; but I hope at least that he is always a sportsman. Permit me, here and now, to swear as a Christian, and promise as a good comrade and a fellow-artist, that I will not report anything of this, whatever it is, to the police. And now, in the name of Colney Hatch, what is it?'

'I think,' said Gregory, with placid irrelevancy, 'that we will call a cab.'

He gave two long whistles, and a hansom came rattling down the road. The two got into it in silence. Gregory gave through the trap the address of an obscure public-house on the Chiswick bank of the river. The cab whisked itself away again, and in it these two fantastics quitted their fantastic town.

CHAPTER 2

The Secret of Gabriel Syme

The cab pulled up before a particularly dreary and greasy beer shop, into which Gregory rapidly conducted his companion. They seated themselves in a close and dim sort of bar-parlour, at a stained wooden table with one wooden leg. The room was so small and dark, that very little could be seen of the attendant who was summoned, beyond a vague and dark impression of something bulky and bearded.

'Will you take a little supper?' asked Gregory politely. 'The *pâté de foie gras* is not good here, but I can recommend the game.'

Syme received the remark with stolidity, imagining it to be a joke. Accepting the vein of humour, he said, with a well-bred indifference: 'Oh, bring me some lobster mayonnaise.'

To his indescribable astonishment, the man only said 'Certainly, sir!' and went away apparently to get it.

'What will you drink?' resumed Gregory, with the same careless yet apologetic air. 'I shall only have a *crême de menthe* myself; I have dined. But the champagne can really be trusted. Do let me start you with a half-bottle of Pommery at least?'

'Thank you!' said the motionless Syme. 'You are very good.'

His further attempts at conversation, somewhat disorganised in themselves, were cut short finally as by a thunderbolt by the actual appearance of the lobster. Syme tasted it, and found it particularly good. Then he suddenly began to eat with great rapidity and appetite.

'Excuse me if I enjoy myself rather obviously!' he said to Gregory, smiling. 'I don't often have the luck to have a dream like this. It is new to me for a nightmare to lead to a lobster. It is commonly the other way.'

'You are not asleep, I assure you,' said Gregory. 'You are, on the contrary, close to the most actual and rousing moment of your existence. Ah, here comes your champagne! I admit that there may be a slight disproportion, let us say, between the inner arrangements of this excellent hotel and its simple and unpretentious exterior. But that is all our modesty. We are the most modest men that ever lived on earth.'

'And who are *we*?' asked Syme, emptying his champagne glass.

'It is quite simple,' replied Gregory. '*We* are the serious anarchists, in whom you do not believe.'

'Oh!' said Syme shortly. 'You do yourselves well in drinks.'

'Yes, we are serious about everything,' answered Gregory.

Then after a pause he added: 'If in a few moments this table begins to turn round a little, don't put it down to your inroads into the champagne. I don't wish you to do yourself an injustice.'

'Well, if I am not drunk, I am mad,' replied Syme with perfect calm; 'but I trust I can behave like a gentleman in either condition. May I smoke?'

'Certainly!' said Gregory, producing a cigar-case. 'Try one of mine.'

Syme took the cigar, clipped the end off with a cigar-cutter out of his waistcoat pocket, put it in his mouth, lit it slowly, and let out a long cloud of smoke. It is not a little to his credit that he performed these rites with so much composure, for almost before he had begun them the table at which he sat had begun to revolve, first slowly, and then rapidly, as if at an insane séance.

'You must not mind it,' said Gregory; 'it's a kind of screw.'

'Quite so,' said Syme placidly, 'a kind of screw. How simple that is!'

The next moment the smoke of his cigar, which had been wavering across the room in snaky twists, went straight up as if from a factory chimney, and the two, with their chairs and table, shot down through the floor as if the earth had swallowed them. They went rattling down a kind of roaring chimney as rapidly as a lift cut loose, and they came with an abrupt bump to the bottom. But when Gregory threw open a pair of doors and let in a red subterranean light, Syme was still smoking with one leg thrown over the other, and had not turned a yellow hair.

Gregory led him down a low, vaulted passage, at the end of which was the red light. It was an enormous crimson lantern, nearly as big as a fireplace, fixed over a small but heavy iron door. In the door there was a sort of hatchway or grating, and on this Gregory struck five times. A heavy voice with a foreign accent asked him who he was. To this he gave the more or less unexpected reply, 'Mr Joseph Chamberlain.' The heavy hinges began to move; it was obviously some kind of password.

Inside the doorway the passage gleamed as if it were lined with a network of steel. On a second glance, Syme saw that the glittering pattern was really made up of ranks and ranks of rifles and revolvers, closely packed or interlocked.

'I must ask you to forgive me all these formalities,' said Gregory; 'we have to be very strict here.'

'Oh, don't apologise,' said Syme. 'I know your passion for law and order,' and he stepped into the passage lined with the steel weapons. With his long, fair hair and rather foppish frock-coat, he looked a singularly frail and fanciful figure as he walked down that shining avenue of death.

They passed through several such passages, and came out at last into a queer steel chamber with curved walls, almost spherical in shape, but presenting, with its tiers of benches, something of the appearance of a scientific lecture-theatre. There were no rifles or pistols in this apartment, but round the walls of it were hung more dubious and dreadful shapes, things that looked like the bulbs of iron plants, or the eggs of iron birds. They were bombs, and the very room itself seemed like the inside of a bomb. Syme knocked his cigar ash off against the wall, and went in.

'And now, my dear Mr Syme,' said Gregory, throwing himself in an expansive manner on the bench under the largest bomb, 'now we are quite cosy, so let us talk properly. Now, no human words can give you any notion of why I brought you here. It was one of those quite arbitrary emotions, like jumping off a cliff or falling in love. Suffice it to say that you were an inexpressibly irritating fellow, and, to do you justice, you are still. I would break twenty oaths of secrecy for the pleasure of taking you down a peg. That way you have of lighting a cigar would make a priest break the seal of confession. Well, you have said that you were quite certain I was not a serious anarchist. Does this place strike you as being serious?'

'It does seem to have a moral under all its gaiety,' assented Syme; 'but may I ask you two questions? You need not fear to give me information, because, as you remember, you very wisely extorted from me a promise not to tell the police, a promise I shall certainly keep. So it is in mere curiosity that I make my queries. First of all, what is it really all about? What is it you object to? You want to abolish Government?'

'To abolish God!' said Gregory, opening the eyes of a fanatic. 'We do not only want to upset a few despotisms and police regulations; that sort of anarchism does exist, but it is a mere branch of the Nonconformists. We dig deeper and we blow you higher. We wish to deny all those arbitrary distinctions of vice and virtue, honour and treachery, upon which mere rebels base themselves. The silly sentimentalists of the French Revolution talked of the Rights of Man! We hate Rights as we hate Wrongs. We have abolished Right and Wrong.'

'And Right and Left,' said Syme with a simple eagerness. 'I hope you will abolish them too. They are much more troublesome to me.'

'You spoke of a second question,' snapped Gregory.

'With pleasure,' resumed Syme. 'In all your present acts and surroundings there is a scientific attempt at secrecy. I have an aunt who lived over a shop, but this is the first time I have found people living from preference under a public-house. You have a heavy iron door. You cannot pass it without submitting to the humiliation of calling yourself Mr Chamberlain. You surround yourself with steel instruments which make the place, if I may say so, more impressive than homelike. May I ask why, after taking all this trouble to barricade yourselves in the bowels of the earth, you then parade your whole secret by talking about anarchism to every silly woman in Saffron Park?'

Gregory smiled.

'The answer is simple,' he said. 'I told you I was a serious anarchist, and you did not believe me. Nor do *they* believe me. Unless I took them into this infernal room they would not believe me.'

Syme smoked thoughtfully, and looked at him with interest. Gregory went on.

'The history of the thing might amuse you,' he said. 'When first I became one of the New Anarchists I tried all kinds of respectable disguises. I dressed up as a bishop. I read up all about bishops in our anarchist pamphlets, in *Superstition the Vampire* and *Priests of Prey*. I certainly understood from them that bishops are strange and terrible old men keeping a cruel secret from mankind. I was misinformed. When on my first appearing in episcopal gaiters in a drawing-room I cried out in a voice of thunder, "Down! down! presumptuous human reason!" they found out in some way that I was not a bishop at all. I was nabbed at once. Then I made up as a millionaire; but I defended Capital with so much intelligence that a fool could see that I was quite poor. Then I tried being a major. Now, I am a humanitarian myself, but I have, I hope, enough intellectual breadth to understand the position of those who, like Nietzsche, admire violence – the proud, mad war of Nature and all that, you know. I threw myself into the major. I drew my sword and waved it constantly. I called out "Blood!" abstractedly, like a man calling for wine. I often said, "Let the weak perish; it is the Law." Well, well, it seems majors don't do this. I was nabbed again. At last I went in despair to the President of the Central Anarchist Council, who is the greatest man in Europe.'

'What is his name?' asked Syme.

'You would not know it,' answered Gregory. 'That is his greatness. Caesar and Napoleon put all their genius into being heard of, and they *were* heard of. He puts all his genius into not being heard of, and he is not heard of. But you cannot be for five minutes in the room with him without feeling that Caesar and Napoleon would have been children in his hands.'

He was silent and even pale for a moment, and then resumed: 'But whenever he gives advice it is always something as startling as an epigram, and yet as practical as the Bank of England. I said to him, "What disguise will hide me from the world? What can I find more respectable than bishops and majors?" He looked at me with his large but indecipherable face. "You want a safe disguise, do you? You want a dress which will guarantee you harmless; a dress in which no one would ever look for a bomb?" I nodded. He suddenly lifted his lion's voice. "Why, then, dress up as an *anarchist*, you fool!" he roared so that the room shook. "Nobody will ever expect you to do anything dangerous then." And he turned his broad back on me without another word. I took his advice, and have never regretted it. I preached blood and murder to those women day and night, and – by God! – they would let me wheel their perambulators.'

Syme sat watching him with some respect in his large, blue eyes.

'You took me in,' he said. 'It is really a smart dodge.'

Then after a pause he added: 'What do you call this tremendous president of yours?'

'We generally call him Sunday,' replied Gregory with simplicity. 'You see, there are seven members of the Central Anarchist Council, and they are named after days of the week. He is called Sunday, by some of his admirers Bloody Sunday. It is curious you should mention the matter, because the very night you have dropped in (if I may so express it) is the night on which our London branch, which assembles in this room, has to elect its own deputy to fill a vacancy in the council. The gentleman who has for some time past played, with propriety and general applause, the difficult part of Thursday, has died quite suddenly. Consequently, we have called a meeting this very evening to elect a successor.'

He got to his feet and strolled across the room with a sort of smiling embarrassment.

'I feel somehow as if you were my mother, Syme,' he continued casually. 'I feel that I can confide anything to you, as you have promised to tell nobody. In fact, I will confide to you something that I would not say in so many words to the anarchists who will be coming to the room in about ten minutes. We shall, of course, go through a form of election; but I don't mind telling you that it is practically certain what the result will be.' He looked down for a moment modestly. 'It is almost a settled thing that I am to be Thursday.'

'My dear fellow,' said Syme heartily, 'I congratulate you. A great career!'

Gregory smiled in deprecation, and walked across the room, talking rapidly.

'As a matter of fact, everything is ready for me on this table,' he said, 'and the ceremony will probably be the shortest possible.'

Syme also strolled across to the table, and found lying across it a walking-stick, which turned out on examination to be a sword-stick, a large Colt's revolver, a sandwich case, and a formidable flask of brandy. Over the chair, beside the table, was thrown a heavy-looking cape or cloak.

'I have only to get the form of election finished,' continued Gregory with animation, 'then I snatch up this cloak and stick, stuff these other things into my pocket, step out of a door in this cavern, which opens on the river, where there is a steam-tug already waiting for me, and then – then – oh, the wild joy of being Thursday!' And he clasped his hands.

Syme, who had sat down once more with his usual insolent languor, got to his feet with an unusual air of hesitation.

'Why is it,' he asked vaguely, 'that I think you are quite a decent fellow? Why do I positively like you, Gregory?' He paused a moment, and then added with a sort of fresh curiosity, 'Is it because you are such an ass?'

There was a thoughtful silence again, and then he cried out: 'Well, damn it all! this is the funniest situation I have ever been in in my life, and I am going to act accordingly. Gregory, I gave you a promise before I came into this place. That promise I would keep under red-hot pincers. Would you give me, for my own safety, a little promise of the same kind?'

'A promise?' asked Gregory, wondering.

'Yes,' said Syme very seriously, 'a promise. I swore before God that I would not tell your secret to the police. Will you swear by Humanity, or whatever beastly thing you believe in, that you will not tell my secret to the anarchists?'

'Your secret?' asked the staring Gregory. 'Have you got a secret?'

'Yes,' said Syme, 'I have a secret.' Then after a pause, 'Will you swear?'

Gregory glared at him gravely for a few moments, and then said abruptly: 'You must have bewitched me, but I feel a furious curiosity about you. Yes, I will swear not to tell the anarchists anything you tell me. But look sharp, for they will be here in a couple of minutes.'

Syme rose slowly to his feet and thrust his long, white hands into his long, grey trousers' pockets. Almost as he did so there came five knocks on the outer grating, proclaiming the arrival of the first of the conspirators.

'Well,' said Syme slowly, 'I don't know how to tell you the truth more shortly than by saying that your expedient of dressing up as an aimless poet is not confined to you or your president. We have known the dodge for some time at Scotland Yard.'

Gregory tried to spring up straight, but he swayed thrice.

'What do you say?' he asked in an inhuman voice.

'Yes,' said Syme simply, 'I am a police detective. But I think I hear your friends coming.'

From the doorway there came a murmur of 'Mr Joseph Chamberlain.' It was repeated twice and thrice, and then thirty times, and the crowd of Joseph Chamberlains (a solemn thought) could be heard trampling down the corridor.

CHAPTER 3

The Man Who Was Thursday

Before one of the fresh faces could appear at the doorway, Gregory's stunned surprise had fallen from him. He was beside the table with a bound, and a noise in his throat like a wild beast. He caught up the Colt's revolver and took aim at Syme. Syme did not flinch, but he put up a pale and polite hand.

'Don't be such a silly man,' he said, with the effeminate dignity of a curate. 'Don't you see it's not necessary? Don't you see that we're both in the same boat? Yes, and jolly seasick.'

Gregory could not speak, but he could not fire either, and he looked his question.

'Don't you see we've checkmated each other?' cried Syme. 'I can't tell the police you are an anarchist. You can't tell the anarchists I'm a policeman. I can only watch you, knowing what you are; you can only watch me, knowing what I am. In short, it's a lonely, intellectual duel, my head against yours. I'm a policeman deprived of the help of the police. You, my poor fellow, are an anarchist deprived of the help of that law and organisation which is so essential to anarchy. The one solitary difference is in your favour. You are not surrounded by inquisitive policemen; I am surrounded by inquisitive anarchists. I cannot betray you, but I might betray myself. Come, come! wait and see me betray myself. I shall do it so nicely.'

Gregory put the pistol slowly down, still staring at Syme as if he were a sea-monster.

'I don't believe in immortality,' he said at last, 'but if, after all this, you were to break your word, God would make a hell only for you, to howl in for ever.'

'I shall not break my word,' said Syme sternly, 'nor will you break yours. Here are your friends.'

The mass of the anarchists entered the room heavily, with a slouching and somewhat weary gait; but one little man, with a black beard and glasses – a man somewhat of the type of Mr Tim Healy – detached himself, and bustled forward with some papers in his hand.

'Comrade Gregory,' he said, 'I suppose this man is a delegate?'

Gregory, taken by surprise, looked down and muttered the name of Syme; but Syme replied almost pertly: 'I am glad to see that your gate is well enough guarded to make it hard for anyone to be here who was not a delegate.'

The brow of the little man with the black beard was, however, still contracted with something like suspicion.

'What branch do you represent?' he asked sharply.

'I should hardly call it a branch,' said Syme, laughing; 'I should call it at the very least a root.'

'What do you mean?'

'The fact is,' said Syme serenely, 'the truth is I am a Sabbatarian. I have been specially sent here to see that you show a due observance of Sunday.'

The little man dropped one of his papers, and a flicker of fear went over all the faces of the group. Evidently the awful president, whose name was Sunday, did sometimes send down such irregular ambassadors to such branch meetings.

'Well, comrade,' said the man with the papers after a pause, 'I suppose we'd better give you a seat in the meeting?'

'If you ask my advice as a friend,' said Syme with severe benevolence, 'I think you'd better.'

When Gregory heard the dangerous dialogue end, with a sudden safety for his rival, he rose abruptly and paced the floor in painful thought. He was, indeed, in an agony of diplomacy. It was clear that Syme's inspired impudence was likely to bring him out of all merely accidental dilemmas. Little was to be hoped from them. He could not himself betray Syme, partly from honour, but partly also because, if he betrayed him and for some reason failed to destroy him, the Syme who escaped would be a Syme freed from all obligation of secrecy, a Syme who would simply walk to the nearest police station. After all, it was only one night's discussion, and only one detective who would know of it. He would let out as little as possible of their plans that night, and then let Syme go, and chance it.

He strode across to the group of anarchists, which was already distributing itself along the benches.

'I think it is time we began,' he said; 'the steam-tug is waiting on the river already. I move that Comrade Buttons takes the chair.'

This being approved by a show of hands, the little man with the papers slipped into the presidential seat.

'Comrades,' he began, as sharp as a pistol-shot, 'our meeting tonight is important, though it need not be long. This branch has always had the honour of electing Thursdays for the Central European Council. We have elected many and splendid Thursdays. We all lament the sad decease of the heroic worker who occupied the post until last week. As you know, his services to the cause were considerable. He organised the great dynamite coup of Brighton which, under happier circumstances, ought to have killed everybody on the pier. As you also know, his death was as self-denying as his life, for he died through his faith in a hygienic mixture of chalk and water as a substitute for milk, which beverage he regarded as barbaric, and as involving cruelty to the cow. Cruelty, or anything approaching to cruelty, revolted him always. But it is not to acclaim his virtues that we are met, but for a harder task. It is difficult properly to praise his qualities, but it is more difficult to replace them. Upon you, comrades, it devolves this evening to choose out of the company present the man who shall be Thursday. If any comrade suggests a name I will put it to the vote. If no comrade suggests a name, I can only tell myself that that dear dynamiter, who is gone from us, has carried into the unknowable abysses the last secret of his virtue and his innocence.'

There was a stir of almost inaudible applause, such as is sometimes heard in church. Then a large old man, with a long and venerable white beard, perhaps the only real working-man present, rose lumberingly and said: 'I move that Comrade Gregory be elected Thursday,' and sat lumberingly down again.

'Does anyone second?' asked the chairman.

A little man with a velvet coat and pointed beard seconded.

'Before I put the matter to the vote,' said the chairman, 'I will call on Comrade Gregory to make a statement.'

Gregory rose amid a great rumble of applause. His face was deadly pale, so that by contrast his queer red hair looked almost scarlet. But he was smiling and altogether at ease. He had made up his mind, and he saw his best policy quite plain in front of him like a white road. His best chance was to make a softened and ambiguous speech, such as would leave on the detective's mind the impression that the anarchist brotherhood was a very mild affair after all. He believed in his own literary power, his capacity for suggesting fine shades and picking perfect words. He thought that with care he could succeed, in spite of all the people around him, in conveying an impression of the institution, subtly and delicately false. Syme had once thought that anarchists, under all their bravado, were only playing the fool. Could he not now, in the hour of peril, make Syme think so again?

'Comrades,' began Gregory, in a low but penetrating voice, 'it is not necessary for me to tell you what is my policy, for it is your policy also. Our belief has been slandered, it has been disfigured, it has been utterly confused and concealed, but it has never been altered. Those who talk about anarchism and its dangers go everywhere and anywhere to get their information, except to us, except to the fountain head. They learn about anarchists from sixpenny novels; they learn about anarchists from tradesmen's newspapers; they learn about anarchists from *Ally Sloper's Half-Holiday* and the *Sporting Times*. They never learn about anarchists from anarchists. We have no chance of denying the mountainous slanders which are heaped upon our heads from one end of Europe to another. The man who has always heard that we are walking plagues has never heard our reply. I know that he will not hear it tonight, though my passion were to rend the roof. For it is deep, deep under the earth that the persecuted are permitted to assemble, as the Christians assembled in the Catacombs. But if, by some incredible accident, there were here tonight a man who all his life had thus immensely misunderstood us, I would put this question to him: "When those Christians met in those Catacombs, what sort of moral reputation had they in the streets above? What tales were told of their atrocities by one educated Roman to another? Suppose" (I would say to him), "suppose that we are only repeating that still mysterious paradox of history. Suppose we seem as shocking as the Christians because we are really as harmless as the Christians. Suppose we seem as mad as the Christians because we are really as meek." '

The applause that had greeted the opening sentences had been gradually growing fainter, and at the last word it stopped suddenly. In the abrupt silence, the man with the velvet jacket said, in a high, squeaky voice: 'I'm not meek!'

'Comrade Witherspoon tells us,' resumed Gregory, 'that he is not meek. Ah, how little he knows himself! His words are, indeed, extravagant; his appearance is ferocious, and even (to an ordinary taste) unattractive. But only the eye of a friendship as deep and delicate as mine can perceive the deep foundation of solid meekness which lies at the base of him, too deep even for himself to see. I repeat, we are the true early Christians, only that we come too late. We are simple, as they revere simple – look at Comrade Witherspoon. We are modest, as they were modest – look at me. We are merciful – '

'No, no!' called out Mr Witherspoon with the velvet jacket.

'I say we are merciful,' repeated Gregory furiously, 'as the early Christians were merciful. Yet this did not prevent their being accused of eating human flesh. We do not eat human flesh – '

'Shame!' cried Witherspoon. 'Why not?'

'Comrade Witherspoon,' said Gregory, with a feverish gaiety, 'is anxious to know why nobody eats him (laughter). In our society, at any rate, which loves him sincerely, which is founded upon love – '

'No, no!' said Witherspoon, 'down with love.'

'Which is founded upon love,' repeated Gregory, grinding his teeth, 'there will be no difficulty about the aims which we shall pursue as a body, or which I should pursue were I chosen as the representative of that body. Superbly careless of the slanders that represent us as assassins and enemies of human society, we shall pursue with moral courage and quiet intellectual pressure, the permanent ideals of brotherhood and simplicity.'

Gregory resumed his seat and passed his hand across his forehead. The silence was sudden and awkward, but the chairman rose like an automaton, and said in a colourless voice: 'Does anyone oppose the election of Comrade Gregory?'

The assembly seemed vague and subconsciously disappointed, and Comrade Witherspoon moved restlessly on his seat and muttered in his thick beard. By the sheer rush of routine, however, the motion would have been put and carried. But as the chairman was opening his mouth to put it, Syme sprang to his feet and said in a small and quiet voice: 'Yes, Mr Chairman, I oppose.'

The most effective fact in oratory is an unexpected change in the voice. Mr Gabriel Syme evidently understood oratory. Having said these first formal words in a moderated tone and with a brief simplicity, he made his next word ring and volley in the vault as if one of the guns had gone off.

'Comrades!' he cried, in a voice that made every man jump out of his boots, 'have we come here for this? Do we live underground like rats in order to listen to talk like this? This is talk we might listen to while eating buns at a Sunday School treat. Do we line these walls with weapons and bar that door with death lest anyone should come and hear Comrade Gregory saying to us, "Be good, and you will be happy," "Honesty is the best policy," and "Virtue is its own reward"? There was not a word in Comrade Gregory's address to which a curate could not have listened with pleasure (hear, hear). But I am not a curate (loud cheers), and I did not listen to it with pleasure (renewed cheers). The man who is fitted to make a good curate is not fitted to make a resolute, forcible, and efficient Thursday (hear, hear).

'Comrade Gregory has told us, in only too apologetic a tone, that we are not the enemies of society. But I say that we are the enemies of society, and so much the worse for society. We are the enemies of society, for society is the enemy of humanity, its oldest and its most pitiless enemy (hear, hear). Comrade Gregory has told us (apologetically again) that we are not murderers. There I agree. We are not murderers, we are executioners (cheers).'

Ever since Syme had risen Gregory had sat staring at him, his face idiotic with astonishment. Now in the pause his lips of clay parted, and he said, with an automatic and lifeless distinctness: 'You damnable hypocrite!'

Syme looked straight into those frightful eyes with his own pale blue ones, and said with dignity: 'Comrade Gregory accuses me of hypocrisy. He knows as well as I do that I am keeping all my engagements and doing nothing but my duty. I do not mince words. I do not pretend to. I say that Comrade Gregory is unfit to be Thursday for all his amiable qualities. He is unfit to be Thursday because of his amiable qualities. We do not want the Supreme Council of Anarchy infected with a maudlin mercy (hear, hear). This is no time for ceremonial politeness, neither is it a time for ceremonial modesty. I set myself against Comrade Gregory as I would set myself against all the Governments of Europe, because the anarchist who has given himself to anarchy has forgotten modesty as much as he has forgotten pride (cheers). I am not a man at all. I am a cause (renewed cheers). I set myself against Comrade Gregory as impersonally and as calmly as I should choose one pistol rather than another out of that rack upon the wall; and I say that rather than have Gregory and his milk-and-water methods on the Supreme Council, I would offer myself for election – '

His sentence was drowned in a deafening cataract of applause. The faces, that had grown fiercer and fiercer with approval as his tirade grew more and more uncompromising, were now distorted with grins of anticipation or cloven with delighted cries. At the moment when he announced himself as ready to stand for the post of Thursday, a roar of excitement and assent broke forth, and became uncontrollable, and at the same moment Gregory sprang to his feet, with foam upon his mouth, and shouted against the shouting.

'Stop, you blasted madmen!' he cried, at the top of a voice that tore his throat. 'Stop, you – '

But louder than Gregory's shouting and louder than the roar of the room came the voice of Syme, still speaking in a peal of pitiless thunder: 'I do not go to the council to rebut that slander that calls us murderers; I go to earn it (loud and prolonged cheering). To the priest who says these men are the enemies of religion, to the judge who says these men are the enemies of law, to the fat parliamentarian who says these men are the enemies of order and public decency, to all these I will reply, "You are false kings, but you are true prophets. I am come to destroy you, and to fulfil your prophecies." '

The heavy clamour gradually died away, but before it had ceased Witherspoon had jumped to his feet, his hair and beard all on end, and had said: 'I move, as an amendment, that Comrade Syme be appointed to the post.'

'Stop all this, I tell you!' cried Gregory, with frantic face and hands. 'Stop it, it is all – '

The voice of the chairman clove his speech with a cold accent.

'Does anyone second this amendment?' he said. A tall, tired man, with melancholy eyes and an American chin beard, was observed on the back bench to be slowly rising to his feet. Gregory had been screaming for some time past; now there was a change in his accent, more shocking than any scream. 'I end all this!' he said, in a voice as heavy as stone. 'This man cannot be elected. He is a – '

'Yes,' said Syme, quite motionless, 'what is he?'

Gregory's mouth worked twice without sound; then slowly the blood began to crawl back into his dead face. 'He is a man quite inexperienced in our work,' he said, and sat down abruptly.

Before he had done so, the long, lean man with the American beard was again upon his feet, and was repeating in a high American monotone: 'I beg to second the election of Comrade Syme.'

'The amendment will, as usual, be put first,' said Mr Buttons, the chairman, with mechanical rapidity. 'The question is that Comrade Syme – '

Gregory had again sprung to his feet, panting and passionate.

'Comrades,' he cried out, 'I am not a madman.'

'Oh, oh!' said Mr Witherspoon.

'I am not a madman,' reiterated Gregory, with a frightful sincerity which for a moment staggered the room, 'but I give you a counsel which you can call mad if you like. No, I will not call it a counsel, for I can give you no reason for it. I will call it a command. Call it a mad command, but act upon it. Strike, but hear me! Kill me, but obey me! Do not elect this man.'

Truth is so terrible, even in fetters, that for a moment Syme's slender and insane victory swayed like a reed. But you could not have guessed it from Syme's bleak blue eyes. He merely began: 'Comrade Gregory commands – '

Then the spell was snapped, and one anarchist called out to Gregory: 'Who are you? You are not Sunday'; and another anarchist added in a heavier voice, 'And you are not Thursday.'

'Comrades,' cried Gregory, in a voice like that of a martyr who in an ecstasy of pain has passed beyond pain, 'it is nothing to me whether you detest me as a tyrant or detest me as a slave. If you will not take my command, accept my degradation. I kneel to you. I throw myself at your feet. I implore you. Do not elect this man.'

'Comrade Gregory,' said the chairman after a painful pause, 'this is really not quite dignified.'

For the first time in the proceedings there was for a few seconds a real silence. Then Gregory fell back in his seat, a pale wreck of a man, and the chairman repeated, like a piece of clockwork suddenly started again: 'The question is that Comrade Syme be elected to the post of Thursday on the General Council.'

The roar rose like the sea, the hands rose like a forest, and three minutes afterwards Mr Gabriel Syme, of the Secret Police Service, was elected to the post of Thursday on the General Council of the Anarchists of Europe.

Everyone in the room seemed to feel the tug waiting on the river, the sword-stick and the revolver waiting on the table. The instant the election was ended and irrevocable, and Syme had received the paper proving his election, they all sprang to their feet, and the fiery groups moved and mixed in the room. Syme found himself, somehow or other, face to face with Gregory, who still regarded him with a stare of stunned hatred. They were silent for many minutes.

'You are a devil!' said Gregory at last.

'And you are a gentleman,' said Syme with gravity.

'It was you that entrapped me,' began Gregory, shaking from head to foot, 'entrapped me into – '

'Talk sense,' said Syme shortly. 'Into what sort of devils' parliament have you entrapped me, if it comes to that? You made me swear before I made you. Perhaps we are both doing what we think right. But what we think right is so damned different that there can be nothing between us in the way of concession. There is nothing possible between us but honour and death,' and he pulled the great cloak about his shoulders and picked up the flask from the table.

'The boat is quite ready,' said Mr Buttons, bustling up. 'Be good enough to step this way.'

With a gesture that revealed the shopwalker, he led Syme down a short, iron-bound passage, the still agonised Gregory following feverishly at their heels. At the end of the passage was a door, which Buttons opened sharply, showing a sudden blue and silver picture of the moonlit river, that looked like a scene in a theatre. Close to the opening lay a dark, dwarfish steam-launch, like a baby dragon with one red eye.

Almost in the act of stepping on board, Gabriel Syme turned to the gaping Gregory.

'You have kept your word,' he said gently, with his face in shadow. 'You are a man of honour, and I thank you. You have kept it even down to a small particular. There was one special thing you promised me at the beginning of the affair, and which you have certainly given me by the end of it.'

'What do you mean?' cried the chaotic Gregory. 'What did I promise you?'

'A very entertaining evening,' said Syme, and he made a military salute with the sword-stick as the steamboat slid away.

CHAPTER 4

The Tale of a Detective

Gabriel Syme was not merely a detective who pretended to be a poet; he was really a poet who had become a detective. Nor was his hatred of anarchy hypocritical. He was one of those who are driven early in life into too conservative an attitude by the bewildering folly of most revolutionists. He had not attained it by any tame tradition. His respectability was spontaneous and sudden, a rebellion against rebellion. He came of a family of cranks, in which all the oldest people had all the newest notions. One of his uncles always walked about without a hat, and another had made an unsuccessful attempt to walk about with a hat and nothing else. His father cultivated art and self-realisation; his mother went in for simplicity and hygiene. Hence the child, during his tenderer years, was wholly unacquainted with any drink between the extremes of absinth and cocoa, of both of which he had a healthy dislike. The more his mother preached a more than Puritan abstinence the more did his father expand into a more than pagan latitude; and by the time the former had come to enforcing vegetarianism, the latter had pretty well reached the point of defending cannibalism.

Being surrounded with every conceivable kind of revolt from infancy, Gabriel had to revolt into something, so he revolted into the only thing left – sanity. But there was just enough in him of the blood of these fanatics to make even his protest for common sense a little too fierce to be sensible. His hatred of modern lawlessness had been crowned also by an accident. It happened that he was walking in a side street at the instant of a dynamite outrage. He had been blind and deaf for a moment, and then seen, the smoke clearing, the broken windows and the bleeding faces. After that he went about as usual – quiet, courteous, rather gentle; but there was a spot on his mind that was not sane. He did not regard anarchists, as most of us do, as a handful of morbid men, combining ignorance with intellectualism. He regarded them as a huge and pitiless peril, like a Chinese invasion.

He poured perpetually into newspapers and their wastepaper baskets a torrent of tales, verses and violent articles, warning men of this deluge of barbaric denial. But he seemed to be getting no nearer his enemy, and, what was worse, no nearer a living. As he paced the Thames Embankment, bitterly biting a cheap cigar and brooding on the advance of Anarchy, there was no anarchist with a bomb in his pocket so savage or so solitary as he. Indeed, he always felt that Government stood alone and desperate, with its back to the wall. He was too quixotic to have cared for it otherwise.

He walked on the Embankment once under a dark red sunset. The red river reflected the red sky, and they both reflected his anger. The sky, indeed, was so swarthy, and the light on the river relatively so lurid, that the water almost seemed of fiercer flame than the sunset it mirrored. It looked like a stream of literal fire winding under the vast caverns of a subterranean country.

Syme was shabby in those days. He wore an old-fashioned black chimney-pot hat; he was wrapped in a yet more old-fashioned cloak, black and ragged; and the combination gave him the look of the early villains in Dickens and Bulwer Lytton. Also his yellow beard and hair were more unkempt and leonine than when they appeared long afterwards, cut and pointed, on the lawns of Saffron Park. A long, lean, black cigar, bought in Soho for two-pence, stood out from between his tightened teeth, and altogether he looked a very satisfactory specimen of the anarchists upon whom he had vowed a holy war. Perhaps this was why a policeman on the Embankment spoke to him, and said 'Good-evening.'

Syme, at a crisis of his morbid fears for humanity, seemed stung by the mere stolidity of the automatic official, a mere bulk of blue in the twilight.

'A good evening is it?' he said sharply. 'You fellows would call the end of the world a good evening. Look at that bloody red sun and that bloody river! I tell you that if that were literally human blood, spilt and shining, you would still be standing here as solid as ever, looking out for some poor harmless tramp whom you could move on. You policemen are cruel to the poor, but I could forgive you even your cruelty if it were not for your calm.'

'If we are calm,' replied the policeman, 'it is the calm of organised resistance.'

'Eh?' said Syme, staring.

'The soldier must be calm in the thick of the battle,' pursued the policeman. 'The composure of an army is the anger of a nation.'

'Good God, the Board Schools!' said Syme. 'Is this undenominational education?'

'No,' said the policeman sadly, 'I never had any of those advantages. The Board Schools came after my time. What education I had was very rough and old-fashioned, I am afraid.'

'Where did you have it?' asked Syme, wondering.

'Oh, at Harrow,' said the policeman.

The class sympathies which, false as they are, are the truest things in so many men, broke out of Syme before he could control them.

'But, good Lord, man,' he said, 'you oughtn't to be a policeman!'

The policeman sighed and shook his head.

'I know,' he said solemnly, 'I know I am not worthy.'

'But why did you join the police?' asked Syme with rude curiosity.

'For much the same reason that you abused the police,' replied the other. 'I found that there was a special opening in the service for those whose fears for humanity were concerned rather with the aberrations of the scientific intellect than with the normal and excusable, though excessive, outbreaks of the human will. I trust I make myself clear.'

'If you mean that you make your opinion clear,' said Syme, 'I suppose you do. But as for making yourself clear, it is the last thing you do. How comes a man like you to be talking philosophy in a blue helmet on the Thames Embankment?'

'You have evidently not heard of the latest development in our police system,' replied the other. 'I am not surprised at it. We are keeping it rather dark from the educated class, because that class contains most of our enemies. But you seem to be exactly in the right frame of mind. I think you might almost join us.'

'Join you in what?' asked Syme.

'I will tell you,' said the policeman slowly. 'This is the situation. The head of one of our departments, one of the most celebrated detectives in Europe, has long been of opinion that a purely intellectual conspiracy would soon threaten the very existence of civilisation. He is certain that the scientific and artistic worlds are silently bound in a crusade against the Family and the State. He has, therefore, formed a special corps of policemen, policemen who are also philosophers. It is their business to watch the beginnings of this conspiracy, not merely in a criminal but in a controversial sense. I am a democrat myself, and I am fully aware of the value of the ordinary man in matters of ordinary valour or virtue. But it would obviously be undesirable to employ the common policeman in an investigation which is also a heresy hunt.'

Syme's eyes were bright with a sympathetic curiosity.

'What do you do, then?' he said.

'The work of the philosophical policeman,' replied the man in blue, 'is at once bolder and more subtle than that of the ordinary detective. The ordinary detective goes to pot-houses to arrest thieves; we go to artistic tea-parties to detect pessimists. The ordinary detective discovers from a ledger or a diary that a crime has been committed. We discover from a book of sonnets that a crime will be committed. We have to trace the origin of those dreadful thoughts that drive men on at last to intellectual fanaticism and intellectual crime. We were only just in time to prevent the assassination at Hartlepool, and that was entirely due to the fact that our Mr Wilks (a smart young fellow) thoroughly understood a triolet.'

'Do you mean,' asked Syme, 'that there is really as much connection between crime and the modern intellect as all that?'

'You are not sufficiently democratic,' answered the policeman, 'but you were right when you said just now that our ordinary treatment of the poor criminal was a pretty brutal business. I tell you I am sometimes sick of my trade when I see how perpetually it means merely a war upon the ignorant and the desperate. But this new movement of ours is a very different affair. We deny the snobbish English assumption that the uneducated are the dangerous criminals. We remember the Roman Emperors. We remember the great poisoning princes of the Renaissance. We say that the dangerous criminal is the educated criminal. We say that the most dangerous criminal now is the entirely lawless modern philosopher. Compared to him, burglars and bigamists are essentially moral men; my heart goes out to them. They accept the essential ideal of man; they merely seek it wrongly. Thieves respect property. They merely wish the property to become their property that they may more perfectly respect it. But philosophers dislike property as property; they wish to destroy the very idea of personal possession. Bigamists respect marriage, or they would not go through the highly ceremonial and even ritualistic formality of bigamy. But philosophers despise marriage as marriage.

Murderers respect human life; they merely wish to attain a greater fullness of human life in themselves by the sacrifice of what seems to them to be lesser lives. But philosophers hate life itself, their own as much as other people's.'

Syme struck his hands together.

'How true that is,' he cried. 'I have felt it from my boyhood, but never could state the verbal antithesis. The common criminal is a bad man, but at least he is, as it were, a conditional good man. He says that if only a certain obstacle be removed – say a wealthy uncle – he is then prepared to accept the universe and to praise God. He is a reformer, but not an anarchist. He wishes to cleanse the edifice, but not to destroy it. But the evil philosopher is not trying to alter things, but to annihilate them. Yes, the modern world has retained all those parts of police work which are really oppressive and ignominious, the harrying of the poor, the spying upon the unfortunate. It has given up its more dignified work, the punishment of powerful traitors in the State and powerful heresiarchs in the Church. The moderns say we must not punish heretics. My only doubt is whether we have a right to punish anybody else.'

'But this is absurd!' cried the policeman, clasping his hands with an excitement uncommon in persons of his figure and costume, 'but this is intolerable! I don't know what you're doing, but you're wasting your life. You must, you shall, join our special army against anarchy. Their armies are on our frontiers. Their bolt is ready to fall. A moment more, and you may lose the glory of working with us, perhaps the glory of dying with the last heroes of the world.'

'It is a chance not to be missed, certainly,' assented Syme, 'but still I do not quite understand. I know as well as anybody that the modern world is full of lawless little men and mad little movements. But, beastly as they are, they generally have the one merit of disagreeing with each other. How can you talk of their leading one army or hurling one bolt? What is this anarchy?'

'Do not confuse it,' replied the constable, 'with those chance dynamite outbreaks from Russia or from Ireland, which are really the outbreaks of oppressed, if mistaken, men. This is a vast philosophic movement, consisting of an outer and an inner ring. You might even call the outer ring the laity and the inner ring the priesthood. I prefer to call the outer ring the innocent section, the inner ring the supremely guilty section. The outer ring – the main mass of their supporters – are merely anarchists; that is, men who believe that rules and formulas have destroyed human happiness. They believe that all the evil results of human crime are the results of the system that has called it crime. They do not believe that the crime creates the punishment. They believe that the punishment has created the crime. They believe that if a man seduced seven women he would naturally walk away as blameless as the flowers of spring. They believe that if a man picked a pocket he would naturally feel exquisitely good. These I call the innocent section.'

'Oh!' said Syme.

'Naturally, therefore, these people talk about "a happy time coming"; "the paradise of the future"; "mankind freed from the bondage of vice and the bondage of virtue", and so on. And so also the men of the inner circle speak – the sacred priesthood. They also speak to applauding crowds of the happiness of the future, and of mankind freed at last. But in their mouths' – and the policeman lowered his voice – 'in their mouths these happy phrases have a horrible meaning. They are under no illusions; they are too intellectual to think that man upon this earth can ever be quite free of original sin and the struggle. And they mean death. When they say that mankind shall be free at last, they mean that mankind shall commit suicide. When they talk of a paradise without right or wrong, they mean the grave.

'They have but two objects, to destroy first humanity and then themselves. That is why they throw bombs instead of firing pistols. The innocent rank and file are disappointed because the bomb has not killed the king; but the high-priesthood are happy because it has killed somebody.'

'How can I join you?' asked Syme, with a sort of passion.

'I know for a fact that there is a vacancy at the moment,' said the policeman, 'as I have the honour to be somewhat in the confidence of the chief of whom I have spoken. You should really come and see him. Or rather, I should not say see him, nobody ever sees him; but you can talk to him if you like.'

'Telephone?' enquired Syme, with interest.

'No,' said the policeman placidly, 'he has a fancy for always sitting in a pitch-dark room. He says it makes his thoughts brighter. Do come along.'

Somewhat dazed and considerably excited, Syme allowed himself to be led to a side door in the long row of buildings of Scotland Yard. Almost before he knew what he was doing, he had been passed through the hands of about four intermediate officials, and was suddenly shown into a room, the abrupt blackness of which startled him like a blaze of light. It was not the ordinary darkness, in which forms can be faintly traced; it was like going suddenly stone-blind.

'Are you the new recruit?' asked a heavy voice.

And in some strange way, though there was not the shadow of a shape in the gloom, Syme knew two things: first, that it came from a man of massive stature; and second, that the man had his back to him.

'Are you the new recruit?' said the invisible chief, who seemed to have heard all about it. 'All right. You are engaged.'

Syme, quite swept off his feet, made a feeble fight against this irrevocable phrase.

'I really have no experience,' he began.

'No one has any experience,' said the other, 'of the Battle of Armageddon.'

'But I am really unfit – '

'You are willing, that is enough,' said the unknown.

'Well, really,' said Syme, 'I don't know any profession of which mere willingness is the final test.'

'I do,' said the other – 'martyrs. I am condemning you to death. Good-day.'

Thus it was that when Gabriel Syme came out again into the crimson light of evening, in his shabby black hat and shabby, lawless cloak, he came out a member of the New Detective Corps for the frustration of the great conspiracy. Acting under the advice of his friend the policeman (who was professionally inclined to neatness), he trimmed his hair and beard, bought a good hat, clad himself in an exquisite summer suit of light blue-grey, with a pale yellow flower in the buttonhole, and, in short, became that elegant and rather insupportable person whom Gregory had first encountered in the little garden of Saffron Park. Before he finally left the police premises his friend provided him with a small blue card, on which was written, 'The Last Crusade', and a number, the sign of his official authority. He put this carefully in his upper waistcoat pocket, lit a cigarette, and went forth to track and fight the enemy in all the drawing-rooms of London. Where his adventure ultimately led him we have already seen. At about half-past one on a February night he found himself steaming in a small tug up the silent Thames, armed with sword-stick and revolver, the duly elected Thursday of the Central Council of Anarchists.

When Syme stepped out on to the steam-tug he had a singular sensation of stepping out into something entirely new; not merely into the landscape of a new land, but even into the landscape of a new planet. This was mainly due to the insane yet solid decision of that evening, though partly also to an entire change in the weather and the sky since he entered the little tavern some two hours before. Every trace of the passionate plumage of the cloudy sunset had been swept away, and a naked moon stood in a naked sky. The moon was so strong and full that (by a paradox often to be noticed) it seemed like a weaker sun. It gave, not the sense of bright moonshine, but rather of a dead daylight.

Over the whole landscape lay a luminous and unnatural discolouration, as of that disastrous twilight which Milton spoke of as shed by the sun in eclipse; so that Syme fell easily into his first thought, that he was actually on some other and emptier planet, which circled round some sadder star. But the more he felt this glittering desolation in the moonlit land, the more his own chivalric folly glowed in the night like a great fire. Even the common things he carried with him – the food and the brandy and the loaded pistol –

took on exactly that concrete and material poetry which a child feels when he takes a gun upon a journey or a bun with him to bed. The sword-stick and the brandy-flask, though in themselves only the tools of morbid conspirators, became the expressions of his own more healthy romance. The sword-stick became almost the sword of chivalry, and the brandy the wine of the stirrup-cup. For even the most dehumanised modern fantasies depend on some older and simpler figure; the adventures may be mad, but the adventurer must be sane. The dragon without St George would not even be grotesque. So this inhuman landscape was only imaginative by the presence of a man really human. To Syme's exaggerative mind the bright, bleak houses and terraces by the Thames looked as empty as the mountains of the moon. But even the moon is only poetical because there is a man in the moon.

The tug was worked by two men, and with much toil went comparatively slowly. The clear moon that had lit up Chiswick had gone down by the time that they passed Battersea, and when they came under the enormous bulk of Westminster day had already begun to break. It broke like the splitting of great bars of lead, showing bars of silver; and these had brightened like white fire when the tug, changing its onward course, turned inward to a large landing stage rather beyond Charing Cross.

The great stones of the Embankment seemed equally dark and gigantic as Syme looked up at them. They were big and black against the huge white dawn. They made him feel that he was landing on the colossal steps of some Egyptian palace; and, indeed, the thing suited his mood, for he was, in his own mind, mounting to attack the solid thrones of horrible and heathen kings. He leapt out of the boat on to one slimy step, and stood, a dark and slender figure, amid the enormous masonry. The two men in the tug put her off again and turned up stream. They had never spoken a word.

CHAPTER 5

The Feast of Fear

At first the large stone stair seemed to Syme as deserted as a pyramid; but before he reached the top he had realised that there was a man leaning over the parapet of the Embankment and looking out across the river. As a figure he was quite conventional, clad in a silk hat and frock-coat of the more formal type of fashion; he had a red flower in his buttonhole. As Syme drew nearer to him step by step, he did not even move a hair; and Syme could come close enough to notice even in the dim, pale morning light that his face was long, pale and intellectual, and ended in a small triangular tuft of dark beard at the very point of the chin, all else being clean-shaven. This scrap of hair almost seemed a mere oversight; the rest of the face was of the type that is best shaven – clear-cut, ascetic, and in its way noble. Syme drew closer and closer, noting all this, and still the figure did not stir.

At first an instinct had told Syme that this was the man whom he was meant to meet. Then, seeing that the man made no sign, he had concluded that he was not. And now again he had come back to a certainty that the man had something to do with his mad adventure. For the man remained more still than would have been natural if a stranger had come so close. He was as motionless as a waxwork, and got on the nerves somewhat in the same way. Syme looked again and again at the pale, dignified and delicate face, and the face still looked blankly across the river. Then he took out of his pocket the note from Buttons proving his election, and put it before that sad and beautiful face. Then the man smiled, and his smile was a shock, for it was all on one side, going up in the right cheek and down in the left.

There was nothing, rationally speaking, to scare anyone about this. Many people have this nervous trick of a crooked smile, and in many it is even attractive. But in all Syme's circumstances, with the dark dawn and the deadly errand and the loneliness on the great dripping stones, there was something unnerving in it.

There was the silent river and the silent man, a man of even classic face. And there was the last nightmare touch that his smile suddenly went wrong.

The spasm of smile was instantaneous, and the man's face dropped at once into its harmonious melancholy. He spoke without further explanation or enquiry, like a man speaking to an old colleague.

'If we walk up towards Leicester Square,' he said, 'we shall just be in time for breakfast. Sunday always insists on an early breakfast. Have you had any sleep?'

'No,' said Syme.

'Nor have I,' answered the man in an ordinary tone. 'I shall try to get to bed after breakfast.'

He spoke with casual civility, but in an utterly dead voice that contradicted the fanaticism of his face. It seemed almost as if all friendly words were to him lifeless conveniences, and that his only life was hate. After a pause the man spoke again.

'Of course, the secretary of the branch told you everything that can be told. But the one thing that can never be told is the last notion of the president, for his notions grow like a tropical forest. So in case you don't know, I'd better tell you that he is carrying out his notion of concealing ourselves by not concealing ourselves to the most extraordinary lengths just now. Originally, of course, we met in a cell underground, just as your branch does. Then Sunday made us take a private room at an ordinary restaurant. He said that if you didn't seem to be hiding nobody hunted you out. Well, he is the only man on earth, I know; but sometimes I really think that his huge brain is going a little mad in its old age. For now we flaunt ourselves before the public. We have our breakfast on a balcony – on a balcony, if you please – overlooking Leicester Square.'

'And what do the people say?' asked Syme.

'It's quite simple what they say,' answered his guide. 'They say we are a lot of jolly gentlemen who pretend they are anarchists.'

'It seems to me a very clever idea,' said Syme.

'Clever! God blast your impudence! Clever!' cried out the other in a sudden, shrill voice which was as startling and discordant as his crooked smile. 'When you've seen Sunday for a split second you'll leave off calling him clever.'

With this they emerged out of a narrow street, and saw the early sunlight filling Leicester Square. It will never be known, I suppose, why this square itself should look so alien and in some ways so continental. It will never be known whether it was the foreign look that attracted the foreigners or the foreigners who gave it the foreign look. But on this particular morning the effect seemed singularly bright and clear. Between the open square and the sunlit leaves and the statue and the Saracenic outlines of the Alhambra, it looked the replica of some French or even Spanish public place. And this effect increased in Syme the sensation, which in many shapes he had had through the whole adventure, the eerie sensation of having strayed into a new world. As a fact, he had bought bad cigars round Leicester Square ever since he was a boy. But as he turned that corner, and saw the trees and the Moorish cupolas, he could have sworn that he was turning into an unknown Place de something or other in some foreign town.

At one corner of the square there projected a kind of angle of a prosperous but quiet hotel, the bulk of which belonged to a street behind. In the wall there was one large French window, probably the window of a large coffee-room; and outside this window, almost literally overhanging the square, was a formidably buttressed balcony, big enough to contain a dining-table. In fact, it did contain a dining-table, or more strictly a breakfast-table; and round the breakfast-table, glowing in the sunlight and evident to the street, were a group of noisy and talkative men, all dressed in the insolence of fashion, with white waistcoats and expensive button-holes. Some of their jokes could almost be heard across the square. Then the grave secretary gave his unnatural smile, and Syme knew that this boisterous breakfast party was the secret conclave of the European Dynamiters.

Then, as Syme continued to stare at them, he saw something that he had not seen before. He had not seen it literally because it was too large to see. At the nearest end of the balcony, blocking up a great part of the perspective, was the back of a great mountain of a man. When Syme had seen him, his first thought was that the weight of him must break down the balcony of stone. His vastness did not lie only in the fact that he was abnormally tall and quite incredibly fat. This man was planned enormously in his original proportions, like a statue carved deliberately as colossal. His head, crowned with white hair, as seen from behind looked bigger than a head ought to be. The ears that stood out from it looked larger than human ears. He was enlarged terribly to scale; and this sense of size was so staggering, that when Syme saw him all the other figures seemed quite suddenly to dwindle and become dwarfish. They were still sitting there as before with their flowers and frock-coats, but now it looked as if the big man was entertaining five children to tea.

As Syme and the guide approached the side door of the hotel, a waiter came out smiling with every tooth in his head.

'The gentlemen are up there, sare,' he said. 'They do talk and they do laugh at what they talk. They do say they will throw bombs at ze king.'

And the waiter hurried away with a napkin over his arm, much pleased with the singular frivolity of the gentlemen upstairs.

The two men mounted the stairs in silence.

Syme had never thought of asking whether the monstrous man who almost filled and broke the balcony was the great president of whom the others stood in awe. He knew it was so, with an unaccountable but instantaneous certainty. Syme, indeed, was one of those men who are open to all the more nameless psychological influences in a degree a little dangerous to mental health. Utterly devoid of fear in physical dangers, he was a great deal too sensitive to the smell of spiritual evil. Twice already that night little unmeaning things had peeped out at him almost pruriently, and given him a sense of drawing nearer and nearer to the headquarters of hell. And this sense became overpowering as he drew nearer to the great president.

The form it took was a childish and yet hateful fancy. As he walked across the inner room towards the balcony, the large face of Sunday grew larger and larger; and Syme was gripped with a fear that when he was quite close the face would be too big to be possible, and that he would scream aloud. He remembered that as a child he would not look at the mask of Memnon in the British Museum, because it was a face, and so large.

By an effort, braver than that of leaping over a cliff, he went to an empty seat at the breakfast-table and sat down. The men greeted him with good-humoured raillery as if they had always known him. He sobered himself a little by looking at their conventional coats and solid, shining coffeepot; then he looked again at Sunday. His face was very large, but it was still possible to humanity.

In the presence of the president the whole company looked sufficiently commonplace; nothing about them caught the eye at first, except that by the president's caprice they had been dressed up with a festive respectability, which gave the meal the look of a wedding breakfast. One man indeed stood out at even a superficial glance. He at least was the common or garden dynamiter. He wore, indeed, the high white collar and satin tie that were the uniform of the occasion; but out of this collar there sprang a head quite unmanageable and quite unmistakable, a bewildering bush of brown hair and beard that almost obscured the eyes like those of a Skye terrier. But the eyes did look out of the tangle, and they were the sad eyes of some Russian serf. The effect of this figure was not terrible like that of the president, but it had every diablerie that can come from the utterly grotesque. If out of that stiff tie and collar there had come abruptly the head of a cat or a dog, it could not have been a more idiotic contrast.

The man's name, it seemed, was Gogol; he was a Pole, and in this circle of days he was called Tuesday. His soul and speech were incurably tragic; he could not force himself to play the prosperous and frivolous part demanded of him by President Sunday. And, indeed, when Syme came in the president, with that daring disregard of public suspicion which was his policy, was actually chaffing Gogol upon his inability to assume conventional graces.

'Our friend Tuesday,' said the president in a deep voice at once of quietude and volume, 'our friend Tuesday doesn't seem to grasp the idea. He dresses up like a gentleman, but he seems to be too great a soul to behave like one. He insists on the ways of the stage conspirator. Now if a gentleman goes about London in a top hat and a frock-coat, no one need know that he is an anarchist. But if a gentleman puts on a top hat and a frock-coat, and then goes about on his hands and knees – well, he may attract attention. That's what Brother Gogol does. He goes about on his hands and knees with such inexhaustible diplomacy, that by this time he finds it quite difficult to walk upright.'

'I am not good at goncealment,' said Gogol sulkily, with a thick foreign accent; 'I am not ashamed of the cause.'

'Yes you are, my boy, and so is the cause of you,' said the president good-naturedly. 'You hide as much as anybody; but you can't do it, you see, you're such an ass! You try to combine two inconsistent methods. When a householder finds a man under his bed, he will probably pause to note the circumstance. But if he finds a man under his bed in a top hat, you will agree with me, my dear Tuesday, that he is not likely ever to forget it. Now when you were found under Admiral Biffin's bed –'

'I am not good at deception,' said Tuesday gloomily, flushing.

'Right, my boy, right,' said the president with a ponderous heartiness, 'you aren't good at anything.'

While this stream of conversation continued, Syme was looking more steadily at the men around him. As he did so, he gradually felt all his sense of something spiritually queer return.

He had thought at first that they were all of common stature and costume, with the evident exception of the hairy Gogol. But as he looked at the others, he began to see in each of them exactly what he had seen in the man by the river, a demoniac detail somewhere. That lop-sided laugh, which would suddenly disfigure the fine face of his original guide, was typical of all these types. Each man had something about him, perceived perhaps at the tenth or twentieth glance, which was not normal, and which seemed hardly human. The only metaphor he could think of was this, that they all looked as men of fashion and presence would look, with the additional twist given in a false and curved mirror.

Only the individual examples will express this half-concealed eccentricity. Syme's original cicerone bore the title of Monday; he was the secretary of the council, and his twisted smile was regarded with more terror than anything, except the president's horrible, happy laughter. But now that Syme had more space and light to observe him, there were other touches. His fine face was so emaciated, that Syme thought it must be wasted with some disease; yet somehow the very distress of his dark eyes denied this. It was no physical ill that troubled him. His eyes were alive with intellectual torture, as if pure thought was pain.

He was typical of each of the tribe; each man was subtly and differently wrong. Next to him sat Tuesday, the tousle-headed Gogol, a man more obviously mad. Next was Wednesday, a certain Marquis de St Eustache, a sufficiently characteristic figure. The first few glances found nothing unusual about him, except that he was the only man at table who wore the fashionable clothes as if they were really his own. He had a black French beard cut square and a black English frock-coat cut even squarer. But Syme, sensitive to such things, felt somehow that the man carried a rich atmosphere with him, a rich atmosphere that suffocated. It reminded one irrationally of drowsy odours and of dying lamps in the darker poems of Byron and Poe. With this went a sense of his being clad, not in lighter colours, but in softer materials; his black seemed richer and warmer than the black shades about him, as if it were compounded of profound colour. His black coat looked as if it were only black by being too dense a purple. His black beard looked as if it were only black by being too deep a blue. And in the gloom and thickness of the beard his dark red mouth showed sensual and scornful. Whatever he was he was not a Frenchman; he might be a Jew; he might be something deeper yet in the dark heart of the East. In the bright coloured Persian tiles and pictures showing tyrants hunting, you may see just those almond eyes, those blue-black beards, those cruel, crimson lips.

Then came Syme, and next a very old man, Professor de Worms, who still kept the chair of Friday, though every day it was expected that his death would leave it empty. Save for his intellect, he was in the last dissolution of senile decay. His face was as grey as his long grey beard, his forehead was lifted and fixed finally in a furrow of mild despair. In no other case, not even that of Gogol, did the bridegroom brilliancy of the morning dress express a more painful contrast. For the red flower in his buttonhole showed up against a face that was literally discoloured like lead; the whole hideous effect was as if some drunken dandies had put their clothes upon a corpse. When he rose or sat down, which was with long labour and peril, something worse was expressed than mere weakness, something indefinably connected with the horror of the whole scene. It did not express decrepitude merely, but corruption. Another hateful fancy crossed Syme's quivering mind. He could not help thinking that whenever the man moved a leg or arm might fall off.

Right at the end sat the man called Saturday, the simplest and the most baffling of all. He was a short, square man with a dark, square face clean-shaven, a medical practitioner going by the name of Bull. He had that combination of *savoir-faire* with a sort of well-groomed coarseness which is not uncommon in young doctors. He carried his fine clothes with confidence rather than ease, and he mostly wore a set smile. There was nothing whatever odd about him, except that he wore a pair of dark, almost opaque spectacles. It may have been merely a crescendo of nervous fancy that had gone before, but those black discs were dreadful to Syme; they reminded him of half-remembered ugly tales, of some story about pennies being put on the eyes of the dead. Syme's eye always caught the black glasses and the blind grin. Had the dying professor worn them, or even the pale secretary, they would have been appropriate. But on the younger and grosser man they seemed only an enigma. They took away the key of the face. You could not tell what his smile or his gravity meant. Partly from this, and partly because he had a vulgar virility wanting in most of the others it seemed to Syme that he might be the wickedest of all those wicked men. Syme even had the thought that his eyes might be covered up because they were too frightful to see.

CHAPTER 6

The Exposure

Such were the six men who had sworn to destroy the world. Again and again Syme strove to pull together his common sense in their presence. Sometimes he saw for an instant that these notions were subjective, that he was only looking at ordinary men, one of whom was old, another nervous, another short-sighted. The sense of an unnatural symbolism always settled back on him again. Each figure seemed to be, somehow, on the borderland of things, just as their theory was on the borderland of thought. He knew that each one of these men stood at the extreme end, so to speak, of some wild road of reasoning. He could only fancy, as in some old-world fable, that if a man went westward to the end of the world he would find something – say a tree – that was more or less than a tree, a tree possessed by a spirit; and that if he went east to the end of the world he would find something else that was not wholly itself – a tower, perhaps, of which the very shape was wicked. So these figures seemed to stand up, violent and unaccountable, against an ultimate horizon, visions from the verge. The ends of the earth were closing in.

Talk had been going on steadily as he took in the scene; and not the least of the contrasts of that bewildering breakfast-table was the contrast between the easy and unobtrusive tone of talk and its terrible purport. They were deep in the discussion of an actual and immediate plot. The waiter downstairs had spoken quite correctly when he said that they were talking about bombs and kings. Only three days afterwards the Czar was to meet the President of the French Republic in Paris, and over their bacon and eggs upon their sunny balcony these beaming gentlemen had decided how both should die. Even the instrument was chosen; the black-bearded marquis, it appeared, was to carry the bomb.

Ordinarily speaking, the proximity of this positive and objective crime would have sobered Syme, and cured him of all his merely mystical tremors. He would have thought of nothing but the need of saving at least two human bodies from being ripped in pieces with iron and roaring gas. But the truth was that by this time he had begun to feel a third kind of fear, more piercing and practical than either his moral revulsion or his social responsibility. Very simply, he had no fear to spare for the French President or the Czar; he had begun to fear for himself. Most of the talkers took little heed of him, debating now with their faces closer together, and almost uniformly grave, save when for an instant the smile of the secretary ran aslant across his face as the jagged lightning runs aslant across the sky. But there was one persistent thing which first troubled Syme and at last terrified him. The president was always looking at him, steadily, and with a great and baffling interest. The enormous man was quite quiet, but his blue eyes stood out of his head. And they were always fixed on Syme.

Syme felt moved to spring up and leap over the balcony. When the president's eyes were on him he felt as if he were made of glass. He had hardly the shred of a doubt that in some silent and extraordinary way Sunday had found out that he was a spy. He looked over the edge of the balcony, and saw a policeman, standing abstractedly just beneath, staring at the bright railings and the sunlit trees.

Then there fell upon him the great temptation that was to torment him for many days. In the presence of these powerful and repulsive men, who were the princes of anarchy, he had almost forgotten the frail and fanciful figure of the poet Gregory, the mere aesthete of anarchism. He even thought of him now with an old kindness, as if they had played together when children. But he remembered that he was still tied to Gregory by a great promise. He had promised never to do the very thing that he now felt himself almost in the act of doing. He had promised not to jump over that balcony and speak to that policeman. He took his cold hand off the cold stone balustrade. His soul swayed in a vertigo of moral indecision. He had only to snap the thread of a rash vow made to a villainous society, and all his life could be as open and sunny as the square beneath him. He had, on the other hand, only to keep his antiquated honour, and be delivered inch by inch into the power of this great enemy of mankind, whose very intellect was a torture-chamber. Whenever he looked down into the square he saw the comfortable policeman, a pillar of common sense and common order. Whenever he looked back at the breakfast-table he saw the president still quietly studying him with big, unbearable eyes.

In all the torrent of his thought there were two thoughts that never crossed his mind. First, it never occurred to him to doubt that the president and his council could crush him if he continued to stand alone. The place might be public, the project might seem impossible. But Sunday was not the man who would carry himself thus easily without having, somehow or somewhere, set open his iron trap. Either by anonymous poison or sudden street accident, by hypnotism or by fire from hell, Sunday could certainly strike him. If he defied the man he was probably dead, either struck stiff there in his chair or long afterwards as by an innocent ailment. If he called in the police promptly, arrested everyone, told all, and set against them the whole energy of England, he would probably escape; certainly not otherwise. They were a balconyful of gentlemen overlooking a bright and busy square; but he felt no more safe with them than if they had been a boatful of armed pirates overlooking an empty sea.

There was a second thought that never came to him. It never occurred to him to be spiritually won over to the enemy. Many moderns, inured to a weak worship of intellect and force, might have wavered in their allegiance under this oppression of a great personality. They might have called Sunday the superman. If any such creature be conceivable, he looked, indeed, somewhat like it, with his earth-shaking abstraction, as of a stone statue walking. He might have been called something above man, with his large plans, which were too obvious to be detected, with his large face, which was too frank to be understood. But this was a kind of modern meanness to which Syme could not sink even in his extreme morbidity. Like any man, he was coward enough to fear great force; but he was not quite coward enough to admire it.

The men were eating as they talked, and even in this they were typical. Dr Bull and the marquis ate casually and conventionally of the best things on the table – cold pheasant or Strasbourg pie. But the secretary was a vegetarian, and he spoke earnestly of the projected murder over half a raw tomato and three-quarters of a glass of tepid water. The old professor had such slops as suggested a sickening second childhood. And even in this President Sunday preserved his curious predominance of mere mass. For he ate like twenty men; he ate incredibly, with a frightful freshness of appetite, so that it was like watching a sausage factory. Yet continually, when he had swallowed a dozen crumpets or drunk a quart of coffee, he would be found with his great head on one side staring at Syme.

'I have often wondered,' said the marquis, taking a great bite out of a slice of bread and jam, 'whether it wouldn't be better for me to do it with a knife. Most of the best things have been brought off with a knife. And it would be a new emotion to get a knife into a French President and wriggle it round.'

'You are wrong,' said the secretary, drawing his black brows together. 'The knife was merely the expression of the old personal quarrel with a personal tyrant. Dynamite is not only our best tool, but our best symbol. It is as perfect a symbol of us as is incense of the prayers of the Christians. It expands; it only destroys because it broadens; even so, thought only destroys because it broadens. A man's brain is a bomb,' he cried out, loosening suddenly his strange passion and striking his own skull with violence. 'My brain feels like a bomb, night and day. It must expand! It must expand! A man's brain must expand, if it breaks up the universe.'

'I don't want the universe broken up just yet,' drawled the marquis. 'I want to do a lot of beastly things before I die. I thought of one yesterday in bed.'

'No, if the only end of the thing is nothing,' said Dr Bull with his sphinx-like smile, 'it hardly seems worth doing.'

The old professor was staring at the ceiling with dull eyes.

'Every man knows in his heart,' he said, 'that nothing is worth doing.'

There was a singular silence, and then the secretary said: 'We are wandering, however, from the point. The only question is how Wednesday is to strike the blow. I take it we should all agree with the original notion of a bomb. As to the actual arrangements, I should suggest that tomorrow morning he should go first of all to – '

The speech was broken off short under a vast shadow. President Sunday had risen to his feet, seeming to fill the sky above them.

'Before we discuss that,' he said in a small, quiet voice, 'let us go into a private room. I have something very particular to say.'

Syme stood up before any of the others. The instant of choice had come at last, the pistol was at his head. On the pavement below he could hear the policeman idly stir and stamp, for the morning, though bright, was cold.

A barrel-organ in the street suddenly sprang with a jerk into a jovial tune. Syme stood up taut, as if it had been a bugle before the battle. He found himself filled with a supernatural courage that came from nowhere. That jingling music seemed full of the vivacity, the vulgarity, and the irrational valour of the poor, who in all those unclean streets were all clinging to the decencies and the charities of Christendom. His youthful prank of being a policeman had faded from his mind; he did not think of himself as the representative of the corps of gentlemen turned into fancy constables, or of the old eccentric who lived in the dark room. But he did feel himself as the ambassador of all these common and kindly people in the street, who every day marched into battle to the music of the barrel-organ. And this high pride in being human had lifted him unaccountably to an infinite height above the monstrous men around him. For an instant, at least, he looked down upon all their sprawling eccentricities from the starry pinnacle of the commonplace. He felt towards them all that unconscious and elementary superiority that a brave man feels over powerful beasts or a wise man over powerful errors. He knew that he had neither the intellectual nor the physical strength of President Sunday; but in that moment he minded it no more than the fact that he had not the muscles of a tiger or a horn on his nose like a rhinoceros. All was swallowed up in an ultimate certainty that the president was wrong and that the barrel-organ was right. There clanged in his mind that unanswerable and terrible truism in the song of Roland: '*Païens ont tort et Chrétiens ont droit*,' which in the old nasal French has the clang and groan of great iron. This liberation of his spirit from the load of his weakness went with a quite clear decision to embrace death. If the people of the barrel-organ could keep their old-world obligations, so could he. This very pride in keeping his word was that he was keeping it to miscreants. It was his last triumph over these lunatics to go down into their dark room and die for something that they could not even understand. The barrel-organ seemed to give the marching tune with the energy and the mingled noises of a whole orchestra; and he could hear deep and rolling, under all the trumpets of the pride of life, the drums of the pride of death.

The conspirators were already filing through the open window and into the rooms behind. Syme went last, outwardly calm, but with all his brain and body throbbing with romantic rhythm. The president led them down an irregular side stair, such as might be used by servants, and into a dim, cold, empty room, with a table and benches, like an abandoned boardroom. When they were all in, he closed and locked the door.

The first to speak was Gogol, the irreconcilable, who seemed bursting with inarticulate grievance.

'Zso! Zso!' he cried, with an obscure excitement, his heavy Polish accent becoming almost impenetrable. 'You zay you nod 'ide. You zay you show himselves. It is all nuzzinks. Ven you vant talk importance you run yourselves in a dark box!'

The president seemed to take the foreigner's incoherent satire with entire good humour.

'You can't get hold of it yet, Gogol,' he said in a fatherly way. 'When once they have heard us talking nonsense on that balcony they will not care where we go afterwards. If we had come here first, we should have had the whole staff at the keyhole. You don't seem to know anything about mankind.'

'I die for zem,' cried the Pole in thick excitement, 'and I slay zare oppressors. I care not for these games of gonzealment. I would zmite ze tyrant in ze open square.'

'I see, I see,' said the president, nodding kindly as he seated himself at the top of a long table. 'You die for mankind first, and then you get up and smite their oppressors. So that's all right. And now may I ask you to control your beautiful sentiments, and sit down with the other gentlemen at this table. For the first time this morning something intelligent is going to be said.'

Syme, with the perturbed promptitude he had shown since the original summons, sat down first. Gogol sat down last, grumbling in his brown beard about gombromise. No one except Syme seemed to have any notion of the blow that was about to fall. As for him, he had merely the feeling of a man mounting the scaffold with the intention, at any rate, of making a good speech.

'Comrades,' said the president, suddenly rising, 'we have spun out this farce long enough. I have called you down here to tell you something so simple and shocking that even the waiters upstairs (long inured to our levities) might hear some new seriousness in my voice. Comrades, we were discussing plans and naming places. I propose, before saying anything else, that those plans and places should not be voted by this meeting, but should be left wholly in the control of some one reliable member. I suggest Comrade Saturday, Dr Bull.'

They all stared at him; then they all started in their seats, for the next words, though not loud, had a living and sensational emphasis. Sunday struck the table.

'Not one word more about the plans and places must be said at this meeting. Not one tiny detail more about what we mean to do must be mentioned in this company.'

Sunday had spent his life in astonishing his followers; but it seemed as if he had never really astonished them until now. They all moved feverishly in their seats, except Syme. He sat stiff in his, with his hand in his pocket, and on the handle of his loaded revolver. When the attack on him came he would sell his life dear. He would find out at least if the president was mortal.

Sunday went on smoothly: 'You will probably understand that there is only one possible motive for forbidding free speech at this festival of freedom. Strangers overhearing us matters nothing. They assume that we are joking. But what would matter, even unto death, is this, that there should be one actually among us who is not of us, who knows our grave purpose, but does not share it, who – '

The secretary screamed out suddenly like a woman.

'It can't be!' he cried, leaping. 'There can't – '

The president flapped his large flat hand on the table like the fin of some huge fish.

'Yes,' he said slowly, 'there is a spy in this room. There is a traitor at this table. I will waste no more words. His name – '

Syme half rose from his seat, his finger firm on the trigger.

'His name is Gogol,' said the president. 'He is that hairy humbug over there who pretends to be a Pole.'

Gogol sprang to his feet, a pistol in each hand. With the same flash three men sprang at his throat. Even the professor made an effort to rise. But Syme saw little of the scene, for he was blinded with a beneficent darkness; he had sunk down into his seat shuddering, in a palsy of passionate relief.

CHAPTER 7

The Unaccountable Conduct of Professor de Worms

'Sit down!' said Sunday in a voice that he used once or twice in his life, a voice that made men drop drawn swords.

The three who had risen fell away from Gogol, and that equivocal person himself resumed his seat.

'Well, my man,' said the president briskly, addressing him as one addresses a total stranger, 'will you oblige me by putting your hand in your upper waistcoat pocket and showing me what you have there?'

The alleged Pole was a little pale under his tangle of dark hair, but he put two fingers into the pocket with apparent coolness and pulled out a blue strip of card. When Syme saw it lying on the table, he woke up again to the world outside him. For although the card lay at the other extreme of the table, and he could read nothing of the inscription on it, it bore a startling resemblance to the blue card in his own pocket, the card which had been given to him when he joined the anti-anarchist constabulary.

'Pathetic Slav,' said the president, 'tragic child of Poland, are you prepared in the presence of that card to deny that you are in this company – shall we say *de trop*?'

'Right oh!' said the late Gogol. It made everyone jump to hear a clear, commercial and somewhat cockney voice coming out of that forest of foreign hair. It was irrational, as if a Chinaman had suddenly spoken with a Scotch accent.

'I gather that you fully understand your position,' said Sunday.

'You bet,' answered the Pole. 'I see it's a fair cop. All I say is, I don't believe any Pole could have imitated my accent like I did his.'

'I concede the point,' said Sunday. 'I believe your own accent to be inimitable, though I shall practise it in my bath. Do you mind leaving your beard with your card?'

'Not a bit,' answered Gogol; and with one finger he ripped off the whole of his shaggy head-covering, emerging with thin red hair and a pale, pert face. 'It was hot,' he added.

'I will do you the justice to say,' said Sunday, not without a sort of brutal admiration, 'that you seem to have kept pretty cool under it. Now listen to me. I like you. The consequence is that it would annoy me for just about two and a half minutes if I heard that you had died in torments. Well, if you ever tell the police or any human soul about us, I shall have that two and a half minutes of discomfort. On your discomfort I will not dwell. Good-day. Mind the step.'

The red-haired detective who had masqueraded as Gogol rose to his feet without a word, and walked out of the room with an air of perfect nonchalance. Yet the astonished Syme was able to realise that this ease was suddenly assumed; for there was a slight stumble outside the door, which showed that the departing detective had not minded the step.

'Time is flying,' said the president in his gayest manner, after glancing at his watch, which like everything about him seemed bigger than it ought to be. 'I must go off at once; I have to take the chair at a Humanitarian meeting.'

The secretary turned to him with working eyebrows.

'Would it not be better,' he said a little sharply, 'to discuss further the details of our project, now that the spy has left us?'

'No, I think not,' said the president with a yawn like an unobtrusive earthquake. 'Leave it as it is. Let Saturday settle it. I must be off. Breakfast here next Sunday.'

But the late loud scenes had whipped up the almost naked nerves of the secretary. He was one of those men who are conscientious even in crime.

'I must protest, president, that the thing is irregular,' he said. 'It is a fundamental rule of our society that all plans shall be debated in full council. Of course, I fully appreciate your forethought when in the actual presence of a traitor – '

'Secretary,' said the president seriously, 'if you'd take your head home and boil it for a turnip it might be useful. I can't say. But it might.'

The secretary reared back in a kind of equine anger.

'I really fail to understand – ' he began in high offence.

'That's it, that's it,' said the president, nodding a great many times. 'That's where you fail right enough. You fail to understand. Why, you dancing donkey,' he roared, rising, 'you didn't want to be overheard by a spy, didn't you? How do you know you aren't overheard now?'

And with these words he shouldered his way out of the room, shaking with incomprehensible scorn.

Four of the men left behind gaped after him without any apparent glimmering of his meaning. Syme alone had even a glimmering, and such as it was it froze him to the bone. If the last words of the president meant anything, they meant that he had not after all passed unsuspected. They meant that while Sunday could not denounce him like Gogol, he still could not trust him like the others.

The other four got to their feet grumbling more or less, and betook themselves elsewhere to find lunch, for it was already well past midday. The professor went last, very slowly and painfully. Syme sat long after the rest had gone, revolving his strange position. He had escaped a thunderbolt, but he was still under a cloud. At last he rose and made his way out of the hotel into Leicester Square. The bright, cold day had grown increasingly colder, and when he came out into the street he was surprised by a few flakes of snow. While he still carried the sword-stick and the rest of Gregory's portable luggage, he had thrown the cloak down and left it somewhere, perhaps on the steam-tug, perhaps on the balcony. Hoping, therefore, that the snow-shower might be slight, he stepped back out of the street for a moment and stood up under the doorway of a small and greasy hairdresser's shop, the front window of which was empty, except for a sickly wax lady in evening dress.

Snow, however, began to thicken and fall fast; and Syme, having found one glance at the wax lady quite sufficient to depress his spirits, stared out instead into the white and empty street. He was considerably astonished to see, standing quite still outside the shop and staring into the window, a man. His top hat was loaded with snow like the hat of Father Christmas, the white drift was rising round his boots and ankles; but it seemed as if nothing could tear him away from the contemplation of the colourless wax doll in dirty evening dress. That any human being should stand in such weather looking into such a shop was a matter of sufficient wonder to Syme; but his idle wonder turned suddenly into a personal shock; for he realised that the man standing there was the paralytic old Professor de Worms. It scarcely seemed the place for a person of his years and infirmities.

Syme was ready to believe anything about the perversions of this dehumanised brotherhood; but even he could not believe that the professor had fallen in love with that particular wax lady. He could only suppose that the man's malady (whatever it was) involved some momentary fits of rigidity or trance. He was not inclined, however, to feel in this case any very compassionate concern. On the contrary, he rather congratulated himself that the professor's stroke and his elaborate and limping walk would make it easy to escape from him and leave him miles behind. For Syme thirsted first and last to get clear of the whole poisonous atmosphere, if only for an hour. Then he could collect his thoughts, formulate his policy, and decide finally whether he should or should not keep faith with Gregory.

He strolled away through the dancing snow, turned up two or three streets, down through two or three others, and entered a small Soho restaurant for lunch. He partook reflectively of four small and quaint courses, drank half a bottle of red wine, and ended up over black coffee and a black cigar, still thinking. He had taken his seat in the upper room of the restaurant, which was full of the chink of knives and the chatter of foreigners. He remembered that in old days he had imagined that all these harmless and kindly aliens were anarchists. He shuddered, remembering the real thing. But even the shudder had the delightful shame of escape. The wine, the common food, the familiar place, the faces of natural and talkative men, made him almost feel as if the Council of the Seven Days had been a bad dream; and although he knew it was nevertheless an objective reality, it was at least a distant one. Tall houses and populous streets lay between him and his last sight of the shameful seven; he was free in free London, and drinking wine among the free. With a somewhat easier action, he took his hat and stick and strolled down the stair into the shop below.

When he entered that lower room he stood stricken and rooted to the spot. At a small table, close up to the blank window and the white street of snow, sat the old anarchist professor over a glass of milk, with his lifted livid face and pendent eyelids. For an instant Syme stood as rigid as the stick he leant upon. Then with a gesture as of blind hurry, he brushed past the professor, dashing open the door and slamming it behind him, and stood outside in the snow.

'Can that old corpse be following me?' he asked himself, biting his yellow moustache. 'I stopped too long up in that room, so that even such leaden feet could catch me up. One comfort is, with a little brisk walking I can put a man like that as far away as Timbuctoo. Or am I too fanciful? Was he really following me? Surely Sunday would not be such a fool as to send a lame man?'

He set off at a smart pace, twisting and whirling his stick, in the direction of Covent Garden. As he crossed the great market the snow increased, growing blinding and bewildering as the afternoon began to darken. The snowflakes tormented him like a swarm of silver bees. Getting into his eyes and beard, they added their unremitting futility to his already irritated nerves; and by the time that he had come at a swinging pace to the beginning of Fleet Street, he lost patience, and finding a Sunday teashop, turned into it to take shelter. He ordered another cup of black coffee as an excuse. Scarcely had he done so, when Professor de Worms hobbled heavily into the shop, sat down with difficulty and ordered a glass of milk.

Syme's walking-stick had fallen from his hand with a great clang, which confessed the concealed steel. But the professor did not look round. Syme, who was commonly a cool character, was literally gaping as a rustic gapes at a conjuring trick. He had seen no cab following; he had heard no wheels outside the shop; to all mortal appearances the man had come on foot. But the old man could only walk like a snail, and Syme had walked like the wind. He started up and snatched his stick, half crazy with the contradiction in mere arithmetic, and swung out of the swinging doors, leaving his coffee untasted. An omnibus going to the Bank went rattling by with an unusual rapidity. He had a violent run of a hundred yards to reach it; but he managed to spring, swaying upon the splash-board and, pausing for an instant to pant, he climbed on to the top. When he had been seated for about half a minute, he heard behind him a sort of heavy and asthmatic breathing.

Turning sharply, he saw rising gradually higher and higher up the omnibus steps a top hat soiled and dripping with snow, and under the shadow of its brim the short-sighted face and shaky shoulders of Professor de Worms. He let himself into a seat with characteristic care, and wrapped himself up to the chin in the mackintosh rug.

Every movement of the old man's tottering figure and vague hands, every uncertain gesture and panic-stricken pause, seemed to put it beyond question that he was helpless, that he was in the last imbecility of the body. He moved by inches, he let himself down with little gasps of caution. And yet, unless the philosophical entities called time and space have no vestige even of a practical existence, it appeared quite unquestionable that he had run after the omnibus.

Syme sprang erect upon the rocking car, and after staring wildly at the wintry sky, that grew gloomier every moment, he ran down the steps. He had repressed an elemental impulse to leap over the side.

Too bewildered to look back or to reason, he rushed into one of the little courts at the side of Fleet Street as a rabbit rushes into a hole. He had a vague idea, if this incomprehensible old Jack-in-the-box was really pursuing him, that in that labyrinth of little streets he could soon throw him off the scent. He dived in and out of those crooked lanes, which were more like cracks than thoroughfares; and by the time that he had completed about twenty alternate angles and described an unthinkable polygon, he paused to listen for any sound of pursuit. There was none; there could not in any case have been much, for the little streets were thick with the soundless snow. Somewhere behind Red Lion Court, however, he noticed a place where some energetic citizen had cleared away the snow for a space of about twenty yards, leaving the wet, glistening cobblestones. He thought little of this as he passed it, only plunging into yet another arm of the maze. But when a few hundred yards farther on he stood still again to listen, his heart stood still also, for he heard from that space of rugged stones the clinking crutch and labouring feet of the infernal cripple.

The sky above was loaded with the clouds of snow, leaving London in a darkness and oppression premature for that hour of the evening. On each side of Syme the walls of the alley were blind and featureless; there was no little window or any kind of eye. He felt a new impulse to break out of this hive of houses, and to get once more into the open and lamp-lit street. Yet he rambled and dodged for a long time before he struck the main thoroughfare. When he did so, he struck it much farther up than he had fancied. He came out into what seemed the vast and void of Ludgate Circus, and saw St Paul's Cathedral sitting in the sky.

At first he was startled to find these great roads so empty, as if a pestilence had swept through the city. Then he told himself that some degree of emptiness was natural; first because the snowstorm was even dangerously deep, and secondly because it was Sunday. And at the very word Sunday he bit his lip; the word was henceforth for hire like some indecent pun. Under the white fog of snow high up in the heaven the whole atmosphere of the city was turned to a very queer kind of green twilight, as of men under the sea. The sealed and sullen sunset behind the dark dome of St Paul's had in it smoky and sinister colours – colours of sickly green, dead red or decaying bronze, that were just bright enough to emphasise the solid whiteness of the snow. But right up against these dreary colours rose the black bulk of the cathedral; and upon the top of the cathedral was a random splash and great stain of snow, still clinging as to an Alpine peak. It had fallen accidentally, but just so fallen as to half drape the dome from its very topmost point, and to pick out in perfect silver the great orb and the cross. When Syme saw it he suddenly straightened himself, and made with his sword-stick an involuntary salute.

He knew that that evil figure, his shadow, was creeping quickly or slowly behind him, and he did not care.

It seemed a symbol of human faith and valour that while the skies were darkening that high place of the earth was bright. The devils might have captured heaven, but they had not yet captured the cross. He had a new impulse to tear out the secret of this dancing, jumping and pursuing paralytic; and at the entrance of the court as it opened upon the Circus he turned, stick in hand, to face his pursuer.

Professor de Worms came slowly round the corner of the irregular alley behind him, his unnatural form outlined against a lonely gas-lamp, irresistibly recalling that very imaginative figure in the nursery rhymes, 'the crooked man who went a crooked mile'. He really looked as if he had been twisted out of shape by the tortuous streets he had been threading. He came nearer and nearer, the lamplight shining on his lifted spectacles, his lifted, patient face. Syme waited for him as St George waited for the dragon, as a man waits for a final explanation or for death. And the old professor came right up to him and passed him like a total stranger, without even a blink of his mournful eyelids.

There was something in this silent and unexpected innocence that left Syme in a final fury. The man's colourless face and manner seemed to assert that the whole following had been an accident. Syme was galvanised with an energy that was something between bitterness and a burst of boyish derision. He made a wild gesture as if to knock the old man's hat off, called out something like 'Catch me if you can,' and went racing away across the white, open Circus. Concealment was impossible now; and looking back over his shoulder, he could see the black figure of the old gentleman coming after him with long, swinging strides like a man winning a mile race. But the head upon that bounding body was still pale, grave and professional, like the head of a lecturer upon the body of a harlequin.

This outrageous chase sped across Ludgate Circus, up Ludgate Hill, round St Paul's Cathedral, along Cheapside, Syme remembering all the nightmares he had ever known. Then Syme broke away towards the river, and ended almost down by the docks. He saw the yellow panes of a low, lighted public-house, flung himself into it and ordered beer. It was a foul tavern, sprinkled with foreign sailors, a place where opium might be smoked or knives drawn.

A moment later Professor de Worms entered the place, sat down carefully, and asked for a glass of milk.

CHAPTER 8

The Professor Explains

When Gabriel Syme found himself finally established in a chair, and opposite to him, fixed and final also, the lifted eyebrows and leaden eyelids of the professor, his fears fully returned. This incomprehensible man from the fierce council, after all, had certainly pursued him. If the man had one character as a paralytic and another character as a pursuer, the antithesis might make him more interesting, but scarcely more soothing. It would be a very small comfort that he could not find the professor out, if by some serious accident the professor should find him out. He emptied a whole pewter pot of ale before the professor had touched his milk.

One possibility, however, kept him hopeful and yet helpless. It was just possible that this escapade signified something other than even a slight suspicion of him. Perhaps it was some regular form or sign. Perhaps the foolish scamper was some sort of friendly signal that he ought to have understood. Perhaps it was a ritual. Perhaps the new Thursday was always chased along Cheapside, as the new Lord Mayor is always escorted along it. He was just selecting a tentative enquiry, when the old professor opposite suddenly and simply cut him short. Before Syme could ask the first diplomatic question, the old anarchist had asked suddenly, without any sort of preparation: 'Are you a policeman?'

Whatever else Syme had expected, he had never expected anything so brutal and actual as this. Even his great presence of mind could only manage a reply with an air of rather blundering jocularity.

'A policeman?' he said, laughing vaguely. 'Whatever made you think of a policeman in connection with me?'

'The process was simple enough,' answered the professor patiently. 'I thought you looked like a policeman. I think so now.'

'Did I take a policeman's hat by mistake out of the restaurant?' asked Syme, smiling wildly. 'Have I by any chance got a number stuck on to me somewhere? Have my boots got that watchful look? Why must I be a policeman? Do, do let me be a postman.'

The old professor shook his head with a gravity that gave no hope, but Syme ran on with a feverish irony.

'But perhaps I misunderstood the delicacies of your German philosophy. Perhaps policeman is a relative term. In an evolutionary sense, sir, the ape fades so gradually into the policeman, that I myself can never detect the shade. The monkey is only the policeman that may be. Perhaps a maiden lady on Clapham Common is only the policeman that might have been. I don't mind being the policeman that might have been. I don't mind being anything in German thought.'

'Are you in the police service?' said the old man, ignoring all Syme's improvised and desperate raillery. 'Are you a detective?'

Syme's heart turned to stone, but his face never changed.

'Your suggestion is ridiculous,' he began. 'Why on earth – '

The old man struck his palsied hand passionately on the rickety table, nearly breaking it.

'Did you hear me ask a plain question, you paltering spy?' he shrieked in a high, crazy voice. 'Are you, or are you not, a police detective?'

'No!' answered Syme, like a man standing on the hangman's drop.

'You swear it,' said the old man, leaning across to him, his dead face becoming as it were loathsomely alive. 'You swear it! You swear it! If you swear falsely, will you be damned? Will you be sure that the devil dances at your funeral? Will you see that the nightmare sits on your grave? Will there really be no mistake? You are an anarchist, you are a dynamiter! Above all, you are not in any sense a detective? You are not in the British police?'

He leant his angular elbow far across the table, and put up his large loose hand like a flap to his ear.

'I am not in the British police,' said Syme with insane calm.

Professor de Worms fell back in his chair with a curious air of kindly collapse.

'That's a pity,' he said, 'because I am.'

Syme sprang up straight, sending back the bench behind him with a crash.

'Because you are what?' he said thickly. 'You are what?'

'I am a policeman,' said the professor with his first broad smile, and beaming through his spectacles. 'But as you think policeman only a relative term, of course I have nothing to do with you. I am in the British police force; but as you tell me you are not in the British police force, I can only say that I met you in a dynamiters' club. I suppose I ought to arrest you.' And with these words he laid on the table before Syme an exact facsimile of the blue card which Syme had in his own waistcoat pocket, the symbol of his power from the police.

Syme had for a flash the sensation that the cosmos had turned exactly upside down, that all trees were growing downwards and that all stars were under his feet. Then came slowly the opposite conviction. For the last twenty-four hours the cosmos had really been upside down, but now the capsized universe had come right side up again. This devil from whom he had been fleeing all day was only an elder brother of his own house, who on the other side of the table lay back and laughed at him. He did not for the moment ask any questions of detail; he only knew the happy and silly fact that this shadow, which had pursued him with an intolerable oppression of peril, was only the shadow of a friend trying to catch him up. He knew simultaneously that he was a fool and a free man. For with any recovery from morbidity there must go a certain healthy humiliation. There comes a certain point in such conditions when only three things are possible: first a perpetuation of Satanic pride, secondly tears, and third laughter. Syme's egotism held hard to the first course for a few seconds, and then suddenly adopted the third. Taking his own blue police ticket from his own waistcoat pocket, he tossed it on to the table; then he flung his head back until his spike of yellow beard almost pointed at the ceiling, and shouted with a barbaric laughter.

Even in that close den, perpetually filled with the din of knives, plates, cans, clamorous voices, sudden struggles and stampedes, there was something Homeric in Syme's mirth which made many half-drunken men look round.

'What yer laughing at, guv'nor?' asked one wondering labourer from the docks.

'At myself,' answered Syme, and went off again into the agony of his ecstatic reaction.

'Pull yourself together,' said the professor, 'or you'll get hysterical. Have some more beer. I'll join you.'

'You haven't drunk your milk,' said Syme.

'My milk!' said the other, in tones of withering and unfathomable contempt, 'my milk! Do you think I'd look at the beastly stuff when I'm out of sight of the bloody anarchists? We're all Christians in this room, though perhaps,' he added, glancing around at the reeling crowd, 'not strict ones. Finish my milk? Great blazes! yes, I'll finish it right enough!' and he knocked the tumbler off the table, making a crash of glass and a splash of silver fluid.

Syme was staring at him with a happy curiosity.

'I understand now,' he cried; 'of course, you're not an old man at all.'

'I can't take my face off here,' replied Professor de Worms. 'It's rather an elaborate make-up. As to whether I'm an old man, that's not for me to say. I was thirty-eight last birthday.'

'Yes, but I mean,' said Syme impatiently, 'there's nothing the matter with you.'

'Yes,' answered the other dispassionately. 'I am subject to colds.'

Syme's laughter at all this had about it a wild weakness of relief. He laughed at the idea of the paralytic professor being really a young actor dressed up as if for the footlights. But he felt that he would have laughed as loudly if a pepperpot had fallen over.

The false professor drank and wiped his false beard.

'Did you know,' he asked, 'that that man Gogol was one of us?'

'I? No, I didn't know it,' answered Syme in some surprise. 'But didn't you?'

'I knew no more than the dead,' replied the man who called himself de Worms. 'I thought the president was talking about me, and I rattled in my boots.'

'And I thought he was talking about me,' said Syme, with his rather reckless laughter. 'I had my hand on my revolver all the time.'

'So had I,' said the professor grimly; 'so had Gogol evidently.'

Syme struck the table with an exclamation.

'Why, there were three of us there!' he cried. 'Three out of seven is a fighting number. If we had only known that we were three!'

The face of Professor de Worms darkened, and he did not look up.

'We were three,' he said. 'If we had been three hundred we could still have done nothing.'

'Not if we were three hundred against four?' asked Syme, jeering rather boisterously.

'No,' said the professor with sobriety, 'not if we were three hundred against Sunday.'

And the mere name struck Syme cold and serious; his laughter had died in his heart before it could die on his lips. The face of the unforgettable president sprang into his mind as startling as a coloured photograph, and he remarked this difference between Sunday and all his satellites, that their faces, however fierce or sinister, became gradually blurred by memory like other human faces, whereas Sunday's seemed almost to grow more actual during absence, as if a man's painted portrait should slowly come alive.

They were both silent for a measure of moments, and then Syme's speech came with a rush, like the sudden foaming of champagne.

'Professor,' he cried, 'it is intolerable. Are you afraid of this man?'

The professor lifted his heavy lids, and gazed at Syme with large, wide-open, blue eyes of an almost ethereal honesty.

'Yes, I am,' he said mildly. 'So are you.'

Syme was dumb for an instant. Then he rose to his feet erect, like an insulted man, and thrust the chair away from him.

'Yes,' he said in a voice indescribable, 'you are right. I am afraid of him. Therefore I swear by God that I will seek out this man whom I fear until I find him, and strike him on the mouth. If heaven were his throne and the earth his footstool, I swear that I would pull him down.'

'How?' asked the staring professor. 'Why?'

'Because I am afraid of him,' said Syme; 'and no man should leave in the universe anything of which he is afraid.'

De Worms blinked at him with a sort of blind wonder. He made an effort to speak, but Syme went on in a low voice, but with an undercurrent of inhuman exaltation: 'Who would condescend to strike down the mere things that he does not fear? Who would debase himself to be merely brave, like any common prizefighter? Who would stoop to be fearless – like a tree? Fight the thing that you fear. You remember the old tale of the English clergyman who gave the last rites to the brigand of Sicily, and how on his deathbed the great robber said, "I can give you no money, but I can give you advice for a lifetime: your thumb on the blade, and strike upwards." So I say to you, strike upwards, if you strike at the stars.'

The other looked at the ceiling, one of the tricks of his pose.

'Sunday is a fixed star,' he said.

'You shall see him a falling star,' said Syme, and put on his hat.

The decision of his gesture drew the professor vaguely to his feet.

'Have you any idea,' he asked, with a sort of benevolent bewilderment, 'exactly where you are going?'

'Yes,' replied Syme shortly, 'I am going to prevent this bomb being thrown in Paris.'

'Have you any conception how?' enquired the other.

'No,' said Syme with equal decision.

'You remember, of course,' resumed the soi-disant de Worms, pulling his beard and looking out of the window, 'that when we broke up rather hurriedly the whole arrangements for the atrocity were left in the private hands of the marquis and Dr Bull. The marquis is by this time probably crossing the Channel. But where he will go and what he will do it is doubtful whether even the president knows; certainly we don't know. The only man who does know is Dr Bull.'

'Confound it!' cried Syme. 'And we don't know where he is.'

'Yes,' said the other in his curious, absent-minded way, 'I know where he is myself.'

'Will you tell me?' asked Syme with eager eyes.

'I will take you there,' said the professor, and took down his own hat from a peg.

Syme stood looking at him with a sort of rigid excitement.

'What do you mean?' he asked sharply. 'Will you join me? Will you take the risk?'

'Young man,' said the professor pleasantly, 'I am amused to observe that you think I am a coward. As to that I will say only one word, and that shall be entirely in the manner of your own philosophical rhetoric. You think that it is possible to pull down the president. I know that it is impossible, and I am going to try it,' and opening the tavern door, which let in a blast of bitter air, they went out together into the dark streets by the docks.

Most of the snow was melted or trampled to mud, but here and there a clot of it still showed grey rather than white in the gloom. The small streets were sloppy and full of pools, which reflected the flaming lamps irregularly, and by accident, like fragments of some other and fallen world. Syme felt almost dazed as he stepped through this growing confusion of lights and shadows; but his companion walked on with a certain briskness, towards where, at the end of the street, an inch or two of the lamp-lit river looked like a bar of flame.

'Where are you going?' Syme enquired.

'Just now,' answered the professor, 'I am going just round the corner to see whether Dr Bull has gone to bed. He is hygienic, and retires early.'

'Dr Bull!' exclaimed Syme. 'Does he live round the corner?'

'No,' answered his friend. 'As a matter of fact he lives some way off, on the other side of the river, but we can tell from here whether he has gone to bed.'

Turning the corner as he spoke, and facing the dim river, flecked with flame, he pointed with his stick to the other bank. On the Surrey side at this point there ran out into the Thames, seeming almost to overhang it, a bulk and cluster of those tall tenements, dotted with lighted windows, and rising like factory chimneys to an almost insane height. Their special poise and position made one block of buildings especially look like a Tower of Babel with a hundred eyes. Syme had never seen any of the sky-scraping buildings in America, so he could only think of the buildings in a dream.

Even as he stared, the highest light in this innumerably lighted turret abruptly went out, as if this black Argus had winked at him with one of his innumerable eyes.

Professor de Worms swung round on his heel, and struck his stick against his boot.

'We are too late,' he said, 'the hygienic doctor has gone to bed.'

'What do you mean?' asked Syme. 'Does he live over there, then?'

'Yes,' said de Worms, 'behind that particular window which you can't see. Come along and get some dinner. We must call on him tomorrow morning.'

Without further parley, he led the way through several byways until they came out into the flare and clamour of the East India Dock Road. The professor, who seemed to know his way about the neighbourhood, proceeded to a place where the line of lighted shops fell back into a sort of abrupt twilight and quiet, in which an old white inn, all out of repair, stood back some twenty feet from the road.

'You can find good English inns left by accident everywhere, like fossils,' explained the professor. 'I once found a decent place in the West End.'

'I suppose,' said Syme, smiling, 'that this is the corresponding decent place in the East End?'

'It is,' said the professor reverently, and went in.

In that place they dined and slept, both very thoroughly. The beans and bacon, which these unaccountable people cooked well, the astonishing emergence of Burgundy from their cellars, crowned Syme's sense of a new comradeship and comfort. Through all this ordeal his root horror had been isolation, and there are no words to express the abyss between isolation and having one ally. It may be conceded to the mathematicians that four is twice two. But two is not twice one; two is two thousand times one. That is why, in spite of a hundred disadvantages, the world will always return to monogamy.

Syme was able to pour out for the first time the whole of his outrageous tale, from the time when Gregory had taken him to the little tavern by the river. He did it idly and amply, in a luxuriant monologue, as a man speaks with very old friends. On his side, also, the man who had impersonated Professor de Worms was not less communicative. His own story was almost as silly as Syme's.

'That's a good get-up of yours,' said Syme, draining a glass of Mâcon; 'a lot better than old Gogol's. Even at the start I thought he was a bit too hairy.'

'A difference of artistic theory,' replied the professor pensively. 'Gogol was an idealist. He made up as the abstract or platonic ideal of an anarchist. But I am a realist. I am a portrait painter. But, indeed, to say that I am a portrait painter is an inadequate expression. I am a portrait.'

'I don't understand you,' said Syme.

'I am a portrait,' repeated the professor. 'I am a portrait of the celebrated Professor de Worms, who is, I believe, in Naples.'

'You mean you are made up like him,' said Syme. 'But doesn't he know that you are taking his nose in vain?'

'He knows it right enough,' replied his friend cheerfully.

'Then why doesn't he denounce you?'

'I have denounced him,' answered the professor.

'Do explain yourself,' said Syme.

'With pleasure, if you don't mind hearing my story,' replied the eminent foreign philosopher. 'I am by profession an actor, and my name is Wilks. When I was on the stage I mixed with all sorts of Bohemian and blackguard company. Sometimes I touched the edge of the turf, sometimes the riff-raff of the arts, and occasionally the political refugee. In some den of exiled dreamers I was introduced to the great German Nihilist philosopher, Professor de Worms. I did not gather much about him beyond his appearance, which was very disgusting, and which I studied carefully. I understood that he had proved that the destructive principle in the universe was God; hence he insisted on the need for a furious and incessant energy, rending all things in pieces. Energy, he said, was the All. He was lame, shortsighted, and partially paralytic. When I met him I was in a frivolous mood, and I disliked him so much that I resolved to imitate him. If I had been a draughtsman I would have drawn a caricature. I was only an actor, I could only act a caricature. I made myself up into what was meant for a wild exaggeration of the old professor's dirty old self. When I went into the room full of his supporters I expected to be received with a roar of laughter, or (if they were too far gone) with a roar of indignation at the insult. I cannot describe the surprise I felt when my entrance was received with a respectful silence, followed (when I had first opened my lips) with a murmur of admiration. The curse of the perfect artist had fallen upon me. I had been too subtle, I had been too true. They thought I really was the great Nihilist professor. I was a healthy-minded young man at the time, and I confess that it was a blow. Before I could fully recover, however, two or three of these admirers ran up to me radiating indignation, and told me that a public insult had been put upon me in the next room. I enquired its nature. It seemed that an impertinent fellow had dressed himself up as a preposterous parody of myself. I had drunk more champagne than was good for me, and in a flash of folly I decided to see the situation through. Consequently it was to meet the glare of the company and my own lifted eyebrows and freezing eyes that the real professor came into the room.

'I need hardly say there was a collision. The pessimists all round me looked anxiously from one professor to the other professor to see which was really the more feeble. But I won. An old man in poor health, like my rival, could not be expected to be so impressively feeble as a young actor in the prime of life. You see, he really had paralysis, and working within this definite limitation, he couldn't be so jolly paralytic as I was. Then he tried to blast my claims intellectually. I countered that by a very simple dodge. Whenever he said something that nobody but he could understand, I replied with something which I could not even understand myself. "I don't fancy," he said, "that you could have worked out the principle that evolution is only negation, since there inheres in it the introduction of lacuna, which are an essential of differentiation." I replied quite scornfully, "You read all that up in Pinckwerts; the notion that involution functioned eugenically was exposed long ago by Glumpe." It is unnecessary for me to say that there never were such people as Pinckwerts and Glumpe. But the people all round (rather to my surprise) seemed to remember them quite well, and the professor, finding that the learned and mysterious method left him rather at the mercy of an enemy slightly deficient in scruples, fell back upon a more popular form of wit. "I see," he sneered, "you prevail like the false pig in Aesop." "And you fail," I answered, smiling, "like the hedgehog in Montaigne." Need I say that there is no hedgehog in Montaigne? "Your claptrap comes off," he said; "so would your beard." I had no intelligent answer to this, which was quite true and rather witty. But I laughed heartily, answered, "Like the Pantheist's boots," at random, and turned on my heel with all the honours of victory. The real professor was thrown out, but not with violence, though one man tried very patiently to pull off his nose. He is now, I believe, received everywhere in Europe as a delightful impostor. His apparent earnestness and anger, you see, make him all the more entertaining.'

'Well,' said Syme, 'I can understand your putting on his dirty old beard for a night's practical joke, but I don't understand your never taking it off again.'

'That is the rest of the story,' said the impersonator. 'When I myself left the company, followed by reverent applause, I went limping down the dark street, hoping that I should soon be far enough away to be able to walk like a human being. To my astonishment, as I was turning the corner, I felt a touch on the shoulder, and turning, found myself under the shadow of an enormous policeman. He told me I was wanted. I struck a sort of paralytic attitude, and cried in a high German accent, "Yes, I am wanted – by the oppressed of the world. You are arresting me on the charge of being the great anarchist, Professor de Worms." The policeman impassively consulted a paper in his hand. "No, sir," he said civilly, "at least, not exactly, sir. I am arresting you on the charge of not being the celebrated anarchist, Professor de Worms." This charge, if it was criminal at all, was certainly the lighter of the two, and I went along with the man, doubtful, but not greatly dismayed. I was shown into a number of rooms, and eventually into the presence of a police officer, who explained that a serious campaign had been opened against the centres of anarchy, and that this, my successful masquerade, might be of considerable value to the public safety. He offered me a good salary and this little blue card. Though our conversation was short, he struck me as a man of very massive common sense and humour; but I cannot tell you much about him personally, because – '

Syme laid down his knife and fork.

'I know,' he said, 'because you talked to him in a dark room.'

Professor de Worms nodded and drained his glass.

CHAPTER 9

The Man in Spectacles

'Burgundy is a jolly thing,' said the professor sadly, as he set his glass down.

'You don't look as if it were,' said Syme; 'you drink it as if it were medicine.'

'You must excuse my manner,' said the professor dismally, 'my position is rather a curious one. Inside I am really bursting with boyish merriment; but I acted the paralytic professor so well, that now I can't leave off. So that when I am among friends, and have no need at all to disguise myself, I still can't help speaking slow and wrinkling my forehead – just as if it were my forehead. I can be quite happy, you understand, but only in a paralytic sort of way. The most buoyant exclamations leap up in my heart, but they come out of my mouth quite different. You should hear me say, "Buck up, old cock!" It would bring tears to your eyes.'

'It does,' said Syme; 'but I cannot help thinking that apart from all that you are really a bit worried.'

The professor started a little and looked at him steadily.

'You are a very clever fellow,' he said, 'it is a pleasure to work with you. Yes, I have rather a heavy cloud in my head. There is a great problem to face,' and he sank his bald brow in his two hands.

Then he said in a low voice: 'Can you play the piano?'

'Yes,' said Syme in simple wonder, 'I'm supposed to have a good touch.'

Then, as the other did not speak, he added: 'I trust the great cloud is lifted.'

After a long silence, the professor said out of the cavernous shadow of his hands: 'It would have done just as well if you could work a typewriter.'

'Thank you,' said Syme, 'you flatter me.'

'Listen to me,' said the other, 'and remember whom we have to see tomorrow. You and I are going tomorrow to attempt something which is very much more dangerous than trying to steal the Crown Jewels out of the Tower. We are trying to steal a secret from a very sharp, very strong, and very wicked man. I believe there is no man, except the president, of course, who is so seriously startling and formidable as that little grinning fellow in goggles. He has not perhaps the white-hot enthusiasm unto death, the mad martyrdom for anarchy, which marks the secretary. But then that very fanaticism in the secretary has a human pathos, and is almost a redeeming trait. But the little doctor has a brutal sanity that is more shocking than the secretary's disease. Don't you notice his detestable virility and vitality? He bounces like an india-rubber ball. Depend on it, Sunday was not asleep (I wonder if he ever sleeps?) when he locked up all the plans of this outrage in the round, black head of Dr Bull.'

'And you think,' said Syme, 'that this unique monster will be soothed if I play the piano to him?'

'Don't be an ass,' said his mentor. 'I mentioned the piano because it gives one quick and independent fingers. Syme, if we are to go through this interview and come out sane or alive, we must have some code of signals between us that this brute will not see. I have made a rough alphabetical cypher corresponding to the five fingers – like this, see,' and he rippled with his fingers on the wooden table – 'B A D, bad, a word we may frequently require.'

Syme poured himself out another glass of wine, and began to study the scheme. He was abnormally quick with his brains at puzzles, and with his hands at conjuring, and it did not take him long to learn how he might convey simple messages by what would seem to be idle taps upon a table or knee. But wine and companionship had always the effect of inspiring him to a farcical ingenuity, and the professor soon found himself struggling with the too vast energy of the new language, as it passed through the heated brain of Syme.

'We must have several word-signs,' said Syme seriously – 'words that we are likely to want, fine shades of meaning. My favourite word is "coeval". What's yours?'

'Do stop playing the goat,' said the professor plaintively. 'You don't know how serious this is.'

' "Lush" too,' said Syme, shaking his head sagaciously, 'we must have "lush" – word applied to grass, don't you know?'

'Do you imagine,' asked the professor furiously, 'that we are going to talk to Dr Bull about grass?'

'There are several ways in which the subject could be approached,' said Syme reflectively, 'and the word introduced without appearing forced. We might say, "Dr Bull, as a revolutionist, you remember that a tyrant once advised us to eat grass; and indeed many of us, looking on the fresh lush grass of summer – " '

'Do you understand,' said the other, 'that this is a tragedy?'

'Perfectly,' replied Syme; 'always be comic in a tragedy. What the deuce else can you do? I wish this language of yours had a wider scope. I suppose we could not extend it from the fingers to the toes? That would involve pulling off our boots and socks during the conversation, which however unobtrusively performed – '

'Syme,' said his friend with a stern simplicity, 'go to bed!'

Syme, however, sat up in bed for a considerable time mastering the new code. He was awakened next morning while the east was still sealed with darkness, and found his grey-bearded ally standing like a ghost beside his bed.

Syme sat up in bed blinking; then slowly collected his thoughts, threw off the bedclothes, and stood up. It seemed to him in some curious way that all the safety and sociability of the night before fell with the bedclothes off him, and he stood up in an air of cold danger. He still felt an entire trust and loyalty towards his companion; but it was the trust between two men going to the scaffold.

'Well,' said Syme with a forced cheerfulness as he pulled on his trousers, 'I dreamt of that alphabet of yours. Did it take you long to make it up?'

The professor made no answer, but gazed in front of him with eyes the colour of a wintry sea; so Syme repeated his question.

'I say, did it take you long to invent all this? I'm considered good at these things, and it was a good hour's grind. Did you learn it all on the spot?'

The professor was silent; his eyes were wide open, and he wore a fixed but very small smile.

'How long did it take you?'

The professor did not move.

'Confound you, can't you answer?' called out Syme, in a sudden anger that had something like fear underneath. Whether or no the professor could answer, he did not.

Syme stood staring back at the stiff face like parchment and the blank, blue eyes. His first thought was that the professor had gone mad, but his second thought was more frightful. After all, what did he know about this queer creature whom he had heedlessly accepted as a friend? What did he know, except that the man had been at the anarchist breakfast and had told him a ridiculous tale? How improbable it was that there should be another friend there beside Gogol! Was this man's silence a sensational way of declaring war? Was this adamantine stare after all only the awful sneer of some threefold traitor, who had turned for the last time? He stood and strained his ears in this heartless silence. He almost fancied he could hear dynamiters come to capture him shifting softly in the corridor outside.

Then his eye strayed downwards, and he burst out laughing. Though the professor himself stood there as voiceless as a statue, his five dumb fingers were dancing alive upon the dead table. Syme watched the twinkling movements of the talking hand, and read clearly the message: 'I will only talk like this. We must get used to it.'

He rapped out the answer with the impatience of relief: 'All right. Let's get out to breakfast.'

They took their hats and sticks in silence; but as Syme took his sword-stick, he held it hard.

They paused for a few minutes only to stuff down coffee and coarse thick sandwiches at a coffee stall, and then made their way across the river, which under the grey and growing light looked as desolate as Acheron. They reached the bottom of the huge block of buildings which they had seen from across the river, and began in silence to mount the naked and numberless stone steps, only pausing now and then to make short remarks on the rail of the banister. At about every other flight they passed a window; each window showed them a pale and tragic dawn lifting itself laboriously over London. From each the innumerable roofs of slate looked like the leaden surges of a grey, troubled sea after rain. Syme was increasingly conscious that his new adventure had somehow a quality of cold sanity worse than the wild adventures of the past. Last night, for instance, the tall tenements had seemed to him like a tower in a dream. As he now went up the weary and perpetual steps, he was daunted and bewildered by their almost infinite series. But it was not the hot horror of a dream or of anything that might be exaggeration or delusion. Their infinity was more like the empty infinity of arithmetic, something unthinkable, yet necessary to thought. Or it was like the stunning statements of astronomy about the distance of the fixed stars. He was ascending the house of reason, a thing more hideous than unreason itself.

By the time they reached Dr Bull's landing, a last window showed them a harsh, white dawn edged with banks of a kind of coarse red, more like red clay than red cloud. And when they entered Dr Bull's bare garret it was full of light.

Syme had been haunted by a half historic memory in connection with these empty rooms and that austere daybreak. The moment he saw the garret and Dr Bull sitting writing at a table, he remembered what the memory was – the French Revolution. There should have been the black outline of a guillotine against that heavy red and white of the morning. Dr Bull was in his white shirt and black breeches only; his cropped, dark head might well have just come out of its wig; he might have been Marat or a more slipshod Robespierre.

Yet when he was seen properly, the French fancy fell away. The Jacobins were idealists; there was about this man a murderous materialism. His position gave him a somewhat new appearance. The strong, white light of morning coming from one side creating sharp shadows, made him seem both more pale and more angular than he had looked at the breakfast on the balcony. Thus the two black glasses that encased his eyes might really have been black cavities in his skull, making him look like a death's-head. And, indeed, if ever Death himself sat writing at a wooden table, it might have been he.

He looked up and smiled brightly enough as the men came in, and rose with the resilient rapidity of which the professor had spoken. He set chairs for both of them, and going to a peg behind the door, proceeded to put on a coat and waistcoat of rough, dark tweed; he buttoned it up neatly, and came back to sit down at his table.

The quiet good humour of his manner left his two opponents helpless. It was with some momentary difficulty that the professor broke silence and began, 'I'm sorry to disturb you so early, comrade,' said he, with a careful resumption of the slow de Worms manner. 'You have no doubt made all the arrangements for the Paris affair?' Then he added with infinite slowness, 'We have information which renders intolerable anything in the nature of a moment's delay.'

Dr Bull smiled again, but continued to gaze on them without speaking. The professor resumed, a pause before each weary word: 'Please do not think me excessively abrupt; but I advise you to alter those plans, or if it is too late for that, to follow your agent with all the support you can get for him. Comrade Syme and I have had an experience which it would take more time to recount than we can afford, if we are to act on it. I will, however, relate the occurrence in detail, even at the risk of losing time, if you really feel that it is essential to the understanding of the problem we have to discuss.'

He was spinning out his sentences, making them intolerably long and lingering, in the hope of maddening the practical little doctor into an explosion of impatience which might show his hand. But the little doctor continued only to stare and smile, and the monologue was uphill work. Syme began to feel a new sickness and despair. The doctor's smile and silence were not at all like the cataleptic stare and horrible silence which he had confronted in the professor half an hour before. About the professor's makeup and all his antics there was always something merely grotesque, like a gollywog. Syme remembered those wild woes of yesterday as one remembers being afraid of Bogy in childhood. But here was daylight; here was a healthy, square-shouldered man in tweeds, not odd save for the accident of his ugly spectacles, not glaring or grinning at all, but smiling steadily and not saying a word. The whole had a sense of unbearable reality. Under the increasing sunlight the colours of the doctor's complexion, the pattern of his tweeds, grew and expanded outrageously, as such things grow too important in a realistic novel. But his smile was quite slight, the pose of his head polite; the only uncanny thing was his silence.

'As I say,' resumed the professor, like a man toiling through heavy sand, 'the incident that has occurred to us and has led us to ask for information about the marquis is one which you may think it better to have narrated; but as it came in the way of Comrade Syme rather than me – '

His words he seemed to be dragging out like words in an anthem; but Syme, who was watching, saw his long fingers rattle quickly on the edge of the crazy table. He read the message, 'You must go on. This devil has sucked me dry!'

Syme plunged into the breach with that bravado of improvisation which always came to him when he was alarmed.

'Yes, the thing really happened to me,' he said hastily. 'I had the good fortune to fall into conversation with a detective who took me, thanks to my hat, for a respectable person. Wishing to clinch my reputation for respectability, I took him and made him very drunk at the Savoy. Under this influence he became friendly, and told me in so many words that within a day or two they hope to arrest the marquis in France. 'So unless you or I can get on his track – '

The doctor was still smiling in the most friendly way, and his protected eyes were still impenetrable. The professor signalled to Syme that he would resume his explanation, and he began again with the same elaborate calm.

'Syme immediately brought this information to me, and we came here together to see what use you would be inclined to make of it. It seems to me unquestionably urgent that – '

All this time Syme had been staring at the doctor almost as steadily as the doctor stared at the professor, but quite without the smile. The nerves of both comrades-in-arms were near snapping under that strain of motionless amiability, when Syme suddenly leant forward and idly tapped the edge of the table. His message to his ally ran, 'I have an intuition.'

The professor, with scarcely a pause in his monologue, signalled back, 'Then sit on it.'

Syme telegraphed, 'It is quite extraordinary.'

The other answered, 'Extraordinary rot!'

Syme said, 'I am a poet.'

The other retorted, 'You are a dead man.'

Syme had gone quite red up to his yellow hair, and his eyes were burning feverishly. As he said, he had an intuition, and it had risen to a sort of lightheaded certainty. Resuming his symbolic taps, he signalled to his friend, 'You scarcely realise how poetic my intuition is. It has that sudden quality we sometimes feel in the coming of spring.'

He then studied the answer on his friend's fingers. The answer was, 'Go to hell!'

The professor then resumed his merely verbal monologue addressed to the doctor.

'Perhaps I should rather say,' said Syme on his fingers, 'that it resembles that sudden smell of the sea which may be found in the heart of lush woods.'

His companion disdained to reply.

'Or yet again,' tapped Syme, 'it is positive, as is the passionate red hair of a beautiful woman.'

The professor was continuing his speech, but in the middle of it Syme decided to act. He leant across the table, and said in a voice that could not be neglected: 'Dr Bull!'

The doctor's sleek and smiling head did not move, but they could have sworn that under his dark glasses his eyes darted towards Syme.

'Dr Bull,' said Syme, in a voice peculiarly precise and courteous, 'would you do me a small favour? Would you be so kind as to take off your spectacles?'

The professor swung round on his seat, and stared at Syme with a sort of frozen fury of astonishment. Syme, like a man who has thrown his life and fortune on the table, leaned forward with a fiery face. The doctor did not move.

For a few seconds there was a silence in which one could hear a pin drop, split once by the single hoot of a distant steamer on the Thames. Then Dr Bull rose slowly, still smiling, and took off his spectacles.

Syme sprang to his feet, stepping backwards a little, like a chemical lecturer from a successful explosion. His eyes were like stars, and for an instant he could only point without speaking.

The professor had also started to his feet, forgetful of his supposed paralysis. He leant on the back of the chair and stared doubtfully at Dr Bull, as if the doctor had been turned into a toad before his eyes. And indeed it was almost as great a transformation scene.

The two detectives saw sitting in the chair before them a very boyish-looking young man, with very frank and happy hazel eyes, an open expression, cockney clothes like those of a city clerk, and an unquestionable breath about him of being very good and rather commonplace. The smile was still there, but it might have been the first smile of a baby.

'I knew I was a poet,' cried Syme in a sort of ecstasy. 'I knew my intuition was as infallible as the Pope. It was the spectacles that did it! It was all the spectacles. Given those beastly black eyes, and all the rest of him, his health and his jolly looks, made him a live devil among dead ones.'

'It certainly does make a queer difference,' said the professor shakily. 'But as regards the project of Dr Bull – '

'Project be damned!' roared Syme, beside himself. 'Look at him! Look at his face, look at his collar, look at his blessed boots! You don't suppose, do you, that that thing's an anarchist?'

'Syme!' cried the other in an apprehensive agony.

'Why, by God,' said Syme, 'I'll take the risk of that myself! Dr Bull, I am a police officer. There's my card,' and he flung down the blue card upon the table.

The professor still feared that all was lost; but he was loyal. He pulled out his own official card and put it beside his friend's. Then the third man burst out laughing, and for the first time that morning they heard his voice.

'I'm awfully glad you chaps have come so early,' he said, with a sort of schoolboy flippancy, 'for we can all start for France together. Yes, I'm in the force right enough,' and he flicked a blue card towards them lightly as a matter of form.

Clapping a brisk bowler on his head and resuming his goblin glasses, the doctor moved so quickly towards the door that the others instinctively followed him. Syme seemed a little distrait, and as he passed under the doorway he suddenly struck his stick on the stone passage so that it rang.

'But Lord God Almighty,' he cried out, 'if this is all right, there were more damned detectives than there were damned dynamiters at the damned council!'

'We might have fought easily,' said Bull; 'we were four against three.'

The professor was descending the stairs, but his voice came up from below.

'No,' said the voice, 'we were not four against three – we were not so lucky. We were four against one.'

The others went down the stairs in silence.

The young man called Bull, with an innocent courtesy characteristic of him, insisted on going last until they reached the street; but there his own robust rapidity asserted itself unconsciously, and he walked quickly on ahead towards a railway enquiry office, talking to the others over his shoulder.

'It is jolly to get some pals,' he said. 'I've been half dead with the jumps, being quite alone. I nearly flung my arms round Gogol and embraced him, which would have been imprudent. I hope you won't despise me for having been in a blue funk.'

'All the blue devils in blue hell,' said Syme, 'contributed to my blue funk! But the worst devil was you and your infernal goggles.'

The young man laughed delightedly.

'Wasn't it a rag?' he said. 'Such a simple idea – not my own. I haven't got the brains. You see, I wanted to go into the detective service, especially the anti-dynamite business. But for that purpose they wanted someone to dress up as a dynamiter; and they all swore by blazes that I could never look like a dynamiter. They said my very walk was respectable, and that seen from behind I looked like the British Constitution. They said I looked too healthy and too optimistic, and too reliable and benevolent; they called me all sorts of names at Scotland Yard. They said that if I had been a criminal, I might have made my fortune by looking so like an honest man; but as I had the misfortune to be an honest man, there was not even the remotest chance of my assisting them by ever looking like a criminal. But at last I was brought before some old josser who was high up in the force, and who seemed to have no end of a head on his shoulders. And there the others all talked hopelessly. One asked whether a bushy beard would hide my nice smile; another said that if they blacked my face I might look like a negro anarchist; but this old chap chipped in with a most extraordinary remark. "A pair of smoked spectacles will do it," he said positively. "Look at him now; he looks like an angelic office boy. Put him on a pair of smoked spectacles, and children will scream at the sight of him." And so it was, by George! When once my eyes were covered, all the rest, smile and big shoulders and short hair, made me look a perfect little devil. As I say, it was simple enough when it was done, like miracles; but that wasn't the really miraculous part of it. There was one really staggering thing about the business, and my head still turns at it.'

'What was that?' asked Syme.

'I'll tell you,' answered the man in spectacles. 'This big pot in the police who sized me up so that he knew how the goggles would go with my hair and socks – by God, he never saw me at all!'

Syme's eyes suddenly flashed on him.

'How was that?' he asked. 'I thought you talked to him.'

'So I did,' said Bull brightly; 'but we talked in a pitch-dark room like a coal cellar. There, you would never have guessed that.'

'I could not have conceived it,' said Syme gravely.

'It is indeed a new idea,' said the professor.

Their new ally was in practical matters a whirlwind. At the enquiry office he asked with businesslike brevity about the trains for Dover. Having got his information, he bundled the company into a cab, and put them and himself inside a railway carriage before they had properly realised the breathless process. They were already on the Calais boat before conversation flowed freely.

'I had already arranged,' he explained, 'to go to France for my lunch; but I am delighted to have someone to lunch with me. You see, I had to send that beast, the marquis, over with his bomb, because the president had his eye on me, though God knows how. I'll tell you the story someday. It was perfectly choking. Whenever I tried to slip out of it I saw the president somewhere, smiling out of the bow-window of a club, or taking off his hat to me from the top of an omnibus. I tell you, you can say what you like, that fellow sold himself to the devil; he can be in six places at once.'

'So you sent the marquis off, I understand,' asked the professor. 'Was it long ago? Shall we be in time to catch him?'

'Yes,' answered the new guide, 'I've timed it all. He'll still be at Calais when we arrive.'

'But when we do catch him at Calais,' said the professor, 'what are we going to do?'

At this question the countenance of Dr Bull fell for the first time. He reflected a little, and then said: 'Theoretically, I suppose, we ought to call the police.'

'Not I,' said Syme. 'Theoretically I ought to drown myself first. I promised a poor fellow, who was a real modern pessimist, on my word of honour not to tell the police. I'm no hand at casuistry, but I can't break my word to a modern pessimist. It's like breaking one's word to a child.'

'I'm in the same boat,' said the professor. 'I tried to tell the police and I couldn't, because of some silly oath I took. You see, when I was an actor I was a sort of all-round beast. Perjury or treason is the only crime I haven't committed. If I did that I shouldn't know the difference between right and wrong.'

'I've been through all that,' said Dr Bull, 'and I've made up my mind. I gave my promise to the secretary – you know him, man who smiles upside down. My friends, that man is the most utterly unhappy man that was ever human. It may be his digestion, or his conscience, or his nerves, or his philosophy of the universe, but he's damned, he's in hell! Well, I can't turn on a man like that, and hunt him down. It's like whipping a leper. I may be mad, but that's how I feel; and there's jolly well the end of it.'

'I don't think you're mad,' said Syme. 'I knew you would decide like that when first you – '

'Eh?' said Dr Bull.

'When first you took off your spectacles.'

Dr Bull smiled a little, and strolled across the deck to look at the sunlit sea. Then he strolled back again, kicking his heels carelessly, and a companionable silence fell between the three men.

'Well,' said Syme, 'it seems that we have all the same kind of morality or immorality, so we had better face the fact that comes of it.'

'Yes,' assented the professor, 'you're quite right; and we must hurry up, for I can see the Grey Nose standing out from France.'

'The fact that comes of it,' said Syme seriously, 'is this, that we three are alone on this planet. Gogol has gone, God knows where; perhaps the president has smashed him like a fly. On the council we are three men against three, like the Romans who held the bridge. But we are worse off than that, first because they can appeal to their organisation and we cannot appeal to ours, and second because – '

'Because one of those other three men,' said the professor, 'is not a man.'

Syme nodded and was silent for a second or two, then he said: 'My idea is this. We must do something to keep the marquis in Calais till tomorrow midday. I have turned over twenty schemes in my head. We cannot denounce him as a dynamiter; that is agreed. We cannot get him detained on some trivial charge, for we should have to appear; he knows us, and he would smell a rat. We cannot pretend to keep him on anarchist business; he might swallow much in that way, but not the notion of stopping in Calais while the Czar went safely through Paris. We might try to kidnap him, and lock him up ourselves; but he is a well-known man here. He has a whole bodyguard of friends; he is very strong and brave, and the event is doubtful. The only thing I can see to do is actually to take advantage of the very things that are in the marquis's favour. I am going to profit by the fact that he is a highly respected nobleman. I am going to profit by the fact that he has many friends and moves in the best society.'

'What the devil are you talking about?' asked the professor.

'The Symes are first mentioned in the fourteenth century,' said Syme; 'but there is a tradition that one of them rode behind Bruce at Bannockburn. Since 1350 the tree is quite clear.'

'He's gone off his head,' said the little doctor, staring.

'Our bearings,' continued Syme calmly, 'are "argent a chevron gules charged with three cross crosslets of the field". The motto varies.'

The professor seized Syme roughly by the waistcoat.

'We are just inshore,' he said. 'Are you seasick or joking in the wrong place?'

'My remarks are almost painfully practical,' answered Syme, in an unhurried manner. 'The house of St Eustache also is very ancient. The marquis cannot deny that he is a gentleman. He cannot deny that I am a gentleman. And in order to put the matter of my social position quite beyond a doubt, I propose at the earliest opportunity to knock his hat off. But here we are in the harbour.'

They went on shore under the strong sun in a sort of daze. Syme, who had now taken the lead as Bull had taken it in London, led them along a kind of marine parade until he came to some cafés, embowered in a bulk of greenery and overlooking the sea. As he went before them his step was slightly swaggering, and he swung his stick like a sword. He was making apparently for the extreme end of the line of cafés, but he stopped abruptly. With a sharp gesture he motioned them to silence, but he pointed with one gloved finger to a café table under a bank of flowering foliage at which sat the Marquis de St Eustache, his teeth shining in his thick, black beard, and his bold, brown face shadowed by a light yellow straw hat and outlined against the violet sea.

CHAPTER 10

The Duel

Syme sat down at a café table with his companions, his blue eyes sparkling like the bright sea below, and ordered a bottle of Saumur with a pleased impatience. He was for some reason in a condition of curious hilarity. His spirits were already unnaturally high; they rose as the Saumur sank, and in half an hour his talk was a torrent of nonsense. He professed to be making out a plan of the conversation which was going to ensue between himself and the deadly marquis. He jotted it down wildly with a pencil. It was arranged like a printed catechism, with questions and answers, and was delivered with an extraordinary rapidity of utterance.

'I shall approach. Before taking off his hat, I shall take off my own. I shall say, "The Marquis de Saint Eustache, I believe." He will say, "The celebrated Mr Syme, I presume." He will say in the most exquisite French, "How are you?" I shall reply in the most exquisite Cockney, "Oh, just the Syme – " '

'Oh, shut it,' said the man in spectacles. 'Pull yourself together, and chuck away that bit of paper. What are you really going to do?'

'But it was a lovely catechism,' said Syme pathetically. 'Do let me read it you. It has only forty-three questions and answers, and some of the marquis's answers are wonderfully witty. I like to be just to my enemy.'

'But what's the good of it all?' asked Dr Bull in exasperation.

'It leads up to my challenge, don't you see,' said Syme, beaming. 'When the marquis has given the thirty-ninth reply, which runs – '

'Has it by any chance occurred to you,' asked the professor, with a ponderous simplicity, 'that the marquis may not say all the forty-three things you have put down for him? In that case, I understand, your own epigrams may appear somewhat more forced.'

Syme struck the table with a radiant face.

'Why, how true that is,' he said, 'and I never thought of it. Sir, you have an intellect beyond the common. You will make a name.'

'Oh, you're as drunk as an owl!' said the doctor.

'It only remains,' continued Syme quite unperturbed, 'to adopt some other method of breaking the ice (if I may so express it) between myself and the man I wish to kill. And since the course of a dialogue cannot be predicted by one of its parties alone (as you have pointed out with such recondite acumen), the only thing to be done, I suppose, is for the one party, as far as possible, to do all the dialogue by himself. And so I will, by George!' And he stood up suddenly, his yellow hair blowing in the slight sea breeze.

A band was playing in a *café chantant* hidden somewhere among the trees, and a woman had just stopped singing. On Syme's heated head the bray of the brass band seemed like the jar and jingle of that barrel-organ in Leicester Square, to the tune of which he had once stood up to die. He looked across to the little table where the marquis sat. The man had two companions now, solemn Frenchmen in frock-coats and silk hats, one of them with the red rosette of the Legion of Honour, evidently people of a solid social position. Besides these black, cylindrical costumes, the marquis, in his loose straw hat and light spring clothes, looked Bohemian and even barbaric; but he looked the marquis. Indeed, one might say that he looked the king, with his animal elegance, his scornful eyes, and his proud head lifted against the purple sea. But he was no Christian king, at any rate; he was, rather, some swarthy despot, half Greek, half Asiatic, who in the days when slavery seemed natural looked down on the Mediterranean, on his galley and his groaning slaves. Just so, Syme thought, would the brown-gold face of such a tyrant have shown against the dark green olives and the burning blue.

'Are you going to address the meeting?' asked the professor peevishly, seeing that Syme still stood up without moving.

Syme drained his last glass of sparkling wine.

'I am,' he said, pointing across to the marquis and his companions, 'that meeting. That meeting displeases me. I am going to pull that meeting's great ugly, mahogany-coloured nose.'

He stepped across swiftly, if not quite steadily. The marquis, seeing him, arched his black Assyrian eyebrows in surprise, but smiled politely.

'You are Mr Syme, I think,' he said.

Syme bowed.

'And you are the Marquis de Saint Eustache,' he said gracefully. 'Permit me to pull your nose.'

He leant over to do so, but the marquis started backwards, upsetting his chair, and the two men in top hats held Syme back by the shoulders.

'This man has insulted me!' said Syme, with gestures of explanation.

'Insulted you?' cried the gentleman with the red rosette, 'when?'

'Oh, just now,' said Syme recklessly. 'He insulted my mother.'

'Insulted your mother!' exclaimed the gentleman incredulously.

'Well, anyhow,' said Syme, conceding a point, 'my aunt.'

'But how can the marquis have insulted your aunt just now?' said the second gentleman with some legitimate wonder. 'He has been sitting here all the time.'

'Ah, it was what he said!' said Syme darkly.

'I said nothing at all,' said the marquis, 'except something about the band. I only said that I liked Wagner played well.'

'It was an allusion to my family,' said Syme firmly. 'My aunt played Wagner badly. It was a painful subject. We are always being insulted about it.'

'This seems most extraordinary,' said the gentleman who was *décoré*, looking doubtfully at the marquis.

'Oh, I assure you,' said Syme earnestly, 'the whole of your conversation was simply packed with sinister allusions to my aunt's weaknesses.'

'This is nonsense!' said the second gentleman. 'I for one have said nothing for half an hour except that I liked the singing of that girl with black hair.'

'Well, there you are again!' said Syme indignantly. 'My aunt's was red.'

'It seems to me,' said the other, 'that you are simply seeking a pretext to insult the marquis.'

'By George!' said Syme, facing round and looking at him, 'what a clever chap you are!'

The marquis started up with eyes flaming like a tiger's.

'Seeking a quarrel with me!' he cried. 'Seeking a fight with me! By God! there was never a man who had to seek long. These gentlemen will perhaps act for me. There are still four hours of daylight. Let us fight this evening.'

Syme bowed with a quite beautiful graciousness.

'Marquis,' he said, 'your action is worthy of your fame and blood. Permit me to consult for a moment with the gentlemen in whose hands I shall place myself.'

In three long strides he rejoined his companions, and they, who had seen his champagne-inspired attack and listened to his idiotic explanations, were quite startled at the look of him. For now that he came back to them he was quite sober, a little pale, and he spoke in a low voice of passionate practicality.

'I have done it,' he said hoarsely. 'I have fixed a fight on the beast. But look here, and listen carefully. There is no time for talk. You are my seconds, and everything must come from you. Now you must insist, and insist absolutely, on the duel coming off after seven tomorrow, so as to give me the chance of preventing him from catching the 7.45 for Paris. If he misses that he misses his crime. He can't refuse to meet you on such a small point of time and place. But this is what he will do. He will choose a field somewhere near a wayside station, where he can pick up the train. He is a very good swordsman, and he will trust to killing me in time to catch it. But I can fence well too, and I think I can keep him in play, at any rate, until the train is lost. Then perhaps he may kill me to console his feelings. You understand? Very well then, let me introduce you to some charming friends of mine,' and leading them quickly across the parade, he presented them to the marquis's seconds by two very aristocratic names of which they had not previously heard.

Syme was subject to spasms of singular common sense, not otherwise a part of his character. They were (as he said of his impulse about the spectacles) poetic intuitions, and they sometimes rose to the exaltation of prophecy.

He had correctly calculated in this case the policy of his opponent. When the marquis was informed by his seconds that Syme could only fight in the morning, he must fully have realised that an obstacle had suddenly arisen between him and his bomb-throwing business in the capital. Naturally he could not explain this objection to his friends, so he chose the course which Syme had predicted. He induced his seconds to settle on a small meadow not far from the railway, and he trusted to the fatality of the first engagement.

When he came down very coolly to the field of honour, no one could have guessed that he had any anxiety about a journey; his hands were in his pockets, his straw hat on the back of his head, his handsome face brazen in the sun. But it might have struck a stranger as odd that there appeared in his train, not only his seconds carrying the sword-case, but two of his servants carrying a portmanteau and a luncheon basket.

Early as was the hour, the sun soaked everything in warmth, and Syme was vaguely surprised to see so many spring flowers burning gold and silver in the tall grass in which the whole company stood almost knee-deep.

With the exception of the marquis, all the men were in sombre and solemn morning-dress, with hats like black chimney-pots; the little doctor especially, with the addition of his black spectacles, looked like an undertaker in a farce. Syme could not help feeling a comic contrast between this funereal church parade of apparel and the rich and glistening meadow, growing wild flowers everywhere. But, indeed, this comic contrast between the yellow blossoms and the black hats was but a symbol of the tragic contrast between the yellow blossoms and the black business. On his right was a little wood; far away to his left lay the long curve of the railway line, which he was, so to speak, guarding from the marquis, whose goal and escape it was. In front of him, behind the black group of his opponents, he could see, like a tinted cloud, a small almond bush in flower against the faint line of the sea.

The member of the Legion of Honour, whose name it seemed was Colonel Ducroix, approached the professor and Dr Bull with great politeness, and suggested that the play should terminate with the first considerable hurt.

Dr Bull, however, having been carefully coached by Syme upon this point of policy, insisted, with great dignity and in very bad French, that it should continue until one of the combatants was disabled. Syme had made up his mind that he could avoid disabling the marquis and prevent the marquis from disabling him for at least twenty minutes. In twenty minutes the Paris train would have gone by.

'To a man of the well-known skill and valour of Monsieur de St Eustache,' said the professor solemnly, 'it must be a matter of indifference which method is adopted, and our principal has strong reasons for demanding the longer encounter, reasons the delicacy of which prevent me from being explicit, but for the just and honourable nature of which I can – '

'*Peste!*' broke from the marquis behind, whose face had suddenly darkened, 'let us stop talking and begin,' and he slashed off the head of a tall flower with his stick.

Syme understood his rude impatience and instinctively looked over his shoulder to see whether the train was coming in sight. But there was no smoke on the horizon.

Colonel Ducroix knelt down and unlocked the case, taking out a pair of twin swords, which took the sunlight and turned to two streaks of white fire. He offered one to the marquis, who snatched it without ceremony, and another to Syme, who took it, bent it, and poised it with as much delay as was consistent with dignity. Then the colonel took out another pair of blades, and taking one himself and giving another to Dr Bull, proceeded to place the men.

Both combatants had thrown off their coats and waistcoats, and stood sword in hand. The seconds stood on each side of the line of fight with drawn swords also, but still sombre in their dark frock-coats and hats. The principals saluted. The colonel said quietly, 'Engage!' and the two blades touched and tingled.

When the jar of the joined iron ran up Syme's arm, all the fantastic fears that have been the subject of this story fell from him like dreams from a man waking up in bed. He remembered them clearly and in order as mere delusions of the nerves – how the fear of the professor had been the fear of the tyrannic accidents of nightmare, and how the fear of the doctor had been the fear of the airless vacuum of science. The first was the old fear that any miracle might happen, the second the more hopeless modern fear that no miracle can ever happen. But he saw that these fears were fancies, for he found himself in the presence of the great fact of the fear of death, with its coarse and pitiless common sense. He felt like a man who had dreamed all night of falling over precipices, and had woke up on the morning when he was to be hanged. For as soon as he had seen the sunlight run down the channel of his foe's foreshortened blade, and as soon as he had felt the two tongues of steel touch, vibrating like two living things, he knew that his enemy was a terrible fighter, and that probably his last hour had come.

He felt a strange and vivid value in all the earth around him, in the grass under his feet; he felt the love of life in all living things. He could almost fancy that he heard the grass growing; he could almost fancy that even as he stood fresh flowers were springing up and breaking into blossom in the meadow – flowers blood red and burning gold and blue, fulfilling the whole pageant of the spring. And whenever his eyes strayed for a flash from the calm, staring, hypnotic eyes of the marquis, they saw the little tuft of almond tree against the skyline. He had the feeling that if by some miracle he escaped he would be ready to sit for ever before that almond tree, desiring nothing else in the world.

But while earth and sky and everything had the living beauty of a thing lost, the other half of his head was as clear as glass, and he was parrying his enemy's point with a kind of clockwork skill of which he had hardly supposed himself capable. Once his enemy's point ran along his wrist, leaving a slight streak of blood, but it either was not noticed or was tacitly ignored. Every now and then he riposted, and once or twice he could almost fancy that he felt his point go home, but as there was no blood on blade or shirt he supposed he was mistaken. Then came an interruption and a change.

At the risk of losing all, the marquis, interrupting his quiet stare, flashed one glance over his shoulder at the line of railway on his right. Then he turned on Syme a face transfigured to that of a fiend, and began to fight as if with twenty weapons. The attack came so fast and furious, that the one shining sword seemed a shower of shining arrows. Syme had no chance to look at the railway; but also he had no need. He could guess the reason of the marquis's sudden madness of battle – the Paris train was in sight.

But the marquis's morbid energy over-reached itself. Twice Syme, parrying, knocked his opponent's point far out of the fighting circle; and the third time his riposte was so rapid, that there was no doubt about the hit this time. Syme's sword actually bent under the weight of the marquis's body, which it had pierced.

Syme was as certain that he had stuck his blade into his enemy as a gardener that he has stuck his spade into the ground. Yet the marquis sprang back from the stroke without a stagger, and Syme stood staring at his own sword-point like an idiot. There was no blood on it at all.

There was an instant of rigid silence, and then Syme in his turn fell furiously on the other, filled with a flaming curiosity. The marquis was probably, in a general sense, a better fencer than he, as he had surmised at the beginning, but at the moment the marquis seemed distraught and at a disadvantage. He fought wildly and even weakly, and he constantly looked away at the railway line, almost as if he feared the train more than the pointed steel. Syme, on the other hand, fought fiercely but still carefully, in an intellectual fury, eager to solve the riddle of his own bloodless sword. For this purpose, he aimed less at the marquis's body, and more at his throat and head. A minute and a half afterwards he felt his point enter the man's neck below the jaw. It came out clean. Half mad, he thrust again, and made what should have been a bloody scar on the marquis's cheek. But there was no scar.

For one moment the heaven of Syme again grew black with supernatural terrors. Surely the man had a charmed life. But this new spiritual dread was a more awful thing than had been the mere spiritual topsy-turvydom symbolised by the paralytic who pursued him. The professor was only a goblin; this man was a devil – perhaps he was the Devil! Anyhow, this was certain, that three times had a human sword been driven into him and made no mark. When Syme had that thought he drew himself up, and all that was good in him sang high up in the air as a high wind sings in the trees. He thought of all the human things in his story – of the Chinese lanterns in Saffron Park, of the girl's red hair in the garden, of the honest, beer-swilling sailors down by the dock, of his loyal companions standing by. Perhaps he had been chosen as a champion of all these fresh and kindly things to cross swords with the enemy of all creation. 'After all,' he said to himself, 'I am more than a devil; I am a man. I can do the one thing which Satan himself cannot do – I can die,' and as the word went through his head, he heard a faint and far-off hoot, which would soon be the roar of the Paris train.

He fell to fighting again with a supernatural levity, like a Mohammedan panting for Paradise. As the train came nearer and nearer he fancied he could see people putting up the floral arches in Paris; he joined in the growing noise and the glory of the great Republic whose gate he was guarding against Hell. His thoughts rose higher and higher with the rising roar of the train, which ended, as if proudly, in a long and piercing whistle. The train stopped.

Suddenly, to the astonishment of everyone the marquis sprang back quite out of sword reach and threw down his sword. The leap was wonderful, and not the less wonderful because Syme had plunged his sword a moment before into the man's thigh.

'Stop!' said the marquis in a voice that compelled a momentary obedience. 'I want to say something.'

'What is the matter?' asked Colonel Ducroix, staring. 'Has there been foul play?'

'There has been foul play somewhere,' said Dr Bull, who was a little pale. 'Our principal has wounded the marquis four times at least, and he is none the worse.'

The marquis put up his hand with a curious air of ghastly patience.

'Please let me speak,' he said. 'It is rather important. Mr Syme,' he continued, turning to his opponent, 'we are fighting today, if I remember right, because you expressed a wish (which I thought irrational) to pull my nose. Would you oblige me by pulling my nose now as quickly as possible? I have to catch a train.'

'I protest that this is most irregular,' said Dr Bull indignantly.

'It is certainly somewhat opposed to precedent,' said Colonel Ducroix, looking wistfully at his principal. 'There is, I think, one case on record (Captain Bellegarde and the Baron Zumpt) in which the weapons were changed in the middle of the encounter at the request of one of the combatants. But one can hardly call one's nose a weapon.'

'Will you or will you not pull my nose?' said the marquis in exasperation. 'Come, come, Mr Syme! You wanted to do it, do it! You can have no conception of how important it is to me. Don't be so selfish! Pull my nose at once, when I ask you!' and he bent slightly forward with a fascinating smile. The Paris train, panting and groaning, had grated into a little station behind the neighbouring hill.

Syme had the feeling he had more than once had in these adventures – the sense that a horrible and sublime wave lifted to heaven was just toppling over. Walking in a world he half understood, he took two paces forward and seized the Roman nose of this remarkable nobleman. He pulled it hard, and it came off in his hand.

He stood for some seconds with a foolish solemnity, with the pasteboard proboscis still between his fingers, looking at it, while the sun and the clouds and the wooded hills looked down upon this imbecile scene.

The marquis broke the silence in a loud and cheerful voice.

'If anyone has any use for my left eyebrow,' he said, 'he can have it. Colonel Ducroix, do accept my left eyebrow! It's the kind of thing that might come in useful any day,' and he gravely tore off one of his swarthy Assyrian brows, bringing about half his brown forehead with it, and politely offered it to the colonel, who stood crimson and speechless with rage.

'If I had known,' he spluttered, 'that I was acting for a poltroon who pads himself to fight – '

'Oh, I know, I know!' said the marquis, recklessly throwing various parts of himself right and left about the field. 'You are making a mistake; but it can't be explained just now. I tell you the train has come into the station!'

'Yes,' said Dr Bull fiercely, 'and the train shall go out of the station. It shall go out without you. We know well enough for what devil's work – '

The mysterious marquis lifted his hands with a desperate gesture. He was a strange scarecrow standing there in the sun with half his old face peeled off, and half another face glaring and grinning from underneath.

'Will you drive me mad?' he cried. 'The train – '

'You shall not go by the train,' said Syme firmly, and grasped his sword.

The wild figure turned towards Syme, and seemed to be gathering itself for a sublime effort before speaking.

'You great fat, blasted, blear-eyed, blundering, thundering, brainless, God-forsaken, doddering, damned fool!' he said without taking breath. 'You great silly, pink-faced, tow-headed turnip! You – '

'You shall not go by this train,' repeated Syme.

'And why the infernal blazes,' roared the other, 'should I want to go by the train?'

'We know all,' said the professor sternly. 'You are going to Paris to throw a bomb!'

'Going to Jericho to throw a Jabberwock!' cried the other, tearing his hair, which came off easily. 'Have you all got softening of the brain, that you don't realise what I am? Did you really think I wanted to catch that train? Twenty Paris trains might go by for me. Damn Paris trains!'

'Then what did you care about?' began the professor.

'What did I care about? I didn't care about catching the train; I cared about whether the train caught me, and now, by God! it has caught me.'

'I regret to inform you,' said Syme with restraint, 'that your remarks convey no impression to my mind. Perhaps if you were to remove the remains of your original forehead and some portion of what was once your chin, your meaning would become clearer. Mental lucidity fulfils itself in many ways. What do you mean by saying that the train has caught you? It may be my literary fancy, but somehow I feel that it ought to mean something.'

'It means everything,' said the other, 'and the end of everything. Sunday has us now in the hollow of his hand.'

'Us!' repeated the professor, as if stupefied. 'What do you mean by "us"?'

'The police, of course!' said the marquis, and tore off his scalp and half his face.

The head which emerged was the blonde, well brushed, smooth-haired head which is common in the English constabulary, but the face was terribly pale.

'I am Inspector Ratcliffe,' he said, with a sort of haste that verged on harshness. 'My name is pretty well known to the police, and I can see well enough that you belong to them. But if there is any doubt about my position, I have a card – ' and he began to pull a blue card from his pocket.

The professor gave a tired gesture.

'Oh, don't show it us,' he said wearily; 'we've got enough of them to equip a paper-chase.'

The little man named Bull had, like many men who seem to be of a mere vivacious vulgarity, sudden movements of good taste. Here he certainly saved the situation. In the midst of this staggering transformation scene he stepped forward with all the gravity and responsibility of a second, and addressed the two seconds of the marquis.

'Gentlemen,' he said, 'we all owe you a serious apology; but I assure you that you have not been made the victims of such a low joke as you imagine, or indeed of anything undignified in a man of honour. You have not wasted your time; you have helped to save the world. We are not buffoons, but very desperate men at war with a vast conspiracy. A secret society of anarchists is hunting us like hares; not such unfortunate madmen as may here or there throw a bomb through starvation or German philosophy, but a rich and powerful and fanatical church, a church of eastern pessimism, which holds it holy to destroy mankind like vermin. How hard they hunt us you can gather from the fact that we are driven to such disguises as those for which I apologise, and to such pranks as this one by which you suffer.'

The younger second of the marquis, a short man with a black moustache, bowed politely, and said: 'Of course, I accept the apology; but you will in your turn forgive me if I decline to follow you further into your difficulties, and permit myself to say good-morning! The sight of an acquaintance and distinguished fellow-townsman coming to pieces in the open air is unusual, and, upon the whole, sufficient for one day. Colonel Ducroix, I would in no way influence your actions, but if you feel with me that our present society is a little abnormal, I am now going to walk back to the town.'

Colonel Ducroix moved mechanically, but then tugged abruptly at his white moustache and broke out: 'No, by George! I won't. If these gentlemen are really in a mess with a lot of low wreckers like that, I'll see them through it. I have fought for France, and it is hard if I can't fight for civilisation.'

Dr Bull took off his hat and waved it, cheering as at a public meeting.

'Don't make too much noise,' said Inspector Ratcliffe, 'Sunday may hear you.'

'Sunday!' cried Bull, and dropped his hat.

'Yes,' retorted Ratcliffe, 'he may be with them.'

'With whom?' asked Syme.

'With the people out of that train,' said the other.

'What you say seems utterly wild,' began Syme. 'Why, as a matter of fact – But, my God,' he cried out suddenly, like a man who sees an explosion a long way off, 'by God! if this is true the whole bally lot of us on the Anarchist Council were against anarchy! Every born man was a detective except the president and his personal secretary. What can it mean?'

'Mean!' said the new policeman with incredible violence. 'It means that we are struck dead! Don't you know Sunday? Don't you know that his jokes are always so big and simple that one has never thought of them? Can you think of anything more like Sunday than this, that he should put all his powerful enemies on the Supreme Council, and then take care that it was not supreme? I tell you he has bought every trust, he has captured every cable, he has control of every railway line – especially of that railway line!' and he pointed a shaking finger towards the small wayside station. 'The whole movement was controlled by him; half the world was ready to rise for him. But there were just five people, perhaps, who would have resisted him . . . and the old devil put them on the Supreme Council, to waste their time in watching each other. Idiots that we are, he planned the whole of our idiocies! Sunday knew that the professor would chase Syme through London, and that Syme would fight me in France. And he was combining great masses of capital, and seizing great lines of telegraphy, while we five idiots were running after each other like a lot of confounded babies playing blind man's buff.'

'Well?' asked Syme with a sort of steadiness.

'Well,' replied the other with sudden serenity, 'he has found us playing blind man's buff today in a field of great rustic beauty and extreme solitude. He has probably captured the world; it only remains to him to capture this field and all the fools in it. And since you really want to know what was my objection to the arrival of that train, I will tell you. My objection was that Sunday or his secretary has just this moment got out of it.'

Syme uttered an involuntary cry, and they all turned their eyes towards the far-off station. It was quite true that a considerable bulk of people seemed to be moving in their direction. But they were too distant to be distinguished in any way.

'It was a habit of the late Marquis de St Eustache,' said the new policeman, producing a leather case, 'always to carry a pair of opera glasses. Either the president or the secretary is coming after us with that mob. They have caught us in a nice quiet place where we are under no temptations to break our oaths by calling the police. Dr Bull, I have a suspicion that you will see better through these than through your own highly decorative spectacles.'

He handed the field-glasses to the doctor, who immediately took off his spectacles and put the apparatus to his eyes.

'It cannot be as bad as you say,' said the professor, somewhat shaken. 'There are a good number of them certainly, but they may easily be ordinary tourists.'

'Do ordinary tourists,' asked Bull, with the field-glasses to his eyes, 'wear black masks halfway down the face?'

Syme almost tore the glasses out of his hand, and looked through them. Most men in the advancing mob really looked ordinary enough; but it was quite true that two or three of the leaders in front wore black half-masks almost down to their mouths. This disguise is very complete, especially at such a distance, and Syme found it impossible to conclude anything from the clean-shaven jaws and chins of the men talking in the front. But presently as they talked they all smiled and one of them smiled on one side.

CHAPTER II

The Criminals Chase the Police

Syme put the field-glasses from his eyes with an almost ghastly relief.

'The president is not with them, anyhow,' he said, and wiped his forehead.

'But surely they are right away on the horizon,' said the bewildered colonel, blinking and but half recovered from Bull's hasty though polite explanation. 'Could you possibly know your president among all those people?'

'Could I know a white elephant among all those people!' answered Syme, somewhat irritably. 'As you very truly say, they are on the horizon; but if he were walking with them . . . by God! I believe this ground would shake.'

After an instant's pause the new man called Ratcliffe said with gloomy decision: 'Of course the president isn't with them. I wish to Gemini he were. Much more likely the president is riding in triumph through Paris, or sitting on the ruins of St Paul's Cathedral.'

'This is absurd!' said Syme. 'Something may have happened in our absence; but he cannot have carried the world with a rush like that. It is quite true,' he added, frowning dubiously at the distant fields that lay towards the little station, 'it is certainly true that there seems to be a crowd coming this way; but they are not all the army that you make out.'

'Oh, they,' said the new detective contemptuously; 'no, they are not a very valuable force. But let me tell you frankly that they are precisely calculated to our value – we are not much, my boy, in Sunday's universe. He has got hold of all the cables and telegraphs himself. But to kill the Supreme Council he regards as a trivial matter, like a postcard; it may be left to his private secretary,' and he spat on the grass.

Then he turned to the others and said somewhat austerely: 'There is a great deal to be said for death; but if anyone has any preference for the other alternative, I strongly advise him to walk after me.'

With these words, he turned his broad back and strode with silent energy towards the wood. The others gave one glance over their shoulders, and saw that the dark cloud of men had detached itself from the station and was moving with a mysterious discipline across the plain. They saw already, even with the naked eye, black blots on the foremost faces, which marked the masks they wore. They turned and followed their leader, who had already struck the wood, and disappeared among the twinkling trees.

The sun on the grass was dry and hot. So in plunging into the wood they had a cool shock of shadow, as of divers who plunge into a dim pool. The inside of the wood was full of shattered sunlight and shaken shadows. They made a sort of shuddering veil, almost recalling the dizziness of a cinematograph. Even the solid figures walking with him Syme could hardly see for the patterns of sun and shade that danced upon them. Now a man's head was lit as with a light of Rembrandt, leaving all else obliterated; now again he had strong and staring white hands with the face of a negro. The ex-marquis had pulled the old straw hat over his eyes, and the black shade of the brim cut his face so squarely in two that it seemed to be wearing one of the black half-masks of their pursuers. The fancy tinted Syme's overwhelming sense of wonder. Was he wearing a mask? Was anyone wearing a mask? Was anyone anything? This wood of witchery, in which men's faces turned black and white by turns, in which their figures first swelled into sunlight and then faded into formless night, this mere chaos of chiaroscuro (after the clear daylight outside), seemed to Syme a perfect symbol of the world in which he had been moving for three days, this world where men took off their beards and their spectacles and their noses, and turned into other people. That tragic self-confidence which he had felt when he believed that the marquis was a devil had strangely disappeared now that he knew that the marquis was a friend. He felt almost inclined to ask after all these bewilderments what was a friend and what an enemy. Was there anything that was apart from what it seemed? The marquis had taken off his nose and turned out to be a detective. Might he not just as well take off his head and turn out to be a hobgoblin? Was not everything, after all, like this bewildering woodland, this dance of dark and light? Everything only a glimpse, the glimpse always unforeseen, and always forgotten. For Gabriel Syme had found in the heart of that sun-splashed wood what many modern painters had found there. He had found the thing which the modern people call Impressionism, which is another name for that final scepticism which can find no floor to the universe.

As a man in an evil dream strains himself to scream and wake, Syme strove with a sudden effort to fling off this last and worst of his fancies. With two impatient strides he overtook the man in the marquis's straw hat, the man whom he had come to address as Ratcliffe. In a voice exaggeratively loud and cheerful, he broke the bottomless silence and made conversation.

'May I ask,' he said, 'where on earth we are all going to?'

So genuine had been the doubts of his soul, that he was quite glad to hear his companion speak in an easy, human voice.

'We must get down through the town of Lancy to the sea,' he said. 'I think that part of the country is least likely to be with them.'

'What can you mean by all this?' cried Syme. 'They can't be running the real world in that way. Surely not many working-men are anarchists, and surely if they were, mere mobs could not beat modern armies and police.'

'Mere mobs!' repeated his new friend with a snort of scorn. 'So you talk about mobs and the working classes as if they were the question. You've got that eternal idiotic idea that if anarchy came it would come from the poor. Why should it? The poor have been rebels, but they have never been anarchists; they have more interest than anyone else in there being some decent government. The poor man really has a stake in the country. The rich man hasn't; he can go away to New Guinea in a yacht. The poor have sometimes objected to being governed badly; the rich have always objected to being governed at all. Aristocrats were always anarchists, as you can see from the barons' wars.'

'As a lecture on English history for the little ones,' said Syme, 'this is all very nice; but I have not yet grasped its application.'

'Its application is,' said his informant, 'that most of old Sunday's right-hand men are South African and American millionaires. That is why he has got hold of all the communications; and that is why the last four champions of the anti-anarchist police force are running through a wood like rabbits.'

'Millionaires I can understand,' said Syme thoughtfully, 'they are nearly all mad. But getting hold of a few wicked old gentlemen with hobbies is one thing; getting hold of great Christian nations is another. I would bet the nose off my face (forgive the allusion) that Sunday would stand perfectly helpless before the task of converting any ordinary healthy person anywhere.'

'Well,' said the other, 'it rather depends what sort of person you mean.'

'Well, for instance,' said Syme, 'he could never convert that person,' and he pointed straight in front of him.

They had come to an open space of sunlight, which seemed to express to Syme the final return of his own good sense; and in the middle of this forest clearing was a figure that might well stand for that common sense in an almost awful actuality. Burnt by the sun and stained with perspiration, and grave with the bottomless gravity of small necessary toils, a heavy French peasant was cutting wood with a hatchet. His cart stood a few yards off, already half full of timber; and the horse that cropped the grass was, like his master, valorous but not desperate; like his master, he was even prosperous, but yet was almost sad. The man was a Norman, taller than the average of the French and very angular; and his swarthy figure stood dark against a square of sunlight, almost like some allegoric figure of labour frescoed on a ground of gold.

'Mr Syme is saying,' called out Ratcliffe to the French colonel, 'that this man, at least, will never be an anarchist.'

'Mr Syme is right enough there,' answered Colonel Ducroix, laughing, 'if only for the reason that he has plenty of property to defend. But I forgot that in your country you are not used to peasants being wealthy.'

'He looks poor,' said Dr Bull doubtfully.

'Quite so,' said the colonel; 'that is why he is rich.'

'I have an idea,' called out Dr Bull suddenly; 'how much would he take to give us a lift in his cart? Those dogs are all on foot, and we could soon leave them behind.'

'Oh, give him anything!' said Syme eagerly. 'I have piles of money on me.'

'That will never do,' said the colonel; 'he will never have any respect for you unless you drive a bargain.'

'Oh, if he haggles!' began Bull impatiently.

'He haggles because he is a free man,' said the other. 'You do not understand; he would not see the meaning of generosity. He is not being tipped.'

And even while they seemed to hear the heavy feet of their strange pursuers behind them, they had to stand and stamp while the French colonel talked to the French woodcutter with all the leisurely badinage and bickering of market-day. At the end of the four minutes, however, they saw that the colonel was right, for the woodcutter entered into their plans, not with the vague servility of a tout too well paid, but with the seriousness of a solicitor who had been paid the proper fee. He told them that the best thing they could do was to make their way down to the little inn on the hills above Lancy, where the innkeeper, an old soldier who had become *dévot* in his latter years, would be certain to sympathise with them, and even to take risks in their support. The whole company, therefore, piled themselves on top of the stacks of wood, and went rocking in the rude cart down the other and steeper side of the woodland. Heavy and ramshackle as was the vehicle, it was driven quickly enough, and they soon had the exhilarating impression of distancing altogether those, whoever they were, who were hunting them. For, after all, the riddle as to where the anarchists had got all these followers was still unsolved. One man's presence had sufficed for them; they had fled at the first sight of the deformed smile of the secretary. Syme every now and then looked back over his shoulder at the army on their track.

As the wood grew first thinner and then smaller with distance, he could see the sunlit slopes beyond it and above it; and across these was still moving the square black mob like one monstrous beetle. In the very strong sunlight and with his own very strong eyes, which were almost telescopic, Syme could see this mass of men quite plainly. He could see them as separate human figures; but he was increasingly surprised by the way in which they moved as one man. They seemed to be dressed in dark clothes and plain hats, like any common crowd out of the streets; but they did not spread and sprawl and trail by various lines to the attack, as would be natural in an ordinary mob. They moved with a sort of dreadful and wicked woodenness, like a staring army of automatons.

Syme pointed this out to Ratcliffe.

'Yes,' replied the policeman, 'that's discipline. That's Sunday. He is perhaps five hundred miles off, but the fear of him is on all of them, like the finger of God. Yes, they are walking regularly; and you bet your boots that they are talking regularly, yes, and thinking regularly. But the one important thing for us is that they are disappearing regularly.'

Syme nodded. It was true that the black patch of the pursuing men was growing smaller and smaller as the peasant belaboured his horse.

The level of the sunlit landscape, though flat as a whole, fell away on the farther side of the wood in billows of heavy slope towards the sea, in a way not unlike the lower slopes of the Sussex downs. The only difference was that in Sussex the road would have been broken and angular like a little brook, but here the white French road fell sheer in front of them like a waterfall. Down this direct descent the cart clattered at a considerable angle, and in a few minutes, the road growing yet steeper, they saw below them the little harbour of Lancy and a great blue arc of the sea. The travelling cloud of their enemies had wholly disappeared from the horizon.

The horse and cart took a sharp turn round a clump of elms, and the horse's nose nearly struck the face of an old gentleman who was sitting on the benches outside the little café of Le Soleil d'Or. The peasant grunted an apology, and got down from his seat. The others also descended one by one, and spoke to the old gentleman with fragmentary phrases of courtesy, for it was quite evident from his expansive manner that he was the owner of the little tavern.

He was a white-haired, apple-faced old boy, with sleepy eyes and a grey moustache; stout, sedentary, and very innocent, of a type that may often be found in France, but is still commoner in Catholic Germany. Everything about him, his pipe, his pot of beer, his flowers, and his beehive, suggested an ancestral peace; only when his visitors looked up as they entered the inn-parlour, they saw the sword upon the wall.

The colonel, who greeted the innkeeper as an old friend, passed rapidly into the inn-parlour, and sat down, ordering some ritual refreshment. The military decision of his action interested Syme, who sat next to him, and he took the opportunity when the old innkeeper had gone out of satisfying his curiosity.

'May I ask you, colonel,' he said in a low voice, 'why we have come here?'

Colonel Ducroix smiled behind his bristly white moustache.

'For two reasons, sir,' he said; 'and I will give first, not the most important, but the most utilitarian. We came here because this is the only place within twenty miles in which we can get horses.'

'Horses!' repeated Syme, looking up quickly.

'Yes,' replied the other; 'if you people are really to distance your enemies it is horses or nothing for you, unless of course you have bicycles and motorcars in your pocket.'

'And where do you advise us to make for?' asked Syme doubtfully.

'Beyond question,' replied the colonel, 'you had better make all haste to the police station beyond the town. My friend, whom I seconded under somewhat deceptive circumstances, seems to me to exaggerate very much the possibilities of a general rising; but even he would hardly maintain, I suppose, that you were not safe with the gendarmes.'

Syme nodded gravely; then he said abruptly: 'And your other reason for coming here?'

'My other reason for coming here,' said Ducroix soberly, 'is that it is just as well to see a good man or two when one is possibly near to death.'

Syme looked up at the wall, and saw a crudely painted and pathetic religious picture. Then he said: 'You are right,' and then almost immediately afterwards, 'Has anyone seen about the horses?'

'Yes,' answered Ducroix, 'you may be quite certain that I gave orders the moment I came in. Those enemies of yours gave no impression of hurry, but they were really moving wonderfully fast, like a well-trained army. I had no idea that the anarchists had so much discipline. You have not a moment to waste.'

Almost as he spoke, the old innkeeper with the blue eyes and white hair came ambling into the room, and announced that six horses were saddled outside.

By Ducroix's advice the five others equipped themselves with some portable form of food and wine, and keeping their duelling swords as the only weapons available, they clattered away down the steep, white road. The two servants, who had carried the marquis's luggage when he was a marquis, were left behind to drink at the café by common consent, and not at all against their own inclination.

By this time the afternoon sun was slanting westward, and by its rays Syme could see the sturdy figure of the old innkeeper growing smaller and smaller, but still standing and looking after them quite silently, the sunshine in his silver hair. Syme had a fixed, superstitious fancy, left in his mind by the chance phrase of the colonel, that this was indeed, perhaps, the last honest stranger whom he should ever see upon the earth.

He was still looking at this dwindling figure, which stood as a mere grey blot touched with a white flame against the great green wall of the steep down behind him. And as he stared over the top of the down behind the innkeeper, there appeared an army of black-clad and marching men. They seemed to hang above the good man and his house like a black cloud of locusts. The horses had been saddled none too soon.

CHAPTER 12

The Earth in Anarchy

Urging the horses to a gallop, without respect to the rather rugged descent of the road, the horsemen soon regained their advantage over the men on the march, and at last the bulk of the first buildings of Lancy cut off the sight of their pursuers. Nevertheless, the ride had been a long one, and by the time they reached the real town the west was warming with the colour and quality of sunset. The colonel suggested that, before making finally for the police station, they should make the effort, in passing, to attach to themselves one more individual who might be useful.

'Four out of the five rich men in this town,' he said, 'are common swindlers. I suppose the proportion is pretty equal all over the world. The fifth is a friend of mine, and a very fine fellow; and what is even more important from our point of view, he owns a motorcar.'

'I am afraid,' said the professor in his mirthful way, looking back along the white road on which the black, crawling patch might appear at any moment, 'I am afraid we have hardly time for afternoon calls.'

'Dr Renard's house is only three minutes off,' said the colonel.

'Our danger,' said Dr Bull, 'is not two minutes off.'

'Yes,' said Syme, 'if we ride on fast we must leave them behind, for they are on foot.'

'He has a motorcar,' said the colonel.

'But we may not get it,' said Bull.

'Yes, he is quite on your side.'

'But he might be out.'

'Hold your tongue,' said Syme suddenly. 'What is that noise?'

For a second they all sat as still as equestrian statues, and for a second – for two or three or four seconds – heaven and earth seemed equally still. Then all their ears, in an agony of attention, heard along the road that indescribable thrill and throb that means only one thing – horses!

The colonel's face had an instantaneous change, as if lightning had struck it, and yet left it scatheless.

'They have done us,' he said, with brief military irony. 'Prepare to receive cavalry!'

'Where can they have got the horses?' asked Syme, as he mechanically urged his steed to a canter.

The colonel was silent for a little, then he said in a strained voice: 'I was speaking with strict accuracy when I said that the Soleil d'Or was the only place where one can get horses within twenty miles.'

'No!' said Syme violently, 'I don't believe he'd do it. Not with all that white hair.'

'He may have been forced,' said the colonel gently. 'They must be at least a hundred strong, for which reason we are all going to see my friend Renard, who has a motorcar.'

With these words he swung his horse suddenly round a street corner, and went down the street with such thundering speed, that the others, though already well at the gallop, had difficulty in following the flying tail of his horse.

Dr Renard inhabited a high and comfortable house at the top of a steep street, so that when the riders alighted at his door they could once more see the solid green ridge of the hill, with the white road across it, standing up above all the roofs of the town. They breathed again to see that the road as yet was clear, and they rang the bell.

Dr Renard was a beaming, brown-bearded man, a good example of that silent but very busy professional class which France has preserved even more perfectly than England. When the matter was explained to him he pooh-poohed the panic of the ex-marquis altogether; he said, with the solid French scepticism, that there was no conceivable probability of a general anarchist rising. 'Anarchy,' he said, shrugging his shoulders, 'it is childishness!'

'*Et ça*,' cried out the colonel suddenly, pointing over the other's shoulder, 'and that is childishness, isn't it?'

They all looked round, and saw a curve of black cavalry come sweeping over the top of the hill with all the energy of Attila. Swiftly as they rode, however, the whole rank still kept well together, and they could see the black vizards of the first line as level as a line of uniforms. But although the main black square was the same, though travelling faster, there was now one sensational difference which they could see clearly upon the slope of the hill, as if upon a slanted map. The bulk of the riders were in one block; but one rider flew far ahead of the column, and with frantic movements of hand and heel urged his horse faster and faster, so that one might have fancied that he was not the pursuer but the pursued. But even at that great distance they could see something so fanatical, so unquestionable in his figure, that they knew it was the secretary himself. 'I am sorry to cut short a cultured discussion,' said the colonel, 'but can you lend me your motorcar now, in two minutes?'

'I have a suspicion that you are all mad,' said Dr Renard, smiling sociably; 'but God forbid that madness should in any way interrupt friendship. Let us go round to the garage.'

Dr Renard was a mild man with monstrous wealth; his rooms were like the

Musée de Cluny, and he had three motorcars. These, however, he seemed to use very sparingly, having the simple tastes of the French middle class, and when his impatient friends came to examine them, it took them some time to assure themselves that one of them even could be made to work. This with some difficulty they brought round into the street before the doctor's house. When they came out of the dim garage they were startled to find that twilight had already fallen with the abruptness of night in the tropics. Either they had been longer in the place than they imagined, or some unusual canopy of cloud had gathered over the town. They looked down the steep streets, and seemed to see a slight mist coming up from the sea.

'It is now or never,' said Dr Bull. 'I hear horses.'

'No,' corrected the professor, 'a horse.'

And as they listened, it was evident that the noise, rapidly coming nearer on the rattling stones, was not the noise of the whole cavalcade but that of the one horseman, who had left it far behind – the insane secretary.

Syme's family, like most of those who end in the simple life, had once owned a motor, and he knew all about them. He had leapt at once into the chauffeur's seat, and with flushed face was wrenching and tugging at the disused machinery. He bent his strength upon one handle, and then said quite quietly: 'I am afraid it's no go.'

As he spoke, there swept round the corner a man rigid on his rushing horse, with the rush and rigidity of an arrow. He had a smile that thrust out his chin as if it were dislocated. He swept alongside of the stationary car, into which its company had crowded, and laid his hand on the front. It was the secretary, and his mouth went quite straight in the solemnity of triumph.

Syme was leaning hard upon the steering wheel, and there was no sound but the rumble of the other pursuers riding into the town. Then there came quite suddenly a scream of scraping iron, and the car leapt forward. It plucked the secretary clean out of his saddle, as a knife is whipped out of its sheath, trailed him kicking terribly for twenty yards, and left him flung flat upon the road far in front of his frightened horse. As the car took the corner of the street with a splendid curve, they could just see the other anarchists filling the street and raising their fallen leader.

'I can't understand why it has grown so dark,' said the professor at last in a low voice.

'Going to be a storm, I think,' said Dr Bull. 'I say, it's a pity we haven't got a light on this car, if only to see by.'

'We have,' said the colonel, and from the floor of the car he fished up a heavy, old-fashioned, carved iron lantern with a light inside it. It was obviously an antique, and it would seem as if its original use had been in some way semi-religious, for there was a rude moulding of a cross upon one of its sides.

'Where on earth did you get that?' asked the professor.

'I got it where I got the car,' answered the colonel, chuckling, 'from my best friend. While our friend here was fighting with the steering wheel, I ran up the front steps of the house and spoke to Renard, who was standing in his own porch, you will remember. "I suppose," I said, "there's no time to get a lamp." He looked up, blinking amiably at the beautiful arched ceiling of his own front hall. From this was suspended, by chains of exquisite ironwork, this lantern, one of the hundred treasures of his treasure house. By sheer force he tore the lamp out of his own ceiling, shattering the painted panels, and bringing down two blue vases with his violence. Then he handed me the iron lantern, and I put it in the car. Was I not right when I said that Dr Renard was worth knowing?'

'You were,' said Syme seriously, and hung the heavy lantern over the front. There was a certain allegory of their whole position in the contrast between the modern automobile and its strange ecclesiastical lamp. Hitherto they had passed through the quietest part of the town, meeting at most one or two pedestrians, who could give them no hint of the peace or the hostility of the place. Now, however, the windows in the houses began one by one to be lit up, giving a greater sense of habitation and humanity. Dr Bull turned to the new detective who had led their flight, and permitted himself one of his natural and friendly smiles.

'These lights make one feel more cheerful.'

Inspector Ratcliffe drew his brows together.

'There is only one set of lights that make me more cheerful,' he said, 'and they are those lights of the police station which I can see beyond the town. Please God we may be there in ten minutes.'

Then all Bull's boiling good sense and optimism broke suddenly out of him.

'Oh, this is all raving nonsense!' he cried. 'If you really think that ordinary people in ordinary houses are anarchists, you must be madder than an anarchist yourself. If we turned and fought these fellows, the whole town would fight for us.'

'No,' said the other with an immovable simplicity, 'the whole town would fight for them. We shall see.'

While they were speaking the professor had leant forward with sudden excitement.

'What is that noise?' he said.

'Oh, the horses behind us, I suppose,' said the colonel. 'I thought we had got clear of them.'

'The horses behind us! No,' said the professor, 'it is not horses, and it is not behind us.'

Almost as he spoke, across the end of the street before them two shining and rattling shapes shot past. They were gone almost in a flash, but everyone could see that they were motorcars, and the professor stood up with a pale face and swore that they were the other two motorcars from Dr Renard's garage.

'I tell you they were his,' he repeated, with wild eyes, 'and they were full of men in masks!'

'Absurd!' said the colonel angrily. 'Dr Renard would never give them his cars.'

'He may have been forced,' said Ratcliffe quietly. 'The whole town is on their side.'

'You still believe that?' asked the colonel incredulously.

'You will all believe it soon,' said the other with a hopeless calm.

There was a puzzled pause for some little time, and then the colonel began again abruptly: 'No, I can't believe it. The thing is nonsense. The plain people of a peaceable French town – '

He was cut short by a bang and a blaze of light, which seemed close to his eyes. As the car sped on it left a floating patch of white smoke behind it, and Syme had heard a shot shriek past his ear.

'My God!' said the colonel, 'someone has shot at us.'

'It need not interrupt conversation,' said the gloomy Ratcliffe. 'Pray resume your remarks, colonel. You were talking, I think, about the plain people of a peaceable French town.'

The staring colonel was long past minding satire. He rolled his eyes all round the street.

'It is extraordinary,' he said, 'most extraordinary.'

'A fastidious person,' said Syme, 'might even call it unpleasant. However, I suppose those lights out in the field beyond this street are the gendarmerie. We shall soon get there.'

'No,' said Inspector Ratcliffe, 'we shall never get there.'

He had been standing up and looking keenly ahead of him. Now he sat down and smoothed his sleek hair with a weary gesture.

'What do you mean?' asked Bull sharply.

'I mean that we shall never get there,' said the pessimist placidly. 'They have two rows of armed men across the road already; I can see them from here. The town is in arms, as I said it was. I can only wallow in the exquisite comfort of my own exactitude.'

And Ratcliffe sat down comfortably in the car and lit a cigarette, but the others rose excitedly and stared down the road. Syme had slowed down the car as their plans became doubtful, and he brought it finally to a standstill just at the corner of a side street that ran down very steeply to the sea.

The town was mostly in shadow, but the sun had not sunk; wherever its level light could break through, it painted everything a burning gold. Up this side street the last sunset light shone as sharp and narrow as the shaft of artificial light at the theatre. It struck the car of the five friends, and lit it like a burning chariot. But the rest of the street, especially the two ends of it, was in the deepest twilight, and for some seconds they could see nothing. Then Syme, whose eyes were the keenest, broke into a little bitter whistle, and he said: 'It is quite true. There is a crowd or an army or some such thing across the end of that street.'

'Well, if there is,' said Bull impatiently, 'it must be something else – a sham fight or the mayor's birthday or something. I cannot and will not believe that plain, jolly people in a place like this walk about with dynamite in their pockets. Get on a bit, Syme, and let us look at them.'

The car crawled about a hundred yards farther, and then they were all startled by Dr Bull breaking into a high crow of laughter.

'Why, you silly mugs!' he cried, 'what did I tell you? That crowd's as law-abiding as a cow, and if it weren't, it's on our side.'

'How do you know?' asked the professor, staring.

'You blind bat,' cried Bull, 'don't you see who is leading them?'

They peered again, and then the colonel, with a catch in his voice, cried out: 'Why, it's Renard!'

There was, indeed, a rank of dim figures running across the road, and they could not be clearly seen; but far enough in front to catch the accident of the evening light was stalking up and down the unmistakable Dr Renard, in a white hat, stroking his long brown beard, and holding a revolver in his left hand.

'What a fool I've been!' exclaimed the colonel. 'Of course, the dear old boy has turned out to help us.'

Dr Bull was bubbling over with laughter, swinging the sword in his hand as carelessly as a cane. He jumped out of the car and ran across the intervening space, calling out: 'Dr Renard! Dr Renard!'

An instant after Syme thought his own eyes had gone mad in his head. For the philanthropic Dr Renard had deliberately raised his revolver and fired twice at Bull, so that the shots rang down the road.

Almost at the same second as the puff of white cloud went up from this atrocious explosion a long puff of white cloud went up also from the cigarette of the cynical Ratcliffe. Like all the rest he turned a little pale, but he smiled. Dr Bull, at whom the bullets had been fired, just missing his scalp, stood quite still in the middle of the road without a sign of fear, and then turned very slowly and crawled back to the car, and climbed in with two holes through his hat.

'Well,' said the cigarette smoker slowly, 'what do you think now?'

'I think,' said Dr Bull with precision, 'that I am lying in bed at No. 217 Peabody Buildings, and that I shall soon wake up with a jump; or, if that's not it, I think that I am sitting in a small cushioned cell in Hanwell, and that the doctor can't make much of my case. But if you want to know what I don't think, I'll tell you. I don't think what you think. I don't think, and I never shall think, that the mass of ordinary men are a pack of dirty modern thinkers. No, sir, I'm a democrat, and I still don't believe that Sunday could convert one average navvy or counter-jumper. No, I may be mad, but humanity isn't.'

Syme turned his bright blue eyes on Bull with an earnestness which he did not commonly make clear.

'You are a very fine fellow,' he said. 'You can believe in a sanity which is not merely your sanity. And you're right enough about humanity, about peasants and people like that jolly old innkeeper. But you're not right about Renard. I suspected him from the first. He's rationalistic, and, what's worse, he's rich. When duty and religion are really destroyed, it will be by the rich.'

'They are really destroyed now,' said the man with a cigarette, and rose with his hands in his pockets. 'The devils are coming on!'

The men in the motorcar looked anxiously in the direction of his dreamy gaze, and they saw that the whole regiment at the end of the road was advancing upon them, Dr Renard marching furiously in front, his beard flying in the breeze.

The colonel sprang out of the car with an intolerant exclamation.

'Gentlemen,' he cried, 'the thing is incredible. It must be a practical joke. If you knew Renard as I do – it's like calling Queen Victoria a dynamiter. If you had got the man's character into your head – '

'Dr Bull,' said Syme sardonically, 'has at least got it into his hat.'

'I tell you it can't be!' cried the colonel, stamping. 'Renard shall explain it. He shall explain it to me,' and he strode forward.

'Don't be in such a hurry,' drawled the smoker. 'He will very soon explain it to all of us.'

But the impatient colonel was already out of earshot, advancing towards the advancing enemy. The excited Dr Renard lifted his pistol again, but perceiving his opponent, hesitated, and the colonel came face to face with him with frantic gestures of remonstrance.

'It is no good,' said Syme. 'He will never get anything out of that old heathen. I vote we drive bang through the thick of them, bang as the bullets went through Bull's hat. We may all be killed, but we must kill a tidy number of them.'

'I won't 'ave it,' said Dr Bull, growing more vulgar in the sincerity of his virtue. 'The poor chaps may be making a mistake. Give the colonel a chance.'

'Shall we go back, then?' asked the professor.

'No,' said Ratcliffe in a cold voice, 'the street behind us is held too. In fact, I seem to see there another friend of yours, Syme.'

Syme spun round smartly, and stared backwards at the track which they had travelled. He saw an irregular body of horsemen gathering and galloping towards them in the gloom. He saw above the foremost saddle the silver gleam of a sword, and then as it grew nearer the silver gleam of an old man's hair. The next moment, with shattering violence, he had swung the motor round and sent it dashing down the steep side street to the sea, like a man that desired only to die.

'What the devil is up?' cried the professor, seizing his arm.

'The morning star has fallen!' said Syme, as his own car went down the darkness like a falling star.

The others did not understand his words, but when they looked back at the street above they saw the hostile cavalry coming round the corner and down the slopes after them; and foremost of all rode the good innkeeper, flushed with the fiery innocence of the evening light.

'The world is insane!' said the professor, and buried his face in his hands.

'No,' said Dr Bull in adamantine humility, 'it is I.'

'What are we going to do?' asked the professor.

'At this moment,' said Syme, with a scientific detachment, 'I think we are going to smash into a lamppost.'

The next instant the automobile had come with a catastrophic jar against an iron object. The instant after that four men had crawled out from under a chaos of metal, and a tall lean lamppost that had stood up straight on the edge of the marine parade stood out, bent and twisted, like the branch of a broken tree.

'Well, we smashed something,' said the professor, with a faint smile. 'That's some comfort.'

'You're becoming an anarchist,' said Syme, dusting his clothes with his instinct of daintiness.

'Everyone is,' said Ratcliffe.

As they spoke, the white-haired horseman and his followers came thundering from above, and almost at the same moment a dark string of men ran shouting along the seafront. Syme snatched a sword, and took it in his teeth; he stuck two others under his armpits, took a fourth in his left hand and the lantern in his right, and leapt off the high parade on to the beach below.

The others leapt after him, with a common acceptance of such decisive action, leaving the debris and the gathering mob above them.

'We have one more chance,' said Syme, taking the steel out of his mouth. 'Whatever all this pandemonium means, I suppose the police station will help us. We can't get there, for they hold the way. But there's a pier or breakwater runs out into the sea just here, which we could defend longer than anything else, like Horatius and his bridge. We must defend it till the gendarmerie turn out. Keep after me.'

They followed him as he went crunching down the beach, and in a second or two their boots broke not on the sea gravel, but on broad, flat stones. They marched down a long, low jetty, running out in one arm into the dim, boiling sea, and when they came to the end of it they felt that they had come to the end of their story. They turned and faced the town.

That town was transfigured with uproar. All along the high parade from which they had just descended was a dark and roaring stream of humanity, with tossing arms and fiery faces, groping and glaring towards them. The long dark line was dotted with torches and lanterns; but even where no flame lit up a furious face, they could see in the farthest figure, in the most shadowy gesture, an organised hate. It was clear that they were the accursed of all men, and they knew not why.

Two or three men, looking little and black like monkeys, leapt over the edge as they had done and dropped on to the beach. These came ploughing down the deep sand, shouting horribly, and strove to wade into the sea at random. The example was followed, and the whole black mass of men began to run and drip over the edge like black treacle.

Foremost among the men on the beach Syme saw the peasant who had driven their cart. He splashed into the surf on a huge carthorse, and shook his axe at them.

'The peasant!' cried Syme. 'They have not risen since the Middle Ages.'

'Even if the police do come now,' said the professor mournfully, 'they can do nothing with this mob.'

'Nonsense!' said Bull desperately; 'there must be some people left in the town who are human.'

'No,' said the hopeless inspector, 'the human being will soon be extinct. We are the last of mankind.'

'It may be,' said the professor absently. Then he added in his dreamy voice, 'What is all that at the end of the *Dunciad*?

> 'Nor public flame; nor private, dare to shine;
> Nor human light is left, nor glimpse divine!
> Lo! thy dread Empire, Chaos, is restored;
> Light dies before thine uncreating word:
> Thy hand, great Anarch, lets the curtain fall;
> And universal darkness buries all.'

'Stop!' cried Bull suddenly, 'the gendarmes are out.'

The low lights of the police station were indeed blotted and broken with hurrying figures, and they heard through the darkness the clash and jingle of a disciplined cavalry.

'They are charging the mob!' cried Bull in ecstasy or alarm.

'No,' said Syme, 'they are formed along the parade.'

'They have unslung their carbines,' cried Bull, dancing with excitement.

'Yes,' said Ratcliffe, 'and they are going to fire on us.'

As he spoke there came a long crackle of musketry, and bullets seemed to hop like hailstones on the stones in front of them.

'The gendarmes have joined them!' cried the professor, and struck his forehead.

'I am in a padded cell,' said Bull stolidly.

There was a long silence, and then Ratcliffe said, looking out over the swollen sea, all a sort of grey purple: 'What does it matter who is mad or who is sane? We shall all be dead soon.'

Syme turned to him and said: 'You are quite hopeless, then?'

Mr Ratcliffe kept a stony silence; then at last he said quietly: 'No; oddly enough I am not quite hopeless. There is one insane little hope that I cannot get out of my mind. The power of this whole planet is against us, yet I cannot help wondering whether this one silly little hope is hopeless yet.'

'In what or whom is your hope?' asked Syme with curiosity.

'In a man I never saw,' said the other, looking at the leaden sea.

'I know what you mean,' said Syme in a low voice, 'the man in the dark room. But Sunday must have killed him by now.'

'Perhaps,' said the other steadily; 'but if so, he was the only man whom Sunday found it hard to kill.'

'I heard what you said,' said the professor, with his back turned. 'I also am holding hard on to the thing I never saw.'

All of a sudden Syme, who was standing as if blind with introspective thought, swung round and cried out, like a man waking from sleep: 'Where is the colonel? I thought he was with us!'

'The colonel! Yes,' cried Bull, 'where on earth is the colonel?'

'He went to speak to Renard,' said the professor.

'We cannot leave him among all those beasts,' cried Syme. 'Let us die like gentlemen if – '

'Do not pity the colonel,' said Ratcliffe, with a pale sneer. 'He is extremely comfortable. He is – '

'No! no! no!' cried Syme in a kind of frenzy, 'not the colonel too! I will never believe it!'

'Will you believe your eyes?' asked the other, and pointed to the beach.

Many of their pursuers had waded into the water shaking their fists, but the sea was rough, and they could not reach the pier. Two or three figures, however, stood on the beginning of the stone footway, and seemed to be cautiously advancing down it. The glare of a chance lantern lit up the faces of the two foremost. One face wore a black half-mask, and under it the mouth was twisting about in such a madness of nerves that the black tuft of beard wriggled round and round like a restless, living thing. The other was the red face and white moustache of Colonel Ducroix. They were in earnest consultation.

'Yes, he is gone too,' said the professor, and sat down on a stone. 'Everything's gone. I'm gone! I can't trust my own bodily machinery. I feel as if my own hand might fly up and strike me.'

'When my hand flies up,' said Syme, 'it will strike somebody else,' and he strode along the pier towards the colonel, the sword in one hand and the lantern in the other.

As if to destroy the last hope or doubt, the colonel, who saw him coming, pointed his revolver at him and fired. The shot missed Syme, but struck his sword, breaking it short at the hilt. Syme rushed on, and swung the iron lantern above his head.

'Judas before Herod!' he said, and struck the colonel down upon the stones. Then he turned to the secretary, whose frightful mouth was almost foaming now, and held the lamp high with so rigid and arresting a gesture, that the man was, as it were, frozen for a moment, and forced to hear.

'Do you see this lantern?' cried Syme in a terrible voice. 'Do you see the cross carved on it, and the flame inside? You did not make it. You did not light it. Better men than you, men who could believe and obey, twisted the entrails of iron and preserved the legend of fire. There is not a street you walk on, there is not a thread you wear, that was not made as this lantern was, by denying your philosophy of dirt and rats. You can make nothing. You can only destroy. You will destroy mankind; you will destroy the world. Let that suffice you. Yet this one old Christian lantern you shall not destroy. It shall go where your empire of apes will never have the wit to find it.'

He struck the secretary once with the lantern so that he staggered; and then, whirling it twice round his head, sent it flying far out to sea, where it flared like a roaring rocket and fell.

'Swords!' shouted Syme, turning his flaming face to the three behind him. 'Let us charge these dogs, for our time has come to die.'

His three companions came after him sword in hand. Syme's sword was broken, but he rent a bludgeon from the fist of a fisherman, flinging him down. In a moment they would have flung themselves upon the face of the mob and perished, when an interruption came. The secretary, ever since Syme's speech, had stood with his hand to his stricken head as if dazed; now he suddenly pulled off his black mask.

The pale face thus peeled in the lamplight revealed not so much rage as astonishment. He put up his hand with an anxious authority.

'There is some mistake,' he said. 'Mr Syme, I hardly think you understand your position. I arrest you in the name of the law.'

'Of the law?' said Syme, and dropped his stick.

'Certainly!' said the secretary. 'I am a detective from Scotland Yard,' and he took a small blue card from his pocket.

'And what do you suppose we are?' asked the professor, and threw up his arms.

'You,' said the secretary stiffly, 'are, as I know for a fact, members of the Supreme Anarchist Council. Disguised as one of you, I – '

Dr Bull tossed his sword into the sea.

'There never was any Supreme Anarchist Council,' he said. 'We were all a lot of silly policemen looking at each other. And all these nice people who have been peppering us with shot thought we were the dynamiters. I knew I couldn't be wrong about the mob,' he said, beaming over the enormous multitude, which stretched away to the distance on both sides. 'Vulgar people are never mad. I'm vulgar myself, and I know. I am now going on shore to stand a drink to everybody here.'

CHAPTER 13
The Pursuit of the President

Next morning five bewildered but hilarious people took the boat for Dover. The poor old colonel might have had some cause to complain, having been first forced to fight for two factions that didn't exist, and then knocked down with an iron lantern. But he was a magnanimous old gentleman, and being much relieved that neither party had anything to do with dynamite, he saw them off on the pier with great geniality.

The five reconciled detectives had a hundred details to explain to each other. The secretary had to tell Syme how they had come to wear masks originally in order to approach the supposed enemy as fellow-conspirators; Syme had to explain how they had fled with such swiftness through a civilised country. But above all these matters of detail which could be explained rose the central mountain of the matter that they could not explain. What did it all mean? If they were all harmless officers, what was Sunday? If he had not seized the world, what on earth had he been up to? Inspector Ratcliffe was still gloomy about this.

'I can't make head or tail of old Sunday's little game any more than you can,' he said. 'But whatever else Sunday is, he isn't a blameless citizen. Damn it! do you remember his face?'

'I grant you,' answered Syme, 'that I have never been able to forget it.'

'Well,' said the secretary, 'I suppose we can find out soon, for tomorrow we have our next general meeting. You will excuse me,' he said, with a rather ghastly smile, 'for being well acquainted with my secretarial duties.'

'I suppose you are right,' said the professor reflectively. 'I suppose we might find it out from him; but I confess that I should feel a bit afraid of asking Sunday who he really is.'

'Why,' asked the secretary, 'for fear of bombs?'

'No,' said the professor, 'for fear he might tell me.'

'Let us have some drinks,' said Dr Bull, after a silence.

Throughout their whole journey by boat and train they were highly convivial, but they instinctively kept together. Dr Bull, who had always been the optimist of the party, endeavoured to persuade the other four that the whole company could take the same hansom cab from Victoria; but this was overruled, and they went in a four-wheeler, with Dr Bull on the box, singing. They finished their journey at an hotel in Piccadilly Circus, so as to be close to the early breakfast next morning in Leicester Square. Yet even then the adventures of the day were not entirely over. Dr Bull, discontented with the general proposal to go to bed, had strolled out of the hotel at about eleven to see and taste some of the beauties of London. Twenty minutes afterwards, however, he came back and made quite a clamour in the hall. Syme, who tried at first to soothe him, was forced at last to listen to his communication with quite new attention.

'I tell you I've seen him!' said Dr Bull, with thick emphasis.

'Whom?' asked Syme quickly. 'Not the president?'

'Not so bad as that,' said Dr Bull, with unnecessary laughter, 'not so bad as that. I've got him here.'

'Got whom here?' asked Syme impatiently.

'Hairy man,' said the other lucidly, 'man that used to be hairy man – Gogol. Here he is,' and he pulled forward by a reluctant elbow the identical young man who five days before had marched out of the council with thin red hair and a pale face, the first of all the sham anarchists who had been exposed.

'Why do you worry with me?' he cried. 'You have expelled me as a spy.'

'We are all spies!' whispered Syme.

'We're all spies!' shouted Dr Bull. 'Come and have a drink.'

Next morning the battalion of the reunited six marched stolidly towards the hotel in Leicester Square.

'This is more cheerful,' said Dr Bull; 'we are six men going to ask one man what he means.'

'I think it is a bit queerer than that,' said Syme. 'I think it is six men going to ask one man what they mean.'

They turned in silence into the square, and though the hotel was in the opposite corner, they saw at once the little balcony and a figure that looked too big for it. He was sitting alone with bent head, poring over a newspaper. But all his councillors, who had come to vote him down, crossed that square as if they were watched out of heaven by a hundred eyes.

They had disputed much upon their policy, about whether they should leave the unmasked Gogol without and begin diplomatically, or whether they should bring him in and blow up the gunpowder at once. The influence of Syme and Bull prevailed for the latter course, though the secretary to the last asked them why they attacked Sunday so rashly.

'My reason is quite simple,' said Syme. 'I attack him rashly because I am afraid of him.'

They followed Syme up the dark stair in silence, and they all came out simultaneously into the broad sunlight of the morning and the broad sunlight of Sunday's smile.

'Delightful!' he said. 'So pleased to see you all. What an exquisite day it is. Is the Czar dead?'

The secretary, who happened to be foremost, drew himself together for a dignified outburst.

'No, sir,' he said sternly 'there has been no massacre. I bring you news of no such disgusting spectacles.'

'Disgusting spectacles?' repeated the president, with a bright, enquiring smile. 'You mean Dr Bull's spectacles?'

The secretary choked for a moment, and the president went on with a sort of smooth appeal: 'Of course, we all have our opinions and even our eyes, but really to call them disgusting before the man himself – '

Dr Bull tore off his spectacles and broke them on the table.

'My spectacles are blackguardly,' he said, 'but I'm not. Look at my face.'

'I dare say it's the sort of face that grows on one,' said the president, 'in fact, it grows on you; and who am I to quarrel with the wild fruits upon the Tree of Life? I dare say it will grow on me someday.'

'We have no time for tomfoolery,' said the secretary, breaking in savagely. 'We have come to know what all this means. Who are you? What are you? Why did you get us all here? Do you know who and what we are? Are you a half-witted man playing the conspirator, or are you a clever man playing the fool? Answer me, I tell you.'

'Candidates,' murmured Sunday, 'are only required to answer eight out of the seventeen questions on the paper. As far as I can make out, you want me to tell you what I am, and what you are, and what this table is, and what this council is, and what this world is for all I know. Well, I will go so far as to rend the veil of one mystery. If you want to know what you are, you are a set of highly well-intentioned young jackasses.'

'And you,' said Syme, leaning forward, 'what are you?'

'I? What am I?' roared the president, and he rose slowly to an incredible height, like some enormous wave about to arch above them and break. 'You want to know what I am, do you? Bull, you are a man of science. Grub in the roots of those trees and find out the truth about them. Syme, you are a poet. Stare at those morning clouds. But I tell you this, that you will have found out the truth of the last tree and the topmost cloud before the truth about me. You will understand the sea, and I shall be still a riddle; you shall know what the stars are, and not know what I am. Since the beginning of the world all men have hunted me like a wolf – kings and sages, and poets and law-givers, all the churches, and all the philosophers. But I have never been caught yet, and the skies will fall in the time I turn to bay. I have given them a good run for their money, and I will now.'

Before one of them could move, the monstrous man had swung himself like some huge orang-outang over the balustrade of the balcony. Yet before he dropped he pulled himself up again as on a horizontal bar, and thrusting his great chin over the edge of the balcony, said solemnly: 'There's one thing I'll tell you though about who I am. I am the man in the dark room, who made you all policemen.'

With that he fell from the balcony, bouncing on the stones below like a great ball of india-rubber, and went bounding off towards the corner of the Alhambra, where he hailed a hansom-cab and sprang inside it. The six detectives had been standing thunderstruck and livid in the light of his last assertion; but when he disappeared into the cab, Syme's practical senses returned to him, and leaping over the balcony so recklessly as almost to break his legs, he called another cab.

He and Bull sprang into the cab together, the professor and the inspector into another, while the secretary and the late Gogol scrambled into a third just in time to pursue the flying Syme, who was pursuing the flying president. Sunday led them a wild chase towards the north-west, his cab-man, evidently under the influence of more than common inducements, urging the horse at breakneck speed. But Syme was in no mood for delicacies, and he stood up in his own cab shouting, 'Stop thief!' until crowds ran along beside his cab, and policemen began to stop and ask questions. All this had its influence upon the president's cabman, who began to look dubious, and to slow down to a trot. He opened the trap to talk reasonably to his fare, and in so doing let the long whip droop over the front of the cab. Sunday leant forward, seized it, and jerked it violently out of the man's hand. Then standing up in front of the cab himself, he lashed the horse and roared aloud, so that they went down the streets like a flying storm. Through street after street and square after square went whirling this preposterous vehicle, in which the fare was urging the horse and the driver trying desperately to stop it. The other three cabs came after it (if the phrase be permissible of a cab) like panting hounds. Shops and streets shot by like rattling arrows.

At the highest ecstasy of speed, Sunday turned round on the splashboard where he stood, and sticking his great grinning head out of the cab, with white hair whistling in the wind, he made a horrible face at his pursuers, like some colossal urchin. Then raising his right hand swiftly, he flung a ball of paper in Syme's face and vanished. Syme caught the thing while instinctively warding it off, and discovered that it consisted of two crumpled papers. One was addressed to himself, and the other to Dr Bull, with a very long, and it is to be feared partly ironical, string of letters after his name. Dr Bull's address was, at any rate, considerably longer than his communication, for the communication consisted entirely of the words: 'What about Martin Tupper now?'

'What does the old maniac mean?' asked Bull, staring at the words. 'What does yours say, Syme?'

Syme's message was, at any rate, longer, and ran as follows:

> No one would regret anything in the nature of an interference by the Archdeacon more than I. I trust it will not come to that. But, for the last time, where are your goloshes? The thing is too bad, especially after what uncle said.

The president's cabman seemed to be regaining some control over his horse, and the pursuers gained a little as they swept round into the Edgware Road. And here there occurred what seemed to the allies a providential stoppage. Traffic of every kind was swerving to right or left or stopping, for down the long road was coming the unmistakable roar announcing the fire-engine, which in a few seconds went by like a brazen thunderbolt. But quick as it went by, Sunday had bounded out of his cab, sprung at the fire-engine, caught it, slung himself on to it, and was seen as he disappeared in the noisy distance talking to the astonished fireman with explanatory gestures.

'After him!' howled Syme. 'He can't go astray now. There's no mistaking a fire-engine.'

The three cabmen, who had been stunned for a moment, whipped up their horses and slightly decreased the distance between themselves and their disappearing prey. The president acknowledged this proximity by coming to the back of the car, bowing repeatedly, kissing his hand, and finally flinging a neatly folded note into the bosom of Inspector Ratcliffe. When that gentleman opened it, not without impatience, he found it contained the words:

> Fly at once. The truth about your trouser-stretchers is known.
>
> A Friend.

The fire-engine had struck still farther to the north, into a region that they did not recognise; and as it ran by a line of high railings shadowed with trees, the six friends were startled, but somewhat relieved, to see the president leap from the fire-engine, though whether through another whim or the increasing protest of his entertainers they could not see. Before the three cabs, however, could reach the spot, he had gone up the high railings like a huge grey cat, tossed himself over, and vanished in a darkness of leaves.

Syme with a furious gesture stopped his cab, jumped out, and sprang also to the escalade. When he had one leg over the fence and his friends were following, he turned a face on them which shone quite pale in the shadow.

'What place can this be?' he asked. 'Can it be the old devil's house? I've heard he has a house in North London.'

'All the better,' said the secretary grimly, planting a foot in a foothold, 'we shall find him at home.'

'No, but it isn't that,' said Syme, knitting his brows. 'I hear the most horrible noises, like devils laughing and sneezing and blowing their devilish noses!'

'His dogs barking, of course,' said the secretary.

'Why not say his black-beetles barking!' said Syme furiously, 'snails barking! geraniums barking! Did you ever hear a dog bark like that?'

He held up his hand, and there came out of the thicket a long growling roar that seemed to get under the skin and freeze the flesh – a low thrilling roar that made a throbbing in the air all about them.

'The dogs of Sunday would be no ordinary dogs,' said Gogol, and shuddered.

Syme had jumped down on the other side, but he still stood listening impatiently.

'Well, listen to that,' he said, 'is that a dog – anybody's dog?'

There broke upon their ear a hoarse screaming as of things protesting and clamouring in sudden pain; and then, far off like an echo, what sounded like a long nasal trumpet.

'Well, his house ought to be hell!' said the secretary; 'and if it is hell, I'm going in!' and he sprang over the tall railings almost with one swing.

The others followed. They broke through a tangle of plants and shrubs, and came out on an open path. Nothing was in sight, but Dr Bull suddenly struck his hands together.

'Why, you asses,' he cried, 'it's the Zoo!'

As they were looking round wildly for any trace of their wild quarry, a keeper in uniform came running along the path with a man in plain clothes.

'Has it come this way?' gasped the keeper.

'Has what?' asked Syme.

'The elephant!' cried the keeper. 'An elephant has gone mad and run away!'

'He has run away with an old gentleman,' said the other stranger breathlessly, 'a poor old gentleman with white hair!'

'What sort of old gentleman?' asked Syme, with great curiosity.

'A very large and fat old gentleman in light grey clothes,' said the keeper eagerly.

'Well,' said Syme, 'if he's that particular kind of old gentleman, if you're quite sure that he's a large and fat old gentleman in grey clothes, you may take my word for it that the elephant has not run away with him. He has run away with the elephant. The elephant is not made by God that could run away with him if he did not consent to the elopement. And, by thunder, there he is!'

There was no doubt about it this time. Clean across the space of grass, about two hundred yards away, with a crowd screaming and scampering vainly at his heels, went a huge grey elephant at an awful stride, with his trunk thrown out as rigid as a ship's bowsprit, and trumpeting like the trumpet of doom. On the back of the bellowing and plunging animal sat President Sunday with all the placidity of a sultan, but goading the animal to a furious speed with some sharp object in his hand.

'Stop him!' screamed the populace. 'He'll be out of the gate!'

'Stop a landslide!' said the keeper. 'He is out of the gate!'

And even as he spoke, a final crash and roar of terror announced that the great grey elephant had broken out of the gates of the Zoological Gardens, and was careening down Albany Street like a new and swift sort of omnibus.

'Great Lord!' cried Bull, 'I never knew an elephant could go so fast. Well, it must be hansom-cabs again if we are to keep him in sight.'

As they raced along to the gate out of which the elephant had vanished, Syme felt a glaring panorama of the strange animals in the cages which they passed. Afterwards he thought it queer that he should have seen them so clearly. He remembered especially seeing pelicans, with their preposterous, pendent throats. He wondered why the pelican was the symbol of charity, except it was that it wanted a good deal of charity to admire a pelican. He remembered a hornbill, which was simply a huge yellow beak with a small bird tied on behind it. The whole gave him a sensation, the vividness of which he could not explain, that Nature was always making quite mysterious jokes. Sunday had told them that they would understand him when they had understood the stars. He wondered whether even the archangels understood the hornbill.

The six unhappy detectives flung themselves into cabs and followed the elephant, sharing the terror which he spread through the long stretch of the streets. This time Sunday did not turn round, but offered them the solid stretch of his unconscious back, which maddened them, if possible, more than his previous mockeries. Just before they came to Baker Street, however, he was seen to throw something far up into the air, as a boy does a ball, meaning to catch it again. But at their rate of racing it fell far behind, just by the cab containing Gogol; and in faint hope of a clue or for some impulse unexplainable, he stopped his cab so as to pick it up. It was addressed to himself, and was quite a bulky parcel. On examination, however, its bulk was found to consist of thirty-three pieces of paper of no value wrapped one round the other. When the last covering was torn away it reduced itself to a small slip of paper, on which was written: 'The word, I fancy, should be "pink".'

The man once known as Gogol said nothing, but the movements of his hands and feet were like those of a man urging a horse to renewed efforts.

Through street after street, through district after district, went the prodigy of the flying elephant, calling crowds to every window, and driving the traffic left and right. And still through all this insane publicity the three cabs toiled after it, until they came to be regarded as part of a procession, and perhaps the advertisement of a circus. They went at such a rate that distances were shortened beyond belief, and Syme saw the Albert Hall in Kensington when he thought that he was still in Paddington. The animal's pace was even more fast and free through the empty, aristocratic streets of South Kensington, and he finally headed towards that part of the skyline where the enormous Wheel of Earl's Court stood up in the sky. The wheel grew larger and larger, till it filled heaven like the wheel of stars.

The beast outstripped the cabs. They lost him round several corners, and when they came to one of the gates of the Earl's Court Exhibition they found themselves finally blocked. In front of them was an enormous crowd; in the midst of it was an enormous elephant, heaving and shuddering as such shapeless creatures do. But the president had disappeared.

'Where has he gone to?' asked Syme, slipping to the ground.

'Gentleman rushed into the Exhibition, sir!' said an official in a dazed manner. Then he added in an injured voice: 'Funny gentleman, sir. Asked me to hold his horse, and gave me this.'

He held out with distaste a piece of folded paper, addressed: 'To the Secretary of the Central Anarchist Council.'

The secretary, raging, rent it open, and found written inside it:

> When the herring runs a mile,
> Let the secretary smile;
> When the herring tries to *fly*,
> Let the secretary die.
>
> Rustic Proverb

'Why the eternal crikey,' began the secretary, 'did you let the man in? Do people commonly come to your Exhibition riding on mad elephants? Do –'

'Look!' shouted Syme suddenly. 'Look over there!'

'Look at what?' asked the secretary savagely.

'Look at the captive balloon!' said Syme, and pointed in a frenzy.

'Why the blazes should I look at a captive balloon?' demanded the secretary. 'What is there queer about a captive balloon?'

'Nothing,' said Syme, 'except that it isn't captive!'

They all turned their eyes to where the balloon swung and swelled above the Exhibition on a string, like a child's balloon. A second afterwards the string came in two just under the car, and the balloon, broken loose, floated away with the freedom of a soap bubble.

'Ten thousand devils!' shrieked the secretary. 'He's got into it!' and he shook his fists at the sky.

The balloon, borne by some chance wind, came right above them, and they could see the great white head of the president peering over the side and looking benevolently down on them.

'God bless my soul!' said the professor with the elderly manner that he could never disconnect from his bleached beard and parchment face. 'God bless my soul! I seemed to fancy that something fell on the top of my hat!'

He put up a trembling hand and took from that shelf a piece of twisted paper, which he opened absently only to find it inscribed with a true lover's knot and, the words:

Your beauty has not left me indifferent. – from LITTLE SNOWDROP

There was a short silence, and then Syme said, biting his beard: 'I'm not beaten yet. The blasted thing must come down somewhere. Let's follow it!'

CHAPTER 14

The Six Philosophers

Across green fields, and breaking through blooming hedges, toiled six draggled detectives, about five miles out of London. The optimist of the party had at first proposed that they should follow the balloon across South England in hansom-cabs. But he was ultimately convinced of the persistent refusal of the balloon to follow the roads, and the still more persistent refusal of the cabmen to follow the balloon. Consequently the tireless though exasperated travellers broke through black thickets and ploughed through ploughed fields till each was turned into a figure too outrageous to be mistaken for a tramp. Those green hills of Surrey saw the final collapse and tragedy of the admirable light grey suit in which Syme had set out from

Saffron Park. His silk hat was broken over his nose by a swinging bough, his coat-tails were torn to the shoulder by arresting thorns, the clay of England was splashed up to his collar; but he still carried his yellow beard forward with a silent and furious determination, and his eyes were still fixed on that floating ball of gas, which in the full flush of sunset seemed coloured like a sunset cloud.

'After all,' he said, 'it is very beautiful!'

'It is singularly and strangely beautiful!' said the professor. 'I wish the beastly gas-bag would burst!'

'No,' said Dr Bull, 'I hope it won't. It might hurt the old boy.'

'Hurt him!' said the vindictive professor, 'hurt him! Not as much as I'd hurt him if I could get up with him. Little Snowdrop!'

'I don't want him hurt, somehow,' said Dr Bull.

'What!' cried the secretary bitterly. 'Do you believe all that tale about his being our man in the dark room? Sunday would say he was anybody.'

'I don't know whether I believe it or not,' said Dr Bull. 'But it isn't that that I mean. I can't wish old Sunday's balloon to burst because – '

'Well,' said Syme impatiently, 'because?'

'Well, because he's so jolly like a balloon himself,' said Dr Bull desperately. 'I don't understand a word of all that idea of his being the same man who gave us all our blue cards. It seems to make everything nonsense. But I don't care who knows it, I always had a sympathy for old Sunday himself, wicked as he was. Just as if he was a great bouncing baby. How can I explain what my queer sympathy was? It didn't prevent my fighting him like hell! Shall I make it clear if I say that I liked him because he was so fat?'

'You will not,' said the secretary.

'I've got it now,' cried Bull, 'it was because he was so fat and so light. Just like a balloon. We always think of fat people as heavy, but he could have danced against a sylph. I see now what I mean. Moderate strength is shown in violence, supreme strength is shown in levity. It was like the old speculations – what would happen if an elephant could leap up in the sky like a grasshopper?'

'Our elephant,' said Syme, looking upwards, 'has leapt into the sky like a grasshopper.'

'And somehow,' concluded Bull, 'that's why I can't help liking old Sunday. No, it's not an admiration of force, or any silly thing like that. There is a kind of gaiety in the thing, as if he were bursting with some good news. Haven't you sometimes felt it on a spring day? You know Nature plays tricks, but somehow that day proves they are good-natured tricks. I never read the Bible myself, but that part they laugh at is literal truth, "Why leap ye, ye high hills?" The hills do leap – at least, they try to . . . Why do I like Sunday? . . . how can I tell you? . . . because he's such a bounder.'

There was a long silence, and then the secretary said in a curious, strained voice: 'You do not know Sunday at all. Perhaps it is because you are better than I, and do not know hell. I was a fierce fellow, and a trifle morbid from the first. The man who sits in darkness, and who chose us all, chose me because I had all the crazy look of a conspirator – because my smile went crooked, and my eyes were gloomy, even when I smiled. But there must have been something in me that answered to the nerves in all these anarchic men. For when I first saw Sunday he expressed to me, not your airy vitality, but something both gross and sad in the Nature of Things. I found him smoking in a twilight room, a room with brown blind down, infinitely more depressing than the genial darkness in which our master lives. He sat there on a bench, a huge heap of a man, dark and out of shape. He listened to all my words without speaking or even stirring. I poured out my most passionate appeals, and asked my most eloquent questions. Then, after a long silence, the Thing began to shake, and I thought it was shaken by some secret malady. It shook like a loathsome and living jelly. It reminded me of everything I had ever read about the base bodies that are the origin of life – the deep sea lumps and protoplasm. It seemed like the final form of matter, the most shapeless and the most shameful. I could only tell myself, from its shudderings, that it was something at least that such a monster could be miserable. And then it broke upon me that the bestial mountain was shaking with a lonely laughter, and the laughter was at me. Do you ask me to forgive him that? It is no small thing to be laughed at by something at once lower and stronger than oneself.'

'Surely you fellows are exaggerating wildly,' cut in the clear voice of Inspector Ratcliffe. 'President Sunday is a terrible fellow for one's intellect, but he is not such a Barnum's freak physically as you make out. He received me in an ordinary office, in a grey check coat, in broad daylight. He talked to me in an ordinary way. But I'll tell you what is a trifle creepy about Sunday. His room is neat, his clothes are neat, everything seems in order; but he's absent-minded. Sometimes his great bright eyes go quite blind. For hours he forgets that you are there. Now absent-mindedness is just a bit too awful in a bad man. We think of a wicked man as vigilant. We can't think of a wicked man who is honestly and sincerely dreamy, because we daren't think of a wicked man alone with himself. An absentminded man means a good-natured man. It means a man who, if he happens to see you, will apologise. But how will you bear an absent-minded man who, if he happens to see you, will kill you? That is what tries the nerves, abstraction combined with cruelty. Men have felt it sometimes when they went through wild forests, and felt that the animals there were at once innocent and pitiless. They might ignore or slay. How would you like to pass ten mortal hours in a parlour with an absent-minded tiger?'

'And what do you think of Sunday, Gogol?' asked Syme.

'I don't think of Sunday on principle,' said Gogol simply, 'any more than I stare at the sun at noonday.'

'Well, that is a point of view,' said Syme thoughtfully. 'What do you say, professor?'

The professor was walking with bent head and trailing stick, and he did not answer at all.

'Wake up, professor!' said Syme genially. 'Tell us what you think of Sunday.'

The professor spoke at last very slowly.

'I think something,' he said, 'that I cannot say clearly. Or, rather, I think something that I cannot even think clearly. But it is something like this. My early life, as you know, was a bit too large and loose. Well, when I saw Sunday's face I thought it was too large – everybody does, but I also thought it was too loose. The face was so big that one couldn't focus it or make it a face at all. The eye was so far away from the nose that it wasn't an eye. The mouth was so much by itself that one had to think of it by itself. The whole thing is too hard to explain.'

He paused for a little, still trailing his stick, and then went on: 'But put it this way. Walking up a road at night, I have seen a lamp and a lighted window and a cloud make together a most complete and unmistakable face. If anyone in heaven has that face I shall know him again. Yet when I walked a little farther I found that there was no face, that the window was ten yards away, the lamp ten hundred yards, the cloud beyond the world. Well, Sunday's face escaped me; it ran away to right and left, as such chance pictures run away. And so his face has made me, somehow, doubt whether there are any faces. I don't know whether your face, Bull, is a face or a combination in perspective. Perhaps one black disc of your beastly glasses is quite close and another fifty miles away. Oh, the doubts of a materialist are not worth a dump. Sunday has taught me the last and the worst doubts, the doubts of a spiritualist. I am a Buddhist, I suppose; and Buddhism is not a creed, it is a doubt. My poor dear Bull, I do not believe that you really have a face. I have not faith enough to believe in matter.'

Syme's eyes were still fixed upon the errant orb, which, reddened in the evening light, looked like some rosier and more innocent world.

'Have you noticed an odd thing,' he said, 'about all your descriptions? Each man of you finds Sunday quite different, yet each man of you can only find one thing to compare him to – the universe itself. Bull finds him like the earth in spring, Gogol like the sun at noonday. The secretary is reminded of the shapeless protoplasm, and the inspector of the carelessness of virgin forests. The professor says he is like a changing landscape. This is queer, but it is queerer still that I also have had my odd notion about the president, and I also find that I think of Sunday as I think of the whole world.'

'Get on a little faster, Syme,' said Bull; 'never mind the balloon.'

'When I first saw Sunday,' said Syme slowly, 'I only saw his back; and when I saw his back, I knew he was the worst man in the world. His neck and shoulders were brutal, like those of some apish god. His head had a stoop that was hardly human, like the stoop of an ox. In fact, I had at once the revolting fancy that this was not a man at all, but a beast dressed up in men's clothes.'

'Get on,' said Dr Bull.

'And then the queer thing happened. I had seen his back from the street, as he sat in the balcony. Then I entered the hotel, and coming round the other side of him, saw his face in the sunlight. His face frightened me, as it did everyone; but not because it was brutal, not because it was evil. On the contrary, it frightened me because it was so beautiful, because it was so good.'

'Syme,' exclaimed the secretary, 'are you ill?'

'It was like the face of some ancient archangel, judging justly after heroic wars. There was laughter in the eyes, and in the mouth honour and sorrow. There was the same white hair, the same great, grey-clad shoulders that I had seen from behind. But when I saw him from behind I was certain he was an animal, and when I saw him in front I knew he was a god.'

'Pan,' said the professor dreamily, 'was a god and an animal.'

'Then, and again and always,' went on Syme like a man talking to himself, 'that has been for me the mystery of Sunday, and it is also the mystery of the world. When I see the horrible back, I am sure the noble face is but a mask. When I see the face but for an instant, I know the back is only a jest. Bad is so bad, that we cannot but think good an accident; good is so good, that we feel certain that evil could be explained. But the whole came to a kind of crest yesterday when I raced Sunday for the cab, and was just behind him all the way.'

'Had you time for thinking then?' asked Ratcliffe.

'Time,' replied Syme, 'for one outrageous thought. I was suddenly possessed with the idea that the blind, blank back of his head really was his face – an awful, eyeless face staring at me! And I fancied that the figure running in front of me was really a figure running backwards, and dancing as he ran.'

'Horrible!' said Dr Bull, and shuddered.

'Horrible is not the word,' said Syme. 'It was exactly the worst instant of my life. And yet ten minutes afterwards, when he put his head out of the cab and made a grimace like a gargoyle, I knew that he was only like a father playing hide-and-seek with his children.'

'It is a long game,' said the secretary, and frowned at his broken boots.

'Listen to me,' cried Syme with extraordinary emphasis. 'Shall I tell you the secret of the whole world? It is that we have only known the back of the world. We see everything from behind, and it looks brutal. That is not a tree, but the back of a tree. That is not a cloud, but the back of a cloud. Cannot you see that everything is stooping and hiding a face? If we could only get round in front – '

'Look!' cried out Bull clamorously, 'the balloon is coming down!'

There was no need to cry out to Syme, who had never taken his eyes off it. He saw the great luminous globe suddenly stagger in the sky, right itself, and then sink slowly behind the trees like a setting sun.

The man called Gogol, who had hardly spoken through all their weary travels, suddenly threw up his hands like a lost spirit.

'He is dead!' he cried. 'And now I know he was my friend – my friend in the dark!'

'Dead!' snorted the secretary. 'You will not find him dead easily. If he has been tipped out of the car, we shall find him rolling as a colt rolls in a field, kicking his legs for fun.'

'Clashing his hoofs,' said the professor. 'The colts do, and so did Pan.'

'Pan again!' said Dr Bull irritably. 'You seem to think Pan is everything.'

'So he is,' said the professor, 'in Greek. He means everything.'

'Don't forget,' said the secretary, looking down, 'that he also means panic.'

Syme had stood without hearing any of the exclamations.

'It fell over there,' he said shortly. 'Let us follow it!'

Then he added with an indescribable gesture: 'Oh, if he has cheated us all by getting killed! It would be like one of his larks.'

He strode off towards the distant trees with a new energy, his rags and ribbons fluttering in the wind. The others followed him in a more footsore and dubious manner. And almost at the same moment all six men realised that they were not alone in the little field.

Across the square of turf a tall man was advancing towards them, leaning on a strange long staff like a sceptre. He was clad in a fine but old-fashioned suit with knee-breeches; its colour was that shade between blue, violet and grey which can be seen in certain shadows of the woodland. His hair was whitish grey, and at the first glance, taken along with his knee-breeches, looked as if it was powdered. His advance was very quiet; but for the silver frost upon his head, he might have been one of the shadows of the wood.

'Gentlemen,' he said, 'my master has a carriage waiting for you in the road just by.'

'Who is your master?' asked Syme, standing quite still.

'I was told you knew his name,' said the man respectfully.

There was a silence, and then the secretary said: 'Where is this carriage?'

'It has been waiting only a few moments,' said the stranger. 'My master has only just come home.'

Syme looked left and right upon the patch of green field in which he found himself. The hedges were ordinary hedges, the trees seemed ordinary trees; yet he felt like a man entrapped in fairyland.

He looked the mysterious ambassador up and down, but he could discover nothing except that the man's coat was the exact colour of the purple shadows, and that the man's face was the exact colour of the red and brown and golden sky.

'Show us the place,' Syme said briefly, and without a word the man in the violet coat turned his back and walked towards a gap in the hedge, which let in suddenly the light of a white road.

As the six wanderers broke out upon this thoroughfare, they saw the white road blocked by what looked like a long row of carriages, such a row of carriages as might close the approach to some house in Park Lane. Along the side of these carriages stood a rank of splendid servants, all dressed in the grey-blue uniform, and all having a certain quality of stateliness and freedom which would not commonly belong to the servants of a gentleman, but rather to the officials and ambassadors of a great king. There were no less than six carriages waiting, one for each of the tattered and miserable band. All the attendants (as if in court-dress) wore swords, and as each man crawled into his carriage they drew them, and saluted with a sudden blaze of steel.

'What can it all mean?' asked Bull of Syme as they separated. 'Is this another joke of Sunday's?'

'I don't know,' said Syme as he sank wearily back in the cushions of his carriage; 'but if it is, it's one of the jokes you talk about. It's a good-natured one.'

The six adventurers had passed through many adventures, but not one had carried them so utterly off their feet as this last adventure of comfort. They had all become inured to things going roughly; but things suddenly going smoothly swamped them. They could not even feebly imagine what the carriages were; it was enough for them to know that they were carriages, and carriages with cushions. They could not conceive who the old man was who had led them; but it was quite enough that he had certainly led them to the carriages.

Syme drove through a drifting darkness of trees in utter abandonment. It was typical of him that while he had carried his bearded chin forward fiercely so long as anything could be done, when the whole business was taken out of his hands he fell back on the cushions in a frank collapse.

Very gradually and very vaguely he realised into what rich roads the carriage was carrying him. He saw that they passed the stone gates of what might have been a park, that they began gradually to climb a hill which, while wooded on both sides, was somewhat more orderly than a forest.

Then there began to grow upon him, as upon a man slowly waking from a healthy sleep, a pleasure in everything. He felt that the hedges were what hedges should be, living walls; that a hedge is like a human army, disciplined, but all the more alive. He saw high elms behind the hedges, and vaguely thought how happy boys would be climbing there. Then his carriage took a turn of the path, and he saw suddenly and quietly, like a long, low, sunset cloud, a long, low house, mellow in the mild light of sunset. All the six friends compared notes afterwards and quarrelled; but they all agreed that in some unaccountable way the place reminded them of their boyhood. It was either this elm-top or that crooked path, it was either this scrap of orchard or that shape of a window; but each man of them declared that he could remember this place before he could remember his mother.

When the carriages eventually rolled up to a large, low, cavernous gateway, another man in the same uniform, but wearing a silver star on the grey breast of his coat, came out to meet them. This impressive person said to the bewildered Syme: 'Refreshments are provided for you in your room.'

Syme, under the influence of the same mesmeric sleep of amazement, went up the large oaken stairs after the respectful attendant. He entered a splendid suite of apartments that seemed to be designed specially for him. He walked up to a long mirror with the ordinary instinct of his class, to pull his tie straight or to smooth his hair; and there he saw the frightful figure that he was – blood running down his face from where the bough had struck him, his hair standing out like yellow rags of rank grass, his clothes torn into long, wavering tatters. At once the whole enigma sprang up, simply as the question of how he had got there, and how he was to get out again. Exactly at the same moment a man in blue, who had been appointed as his valet, said very solemnly: 'I have put out your clothes, sir.'

'Clothes!' said Syme sardonically. 'I have no clothes except these,' and he lifted two long strips of his frock-coat in fascinating festoons, and made a movement as if to twirl like a ballet girl.

'My master asks me to say,' said the attendant, 'that there is a fancy dress ball tonight, and that he desires you to put on the costume that I have laid out. Meanwhile, sir, there is a bottle of Burgundy and some cold pheasant, which he hopes you will not refuse, as it is some hours before supper.'

'Cold pheasant is a good thing,' said Syme reflectively, 'and Burgundy is a spanking good thing. But really I do not want either of them so much as I want to know what the devil all this means, and what sort of costume you have got laid out for me. Where is it?'

The servant lifted off a kind of ottoman a long peacock-blue drapery, rather of the nature of a domino, on the front of which was emblazoned a large golden sun, and which was splashed here and there with flaming stars and crescents.

'You're to be dressed as Thursday, sir,' said the valet somewhat affably.

'Dressed as Thursday!' said Syme in meditation. 'It doesn't sound a warm costume.'

'Oh, yes, sir,' said the other eagerly, 'the Thursday costume is quite warm, sir. It fastens up to the chin.'

'Well, I don't understand anything,' said Syme, sighing. 'I have been used so long to uncomfortable adventures that comfortable adventures knock me out. Still, I may be allowed to ask why I should be particularly like Thursday in a green frock spotted all over with the sun and moon. Those orbs, I think, shine on other days. I once saw the moon on Tuesday, I remember.'

'Beg pardon, sir,' said the valet, 'Bible also provided for you,' and with a respectful and rigid finger he pointed out a passage in the first chapter of Genesis. Syme read it wondering. It was that in which the fourth day of the week is associated with the creation of the sun and moon. Here, however, they reckoned from a Christian Sunday.

'This is getting wilder and wilder,' said Syme, as he sat down in a chair. 'Who are these people who provide cold pheasant and Burgundy, and green clothes and Bibles? Do they provide everything?'

'Yes, sir, everything,' said the attendant gravely. 'Shall I help you on with your costume?'

'Oh, hitch the bally thing on!' said Syme impatiently.

But though he affected to despise the mummery, he felt a curious freedom and naturalness in his movements as the blue and gold garment fell about him; and when he found that he had to wear a sword, it stirred a boyish dream. As he passed out of the room he flung the folds across his shoulder with a gesture, his sword stood out at an angle, and he had all the swagger of a troubadour. For these disguises did not disguise, but reveal.

CHAPTER 15

The Accuser

As Syme strode along the corridor he saw the secretary standing at the top of a great flight of stairs. The man had never looked so noble. He was draped in a long robe of starless black, down the centre of which fell a band or broad stripe of pure white, like a single shaft of light. The whole looked like some very severe ecclesiastical vestment. There was no need for Syme to search his memory or the Bible in order to remember that the first day of creation marked the mere creation of light out of darkness. The vestment itself would alone have suggested the symbol; and Syme felt also how perfectly this pattern of pure white and black expressed the soul of the pale and austere secretary, with his inhuman veracity and his cold frenzy, which made him so easily make war on the anarchists, and yet so easily pass for one of them. Syme was scarcely surprised to notice that, amid all the ease and hospitality of their new surroundings, this man's eyes were still stern. No smell of ale or orchards could make the secretary cease to ask a reasonable question.

If Syme had been able to see himself, he would have realised that he, too, seemed to be for the first time himself and no one else. For if the secretary stood for that philosopher who loves the original and formless light, Syme was a type of the poet who seeks always to make the light in special shapes, to split it up into sun and star. The philosopher may sometimes love the infinite; the poet always loves the finite. For him the great moment is not the creation of light, but the creation of the sun and moon.

As they descended the broad stairs together they overtook Ratcliffe, who was clad in spring green like a huntsman, and the pattern upon whose garment was a green tangle of trees. For he stood for that third day on which the earth and green things were made, and his square, sensible face, with its not unfriendly cynicism, seemed appropriate enough to it.

They were led out of another broad and low gateway into a very large old English garden, full of torches and bonfires, by the broken light of which a vast carnival of people were dancing in motley dress. Syme seemed to see every shape in Nature imitated in some crazy costume. There was a man dressed as a windmill with enormous sails, a man dressed as an elephant, a man dressed as a balloon; the two last, together, seemed to keep the thread of their farcical adventures. Syme even saw, with a queer thrill, one dancer dressed like an enormous hornbill, with a beak twice as big as himself – the queer bird which had fixed itself on his fancy like a living question while he was rushing down the long road at the Zoological Gardens. There were a thousand other such objects, however. There was a dancing lamppost, a dancing apple tree, a dancing ship. One would have thought that the untamable tune of some mad musician had set all the common objects of field and street dancing an eternal jig. And long afterwards, when Syme was middle-aged and at rest, he could never see one of those particular objects – a lamppost, or an apple tree, or a windmill – without thinking that it was a strayed reveller from that revel of masquerade.

On one side of this lawn, alive with dancers, was a sort of green bank, like the terrace in such old-fashioned gardens.

Along this, in a kind of crescent, stood seven great chairs, the thrones of the seven days. Gogol and Dr Bull were already in their seats; the professor was just mounting to his. Gogol, or Tuesday, had his simplicity well symbolised by a dress designed upon the division of the waters, a dress that separated upon his forehead and fell to his feet, grey and silver, like a sheet of rain. The professor, whose day was that on which the birds and fishes – the ruder forms of life – were created, had a dress of dim purple, over which sprawled goggle-eyed fishes and outrageous tropical birds, the union in him of unfathomable fancy and of doubt. Dr Bull, the last day of Creation, wore a coat covered with heraldic animals in red and gold, and on his crest a man rampant. He lay back in his chair with a broad smile, the picture of an optimist in his element.

One by one the wanderers ascended the bank and sat in their strange seats. As each of them sat down a roar of enthusiasm rose from the carnival, such as that with which crowds receive kings. Cups were clashed and torches shaken, and feathered hats flung in the air. The men for whom these thrones were reserved were men crowned with some extraordinary laurels. But the central chair was empty.

Syme was on the left hand of it and the secretary on the right. The secretary looked across the empty throne at Syme, and said, compressing his lips: 'We do not know yet that he is not dead in a field.'

Almost as Syme heard the words, he saw on the sea of human faces in front of him a frightful and beautiful alteration, as if heaven had opened behind his head. But Sunday had only passed silently along the front like a shadow, and had sat in the central seat. He was draped plainly, in a pure and terrible white, and his hair was like a silver flame on his forehead.

For a long time – it seemed for hours – that huge masquerade of mankind swayed and stamped in front of them to marching and exultant music. Every couple dancing seemed a separate romance; it might be a fairy dancing with a pillar-box, or a peasant girl dancing with the moon; but in each case it was, somehow, as absurd as Alice in Wonderland, yet as grave and kind as a love story. At last, however, the thick crowd began to thin itself. Couples strolled away into the garden-walks, or began to drift towards that end of the building where stood smoking, in huge pots like fish-kettles, some hot and scented mixtures of old ale or wine. Above all these, upon a sort of black framework on the roof of the house, roared in its iron basket a gigantic bonfire, which lit up the land for miles. It flung the homely effect of firelight over the face of vast forests of grey or brown, and it seemed to fill with warmth even the emptiness of upper night. Yet this also, after a time, was allowed to grow fainter; the dim groups gathered more and more round the great cauldrons, or passed, laughing and clattering, into the inner passages of that ancient house. Soon there were only some ten loiterers in the garden; soon only four. Finally the last stray merry-maker ran into the house whooping to his companions. The fire faded, and the slow, strong stars came out. And the seven strange men were left alone, like seven stone statues on their chairs of stone. Not one of them had spoken a word.

They seemed in no haste to do so, but heard in silence the hum of insects and the distant song of one bird. Then Sunday spoke, but so dreamily that he might have been continuing a conversation rather than beginning one.

'We will eat and drink later,' he said. 'Let us remain together a little, we who have loved each other so sadly, and have fought so long. I seem to remember only centuries of heroic war, in which you were always heroes – epic on epic, iliad on iliad, and you always brothers in arms. Whether it was but recently (for time is nothing), or at the beginning of the world, I sent you out to war. I sat in the darkness, where there is not any created thing, and to you I was only a voice commanding valour and an unnatural virtue. You heard the voice in the dark, and you never heard it again. The sun in heaven denied it, the earth and sky denied it, all human wisdom denied it. And when I met you in the daylight I denied it myself.'

Syme stirred sharply in his seat, but otherwise there was silence, and the incomprehensible went on.

'But you were men. You did not forget your secret honour, though the whole cosmos turned an engine of torture to tear it out of you. I knew how near you were to hell. I know how you, Thursday, crossed swords with King Satan, and how you, Wednesday, named me in the hour without hope.'

There was complete silence in the starlit garden, and then the black-browed secretary, implacable, turned in his chair towards Sunday, and said in a harsh voice: 'Who and what are you?'

'I am the Sabbath,' said the other without moving. 'I am the peace of God.'

The secretary started up, and stood crushing his costly robe in his hand.

'I know what you mean,' he cried, 'and it is exactly that that I cannot forgive you. I know you are contentment, optimism, what do they call the thing, an ultimate reconciliation. Well, I am not reconciled. If you were the man in the dark room, why were you also Sunday, an offence to the sunlight? If you were from the first our father and our friend, why were you also our greatest enemy? We wept, we fled in terror; the iron entered into our souls – and you are the peace of God! Oh, I can forgive God His anger, though it destroyed nations; but I cannot forgive Him His peace.'

Sunday answered not a word, but very slowly he turned his face of stone upon Syme as if asking a question.

'No,' said Syme, 'I do not feel fierce like that. I am grateful to you, not only for wine and hospitality here, but for many a fine scamper and free fight. But I should like to know. My soul and heart are as happy and quiet here as this old garden, but my reason is still crying out. I should like to know.'

Sunday looked at Ratcliffe, whose clear voice said: 'It seems so *silly* that you should have been on both sides and fought yourself.'

Bull said: 'I understand nothing, but I am happy. In fact, I am going to sleep.'

'I am not happy,' said the professor with his head in his hands, 'because I do not understand. You let me stray a little too near to hell.'

And then Gogol said, with the absolute simplicity of a child: 'I wish I knew why I was hurt so much.'

Still Sunday said nothing, but only sat with his mighty chin upon his hand, and gazed at the distance. Then at last he said: 'I have heard your complaints in order. And here, I think, comes another to complain, and we will hear him also.'

The falling fire in the great cresset threw a last long gleam, like a bar of burning gold, across the dim grass. Against this fiery band was outlined in utter black the advancing legs of a black-clad figure. He seemed to have a fine close suit with knee-breeches such as that which was worn by the servants of the house, only that it was not blue, but of this absolute sable. He had, like the servants, a kind of sword by his side. It was only when he had come quite close to the crescent of the seven and flung up his face to look at them, that Syme saw, with thunder-struck clearness, that the face was the broad, almost apelike face of his old friend Gregory, with its rank red hair and its insulting smile.

'Gregory!' gasped Syme, half-rising from his seat. 'Why, this is the real anarchist!'

'Yes,' said Gregory, with a great and dangerous restraint, 'I am the real anarchist.'

' "Now there was a day," ' murmured Bull, who seemed really to have fallen asleep, ' "when the sons of God came to present themselves before the Lord, and Satan came also among them." '

'You are right,' said Gregory, and gazed all round. 'I am a destroyer. I would destroy the world if I could.'

A sense of a pathos far under the earth stirred up in Syme, and he spoke brokenly and without sequence.

'Oh, most unhappy man,' he cried, 'try to be happy! You have red hair like your sister.'

'My red hair, like red flames, shall burn up the world,' said Gregory. 'I thought I hated everything more than common men can hate anything; but I find that I do not hate everything as much as I hate you!'

'I never hated you,' said Syme very sadly.

Then out of this unintelligible creature the last thunders broke.

'You!' he cried. 'You never hated because you never lived. I know what you are, all of you, from first to last – you are the people in power! You are the police – the great fat, smiling men in blue and buttons! You are the Law, and you have never been broken. But is there a free soul alive that does not long to break you, only because you have never been broken? We in revolt talk all kind of nonsense doubtless about this crime or that crime of the

Government. It is all folly! The only crime of the Government is that it governs. The unpardonable sin of the supreme power is that it is supreme. I do not curse you for being cruel. I do not curse you (though I might) for being kind. I curse you for being safe! You sit in your chairs of stone, and have never come down from them. You are the seven angels of heaven, and you have had no troubles. Oh, I could forgive you everything, you that rule all mankind, if I could feel for once that you had suffered for one hour a real agony such as I – '

Syme sprang to his feet, shaking from head to foot.

'I see everything,' he cried, 'everything that there is. Why does each thing on the earth war against each other thing? Why does each small thing in the world have to fight against the world itself? Why does a fly have to fight the whole universe? Why does a dandelion have to fight the whole universe? For the same reason that I had to be alone in the dreadful Council of the Days. So that each thing that obeys law may have the glory and isolation of the anarchist. So that each man fighting for order may be as brave and good a man as the dynamiter. So that the real lie of Satan may be flung back in the face of this blasphemer, so that by tears and torture we may earn the right to say to this man, "You lie!" No agonies can be too great to buy the right to say to this accuser, "We also have suffered."

'It is not true that we have never been broken. We have been broken upon the wheel. It is not true that we have never descended from these thrones. We have descended into hell. We were complaining of unforgettable miseries even at the very moment when this man entered insolently to accuse us of happiness. I repel the slander; we have not been happy. I can answer for every one of the great guards of Law whom he has accused. At least – '

He had turned his eyes so as to see suddenly the great face of Sunday, which wore a strange smile.

'Have you,' he cried in a dreadful voice, 'have you ever suffered?'

As he gazed, the great face grew to an awful size, grew larger than the colossal mask of Memnon, which had made him scream as a child. It grew larger and larger, filling the whole sky; then everything went black. Only in the blackness before it entirely destroyed his brain he seemed to hear a distant voice saying a commonplace text that he had heard somewhere, 'Can ye drink of the cup that I drink of?'

* * *

When men in books awake from a vision, they commonly find themselves in some place in which they might have fallen asleep; they yawn in a chair, or lift themselves with bruised limbs from a field. Syme's experience was something much more psychologically strange if there was indeed anything unreal, in the earthly sense, about the things he had gone through. For while he could always remember afterwards that he had swooned before the face of Sunday, he could not remember having ever come to at all. He could only remember that gradually and naturally he knew that he was and had been walking along a country lane with an easy and conversational companion. That companion had been a part of his recent drama; it was the red-haired poet Gregory. They were walking like old friends, and were in the middle of a conversation about some triviality. But Syme could only feel an unnatural buoyancy in his body and a crystal simplicity in his mind that seemed to be superior to everything that he said or did. He felt he was in possession of some impossible good news, which made every other thing a triviality, but an adorable triviality.

Dawn was breaking over everything in colours at once clear and timid; as if Nature made a first attempt at yellow and a first attempt at rose. A breeze blew so clean and sweet, that one could not think that it blew from the sky; it blew rather through some hole in the sky. Syme felt a simple surprise when he saw rising all round him on both sides of the road the red, irregular buildings of Saffron Park. He had no idea that he had walked so near London. He walked by instinct along one white road, on which early birds hopped and sang, and found himself outside a fenced garden. There he saw the sister of Gregory, the girl with the gold-red hair, cutting lilac before breakfast, with the great unconscious gravity of a girl.

THE INNOCENCE OF FATHER BROWN

The Innocence of Father Brown

Contents

The Blue Cross

Between the silver ribbon of morning and the green glittering ribbon of sea, the boat touched Harwich and let loose a swarm of folk like flies, among whom the man we must follow was by no means conspicuous – nor wished to be. There was nothing notable about him, except a slight contrast between the holiday gaiety of his clothes and the official gravity of his face. His clothes included a slight, pale grey jacket, a white waistcoat, and a silver straw hat with a grey-blue ribbon. His lean face was dark by contrast, and ended in a curt black beard that looked Spanish and suggested an Elizabethan ruff. He was smoking a cigarette with the seriousness of an idler. There was nothing about him to indicate the fact that the grey jacket covered a loaded revolver, that the white waistcoat covered a police card, or that the straw hat covered one of the most powerful intellects in Europe. For this was Valentin himself, the head of the Paris police and the most famous investigator of the world; and he was coming from Brussels to London to make the greatest arrest of the century.

Flambeau was in England. The police of three countries had tracked the great criminal at last from Ghent to Brussels, from Brussels to the Hook of Holland; and it was conjectured that he would take some advantage of the unfamiliarity and confusion of the Eucharistic Congress, then taking place in London. Probably he would travel as some minor clerk or secretary connected with it; but, of course, Valentin could not be certain; nobody could be certain about Flambeau.

It is many years now since this colossus of crime suddenly ceased keeping the world in a turmoil; and when he ceased, as they said after the death of Roland, there was a great quiet upon the earth. But in his best days (I mean, of course, his worst) Flambeau was a figure as statuesque and international as the Kaiser. Almost every morning the daily paper announced that he had escaped the consequences of one extraordinary crime by committing another. He was a Gascon of gigantic stature and bodily daring; and the wildest tales were told of his outbursts of athletic humour; how he turned the *juge d'instruction* upside down and stood him on his head, 'to clear his mind'; how he ran down the Rue de Rivoli with a policeman under each arm. It is due to him to say that his fantastic physical strength was generally employed in such bloodless though undignified scenes; his real crimes were chiefly those of ingenious and wholesale robbery. But each of his thefts was almost a new sin, and would make a story by itself. It was he who ran the great Tyrolean Dairy Company in London, with no dairies, no cows, no carts, no milk, but with some thousand subscribers. These he served by the simple operation of moving the little milk cans outside people's doors to the doors of his own customers. It was he who had kept up an unaccountable and close correspondence with a young lady whose whole letter-bag was intercepted, by the extraordinary trick of photographing his messages infinitesimally small upon the slides of a microscope. A sweeping simplicity, however, marked many of his experiments. It is said that he once repainted all the numbers in a street in the dead of night merely to divert one traveller into a trap. It is quite certain that he invented a portable pillar-box, which he put up at corners in quiet suburbs on the chance of strangers dropping postal orders into it. Lastly, he was known to be a startling acrobat; despite his huge figure, he could leap like a grasshopper and melt into the tree-tops like a monkey. Hence the great Valentin, when he set out to find Flambeau, was perfectly aware that his adventures would not end when he had found him.

But how was he to find him? On this the great Valentin's ideas were still in process of settlement.

There was one thing which Flambeau, with all his dexterity of disguise, could not cover, and that was his singular height. If Valentin's quick eye had caught a tall apple-woman, a tall grenadier, or even a tolerably tall duchess, he might have arrested them on the spot. But all along his train there was nobody that could be a disguised Flambeau, any more than a cat could be a disguised giraffe. About the people on the boat he had already satisfied himself; and the people picked up at Harwich or on the journey limited themselves with certainty to six. There was a short railway official travelling up to the terminus, three fairly short market gardeners picked up two stations afterwards, one very short widow lady going up from a small Essex town, and a very short Roman Catholic priest going up from a small Essex village. When it came to the last case, Valentin gave it up and almost laughed. The little priest was so much the essence of those Eastern flats; he had a face as round and dull as a Norfolk dumpling; he had eyes as empty as the North Sea; he had several brown paper parcels, which he was quite incapable of collecting. The Eucharistic Congress had doubtless sucked out of their local stagnation many such creatures, blind and helpless, like moles disinterred. Valentin was a sceptic in the severe style of France, and could have no love for priests. But he could have pity for them, and this one might have provoked pity in anybody. He had a large, shabby umbrella, which constantly fell on the floor. He did not seem to know which was the right end of his return ticket. He explained with a moon-calf simplicity to everybody in the carriage that he had to be careful, because he had something made of real silver 'with blue stones' in one of his brown-paper parcels. His quaint blending of Essex flatness with saintly simplicity continuously amused the Frenchman till the priest arrived (somehow) at Tottenham with all his parcels, and came back for his umbrella. When he did the last, Valentin even had the good nature to warn him not to take care of the silver by telling everybody about it. But to whomever he talked, Valentin kept his eye open for someone else; he looked out steadily for anyone, rich or poor, male or female, who was well up to six feet; for Flambeau was four inches above it.

He alighted at Liverpool Street, however, quite conscientiously secure that he had not missed the criminal so far. He then went to Scotland Yard to regularise his position and arrange for help in case of need; he then lit another cigarette and went for a long stroll in the streets of London. As he was walking in the streets and squares beyond Victoria, he paused suddenly and stood. It was a quaint, quiet square, very typical of London, full of an accidental stillness. The tall, flat houses round looked at once prosperous and uninhabited; the square of shrubbery in the centre looked as deserted as a green Pacific islet. One of the four sides was much higher than the rest, like a dais; and the line of this side was broken by one of London's admirable accidents – a restaurant that looked as if it had strayed from Soho. It was an unreasonably attractive object, with dwarf plants in pots and long, striped blinds of lemon yellow and white. It stood specially high above the street, and in the usual patchwork way of London, a flight of steps from the street ran up to meet the front door almost as a fire-escape might run up to a first-floor window. Valentin stood and smoked in front of the yellow-white blinds and considered them long.

The most incredible thing about miracles is that they happen. A few clouds in heaven do come together into the staring shape of one human eye. A tree does stand up in the landscape of a doubtful journey in the exact and elaborate shape of a note of interrogation. I have seen both these things myself within the last few days. Nelson does die in the instant of victory; and a man named Williams does quite accidentally murder a man named Williamson; it sounds like a sort of infanticide. In short, there is in life an element of elfin coincidence which people reckoning on the prosaic may perpetually miss. As it has been well expressed in the paradox of Poe, wisdom should reckon on the unforeseen.

Aristide Valentin was unfathomably French; and the French intelligence is intelligence specially and solely. He was not 'a thinking machine'; for that is a brainless phrase of modern fatalism and materialism. A machine only *is* a machine because it cannot think. But he was a thinking man, and a plain man at the same time. All his wonderful successes, that looked like conjuring, had been gained by plodding logic, by clear and commonplace French thought. The French electrify the world not by starting any paradox, they electrify it by carrying out a truism. They carry a truism so far – as in the French Revolution. But exactly because Valentin understood reason, he understood the limits of reason. Only a man who knows nothing of motors talks of motoring without petrol; only a man who knows nothing of reason talks of reasoning without strong, undisputed first principles. Here he had no strong first principles. Flambeau had been missed at Harwich; and if he was in London at all, he might be anything from a tall tramp on Wimbledon Common to a tall toast-master at the Hotel Metropole. In such a naked state of nescience, Valentin had a view and a method of his own.

In such cases he reckoned on the unforeseen. In such cases, when he could not follow the train of the reasonable, he coldly and carefully followed the train of the unreasonable. Instead of going to the right places – banks, police stations, rendezvous – he systematically went to the wrong places; knocked at every empty house, turned down every cul-de-sac, went up every lane blocked with rubbish, went round every crescent that led him uselessly out of the way. He defended this crazy course quite logically. He said that if one had a clue this was the worst way; but if one had no clue at all it was the best, because there was just the chance that any oddity that caught the eye of the pursuer might be the same that had caught the eye of the pursued. Somewhere a man must begin, and it had better be just where another man might stop. Something about that flight of steps up to the shop, something about the quietude and quaintness of the restaurant, roused all the detective's rare romantic fancy and made him resolve to strike at random. He went up the steps, and sitting down at a table by the window, asked for a cup of black coffee.

It was halfway through the morning, and he had not breakfasted; the slight litter of other breakfasts stood about on the table to remind him of his hunger; and adding a poached egg to his order, he proceeded musingly to shake some white sugar into his coffee, thinking all the time about Flambeau. He remembered how Flambeau had escaped, once by a pair of nail scissors, and once by a house on fire; once by having to pay for an unstamped letter, and once by getting people to look through a telescope at a comet that might destroy the world. He thought his detective brain as good as the criminal's, which was true. But he fully realised the disadvantage. 'The criminal is the creative artist; the detective only the critic,' he said with a sour smile, and lifted his coffee cup to his lips slowly, and put it down very quickly. He had put salt in it.

He looked at the vessel from which the silvery powder had come; it was certainly a sugar-basin; as unmistakably meant for sugar as a champagne-bottle for champagne. He wondered why they should keep salt in it. He looked to see if there were any more orthodox vessels. Yes; there were two salt-cellars quite full. Perhaps there was some speciality in the condiment in the salt-cellars. He tasted it; it was sugar. Then he looked round at the restaurant with a refreshed air of interest, to see if there were any other traces of that singular artistic taste which puts the sugar in the salt-cellars and the salt in the sugar-basin. Except for an odd splash of some dark fluid on one of the white-papered walls, the whole place appeared neat, cheerful and ordinary. He rang the bell for the waiter.

When that official hurried up, fuzzy-haired and somewhat blear-eyed at that early hour, the detective (who was not without an appreciation of the simpler forms of humour) asked him to taste the sugar and see if it was up to the high reputation of the hotel. The result was that the waiter yawned suddenly and woke up.

'Do you play this delicate joke on your customers every morning?' enquired Valentin. 'Does changing the salt and sugar never pall on you as a jest?'

The waiter, when this irony grew clearer, stammeringly assured him that the establishment had certainly no such intention; it must be a most curious mistake. He picked up the sugar-basin and looked at it; he picked up the salt-cellar and looked at that, his face growing more and more bewildered. At last he abruptly excused himself, and hurrying away, returned in a few seconds with the proprietor. The proprietor also examined the sugar-basin and then the salt-cellar; the proprietor also looked bewildered.

Suddenly the waiter seemed to grow inarticulate with a rush of words.

'I zink,' he stuttered eagerly, 'I zink it is those two clergymen.'

'What two clergymen?'

'The two clergymen,' said the waiter, 'that threw soup at the wall.'

'Threw soup at the wall?' repeated Valentin, feeling sure this must be some singular Italian metaphor.

'Yes, yes,' said the attendant excitedly, and pointed at the dark splash on the white paper; 'threw it over there on the wall.'

Valentin looked his query at the proprietor, who came to his rescue with fuller reports.

'Yes, sir,' he said, 'it's quite true, though I don't suppose it has anything to do with the sugar and salt. Two clergymen came in and drank soup here very early, as soon as the shutters were taken down. They were both very quiet, respectable people; one of them paid the bill and went out; the other, who seemed a slower coach altogether, was some minutes longer getting his things together. But he went at last. Only, the instant before he stepped into the street he deliberately picked up his cup, which he had only half emptied, and threw the soup slap on the wall. I was in the back room myself, and so was the waiter; so I could only rush out in time to find the wall splashed and the shop empty. It didn't do any particular damage, but it was confounded cheek; and I tried to catch the men in the street. They were too far off though; I only noticed they went round the next corner into Carstairs Street.'

The detective was on his feet, hat settled and stick in hand. He had already decided that in the universal darkness of his mind he could only follow the first odd finger that pointed; and this finger was odd enough. Paying his bill and clashing the glass doors behind him, he was soon swinging round into the other street.

It was fortunate that even in such fevered moments his eye was cool and quick. Something in a shop-front went by him like a mere flash; yet he went back to look at it. The shop was a popular greengrocer and fruiterer's, an array of goods set out in the open air and plainly ticketed with their names and prices. In the two most prominent compartments were two heaps, of oranges and of nuts respectively. On the heap of nuts lay a scrap of cardboard, on which was written in bold, blue chalk, 'Best tangerine oranges, two a penny.' On the oranges was the equally clear and exact description, 'Finest Brazil nuts, *4d.* a lb.' M. Valentin looked at these two placards and fancied he had met this highly subtle form of humour before, and that somewhat recently. He drew the attention of the red-faced fruiterer, who was looking rather sullenly up and down the street, to this inaccuracy in his advertisements. The fruiterer said nothing, but sharply put each card into its proper place. The detective, leaning elegantly on his walking-cane, continued to scrutinise the shop. At last he said, 'Pray excuse my apparent irrelevance, my good sir, but I should like to ask you a question in experimental psychology and the association of ideas.'

The red-faced shopman regarded him with an eye of menace; but he continued gaily, swinging his cane. 'Why,' he pursued, 'why are two tickets wrongly placed in a greengrocer's shop like a shovel hat that has come to London for a holiday? Or, in case I do not make myself clear, what is the mystical association which connects the idea of nuts marked as oranges with the idea of two clergymen, one tall and the other short?'

The eyes of the tradesman stood out of his head like a snail's; he really seemed for an instant likely to fling himself upon the stranger. At last he stammered angrily: 'I don't know what you 'ave to do with it, but if you're one of their friends, you can tell 'em from me that I'll knock their silly 'eads off, parsons or no parsons, if they upset my apples again.'

'Indeed?' asked the detective, with great sympathy. 'Did they upset your apples?'

'One of 'em did,' said the heated shopman; 'rolled 'em all over the street. I'd 'ave caught the fool but for havin' to pick 'em up.'

'Which way did these parsons go?' asked Valentin.

'Up that second road on the left-hand side, and then across the square,' said the other promptly.

'Thanks,' replied Valentin, and vanished like a fairy. On the other side of the second square he found a policeman, and said: 'This is urgent, constable; have you seen two clergymen in shovel hats?'

The policeman began to chuckle heavily. 'I 'ave, sir; and if you arst me, one of 'em was drunk. He stood in the middle of the road that bewildered that – '

'Which way did they go?' snapped Valentin.

'They took one of them yellow buses over there,' answered the man; 'them that go to Hampstead.'

Valentin produced his official card and said very rapidly: 'Call up two of your men to come with me in pursuit,' and crossed the road with such contagious energy that the ponderous policeman was moved to almost agile obedience. In a minute and a half the French detective was joined on the opposite pavement by an inspector and a man in plain clothes.

'Well, sir,' began the former, with smiling importance, 'and what may – ?'

Valentin pointed suddenly with his cane. 'I'll tell you on the top of that omnibus,' he said, and was darting and dodging across the tangle of the traffic. When all three sank panting on the top seats of the yellow vehicle, the inspector said: 'We could go four times as quick in a taxi.'

'Quite true,' replied their leader placidly, 'if we only had an idea of where we were going.'

'Well, where are you going?' asked the other, staring.

Valentin smoked frowningly for a few seconds; then, removing his cigarette, he said: 'If you know what a man's doing, get in front of him; but if you want to guess what he's doing, keep behind him. Stray when he strays; stop when he stops; travel as slowly as he. Then you may see what he saw and may act as he acted. All we can do is to keep our eyes skinned for a queer thing.'

'What sort of queer thing do you mean?' asked the inspector.

'Any sort of queer thing,' answered Valentin, and relapsed into obstinate silence.

The yellow omnibus crawled up the northern roads for what seemed like hours on end; the great detective would not explain further, and perhaps his assistants felt a silent and growing doubt of his errand. Perhaps, also, they felt a silent and growing desire for lunch, for the hours crept long past the normal luncheon hour, and the long roads of the North London suburbs seemed to shoot out into length after length like an infernal telescope. It was one of those journeys on which a man perpetually feels that now at last he must have come to the end of the universe, and then finds he has only come to the beginning of Tufnell Park. London died away in draggled taverns and dreary scrubs, and then was unaccountably born again in blazing high streets and blatant hotels. It was like passing through thirteen separate vulgar cities all just touching each other. But though the winter twilight was already threatening the road ahead of them, the Parisian detective still sat silent and watchful, eyeing the frontage of the streets that slid by on either side. By the time they had left Camden Town behind, the policemen were nearly asleep; at least, they gave something like a jump as Valentin leapt erect, struck a hand on each man's shoulder, and shouted to the driver to stop.

They tumbled down the steps into the road without realising why they had been dislodged; when they looked round for enlightenment they found Valentin triumphantly pointing his finger towards a window on the left side of the road. It was a large window, forming part of the long façade of a gilt and palatial public-house; it was the part reserved for respectable dining, and labelled 'Restaurant'. This window, like all the rest along the frontage of the hotel, was of frosted and figured glass; but in the middle of it was a big, black smash, like a star in the ice.

'Our cue at last,' cried Valentin, waving his stick; 'the place with the broken window.'

'What window? What cue?' asked his principal assistant. 'Why, what proof is there that this has anything to do with them?'

Valentin almost broke his bamboo stick with rage.

'Proof!' he cried. 'Good God! the man is looking for proof! Why, of course, the chances are twenty to one that it has nothing to do with them. But what else can we do? Don't you see we must either follow one wild possibility or else go home to bed?' He banged his way into the restaurant, followed by his companions, and they were soon seated at a late luncheon at a little table, and looked at the star of smashed glass from the inside. Not that it was very informative to them even then.

'Got your window broken, I see,' said Valentin to the waiter as he paid the bill.

'Yes, sir,' answered the attendant, bending busily over the change, to which Valentin silently added an enormous tip. The waiter straightened himself with mild but unmistakable animation.

'Ah, yes, sir,' he said. 'Very odd thing, that, sir.'

'Indeed? Tell us about it,' said the detective with careless curiosity.

'Well, two gents in black came in,' said the waiter; 'two of those foreign parsons that are running about. They had a cheap and quiet little lunch, and one of them paid for it and went out. The other was just going out to join him when I looked at my change again and found he'd paid me more than three times too much. "Here," I says to the chap who was nearly out of the door, "you've paid too much." "Oh," he says, very cool, "have we?" "Yes," I says, and picks up the bill to show him. Well, that was a knock-out.'

'What do you mean?' asked his interlocutor.

'Well, I'd have sworn on seven Bibles that I'd put 4*s*. on that bill. But now I saw I'd put 14*s*., as plain as paint.'

'Well?' cried Valentin, moving slowly, but with burning eyes, 'and then?'

'The parson at the door he says, all serene, "Sorry to confuse your accounts, but it'll pay for the window." "What window?" I says. "The one I'm going to break," he says, and smashed that blessed pane with his umbrella.'

All three enquirers made an exclamation; and the inspector said under his breath, 'Are we after escaped lunatics?' The waiter went on with some relish for the ridiculous story: 'I was so knocked silly for a second, I couldn't do anything. The man marched out of the place and joined his friend just round the corner. Then they went so quick up Bullock Street that I couldn't catch them, though I ran round the bars to do it.'

'Bullock Street,' said the detective, and shot up that thoroughfare as quickly as the strange couple he pursued.

Their journey now took them through bare brick ways like tunnels; streets with few lights and even with few windows; streets that seemed built out of the blank backs of everything and everywhere. Dusk was deepening, and it was not easy even for the London policemen to guess in what exact direction they were treading. The inspector, however, was pretty certain that they would eventually strike some part of Hampstead Heath. Abruptly one bulging gas-lit window broke the blue twilight like a bull's-eye lantern; and Valentin stopped an instant before a little garish sweet-stuff shop. After an instant's hesitation he went in; he stood amid the gaudy colours of the confectionery with entire gravity and bought thirteen chocolate cigars with a certain care. He was clearly preparing an opening; but he did not need one.

An angular, elderly young woman in the shop had regarded his elegant appearance with a merely automatic enquiry; but when she saw the door behind him blocked with the blue uniform of the inspector, her eyes seemed to wake up.

'Oh,' she said, 'if you've come about that parcel, I've sent it off already.'

'Parcel?' repeated Valentin; and it was his turn to look enquiring.

'I mean the parcel the gentleman left – the clergyman gentleman.'

'For goodness' sake,' said Valentin, leaning forward with his first real confession of eagerness, 'for Heaven's sake tell us what happened exactly.'

'Well,' said the woman a little doubtfully, 'the clergymen came in about half an hour ago and bought some peppermints and talked a bit, and then went off towards the Heath. But a second after, one of them runs back into the shop and says, "Have I left a parcel?" Well, I looked everywhere and couldn't see one; so he says, "Never mind; but if it should turn up, please post it to this address," and he left me the address and a shilling for my trouble. And sure enough, though I thought I'd looked everywhere, I found he'd left a brown-paper parcel, so I posted it to the place he said. I can't remember the address now; it was somewhere in Westminster. But as the thing seemed so important, I thought perhaps the police had come about it.'

'So they have,' said Valentin shortly. 'Is Hampstead Heath near here?'

'Straight on for fifteen minutes,' said the woman, 'and you'll come right out on the open.' Valentin sprang out of the shop and began to run. The other detectives followed him at a reluctant trot.

The street they threaded was so narrow and shut in by shadows that when they came out unexpectedly into the void common and vast sky they were startled to find the evening still so light and clear. A perfect dome of peacock-green sank into gold amid the blackening trees and the dark violet distances. The glowing green tint was just deep enough to pick out in points of crystal one or two stars. All that was left of the daylight lay in a golden glitter across the edge of Hampstead and that popular hollow which is called the Vale of Health. The holiday makers who roam this region had not wholly dispersed; a few couples sat shapelessly on benches; and here and there a distant girl still shrieked in one of the swings. The glory of heaven deepened and darkened around the sublime vulgarity of man; and standing on the slope and looking across the valley, Valentin beheld the thing which he sought.

Among the black and breaking groups in that distance was one especially black which did not break – a group of two figures clerically clad. Though they seemed as small as insects, Valentin could see that one of them was much smaller than the other. Though the other had a student's stoop and an inconspicuous manner, he could see that the man was well over six feet high. He shut his teeth and went forward, whirling his stick impatiently. By the time he had substantially diminished the distance and magnified the two black figures as in a vast microscope, he had perceived something else; something which startled him, and yet which he had somehow expected. Whoever was the tall priest, there could be no doubt about the identity of the short one. It was his friend of the Harwich train, the stumpy little *curé* of Essex whom he had warned about his brown-paper parcels.

Now, so far as this went, everything fitted in finally and rationally enough. Valentin had learned by his enquiries that morning that a Father Brown from Essex was bringing up a silver cross with sapphires, a relic of considerable value, to show some of the foreign priests at the congress. This undoubtedly was the 'silver with blue stones'; and Father Brown undoubtedly was the little greenhorn in the train. Now there was nothing wonderful about the fact that what Valentin had found out Flambeau had also found out; Flambeau found out everything. Also there was nothing wonderful in the fact that when Flambeau heard of a sapphire cross he should try to steal it; that was the most natural thing in all natural history. And most certainly there was nothing wonderful about the fact that Flambeau should have it all his own way with such a silly sheep as the man with the umbrella and the parcels. He was the sort of man whom anybody could lead on a string to the North Pole; it was not surprising that an actor like Flambeau, dressed as another priest, could lead him to Hampstead Heath.

So far the crime seemed clear enough; and while the detective pitied the priest for his helplessness, he almost despised Flambeau for condescending to so gullible a victim. But when Valentin thought of all that had happened in between, of all that had led him to his triumph, he racked his brains for the smallest rhyme or reason in it. What had the stealing of a blue-and-silver cross from a priest from Essex to do with chucking soup at wallpaper? What had it to do with calling nuts oranges, or with paying for windows first and breaking them afterwards? He had come to the end of his chase; yet somehow he had missed the middle of it. When he failed (which was seldom), he had usually grasped the clue, but nevertheless missed the criminal. Here he had grasped the criminal, but still he could not grasp the clue.

The two figures that they followed were crawling like black flies across the huge green contour of a hill. They were evidently sunk in conversation, and perhaps did not notice where they were going; but they were certainly going to the wilder and more silent heights of the Heath. As their pursuers gained on them, the latter had to use the undignified attitudes of the deerstalker, to crouch behind clumps of trees and even to crawl prostrate in deep grass. By these ungainly ingenuities the hunters even came close enough to the quarry to hear the murmur of the discussion, but no word could be distinguished except the word 'reason' recurring frequently in a high and almost childish voice. Once over an abrupt dip of land and a dense tangle of thickets, the detectives actually lost the two figures they were following. They did not find the trail again for an agonising ten minutes, and then it led round the brow of a great dome of hill overlooking an amphitheatre of rich and desolate sunset scenery. Under a tree in this commanding yet neglected spot was an old ramshackle wooden seat. On this seat sat the two priests still in serious speech together. The gorgeous green and gold still clung to the darkening horizon; but the dome above was turning slowly from peacock-green to peacock-blue, and the stars detached themselves more and more like solid jewels. Mutely motioning to his followers, Valentin contrived to creep up behind the big branching tree, and, standing there in deathly silence, heard the words of the strange priests for the first time.

After he had listened for a minute and a half, he was gripped by a devilish doubt. Perhaps he had dragged the two English policemen to the wastes of a nocturnal heath on an errand no saner than seeking figs on its thistles. For the two priests were talking exactly like priests, piously, with learning and leisure, about the most aerial enigmas of theology. The little Essex priest spoke the more simply, with his round face turned to the strengthening stars; the other talked with his head bowed, as if he were not even worthy to look at them. But no more innocently clerical conversation could have been heard in any white Italian cloister or black Spanish cathedral.

The first he heard was the tail of one of Father Brown's sentences, which ended: '... what they really meant in the Middle Ages by the heavens being incorruptible.'

The taller priest nodded his bowed head and said: 'Ah, yes, these modern infidels appeal to their reason; but who can look at those millions of worlds and not feel that there may well be wonderful universes above us where reason is utterly unreasonable?'

'No,' said the other priest; 'reason is always reasonable, even in the last limbo, in the lost borderland of things. I know that people charge the Church with lowering reason, but it is just the other way. Alone on earth, the Church makes reason really supreme. Alone on earth, the Church affirms that God himself is bound by reason.'

The other priest raised his austere face to the spangled sky and said: 'Yet who knows if in that infinite universe – ?'

'Only infinite physically,' said the little priest, turning sharply in his seat, 'not infinite in the sense of escaping from the laws of truth.'

Valentin behind his tree was tearing his fingernails with silent fury. He seemed almost to hear the sniggers of the English detectives whom he had brought so far on a fantastic guess only to listen to the metaphysical gossip of two mild old parsons. In his impatience he lost the equally elaborate answer of the tall cleric, and when he listened again it was again Father Brown who was speaking: 'Reason and justice grip the remotest and the loneliest star. Look at those stars. Don't they look as if they were single diamonds and sapphires? Well, you can imagine any mad botany or geology you please. Think of forests of adamant with leaves of brilliants. Think the moon is a blue moon, a single elephantine sapphire. But don't fancy that all that frantic astronomy would make the smallest difference to the reason and justice of conduct. On plains of opal, under cliffs cut out of pearl, you would still find a noticeboard, "Thou shalt not steal".'

Valentin was just in the act of rising from his rigid and crouching attitude and creeping away as softly as might be, felled by the one great folly of his life. But something in the very silence of the tall priest made him stop until the latter spoke. When at last he did speak, he said simply, his head bowed and his hands on his knees: 'Well, I think that other worlds may perhaps rise higher than our reason. The mystery of heaven is unfathomable, and I for one can only bow my head.'

Then, with brow yet bent and without changing by the faintest shade his attitude or voice, he added: 'Just hand over that sapphire cross of yours, will you? We're all alone here, and I could pull you to pieces like a straw doll.'

The utterly unaltered voice and attitude added a strange violence to that shocking change of speech. But the guarder of the relic only seemed to turn his head by the smallest section of the compass. He seemed still to have a somewhat foolish face turned to the stars. Perhaps he had not understood. Or, perhaps, he had understood and sat rigid with terror.

'Yes,' said the tall priest, in the same low voice and in the same still posture, 'yes, I am Flambeau.'

Then, after a pause, he said: 'Come, will you give me that cross?'

'No,' said the other, and the monosyllable had an odd sound.

Flambeau suddenly flung off all his pontifical pretensions. The great robber leaned back in his seat and laughed low but long.

'No,' he cried, 'you won't give it me, you proud prelate. You won't give it me, you little celibate simpleton. Shall I tell you why you won't give it me? Because I've got it already in my own breast-pocket.'

The small man from Essex turned what seemed to be a dazed face in the dusk, and said, with the timid eagerness of 'The Private Secretary': 'Are – are you sure?'

Flambeau yelled with delight.

'Really, you're as good as a three-act farce,' he cried. 'Yes, you turnip, I am quite sure. I had the sense to make a duplicate of the right parcel, and now, my friend, you've got the duplicate and I've got the jewels. An old dodge, Father Brown – a very old dodge.'

'Yes,' said Father Brown, and passed his hand through his hair with the same strange vagueness of manner. 'Yes, I've heard of it before.'

The colossus of crime leaned over to the little rustic priest with a sort of sudden interest.

'You have heard of it?' he asked. 'Where have you heard of it?'

'Well, I mustn't tell you his name, of course,' said the little man simply. 'He was a penitent, you know. He had lived prosperously for about twenty years entirely on duplicate brown-paper parcels. And so, you see, when I began to suspect you, I thought of this poor chap's way of doing it at once.'

'Began to suspect me?' repeated the outlaw with increased intensity. 'Did you really have the gumption to suspect me just because I brought you up to this bare part of the heath?'

'No, no,' said Brown with an air of apology. 'You see, I suspected you when we first met. It's that little bulge up the sleeve where you people have the spiked bracelet.'

'How in Tartarus,' cried Flambeau, 'did you ever hear of the spiked bracelet?'

'Oh, one's little flock, you know!' said Father Brown, arching his eyebrows rather blankly. 'When I was a curate in Hartlepool, there were three of them with spiked bracelets. So, as I suspected you from the first, don't you see, I made sure that the cross should go safe, anyhow. I'm afraid I watched you, you know. So at last I saw you change the parcels. Then, don't you see, I changed them back again. And then I left the right one behind.'

'Left it behind?' repeated Flambeau, and for the first time there was another note in his voice beside his triumph.

'Well, it was like this,' said the little priest, speaking in the same unaffected way. 'I went back to that sweet-shop and asked if I'd left a parcel, and gave them a particular address if it turned up. Well, I knew I hadn't; but when I went away again I did. So, instead of running after me with that valuable parcel, they have sent it flying to a friend of mine in Westminster.' Then he added rather sadly: 'I learnt that, too, from a poor fellow in Hartlepool. He used to do it with handbags he stole at railway stations, but he's in a monastery now. Oh, one gets to know, you know,' he added, rubbing his head again with the same sort of desperate apology. 'We can't help being priests. People come and tell us these things.'

Flambeau tore a brown-paper parcel out of his inner pocket and rent it in pieces. There was nothing but paper and sticks of lead inside it. He sprang to his feet with a gigantic gesture, and cried: 'I don't believe you. I don't believe a bumpkin like you could manage all that. I believe you've still got the stuff on you, and if you don't give it up – why, we're all alone, and I'll take it by force!'

'No,' said Father Brown simply, and stood up also, 'you won't take it by force. First, because I really haven't still got it. And, second, because we are not alone.'

Flambeau stopped in his stride forward.

'Behind that tree,' said Father Brown, pointing, 'are two strong policemen and the greatest detective alive. How did they come here, do you ask? Why, I brought them, of course! How did I do it? Why, I'll tell you if you like! Lord bless you, we have to know twenty such things when we work among the criminal classes! Well, I wasn't sure you were a thief, and it would never do to make a scandal against one of our own clergy. So I just tested you to see if anything would make you show yourself. A man generally makes a small scene if he finds salt in his coffee; if he doesn't, he has some reason for keeping quiet. I changed the salt and sugar, and *you* kept quiet. A man generally objects if his bill is three times too big. If he pays it, he has some motive for passing unnoticed. I altered your bill, and *you* paid it.'

The world seemed waiting for Flambeau to leap like a tiger. But he was held back as by a spell; he was stunned with the utmost curiosity.

'Well,' went on Father Brown, with lumbering lucidity, 'as you wouldn't leave any tracks for the police, of course somebody had to. At every place we went to, I took care to do something that would get us talked about for the rest of the day. I didn't do much harm – a splashed wall, spilt apples, a broken window; but I saved the cross, as the cross will always be saved. It is at Westminster by now. I rather wonder you didn't stop it with the Donkey's Whistle.'

'With the what?' asked Flambeau.

'I'm glad you've never heard of it,' said the priest, making a face. 'It's a foul thing. I'm sure you're too good a man for a Whistler. I couldn't have countered it even with the Spots myself; I'm not strong enough in the legs.'

'What on earth are you talking about?' asked the other.

'Well, I did think you'd know the Spots,' said Father Brown, agreeably surprised. 'Oh, you can't have gone so very wrong yet!'

'How in blazes do you know all these horrors?' cried Flambeau.

The shadow of a smile crossed the round, simple face of his clerical opponent.

'Oh, by being a celibate simpleton, I suppose,' he said. 'Has it never struck you that a man who does next to nothing but hear men's real sins is not likely to be wholly unaware of human evil? But, as a matter of fact, another part of my trade, too, made me sure you weren't a priest.'

'What?' asked the thief, almost gaping.

'You attacked reason,' said Father Brown. 'It's bad theology.'

And even as he turned away to collect his property, the three policemen came out from under the twilight trees. Flambeau was an artist and a sportsman. He stepped back and swept Valentin a great bow.

'Do not bow to me, *mon ami*,' said Valentin with silver clearness. 'Let us both bow to our master.'

And they both stood an instant uncovered, while the little Essex priest blinked about for his umbrella.

The Secret Garden

Aristide Valentin, Chief of the Paris Police, was late for his dinner, and some of his guests began to arrive before him. These were, however, reassured by his confidential servant, Ivan, the old man with a scar, and a face almost as grey as his moustaches, who always sat at a table in the entrance hall – a hall hung with weapons. Valentin's house was perhaps as peculiar and celebrated as its master. It was an old house, with high walls and tall poplars almost overhanging the Seine; but the oddity – and perhaps the police value – of its architecture was this: that there was no ultimate exit at all except through this front door, which was guarded by Ivan and the armoury. The garden was large and elaborate, and there were many exits from the house into the garden. But there was no exit from the garden into the world outside; all round it ran a tall, smooth, unscalable wall with special spikes at the top; no bad garden, perhaps, for a man to reflect in whom some hundred criminals had sworn to kill.

As Ivan explained to the guests, their host had telephoned that he was detained for ten minutes. He was, in truth, making some last arrangements about executions and such ugly things; and though these duties were rootedly repulsive to him, he always performed them with precision. Ruthless in the pursuit of criminals, he was very mild about their punishment. Since he had been supreme over French – and largely over European – police methods, his great influence had been honourably used for the mitigation of sentences and the purification of prisons. He was one of the great humanitarian French freethinkers; and the only thing wrong with them is that they make mercy even colder than justice.

When Valentin arrived he was already dressed in black clothes and the red rosette – an elegant figure, his dark beard already streaked with grey. He went straight through his house to his study, which opened on the grounds behind. The garden door of it was open, and after he had carefully locked his box in its official place, he stood for a few seconds at the open door looking out upon the garden. A sharp moon was fighting with the flying rags and tatters of a storm, and Valentin regarded it with a wistfulness unusual in such scientific natures as his. Perhaps such scientific natures have some psychic prevision of the most tremendous problem of their lives. From any such occult mood, at least, he quickly recovered, for he knew he was late, and that his guests had already begun to arrive. A glance at his drawing-room when he entered it was enough to make certain that his principal guest was not there, at any rate. He saw all the other pillars of the little party; he saw Lord

Galloway, the English Ambassador – a choleric old man with a russet face like an apple, wearing the blue ribbon of the Garter. He saw Lady Galloway, slim and threadlike, with silver hair and a face sensitive and superior. He saw her daughter, Lady Margaret Graham, a pale and pretty girl with an elfish face and copper-coloured hair. He saw the Duchess of Mont St Michel, black-eyed and opulent, and with her her two daughters, black-eyed and opulent also. He saw Dr Simon, a typical French scientist, with glasses, a pointed brown beard, and a forehead barred with those parallel wrinkles which are the penalty of superciliousness, since they come through constantly elevating the eyebrows. He saw Father Brown, of Cobhole, in Essex, whom he had recently met in England. He saw – perhaps with more interest than any of these – a tall man in uniform, who had bowed to the Galloways without receiving any very hearty acknowledgement, and who now advanced alone to pay his respects to his host. This was Commandant O'Brien, of the French Foreign Legion. He was a slim yet somewhat swaggering figure, clean-shaven, dark-haired, and blue-eyed, and, as seemed natural in an officer of that famous regiment of victorious failures and successful suicides, he had an air at once dashing and melancholy. He was by birth an Irish gentleman, and in boyhood had known the Galloways – especially Margaret Graham. He had left his country after some crash of debts, and now expressed his complete freedom from British etiquette by swinging about in uniform, sabre and spurs. When he bowed to the Ambassador's family, Lord and Lady Galloway bent stiffly, and Lady Margaret looked away.

But for whatever old causes such people might be interested in each other, their distinguished host was not specially interested in them. No one of them at least was in his eyes the guest of the evening. Valentin was expecting, for special reasons, a man of world-wide fame, whose friendship he had secured during some of his great detective tours and triumphs in the United States. He was expecting Julius K. Brayne, that multi-millionaire whose colossal and even crushing endowments of small religions have occasioned so much easy sport and easier solemnity for the American and English papers. Nobody could quite make out whether Mr Brayne was an atheist or a Mormon or a Christian Scientist; but he was ready to pour money into any intellectual vessel, so long as it was an untried vessel. One of his hobbies was to wait for the American Shakespeare – a hobby more patient than angling. He admired Walt Whitman, but thought that Luke P. Tanner, of Paris, Pa., was more 'progressive' than Whitman any day. He liked anything that he thought 'progressive'. He thought Valentin 'progressive', thereby doing him a grave injustice.

The solid appearance of Julius K. Brayne in the room was as decisive as a dinner bell. He had this great quality, which very few of us can claim, that his presence was as big as his absence. He was a huge fellow, as fat as he was tall, clad in complete evening black, without so much relief as a watch-chain or a ring. His hair was white and well brushed back like a German's; his face was red, fierce and cherubic, with one dark tuft under the lower lip that threw up that otherwise infantile visage with an effect theatrical and even Mephistophelean. Not long, however, did that salon merely stare at the celebrated American; his lateness had already become a domestic problem, and he was sent with all speed into the dining-room with Lady Galloway on his arm.

Except on one point the Galloways were genial and casual enough. So long as Lady Margaret did not take the arm of that adventurer O'Brien, her father was quite satisfied; and she had not done so, she had decorously gone in with Dr Simon. Nevertheless, old Lord Galloway was restless and almost rude. He was diplomatic enough during dinner, but when, over the cigars, three of the younger men – Simon the doctor, Brown the priest, and the detrimental O'Brien, the exile in a foreign uniform – all melted away to mix with the ladies or smoke in the conservatory, then the English diplomatist grew very undiplomatic indeed. He was stung every sixty seconds with the thought that the scamp O'Brien might be signalling to Margaret somehow; he did not attempt to imagine how. He was left over the coffee with Brayne, the hoary Yankee who believed in all religions, and Valentin, the grizzled Frenchman who believed in none. They could argue with each other, but neither could appeal to him. After a time this 'progressive' logomachy had reached a crisis of tedium; Lord Galloway got up also and sought the drawing-room. He lost his way in long passages for some six or eight minutes: till he heard the high-pitched, didactic voice of the doctor, and then the dull voice of the priest, followed by general laughter. They also, he thought with a curse, were probably arguing about 'science and religion'. But the instant he opened the salon door he saw only one thing – he saw what was not there. He saw that Commandant O'Brien was absent, and that Lady Margaret was absent too.

Rising impatiently from the drawing-room, as he had from the dining-room, he stamped along the passage once more. His notion of protecting his daughter from the Irish-Algerian ne'er-do-well had become something central and even mad in his mind. As he went towards the back of the house, where was Valentin's study, he was surprised to meet his daughter, who swept past with a white, scornful face, which was a second enigma. If she had been with O'Brien, where was O'Brien? If she had not been with O'Brien, where had she been? With a sort of senile and passionate suspicion he groped his way to the dark back parts of the mansion, and eventually found a servants' entrance that opened on to the garden. The moon with her scimitar had now ripped up and rolled away all the storm-wrack. The argent light lit up all four corners of the garden. A tall figure in blue was striding across the lawn towards the study door; a glint of moonlit silver on his facings picked him out as Commandant O'Brien.

He vanished through the french windows into the house, leaving Lord Galloway in an indescribable temper, at once virulent and vague. The blue-and-silver garden, like a scene in a theatre, seemed to taunt him with all that tyrannic tenderness against which his worldly authority was at war. The length and grace of the Irishman's stride enraged him as if he were a rival instead of a father; the moonlight maddened him. He was trapped as if by magic into a garden of troubadours, a Watteau fairyland; and, willing to shake off such amorous imbecilities by speech, he stepped briskly after his enemy. As he did so he tripped over some tree or stone in the grass; looked down at it first with irritation and then a second time with curiosity. The next instant the moon and the tall poplars looked at an unusual sight – an elderly English diplomatist running hard and crying or bellowing as he ran.

His hoarse shouts brought a pale face to the study door, the beaming glasses and worried brow of Dr Simon, who heard the nobleman's first clear words. Lord Galloway was crying: 'A corpse in the grass – a blood-stained corpse.' O'Brien at least had gone utterly from his mind.

'We must tell Valentin at once,' said the doctor, when the other had brokenly described all that he had dared to examine. 'It is fortunate that he is here'; and even as he spoke the great detective entered the study, attracted by the cry. It was almost amusing to note his typical transformation; he had come with the common concern of a host and a gentleman, fearing that some guest or servant was ill. When he was told the gory fact, he turned with all his gravity instantly bright and businesslike; for this, however abrupt and awful, was his business.

'Strange, gentlemen,' he said as they hurried out into the garden, 'that I should have hunted mysteries all over the earth, and now one comes and settles in my own backyard. But where is the place?' They crossed the lawn less easily, as a slight mist had begun to rise from the river; but under the guidance of the shaken Galloway they found the body sunken in deep grass – the body of a very tall and broad-shouldered man. He lay face downwards, so they could only see that his big shoulders were clad in black cloth, and that his big head was bald, except for a wisp or two of brown hair that clung to his skull like wet seaweed. A scarlet serpent of blood crawled from under his fallen face.

'At least,' said Simon, with a deep and singular intonation, 'he is none of our party.'

'Examine him, doctor,' cried Valentin rather sharply. 'He may not be dead.'

The doctor bent down. 'He is not quite cold, but I am afraid he is dead enough,' he answered. 'Just help me to lift him up.'

They lifted him carefully an inch from the ground, and all doubts as to his being really dead were settled at once and frightfully. The head fell away. It had been entirely sundered from the body; whoever had cut his throat had managed to sever the neck as well. Even Valentin was slightly shocked. 'He must have been as strong as a gorilla,' he muttered.

Not without a shiver, though he was used to anatomical abortions, Dr Simon lifted the head. It was slightly slashed about the neck and jaw, but the face was substantially unhurt. It was a ponderous, yellow face, at once sunken and swollen, with a hawklike nose and heavy lids – a face of a wicked Roman emperor, with, perhaps, a distant touch of a Chinese emperor. All present seemed to look at it with the coldest eye of ignorance. Nothing else could be noted about the man except that, as they had lifted his body, they had seen underneath it the white gleam of a shirt-front defaced with a red gleam of blood. As Dr Simon said, the man had never been of their party. But he might very well have been trying to join it, for he had come dressed for such an occasion.

Valentin went down on his hands and knees and examined with his closest professional attention the grass and ground for some twenty yards round the body, in which he was assisted less skilfully by the doctor, and quite vaguely by the English lord. Nothing rewarded their grovellings except a few twigs, snapped or chopped into very small lengths, which Valentin lifted for an instant's examination and then tossed away.

'Twigs,' he said gravely; 'twigs, and a total stranger with his head cut off; that is all there is on this lawn.'

There was an almost creepy stillness, and then the unnerved Galloway called out sharply: 'Who's that! Who's that over there by the garden wall!'

A small figure with a foolishly large head drew waveringly near them in the moonlit haze; looked for an instant like a goblin, but turned out to be the harmless little priest whom they had left in the drawing-room.

'I say,' he said meekly, 'there are no gates to this garden, do you know.'

Valentin's black brows had come together somewhat crossly, as they did on principle at the sight of the cassock. But he was far too just a man to deny the relevance of the remark. 'You are right,' he said. 'Before we find out how he came to be killed, we may have to find out how he came to be here. Now listen to me, gentlemen. If it can be done without prejudice to my position and duty, we shall all agree that certain distinguished names might well be kept out of this. There are ladies, gentlemen, and there is a foreign ambassador. If we must mark it down as a crime, then it must be followed up as a crime. But till then I can use my own discretion. I am the head of the police; I am so public that I can afford to be private. Please Heaven, I will clear every one of my own guests before I call in my men to look for anybody else. Gentlemen, upon your honour, you will none of you leave the house till tomorrow at noon; there are bedrooms for all. Simon, I think you know where to find my man, Ivan, in the front hall; he is a confidential man. Tell him to leave another servant on guard and come to me at once. Lord Galloway, you are certainly the best person to tell the ladies what has happened, and prevent a panic. They also must stay. Father Brown and I will remain with the body.'

When this spirit of the captain spoke in Valentin he was obeyed like a bugle. Dr Simon went through to the armoury and routed out Ivan, the public detective's private detective. Galloway went to the drawing-room and told the terrible news tactfully enough, so that by the time the company assembled there the ladies were already startled and already soothed. Meanwhile the good priest and the good atheist stood at the head and foot of the dead man motionless in the moonlight, like symbolic statues of their two philosophies of death.

Ivan, the confidential man with the scar and the moustaches, came out of the house like a cannon ball, and came racing across the lawn to Valentin like a dog to his master. His livid face was quite lively with the glow of this domestic detective story, and it was with almost unpleasant eagerness that he asked his master's permission to examine the remains.

'Yes; look, if you like, Ivan,' said Valentin, 'but don't be long. We must go in and thrash this out in the house.'

Ivan lifted the head, and then almost let it drop.

'Why,' he gasped, 'it's – no, it isn't; it can't be. Do you know this man, sir?'

'No,' said Valentin indifferently; 'we had better go inside.'

Between them they carried the corpse to a sofa in the study, and then all made their way to the drawing-room.

The detective sat down at a desk quietly, and even with hesitation; but his eye was the iron eye of a judge at assize. He made a few rapid notes upon paper in front of him, and then said shortly: 'Is everybody here?'

'Not Mr Brayne,' said the Duchess of Mont St Michel, looking round.

'No,' said Lord Galloway in a hoarse, harsh voice. 'And not Mr Neil O'Brien, I fancy. I saw that gentleman walking in the garden when the corpse was still warm.'

'Ivan,' said the detective, 'go and fetch Commandant O'Brien and Mr Brayne. Mr Brayne, I know, is finishing a cigar in the dining-room; Commandant O'Brien, I think, is walking up and down the conservatory. I am not sure.'

The faithful attendant flashed from the room, and before anyone could stir or speak Valentin went on with the same soldierly swiftness of exposition.

'Everyone here knows that a dead man has been found in the garden, his head cut clean from his body. Dr Simon, you have examined it. Do you think that to cut a man's throat like that would need great force? Or, perhaps, only a very sharp knife?'

'I should say that it could not be done with a knife at all,' said the pale doctor.

'Have you any thought,' resumed Valentin, 'of a tool with which it could be done?'

'Speaking within modern probabilities, I really haven't,' said the doctor, arching his painful brows. 'It's not easy to hack a neck through even clumsily, and this was a very clean cut. It could be done with a battle-axe or an old headsman's axe, or an old two-handed sword.'

'But, good heavens!' cried the Duchess, almost in hysterics, 'there aren't any two-handed swords and battle-axes round here.'

Valentin was still busy with the paper in front of him. 'Tell me,' he said, still writing rapidly, 'could it have been done with a long French cavalry sabre?'

A low knocking came at the door, which, for some unreasonable reason, curdled everyone's blood like the knocking in *Macbeth*. Amid that frozen silence Dr Simon managed to say: 'A sabre – yes, I suppose it could.'

'Thank you,' said Valentin. 'Come in, Ivan.'

The confidential Ivan opened the door and ushered in Commandant Neil O'Brien, whom he had found at last pacing the garden again.

The Irish officer stood up disordered and defiant on the threshold. 'What do you want with me?' he cried.

'Please sit down,' said Valentin in pleasant, level tones. 'Why, you aren't wearing your sword. Where is it?'

'I left it on the library table,' said O'Brien, his brogue deepening in his disturbed mood. 'It was a nuisance, it was getting – '

'Ivan,' said Valentin, 'please go and get the Commandant's sword from the library.' Then, as the servant vanished, 'Lord Galloway says he saw you leaving the garden just before he found the corpse. What were you doing in the garden?'

The Commandant flung himself recklessly into a chair. 'Oh,' he cried in pure Irish, 'admirin' the moon. Communing with Nature, me boy.'

A heavy silence sank and endured, and at the end of it came again that trivial and terrible knocking. Ivan reappeared, carrying an empty steel scabbard. 'This is all I can find,' he said.

'Put it on the table,' said Valentin, without looking up.

There was an inhuman silence in the room, like that sea of inhuman silence round the dock of the condemned murderer. The Duchess's weak exclamations had long ago died away. Lord Galloway's swollen hatred was satisfied and even sobered. The voice that came was quite unexpected.

'I think I can tell you,' cried Lady Margaret, in that clear, quivering voice with which a courageous woman speaks publicly. 'I can tell you what Mr O'Brien was doing in the garden, since he is bound to silence. He was asking me to marry him. I refused; I said in my family circumstances I could give him nothing but my respect. He was a little angry at that; he did not seem to think much of my respect. I wonder,' she added, with rather a wan smile, 'if he will care at all for it now. For I offer it him now. I will swear anywhere that he never did a thing like this.'

Lord Galloway had edged up to his daughter, and was intimidating her in what he imagined to be an undertone. 'Hold your tongue, Maggie,' he said in a thunderous whisper. 'Why should you shield the fellow? Where's his sword? Where's his confounded cavalry – '

He stopped because of the singular stare with which his daughter was regarding him, a look that was indeed a lurid magnet for the whole group.

'You old fool!' she said in a low voice without pretence of piety; 'what do you suppose you are trying to prove? I tell you this man was innocent while with me. But if he wasn't innocent, he was still with me. If he murdered a man in the garden, who was it who must have seen – who must at least have known? Do you hate Neil so much as to put your own daughter – '

Lady Galloway screamed. Everyone else sat tingling at the touch of those satanic tragedies that have been between lovers before now. They saw the proud, white face of the Scotch aristocrat and her lover, the Irish adventurer, like old portraits in a dark house. The long silence was full of formless historical memories of murdered husbands and poisonous paramours.

In the centre of this morbid silence an innocent voice said: 'Was it a very long cigar?'

The change of thought was so sharp that they had to look round to see who had spoken.

'I mean,' said little Father Brown, from the corner of the room, 'I mean that cigar Mr Brayne is finishing. It seems nearly as long as a walking-stick.'

Despite the irrelevance there was assent as well as irritation in Valentin's face as he lifted his head.

'Quite right,' he remarked sharply. 'Ivan, go and see about Mr Brayne again, and bring him here at once.'

The instant the factotum had closed the door, Valentin addressed the girl with an entirely new earnestness.

'Lady Margaret,' he said, 'we all feel, I am sure, both gratitude and admiration for your act in rising above your lower dignity and explaining the Commandant's conduct. But there is a hiatus still. Lord Galloway, I understand, met you passing from the study to the drawing-room, and it was only some minutes afterwards that he found the garden and the Commandant still walking there.'

'You have to remember,' replied Margaret, with a faint irony in her voice, 'that I had just refused him, so we should scarcely have come back arm in arm. He is a gentleman, anyhow; and he loitered behind – and so got charged with murder.'

'In those few moments,' said Valentin gravely, 'he might really – '

The knock came again, and Ivan put in his scarred face.

'Beg pardon, sir,' he said, 'but Mr Brayne has left the house.'

'Left!' cried Valentin, and rose for the first time to his feet.

'Gone. Scooted. Evaporated,' replied Ivan in humorous French. 'His hat and coat are gone, too, and I'll tell you something to cap it all. I ran outside the house to find any traces of him, and I found one, and a big trace, too.'

'What do you mean?' asked Valentin.

'I'll show you,' said his servant, and reappeared with a flashing naked cavalry sabre, streaked with blood about the point and edge. Everyone in the room eyed it as if it were a thunderbolt; but the experienced Ivan went on quite quietly: 'I found this,' he said, 'flung among the bushes fifty yards up the road to Paris. In other words, I found it just where your respectable Mr Brayne threw it when he ran away.'

There was again a silence, but of a new sort. Valentin took the sabre, examined it, reflected with unaffected concentration of thought, and then turned a respectful face to O'Brien. 'Commandant,' he said, 'we trust you will always produce this weapon if it is wanted for police examination. Meanwhile,' he added, slapping the steel back in the ringing scabbard, 'let me return you your sword.'

At the military symbolism of the action the audience could hardly refrain from applause.

For Neil O'Brien, indeed, that gesture was the turning-point of existence. By the time he was wandering in the mysterious garden again in the colours of the morning the tragic futility of his ordinary mien had fallen from him; he was a man with many reasons for happiness. Lord Galloway was a gentleman, and had offered him an apology. Lady Margaret was something better than a lady, a woman at least, and had perhaps given him something better than an apology, as they drifted among the old flowerbeds before breakfast. The whole company was more light-hearted and humane, for though the riddle of the death remained, the load of suspicion was lifted off them all, and sent flying off to Paris with the strange millionaire – a man they hardly knew. The devil was cast out of the house – he had cast himself out.

Still, the riddle remained; and when O'Brien threw himself on a garden seat beside Dr Simon, that keenly scientific person at once resumed it. He did not get much talk out of O'Brien, whose thoughts were on pleasanter things.

'I can't say it interests me much,' said the Irishman frankly, 'especially as it seems pretty plain now. Apparently Brayne hated this stranger for some reason; lured him into the garden, and killed him with my sword. Then he fled to the city, tossing the sword away as he went. By the way, Ivan tells me the dead man had a Yankee dollar in his pocket. So he was a countryman of Brayne's, and that seems to clinch it. I don't see any difficulties about the business.'

'There are five colossal difficulties,' said the doctor quietly; 'like high walls within walls. Don't mistake me. I don't doubt that Brayne did it; his flight, I fancy, proves that. But as to how he did it. First difficulty: Why should a man kill another man with a great hulking sabre, when he can almost kill him with a pocket knife and put it back in his pocket? Second difficulty: Why was there no noise or outcry? Does a man commonly see another come up waving a scimitar and offer no remarks? Third difficulty: A servant watched the front door all the evening; and a rat cannot get into Valentin's garden anywhere. How did the dead man get into the garden? Fourth difficulty: Given the same conditions, how did Brayne get out of the garden?'

'And the fifth,' said Neil, with eyes fixed on the English priest who was coming slowly up the path.

'Is a trifle, I suppose,' said the doctor, 'but I think an odd one. When I first saw how the head had been slashed, I supposed the assassin had struck more than once. But on examination I found many cuts across the truncated section; in other words, they were struck *after* the head was off. Did Brayne hate his foe so fiendishly that he stood sabring his body in the moonlight?'

'Horrible!' said O'Brien, and shuddered.

The little priest, Brown, had arrived while they were talking, and had waited, with characteristic shyness, till they had finished. Then he said awkwardly: 'I say, I'm sorry to interrupt. But I was sent to tell you the news!'

'News?' repeated Simon, and stared at him rather painfully through his glasses.

'Yes, I'm sorry,' said Father Brown mildly. 'There's been another murder, you know.'

Both men on the seat sprang up, leaving it rocking.

'And, what's stranger still,' continued the priest, with his dull eye on the rhododendrons, 'it's the same disgusting sort; it's another beheading. They found the second head actually bleeding into the river, a few yards along Brayne's road to Paris; so they suppose that he – '

'Great Heaven!' cried O'Brien. 'Is Brayne a monomaniac?'

'There are American vendettas,' said the priest impassively. Then he added: 'They want you to come to the library and see it.'

Commandant O'Brien followed the others towards the inquest, feeling decidedly sick. As a soldier, he loathed all this secretive carnage; where were these extravagant amputations going to stop? First one head was hacked off, and then another; in this case (he told himself bitterly) it was not true that two heads were better than one. As he crossed the study he almost staggered at a shocking coincidence. Upon Valentin's table lay the coloured picture of yet a third bleeding head; and it was the head of Valentin himself. A second glance showed him it was only a Nationalist paper, called *The Guillotine*, which every week showed one of its political opponents with rolling eyes and writhing features just after execution; for Valentin was an anti-clerical of some note. But O'Brien was an Irishman, with a kind of chastity even in his sins; and his gorge rose against that great brutality of the intellect which belongs only to France. He felt Paris as a whole, from the grotesques on the Gothic churches to the gross caricatures in the newspapers. He remembered the gigantic jests of the Revolution. He saw the whole city as one ugly energy, from the sanguinary sketch lying on Valentin's table up to where, above a mountain and forest of gargoyles, the great devil grins on Notre Dame.

The library was long, low, and dark; what light entered it shot from under low blinds and had still some of the ruddy tinge of morning. Valentin and his servant Ivan were waiting for them at the upper end of a long, slightly sloping desk, on which lay the mortal remains, looking enormous in the twilight. The big black figure and yellow face of the man found in the garden confronted them essentially unchanged. The second head, which had been fished from among the river reeds that morning, lay streaming and dripping beside it; Valentin's men were still seeking to recover the rest of this second corpse, which was supposed to be afloat. Father Brown, who did not seem to share O'Brien's sensibilities in the least, went up to the second head and examined it with his blinking care. It was little more than a mop of wet white hair, fringed with silver fire in the red and level morning light; the face, which seemed of an ugly, empurpled and perhaps criminal type, had been much battered against trees or stones as it tossed in the water.

'Good-morning, Commandant O'Brien,' said Valentin, with quiet cordiality. 'You have heard of Brayne's last experiment in butchery, I suppose?'

Father Brown was still bending over the head with white hair, and he said, without looking up: 'I suppose it is quite certain that Brayne cut off this head, too.'

'Well, it seems common sense,' said Valentin, with his hands in his pockets. 'Killed in the same way as the other. Found within a few yards of the other. And sliced by the same weapon which we know he carried away.'

'Yes, yes; I know,' replied Father Brown submissively. 'Yet, you know, I doubt whether Brayne could have cut off this head.'

'Why not?' enquired Dr Simon, with a rational stare.

'Well, doctor,' said the priest, looking up blinking, 'can a man cut off his own head? I don't know.'

O'Brien felt an insane universe crashing about his ears; but the doctor sprang forward with impetuous practicality and pushed back the wet white hair.

'Oh, there's no doubt it's Brayne,' said the priest quietly. 'He had exactly that chip in the left ear.'

The detective, who had been regarding the priest with steady and glittering eyes, opened his clenched mouth and said sharply: 'You seem to know a lot about him, Father Brown.'

'I do,' said the little man simply. 'I've been about with him for some weeks. He was thinking of joining our church.'

The star of the fanatic sprang into Valentin's eyes; he strode towards the priest with clenched hands. 'And, perhaps,' he cried, with a blasting sneer, 'perhaps he was also thinking of leaving all his money to your church.'

'Perhaps he was,' said Brown stolidly; 'it is possible.'

'In that case,' cried Valentin, with a dreadful smile, 'you may indeed know a great deal about him. About his life and about his – '

Commandant O'Brien laid a hand on Valentin's arm. 'Drop that slanderous rubbish, Valentin,' he said, 'or there may be more swords yet.'

But Valentin (under the steady, humble gaze of the priest) had already recovered himself. 'Well,' he said shortly, 'people's private opinions can wait. You gentlemen are still bound by your promise to stay; you must enforce it on yourselves – and on each other. Ivan here will tell you anything more you want to know; I must get to business and write to the authorities. We can't keep this quiet any longer. I shall be writing in my study if there is any more news.'

'Is there any more news, Ivan?' asked Dr Simon, as the chief of police strode out of the room.

'Only one more thing, I think, sir,' said Ivan, wrinkling up his grey old face, 'but that's important, too, in its way. There's that old buffer you found on the lawn,' and he pointed without pretence of reverence at the big black body with the yellow head. 'We've found out who he is, anyhow.'

'Indeed!' cried the astonished doctor, 'and who is he?'

'His name was Arnold Becker,' said the under-detective, 'though he went by many aliases. He was a wandering sort of scamp, and is known to have been in America; so that was where Brayne got his knife into him. We didn't have much to do with him ourselves, for he worked mostly in Germany. We've communicated, of course, with the German police. But, oddly enough, there was a twin brother of his, named Louis Becker, whom we had a great deal to do with. In fact, we found it necessary to guillotine him only yesterday. Well, it's a rum thing, gentlemen, but when I saw that fellow flat on the lawn I had the greatest jump of my life. If I hadn't seen Louis Becker guillotined with my own eyes, I'd have sworn it was Louis

Becker lying there in the grass. Then, of course, I remembered his twin brother in Germany, and following up the clue – '

The explanatory Ivan stopped, for the excellent reason that nobody was listening to him. The Commandant and the doctor were both staring at Father Brown, who had sprung stiffly to his feet, and was holding his temples tight like a man in sudden and violent pain.

'Stop, stop, stop!' he cried; 'stop talking a minute, for I see half. Will God give me strength? Will my brain make the one jump and see all? Heaven help me! I used to be fairly good at thinking. I could paraphrase any page in Aquinas once. Will my head split – or will it see? I see half – I only see half.'

He buried his head in his hands, and stood in a sort of rigid torture of thought or prayer, while the other three could only go on staring at this last prodigy of their wild twelve hours.

When Father Brown's hands fell they showed a face quite fresh and serious, like a child's. He heaved a huge sigh, and said: 'Let us get this said and done with as quickly as possible. Look here, this will be the quickest way to convince you all of the truth.' He turned to the doctor. 'Dr Simon,' he said, 'you have a strong head-piece, and I heard you this morning asking the five hardest questions about this business. Well, if you will ask them again, I will answer them.'

Simon's pince-nez dropped from his nose in his doubt and wonder, but he answered at once. 'Well, the first question, you know, is why a man should kill another with a clumsy sabre at all when a man can kill with a bodkin?'

'A man cannot behead with a bodkin,' said Brown calmly, 'and for *this* murder beheading was absolutely necessary.'

'Why?' asked O'Brien, with interest.

'And the next question?' asked Father Brown.

'Well, why didn't the man cry out or anything?' asked the doctor; 'sabres in gardens are certainly unusual.'

'Twigs,' said the priest gloomily, and turned to the window which looked on the scene of death. 'No one saw the point of the twigs. Why should they lie on that lawn (look at it) so far from any tree? They were not snapped off; they were chopped off. The murderer occupied his enemy with some tricks with the sabre, showing how he could cut a branch in mid-air, or what-not. Then, while his enemy bent down to see the result, a silent slash, and the head fell.'

'Well,' said the doctor slowly, 'that seems plausible enough. But my next two questions will stump anyone.'

The priest still stood looking critically out of the window and waited.

'You know how all the garden was sealed up like an airtight chamber,' went on the doctor. 'Well, how did the strange man get into the garden?'

Without turning round, the little priest answered: 'There never was any strange man in the garden.'

There was a silence, and then a sudden cackle of almost childish laughter relieved the strain. The absurdity of Brown's remark moved Ivan to open taunts.

'Oh!' he cried; 'then we didn't lug a great fat corpse on to a sofa last night? He hadn't got into the garden, I suppose?'

'Got into the garden?' repeated Brown reflectively. 'No, not entirely.'

'Hang it all,' cried Simon, 'a man gets into a garden, or he doesn't.'

'Not necessarily,' said the priest, with a faint smile. 'What is the next question, doctor?'

'I fancy you're ill,' exclaimed Dr Simon sharply; 'but I'll ask the next question if you like. How did Brayne get out of the garden?'

'He didn't get out of the garden,' said the priest, still looking out of the window.

'Didn't get out of the garden?' exploded Simon.

'Not completely,' said Father Brown.

Simon shook his fists in a frenzy of French logic. 'A man gets out of a garden, or he doesn't,' he cried.

'Not always,' said Father Brown.

Dr Simon sprang to his feet impatiently. 'I have no time to spare on such senseless talk,' he cried angrily. 'If you can't understand a man being on one side of a wall or the other, I won't trouble you further.'

'Doctor,' said the cleric very gently, 'we have always got on very pleasantly together. If only for the sake of old friendship, stop and tell me your fifth question.'

The impatient Simon sank into a chair by the door and said briefly: 'The head and shoulders were cut about in a queer way. It seemed to be done after death.'

'Yes,' said the motionless priest, 'it was done so as to make you assume exactly the one simple falsehood that you did assume. It was done to make you take for granted that the head belonged to the body.'

The borderland of the brain, where all the monsters are made, moved horribly in the Gaelic O'Brien. He felt the chaotic presence of all the horsemen and fish-women that man's unnatural fancy has begotten. A voice older than his first fathers seemed saying in his ear: 'Keep out of the monstrous garden where grows the tree with double fruit. Avoid the evil garden where died the man with two heads.' Yet, while these shameful symbolic shapes passed across the ancient mirror of his Irish soul, his Frenchified intellect was quite alert, and was watching the odd priest as closely and incredulously as all the rest.

Father Brown had turned round at last, and stood against the window, with his face in dense shadow; but even in that shadow they could see it was pale as ashes. Nevertheless, he spoke quite sensibly, as if there were no Gaelic souls on earth.

'Gentlemen,' he said, 'you did not find the strange body of Becker in the garden. You did not find any strange body in the garden. In face of Dr Simon's rationalism, I still affirm that Becker was only partly present. Look here!' (pointing to the black bulk of the mysterious corpse); 'you never saw that man in your lives. Did you ever see this man?'

He rapidly rolled away the bald, yellow head of the unknown, and put in its place the white-maned head beside it. And there, complete, unified, unmistakable, lay Julius K. Brayne.

'The murderer,' went on Brown quietly, 'hacked off his enemy's head and flung the sword far over the wall. But he was too clever to fling the sword only. He flung the *head* over the wall also. Then he had only to clap on another head to the corpse, and (as he insisted on a private inquest) you all imagined a totally new man.'

'Clap on another head!' said O'Brien staring. 'What other head? Heads don't grow on garden bushes, do they?'

'No,' said Father Brown huskily, and looking at his boots; 'there is only one place where they grow. They grow in the basket of the guillotine, beside which the chief of police, Aristide Valentin, was standing not an hour before the murder. Oh, my friends, hear me a minute more before you tear me in pieces. Valentin is an honest man, if being mad for an arguable cause is honesty. But did you never see in that cold, grey eye of his that he is mad! He would do anything, *anything*, to break what he calls the superstition of the Cross. He has fought for it and starved for it, and now he has murdered for it. Brayne's crazy millions had hitherto been scattered among so many sects that they did little to alter the balance of things. But Valentin heard a whisper that Brayne, like so many scatter-brained sceptics, was drifting to us; and that was quite a different thing. Brayne would pour supplies into the impoverished and pugnacious Church of France; he would support six Nationalist newspapers like *The Guillotine*. The battle was already balanced on a point, and the fanatic took flame at the risk. He resolved to destroy the millionaire, and he did it as one would expect the greatest of detectives to commit his only crime. He abstracted the severed head of Becker on some criminological excuse, and took it home in his official box. He had that last argument with Brayne, that Lord Galloway did not hear the end of; that failing, he led him out into the sealed garden, talked about swordsmanship, used twigs and a sabre for illustration, and – '

Ivan of the Scar sprang up. 'You lunatic,' he yelled; 'you'll go to my master now, if I take you by – '

'Why, I was going there,' said Brown heavily; 'I must ask him to confess, and all that.'

Driving the unhappy Brown before them like a hostage or sacrifice, they rushed together into the sudden stillness of Valentin's study.

The great detective sat at his desk apparently too occupied to hear their turbulent entrance. They paused a moment, and then something in the look of that upright and elegant back made the doctor run forward suddenly. A touch and a glance showed him that there was a small box of pills at Valentin's elbow, and that Valentin was dead in his chair; and on the blind face of the suicide was more than the pride of Cato.

The Queer Feet

If you meet a member of that select club, 'The Twelve True Fishermen', entering the Vernon Hotel for the annual club dinner, you will observe, as he takes off his overcoat, that his evening coat is green and not black. If (supposing that you have the star-defying audacity to address such a being) you ask him why, he will probably answer that he does it to avoid being mistaken for a waiter. You will then retire crushed. But you will leave behind you a mystery as yet unsolved and a tale worth telling.

If (to pursue the same vein of improbable conjecture) you were to meet a mild, hard-working little priest, named Father Brown, and were to ask him what he thought was the most singular luck of his life, he would probably reply that upon the whole his best stroke was at the Vernon Hotel, where he had averted a crime and, perhaps, saved a soul, merely by listening to a few footsteps in a passage. He is perhaps a little proud of this wild and wonderful guess of his, and it is possible that he might refer to it. But since it is immeasurably unlikely that you will ever rise high enough in the social world to find 'The Twelve True Fishermen', or that you will ever sink low enough among slums and criminals to find Father Brown, I fear you will never hear the story at all unless you hear it from me.

The Vernon Hotel, at which The Twelve True Fishermen held their annual dinners, was an institution such as can only exist in an oligarchical society which has almost gone mad on good manners. It was that topsy-turvy product – an 'exclusive' commercial enterprise. That is, it was a thing which paid not by attracting people, but actually by turning people away. In the heart of a plutocracy tradesmen become cunning enough to be more fastidious than their customers. They positively create difficulties so that their wealthy and weary clients may spend money and diplomacy in overcoming them. If there were a fashionable hotel in London which no man could enter who was under six foot, society would meekly make up parties of six-foot men to dine in it. If there were an expensive restaurant which by a mere caprice of its proprietor was only open on Thursday afternoon, it would be crowded on Thursday afternoon. The Vernon Hotel stood, as if by accident, in the corner of a square in Belgravia. It was a small hotel; and a very inconvenient one. But its very inconveniences were considered as walls protecting a particular class. One inconvenience, in particular, was held to be of vital importance: the fact that practically only twenty-four people could dine in the place at once. The only big dinner table was the celebrated terrace table, which stood open to the air on a sort of veranda overlooking one of the most exquisite old gardens in London. Thus it happened that even the twenty-four seats at this table could only be enjoyed in warm weather; and this making the enjoyment yet more difficult made it yet more desired. The existing owner of the hotel was a Jew named Lever; and he made nearly a million out of it, by making it difficult to get into. Of course he combined with this limitation in the scope of his enterprise the most careful polish in its performance. The wines and cooking were really as good as any in Europe, and the demeanour of the attendants exactly mirrored the fixed mood of the English upper class. The proprietor knew all his waiters like the fingers on his hand; there were only fifteen of them all told. It was much easier to become a Member of Parliament than to become a waiter in that hotel. Each waiter was trained in terrible silence and smoothness, as if he were a gentleman's servant. And, indeed, there was generally at least one waiter to every gentleman who dined.

The club of The Twelve True Fishermen would not have consented to dine anywhere but in such a place, for it insisted on a luxurious privacy; and would have been quite upset by the mere thought that any other club was even dining in the same building. On the occasion of their annual dinner the Fishermen were in the habit of exposing all their treasures, as if they were in a private house, especially the celebrated set of fish knives and forks which were, as it were, the insignia of the society, each being exquisitely wrought in silver in the form of a fish, and each loaded at the hilt with one large pearl. These were always laid out for the fish course, and the fish course was always the most magnificent in that magnificent repast. The society had a vast number of ceremonies and observances, but it had no history and no object; that was where it was so very aristocratic. You did not have to be anything in order to be one of the Twelve Fishers; unless you were already a certain sort of person, you never even heard of them. It had been in existence twelve years. Its president was Mr Audley. Its vice-president was the Duke of Chester.

If I have in any degree conveyed the atmosphere of this appalling hotel, the reader may feel a natural wonder as to how I came to know anything about it, and may even speculate as to how so ordinary a person as my friend Father Brown came to find himself in that golden gallery. As far as that is concerned, my story is simple, or even vulgar. There is in the world a very aged rioter and demagogue who breaks into the most refined retreats with the dreadful information that all men are brothers, and wherever this leveller went on his pale horse it was Father Brown's trade to follow. One of the waiters, an Italian, had been struck down with a paralytic stroke that afternoon; and his Jewish employer, marvelling mildly at such superstitions, had consented to send for the nearest Popish priest. With what the waiter confessed to Father Brown we are not concerned, for the excellent reason that that cleric kept it to himself; but apparently it involved him in writing out a note or statement for the conveying of some message or the righting of some wrong. Father Brown, therefore, with a meek impudence which he would have shown equally in Buckingham Palace, asked to be provided with a room and writing materials. Mr Lever was torn in two. He was a kind man, and had also that bad imitation of kindness, the dislike of any difficulty or scene. At the same time the presence of one unusual stranger in his hotel that evening was like a speck of dirt on something just cleaned. There was never any borderland or anteroom in the Vernon Hotel, no people waiting in the hall, no customers coming in on chance. There were fifteen waiters. There were twelve guests. It would be as startling to find a new guest in the hotel that night as to find a new brother taking breakfast or tea in one's own family. Moreover, the priest's appearance was second-rate and his clothes muddy; a mere glimpse of him afar off might precipitate a crisis in the club. Mr Lever at last hit on a plan to cover, since he might not obliterate, the disgrace. When you enter (as you never will) the Vernon Hotel, you pass down a short passage decorated with a few dingy but important pictures, and come to the main vestibule and lounge which opens on your right into passages leading to the public rooms, and on your left to a similar passage pointing to the kitchens and offices of the hotel. Immediately on your left hand is the corner of a glass office, which abuts upon the lounge – a house within a house, so to speak, like the old hotel bar which probably once occupied its place.

In this office sat the representative of the proprietor (nobody in this place ever appeared in person if he could help it), and just beyond the office, on the way to the servants' quarters, was the gentlemen's cloak room, the last boundary of the gentlemen's domain. But between the office and the cloak room was a small private room without other outlet, sometimes used by the proprietor for delicate and important matters, such as lending a duke a thousand pounds or declining to lend him sixpence. It is a mark of the magnificent tolerance of Mr Lever that he permitted this holy place to be for about half an hour profaned by a mere priest, scribbling away on a piece of paper. The story which Father Brown was writing down was very likely a much better story than this one, only it will never be known. I can merely state that it was very nearly as long, and that the last two or three paragraphs of it were the least exciting and absorbing.

For it was by the time that he had reached these that the priest began a little to allow his thoughts to wander and his animal senses, which were commonly keen, to awaken. The time of darkness and dinner was drawing on; his own forgotten little room was without a light, and perhaps the gathering gloom, as occasionally happens, sharpened the sense of sound. As Father Brown wrote the last and least essential part of his document, he caught himself writing to the rhythm of a recurrent noise outside, just as one sometimes thinks to the tune of a railway train. When he became conscious of the thing he found what it was: only the ordinary patter of feet passing the door, which in an hotel was no very unlikely matter. Nevertheless, he stared at the darkened ceiling, and listened to the sound. After he had listened for a few seconds dreamily, he got to his feet and listened intently, with his head a little on one side. Then he sat down again and buried his brow in his hands, now not merely listening, but listening and thinking also.

The footsteps outside at any given moment were such as one might hear in any hotel; and yet, taken as a whole, there was something very strange about them. There were no other footsteps. It was always a very silent house, for the few familiar guests went at once to their own apartments, and the well-trained waiters were told to be almost invisible until they were wanted. One could not conceive any place where there was less reason to apprehend anything irregular. But these footsteps were so odd that one could not decide to call them regular or irregular. Father Brown followed them with his finger on the edge of the table, like a man trying to learn a tune on the piano.

First, there came a long rush of rapid little steps, such as a light man might make in winning a walking race. At a certain point they stopped and changed to a sort of slow, swinging stamp, numbering not a quarter of the steps, but occupying about the same time. The moment the last echoing stamp had died away would come again the run or ripple of light, hurrying feet, and then again the thud of the heavier walking. It was certainly the same pair of boots, partly because (as has been said) there were no other boots about, and partly because they had a small but unmistakable creak in them. Father Brown had the kind of head that cannot help asking questions; and on this apparently trivial question his head almost split. He had seen men run in order to jump. He had seen men run in order to slide. But why on earth should a man run in order to walk? Or, again, why should he walk in order to run? Yet no other description would cover the antics of this invisible pair of legs. The man was either walking very fast down one-half of the corridor in order to walk very slow down the other half; or he was walking very slow at one end to have the rapture of walking fast at the other. Neither suggestion seemed to make much sense. His brain was growing darker and darker, like his room.

Yet, as he began to think steadily, the very blackness of his cell seemed to make his thoughts more vivid; he began to see as in a kind of vision the fantastic feet capering along the corridor in unnatural or symbolic attitudes. Was it a heathen religious dance? Or some entirely new kind of scientific exercise? Father Brown began to ask himself with more exactness what the steps suggested. Taking the slow step first: it certainly was not the step of the proprietor. Men of his type walk with a rapid waddle, or they sit still. It could not be any servant or messenger waiting for directions. It did not sound like it. The poorer orders (in an oligarchy) sometimes lurch about when they are slightly drunk, but generally, and especially in such gorgeous scenes, they stand or sit in constrained attitudes. No; that heavy yet springy step, with a kind of careless emphasis, not specially noisy, yet not caring what noise it made, belonged to only one of the animals of this earth. It was a gentleman of western Europe, and probably one who had never worked for his living.

Just as he came to this solid certainty, the step changed to the quicker one, and ran past the door as feverishly as a rat. The listener remarked that though this step was much swifter it was also much more noiseless, almost as if the man were walking on tiptoe. Yet it was not associated in his mind with secrecy, but with something else – something that he could not remember. He was maddened by one of those half-memories that make a man feel half-witted. Surely he had heard that strange, swift walking somewhere. Suddenly he sprang to his feet with a new idea in his head, and walked to the door. His room had no direct outlet on the passage, but let on one side into the glass office, and on the other into the cloak room beyond. He tried the door into the office, and found it locked. Then he looked at the window, now a square pane full of purple cloud cleft by livid sunset, and for an instant he smelt evil as a dog smells rats.

The rational part of him (whether the wiser or not) regained its supremacy. He remembered that the proprietor had told him that he should lock the door, and would come later to release him. He told himself that twenty things he had not thought of might explain the eccentric sounds outside; he reminded himself that there was just enough light left to finish his own proper work. Bringing his paper to the window so as to catch the last stormy evening light, he resolutely plunged once more into the almost completed record. He had written for about twenty minutes, bending closer and closer to his paper in the lessening light; then suddenly he sat upright. He had heard the strange feet once more.

This time they had a third oddity. Previously the unknown man had walked, with levity indeed and lightning quickness, but he had walked. This time he ran. One could hear the swift, soft, bounding steps coming along the corridor, like the pads of a fleeing and leaping panther. Whoever was coming was a very strong, active man, in still yet tearing excitement. Yet, when the sound had swept up to the office like a sort of whispering whirlwind, it suddenly changed again to the old slow, swaggering stamp.

Father Brown flung down his paper, and, knowing the office door to be locked, went at once into the cloak room on the other side. The attendant of this place was temporarily absent, probably because the only guests were at dinner and his office was a sinecure. After groping through a grey forest of overcoats, he found that the dim cloak room opened on the lighted corridor in the form of a sort of counter or half-door, like most of the counters across which we have all handed umbrellas and received tickets. There was a light immediately above the semicircular arch of this opening. It threw little illumination on Father Brown himself, who seemed a mere dark outline against the dim sunset window behind him. But it threw an almost theatrical light on the man who stood outside the cloak room in the corridor.

He was an elegant man in very plain evening dress; tall, but with an air of not taking up much room; one felt that he could have slid along like a shadow where many smaller men would have been obvious and obstructive. His face, now flung back in the lamplight, was swarthy and vivacious, the face of a foreigner. His figure was good, his manners good-humoured and confident; a critic could only say that his black coat was a shade below his figure and manners, and even bulged and bagged in an odd way. The moment he caught sight of Brown's black silhouette against the sunset, he tossed down a scrap of paper with a number and called out with amiable authority: 'I want my hat and coat, please; I find I have to go away at once.'

Father Brown took the paper without a word, and obediently went to look for the coat; it was not the first menial work he had done in his life. He brought it and laid it on the counter; meanwhile, the strange gentleman who had been feeling in his waistcoat pocket, said laughing: 'I haven't got any silver; you can keep this.' And he threw down half a sovereign, and caught up his coat.

Father Brown's figure remained quite dark and still; but in that instant he had lost his head. His head was always most valuable when he had lost it. In such moments he put two and two together and made four million. Often the Catholic Church (which is wedded to common sense) did not approve of it. Often he did not approve of it himself. But it was real inspiration – important at rare crises – when whosoever shall lose his head the same shall save it.

'I think, sir,' he said civilly, 'that you have some silver in your pocket.'

The tall gentleman stared. 'Hang it,' he cried, 'if I choose to give you gold, why should you complain?'

'Because silver is sometimes more valuable than gold,' said the priest mildly; 'that is, in large quantities.'

The stranger looked at him curiously. Then he looked still more curiously up the passage towards the main entrance. Then he looked back at Brown again, and then he looked very carefully at the window beyond Brown's head, still coloured with the afterglow of the storm. Then he seemed to make up his mind. He put one hand on the counter, vaulted over as easily as an acrobat and towered above the priest, putting one tremendous hand upon his collar.

'Stand still,' he said, in a hacking whisper. 'I don't want to threaten you, but – '

'I do want to threaten you,' said Father Brown, in a voice like a rolling drum, 'I want to threaten you with the worm that dieth not, and the fire that is not quenched.'

'You're a rum sort of cloakroom clerk,' said the other.

'I am a priest, Monsieur Flambeau,' said Brown, 'and I am ready to hear your confession.'

The other stood gasping for a few moments, and then staggered back into a chair.

* * *

The first two courses of the dinner of the Twelve True Fishermen had proceeded with placid success. I do not possess a copy of the menu; and if I did it would not convey anything to anybody. It was written in a sort of super-French employed by cooks, but quite unintelligible to Frenchmen. There was a tradition in the club that the *hors d'oeuvres* should be various and manifold to the point of madness. They were taken seriously because they were avowedly useless extras, like the whole dinner and the whole club. There was also a tradition that the soup course should be light and unpretending – a sort of simple and austere vigil for the feast of fish that was to come. The talk was that strange, slight talk which governs the British Empire, which governs it in secret, and yet would scarcely enlighten an ordinary Englishman even if he could overhear it. Cabinet ministers on both sides were alluded to by their Christian names with a sort of bored benignity. The Radical Chancellor of the Exchequer, whom the whole Tory party was supposed to be cursing for his extortions, was praised for his minor poetry, or his saddle in the hunting field. The Tory leader, whom all Liberals were supposed to hate as a tyrant, was discussed and, on the whole, praised – as a Liberal. It seemed somehow that politicians were very important. And yet, anything seemed important about them except their politics. Mr Audley, the chairman, was an amiable, elderly man who still wore Gladstone collars; he was a kind of symbol of all that phantasmal and yet fixed society. He had never done anything – not even anything wrong. He was not fast; he was not even particularly rich. He was simply in the thing; and there was an end of it. No party could ignore him, and if he had wished to be in the Cabinet he certainly would have been put there. The Duke of Chester, the vice-president, was a young and rising politician. That is to say, he was a pleasant youth, with flat, fair hair and a freckled face, with moderate intelligence and enormous estates. In public his appearances were always successful and his principle was simple enough. When he thought of a joke he made it, and was called brilliant. When he could not think of a joke he said that this was no time for trifling, and was called able. In private, in a club of his own class, he was simply quite pleasantly frank and silly, like a schoolboy. Mr Audley, never having been in politics, treated them a little more seriously. Sometimes he even embarrassed the company by phrases suggesting that there was some difference between a Liberal and a Conservative. He himself was a Conservative, even in private life. He had a roll of grey hair over the back of his collar, like certain old-fashioned statesmen, and seen from behind he looked like the man the empire wants. Seen from the front he looked like a mild, self-indulgent bachelor, with rooms in the Albany – which he was.

As has been remarked, there were twenty-four seats at the terrace table, and only twelve members of the club. Thus they could occupy the terrace in the most luxurious style of all, being ranged along the inner side of the table, with no one opposite, commanding an uninterrupted view of the garden, the colours of which were still vivid, though evening was closing in somewhat luridly for the time of year. The chairman sat in the centre of the line, and the vice-president at the right-hand end of it. When the twelve guests first trooped into their seats it was the custom (for some unknown reason) for all the fifteen waiters to stand lining the wall like troops presenting arms to the king, while the fat proprietor stood and bowed to the club with radiant surprise, as if he had never heard of them before. But before the first chink of knife and fork this army of retainers had vanished, only the one or two required to collect and distribute the plates darting about in deathly silence. Mr Lever, the proprietor, of course had disappeared in convulsions of courtesy long before. It would be exaggerative, indeed irreverent, to say that he ever positively appeared again. But when the important course, the fish course, was being brought on, there was – how shall I put it? – a vivid shadow, a projection of his personality, which told that he was hovering near. The sacred fish course consisted (to the eyes of the vulgar) in a sort of monstrous pudding, about the size and shape of a wedding cake, in which some considerable number of interesting fishes had finally lost the shapes which God had given to them. The Twelve True Fishermen took up their celebrated fish knives and fish forks, and approached it as gravely as if every inch of the pudding cost as much as the silver fork it was eaten with. So it did, for all I know. This course was dealt with in eager and devouring silence; and it was only when his plate was nearly empty that the young duke made the ritual remark: 'They can't do this anywhere but here.'

'Nowhere,' said Mr Audley, in a deep bass voice, turning to the speaker and nodding his venerable head a number of times. 'Nowhere, assuredly, except here. It was represented to me that at the Café Anglais – '

Here he was interrupted and even agitated for a moment by the removal of his plate, but he recaptured the valuable thread of his thoughts. 'It was represented to me that the same could be done at the Café Anglais. Nothing like it, sir,' he said, shaking his head ruthlessly, like a hanging judge. 'Nothing like it.'

'Overrated place,' said a certain Colonel Pound, speaking (by the look of him) for the first time for some months.

'Oh, I don't know,' said the Duke of Chester, who was an optimist, 'it's jolly good for some things. You can't beat it at – '

A waiter came swiftly along the room, and then stopped dead. His stoppage was as silent as his tread; but all those vague and kindly gentlemen were so used to the utter smoothness of the unseen machinery which surrounded and supported their lives, that a waiter doing anything unexpected was a start and a jar. They felt as you and I would feel if the inanimate world disobeyed – if a chair ran away from us.

The waiter stood staring a few seconds, while there deepened on every face at table a strange shame which is wholly the product of our time. It is the combination of modern humanitarianism with the horrible modern abyss between the souls of the rich and poor. A genuine historic aristocrat would have thrown things at the waiter, beginning with empty bottles, and very probably ending with money. A genuine democrat would have asked him, with comrade-like clearness of speech, what the devil he was doing. But these modern plutocrats could not bear a poor man near to them, either as a slave or as a friend. That something had gone wrong with the servants was merely a dull, hot embarrassment. They did not want to be brutal, and they dreaded the need to be benevolent. They wanted the thing, whatever it was, to be over. It was over. The waiter, after standing for some seconds rigid, like a cataleptic, turned round and ran madly out of the room.

When he reappeared in the room, or rather in the doorway, it was in company with another waiter, with whom he whispered and gesticulated with southern fierceness. Then the first waiter went away, leaving the second waiter, and reappeared with a third waiter. By the time a fourth waiter had joined this hurried synod, Mr Audley felt it necessary to break the silence in the interests of Tact. He used a very loud cough, instead of a presidential hammer, and said: 'Splendid work young Moocher's doing in Burmah. Now, no other nation in the world could have – '

A fifth waiter had sped towards him like an arrow, and was whispering in his ear: 'So sorry. Important! Might the proprietor speak to you?'

The chairman turned in disorder, and with a dazed stare saw Mr Lever coming towards them with his lumbering quickness. The gait of the good proprietor was indeed his usual gait, but his face was by no means usual. Generally it was a genial copper-brown; now it was a sickly yellow.

'You will pardon me, Mr Audley,' he said, with asthmatic breathlessness. 'I have great apprehensions. Your fish plates, they are cleared away with the knife and fork on them!'

'Well, I hope so,' said the chairman, with some warmth.

'You see him?' panted the excited hotel keeper; 'you see the waiter who took them away? You know him?'

'Know the waiter?' answered Mr Audley indignantly. 'Certainly not!'

Mr Lever opened his hands with a gesture of agony. 'I never send him,' he said. 'I know not when or why he come. I send my waiter to take away the plates, and he find them already away.'

Mr Audley still looked rather too bewildered to be really the man the empire wants; none of the company could say anything except the man of wood – Colonel Pound – who seemed galvanised into an unnatural life. He rose rigidly from his chair, leaving all the rest sitting, screwed his eyeglass into his eye, and spoke in a raucous undertone as if he had half-forgotten how to speak. 'Do you mean,' he said, 'that somebody has stolen our silver fish service?'

The proprietor repeated the open-handed gesture with even greater helplessness and in a flash all the men at the table were on their feet.

'Are all your waiters here?' demanded the colonel, in his low, harsh accent.

'Yes; they're all here. I noticed it myself,' cried the young duke, pushing his boyish face into the inmost ring. 'Always count 'em as I come in; they look so queer standing up against the wall.'

'But surely one cannot exactly remember,' began Mr Audley, with heavy hesitation.

'I remember exactly, I tell you,' cried the duke excitedly. 'There never have been more than fifteen waiters at this place, and there were no more than fifteen tonight, I'll swear; no more and no less.'

The proprietor turned upon him, quaking in a kind of palsy of surprise. 'You say – you say,' he stammered, 'that you see all my fifteen waiters?'

'As usual,' assented the duke. 'What is the matter with that?'

'Nothing,' said Lever, with a deepening accent, 'only you did not. For one of zem is dead upstairs.'

There was a shocking stillness for an instant in that room. It may be (so supernatural is the word death) that each of those idle men looked for a second at his soul, and saw it as a small dried pea. One of them – the duke, I think – even said with the idiotic kindness of wealth: 'Is there anything we can do?'

'He has had a priest,' said the Jew, not untouched.

Then, as to the clang of doom, they awoke to their own position. For a few weird seconds they had really felt as if the fifteenth waiter might be the ghost of the dead man upstairs. They had been dumb under that oppression, for ghosts were to them an embarrassment, like beggars. But the remembrance of the silver broke the spell of the miraculous; broke it abruptly and with a brutal reaction. The colonel flung over his chair and strode to the door. 'If there was a fifteenth man here, friends,' he said, 'that fifteenth fellow was a thief. Down at once to the front and back doors and secure everything; then we'll talk. The twenty-four pearls of the club are worth recovering.'

Mr Audley seemed at first to hesitate about whether it was gentlemanly to be in such a hurry about anything; but, seeing the duke dash down the stairs with youthful energy, he followed with a more mature motion.

At the same instant a sixth waiter ran into the room, and declared that he had found the pile of fish plates on a sideboard, with no trace of the silver.

The crowd of diners and attendants that tumbled helter-skelter down the passages divided into two groups. Most of the Fishermen followed the proprietor to the front room to demand news of any exit. Colonel Pound, with the chairman, the vice-president, and one or two others, darted down the corridor leading to the servants' quarters, as the more likely line of escape. As they did so they passed the dim alcove or cavern of the cloak room, and saw a short, black-coated figure, presumably an attendant, standing a little way back in the shadow of it.

'Hallo, there!' called out the duke. 'Have you seen anyone pass?'

The short figure did not answer the question directly, but merely said: 'Perhaps I have got what you are looking for, gentlemen.'

They paused, wavering and wondering, while he quietly went to the back of the cloak room, and came back with both hands full of shining silver, which he laid out on the counter as calmly as a salesman. It took the form of a dozen quaintly shaped forks and knives.

'You – you – ' began the colonel, quite thrown off his balance at last. Then he peered into the dim little room and saw two things: first, that the short, black-clad man was dressed like a clergyman; and, second, that the window of the room behind him was burst, as if someone had passed violently through. 'Valuable things to deposit in a cloak room, aren't they?' remarked the clergyman, with cheerful composure.

'Did – did you steal those things?' stammered Mr Audley, with staring eyes.

'If I did,' said the cleric pleasantly, 'at least I am bringing them back again.'

'But you didn't,' said Colonel Pound, still staring at the broken window.

'To make a clean breast of it, I didn't,' said the other, with some humour. And he seated himself quite gravely on a stool. 'But you know who did,' said the colonel.

'I don't know his real name,' said the priest placidly, 'but I know something of his fighting weight, and a great deal about his spiritual difficulties. I formed the physical estimate when he was trying to throttle me, and the moral estimate when he repented.'

'Oh, I say – repented!' cried young Chester, with a sort of crow of laughter.

Father Brown got to his feet, putting his hands behind him. 'Odd, isn't it,' he said, 'that a thief and a vagabond should repent, when so many who are rich and secure remain hard and frivolous, and without fruit for God or man? But there, if you will excuse me, you trespass a little upon my province. If you doubt the penitence as a practical fact, there are your knives and forks. You are The Twelve True Fishers, and there are all your silver fish. But He has made me a fisher of men.'

'Did you catch this man?' asked the colonel, frowning.

Father Brown looked him full in his frowning face. 'Yes,' he said, 'I caught him, with an unseen hook and an invisible line which is long enough to let him wander to the ends of the world, and still to bring him back with a twitch upon the thread.'

There was a long silence. All the other men present drifted away to carry the recovered silver to their comrades, or to consult the proprietor about the queer condition of affairs. But the grim-faced colonel still sat sideways on the counter, swinging his long, lank legs and biting his dark moustache.

At last he said quietly to the priest: 'He must have been a clever fellow, but I think I know a cleverer.'

'He was a clever fellow,' answered the other, 'but I am not quite sure of what other you mean.'

'I mean you,' said the colonel, with a short laugh. 'I don't want to get the fellow jailed; make yourself easy about that. But I'd give a good many silver forks to know exactly how you fell into this affair, and how you got the stuff out of him. I reckon you're the most up-to-date devil of the present company.'

Father Brown seemed rather to like the saturnine candour of the soldier. 'Well,' he said, smiling, 'I mustn't tell you anything of the man's identity, or his own story, of course; but there's no particular reason why I shouldn't tell you of the mere outside facts which I found out for myself.'

He hopped over the barrier with unexpected activity, and sat beside Colonel Pound, kicking his short legs like a little boy on a gate. He began to tell the story as easily as if he were telling it to an old friend by a Christmas fire.

'You see, colonel,' he said, 'I was shut up in that small room there doing some writing, when I heard a pair of feet in this passage doing a dance that was as queer as the dance of death. First came quick, funny little steps, like a man walking on tiptoe for a wager; then came slow, careless, creaking steps, as of a big man walking about with a cigar. But they were both made by the same feet, I swear, and they came in rotation; first the run and then the walk, and then the run again. I wondered at first idly and then wildly why a man should act these two parts at once. One walk I knew; it was just like yours, colonel. It was the walk of a well-fed gentleman waiting for something, who strolls about rather because he is physically alert than because he is mentally impatient. I knew that I knew the other walk, too, but I could not remember what it was. What wild creature had I met on my travels that tore along on tiptoe in that extraordinary style? Then I heard a clink of plates somewhere; and the answer stood up as plain as St Peter's. It was the walk of a waiter – that walk with the body slanted forward, the eyes looking down, the ball of the toe spurning away the ground, the coat tails and napkin flying. Then I thought for a minute and a half more. And I believe I saw the manner of the crime, as clearly as if I were going to commit it.'

Colonel Pound looked at him keenly, but the speaker's mild grey eyes were fixed upon the ceiling with almost empty wistfulness.

'A crime,' he said slowly, 'is like any other work of art. Don't look surprised; crimes are by no means the only works of art that come from an infernal workshop. But every work of art, divine or diabolic, has one indispensable mark – I mean, that the centre of it is simple, however much the fulfilment may be complicated. Thus, in *Hamlet*, let us say, the grotesqueness of the grave-digger, the flowers of the mad girl, the fantastic finery of Osric, the pallor of the ghost and the grin of the skull are all oddities in a sort of tangled wreath round one plain tragic figure of a man in black. Well, this also,' he said, getting slowly down from his seat with a smile, 'this also is the plain tragedy of a man in black. Yes,' he went on, seeing the colonel look up in some wonder, 'the whole of this tale turns on a black coat. In this, as in *Hamlet*, there are the rococo excrescences – yourselves, let us say. There is the dead waiter, who was there when he could not be there. There is the invisible hand that swept your table clear of silver and melted into air. But every clever crime is founded ultimately on some one quite simple fact – some fact that is not itself mysterious. The mystification comes in covering it up, in leading men's thoughts away from it. This large and subtle and (in the ordinary course) most profitable crime, was built on the plain fact that a gentleman's evening dress is the same as a waiter's. All the rest was acting, and thundering good acting, too.'

'Still,' said the colonel, getting up and frowning at his boots, 'I am not sure that I understand.'

'Colonel,' said Father Brown, 'I tell you that this archangel of impudence who stole your forks walked up and down this passage twenty times in the blaze of all the lamps, in the glare of all the eyes. He did not go and hide in dim corners where suspicion might have searched for him. He kept constantly on the move in the lighted corridors, and everywhere that he went he seemed to be there by right. Don't ask me what he was like; you have seen him yourself six or seven times tonight. You were waiting with all the other grand people in the reception room at the end of the passage there, with the terrace just beyond. Whenever he came among you gentlemen, he came in the lightning style of a waiter, with bent head, flapping napkin and flying feet. He shot out on to the terrace, did something to the tablecloth, and shot back again towards the office and the waiters' quarters. By the time he had come under the eye of the office clerk and the waiters he had become another man in every inch of his body, in every instinctive gesture. He strolled among the servants with the absent-minded insolence which they have all seen in their patrons. It was no new thing to them that a swell from the dinner party should pace all parts of the house like an animal at the Zoo; they know that nothing marks the Smart Set more than a habit of walking where one chooses. When he was magnificently weary of walking down that particular passage he would wheel round and pace back past the office; in the shadow of the arch just beyond he was altered as by a blast of magic, and went hurrying forward again among the Twelve Fishermen, an obsequious attendant. Why should the gentlemen look at a chance waiter? Why should the waiters suspect a first-rate walking gentleman? Once or twice he played the coolest tricks. In the proprietor's private quarters he called out breezily for a syphon of soda water, saying he was thirsty. He said genially that he would carry it himself, and he did; he carried it quickly and correctly through the thick of you, a waiter with an obvious errand. Of course, it could not have been kept up long, but it only had to be kept up till the end of the fish course.

'His worst moment was when the waiters stood in a row; but even then he contrived to lean against the wall just round the corner in such a way that for that important instant the waiters thought him a gentleman, while the gentlemen thought him a waiter. The rest went like winking. If any waiter caught him away from the table, that waiter caught a languid aristocrat. He had only to time himself two minutes before the fish was cleared, become a swift servant, and clear it himself. He put the plates down on a sideboard, stuffed the silver in his breast pocket, giving it a bulgy look, and ran like a hare (I heard him coming) till he came to the cloak room. There he had only to be a plutocrat again – a plutocrat called away suddenly on business. He had only to give his ticket to the cloakroom attendant, and go out again elegantly as he had come in. Only – only I happened to be the cloakroom attendant.'

'What did you do to him?' cried the colonel, with unusual intensity. 'What did he tell you?'

'I beg your pardon,' said the priest immovably, 'that is where the story ends.'

'And the interesting story begins,' muttered Pound. 'I think I understand his professional trick. But I don't seem to have got hold of yours.'

'I must be going,' said Father Brown.

They walked together along the passage to the entrance hall, where they saw the fresh, freckled face of the Duke of Chester, who was bounding buoyantly along towards them.

'Come along, Pound,' he cried breathlessly. 'I've been looking for you everywhere. The dinner's going again in spanking style, and old Audley has got to make a speech in honour of the forks being saved. We want to start some new ceremony, don't you know, to commemorate the occasion. I say, you really got the goods back, what do you suggest?'

'Why,' said the colonel, eyeing him with a certain sardonic approval, 'I should suggest that henceforward we wear green coats, instead of black. One never knows what mistakes may arise when one looks so like a waiter.'

'Oh, hang it all!' said the young man, 'a gentleman never looks like a waiter.'

'Nor a waiter like a gentleman, I suppose,' said Colonel Pound, with the same lowering laughter on his face. 'Reverend sir, your friend must have been very smart to act the gentleman.'

Father Brown buttoned up his commonplace overcoat to the neck, for the night was stormy, and took his commonplace umbrella from the stand.

'Yes,' he said; 'it must be very hard work to be a gentleman; but, do you know, I have sometimes thought that it may be almost as laborious to be a waiter.'

And saying 'Good-evening,' he pushed open the heavy doors of that palace of pleasures. The golden gates closed behind him, and he went at a brisk walk through the damp, dark streets in search of a penny omnibus.

The Flying Stars

'The most beautiful crime I ever committed,' Flambeau would say in his highly moral old age, 'was also, by a singular coincidence, my last. It was committed at Christmas. As an artist I had always attempted to provide crimes suitable to the special season or landscapes in which I found myself, choosing this or that terrace or garden for a catastrophe, as if for a statuary group. Thus squires should be swindled in long rooms panelled with oak; while Jews, on the other hand, should rather find themselves unexpectedly penniless among the lights and screens of the Café Riche. Thus, in England, if I wished to relieve a dean of his riches (which is not so easy as you might suppose), I wished to frame him, if I make myself clear, in the green lawns and grey towers of some cathedral town. Similarly, in France, when I had got money out of a rich and wicked peasant (which is almost impossible), it gratified me to get his indignant head relieved against a grey line of clipped poplars, and those solemn plains of Gaul over which broods the mighty spirit of Millet.

'Well, my last crime was a Christmas crime, a cheery, cosy, English middle-class crime; a crime of Charles Dickens. I did it in a good old middle-class house near Putney, a house with a crescent of carriage drive, a house with a stable by the side of it, a house with the name on the two outer gates, a house with a monkey tree. Enough, you know the species. I really think my imitation of Dickens's style was dexterous and literary. It seems almost a pity I repented the same evening.'

Flambeau would then proceed to tell the story from the inside; and even from the inside it was odd. Seen from the outside it was perfectly incomprehensible, and it is from the outside that the stranger must study it. From this standpoint the drama may be said to have begun when the front doors of the house with the stable opened on the garden with the monkey tree, and a young girl came out with bread to feed the birds on the afternoon of Boxing Day. She had a pretty face, with brave brown eyes; but her figure was beyond conjecture, for she was so wrapped up in brown furs that it was hard to say which was hair and which was fur. But for the attractive face she might have been a small toddling bear.

The winter afternoon was reddening towards evening, and already a ruby light was rolled over the bloomless beds, filling them, as it were, with the ghosts of the dead roses. On one side of the house stood the stable, on the other an alley or cloister of laurels led to the larger garden behind. The young lady, having scattered bread for the birds (for the fourth or fifth time that day, because the dog ate it), passed unobtrusively down the lane of laurels and into a glimmering plantation of evergreens behind. Here she gave an exclamation of wonder, real or ritual, and looking up at the high garden wall above her, beheld it fantastically bestridden by a somewhat fantastic figure.

'Oh, don't jump, Mr Crook,' she called out in some alarm; 'it's much too high.'

The individual riding the party wall like an aerial horse was a tall, angular young man, with dark hair sticking up like a hair brush, intelligent and even distinguished lineaments, but a sallow and almost alien complexion. This showed the more plainly because he wore an aggressive red tie, the only part of his costume of which he seemed to take any care. Perhaps it was a symbol. He took no notice of the girl's alarmed adjuration, but leapt like a grasshopper to the ground beside her, where he might very well have broken his legs.

'I think I was meant to be a burglar,' he said placidly, 'and I have no doubt I should have been if I hadn't happened to be born in that nice house next door. I can't see any harm in it, anyhow.'

'How can you say such things!' she remonstrated.

'Well,' said the young man, 'if you're born on the wrong side of the wall, I can't see that it's wrong to climb over it.'

'I never know what you will say or do next,' she said.

'I don't often know myself,' replied Mr Crook; 'but then I am on the right side of the wall now.'

'And which is the right side of the wall?' asked the young lady, smiling.

'Whichever side you are on,' said the young man named Crook.

As they went together through the laurels towards the front garden a motor horn sounded thrice, coming nearer and nearer, and a car of splendid speed, great elegance, and a pale green colour swept up to the front doors like a bird and stood throbbing.

'Hullo, hullo!' said the young man with the red tie, 'here's somebody born on the right side, anyhow. I didn't know, Miss Adams, that your Santa Claus was so modern as this.'

'Oh, that's my godfather, Sir Leopold Fischer. He always comes on Boxing Day.'

Then, after an innocent pause, which unconsciously betrayed some lack of enthusiasm, Ruby Adams added: 'He is very kind.'

John Crook, journalist, had heard of that eminent City magnate; and it was not his fault if the City magnate had not heard of him; for in certain articles in *The Clarion* or *The New Age* Sir Leopold had been dealt with austerely. But he said nothing and grimly watched the unloading of the motor car, which was rather a long process. A large, neat chauffeur in green got out from the front, and a small, neat manservant in grey got out from the back, and between them they deposited Sir Leopold on the doorstep and began to unpack him, like some very carefully protected parcel. Rugs enough to stock a bazaar, furs of all the beasts of the forest, and scarves of all the colours of the rainbow were unwrapped one by one, till they revealed something resembling the human form; the form of a friendly, but foreign-looking old gentleman, with a grey goatlike beard and a beaming smile, who rubbed his big fur gloves together.

Long before this revelation was complete the two big doors of the porch had opened in the middle, and Colonel Adams (father of the furry young lady) had come out himself to invite his eminent guest inside. He was a tall, sunburnt, and very silent man, who wore a red smoking-cap like a fez, making him look like one of the English Sirdars or Pashas in Egypt. With him was his brother-in-law, lately come from Canada, a big and rather boisterous young gentleman-farmer, with a yellow beard, by name James Blount. With him also was the more insignificant figure of the priest from the neighbouring Roman Church; for the colonel's late wife had been a Catholic, and the children, as is common in such cases, had been trained to follow her. Everything seemed undistinguished about the priest, even down to his name, which was Brown; yet the colonel had always found something companionable about him, and frequently asked him to such family gatherings.

In the large entrance hall of the house there was ample room even for Sir Leopold and the removal of his wraps. Porch and vestibule, indeed, were unduly large in proportion to the house, and formed, as it were, a big room with the front door at one end, and the bottom of the staircase at the other. In front of the large hall fire, over which hung the colonel's sword, the process was completed and the company, including the saturnine Crook, presented to Sir Leopold Fischer. That venerable financier, however, still seemed struggling with portions of his well-lined attire, and at length produced from a very interior tail-coat pocket, a black oval case which he radiantly explained to be his Christmas present for his god-daughter. With an unaffected vain-glory that had something disarming about it he held out the case before them all; it flew open at a touch and half-blinded them. It was just as if a crystal fountain had spurted in their eyes. In a nest of orange velvet lay like three eggs, three white and vivid diamonds that seemed to set the very air on fire all round them. Fischer stood beaming benevolently and drinking deep of the astonishment and ecstasy of the girl, the grim admiration and gruff thanks of the colonel, the wonder of the whole group.

'I'll put 'em back now, my dear,' said Fischer, returning the case to the tails of his coat. 'I had to be careful of 'em coming down. They're the three great African diamonds called "The Flying Stars", because they've been stolen so often. All the big criminals are on the track; but even the rough men about in the streets and hotels could hardly have kept their hands off them. I might have lost them on the road here. It was quite possible.'

'Quite natural, I should say,' growled the man in the red tie. 'I shouldn't blame 'em if they had taken 'em. When they ask for bread, and you don't even give them a stone, I think they might take the stone for themselves.'

'I won't have you talking like that,' cried the girl, who was in a curious glow. 'You've only talked like that since you became a horrid what's-his-name. You know what I mean. What do you call a man who wants to embrace the chimney-sweep?'

'A saint,' said Father Brown.

'I think,' said Sir Leopold, with a supercilious smile, 'that Ruby means a Socialist.'

'A Radical does not mean a man who lives on radishes,' remarked Crook, with some impatience; 'and a Conservative does not mean a man who preserves jam. Neither, I assure you, does a Socialist mean a man who desires a social evening with the chimney-sweep. A Socialist means a man who wants all the chimneys swept and all the chimney-sweeps paid for it.'

'But who won't allow you,' put in the priest in a low voice, 'to own your own soot.'

Crook looked at him with an eye of interest and even respect. 'Does one want to own soot?' he asked.

'One might,' answered Brown, with speculation in his eye. 'I've heard that gardeners use it. And I once made six children happy at Christmas when the conjuror didn't come, entirely with soot – applied externally.'

'Oh, splendid,' cried Ruby. 'Oh, I wish you'd do it to this company.'

The boisterous Canadian, Mr Blount, was lifting his loud voice in applause, and the astonished financier his (in some considerable deprecation), when a knock sounded at the double front doors. The priest opened them, and they showed again the front garden of evergreens, monkey tree and all, now gathering gloom against a gorgeous violet sunset. The scene thus framed was so coloured and quaint, like a back scene in a play, that they forgot a moment the insignificant figure standing in the door. He was dusty-looking and in a frayed coat, evidently a common messenger. 'Any of you gentlemen Mr Blount?' he asked, and held forward a letter doubtfully. Mr Blount started, and stopped in his shout of assent. Ripping up the envelope with evident astonishment he read it; his face clouded a little, and then cleared, and he turned to his brother-in-law and host.

'I'm sick at being such a nuisance, colonel,' he said, with the cheery colonial convention; 'but would it upset you if an old acquaintance called on me here tonight on business? In point of fact it's Florian, that famous French acrobat and comic actor; I knew him years ago out West (he was a French-

Canadian by birth), and he seems to have business for me, though I hardly guess what.'

'Of course, of course,' replied the colonel carelessly. 'My dear chap, any friend of yours. No doubt he will prove an acquisition.'

'He'll black his face, if that's what you mean,' cried Blount, laughing. 'I don't doubt he'd black everyone else's eyes. I don't care; I'm not refined. I like the jolly old pantomime where a man sits on his top hat.'

'Not on mine, please,' said Sir Leopold Fischer, with dignity.

'Well, well,' observed Crook, airily, 'don't let's quarrel. There are lower jokes than sitting on a top hat.'

Dislike of the red-tied youth, born of his predatory opinions and evident intimacy with the pretty godchild, led Fischer to say, in his most sarcastic, magisterial manner: 'No doubt you have found something much lower than sitting on a top hat. What is it, pray?'

'Letting a top hat sit on you, for instance,' said the Socialist.

'Now, now, now,' cried the Canadian farmer with his barbarian benevolence, 'don't let's spoil a jolly evening. What I say is, let's do something for the company tonight. Not blacking faces or sitting on hats, if you don't like those – but something of the sort. Why couldn't we have a proper old English pantomime – clown, columbine, and so on. I saw one when I left England at twelve years old, and it's blazed in my brain like a bonfire ever since. I came back to the old country only last year, and I find the thing's extinct. Nothing but a lot of snivelling fairy plays. I want a hot poker and a policeman made into sausages, and they give me princesses moralising by moonlight, Blue Birds, or something. Blue Beard's more in my line, and him I liked best when he turned into the pantaloon.'

'I'm all for making a policeman into sausages,' said John Crook. 'It's a better definition of Socialism than some recently given. But surely the get-up would be too big a business.'

'Not a scrap,' cried Blount, quite carried away. 'A harlequinade's the quickest thing we can do, for two reasons. First, one can gag to any degree; and, second, all the objects are household things – tables and towel-horses and washing baskets, and things like that.'

'That's true,' admitted Crook, nodding eagerly and walking about. 'But I'm afraid I can't have my policeman's uniform! Haven't killed a policeman lately.'

Blount frowned thoughtfully a space, and then smote his thigh. 'Yes, we can!' he cried. 'I've got Florian's address here, and he knows every costumier in London. I'll phone him to bring a police dress when he comes.' And he went bounding away to the telephone.

'Oh, it's glorious, godfather,' cried Ruby, almost dancing. 'I'll be columbine and you shall be pantaloon.'

The millionaire held himself stiff with a sort of heathen solemnity. 'I think, my dear,' he said, 'you must get someone else for pantaloon.'

'I will be pantaloon, if you like,' said Colonel Adams, taking his cigar out of his mouth, and speaking for the first and last time.

'You ought to have a statue,' cried the Canadian, as he came back, radiant, from the telephone. 'There, we are all fitted. Mr Crook shall be clown; he's a journalist and knows all the oldest jokes. I can be harlequin, that only wants long legs and jumping about. My friend Florian phones he's bringing the police costume; he's changing on the way. We can act it in this very hall, the audience sitting on those broad stairs opposite, one row above another. These front doors can be the back scene, either open or shut. Shut, you see an English interior. Open, a moonlit garden. It all goes by magic.' And snatching a chance piece of billiard chalk from his pocket, he ran it across the hall floor, halfway between the front door and the staircase, to mark the line of the footlights.

How even such a banquet of bosh was got ready in the time remained a riddle. But they went at it with that mixture of recklessness and industry that lives when youth is in a house; and youth was in that house that night, though not all may have isolated the two faces and hearts from which it flamed. As always happens, the invention grew wilder and wilder through the very tameness of the bourgeois conventions from which it had to create. The columbine looked charming in an outstanding skirt that strangely resembled the large lampshade in the drawing-room. The clown and pantaloon made themselves white with flour from the cook, and red with rouge from some other domestic, who remained (like all true Christian benefactors) anonymous. The harlequin, already clad in silver paper out of cigar boxes, was, with difficulty, prevented from smashing the old Victorian lustre chandeliers, that he might cover himself with resplendent crystals. In fact he would certainly have done so, had not Ruby unearthed some old pantomime paste jewels she had worn at a fancy-dress party as the Queen of Diamonds. Indeed, her uncle, James Blount, was getting almost out of hand in his excitement; he was like a schoolboy. He put a paper donkey's head unexpectedly on Father Brown, who bore it patiently, and even found some private manner of moving his ears. He even essayed to put the paper donkey's tail to the coat-tails of Sir Leopold Fischer. This, however, was frowned down. 'Uncle is too absurd,' cried Ruby to Crook, round whose shoulders she had seriously placed a string of sausages. 'Why is he so wild?'

'He is harlequin to your columbine,' said Crook. 'I am only the clown who makes the old jokes.'

'I wish you were the harlequin,' she said, and left the string of sausages swinging.

Father Brown, though he knew every detail done behind the scenes, and had even evoked applause by his transformation of a pillow into a pantomime baby, went round to the front and sat among the audience with all the solemn expectation of a child at his first matinee. The spectators were few, relations, one or two local friends, and the servants; Sir Leopold sat in the front seat, his full and still fur-collared figure largely obscuring the view of the little cleric behind him; but it has never been settled by artistic authorities whether the cleric lost much. The pantomime was utterly chaotic, yet not contemptible; there ran through it a rage of improvisation which came chiefly from Crook the clown. Commonly he was a clever man, and he was inspired tonight with a wild omniscience, a folly wiser than the world, that which comes to a young man who has seen for an instant a particular expression on a particular face. He was supposed to be the clown, but he was really almost everything else, the author (so far as there was an author), the prompter, the scene-painter, the scene-shifter, and, above all, the orchestra. At abrupt intervals in the outrageous performance he would hurl himself in full costume at the piano and bang out some popular music equally absurd and appropriate.

The climax of this, as of all else, was the moment when the two front doors at the back of the scene flew open, showing the lovely moonlit garden, but showing more prominently the famous professional guest; the great Florian, dressed up as a policeman. The clown at the piano played the constabulary chorus in the *Pirates of Penzance*, but it was drowned in the deafening applause, for every gesture of the great comic actor was an admirable though restrained version of the carriage and manner of the police. The harlequin leapt upon him and hit him over the helmet; the pianist playing 'Where did you get that hat?' he faced about in admirably simulated astonishment, and then the leaping harlequin hit him again (the pianist suggesting a few bars of 'Then we had another one'). Then the harlequin rushed right into the arms of the policeman and fell on top of him, amid a roar of applause. Then it was that the strange actor gave that celebrated imitation of a dead man, of which the fame still lingers round Putney. It was almost impossible to believe that a living person could appear so limp.

The athletic harlequin swung him about like a sack or twisted or tossed him like an Indian club; all the time to the most maddeningly ludicrous tunes from the piano. When the harlequin heaved the comic constable heavily off the floor the clown played 'I arise from dreams of thee'. When he shuffled him across his back, 'With my bundle on my shoulder', and when the harlequin finally let fall the policeman with a most convincing thud, the lunatic at the instrument struck into a jingling measure with some words which are still believed to have been, 'I sent a letter to my love and on the way I dropped it'.

At about this limit of mental anarchy Father Brown's view was obscured altogether; for the City magnate in front of him rose to his full height and thrust his hands savagely into all his pockets. Then he sat down nervously, still fumbling, and then stood up again. For an instant it seemed seriously likely that he would stride across the footlights; then he turned a glare at the clown playing the piano; and then he burst in silence out of the room.

The priest had only watched for a few more minutes the absurd but not inelegant dance of the amateur harlequin over his splendidly unconscious foe. With real though rude art, the harlequin danced slowly backwards out of the door into the garden, which was full of moonlight and stillness. The vamped dress of silver paper and paste, which had been too glaring in the footlights, looked more and more magical and silvery as it danced away under a brilliant moon. The audience was closing in with a cataract of applause, when Brown felt his arm abruptly touched, and he was asked in a whisper to come into the colonel's study.

He followed his summoner with increasing doubt, which was not dispelled by a solemn comicality in the scene of the study. There sat Colonel Adams, still unaffectedly dressed as a pantaloon, with the knobbed whalebone nodding above his brow, but with his poor old eyes sad enough to have sobered a Saturnalia. Sir Leopold Fischer was leaning against the mantelpiece and heaving with all the importance of panic.

'This is a very painful matter, Father Brown,' said Adams. 'The truth is, those diamonds we all saw this afternoon seem to have vanished from my friend's tail-coat pocket. And as you – '

'As I,' supplemented Father Brown, with a broad grin, 'was sitting just behind him – '

'Nothing of the sort shall be suggested,' said Colonel Adams, with a firm look at Fischer, which rather implied that some such thing had been suggested. 'I only ask you to give me the assistance that any gentleman might give.'

'Which is turning out his pockets,' said Father Brown, and proceeded to do so, displaying seven and sixpence, a return ticket, a small silver crucifix, a small breviary, and a stick of chocolate.

The colonel looked at him long, and then said, 'Do you know, I should like to see the inside of your head more than the inside of your pockets. My daughter is one of your people, I know; well, she has lately – ' and he stopped.

'She has lately,' cried out old Fischer, 'opened her father's house to a cut-throat Socialist, who says openly he would steal anything from a richer man. This is the end of it. Here is the richer man – and none the richer.'

'If you want the inside of my head you can have it,' said Father Brown rather wearily. 'What it's worth you can say afterwards. But the first thing I find in that disused pocket is this: that men who mean to steal diamonds don't talk Socialism. They are more likely,' he added demurely, 'to denounce it.'

Both the others shifted sharply and the priest went on: 'You see, we know these people, more or less. That Socialist would no more steal a diamond than a Pyramid. We ought to look at once to the one man we don't know. The fellow acting the policeman – Florian. Where is he exactly at this minute, I wonder?'

The pantaloon sprang erect and strode out of the room. An interlude ensued, during which the millionaire stared at the priest, and the priest at his breviary; then the pantaloon returned and said, with staccato gravity, 'The policeman is still lying on the stage. The curtain has gone up and down six times; he is still lying there.'

Father Brown dropped his book and stood staring with a look of blank mental ruin. Very slowly a light began to creep in his grey eyes, and then he made the scarcely obvious answer.

'Please forgive me, colonel, but when did your wife die?'

'Wife!' replied the staring soldier, 'she died this year two months. Her brother James arrived just a week too late to see her.'

The little priest bounded like a rabbit shot. 'Come on!' he cried in quite unusual excitement. 'Come on! We've got to go and look at that policeman!'

They rushed on to the now curtained stage, breaking rudely past the columbine and clown (who seemed whispering quite contentedly), and Father Brown bent over the prostrate comic policeman.

'Chloroform,' he said as he rose; 'I only guessed it just now.'

There was a startled stillness, and then the colonel said slowly, 'Please say seriously what all this means.'

Father Brown suddenly shouted with laughter, then stopped, and only struggled with it for instants during the rest of his speech. 'Gentlemen,' he gasped, 'there's not much time to talk. I must run after the criminal. But this great French actor who played the policeman – this clever corpse the harlequin waltzed with and dandled and threw about – he was – ' His voice again failed him, and he turned his back to run.

'He was?' called Fischer enquiringly.

'A real policeman,' said Father Brown, and ran away into the dark.

There were hollows and bowers at the extreme end of that leafy garden, in which the laurels and other immortal shrubs showed against sapphire sky and silver moon, even in that midwinter, warm colours as of the south. The green gaiety of the waving laurels, the rich purple indigo of the night, the moon like a monstrous crystal, make an almost irresponsible romantic picture; and among the top branches of the garden trees a strange figure is climbing, who looks not so much romantic as impossible. He sparkles from head to heel, as if clad in ten million moons; the real moon catches him at every movement and sets a new inch of him on fire. But he swings, flashing and successful, from the short tree in this garden to the tall, rambling tree in the other, and only stops there because a shade has slid under the smaller tree and has unmistakably called up to him.

'Well, Flambeau,' says the voice, 'you really look like a Flying Star; but that always means a Falling Star at last.'

The silver, sparkling figure above seems to lean forward in the laurels and, confident of escape, listens to the little figure below.

'You never did anything better, Flambeau. It was clever to come from Canada (with a Paris ticket, I suppose) just a week after Mrs Adams died, when no one was in a mood to ask questions. It was cleverer to have marked down the Flying Stars and the very day of Fischer's coming. But there's no cleverness, but mere genius, in what followed. Stealing the stones, I suppose, was nothing to you. You could have done it by sleight of hand in a hundred other ways besides that pretence of putting a paper donkey's tail to Fischer's coat. But in the rest you eclipsed yourself.'

The silvery figure among the green leaves seems to linger as if hypnotised, though his escape is easy behind him; he is staring at the man below.

'Oh, yes,' says the man below, 'I know all about it. I know you not only forced the pantomime, but put it to a double use. You were going to steal the stones quietly; news came by an accomplice that you were already suspected, and a capable police officer was coming to rout you up that very night. A common thief would have been thankful for the warning and fled; but you are a poet. You already had the clever notion of hiding the jewels in a blaze of false stage jewellery. Now, you saw that if the dress were a harlequin's the appearance of a policeman would be quite in keeping. The worthy officer started from Putney police station to find you, and walked into the queerest trap ever set in this world. When the front door opened he walked straight on to the stage of a Christmas pantomime, where he could be kicked, clubbed, stunned and drugged by the dancing harlequin, amid roars of laughter from all the most respectable people in Putney. Oh, you will never do anything better. And now, by the way, you might give me back those diamonds.'

The green branch on which the glittering figure swung, rustled as if in astonishment; but the voice went on: 'I want you to give them back, Flambeau, and I want you to give up this life. There is still youth and honour and humour in you; don't fancy they will last in that trade. Men may keep a sort of level of good, but no man has ever been able to keep on one level of evil. That road goes down and down. The kind man drinks and turns cruel; the frank man kills and lies about it. Many a man I've known started like you to be an honest outlaw, a merry robber of the rich, and ended stamped into slime. Maurice Blum started out as an anarchist of principle, a father of the poor; he ended a greasy spy and tale-bearer that both sides used and despised. Harry Burke started his free money movement sincerely enough; now he's sponging on a half-starved sister for endless brandies and sodas. Lord Amber went into wild society in a sort of chivalry; now he's paying blackmail to the lowest vultures in London. Captain Barillon was the great gentleman-apache before your time; he died in a madhouse, screaming with fear of the "narks" and receivers that had betrayed him and hunted him down. I know the woods look very free behind you, Flambeau; I know that in a flash you could melt into them like a monkey. But someday you will be an old grey monkey, Flambeau. You will sit up in your free forest cold at heart and close to death, and the tree-tops will be very bare.'

Everything continued still, as if the small man below held the other in the tree in some long invisible leash; and he went on: 'Your downward steps have begun. You used to boast of doing nothing mean, but you are doing something mean tonight. You are leaving suspicion on an honest boy with a good deal against him already; you are separating him from the woman he loves and who loves him. But you will do meaner things than that before you die.'

Three flashing diamonds fell from the tree to the turf. The small man stooped to pick them up, and when he looked up again the green cage of the tree was emptied of its silver bird.

The restoration of the gems (accidentally picked up by Father Brown, of all people) ended the evening in uproarious triumph; and Sir Leopold, in his height of good humour, even told the priest that though he himself had broader views, he could respect those whose creed required them to be cloistered and ignorant of this world.

The Invisible Man

In the cool blue twilight of two steep streets in Camden Town, the shop at the corner, a confectioner's, glowed like the butt of a cigar. One should rather say, perhaps, like the butt of a firework, for the light was of many colours and some complexity, broken up by many mirrors and dancing on many gilt and gaily-coloured cakes and sweetmeats. Against this one fiery glass were glued the noses of many guttersnipes, for the chocolates were all wrapped in those red and gold and green metallic colours which are almost better than chocolate itself; and the huge white wedding-cake in the window was somehow at once remote and satisfying, just as if the whole North Pole were good to eat. Such rainbow provocations could naturally collect the youth of the neighbourhood up to the ages of ten or twelve. But this corner was also attractive to youth at a later stage; and a young man, not less than twenty-four, was staring into the same shop-window. To him, also, the shop was of fiery charm, but this attraction was not wholly to be explained by chocolates; which, however, he was far from despising.

He was a tall, burly, red-haired young man, with a resolute face but a listless manner. He carried under his arm a flat, grey portfolio of black-and-white sketches, which he had sold with more or less success to publishers ever since his uncle (who was an admiral) had disinherited him for Socialism, because of a lecture which he had delivered against that economic theory. His name was John Turnbull Angus.

Entering at last, he walked through the confectioner's shop to the back room, which was a sort of pastry-cook restaurant, merely raising his hat to the young lady who was serving there. She was a dark, elegant, alert girl in black, with a high colour and very quick, dark eyes; and after the ordinary interval she followed him into the inner room to take his order.

His order was evidently a usual one. 'I want, please,' he said with precision, 'one halfpenny bun and a small cup of black coffee.' An instant before the girl could turn away he added, 'Also, I want you to marry me.'

The young lady of the shop stiffened suddenly and said, 'Those are jokes I don't allow.'

The red-haired young man lifted grey eyes of an unexpected gravity.

'Really and truly,' he said, 'it's as serious – as serious as the halfpenny bun. It is expensive, like the bun; one pays for it. It is indigestible, like the bun. It hurts.'

The dark young lady had never taken her dark eyes off him, but seemed to be studying him with almost tragic exactitude. At the end of her scrutiny she had something like the shadow of a smile, and she sat down in a chair.

'Don't you think,' observed Angus, absently, 'that it's rather cruel to eat these halfpenny buns? They might grow up into penny buns. I shall give up these brutal sports when we are married.'

The dark young lady rose from her chair and walked to the window, evidently in a state of strong but not unsympathetic cogitation. When at last she swung round again with an air of resolution she was bewildered to observe that the young man was carefully laying out on the table various objects from the shop-window. They included a pyramid of highly coloured sweets, several plates of sandwiches, and the two decanters containing that mysterious port and sherry which are peculiar to pastry-cooks. In the middle of this neat arrangement he had carefully let down the enormous load of white sugared cake which had been the huge ornament of the window.

'What on earth are you doing?' she asked.

'Duty, my dear Laura,' he began.

'Oh, for the Lord's sake, stop a minute,' she cried, 'and don't talk to me in that way. I mean, what is all that?'

'A ceremonial meal, Miss Hope.'

'And what is that?' she asked impatiently, pointing to the mountain of sugar.

'The wedding-cake, Mrs Angus,' he said.

The girl marched to that article, removed it with some clatter, and put it back in the shop-window; she then returned, and, putting her elegant elbows on the table, regarded the young man not unfavourably but with considerable exasperation.

'You don't give me any time to think,' she said.

'I'm not such a fool,' he answered; 'that's my Christian humility.'

She was still looking at him; but she had grown considerably graver behind the smile.

'Mr Angus,' she said steadily, 'before there is a minute more of this nonsense I must tell you something about myself as shortly as I can.'

'Delighted,' replied Angus gravely. 'You might tell me something about myself, too, while you are about it.'

'Oh, do hold your tongue and listen,' she said. 'It's nothing that I'm ashamed of, and it isn't even anything that I'm specially sorry about. But what would you say if there were something that is no business of mine and yet is my nightmare?'

'In that case,' said the man seriously, 'I should suggest that you bring back the cake.'

'Well, you must listen to the story first,' said Laura, persistently. 'To begin with, I must tell you that my father owned the inn called the Red Fish at Ludbury, and I used to serve people in the bar.'

'I have often wondered,' he said, 'why there was a kind of a Christian air about this one confectioner's shop.'

'Ludbury is a sleepy, grassy little hole in the Eastern Counties, and the only kind of people who ever came to the Red Fish were occasional commercial travellers, and for the rest, the most awful people you can see, only you've never seen them. I mean little, loungy men, who had just enough to live on and had nothing to do but lean about in bar-rooms and bet on horses, in bad clothes that were just too good for them. Even these wretched young rotters were not very common at our house; but there were two of them that were a lot too common – common in every sort of way. They both lived on money of their own, and were wearisomely idle and overdressed. But yet I was a bit sorry for them, because I half believe they slunk into our little empty bar because each of them had a slight deformity; the sort of thing that some yokels laugh at. It wasn't exactly a deformity either; it was more an oddity. One of them was a surprisingly small man, something like a dwarf, or at least like a jockey. He was not at all jockeyish to look at, though; he had a round black head and a well-trimmed black beard, bright eyes like a bird's; he jingled money in his pockets; he jangled a great gold watch chain; and he never turned up except dressed just too much like a gentleman to be one. He was no fool though, though a futile idler; he was curiously clever at all kinds of things that couldn't be the slightest use; a sort of impromptu conjuring; making fifteen matches set fire to each other like a regular firework; or cutting a banana or some such thing into a dancing doll. His name was Isidore Smythe; and I can see him still, with his little dark face, just coming up to the counter, making a jumping kangaroo out of five cigars.

'The other fellow was more silent and more ordinary; but somehow he alarmed me much more than poor little Smythe. He was very tall and slight, and light-haired; his nose had a high bridge, and he might almost have been handsome in a spectral sort of way; but he had one of the most appalling squints I have ever seen or heard of. When he looked straight at you, you didn't know where you were yourself, let alone what he was looking at. I fancy this sort of disfigurement embittered the poor chap a little; for while Smythe was ready to show off his monkey tricks anywhere, James Welkin (that was the squinting man's name) never did anything except soak in our bar parlour, and go for great walks by himself in the flat, grey country all round. All the same, I think Smythe, too, was a little sensitive about being so small, though he carried it off more smartly. And so it was that I was really puzzled, as well as startled, and very sorry, when they both offered to marry me in the same week.

'Well, I did what I've since thought was perhaps a silly thing. But, after all, these freaks were my friends in a way; and I had a horror of their thinking I refused them for the real reason, which was that they were so impossibly ugly. So I made up some gas of another sort, about never meaning to marry anyone who hadn't carved his way in the world. I said it was a point of principle with me not to live on money that was just inherited like theirs. Two days after I had talked in this well-meaning sort of way, the whole trouble began. The first thing I heard was that both of them had gone off to seek their fortunes, as if they were in some silly fairytale.

'Well, I've never seen either of them from that day to this. But I've had two letters from the little man called Smythe, and really they were rather exciting.'

'Ever heard of the other man?' asked Angus.

'No, he never wrote,' said the girl, after an instant's hesitation. 'Smythe's first letter was simply to say that he had started out walking with Welkin to London; but Welkin was such a good walker that the little man dropped out of it, and took a rest by the roadside. He happened to be picked up by some travelling show, and, partly because he was nearly a dwarf, and partly because he was really a clever little wretch, he got on quite well in the show business, and was soon sent up to the Aquarium, to do some tricks that I forget. That was his first letter. His second was much more of a startler, and I only got it last week.'

The man called Angus emptied his coffee-cup and regarded her with mild and patient eyes. Her own mouth took a slight twist of laughter as she resumed, 'I suppose you've seen on the hoardings all about this "Smythe's Silent Service"? Or you must be the only person that hasn't. Oh, I don't know much about it, it's some clockwork invention for doing all the housework by machinery. You know the sort of thing: "Press a Button – A Butler who Never Drinks". "Turn a Handle – Ten Housemaids who Never Flirt". You must have seen the advertisements. Well, whatever these machines are, they are making pots of money; and they are making it all for that little imp whom I knew down in Ludbury. I can't help feeling pleased the poor little chap has fallen on his feet; but the plain fact is, I'm in terror of his turning up any minute and telling me he's carved his way in the world – as he certainly has.'

'And the other man?' repeated Angus with a sort of obstinate quietude.

Laura Hope got to her feet suddenly. 'My friend,' she said, 'I think you are a witch. Yes, you are quite right. I have not seen a line of the other man's writing; and I have no more notion than the dead of what or where he is. But it is of him that I am frightened. It is he who is all about my path. It is he who has half driven me mad. Indeed, I think he has driven me mad; for I have felt him where he could not have been, and I have heard his voice when he could not have spoken.'

'Well, my dear,' said the young man, cheerfully, 'if he were Satan himself, he is done for now you have told somebody. One goes mad all alone, old girl. But when was it you fancied you felt and heard our squinting friend?'

'I heard James Welkin laugh as plainly as I hear you speak,' said the girl, steadily. 'There was nobody there, for I stood just outside the shop at the corner, and could see down both streets at once. I had forgotten how he laughed, though his laugh was as odd as his squint. I had not thought of him for nearly a year. But it's a solemn truth that a few seconds later the first letter came from his rival.'

'Did you ever make the spectre speak or squeak, or anything?' asked Angus, with some interest.

Laura suddenly shuddered, and then said, with an unshaken voice, 'Yes. Just when I had finished reading the second letter from Isidore Smythe announcing his success. Just then, I heard Welkin say, "He shan't have you, though." It was quite plain, as if he were in the room. It is awful; I think I must be mad.'

'If you really were mad,' said the young man, 'you would think you must be sane. But certainly there seems to me to be something a little rum about this unseen gentleman. Two heads are better than one – I spare you allusions to any other organs and really, if you would allow me, as a sturdy, practical man, to bring back the wedding-cake out of the window –'

Even as he spoke, there was a sort of steely shriek in the street outside, and a small motor, driven at devilish speed, shot up to the door of the shop and stuck there. In the same flash of time a small man in a shiny top hat stood stamping in the outer room.

Angus, who had hitherto maintained hilarious ease from motives of mental hygiene, revealed the strain of his soul by striding abruptly out of the inner room and confronting the newcomer. A glance at him was quite sufficient to confirm the savage guesswork of a man in love. This very dapper but dwarfish figure, with the spike of black beard carried insolently forward, the clever unrestful eyes, the neat but very nervous fingers, could be none other than the man just described to him: Isidore Smythe, who made dolls out of banana skins and matchboxes; Isidore Smythe, who made millions out of undrinking butlers and unflirting housemaids of metal. For a moment the two men, instinctively understanding each other's air of possession, looked at each other with that curious cold generosity which is the soul of rivalry.

Mr Smythe, however, made no allusion to the ultimate ground of their antagonism, but said simply and explosively, 'Has Miss Hope seen that thing on the window?'

'On the window?' repeated the staring Angus.

'There's no time to explain other things,' said the small millionaire shortly. 'There's some tomfoolery going on here that has to be investigated.'

He pointed his polished walking-stick at the window, recently depleted by the bridal preparations of Mr Angus; and that gentleman was astonished to see along the front of the glass a long strip of paper pasted, which had certainly not been on the window when he looked through it some time before. Following the energetic Smythe outside into the street, he found that some yard and a half of stamp-paper had been carefully gummed along the glass outside, and on this was written in straggly characters, 'If you marry Smythe, he will die.'

'Laura,' said Angus, putting his big red head into the shop, 'you're not mad.'

'It's the writing of that fellow Welkin,' said Smythe gruffly. 'I haven't seen him for years, but he's always bothering me. Five times in the last fortnight he's had threatening letters left at my flat, and I can't even find out who leaves them, let alone if it is Welkin himself. The porter of the flats swears that no suspicious characters have been seen, and here he has pasted up a sort of dado on a public shop-window, while the people in the shop – '

'Quite so,' said Angus modestly, 'while the people in the shop were having tea. Well, sir, I can assure you I appreciate your common sense in dealing so directly with the matter. We can talk about other things afterwards. The fellow cannot be very far off yet, for I swear there was no paper there when I went last to the window, ten or fifteen minutes ago. On the other hand, he's too far off to be chased, as we don't even know the direction. If you'll take my advice, Mr Smythe, you'll put this at once in the hands of some energetic enquiry man, private rather than public. I know an extremely clever fellow, who has set up in business five minutes from here in your car. His name's Flambeau, and though his youth was a bit stormy, he's a strictly honest man now, and his brains are worth money. He lives in Lucknow Mansions, Hampstead.'

'That is odd,' said the little man, arching his black eyebrows. 'I live, myself, in Himalaya Mansions, round the corner. Perhaps you might care to come with me; I can go to my rooms and sort out these queer Welkin documents, while you run round and get your friend the detective.'

'You are very good,' said Angus politely. 'Well, the sooner we act the better.'

Both men, with a queer kind of impromptu fairness, took the same sort of formal farewell of the lady, and both jumped into the brisk little car. As Smythe took the wheel and they turned the great corner of the street, Angus was amused to see a gigantesque poster of 'Smythe's Silent Service', with a picture of a huge headless iron doll, carrying a saucepan with the legend, 'A Cook who is Never Cross'.

'I use them in my own flat,' said the little black-bearded man, laughing, 'partly for advertisements, and partly for real convenience. Honestly, and all above board, those big clockwork dolls of mine do bring your coals or claret or a timetable quicker than any live servants I've ever known, if you know which knob to press. But I'll never deny, between ourselves, that such servants have their disadvantages, too.'

'Indeed?' said Angus; 'is there something they can't do?'

'Yes,' replied Smythe coolly; 'they can't tell me who left those threatening letters at my flat.'

The man's motor was small and swift like himself; in fact, like his domestic service, it was of his own invention. If he was an advertising quack, he was one who believed in his own wares. The sense of something tiny and flying was accentuated as they swept up long white curves of road in the dead but open daylight of evening. Soon the white curves came sharper and dizzier; they were upon ascending spirals, as they say in the modern religions. For, indeed, they were cresting a corner of London which is almost as precipitous as Edinburgh, if not quite so picturesque. Terrace rose above terrace, and the special tower of flats they sought, rose above them all to almost Egyptian height, gilt by the level sunset. The change, as they turned the corner and entered the crescent known as Himalaya Mansions, was as abrupt as the opening of a window; for they found that pile of flats sitting above London as above a green sea of slate. Opposite to the mansions, on the other side of the gravel crescent, was a bushy enclosure more like a steep hedge or dyke than a garden, and some way below that ran a strip of artificial water, a sort of canal, like the moat of that embowered fortress. As the car swept round the crescent it passed, at one corner, the stray stall of a man selling chestnuts; and right away at the other end of the curve, Angus could see a dim blue policeman walking slowly. These were the only human shapes in that high suburban solitude; but he had an irrational sense that they expressed the speechless poetry of London. He felt as if they were figures in a story.

The little car shot up to the right house like a bullet, and shot out its owner like a bomb shell. He was immediately enquiring of a tall commissionaire in shining braid, and a short porter in shirt sleeves, whether anybody or anything had been seeking his apartments. He was assured that nobody and nothing had passed these officials since his last enquiries; whereupon he and the slightly bewildered Angus were shot up in the lift like a rocket, till they reached the top floor.

'Just come in for a minute,' said the breathless Smythe. 'I want to show you those Welkin letters. Then you might run round the corner and fetch your friend.' He pressed a button concealed in the wall, and the door opened of itself.

It opened on a long, commodious ante-room, of which the only arresting features, ordinarily speaking, were the rows of tall half-human mechanical figures that stood up on both sides like tailors' dummies. Like tailors' dummies they were headless; and like tailors' dummies they had a handsome unnecessary humpiness in the shoulders, and a pigeon-breasted protuberance of chest; but barring this, they were not much more like a human figure than any automatic machine at a station that is about the human height. They had two great hooks like arms, for carrying trays; and they were painted pea-green, or vermilion, or black for convenience of distinction; in every other way they were only automatic machines and nobody would have looked twice at them. On this occasion, at least, nobody did. For between the two rows of these domestic dummies lay something more interesting than most of the mechanics of the world. It was a white, tattered scrap of paper scrawled with red ink; and the agile inventor had snatched it up almost as soon as the door flew open. He handed it to Angus without a word. The red ink on it actually was not dry, and the message ran, 'If you have been to see her today, I shall kill you.'

There was a short silence, and then Isidore Smythe said quietly, 'Would you like a little whisky? I rather feel as if I should.'

'Thank you; I should like a little Flambeau,' said Angus, gloomily. 'This business seems to me to be getting rather grave. I'm going round at once to fetch him.'

'Right you are,' said the other, with admirable cheerfulness. 'Bring him round here as quick as you can.'

But as Angus closed the front door behind him he saw Smythe push back a button, and one of the clockwork images glided from its place and slid along a groove in the floor carrying a tray with syphon and decanter. There did seem something a trifle weird about leaving the little man alone among those dead servants, who were coming to life as the door closed.

Six steps down from Smythe's landing the man in shirt sleeves was doing something with a pail. Angus stopped to extract a promise, fortified with a prospective bribe, that he would remain in that place until the return with the detective, and would keep count of any kind of stranger coming up those stairs. Dashing down to the front hall he then laid similar charges of vigilance on the commissionaire at the front door, from whom he learned the simplifying circumstances that there was no back door. Not content with this, he captured the floating policeman and induced him to stand opposite the entrance and watch it; and finally paused an instant for a pennyworth of chestnuts, and an enquiry as to the probable length of the merchant's stay in the neighbourhood.

The chestnut seller, turning up the collar of his coat, told him he should probably be moving shortly, as he thought it was going to snow. Indeed, the evening was growing grey and bitter, but Angus, with all his eloquence, proceeded to nail the chestnut man to his post.

'Keep yourself warm on your own chestnuts,' he said earnestly. 'Eat up your whole stock; I'll make it worth your while. I'll give you a sovereign if you'll wait here till I come back, and then tell me whether any man, woman, or child has gone into that house where the commissionaire is standing.'

He then walked away smartly, with a last look at the besieged tower.

'I've made a ring round that room, anyhow,' he said. 'They can't all four of them be Mr Welkin's accomplices.'

Lucknow Mansions were, so to speak, on a lower platform of that hill of houses, of which Himylaya Mansions might be called the peak. Mr Flambeau's semi-official flat was on the ground floor, and presented in every way a marked contrast to the American machinery and cold hotel-like luxury of the flat of the Silent Service. Flambeau, who was a friend of Angus, received him in a rococo artistic den behind his office, of which the ornaments were sabres, harquebuses, Eastern curiosities, flasks of Italian wine, savage cooking-pots, a plumy Persian cat, and a small dusty-looking Roman Catholic priest, who looked particularly out of place.

'This is my friend Father Brown,' said Flambeau. 'I've often wanted you to meet him. Splendid weather, this; a little cold for Southerners like me.'

'Yes, I think it will keep clear,' said Angus, sitting down on a violet-striped Eastern ottoman.

'No,' said the priest quietly, 'it has begun to snow.'

And, indeed, as he spoke, the first few flakes, foreseen by the man of chestnuts, began to drift across the darkening windowpane.

'Well,' said Angus heavily. 'I'm afraid I've come on business, and rather jumpy business at that. The fact is, Flambeau, within a stone's throw of your house is a fellow who badly wants your help; he's perpetually being haunted and threatened by an invisible enemy – a scoundrel whom nobody has even seen.' As Angus proceeded to tell the whole tale of Smythe and Welkin, beginning with Laura's story, and going on with his own, the supernatural laugh at the corner of two empty streets, the strange distinct words spoken in an empty room, Flambeau grew more and more vividly concerned, and the little priest seemed to be left out of it, like a piece of furniture. When it came to the scribbled stamp-paper pasted on the window, Flambeau rose, seeming to fill the room with his huge shoulders.

'If you don't mind,' he said, 'I think you had better tell me the rest on the nearest road to this man's house. It strikes me, somehow, that there is no time to be lost.'

'Delighted,' said Angus, rising also, 'though he's safe enough for the present, for I've set four men to watch the only hole to his burrow.'

They turned out into the street, the small priest trundling after them with the docility of a small dog. He merely said, in a cheerful way, like one making conversation, 'How quick the snow gets thick on the ground.'

As they threaded the steep side streets already powdered with silver, Angus finished his story; and by the time they reached the crescent with the towering flats, he had leisure to turn his attention to the four sentinels. The chestnut seller, both before and after receiving a sovereign, swore stubbornly that he had watched the door and seen no visitor enter. The policeman was even more emphatic. He said he had had experience of crooks of all kinds, in top hats and in rags; he wasn't so green as to expect suspicious characters to look suspicious; he looked out for anybody, and, so help him, there had been nobody. And when all three men gathered round the gilded commissionaire, who still stood smiling astride of the porch, the verdict was more final still.

'I've got a right to ask any man, duke or dustman, what he wants in these flats,' said the genial and gold-laced giant, 'and I'll swear there's been nobody to ask since this gentleman went away.'

The unimportant Father Brown, who stood back, looking modestly at the pavement, here ventured to say meekly, 'Has nobody been up and down stairs, then, since the snow began to fall? It began while we were all round at Flambeau's.'

'Nobody's been in here, sir, you can take it from me,' said the official, with beaming authority.

'Then I wonder what that is?' said the priest, and stared at the ground blankly like a fish.

The others all looked down also; and Flambeau used a fierce exclamation and a French gesture. For it was unquestionably true that down the middle of the entrance guarded by the man in gold lace, actually between the arrogant, stretched legs of that colossus, ran a stringy pattern of grey footprints stamped upon the white snow.

'God!' cried Angus involuntarily, 'the Invisible Man!'

Without another word he turned and dashed up the stairs, with Flambeau following; but Father Brown still stood looking about him in the snow-clad street as if he had lost interest in his query.

Flambeau was plainly in a mood to break down the door with his big shoulders; but the Scotchman, with more reason, if less intuition, fumbled about on the frame of the door till he found the invisible button; and the door swung slowly open.

It showed substantially the same serried interior; the hall had grown darker, though it was still struck here and there with the last crimson shafts of sunset, and one or two of the headless machines had been moved from their places for this or that purpose, and stood here and there about the twilit place. The green and red of their coats were all darkened in the dusk; and their likeness to human shapes slightly increased by their very shapelessness. But in the middle of them all, exactly where the paper with the red ink had lain, there lay something that looked like red ink spilt out of its bottle. But it was not red ink.

With a French combination of reason and violence Flambeau simply said

'Murder!' and, plunging into the flat, had explored every corner and cupboard of it in five minutes. But if he expected to find a corpse he found none. Isidore Smythe was not in the place, either dead or alive. After the most tearing search the two men met each other in the outer hall, with streaming faces and staring eyes. 'My friend,' said Flambeau, talking French in his excitement, 'not only is your murderer invisible, but he makes invisible also the murdered man.'

Angus looked round at the dim room full of dummies, and in some Celtic corner of his Scotch soul a shudder started. One of the life-size dolls stood immediately overshadowing the blood stain, summoned, perhaps, by the slain man an instant before he fell. One of the high-shouldered hooks that served the thing for arms, was a little lifted, and Angus had suddenly the horrid fancy that poor Smythe's own iron child had struck him down. Matter had rebelled, and these machines had killed their master. But even so, what had they done with him?

'Eaten him?' said the nightmare at his ear; and he sickened for an instant at the idea of rent, human remains absorbed and crushed into all that acephalous clockwork.

He recovered his mental health by an emphatic effort, and said to Flambeau, 'Well, there it is. The poor fellow has evaporated like a cloud and left a red streak on the floor. The tale does not belong to this world.'

'There is only one thing to be done,' said Flambeau, 'whether it belongs to this world or the other. I must go down and talk to my friend.'

They descended, passing the man with the pail, who again asseverated that he had let no intruder pass, down to the commissionaire and the hovering chestnut man, who rigidly reasserted their own watchfulness. But when Angus looked round for his fourth confirmation he could not see it, and called out with some nervousness, 'Where is the policeman?'

'I beg your pardon,' said Father Brown; 'that is my fault. I just sent him down the road to investigate something – that I just thought worth investigating.'

'Well, we want him back pretty soon,' said Angus abruptly, 'for the wretched man upstairs has not only been murdered, but wiped out.'

'How?' asked the priest.

'Father,' said Flambeau, after a pause, 'upon my soul I believe it is more in your department than mine. No friend or foe has entered the house, but Smythe is gone, as if stolen by the fairies. If that is not supernatural, I – '

As he spoke they were all checked by an unusual sight; the big blue policeman came round the corner of the crescent, running. He came straight up to Brown.

'You're right, sir,' he panted, 'they've just found poor Mr Smythe's body in the canal down below.'

Angus put his hand wildly to his head. 'Did he run down and drown himself?' he asked.

'He never came down, I'll swear,' said the constable, 'and he wasn't drowned either, for he died of a great stab over the heart.'

'And yet you saw no one enter?' said Flambeau in a grave voice.

'Let us walk down the road a little,' said the priest.

As they reached the other end of the crescent he observed abruptly, 'Stupid of me! I forgot to ask the policeman something. I wonder if they found a light brown sack.'

'Why a light brown sack?' asked Angus, astonished.

'Because if it was any other coloured sack, the case must begin over again,' said Father Brown; 'but if it was a light brown sack, why, the case is finished.'

'I am pleased to hear it,' said Angus with hearty irony. 'It hasn't begun, so far as I am concerned.'

'You must tell us all about it,' said Flambeau with a strange heavy simplicity, like a child.

Unconsciously they were walking with quickening steps down the long sweep of road on the other side of the high crescent, Father Brown leading briskly, though in silence. At last he said with an almost touching vagueness, 'Well, I'm afraid you'll think it so prosy. We always begin at the abstract end of things, and you can't begin this story anywhere else.

'Have you ever noticed this – that people never answer what you say? They answer what you mean – or what they think you mean. Suppose one lady says to another in a country house, "Is anybody staying with you?" the lady doesn't answer "Yes; the butler, the three footmen, the parlourmaid, and so on," though the parlourmaid may be in the room, or the butler behind her chair. She says "There is nobody staying with us," meaning nobody of the sort you mean. But suppose a doctor enquiring into an epidemic asks, "Who is staying in the house?" then the lady will remember the butler, the parlourmaid, and the rest. All language is used like that; you never get a question answered literally, even when you get it answered truly. When those four quite honest men said that no man had gone into the Mansions, they did not really mean that no man had gone into them. They meant no man whom they could suspect of being your man. A man did go into the house, and did come out of it, but they never noticed him.'

'An invisible man?' enquired Angus, raising his red eyebrows. 'A mentally invisible man,' said Father Brown.

A minute or two after he resumed in the same unassuming voice, like a man thinking his way. 'Of course you can't think of such a man, until you do think of him. That's where his cleverness comes in. But I came to think of him through two or three little things in the tale Mr Angus told us. First, there was the fact that this Welkin went for long walks. And then there was the vast lot of stamp-paper on the window. And then, most of all, there were the two things the young lady said – things that couldn't be true. Don't get annoyed,' he added hastily, noting a sudden movement of the Scotchman's head; 'she thought they were true. A person can't be quite alone in a street a second before she receives a letter. She can't be quite alone in a street when she starts reading a letter just received. There must be somebody pretty near her; he must be mentally invisible.'

'Why must there be somebody near her?' asked Angus.

'Because,' said Father Brown, 'barring carrier-pigeons, somebody must have brought her the letter.'

'Do you really mean to say,' asked Flambeau, with energy, 'that Welkin carried his rival's letters to his lady?'

'Yes,' said the priest. 'Welkin carried his rival's letters to his lady. You see, he had to.'

'Oh, I can't stand much more of this,' exploded Flambeau. 'Who is this fellow? What does he look like? What is the usual get-up of a mentally invisible man?'

'He is dressed rather handsomely in red, blue and gold,' replied the priest promptly with precision, 'and in this striking, and even showy, costume he entered Himalaya Mansions under eight human eyes; he killed Smythe in cold blood, and came down into the street again carrying the dead body in his arms –'

'Reverend sir,' cried Angus, standing still, 'are you raving mad, or am I?'

'You are not mad,' said Brown, 'only a little unobservant. You have not noticed such a man as this, for example.'

He took three quick strides forward, and put his hand on the shoulder of an ordinary passing postman who had bustled by them unnoticed under the shade of the trees.

'Nobody ever notices postmen, somehow,' he said thoughtfully; 'yet they have passions like other men, and even carry large bags where a small corpse can be stowed quite easily.'

The postman, instead of turning naturally, had ducked and tumbled against the garden fence. He was a lean fair-bearded man of very ordinary appearance, but as he turned an alarmed face over his shoulder, all three men were fixed with an almost fiendish squint.

Flambeau went back to his sabres, purple rugs and Persian cat, having many things to attend to. John Turnbull Angus went back to the lady at the shop, with whom that imprudent young man contrives to be extremely comfortable. But Father Brown walked those snow-covered hills under the stars for many hours with a murderer, and what they said to each other will never be known.

The Honour of Israel Gow

A stormy evening of olive and silver was closing in, as Father Brown, wrapped in a grey Scotch plaid, came to the end of a grey Scotch valley and beheld the strange castle of Glengyle. It stopped one end of the glen or hollow like a blind alley; and it looked like the end of the world. Rising in steep roofs and spires of sea-green slate in the manner of the old French-Scottish châteaux, it reminded an Englishman of the sinister steeple-hats of witches in fairy tales; and the pine woods that rocked round the green turrets looked, by comparison, as black as numberless flocks of ravens. This note of a dreamy, almost a sleepy devilry, was no mere fancy from the landscape. For there did rest on the place one of those clouds of pride and madness and mysterious sorrow which lie more heavily on the noble houses of Scotland than on any other of the children of men. For Scotland has a double dose of the poison called heredity; the sense of blood in the aristocrat, and the sense of doom in the Calvinist.

The priest had snatched a day from his business at Glasgow to meet his friend Flambeau, the amateur detective, who was at Glengyle Castle with another more formal officer investigating the life and death of the late Earl of Glengyle. That mysterious person was the last representative of a race whose valour, insanity, and violent cunning had made them terrible even among the sinister nobility of their nation in the sixteenth century. None were deeper in that labyrinthine ambition, in chamber within chamber of that palace of lies that was built up around Mary Queen of Scots.

The rhyme in the countryside attested the motive and the result of their machinations candidly:

As green sap to the simmer trees
Is red gold to the Ogilvies.

For many centuries there had never been a decent lord in Glengyle Castle; and with the Victorian era one would have thought that all eccentricities were exhausted. The last Glengyle, however, satisfied his tribal tradition by doing the only thing that was left for him to do; he disappeared. I do not mean that he went abroad; by all accounts he was still in the castle, if he was anywhere. But though his name was in the church register and the big red Peerage, nobody ever saw him under the sun.

If anyone saw him it was a solitary manservant, something between a groom and a gardener. He was so deaf that the more businesslike assumed him to be dumb; while the more penetrating declared him to be half-witted.

A gaunt, red-haired labourer, with a dogged jaw and chin, but quite blank blue eyes, he went by the name of Israel Gow, and was the one silent servant on that deserted estate. But the energy with which he dug potatoes, and the regularity with which he disappeared into the kitchen gave people an impression that he was providing for the meals of a superior, and that the strange earl was still concealed in the castle. If society needed any further proof that he was there, the servant persistently asserted that he was not at home. One morning the provost and the minister (for the Glengyles were Presbyterian) were summoned to the castle. There they found that the gardener, groom and cook had added to his many professions that of an undertaker, and had nailed up his noble master in a coffin. With how much or how little further enquiry this odd fact was passed, did not as yet very plainly appear; for the thing had never been legally investigated till Flambeau had gone north two or three days before. By then the body of Lord Glengyle (if it was the body) had lain for some time in the little churchyard on the hill.

As Father Brown passed through the dim garden and came under the shadow of the château, the clouds were thick and the whole air damp and thundery. Against the last stripe of the green-gold sunset he saw a black human silhouette; a man in a chimney-pot hat, with a big spade over his shoulder. The combination was queerly suggestive of a sexton; but when Brown remembered the deaf servant who dug potatoes, he thought it natural enough. He knew something of the Scotch peasant; he knew the respectability which might well feel it necessary to wear 'blacks' for an official enquiry; he knew also the economy that would not lose an hour's digging for that. Even the man's start and suspicious stare as the priest went by were consonant enough with the vigilance and jealousy of such a type.

The great door was opened by Flambeau himself, who had with him a lean man with iron-grey hair and papers in his hand: Inspector Craven from Scotland Yard. The entrance hall was mostly stripped and empty; but the pale, sneering faces of one or two of the wicked Ogilvies looked down out of the black periwigs and blackening canvas.

Following them into an inner room, Father Brown found that the allies had been seated at a long oak table, of which their end was covered with scribbled papers, flanked with whisky and cigars. Through the whole of its remaining length it was occupied by detached objects arranged at intervals; objects about as inexplicable as any objects could be. One looked like a small heap of glittering broken glass. Another looked like a high heap of brown dust. A third appeared to be a plain stick of wood.

'You seem to have a sort of geological museum here,' he said, as he sat down, jerking his head briefly in the direction of the brown dust and the crystalline fragments.

'Not a geological museum,' replied Flambeau; 'say a psychological museum.'

'Oh, for the Lord's sake,' cried the police detective, laughing, 'don't let's begin with such long words.'

'Don't you know what psychology means?' asked Flambeau with friendly surprise. 'Psychology means being off your chump.'

'Still I hardly follow,' replied the official.

'Well,' said Flambeau, with decision, 'I mean that we've only found out one thing about Lord Glengyle. He was a maniac.'

The black silhouette of Gow with his top hat and spade passed the window, dimly outlined against the darkening sky. Father Brown stared passively at it and answered: 'I can understand there must have been something odd about the man, or he wouldn't have buried himself alive – nor been in such a hurry to bury himself dead. But what makes you think it was lunacy?'

'Well,' said Flambeau, 'you just listen to the list of things Mr Craven has found in the house.'

'We must get a candle,' said Craven, suddenly. 'A storm is getting up, and it's too dark to read.'

'Have you found any candles,' asked Brown smiling, 'among your oddities?'

Flambeau raised a grave face, and fixed his dark eyes on his friend.

'That is curious, too,' he said. 'Twenty-five candles, and not a trace of a candlestick.'

In the rapidly darkening room and rapidly rising wind, Brown went along the table to where a bundle of wax candles lay among the other scrappy exhibits. As he did so he bent accidentally over the heap of red-brown dust; and a sharp sneeze cracked the silence.

'Hullo!' he said, 'snuff!'

He took one of the candles, lit it carefully, came back and stuck it in the neck of the whisky bottle. The unrestful night air, blowing through the crazy window, waved the long flame like a banner. And on every side of the castle they could hear the miles and miles of black pine wood seething like a black sea around a rock.

'I will read the inventory,' began Craven gravely, picking up one of the papers, 'the inventory of what we found loose and unexplained in the castle. You are to understand that the place generally was dismantled and neglected; but one or two rooms had plainly been inhabited in a simple but not squalid style by somebody; somebody who was not the servant Gow. The list is as follows: First item. A very considerable hoard of precious stones, nearly all diamonds, and all of them loose, without any setting whatever. Of course, it is natural that the Ogilvies should have family jewels; but those are exactly the jewels that are almost always set in particular articles of ornament. The

Ogilvies would seem to have kept theirs loose in their pockets, like coppers.

'Second item. Heaps and heaps of loose snuff, not kept in a horn, or even a pouch, but lying in heaps on the mantelpieces, on the sideboard, on the piano, anywhere. It looks as if the old gentleman would not take the trouble to look in a pocket or lift a lid.

'Third item. Here and there about the house curious little heaps of minute pieces of metal, some like steel springs and some in the form of microscopic wheels. As if they had gutted some mechanical toy.

'Fourth item. The wax candles, which have to be stuck in bottle necks because there is nothing else to stick them in. Now I wish you to note how very much queerer all this is than anything we anticipated. For the central riddle we are prepared; we have all seen at a glance that there was something wrong about the last earl. We have come here to find out whether he really lived here, whether he really died here, whether that red-haired scarecrow who did his burying had anything to do with his dying. But suppose the worst in all this, the most lurid or melodramatic solution you like. Suppose the servant really killed the master, or suppose the master isn't really dead, or suppose the master is dressed up as the servant, or suppose the servant is buried for the master; invent what Wilkie Collins' tragedy you like, and you still have not explained a candle without a candlestick, or why an elderly gentleman of good family should habitually spill snuff on the piano. The core of the tale we could imagine; it is the fringes that are mysterious. By no stretch of fancy can the human mind connect together snuff and diamonds and wax and loose clockwork.'

'I think I see the connection,' said the priest. 'This Glengyle was mad against the French Revolution. He was an enthusiast for the *ancien régime*, and was trying to re-enact literally the family life of the last Bourbons. He had snuff because it was the eighteenth-century luxury; wax candles, because they were the eighteenth-century lighting; the mechanical bits of iron represent the locksmith hobby of Louis XVI; the diamonds are for the Diamond Necklace of Marie Antoinette.'

Both the other men were staring at him with round eyes. 'What a perfectly extraordinary notion!' cried Flambeau. 'Do you really think that is the truth?'

'I am perfectly sure it isn't,' answered Father Brown, 'only you said that nobody could connect snuff and diamonds and clockwork and candles. I give you that connection offhand. The real truth, I am very sure, lies deeper.'

He paused a moment and listened to the wailing of the wind in the turrets. Then he said, 'The late Earl of Glengyle was a thief. He lived a second and darker life as a desperate housebreaker. He did not have any candlesticks because he only used these candles cut short in the little lantern he carried. The snuff he employed as the fiercest French criminals have used pepper: to fling it suddenly in dense masses in the face of a captor or pursuer. But the final proof is in the curious coincidence of the diamonds and the small steel wheels. Surely that makes everything plain to you? Diamonds and small steel wheels are the only two instruments with which you can cut out a pane of glass.'

The bough of a broken pine tree lashed heavily in the blast against the windowpane behind them, as if in parody of a burglar, but they did not turn round. Their eyes were fastened on Father Brown.

'Diamonds and small wheels,' repeated Craven ruminating. 'Is that all that makes you think it the true explanation?'

'I don't think it the true explanation,' replied the priest placidly; 'but you said that nobody could connect the four things. The true tale, of course, is something much more humdrum. Glengyle had found, or thought he had found, precious stones on his estate. Somebody had bamboozled him with those loose brilliants, saying they were found in the castle caverns. The little wheels are some diamond-cutting affair. He had to do the thing very roughly and in a small way, with the help of a few shepherds or rude fellows on these hills. Snuff is the one great luxury of such Scotch shepherds; it's the one thing with which you can bribe them. They didn't have candlesticks because they didn't want them; they held the candles in their hands when they explored the caves.'

'Is that all?' asked Flambeau after a long pause. 'Have we got to the dull truth at last?'

'Oh, no,' said Father Brown.

As the wind died in the most distant pine woods with a long hoot as of mockery, Father Brown, with an utterly impassive face, went on: 'I only suggested that because you said one could not plausibly connect snuff with clockwork or candles with bright stones. Ten false philosophies will fit the universe; ten false theories will fit Glengyle Castle. But we want the real explanation of the castle and the universe. But are there no other exhibits?'

Craven laughed, and Flambeau rose smiling to his feet and strolled down the long table.

'Items five, six, seven, etc.,' he said, 'and certainly more varied than instructive. A curious collection, not of lead pencils, but of the lead out of lead pencils. A senseless stick of bamboo, with the top rather splintered. It might be the instrument of the crime. Only, there isn't any crime. The only other things are a few old missals and little Catholic pictures, which the Ogilvies kept, I suppose, from the Middle Ages – their family pride being stronger than their Puritanism. We only put them in the museum because they seem curiously cut about and defaced.'

The heady tempest without drove a dreadful wrack of clouds across Glengyle and threw the long room into darkness as Father Brown picked up the little illuminated pages to examine them. He spoke before the drift of darkness had passed; but it was the voice of an utterly new man.

'Mr Craven,' said he, talking like a man ten years younger, 'you have got a legal warrant, haven't you, to go up and examine that grave? The sooner we do it the better, and get to the bottom of this horrible affair. If I were you I should start now.'

'Now,' repeated the astonished detective, 'and why now?'

'Because this is serious,' answered Brown; 'this is not spilt snuff or loose pebbles, that might be there for a hundred reasons. There is only one reason I know of for this being done; and the reason goes down to the roots of the world. These religious pictures are not just dirtied or torn or scrawled over, which might be done in idleness or bigotry, by children or by Protestants. These have been treated very carefully – and very queerly. In every place where the great ornamented name of God comes in the old illuminations it has been elaborately taken out. The only other thing that has been removed is the halo round the head of the Child Jesus. Therefore, I say, let us get our warrant and our spade and our hatchet, and go up and break open that coffin.'

'What *do* you mean?' demanded the London officer.

'I mean,' answered the little priest, and his voice seemed to rise slightly in the roar of the gale. 'I mean that the great devil of the universe may be sitting on the top tower of this castle at this moment, as big as a hundred elephants, and roaring like the Apocalypse. There is black magic somewhere at the bottom of this.'

'Black magic,' repeated Flambeau in a low voice, for he was too enlightened a man not to know of such things; 'but what can these other things mean?'

'Oh, something damnable, I suppose,' replied Brown impatiently. 'How should I know? How can I guess all their mazes down below? Perhaps you can make a torture out of snuff and bamboo. Perhaps lunatics lust after wax and steel filings. Perhaps there is a maddening drug made of lead pencils! Our shortest cut to the mystery is up the hill to the grave.'

His comrades hardly knew that they had obeyed and followed him till a blast of the night wind nearly flung them on their faces in the garden. Nevertheless they had obeyed him like automata; for Craven found a hatchet in his hand, and the warrant in his pocket; Flambeau was carrying the heavy spade of the strange gardener; Father Brown was carrying the little gilt book from which had been torn the name of God.

The path up the hill to the churchyard was crooked but short; only under that stress of wind it seemed laborious and long. Far as the eye could see, farther and farther as they mounted the slope, were seas beyond seas of pines, now all aslope one way under the wind. And that universal gesture seemed as vain as it was vast, as vain as if that wind were whistling about some unpeopled and purposeless planet. Through all that infinite growth of grey-blue forests sang, shrill and high, that ancient sorrow that is in the heart of all heathen things. One could fancy that the voices from the underworld of unfathomable foliage were cries of the lost and wandering pagan gods: gods who had gone roaming in that irrational forest, and who will never find their way back to heaven.

'You see,' said Father Brown in low but easy tone, 'Scotch people before Scotland existed were a curious lot. In fact, they're a curious lot still. But in the prehistoric times I fancy they really worshipped demons. That,' he added genially, 'is why they jumped at the Puritan theology.'

'My friend,' said Flambeau, turning in a kind of fury, 'what does all that snuff mean?'

'My friend,' replied Brown, with equal seriousness, 'there is one mark of all genuine religions: materialism. Now, devil-worship is a perfectly genuine religion.'

They had come up on the grassy scalp of the hill, one of the few bald spots that stood clear of the crashing and roaring pine forest. A mean enclosure, partly timber and partly wire, rattled in the tempest to tell them the border of the graveyard. But by the time Inspector Craven had come to the corner of the grave, and Flambeau had planted his spade point downwards and leaned on it, they were both almost as shaken as the shaky wood and wire. At the foot of the grave grew great tall thistles, grey and silver in their decay. Once or twice, when a ball of thistledown broke under the breeze and flew past him, Craven jumped slightly as if it had been an arrow.

Flambeau drove the blade of his spade through the whistling grass into the wet clay below. Then he seemed to stop and lean on it as on a staff.

'Go on,' said the priest very gently. 'We are only trying to find the truth. What are you afraid of?'

'I am afraid of finding it,' said Flambeau.

The London detective spoke suddenly in a high crowing voice that was meant to be conversational and cheery. 'I wonder why he really did hide himself like that. Something nasty, I suppose; was he a leper?'

'Something worse than that,' said Flambeau.

'And what do you imagine,' asked the other, 'would be worse than a leper?'

'I don't imagine it,' said Flambeau.

He dug for some dreadful minutes in silence, and then said in a choked voice, 'I'm afraid of his not being the right shape.'

'Nor was that piece of paper, you know,' said Father Brown quietly, 'and we survived even that piece of paper.'

Flambeau dug on with a blind energy. But the tempest had shouldered away the choking grey clouds that clung to the hills like smoke and revealed grey fields of faint starlight before he cleared the shape of a rude timber coffin, and somehow tipped it up upon the turf. Craven stepped forward with his axe; a thistle-top touched him, and he flinched. Then he took a firmer stride, and hacked and wrenched with an energy like Flambeau's till the lid was torn off, and all that was there lay glimmering in the grey starlight.

'Bones,' said Craven; and then he added, 'but it is a man,' as if that were something unexpected.

'Is he,' asked Flambeau in a voice that went oddly up and down, 'is he all right?'

'Seems so,' said the officer huskily, bending over the obscure and decaying skeleton in the box. 'Wait a minute.'

A vast heave went over Flambeau's huge figure. 'And now I come to think of it,' he cried, 'why in the name of madness shouldn't he be all right? What is it gets hold of a man on these cursed cold mountains? I think it's the black, brainless repetition; all these forests, and over all an ancient horror of unconsciousness. It's like the dream of an atheist. Pine trees and more pine trees and millions more pine trees – '

'God!' cried the man by the coffin, 'but he hasn't got a head.'

While the others stood rigid the priest, for the first time, showed a leap of startled concern.

'No head!' he repeated. '*No head?*' as if he had almost expected some other deficiency.

Half-witted visions of a headless baby born to Glengyle, of a headless youth hiding himself in the castle, of a headless man pacing those ancient halls or that gorgeous garden, passed in panorama through their minds. But even in that stiffened instant the tale took no root in them and seemed to have no reason in it. They stood listening to the loud woods and the shrieking sky quite foolishly, like exhausted animals. Thought seemed to be something enormous that had suddenly slipped out of their grasp.

'There are three headless men,' said Father Brown, 'standing round this open grave.'

The pale detective from London opened his mouth to speak, and left it open like a yokel, while a long scream of wind tore the sky; then he looked at the axe in his hands as if it did not belong to him, and dropped it.

'Father,' said Flambeau in that infantile and heavy voice he used very seldom, 'what are we to do?'

His friend's reply came with the pent promptitude of a gun going off.

'Sleep!' cried Father Brown. 'Sleep. We have come to the end of the ways. Do you know what sleep is? Do you know that every man who sleeps believes in God? It is a sacrament; for it is an act of faith and it is a food. And we need a sacrament, if only a natural one. Something has fallen on us that falls very seldom on men; perhaps the worst thing that can fall on them.'

Craven's parted lips came together to say, 'What do you mean?'

The priest had turned his face to the castle as he answered: 'We have found the truth; and the truth makes no sense.'

He went down the path in front of them with a plunging and reckless step very rare with him, and when they reached the castle again he threw himself upon sleep with the simplicity of a dog.

Despite his mystic praise of slumber, Father Brown was up earlier than anyone else except the silent gardener; and was found smoking a big pipe and watching that expert at his speechless labours in the kitchen garden. Towards daybreak the rocking storm had ended in roaring rains, and the day came with a curious freshness. The gardener seemed even to have been conversing, but at sight of the detectives he planted his spade sullenly in a bed and, saying something about his breakfast, shifted along the lines of cabbages and shut himself in the kitchen. 'He's a valuable man, that,' said Father Brown. 'He does the potatoes amazingly. Still,' he added, with a dispassionate charity, 'he has his faults; which of us hasn't? He doesn't dig this bank quite regularly. There, for instance,' and he stamped suddenly on one spot. 'I'm really very doubtful about that potato.'

'And why?' asked Craven, amused with the little man's hobby.

'I'm doubtful about it,' said the other, 'because old Gow was doubtful about it himself. He put his spade in methodically in every place but just this. There must be a mighty fine potato just here.'

Flambeau pulled up the spade and impetuously drove it into the place. He turned up, under a load of soil, something that did not look like a potato, but rather like a monstrous, over-domed mushroom. But it struck the spade with a cold click; it rolled over like a ball, and grinned up at them.

'The Earl of Glengyle,' said Brown sadly, and looked down heavily at the skull.

Then, after a momentary meditation, he plucked the spade from Flambeau, and, saying 'We must hide it again,' clamped the skull down in the earth. Then he leaned his little body and huge head on the great handle of the spade, that stood up stiffly in the earth, and his eyes were empty and his forehead full of wrinkles. 'If one could only conceive,' he muttered, 'the meaning of this last monstrosity.' And leaning on the large spade handle, he buried his brows in his hands, as men do in church.

All the corners of the sky were brightening into blue and silver; the birds were chattering in the tiny garden trees; so loud it seemed as if the trees themselves were talking. But the three men were silent enough.

'Well, I give it all up,' said Flambeau at last boisterously. 'My brain and this world don't fit each other; and there's an end of it. Snuff, spoilt Prayer Books, and the insides of musical boxes – what – '

Brown threw up his bothered brow and rapped on the spade handle with an intolerance quite unusual with him. 'Oh, tut, tut, tut, tut!' he cried. 'All that is as plain as a pikestaff. I understood the snuff and clockwork, and so on, when I first opened my eyes this morning. And since then I've had it out with old Gow, the gardener, who is neither so deaf nor so stupid as he pretends. There's nothing amiss about the loose items. I was wrong about the torn mass-book, too; there's no harm in that. But it's this last business. Desecrating graves and stealing dead men's heads – surely there's harm in that? Surely there's black magic still in that? That doesn't fit in to the quite simple story of the snuff and the candles.' And, striding about again, he smoked moodily.

'My friend,' said Flambeau, with a grim humour, 'you must be careful with me and remember I was once a criminal. The great advantage of that estate was that I always made up the story myself, and acted it as quick as I chose. This detective business of waiting about is too much for my French impatience. All my life, for good or evil, I have done things at the instant; I always fought duels the next morning; I always paid bills on the nail; I never even put off a visit to the dentist – '

Father Brown's pipe fell out of his mouth and broke into three pieces on the gravel path. He stood rolling his eyes, the exact picture of an idiot. 'Lord, what a turnip I am!' he kept saying. 'Lord, what a turnip!' Then, in a somewhat groggy kind of way, he began to laugh.

'The dentist!' he repeated. 'Six hours in the spiritual abyss, and all because I never thought of the dentist! Such a simple, such a beautiful and peaceful thought! Friends, we have passed a night in hell; but now the sun is risen, the birds are singing, and the radiant form of the dentist consoles the world.'

'I will get some sense out of this,' cried Flambeau, striding forward, 'if I use the tortures of the Inquisition.'

Father Brown repressed what appeared to be a momentary disposition to dance on the now sunlit lawn and cried quite piteously, like a child, 'Oh, let me be silly a little. You don't know how unhappy I have been. And now I know that there has been no deep sin in this business at all. Only a little lunacy, perhaps – and who minds that?'

He spun round once more, then faced them with gravity.

'This is not a story of crime,' he said; 'rather it is the story of a strange and crooked honesty. We are dealing with the one man on earth, perhaps, who has taken no more than his due. It is a study in the savage living logic that has been the religion of this race.

'That old local rhyme about the house of Glengyle –

> As green sap to the simmer trees
> Is red gold to the Ogilvies –

was literal as well as metaphorical. It did not merely mean that the Glengyles sought for wealth; it was also true that they literally gathered gold; they had a huge collection of ornaments and utensils in that metal. They were, in fact, misers whose mania took that turn. In the light of that fact, run through all the things we found in the castle. Diamonds without their gold rings; candles without their gold candlesticks; snuff without the gold snuff-boxes; pencil-leads without the gold pencil-cases; a walking stick without its gold top; clockwork without the gold clocks – or rather watches. And, mad as it sounds, because the halos and the name of God in the old missals were of real gold, these also were taken away.'

The garden seemed to brighten, the grass to grow gayer in the strengthening sun, as the crazy truth was told. Flambeau lit a cigarette as his friend went on.

'Were taken away,' continued Father Brown; 'were taken away – but not stolen. Thieves would never have left this mystery. Thieves would have taken the gold snuff-boxes, snuff and all; the gold pencil-cases, lead and all. We have to deal with a man with a peculiar conscience, but certainly a conscience. I found that mad moralist this morning in the kitchen garden yonder, and I heard the whole story.

'The late Archibald Ogilvie was the nearest approach to a good man ever born at Glengyle. But his bitter virtue took the turn of the misanthrope; he moped over the dishonesty of his ancestors, from which, somehow, he generalised a dishonesty of all men. More especially he distrusted philanthropy or free-giving; and he swore if he could find one man who took his exact rights he should have all the gold of Glengyle. Having delivered this defiance to humanity he shut himself up, without the smallest expectation of its being answered. One day, however, a deaf and seemingly senseless lad from a distant village brought him a belated telegram; and Glengyle, in his acrid pleasantry, gave him a new farthing. At least he thought he had done so, but when he turned over his change he found the new farthing still there and a sovereign gone. The accident offered him vistas of sneering speculation. Either way, the boy would show the greasy greed of the species. Either he would vanish, a thief stealing a coin; or he would sneak back with it virtuously, a snob seeking a reward. In the middle of that night Lord Glengyle was knocked up out of his bed – for he lived alone – and forced to open the door to the deaf idiot. The idiot brought with him, not the sovereign, but exactly nineteen shillings and eleven-pence three-farthings in change.

'Then the wild exactitude of this action took hold of the mad lord's brain like fire. He swore he was Diogenes, that had long sought an honest man, and at last had found one. He made a new will, which I have seen. He took the literal youth into his huge, neglected house, and trained him up as his solitary servant and – after an odd manner – his heir. And whatever that queer creature understands, he understood absolutely his lord's two fixed ideas: first, that the letter of right is everything; and second, that he himself was to have the gold of Glengyle. So far, that is all; and that is simple. He has stripped the house of gold, and taken not a grain that was not gold; not so much as a grain of snuff. He lifted the gold leaf off an old illumination, fully satisfied that he left the rest unspoilt. All that I understood; but I could not understand this skull business. I was really uneasy about that human head buried among the potatoes. It distressed me – till Flambeau said the word.

'It will be all right. He will put the skull back in the grave, when he has taken the gold out of the tooth.'

And, indeed, when Flambeau crossed the hill that morning, he saw that strange being, the just miser, digging at the desecrated grave, the plaid round his throat thrashing out in the mountain wind; the sober top hat on his head.

The Wrong Shape

Certain of the great roads going north out of London continue far into the country a sort of attenuated and interrupted spectre of a street, with great gaps in the building, but preserving the line. Here will be a group of shops, followed by a fenced field or paddock, and then a famous public-house, and then perhaps a market garden or a nursery garden, and then one large private house, and then another field and another inn, and so on. If anyone walks along one of these roads he will pass a house which will probably catch his eye, though he may not be able to explain its attraction. It is a long, low house, running parallel with the road, painted mostly white and pale green, with a veranda and sun-blinds, and porches capped with those quaint sort of cupolas like wooden umbrellas that one sees in some old-fashioned houses. In fact, it is an old-fashioned house, very English and very suburban in the good old wealthy Clapham sense. And yet the house has a look of having been built chiefly for the hot weather. Looking at its white paint and sun-blinds one thinks vaguely of pugarees and even of palm trees. I cannot trace the feeling to its root; perhaps the place was built by an Anglo-Indian.

Anyone passing this house, I say, would be namelessly fascinated by it; would feel that it was a place about which some story was to be told. And he would have been right, as you shall shortly hear. For this is the story – the story of the strange things that did really happen in it in the Whitsuntide of the year 18—:

Anyone passing the house on the Thursday before Whit Sunday at about half-past four in the afternoon would have seen the front door open, and Father Brown, of the small church of St Mungo, come out smoking a large pipe in company with a very tall French friend of his called Flambeau, who was smoking a very small cigarette. These persons may or may not be of interest to the reader, but the truth is that they were not the only interesting things that were displayed when the front door of the white-and-green house was opened. There are further peculiarities about this house, which must be described to start with, not only that the reader may understand this tragic tale, but also that he may realise what it was that the opening of the door revealed.

The whole house was built upon the plan of a T, but a T with a very long cross piece and a very short tail piece. The long cross piece was the frontage that ran along in face of the street, with the front door in the middle; it was two stories high, and contained nearly all the important rooms. The short tail piece, which ran out at the back immediately opposite the front door, was one story high, and consisted only of two long rooms, the one leading into the other. The first of these two rooms was the study in which the celebrated Mr Quinton wrote his wild Oriental poems and romances. The farther room was a glass conservatory full of tropical blossoms of quite unique and almost monstrous beauty, and on such afternoons as these glowing with gorgeous sunlight. Thus when the hall door was open, many a passer-by literally stopped to stare and gasp; for he looked down a perspective of rich apartments to something really like a transformation scene in a fairy play: purple clouds and golden suns and crimson stars that were at once scorchingly vivid and yet transparent and far away.

Leonard Quinton, the poet, had himself most carefully arranged this effect; and it is doubtful whether he so perfectly expressed his personality in any of his poems. For he was a man who drank and bathed in colours, who indulged his lust for colour somewhat to the neglect of form – even of good form. This it was that had turned his genius so wholly to eastern art and imagery; to those bewildering carpets or blinding embroideries in which all the colours seem fallen into a fortunate chaos, having nothing to typify or to teach. He had attempted, not perhaps with complete artistic success, but with acknowledged imagination and invention, to compose epics and love stories reflecting the riot of violent and even cruel colour; tales of tropical heavens of burning gold or blood-red copper; of eastern heroes who rode with twelve-turbaned mitres upon elephants painted purple or peacock green; of gigantic jewels that a hundred Negroes could not carry, but which burned with ancient and strange-hued fires.

In short (to put the matter from the more common point of view), he dealt much in eastern heavens, rather worse than most western hells; in eastern monarchs, whom we might possibly call maniacs; and in eastern jewels which a Bond Street jeweller (if the hundred staggering Negroes brought them into his shop) might possibly not regard as genuine. Quinton was a genius, if a morbid one; and even his morbidity appeared more in his life than in his work. In temperament he was weak and waspish, and his health had suffered heavily from oriental experiments with opium. His wife – a handsome, hard-working, and, indeed, overworked woman – objected to the opium, but objected much more to a live Indian hermit in white and yellow robes, whom her husband insisted on entertaining for months together, a Virgil to guide his spirit through the heavens and the hells of the east.

It was out of this artistic household that Father Brown and his friend stepped on to the doorstep; and to judge from their faces, they stepped out of it with much relief. Flambeau had known Quinton in wild student days in Paris, and they had renewed the acquaintance for a weekend; but apart from Flambeau's more responsible developments of late, he did not get on well with the poet now. Choking oneself with opium and writing little erotic verses on vellum was not his notion of how a gentleman should go to the devil. As the two paused on the doorstep, before taking a turn in the garden, the front garden gate was thrown open with violence, and a young man with a billycock hat on the back of his head tumbled up the steps in his eagerness. He was a dissipated-looking youth with a gorgeous red necktie all awry, as if he had slept in it, and he kept fidgeting and lashing about with one of those little jointed canes.

'I say,' he said breathlessly, 'I want to see old Quinton. I must see him. Has he gone?'

'Mr Quinton is in, I believe,' said Father Brown, cleaning his pipe, 'but I do not know if you can see him. The doctor is with him at present.'

The young man, who seemed not to be perfectly sober, stumbled into the hall; and at the same moment the doctor came out of Quinton's study, shutting the door and beginning to put on his gloves.

'See Mr Quinton?' said the doctor coolly. 'No, I'm afraid you can't. In fact, you mustn't on any account. Nobody must see him; I've just given him his sleeping draught.'

'No, but look here, old chap,' said the youth in the red tie, trying affectionately to capture the doctor by the lapels of his coat. 'Look here. I'm simply sewn up, I tell you. I – '

'It's no good, Mr Atkinson,' said the doctor, forcing him to fall back; 'when you can alter the effects of a drug I'll alter my decision,' and, settling on his hat, he stepped out into the sunlight with the other two. He was a bull-necked, good-tempered little man with a small moustache, inexpressibly ordinary, yet giving an impression of capacity.

The young man in the billycock, who did not seem to be gifted with any tact in dealing with people beyond the general idea of clutching hold of their coats, stood outside the door, as dazed as if he had been thrown out bodily, and silently watched the other three walk away together through the garden.

'That was a sound, spanking lie I told just now,' remarked the medical man, laughing. 'In point of fact, poor Quinton doesn't have his sleeping draught for nearly half an hour. But I'm not going to have him bothered with that little beast, who only wants to borrow money that he wouldn't pay back if he could. He's a dirty little scamp, though he is Mrs Quinton's brother, and she's as fine a woman as ever walked.'

'Yes,' said Father Brown. 'She's a good woman.'

'So I propose to hang about the garden till the creature has cleared off,' went on the doctor, 'and then I'll go in to Quinton with the medicine. Atkinson can't get in, because I locked the door.'

'In that case, Dr Harris,' said Flambeau, 'we might as well walk round at the back by the end of the conservatory. There's no entrance to it that way, but it's worth seeing, even from the outside.'

'Yes, and I might get a squint at my patient,' laughed the doctor, 'for he prefers to lie on an ottoman right at the end of the conservatory amid all those blood-red poinsettias; it would give me the creeps. But what are you doing?'

Father Brown had stopped for a moment, and picked up out of the long grass, where it had almost been wholly hidden, a queer, crooked Oriental knife, inlaid exquisitely in coloured stones and metals.

'What is this?' asked Father Brown, regarding it with some disfavour.

'Oh, Quinton's, I suppose,' said Dr Harris carelessly; 'he has all sorts of Chinese knickknacks about the place. Or perhaps it belongs to that mild Hindu of his whom he keeps on a string.'

'What Hindu?' asked Father Brown, still staring at the dagger in his hand.

'Oh, some Indian conjuror,' said the doctor lightly; 'a fraud, of course.'

'You don't believe in magic?' asked Father Brown, without looking up.

'O crikey! magic!' said the doctor.

'It's very beautiful,' said the priest in a low, dreaming voice; 'the colours are very beautiful. But it's the wrong shape.'

'What for?' asked Flambeau, staring.

'For anything. It's the wrong shape in the abstract. Don't you ever feel that about Eastern art? The colours are intoxicatingly lovely; but the shapes are mean and bad – deliberately mean and bad. I have seen wicked things in a Turkey carpet.'

'Mon Dieu!' cried Flambeau, laughing.

'They are letters and symbols in a language I don't know; but I know they stand for evil words,' went on the priest, his voice growing lower and lower. 'The lines go wrong on purpose – like serpents doubling to escape.'

'What the devil are you talking about?' said the doctor with a loud laugh.

Flambeau spoke quietly to him in answer. 'The Father sometimes gets this mystic's cloud on him,' he said; 'but I give you fair warning that I have never known him to have it except when there was some evil quite near.'

'Oh, rats!' said the scientist.

'Why, look at it,' cried Father Brown, holding out the crooked knife at arm's length, as if it were some glittering snake. 'Don't you see it is the wrong shape? Don't you see that it has no hearty and plain purpose? It does not point like a spear. It does not sweep like a scythe. It does not look like a weapon. It looks like an instrument of torture.'

'Well, as you don't seem to like it,' said the jolly Harris, 'it had better be taken back to its owner. Haven't we come to the end of this confounded conservatory yet? This house is the wrong shape, if you like.'

'You don't understand,' said Father Brown, shaking his head. 'The shape of this house is quaint – it is even laughable. But there is nothing wrong about it.'

As they spoke they came round the curve of glass that ended the conservatory, an uninterrupted curve, for there was neither door nor window by which to enter at that end. The glass, however, was clear, and the sun still bright, though beginning to set; and they could see not only the flamboyant blossoms inside, but the frail figure of the poet in a brown velvet coat lying languidly on the sofa, having, apparently, fallen half asleep over a book. He was a pale, slight man, with loose, chestnut hair and a fringe of beard that was the paradox of his face, for the beard made him look less manly. These traits were well known to all three of them; but even had it not been so, it may be doubted whether they would have looked at Quinton just then. Their eyes were riveted on another object.

Exactly in their path, immediately outside the round end of the glass building, was standing a tall man, whose drapery fell to his feet in faultless white, and whose bare, brown skull, face, and neck gleamed in the setting sun like splendid bronze. He was looking through the glass at the sleeper, and he was more motionless than a mountain.

'Who is that?' cried Father Brown, stepping back with a hissing intake of his breath.

'Oh, it is only that Hindu humbug,' growled Harris; 'but I don't know what the deuce he's doing here.'

'It looks like hypnotism,' said Flambeau, biting his black moustache.

'Why are you unmedical fellows always talking bosh about hypnotism?' cried the doctor. 'It looks a deal more like burglary.'

'Well, we will speak to it, at any rate,' said Flambeau, who was always for action. One long stride took him to the place where the Indian stood. Bowing from his great height, which over-topped even the Oriental's, he said with placid impudence: 'Good-evening, sir. Do you want anything?'

Quite slowly, like a great ship turning into a harbour, the great yellow face turned, and looked at last over its white shoulder. They were startled to see that its yellow eyelids were quite sealed, as in sleep. 'Thank you,' said the face in excellent English. 'I want nothing.' Then, half opening the lids, so as to show a slit of opalescent eyeball, he repeated, 'I want nothing.' Then he opened his eyes wide with a startling stare, said, 'I want nothing,' and went rustling away into the rapidly darkening garden.

'The Christian is more modest,' muttered Father Brown; 'he wants something.'

'What on earth was he doing?' asked Flambeau, knitting his black brows and lowering his voice.

'I should like to talk to you later,' said Father Brown.

The sunlight was still a reality, but it was the red light of evening, and the bulk of the garden trees and bushes grew blacker and blacker against it. They turned round the end of the conservatory, and walked in silence down the other side to get round to the front door. As they went they seemed to wake something, as one startles a bird, in the deeper corner between the study and the main building; and again they saw the white-robed fakir slide out of the shadow, and slip round towards the front door. To their surprise, however, he had not been alone. They found themselves abruptly pulled up and forced to banish their bewilderment by the appearance of Mrs Quinton, with her heavy golden hair and square pale face, advancing on them out of the twilight. She looked a little stern, but was entirely courteous.

'Good-evening, Dr Harris,' was all she said.

'Good-evening, Mrs Quinton,' said the little doctor heartily. 'I am just going to give your husband his sleeping draught.'

'Yes,' she said in a clear voice. 'I think it is quite time.' And she smiled at them, and went sweeping into the house.

'That woman's over-driven,' said Father Brown; 'that's the kind of woman that does her duty for twenty years, and then does something dreadful.'

The little doctor looked at him for the first time with an eye of interest. 'Did you ever study medicine?' he asked.

'You have to know something of the mind as well as the body,' answered the priest; 'we have to know something of the body as well as the mind.'

'Well,' said the doctor, 'I think I'll go and give Quinton his stuff.'

They had turned the corner of the front façade, and were approaching the front doorway. As they turned into it they saw the man in the white robe for the third time. He came so straight towards the front door that it seemed quite incredible that he had not just come out of the study opposite to it. Yet they knew that the study door was locked.

Father Brown and Flambeau, however, kept this weird contradiction to themselves, and Dr Harris was not a man to waste his thoughts on the impossible. He permitted the omnipresent Asiatic to make his exit, and then stepped briskly into the hall. There he found a figure which he had already forgotten. The inane Atkinson was still hanging about, humming and poking things with his knobby cane. The doctor's face had a spasm of disgust and decision, and he whispered rapidly to his companion: 'I must lock the door again, or this rat will get in. But I shall be out again in two minutes.'

He rapidly unlocked the door and locked it again behind him, just balking a blundering charge from the young man in the billycock. The young man threw himself impatiently on a hall chair. Flambeau looked at a Persian illumination on the wall; Father Brown, who seemed in a sort of daze, dully eyed the door. In about four minutes the door was opened again. Atkinson was quicker this time. He sprang forward, held the door open for an instant, and called out: 'Oh, I say, Quinton, I want – '

From the other end of the study came the clear voice of Quinton, in something between a yawn and a yell of weary laughter.

'Oh, I know what you want. Take it, and leave me in peace. I'm writing a song about peacocks.'

Before the door closed half a sovereign came flying through the aperture; and Atkinson, stumbling forward, caught it with singular dexterity.

'So that's settled,' said the doctor, and, locking the door savagely, he led the way out into the garden.

'Poor Leonard can get a little peace now,' he added to Father Brown; 'he's locked in all by himself for an hour or two.'

'Yes,' answered the priest; 'and his voice sounded jolly enough when we left him.' Then he looked gravely round the garden, and saw the loose figure of Atkinson standing and jingling the half-sovereign in his pocket, and beyond, in the purple twilight, the figure of the Indian sitting bolt upright upon a bank of grass with his face turned towards the setting sun. Then he said abruptly: 'Where is Mrs Quinton?'

'She has gone up to her room,' said the doctor. 'That is her shadow on the blind.'

Father Brown looked up, and frowningly scrutinised a dark outline at the gas-lit window.

'Yes,' he said, 'that is her shadow,' and he walked a yard or two and threw himself upon a garden seat.

Flambeau sat down beside him; but the doctor was one of those energetic people who live naturally on their legs. He walked away, smoking, into the twilight, and the two friends were left together.

'My father,' said Flambeau in French, 'what is the matter with you?'

Father Brown was silent and motionless for half a minute, then he said: 'Superstition is irreligious, but there is something in the air of this place. I think it's that Indian – at least, partly.'

He sank into silence, and watched the distant outline of the Indian, who still sat rigid as if in prayer. At first sight he seemed motionless, but as Father Brown watched him he saw that the man swayed ever so slightly with a rhythmic movement, just as the dark tree-tops swayed ever so slightly in the wind that was creeping up the dim garden paths and shuffling the fallen leaves a little.

The landscape was growing rapidly dark, as if for a storm, but they could still see all the figures in their various places. Atkinson was leaning against a tree with a listless face; Quinton's wife was still at her window; the doctor had gone strolling round the end of the conservatory; they could see his cigar like a will-o'-the-wisp; and the fakir still sat rigid and yet rocking, while the trees above him began to rock and almost to roar. Storm was certainly coming.

'When that Indian spoke to us,' went on Brown in a conversational undertone, 'I had a sort of vision, a vision of him and all his universe. Yet he only said the same thing three times. When first he said "I want nothing," it meant only that he was impenetrable, that Asia does not give itself away. Then he said again, "I want nothing," and I knew that he meant that he was sufficient to himself, like a cosmos, that he needed no God, neither admitted any sins. And when he said the third time, "I want nothing," he said it with blazing eyes. And I knew that he meant literally what he said; that nothing was his desire and his home; that he was weary for nothing as for wine; that annihilation, the mere destruction of everything or anything – '

Two drops of rain fell; and for some reason Flambeau started and looked up, as if they had stung him. And the same instant the doctor down by the end of the conservatory began running towards them, calling out something as he ran.

As he came among them like a bombshell the restless Atkinson happened to be taking a turn nearer to the house front; and the doctor clutched him by the collar in a convulsive grip. 'Foul play!' he cried; 'what have you been doing to him, you dog?'

The priest had sprung erect, and had the voice of steel of a soldier in command.

'No fighting,' he cried coolly; 'we are enough to hold anyone we want to. What is the matter, doctor?'

'Things are not right with Quinton,' said the doctor, quite white. 'I could just see him through the glass, and I don't like the way he's lying. It's not as I left him, anyhow.'

'Let us go in to him,' said Father Brown shortly. 'You can leave Mr Atkinson alone. I have had him in sight since we heard Quinton's voice.'

'I will stop here and watch him,' said Flambeau hurriedly. 'You go in and see.'

The doctor and the priest flew to the study door, unlocked it, and fell into the room. In doing so they nearly fell over the large mahogany table in the centre at which the poet usually wrote; for the place was lit only by a small fire kept for the invalid. In the middle of this table lay a single sheet of paper, evidently left there on purpose. The doctor snatched it up, glanced at it, handed it to Father Brown, and crying, 'Good God, look at that!' plunged towards the glass room beyond, where the terrible tropic flowers still seemed to keep a crimson memory of the sunset.

Father Brown read the words three times before he put down the paper. The words were: 'I die by my own hand; yet I die murdered!' They were in the quite inimitable, not to say illegible, handwriting of Leonard Quinton.

Then Father Brown, still keeping the paper in his hand, strode towards the conservatory, only to meet his medical friend coming back with a face of assurance and collapse. 'He's done it,' said Harris.

They went together through the gorgeous unnatural beauty of cactus and azalea and found Leonard Quinton, poet and romancer, with his head hanging downward off his ottoman and his red curls sweeping the ground. Into his left side was thrust the queer dagger that they had picked up in the garden, and his limp hand still rested on the hilt.

Outside the storm had come at one stride, like the night in Coleridge, and garden and glass roof were darkened with driving rain. Father Brown seemed to be studying the paper more than the corpse; he held it close to his eyes; and seemed trying to read it in the twilight. Then he held it up against the faint light, and, as he did so, lightning stared at them for an instant so white that the paper looked black against it.

Darkness full of thunder followed, and after the thunder Father Brown's voice said out of the dark: 'Doctor, this paper is the wrong shape.'

'What do you mean?' asked Doctor Harris, with a frowning stare.

'It isn't square,' answered Brown. 'It has a sort of edge snipped off at the corner. What does it mean?'

'How the deuce should I know?' growled the doctor. 'Shall we move this poor chap, do you think? He's quite dead.'

'No,' answered the priest; 'we must leave him as he lies and send for the police.' But he was still scrutinising the paper.

As they went back through the study he stopped by the table and picked up a small pair of nail scissors. 'Ah,' he said, with a sort of relief, 'this is what he did it with. But yet – ' And he knitted his brows.

'Oh, stop fooling with that scrap of paper,' said the doctor emphatically. 'It was a fad of his. He had hundreds of them. He cut all his paper like that,' as he pointed to a stack of sermon paper still unused on another and smaller table. Father Brown went up to it and held up a sheet. It was the same irregular shape.

'Quite so,' he said. 'And here I see the corners that were snipped off.' And to the indignation of his colleague he began to count them.

'That's all right,' he said, with an apologetic smile. 'Twenty-three sheets cut and twenty-two corners cut off them. And as I see you are impatient we will rejoin the others.'

'Who is to tell his wife?' asked Dr Harris. 'Will you go and tell her now, while I send a servant for the police?'

'As you will,' said Father Brown indifferently. And he went out to the hall door.

Here also he found a drama, though of a more grotesque sort. It showed nothing less than his big friend Flambeau in an attitude to which he had long been unaccustomed, while upon the pathway at the bottom of the steps was sprawling with his boots in the air the amiable Atkinson, his billycock hat and walking cane sent flying in opposite directions along the path. Atkinson had at length wearied of Flambeau's almost paternal custody, and had endeavoured to knock him down, which was by no means a smooth game to play with the Roi des Apaches, even after that monarch's abdication.

Flambeau was about to leap upon his enemy and secure him once more, when the priest patted him easily on the shoulder.

'Make it up with Mr Atkinson, my friend,' he said. 'Beg a mutual pardon and say "Good-night." We need not detain him any longer.' Then, as Atkinson rose somewhat doubtfully and gathered his hat and stick and went towards the garden gate, Father Brown said in a more serious voice: 'Where is that Indian?'

They all three (for the doctor had joined them) turned involuntarily towards the dim grassy bank amid the tossing trees, purple with twilight, where they had last seen the brown man swaying in his strange prayers. The Indian was gone.

'Confound him,' cried the doctor, stamping furiously. 'Now I know that it was that nigger that did it.'

'I thought you didn't believe in magic,' said Father Brown quietly.

'No more I did,' said the doctor, rolling his eyes. 'I only know that I loathed that yellow devil when I thought he was a sham wizard. And I shall loathe him more if I come to think he was a real one.'

'Well, his having escaped is nothing,' said Flambeau. 'For we could have proved nothing and done nothing against him. One hardly goes to the parish constable with a story of suicide imposed by witchcraft or auto-suggestion.'

Meanwhile Father Brown had made his way into the house, and now went to break the news to the wife of the dead man.

When he came out again he looked a little pale and tragic, but what passed between them in that interview was never known, even when all was known.

Flambeau, who was talking quietly with the doctor, was surprised to see his friend reappear so soon at his elbow; but Brown took no notice, and merely drew the doctor apart. 'You have sent for the police, haven't you?' he asked.

'Yes,' answered Harris. 'They ought to be here in ten minutes.'

'Will you do me a favour?' said the priest quietly. 'The truth is, I make a collection of these curious stories, which often contain, as in the case of our Hindu friend, elements which can hardly be put into a police report. Now, I want you to write out a report of this case for my private use. Yours is a clever trade,' he said, looking the doctor gravely and steadily in the face. 'I sometimes think that you know some details of this matter which you have not thought fit to mention. Mine is a confidential trade like yours, and I will treat anything you write for me in strict confidence. But write the whole.'

The doctor, who had been listening thoughtfully with his head a little on one side, looked the priest in the face for an instant, and said: 'All right,' and went into the study, closing the door behind him.

'Flambeau,' said Father Brown, 'there is a long seat there under the veranda, where we can smoke out of the rain. You are my only friend in the world, and I want to talk to you. Or, perhaps, be silent with you.'

They established themselves comfortably in the veranda seat; Father Brown, against his common habit, accepted a good cigar and smoked it steadily in silence, while the rain shrieked and rattled on the roof of the veranda.

'My friend,' he said at length, 'this is a very queer case. A very queer case.'

'I should think it was,' said Flambeau, with something like a shudder.

'You call it queer, and I call it queer,' said the other, 'and yet we mean quite opposite things. The modern mind always mixes up two different ideas: mystery in the sense of what is marvellous, and mystery in the sense of what is complicated. That is half its difficulty about miracles. A miracle is startling; but it is simple. It is simple because it is a miracle. It is power coming directly from God (or the devil) instead of indirectly through nature or human wills. Now, you mean that this business is marvellous because it is miraculous, because it is witchcraft worked by a wicked Indian. Understand, I do not say that it was not spiritual or diabolic. Heaven and hell only know by what surrounding influences strange sins come into the lives of men. But for the present my point is this: if it was pure magic, as you think, then it is marvellous; but it is not mysterious – that is, it is not complicated. The quality of a miracle is mysterious, but its manner is simple. Now, the manner of this business has been the reverse of simple.'

The storm that had slackened for a little seemed to be swelling again, and there came heavy movements as of faint thunder. Father Brown let fall the ash of his cigar and went on: 'There has been in this incident,' he said, 'a twisted, ugly, complex quality that does not belong to the straight bolts either of heaven or hell. As one knows the crooked track of a snail, I know the crooked track of a man.'

The white lightning opened its enormous eye in one wink, the sky shut up again, and the priest went on: 'Of all these crooked things, the crookedest was the shape of that piece of paper. It was crookeder than the dagger that killed him.'

'You mean the paper on which Quinton confessed his suicide,' said Flambeau.

'I mean the paper on which Quinton wrote, "I die by my own hand",' answered Father Brown. 'The shape of that paper, my friend, was the wrong shape; the wrong shape, if ever I have seen it in this wicked world.'

'It only had a corner snipped off,' said Flambeau, 'and I understand that all Quinton's paper was cut that way.'

'It was a very odd way,' said the other, 'and a very bad way, to my taste and fancy. Look here, Flambeau, this Quinton – God receive his soul! – was perhaps a bit of a cur in some ways, but he really was an artist, with the pencil as well as the pen. His handwriting, though hard to read, was bold and beautiful. I can't prove what I say; I can't prove anything. But I tell you with the full force of conviction that he could never have cut that mean little piece off a sheet of paper. If he had wanted to cut down paper for some purpose of fitting in, or binding up, or what not, he would have made quite a different slash with the scissors. Do you remember the shape? It was a mean shape. It was a wrong shape. Like this. Don't you remember?'

And he waved his burning cigar before him in the darkness, making irregular squares so rapidly that Flambeau really seemed to see them as fiery hieroglyphics upon the darkness – hieroglyphics such as his friend had spoken of, which are undecipherable, yet can have no good meaning.

'But,' said Flambeau, as the priest put his cigar in his mouth again and leaned back, staring at the roof, 'suppose somebody else did use the scissors. Why should somebody else, cutting pieces off his sermon paper, make Quinton commit suicide?'

Father Brown was still leaning back and staring at the roof, but he took his cigar out of his mouth and said: 'Quinton never did commit suicide.'

Flambeau stared at him. 'Why, confound it all,' he cried, 'then why did he confess to suicide?'

The priest leant forward again, settled his elbows on his knees, looked at the ground, and said, in a low, distinct voice: 'He never did confess to suicide.'

Flambeau laid his cigar down. 'You mean,' he said, 'that the writing was forged?'

'No,' said Father Brown. 'Quinton wrote it all right.'

'Well, there you are,' said the aggravated Flambeau; 'Quinton wrote, "I die by my own hand", with his own hand on a plain piece of paper.'

'Of the wrong shape,' said the priest calmly.

'Oh, the shape be damned!' cried Flambeau. 'What has the shape to do with it?'

'There were twenty-three snipped papers,' resumed Brown unmoved, 'and only twenty-two pieces snipped off. Therefore one of the pieces had been destroyed, probably that from the written paper. Does that suggest anything to you?'

A light dawned on Flambeau's face, and he said: 'There was something else written by Quinton, some other words. "They will tell you I die by my own hand", or "Do not believe that – " '

'Hotter, as the children say,' said his friend. 'But the piece was hardly half an inch across; there was no room for one word, let alone five. Can you think of anything hardly bigger than a comma which the man with hell in his heart had to tear away as a testimony against him?'

'I can think of nothing,' said Flambeau at last.

'What about quotation marks?' said the priest, and flung his cigar far into the darkness like a shooting star.

All words had left the other man's mouth, and Father Brown said, like one going back to fundamentals: 'Leonard Quinton was a romancer, and was writing an Oriental romance about wizardry and hypnotism. He – '

At this moment the door opened briskly behind them, and the doctor came out with his hat on. He put a long envelope into the priest's hands.

'That's the document you wanted,' he said, 'and I must be getting home. Good-night.'

'Good-night,' said Father Brown, as the doctor walked briskly to the gate. He had left the front door open, so that a shaft of gaslight fell upon them. In the light of this Brown opened the envelope and read the following words:

Dear Father Brown – *Vicisti Galilae!* Otherwise, damn your eyes, which are very penetrating ones. Can it be possible that there is something in all that stuff of yours after all?

I am a man who has ever since boyhood believed in Nature and in all natural functions and instincts, whether men called them moral or immoral. Long before I became a doctor, when I was a schoolboy keeping mice and spiders, I believed that to be a good animal is the best thing in the world. But just now I am shaken; I have believed in Nature; but it seems as if Nature could betray a man. Can there be anything in your bosh? I am really getting morbid.

I loved Quinton's wife. What was there wrong in that? Nature told me to, and it's love that makes the world go round. I also thought quite sincerely that she would be happier with a clean animal like me than with that tormenting little lunatic. What was there wrong in that? I was only facing facts, like a man of science. She would have been happier.

According to my own creed I was quite free to kill Quinton, which was the best thing for everybody, even himself. But as a healthy animal I had no notion of killing myself. I resolved, therefore, that I would never do it until I saw a chance that would leave me scot free. I saw that chance this morning.

I have been three times, all told, into Quinton's study today. The first time I went in he would talk about nothing but the weird tale, called 'The Curse of a Saint', which he was writing, which was all about how some Indian hermit made an English colonel kill himself by thinking about him. He showed me the last sheets, and even read me the last paragraph, which was something like this: 'The conqueror of the Punjab, a mere yellow skeleton, but still gigantic, managed to lift himself on his elbow and gasp in his nephew's ear: "I die by my own hand, yet I die murdered!" ' It so happened by one chance out of a hundred, that those last words were written at the top of a new sheet of paper. I left the room, and went out into the garden intoxicated with a frightful opportunity.

We walked round the house; and two more things happened in my favour. You suspected an Indian, and you found a dagger which the Indian might most probably use. Taking the opportunity to stuff it in my pocket I went back to Quinton's study, locked the door, and gave him his sleeping draught. He was against answering Atkinson at all, but I urged him to call out and quiet the fellow, because I wanted a clear proof that Quinton was alive when I left the room for the second time. Quinton lay down in the conservatory, and I came through the study. I am a quick man with my hands, and in a minute and a half I had done what I wanted to do. I had emptied all the first part of Quinton's romance into the fireplace, where it burnt to ashes. Then I saw that the quotation marks wouldn't do, so I snipped them off, and to make it seem likelier, snipped the whole quire to match. Then I came out with the knowledge that Quinton's confession of suicide lay on the front table, while Quinton lay alive but asleep in the conservatory beyond.

The last act was a desperate one; you can guess it: I pretended to have seen Quinton dead and rushed to his room. I delayed you with the paper, and, being a quick man with my hands, killed Quinton while you were looking at his confession of suicide. He was half-asleep, being drugged, and I put his own hand on the knife and drove it into his body. The knife was of so queer a shape that no one but an operator could have calculated the angle that would reach his heart. I wonder if you noticed this.

When I had done it, the extraordinary thing happened. Nature deserted me. I felt ill. I felt just as if I had done something wrong. I think my brain is breaking up; I feel some sort of desperate pleasure in thinking I have told the thing to somebody; that I shall not have to be alone with it if I marry and have children. What is the matter with me? . . . Madness . . . or can one have remorse, just as if one were in Byron's poems! I cannot write any more.

James Erskine Harris

* * *

Father Brown carefully folded up the letter, and put it in his breast pocket just as there came a loud peal at the gate bell, and the wet waterproofs of several policemen gleamed in the road outside.

The Sins of Prince Saradine

When Flambeau took his month's holiday from his office in Westminster he took it in a small sailing-boat, so small that it passed much of its time as a rowing-boat. He took it, moreover, in little rivers in the Eastern Counties, rivers so small that the boat looked like a magic boat, sailing on land through meadows and cornfields. The vessel was just comfortable for two people; there was room only for necessities, and Flambeau had stocked it with such things as his special philosophy considered necessary. They reduced themselves, apparently, to four essentials: tins of salmon, if he should want to eat; loaded revolvers, if he should want to fight; a bottle of brandy, presumably in case he should faint; and a priest, presumably in case he should die. With this light luggage he crawled down the little Norfolk rivers, intending to reach the Broads at last, but meanwhile delighting in the overhanging gardens and meadows, the mirrored mansions or villages, lingering to fish in the pools and corners, and in some sense hugging the shore.

Like a true philosopher, Flambeau had no aim in his holiday; but, like a true philosopher, he had an excuse. He had a sort of half purpose, which he took just so seriously that its success would crown the holiday, but just so lightly that its failure would not spoil it. Years ago, when he had been a king of thieves and the most famous figure in Paris, he had often received wild communications of approval, denunciation, or even love; but one had, somehow, stuck in his memory. It consisted simply of a visiting-card, in an envelope with an English postmark. On the back of the card was written in French and in green ink: 'If you ever retire and become respectable, come and see me. I want to meet you, for I have met all the other great men of my time. That trick of yours of getting one detective to arrest the other was the most splendid scene in French history.' On the front of the card was engraved in the formal fashion, 'Prince Saradine, Reed House, Reed Island, Norfolk'.

He had not troubled much about the prince then, beyond ascertaining that he had been a brilliant and fashionable figure in southern Italy. In his youth, it was said, he had eloped with a married woman of high rank; the escapade was scarcely startling in his social world, but it had clung to men's minds because of an additional tragedy: the alleged suicide of the insulted husband, who appeared to have flung himself over a precipice in Sicily. The prince then lived in Vienna for a time, but his more recent years seemed to have been passed in perpetual and restless travel. But when Flambeau, like the prince himself, had left European celebrity and settled in England, it occurred to him that he might pay a surprise visit to this eminent exile in the Norfolk Broads. Whether he should find the place he had no idea; and, indeed, it was sufficiently small and forgotten. But, as things fell out, he found it much sooner than he expected.

They had moored their boat one night under a bank veiled in high grasses and short pollarded trees. Sleep, after heavy sculling, had come to them early, and by a corresponding accident they awoke before it was light. To speak more strictly, they awoke before it was daylight; for a large lemon moon was only just setting in the forest of high grass above their heads, and the sky was of a vivid violet-blue, nocturnal but bright. Both men had simultaneously a reminiscence of childhood, of the elfin and adventurous time when tall weeds close over us like woods. Standing up thus against the large low moon, the daisies really seemed to be giant daisies, the dandelions to be giant dandelions. Somehow it reminded them of the dado of a nursery wallpaper. The drop of the riverbed sufficed to sink them under the roots of all shrubs and flowers and make them gaze upwards at the grass.

'By Jove!' said Flambeau, 'it's like being in fairyland.'

Father Brown sat bolt upright in the boat and crossed himself. His movement was so abrupt that his friend asked him, with a mild stare, what was the matter.

'The people who wrote the mediaeval ballads,' answered the priest, 'knew more about fairies than you do. It isn't only nice things that happen in fairyland.'

'Oh, bosh!' said Flambeau. 'Only nice things could happen under such an innocent moon. I am for pushing on now and seeing what does really come. We may die and rot before we ever see again such a moon or such a mood.'

'All right,' said Father Brown. 'I never said it was always wrong to enter fairyland. I only said it was always dangerous.'

They pushed slowly up the brightening river; the glowing violet of the sky and the pale gold of the moon grew fainter and fainter, and faded into that vast colourless cosmos that precedes the colours of the dawn. When the first faint stripes of red and gold and grey split the horizon from end to end they were broken by the black bulk of a town or village which sat on the river just ahead of them. It was already an easy twilight, in which all things were visible, when they came under the hanging roofs and bridges of this riverside hamlet. The houses, with their long, low, stooping roofs, seemed to come down to drink at the river, like huge grey and red cattle. The broadening and whitening dawn had already turned to working daylight before they saw any living creature on the wharves and bridges of that silent town. Eventually they saw a very placid and prosperous man in his shirt sleeves, with a face as round as the recently sunken moon, and rays of red whisker around the low arc of it, who was leaning on a post above the sluggish tide. By an impulse not to be analysed, Flambeau rose to his full height in the swaying boat and shouted at the man to ask if he knew Reed Island or Reed House. The prosperous man's smile grew slightly more expansive, and he simply pointed up the river towards the next bend of it. Flambeau went ahead without further speech.

The boat took many such grassy corners and followed many such reedy and silent reaches of river; but before the search had become monotonous they had swung round a specially sharp angle and come into the silence of a sort of pool or lake, the sight of which instinctively arrested them. For in the middle of this wider piece of water, fringed on every side with rushes, lay a long, low islet, along which ran a long, low house or bungalow built of bamboo or some kind of tough tropic cane. The upstanding rods of bamboo which made the walls were pale yellow, the sloping rods that made the roof were of darker red or brown, otherwise the long house was a thing of repetition and monotony. The early morning breeze rustled the reeds round the island and sang in the strange ribbed house as in a giant pan-pipe.

'By George!' cried Flambeau; 'here is the place, after all! Here is Reed Island, if ever there was one. Here is Reed House, if it is anywhere. I believe that fat man with whiskers was a fairy.'

'Perhaps,' remarked Father Brown impartially. 'If he was, he was a bad fairy.'

But even as he spoke the impetuous Flambeau had run his boat ashore in the rattling reeds, and they stood in the long, quaint islet beside the old and silent house.

The house stood with its back, as it were, to the river and the only landing-stage; the main entrance was on the other side, and looked down the long island garden. The visitors approached it, therefore, by a small path running round nearly three sides of the house, close under the low eaves. Through three different windows on three different sides they looked in on the same long, well-lit room, panelled in light wood, with a large number of looking-glasses, and laid out as for an elegant lunch. The front door, when they came round to it at last, was flanked by two turquoise-blue flower pots. It was opened by a butler of the drearier type – long, lean, grey and listless – who murmured that Prince Saradine was from home at present, but was expected hourly; the house being kept ready for him and his guests. The exhibition of the card with the scrawl of green ink awoke a flicker of life in the parchment face of the depressed retainer, and it was with a certain shaky courtesy that he suggested that the strangers should remain. 'His Highness may be here any minute,' he said, 'and would be distressed to have just missed any gentleman he had invited. We have orders always to keep a little cold lunch for him and his friends, and I am sure he would wish it to be offered.'

Moved with curiosity to this minor adventure, Flambeau assented gracefully, and followed the old man, who ushered him ceremoniously into the long, lightly panelled room. There was nothing very notable about it, except the rather unusual alternation of many long, low windows with many long, low oblongs of looking-glass, which gave a singular air of lightness and unsubstantialness to the place. It was somehow like lunching out of doors. One or two pictures of a quiet kind hung in the corners, one a large grey photograph of a very young man in uniform, another a red chalk sketch of two long-haired boys. Asked by Flambeau whether the soldierly person was the prince, the butler answered shortly in the negative; it was the prince's younger brother, Captain Stephen Saradine, he said. And with that the old man seemed to dry up suddenly and lose all taste for conversation.

After lunch had tailed off with exquisite coffee and liqueurs, the guests were introduced to the garden, the library, and the housekeeper – a dark, handsome lady, of no little majesty, and rather like a plutonic Madonna. It appeared that she and the butler were the only survivors of the prince's original foreign *ménage*, all the other servants now in the house being new and collected in Norfolk by the housekeeper. This latter lady went by the name of Mrs Anthony, but she spoke with a slight Italian accent, and Flambeau did not doubt that Anthony was a Norfolk version of some more Latin name. Mr Paul, the butler, also had a faintly foreign air, but he was in tongue and training English, as are many of the most polished menservants of the cosmopolitan nobility.

Pretty and unique as it was, the place had about it a curious luminous sadness. Hours passed in it like days. The long, well-windowed rooms were full of daylight, but it seemed a dead daylight. And through all other incidental noises, the sound of talk, the clink of glasses, or the passing feet of servants, they could hear on all sides of the house the melancholy noise of the river.

'We have taken a wrong turning, and come to a wrong place,' said Father Brown, looking out of the window at the grey-green sedges and the silver flood. 'Never mind; one can sometimes do good by being the right person in the wrong place.'

Father Brown, though commonly a silent, was an oddly sympathetic little man, and in those few but endless hours he unconsciously sank deeper into the secrets of Reed House than his professional friend. He had that knack of friendly silence which is so essential to gossip; and saying scarcely a word, he probably obtained from his new acquaintances all that in any case they would have told. The butler indeed was naturally uncommunicative. He betrayed a sullen and almost animal affection for his master; who, he said, had been very badly treated. The chief offender seemed to be his highness's brother, whose name alone would lengthen the old man's lantern jaws and pucker his parrot nose into a sneer. Captain Stephen was a ne'er-do-well, apparently, and had drained his benevolent brother of hundreds and thousands; forced him to fly from fashionable life and live quietly in this retreat. That was all Paul, the butler, would say, and Paul was obviously a partisan.

The Italian housekeeper was somewhat more communicative, being, as Brown fancied, somewhat less content. Her tone about her master was faintly acid; though not without a certain awe. Flambeau and his friend were standing in the room of the looking-glasses examining the red sketch of the two boys, when the housekeeper swept in swiftly on some domestic errand. It was a peculiarity of this glittering, glass-panelled place that anyone entering was reflected in four or five mirrors at once; and Father Brown, without turning round, stopped in the middle of a sentence of family criticism. But Flambeau, who had his face close up to the picture, was already saying in a loud voice, 'The brothers Saradine, I suppose. They both look innocent enough. It would be hard to say which is the good brother and which the bad.' Then, realising the lady's presence, he turned the conversation with some triviality, and strolled out into the garden. But Father Brown still gazed steadily at the red crayon sketch; and Mrs Anthony still gazed steadily at Father Brown.

She had large and tragic brown eyes, and her olive face glowed darkly with a curious and painful wonder – as of one doubtful of a stranger's identity or purpose. Whether the little priest's coat and creed touched some southern memories of confession, or whether she fancied he knew more than he did, she said to him in a low voice as to a fellow plotter, 'He is right enough in one way, your friend. He says it would be hard to pick out the good and bad brothers. Oh, it would be hard, it would be mighty hard, to pick out the good one.'

'I don't understand you,' said Father Brown, and began to move away.

The woman took a step nearer to him, with thunderous brows and a sort of savage stoop, like a bull lowering his horns.

'There isn't a good one,' she hissed. 'There was badness enough in the captain taking all that money, but I don't think there was much goodness in the prince giving it. The captain's not the only one with something against him.'

A light dawned on the cleric's averted face, and his mouth formed silently the word 'blackmail'. Even as he did so the woman turned an abrupt white face over her shoulder and almost fell. The door had opened soundlessly and the pale Paul stood like a ghost in the doorway. By the weird trick of the reflecting walls, it seemed as if five Pauls had entered by five doors simultaneously.

'His Highness,' he said, 'has just arrived.'

In the same flash the figure of a man had passed outside the first window, crossing the sunlit pane like a lighted stage. An instant later he passed at the second window and the many mirrors repainted in successive frames the same eagle profile and marching figure. He was erect and alert, but his hair was white and his complexion of an odd ivory yellow. He had that short, curved Roman nose which generally goes with long, lean cheeks and chin, but these were partly masked by moustache and imperial. The moustache was much darker than the beard, giving an effect slightly theatrical, and he was dressed up to the same dashing part, having a white top hat, an orchid in his coat, a yellow waistcoat and yellow gloves which he flapped and swung as he walked. When he came round to the front door they heard the stiff Paul open it, and heard the new arrival say cheerfully, 'Well, you see I have come.' The stiff Mr Paul bowed and answered in his inaudible manner; for a few minutes their conversation could not be heard. Then the butler said, 'Everything is at your disposal'; and the glove-flapping Prince Saradine came gaily into the room to greet them. They beheld once more that spectral scene – five princes entering a room with five doors.

The prince put the white hat and yellow gloves on the table and offered his hand quite cordially.

'Delighted to see you here, Mr Flambeau,' he said. 'Knowing you very well by reputation, if that's not an indiscreet remark.'

'Not at all,' answered Flambeau, laughing. 'I am not sensitive. Very few reputations are gained by unsullied virtue.'

The prince flashed a sharp look at him to see if the retort had any personal point; then he laughed also and offered chairs to everyone, including himself.

'Pleasant little place, this, I think,' he said with a detached air. 'Not much to do, I fear; but the fishing is really good.'

The priest, who was staring at him with the grave stare of a baby, was haunted by some fancy that escaped definition. He looked at the grey, carefully curled hair, yellow-white visage, and slim, somewhat foppish figure. These were not unnatural, though perhaps a shade *prononcé*, like the outfit of a figure behind the footlights. The nameless interest lay in something else, in the very framework of the face; Brown was tormented with a half memory of having seen it somewhere before. The man looked like some old friend of his dressed up. Then he suddenly remembered the mirrors, and put his fancy down to some psychological effect of that multiplication of human masks.

Prince Saradine distributed his social attentions between his guests with great gaiety and tact. Finding the detective of a sporting turn and eager to employ his holiday, he guided Flambeau and Flambeau's boat down to the best fishing spot in the stream, and was back in his own canoe in twenty minutes to join Father Brown in the library and plunge equally politely into the priest's more philosophic pleasures. He seemed to know a great deal both about the fishing and the books, though of these not the most edifying; he spoke five or six languages, though chiefly the slang of each. He had evidently lived in varied cities and very motley societies, for some of his cheerfullest stories were about gambling hells and opium dens, Australian bushrangers or Italian brigands. Father Brown knew that the once-celebrated Saradine had spent his last few years in almost ceaseless travel, but he had not guessed that the travels were so disreputable or so amusing.

Indeed, with all his dignity of a man of the world, Prince Saradine radiated, to such sensitive observers as the priest, a certain atmosphere of the restless and even the unreliable. His face was fastidious, but his eye was wild; he had little nervous tricks, like a man shaken by drink or drugs, and he neither had, nor professed to have, his hand on the helm of household affairs. All these were left to the two old servants, especially to the butler, who was plainly the central pillar of the house. Mr Paul, indeed, was not so much a butler as a sort of steward or, even, chamberlain; he dined privately, but with almost as much pomp as his master; he was feared by all the servants; and he consulted with the prince decorously, but somewhat unbendingly – rather as if he were the prince's solicitor. The sombre housekeeper was a mere shadow in comparison; indeed, she seemed to efface herself and wait only on the butler, and Brown heard no more of those volcanic whispers which had half told him of the younger brother who blackmailed the elder. Whether the prince was really being thus bled by the absent captain, he could not be certain, but there was something insecure and secretive about Saradine that made the tale by no means incredible.

When they went once more into the long hall with the windows and the mirrors, yellow evening was dropping over the waters and the willowy banks; and a bittern sounded in the distance like an elf upon his dwarfish drum. The same singular sentiment of some sad and evil fairyland crossed the priest's mind again like a little grey cloud. 'I wish Flambeau were back,' he muttered.

'Do you believe in doom?' asked the restless Prince Saradine suddenly.

'No,' answered his guest. 'I believe in Doomsday.'

The prince turned from the window and stared at him in a singular manner, his face in shadow against the sunset. 'What do you mean?' he asked.

'I mean that we here are on the wrong side of the tapestry,' answered Father Brown. 'The things that happen here do not seem to mean anything; they mean something somewhere else. Somewhere else retribution will come on the real offender. Here it often seems to fall on the wrong person.'

The prince made an inexplicable noise like an animal; in his shadowed face the eyes were shining queerly. A new and shrewd thought exploded silently in the other's mind. Was there another meaning in Saradine's blend of brilliancy and abruptness? Was the prince – Was he perfectly sane? He was repeating, 'The wrong person – the wrong person,' many more times than was natural in a social exclamation.

Then Father Brown awoke tardily to a second truth. In the mirrors before him he could see the silent door standing open, and the silent Mr Paul standing in it, with his usual pallid impassiveness.

'I thought it better to announce at once,' he said, with the same stiff respectfulness as of an old family lawyer, 'a boat rowed by six men has come to the landing-stage, and there's a gentleman sitting in the stern.'

'A boat!' repeated the prince; 'a gentleman?' and he rose to his feet.

There was a startled silence punctuated only by the odd noise of the bird in the sedge; and then, before anyone could speak again, a new face and figure passed in profile round the three sunlit windows, as the prince had passed an hour or two before. But except for the accident that both outlines were aquiline, they had little in common. Instead of the new white topper of Saradine, was a black one of antiquated or foreign shape; under it was a young and very solemn face, clean shaven, blue about its resolute chin, and carrying a faint suggestion of the young Napoleon. The association was assisted by something old and odd about the whole get-up, as of a man who had never troubled to change the fashions of his fathers. He had a shabby blue frock coat, a red, soldierly-looking waistcoat, and a kind of coarse white trousers common among the early Victorians, but strangely incongruous today. From all this old clothes-shop his olive face stood out strangely young and monstrously sincere.

'The deuce!' said Prince Saradine, and clapping on his white hat he went to the front door himself, flinging it open on the sunset garden.

By that time the newcomer and his followers were drawn up on the lawn like a small stage army. The six boatmen had pulled the boat well up on shore, and were guarding it almost menacingly, holding their oars erect like spears. They were swarthy men, and some of them wore earrings. But one of them stood forward beside the olive-faced young man in the red waistcoat, and carried a large black case of unfamiliar form.

'Your name,' said the young man, 'is Saradine?'

Saradine assented rather negligently.

The newcomer had dull, doglike brown eyes, as different as possible from the restless and glittering grey eyes of the prince. But once again Father Brown was tortured with a sense of having seen somewhere a replica of the face; and once again he remembered the repetitions of the glass-panelled room, and put down the coincidence to that. 'Confound this crystal palace!' he muttered. 'One sees everything too many times. It's like a dream.'

'If you are Prince Saradine,' said the young man, 'I may tell you that my name is Antonelli.'

'Antonelli,' repeated the prince languidly. 'Somehow I remember the name.'

'Permit me to present myself,' said the young Italian.

With his left hand he politely took off his old-fashioned top hat; with his right he caught Prince Saradine so ringing a crack across the face that the white top hat rolled down the steps and one of the blue flowerpots rocked upon its pedestal.

The prince, whatever he was, was evidently not a coward; he sprang at his enemy's throat and almost bore him backwards to the grass. But his enemy extricated himself with a singularly inappropriate air of hurried politeness.

'That is all right,' he said, panting and in halting English. 'I have insulted. I will give satisfaction. Marco, open the case.'

The man beside him with the earrings and the big black case proceeded to unlock it. He took out of it two long Italian rapiers, with splendid steel hilts and blades, which he planted point downwards in the lawn. The strange young man standing facing the entrance with his yellow and vindictive face, the two swords standing up in the turf like two crosses in a cemetery, and the line of the ranked towers behind, gave it all an odd appearance of being some barbaric court of justice. But everything else was unchanged, so sudden had been the interruption. The sunset gold still glowed on the lawn, and the bittern still boomed as announcing some small but dreadful destiny.

'Prince Saradine,' said the man called Antonelli, 'when I was an infant in the cradle you killed my father and stole my mother; my father was the more fortunate. You did not kill him fairly, as I am going to kill you. You and my wicked mother took him driving to a lonely pass in Sicily, flung him down a cliff, and went on your way. I could imitate you if I chose, but imitating you is too vile. I have followed you all over the world, and you have always fled from me. But this is the end of the world – and of you. I have you now, and I give you the chance you never gave my father. Choose one of those swords.'

Prince Saradine, with contracted brows, seemed to hesitate a moment, but his ears were still singing with the blow, and he sprang forward and snatched at one of the hilts. Father Brown had also sprung forward, striving to compose the dispute; but he soon found his personal presence made matters worse. Saradine was a French freemason and a fierce atheist, and a priest moved him by the law of contraries. And for the other man neither priest nor layman moved him at all. This young man with the Bonaparte face and the brown eyes was something far sterner than a puritan – a pagan. He was a simple slayer from the morning of the earth; a man of the stone age – a man of stone.

One hope remained, the summoning of the household; and Father Brown ran back into the house. He found, however, that all the under servants had been given a holiday ashore by the autocrat Paul, and that only the sombre

Mrs Anthony moved uneasily about the long rooms. But the moment she turned a ghastly face upon him, he resolved one of the riddles of the house of mirrors. The heavy brown eyes of Antonelli were the heavy brown eyes of Mrs Anthony; and in a flash he saw half the story.

'Your son is outside,' he said without wasting words; 'either he or the prince will be killed. Where is Mr Paul?'

'He is at the landing-stage,' said the woman faintly. 'He is – he is – signalling for help.'

'Mrs Anthony,' said Father Brown seriously, 'there is no time for nonsense. My friend has his boat down the river fishing. Your son's boat is guarded by your son's men. There is only this one canoe; what is Mr Paul doing with it?'

'Santa Maria! I do not know,' she said; and swooned all her length on the matted floor.

Father Brown lifted her to a sofa, flung a pot of water over her, shouted for help, and then rushed down to the landing-stage of the little island. But the canoe was already in midstream, and old Paul was pulling and pushing it up the river with an energy incredible at his years.

'I will save my master,' he cried, his eyes blazing maniacally. 'I will save him yet!'

Father Brown could do nothing but gaze after the boat as it struggled upstream and pray that the old man might waken the little town in time.

'A duel is bad enough,' he muttered, rubbing up his rough dust-coloured hair, 'but there's something wrong about this duel, even as a duel. I feel it in my bones. But what can it be?'

As he stood staring at the water, a wavering mirror of sunset, he heard from the other end of the island garden a small but unmistakable sound – the cold concussion of steel. He turned his head.

Away on the farthest cape or headland of the long islet, on a strip of turf beyond the last rank of roses, the duellists had already crossed swords. Evening above them was a dome of virgin gold, and, distant as they were, every detail was picked out. They had cast off their coats, but the yellow waistcoat and white hair of Saradine, the red waistcoat and white trousers of Antonelli, glittered in the level light like the colours of the dancing clockwork dolls. The two swords sparkled from point to pommel like two diamond pins. There was something frightful in the two figures appearing so little and so gay. They looked like two butterflies trying to pin each other to a cork.

Father Brown ran as hard as he could, his little legs going like a wheel. But when he came to the field of combat he found he was both too late and too early – too late to stop the strife, under the shadow of the grim Sicilians leaning on their oars, and too early to anticipate any disastrous issue of it.

For the two men were singularly well matched, the prince using his skill with a sort of cynical confidence, the Sicilian using his with a murderous care. Few finer fencing matches can ever have been seen in crowded amphitheatres than that which tinkled and sparkled on that forgotten island in the reedy river. The dizzy fight was balanced so long that hope began to revive in the protesting priest; by all common probability Paul must soon come back with the police. It would be some comfort even if Flambeau came back from his fishing, for Flambeau, physically speaking, was worth four other men. But there was no sign of Flambeau, and, what was much queerer, no sign of Paul or the police. No other raft or stick was left to float on; in that lost island in that vast nameless pool, they were cut off as on a rock in the Pacific.

Almost as he had the thought the ringing of the rapiers quickened to a rattle, the prince's arms flew up, and the point shot out behind between his shoulder-blades. He went over with a great whirling movement, almost like one throwing the half of a boy's cartwheel. The sword flew from his hand like a shooting star, and dived into the distant river. And he himself sank with so earth-shaking a subsidence that he broke a big rose tree with his body and shook up into the sky a cloud of red earth – like the smoke of some heathen sacrifice. The Sicilian had made blood-offering to the ghost of his father.

The priest was instantly on his knees by the corpse; but only to make too sure that it was a corpse. As he was still trying some last hopeless tests he heard for the first time voices from farther up the river, and saw a police boat shoot up to the landing-stage, with constables and other important people, including the excited Paul. The little priest rose with a distinctly dubious grimace.

'Now, why on earth,' he muttered, 'why on earth couldn't he have come before?'

Some seven minutes later the island was occupied by an invasion of townsfolk and police, and the latter had put their hands on the victorious duellist, ritually reminding him that anything he said might be used against him.

'I shall not say anything,' said the monomaniac, with a wonderful and peaceful face. 'I shall never say anything more. I am very happy, and I only want to be hanged.'

Then he shut his mouth as they led him away, and it is the strange but certain truth that he never opened it again in this world, except to say 'Guilty' at his trial.

Father Brown had stared at the suddenly crowded garden, the arrest of the man of blood, the carrying away of the corpse after its examination by the doctor, rather as one watches the break-up of some ugly dream; he was motionless, like a man in a nightmare. He gave his name and address as a witness, but declined their offer of a boat to the shore, and remained alone in the island garden, gazing at the broken rose bush and the whole green theatre of that swift and inexplicable tragedy. The light died along the river; mist rose in the marshy banks; a few belated birds flitted fitfully across.

Stuck stubbornly in his subconsciousness (which was an unusually lively one) was an unspeakable certainty that there was something still unexplained. This sense that had clung to him all day could not be fully explained by his fancy about 'looking-glass land'. Somehow he had not seen the real story, but some game or masque. And yet people do not get hanged or run through the body for the sake of a charade.

As he sat on the steps of the landing-stage ruminating he grew conscious of the tall, dark streak of a sail coming silently down the shining river, and sprang to his feet with such a back-rush of feeling that he almost wept.

'Flambeau!' he cried, and shook his friend by both hands again and again, much to the astonishment of that sportsman, as he came on shore with his fishing tackle. 'Flambeau,' he said, 'so you're not killed?'

'Killed!' repeated the angler in great astonishment. 'And why should I be killed?'

'Oh, because nearly everybody else is,' said his companion rather wildly. 'Saradine got murdered, and Antonelli wants to be hanged, and his mother's fainted, and I, for one, don't know whether I'm in this world or the next. But, thank God, you're in the same one.' And he took the bewildered Flambeau's arm.

As they turned from the landing-stage they came under the eaves of the low bamboo house, and looked in through one of the windows, as they had done on their first arrival. They beheld a lamp-lit interior well calculated to arrest their eyes. The table in the long dining-room had been laid for dinner when Saradine's destroyer had fallen like a storm-bolt on the island. And the dinner was now in placid progress, for Mrs Anthony sat somewhat sullenly at the foot of the table, while at the head of it was Mr Paul, the major domo, eating and drinking of the best, his bleared, bluish eyes standing queerly out of his face, his gaunt countenance inscrutable, but by no means devoid of satisfaction.

With a gesture of powerful impatience, Flambeau rattled at the window, wrenched it open, and put an indignant head into the lamp-lit room.

'Well!' he cried. 'I can understand you may need some refreshment, but really to steal your master's dinner while he lies murdered in the garden – '

'I have stolen a great many things in a long and pleasant life,' replied the strange old gentleman placidly; 'this dinner is one of the few things I have not stolen. This dinner and this house and garden happen to belong to me.'

A thought flashed across Flambeau's face. 'You mean to say,' he began, 'that the will of Prince Saradine – '

'I am Prince Saradine,' said the old man, munching a salted almond.

Father Brown, who was looking at the birds outside, jumped as if he were shot, and put in at the window a pale face like a turnip.

'You are what?' he repeated in a shrill voice.

'Paul, Prince Saradine, *à vos ordres*,' said the venerable person politely, lifting a glass of sherry. 'I live here very quietly, being a domestic kind of fellow; and for the sake of modesty I am called Mr Paul, to distinguish me from my unfortunate brother Mr Stephen. He died, I hear, recently – in the garden. Of course, it is not my fault if enemies pursue him to this place. It is owing to the regrettable irregularity of his life. He was not a domestic character.'

He relapsed into silence, and continued to gaze at the opposite wall just above the bowed and sombre head of the woman. They saw plainly the family likeness that had haunted them in the dead man. Then his old shoulders began to heave and shake a little, as if he were choking, but his face did not alter.

'My God!' cried Flambeau after a pause, 'he's laughing!'

'Come away,' said Father Brown, who was quite white. 'Come away from this house of hell. Let us get into an honest boat again.'

Night had sunk on rushes and river by the time they had pushed off from the island, and they went downstream in the dark, warming themselves with two big cigars that glowed like crimson ships' lanterns. Father Brown took his cigar out of his mouth and said: 'I suppose you can guess the whole story now? After all, it's a primitive story. A man had two enemies. He was a wise man. And so he discovered that two enemies are better than one.'

'I do not follow that,' answered Flambeau.

'Oh, it's really simple,' rejoined his friend. 'Simple, though anything but innocent. Both the Saradines were scamps, but the prince, the elder, was the sort of scamp that gets to the top, and the younger, the captain, was the sort that sinks to the bottom. This squalid officer fell from beggar to blackmailer, and one ugly day he got his hold upon his brother, the prince. Obviously it was for no light matter, for Prince Paul Saradine was frankly "fast", and had no reputation to lose as to the mere sins of society. In plain fact, it was a hanging matter, and Stephen literally had a rope round his brother's neck. He had somehow discovered the truth about the Sicilian affair, and could prove that Paul murdered old Antonelli in the mountains. The captain raked in the hush money heavily for ten years, until even the prince's splendid fortune began to look a little foolish.

'But Prince Saradine bore another burden besides his blood-sucking brother. He knew that the son of Antonelli, a mere child at the time of the murder, had been trained in savage Sicilian loyalty, and lived only to avenge his father, not with the gibbet (for he lacked Stephen's legal proof), but with the old weapons of vendetta. The boy had practised arms with a deadly perfection, and about the time that he was old enough to use them Prince Saradine began, as the society papers said, to travel. The fact is that he began to flee for his life, passing from place to place like a hunted criminal; but with one relentless man upon his trail. That was Prince Paul's position, and by no means a pretty one. The more money he spent on eluding Antonelli the less he had to silence Stephen. The more he gave to silence Stephen the less chance there was of finally escaping Antonelli. Then it was that he showed himself a great man – a genius like Napoleon.

'Instead of resisting his two antagonists, he surrendered suddenly to both of them. He gave way like a Japanese wrestler, and his foes fell prostrate before him. He gave up the race round the world, and he gave up his address to young Antonelli; then he gave up everything to his brother. He sent Stephen money enough for smart clothes and easy travel, with a letter saying roughly: "This is all I have left. You have cleaned me out. I still have a little house in Norfolk, with servants and a cellar, and if you want more from me you must take that. Come and take possession if you like, and I will live there quietly as your friend or agent or anything." He knew that the Sicilian had never seen the Saradine brothers save, perhaps, in pictures; he knew they were somewhat alike, both having grey, pointed beards. Then he shaved his own face and waited. The trap worked. The unhappy captain, in his new clothes, entered the house in triumph as a prince, and walked upon the Sicilian's sword.

'There was one hitch, and it is to the honour of human nature. Evil spirits like Saradine often blunder by never expecting the virtues of mankind. He took it for granted that the Italian's blow, when it came, would be dark, violent and nameless, like the blow it avenged; that the victim would be knifed at night, or shot from behind a hedge, and so die without speech. It was a bad minute for Prince Paul when Antonelli's chivalry proposed a formal duel, with all its possible explanations. It was then that I found him putting off in his boat with wild eyes. He was fleeing, bareheaded, in an open boat before Antonelli should learn who he was.

'But, however agitated, he was not hopeless. He knew the adventurer and he knew the fanatic. It was quite probable that Stephen, the adventurer, would hold his tongue, through his mere histrionic pleasure in playing a part, his lust for clinging to his new cosy quarters, his rascal's trust in luck, and his fine fencing. It was certain that Antonelli, the fanatic, would hold his tongue, and be hanged without telling tales of his family. Paul hung about on the river till he knew the fight was over. Then he roused the town, brought the police, saw his two vanquished enemies taken away for ever, and sat down smiling to his dinner.'

'Laughing, God help us!' said Flambeau with a strong shudder. 'Do they get such ideas from Satan?'

'He got that idea from you,' answered the priest.

'God forbid!' ejaculated Flambeau. 'From me! What do you mean!'

The priest pulled a visiting-card from his pocket and held it up in the faint glow of his cigar; it was scrawled with green ink.

'Don't you remember his original invitation to you?' he asked, 'and the compliment to your criminal exploit? "That trick of yours," he says, "of getting one detective to arrest the other?" He has just copied your trick. With an enemy on each side of him, he slipped swiftly out of the way and let them collide and kill each other.'

Flambeau tore Prince Saradine's card from the priest's hands and rent it savagely in small pieces.

'There's the last of that old skull and crossbones,' he said as he scattered the pieces upon the dark and disappearing waves of the stream; 'but I should think it would poison the fishes.'

The last gleam of white card and green ink was drowned and darkened; a faint and vibrant colour as of morning changed the sky, and the moon behind the grasses grew paler. They drifted in silence.

'Father,' said Flambeau suddenly, 'do you think it was all a dream?'

The priest shook his head, whether in dissent or agnosticism, but remained mute. A smell of hawthorn and of orchards came to them through the darkness, telling them that a wind was awake; the next moment it swayed their little boat and swelled their sail, and carried them onward down the winding river to happier places and the homes of harmless men.

The Hammer of God

The little village of Bohun Beacon was perched on a hill so steep that the tall spire of its church seemed only like the peak of a small mountain. At the foot of the church stood a smithy, generally red with fires and always littered with hammers and scraps of iron; opposite to this, over a rude cross of cobbled paths, was the Blue Boar, the only inn of the place. It was upon this crossway, in the lifting of a leaden and silver daybreak, that two brothers met in the street and spoke; though one was beginning the day and the other finishing it. The Revd and Hon. Wilfred Bohun was very devout, and was making his way to some austere exercises of prayer or contemplation at dawn. Colonel the Hon. Norman Bohun, his elder brother, was by no means devout, and was sitting in evening dress on the bench outside the Blue Boar, drinking what the philosophic observer was free to regard either as his last glass on Tuesday or his first on Wednesday. The colonel was not particular.

The Bohuns were one of the very few aristocratic families really dating from the Middle Ages, and their pennon had actually seen Palestine. But it is a great mistake to suppose that such houses stand high in chivalric tradition. Few except the poor preserve traditions. Aristocrats live not in traditions but in fashions. The Bohuns had been Mohocks under Queen Anne and Mashers under Queen Victoria. But like more than one of the really ancient houses, they had rotted in the last two centuries into mere drunkards and dandy degenerates, till there had even come a whisper of insanity. Certainly there was something hardly human about the colonel's wolfish pursuit of pleasure, and his chronic resolution not to go home till morning had a touch of the hideous clarity of insomnia. He was a tall, fine animal, elderly, but with hair still startlingly yellow. He would have looked merely blond and leonine, but his blue eyes were sunk so deep in his face that they looked black. They were a little too close together. He had very long yellow moustaches; on each side of them a fold or furrow from nostril to jaw, so that a sneer seemed cut into his face. Over his evening clothes he wore a curious pale yellow coat that looked more like a very light dressing gown than an overcoat, and on the back of his head was stuck an extraordinary broad-brimmed hat of a bright green colour, evidently some oriental curiosity caught up at random. He was proud of appearing in such incongruous attires – proud of the fact that he always made them look congruous.

His brother the curate had also the yellow hair and the elegance, but he was buttoned up to the chin in black, and his face was clean-shaven, cultivated, and a little nervous. He seemed to live for nothing but his religion; but there were some who said (notably the blacksmith, who was a Presbyterian) that it was a love of Gothic architecture rather than of God, and that his haunting of the church like a ghost was only another and purer turn of the almost morbid thirst for beauty which sent his brother raging after women and wine. This charge was doubtful, while the man's practical piety was indubitable. Indeed, the charge was mostly an ignorant misunderstanding of the love of solitude and secret prayer, and was founded on his being often found kneeling, not before the altar, but in peculiar places, in the crypts or gallery, or even in the belfry. He was at the moment about to enter the church through the yard of the smithy, but stopped and frowned a little as he saw his brother's cavernous eyes staring in the same direction. On the hypothesis that the colonel was interested in the church he did not waste any speculations. There only remained the blacksmith's shop, and though the blacksmith was a Puritan and none of his people, Wilfred Bohun had heard some scandals about a beautiful and rather celebrated wife. He flung a suspicious look across the shed, and the colonel stood up laughing to speak to him.

'Good-morning, Wilfred,' he said. 'Like a good landlord I am watching sleeplessly over my people. I am going to call on the blacksmith.'

Wilfred looked at the ground, and said: 'The blacksmith is out. He is over at Greenford.'

'I know,' answered the other with silent laughter; 'that is why I am calling on him.'

'Norman,' said the cleric, with his eye on a pebble in the road, 'are you ever afraid of thunderbolts?'

'What do you mean?' asked the colonel. 'Is your hobby meteorology?'

'I mean,' said Wilfred, without looking up, 'do you ever think that God might strike you in the street?'

'I beg your pardon,' said the colonel; 'I see your hobby is folklore.'

'I know your hobby is blasphemy,' retorted the religious man, stung in the one live place of his nature. 'But if you do not fear God, you have good reason to fear man.'

The elder raised his eyebrows politely. 'Fear man?' he said.

'Barnes the blacksmith is the biggest and strongest man for forty miles round,' said the clergyman sternly. 'I know you are no coward or weakling, but he could throw you over the wall.'

This struck home, being true, and the lowering line by mouth and nostril darkened and deepened. For a moment he stood with the heavy sneer on his face. But in an instant Colonel Bohun had recovered his own cruel good humour and laughed, showing two doglike front teeth under his yellow moustache. 'In that case, my dear Wilfred,' he said quite carelessly, 'it was wise for the last of the Bohuns to come out partially in armour.'

And he took off the queer round hat covered with green, showing that it was lined within with steel. Wilfred recognised it indeed as a light Japanese or Chinese helmet torn down from a trophy that hung in the old family hall.

'It was the first hat to hand,' explained his brother airily; 'always the nearest hat – and the nearest woman.'

'The blacksmith is away at Greenford,' said Wilfred quietly; 'the time of his return is unsettled.'

And with that he turned and went into the church with bowed head, crossing himself like one who wishes to be quit of an unclean spirit. He was anxious to forget such grossness in the cool twilight of his tall Gothic cloisters; but on that morning it was fated that his still round of religious exercises should be everywhere arrested by small shocks. As he entered the church, hitherto always empty at that hour, a kneeling figure rose hastily to its feet and came towards the full daylight of the doorway. When the curate saw it he stood still with surprise. For the early worshipper was none other than the village idiot, a nephew of the blacksmith, one who neither would nor could care for the church or for anything else. He was always called 'Mad Joe', and seemed to have no other name; he was a dark, strong, slouching lad, with a heavy white face, dark straight hair, and a mouth always open. As he passed the priest, his moon-calf countenance gave no hint of what he had been doing or thinking of. He had never been known to pray before. What sort of prayers was he saying now? Extraordinary prayers surely.

Wilfred Bohun stood rooted to the spot long enough to see the idiot go out into the sunshine, and even to see his dissolute brother hail him with a sort of avuncular jocularity. The last thing he saw was the colonel throwing pennies at the open mouth of Joe, with the serious appearance of trying to hit it.

This ugly sunlit picture of the stupidity and cruelty of the earth sent the ascetic finally to his prayers for purification and new thoughts. He went up to a pew in the gallery, which brought him under a coloured window which he loved and which always quieted his spirit; a blue window with an angel carrying lilies. There he began to think less about the half-wit, with his livid face and mouth like a fish. He began to think less of his evil brother, pacing like a lean lion in his horrible hunger. He sank deeper and deeper into those cold and sweet colours of silver blossoms and sapphire sky.

In this place half an hour afterwards he was found by Gibbs, the village cobbler, who had been sent for him in some haste. He got to his feet with promptitude, for he knew that no small matter would have brought Gibbs into such a place at all. The cobbler was, as in many villages, an atheist, and his appearance in church was a shade more extraordinary than Mad Joe's. It was a morning of theological enigmas.

'What is it?' asked Wilfred Bohun rather stiffly, but putting out a trembling hand for his hat.

The atheist spoke in a tone that, coming from him, was quite startlingly respectful, and even, as it were, huskily sympathetic.

'You must excuse me, sir,' he said in a hoarse whisper, 'but we didn't think it right not to let you know at once. I'm afraid a rather dreadful thing has happened, sir. I'm afraid your brother – '

Wilfred clenched his frail hands. 'What devilry has he done now?' he cried in involuntary passion.

'Why, sir,' said the cobbler, coughing, 'I'm afraid he's done nothing, and won't do anything. I'm afraid he's done for. You had really better come down, sir.'

The curate followed the cobbler down a short winding stair which brought them out at an entrance rather higher than the street. Bohun saw the tragedy in one glance, flat underneath him like a plan. In the yard of the smithy were standing five or six men mostly in black, one in an inspector's uniform. They included the doctor, the Presbyterian minister, and the priest from the Roman Catholic chapel, to which the blacksmith's wife belonged. The latter was speaking to her, indeed, very rapidly, in an undertone, as she, a magnificent woman with red-gold hair, was sobbing blindly on a bench. Between these two groups, and just clear of the main heap of hammers, lay a man in evening dress, spread-eagled and flat on his face. From the height above Wilfred could have sworn to every item of his costume and appearance, down to the Bohun rings upon his fingers; but the skull was only a hideous splash, like a star of blackness and blood.

Wilfred Bohun gave but one glance, and ran down the steps into the yard. The doctor, who was the family physician, saluted him, but he scarcely took any notice. He could only stammer out: 'My brother is dead. What does it mean? What is this horrible mystery?' There was an unhappy silence; and then the cobbler, the most outspoken man present, answered: 'Plenty of horror, sir,' he said; 'but not much mystery.'

'What do you mean?' asked Wilfred, with a white face.

'It's plain enough,' answered Gibbs. 'There is only one man for forty miles round that could have struck such a blow as that, and he's the man that had most reason to.'

'We must not prejudge anything,' put in the doctor, a tall, black-bearded man, rather nervously; 'but it is competent for me to corroborate what Mr Gibbs says about the nature of the blow, sir; it is an incredible blow. Mr Gibbs says that only one man in this district could have done it. I should have said myself that nobody could have done it.'

A shudder of superstition went through the slight figure of the curate. 'I can hardly understand,' he said.

'Mr Bohun,' said the doctor in a low voice, 'metaphors literally fail me. It is inadequate to say that the skull was smashed to bits like an eggshell. Fragments of bone were driven into the body and the ground like bullets into a mud wall. It was the hand of a giant.'

He was silent a moment, looking grimly through his glasses; then he added: 'The thing has one advantage – that it clears most people of suspicion at one stroke. If you or I or any normally made man in the country were accused of this crime, we should be acquitted as an infant would be acquitted of stealing the Nelson Column.'

'That's what I say,' repeated the cobbler obstinately; 'there's only one man that could have done it, and he's the man that would have done it. Where's Simeon Barnes, the blacksmith?'

'He's over at Greenford,' faltered the curate.

'More likely over in France,' muttered the cobbler.

'No; he is in neither of those places,' said a small and colourless voice, which came from the little Roman priest who had joined the group. 'As a matter of fact, he is coming up the road at this moment.'

The little priest was not an interesting man to look at, having stubbly brown hair and a round and stolid face. But if he had been as splendid as Apollo no one would have looked at him at that moment. Everyone turned round and peered at the pathway which wound across the plain below, along which was indeed walking, at his own huge stride and with a hammer on his shoulder, Simeon the smith. He was a bony and gigantic man, with deep, dark, sinister eyes and a dark chin beard. He was walking and talking quietly with two other men; and though he was never specially cheerful, he seemed quite at his ease.

'My God!' cried the atheistic cobbler, 'and there's the hammer he did it with.'

'No,' said the inspector, a sensible-looking man with a sandy moustache, speaking for the first time. 'There's the hammer he did it with over there by the church wall. We have left it and the body exactly as they are.'

All glanced round and the short priest went across and looked down in silence at the tool where it lay. It was one of the smallest and the lightest of the hammers, and would not have caught the eye among the rest; but on the iron edge of it were blood and yellow hair.

After a silence the short priest spoke without looking up, and there was a new note in his dull voice. 'Mr Gibbs was hardly right,' he said, 'in saying that there is no mystery. There is at least the mystery of why so big a man should attempt so big a blow with so little a hammer.'

'Oh, never mind that,' cried Gibbs, in a fever. 'What are we to do with Simeon Barnes?'

'Leave him alone,' said the priest quietly. 'He is coming here of himself. I know those two men with him. They are very good fellows from Greenford, and they have come over about the Presbyterian chapel.'

Even as he spoke the tall smith swung round the corner of the church, and strode into his own yard. Then he stood there quite still, and the hammer fell from his hand. The inspector, who had preserved impenetrable propriety, immediately went up to him.

'I won't ask you, Mr Barnes,' he said, 'whether you know anything about what has happened here. You are not bound to say. I hope you don't know, and that you will be able to prove it. But I must go through the form of arresting you in the King's name for the murder of Colonel Norman Bohun.'

'You are not bound to say anything,' said the cobbler in officious excitement. 'They've got to prove everything. They haven't proved yet that it is Colonel Bohun, with the head all smashed up like that.'

'That won't wash,' said the doctor aside to the priest. 'That's out of the detective stories. I was the colonel's medical man, and I knew his body better than he did. He had very fine hands, but quite peculiar ones. The second and third fingers were the same length. Oh, that's the colonel right enough.'

As he glanced at the brained corpse upon the ground the iron eyes of the motionless blacksmith followed them and rested there also.

'Is Colonel Bohun dead?' said the smith quite calmly. 'Then he's damned.'

'Don't say anything! Oh, don't say anything,' cried the atheist cobbler, dancing about in an ecstasy of admiration of the English legal system. For no man is such a legalist as the good Secularist.

The blacksmith turned on him over his shoulder the august face of a fanatic.

'It's well for you infidels to dodge like foxes because the world's law favours you,' he said; 'but God guards His own in His pocket, as you shall see this day.'

Then he pointed to the colonel and said: 'When did this dog die in his sins?'

'Moderate your language,' said the doctor.

'Moderate the Bible's language, and I'll moderate mine. When did he die?'

'I saw him alive at six o'clock this morning,' stammered Wilfred Bohun.

'God is good,' said the smith. 'Mr Inspector, I have not the slightest objection to being arrested. It is you who may object to arresting me. I don't mind leaving the court without a stain on my character. You do mind perhaps leaving the court with a bad setback in your career.'

The solid inspector for the first time looked at the blacksmith with a lively eye; as did everybody else, except the short, strange priest, who was still looking down at the little hammer that had dealt the dreadful blow.

'There are two men standing outside this shop,' went on the blacksmith with ponderous lucidity, 'good tradesmen in Greenford whom you all know, who will swear that they saw me from before midnight till daybreak and long after in the committee room of our Revival Mission, which sits all night, we save souls so fast. In Greenford itself twenty people could swear to me for all that time. If I were a heathen, Mr Inspector, I would let you walk on to your downfall. But as a Christian man I feel bound to give you your chance, and ask you whether you will hear my alibi now or in court.'

The inspector seemed for the first time disturbed, and said, 'Of course I should be glad to clear you altogether now.'

The smith walked out of his yard with the same long and easy stride, and returned to his two friends from Greenford, who were indeed friends of nearly everyone present. Each of them said a few words which no one ever thought of disbelieving. When they had spoken, the innocence of Simeon stood up as solid as the great church above them.

One of those silences struck the group which are more strange and insufferable than any speech. Madly, in order to make conversation, the curate said to the Catholic priest: 'You seem very much interested in that hammer, Father Brown.'

'Yes, I am,' said Father Brown; 'why is it such a small hammer?'

The doctor swung round on him.

'By George, that's true,' he cried; 'who would use a little hammer with ten larger hammers lying about?'

Then he lowered his voice in the curate's ear and said: 'Only the kind of person that can't lift a large hammer. It is not a question of force or courage between the sexes. It's a question of lifting power in the shoulders. A bold woman could commit ten murders with a light hammer and never turn a hair. She could not kill a beetle with a heavy one.'

Wilfred Bohun was staring at him with a sort of hypnotised horror, while Father Brown listened with his head a little on one side, really interested and attentive. The doctor went on with more hissing emphasis: 'Why do these idiots always assume that the only person who hates the wife's lover is the wife's husband? Nine times out of ten the person who most hates the wife's lover is the wife. Who knows what insolence or treachery he had shown her – look there!'

He made a momentary gesture towards the red-haired woman on the bench. She had lifted her head at last and the tears were drying on her splendid face. But the eyes were fixed on the corpse with an electric glare that had in it something of idiocy.

The Revd Wilfred Bohun made a limp gesture as if waving away all desire to know; but Father Brown, dusting off his sleeve some ashes blown from the furnace, spoke in his indifferent way.

'You are like so many doctors,' he said; 'your mental science is really suggestive. It is your physical science that is utterly impossible. I agree that the woman wants to kill the co-respondent much more than the petitioner does. And I agree that a woman will always pick up a small hammer instead of a big one. But the difficulty is one of physical impossibility. No woman ever born could have smashed a man's skull out flat like that.' Then he added reflectively, after a pause: 'These people haven't grasped the whole of it. The man was actually wearing an iron helmet, and the blow scattered it like broken glass. Look at that woman. Look at her arms.'

Silence held them all up again, and then the doctor said rather sulkily: 'Well, I may be wrong; there are objections to everything. But I stick to the main point. No man but an idiot would pick up that little hammer if he could use a big hammer.'

With that the lean and quivering hands of Wilfred Bohun went up to his head and seemed to clutch his scanty yellow hair. After an instant they dropped, and he cried: 'That was the word I wanted; you have said the word.'

Then he continued, mastering his discomposure: 'The words you said were, "No man but an idiot would pick up the small hammer." '

'Yes,' said the doctor. 'Well?'

'Well,' said the curate, 'no man but an idiot did.' The rest stared at him with eyes arrested and riveted, and he went on in a febrile and feminine agitation.

'I am a priest,' he cried unsteadily, 'and a priest should be no shedder of blood. I – I mean that he should bring no one to the gallows. And I thank God that I see the criminal clearly now – because he is a criminal who cannot be brought to the gallows.'

'You will not denounce him?' enquired the doctor.

'He would not be hanged if I did denounce him,' answered Wilfred with a wild but curiously happy smile. 'When I went into the church this morning I found a madman praying there – that poor Joe, who has been wrong all his life. God knows what he prayed; but with such strange folk it is not incredible to suppose that their prayers are all upside down. Very likely a lunatic would pray before killing a man. When I last saw poor Joe he was with my brother. My brother was mocking him.'

'By Jove!' cried the doctor, 'this is talking at last. But how do you explain – '

The Revd Wilfred was almost trembling with the excitement of his own glimpse of the truth. 'Don't you see; don't you see,' he cried feverishly; 'that is the only theory that covers both the queer things, that answers both the riddles. The two riddles are the little hammer and the big blow. The smith might have struck the big blow, but would not have chosen the little hammer. His wife would have chosen the little hammer, but she could not have struck the big blow. But the madman might have done both. As for the little hammer – why, he was mad and might have picked up anything. And for the big blow, have you never heard, doctor, that a maniac in his paroxysm may have the strength of ten men?'

The doctor drew a deep breath and then said, 'By golly, I believe you've got it.'

Father Brown had fixed his eyes on the speaker so long and steadily as to prove that his large grey, ox-like eyes were not quite so insignificant as the rest of his face. When silence had fallen he said with marked respect: 'Mr Bohun, yours is the only theory yet propounded which holds water every way and is essentially unassailable. I think, therefore, that you deserve to be told, on my positive knowledge, that it is not the true one.' And with that the odd little man walked away and stared again at the hammer.

'That fellow seems to know more than he ought to,' whispered the doctor peevishly to Wilfred. 'Those popish priests are deucedly sly.'

'No, no,' said Bohun, with a sort of wild fatigue. 'It was the lunatic. It was the lunatic.'

The group of the two clerics and the doctor had fallen away from the more official group containing the inspector and the man he had arrested. Now, however, that their own party had broken up, they heard voices from the others. The priest looked up quietly and then looked down again as he heard the blacksmith say in a loud voice: 'I hope I've convinced you, Mr Inspector. I'm a strong man, as you say, but I couldn't have flung my hammer bang here from Greenford. My hammer hasn't got wings that it should come flying half a mile over hedges and fields.'

The inspector laughed amicably and said: 'No, I think you can be considered out of it, though it's one of the rummiest coincidences I ever saw. I can only ask you to give us all the assistance you can in finding a man as big and strong as yourself. By George! you might be useful, if only to hold him! I suppose you yourself have no guess at the man?'

'I may have a guess,' said the pale smith, 'but it is not at a man.' Then, seeing the scared eyes turn towards his wife on the bench, he put his huge hand on her shoulder and said: 'Nor a woman either.'

'What do you mean?' asked the inspector jocularly. 'You don't think cows use hammers, do you?'

'I think no thing of flesh held that hammer,' said the blacksmith in a stifled voice; 'mortally speaking, I think the man died alone.'

Wilfred made a sudden forward movement and peered at him with burning eyes.

'Do you mean to say, Barnes,' came the sharp voice of the cobbler, 'that the hammer jumped up of itself and knocked the man down?'

'Oh, you gentlemen may stare and snigger,' cried Simeon; 'you clergymen who tell us on Sunday in what a stillness the Lord smote Sennacherib. I believe that One who walks invisible in every house defended the honour of mine, and laid the defiler dead before the door of it. I believe the force in that blow was just the force there is in earthquakes, and no force less.'

Wilfred said, with a voice utterly indescribable: 'I told Norman myself to beware of the thunderbolt.'

'That agent is outside my jurisdiction,' said the inspector with a slight smile.

'You are not outside His,' answered the smith; 'see you to it,' and, turning his broad back, he went into the house.

The shaken Wilfred was led away by Father Brown, who had an easy and friendly way with him. 'Let us get out of this horrid place, Mr Bohun,' he said. 'May I look inside your church? I hear it's one of the oldest in England. We take some interest, you know,' he added with a comical grimace, 'in old English churches.'

Wilfred Bohun did not smile, for humour was never his strong point. But he nodded rather eagerly, being only too ready to explain the Gothic splendours to someone more likely to be sympathetic than the Presbyterian blacksmith or the atheist cobbler.

'By all means,' he said; 'let us go in at this side.' And he led the way into the high side entrance at the top of the flight of steps. Father Brown was mounting the first step to follow him when he felt a hand on his shoulder, and turned to behold the dark, thin figure of the doctor, his face darker yet with suspicion.

'Sir,' said the physician harshly, 'you appear to know some secrets in this black business. May I ask if you are going to keep them to yourself?'

'Why, doctor,' answered the priest, smiling quite pleasantly, 'there is one very good reason why a man of my trade should keep things to himself when he is not sure of them, and that is that it is so constantly his duty to keep them to himself when he is sure of them. But if you think I have been discourteously reticent with you or anyone, I will go to the extreme limit of my custom. I will give you two very large hints.'

'Well, sir?' said the doctor gloomily.

'First,' said Father Brown quietly, 'the thing is quite in your own province. It is a matter of physical science. The blacksmith is mistaken, not perhaps in saying that the blow was divine, but certainly in saying that it came by a miracle. It was no miracle, doctor, except in so far as man is himself a miracle, with his strange and wicked and yet half-heroic heart. The force that smashed that skull was a force well known to scientists – one of the most frequently debated of the laws of nature.'

The doctor, who was looking at him with frowning intentness, only said: 'And the other hint?'

'The other hint is this,' said the priest. 'Do you remember the blacksmith, though he believes in miracles, talking scornfully of the impossible fairy tale that his hammer had wings and flew half a mile across country?'

'Yes,' said the doctor, 'I remember that.'

'Well,' added Father Brown, with a broad smile, 'that fairy tale was the nearest thing to the real truth that has been said today.' And with that he turned his back and stumped up the steps after the curate.

The Revd Wilfred, who had been waiting for him, pale and impatient, as if this little delay were the last straw for his nerves, led him immediately to his favourite corner of the church, that part of the gallery closest to the carved roof and lit by the wonderful window with the angel. The little Latin priest explored and admired everything exhaustively, talking cheerfully but in a low voice all the time. When in the course of his investigation he found the side exit and the winding stair down which Wilfred had rushed to find his brother dead, Father Brown ran not down but up, with the agility of a monkey, and his clear voice came from an outer platform above.

'Come up here, Mr Bohun,' he called. 'The air will do you good.'

Bohun followed him, and came out on a kind of stone gallery or balcony outside the building, from which one could see the illimitable plain in which their small hill stood, wooded away to the purple horizon and dotted with villages and farms. Clear and square, but quite small beneath them, was the blacksmith's yard, where the inspector still stood taking notes and the corpse still lay like a smashed fly.

'Might be the map of the world, mightn't it?' said Father Brown.

'Yes,' said Bohun very gravely, and nodded his head.

Immediately beneath and about them the lines of the Gothic building plunged outwards into the void with a sickening swiftness akin to suicide. There is that element of Titan energy in the architecture of the Middle Ages that, from whatever aspect it be seen, it always seems to be rushing away, like the strong back of some maddened horse. This church was hewn out of ancient and silent stone, bearded with old fungoids and stained with the nests of birds. And yet, when they saw it from below, it sprang like a fountain at the stars; and when they saw it, as now, from above, it poured like a cataract into a voiceless pit. For these two men on the tower were left alone with the most terrible aspect of Gothic; the monstrous foreshortening and disproportion, the dizzy perspectives, the glimpses of great things small and small things great; a topsy-turvydom of stone in the mid-air. Details of stone, enormous by their proximity, were relieved against a pattern of fields and farms, pygmy in their distance. A carved bird or beast at a corner seemed like some vast walking or flying dragon wasting the pastures and villages below. The whole atmosphere was dizzy and dangerous, as if men were upheld in air amid the gyrating wings of colossal genii; and the whole of that old church, as tall and rich as a cathedral, seemed to sit upon the sunlit country like a cloudburst.

'I think there is something rather dangerous about standing on these high places even to pray,' said Father Brown. 'Heights were made to be looked at, not to be looked from.'

'Do you mean that one may fall over?' asked Wilfred.

'I mean that one's soul may fall if one's body doesn't,' said the other priest.

'I scarcely understand you,' remarked Bohun indistinctly.

'Look at that blacksmith, for instance,' went on Father Brown calmly; 'a good man, but not a Christian – hard, imperious, unforgiving. Well, his Scotch religion was made up by men who prayed on hills and high crags, and learnt to look down on the world more than to look up at heaven. Humility is the mother of giants. One sees great things from the valley; only small things from the peak.'

'But he – he didn't do it,' said Bohun tremulously.

'No,' said the other in an odd voice; 'we know he didn't do it.'

After a moment he resumed, looking tranquilly out over the plain with his pale grey eyes. 'I knew a man,' he said, 'who began by worshipping with others before the altar, but who grew fond of high and lonely places to pray from, corners or niches in the belfry or the spire. And once in one of those dizzy places, where the whole world seemed to turn under him like a wheel, his brain turned also, and he fancied he was God. So that, though he was a good man, he committed a great crime.'

Wilfred's face was turned away, but his bony hands turned blue and white as they tightened on the parapet of stone.

'He thought it was given to him to judge the world and strike down the sinner. He would never have had such a thought if he had been kneeling with other men upon a floor. But he saw all men walking about like insects. He saw one especially strutting just below him, insolent and evident by a bright green hat – a poisonous insect.'

Rooks cawed round the corners of the belfry; but there was no other sound till Father Brown went on.

'This also tempted him, that he had in his hand one of the most awful engines of nature; I mean gravitation, that mad and quickening rush by which all earth's creatures fly back to her heart when released. See, the inspector is strutting just below us in the smithy. If I were to toss a pebble over this parapet it would be something like a bullet by the time it struck him. If I were to drop a hammer – even a small hammer – '

Wilfred Bohun threw one leg over the parapet, and Father Brown had him in a minute by the collar.

'Not by that door,' he said quite gently; 'that door leads to hell.'

Bohun staggered back against the wall, and stared at him with frightful eyes.

'How do you know all this?' he cried. 'Are you a devil?'

'I am a man,' answered Father Brown gravely; 'and therefore have all devils in my heart. Listen to me,' he said after a short pause. 'I know what you did – at least, I can guess the great part of it. When you left your brother you were racked with no unrighteous rage, to the extent even that you snatched up a small hammer, half inclined to kill him with his foulness on his mouth. Recoiling, you thrust it under your buttoned coat instead, and rushed into the church. You pray wildly in many places, under the angel window, upon the platform above, and a higher platform still, from which you could see the colonel's Eastern hat like the back of a green beetle crawling about. Then something snapped in your soul, and you let God's thunderbolt fall.'

Wilfred put a weak hand to his head, and asked in a low voice: 'How did you know that his hat looked like a green beetle?'

'Oh, that,' said the other with the shadow of a smile, 'that was common sense. But hear me further. I say I know all this; but no one else shall know it. The next step is for you; I shall take no more steps; I will seal this with the seal of confession. If you ask me why, there are many reasons, and only one that concerns you. I leave things to you because you have not yet gone very far wrong, as assassins go. You did not help to fix the crime on the smith when it was easy; or on his wife, when that was easy. You tried to fix it on the imbecile because you knew that he could not suffer. That was one of the gleams that it is my business to find in assassins. And now come down into the village, and go your own way as free as the wind; for I have said my last word.'

They went down the winding stairs in utter silence, and came out into the sunlight by the smithy. Wilfred Bohun carefully unlatched the wooden gate of the yard, and going up to the inspector, said: 'I wish to give myself up; I have killed my brother.'

The Eye of Apollo

That singular smoky sparkle, at once a confusion and a transparency, which is the strange secret of the Thames, was changing more and more from its grey to its glittering extreme as the sun climbed to the zenith over Westminster, and two men crossed Westminster Bridge. One man was very tall and the other very short; they might even have been fantastically compared to the arrogant clock-tower of Parliament and the humbler humped shoulders of the Abbey, for the short man was in clerical dress. The official description of the tall man was M. Hercule Flambeau, private detective, and he was going to his new offices in a new pile of flats facing the Abbey entrance. The official description of the short man was the Revd J. Brown, attached to St Francis Xavier's Church, Camberwell, and he was coming from a Camberwell deathbed to see the new offices of his friend.

The building was American in its sky-scraping altitude, and American also in the oiled elaboration of its machinery of telephones and lifts. But it was barely finished and still understaffed; only three tenants had moved in; the office just above Flambeau was occupied, as also was the office just below him; the two floors above that and the three floors below were entirely bare. But the first glance at the new tower of flats caught something much more arresting. Save for a few relics of scaffolding, the one glaring object was erected outside the office just above Flambeau's. It was an enormous gilt effigy of the human eye, surrounded with rays of gold, and taking up as much room as two or three of the office windows.

'What on earth is that?' asked Father Brown, and stood still.

'Oh, a new religion,' said Flambeau, laughing; 'one of those new religions that forgive your sins by saying you never had any. Rather like Christian Science. The fact is that a fellow calling himself Kalon (I don't know what his name is, except that it can't be that) has taken the flat just above me. I have two lady typewriters underneath me, and this enthusiastic old humbug on top. He calls himself the New Priest of Apollo, and worships the sun.'

'Let him look out,' said Father Brown. 'The sun was the cruellest of all the gods. But what does that monstrous eye mean?'

'As I understand it, it is a theory of theirs,' answered Flambeau, 'that a man can endure anything if his mind is quite steady. Their two great symbols are the sun and the open eye; for they say that if a man were really healthy he could stare at the sun.'

'If a man were really healthy,' said Father Brown, 'he wouldn't bother to stare at it.'

'Well, that's all I can tell you about the new religion,' went on Flambeau carelessly. 'It claims, of course, that it can cure all physical diseases.'

'Can it cure the one spiritual disease?' asked Father Brown, with a serious curiosity.

'And what is the one spiritual disease?' asked Flambeau, smiling.

'Oh, thinking one is quite well,' said his friend.

Flambeau was more interested in the quiet little office below him than in the flamboyant temple above. He was a lucid Southerner, incapable of conceiving himself as anything but a Catholic or an atheist; and new religions of a bright and pallid sort were not much in his line. But humanity was always in his line, especially when it was good-looking; moreover, the ladies downstairs were characters in their way. The office was kept by two sisters, both slight and dark, one of them tall and striking. She had a dark, eager and aquiline profile, and was one of those women whom one always thinks of in profile, as of the clean-cut edge of some weapon. She seemed to cleave her way through life. She had eyes of startling brilliancy, but it was the brilliancy of steel rather than of diamonds; and her straight, slim figure was a shade too stiff for its grace. Her younger sister was like her shortened shadow, a little greyer, paler, and more insignificant. They both wore a businesslike black, with little masculine cuffs and collars. There are thousands of such curt, strenuous ladies in the offices of London, but the interest of these lay rather in their real than their apparent position.

For Pauline Stacey, the elder, was actually the heiress of a crest and half a county, as well as great wealth; she had been brought up in castles and gardens, before a frigid fierceness (peculiar to the modern woman) had driven her to what she considered a harsher and a higher existence. She had not, indeed, surrendered her money; in that there would have been a romantic or monkish abandon quite alien to her masterful utilitarianism. She held her wealth, she would say, for use upon practical social objects. Part of it she had put into her business, the nucleus of a model typewriting emporium; part of it was distributed in various leagues and causes for the advancement of such work among women. How far Joan, her sister and partner, shared this slightly prosaic idealism no one could be very sure. But she followed her leader with a doglike affection which was somehow more attractive, with its touch of tragedy, than the hard, high spirits of the elder. For Pauline Stacey had nothing to say to tragedy; she was understood to deny its existence.

Her rigid rapidity and cold impatience had amused Flambeau very much on the first occasion of his entering the flats. He had lingered outside the lift in the entrance hall waiting for the lift-boy, who generally conducts strangers to the various floors. But this bright-eyed falcon of a girl had openly refused to endure such official delay. She said sharply that she knew all about the lift, and was not dependent on boys – or men either. Though her flat was only three floors above, she managed in the few seconds of ascent to give Flambeau a great many of her fundamental views in an offhand manner; they were to the general effect that she was a modern working woman and loved modern working machinery. Her bright black eyes blazed with abstract anger against those who rebuke mechanic science and ask for the return of romance. Everyone, she said, ought to be able to manage machines, just as she could manage the lift. She seemed almost to resent the fact of Flambeau opening the lift-door for her; and that gentleman went up to his own apartments smiling with somewhat mingled feelings at the memory of such spitfire self-dependence.

She certainly had a temper, of a snappy, practical sort; the gestures of her thin, elegant hands were abrupt or even destructive. Once Flambeau entered her office on some typewriting business, and found she had just flung a pair of spectacles belonging to her sister into the middle of the floor and stamped on them. She was already in the rapids of an ethical tirade about the 'sickly medical notions' and the morbid admission of weakness implied in such an apparatus. She dared her sister to bring such artificial, unhealthy rubbish into the place again. She asked if she was expected to wear wooden legs or false hair or glass eyes; and as she spoke her eyes sparkled like the terrible crystal.

Flambeau, quite bewildered with this fanaticism, could not refrain from asking Miss Pauline (with direct French logic) why a pair of spectacles was a more morbid sign of weakness than a lift, and why, if science might help us in the one effort, it might not help us in the other.

'That is so different,' said Pauline Stacey, loftily. 'Batteries and motors and all those things are marks of the force of man – yes, Mr Flambeau, and the force of woman, too! We shall take our turn at these great engines that devour distance and defy time. That is high and splendid – that is really science. But these nasty props and plasters the doctors sell – why, they are just badges of poltroonery. Doctors stick on legs and arms as if we were born cripples and sick slaves. But I was free-born, Mr Flambeau! People only think they need these things because they have been trained in fear instead of being trained in power and courage, just as the silly nurses tell children not to stare at the sun, and so they can't do it without blinking. But why among the stars should there be one star I may not see? The sun is not my master, and I will open my eyes and stare at him whenever I choose.'

'Your eyes,' said Flambeau, with a foreign bow, 'will dazzle the sun.' He took pleasure in complimenting this strange stiff beauty, partly because it threw her a little off her balance. But as he went upstairs to his floor he drew a deep breath and whistled, saying to himself: 'So she has got into the hands of that conjurer upstairs with his golden eye.' For, little as he knew or cared about the new religion of Kalon, he had heard of his special notion about sun-gazing.

He soon discovered that the spiritual bond between the floors above and below him was close and increasing. The man who called himself Kalon was a magnificent creature, worthy, in a physical sense, to be the pontiff of Apollo. He was nearly as tall even as Flambeau, and very much better looking, with a golden beard, strong blue eyes, and a mane flung back like a lion's. In structure he was the blond beast of Nietzsche, but all this animal beauty was heightened, brightened and softened by genuine intellect and spirituality. If he looked like one of the great Saxon kings, he looked like one of the kings that were also saints. And this despite the cockney incongruity of his surroundings; the fact that he had an office halfway up a building in Victoria Street; that the clerk (a commonplace youth in cuffs and collars) sat in the outer room, between him and the corridor; that his name was on a brass plate, and the gilt emblem of his creed hung above his street, like the advertisement of an oculist. All this vulgarity could not take away from the man called Kalon the vivid oppression and inspiration that came from his soul and body. When all was said, a man in the presence of this quack did feel in the presence of a great man. Even in the loose jacket-suit of linen that he wore as a workshop dress in his office he was a fascinating and formidable figure; and when robed in the white vestments and crowned with the golden circlet, in which he daily saluted the sun, he really looked so splendid that the laughter of the street people sometimes died suddenly on their lips. For three times in the day the new sun-worshipper went out on his little balcony, in the face of all Westminster, to say some litany to his shining lord: once at daybreak, once at sunset, and once at the shock of noon. And it was while the shock of noon still shook faintly from the towers of Parliament and parish church that Father Brown, the friend of Flambeau, first looked up and saw the white priest of Apollo.

Flambeau had seen quite enough of these daily salutations of Phoebus, and plunged into the porch of the tall building without even looking for his clerical friend to follow. But Father Brown, whether from a professional interest in ritual or a strong individual interest in tomfoolery, stopped and stared up at the balcony of the sun-worshipper, just as he might have stopped and stared up at a Punch and Judy. Kalon the Prophet was already erect, with argent garments and uplifted hands, and the sound of his strangely penetrating voice could be heard all the way down the busy street uttering his solar litany. He was already in the middle of it; his eyes were fixed upon the flaming disc. It is doubtful if he saw anything or anyone on this earth; it is substantially certain that he did not see a stunted, round-faced priest who, in the crowd below, looked up at him with blinking eyes. That was perhaps the most startling difference between even these two far-divided men. Father Brown could not look at anything without blinking; but the priest of Apollo could look on the blaze at noon without a quiver of the eyelid.

'O sun,' cried the prophet, 'O star that art too great to be allowed among the stars! O fountain that flowest quietly in that secret spot that is called space. White Father of all white unwearied things, white flames and white flowers and white peaks. Father, who art more innocent than all thy most innocent and quiet children; primal purity, into the peace of which –'

A rush and crash like the reversed rush of a rocket was cloven with a strident and incessant yelling. Five people rushed into the gate of the mansions as three people rushed out, and for an instant they all deafened each other. The sense of some utterly abrupt horror seemed for a moment to fill half the street with bad news – bad news that was all the worse because no one knew what it was. Two figures remained still after the crash of commotion: the fair priest of Apollo on the balcony above, and the ugly priest of Christ below him.

At last the tall figure and titanic energy of Flambeau appeared in the doorway of the mansions and dominated the little mob. Talking at the top of his voice like a fog-horn, he told somebody or anybody to go for a surgeon; and as he turned back into the dark and thronged entrance his friend Father Brown slipped in insignificantly after him. Even as he ducked and dived through the crowd he could still hear the magnificent melody and monotony of the solar priest still calling on the happy god who is the friend of fountains and flowers.

Father Brown found Flambeau and some six other people standing round the enclosed space into which the lift commonly descended. But the lift had not descended. Something else had descended; something that ought to have come by a lift.

For the last four minutes Flambeau had looked down on it; had seen the brained and bleeding figure of that beautiful woman who denied the existence of tragedy. He had never had the slightest doubt that it was Pauline Stacey; and, though he had sent for a doctor, he had not the slightest doubt that she was dead.

He could not remember for certain whether he had liked her or disliked her; there was so much both to like and dislike. But she had been a person to him, and the unbearable pathos of details and habit stabbed him with all the small daggers of bereavement. He remembered her pretty face and priggish speeches with a sudden secret vividness which is all the bitterness of death. In an instant like a bolt from the blue, like a thunderbolt from nowhere, that beautiful and defiant body had been dashed down the open well of the lift to death at the bottom. Was it suicide? With so insolent an optimist it seemed impossible. Was it murder? But who was there in those hardly inhabited flats to murder anybody? In a rush of raucous words, which he meant to be strong and suddenly found weak, he asked where was that fellow Kalon. A voice, habitually heavy, quiet and full, assured him that Kalon for the last fifteen minutes had been away up on his balcony worshipping his god. When Flambeau heard the voice, and felt the hand of Father Brown, he turned his swarthy face and said abruptly: 'Then, if he has been up there all the time, who can have done it?'

'Perhaps,' said the other, 'we might go upstairs and find out. We have half an hour before the police will move.'

Leaving the body of the slain heiress in charge of the surgeons, Flambeau dashed up the stairs to the typewriting office, found it utterly empty, and then dashed up to his own. Having entered that, he abruptly returned with a new and white face to his friend.

'Her sister,' he said, with an unpleasant seriousness, 'her sister seems to have gone out for a walk.'

Father Brown nodded. 'Or, she may have gone up to the office of that sun man,' he said. 'If I were you I should just verify that, and then let us all talk it over in your office. No,' he added suddenly, as if remembering something, 'shall I ever get over that stupidity of mine? Of course, in their office downstairs.'

Flambeau stared; but he followed the little father downstairs to the empty flat of the Staceys, where that impenetrable pastor took a large red-leather chair in the very entrance, from which he could see the stairs and landings, and waited. He did not wait very long. In about four minutes three figures descended the stairs, alike only in their solemnity. The first was Joan Stacey, the sister of the dead woman – evidently she had been upstairs in the temporary temple of Apollo; the second was the priest of Apollo himself, his litany finished, sweeping down the empty stairs in utter magnificence – something in his white robes, beard and parted hair had the look of Doré's Christ leaving the Pretorium; the third was Flambeau, black-browed and somewhat bewildered.

Miss Joan Stacey, dark, with a drawn face and hair prematurely touched with grey, walked straight to her own desk and set out her papers with a practical flap. The mere action rallied everyone else to sanity. If Miss Joan Stacey was a criminal, she was a cool one. Father Brown regarded her for some time with an odd little smile, and then, without taking his eyes off her, addressed himself to somebody else.

'Prophet,' he said, presumably addressing Kalon, 'I wish you would tell me a lot about your religion.'

'I shall be proud to do it,' said Kalon, inclining his still crowned head, 'but I am not sure that I understand.'

'Why, it's like this,' said Father Brown, in his frankly doubtful way. 'We are taught that if a man has really bad first principles, that must be partly his fault. But, for all that, we can make some difference between a man who insults his quite clear conscience and a man with a conscience more or less clouded with sophistries. Now, do you really think that murder is wrong at all?'

'Is this an accusation?' asked Kalon very quietly.

'No,' answered Brown, equally gently, 'it is the speech for the defence.'

In the long and startled stillness of the room the prophet of Apollo slowly rose; and really it was like the rising of the sun. He filled that room with his light and life in such a manner that a man felt he could as easily have filled Salisbury Plain. His robed form seemed to hang the whole room with classic draperies; his epic gesture seemed to extend it into grander perspectives, till the little black figure of the modern cleric seemed to be a fault and an intrusion, a round, black blot upon some splendour of Hellas.

'We meet at last, Caiaphas,' said the prophet. 'Your church and mine are the only realities on this earth. I adore the sun, and you the darkening of the sun; you are the priest of the dying and I of the living God. Your present work of suspicion and slander is worthy of your coat and creed. All your church is but a black police; you are only spies and detectives seeking to tear from men confessions of guilt, whether by treachery or torture. You would convict men of crime, I would convict them of innocence. You would convince them of sin, I would convince them of virtue.

'Reader of the books of evil, one more word before I blow away your baseless nightmares for ever. Not even faintly could you understand how little I care whether you can convict me or no. The things you call disgrace and horrible hanging are to me no more than an ogre in a child's toy-book to a man once grown up. You said you were offering the speech for the defence. I care so little for the cloud-land of this life that I will offer you the speech for the prosecution. There is but one thing that can be said against me in this matter, and I will say it myself. The woman that is dead was my love and my bride; not after such manner as your tin chapels call lawful, but by a law purer and sterner than you will ever understand. She and I walked another world from yours, and trod palaces of crystal while you were plodding through tunnels and corridors of brick. Well, I know that policemen, theological and otherwise, always fancy that where there has been love there must soon be hatred; so there you have the first point made for the prosecution. But the second point is stronger; I do not grudge it you. Not only is it true that Pauline loved me, but it is also true that this very morning, before she died, she wrote at that table a will leaving me and my new church half a million. Come, where are the handcuffs? Do you suppose I care what foolish things you do with me? Penal servitude will only be like waiting for her at a wayside station. The gallows will only be going to her in a headlong car.'

He spoke with the brain-shaking authority of an orator, and Flambeau and Joan Stacey stared at him in amazed admiration. Father Brown's face seemed to express nothing but extreme distress; he looked at the ground with one wrinkle of pain across his forehead. The prophet of the sun leaned easily against the mantelpiece and resumed: 'In a few words I have put before you the whole case against me – the only possible case against me. In fewer words still I will blow it to pieces, so that not a trace of it remains. As to whether I have committed this crime, the truth is in one sentence: I could not have committed this crime. Pauline Stacey fell from this floor to the ground at five minutes past twelve. A hundred people will go into the witness-box and say that I was standing out upon the balcony of my own rooms above from just before the stroke of noon to a quarter-past – the usual period of my public prayers. My clerk (a respectable youth from Clapham, with no sort of connection with me) will swear that he sat in my outer office all the morning, and that no communication passed through. He will swear that I arrived a full ten minutes before the hour, fifteen minutes before any whisper of the accident, and that I did not leave the office or the balcony all that time. No one ever had so complete an alibi; I could subpoena half Westminster. I think you had better put the handcuffs away again. The case is at an end.

'But last of all, that no breath of this idiotic suspicion remain in the air, I will tell you all you want to know. I believe I do know how my unhappy friend came by her death. You can, if you choose, blame me for it, or my faith and philosophy at least; but you certainly cannot lock me up. It is well known to all students of the higher truths that certain adepts and illuminati have in history attained the power of levitation – that is, of being self-sustained upon the empty air. It is but a part of that general conquest of matter which is the main element in our occult wisdom. Poor Pauline was of an impulsive and ambitious temper. I think, to tell the truth, she thought herself somewhat deeper in the mysteries than she was; and she has often said to me, as we went down in the lift together, that if one's will were strong enough, one could float down as harmlessly as a feather. I solemnly believe that in some ecstasy of noble thoughts she attempted the miracle. Her will, or faith, must have failed her at the crucial instant, and the lower law of matter had its horrible revenge. There is the whole story, gentlemen, very sad and, as you think, very presumptuous and wicked, but certainly not criminal or in any way connected with me. In the shorthand of the police-courts, you had better call it suicide. I shall always call it heroic failure for the advance of science and the slow scaling of heaven.'

It was the first time Flambeau had ever seen Father Brown vanquished. He still sat looking at the ground, with a painful and corrugated brow, as if in shame. It was impossible to avoid the feeling which the prophet's winged words had fanned, that here was a sullen, professional suspecter of men overwhelmed by a prouder and purer spirit of natural liberty and health. At last he said, blinking as if in bodily distress: 'Well, if that is so, sir, you need do no more than take the testamentary paper you spoke of and go. I wonder where the poor lady left it.'

'It will be over there on her desk by the door, I think,' said Kalon, with that massive innocence of manner that seemed to acquit him wholly. 'She told me specially she would write it this morning, and I actually saw her writing as I went up in the lift to my own room.'

'Was her door open then?' asked the priest, with his eye on the corner of the matting.

'Yes,' said Kalon calmly.

'Ah! it has been open ever since,' said the other, and resumed his silent study of the mat.

'There is a paper over here,' said the grim Miss Joan, in a somewhat singular voice. She had passed over to her sister's desk by the doorway, and was holding a sheet of blue foolscap in her hand. There was a sour smile on her face that seemed unfit for such a scene or occasion, and Flambeau looked at her with a darkening brow.

Kalon the prophet stood away from the paper with that loyal unconsciousness that had carried him through. But Flambeau took it out of the lady's hand, and read it with the utmost amazement. It did, indeed, begin in the formal manner of a will, but after the words 'I give and bequeath all of which I die possessed' the writing abruptly stopped with a set of scratches, and there was no trace of the name of any legatee. Flambeau, in wonder, handed this truncated testament to his clerical friend, who glanced at it and silently gave it to the priest of the sun.

An instant afterwards that pontiff, in his splendid sweeping draperies, had crossed the room in two great strides, and was towering over Joan Stacey, his blue eyes standing from his head.

'What monkey tricks have you been playing here?' he cried. 'That's not all Pauline wrote.'

They were startled to hear him speak in quite a new voice, with a Yankee shrillness in it; all his grandeur and good English had fallen from him like a cloak.

'That is the only thing on her desk,' said Joan, and confronted him steadily with the same smile of evil favour.

Of a sudden the man broke out into blasphemies and cataracts of incredulous words. There was something shocking about the dropping of his mask; it was like a man's real face falling off.

'See here!' he cried in broad American, when he was breathless with cursing, 'I may be an adventurer, but I guess you're a murderess. Yes, gentlemen, here's your death explained, and without any levitation. The poor girl is writing a will in my favour; her cursed sister comes in, struggles for the pen, drags her to the well, and throws her down before she can finish it. Sakes! I reckon we want the handcuffs after all.'

'As you have truly remarked,' replied Joan, with ugly calm, 'your clerk is a very respectable young man, who knows the nature of an oath; and he will swear in any court that I was up in your office arranging some typewriting work for five minutes before and five minutes after my sister fell. Mr Flambeau will tell you that he found me there.'

There was a silence.

'Why, then,' cried Flambeau, 'Pauline was alone when she fell, and it was suicide!'

'She was alone when she fell,' said Father Brown, 'but it was not suicide.'

'Then how did she die?' asked Flambeau impatiently.

'She was murdered.'

'But she was alone,' objected the detective.

'She was murdered when she was all alone,' answered the priest.

All the rest stared at him, but he remained sitting in the same old dejected attitude, with a wrinkle in his round forehead and an appearance of impersonal shame and sorrow; his voice was colourless and sad.

'What I want to know,' cried Kalon, with an oath, 'is when the police are coming for this bloody and wicked sister. She's killed her flesh and blood; she's robbed me of half a million that was just as sacredly mine as – '

'Come, come, prophet,' interrupted Flambeau, with a kind of sneer; 'remember that all this world is a cloud-land.'

The hierophant of the sun-god made an effort to climb back on his pedestal. 'It is not the mere money,' he cried, 'though that would equip the cause throughout the world. It is also my beloved one's wishes. To Pauline all this was holy. In Pauline's eyes – '

Father Brown suddenly sprang erect, so that his chair fell over flat behind him. He was deathly pale, yet he seemed fired with a hope; his eyes shone.

'That's it!' he cried in a clear voice. 'That's the way to begin. In Pauline's eyes – '

The tall prophet retreated before the tiny priest in an almost mad disorder. 'What do you mean? How dare you?' he cried repeatedly.

'In Pauline's eyes,' repeated the priest, his own shining more and more. 'Go on – in God's name, go on. The foulest crime the fiends ever prompted feels lighter after confession; and I implore you to confess. Go on, go on – in Pauline's eyes – '

'Let me go, you devil!' thundered Kalon, struggling like a giant in bonds. 'Who are you, you cursed spy, to weave your spiders' webs round me, and peep and peer? Let me go.'

'Shall I stop him?' asked Flambeau, bounding towards the exit, for Kalon had already thrown the door wide open.

'No; let him pass,' said Father Brown, with a strange deep sigh that seemed to come from the depths of the universe. 'Let Cain pass by, for he belongs to God.'

There was a long-drawn silence in the room when he had left it, which was to Flambeau's fierce wits one long agony of interrogation. Miss Joan Stacey very coolly tidied up the papers on her desk.

'Father,' said Flambeau at last, 'it is my duty, not my curiosity only – it is my duty to find out, if I can, who committed the crime.'

'Which crime?' asked Father Brown.

'The one we are dealing with, of course,' replied his impatient friend.

'We are dealing with two crimes,' said Brown, 'crimes of very different weight – and by very different criminals.'

Miss Joan Stacey, having collected and put away her papers, proceeded to lock up her drawer. Father Brown went on, noticing her as little as she noticed him.

'The two crimes,' he observed, 'were committed against the same weakness of the same person, in a struggle for her money. The author of the larger crime found himself thwarted by the smaller crime; the author of the smaller crime got the money.'

'Oh, don't go on like a lecturer,' groaned Flambeau; 'put it in a few words.'

'I can put it in one word,' answered his friend.

Miss Joan Stacey skewered her businesslike black hat on to her head with a businesslike black frown before a little mirror, and, as the conversation proceeded, took her handbag and umbrella in an unhurried style, and left the room.

'The truth is one word, and a short one,' said Father Brown. 'Pauline Stacey was blind.'

'Blind!' repeated Flambeau, and rose slowly to his whole huge stature.

'She was subject to it by blood,' Brown proceeded. 'Her sister would have started eyeglasses if Pauline would have let her; but it was her special philosophy or fad that one must not encourage such diseases by yielding to them. She would not admit the cloud; or she tried to dispel it by will. So her eyes got worse and worse with straining; but the worst strain was to come. It came with this precious prophet, or whatever he calls himself, who taught her to stare at the hot sun with the naked eye. It was called accepting Apollo. Oh, if these new pagans would only be old pagans, they would be a little wiser! The old pagans knew that mere naked Nature-worship must have a cruel side. They knew that the eye of Apollo can blast and blind.'

There was a pause, and the priest went on in a gentle and even broken voice. 'Whether or no that devil deliberately made her blind, there is no doubt that he deliberately killed her through her blindness. The very simplicity of the crime is sickening. You know he and she went up and down in those lifts without official help; you know also how smoothly and silently the lifts slide. Kalon brought the lift to the girl's landing, and saw her, through the open door, writing in her slow, sightless way the will she had promised him. He called out to her cheerily that he had the lift ready for her, and she was to come out when she was ready. Then he pressed a button and shot soundlessly up to his own floor, walked through his own office, out on to his own balcony, and was safely praying before the crowded street when the poor girl, having finished her work, ran gaily out to where lover and lift were to receive her, and stepped – '

'Don't!' cried Flambeau.

'He ought to have got half a million by pressing that button,' continued the little father, in the colourless voice in which he talked of such horrors. 'But that went smash. It went smash because there happened to be another person who also wanted the money, and who also knew the secret about poor Pauline's sight. There was one thing about that will that I think nobody noticed: although it was unfinished and without signature, the other Miss Stacey and some servant of hers had already signed it as witnesses. Joan had signed first, saying Pauline could finish it later, with a typical feminine contempt for legal forms. Therefore, Joan wanted her sister to sign the will without real witnesses. Why? I thought of the blindness, and felt sure she had wanted Pauline to sign in solitude because she had wanted her not to sign at all.

'People like the Staceys always use fountain pens; but this was specially natural to Pauline. By habit and her strong will and memory she could still write almost as well as if she saw; but she could not tell when her pen needed dipping. Therefore, her fountain pens were carefully filled by her sister – all except this fountain pen. This was carefully not filled by her sister; the remains of the ink held out for a few lines and then failed altogether. And the prophet lost five hundred thousand pounds and committed one of the most brutal and brilliant murders in human history for nothing.'

Flambeau went to the open door and heard the official police ascending the stairs. He turned and said: 'You must have followed everything devilish close to have traced the crime to Kalon in ten minutes.'

Father Brown gave a sort of start.

'Oh! to him,' he said. 'No; I had to follow rather close to find out about Miss Joan and the fountain pen. But I knew Kalon was the criminal before I came into the front door.'

'You must be joking!' cried Flambeau.

'I'm quite serious,' answered the priest. 'I tell you I knew he had done it, even before I knew what he had done.'

'But why?'

'These pagan stoics,' said Brown reflectively, 'always fail by their strength. There came a crash and a scream down the street, and the priest of Apollo did not start or look round. I did not know what it was. But I knew that he was expecting it.'

The Sign of the Broken Sword

The thousand arms of the forest were grey, and its million fingers silver. In a sky of dark green-blue-like slate the stars were bleak and brilliant like splintered ice. All that thickly wooded and sparsely tenanted countryside was stiff with a bitter and brittle frost. The black hollows between the trunks of the trees looked like bottomless, black caverns of that Scandinavian hell, a hell of incalculable cold. Even the square stone tower of the church looked northern to the point of heathenry, as if it were some barbaric tower among the sea rocks of Iceland. It was a queer night for anyone to explore a churchyard. But, on the other hand, perhaps it was worth exploring.

It rose abruptly out of the ashen wastes of forest in a sort of hump or shoulder of green turf that looked grey in the starlight. Most of the graves were on a slant, and the path leading up to the church was as steep as a staircase. On the top of the hill, in the one flat and prominent place, was the monument for which the place was famous. It contrasted strangely with the featureless graves all round, for it was the work of one of the greatest sculptors of modern Europe; and yet his fame was at once forgotten in the fame of the man whose image he had made. It showed, by touches of the small silver pencil of starlight, the massive metal figure of a soldier recumbent, the strong hands sealed in an everlasting worship, the great head pillowed upon a gun. The venerable face was bearded, or rather whiskered, in the old, heavy Colonel Newcome fashion. The uniform, though suggested with the few strokes of simplicity, was that of modern war. By his right side lay a sword, of which the tip was broken off; on the left side lay a Bible. On glowing summer afternoons wagonettes came full of Americans and cultured suburbans to see the sepulchre; but even then they felt the vast forest land with its one dumpy dome of churchyard and church as a place oddly dumb and neglected. In this freezing darkness of midwinter one would think he might be left alone with the stars. Nevertheless, in the stillness of those stiff woods a wooden gate creaked, and two dim figures dressed in black climbed up the little path to the tomb.

So faint was that frigid starlight that nothing could have been traced about them except that while they both wore black, one man was enormously big, and the other (perhaps by contrast) almost startlingly small. They went up to the great graven tomb of the historic warrior, and stood for a few minutes staring at it. There was no human, perhaps no living, thing for a wide circle; and a morbid fancy might well have wondered if they were human themselves. In any case, the beginning of their conversation might have seemed strange.

After the first silence the small man said to the other: 'Where does a wise man hide a pebble?'

And the tall man answered in a low voice: 'On the beach.'

The small man nodded, and after a short silence said: 'Where does a wise man hide a leaf?'

And the other answered: 'In the forest.'

There was another stillness, and then the tall man resumed: 'Do you mean that when a wise man has to hide a real diamond he has been known to hide it among sham ones?'

'No, no,' said the little man with a laugh, 'we will let bygones be bygones.'

He stamped his cold feet for a second or two, and then said: 'I'm not thinking of that at all, but of something else; something rather peculiar. Just strike a match, will you?'

The big man fumbled in his pocket, and soon a scratch and a flare painted gold the whole flat side of the monument. On it was cut in black letters the well-known words which so many Americans had reverently read: 'Sacred to the Memory of General Sir Arthur St Clare, Hero and Martyr, who Always Vanquished his Enemies and Always Spared Them, and Was Treacherously Slain by Them at Last. May God in Whom he Trusted both Reward and Revenge him.'

The match burnt the big man's fingers, blackened, and dropped. He was about to strike another, but his small companion stopped him. 'That's all right, Flambeau, old man; I saw what I wanted. Or, rather, I didn't see what I didn't want. And now we must walk a mile and a half along the road to the next inn, and I will try to tell you all about it. For Heaven knows a man should have a fire and ale when he dares tell such a story.'

They descended the precipitous path, they relatched the rusty gate, and set off at a stamping, ringing walk down the frozen forest road. They had gone a full quarter of a mile before the smaller man spoke again. He said: 'Yes; the wise man hides a pebble on the beach. But what does he do if there is no beach? Do you know anything of that great St Clare trouble?'

'I know nothing about English generals, Father Brown,' answered the large man, laughing, 'though a little about English policemen. I only know that you have dragged me a precious long dance to all the shrines of this fellow, whoever he is. One would think he got buried in six different places. I've seen a memorial to General St Clare in Westminster Abbey. I've seen a ramping equestrian statue of General St Clare on the Embankment. I've seen a medallion of St Clare in the street he was born in, and another in the street he lived in; and now you drag me after dark to his coffin in the village churchyard. I am beginning to be a bit tired of his magnificent personality, especially as I don't in the least know who he was. What are you hunting for in all these crypts and effigies?'

'I am only looking for one word,' said Father Brown. 'A word that isn't there.'

'Well,' asked Flambeau; 'are you going to tell me anything about it?'

'I must divide it into two parts,' remarked the priest. 'First there is what everybody knows; and then there is what I know. Now, what everybody knows is short and plain enough. It is also entirely wrong.'

'Right you are,' said the big man called Flambeau cheerfully. 'Let's begin at the wrong end. Let's begin with what everybody knows, which isn't true.'

'If not wholly untrue, it is at least very inadequate,' continued Brown; 'for in point of fact, all that the public knows amounts precisely to this: the public knows that Arthur St Clare was a great and successful English general. It knows that after splendid yet careful campaigns both in India and Africa he was in command against Brazil when the great Brazilian patriot Olivier issued his ultimatum. It knows that on that occasion St Clare with a very small force attacked Olivier with a very large one, and was captured after heroic resistance. And it knows that after his capture, and to the abhorrence of the civilised world, St Clare was hanged on the nearest tree. He was found swinging there after the Brazilians had retired, with his broken sword hung round his neck.'

'And that popular story is untrue?' suggested Flambeau.

'No,' said his friend quietly, 'that story is quite true, so far as it goes.'

'Well, I think it goes far enough!' said Flambeau; 'but if the popular story is true, what is the mystery?'

They had passed many hundreds of grey and ghostly trees before the little priest answered. Then he bit his finger reflectively and said: 'Why, the mystery is a mystery of psychology. Or, rather, it is a mystery of two psychologies. In that Brazilian business two of the most famous men of modern history acted flat against their characters. Mind you, Olivier and St Clare were both heroes – the old thing, and no mistake; it was like the fight between Hector and Achilles. Now, what would you say to an affair in which Achilles was timid and Hector was treacherous?'

'Go on,' said the large man impatiently as the other bit his finger again.

'Sir Arthur St Clare was a soldier of the old religious type – the type that saved us during the Mutiny,' continued Brown. 'He was always more for duty than for dash; and with all his personal courage was decidedly a prudent commander, particularly indignant at any needless waste of soldiers. Yet in this last battle he attempted something that a baby could see was absurd. One need not be a strategist to see it was as wild as wind; just as one need not be a strategist to keep out of the way of a motor bus. Well, that is the first mystery; what had become of the English general's head? The second riddle is, what had become of the Brazilian general's heart? President Olivier might be called a visionary or a nuisance; but even his enemies admitted that he was magnanimous to the point of knight errantry. Almost every other prisoner he had ever captured had been set free or even loaded with benefits. Men who had really wronged him came away touched by his simplicity and sweetness. Why the deuce should he diabolically revenge himself only once in his life; and that for the one particular blow that could not have hurt him? Well, there you have it. One of the wisest men in the world acted like an idiot for no reason. One of the best men in the world acted like a fiend for no reason. That's the long and the short of it; and I leave it to you, my boy.'

'No, you don't,' said the other with a snort. 'I leave it to you; and you jolly well tell me all about it.'

'Well,' resumed Father Brown, 'it's not fair to say that the public impression is just what I've said, without adding that two things have happened since. I can't say they threw a new light; for nobody can make sense of them. But they threw a new kind of darkness; they threw the darkness in new directions. The first was this. The family physician of the St Clares quarrelled with that family, and began publishing a violent series of articles, in which he said that the late general was a religious maniac; but as far as the tale went, this seemed to mean little more than a religious man.

'Anyhow, the story fizzled out. Everyone knew, of course, that St Clare had some of the eccentricities of puritan piety. The second incident was much more arresting. In the luckless and unsupported regiment which made that rash attempt at the Black River there was a certain Captain Keith, who was at that time engaged to St Clare's daughter, and who afterwards married her. He was one of those who were captured by Olivier, and, like all the rest except the general, appears to have been bounteously treated and promptly set free. Some twenty years afterwards this man, then Lieutenant-Colonel Keith, published a sort of autobiography called "A British Officer in Burmah and Brazil". In the place where the reader looks eagerly for some account of the mystery of St Clare's disaster may be found the following words: "Everywhere else in this book I have narrated things exactly as they occurred, holding as I do the old-fashioned opinion that the glory of England is old enough to take care of itself. The exception I shall make is in this matter of the defeat by the Black River; and my reasons, though private, are honourable and compelling. I will, however, add this in justice to the memories of two distinguished men. General St Clare has been accused of incapacity on this occasion; I can at least testify that this action, properly understood, was one of the most brilliant and sagacious of his life. President Olivier by similar report is charged with savage injustice. I think it due to the honour of an enemy to say that he acted on this occasion with even more than his characteristic good feeling. To put the matter popularly, I can assure my countrymen that St Clare was by no means such a fool nor Olivier such a brute as he looked. This is all I have to say; nor shall any earthly consideration induce me to add a word to it." '

A large frozen moon like a lustrous snowball began to show through the tangle of twigs in front of them, and by its light the narrator had been able to refresh his memory of Captain Keith's text from a scrap of printed paper. As he folded it up and put it back in his pocket Flambeau threw up his hand with a French gesture.

'Wait a bit, wait a bit,' he cried excitedly. 'I believe I can guess it at the first go.'

He strode on, breathing hard, his black head and bull neck forward, like a man winning a walking race. The little priest, amused and interested, had some trouble in trotting beside him. Just before them the trees fell back a little to left and right, and the road swept downwards across a clear, moonlit valley, till it dived again like a rabbit into the wall of another wood. The entrance to the farther forest looked small and round, like the black hole of a remote railway tunnel. But it was within some hundred yards, and gaped like a cavern before Flambeau spoke again.

'I've got it,' he cried at last, slapping his thigh with his great hand. 'Four minutes' thinking, and I can tell your whole story myself.'

'All right,' assented his friend. 'You tell it.'

Flambeau lifted his head, but lowered his voice. 'General Sir Arthur St Clare,' he said, 'came of a family in which madness was hereditary; and his whole aim was to keep this from his daughter, and even, if possible, from his future son-in-law. Rightly or wrongly, he thought the final collapse was close, and resolved on suicide. Yet ordinary suicide would blazon the very idea he dreaded. As the campaign approached the clouds came thicker on his brain; and at last in a mad moment he sacrificed his public duty to his private. He rushed rashly into battle, hoping to fall by the first shot. When he found that he had only attained capture and discredit, the sealed bomb in his brain burst, and he broke his own sword and hanged himself.'

He stared firmly at the grey façade of forest in front of him, with the one black gap in it, like the mouth of the grave, into which their path plunged. Perhaps something menacing in the road thus suddenly swallowed reinforced his vivid vision of the tragedy, for he shuddered.

'A horrid story,' he said.

'A horrid story,' repeated the priest with bent head. 'But not the real story.'

Then he threw back his head with a sort of despair and cried: 'Oh, I wish it had been.'

The tall Flambeau faced round and stared at him.

'Yours is a clean story,' cried Father Brown, deeply moved. 'A sweet, pure, honest story, as open and white as that moon. Madness and despair are innocent enough. There are worse things, Flambeau.'

Flambeau looked up wildly at the moon thus invoked; and from where he stood one black tree-bough curved across it exactly like a devil's horn.

'Father – father,' cried Flambeau with the French gesture and stepping yet more rapidly forward, 'do you mean it was worse than that?'

'Worse than that,' said the other like a grave echo. And they plunged into the black cloister of the woodland, which ran by them in a dim tapestry of trunks, like one of the dark corridors in a dream.

They were soon in the most secret entrails of the wood, and felt close about them foliage that they could not see, when the priest said again: 'Where does a wise man hide a leaf? In the forest. But what does he do if there is no forest?'

'Well, well,' cried Flambeau irritably, 'what does he do?'

'He grows a forest to hide it in,' said the priest in an obscure voice. 'A fearful sin.'

'Look here,' cried his friend impatiently, for the dark wood and the dark saying got a little on his nerves; 'will you tell me this story or not? What other evidence is there to go on?'

'There are three more bits of evidence,' said the other, 'that I have dug up in holes and corners; and I will give them in logical rather than chronological order. First of all, of course, our authority for the issue and event of the battle is in Olivier's own dispatches, which are lucid enough. He was entrenched with two or three regiments on the heights that swept down to the Black River, on the other side of which was lower and more marshy ground. Beyond this again was gently rising country, on which was the first English outpost, supported by others which lay, however, considerably in its rear. The British forces as a whole were greatly superior in numbers; but this particular regiment was just far enough from its base to make Olivier consider the project of crossing the river to cut it off. By sunset, however, he had decided to retain his own position, which was a specially strong one. At daybreak next morning he was thunderstruck to see that this stray handful of English, entirely unsupported from their rear, had flung themselves across the river, half by a bridge to the right, and the other half by a ford higher up, and were massed upon the marshy bank below him.

'That they should attempt an attack with such numbers against such a position was incredible enough; but Olivier noticed something yet more extraordinary. For instead of attempting to seize more solid ground, this mad regiment, having put the river in its rear by one wild charge, did nothing more, but stuck there in the mire like flies in treacle. Needless to say, the Brazilians blew great gaps in them with artillery, which they could only return with spirited but lessening rifle fire. Yet they never broke; and

Olivier's curt account ends with a strong tribute of admiration for the mystic valour of these imbeciles. "Our line then advanced finally," writes Olivier, "and drove them into the river; we captured General St Clare himself and several other officers. The colonel and the major had both fallen in the battle. I cannot resist saying that few finer sights can have been seen in history than the last stand of this extraordinary regiment; wounded officers picking up the rifles of dead soldiers, and the general himself facing us on horseback bareheaded and with a broken sword." On what happened to the general afterwards Olivier is as silent as Captain Keith.'

'Well,' grunted Flambeau, 'get on to the next bit of evidence.'

'The next evidence,' said Father Brown, 'took some time to find, but it will not take long to tell. I found at last in an almshouse down in the Lincolnshire Fens an old soldier who not only was wounded at the Black River, but had actually knelt beside the colonel of the regiment when he died. This latter was a certain Colonel Clancy, a big bull of an Irishman; and it would seem that he died almost as much of rage as of bullets. He, at any rate, was not responsible for that ridiculous raid; it must have been imposed on him by the general. His last edifying words, according to my informant, were these: "And there goes the damned old donkey with the end of his sword knocked off. I wish it was his head." You will remark that everyone seems to have noticed this detail about the broken sword blade, though most people regard it somewhat more reverently than did the late Colonel Clancy. And now for the third fragment.'

Their path through the woodland began to go upward, and the speaker paused a little for breath before he went on. Then he continued in the same businesslike tone: 'Only a month or two ago a certain Brazilian official died in England, having quarrelled with Olivier and left his country. He was a well-known figure both here and on the Continent, a Spaniard named Espado; I knew him myself, a yellow-faced old dandy, with a hooked nose. For various private reasons I had permission to see the documents he had left; he was a Catholic, of course, and I had been with him towards the end. There was nothing of his that lit up any corner of the black St Clare business, except five or six common exercise books filled with the diary of some English soldier. I can only suppose that it was found by the Brazilians on one of those that fell. Anyhow, it stopped abruptly the night before the battle.

'But the account of that last day in the poor fellow's life was certainly worth reading. I have it on me; but it's too dark to read it here, and I will give you a résumé. The first part of that entry is full of jokes, evidently flung about among the men, about somebody called the Vulture. It does not seem as if this person, whoever he was, was one of themselves, nor even an Englishman; neither is he exactly spoken of as one of the enemy. It sounds rather as if he were some local go-between and non-combatant; perhaps a guide or a journalist. He has been closeted with old Colonel Clancy; but is more often seen talking to the major. Indeed, the major is somewhat prominent in this soldier's narrative; a lean, dark-haired man, apparently, of the name of Murray – a north of Ireland man and a Puritan. There are continual jests about the contrast between this Ulsterman's austerity and the conviviality of Colonel Clancy. There is also some joke about the Vulture wearing bright-coloured clothes.

'But all these levities are scattered by what may well be called the note of a bugle. Behind the English camp and almost parallel to the river ran one of the few great roads of that district. Westward the road curved round towards the river, which it crossed by the bridge before mentioned. To the east the road swept backwards into the wilds, and some two miles along it was the next English outpost. From this direction there came along the road that evening a glitter and clatter of light cavalry, in which even the simple diarist could recognise with astonishment the general with his staff. He rode the great white horse which you have seen so often in illustrated papers and Academy pictures; and you may be sure that the salute they gave him was not merely ceremonial. He, at least, wasted no time on ceremony, but, springing from the saddle immediately, mixed with the group of officers, and fell into emphatic though confidential speech. What struck our friend the diarist most was his special disposition to discuss matters with Major Murray; but, indeed, such a selection, so long as it was not marked, was in no way unnatural. The two men were made for sympathy; they were men who "read their Bibles"; they were both the old Evangelical type of officer. However this may be, it is certain that when the general mounted again he was still talking earnestly to Murray; and that as he walked his horse slowly down the road towards the river, the tall Ulsterman still walked by his bridle rein in earnest debate. The soldiers watched the two until they vanished behind a clump of trees where the road turned towards the river. The colonel had gone back to his tent, and the men to their pickets; the man with the diary lingered for another four minutes, and saw a marvellous sight.

'The great white horse which had marched slowly down the road, as it had marched in so many processions, flew back, galloping up the road towards them as if it were mad to win a race. At first they thought it had run away with the man on its back; but they soon saw that the general, a fine rider, was himself urging it to full speed. Horse and man swept up to them like a whirlwind; and then, reining up the reeling charger, the general turned on them a face like flame, and called for the colonel like the trumpet that wakes the dead.

'I conceive that all the earthquake events of that catastrophe tumbled on top of each other rather like lumber in the minds of men such as our friend with the diary. With the dazed excitement of a dream, they found themselves falling – literally falling – into their ranks, and learned that an attack was to be led at once across the river. The general and the major, it was said, had found out something at the bridge, and there was only just time to strike for life. The major had gone back at once to call up the reserve along the road behind; it was doubtful if even with that prompt appeal help could reach them in time. But they must pass the stream that night, and seize the heights by morning. It is with the very stir and throb of that romantic nocturnal march that the diary suddenly ends.'

Father Brown had mounted ahead; for the woodland path grew smaller, steeper, and more twisted, till they felt as if they were ascending a winding staircase. The priest's voice came from above out of the darkness.

'There was one other little and enormous thing. When the general urged them to their chivalric charge he half drew his sword from the scabbard; and then, as if ashamed of such melodrama, thrust it back again. The sword again, you see.'

A half-light broke through the network of boughs above them, flinging the ghost of a net about their feet; for they were mounting again to the faint luminosity of the naked night. Flambeau felt truth all round him as an atmosphere, but not as an idea. He answered with bewildered brain: 'Well, what's the matter with the sword? Officers generally have swords, don't they?'

'They are not often mentioned in modern war,' said the other dispassionately; 'but in this affair one falls over the blessed sword everywhere.'

'Well, what is there in that?' growled Flambeau; 'it was a twopence coloured sort of incident; the old man's blade breaking in his last battle. Anyone might bet the papers would get hold of it, as they have. On all these tombs and things it's shown broken at the point. I hope you haven't dragged me through this Polar expedition merely because two men with an eye for a picture saw St Clare's broken sword.'

'No,' cried Father Brown, with a sharp voice like a pistol shot; 'but who saw his unbroken sword?'

'What do you mean?' cried the other, and stood still under the stars. They had come abruptly out of the grey gates of the wood.

'I say, who saw his unbroken sword?' repeated Father Brown obstinately. 'Not the writer of the diary, anyhow; the general sheathed it in time.'

Flambeau looked about him in the moonlight, as a man struck blind might look in the sun; and his friend went on, for the first time with eagerness: 'Flambeau,' he cried, 'I cannot prove it, even after hunting through the tombs. But I am sure of it. Let me add just one more tiny fact that tips the whole thing over. The colonel, by a strange chance, was one of the first struck by a bullet. He was struck long before the troops came to close quarters. But he saw St Clare's sword broken. Why was it broken? How was it broken? My friend, it was broken before the battle.'

'Oh!' said his friend, with a sort of forlorn jocularity; 'and pray where is the other piece?'

'I can tell you,' said the priest promptly. 'In the north-east corner of the cemetery of the Protestant Cathedral at Belfast.'

'Indeed?' enquired the other. 'Have you looked for it?'

'I couldn't,' replied Brown, with frank regret. 'There's a great marble monument on top of it; a monument to the heroic Major Murray, who fell fighting gloriously at the famous Battle of the Black River.'

Flambeau seemed suddenly galvanised into existence. 'You mean,' he cried hoarsely, 'that General St Clare hated Murray, and murdered him on the field of battle because – '

'You are still full of good and pure thoughts,' said the other. 'It was worse than that.'

'Well,' said the large man, 'my stock of evil imagination is used up.'

The priest seemed really doubtful where to begin, and at last he said again: 'Where would a wise man hide a leaf? In the forest.'

The other did not answer.

'If there were no forest, he would make a forest. And if he wished to hide a dead leaf, he would make a dead forest.'

There was still no reply, and the priest added still more mildly and quietly: 'And if a man had to hide a dead body, he would make a field of dead bodies to hide it in.'

Flambeau began to stamp forward with an intolerance of delay in time or space; but Father Brown went on as if he were continuing the last sentence: 'Sir Arthur St Clare, as I have already said, was a man who read his Bible. That was what was the matter with him. When will people understand that it is useless for a man to read his Bible unless he also reads everybody else's Bible? A printer reads a Bible for misprints. A Mormon reads his Bible, and finds polygamy; a Christian Scientist reads his, and finds we have no arms and legs. St Clare was an old Anglo-Indian Protestant soldier. Now, just think what that might mean; and, for Heaven's sake, don't cant about it. It might mean a man physically formidable living under a tropic sun in an Oriental society, and soaking himself without sense or guidance in an Oriental book. Of course, he read the Old Testament rather than the New. Of course, he found in the Old Testament anything that he wanted – lust, tyranny, treason. Oh, I dare say he was honest, as you call it. But what is the good of a man being honest in his worship of dishonesty?

'In each of the hot and secret countries to which the man went he kept a harem, he tortured witnesses, he amassed shameful gold; but certainly he would have said with steady eyes that he did it to the glory of the Lord. My own theology is sufficiently expressed by asking which Lord? Anyhow, there is this about such evil, that it opens door after door in hell, and always into smaller and smaller chambers. This is the real case against crime, that a man does not become wilder and wilder, but only meaner and meaner. St Clare was soon suffocated by difficulties of bribery and blackmail; and needed more and more cash. And by the time of the Battle of the Black River he had fallen from world to world to that place which Dante makes the lowest floor of the universe.'

'What do you mean?' asked his friend again.

'I mean that,' retorted the cleric, and suddenly pointed at a puddle sealed with ice that shone in the moon. 'Do you remember whom Dante put in the last circle of ice?'

'The traitors,' said Flambeau, and shuddered. As he looked around at the inhuman landscape of trees, with taunting and almost obscene outlines, he could almost fancy he was Dante, and the priest with the rivulet of a voice was, indeed, a Virgil leading him through a land of eternal sins.

The voice went on: 'Olivier, as you know, was quixotic, and would not permit a secret service and spies. The thing, however, was done, like many other things, behind his back. It was managed by my old friend Espado; he was the bright-clad fop, whose hook nose got him called the Vulture. Posing as a sort of philanthropist at the front, he felt his way through the English Army, and at last got his fingers on its one corrupt man – please God! – and that man at the top. St Clare was in foul need of money, and mountains of it. The discredited family doctor was threatening those extraordinary exposures that afterwards began and were broken off; tales of monstrous and prehistoric things in Park Lane; things done by an English Evangelical that smelt like human sacrifice and hordes of slaves. Money was wanted, too, for his daughter's dowry; for to him the fame of wealth was as sweet as wealth itself. He snapped the last thread, whispered the word to Brazil, and wealth poured in from the enemies of England. But another man had talked to Espado the Vulture as well as he. Somehow the dark, grim young major from Ulster had guessed the hideous truth; and when they walked slowly together down that road towards the bridge Murray was telling the general that he must resign instantly, or be court-martialled and shot. The general temporised with him till they came to the fringe of tropic trees by the bridge; and there by the singing river and the sunlit palms (for I can see the picture) the general drew his sabre and plunged it through the body of the major.'

The wintry road curved over a ridge in cutting frost, with cruel black shapes of bush and thicket; but Flambeau fancied that he saw beyond it faintly the edge of an aureole that was not starlight and moonlight, but some fire such as is made by men. He watched it as the tale drew to its close.

'St Clare was a hell-hound, but he was a hound of breed. Never, I'll swear, was he so lucid and so strong as when poor Murray lay a cold lump at his feet. Never in all his triumphs, as Captain Keith said truly, was the great man so great as he was in this last world-despised defeat. He looked coolly at his weapon to wipe off the blood; he saw the point he had planted between his victim's shoulders had broken off in the body. He saw quite calmly, as through a club windowpane, all that must follow. He saw that men must find the unaccountable corpse; must extract the unaccountable sword-point; must notice the unaccountable broken sword – or absence of sword. He had killed, but not silenced. But his imperious intellect rose against the facer; there was one way yet. He could make the corpse less unaccountable. He could create a hill of corpses to cover this one. In twenty minutes eight hundred English soldiers were marching down to their death.'

The warmer glow behind the black winter wood grew richer and brighter, and Flambeau strode on to reach it. Father Brown also quickened his stride; but he seemed merely absorbed in his tale.

'Such was the valour of that English thousand, and such the genius of their commander, that if they had at once attacked the hill, even their mad march might have met some luck. But the evil mind that played with them like pawns had other aims and reasons. They must remain in the marshes by the bridge at least till British corpses should be a common sight there. Then for the last grand scene; the silver-haired soldier-saint would give up his shattered sword to save further slaughter. Oh, it was well organised for an impromptu. But I think (I cannot prove), I think that it was while they stuck there in the bloody mire that someone doubted – and someone guessed.'

He was mute a moment, and then said: 'There is a voice from nowhere that tells me the man who guessed was the lover . . . the man to wed the old man's child.'

'But what about Olivier and the hanging?' asked Flambeau.

'Olivier, partly from chivalry, partly from policy, seldom encumbered his march with captives,' explained the narrator. 'He released everybody in most cases. He released everybody in this case.'

'Everybody but the general,' said the tall man.

'Everybody,' said the priest.

Flambeau knit his black brows. 'I don't grasp it all yet,' he said.

'There is another picture, Flambeau,' said Brown in his more mystical undertone. 'I can't prove it; but I can do more – I can see it. There is a camp breaking up on the bare, torrid hills at morning, and Brazilian uniforms massed in blocks and columns to march. There is the red shirt and long black beard of Olivier, which blows as he stands, his broad-brimmed hat in his hand. He is saying farewell to the great enemy he is setting free – the simple, snow-headed English veteran, who thanks him in the name of his men. The English remnant stand behind at attention; beside them are stores and vehicles for the retreat. The drums roll; the Brazilians are moving; the English are still like statues. So they abide till the last hum and flash of the enemy have faded from the tropic horizon. Then they alter their postures all at once, like dead men coming to life; they turn their fifty faces upon the general – faces not to be forgotten.'

Flambeau gave a great jump. 'Ah,' he cried, 'you don't mean – '

'Yes,' said Father Brown in a deep, moving voice. 'It was an English hand that put the rope round St Clare's neck; I believe the hand that put the ring on his daughter's finger. They were English hands that dragged him up to the tree of shame; the hands of men that had adored him and followed him to victory. And they were English souls (God pardon and endure us all!) who stared at him swinging in that foreign sun on the green gallows of palm, and prayed in their hatred that he might drop off it into hell.'

As the two topped the ridge there burst on them the strong scarlet light of a red-curtained English inn. It stood sideways in the road, as if standing aside in the amplitude of hospitality. Its three doors stood open with invitation; and even where they stood they could hear the hum and laughter of humanity happy for a night.

'I need not tell you more,' said Father Brown. 'They tried him in the wilderness and destroyed him; and then, for the honour of England and of his daughter, they took an oath to seal up for ever the story of the traitor's purse and the assassin's sword blade. Perhaps – Heaven help them – they tried to forget it. Let us try to forget it, anyhow; here is our inn.'

'With all my heart,' said Flambeau, and was just striding into the bright, noisy bar when he stepped back and almost fell on the road.

'Look there, in the devil's name!' he cried, and pointed rigidly at the square wooden sign that overhung the road. It showed dimly the crude shape of a sabre hilt and a shortened blade; and was inscribed in false archaic lettering, 'The Sign of the Broken Sword'.

'Were you not prepared?' asked Father Brown gently. 'He is the god of this country; half the inns and parks and streets are named after him and his story.'

'I thought we had done with the leper,' cried Flambeau, and spat on the road.

'You will never have done with him in England,' said the priest, looking down, 'while brass is strong and stone abides. His marble statues will erect the souls of proud, innocent boys for centuries, his village tomb will smell of loyalty as of lilies. Millions who never knew him shall love him like a father – this man whom the last few that knew him dealt with like dung. He shall be a saint; and the truth shall never be told of him, because I have made up my mind at last. There is so much good and evil in breaking secrets, that I put my conduct to a test. All these newspapers will perish; the anti-Brazil boom is already over; Olivier is already honoured everywhere. But I told myself that if anywhere, by name, in metal or marble that will endure like the pyramids, Colonel Clancy, or Captain Keith, or President Olivier, or any innocent man was wrongly blamed, then I would speak. If it were only that St Clare was wrongly praised, I would be silent. And I will.'

They plunged into the red-curtained tavern, which was not only cosy, but even luxurious inside. On a table stood a silver model of the tomb of St Clare, the silver head bowed, the silver sword broken. On the walls were coloured photographs of the same scene, and of the system of wagonettes that took tourists to see it. They sat down on the comfortable padded benches.

'Come, it's cold,' cried Father Brown; 'let's have some wine or beer.'

'Or brandy,' said Flambeau.

The Three Tools of Death

Both by calling and conviction Father Brown knew better than most of us that every man is dignified when he is dead. But even he felt a pang of incongruity when he was knocked up at daybreak and told that Sir Aaron Armstrong had been murdered. There was something absurd and unseemly about secret violence in connection with so entirely entertaining and popular a figure. For Sir Aaron Armstrong was entertaining to the point of being comic; and popular in such a manner as to be almost legendary. It was like hearing that Sunny Jim had hanged himself; or that Mr Pickwick had died in Hanwell. For though Sir Aaron was a philanthropist, and thus dealt with the darker side of our society, he prided himself on dealing with it in the brightest possible style. His political and social speeches were cataracts of anecdotes and 'loud laughter'; his bodily health was of a bursting sort; his ethics were all optimism; and he dealt with the Drink problem (his favourite topic) with that immortal or even monotonous gaiety which is so often a mark of the prosperous total abstainer.

The established story of his conversion was familiar on the more puritanic platforms and pulpits, how he had been, when only a boy, drawn away from Scotch theology to Scotch whisky, and how he had risen out of both and become (as he modestly put it) what he was. Yet his wide white beard, cherubic face, and sparkling spectacles, at the numberless dinners and congresses where they appeared, made it hard to believe, somehow, that he had ever been anything so morbid as either a dram-drinker or a Calvinist. He was, one felt, the most seriously merry of all the sons of men.

He had lived on the rural skirt of Hampstead in a handsome house, high but not broad, a modern and prosaic tower. The narrowest of its narrow sides overhung the steep green bank of a railway, and was shaken by passing trains. Sir Aaron Armstrong, as he boisterously explained, had no nerves. But if the train had often given a shock to the house, that morning the tables were turned, and it was the house that gave a shock to the train.

The engine slowed down and stopped just beyond that point where an angle of the house impinged upon the sharp slope of turf. The arrest of most mechanical things must be slow; but the living cause of this had been very rapid. A man clad completely in black, even (it was remembered) to the dreadful detail of black gloves, appeared on the ridge above the engine, and waved his black hands like some sable windmill. This in itself would hardly have stopped even a lingering train. But there came out of him a cry which was talked of afterwards as something utterly unnatural and new. It was one of those shouts that are horridly distinct even when we cannot hear what is shouted. The word in this case was 'Murder!'

But the engine-driver swears he would have pulled up just the same if he had heard only the dreadful and definite accent and not the word.

The train once arrested, the most superficial stare could take in many features of the tragedy. The man in black on the green bank was Sir Aaron Armstrong's manservant Magnus. The baronet in his optimism had often laughed at the black gloves of this dismal attendant; but no one was likely to laugh at him just now.

So soon as an enquirer or two had stepped off the line and across the smoky hedge, they saw, rolled down almost to the bottom of the bank, the body of an old man in a yellow dressing-gown with a very vivid scarlet lining. A scrap of rope seemed caught about his leg, entangled presumably in a struggle. There was a smear or so of blood, though very little; but the body was bent or broken into a posture impossible to any living thing. It was Sir Aaron Armstrong. A few more bewildered moments brought out a big fair-bearded man, whom some travellers could salute as the dead man's secretary, Patrick Royce, once well known in Bohemian society and even famous in the Bohemian arts. In a manner more vague, but even more convincing, he echoed the agony of the servant. By the time the third figure of that household, Alice Armstrong, daughter of the dead man, had come already tottering and waving into the garden, the engine-driver had put a stop to his stoppage. The whistle had blown and the train had panted on to get help from the next station.

Father Brown had been thus rapidly summoned at the request of Patrick Royce, the big ex-Bohemian secretary. Royce was an Irishman by birth; and that casual kind of Catholic that never remembers his religion until he is really in a hole. But Royce's request might have been less promptly complied with if one of the official detectives had not been a friend and admirer of the unofficial Flambeau; and it was impossible to be a friend of Flambeau without hearing numberless stories about Father Brown. Hence, while the young detective (whose name was Merton) led the little priest across the fields to the railway, their talk was more confidential than could be expected between two total strangers.

'As far as I can see,' said Mr Merton candidly, 'there is no sense to be made of it at all. There is nobody one can suspect. Magnus is a solemn old fool; far too much of a fool to be an assassin. Royce has been the baronet's best friend for years; and his daughter undoubtedly adored him. Besides, it's all too absurd. Who would kill such a cheery old chap as Armstrong? Who could dip his hands in the gore of an after-dinner speaker? It would be like killing Father Christmas.'

'Yes, it was a cheery house,' assented Father Brown. 'It was a cheery house while he was alive. Do you think it will be cheery now he is dead?'

Merton started a little and regarded his companion with an enlivened eye. 'Now he is dead?' he repeated.

'Yes,' continued the priest stolidly, 'he was cheerful. But did he communicate his cheerfulness? Frankly, was anyone else in the house cheerful but he?'

A window in Merton's mind let in that strange light of surprise in which we see for the first time things we have known all along. He had often been to the Armstrongs', on little police jobs of the philanthropist; and, now he came to think of it, it was in itself a depressing house. The rooms were very high and very cold; the decoration mean and provincial; the draughty corridors were lit by electricity that was bleaker than moonlight. And though the old man's scarlet face and silver beard had blazed like a bonfire in each room or passage in turn, it did not leave any warmth behind it. Doubtless this spectral discomfort in the place was partly due to the very vitality and exuberance of its owner; he needed no stoves or lamps, he would say, but carried his own warmth with him. But when Merton recalled the other inmates, he was compelled to confess that they also were as shadows of their lord. The moody manservant, with his monstrous black gloves, was almost a nightmare; Royce, the secretary, was solid enough, a big bull of a man, in tweeds, with a short beard; but the straw-coloured beard was startlingly salted with grey like the tweeds, and the broad forehead was barred with premature wrinkles. He was good-natured enough also, but it was a sad sort of good-nature, almost a heart-broken sort – he had the general air of being some sort of failure in life. As for Armstrong's daughter, it was almost incredible that she was his daughter; she was so pallid in colour and sensitive in outline. She was graceful, but there was a quiver in the very shape of her that was like the lines of an aspen. Merton had sometimes wondered if she had learnt to quail at the crash of the passing trains.

'You see,' said Father Brown, blinking modestly, 'I'm not sure that the Armstrong cheerfulness is so very cheerful – for other people. You say that nobody could kill such a happy old man, but I'm not sure; *ne nos inducas in tentationem*. If ever I murdered somebody,' he added quite simply, 'I dare say it might be an Optimist.'

'Why?' cried Merton, amused, 'Do you think people dislike cheerfulness?'

'People like frequent laughter,' answered Father Brown, 'but I don't think they like a permanent smile. Cheerfulness without humour is a very trying thing.'

They walked some way in silence along the windy grassy bank by the rail, and just as they came under the far-flung shadow of the tall Armstrong house, Father Brown said suddenly, like a man throwing away a troublesome thought rather than offering it seriously: 'Of course, drink is neither good nor bad in itself. But I can't help sometimes feeling that men like Armstrong want an occasional glass of wine to sadden them.'

Merton's official superior, a grizzled and capable detective named Gilder, was standing on the green bank waiting for the coroner, talking to Patrick Royce, whose big shoulders and bristly beard and hair towered above him. This was the more noticeable because Royce walked always with a sort of powerful stoop, and seemed to be going about his small clerical and domestic duties in a heavy and humbled style, like a buffalo drawing a go-cart.

He raised his head with unusual pleasure at the sight of the priest, and took him a few paces apart. Meanwhile Merton was addressing the older detective respectfully indeed, but not without a certain boyish impatience.

'Well, Mr Gilder, have you got much farther with the mystery?'

'There is no mystery,' replied Gilder, as he looked under dreamy eyelids at the rooks.

'Well, there is for me, at any rate,' said Merton, smiling.

'It is simple enough, my boy,' observed the senior investigator, stroking his grey, pointed beard. 'Three minutes after you'd gone for Mr Royce's parson the whole thing came out. You know that pasty-faced servant in the black gloves who stopped the train?'

'I should know him anywhere. Somehow he rather gave me the creeps.'

'Well,' drawled Gilder, 'when the train had gone on again, that man had gone too. Rather a cool criminal, don't you think, to escape by the very train that went off for the police?'

'You're pretty sure, I suppose,' remarked the young man, 'that he really did kill his master?'

'Yes, my son, I'm pretty sure,' replied Gilder drily, 'for the trifling reason that he has gone off with twenty thousand pounds in papers that were in his master's desk. No, the only thing worth calling a difficulty is how he killed him. The skull seems broken as with some big weapon, but there's no weapon at all lying about, and the murderer would have found it awkward to carry it away, unless the weapon was too small to be noticed.'

'Perhaps the weapon was too big to be noticed,' said the priest, with an odd little giggle.

Gilder looked round at this wild remark, and rather sternly asked Brown what he meant.

'Silly way of putting it, I know,' said Father Brown apologetically. 'Sounds like a fairy tale. But poor Armstrong was killed with a giant's club, a great green club, too big to be seen, and which we call the earth. He was broken against this green bank we are standing on.'

'How do you mean?' asked the detective quickly.

Father Brown turned his moon face up to the narrow façade of the house and blinked hopelessly up. Following his eyes, they saw that right at the top of this otherwise blind back quarter of the building, an attic window stood open.

'Don't you see,' he explained, pointing a little awkwardly like a child, 'he was thrown down from there?'

Gilder frowningly scrutinised the window, and then said: 'Well, it is certainly possible. But I don't see why you are so sure about it.'

Brown opened his grey eyes wide. 'Why,' he said, 'there's a bit of rope round the dead man's leg. Don't you see that other bit of rope up there caught at the corner of the window?'

At that height the thing looked like the faintest particle of dust or hair, but the shrewd old investigator was satisfied. 'You're quite right, sir,' he said to Father Brown; 'that is certainly one to you.'

Almost as he spoke a special train with one carriage took the curve of the line on their left, and, stopping, disgorged another group of policemen, in whose midst was the hangdog visage of Magnus, the absconded servant.

'By Jove! they've got him,' cried Gilder, and stepped forward with quite a new alertness.

'Have you got the money?' he cried to the first policeman.

The man looked him in the face with a rather curious expression and said: 'No.' Then he added: 'At least, not here.'

'Which is the inspector, please?' asked the man called Magnus.

When he spoke everyone instantly understood how this voice had stopped a train. He was a dull-looking man with flat black hair, a colourless face, and a faint suggestion of the East in the level slits in his eyes and mouth. His blood and name, indeed, had remained dubious, ever since Sir Aaron had 'rescued' him from a waitership in a London restaurant, and (as some said) from more infamous things. But his voice was as vivid as his face was dead. Whether through exactitude in a foreign language, or in deference to his master (who had been somewhat deaf), Magnus's tones had a peculiarly ringing and piercing quality, and the whole group quite jumped when he spoke.

'I always knew this would happen,' he said aloud with brazen blandness. 'My poor old master made game of me for wearing black; but I always said I should be ready for his funeral.'

And he made a momentary movement with his two dark-gloved hands.

'Sergeant,' said Inspector Gilder, eyeing the black hands with wrath, 'aren't you putting the bracelets on this fellow? He looks pretty dangerous.'

'Well, sir,' said the sergeant, with the same odd look of wonder, 'I don't know that we can.'

'What do you mean?' asked the other sharply. 'Haven't you arrested him?'

A faint scorn widened the slit-like mouth, and the whistle of an approaching train seemed oddly to echo the mockery.

'We arrested him,' replied the sergeant gravely, 'just as he was coming out of the police station at Highgate, where he had deposited all his master's money in the care of Inspector Robinson.'

Gilder looked at the manservant in utter amazement. 'Why on earth did you do that?' he asked of Magnus.

'To keep it safe from the criminal, of course,' replied that person placidly.

'Surely,' said Gilder, 'Sir Aaron's money might have been safely left with Sir Aaron's family.'

The tail of his sentence was drowned in the roar of the train as it went rocking and clanking; but through all the hell of noises to which that unhappy house was periodically subject, they could hear the syllables of Magnus's answer, in all their bell-like distinctness: 'I have no reason to feel confidence in Sir Aaron's family.'

All the motionless men had the ghostly sensation of the presence of some new person; and Merton was scarcely surprised when he looked up and saw the pale face of Armstrong's daughter over Father Brown's shoulder. She was still young and beautiful in a silvery style, but her hair was of so dusty and hueless a brown that in some shadows it seemed to have turned totally grey.

'Be careful what you say,' said Royce gruffly, 'you'll frighten Miss Armstrong.'

'I hope so,' said the man with the clear voice.

As the woman winced and everyone else wondered, he went on: 'I am somewhat used to Miss Armstrong's tremors. I have seen her trembling off and on for years. And some said she was shaking with cold and some she was shaking with fear, but I know she was shaking with hate and wicked anger – fiends that have had their feast this morning. She would have been away by now with her lover and all the money but for me. Ever since my poor old master prevented her from marrying that tipsy blackguard – '

'Stop,' said Gilder very sternly. 'We have nothing to do with your family fancies or suspicions. Unless you have some practical evidence, your mere opinions – '

'Oh! I'll give you practical evidence,' cut in Magnus, in his hacking accent. 'You'll have to subpoena me, Mr Inspector, and I shall have to tell the truth. And the truth is this: an instant after the old man was pitched bleeding out of the window, I ran into the attic, and found his daughter swooning on the floor with a red dagger still in her hand. Allow me to hand that also to the proper authorities.' He took from his tail-pocket a long horn-hilted knife with a red smear on it, and handed it politely to the sergeant. Then he stood back again, and his slits of eyes almost faded from his face in one fat Chinese sneer.

Merton felt an almost bodily sickness at the sight of him; and he muttered to Gilder: 'Surely you would take Miss Armstrong's word against his?'

Father Brown suddenly lifted a face so absurdly fresh that it looked somehow as if he had just washed it. 'Yes,' he said, radiating innocence, 'but is Miss Armstrong's word against his?'

The girl uttered a startled, singular little cry; everyone looked at her. Her figure was rigid as if paralysed; only her face within its frame of faint brown hair was alive with an appalling surprise. She stood like one of a sudden lassooed and throttled.

'This man,' said Mr Gilder gravely, 'actually says that you were found grasping a knife, insensible, after the murder.'

'He says the truth,' answered Alice.

The next fact of which they were conscious was that Patrick Royce strode with his great stooping head into their ring and uttered the singular words: 'Well, if I've got to go, I'll have a bit of pleasure first.'

His huge shoulder heaved and he sent an iron fist smash into Magnus's bland Mongolian visage, laying him on the lawn as flat as a starfish. Two or three of the police instantly put their hands on Royce; but to the rest it seemed as if all reason had broken up and the universe were turning into a brainless harlequinade.

'None of that, Mr Royce,' Gilder had called out authoritatively. 'I shall arrest you for assault.'

'No, you won't,' answered the secretary in a voice like an iron gong, 'you will arrest me for murder.'

Gilder threw an alarmed glance at the man knocked down; but since that outraged person was already sitting up and wiping a little blood off a substantially uninjured face, he only said shortly: 'What do you mean?'

'It is quite true, as this fellow says,' explained Royce, 'that Miss Armstrong fainted with a knife in her hand. But she had not snatched the knife to attack her father, but to defend him.'

'To defend him,' repeated Gilder gravely. 'Against whom?'

'Against me,' answered the secretary.

Alice looked at him with a complex and baffling face; then she said in a low voice: 'After it all, I am still glad you are brave.'

'Come upstairs,' said Patrick Royce heavily, 'and I will show you the whole cursed thing.'

The attic, which was the secretary's private place (and rather a small cell for so large a hermit), had indeed all the vestiges of a violent drama. Near the centre of the floor lay a large revolver as if flung away; nearer to the left was rolled a whisky bottle, open but not quite empty. The cloth of the little table lay dragged and trampled, and a length of cord, like that found on the corpse, was cast wildly across the windowsill. Two vases were smashed on the mantelpiece and one on the carpet.

'I was drunk,' said Royce; and this simplicity in the prematurely battered man somehow had the pathos of the first sin of a baby.

'You all know about me,' he continued huskily; 'everybody knows how my story began, and it may as well end like that too. I was called a clever man once, and might have been a happy one; Armstrong saved the remains of a brain and body from the taverns, and was always kind to me in his own way, poor fellow! Only he wouldn't let me marry Alice here; and it will always be said that he was right enough. Well, you can form your own conclusions, and you won't want me to go into details. That is my whisky bottle half emptied in the corner; that is my revolver quite emptied on the carpet. It was the rope from my box that was found on the corpse, and it was from my window the corpse was thrown. You need not set detectives to grub up my tragedy; it is a common enough weed in this world. I give myself to the gallows; and, by God, that is enough!'

At a sufficiently delicate sign, the police gathered round the large man to lead him away; but their unobtrusiveness was somewhat staggered by the remarkable appearance of Father Brown, who was on his hands and knees on the carpet in the doorway, as if engaged in some kind of undignified prayers. Being a person utterly insensible to the social figure he cut, he remained in this posture, but turned a bright round face up at the company, presenting the appearance of a quadruped with a very comic human head.

'I say,' he said good-naturedly, 'this really won't do at all, you know. At the beginning you said we'd found no weapon. But now we're finding too many; there's the knife to stab, and the rope to strangle, and the pistol to shoot; and after all he broke his neck by falling out of a window! It won't do. It's not economical.' And he shook his head at the ground as a horse does grazing.

Inspector Gilder had opened his mouth with serious intentions, but before he could speak the grotesque figure on the floor had gone on quite volubly.

'And now three quite impossible things. First, these holes in the carpet, where the six bullets have gone in. Why on earth should anybody fire at the carpet? A drunken man lets fly at his enemy's head, the thing that's grinning at him. He doesn't pick a quarrel with his feet, or lay siege to his slippers. And then there's the rope' – and having done with the carpet the speaker lifted his hands and put them in his pockets, but continued unaffectedly on his knees – 'in what conceivable intoxication would anybody try to put a rope round a man's neck and finally put it round his leg? Royce, anyhow, was not so drunk as that, or he would be sleeping like a log by now. And, plainest of all, the whisky bottle. You suggest a dipsomaniac fought for the whisky bottle, and then having won, rolled it away in a corner, spilling one half and leaving the other. That is the very last thing a dipsomaniac would do.'

He scrambled awkwardly to his feet, and said to the self-accused murderer in tones of limpid penitence: 'I'm awfully sorry, my dear sir, but your tale is really rubbish.'

'Sir,' said Alice Armstrong in a low tone to the priest, 'can I speak to you alone for a moment?'

This request forced the communicative cleric out of the gangway, and before he could speak in the next room, the girl was talking with strange incisiveness.

'You are a clever man,' she said, 'and you are trying to save Patrick, I know. But it's no use. The core of all this is black, and the more things you find out the more there will be against the miserable man I love.'

'Why?' asked Brown, looking at her steadily.

'Because,' she answered equally steadily, 'I saw him commit the crime myself.'

'Ah!' said the unmoved Brown, 'and what did he do?'

'I was in this room next to them,' she explained; 'both doors were closed, but I suddenly heard a voice, such as I had never heard on earth, roaring "Hell, hell, hell," again and again, and then the two doors shook with the first explosion of the revolver. Thrice again the thing banged before I got the two doors open and found the room full of smoke; but the pistol was smoking in my poor, mad Patrick's hand; and I saw him fire the last murderous volley with my own eyes. Then he leapt on my father, who was clinging in terror to the window-sill, and, grappling, tried to strangle him with the rope, which he threw over his head, but which slipped over his struggling shoulders to his feet. Then it tightened round one leg and Patrick dragged him along like a maniac. I snatched a knife from the mat, and, rushing between them, managed to cut the rope before I fainted.'

'I see,' said Father Brown, with the same wooden civility. 'Thank you.'

As the girl collapsed under her memories, the priest passed stiffly into the next room, where he found Gilder and Merton alone with Patrick Royce, who sat in a chair, handcuffed. There he said to the Inspector submissively: 'Might I say a word to the prisoner in your presence; and might he take off those funny cuffs for a minute?'

'He is a very powerful man,' said Merton in an undertone. 'Why do you want them taken off?'

'Why, I thought,' replied the priest humbly, 'that perhaps I might have the very great honour of shaking hands with him.'

Both detectives stared, and Father Brown added: 'Won't you tell them about it, sir?'

The man on the chair shook his tousled head, and the priest turned impatiently.

'Then I will,' he said. 'Private lives are more important than public reputations. I am going to save the living, and let the dead bury their dead.'

He went to the fatal window, and blinked out of it as he went on talking.

'I told you that in this case there were too many weapons and only one death. I tell you now that they were not weapons, and were not used to cause death. All those grisly tools, the noose, the bloody knife, the exploding pistol, were instruments of a curious mercy. They were not used to kill Sir Aaron, but to save him.'

'To save him!' repeated Gilder. 'And from what?'

'From himself,' said Father Brown. 'He was a suicidal maniac.'

'*What?*' cried Merton in an incredulous tone. 'And the Religion of Cheerfulness – '

'It is a cruel religion,' said the priest, looking out of the window. 'Why couldn't they let him weep a little, like his fathers before him? His plans stiffened, his views grew cold; behind that merry mask was the empty mind of the atheist. At last, to keep up his hilarious public level, he fell back on that dram-drinking he had abandoned long ago. But there is this horror about alcoholism in a sincere teetotaller: that he pictures and expects that psychological inferno from which he has warned others. It leapt upon poor Armstrong prematurely, and by this morning he was in such a case that he sat here and cried he was in hell, in so crazy a voice that his daughter did not know it. He was mad for death, and with the monkey tricks of the mad he had scattered round him death in many shapes – a running noose and his friend's revolver and a knife. Royce entered accidentally and acted in a flash. He flung the knife on the mat behind him, snatched up the revolver, and having no time to unload it, emptied it shot after shot all over the floor. The suicide saw a fourth shape of death, and made a dash for the window. The rescuer did the only thing he could – ran after him with the rope and tried to tie him hand and foot. Then it was that the unlucky girl ran in, and misunderstanding the struggle, strove to slash her father free. At first she only slashed poor Royce's knuckles, from which has come all the little blood in this affair. But, of course, you noticed that he left blood, but no wound, on that servant's face? Only before the poor woman swooned, she did hack her father loose, so that he went crashing through that window into eternity.'

There was a long stillness slowly broken by the metallic noises of Gilder unlocking the handcuffs of Patrick Royce, to whom he said: 'I think I should have told the truth, sir. You and the young lady are worth more than Armstrong's obituary notices.'

'Confound Armstrong's notices,' cried Royce roughly. 'Don't you see it was because she mustn't know?'

'Mustn't know what?' asked Merton.

'Why, that she killed her father, you fool!' roared the other. 'He'd have been alive now but for her. It might craze her to know that.'

'No, I don't think it would,' remarked Father Brown, as he picked up his hat. 'I rather think I should tell her. Even the most murderous blunders don't poison life like sins; anyhow, I think you may both be the happier now. I've got to go back to the Deaf School.'

As he went out on to the gusty grass an acquaintance from Highgate stopped him and said: 'The Coroner has arrived. The inquiry is just going to begin.'

'I've got to get back to the Deaf School,' said Father Brown. 'I'm sorry I can't stop for the inquiry.'

MANALIVE

Manalive

Contents

PART ONE

The Enigmas of Innocent Smith

CHAPTER I

How the Great Wind Came to Beacon House

A wind sprang high in the west, like a wave of unreasonable happiness, and tore eastward across England, trailing with it the frosty scent of forests and the cold intoxication of the sea. In a million holes and corners it refreshed a man like a flagon, and astonished him like a blow. In the inmost chambers of intricate and embowered houses it woke like a domestic explosion, littering the floor with some professor's papers till they seemed as precious as fugitive, or blowing out the candle by which a boy read *Treasure Island* and wrapping him in roaring dark. But everywhere it bore drama into undramatic lives, and carried the trump of crisis across the world. Many a harassed mother in a mean backyard had looked at five dwarfish shirts on the clothesline as at some small, sick tragedy; it was as if she had hanged her five children. The wind came, and they were full and kicking as if five fat imps had sprung into them; and far down in her oppressed subconscious she half-remembered those coarse comedies of her fathers when the elves still dwelt in the homes of men. Many an unnoticed girl in a dank walled garden had tossed herself into the hammock with the same intolerant gesture with which she might have tossed herself into the Thames; and that wind rent the waving wall of woods and lifted the hammock like a balloon, and showed her shapes of quaint clouds far beyond, and pictures of bright villages far below, as if she rode heaven in a fairy boat. Many a dusty clerk or cleric, plodding a telescopic road of poplars, thought for the hundredth time that they were like the plumes of a hearse; when this invisible energy caught and swung and clashed them round his head like a wreath or salutation of seraphic wings. There was in it something more inspired and authoritative even than the old wind of the proverb; for this was the good wind that blows nobody harm.

The flying blast struck London just where it scales the northern heights, terrace above terrace, as precipitous as Edinburgh. It was round about this place that some poet, probably drunk, looked up astonished at all those streets gone skywards, and (thinking vaguely of glaciers and roped mountaineers) gave it the name of Swiss Cottage, which it has never been able to shake off. At some stage of those heights a terrace of tall grey houses, mostly empty and almost as desolate as the Grampians, curved round at the western end, so that the last building, a boarding establishment called 'Beacon House', offered abruptly to the sunset its high, narrow and towering termination, like the prow of some deserted ship.

The ship, however, was not wholly deserted. The proprietor of the boarding-house, a Mrs Duke, was one of those helpless persons against whom fate wars in vain; she smiled vaguely both before and after all her calamities; she was too soft to be hurt. But by the aid (or rather under the orders) of a strenuous niece she always kept the remains of a clientele, mostly of young but listless folks. And there were actually five inmates standing disconsolately about the garden when the great gale broke at the base of the terminal tower behind them, as the sea bursts against the base of an outstanding cliff.

All day that hill of houses over London had been domed and sealed up with cold cloud. Yet three men and two girls had at last found even the grey and chilly garden more tolerable than the black and cheerless interior. When the wind came it split the sky and shouldered the cloudland left and right, unbarring great clear furnaces of evening gold. The burst of light released and the burst of air blowing seemed to come almost simultaneously; and the wind especially caught everything in a throttling violence. The bright short grass lay all one way like brushed hair. Every shrub in the garden tugged at its roots like a dog at the collar, and strained every leaping leaf after the hunting and exterminating element. Now and again a twig would snap and fly like a bolt from an arbalist. The three men stood stiffly and aslant against the wind, as if leaning against a wall. The two ladies disappeared into the house; rather, to speak truly, they were blown into the house. Their two frocks, blue and white, looked like two big broken flowers, driving and drifting upon the gale. Nor is such a poetic fancy inappropriate, for there was something oddly romantic about this inrush of air and light after a long, leaden and unlifting day. Grass and garden trees seemed glittering with something at once good and unnatural, like a fire from fairyland. It seemed like a strange sunrise at the wrong end of the day.

The girl in white dived in quickly enough, for she wore a white hat of the proportions of a parachute, which might have wafted her away into the coloured clouds of evening. She was their one splash of splendour, and irradiated wealth in that impecunious place (staying there temporarily with a friend), an heiress in a small way, by name Rosamund Hunt, brown-eyed, round-faced, but resolute and rather boisterous. On top of her wealth she was good-humoured and rather good-looking; but she had not married, perhaps because there was always a crowd of men around her. She was not fast (though some might have called her vulgar), but she gave irresolute youths an impression of being at once popular and inaccessible. A man felt as if he had fallen in love with Cleopatra, or as if he were asking for a great actress at the stage door. Indeed, some theatrical spangles seemed to cling about Miss Hunt; she played the guitar and the mandoline; she always wanted charades; and with that great rending of the sky by sun and storm, she felt a girlish melodrama swell again within her. To the crashing orchestration of the air the clouds rose like the curtain of some long-expected pantomime.

Nor, oddly enough, was the girl in blue entirely unimpressed by this apocalypse in a private garden; though she was one of the most prosaic and practical creatures alive. She was, indeed, no other than the strenuous niece whose strength alone upheld that mansion of decay. But as the gale swung and swelled the blue and white skirts till they took on the monstrous contours of Victorian crinolines, a sunken memory stirred in her that was almost romance – a memory of a dusty volume of *Punch* in an aunt's house in infancy: pictures of crinoline hoops and croquet hoops and some pretty story, of which perhaps they were a part. This half-perceptible fragrance in her thoughts faded almost instantly, and Diana Duke entered the house even more promptly than her companion. Tall, slim, aquiline, and dark, she seemed made for such swiftness. In body she was of the breed of those birds and beasts that are at once long and alert, like greyhounds or herons or even like an innocent snake. The whole house revolved on her as on a rod of steel. It would be wrong to say that she commanded; for her own efficiency was so impatient that she obeyed herself before anyone else obeyed her. Before electricians could mend a bell or locksmiths open a door, before dentists could pluck a tooth or butlers draw a tight cork, it was done already with the silent violence of her slim hands. She was light; but there was nothing leaping about her lightness. She spurned the ground, and she meant to spurn it. People talk of the pathos and failure of plain women; but it is a more terrible thing that a beautiful woman may succeed in everything but womanhood.

'It's enough to blow your head off,' said the young woman in white, going to the looking-glass.

The young woman in blue made no reply, but put away her gardening gloves, and then went to the sideboard and began to spread out an afternoon cloth for tea.

'Enough to blow your head off, I say,' said Miss Rosamund Hunt, with the unruffled cheeriness of one whose songs and speeches had always been safe for an encore.

'Only your hat, I think,' said Diana Duke, 'but I dare say that is sometimes more important.'

Rosamund's face showed for an instant the offence of a spoilt child, and then the humour of a very healthy person. She broke into a laugh and said, 'Well, it would have to be a big wind to blow your head off.'

There was another silence; and the sunset breaking more and more from the sundering clouds, filled the room with soft fire and painted the dull walls with ruby and gold.

'Somebody once told me,' said Rosamund Hunt, 'that it's easier to keep one's head when one has lost one's heart.'

'Oh, don't talk such rubbish,' said Diana with savage sharpness.

Outside, the garden was clad in a golden splendour; but the wind was still stiffly blowing, and the three men who stood their ground might also have considered the problem of hats and heads. And, indeed, their position, touching hats, was somewhat typical of them. The tallest of the three abode the blast in a high silk hat, which the wind seemed to charge as vainly as that other sullen tower, the house behind him. The second man tried to hold on a stiff straw hat at all angles, and ultimately held it in his hand. The third had no hat, and, by his attitude, seemed never to have had one in his life. Perhaps this wind was a kind of fairy wand to test men and women, for there was much of the three men in this difference.

The man in the solid silk hat was the embodiment of silkiness and solidity. He was a big, bland, bored and (as some said) boring man, with flat fair hair and handsome heavy features; a prosperous young doctor by the name of Warner. But if his blondness and blandness seemed at first a little fatuous, it is certain that he was no fool. If Rosamund Hunt was the only person there with much money, he was the only person who had as yet found any kind of fame. His treatise on 'The Probable Existence of Pain in the Lowest Organisms' had been universally hailed by the scientific world as at once solid and daring. In short, he undoubtedly had brains; and perhaps it was not his fault if they were the kind of brains that most men desire to analyse with a poker.

The young man who put his hat off and on was a scientific amateur in a small way, and worshipped the great Warner with a solemn freshness. It was, in fact, at his invitation that the distinguished doctor was present; for Warner lived in no such ramshackle lodging-house, but in a professional palace in Harley Street. This young man was really the youngest and best-looking of the three. But he was one of those persons, both male and female, who seem doomed to be good-looking and insignificant. Brown-haired, high-coloured, and shy, he seemed to lose the delicacy of his features in a sort of blur of brown and red as he stood blushing and blinking against the wind. He was one of those obvious unnoticeable people: everyone knew that he was Arthur Inglewood, unmarried, moral, decidedly intelligent, living on a little money of his own, and hiding himself in the two hobbies of photography and cycling. Everybody knew him and forgot him; even as he stood there in the glare of golden sunset there was something about him indistinct, like one of his own red-brown amateur photographs.

The third man had no hat; he was lean, in light, vaguely sporting clothes, and the large pipe in his mouth made him look all the leaner. He had a long ironical face, blue-black hair, the blue eyes of an Irishman, and the blue chin of an actor. An Irishman he was, an actor he was not, except in the old days of Miss Hunt's charades, being, as a matter of fact, an obscure and flippant journalist named Michael Moon. He had once been hazily supposed to be reading for the Bar; but (as Warner would say with his rather elephantine wit) it was mostly at another kind of bar that his friends found him. Moon, however, did not drink, nor even frequently get drunk; he simply was a gentleman who liked low company. This was partly because company is quieter than society: and if he enjoyed talking to a barmaid (as apparently he did), it was chiefly because the barmaid did the talking. Moreover he would often bring other talent to assist her. He shared that strange trick of all men of his type, intellectual and without ambition – the trick of going about with his mental inferiors. There was a small resilient Jew named Moses Gould in the same boarding-house, a little man whose negro vitality and vulgarity amused Michael so much that he went round with him from bar to bar, like the owner of a performing monkey.

The colossal clearance which the wind had made of that cloudy sky grew clearer and clearer; chamber within chamber seemed to open in heaven. One felt one might at last find something lighter than light. In the fullness of this silent effulgence all things collected their colours again: the grey trunks turned silver, and the drab gravel gold. One bird fluttered like a loosened leaf from one tree to another, and his brown feathers were brushed with fire.

'Inglewood,' said Michael Moon, with his blue eye on the bird, 'have you any friends?'

Dr Warner mistook the person addressed, and turning a broad beaming face, said: 'Oh yes, I go out a great deal.'

Michael Moon gave a tragic grin, and waited for his real informant, who spoke a moment after in a voice curiously cool, fresh and young, as coming out of that brown and even dusty interior.

'Really,' answered Inglewood, 'I'm afraid I've lost touch with my old friends. The greatest friend I ever had was at school, a fellow named Smith. It's odd you should mention it, because I was thinking of him today, though I haven't seen him for seven or eight years. He was on the science side with me at school – a clever fellow though queer; and he went up to Oxford when I went to Germany. The fact is, it's rather a sad story. I often asked him to come and see me, and when I heard nothing I made enquiries, you know. I was shocked to learn that poor Smith had gone off his head. The accounts were a bit cloudy, of course, some saying that he had recovered again; but they always say that. About a year ago I got a telegram from him myself. The telegram, I'm sorry to say, put the matter beyond a doubt.'

'Quite so,' assented Dr Warner stolidly; 'insanity is generally incurable.'

'So is sanity,' said the Irishman, and studied him with a dreary eye.

'Symptoms?' asked the doctor. 'What was this telegram?'

'It's a shame to joke about such things,' said Inglewood, in his honest, embarrassed way; 'the telegram was Smith's illness, not Smith. The actual words were, "Man found alive with two legs." '

'Alive with two legs,' repeated Michael, frowning. 'Perhaps a version of alive and kicking? I don't know much about people out of their senses; but I suppose they ought to be kicking.'

'And people in their senses?' asked Warner, smiling.

'Oh, they ought to be kicked,' said Michael with sudden heartiness.

'The message is clearly insane,' continued the impenetrable Warner. 'The best test is a reference to the undeveloped normal type. Even a baby does not expect to find a man with three legs.'

'Three legs,' said Michael Moon, 'would be very convenient in this wind.'

A fresh eruption of the atmosphere had indeed almost thrown them off their balance and broken the blackened trees in the garden. Beyond, all sorts of accidental objects could be seen scouring the wind-scoured sky – straws, sticks, rags, papers, and, in the distance, a disappearing hat. Its disappearance, however, was not final; after an interval of minutes they saw it again, much larger and closer, a white panama, towering up into the heavens like a balloon, staggering to and fro for an instant like a stricken kite, and then settling in the centre of their own lawn as falteringly as a fallen leaf.

'Somebody's lost a good hat,' said Dr Warner shortly.

Almost as he spoke, another object came over the garden wall, flying after the fluttering panama. It was a big green umbrella. After that came hurtling a huge yellow Gladstone bag, and after that came a figure like a flying wheel of legs, as in the shield of the Isle of Man.

But though for a flash it seemed to have five or six legs, it alighted upon two, like the man in the queer telegram. It took the form of a large light-haired man in gay green holiday clothes. He had bright blond hair that the wind brushed back like a German's, a flushed eager face like a cherub's, and a prominent pointing nose, a little like a dog's. His head, however, was by no means cherubic in the sense of being without a body. On the contrary, on his vast shoulders and shape generally gigantesque, his head looked oddly and unnaturally small. This gave rise to a scientific theory (which his conduct fully supported) that he was an idiot.

Inglewood had a politeness instinctive and yet awkward. His life was full of arrested half gestures of assistance. And even this prodigy of a big man in green, leaping the wall like a bright green grasshopper, did not paralyse that small altruism of his habits in such a matter as a lost hat. He was stepping forward to recover the green gentleman's headgear, when he was struck rigid with a roar like a bull's.

'Unsportsmanlike!' bellowed the big man. 'Give it fair play, give it fair play!' And he came after his own hat quickly but cautiously, with burning eyes. The hat had seemed at first to droop and dawdle as in ostentatious languor on the sunny lawn; but the wind again freshening and rising, it went dancing down the garden with the devilry of a *pas de quatre*. The eccentric went bounding after it with kangaroo leaps and bursts of breathless speech, of which it was not always easy to pick up the thread: 'Fair play, fair play . . . sport of kings . . . chase their crowns . . . quite humane . . . tramontana . . . cardinals chase red hats . . . old English hunting . . . started a hat in Bramber Combe . . . hat at bay . . . mangled hounds . . . Got him!'

As the wind rose out of a roar into a shriek, he leapt into the sky on his strong, fantastic legs, snatched at the vanishing hat, missed it, and pitched sprawling face foremost on the grass. The hat rose over him like a bird in triumph. But its triumph was premature; for the lunatic, flung forward on his hands, threw up his boots behind, waved his two legs in the air like symbolic ensigns (so that they actually thought again of the telegram), and actually caught the hat with his feet. A prolonged and piercing yell of wind split the welkin from end to end. The eyes of all the men were blinded by the invisible blast, as by a strange, clear cataract of transparency rushing between them and all objects about them. But as the large man fell back in a sitting posture and solemnly crowned himself with the hat, Michael found, to his incredulous surprise, that he had been holding his breath, like a man watching a duel.

While that tall wind was at the top of its sky-scraping energy, another short cry was heard, beginning very querulous, but ending very quick, swallowed in abrupt silence. The shiny black cylinder of Dr Warner's official hat sailed off his head in the long, smooth parabola of an airship, and in almost cresting a garden tree was caught in the topmost branches. Another hat was gone. Those in that garden felt themselves caught in an unaccustomed eddy of things happening; no one seemed to know what would blow away next. Before they could speculate, the cheering and hallooing hat-hunter was already half-way up the tree, swinging himself from fork to fork with his strong, bent, grasshopper legs, and still giving forth his gasping, mysterious comments.

'Tree of life . . . Ygdrasil . . . climb for centuries perhaps . . . owls nesting in the hat . . . remotest generations of owls . . . still usurpers . . . gone to heaven . . . man in the moon wears it . . . brigand . . . not yours . . . belongs to depressed medical man . . . in garden . . . give it up . . . give it up!'

The tree swung and swept and thrashed to and fro in the thundering wind like a thistle, and flamed in the full sunshine like a bonfire. The green, fantastic human figure, vivid against its autumn red and gold, was already among its highest and craziest branches, which by bare luck did not break with the weight of his big body. He was up there among the last tossing leaves and the first twinkling stars of evening, still talking to himself cheerfully, reasoningly, half apologetically, in little gasps. He might well be out of breath, for his whole preposterous raid had gone with one rush; he had bounded the wall once like a football, swept down the garden like a slide, and shot up the tree like a rocket. The other three men seemed buried under incident piled on incident – a wild world where one thing began before another thing left off. All three had the first thought. The tree had been there for the five years they had known the boarding-house. Each one of them was active and strong. No one of them had even thought of climbing it. Beyond that, Inglewood felt first the mere fact of colour. The bright brisk leaves, the bleak blue sky, the wild green arms and legs, reminded him irrationally of something glowing in his infancy, something akin to a gaudy man on a golden tree; perhaps it was only a painted monkey on a stick. Oddly enough, Michael Moon, though more of a humorist, was touched on a tenderer nerve, half remembered the old, young theatricals with Rosamund, and was amused to find himself almost quoting Shakespeare –

> 'For valour, is not love a Hercules,
> Still climbing trees in the Hesperides?'

Even the immovable man of science had a bright, bewildered sensation that the Time Machine had given a great jerk, and gone forward with rather rattling rapidity.

He was not, however, wholly prepared for what happened next. The man in green, riding the frail topmost bough like a witch on a very risky broomstick, reached up and rent the black hat from its airy nest of twigs. It had been broken across a heavy bough in the first burst of its passage, a tangle of branches had torn and scored and scratched it in every direction, a clap of wind and foliage had flattened it like a concertina; nor can it be said that the obliging gentleman with the sharp nose showed any adequate tenderness for its structure when he finally unhooked it from its place. When he had found it, however, his proceedings were by some counted singular. He waved it with a loud whoop of triumph, and then immediately appeared to fall backwards off the tree, to which, however, he remained attached by his long strong legs, like a monkey swung by his tail. Hanging thus head downwards above the unhelmed Warner, he gravely proceeded to drop the battered silk cylinder upon his brows. 'Every man a king,' explained the inverted philosopher, 'every hat (consequently) a crown. But this is a crown out of heaven.'

And he again attempted the coronation of Warner, who, however, moved away with great abruptness from the hovering diadem; not seeming, strangely enough, to wish for his former decoration in its present state.

'Wrong, wrong!' cried the obliging person hilariously. 'Always wear uniform, even if it's shabby uniform! Ritualists may always be untidy. Go to a dance with soot on your shirt-front; but go with a shirt-front. Huntsman wears old coat, but old pink coat. Wear a topper, even if it's got no top. It's the symbol that counts, old cock. Take your hat, because it is your hat after all; its nap rubbed all off by the bark, dears, and its brim not the least bit curled; but for old sakes' sake it is still, dears, the nobbiest tile in the world.'

Speaking thus, with a wild comfortableness, he settled or smashed the shapeless silk hat over the face of the disturbed physician, and fell on his feet among the other men, still talking, beaming and breathless.

'Why don't they make more games out of the wind?' he asked in some excitement. 'Kites are all right, but why should it only be kites? Why, I thought of three other games for a windy day while I was climbing that tree. Here's one of them: you take a lot of pepper – '

'I think,' interposed Moon, with a sardonic mildness, 'that your games are already sufficiently interesting. Are you, may I ask, a professional acrobat on a tour, or a travelling advertisement of Sunny Jim? How and why do you display all this energy for clearing walls and climbing trees in our melancholy, but at least rational, suburbs?'

The stranger, so far as so loud a person was capable of it, appeared to grow confidential.

'Well, it's a trick of my own,' he confessed candidly. 'I do it by having two legs.'

Arthur Inglewood, who had sunk into the background of this scene of folly, started and stared at the newcomer with his short-sighted eyes screwed up and his high colour slightly heightened.

'Why, I believe you're Smith,' he cried with his fresh, almost boyish voice; and then after an instant's stare, 'and yet I'm not sure.'

'I have a card, I think,' said the unknown, with baffling solemnity – 'a card with my real name, my titles, offices, and true purpose on this earth.'

He drew out slowly from an upper waistcoat pocket a scarlet card-case, and as slowly produced a very large card. Even in the instant of its production, they fancied it was of a queer shape, unlike the cards of ordinary gentlemen. But it was there only for an instant; for as it passed from his fingers to Arthur's, one or another slipped his hold. The strident, tearing gale in that garden carried away the stranger's card to join the wild waste paper of the universe; and that great western wind shook the whole house and passed.

CHAPTER 2

The Luggage of an Optimist

We all remember the fairy tales of science in our infancy, which played with the supposition that large animals could jump in the proportion of small ones. If an elephant were as strong as a grasshopper, he could (I suppose) spring clean out of the Zoological Gardens and alight trumpeting upon Primrose Hill. If a whale could leap from the sea like a trout, perhaps men might look up and see one soaring above Yarmouth like the winged island of Laputa. Such natural energy, though sublime, might certainly be inconvenient, and much of this inconvenience attended the gaiety and good intentions of the man in green. He was too large for everything, because he was lively as well as large. By a fortunate physical provision, most very substantial creatures are also reposeful; and middle-class boarding-houses in the lesser parts of London are not built for a man as big as a bull and as excitable as a kitten.

When Inglewood followed the stranger into the boarding-house, he found him talking earnestly (and in his own opinion privately) to the helpless Mrs Duke. That fat, faint lady could only goggle up like a dying fish at the enormous new gentleman, who politely offered himself as a lodger, with vast gestures of the wide white hat in one hand, and the yellow Gladstone bag in the other. Fortunately, Mrs Duke's more efficient niece and partner was there to complete the contract; for, indeed, all the people of the house had somehow collected in the room. This fact, in truth, was typical of the whole episode. The visitor created an atmosphere of comic crisis; and from the time he came into the house to the time he left it, he somehow got the company to gather and even follow (though in derision) as children gather and follow a Punch and Judy. An hour ago, and for four years previously, these people had avoided each other, even when they had really liked each other. They had slid in and out of dismal and deserted rooms in search of particular newspapers or private needlework. Even now they all came casually, as with varying interests; but they all came. There was the embarrassed Inglewood, still a sort of red shadow; there was the unembarrassed Warner, a pallid but solid substance. There was Michael Moon offering like a riddle the contrast of the horsy crudeness of his clothes and the sombre sagacity of his visage. He was now joined by his yet more comic crony, Moses Gould. Swaggering on short legs with a prosperous purple tie, he was the gayest of godless little dogs; but like a dog also in this, that however he danced and wagged with delight, the two dark eyes on each side of his protuberant nose glistened gloomily like black buttons. There was Miss Rosamund Hunt, still with the fine white hat framing her square, good-looking face, and still with her native air of being dressed for some party that never came off. She also, like Mr Moon, had a new companion, new so far as this narrative goes, but in reality an old friend and a protégée. This was a slight young woman in dark grey, and in no way notable but for a load of dull red hair, of which the shape somehow gave her pale face that triangular, almost peaked, appearance which was given by the lowering headdress and deep rich ruff of the Elizabethan beauties. Her surname seemed to be Grey, and Miss Hunt called her Mary, in that indescribable tone applied to an old dependent who has practically become a friend. She wore a small silver cross on her very businesslike grey clothes, and was the only member of the party who went to church. Last, but the reverse of least, there was Diana Duke, studying the newcomer with eyes of steel, and listening carefully to every idiotic word he said. As for Mrs Duke, she smiled up at him, but never dreamed of listening to him. She had never really listened to anyone in her life; which, some said, was why she had survived.

Nevertheless, Mrs Duke was pleased with her new guest's concentration of courtesy upon herself; for no one ever spoke seriously to her any more than she listened seriously to anyone. And she almost beamed as the stranger, with yet wider and almost whirling gestures of explanation with his huge hat and bag, apologised for having entered by the wall instead of the front door. He was understood to put it down to an unfortunate family tradition of neatness and care of his clothes.

'My mother was rather strict about it, to tell the truth,' he said, lowering his voice, to Mrs Duke. 'She never liked me to lose my cap at school. And when a man's been taught to be tidy and neat it sticks to him.'

Mrs Duke weakly gasped that she was sure he must have had a good mother; but her niece seemed inclined to probe the matter further.

'You've got a funny idea of neatness,' she said, 'if it's jumping garden walls and clambering up garden trees. A man can't very well climb a tree tidily.'

'He can clear a wall neatly,' said Michael Moon; 'I saw him do it.'

Smith seemed to be regarding the girl with genuine astonishment. 'My dear young lady,' he said, 'I was tidying the tree. You don't want last year's hats there, do you, any more than last year's leaves? The wind takes off the leaves, but it couldn't manage the hat; that wind, I suppose, has tidied whole forests today. Rum idea this is, that tidiness is a timid, quiet sort of thing; why, tidiness is a toil for giants. You can't tidy anything without untidying yourself; just look at my trousers. Don't you know that? Haven't you ever had a spring cleaning?'

'Oh yes, sir,' said Mrs Duke, almost eagerly. 'You will find everything of that sort quite nice.' For the first time she had heard two words that she could understand.

Miss Diana Duke seemed to be studying the stranger with a sort of spasm of calculation; then her black eyes snapped with decision, and she said that he could have a particular bedroom on the top floor if he liked: and the silent and sensitive Inglewood, who had been on the rack through these cross-purposes, eagerly offered to show him up to the room. Smith went up the stairs four at a time, and when he bumped his head against the ultimate ceiling, Inglewood had an odd sensation that the tall house was much shorter than it used to be.

Arthur Inglewood followed his old friend – or his new friend, for he did not very clearly know which he was. The face looked very like his old schoolfellow's at one second and very unlike at another. And when Inglewood broke through his native politeness so far as to say suddenly, 'Is your name Smith?' he received only the unenlightening reply, 'Quite right; quite right. Very good. Excellent!' Which appeared to Inglewood, on reflection, rather the speech of a new-born babe accepting a name than of a grown-up man admitting one.

Despite these doubts about identity, the hapless Inglewood watched the other unpack, and stood about his bedroom in all the impotent attitudes of the male friend. Mr Smith unpacked with the same kind of whirling accuracy with which he climbed a tree – throwing things out of his bag as if they were rubbish, yet managing to distribute quite a regular pattern all round him on the floor.

As he did so he continued to talk in the same somewhat gasping manner (he had come upstairs four steps at a time, but even without this his style of speech was breathless and fragmentary), and his remarks were still a string of more or less significant but often separate pictures.

'Like the day of judgement,' he said, throwing a bottle so that it somehow settled, rocking on its right end. 'People say vast universe . . . infinity and astronomy; not sure . . . I think things are too close together . . . packed up; for travelling . . . stars too close, really . . . why, the sun's a star, too close to be seen properly; the earth's a star, too close to be seen at all . . . too many pebbles on the beach; ought all to be put in rings; too many blades of grass to study . . . feathers on a bird make the brain reel; wait till the big bag is unpacked . . . may all be put in our right places then.'

Here he stopped, literally for breath – throwing a shirt to the other end of the room, and then a bottle of ink so that it fell quite neatly beyond it. Inglewood looked round on this strange, half-symmetrical disorder with an increasing doubt.

In fact, the more one explored Mr Smith's holiday luggage, the less one could make anything of it. One peculiarity of it was that almost everything seemed to be there for the wrong reason; what is secondary with everyone else was primary with him. He would wrap up a pot or pan in brown paper;

and the unthinking assistant would discover that the pot was valueless or even unnecessary, and that it was the brown paper that was truly precious. He produced two or three boxes of cigars, and explained with plain and perplexing sincerity that he was no smoker, but that cigar-box wood was by far the best for fretwork. He also exhibited about six small bottles of wine, white and red, and Inglewood, happening to note a Volnay which he knew to be excellent, supposed at first that the stranger was an epicure in vintages. He was therefore surprised to find that the next bottle was a vile sham claret from the colonies, which even colonials (to do them justice) do not drink. It was only then that he observed that all six bottles had those bright metallic seals of various tints, and seemed to have been chosen solely because they gave the three primary and three secondary colours: red, blue, and yellow; green, violet and orange. There grew upon Inglewood an almost creepy sense of the real childishness of this creature. For Smith was really, so far as human psychology can be, innocent. He had the sensualities of innocence: he loved the stickiness of gum, and he cut white wood greedily as if he were cutting a cake. To this man wine was not a doubtful thing to be defended or denounced; it was a quaintly coloured syrup, such as a child sees in a shop window. He talked dominantly and rushed the social situation; but he was not asserting himself, like a superman in a modern play. He was simply forgetting himself, like a little boy at a party. He had somehow made the giant stride from babyhood to manhood, and missed that crisis in youth when most of us grow old.

As he shunted his big bag, Arthur observed the initials I. S. printed on one side of it, and remembered that Smith had been called Innocent Smith at school, though whether as a formal Christian name or a moral description he could not remember. He was just about to venture another question, when there was a knock at the door, and the short figure of Mr Gould offered itself, with the melancholy Moon, standing like his tall crooked shadow, behind him. They had drifted up the stairs after the other two men with the wandering gregariousness of the male.

'Hope there's no intrusion,' said the beaming Moses with a glow of good nature, but not the airiest tinge of apology.

'The truth is,' said Michael Moon with comparative courtesy, 'we thought we might see if they had made you comfortable. Miss Duke is rather – '

'I know,' cried the stranger, looking up radiantly from his bag; 'magnificent, isn't she? Go close to her – hear military music going by, like Joan of Arc.'

Inglewood started and stared at the speaker like one who has just heard a wild fairy tale, which nevertheless contains one small and forgotten fact. For he remembered how he had himself thought of Jeanne d'Arc years ago, when, hardly more than a schoolboy, he had first come to the boarding-house.

Long since the pulverising rationalism of his friend Dr Warner had crushed such youthful ignorances and disproportionate dreams. Under the Warnerian scepticism and science of hopeless human types, Inglewood had long come to regard himself as a timid, insufficient, and 'weak' type, who would never marry; to regard Diana Duke as a materialistic maidservant; and to regard his first fancy for her as the small, dull farce of a collegian kissing his landlady's daughter. And yet the phrase about military music moved him queerly, as if he had heard those distant drums.

'She has to keep things pretty tight, as is only natural,' said Moon, glancing round the rather dwarfish room, with its wedge of slanted ceiling, like the conical hood of a dwarf.

'Rather a small box for you, sir,' said the waggish Mr Gould.

'Splendid room, though,' answered Mr Smith enthusiastically, with his head inside his Gladstone bag. 'I love these pointed sorts of rooms, like Gothic. By the way,' he cried out, pointing in quite a startling way, 'where does that door lead to?'

'To certain death, I should say,' answered Michael Moon, staring up at a dust-stained and disused trapdoor in the sloping roof of the attic. 'I don't think there's a loft there; and I don't know what else it could lead to.' Long before he had finished his sentence the man with the strong green legs had leapt at the door in the ceiling, swung himself somehow on to the ledge beneath it, wrenched it open after a struggle, and clambered through it. For a moment they saw the two symbolic legs standing like a truncated statue; then they vanished. Through the hole thus burst in the roof appeared the empty and lucid sky of evening, with one great many-coloured cloud sailing across it like a whole county upside down.

'Hullo, you fellows!' came the far cry of Innocent Smith, apparently from some remote pinnacle. 'Come up here; and bring some of my things to eat and drink. It's just the spot for a picnic.'

With a sudden impulse Michael snatched two of the small bottles of wine, one in each solid fist; and Arthur Inglewood, as if mesmerised, groped for a biscuit tin and a big jar of ginger. The enormous hand of Innocent Smith appearing through the aperture, like a giant's in a fairy tale, received these tributes and bore them off to the eyrie; then they both hoisted themselves out of the window. They were both athletic, and even gymnastic; Inglewood through his concern for hygiene, and Moon through his concern for sport, which was not quite so idle and inactive as that of the average sportsman. Also they both had a light-headed burst of celestial sensation when the door was burst in the roof, as if a door had been burst in the sky, and they could climb out on to the very roof of the universe. They were both men who had long been unconsciously imprisoned in the commonplace, though one took it comically, and the other seriously. They were both men, nevertheless, in whom sentiment had never died. But Mr Moses Gould had an equal contempt for their suicidal athletics and their subconscious transcendentalism, and he stood and laughed at the thing with the shameless rationality of another race.

When the singular Smith, astride of a chimney-pot, learnt that Gould was not following, his infantile officiousness and good nature forced him to dive back into the attic to comfort or persuade; and Inglewood and Moon were left alone on the long grey-green ridge of the slate roof, with their feet against gutters and their backs against chimney-pots, looking agnostically at each other. Their first feeling was that they had come out into eternity, and that eternity was very like topsy-turvydom. One definition occurred to both of them – that he had come out into the light of that lucid and radiant ignorance in which all beliefs had begun. The sky above them was full of mythology. Heaven seemed deep enough to hold all the gods. The round of the ether turned from green to yellow gradually like a great unripe fruit. All around the sunken sun it was like a lemon; round all the east it was a sort of golden green, more suggestive of a greengage; but the whole had still the emptiness of daylight and none of the secrecy of dusk. Tumbled here and there across this gold and pale green were shards and shattered masses of inky purple cloud, which seemed falling towards the earth in every kind of colossal perspective. One of them really had the character of some many-mitred, many-bearded, many-winged Assyrian image, huge head downwards, hurled out of heaven – a sort of false Jehovah, who was perhaps Satan. All the other clouds had preposterous pinnacled shapes, as if the god's palaces had been flung after him.

And yet, while the empty heaven was full of silent catastrophe, the height of human buildings above which they sat held here and there a tiny trivial noise that was the exact antithesis; and they heard some six streets below a newsboy calling, and a bell bidding to chapel. They could also hear talk out of the garden below; and realised that the irrepressible Smith must have followed Gould downstairs, for his eager and pleading accents could be heard, followed by the half-humorous protests of Miss Duke and the full and very youthful laughter of Rosamund Hunt. The air had that cold kindness that comes after a storm. Michael Moon drank it in with as serious a relish as he had drunk the little bottle of cheap claret, which he had emptied almost at a draught. Inglewood went on eating ginger very slowly and with a solemnity unfathomable as the sky above him. There was still enough stir in the freshness of the atmosphere to make them almost fancy they could smell the garden soil and the last roses of autumn. Suddenly there came from the darkening room a silvery ping and pong which told them that Rosamund had brought out the long-neglected mandoline. After the first few notes there was more of the distant bell-like laughter.

'Inglewood,' said Michael Moon, 'have you ever heard that I am a blackguard?'

'I haven't heard it, and I don't believe it,' answered Inglewood, after an odd pause. 'But I have heard you were – what they call rather wild.'

'If you have heard that I am wild, you can contradict the rumour,' said Moon, with an extraordinary calm; 'I am tame. I am quite tame; I am about the tamest beast that crawls. I drink too much of the same kind of whisky at the same time every night. I even drink about the same amount too much. I go to the same number of public-houses. I meet the same damned women with mauve faces. I hear the same number of dirty stories – generally the same dirty stories. You may assure my friends, Inglewood, that you see before you a person whom civilisation has thoroughly tamed.'

Arthur Inglewood was staring with feelings that made him nearly fall off the roof, for indeed the Irishman's face, always sinister, was now almost demoniacal.

'Christ confound it!' cried out Moon, suddenly clutching the empty claret bottle, 'this is about the thinnest and filthiest wine I ever uncorked, and it's the only drink I have really enjoyed for nine years. I was never wild until just ten minutes ago.' And he sent the bottle whizzing, a wheel of glass, far away beyond the garden into the road, where, in the profound evening silence, they could even hear it break and part upon the stones.

'Moon,' said Arthur Inglewood, rather huskily, 'you mustn't be so bitter about it. Everyone has to take the world as he finds it; of course one often finds it a bit dull – '

'That fellow doesn't,' said Michael decisively; 'I mean that fellow Smith. I have a fancy there's some method in his madness. It looks as if he could turn into a sort of wonderland any minute by taking one step out of the plain road. Who would have thought of that trapdoor? Who would have thought that this cursed colonial claret could taste quite nice among the chimney-pots? Perhaps that is the real key of fairyland. Perhaps Nosey Gould's beastly little Empire Cigarettes ought only to be smoked on stilts, or something of that sort. Perhaps Mrs Duke's cold leg of mutton would seem quite appetising at the top of a tree. Perhaps even my damned, dirty, monotonous drizzle of Old Bill Whisky – '

'Don't be so rough on yourself,' said Inglewood, in serious distress. 'The dullness isn't your fault or the whisky's. Fellows who don't – fellows like me I mean – have just the same feeling that it's all rather flat and a failure. But the world's made like that; it's all survival. Some people are made to get on, like Warner; and some people are made to stick quiet, like me. You can't help your temperament. I know you're much cleverer than I am; but you can't help having all the loose ways of a poor literary chap, and I can't help having all the doubts and helplessness of a small scientific chap, any more than a fish can help floating or a fern can help curling up. Humanity, as Warner said so well in that lecture, really consists of quite different tribes of animals all disguised as men.'

In the dim garden below the buzz of talk was suddenly broken by Miss Hunt's musical instrument banging with the abruptness of artillery into a vulgar but spirited tune.

Rosamund's voice came up rich and strong in the words of some fatuous, fashionable coon song:

> 'Darkies sing a song on the old plantation,
> Sing it as we sang it in the days long since gone by.'

Inglewood's brown eyes softened and saddened still more as he continued his monologue of resignation to such a rollicking and romantic tune. But the blue eyes of Michael Moon brightened and hardened with a light that Inglewood did not understand. Many centuries, and many villages and valleys, would have been happier if Inglewood or Inglewood's countrymen had ever understood that light, or guessed at the first blink that it was the battle star of Ireland.

'Nothing can ever alter it; it's in the wheels of the universe,' went on Inglewood, in a low voice: 'some men are weak and some strong, and the only thing we can do is to know that we are weak. I have been in love lots of times, but I could not do anything, for I remembered my own fickleness. I have formed opinions, but I haven't the cheek to push them, because I've so often changed them. That's the upshot, old fellow. We can't trust ourselves – and we can't help it.'

Michael had risen to his feet, and stood poised in a perilous position at the end of the roof, like some dark statue hung above its gable. Behind him, huge clouds of an almost impossible purple turned slowly topsy-turvy in the silent anarchy of heaven. Their gyration made the dark figure seem yet dizzier.

'Let us . . . ' he said, and was suddenly silent.

'Let us what?' asked Arthur Inglewood, rising equally quick though somewhat more cautiously, for his friend seemed to find some difficulty in speech.

'Let us go and do some of these things we can't do,' said Michael.

At the same moment there burst out of the trapdoor below them the cockatoo hair and flushed face of Innocent Smith, calling to them that they must come down as the 'concert' was in full swing, and Mr Moses Gould was about to recite 'Young Lochinvar'.

As they dropped into Innocent's attic they nearly tumbled over its entertaining impedimenta again. Inglewood, staring at the littered floor, thought instinctively of the littered floor of a nursery. He was therefore the more moved, and even shocked, when his eye fell on a large well-polished American revolver.

'Hullo!' he cried, stepping back from the steely glitter as men step back from a serpent; 'are you afraid of burglars? or when and why do you deal death out of that machine gun?'

'Oh, that!' said Smith, throwing it a single glance; 'I deal life out of that,' and he went bounding down the stairs.

CHAPTER 3

The Banner of Beacon

All next day at Beacon House there was a crazy sense that it was everybody's birthday. It is the fashion to talk of institutions as cold and cramping things. The truth is that when people are in exceptionally high spirits, really wild with freedom and invention, they always must, and they always do, create institutions. When men are weary they fall into anarchy; but while they are gay and vigorous they invariably make rules. This, which is true of all the churches and republics of history, is also true of the most trivial parlour game or the most unsophisticated meadow romp. We are never free until some institution frees us; and liberty cannot exist till it is declared by authority. Even the wild authority of the harlequin Smith was still authority, because it produced everywhere a crop of crazy regulations and conditions. He filled everyone with his own half-lunatic life; but it was not expressed in destruction, but rather in a dizzy and toppling construction. Each person with a hobby found it turning into an institution. Rosamund's songs seemed to coalesce into a kind of opera; Michael's jests and paragraphs into a magazine. His pipe and her mandoline seemed between them to make a sort of smoking concert. The bashful and bewildered Arthur Inglewood almost struggled against his own growing importance. He felt as if, in spite of him, his photographs were turning into a picture gallery, and his bicycle into a gymkhana. But no one had any time to criticise these impromptu estates and offices, for they followed each other in wild succession like the topics of a rambling talker.

Existence with such a man was an obstacle race made out of pleasant obstacles. Out of any homely and trivial object he could drag reels of exaggeration, like a conjurer. Nothing could be more shy and impersonal than poor Arthur's photography. Yet the preposterous Smith was seen assisting him eagerly through sunny morning hours, and an indefensible sequence described as 'Moral Photography' began to unroll about the boarding-house. It was only a version of the old photographer's joke which produces the same figure twice on one plate, making a man play chess with himself, dine with himself, and so on. But these plates were more hysterical and ambitious – as, 'Miss Hunt forgets Herself', showing that lady answering her own too rapturous recognition with a most appalling stare of ignorance; or 'Mr Moon questions Himself', in which Mr Moon appeared as one driven to madness under his own legal cross-examination, which was conducted with a long forefinger and an air of ferocious waggery. One highly successful trilogy – representing Inglewood recognising Inglewood, Inglewood prostrating himself before Inglewood, and Inglewood severely beating Inglewood with an umbrella – Innocent Smith wanted to have enlarged and put up in the hall, like a sort of fresco, with the inscription:

> 'Self-reverence, self-knowledge, self-control –
> These three alone will make a man a prig.'
> TENNYSON

Nothing, again, could be more prosaic and impenetrable than the domestic energies of Miss Diana Duke. But Innocent had somehow blundered on the discovery that her thrifty dressmaking went with a considerable feminine care for dress – the one feminine thing that had never failed her solitary self-respect. In consequence Smith pestered her with a theory (which he really seemed to take seriously) that ladies might combine economy with magnificence if they would draw light chalk patterns on a plain dress and then dust them off again. He set up 'Smith's Lightning Dressmaking Company', with two screens, a cardboard placard, and box of bright soft crayons; and Miss Diana actually threw him an abandoned black overall or working dress on which to exercise the talents of a modiste. He promptly produced for her a garment aflame with red and gold sunflowers; she held it up an instant to her shoulders, and looked like an empress. And Arthur Inglewood, some hours afterwards cleaning his bicycle (with his usual air of being inextricably hidden in it), glanced up; and his hot face grew hotter, for Diana stood laughing for one flash in the doorway, and her dark robe was rich with the green and purple of great decorative peacocks, like a secret garden in the *Arabian Nights*. A pang too swift to be named pain or pleasure went through his heart like an old-world rapier. He remembered how pretty he thought her years ago, when he was ready to fall in love with anybody; but it was like remembering a worship of some Babylonian princess in some previous existence. At his next glimpse of her (and he caught himself awaiting it) the purple and green chalk was dusted off, and she went by quickly in her working clothes.

As for Mrs Duke, none who knew that matron could conceive her as actively resisting this invasion that had turned her house upside down. But among the most exact observers it was seriously believed that she liked it. For she was one of those women who at bottom regard all men as equally mad, wild animals of some utterly separate species. And it is doubtful if she really saw anything more eccentric or inexplicable in Smith's chimney-pot picnics or crimson sunflowers than she had in the chemicals of Inglewood or the sardonic speeches of Moon. Courtesy, on the other hand, is a thing that anybody can understand, and Smith's manners were as courteous as they were unconventional. She said he was 'a real gentleman', by which she simply meant a kind-hearted man, which is a very different thing. She would sit at the head of the table with fat, folded hands and a fat, folded smile for hours and hours, while everyone else was talking at once. At least, the only other exception was Rosamund's companion, Mary Gray, whose silence was of a much more eager sort. Though she never spoke she always looked as if she might speak any minute. Perhaps this is the very definition of a companion. Innocent Smith seemed to throw himself, as into other adventures, into the adventure of making her talk. He never succeeded, yet he was never snubbed; if he achieved anything, it was only to draw attention to this quiet figure, and to turn her, by ever so little, from a modesty to a mystery. But if she was a riddle, everyone recognised that she was a fresh and unspoilt riddle, like the riddle of the sky and the woods in spring. Indeed, though she was rather older than the other two girls, she had an early morning ardour, a fresh earnestness of youth, which Rosamund seemed to have lost in the mere spending of money, and Diana in the mere guarding of it. Smith looked at her again and again. Her eyes and mouth were set in her face the wrong way – which was really the right way. She had the knack of saying everything with her face: her silence was a sort of steady applause.

But among the hilarious experiments of that holiday (which seemed more like a week's holiday than a day's) one experiment towers supreme, not because it was any sillier or more successful than the others, but because out of this particular folly flowed all of the odd events that were to follow. All the other practical jokes exploded of themselves, and left vacancy; all the other fictions returned upon themselves, and were finished like a song. But the string of solid and startling events – which were to include a hansom cab, a detective, a pistol, and a marriage licence – were all made primarily possible by the joke about the High Court of Beacon.

It had originated, not with Innocent Smith, but with Michael Moon. He was in a strange glow and pressure of spirits, and talked incessantly; yet he had never been more sarcastic, and even inhuman. He used his old useless knowledge as a barrister to talk entertainingly of a tribunal that was a parody on the pompous anomalies of English law. The High Court of Beacon, he declared, was a splendid example of our free and sensible constitution. It had been founded by King John in defiance of Magna Carta, and now held absolute power over windmills, wine and spirit licences, ladies travelling in Turkey, revision of sentences for dog-stealing and parricide, as well as anything whatever that happened in the town of Market Bosworth. The whole hundred and nine seneschals of the High Court of Beacon met once in every four centuries; but in the intervals (as Mr Moon explained) the whole powers of the institution were vested in Mrs Duke. Tossed about among the rest of the company, however, the High Court did not retain its historical and legal seriousness, but was used somewhat unscrupulously in a riot of domestic detail. If somebody spilt the Worcester Sauce on the tablecloth, he was quite sure it was a rite without which the sittings and findings of the Court would be invalid; or if somebody wanted a window to remain shut, he would suddenly remember that none but the third son of the lord of the manor of Penge had the right to open it. They even went to the length of making arrests and conducting criminal enquiries. The proposed trial of Moses Gould for patriotism was rather above the heads of the company, especially of the criminal; but the trial of Inglewood on a charge of photographic libel, and his triumphant acquittal upon a plea of insanity, were admitted to be in the best traditions of the Court.

But when Smith was in wild spirits he grew more and more serious, not more and more flippant like Michael Moon. This proposal of a private court of justice, which Moon had thrown off with the detachment of a political humorist, Smith really caught hold of with the eagerness of an abstract philosopher. It was by far the best thing they could do, he declared, to claim sovereign powers even for the individual household.

'You believe in Home Rule for Ireland; I believe in Home Rule for homes,' he cried eagerly to Michael. 'It would be better if every father *could* kill his son, as with the old Romans; it would be better, because nobody would be killed. Let's issue a Declaration of Independence from Beacon House. We could grow enough greens in that garden to support us, and when the tax-collector comes let's tell him we're self-supporting, and play on him with the hose . . . Well, perhaps, as you say, we couldn't very well have a hose, as that comes from the main; but we could sink a well in this chalk, and a lot could be done with water-jugs . . . Let this really be Beacon House. Let's light a bonfire of independence on the roof, and see house after house answering it across the valley of the Thames! Let us begin the League of the Free Families! Away with Local Government! A fig for Local Patriotism! Let every house be a sovereign state as this is, and judge its own children by its own law, as we do by the Court of Beacon. Let us cut the painter, and begin to be happy together, as if we were on a desert island.'

'I know that desert island,' said Michael Moon; 'it only exists in the *Swiss Family Robinson*. A man feels a strange desire for some sort of vegetable milk, and crash comes down some unexpected coconut from some undiscovered monkey. A literary man feels inclined to pen a sonnet, and at once an officious porcupine rushes out of a thicket and shoots out one of his quills.'

'Don't you say a word against the *Swiss Family Robinson*,' cried Innocent with great warmth. 'It mayn't be exact science, but it's dead accurate philosophy. When you're really shipwrecked, you do really find what you want. When you're really on a desert island, you never find it a desert. If we were really besieged in this garden, we'd find a hundred English birds and English berries that we never knew were here. If we were snowed up in this room, we'd be the better for reading scores of books in that bookcase that we don't even know are there; we'd have talks with each other, good, terrible talks, that we shall go to the grave without guessing; we'd find materials for everything – christening, marriage, or funeral; yes, even for a coronation – if we didn't decide to be a republic.'

'A coronation on "Swiss Family" lines, I suppose,' said Michael, laughing. 'Oh, I know you would find everything in that atmosphere. If we wanted such a simple thing, for instance, as a Coronation Canopy, we should walk down beyond the geraniums and find the Canopy Tree in full bloom. If we wanted such a trifle as a crown of gold, why, we should be digging up dandelions, and we should find a gold mine under the lawn. And when we wanted oil for the ceremony, why I suppose a great storm would wash everything on shore, and we should find there was a whale on the premises.'

'And so there *is* a whale on the premises for all you know,' asseverated Smith, striking the table with passion. 'I bet you've never examined the premises! I bet you've never been round at the back as I was this morning – for I found the very thing you say could only grow on a tree. There's an old sort of square tent up against the dustbin; it's got three holes in the canvas, and a pole's broken, so it's not much good as a tent, but as a canopy – ' And his voice quite failed him to express its shining adequacy; then he went on with controversial eagerness: 'You see I take every challenge as you make it. I believe every blessed thing you say couldn't be here has been here all the time. You say you want a whale washed up for oil. Why, there's oil in that cruet-stand at your elbow; and I don't believe anybody has touched it or thought of it for years. And as for your gold crown, we're none of us wealthy here, but we could collect enough ten-shilling bits from our own pockets to string round a man's head for half an hour; or one of Miss Hunt's gold bangles is nearly big enough to – '

The good-humoured Rosamund was almost choking with laughter. 'All is not gold that glitters,' she said, 'and besides – '

'What a mistake that is!' cried Innocent Smith, leaping up in great excitement. 'All is gold that glitters – especially now we are a Sovereign State. What's the good of a Sovereign State if you can't define a sovereign? We can make anything a precious metal, as men could in the morning of the world. They didn't choose gold because it was rare; your scientists can tell you twenty sorts of slime much rarer. They chose gold because it was bright – because it was a hard thing to find, but pretty when you've found it. You can't fight with golden swords or eat golden biscuits; you can only look at it – and you can look at it out here.'

With one of his incalculable motions he sprang back and burst open the doors into the garden. At the same time also, with one of his gestures that never seemed at the instant so unconventional as they were, he stretched out his hand to Mary Gray, and led her out on to the lawn as if for a dance.

The French windows, thus flung open, let in an evening even lovelier than that of the day before. The west was swimming with sanguine colours, and a sort of sleepy flame lay along the lawn. The twisted shadows of the one or two garden trees showed upon this sheen, not grey or black, as in common daylight, but like arabesques written in vivid violet ink on some page of Eastern gold. The sunset was one of those festive and yet mysterious conflagrations in which common things by their colours remind us of costly or curious things. The slates upon the sloping roof burned like the plumes of a vast peacock, in every mysterious blend of blue and green. The red-brown bricks of the wall glowed with all the October tints of strong ruby and tawny wines. The sun seemed to set each object alight with a different coloured flame, like a man lighting fireworks; and even Innocent's hair, which was of a rather colourless fairness, seemed to have a flame of pagan gold on it as he strode across the lawn towards the one tall ridge of rockery.

'What would be the good of gold,' he was saying, 'if it did not glitter? Why should we care for a black sovereign any more than for a black sun at noon? A black button would do just as well. Don't you see that everything in this garden looks like a jewel? And will you kindly tell me what the deuce is the good of a jewel except that it looks like a jewel? Leave off buying and selling, and start looking! Open your eyes, and you'll wake up in the New Jerusalem.

'All is gold that glitters –
    Tree and tower of brass;
Rolls the golden evening air
    Down the golden grass.
Kick the cry to Jericho,
    How yellow mud is sold;
All is gold that glitters,
    For the glitter is the gold.'

'And who wrote that?' asked Rosamund, amused.

'No one will ever write it,' answered Smith, and cleared the rockery with a flying leap.

'Really,' said Rosamund to Michael Moon, 'he ought to be sent to an asylum. Don't you think so?'

'I beg your pardon,' enquired Michael, rather sombrely; his long, swarthy head was dark against the sunset, and, either by accident or mood, he had the look of something isolated and even hostile amid the social extravagance of the garden.

'I only said Mr Smith ought to go to an asylum,' repeated the lady.

The lean face seemed to grow longer and longer, for Moon was unmistakably sneering. 'No,' he said; 'I don't think it's at all necessary.'

'What do you mean?' asked Rosamund quickly. 'Why not?'

'Because he is in one now,' answered Michael Moon, in a quiet but ugly voice. 'Why, didn't you know?'

'What?' cried the girl, and there was a break in her voice; for the Irishman's face and voice were really almost creepy. With his dark figure and dark sayings in all that sunshine he looked like the devil in paradise.

'I'm sorry,' he continued, with a sort of harsh humility. 'Of course we don't talk about it much . . . but I thought we all really knew.'

'Knew what?'

'Well,' answered Moon, 'that Beacon House is a certain rather singular sort of house – a house with the tiles loose, shall we say? Innocent Smith is only the doctor that visits us; hadn't you come when he called before? As most of our maladies are melancholic, of course he has to be extra cheery. Sanity, of course, seems a very bumptious eccentric thing to us. Jumping over a wall, climbing a tree – that's his bedside manner.'

'You daren't say such a thing!' cried Rosamund in a rage. 'You daren't suggest that I – '

'Not more than I am,' said Michael soothingly; 'not more than the rest of us. Haven't you ever noticed that Miss Duke never sits still – a notorious sign? Haven't you ever observed that Inglewood is always washing his hands – a known mark of mental disease? I, of course, am a dipsomaniac.'

'I don't believe you,' broke out his companion, not without agitation. 'I've heard you had some bad habits – '

'All habits are bad habits,' said Michael, with deadly calm. 'Madness does not come by breaking out, but by giving in; by settling down in some dirty, little, self-repeating circle of ideas; by being tamed. *You* went mad about money, because you're an heiress.'

'It's a lie,' cried Rosamund furiously. 'I never was mean about money.'

'You were worse,' said Michael, in a low voice and yet violently. 'You thought that other people were. You thought every man who came near you must be a fortune-hunter; you would not let yourself go and be sane; and now you're mad and I'm mad, and serve us right.'

'You brute!' said Rosamund, quite white. 'And is this true?'

With an intellectual cruelty of which the Celt is capable when his abysses are in revolt, Michael was silent for some seconds, and then stepped back with an ironical bow. 'Not literally true, of course,' he said; 'only really true. An allegory, shall we say? a social satire.'

'And I hate and despise your satires,' cried Rosamund Hunt, letting loose her whole forcible female personality like a cyclone, and speaking every word to wound. 'I despise it as I despise your rank tobacco, and your nasty, loungy ways, and your snarling, and your Radicalism, and your old clothes, and your potty little newspaper, and your rotten failure at everything. I don't care whether you call it snobbishness or not, I like life and success, and jolly things to look at, and action. You won't frighten me with Diogenes; I prefer Alexander.'

'*Victrix causa deae* – ' said Michael gloomily; and this angered her more, as, not knowing what it meant, she imagined it to be witty.

'Oh, I dare say you know Greek,' she said, with cheerful inaccuracy; 'you haven't done much with that either.' And she crossed the garden, pursuing the vanished Innocent and Mary.

In doing so she passed Inglewood, who was returning to the house slowly, and with a thought-clouded brow. He was one of those men who are quite clever, but quite the reverse of quick. As he came back out of the sunset garden into the twilight parlour, Diana Duke slipped swiftly to her feet and began putting away the tea things. But it was not before Inglewood had seen an instantaneous picture so unique that he might well have snapshotted it with his everlasting camera. For Diana had been sitting in front of her unfinished work with her chin on her hand, looking straight out of the window in pure thoughtless thought.

'You are busy,' said Arthur, oddly embarrassed with what he had seen, and wishing to ignore it.

'There's no time for dreaming in this world,' answered the young lady with her back to him.

'I have been thinking lately,' said Inglewood in a low voice, 'that there's no time for waking up.'

She did not reply, and he walked to the window and looked out on the garden.

'I don't smoke or drink, you know,' he said irrelevantly, 'because I think they're drugs. And yet I fancy all hobbies, like my camera and bicycle, are drugs too. Getting under a black hood, getting into a dark room – getting into a hole anyhow. Drugging myself with speed, and sunshine, and fatigue, and fresh air. Pedalling the machine so fast that I turn into a machine myself. That's the matter with all of us. We're too busy to wake up.'

'Well,' said the girl solidly, 'what is there to wake up to?'

'There must be!' cried Inglewood, turning round in a singular excitement – 'there must be something to wake up to! All we do is preparations – your cleanliness, and my healthiness, and Warner's scientific appliances. We're always preparing for something – something that never comes off. I ventilate the house, and you sweep the house; but what is going to *happen* in the house?'

She was looking at him quietly, but with very bright eyes, and seemed to be searching for some form of words which she could not find.

Before she could speak the door burst open, and the boisterous Rosamund Hunt, in her flamboyant white hat, boa, and parasol, stood framed in the doorway. She was in a breathing heat, and on her open face was an expression of the most infantile astonishment.

'Well, here's a fine game!' she said, panting. 'What am I to do now, I wonder? I've wired for Dr Warner; that's all I can think of doing.'

'What is the matter?' asked Diana, rather sharply, but moving forward like one used to be called upon for assistance.

'It's Mary,' said the heiress, 'my companion Mary Gray: that cracked friend of yours called Smith has proposed to her in the garden, after ten hours' acquaintance, and he wants to go off with her now for a special licence.'

Arthur Inglewood walked to the open French windows and looked out on the garden, still golden with evening light. Nothing moved there but a bird or two hopping and twittering; but beyond the hedge and railings, in the road outside the garden gate, a hansom cab was waiting, with the yellow Gladstone bag on top of it.

CHAPTER 4

The Garden of the God

Diana Duke seemed inexplicably irritated at the abrupt entrance and utterance of the other girl.

'Well,' she said shortly, 'I suppose Miss Gray can decline him if she doesn't want to marry him.'

'But she *does* want to marry him!' cried Rosamund in exasperation. 'She's a wild, wicked fool, and I won't be parted from her.'

'Perhaps,' said Diana icily, 'but I really don't see what we can do.'

'But the man's barmy, Diana,' reasoned her friend angrily. 'I can't let my nice governess marry a man that's barmy! You or somebody *must* stop it! – Mr Inglewood, you're a man; go and tell them they simply can't.'

'Unfortunately, it seems to me they simply can,' said Inglewood, with a depressed air. 'I have far less right of intervention than Miss Duke, besides having, of course, far less moral force than she.'

'You haven't either of you got much,' cried Rosamund, the last stays of her formidable temper giving way; 'I think I'll go somewhere else for a little sense and pluck. I think I know someone who will help me more than you do, at any rate . . . he's a cantankerous beast, but he's a man, and has a mind, and knows it . . . ' And she flung out into the garden, with cheeks aflame, and the parasol whirling like a Catherine wheel.

She found Michael Moon standing under the garden tree, looking over the hedge; hunched like a bird of prey, with his large pipe hanging down his long blue chin. The very hardness of his expression pleased her, after the nonsense of the new engagement and the shilly-shallying of her other friends.

'I am sorry I was cross, Mr Moon,' she said frankly. 'I hated you for being a cynic; but I've been well punished, for I want a cynic just now. I've had my fill of sentiment – I'm fed up with it. The world's gone mad, Mr Moon – all except the cynics, I think. That maniac Smith wants to marry my old friend Mary, and she – and she – doesn't seem to mind.'

Seeing his attentive face still undisturbedly smoking, she added smartly, 'I'm not joking; that's Mr Smith's cab outside. He swears he'll take her off now to his aunt's, and go for a special licence. Do give me some practical advice, Mr Moon.'

Mr Moon took his pipe out of his mouth, held it in his hand for an instant reflectively, and then tossed it to the other side of the garden. 'My practical advice to you is this,' he said: 'Let him go for his special licence, and ask him to get another one for you and me.'

'Is that one of your jokes?' asked the young lady. 'Do say what you really mean.'

'I mean that Innocent Smith is a man of business,' said Moon with ponderous precision – 'a plain, practical man: a man of affairs; a man of facts and the daylight. He has let down twenty ton of good building bricks suddenly on my head, and I am glad to say they have woken me up. We went to sleep a little while ago on this very lawn, in this very sunlight. We have had a little nap for five years or so, but now we're going to be married, Rosamund, and I can't see why that cab . . . '

'Really,' said Rosamund stoutly, 'I don't know what you mean.'

'What a lie!' cried Michael, advancing on her with brightening eyes. 'I'm all for lies in an ordinary way; but don't you see that tonight they won't do? We've wandered into a world of facts, old girl. That grass growing, and that sun going down, and that cab at the door, are facts. You used to torment and excuse yourself by saying I was after your money, and didn't really love you. But if I stood here now and told you I didn't love you – you wouldn't believe me: for truth is in this garden tonight.'

'Really, Mr Moon . . . ' said Rosamund, rather more faintly.

He kept two big blue magnetic eyes fixed on her face. 'Is my name Moon?' he asked. 'Is your name Hunt? On my honour, they sound to me as quaint and as distant as Red Indian names. It's as if your name was "Swim" and my name was "Sunrise". But our real names are Husband and Wife, as they were when we fell asleep.'

'It is no good,' said Rosamund, with real tears in her eyes; 'one can never go back.'

'I can go where I damn please,' said Michael, 'and I can carry you on my shoulder.'

'But really, Michael, really, you must stop and think!' cried the girl earnestly. 'You could carry me off my feet, I dare say, soul and body, but it may be bitter bad business for all that. These things done in that romantic rush, like Mr Smith's, they – they do attract women, I don't deny it. As you say, we're all telling the truth tonight. They've attracted poor Mary, for one. They attract me, Michael. But the cold fact remains: imprudent marriages do lead to long unhappiness and disappointment – you've got used to your drinks and things – I shan't be pretty much longer – '

'Imprudent marriages!' roared Michael. 'And pray where in earth or heaven are there any prudent marriages? Might as well talk about prudent suicides. You and I have dawdled round each other long enough, and are we any safer than Smith and Mary Gray, who met last night? You never know a husband till you marry him. Unhappy! of course you'll be unhappy. Who the devil are you that you shouldn't be unhappy, like the mother that bore you? Disappointed! of course we'll be disappointed. I, for one, don't expect till I die to be so good a man as I am at this minute – a tower with all the trumpets shouting.'

'You see all this,' said Rosamund, with a grand sincerity in her solid face, 'and do you really want to marry me?'

'My darling, what else is there to do?' reasoned the Irishman. 'What other occupation is there for an active man on this earth, except to marry you? What's the alternative to marriage, barring sleep? It's not liberty, Rosamund. Unless you marry God, as our nuns do in Ireland, you must marry Man – that is Me. The only third thing is to marry yourself – yourself, yourself, yourself – the only companion that is never satisfied – and never satisfactory.'

'Michael,' said Miss Hunt, in a very soft voice, 'if you won't talk so much, I'll marry you.'

'It's no time for talking,' cried Michael Moon; 'singing is the only thing. Can't you find that mandoline of yours, Rosamund?'

'Go and fetch it for me,' said Rosamund, with crisp and sharp authority.

The lounging Mr Moon stood for one split second astonished; then he shot away across the lawn, as if shod with the feathered shoes out of the Greek fairy tale. He cleared three yards and fifteen daisies at a leap, out of mere bodily levity; but when he came within a yard or two of the open parlour windows, his flying feet fell in their old manner like lead; he twisted round and came back slowly, whistling. The events of that enchanted evening were not at an end.

Inside the dark sitting-room of which Moon had caught a glimpse a curious thing had happened, almost an instant after the intemperate exit of Rosamund. It was something which, occurring in that obscure parlour, seemed to Arthur Inglewood like heaven and earth turning head over heels, the sea being the ceiling and the stars the floor. No words can express how it astonished him, as it astonishes all simple men when it happens. Yet the stiffest female stoicism seems separated from it only by a sheet of paper or a sheet of steel. It indicates no surrender, far less any sympathy. The most rigid and ruthless woman can begin to cry, just as the most effeminate man can grow a beard. It is a separate sexual power, and proves nothing one way or the other about force of character. But to young men ignorant of women, like Arthur Inglewood, to see Diana Duke crying was like seeing a motorcar shedding tears of petrol.

He could never have given (even if his really manly modesty had permitted it) any vaguest vision of what he did when he saw that portent. He acted as men do when a theatre catches fire – very differently from how they would have conceived themselves as acting, whether for better or worse. He had a faint memory of certain half-stifled explanations, that the heiress was the one really paying guest, and she would go, and the bailiffs (in consequence) would come; but after that he knew nothing of his own conduct except by the protests it evoked.

'Leave me alone, Mr Inglewood – leave me alone; that's not the way to help.'

'But I can help you,' said Arthur, with grinding certainty; 'I can, I can, I can . . .'

'Why, you said,' cried the girl, 'that you were much weaker than me.'

'So I am weaker than you,' said Arthur, in a voice that went vibrating through everything, 'but not just now.'

'Let go my hands!' cried Diana. 'I won't be bullied.'

In one element he was much stronger than she – the matter of humour. This leapt up in him suddenly, and he laughed, saying: 'Well, you are mean. You know quite well you'll bully me all the rest of my life. You might allow a man the one minute of his life when he's allowed to bully.'

It was as extraordinary for him to laugh as for her to cry, and for the first time since her childhood Diana was entirely off her guard.

'Do you mean you want to marry me?' she said.

'Why, there's a cab at the door!' cried Inglewood, springing up with an unconscious energy and bursting open the glass doors that led into the garden.

As he led her out by the hand they realised somehow for the first time that the house and garden were on a steep height over London. And yet, though they felt the place to be uplifted, they felt it also to be secret: it was like some round walled garden on the top of one of the turrets of heaven.

Inglewood looked around dreamily, his brown eyes devouring all sorts of details with a senseless delight. He noticed for the first time that the railings of the gate beyond the garden bushes were moulded like little spearheads and painted blue. He noticed that one of the blue spears was loosened in its place, and hung sideways; and this almost made him laugh. He thought it somehow exquisitely harmless and funny that the railing should be crooked; he thought he should like to know how it happened, who did it, and how the man was getting on.

When they were gone a few feet across that fiery grass they realised that they were not alone. Rosamund Hunt and the eccentric Mr Moon, both of whom they had last seen in the blackest temper of detachment, were standing together on the lawn. They were standing in quite an ordinary manner, and yet they looked somehow like people in a book.

'Oh,' said Diana, 'what lovely air!'

'I know,' called out Rosamund, with a pleasure so positive that it rang out like a complaint. 'It's just like that horrid, beastly fizzy stuff they gave me that made me feel happy.'

'Oh, it isn't like anything but itself!' answered Diana, breathing deeply. 'Why, it's all cold, and yet it feels like fire.'

'Barmy is the word we use in Fleet Street,' said Mr Moon. 'Barmy – especially on the crumpet.' And he fanned himself quite unnecessarily with his straw hat. They were all full of little leaps and pulsations of objectless and airy energy. Diana stirred and stretched her long arms rigidly, as if crucified, in a sort of excruciating restfulness; Michael stood still for long intervals, with gathered muscles, then spun round like a teetotum, and stood still again; Rosamund did not trip, for women never trip, except when they fall on their noses, but she struck the ground with her foot as she moved, as if to some inaudible dance tune; and Inglewood, leaning quite quietly against a tree, had unconsciously clutched a branch and shaken it with a creative violence. Those giant gestures of Man, that make the high statues and the strokes of war, tossed and tormented all their limbs. Silently as they strolled and stood they were bursting like batteries with an animal magnetism.

'And now,' cried Moon quite suddenly, stretching out a hand on each side, 'let's dance round that bush!'

'Why, what bush do you mean?' asked Rosamund, looking round with a sort of radiant rudeness.

'The bush that isn't there,' said Michael – 'the Mulberry Bush.'

They had taken each other's hands, half laughing and quite ritually; and before they could disconnect again Michael spun them all round, like a demon spinning the world for a top. Diana felt, as the circle of the horizon flew instantaneously around her, a far aerial sense of the ring of heights beyond London and corners where she had climbed as a child; she seemed almost to hear the rooks cawing about the old pines on Highgate, or to see the glowworms gathering and kindling in the woods of Box Hill.

The circle broke – as all such perfect circles of levity must break – and sent its author, Michael, flying, as by centrifugal force, far away against the blue rails of the gate. When reeling there he suddenly raised shout after shout of a new and quite dramatic character.

'Why, it's Warner!' he shouted, waving his arms. 'It's jolly old Warner – with a new silk hat and the old silk moustache!'

'Is that Dr Warner?' cried Rosamund, bounding forward in a burst of memory, amusement, and distress. 'Oh, I'm so sorry! Oh, do tell him it's all right!'

'Let's take hands and tell him,' said Michael Moon. For indeed, while they were talking, another hansom cab had dashed up behind the one already waiting, and Dr Herbert Warner, leaving a companion in the cab, had carefully deposited himself on the pavement.

Now, when you are an eminent physician and are wired for by an heiress to come to a case of dangerous mania, and when, as you come in through the garden to the house, the heiress and her landlady and two of the gentlemen boarders join hands and dance round you in a ring, calling out, 'It's all right! it's all right!' you are apt to be flustered and even displeased. Dr Warner was a placid but hardly a placable person. The two things are by no means the same; and even when Moon explained to him that he, Warner, with his high hat and tall, solid figure, was just such a classic figure as *ought* to be danced round by a ring of laughing maidens on some old golden Greek seashore – even then he seemed to miss the point of the general rejoicing.

'Inglewood!' cried Dr Warner, fixing his former disciple with a stare, 'are you mad?'

Arthur flushed to the roots of his brown hair, but he answered, easily and quietly enough, 'Not now. The truth is, Warner, I've just made a rather important medical discovery – quite in your line.'

'What do you mean?' asked the great doctor stiffly – 'what discovery?'

'I've discovered that health really is catching, like disease,' answered Arthur.

'Yes; sanity has broken out, and is spreading,' said Michael, performing a *pas seul* with a thoughtful expression. 'Twenty thousand more cases taken to the hospitals; nurses employed night and day.'

Dr Warner studied Michael's grave face and lightly moving legs with an unfathomed wonder. 'And is *this*, may I ask,' he said, 'the sanity that is spreading?'

'You must forgive me, Dr Warner,' cried Rosamund Hunt heartily. 'I know I've treated you badly; but indeed it was all a mistake. I was in a frightfully bad temper when I sent for you, but now it all seems like a dream – and Mr Smith is the sweetest, most sensible, most delightful old thing that ever existed, and he may marry anyone he likes – except me.'

'I should suggest Mrs Duke,' said Michael.

The gravity of Dr Warner's face increased. He took a slip of pink paper from his waistcoat pocket, with his pale blue eyes quietly fixed on Rosamund's face all the time. He spoke with a not inexcusable frigidity.

'Really, Miss Hunt,' he said, 'you are not yet very reassuring. You sent me this wire only half an hour ago: "Come at once, if possible, with another doctor. Man – Innocent Smith – gone mad on premises, and doing dreadful things. Do you know anything of him?" I went round at once to a distinguished colleague of mine, a doctor who is also a private detective and an authority on criminal lunacy; he has come round with me, and is waiting in the cab. Now you calmly tell me that this criminal madman is a highly sweet and sane old thing, with accompaniments that set me speculating on your own definition of sanity. I hardly comprehend the change.'

'Oh, how can one explain a change in sun and moon and everybody's soul?' cried Rosamund, in despair. 'Must I confess we had got so morbid as to think him mad merely because he wanted to get married; and that we didn't even know it was only because we wanted to get married ourselves? We'll humiliate ourselves, if you like, doctor; we're happy enough.'

'Where is Mr Smith?' asked Warner of Inglewood very sharply.

Arthur started; he had forgotten all about the central figure of their farce, who had not been visible for an hour or more.

'I – I think he's on the other side of the house, by the dustbin,' he said.

'He may be on the road to Russia,' said Warner, 'but he must be found.' And he strode away and disappeared round a corner of the house by the sunflowers.

'I hope,' said Rosamund, 'he won't really interfere with Mr Smith.'

'Interfere with the daisies!' said Michael with a snort. 'A man can't be locked up for falling in love – at least I hope not.'

'No; I think even a doctor couldn't make a disease out of him. He'd throw off the doctor like the disease, don't you know? I believe it's a case of a sort of holy well. I believe Innocent Smith is simply innocent, and that is why he is so extraordinary.'

It was Rosamund who spoke, restlessly tracing circles in the grass with the point of her white shoe.

'I think,' said Inglewood, 'that Smith is not extraordinary at all. He's comic just because he's so startlingly commonplace. Don't you know what it is to be all one family circle, with aunts and uncles, when a schoolboy comes home for the holidays? That bag there on the cab is only a schoolboy's hamper. This tree here in the garden is only the sort of tree that any schoolboy would have climbed. Yes, that's the thing that has haunted us all about him, the thing we could never fit a word to. Whether he is my old schoolfellow or no, at least he is all my old schoolfellows. He is the endless bun-eating, ball-throwing animal that we have all been.'

'That is only you absurd boys,' said Diana. 'I don't believe any girl was ever so silly, and I'm sure no girl was ever so happy, except – ' and she stopped.

'I will tell you the truth about Innocent Smith,' said Michael Moon in a low voice. 'Dr Warner has gone to look for him in vain. He is not there. Haven't you noticed that we never saw him since we found ourselves? He was an astral baby born on all four of us; he was only our own youth returned. Long before poor old Warner had clambered out of his cab, the thing we called Smith had dissolved into dew and light on this lawn. Once or twice more, by the mercy of God, we may feel the thing, but the man we shall never see. In a spring garden before breakfast we shall smell the smell called Smith. In the snapping of brisk twigs in tiny fires we shall hear a noise named Smith. Everything insatiable and innocent in the grasses that gobble up the earth like babies at a bun feast, in the white mornings that split the sky as a boy splits up white fir wood, we may feel for one instant the presence of an impetuous purity; but his innocence was too close to the unconsciousness of inanimate things not to melt back at a mere touch into the mild hedges and heavens; he – '

He was interrupted from behind the house by a bang like that of a bomb. Almost at the same instant the stranger in the cab sprang out of it, leaving it rocking upon the stones of the road. He clutched the blue railings of the garden, and peered eagerly over them in the direction of the noise. He was a small, loose, yet alert man, very thin, with a face that seemed made out of fish bones, and a silk hat quite as rigid and resplendent as Warner's, but thrust back recklessly on the hinder part of his head.

'Murder!' he shrieked, in a high and feminine but very penetrating voice. 'Stop that murderer there!'

Even as he shrieked a second shot shook the lower windows of the house, and with the noise of it Dr Herbert Warner came flying round the corner like a leaping rabbit. Yet before he had reached the group a third discharge had deafened them, and they saw with their own eyes two spots of white sky drilled through the second of the unhappy Herbert's high hats. The next moment the fugitive physician fell over a flowerpot, and came down on all fours, staring like a cow. The hat with the two shot-holes in it rolled upon the gravel path before him, and Innocent Smith came round the corner like a railway train. He was looking twice his proper size – a giant clad in green, the big revolver still smoking in his hand, his face sanguine and in shadow, his eyes blazing like all stars, and his yellow hair standing out all ways like Struwelpeter's.

Though this startling scene hung but an instant in stillness, Inglewood had time to feel once more what he had felt when he saw the other lovers standing on the lawn – the sensation of a certain cut and coloured clearness that belongs rather to the things of art than to the things of experience. The broken flowerpot with its red-hot geraniums, the green bulk of Smith and the black bulk of Warner, the blue-spiked railings behind, clutched by the stranger's yellow vulture claws and peered over by his long vulture neck, the silk hat on the gravel, and the little cloudlet of smoke floating across the garden as innocently as the puff of a cigarette – all these seemed unnaturally distinct and definite. They existed, like symbols, in an ecstasy of separation. Indeed, every object grew more and more particular and precious because the whole picture was breaking up. Things look so bright just before they burst.

Long before his fancies had begun, let alone ceased, Arthur had stepped across and taken one of Smith's arms. Simultaneously the little stranger had run up the steps and taken the other. Smith went into peals of laughter, and surrendered his pistol with perfect willingness. Moon raised the doctor to his feet, and then went and leaned sullenly on the garden gate. The girls were quiet and vigilant, as good women mostly are in instants of catastrophe, but their faces showed that, somehow or other, a light had been dashed out of the sky. The doctor himself, when he had risen, collected his hat and wits, and dusting himself down with an air of great disgust, turned to them in brief apology. He was very white with his recent panic, but he spoke with perfect self-control.

'You will excuse us, ladies,' he said; 'my friend and Mr Inglewood are both scientists in their several ways. I think we had better all take Mr Smith indoors, and communicate with you later.'

And under the guard of the three natural philosophers the disarmed Smith was led tactfully into the house, still roaring with laughter.

From time to time during the next twenty minutes his distant boom of mirth could again be heard through the half-open window; but there came no echo of the quiet voices of the physicians. The girls walked about the garden together, rubbing up each other's spirits as best they might; Michael Moon still hung heavily against the gate. Somewhere about the expiration of that time Dr Warner came out of the house with a face less pale but even more stern, and the little man with the fish-bone face advanced gravely in his rear. And if the face of Warner in the sunlight was that of a hanging judge, the face of the little man behind was more like a death's-head.

'Miss Hunt,' said Dr Herbert Warner, 'I only wish to offer you my warm thanks and admiration. By your prompt courage and wisdom in sending for us by wire this evening, you have enabled us to capture and put out of mischief one of the most cruel and terrible of the enemies of humanity – a criminal whose plausibility and pitilessness have never been before combined in flesh.'

Rosamund looked across at him with a white, blank face and blinking eyes. 'What do you mean?' she asked. 'You can't mean Mr Smith?'

'He has gone by many other names,' said the doctor gravely, 'and not one he did not leave to be cursed behind him. That man, Miss Hunt, has left a track of blood and tears across the world. Whether he is mad as well as wicked, we are trying, in the interests of science, to discover. In any case, we shall have to take him to a magistrate first, even if only on the road to a lunatic asylum. But the lunatic asylum in which he is confined will have to be sealed with wall within wall, and ringed with guns like a fortress, or he will break out again to bring forth carnage and darkness on the earth.'

Rosamund looked at the two doctors, her face growing paler and paler. Then her eyes strayed to Michael, who was leaning on the gate; but he continued to lean on it without moving, with his face turned away towards the darkening road.

CHAPTER 5

The Allegorical Practical Joker

The criminal specialist who had come with Dr Warner was a somewhat more urbane and even dapper figure than he had appeared when clutching the railings and craning his neck into the garden. He even looked comparatively young when he took his hat off, having fair hair parted in the middle and carefully curled on each side, and lively movements, especially of the hands. He had a dandified monocle slung round his neck by a broad black ribbon, and a big bow tie, as if a big American moth had alighted on him. His dress and gestures were bright enough for a boy's; it was only when you looked at the fish-bone face that you beheld something acrid and old. His manners were excellent, though hardly English, and he had two half-conscious tricks by which people who only met him once remembered him. One was a trick of closing his eyes when he wished to be particularly polite; the other was one of lifting his joined thumb and forefinger in the air as if holding a pinch of snuff, when he was hesitating or hovering over a word. But those who were longer in his company tended to forget these oddities in the stream of his quaint and solemn conversation and really singular views.

'Miss Hunt,' said Dr Warner, 'this is Dr Cyrus Pym.'

Dr Cyrus Pym shut his eyes during the introduction, rather as if he were 'playing fair' in some child's game, and gave a prompt little bow, which somehow suddenly revealed him as a citizen of the United States.

'Dr Cyrus Pym,' continued Warner (Dr Pym shut his eyes again), 'is perhaps the first criminological expert of America. We are very fortunate to be able to consult with him in this extraordinary case – '

'I can't make head or tail of anything,' said Rosamund. 'How can poor Mr Smith be so dreadful as he is by your account?'

'Or by your telegram,' said Herbert Warner, smiling.

'Oh, you don't understand,' cried the girl impatiently. 'Why, he's done us all more good than going to church.'

'I think I can explain to the young lady,' said Dr Cyrus Pym. 'This criminal or maniac Smith is a very genius of evil, and has a method of his own, a method of the most daring ingenuity. He is popular wherever he goes, for he invades every house as an uproarious child. People are getting suspicious of all the respectable disguises for a scoundrel; so he always uses the disguise of – what shall I say – the Bohemian, the blameless Bohemian. He always carries people off their feet. People are used to the mask of conventional good conduct. He goes in for eccentric good-nature. You expect a Don Juan to dress up as a solemn and solid Spanish merchant; but you're not prepared when he dresses up as Don Quixote. You expect a humbug to behave like Sir Charles Grandison; because (with all respect, Miss Hunt, for the deep, tear-moving tenderness of Samuel Richardson) Sir Charles Grandison so often behaved like a humbug. But no real red-blooded citizen is quite ready for a humbug that models himself not on Sir Charles Grandison but on Sir Roger de Coverly. Setting up to be a good man a little cracked is a new criminal incognito, Miss Hunt. It's been a great notion, and uncommonly successful; but its success just makes it mighty cruel. I can forgive Dick Turpin if he impersonates Dr Busby; I can't forgive him when he impersonates Dr Johnson. The saint with a tile loose is a bit too sacred, I guess, to be parodied.'

'But how do you know,' cried Rosamund desperately, 'that Mr Smith is a known criminal?'

'I collated all the documents,' said the American, 'when my friend Warner knocked me up on receipt of your cable. It is my professional affair to know these facts, Miss Hunt; and there's no more doubt about them than about the Bradshaw down at the depot. This man has hitherto escaped the law, through his admirable affectations of infancy or insanity. But I myself, as a specialist, have privately authenticated notes of some eighteen or twenty crimes attempted or achieved in this manner. He comes to houses as he has to this, and gets a grand popularity. He makes things go. They do go; when he's gone the things are gone. Gone, Miss Hunt, gone, a man's life or a man's spoons, or more often a woman. I assure you I have all the memoranda.'

'I have seen them,' said Warner solidly. 'I can assure you that all this is correct.'

'The most unmanly aspect, according to my feelings,' went on the American doctor, 'is this perpetual deception of innocent women by a wild simulation of innocence. From almost every house where this great imaginative devil has been, he has taken some poor girl away with him; some say he's got a hypnotic eye with his other queer features, and that they go like automata. What's become of all those poor girls nobody knows. Murdered, I dare say; for we've lots of instances, besides this one, of his turning his hand to murder, though none ever brought him under the law. Anyhow, our most modern methods of research can't find any trace of the wretched women. It's when I think of them that I am really moved, Miss Hunt. And I've really nothing else to say just now except what Dr Warner has said.'

'Quite so,' said Warner, with a smile that seemed moulded in marble – 'that we all have to thank you very much for that telegram.'

The little Yankee scientist had been speaking with such evident sincerity that one forgot the tricks of his voice and manner – the falling eyelids, the rising intonation, and the poised finger and thumb – which were at other times a little comic. It was not so much that he was cleverer than Warner; perhaps he was not so clever, though he was more celebrated. But he had what Warner never had, a fresh and unaffected seriousness – the great American virtue of simplicity. Rosamund knitted her brows and looked gloomily towards the darkening house that contained the dark prodigy.

Broad daylight still endured; but it had already changed from gold to silver, and was changing from silver to grey. The long plumy shadows of the one or two trees in the garden faded more and more upon a dead background of dusk. In the sharpest and deepest shadow, which was the entrance to the house by the big French windows, Rosamund could watch a hurried consultation between Inglewood (who was still left in charge of the mysterious captive) and Diana, who had moved to his assistance from without. After a few minutes and gestures they went inside, shutting the glass doors upon the garden; and the garden seemed to grow greyer still.

The American gentleman named Pym seemed to be turning and on the move in the same direction; but before he started he spoke to Rosamund with a flash of that guileless tact which redeemed much of his childish vanity, and with something of that spontaneous poetry which made it difficult, pedantic as he was, to call him a pedant.

'I'm vurry sorry, Miss Hunt,' he said; 'but Dr Warner and I, as two quali-*fied* practitioners, had better take Mr Smith away in that cab, and the less said about it the better. Don't you agitate yourself, Miss Hunt. You've just got to think that we're taking away a monstrosity, something that oughtn't to be at all – something like one of those gods in your Britannic Museum, all wings, and beards, and legs, and eyes, and no shape. That's what Smith is, and you shall soon be quit of him.'

He had already taken a step towards the house, and Warner was about to follow him, when the glass doors were opened again and Diana Duke came out with more than her usual quickness across the lawn. Her face was aquiver with worry and excitement, and her dark earnest eyes fixed only on the other girl.

'Rosamund,' she cried in despair, 'what shall I do with her?'

'With her?' cried Miss Hunt, with a violent jump. 'O lord, he isn't a woman too, is he?'

'No, no, no,' said Dr Pym soothingly, as if in common fairness. 'A woman? no, really, he is not so bad as that.'

'I mean your friend Mary Gray,' retorted Diana with equal tartness. 'What on earth am I to do with her?'

'How can we tell her about Smith, you mean,' answered Rosamund, her face at once clouded and softening. 'Yes, it will be pretty painful.'

'But I *have* told her,' exploded Diana, with more than her congenital exasperation. 'I have told her, and she doesn't seem to mind. She still says she's going away with Smith in that cab.'

'But it's impossible!' ejaculated Rosamund. 'Why, Mary is really religious. She – '

She stopped in time to realise that Mary Gray was comparatively close to her on the lawn. Her quiet companion had come down very quietly into the garden, but dressed very decisively for travel. She had a neat but very ancient blue tam-o'-shanter on her head, and was pulling some rather threadbare grey gloves on to her hands. Yet the two tints fitted excellently with her heavy copper-coloured hair; the more excellently for the touch of shabbiness: for a woman's clothes never suit her so well as when they seem to suit her by accident.

But in this case the woman had a quality yet more unique and attractive. In such grey hours, when the sun is sunk and the skies are already sad, it will often happen that one reflection at some occasional angle will cause to linger the last of the light. A scrap of window, a scrap of water, a scrap of looking-glass, will be full of the fire that is lost to all the rest of the earth. The quaint, almost triangular face of Mary Gray was like some triangular piece of mirror that could still repeat the splendour of hours before. Mary, though she was always graceful, could never before have properly been called beautiful; and yet her happiness amid all that misery was so beautiful as to make a man catch his breath.

'O Diana,' cried Rosamund in a lower voice and altering her phrase; 'but how did you tell her?'

'It is quite easy to tell her,' answered Diana sombrely; 'it makes no impression at all.'

'I'm afraid I've kept everything waiting,' said Mary Gray apologetically, 'and now we must really say goodbye. Innocent is taking me to his aunt's over at Hampstead, and I'm afraid she goes to bed early.'

Her words were quite casual and practical, but there was a sort of sleepy light in her eyes that was more baffling than darkness; she was like one speaking absently with her eye on some very distant object.

'Mary, Mary,' cried Rosamund, almost breaking down, 'I'm so sorry about it, but the thing can't be at all. We – we have found out all about Mr Smith.'

'All?' repeated Mary, with a low and curious intonation; 'why, that must be awfully exciting.'

There was no noise for an instant and no motion except that the silent Michael Moon, leaning on the gate, lifted his head, as it might be to listen. Then Rosamund remaining speechless, Dr Pym came to her rescue in a definite way.

'To begin with,' he said, 'this man Smith is constantly attempting murder. The Warden of Brakespeare College – '

'I know,' said Mary, with a vague but radiant smile. 'Innocent told me.'

'I can't say what he told you,' replied Pym quickly, 'but I'm very much afraid it wasn't true. The plain truth is that the man's stained with every known human crime. I assure you I have all the documents. I have evidence of his committing burglary, signed by a most eminent English curate. I have – '

'Oh, but there were two curates,' cried Mary, with a certain gentle eagerness; 'that was what made it so much funnier.'

The darkened glass doors of the house opened once more, and Inglewood appeared for an instant, making a sort of signal. The American doctor bowed, the English doctor did not, but they both set out stolidly towards the house. No one else moved, not even Michael hanging on the gate; but the back of his head and shoulders had still an indescribable indication that he was listening to every word.

'But don't you understand, Mary,' cried Rosamund in despair; 'don't you know that awful things have happened even before our very eyes. I should have thought you would have heard the revolver shots upstairs.'

'Yes, I heard the shots,' said Mary almost brightly; 'but I was busy packing just then. And Innocent had told me he was going to shoot at Dr Warner; so it wasn't worth while to come down.'

'Oh, I don't understand what you mean,' cried Rosamund Hunt, stamping, 'but you must and shall understand what I mean. I don't care how cruelly I put it, if only I can save you. I mean that your Innocent Smith is the most awfully wicked man in the world. He has sent bullets at lots of other men and gone off in cabs with lots of other women. And he seems to have killed the women too, for nobody can find them.'

'He is really rather naughty sometimes,' said Mary Gray, laughing softly as she buttoned her old grey gloves.

'Oh, this is really mesmerism, or something,' said Rosamund, and burst into tears.

At the same moment the two black-clad doctors appeared out of the house with their great green-clad captive between them. He made no resistance, but was still laughing in a groggy and half-witted style. Arthur Inglewood followed in the rear, a dark and red study in the last shades of distress and shame. In this black, funereal, and painfully realistic style the exit from Beacon House was made by a man whose entrance a day before had been effected by the happy leaping of a wall and the hilarious climbing of a tree. No one moved of the groups in the garden except Mary Gray, who stepped forward quite naturally, calling out, 'Are you ready, Innocent? Our cab's been waiting such a long time.'

'Ladies and gentlemen,' said Dr Warner firmly, 'I must insist on asking this lady to stand aside. We shall have trouble enough as it is, with the three of us in a cab.'

'But it *is* our cab,' persisted Mary. 'Why, there's Innocent's yellow bag on the top of it.'

'Stand aside,' repeated Warner roughly. 'And you, Mr Moon, please be so obliging as to move a moment. Come, come! the sooner this ugly business is over the better – and how can we open the gate if you will keep leaning on it?'

Michael Moon looked at his long lean forefinger, and seemed to consider and reconsider this argument. 'Yes,' he said at last; 'but how can I lean on this gate if you keep on opening it?'

'Oh, get out of the way!' cried Warner, almost good-humouredly. 'You can lean on the gate any time.'

'No,' said Moon reflectively. 'Seldom the time and the place and the blue gate altogether; and it all depends whether you come of an old country family. My ancestors leaned on gates before anyone had discovered how to open them.'

'Michael!' cried Arthur Inglewood in a kind of agony, 'are you going to get out of the way?'

'Why, no; I think not,' said Michael, after some meditation, and swung himself slowly round, so that he confronted the company, while still, in a lounging attitude, occupying the path.

'Hullo!' he called out suddenly; 'what are you doing to Mr Smith?'

'Taking him away,' answered Warner shortly, 'to be examined.'

'Matriculation?' asked Moon brightly.

'By a magistrate,' said the other curtly.

'And what other magistrate,' cried Michael, raising his voice, 'dares to try what befell on this free soil, save only the ancient and independent Dukes of Beacon? What other court dares to try one of our company, save only the High Court of Beacon? Have you forgotten that only this afternoon we flew the flag of independence and severed ourselves from all the nations of the earth?'

'Michael,' cried Rosamund, wringing her hands, 'how can you stand there talking nonsense? Why, you saw the dreadful thing yourself. You were there when he went mad. It was you that helped the doctor up when he fell over the flowerpot.'

'And the High Court of Beacon,' replied Moon with hauteur, 'has special powers in all cases concerning lunatics, flowerpots, and doctors who fall down in gardens. It's in our very first charter from Edward I: "*Si medicus quisquam in horto prostratus* – " '

'Out of the way!' cried Warner with sudden fury, 'or we will force you out of it.'

'What!' cried Michael Moon, with a cry of hilarious fierceness. 'Shall I die in defence of this sacred pale? Will you paint these blue railings red with my gore?' and he laid hold of one of the blue spikes behind him. As Inglewood had noticed earlier in the evening, the railing was loose and crooked at this place, and the painted iron staff and spearhead came away in Michael's hand as he shook it.

'See!' he cried, brandishing this broken javelin in the air, 'the very lances round Beacon Tower leap from their places to defend it. Ah, in such a place and hour it is a fine thing to die alone!' And in a voice like a drum he rolled the noble lines of Ronsard:

> 'Ou pour l'honneur de Dieu, ou pour le droit de mon prince,
> Navré, poitrine ouverte, au bord de mon province.'

'Sakes alive!' said the American gentleman, almost in an awed tone. Then he added, 'Are there two maniacs here?'

'No; there are five,' thundered Moon. 'Smith and I are the only sane people left.'

'Michael!' cried Rosamund; 'Michael, what does it mean?'

'It means bosh!' roared Michael, and slung his painted spear hurtling to the other end of the garden. 'It means that doctors are bosh, and criminology is bosh, and Americans are bosh – much more bosh than our Court of Beacon. It means, you fatheads, that Innocent Smith is no more mad or bad than the bird on that tree.'

'But, my dear Moon,' began Inglewood in his modest manner, 'these gentlemen – '

'On the word of two doctors,' exploded Moon again, without listening to anybody else, 'shut up in a private hell on the word of two doctors! And such doctors! Oh, my hat! Look at 'em! – do just look at 'em! Would you read a book, or buy a dog, or go to a hotel on the advice of twenty such? My people came from Ireland, and were Catholics. What would you say if I called a man wicked on the word of two priests?'

'But it isn't only their word, Michael,' reasoned Rosamund; 'they've got evidence too.'

'Have you looked at it?' asked Moon.

'No,' said Rosamund, with a sort of faint surprise; 'these gentlemen are in charge of it.'

'And of everything else, it seems to me,' said Michael. 'Why, you haven't even had the decency to consult Mrs Duke.'

'Oh, that's no use,' said Diana in an undertone to Rosamund; 'Auntie couldn't say "Bo!" to a goose.'

'I am glad to hear it,' answered Michael, 'for with such a flock of geese to say it to, the horrid expletive might be constantly on her lips. For my part, I simply refuse to let things be done in this light and airy style. I appeal to Mrs Duke – it's her house.'

'Mrs Duke?' repeated Inglewood doubtfully.

'Yes, Mrs Duke,' said Michael firmly, 'commonly called the Iron Duke.'

'If you ask Auntie,' said Diana quietly, 'she'll only be for doing nothing at all. Her only idea is to hush things up or to let things slide. That just suits her.'

'Yes,' replied Michael Moon; 'and, as it happens, it just suits all of us. You are impatient with your elders, Miss Duke; but when you are as old yourself you will know what Napoleon knew – that half one's letters answer themselves if you can only refrain from the fleshly appetite of answering them.'

He was still lounging in the same absurd attitude, with his elbow on the gate, but his voice had altered abruptly for the third time; just as it had changed from the mock heroic to the humanly indignant, it now changed to the airy incisiveness of a lawyer giving good legal advice.

'It isn't only your aunt who wants to keep this quiet if she can,' he said; 'we all want to keep it quiet if we can. Look at the large facts – the big bones of the case. I believe those scientific gentlemen have made a highly scientific mistake. I believe Smith is as blameless as a buttercup. I admit buttercups don't often let off loaded pistols in private houses; I admit there is something demanding explanation. But I am morally certain there's some blunder, or some joke, or some allegory, or some accident behind all this. Well, suppose I'm wrong. We've disarmed him; we're five men to hold him; he may as well go to a lock-up later on as now. But suppose there's even a chance of my being right. Is it anybody's interest here to wash this linen in public?

'Come, I'll take each of you in order. Once take Smith outside that gate, and you take him into the front page of the evening papers. I know; I've written the front page myself. Miss Duke, do you or your aunt want a sort of notice stuck up over your boarding-house – "Doctors shot here."? No, no – doctors are rubbish, as I said; but you don't want the rubbish shot here. Arthur, suppose I am right, or suppose I am wrong. Smith has appeared as an old schoolfellow of yours. Mark my words, if he's proved guilty, the Organs of Public Opinion will say you introduced him. If he's proved innocent, they will say you helped to collar him. Rosamund, my dear, suppose I am right or wrong. If he's proved guilty, they'll say you engaged your companion to him. If he's proved innocent, they'll print that telegram. I know the Organs, damn them.'

He stopped an instant; for this rapid rationalism left him more breathless than had either his theatrical or his real denunciation. But he was plainly in earnest, as well as positive and lucid; as was proved by his proceeding quickly the moment he had found his breath.

'It is just the same,' he cried, 'with our medical friends. You will say that Dr Warner has a grievance. I agree. But does he want specially to be snap-shotted by all the journalists *prostratus in horto*? It was no fault of his, but the scene was not very dignified even for him. He must have justice; but does he want to ask for justice, not only on his knees, but on his hands and knees? Does he want to enter the court of justice on all fours? Doctors are not allowed to advertise; and I'm sure no doctor wants to advertise himself as looking like that. And even for our American guest the interest is the same. Let us suppose that he has conclusive documents. Let us assume that he has revelations really worth reading. Well, in a legal enquiry (or a medical enquiry, for that matter) ten to one he won't be allowed to read them. He'll be tripped up every two or three minutes with some tangle of old rules. A man can't tell the truth in public nowadays. But he can still tell it in private; he can tell it inside that house.'

'It is quite true,' said Dr Cyrus Pym, who had listened throughout the speech with a seriousness which only an American could have retained through such a scene. 'It is true that I have been perceptibly less hampered in private enquiries.'

'Dr Pym!' cried Warner in a sort of sudden anger. 'Dr Pym! you aren't surely going to admit – '

'Smith may be mad,' went on the melancholy Moon in a monologue that seemed as heavy as a hatchet, 'but there was something after all in what he said about Home Rule for every home. Yes, there is something, when all's said and done, in the High Court of Beacon. It is really true that human beings might often get some sort of domestic justice where just now they can only get legal injustice – oh, I am a lawyer too, and I know that as well. It is true that there's too much official and indirect power. Often and often the thing a whole nation can't settle is just the thing a family could settle. Scores of young criminals have been fined and sent to jail when they ought to have been thrashed and sent to bed. Scores of men, I am sure, have had a lifetime at Hanwell when they only wanted a week at Brighton. There *is* something in Smith's notion of domestic self-government; and I propose that we put it into practice. You have the prisoner; you have the documents. Come, we are a company of free, white, Christian people, such as might be besieged in a town or cast up on a desert island. Let us do this thing ourselves. Let us go into that house there and sit down and find out with our own eyes and ears whether this thing is true or not; whether this Smith is a man or a monster. If we can't do a little thing like that, what right have we to put crosses on ballot papers?'

Inglewood and Pym exchanged a glance; and Warner, who was no fool, saw in that glance that Moon was gaining ground. The motives that led Arthur to think of surrender were indeed very different from those which affected Dr Cyrus Pym. All Arthur's instincts were on the side of privacy and polite settlement; he was very English and would often endure wrongs rather than right them by scenes and serious rhetoric. To play at once the buffoon and the knight-errant, like his Irish friend, would have been absolute torture to him; but even the semi-official part he had played that afternoon was very painful. He was not likely to be reluctant if anyone could convince him that his duty was to let sleeping dogs lie.

On the other hand, Cyrus Pym belonged to a country in which things are possible that seem crazy to the English. Regulations and authorities exactly like one of Innocent's pranks or one of Michael's satires really exist, propped by placid policemen and imposed on bustling business men. Pym knew whole States which are vast and yet secret and fanciful; each is as big as a nation yet as private as a lost village, and as unexpected as an apple-pie bed. States where no man may have a cigarette, States where any man may have ten wives, very strict prohibition States, very lax divorce States – all these large local vagaries had prepared Cyrus Pym's mind for small local vagaries in a smaller country. Infinitely more remote from England than any Russian or Italian, utterly incapable of even conceiving what English conventions are, he could not see the social impossibility of the Court of Beacon. It is firmly believed by those who shared the experiment, that to the very end Pym believed in that phantasmal court and supposed it to be some Britannic institution.

Towards the synod thus somewhat at a standstill there approached through the growing haze and gloaming a short dark figure with a walk apparently founded on the imperfect repression of a negro breakdown. Something at once in the familiarity and the incongruity of this being moved Michael to even heartier outbursts of a healthy and humane flippancy.

'Why, here's little Nosey Gould,' he exclaimed. 'Isn't the mere sight of him enough to banish all your morbid reflections?'

'Really,' replied Dr Warner, 'I really fail to see how Mr Gould affects the question; and I once more demand – '

'Hello! what's the funeral, gents?' enquired the newcomer with the air of an uproarious umpire. 'Doctor demandin' something? Always the way at a boarding-house, you know. Always lots of demand. No supply.'

As delicately and impartially as he could, Michael restated his position, and indicated generally that Smith had been guilty of certain dangerous and dubious acts, and that there had even arisen an allegation that he was insane.

'Well, of course he is,' said Moses Gould equably; 'it don't need old 'Olmes to see that. The 'awk-like face of 'Olmes,' he added with abstract relish, 'showed a shide of disappointment, the sleuth-like Gould 'avin' got there before 'im.'

'If he is mad,' began Inglewood.

'Well,' said Moses, 'when a cove gets out on the tiles the first night there's generally a tile loose.'

'You never objected before,' said Diana Duke rather stiffly, 'and you're generally pretty free with your complaints.'

'I don't compline of him,' said Moses magnanimously, 'the poor chap's 'armless enough; you might tie 'im up in the garden here and 'e'd make noises at the burglars.'

'Moses,' said Moon with solemn fervour, 'you are the incarnation of Common Sense. You think Mr Innocent is mad. Let me introduce you to the incarnation of Scientific Theory. He also thinks Mr Innocent is mad. – Doctor, this is my friend Mr Gould. – Moses, this is the celebrated Dr Cyrus Pym.' The celebrated Dr Cyrus Pym closed his eyes and bowed. He also murmured his national war-cry in a low voice, which sounded like 'Pleased to meet you.'

'Now you two people,' said Michael cheerfully, 'who both think our poor friend mad, shall jolly well go into that house over there and prove him mad. What could be more powerful than the combination of Scientific Theory with Common Sense? United you stand; divided you fall. I will not be so uncivil as to suggest that Dr Pym has no common sense; I confine myself to recording the chronological accident that he has not shown us any so far. I take the freedom of an old friend in staking my shirt that Moses has no scientific theory. Yet against this strong coalition I am ready to appear, armed with nothing but an intuition – which is American for a guess.'

'Distinguished by Mr Gould's assistance,' said Pym, opening his eyes suddenly. 'I gather that though he and I are identical in primary di-agnosis there is yet between us something that cannot be called a disagreement, something which we may perhaps call a – ' He put the points of thumb and forefinger together, spreading the other fingers exquisitely in the air, and seemed to be waiting for somebody else to tell him what to say.

'Catchin' flies?' enquired the affable Moses.

'A divergence,' said Dr Pym, with a refined sigh of relief; 'a divergence. Granted that the man in question is deranged, he would not necessarily be all that science requires in a homicidal maniac – '

'Has it occurred to you,' observed Moon, who was leaning on the gate again, and did not turn round, 'that if he were a homicidal maniac he might have killed us all here while we were talking?'

Something exploded silently underneath all their minds, like sealed dynamite in some forgotten cellars. They all remembered for the first time for some hour or two that the monster of whom they were talking was standing quietly among them. They had left him in the garden like a garden statue; there might have been a dolphin coiling round his legs, or a fountain pouring out of his mouth, for all the notice they had taken of Innocent Smith. He stood with his crest of blond, blown hair thrust somewhat forward, his fresh-coloured, rather short-sighted face looking patiently downwards at nothing in particular, his huge shoulders humped, and his hands in his trousers pockets. So far as they could guess he had not moved at all. His green coat might have been cut out of the green turf on which he stood. In his shadow Pym had expounded and Rosamund expostulated, Michael had ranted and Moses had ragged. He had remained like a thing graven; the god of the garden. A sparrow had perched on one of his heavy shoulders; and then, after correcting its costume of feathers, had flown away.

'Why,' cried Michael, with a shout of laughter, 'the Court of Beacon has opened – and shut up again too. You all know now I am right. Your buried common sense has told you what my buried common sense has told me. Smith might have fired off a hundred cannons instead of a pistol, and you would still know he was harmless as I know he is harmless. Back we all go to the house and clear a room for discussion. For the High Court of Beacon, which has already arrived at its decision, is just about to begin its enquiry.'

'Just a goin' to begin!' cried little Mr Moses in an extraordinary sort of disinterested excitement, like that of an animal during music or a thunderstorm. 'Follow on to the 'Igh Court of Eggs and Bacon; 'ave a kipper from the old firm! 'Is Lordship complimented Mr Gould on the 'igh professional delicacy 'e had shown, and which was worthy of the best traditions of the Saloon Bar – and three of Scotch hot, miss! Oh, chase me, girls!'

The girls betraying no temptation to chase him, he went away in a sort of waddling dance of pure excitement; and had made a circuit of the garden before he reappeared, breathless but still beaming. Moon had known his man when he realised that no people presented to Moses Gould could be quite serious, even if they were quite furious. The glass doors stood open on the side nearest to Mr Moses Gould; and as the feet of that festive idiot were evidently turned in the same direction, everybody else went that way with the unanimity of some uproarious procession. Only Diana Duke retained enough rigidity to say the thing that had been boiling at her fierce feminine lips for the last few hours. Under the shadow of tragedy she had kept it back as unsympathetic. 'In that case,' she said sharply, 'these cabs can be sent away.'

'Well, Innocent must have his bag, you know,' said Mary with a smile. 'I dare say the cabman would get it down for us.'

'I'll get the bag,' said Smith, speaking for the first time in hours; his voice sounded remote and rude, like the voice of a statue.

Those who had so long danced and disputed round his immobility were left breathless by his precipitance. With a run and spring he was out of the garden into the street; with a spring and one quivering kick he was actually on the roof of the cab. The cabman happened to be standing by the horse's head, having just removed its emptied nosebag. Smith seemed for an instant to be rolling about on the cab's back in the embraces of his Gladstone bag. The next instant, however, he had rolled, as if by a royal luck, into the high seat behind, and with a shriek of piercing and appalling suddenness had sent the horse flying and scampering far away down the street.

His evanescence was so violent and swift, that this time it was all the other people who were turned into garden statues. Mr Moses Gould, however, being ill-adapted both physically and morally for the purposes of permanent sculpture, came to life some time before the rest, and, turning to Moon, remarked, like a man starting chattily with a stranger on an omnibus, 'Tile loose, eh? Cab loose anyhow.' There followed a fatal silence; and then Dr Warner said, with a sneer like a club of stone: 'This is what comes of the Court of Beacon, Mr Moon. You have let loose a maniac on the whole metropolis.'

Beacon House stood, as has been said, at the end of a long crescent of continuous houses. The little garden that shut it in ran out into a sharp point like a green cape pushed out into the sea of two streets. Smith and his cab shot up one side of the triangle, and certainly most of those standing inside of it never expected to see him again. At the apex, however, he turned the horse sharply round and drove with equal violence up the other side of the garden, visible to all those in the group. With a common impulse the little crowd ran across the lawn as if to stop him, but they soon had reason to duck and recoil. Even as he vanished up the street for the second time, he let the big yellow bag fly from his hand, so that it fell in the centre of the garden, scattering the company like a bomb, and nearly damaging Dr Warner's hat for the third time. Long before they had collected themselves, the cab had shot away with a shriek that went into a whisper.

'Well,' said Michael Moon, with a queer note in his voice; 'you may as well all go inside anyhow. We've got two relics of Mr Smith at least; his fiancée and his trunk.'

'Why do you want us to go inside?' asked Arthur Inglewood, in whose red brow and rough brown hair botheration seemed to have reached its limit.

'I want the rest to go in,' said Michael in a clear voice, 'because I want the whole of this garden in which to talk to you.'

There was an atmosphere of irrational doubt; it was really getting colder, and a night wind had begun to wave the one or two trees in the twilight. Dr Warner, however, spoke in a voice devoid of indecision.

'I refuse to listen to any such proposal,' he said; 'you have lost this ruffian, and I must find him.'

'I don't ask you to listen to any proposal,' answered Moon quietly; 'I only ask you to listen.'

He made a silencing movement with his hand, and immediately the whistling noise that had been lost in the dark streets on one side of the house could be heard from quite a new quarter on the other side. Through the night-maze of streets the noise increased with incredible rapidity, and the next moment the flying hoofs and flashing wheels had swept up to the blue-railed gate at which they had originally stood. Mr Smith got down from his perch with an air of absent-mindedness, and coming back into the garden stood in the same elephantine attitude as before.

'Get inside! get inside!' cried Moon hilariously, with the air of one shooing a company of cats. 'Come, come, be quick about it! Didn't I tell you I wanted to talk to Inglewood?'

How they were all really driven into the house again it would have been difficult afterwards to say. They had reached the point of being exhausted with incongruities, as people at a farce are ill with laughing, and the brisk growth of the storm among the trees seemed like a final gesture of things in general. Inglewood lingered behind them, saying with a certain amicable exasperation, 'I say, do you really want to speak to me?'

'I do,' said Michael, 'very much.'

Night had come as it generally does, quicker than the twilight had seemed to promise. While the human eye still felt the sky as light grey, a very large and lustrous moon appearing abruptly above a bulk of roofs and trees, proved by contrast that the sky was already a very dark grey indeed. A drift of barren leaves across the lawn, a drift of riven clouds across the sky, seemed to be lifted on the same strong and yet laborious wind.

'Arthur,' said Michael, 'I began with an intuition; but now I am sure. You and I are going to defend this friend of yours before the blessed Court of Beacon, and to clear him too – clear him of both crime and lunacy. Just listen to me while I preach to you for a bit.' They walked up and down the darkening garden together as Michael Moon went on.

'Can you,' asked Michael, 'shut your eyes and see some of those queer old hieroglyphics they stuck up on white walls in the old hot countries? How stiff they were in shape and yet how gaudy in colour. Think of some alphabet of arbitrary figures picked out in black and red, or white and green, with some old Semitic crowd of Nosey Gould's ancestors staring at it, and try to think why the people put it up at all.'

Inglewood's first instinct was to think that his perplexing friend had really gone off his head at last; there seemed so reckless a flight of irrelevancy from the tropic-pictured walls he was asked to imagine to the grey, windswept, and somewhat chilly suburban garden in which he was actually kicking his heels. How he could be more happy in one by imagining the other he could not conceive. Both (in themselves) were unpleasant.

'Why does everybody repeat riddles,' went on Moon abruptly, 'even if they've forgotten the answers? Riddles are easy to remember because they are hard to guess. So were those stiff old symbols in black, red, or green easy to remember because they had been hard to guess. Their colours were plain. Their shapes were plain. Everything was plain except the meaning.'

Inglewood was about to open his mouth in an amiable protest, but Moon went on, plunging quicker and quicker up and down the garden and smoking faster and faster. 'Dances, too,' he said; 'dances were not frivolous. Dances were harder to understand than inscriptions and texts. The old dances were stiff, ceremonial, highly coloured but silent. Have you noticed anything odd about Smith?'

'Well, really,' cried Inglewood, left behind in a collapse of humour, 'have I noticed anything else about him?'

'Have you noticed this about him,' asked Moon, with unshaken persistency, 'that he has done so much and said so little? When first he came he talked, but in a gasping, irregular sort of way, as if he wasn't used to it. All he really did was actions – painting red flowers on black gowns or throwing yellow bags on to the grass. I tell you that big green figure is figurative – like any green figure capering on some white Eastern wall.'

'My dear Michael,' cried Inglewood, in a rising irritation which increased with the rising wind, 'you are getting absurdly fanciful.'

'I think of what has just happened,' said Michael steadily. 'The man has not spoken for hours; and yet he has been speaking all the time. He fired three shots from a six-shooter and then gave it up to us, when he might have shot us dead in our boots. How could he express his trust in us better than that? He wanted to be tried by us. How could he have shown it better than by standing quite still and letting us discuss it? He wanted to show that he stood there willingly, and could escape if he liked. How could he have shown it better than by escaping in the cab and coming back again? Innocent Smith is not a madman – he is a ritualist. He wants to express himself, not with his tongue, but with his arms and legs – with my body I thee worship, as it says in the marriage service. I begin to understand the old plays and pageants. I see why the mutes at a funeral were mute. I see why the mummers were mum. They *meant* something; and Smith means something too. All other jokes have to be noisy – like little Nosey Gould's jokes, for instance. The only silent jokes are the practical jokes. Poor Smith, properly considered, is an allegorical practical joker. What he has really done in this house has been as frantic as a war-dance, but as silent as a picture.'

'I suppose you mean,' said the other dubiously, 'that we have got to find out what all these crimes meant, as if they were so many coloured picture-puzzles. But even supposing that they do mean something – why, Lord bless my soul! – '

Taking the turn of the garden quite naturally, he had lifted his eyes to the moon, by this time risen big and luminous, and had seen a huge, half-human figure sitting on the garden wall. It was outlined so sharply against the moon that for the first flash it was hard to be certain even that it was human: the hunched shoulders and outstanding hair had rather the air of a colossal cat. It resembled a cat also in the fact that when first startled it sprang up and ran with easy activity along the top of the wall. As it ran, however, its heavy shoulders and small stooping head rather suggested a baboon. The instant it came within reach of a tree it made an apelike leap and was lost in the branches. The gale, which by this time was shaking every shrub in the garden, made the identification yet more difficult, since it melted the moving limbs of the fugitive in the multitudinous moving limbs of the tree.

'Who is there?' shouted Arthur. 'Who are you? Are you Innocent?'

'Not quite,' answered an obscure voice among the leaves. 'I cheated you once about a penknife.'

The wind in the garden had gathered strength, and was throwing the tree backwards and forwards with the man in the thick of it, just as it had on the gay and golden afternoon when he had first arrived.

'But are you Smith?' asked Inglewood as in an agony.

'Very nearly,' said the voice out of the tossing tree.

'But you must have some real names,' shrieked Inglewood in despair. 'You must call yourself something.'

'Call myself something,' thundered the obscure voice, shaking the tree so that all its ten thousand leaves seemed to be talking at once. 'I call myself Roland Oliver Isaiah Charlemagne Arthur Hildebrand Homer Danton Michaelangelo Shakespeare Brakespeare – '

'But, manalive!' began Inglewood in exasperation.

'That's right! that's right!' came with a roar out of the rocking tree; 'that's my real name.' And he broke a branch, and one or two autumn leaves fluttered away across the moon.

PART TWO

The Explanations of Innocent Smith

CHAPTER I

The Eye of Death; or, the Murder Charge

The dining-room of the Dukes had been set out for the Court of Beacon with a certain impromptu pomposity that seemed somehow to increase its cosiness. The big room was, as it were, cut up into small rooms, with walls only waist high – the sort of separation that children make when they are playing at shops. This had been done by Moses Gould and Michael Moon (the two most active members of this remarkable enquiry) with the ordinary furniture of the place. At one end of the long mahogany table was set the one enormous garden chair, which was surmounted by the old torn tent or umbrella which Smith himself had suggested as a coronation canopy. Inside this erection could be perceived the dumpy form of Mrs Duke, with cushions and a form of countenance that already threatened slumber. At the other end sat the accused Smith, in a kind of dock; for he was carefully fenced in with a quadrilateral of light bedroom chairs, any of which he could have tossed out the window with his big toe. He had been provided with pens and paper, out of the latter of which he made paper boats, paper darts, and paper dolls contentedly throughout the whole proceedings. He never spoke or even looked up, but seemed as unconscious as a child on the floor of an empty nursery.

On a row of chairs raised high on the top of a long settee sat the three young ladies with their backs up against the window, and Mary Gray in the middle; it was something between a jury box and the stall of the Queen of Beauty at a tournament. Down the centre of the long table Moon had built a low barrier out of eight bound volumes of 'Good Words' to express the moral wall that divided the conflicting parties. On the right side sat the two advocates of the prosecution, Dr Pym and Mr Gould; behind, a barricade of books and documents, chiefly (in the case of Dr Pym) solid volumes of criminology. On the other side, Moon and Inglewood, for the defence, were also fortified with books and papers; but as these included several old yellow volumes by Ouida and Wilkie Collins, the hand of Mr Moon seemed to have been somewhat careless and comprehensive. As for the victim and prosecutor,

Dr Warner, Moon wanted at first to have him kept entirely behind a high screen in the corner, urging the indelicacy of his appearance in court, but privately assuring him of an unofficial permission to peep over the top now and then. Dr Warner, however, failed to rise to the chivalry of such a course, and after some little disturbance and discussion he was accommodated with a seat on the right side of the table in a line with his legal advisers.

It was before this solidly established tribunal that Dr Cyrus Pym, after passing a hand through the honey-coloured hair over each ear, rose to open the case. His statement was clear and even restrained, and such flights of imagery as occurred in it only attracted attention by a certain indescribable abruptness, not uncommon in the flowers of American speech.

He planted the points of his ten frail fingers on the mahogany, closed his eyes, and opened his mouth. 'The time has gone by,' he said, 'when murder could be regarded as a moral and individual act, important perhaps to the murderer, perhaps to the murdered. Science has profoundly . . . ' here he paused, poising his compressed finger and thumb in the air as if he were holding an elusive idea very tight by its tail, then he screwed up his eyes and said 'modified,' and let it go – 'has profoundly Modified our view of death. In superstitious ages it was regarded as the termination of life, catastrophic, and even tragic, and was often surrounded by solemnity. Brighter days, however, have dawned, and we now see death as universal and inevitable, as part of that great soul-stirring and heart-upholding average which we call for convenience the order of nature. In the same way we have come to consider murder *socially*. Rising above the mere private feelings of a man while being forcibly deprived of life, we are privileged to behold murder as a mighty whole, to see the rich rotation of the cosmos, bringing, as it brings the golden harvests and the golden-bearded harvesters, the return for ever of the slayers and the slain.'

He looked down, somewhat affected with his own eloquence, coughed slightly, putting up four of his pointed fingers with the excellent manners of Boston, and continued: 'There is but one result of this happier and humaner outlook which concerns the wretched man before us. It is that thoroughly elucidated by a Milwaukee doctor, our great secret-guessing Sonnenschein, in his great work, *The Destructive Type*. We do not denounce Smith as a murderer, but rather as a murderous man. The type is such that its very life – I might say its very health – is in killing. Some hold that it is not properly an aberration, but a newer and even a higher creature. My dear old friend Dr Bulger, who kept ferrets – ' (here Moon suddenly ejaculated a loud 'hurrah!' but so instantaneously resumed his tragic expression that Mrs Duke looked everywhere else for the origin of sound); Dr Pym continued somewhat sternly – 'who, in the interests of knowledge, kept ferrets, felt that the creature's ferocity is not utilitarian, but absolutely an end in itself. However this may be with ferrets, it is certainly so with the prisoner. In his other iniquities you may find the cunning of the maniac; but his acts of blood have almost the simplicity of sanity. But it is the awful sanity of the sun and the elements – a cruel, an evil sanity. As soon stay the iris-leapt cataracts of our virgin West as stay the natural force that sends him forth to slay. No environment, however scientific, could have softened him. Place that man in the silver-silent purity of the palest cloister, and there will be some deed of violence done with the crozier or the alb. Rear him in a happy nursery, amid our brave-browed Anglo-Saxon infancy, and he will find some way to strangle with the skipping-rope or brain with the brick. Circumstances may be favourable, training may be admirable, hopes may be high, but the huge elemental hunger of Innocent Smith for blood will in its appointed season burst like a well-timed bomb.'

Arthur Inglewood glanced curiously for an instant at the huge creature at the foot of the table, who was fitting a paper figure with a cocked hat, and then looked back at Dr Pym, who was concluding in a quieter tone.

'It only remains for us,' he said, 'to bring forward actual evidence of his previous attempts. By an agreement already made with the Court and the leaders of the defence, we are permitted to put in evidence authentic letters from witnesses to these scenes, which the defence is free to examine. Out of several cases of such outrages we have decided to select one – the clearest and most scandalous. I will therefore, without further delay, call on my junior, Mr Gould, to read two letters – one from the Sub-Warden and the other from the porter of Brakespeare College, in Cambridge University.'

Gould jumped up with a jerk like a jack-in-the-box, an academic-looking paper in his hand and a fever of importance on his face. He began in a loud, high, cockney voice that was as abrupt as a cockcrow:

'SIR – Hi am the Sub-Warden of Brikespeare College, Cambridge – '

'Lord have mercy on us,' muttered Moon, making a backward movement as men do when a gun goes off.

'Hi am the Sub-Warden of Brikespeare College, Cambridge,' proclaimed the uncompromising Moses, 'and I can endorse the description you gave of the un'appy Smith. It was not alone my unfortunate duty to rebuke many of the lesser violences of his undergraduate period, but I was actually a witness to the last iniquity which terminated that period. Hi happened to be passing under the house of my friend the Warden of Brikespeare, which is semi-detached from the College and connected with it by two or three very ancient arches or props, like bridges, across a small strip of water connected with the river. To my grive astonishment I be'eld my eminent friend suspended in midair and clinging to one of these pieces of masonry, his appearance and attitude indicatin' that he suffered from the grivest apprehensions. After a short time I heard two very loud shots, and distinctly perceived the unfortunate undergraduate Smith leaning far out of the Warden's window and aiming at the Warden repeatedly with a revolver. Upon seeing me, Smith burst into a loud laugh (in which impertinence was mingled with insanity), and appeared to desist. I sent the college porter for a ladder, and he succeeded in detaching the Warden from his painful position. Smith was sent down. The photograph I enclose is from the group of the University Rifle Club prizemen, and represents him as he was when at the College.

'Hi am, your obedient servant,

'Amos Boulter.'

'The other letter,' continued Gould in a glow of triumph, 'is from the porter, and won't take long to read.

'Dear Sir – It is quite true that I am the porter of Brikespeare College, and that I 'elped the Warden down when the young man was shooting at him, as Mr Boulter has said in his letter. The young man who was shooting at him was Mr Smith, the same that is in the photograph Mr Boulter sends.

'Yours respectfully,

'Samuel Barker.'

Gould handed the two letters across to Moon, who examined them. But for the vocal divergences in the matter of h's and a's, the Sub-Warden's letter was exactly as Gould had rendered it; and both that and the porter's letter were plainly genuine. Moon handed them to Inglewood, who handed them back in silence to Moses Gould.

'So far as this first charge of continual attempted murder is concerned,' said Dr Pym, standing up for the last time, 'that is my case.'

Michael Moon rose for the defence with an air of depression which gave little hope at the outset to the sympathisers with the prisoner. He did not, he said, propose to follow the doctor into the abstract questions. 'I do not know enough to be an agnostic,' he said, rather wearily, 'and I can only master the known and admitted elements in such controversies. As for science and religion, the known and admitted facts are plain enough. All that the parsons say is unproved. All that the doctors say is disproved. That's the only difference between science and religion there's ever been, or will be. Yet these new discoveries touch me, somehow,' he said, looking down sorrowfully at his boots. 'They remind me of a dear old great-aunt of mine who used to enjoy them in her youth. It brings tears to my eyes. I can see the old bucket by the garden fence and the line of shimmering poplars behind – '

'Hi! here, stop the bus a bit,' cried Mr Moses Gould, rising in a sort of perspiration. 'We want to give the defence a fair run – like gents, you know; but any gent would draw the line at shimmering poplars.'

'Well, hang it all,' said Moon, in an injured manner, 'if Dr Pym may have an old friend with ferrets, why mayn't I have an old aunt with poplars?'

'I am sure,' said Mrs Duke, bridling, with something almost like a shaky authority, 'Mr Moon may have what aunts he likes.'

'Why, as to liking her,' began Moon, 'I – but perhaps, as you say, she is scarcely the core of the question. I repeat that I do not mean to follow the abstract speculations. For, indeed, my answer to Dr Pym is simple and severely concrete. Dr Pym has only treated one side of the psychology of murder. If it is true that there is a kind of man who has a natural tendency to murder, is it not equally true' – here he lowered his voice and spoke with a crushing quietude and earnestness – 'is it not equally true that there is a kind of man who has a natural tendency to get murdered? Is it not at least a hypothesis holding the field that Dr Warner is such a man? I do not speak without the book, any more than my learned friend. The whole matter is expounded in Dr Moonenschein's monumental work, *The Destructible Doctor*, with diagrams, showing the various ways in which such a person as Dr Warner may be resolved into his elements. In the light of these facts – '

'Hi, stop the bus! stop the bus!' cried Moses, jumping up and down and gesticulating in great excitement. 'My principal's got something to say! My principal wants to do a bit of talkin'.'

Dr Pym was indeed on his feet, looking pallid and rather vicious. 'I have strictly *con*-fined myself,' he said nasally, 'to books to which immediate reference can be made. I have Sonnenschein's *Destructive Type* here on the table, if the defence wish to see it. Where is this wonderful work on Destructibility Mr Moon is talking about? Does it exist? Can he produce it?'

'Produce it!' cried the Irishman with a rich scorn. 'I'll produce it in a week if you'll pay for the ink and paper.'

'Would it have much authority?' asked Pym, sitting down.

'Oh, authority!' said Moon lightly; 'that depends on a fellow's religion.'

Dr Pym jumped up again. 'Our authority is based on masses of accurate detail,' he said. 'It deals with a region in which things can be handled and tested. My opponent will at least admit that death is a fact of experience.'

'Not of mine,' said Moon mournfully, shaking his head. 'I've never experienced such a thing in all my life.'

'Well, really,' said Dr Pym, and sat down sharply amid a crackle of papers.

'So we see,' resumed Moon, in the same melancholy voice, 'that a man like Dr Warner is, in the mysterious workings of evolution, doomed to such attacks. My client's onslaught, even if it occurred, was not unique. I have in my hand letters from more than one acquaintance of Dr Warner whom that remarkable man has affected in the same way. Following the example of my learned friends I will read only two of them. The first is from an honest and laborious matron living off the Harrow Road.

> 'MR MOON, SIR – Yes, I did throw a sorsepan at him. Wot then? It was all I had to throw, all the soft things being porned, and if your Docter Warner doesn't like having sorsepans thrown at him, don't let him wear his hat in a respectable woman's parler, and tell him to leave orf smiling or tell us the joke.
>
> 'Yours respectfully,
>
> 'HANNAH MILES.

'The other letter is from a physician of some note in Dublin, with whom Dr Warner was once engaged in consultation. He writes as follows:

> 'DEAR SIR – The incident to which you refer is one which I regret, and which, moreover, I have never been able to explain. My own branch of medicine is not mental; and I should be glad to have the view of a mental specialist on my singular momentary and indeed almost automatic action. To say that I "pulled Dr Warner's nose" is, however, inaccurate in a respect that strikes me as important. That I punched his nose I must cheerfully admit (I need not say with what regret); but pulling seems to me to imply a precision of objective with which I cannot reproach myself. In comparison with this, the act of punching was an outward, instantaneous, and even natural gesture.
>
> 'Believe me, yours faithfully,
>
> 'BURTON LESTRANGE.

'I have numberless other letters,' continued Moon, 'all bearing witness to this widespread feeling about my eminent friend; and I therefore think that Dr Pym should have admitted this side of the question in his survey. We are in the presence, as Dr Pym so truly says, of a natural force. As soon stay the cataract of the London waterworks as stay the great tendency of Dr Warner to be assassinated by somebody. Place that man in a Quakers' meeting, among the most peaceful of Christians, and he will immediately be beaten to death with sticks of chocolate. Place him among the angels of the New Jerusalem, and he will be stoned to death with precious stones. Circumstances may be beautiful and wonderful, the average may be heart-upholding, the harvester may be golden-bearded, the doctor may be secret-guessing, the cataract may be iris-leapt, the Anglo-Saxon infant may be brave-browed, but against and above all these prodigies the grand simple tendency of Dr Warner to get murdered will still pursue its way until it happily and triumphantly succeeds at last.'

He pronounced this peroration with an appearance of strong emotion.

But even stronger emotions were manifesting themselves on the other side of the table. Dr Warner had leaned his large body quite across the little figure of Moses Gould and was talking in excited whispers to Dr Pym. That expert nodded a great many times and finally started to his feet with a sincere expression of sternness.

'Ladies and gentlemen,' he cried indignantly, 'as my colleague has said, we should be delighted to give any latitude to the defence – if there were a defence. But Mr Moon seems to think he is there to make jokes – very good jokes I dare say, but not at all adapted to assist his client. He picks holes in science. He picks holes in my client's social popularity. He picks holes in my literary style, which doesn't seem to suit his high-toned European taste. But how does this picking of holes affect the issue? This Smith has picked two holes in my client's hat, and with an inch better aim would have picked two holes in his head. All the jokes in the world won't unpick those holes or be any use for the defence.'

Inglewood looked down in some embarrassment, as if shaken by the evident fairness of this, but Moon still gazed at his opponent in a dreamy way. 'The defence?' he said vaguely – 'oh, I haven't begun that yet.'

'You certainly have not,' said Pym warmly, amid a murmur of applause from his side, which the other side found it impossible to answer. 'Perhaps, if you have any defence, which has been doubtful from the very beginning – '

'While you're standing up,' said Moon, in the same almost sleepy style, 'perhaps I might ask you a question.'

'A question? Certainly,' said Pym stiffly. 'It was distinctly arranged between us that as we could not cross-examine the witnesses, we might vicariously cross-examine each other. We are in a position to invite all such enquiry.'

'I think you said,' observed Moon absently, 'that none of the prisoner's shots really hit the doctor.'

'For the cause of science,' cried the complacent Pym, 'fortunately not.'

'Yet they were fired from a few feet away.'

'Yes; about four feet.'

'And no shots hit the Warden, though they were fired quite close to him too?' asked Moon.

'That is so,' said the witness gravely.

'I think,' said Moon, suppressing a slight yawn, 'that your Sub-Warden mentioned that Smith was one of the University's record men for shooting.'

'Why, as to that – ' began Pym, after an instant of stillness.

'A second question,' continued Moon, comparatively curtly. 'You said there were other cases of the accused trying to kill people. Why have you not got evidence of them?'

The American planted the points of his fingers on the table again. 'In those cases,' he said precisely, 'there was no evidence from outsiders, as in the Cambridge case, but only the evidence of the actual victims.'

'Why didn't you get their evidence?'

'In the case of the actual victims,' said Pym, 'there was some difficulty and reluctance, and – '

'Do you mean,' asked Moon, 'that none of the actual victims would appear against the prisoner?'

'That would be exaggerative,' began the other.

'A third question,' said Moon, so sharply that everyone jumped. 'You've got the evidence of the Sub-Warden who heard some shots; where's the evidence of the Warden himself who was shot at? The Warden of Brakespeare lives, a prosperous gentleman.'

'We did ask for a statement from him,' said Pym a little nervously; 'but it was so eccentrically expressed that we suppressed it out of deference to an old gentleman whose past services to science have been great.'

Moon leaned forward. 'You mean, I suppose,' he said, 'that his statement was favourable to the prisoner.'

'It might be understood so,' replied the American doctor; 'but, really, it was difficult to understand at all. In fact, we sent it back to him.'

'You have no longer, then, any statement signed by the Warden of Brakespeare.'

'No.'

'I only ask,' said Michael quietly, 'because we have. To conclude my case I will ask my junior, Mr Inglewood, to read a statement of the true story – a statement attested as true by the signature of the Warden himself.'

Arthur Inglewood rose with several papers in his hand, and though he looked somewhat refined and self-effacing, as he always did, the spectators were surprised to feel that his presence was, upon the whole, more efficient and sufficing than his leader's. He was, in truth, one of those modest men who cannot speak until they are told to speak; and then can speak well. Moon was entirely the opposite. His own impudences amused him in private, but they slightly embarrassed him in public; he felt a fool while he was speaking, whereas Inglewood felt a fool only because he could not speak. The moment he had anything to say he could speak; and the moment he could speak, speaking seemed quite natural. Nothing in this universe seemed quite natural to Michael Moon.

'As my colleague has just explained,' said Inglewood, 'there are two enigmas or inconsistencies on which we base the defence. The first is a plain physical fact. By the admission of everybody, by the very evidence adduced by the prosecution, it is clear that the accused was celebrated as a specially good shot. Yet on both the occasions complained of he shot from a distance of four or five feet, and shot at him four or five times, and never hit him once. That is the first startling circumstance on which we base our argument. The second, as my colleague has urged, is the curious fact that we cannot find a single victim of these alleged outrages to speak for himself. Subordinates speak for him. Porters climb up ladders to him. But he himself is silent. Ladies and gentlemen, I propose to explain on the spot both the riddle of the shots and the riddle of the silence. I will first of all read the covering letter in which the true account of the Cambridge incident is contained, and then that document itself. When you have heard both, there will be no doubt about your decision. The covering letter runs as follows:

> 'Dear Sir – The following is a very exact and even vivid account of the incident as it really happened at Brakespeare College. We, the undersigned, do not see any particular reason why we should refer it to any isolated authorship. The truth is, it has been a composite production; and we have even had some difference of opinion about the adjectives. But every word of it is true.
>
> 'We are, yours faithfully,
>
> 'Wilfred Emerson Eames,
> '*Warden of Brakespeare College, Cambridge*
> 'Innocent Smith.

'The enclosed statement,' continued Inglewood, 'runs as follows:

> 'A celebrated English university backs so abruptly on the river, that it has, so to speak, to be propped up and patched with all sorts of bridges and semi-detached buildings. The river splits itself into several small streams and canals, so that in one or two corners the place has almost the look of Venice. It was so especially in the case with which we are concerned, in which a few flying buttresses or airy ribs of stone sprang across a strip of water to connect Brakespeare College with the house of the Warden of Brakespeare.
>
> 'The country around these colleges is flat; but it does not seem flat when one is thus in the midst of the colleges. For in these flat fens there are always wandering lakes and lingering rivers of water. And these always change what might have been a scheme of horizontal lines into a scheme of vertical lines. Wherever there is water the height of high buildings is doubled, and a British brick house becomes a Babylonian tower. In that shining unshaken surface the houses hang head downwards exactly to their highest or lowest chimney. The coral-coloured cloud seen in that abyss is as far below the world as its original appears above it. Every scrap of water is not only a window but a skylight. Earth splits under men's feet into precipitous aerial perspectives, into which a bird could as easily wing its way as – '

Dr Cyrus Pym rose in protest. The documents he had put in evidence had been confined to cold affirmation of fact. The defence, in a general way, had an indubitable right to put their case in their own way, but all this landscape gardening seemed to him (Dr Cyrus Pym) to be not up to the business. 'Will the leader of the defence tell me,' he asked, 'how it can possibly affect this case, that a cloud was cor'l-coloured, or that a bird could have winged itself anywhere?'

'Oh, I don't know,' said Michael, lifting himself lazily; 'you see, you don't know yet what our defence is. Till you know that, don't you see, anything may be relevant. Why, suppose,' he said suddenly, as if an idea had struck him, 'suppose we wanted to prove the old Warden colour-blind. Suppose he was shot by a black man with white hair, when he thought he was being shot by a white man with yellow hair! To ascertain if that cloud was really and truly coral-coloured might be of the most massive importance.'

He paused with a seriousness which was hardly generally shared, and continued with the same fluency: 'Or suppose we wanted to maintain that the Warden committed suicide – that he just got Smith to hold the pistol as Brutus's slave held the sword. Why, it would make all the difference whether the Warden could see himself plain in still water. Still water has made hundreds of suicides: one sees oneself so very – well, so very plain.'

'Do you, perhaps,' enquired Pym with austere irony, 'maintain that your client was a bird of some sort – say, a flamingo?'

'In the matter of his being a flamingo,' said Moon with sudden severity, 'my client reserves his defence.'

No one quite knowing what to make of this, Mr Moon resumed his seat and Inglewood resumed the reading of his document:

> 'There is something pleasing to a mystic in such a land of mirrors. For a mystic is one who holds that two worlds are better than one. In the highest sense, indeed, all thought is reflection.
>
> 'This is the real truth, in the saying that second thoughts are best. Animals have no second thoughts; man alone is able to see his own thought double, as a drunkard sees a lamp post; man alone is able to see his own thought upside down as one sees a house in a puddle. This duplication of mentality, as in a mirror, is (we repeat) the inmost thing of human philosophy. There is a mystical, even a monstrous truth, in the statement that two heads are better than one. But they ought both to grow on the same body.'

'I know it's a little transcendental at first,' interposed Inglewood, beaming round with a broad apology, 'but you see this document was written in collaboration by a don and a – '

'Drunkard, eh?' suggested Moses Gould, beginning to enjoy himself.

'I rather think,' proceeded Inglewood with an unruffled and critical air, 'that this part was written by the don. I merely warn the Court that the statement, though indubitably accurate, bears here and there the trace of coming from two authors.'

'In that case,' said Dr Pym, leaning back and sniffing, 'I cannot agree with them that two heads are better than one.'

'The undersigned persons think it needless to touch on a kindred problem so often discussed at committees for University Reform: the question of whether dons see double because they are drunk, or get drunk because they see double. It is enough for them (the undersigned persons) if they are able to pursue their own peculiar and profitable theme – which is puddles. What (the undersigned persons ask themselves) is a puddle? A puddle repeats infinity, and is full of light; nevertheless, if analysed objectively, a puddle is a piece of dirty water spread very thin on mud. The two great historic universities of England have all this large and level and reflective brilliance. Nevertheless, or, rather, on the other hand, they are puddles – puddles, puddles, puddles, puddles. The undersigned persons ask you to excuse an emphasis inseparable from strong conviction.'

Inglewood ignored a somewhat wild expression on the faces of some present, and continued with eminent cheerfulness:

'Such were the thoughts that failed to cross the mind of the undergraduate Smith as he picked his way among the stripes of canal and the glittering rainy gutters into which the water broke up round the back of Brakespeare College. Had these thoughts crossed his mind he would have been much happier than he was. Unfortunately he did not know that his puzzles were puddles. He did not know that the academic mind reflects infinity and is full of light by the simple process of being shallow and standing still. In his case, therefore, there was something solemn, and even evil about the infinity implied. It was halfway through a starry night of bewildering brilliancy; stars were both above and below. To young Smith's sullen fancy the skies below seemed even hollower than the skies above; he had a horrible idea that if he counted the stars he would find one too many in the pool.

'In crossing the little paths and bridges he felt like one stepping on the black and slender ribs of some cosmic Eiffel Tower. For to him, and nearly all the educated youth of that epoch, the stars were cruel things. Though they glowed in the great dome every night, they were an enormous and ugly secret; they uncovered the nakedness of nature; they were a glimpse of the iron wheels and pulleys behind the scenes. For the young men of that sad time thought that the god always comes from the machine. They did not know that in reality the machine only comes from the god. In short, they were all pessimists, and starlight was atrocious to them – atrocious because it was true. All their universe was black with white spots.

'Smith looked up with relief from the glittering pools below to the glittering skies and the great black bulk of the college. The only light other than stars glowed through one peacock-green curtain in the upper part of the building, marking where Dr Emerson Eames always worked till morning and received his friends and favourite pupils at any hour of the night. Indeed, it was to his rooms that the melancholy Smith was bound. Smith had been at Dr Eames's lecture for the first half of the morning, and at pistol practice and fencing in a saloon for the second half. He had been sculling madly for the first half of the afternoon and thinking idly (and still more madly) for the second half. He had gone to a supper where he was uproarious, and on to a debating club where he was perfectly insufferable, and the melancholy Smith was melancholy still. Then, as he was going home to his diggings he remembered the eccentricity of his friend and master, the Warden of Brakespeare, and resolved desperately to turn in to that gentleman's private house.

'Emerson Eames was an eccentric in many ways, but his throne in philosophy and metaphysics was of international eminence; the university could hardly have afforded to lose him, and, moreover, a don has only to continue any of his bad habits long enough to make them a part of the British Constitution. The bad habits of Emerson Eames were to sit up all night and to be a student of Schopenhauer. Personally, he was a lean, lounging sort of man, with a blond pointed beard, not so very much older than his pupil Smith in the matter of mere years, but older by centuries in the two essential respects of having a European reputation and a bald head.

' "I came, against the rules, at this unearthly hour," said Smith, who was nothing to the eye except a very big man trying to make himself small, "because I am coming to the conclusion that existence is really too rotten. I know all the arguments of the thinkers that think otherwise – bishops, and agnostics, and those sort of people. And knowing you were the greatest living authority on the pessimist thinkers – "

' "All thinkers," said Eames, "are pessimist thinkers."

'After a patch of pause, not the first – for this depressing conversation had gone on for some hours with alternations of cynicism and silence – the Warden continued with his air of weary brilliancy: "It's all a question of wrong calculation. The moth flies into the candle because he doesn't happen to know that the game is not worth the candle. The wasp gets into the jam in hearty and hopeful efforts to get the jam into him. In the same way the vulgar people want to enjoy life just as they want to enjoy gin – because they are too stupid to see that they are paying too big a price for it. That they never find happiness – that they don't even know how to look for it – is proved by the paralysing clumsiness and ugliness of everything they do. Their discordant colours are cries of pain. Look at the brick villas beyond the college on this side of the river. There's one with spotted blinds; look at it! just go and look at it!

' "Of course," he went on dreamily, "one or two men see the sober fact a long way off – they go mad. Do you notice that maniacs mostly try either to destroy other things, or (if they are thoughtful) to destroy themselves? The madman is the man behind the scenes, like the man that wanders about the *coulisse* of a theatre. He has only opened the wrong door and come into the right place. He sees things at the right angle. But the common world – "

' "Oh, hang the common world!" said the sullen Smith, letting his fist fall on the table in an idle despair.

' "Let's give it a bad name first," said the Professor calmly, "and then hang it. A puppy with hydrophobia would probably struggle for life while we killed it; but if we were kind we should kill it. So an omniscient god would put us out of our pain. He would strike us dead."

' "Why doesn't he strike us dead?" asked the undergraduate abstractedly, plunging his hands into his pockets.

' "He is dead himself," said the philosopher; "that is where he is really enviable.

' "To anyone who thinks," proceeded Eames, "the pleasures of life, trivial and soon tasteless, are bribes to bring us into a torture chamber. We all see that for any thinking man mere extinction is the . . . What are you doing? . . . Are you mad? . . . Put that thing down."

'Dr Eames had turned his tired but still talkative head over his shoulder, and had found himself looking into a small round black hole, rimmed by a six-sided circlet of steel, with a sort of spike standing up on the top. It fixed him like an iron eye. Through those eternal instants during which the reason is stunned he did not even know what it was. Then he saw behind it the chambered barrel and cocked hammer of a revolver, and behind that the flushed and rather heavy face of Smith, apparently quite unchanged, or even more mild than before.

' "I'll help you out of your hole, old man," said Smith, with rough tenderness. "I'll put the puppy out of his pain."

'Emerson Eames retreated towards the window. "Do you mean to kill me?" he cried.

' "It's not a thing I'd do for everyone," said Smith with emotion; "but you and I seem to have got so intimate tonight, somehow. I know all your troubles now, and the only cure, old chap."

' "Put that thing down," shouted the Warden.

' "It'll soon be over, you know," said Smith with the air of a sympathetic dentist. And as the Warden made a run for the window and balcony, his benefactor followed him with a firm step and a compassionate expression.

'Both men were perhaps surprised to see that the grey and white of early daybreak had already come. One of them, however, had emotions calculated to swallow up surprise. Brakespeare College was one of the few that retained real traces of Gothic ornament, and just beneath Dr Eames's balcony there ran out what had perhaps been a flying buttress, still shapelessly shaped into grey beasts and devils, but blinded with mosses and washed out with rains. With an ungainly and most courageous leap, Eames sprang out on this antique bridge, as the only possible mode of escape from the maniac. He sat astride of it, still in his academic gown, dangling his long thin legs, and considering further chances of flight. The whitening daylight opened under as well as over him that impression of vertical infinity already remarked about the little lakes round Brakespeare. Looking down and seeing the spires and chimneys pendent in the pools, they felt alone in space. They felt as if they were looking over the edge from the North Pole and seeing the South Pole below.

' "Hang the world, we said," observed Smith, "and the world is hanged. 'He has hanged the world upon nothing,' says the Bible. Do you like being hanged upon nothing? I'm going to be hanged upon something myself. I'm going to swing for you . . . Dear, tender old phrase," he murmured; "never true till this moment. I am going to swing for you. For you, dear friend. For your sake. At your express desire."

' "Help!" cried the Warden of Brakespeare College; "help!"

' "The puppy struggles," said the undergraduate, with an eye of pity, "the poor puppy struggles. How fortunate it is that I am wiser and kinder than he," and he sighted his weapon so as exactly to cover the upper part of Eames's bald head.

' "Smith," said the philosopher with a sudden change to a sort of ghastly lucidity, "I shall go mad."

' "And so look at things from the right angle," observed Smith, sighing gently. "Ah, but madness is only a palliative at best, a drug. The only cure is an operation – an operation that is always successful: death."

'As he spoke the sun rose. It seemed to put colour into everything, with the rapidity of a lightning artist. A fleet of little clouds sailing across the sky changed from pigeon-grey to pink. All over the little academic town the tops of different buildings took on different tints: here the sun would pick out the green enamel on a pinnacle, there the scarlet tiles of a villa; here the copper ornament on some artistic shop, and there the sea-blue slates of some old and steep church roof. All these coloured crests seemed to have something oddly individual and significant about them, like crests of famous knights pointed out in a pageant or a battlefield: they each arrested the eye, especially the rolling eye of Emerson Eames as he looked round on the morning and accepted it as his last. Through a narrow chink between a black timber tavern and a big grey college he could see a clock with gilt hands which the sunshine set on fire. He stared at it as though hypnotised; and suddenly the clock began to strike, as if in personal reply. As if at a signal, clock after clock took up the cry: all the churches awoke like chickens at cockcrow. The birds were already noisy in the trees behind the college. The sun rose, gathering glory that seemed too full for the deep skies to hold, and the shallow waters beneath them seemed golden and brimming and deep enough for the thirst of the gods. Just round the corner of the College, and visible from his crazy perch, were the brightest specks on that bright landscape, the villa with the spotted blinds which he had made his text that night. He wondered for the first time what people lived in them.

'Suddenly he called out with mere querulous authority, as he might have called to a student to shut a door.

' "Let me come off this place," he cried; "I can't bear it."

' "I rather doubt if it will bear you," said Smith critically; "but before you break your neck, or I blow out your brains, or let you back into this room (on which complex points I am undecided) I want the metaphysical point cleared up. Do I understand that you want to get back to life?"

' "I'd give anything to get back," replied the unhappy professor.

' "Give anything!" cried Smith; "then, blast your impudence, give us a song!"

' "What song do you mean?" demanded the exasperated Eames; "what song?"

' "A hymn, I think, would be most appropriate," answered the other gravely. "I'll let you off if you'll repeat after me the words –

' "I thank the goodness and the grace
That on my birth have smiled.
And perched me on this curious place,
A happy English child."

'Dr Emerson Eames having briefly complied, his persecutor abruptly told him to hold his hands up in the air. Vaguely connecting this proceeding with the usual conduct of brigands and bushrangers, Mr Eames held them up, very stiffly, but without marked surprise. A bird alighting on his stone seat took no more notice of him than of a comic statue.

' "You are now engaged in public worship," remarked Smith severely, "and before I have done with you, you shall thank God for the very ducks on the pond."

'The celebrated pessimist half articulately expressed his perfect readiness to thank God for the ducks on the pond.

' "Not forgetting the drakes," said Smith sternly. (Eames weakly conceded the drakes.) "Not forgetting anything, please. You shall thank heaven for churches and chapels and villas and vulgar people and puddles and pots and pans and sticks and rags and bones and spotted blinds."

' "All right, all right," repeated the victim in despair; "sticks and rags and bones and blinds."

' "Spotted blinds, I think we said," remarked Smith with a roguish ruthlessness, and wagging the pistol-barrel at him like a long metallic finger.

' "Spotted blinds," said Emerson Eames faintly.

' "You can't say fairer than that," admitted the younger man, "and now I'll just tell you this to wind up with. If you really were what you profess to be, I don't see that it would matter to snail or seraph if you broke your impious stiff neck and dashed out all your drivelling devil-worshipping brains. But in strict biographical fact you are a very nice fellow, addicted to talking putrid nonsense, and I love you like a brother. I shall therefore fire off all my cartridges round your head so as not to hit you (I am a good shot, you may be glad to hear), and then we will go in and have some breakfast."

'He then let off two barrels in the air, which the Professor endured with singular firmness, and then said, "But don't fire them all off."

' "Why not?" asked the other buoyantly.

' "Keep them," asked his companion, "for the next man you meet who talks as we were talking."

'It was at this moment that Smith, looking down, perceived apoplectic terror upon the face of the Sub-Warden, and heard the refined shriek with which he summoned the porter and the ladder.

'It took Dr Eames some little time to disentangle himself from the ladder, and some little time longer to disentangle himself from the Sub-Warden. But as soon as he could do so unobtrusively, he rejoined his companion in the late extraordinary scene. He was astonished to find the gigantic Smith heavily shaken, and sitting with his shaggy head on his hands. When addressed, he lifted a very pale face.

' "Why, what is the matter?" asked Eames, whose own nerves had by this time twittered themselves quiet, like the morning birds.

' "I must ask your indulgence," said Smith, rather brokenly. "I must ask you to realise that I have just had an escape from death."

' "*You* have had an escape from death?" repeated the Professor in not unpardonable irritation. "Well, of all the cheek –"

' "Oh, don't you understand, don't you understand?" cried the pale young man impatiently. "I had to do it, Eames; I had to prove you wrong or die. When a man's young, he nearly always has someone whom he thinks the top-water mark of the mind of man – someone who knows all about it, if anybody knows.

' "Well, you were that to me; you spoke with authority, and not as the scribes. Nobody could comfort me if *you* said there was no comfort. If you really thought there was nothing anywhere, it was because you had been there to see. Don't you see that I *had* to prove you didn't really mean it? – or else drown myself in the canal."

' "Well," said Eames hesitatingly, "I think perhaps you confuse – "

' "Oh, don't tell me that!" cried Smith with the sudden clairvoyance of mental pain; "don't tell me I confuse enjoyment of existence with the Will to Live! That's German, and German is High Dutch, and High Dutch is Double Dutch. The thing I saw shining in your eyes when you dangled on that bridge was enjoyment of life and not 'the Will to Live'. What you knew when you sat on that damned gargoyle was that the world, when all is said and done, is a wonderful and beautiful place; I know it, because I knew it at the same minute. I saw the grey clouds turn pink, and the little gilt clock in the crack between the houses. It was *those things* you hated leaving, not Life, whatever that is. Eames, we've been to the brink of death together; won't you admit I'm right?"

' "Yes," said Eames very slowly, "I think you are right. You shall have a First!"

' "Right!" cried Smith, springing up reanimated. "I've passed with honours, and now let me go and see about being sent down."

' "You needn't be sent down," said Eames with the quiet confidence of twelve years of intrigue. "Everything with us comes from the man on top to the people just round him: I am the man on top, and I shall tell the people round me the truth."

'The massive Mr Smith rose and went firmly to the window, but he spoke with equal firmness. "I must be sent down," he said, "and the people must not be told the truth."

' "And why not?" asked the other.

' "Because I mean to follow your advice," answered the massive youth, "I mean to keep the remaining shots for people in the shameful state you and I were in last night – I wish we could even plead drunkenness. I mean to keep those bullets for pessimists – pills for pale people. And in this way I want to walk the world like a wonderful surprise – to float as idly as the thistledown, and come as silently as the sunrise; not to be expected any more than the thunderbolt, not to be recalled any more than the dying breeze. I don't want people to anticipate me as a well-known practical joke. I want both my gifts to come virgin and violent, the death and the life after death. I am going to hold a pistol to the head of the Modern Man. But I shall not use it to kill him – only to bring him to life. I begin to see a new meaning in being the skeleton at the feast."

' "You can scarcely be called a skeleton," said Dr Eames, smiling.

' "That comes of being so much at the feast," answered the massive youth. "No skeleton can keep his figure if he is always dining out. But that is not quite what I meant: what I mean is that I caught a kind of glimpse of the meaning of death and all that – the skull and cross-bones, the *memento mori*. It isn't only meant to remind us of a future life, but to remind us of a present life too. With our weak spirits we should grow old in eternity if we were not kept young by death. Providence has to cut immortality into lengths for us, as nurses cut the bread and butter into fingers."

'Then he added suddenly in a voice of unnatural actuality, "But I know something now, Eames. I knew it when I saw the clouds turn pink."

' "What do you mean?" asked Eames. "What did you know?"

' "I knew for the first time that murder is really wrong."

'He gripped Dr Eames's hand and groped his way somewhat unsteadily to the door. Before he had vanished through it he had added, "It's very dangerous, though, when a man thinks for a split second that he understands death."

'Dr Eames remained in repose and rumination some hours after his late assailant had left. Then he rose, took his hat and umbrella, and went for a brisk if rotatory walk. Several times, however, he stood outside the villa with the spotted blinds, studying them intently with his head slightly on one side. Some took him for a lunatic and some for an intending purchaser. He is not yet sure that the two characters would be widely different.

'The above narrative has been constructed on a principle which is, in the opinion of the undersigned persons, new in the art of letters. Each of the two actors is described as he appeared to the other. But the undersigned persons absolutely guarantee the exactitude of the story; and if their version of the thing be questioned, they, the undersigned persons, would deucedly well like to know who does know about it if they don't.

'The undersigned persons will now adjourn to the Spotted Dog for beer.

'Farewell.

'(*Signed*) James Emerson Eames,
'*Warden of Brakespeare College, Cambridge.*
'Innocent Smith.'

CHAPTER 2

The Two Curates; or, the Burglary Charge

Arthur Inglewood handed the document he had just read to the leaders of the prosecution, who examined it with their heads together. Both the Jew and the American were of sensitive and excitable stocks, and they revealed by the jumpings and bumpings of the black head and the yellow that nothing could be done in the way of denial of the document. The letter from the Warden was as authentic as the letter from the Sub-Warden, however regrettably different in dignity and social tone.

'Very few words,' said Inglewood, 'are required to conclude our case in this matter. Surely it is now plain that our client carried his pistol about with the eccentric but innocent purpose of giving a wholesome scare to those whom he regarded as blasphemers. In each case the scare was so wholesome that the victim himself has dated from it as from a new birth. Smith, so far from being a madman, is rather a mad doctor – he walks the world curing frenzies and not distributing them. That is the answer to the two unanswerable questions which I put to the prosecutors. That is why they dared not produce a line by anyone who had actually confronted the pistol. All who had actually confronted the pistol confessed that they had profited by it. That was why Smith, though a good shot, never hit anybody. He never hit anybody because he was a good shot. His mind was as clear of murder as his hands are of blood. This, I say, is the only possible explanation of these facts and of all the other facts. No one can possibly explain the Warden's conduct except by believing the Warden's story. Even Dr Pym, who is a very factory of ingenious theories, could find no other theory to cover the case.'

'There are promising perspectives in hypnotism and dual personality,' said Dr Cyrus Pym dreamily; 'the science of criminology is in its infancy, and – '

'Infancy!' cried Moon, jerking his red pencil in the air with a gesture of enlightenment; 'why, that explains it!'

'I repeat,' proceeded Inglewood, 'that neither Dr Pym nor anyone else can account on any other theory but ours for the Warden's signature, for the shots missed and the witnesses missing.'

The little Yankee had slipped to his feet with some return of a cockfighting coolness. 'The defence,' he said, 'omits a coldly colossal fact. They say we produce none of the actual victims. Wal, here is one victim – England's celebrated and stricken Warner. I reckon he is pretty well produced. And they suggest that all the outrages were followed by reconciliation. Wal, there's no flies on England's Warner; and he isn't reconciliated much.'

'My learned friend,' said Moon, getting elaborately to his feet, 'must remember that the science of shooting Dr Warner is in its infancy. Dr Warner would strike the idlest eye as one specially difficult to startle into any recognition of the glory of God. We admit that our client, in this one instance, failed, and that the operation was not successful. But I am empowered to offer, on behalf of my client, a proposal for operating on Dr Warner again, at his earliest convenience, and without further fees.'

' 'Ang it all, Michael,' cried Gould, quite serious for the first time in his life, 'you might give us a bit of bally sense for a chinge.'

'What was Dr Warner talking about just before the first shot?' asked Moon sharply.

'The creature,' said Dr Warner superciliously, 'asked me, with characteristic rationality, whether it was my birthday.'

'And you answered, with characteristic swank,' cried Moon, shooting out a long lean finger, as rigid and arresting as the pistol of Smith, 'that you didn't keep your birthday.'

'Something like that,' assented the doctor.

'Then,' continued Moon, 'he asked you why not, and you said it was because you didn't see that birth was anything to rejoice over. Agreed? Now is there anyone who doubts that our tale is true?'

There was a cold crash of stillness in the room; and Moon said, '*Pax populi vox Dei*; it is the silence of the people that is the voice of God. Or in Dr Pym's more civilised language, it is up to him to open the next charge. On this we claim an acquittal.'

It was about an hour later. Dr Cyrus Pym had remained for an unprecedented time with his eyes closed and his thumb and finger in the air. It almost seemed as if he had been 'struck so', as the nurses say; and in the deathly silence Michael Moon felt forced to relieve the strain with some remark. For the last half-hour or so the eminent criminologist had been explaining that science took the same view of offences against property as it did of offences against life. 'Most murder,' he had said, 'is a variation of homicidal mania, and in the same way most theft is a version of kleptomania. I cannot entertain any doubt that my learned friends opposite adequately conceive how this must involve a scheme of punishment more tol'rant and humane than the cruel methods of ancient codes. They will doubtless exhibit consciousness of a chasm so eminently yawning, so thought-arresting, so – ' It was here that he paused and indulged in the delicate gesture to which allusion has been made; and Michael could bear it no longer.

'Yes, yes,' he said impatiently, 'we admit the chasm. The old cruel codes accuse a man of theft and send him to prison for ten years. The tolerant and humane ticket accuses him of nothing and sends him to prison for ever. We pass the chasm.'

It was characteristic of the eminent Pym, in one of his trances of verbal fastidiousness, that he went on, unconscious not only of his opponent's interruption, but even of his own pause.

'So stock-improving,' continued Dr Cyrus Pym, 'so fraught with real high hopes of the future. Science therefore regards thieves, in the abstract, just as it regards murderers. It regards them not as sinners to be punished for an arbitrary period, but as patients to be detained and cared for' (his first two digits closed again as he hesitated) – 'in short, for the required period. But there is something special in the case we investigate here. Kleptomania commonly conjoins itself – '

'I beg pardon,' said Michael; 'I did not ask just now because, to tell the truth, I really thought Dr Pym, though seemingly vertical, was enjoying well-earned slumber, with a pinch in his fingers of scentless and delicate dust. But now that things are moving a little more, there is something I should really like to know. I have hung on Dr Pym's lips, of course, with an interest that it were weak to call rapture, but I have so far been unable to form any conjecture about what the accused, in the present instance, is supposed to have been and gone and done.'

'If Mr Moon will have patience,' said Pym with dignity, 'he will find that this was the very point to which my exposition was directed. Kleptomania, I say, exhibits itself as a kind of physical attraction to certain defined materials; and it has been held (by no less a man than Harris) that this is the ultimate explanation of the strict specialism and vurry narrow professional outlook of most criminals. One will have an irresistible physical impulsion towards pearl sleeve-links, while he passes over the most elegant and celebrated diamond sleeve-links, placed about in the most con-spicuous locations. Another will impede his flight with no less than forty-seven buttoned boots, while elastic-sided boots leave him cold, and even sarcastic. The specialism of the criminal, I repeat, is a mark rather of insanity than of any brightness of business habits; but there is one kind of depredator to whom this principle is at first sight hard to apply. I allude to our fellow-citizen the housebreaker.

'It has been maintained by some of our boldest young truth-seekers, that the eye of a burglar beyond the back-garden wall could hardly be caught and hypnotised by a fork that is insulated in a locked box under the butler's bed. They have thrown down the gauntlet to American science on this point. They declare that diamond links are not left about in conspicuous locations in the haunts of the lower classes, as they were in the great test experiment of Calypso College. We hope this experiment here will be an answer to that young ringing challenge, and will bring the burglar once more into line and union with his fellow-criminals.'

Moon, whose face had gone through every phase of black bewilderment for five minutes past, suddenly lifted his hand and struck the table in explosive enlightenment.

'Oh, I see!' he cried; 'you mean that Smith is a burglar.'

'I thought I made it quite ad'quately lucid,' said Mr Pym, folding up his eyelids. It was typical of this topsy-turvy private trial that all the eloquent extras, all the rhetoric or digression on either side, was exasperating and unintelligible to the other. Moon could not make head or tail of the solemnity of a new civilisation. Pym could not make head or tail of the gaiety of an old one.

'All the cases in which Smith has figured as an expropriator,' continued the American doctor, 'are cases of burglary. Pursuing the same course as in the previous case, we select the indubitable instance from the rest, and we take the most correct cast-iron evidence. I will now call on my colleague, Mr Gould, to read a letter we have received from the earnest, unspotted Canon of Durham, Canon Hawkins.'

Mr Moses Gould leapt up with his usual alacrity to read the letter from the earnest and unspotted Hawkins. Moses Gould could imitate a farmyard well, Sir Henry Irving not so well, Marie Lloyd to a point of excellence, and the new motor horns in a manner that put him upon the platform of great artists. But his imitation of a Canon of Durham was not convincing; indeed, the sense of the letter was so much obscured by the extraordinary leaps and gasps of his pronunciation that it is perhaps better to print it here as Moon read it when, a little later, it was handed across the table.

'Dear Sir – I can scarcely feel surprise that the incident you mention, private as it was, should have filtered through our omnivorous journals to the mere populace; for the position I have since attained makes me, I conceive, a public character, and this was certainly the most extraordinary incident in a not uneventful and perhaps not an unimportant career. I am by no means without experience in scenes of civil tumult. I have faced many a political crisis in the old Primrose League days at Herne Bay, and, before I broke with the wilder set, have spent many a night at the Christian Social Union. But this other experience was quite inconceivable. I can only describe it as the letting loose of a place which it is not for me, as a clergyman, to mention.

'It occurred in the days when I was, for a short period, a curate at Hoxton; and the other curate, then my colleague, induced me to attend a meeting which he described, I must say profanely described, as calculated to promote the kingdom of God. I found, on the contrary, that it consisted entirely of men in corduroys and greasy clothes whose manners were coarse and their opinions extreme.

'Of my colleague in question I wish to speak with the fullest respect and friendliness, and I will therefore say little. No one can be more convinced than I of the evil of politics in the pulpit; and I never offer my congregation any advice about voting except in cases in which I feel strongly that they are likely to make an erroneous selection. But, while I do not mean to touch at all upon political or social problems, I must say that for a clergyman to countenance, even in jest, such discredited nostrums of dissipated demagogues as Socialism or Radicalism partakes of the character of the betrayal of a sacred trust. Far be it from me to say a word against the Reverend Raymond Percy, the colleague in question. He was brilliant, I suppose, and to some apparently fascinating; but a clergyman who talks like a Socialist, wears his hair like a pianist, and behaves like an intoxicated person, will never rise in his profession, or even obtain the admiration of the good and wise. Nor is it for me to utter my personal judgements of the appearance of the people in the hall. Yet a glance round the room, revealing ranks of debased and envious faces – '

'Adopting,' said Moon explosively, for he was getting restive – 'adopting the reverend gentleman's favourite figure of logic, may I say that while tortures would not tear from me a whisper about his intellect, he is a blasted old jackass.'

'Really!' said Dr Pym; 'I protest.'

'You must keep quiet, Michael,' said Inglewood; 'they have a right to read their story.'

'Chair! Chair! Chair!' cried Gould, rolling about exuberantly in his own; and Pym glanced for a moment towards the canopy which covered all the authority of the Court of Beacon.

'Oh, don't wake the old lady,' said Moon, lowering his voice in a moody good-humour. 'I apologise. I won't interrupt again.'

Before the little eddy of interruption was ended the reading of the clergyman's letter was already continuing.

'The proceedings opened with a speech from my colleague, of which I will say nothing. It was deplorable. Many of the audience were Irish, and showed the weakness of that impetuous people. When gathered together into gangs and conspiracies they seem to lose altogether that lovable good-nature and readiness to accept anything one tells them which distinguishes them as individuals.'

With a slight start, Michael rose to his feet, bowed solemnly, and sat down again.

'These persons, if not silent, were at least applausive during the speech of Mr Percy. He descended to their level with witticisms about rent and a reserve of labour. Confiscation, expropriation, arbitration, and such words with which I cannot soil my lips, recurred constantly. Some hours afterwards the storm broke. I had been addressing the meeting for some time, pointing out the lack of thrift in the working classes, their insufficient attendance at evening service, their neglect of the Harvest Festival, and of many other things that might materially help them to improve their lot. It was, I think, about this time that an extraordinary interruption occurred. An enormous, powerful man, partly concealed with white plaster, arose in the middle of the hall, and offered (in a loud, roaring voice, like a bull's) some observations which seemed to be in a foreign language. Mr Raymond Percy, my colleague, descended to his level by entering into a duel of repartee, in which he appeared to be the victor. The meeting began to behave more respectfully for a little; yet before I had said twelve sentences more the rush was made for the platform. The enormous plasterer, in particular, plunged towards us, shaking the earth like an elephant; and I really do not know what would have happened if a man equally large, but not quite so ill-dressed, had not jumped up also and held him away. This other big man shouted a sort of speech to the mob as he was shoving them back. I don't know what he said, but, what with shouting and shoving and such horseplay, he got us out at a back door, while the wretched people went roaring down another passage.

'Then follows the truly extraordinary part of my story. When he had got us outside, in a mean backyard of blistered grass leading into a lane with a very lonely-looking lamp post, this giant addressed me as follows: "You're well out of that, sir; now you'd better come along with me. I want you to help me in an act of social justice, such as we've all been talking about. Come along!" And turning his big back abruptly, he led us down the lean old lane with the one lean old lamp post, we scarcely knowing what to do but to follow him. He had certainly helped us in a most difficult situation, and, as a gentleman, I could not treat such a benefactor with suspicion without grave grounds. Such also was the view of my Socialistic colleague, who (with all his dreadful talk of arbitration) is a gentleman also. In fact, he comes of the Staffordshire Percys, a branch of the old house, and has the black hair and pale, clear-cut face of the whole family. I cannot but refer it to vanity that he should heighten his personal advantages with black velvet or a red cross of considerable ostentation, and certainly – but I digress.

'A fog was coming up the street, and that last lost lamp post faded behind us in a way that certainly depressed the mind. The large man in front of us looked larger and larger in the haze. He did not turn round, but he said with his huge back to us, "All that talking's no good; we want a little practical Socialism."

' "I quite agree," said Percy; "but I always like to understand things in theory before I put them into practice."

' "Oh, you just leave that to me," said the practical Socialist, or whatever he was, with the most terrifying vagueness. "I have a way with me. I'm a permeator."

'I could not imagine what he meant, but my companion laughed, so I was sufficiently reassured to continue the unaccountable journey for the present. It led us through most singular ways; out of the lane, where we were already rather cramped, into a paved passage, at the end of which we passed through a wooden gate left open. We then found ourselves, in the increasing darkness and vapour, crossing what appeared to be a beaten path across a kitchen garden. I called out to the enormous person going on in front, but he answered obscurely that it was a short cut.

'I was just repeating my very natural doubt to my clerical companion when I was brought up against a short ladder, apparently leading to a higher level of road. My thoughtless colleague ran up it so quickly that I could not do otherwise than follow as best I could. The path on which I then planted my feet was quite unprecedentedly narrow. I had never had to walk along a thoroughfare so exiguous. Along one side of it grew what, in the dark and density of air, I first took to be some short, strong thicket of shrubs. Then I saw that they were not short shrubs; they were the tops of tall trees. I, an English gentleman and clergyman of the Church of England – I was walking along the top of a garden wall like a tom cat.

'I am glad to say that I stopped within my first five steps, and let loose my just reprobation, balancing myself as best I could all the time.

' "It's a right-of-way," declared my indefensible informant. "It's closed to traffic once in a hundred years."

' "Mr Percy, Mr Percy!" I called out; "you are not going on with this blackguard?"

' "Why, I think so," answered my unhappy colleague flippantly. "I think you and I are bigger blackguards than he is, whatever he is."

' "I am a burglar," explained the big creature quite calmly. "I am a member of the Fabian Society. I take back the wealth stolen by the capitalist, not by sweeping civil war and revolution, but by reform fitted to the special occasion – here a little and there a little. Do you see that fifth house along the terrace with the flat roof? I'm permeating that one tonight."

' "Whether this is a crime or a joke," I cried, "I desire to be quit of it."

' "The ladder is just behind you," answered the creature with horrible courtesy; "and, before you go, do let me give you my card."

'If I had had the presence of mind to show any proper spirit I should have flung it away, though any adequate gesture of the kind would have gravely affected my equilibrium upon the wall. As it was, in the wildness of the moment, I put it in my waistcoat pocket, and, picking my way back by wall and ladder, landed in the respectable streets once more. Not before, however, I had seen with my own eyes the two awful and lamentable facts – that the burglar was climbing up a slanting roof towards the chimneys, and that Raymond Percy (a priest of God and, what was worse, a gentleman) was crawling up after him. I have never seen either of them since that day.

'In consequence of this soul-searching experience I severed my connection with the wild set. I am far from saying that every member of the Christian Social Union must necessarily be a burglar. I have no right to bring any such charge. But it gave me a hint of what such courses may lead to in many cases; and I saw them no more.

'I have only to add that the photograph you enclose, taken by a Mr Inglewood, is undoubtedly that of the burglar in question. When I got home that night I looked at his card, and he was inscribed there under the name of Innocent Smith.

'Yours faithfully,

'JOHN CLEMENT HAWKINS.'

Moon merely went through the form of glancing at the paper. He knew that the prosecutors could not have invented so heavy a document; that Moses Gould (for one) could no more write like a canon than he could read like one. After handing it back he rose to open the defence on the burglary charge.

'We wish,' said Michael, 'to give all reasonable facilities to the prosecution; especially as it will save the time of the whole court. The latter object I shall once again pursue by passing over all those points of theory which are so dear to Dr Pym. I know how they are made. Perjury is a variety of aphasia, leading a man to say one thing instead of another. Forgery is a kind of writer's cramp, forcing a man to write his uncle's name instead of his own. Piracy on the high seas is probably a form of seasickness. But it is unnecessary for us to enquire into the causes of a fact which we deny. Innocent Smith never did commit burglary at all.

'I should like to claim the power permitted by our previous arrangement, and ask the prosecution two or three questions.'

Dr Cyrus Pym closed his eyes to indicate a courteous assent.

'In the first place,' continued Moon, 'have you the date of Canon Hawkins's last glimpse of Smith and Percy climbing up the walls and roofs?'

'Ho, yus!' called out Gould smartly. 'November thirteen, eighteen ninety-one.'

'Have you,' continued Moon, 'identified the houses in Hoxton up which they climbed?'

'Must have been Ladysmith Terrace out of the highroad,' answered Gould with the same clockwork readiness.

'Well,' said Michael, cocking an eyebrow at him, 'was there any burglary in that terrace that night? Surely you could find that out.'

'There may well have been,' said the doctor primly, after a pause, 'an unsuccessful one that led to no legalities.'

'Another question,' proceeded Michael. 'Canon Hawkins, in his blood-and-thunder boyish way, left off at the exciting moment. Why don't you produce the evidence of the other clergyman, who actually followed the burglar and presumably was present at the crime?'

Dr Pym rose and planted the points of his fingers on the table, as he did when he was specially confident of the clearness of his reply.

'We have entirely failed,' he said, 'to track the other clergyman, who seems to have melted into the ether after Canon Hawkins had seen him as-cending the gutters and the leads. I am fully aware that this may strike many as sing'lar; yet, upon reflection, I think it will appear pretty natural to a bright thinker. This Mr Raymond Percy is admittedly, by the canon's evidence, a minister of eccentric ways. His con-nection with England's proudest and fairest does not seemingly prevent a taste for the society of the real low-down. On the other hand, the prisoner Smith is, by general agreement, a man of irr'sistible fascination. I entertain no doubt that Smith led the Revered Percy into the crime and forced him to hide his head in the real crim'nal class. That would fully account for his non-appearance, and the failure of all attempts to trace him.'

'It is impossible, then, to trace him?' asked Moon.

'Impossible,' repeated the specialist, shutting his eyes.

'You are sure it's impossible?'

'Oh dry up, Michael,' cried Gould, irritably. 'We'd 'ave found 'im if we could, for you bet 'e saw the burglary. Don't *you* start looking for 'im. Look for your own 'ead in the dustbin. You'll find that – after a bit,' and his voice died away in grumbling.

'Arthur,' directed Michael Moon, sitting down, 'kindly read Mr Raymond Percy's letter to the court.'

'Wishing, as Mr Moon has said, to shorten the proceedings as much as possible,' began Inglewood, 'I will not read the first part of the letter sent to us. It is only fair to the prosecution to admit the account given by the second clergyman fully ratifies, as far as facts are concerned, that given by the first clergyman. We concede, then, the canon's story so far as it goes. This must necessarily be valuable to the prosecutor and also convenient to the court. I begin Mr Percy's letter, then, at the point when all three men were standing on the garden wall:

'As I watched Hawkins wavering on the wall, I made up my own mind not to waver. A cloud of wrath was on my brain, like the cloud of copper fog on the houses and gardens round. My decision was violent and simple; yet the thoughts that led up to it were so complicated and contradictory that I could not retrace them now. I knew Hawkins was a kind, innocent gentleman; and I would have given ten pounds for the pleasure of kicking him down the road. That God should allow good people to be as bestially stupid as that – rose against me like a towering blasphemy.

'At Oxford, I fear, I had the artistic temperament rather badly; and artists love to be limited. I liked the church as a pretty pattern; discipline was mere decoration. I delighted in mere divisions of time; I liked eating fish on Friday. But then I like fish; and the fast was made for men who like meat. Then I came to Hoxton and found men who had fasted for five hundred years; men who had to gnaw fish because they could not get meat – and fish-bones when they could not get fish. As too many British officers treat the army as a review, so I had treated the Church Militant as if it were the Church Pageant. Hoxton cures that. Then I realised that for eighteen hundred years the Church Militant had not been a pageant, but a riot – and a suppressed riot. There, still living patiently in Hoxton, were the people to whom the tremendous promises had been made. In the face of that I had to become a revolutionary if I was to continue to be religious. In Hoxton one cannot be a conservative without being also an atheist – and a pessimist. Nobody but the devil could want to conserve Hoxton.

'On the top of all this comes Hawkins. If he had cursed all the Hoxton men, excommunicated them, and told them they were going to hell, I should have rather admired him. If he had ordered them all to be burned in the marketplace, I should still have had that patience that all good Christians have with the wrongs inflicted on other people. But there is no priestcraft about Hawkins – nor any other kind of craft. He is as perfectly incapable of being a priest as he is of being a carpenter or a cabman or a gardener or a plasterer. He is a perfect gentleman; that is his complaint. He does not impose his creed, but simply his class. He never said a word of religion in the whole of his damnable address. He simply said all the things his brother, the major, would have said. A voice from heaven assures me that he has a brother, and that this brother is a major.

'When this helpless aristocrat had praised cleanliness in the body and convention in the soul to people who could hardly keep body and soul together, the stampede against our platform began. I took part in his undeserved rescue, I followed his obscure deliverer, until (as I have said) we stood together on the wall above the dim gardens, already clouding with fog. Then I looked at the curate and at the burglar, and decided, in a spasm of inspiration, that the burglar was the better man of the two. The burglar seemed quite as kind and human as the curate was – and he was also brave and self-reliant, which the curate was not. I knew there was no virtue in the upper class, for I belong to it myself; I knew there was not so very much in the lower class, for I had lived with it a long time. Many old texts about the despised and persecuted came back to my mind, and I thought that the saints might well be hidden in the criminal class. About the time Hawkins let himself down the ladder I was crawling up a low, sloping, blue-slate roof after the large man, who went leaping in front of me like a gorilla.

'This upward scramble was short, and we soon found ourselves tramping along a broad road of flat roofs, broader than many big thoroughfares, with chimney-pots here and there that seemed in the haze as bulky as small forts. The asphyxiation of the fog seemed to increase the somewhat swollen and morbid anger under which my brain and body laboured. The sky and all those things that are commonly clear seemed overpowered by sinister spirits. Tall spectres with turbans of vapour seemed to stand higher than the sun or moon, eclipsing both. I thought dimly of illustrations to the *Arabian Nights* on brown paper with rich but sombre tints, showing genii gathering round the Seal of Solomon. By the way, what was the Seal of Solomon? Nothing to do with sealing-wax really, I suppose; but my muddled fancy felt the thick clouds as being of that heavy and clinging substance, of strong opaque colour, poured out of boiling pots and stamped into monstrous emblems.

'The first effect of the tall turbaned vapours was that discoloured look of pea-soup or coffee brown of which Londoners commonly speak. But the scene grew subtler with familiarity. We stood above the average of the housetops and saw something of that thing called smoke, which in great cities creates the strange thing called fog. Beneath us rose a forest of chimney-pots. And there stood in every chimney-pot, as if it were a flowerpot, a brief shrub or a tall tree of coloured vapour. The colours of the smoke were various; for some chimneys were from firesides and some from factories, and some again from mere rubbish heaps. And yet, though the tints were all varied, they all seemed unnatural, like fumes from a witch's pot. It was as if the shameful and ugly shapes growing shapeless in the cauldron sent up each its separate spurt of steam, coloured according to the fish or flesh consumed. Here, aglow from underneath, were dark red clouds, such as might drift from dark jars of sacrificial blood; there the vapour was dark indigo grey, like the long hair of witches steeped in the hell-broth. In another place the smoke was of an awful opaque ivory yellow, such as might be the disembodiment of one of their old, leprous waxen images. But right across it ran a line of bright, sinister, sulphurous green, as clear and crooked as Arabic – '

Mr Moses Gould once more attempted the arrest of the bus. He was understood to suggest that the reader should shorten the proceedings by leaving out all the adjectives. Mrs Duke, who had woken up, observed that she was sure it was all very nice, and the decision was duly noted down by Moses with a blue, and by Michael with a red pencil. Inglewood then resumed the reading of the document.

'Then I read the writing of the smoke. Smoke was like the modern city that makes it; it is not always dull or ugly, but it is always wicked and vain.

'Modern England was like a cloud of smoke; it could carry all colours, but it could leave nothing but a stain. It was our weakness and not our strength that put a rich refuse in the sky. These were the rivers of our vanity pouring into the void. We had taken the sacred circle of the whirlwind, and looked down on it, and seen it as a whirlpool. And then we had used it as a sink. It was a good symbol of the mutiny in my own mind. Only our worst things were going to heaven. Only our criminals could still ascend like angels.

'As my brain was blinded with such emotions, my guide stopped by one of the big chimney-pots that stood at the regular intervals like lamp posts along that uplifted and aerial highway. He put his heavy hand upon it, and for the moment I thought he was merely leaning on it, tired with his steep scramble along the terrace. So far as I could guess from the abysses, full of fog on either side, and the veiled lights of red brown and old gold glowing through them now and again, we were on the top of one of those long, consecutive, and genteel rows of houses which are still to be found lifting their heads above poorer districts, the remains of some rage of optimism in earlier speculative builders. Probably enough, they were entirely untenanted, or tenanted only by such small clans of the poor as gather also in the old emptied palaces of Italy. Indeed, some little time later, when the fog had lifted a little, I discovered that we were walking round a semicircle of crescent which fell away below us into one flat square or wide street below another, like a giant stairway, in a manner not unknown in the eccentric building of London, and looking like the last ledges of the land. But a cloud sealed the giant stairway as yet.

'My speculations about the sullen skyscape, however, were interrupted by something as unexpected as the moon falling from the sky. Instead of my burglar lifting his hand from the chimney he leaned on, he leaned on it a little more heavily, and the whole chimney-pot turned over like the opening top of an inkstand. I remembered the short ladder leaning against the low wall and felt sure he had arranged his criminal approach long before.

'The collapse of the big chimney-pot ought to have been the culmination of my chaotic feelings; but, to tell the truth, it produced a sudden sense of comedy and even of comfort. I could not recall what connected this abrupt bit of housebreaking with some quaint but still kindly fancies. Then I remembered the delightful and uproarious scenes of roofs and chimneys in the harlequinades of my childhood, and was darkly and quite irrationally comforted by a sense of unsubstantiality in the scene, as if the houses were of lath and paint and pasteboard, and were only meant to be tumbled in and out of by policemen and pantaloons. The law-breaking of my companion seemed not only seriously excusable, but even comically excusable. Who were all these pompous preposterous people with their footmen and their foot-scrapers, their chimney-pots and their chimney-pot hats, that they should prevent a poor clown from getting sausages if he wanted them? One would suppose that property was a serious thing. I had reached, as it were, a higher level of that mountain of vaporous visions, the heaven of a higher levity.

'My guide had jumped down into the dark cavity revealed by the displaced chimney-pot. He must have landed at a level considerably lower, for, tall as he was, nothing but his weirdly tousled head remained visible. Something again far off, and yet familiar, pleased me about this way of invading the houses of men. I thought of little chimney-sweeps, and *The Water Babies*; but I decided that it was not that. Then I remembered what it was that made me connect such topsy-turvy trespass with ideas quite opposite to the idea of crime. Christmas Eve, of course, and Santa Claus coming down the chimney.

'Almost at the same instant the hairy head disappeared into the black hole; but I heard a voice calling to me from below. A second or two afterwards, the hairy head reappeared; it was dark against the more fiery part of the fog, and nothing could be spelt of its expression, but its voice called on me to follow with that enthusiastic impatience proper only among old friends. I jumped into the gulf, and as blindly as Curtius, for I was still thinking of Santa Claus and the traditional virtue of such vertical entrance.

'In every well-appointed gentleman's house, I reflected, there was the front door for the gentlemen, and the side door for the tradesmen; but there was also the top door for the gods. The chimney is, so to speak, the underground passage between earth and heaven. By this starry tunnel Santa Claus manages – like the skylark – to be true to the kindred points of heaven and home. Nay, owing to certain conventions, and a widely distributed lack of courage for climbing, this door was, perhaps, little used. But Santa Claus's door was really the front door: it was the door fronting the universe.

'I thought this as I groped my way across the black garret, or loft below the roof, and scrambled down the squat ladder that let us down into a yet larger loft below. Yet it was not till I was halfway down the ladder that I suddenly stood still, and thought for an instant of retracing all my steps, as my companion had retraced them from the beginning of the garden wall. The name of Santa Claus had suddenly brought me back to my senses. I remembered why Santa Claus came, and why he was welcome.

'I was brought up in the propertied classes, and with all their horror of offences against property. I had heard all the regular denunciations of robbery, both right and wrong; I had read the Ten Commandments in church a thousand times. And then and there, at the age of thirty-four, halfway down a ladder in a dark room in the bodily act of burglary, I saw suddenly for the first time that theft, after all, is really wrong.

'It was too late to turn back, however, and I followed the strangely soft footsteps of my huge companion across the lower and larger loft, till he knelt down on a part of the bare flooring and, after a few fumbling efforts, lifted a sort of trapdoor. This released a light from below, and we found ourselves looking down into a lamp-lit sitting-room, of the sort that in large houses often leads out of a bedroom, and is an adjunct to it. Light thus breaking from beneath our feet like a soundless explosion, showed that the trapdoor just lifted was clogged with dust and rust, and had doubtless been long disused until the advent of my enterprising friend. But I did not look at this long, for the sight of the shining room underneath us had an almost unnatural attractiveness. To enter a modern interior at so strange an angle, by so forgotten a door, was an epoch in one's psychology. It was like having found a fourth dimension.

'My companion dropped from the aperture into the room so suddenly and soundlessly, that I could do nothing but follow him; though, for lack of practice in crime, I was by no means soundless. Before the echo of my boots had died away, the big burglar had gone quickly to the door, half opened it, and stood looking down the staircase and listening. Then, leaving the door still half open, he came back into the middle of the room, and ran his roving blue eye round its furniture and ornament. The room was comfortably lined with books in that rich and human way that makes the walls seem alive; it was a deep and full, but slovenly, bookcase, of the sort that is constantly ransacked for the purposes of reading in bed. One of those stunted German stoves that look like red goblins stood in a corner, and a sideboard of walnut wood with closed doors in its lower part. There were three windows, high but narrow. After another glance round, my housebreaker plucked the walnut doors open and rummaged inside. He found nothing there, apparently, except an extremely handsome cut-glass decanter, containing what looked like port. Somehow the sight of the thief returning with this ridiculous little luxury in his hand woke within me once more all the revelation and revulsion I had felt above.

‘ “Don’t do it!” I cried quite incoherently, “Santa Claus – ”

‘ “Ah,” said the burglar, as he put the decanter on the table and stood looking at me, “you’ve thought about that, too.”

‘ “I can’t express a millionth part of what I’ve thought of,” I cried, “but it’s something like this . . . oh, can’t you see it? Why are children not afraid of Santa Claus, though he comes like a thief in the night? He is permitted secrecy, trespass, almost treachery – because there are more toys where he has been. What should we feel if there were less? Down what chimney from hell would come the goblin that should take away the children’s balls and dolls while they slept? Could a Greek tragedy be more grey and cruel than that daybreak and awakening? Dog-stealer, horse-stealer, man-stealer – can you think of anything so base as a toy-stealer?”

‘The burglar, as if absently, took a large revolver from his pocket and laid it on the table beside the decanter, but still kept his blue reflective eyes fixed on my face.

‘ “Man!” I said, “all stealing is toy-stealing. That’s why it’s really wrong. The goods of the unhappy children of men should be really respected because of their worthlessness. I know Naboth’s vineyard is as painted as Noah’s Ark. I know Nathan’s ewe-lamb is really a woolly baa-lamb on a wooden stand. That is why I could not take them away. I did not mind so much, as long as I thought of men’s things as their valuables; but I dare not put a hand upon their vanities.”

‘After a moment I added abruptly, “Only saints and sages ought to be robbed. They may be stripped and pillaged; but not the poor little worldly people of the things that are their poor little pride.”

‘He set out two wineglasses from the cupboard, filled them both, and lifted one of them with a salutation towards his lips.

‘ “Don’t do it!” I cried. “It might be the last bottle of some rotten vintage or other. The master of this house may be quite proud of it. Don’t you see there’s something sacred in the silliness of such things?”

‘ “It’s not the last bottle,” answered my criminal calmly; “there’s plenty more in the cellar.”

‘ “You know the house, then?” I said.

‘ “Too well,” he answered, with a sadness so strange as to have something eerie about it. “I am always trying to forget what I know – and to find what I don’t know.” He drained his glass. “Besides,” he added, “it will do him good.”

‘ “What will do him good?”

‘ “The wine I’m drinking,” said the strange person.

‘ “Does he drink too much, then?” I enquired.

' "No," he answered, "not unless I do."

' "Do you mean," I demanded, "that the owner of this house approves of all you do?"

' "God forbid," he answered; "but he has to do the same."

'The dead face of the fog looking in at all the three windows unreasonably increased a sense of riddle, and even terror, about this tall, narrow house we had entered out of the sky. I had once more the notion about the gigantic genii – I fancied that enormous Egyptian faces, of the dead reds and yellows of Egypt, were staring in at each window of our little lamp-lit room as at a lighted stage of marionettes. My companion went on playing with the pistol in front of him, and talking with the same rather creepy confidentialness.

' "I am always trying to find him – to catch him unawares. I come in through skylights and trapdoors to find him; but whenever I find him – he is doing what I am doing."

'I sprang to my feet with a thrill of fear. "There is someone coming," I cried, and my cry had something of a shriek in it. Not from the stairs below, but along the passage from the inner bedchamber (which seemed somehow to make it more alarming), footsteps were coming nearer. I am quite unable to say what mystery, or monster, or double, I expected to see when the door was pushed open from within. I am only quite certain that I did not expect to see what I did see.

'Framed in the open doorway stood, with an air of great serenity, a rather tall young woman, definitely though indefinably artistic – her dress the colour of spring and her hair of autumn leaves, with a face which, though still comparatively young, conveyed experience as well as intelligence. All she said was, "I didn't hear you come in."

' "I came in another way," said the permeator, somewhat vaguely. "I'd left my latchkey at home."

'I got to my feet in a mixture of politeness and mania. "I'm really very sorry," I cried. "I know my position is irregular. Would you be so obliging as to tell me whose house this is?"

' "Mine," said the burglar. "May I present you to my wife?"

'I doubtfully, and somewhat slowly, resumed my seat; and I did not get out of it till nearly morning. Mrs Smith (such was the prosaic name of this far from prosaic household) lingered a little, talking slightly and pleasantly. She left on my mind the impression of a certain odd mixture of shyness and sharpness; as if she knew the world well, but was still a little harmlessly afraid of it. Perhaps the possession of so jumpy and incalculable a husband had left her a little nervous. Anyhow, when she had retired to the inner chamber once more, that extraordinary man poured forth his apologia and autobiography over the dwindling wine.

'He had been sent to Cambridge with a view to a mathematical and scientific, rather than a classical or literary, career. A starless nihilism was then the philosophy of the schools; and it bred in him a war between the members and the spirit, but one in which the members were right. While his brain accepted the black creed, his very body rebelled against it. As he put it, his right hand taught him terrible things. As the authorities of Cambridge University put it, unfortunately, it had taken the form of his right hand flourishing a loaded firearm in the very face of a distinguished don, and driving him to climb out of the window and cling to a water-spout. He had done it solely because the poor don had professed in theory a preference for non-existence. For this very unacademic type of argument he had been sent down. Vomiting as he was with revulsion, from the pessimism that had quailed under his pistol, he made himself a kind of fanatic of the joy of life. He cut across all the associations of serious-minded men. He was gay, but by no means careless. His practical jokes were more in earnest than verbal ones. Though not an optimist in the absurd sense of maintaining that life is all beer and skittles, he did really seem to maintain that beer and skittles are the most serious part of it. "What is more immortal," he would cry, "than love and war? Type of all desire and joy – beer. Type of all battle and conquest – skittles."

'There was something in him of what the old world called the solemnity of revels – when they spoke of "solemnising" a mere masquerade or wedding banquet. Nevertheless he was not a mere pagan any more than he was a mere practical joker. His eccentricities sprang from a static fact of faith, in itself mystical, and even childlike and Christian.

' "I don't deny," he said, "that there should be priests to remind men that they will one day die. I only say that at certain strange epochs it is necessary to have another kind of priests, called poets, actually to remind men that they are not dead yet. The intellectuals among whom I moved were not even alive enough to fear death. They hadn't enough blood in them to be cowards. Until a pistol barrel was poked under their very noses they never even knew they had been born. For ages looking up an eternal perspective it might be true that life is a learning to die. But for these little white rats it was just as true that death was their only chance of learning to live."

'His creed of wonder was Christian by this absolute test; that he felt it continually slipping from himself as much as from others. He had the same pistol for himself, as Brutus said of the dagger. He continually ran preposterous risks of high precipice or headlong speed to keep alive the mere conviction that he was alive. He treasured up trivial and yet insane details that had once reminded him of the awful subconscious reality. When the don had hung on the stone gutter, the sight of his long dangling legs, vibrating in the void like wings, somehow awoke the naked satire of the old definition of man as a two-legged animal without feathers. The wretched professor had been brought into peril by his head, which he had so elaborately cultivated, and only saved by his legs, which he had treated with coldness and neglect. Smith could think of no other way of announcing or recording this, except to send a telegram to an old friend (by this time a total stranger) to say that he had just seen a man with two legs; and that the man was alive.

'The uprush of his released optimism burst into stars like a rocket when he suddenly fell in love. He happened to be shooting a high and very headlong weir in a canoe, by way of proving to himself that he was alive; and he soon found himself involved in some doubt about the continuance of the fact. What was worse, he found he had equally jeopardised a harmless lady alone in a rowing-boat, and one who had provoked death by no professions of philosophic negation. He apologised in wild gasps through all his wild wet labours to bring her to the shore, and when he had done so at last, he seems to have proposed to her on the bank. Anyhow, with the same impetuosity with which he had nearly murdered her, he completely married her; and she was the lady in green to whom I had recently said "good-night".

'They had settled down in these high narrow houses near Highbury. Perhaps, indeed, that is hardly the word. One could strictly say that Smith was married, that he was very happily married, that he not only did not care for any woman but his wife, but did not seem to care for any place but his home; but perhaps one could hardly say that he had settled down. "I am a very domestic fellow," he explained with gravity, "and have often come in through a broken window rather than be late for tea."

'He lashed his soul with laughter to prevent it falling asleep. He lost his wife a series of excellent servants by knocking at the door as a total stranger, and asking if Mr Smith lived there and what kind of a man he was. The London general servant is not used to the master indulging in such transcendental ironies. And it was found impossible to explain to her that he did it in order to feel the same interest in his own affairs that he always felt in other people's.

' "I know there's a fellow called Smith," he said in his rather weird way, "living in one of the tall houses in this terrace. I know he is really happy, and yet I can never catch him at it."

'Sometimes he would, of a sudden, treat his wife with a kind of paralysed politeness, like a young stranger struck with love at first sight. Sometimes he would extend this poetic fear to the very furniture; would seem to apologise to the chair he sat on, and climb the staircase as cautiously as a cragsman, to renew in himself the sense of their skeleton of reality. Every stair is a ladder and every stool a leg, he said. And at other times he would play the stranger exactly in the opposite sense, and would enter by another way, so as to feel like a thief and a robber. He would break and violate his own home, as he had done with me that night. It was near morning before I could tear myself from this queer confidence of the Man Who Would Not Die, and as I shook hands with him on the doorstep the last load of fog was lifting, and rifts of daylight revealed the stairway of irregular street levels that looked like the end of the world.

'It will be enough for many to say that I had passed a night with a maniac. What other term, it will be said, could be applied to such a being? A man who reminds himself that he is married by pretending not to be married! A man who tries to covet his own goods instead of his neighbour's! On this I have but one word to say, and I feel it of my honour to say it, though no one understands. I believe the maniac was one of those who do not merely come, but are sent; sent like a great gale upon ships by Him who made His angels winds and His messengers a flaming fire. This, at least, I know for certain. Whether such men have laughed or wept, we have laughed at their laughter as much as at their weeping. Whether they cursed or blessed the world, they have never fitted it. It is true that men have shrunk from the sting of a great satirist as if from the sting of an adder. But it is equally true that men flee from the embrace of a great optimist as from the embrace of a bear. Nothing brings down more curses than a real benediction. For the goodness of good things, like the badness of bad things, is a prodigy past speech; it is to be pictured rather than spoken. We shall have gone deeper than the deeps of heaven and grown older than the oldest angels before we feel, even in its first faint vibrations, the everlasting violence of that double passion with which God hates and loves the world.

'I am, yours faithfully,

'RAYMOND PERCY.'

'Oh, 'oly, 'oly, 'oly!' said Mr Moses Gould.

The instant he had spoken all the rest knew they had been in an almost religious state of submission and assent. Something had bound them together; something in the sacred tradition of the last two words of the letter; something also in the touching and boyish embarrassment with which Inglewood had read them – for he had all the thin-skinned reverence of the agnostic. Moses Gould was as good a fellow in his way as ever lived; far kinder to his family than more refined men of pleasure, simple and steadfast in his admiration, a thoroughly wholesome animal and a thoroughly genuine character. But wherever there is conflict, crises come in which any soul, personal or racial, unconsciously turns on the world the most hateful of its hundred faces. English reverence, Irish mysticism, American idealism, looked up and saw on the face of Moses a certain smile. It was that smile of the Cynic Triumphant, which has been the tocsin for many a cruel riot in Russian villages or mediaeval towns.

'Oh, 'oly, 'oly, 'oly!' said Moses Gould.

Finding that this was not well received, he explained further, exuberance deepening on his dark exuberant features.

'Always fun to see a bloke swallow a wasp when 'e's corfin' up a fly,' he said pleasantly. 'Don't you see you've bunged up old Smith anyhow. If this parson's tale's OK – why, Smith is 'ot. 'E's pretty 'ot. We find him elopin' with Miss Gray (best respects!) in a cab. Well, what abart this Mrs Smith the curate talks of, with her blarsted shyness – transmigogrified into a blighted sharpness? Miss Gray ain't been very sharp, but I reckon she'll be pretty shy.'

'Don't be a brute,' growled Michael Moon.

None could lift their eyes to look at Mary; but Inglewood sent a glance along the table at Innocent Smith. He was still bowed above his paper toys, and a wrinkle was on his forehead that might have been worry or shame. He carefully plucked out one corner of a complicated paper and tucked it in elsewhere; then the wrinkle vanished and he looked relieved.

CHAPTER 3

The Round Road; or, the Desertion Charge

Pym rose with sincere embarrassment; for he was an American, and his respect for ladies was real, and not at all scientific.

'Ignoring,' he said, 'the delicate and considerable knightly protests that have been called forth by my colleague's native sense of oration, and apologising to all for whom our wild search for truth seems unsuitable to the grand ruins of a feudal land, I still think my colleague's question by no means devoid of rel'vancy. The last charge against the accused was one of burglary; the next charge on the paper is of bigamy and desertion. It does without question appear that the defence, in aspiring to rebut this last charge, have really admitted the next. Either Innocent Smith is still under a charge of attempted burglary, or else that is exploded; but he is pretty well fixed for attempted bigamy. It all depends on what view we take of the alleged letter from Curate Percy. Under these conditions I feel justified in claiming my right to questions. May I ask how the defence got hold of the letter from Curate Percy? Did it come direct from the prisoner?'

'We have had nothing direct from the prisoner,' said Moon quietly. 'The few documents which the defence guarantees came to us from another quarter.'

'From what quarter?' asked Dr Pym.

'If you insist,' answered Moon, 'we had them from Miss Gray.'

Dr Cyrus Pym quite forgot to close his eyes, and, instead, opened them very wide.

'Do you really mean to say,' he said, 'that Miss Gray was in possession of this document testifying to a previous Mrs Smith?'

'Quite so,' said Inglewood, and sat down.

The doctor said something about infatuation in a low and painful voice, and then with visible difficulty continued his opening remarks.

'Unfortunately the tragic truth revealed by Curate Percy's narrative is only too crushingly confirmed by other and shocking documents in our own possession. Of these the principal and most certain is the testimony of Innocent Smith's gardener, who was present at the most dramatic and eye-opening of his many acts of marital infidelity. Mr Gould, the gardener, please.'

Mr Gould, with his tireless cheerfulness, arose to present the gardener. That functionary explained that he had served Mr and Mrs Innocent Smith when they had a little house on the edge of Croydon. From the gardener's tale, with its many small allusions, Inglewood grew certain he had seen the place. It was one of those corners of town or country that one does not forget, for it looked like a frontier. The garden hung very high above the lane, and its end was steep and sharp, like a fortress. Beyond was a roll of real country, with a white path sprawling across it, and the roots, boles, and branches of great grey trees writhing and twisting against the sky. But as if to assert that the lane itself was suburban, were sharply relieved against that grey and tossing upland a lamp post painted a peculiar yellow-green and a red pillar-box that stood exactly at the corner. Inglewood was sure of the place; he had passed it twenty times in his constitutionals on the bicycle; he had always dimly felt it was a place where something might occur. But it gave him quite a shiver to feel that the face of his frightful friend or enemy Smith might at any time have appeared over the garden bushes above. The gardener's account, unlike the curate's, was quite free from decorative adjectives, however many he may have uttered privately when writing it. He simply said that on a particular morning Mr Smith came out and began to play about with a rake, as he often did. Sometimes he would tickle the nose of his eldest child (he had two children); sometimes he would hook the rake on to the branch of a tree, and hoist himself up with horrible gymnastic jerks, like those of a giant frog in its final agony. Never, apparently, did he think of putting the rake to any of its proper uses, and the gardener, in consequence, treated his actions with coldness and brevity. But the gardener was certain that on one particular morning in October he (the gardener) had come round the corner of the house carrying the hose, had seen Mr Smith standing on the lawn in a striped red and white jacket (which might have been his smoking-jacket, but was quite as like a part of his pyjamas), and had heard him then and there call out to his wife, who was looking out of the bedroom window on to the garden, these decisive and very loud expressions –

'I won't stay here any longer. I've got another wife and much better children a long way from here. My other wife's got redder hair than yours, and my other garden's got a much finer situation; and I'm going off to them.'

With these words, apparently, he sent the rake flying far up into the sky, higher than many could have shot an arrow, and caught it again. Then he cleared the hedge at a leap and alighted on his feet down in the lane below, and set off up the road without even a hat. Much of the picture was doubtless supplied by Inglewood's accidental memory of the place. He could see with his mind's eye that big bare-headed figure with the ragged rake swaggering up the crooked woodland road, and leaving lamp post and pillar-box behind. But the gardener, on his own account, was quite prepared to swear to the public confession of bigamy, to the temporary disappearance of the rake in the sky, and the final disappearance of the man up the road. Moreover, being a local man, he could swear that, beyond some local rumours that Smith had embarked on the south-eastern coast, nothing was known of him again.

This impression was somewhat curiously clinched by Michael Moon in the few but clear phrases in which he opened the defence upon the third charge. So far from denying that Smith had fled from Croydon and disappeared on the Continent, he seemed prepared to prove all this on his own account. 'I hope you are not so insular,' he said, 'that you will not respect the word of a French innkeeper as much as that of an English gardener. By Mr Inglewood's favour we will hear the French innkeeper.'

Before the company had decided the delicate point Inglewood was already reading the account in question. It was in French. It seemed to them to run something like this:

'Sir – Yes; I am Durobin of Durobin's Café on the seafront at Gras, rather north of Dunquerque. I am willing to write all I know of the stranger out of the sea.

'I have no sympathy with eccentrics or poets. A man of sense looks for beauty in things deliberately intended to be beautiful, such as a trim flower-bed or an ivory statuette. One does not permit beauty to pervade one's whole life, just as one does not pave all the roads with ivory or cover all the fields with geraniums. My faith, but we should miss the onions!

'But whether I read things backwards through my memory, or whether there are indeed atmospheres of psychology which the eye of science cannot as yet pierce, it is the humiliating fact that on that particular evening I felt like a poet – like any little rascal of a poet who drinks absinthe in the mad Montmartre.

'Positively the sea itself looked like absinthe, green and bitter and poisonous. I had never known it look so unfamiliar before. In the sky was that early and stormy darkness that is so depressing to the mind, and the wind blew shrilly round the little lonely coloured kiosk where they sell the newspapers, and along the sand-hills by the shore. There I saw a fishing-boat with a brown sail standing in silently from the sea. It was already quite close, and out of it clambered a man of monstrous stature, who came wading to shore with the water not up to his knees, though it would have reached the hips of many men. He leaned on a long rake or pole, which looked like a trident, and made him look like a Triton. Wet as he was, and with strips of seaweed clinging to him, he walked across to my café, and, sitting down at a table outside, asked for cherry brandy, a liqueur which I keep, but is seldom demanded. Then the monster, with great politeness, invited me to partake of a vermouth before my dinner, and we fell into conversation. He had apparently crossed from Kent by a small boat got at a private bargain because of some odd fancy he had for passing promptly in an easterly direction, and not waiting for any of the official boats. He was, he somewhat vaguely explained, looking for a house. When I naturally asked him where the house was, he answered that he did not know; it was on an island; it was somewhere to the east; or, as he expressed it with a hazy and yet impatient gesture, "over there".

'I asked him how, if he did not know the place, he would know it when he saw it. Here he suddenly ceased to be hazy, and became alarmingly minute. He gave a description of the house detailed enough for an auctioneer. I have forgotten nearly all the details except the last two, which were that the lamp post was painted green, and that there was a red pillar-box at the corner.

' "A red pillar-box!" I cried in astonishment. "Why, the place must be in England!"

' "I had forgotten," he said, nodding heavily. "That is the island's name."

' "But, *nom du nom*," I cried testily, "you've just come from England, my boy."

' "They *said* it was England," said my imbecile, conspiratorially. "They said it was Kent. But Kentish men are such liars one can't believe anything they say."

' "Monsieur," I said, "you must pardon me. I am elderly, and the *fumisteries* of the young men are beyond me. I go by common sense, or, at the largest, by that extension of applied common sense called science."

' "Science!" cried the stranger. "There is only one good thing science ever discovered – a good thing, good tidings of great joy – that the world is round."

'I told him with civility that his words conveyed no impression to my intelligence. "I mean," he said, "that going right round the world is the shortest way to where you are already."

' "Is it not even shorter," I asked, "to stop where you are?"

' "No, no, no!" he cried emphatically. "That way is long and very weary. At the end of the world, at the back of the dawn, I shall find the wife I really married and the house that is really mine. And that house will have a greener lamp post and a redder pillar-box. Do you," he asked with a sudden intensity, "do you never want to rush out of your house in order to find it?"

' "No, I think not," I replied; "reason tells a man from the first to adapt his desires to the probable supply of life. I remain here, content to fulfil the life of man. All my interests are here, and most of my friends, and – "

' "And yet," he cried, starting to his almost terrific height, "you made the French Revolution!"

' "Pardon me," I said, "I am not quite so elderly. A relative perhaps."

' "I mean your sort did!" exclaimed this personage. "Yes, your damned smug, settled, sensible sort made the French Revolution. Oh! I know some say it was no good, and you're just back where you were before. Why, blast it all, that's just where we all want to be – back where we were before! That is revolution – going right round! Every revolution, like every repentance, is a return."

'He was so excited that I waited till he had taken his seat again, and then said something indifferent and soothing; but he struck the tiny table with his colossal fist and went on.

' "I am going to have a revolution, not a French Revolution, but an English Revolution. God has given to each tribe its own type of mutiny. The Frenchmen march against the citadel of the city together; the Englishman marches to the outskirts of the city, and alone. But I am going to turn the world upside down, too. I'm going to turn myself upside down. I'm going to walk upside down in the cursed upside-downland of the Antipodes, where trees and men hang head downward in the sky. But my revolution, like yours, like the earth's, will end up in the holy, happy place – the celestial, incredible place – the place where we were before."

'With these remarks, which can scarcely be reconciled with reason, he leapt from the seat and strode away into the twilight, swinging his pole and leaving behind him an excessive payment, which also pointed to some loss of mental balance. This is all I know of the episode of the man landed from the fishing-boat, and I hope it may serve the interests of justice.

'Accept, Sir, the assurances of the very high consideration, with which I have the honour to be your obedient servant,

'JULES DUROBIN.'

'The next document in our dossier,' continued Inglewood, 'comes from the town of Crazok, in the central plains of Russia, and runs as follows:

'SIR – My name is Paul Nickolaiovitch: I am the stationmaster at the station near Crazok. The great trains go by across the plains taking people to China, but very few people get down at the platform where I have to watch. This makes my life rather lonely, and I am thrown back much upon the books I have. But I cannot discuss these very much with my neighbours, for enlightened ideas have not spread in this part of Russia so much as in other parts. Many of the peasants round here have never heard of Bernard Shaw.

'I am a Liberal, and do my best to spread Liberal ideas; but since the failure of the revolution this has been even more difficult. The revolutionists committed many acts contrary to the pure principles of humanitarianism, with which indeed, owing to the scarcity of books, they were ill acquainted. I did not approve of these cruel acts, though provoked by the tyranny of the government; but now there is a tendency to reproach all Intelligents with the memory of them. This is very unfortunate for Intelligents.

'It was when the railway strike was almost over, and a few trains came through at long intervals, that I stood one day watching a train that had come in. Only one person got out of the train, far away up at the other end of it, for it was a very long train. It was evening, with a cold, greenish sky. A little snow had fallen, but not enough to whiten the plain, which stretched away a sort of sad purple in all directions, save where the flat tops of some distant tablelands caught the evening light like lakes. As the solitary man came stamping along on the thin snow by the train he grew larger and larger; I thought I had never seen so large a man. But he looked even taller than he was, I think, because his shoulders were very big and his head comparatively little. From the big shoulders hung a tattered old jacket, striped dull red and dirty white, very thin for the winter, and one hand rested on a huge pole such as peasants rake in weeds with to burn them.

'Before he had traversed the full length of the train he was entangled in one of those knots of rowdies that were the embers of the extinct revolution, though they mostly disgraced themselves upon the government side. I was just moving to his assistance, when he whirled up his rake and laid out right and left with such energy that he came through them without scathe and strode right up to me, leaving them staggered and really astonished.

'Yet when he reached me, after so abrupt an assertion of his aim, he could only say rather dubiously in French that he wanted a house.

' "There are not many houses to be had round here," I answered in the same language, "the district has been very disturbed. A revolution, as you know, has recently been suppressed. Any further building – "

' "Oh! I don't mean that," he cried; "I mean a real house – a live house. It really is a live house, for it runs away from me."

'I am ashamed to say that something in his phrase or gesture moved me profoundly. We Russians are brought up in an atmosphere of folklore, and its unfortunate effects can still be seen in the bright colours of the children's dolls and of the ikons. For an instant the idea of a house running away from a man gave me pleasure, for the enlightenment of man moves slowly.

' "Have you no other house of your own?" I asked.

' "I have left it," he said very sadly. "It was not the house that grew dull, but I that grew dull in it. My wife was better than all women, and yet I could not feel it."

' "And so," I said with sympathy, "you walked straight out of the front door, like a masculine Nora."

' "Nora?" he enquired politely, apparently supposing it to be a Russian word.

' "I mean Nora in *A Doll's House*," I replied.

'At this he looked very much astonished, and I knew he was an Englishman; for Englishmen always think that Russians study nothing but "ukases".

' "*A Doll's House*?" he cried vehemently; "why, that is just where Ibsen was so wrong! Why, the whole aim of a house is to be a doll's house. Don't you remember, when you were a child, how those little windows *were* windows, while the big windows weren't. A child has a doll's house, and shrieks when a front door opens inwards. A banker has a real house, yet how numerous are the bankers who fail to emit the faintest shriek when their real front doors open inwards."

'Something from the folklore of my infancy still kept me foolishly silent; and before I could speak, the Englishman had leaned over and was saying in a sort of loud whisper, "I have found out how to make a big thing small. I have found out how to turn a house into a doll's house. Get a long way off it: God lets us turn all things into toys by his great gift of distance. Once let me see my old brick house standing up quite little against the horizon, and I shall want to go back to it again. I shall see the funny little toy lamp post painted green against the gate, and all the dear little people like dolls looking out of the window. For the windows really open in my doll's house.'

' "But why?" I asked, "should you wish to return to that particular doll's house? Having taken, like Nora, the bold step against convention, having made yourself in the conventional sense disreputable, having dared to be free, why should you not take advantage of your freedom? As the greatest modern writers have pointed out, what you called your marriage was only your mood. You have a right to leave it all behind, like the clippings of your hair or the parings of your nails. Having once escaped, you have the world before you. Though the words may seem strange to you, you are free in Russia."

'He sat with his dreamy eyes on the dark circles of the plains, where the only moving thing was the long and labouring trail of smoke out of the railway engine, violet in tint, volcanic in outline, the one hot and heavy cloud of that cold clear evening of pale green.

' "Yes," he said with a huge sigh, "I am free in Russia. You are right. I could really walk into that town over there and have love all over again, and perhaps marry some beautiful woman and begin again, and nobody could ever find me. Yes, you have certainly convinced me of something."

'His tone was so queer and mystical that I felt impelled to ask him what he meant, and of what exactly I had convinced him.

' "You have convinced me," he said with the same dreamy eye, "why it is really wicked and dangerous for a man to run away from his wife."

' "And why is it dangerous?" I enquired.

' "Why, because nobody can find him," answered this odd person, "and we all want to be found."

' "The most original modern thinkers," I remarked, "Ibsen, Gorki, Nietzsche, Shaw, would all rather say that what we want most is to be lost: to find ourselves in untrodden paths, and to do unprecedented things: to break with the past and belong to the future."

'He rose to his whole height somewhat sleepily, and looked round on what was, I confess, a somewhat desolate scene – the dark purple plains, the neglected railroad, the few ragged knots of malcontents. "I shall not find the house here," he said. "It is still eastward – further and further eastward."

'Then he turned upon me with something like fury, and struck the foot of his pole upon the frozen earth.

' "And if I do go back to my country," he cried, "I may be locked up in a madhouse before I reach my own house. I have been a bit unconventional in my time! Why, Nietzsche stood in a row of ramrods in the silly old Prussian army, and Shaw takes temperance beverages in the suburbs; but the things I do are unprecedented things. This round road I am treading is an untrodden path. I do believe in breaking out; I am a revolutionist. But don't you see that all these real leaps and destructions and escapes are only attempts to get back to Eden – to something we have had, to something we at least have heard of? Don't you see one only breaks the fence or shoots the moon in order to get *home*?"

' "No," I answered after due reflection, "I don't think I should accept that."

' "Ah," he said with a sort of a sigh, "then you have explained a second thing to me."

' "What do you mean?" I asked; "what thing?"

' "Why your revolution has failed," he said; and walking across quite suddenly to the train he got into it just as it was steaming away at last. And I saw the long snaky tail of it disappear along the darkening flats.

'I saw no more of him. But though his views were adverse to the best advanced thought, he struck me as an interesting person: I should like to find out if he has produced any literary works.

'Yours, etc.,

'PAUL NICKOLAIOVITCH.'

There was something in this odd set of glimpses into foreign lives which kept the absurd tribunal quieter than it had hitherto been, and it was again without interruption that Inglewood opened another paper upon his pile. 'The Court will be indulgent,' he said, 'if the next note lacks the special ceremonies of our letter-writing. It is ceremonious enough in its own way:

'The Celestial Principles are permanent: Greeting. – I am Wong-Hi, and I tend the temple of all the ancestors of my family in the forest of Fu. The man that broke through the sky and came to me said that it must be very dull, but I showed him the wrongness of his thought. I am indeed in one place, for my uncle took me to this temple when I was a boy, and in this I shall doubtless die. But if a man remain in one place he shall see that the place changes. The pagoda of my temple stands up silently out of all the trees, like a yellow pagoda above many green pagodas. But the skies are sometimes blue like porcelain, and sometimes green like jade, and sometimes red like garnet. But the night is always ebony and always returns, said the Emperor Ho.

'The sky-breaker came at evening very suddenly, for I had hardly seen any stirring in the tops of the green trees over which I look as over a sea, when I go to the top of the temple at morning. And yet when he came, it was as if an elephant had strayed from the armies of the great kings of India. For palms snapped, and bamboos broke, and there came forth in the sunshine before the temple one taller than the sons of men.

'Strips of red and white hung about him like ribbons of a carnival, and he carried a pole with a row of teeth on it like the teeth of a dragon. His face was white and discomposed, after the fashion of the foreigners, so that they look like dead men filled with devils; and he spoke our speech brokenly.

'He said to me, "This is only a temple; I am trying to find a house." And then he told me with indelicate haste that the lamp outside his house was green, and that there was a red post at the corner of it.

' "I have not seen your house nor any houses," I answered. "I dwell in this temple and serve the gods."

' "Do you believe in the gods?" he asked with hunger in his eyes, like the hunger of dogs. And this seemed to me a strange question to ask, for what should a man do except what men have done?

' "My Lord," I said, "it must be good for men to hold up their hands even if the skies are empty. For if there are gods, they will be pleased, and if there are none, then there are none to be displeased. Sometimes the skies are gold and sometimes porphyry and sometimes ebony, but the trees and the temple stand still under it all. So the great Confucius taught us that if we do always the same things with our hands and our feet as do the wise beasts and birds, with our heads we may think many things: yes, my Lord, and doubt many things. So long as men offer rice at the right season, and kindle lanterns at the right hour, it matters little whether there be gods or no. For these things are not to appease gods, but to appease men."

'He came yet closer to me, so that he seemed enormous; yet his look was very gentle.

' "Break your temple," he said, "and your gods will be freed."

'And I, smiling at his simplicity, answered: "And so, if there be no gods, I shall have nothing but a broken temple."

'And at this, that giant from whom the light of reason was withheld threw out his mighty arms and asked me to forgive him. And when I asked him for what he should be forgiven he answered: "For being right."

' "Your idols and emperors are so old and wise and satisfying," he cried, "it is a shame that they should be wrong. We are so vulgar and violent, we have done you so many iniquities – it is a shame we should be right after all."

'And I, still enduring his harmlessness, asked him why he thought that he and his people were right.

'And he answered: "We are right because we are bound where men should be bound, and free where men should be free. We are right because we doubt and destroy laws and customs – but we do not doubt our own right to destroy them. For you live by customs, but we live by creeds. Behold me! In my country I am called Smip. My country is abandoned, my name is defiled, because I pursue around the world what really belongs to me. You are steadfast as the trees because you do not believe. I am as fickle as the tempest because I do believe. I do believe in my own house, which I shall find again. And at the last remaineth the green lantern and the red post."

'I said to him: "At the last remaineth only wisdom."

'But even as I said the word he uttered a horrible shout, and rushing forward disappeared among the trees. I have not seen this man again nor any other man. The virtues of the wise are of fine brass.

'WONG-HI.'

'The next letter I have to read,' proceeded Arthur Inglewood, 'will probably make clear the nature of our client's curious but innocent experiment. It is dated from a mountain village in California, and runs as follows:

'SIR – A person answering to the rather extraordinary description required certainly went, some time ago, over the high pass of the Sierras on which I live and of which I am probably the sole stationary inhabitant. I keep a rudimentary tavern, rather ruder than a hut, on the very top of this specially steep and threatening pass. My name is Louis Hara, and the very name may puzzle you about my nationality. Well, it puzzles me a great deal. When one has been for fifteen years without society it is hard to have patriotism; and where there is not even a hamlet it is difficult to invent a nation. My father was an Irishman of the fiercest and most free-shooting of the old Californian kind. My mother was a Spaniard, proud of descent from the old Spanish families round San Francisco, yet accused for all that of some admixture of Red Indian blood. I was well educated and fond of music and books. But, like many other hybrids, I was too good or too bad for the world; and after attempting many things I was glad enough to get a sufficient though a lonely living in this little cabaret in the mountains. In my solitude I fell into many of the ways of a savage. Like an Eskimo, I was shapeless in winter; like a Red Indian, I wore in hot summers nothing but a pair of leather trousers, with a great straw hat as big as a parasol to defend me from the sun. I had a bowie knife at my belt and a long gun under my arm; and I dare say I produced a pretty wild impression on the few peaceable travellers that could climb up to my place. But I promise you I never looked as mad as that man did. Compared with him I was Fifth Avenue.

'I dare say that living under the very top of the Sierras has an odd effect on the mind; one tends to think of those lonely rocks not as peaks coming to a point, but rather as pillars holding up heaven itself. Straight cliffs sail up and away beyond the hope of the eagles; cliffs so tall that they seem to attract the stars and collect them as sea-crags collect a mere glitter of phosphorous. These terraces and towers of rock do not, like smaller crests, seem to be the end of the world. Rather they seem to be its awful beginning: its huge foundations. We could almost fancy the mountain branching out above us like a tree of stone, and carrying all those cosmic lights like a candelabrum. For just as the peaks failed us, soaring impossibly far, so the stars crowded us (as it seemed), coming impossibly near. The spheres burst about us more like thunderbolts hurled at the earth than planets circling placidly about it.

'All this may have driven me mad; I am not sure. I know there is one angle of the road down the pass where the rock leans out a little, and on windy nights I seem to hear it clashing overhead with other rocks – yes, city against city and citadel against citadel, far up into the night. It was on such an evening that the strange man struggled up the pass. Broadly speaking, only strange men did struggle up the pass. But I had never seen one like this one before.

'He carried (I cannot conceive why) a long, dilapidated garden rake, all bearded and bedraggled with grasses, so that it looked like the ensign of some old barbarian tribe. His hair, which was as long and rank as the grass, hung down below his huge shoulders; and such clothes as clung about him were rags and tongues of red and yellow, so that he had the air of being dressed like an Indian in feathers or autumn leaves. The rake or pitchfork, or whatever it was, he used sometimes as an alpenstock, sometimes (I was told) as a weapon. I do not know why he should have used it as a weapon, for he had, and afterwards showed me, an excellent six-shooter in his pocket. "But *that*," he said, "I use only for peaceful purposes." I have no notion what he meant.

'He sat down on the rough bench outside my inn and drank some wine from the vineyards below, sighing with ecstasy over it like one who had travelled long among alien, cruel things and found at last something that he knew. Then he sat staring rather foolishly at the rude lantern of lead and coloured glass that hangs over my door. It is old, but of no value; my grandmother gave it to me long ago: she was devout, and it happens that the glass is painted with a crude picture of Bethlehem and the Wise Men and the Star. He seemed so mesmerised with the transparent glow of Our Lady's blue gown and the big gold star behind, that he led me also to look at the thing, which I had not done for fourteen years.

'Then he slowly withdrew his eyes from this and looked out eastward where the road fell away below us. The sunset sky was a vault of rich velvet, fading away into mauve and silver round the edges of the dark mountain amphitheatre; and between us and the ravine below rose up out of the deeps and went up into the heights the straight solitary rock we call Green Finger. Of a queer volcanic colour, and wrinkled all over with what looks undecipherable writing, it hung there like a Babylonian pillar or needle.

'The man silently stretched out his rake in that direction, and before he spoke I knew what he meant. Beyond the great green rock in the purple sky hung a single star.

' "A star in the east," he said in a strange hoarse voice like one of our ancient eagles. "The wise men followed the star and found the house. But if I followed the star, should I find the house?"

' "It depends perhaps," I said, smiling, "on whether you are a wise man." I refrained from adding that he certainly didn't look it.

' "You may judge for yourself," he answered. "I am a man who left his own house because he could no longer bear to be away from it."

' "It certainly sounds paradoxical," I said.

' "I heard my wife and children talking and saw them moving about the room," he continued, "and all the time I knew they were walking and talking in another house thousands of miles away, under the light of different skies, and beyond the series of the seas. I loved them with a devouring love, because they seemed not only distant but unattainable. Never did human creatures seem so dear and so desirable: but I seemed like a cold ghost; therefore I cast off their dust from my feet for a testimony. Nay, I did more. I spurned the world under my feet so that it swung full circle like a treadmill."

' "Do you really mean," I cried, "that you have come right round the world? Your speech is English, yet you are coming from the west."

' "My pilgrimage is not yet accomplished," he replied sadly. "I have become a pilgrim to cure myself of being an exile."

'Something in the word "pilgrim" awoke down in the roots of my ruinous experience memories of what my fathers had felt about the world, and of something from whence I came. I looked again at the little pictured lantern at which I had not looked for fourteen years.

' "My grandmother," I said in a low tone, "would have said that we were all in exile, and that no earthly house could cure the holy home-sickness that forbids us rest."

'He was silent a long while, and watched a single eagle drift out beyond the Green Finger into the darkening void.

'Then he said, "I think your grandmother was right," and stood up leaning on his grassy pole. "I think that must be the reason," he said – "the secret of this life of man, so ecstatic and so unappeased. But I think there is more to be said. I think God has given us the love of special places, of a hearth and of a native land, for a good reason."

' "I dare say," I said. "What reason?"

'"Because otherwise," he said, pointing his pole out at the sky and the abyss, "we might worship that."

'"What do you mean?" I demanded.

'"Eternity," he said in his harsh voice, "the largest of the idols – the mightiest of the rivals of God."

'"You mean pantheism and infinity and all that," I suggested.

'"I mean," he said with increasing vehemence, "that if there be a house for me in heaven it will either have a green lamp post and a hedge, or something quite as positive and personal as a green lamp post and a hedge. I mean that God bade me love one spot and serve it, and do all things however wild in praise of it, so that this one spot might be a witness against all the infinities and the sophistries, that Paradise is somewhere and not anywhere, is something and not anything. And I would not be so very much surprised if the house in heaven had a real green lamp post after all."

'With which he shouldered his pole and went striding down the perilous paths below, and left me alone with the eagles. But since he went a fever of homelessness will often shake me. I am troubled by rainy meadows and mud cabins that I have never seen; and I wonder whether America will endure.

'Yours faithfully,

'LOUIS HARA.'

After a short silence Inglewood said: 'And, finally, we desire to put in as evidence the following document:

'This is to say that I am Ruth Davis, and have been housemaid to Mrs I. Smith at "The Laurels" in Croydon for the last six months. When I came the lady was alone, with two children; she was not a widow, but her husband was away. She was left with plenty of money and did not seem disturbed about him, though she often hoped he would be back soon. She said he was rather eccentric and a little change did him good. One evening last week I was bringing the tea-things out on to the lawn when I nearly dropped them. The end of a long rake was suddenly stuck over the hedge, and planted like a jumping-pole; and over the hedge, just like a monkey on a stick, came a huge, horrible man, all hairy and ragged like Robinson Crusoe. I screamed out, but my mistress didn't even get out of her chair, but smiled and said he wanted shaving. Then he sat down quite calmly at the garden table and took a cup of tea, and then I realised that this must be Mr Smith himself. He has stopped here ever since and does not really give much trouble, though I sometimes fancy he is a little weak in his head.

'RUTH DAVIS.

'P.S. – I forgot to say that he looked round at the garden and said, very loud and strong: "Oh, what a lovely place you've got"; just as if he'd never seen it before."

The room had been growing dark and drowsy; the afternoon sun sent one heavy shaft of powdered gold across it, which fell with an intangible solemnity upon the empty seat of Mary Gray, for the younger women had left the court before the more recent of the investigations. Mrs Duke was still asleep, and Innocent Smith, looking like a large hunchback in the twilight, was bending closer and closer to his paper toys. But the five men really engaged in the controversy, and concerned not to convince the tribunal but to convince each other, still sat round the table like the Committee of Public Safety.

Suddenly Moses Gould banged one big scientific book on top of another, cocked his little legs up against the table, tipped his chair backwards so far as to be in direct danger of falling over, emitted a startling and prolonged whistle like a steam engine, and asserted that it was all his eye.

When asked by Moon what was all his eye, he banged down behind the books again and answered with considerable excitement, throwing his papers about. 'All those fairy-tales you've been reading out,' he said. 'Oh! don't talk to me! I ain't littery and that, but I know fairy-tales when I hear 'em. I got a bit stumped in some of the philosophical bits and felt inclined to go out for a B. and S. But we're living in West 'Ampstead and not in 'Ell; and the long and the short of it is that some things 'appen and some things don't 'appen. Those are the things that don't 'appen.'

'I thought,' said Moon gravely, 'that we quite clearly explained – '

'Oh yes, old chap, you quite clearly explained,' assented Mr Gould with extraordinary volubility. 'You'd explain an elephant off the doorstep, you would. I ain't a clever chap like you; but I ain't a born natural, Michael Moon, and when there's an elephant on my doorstep I don't listen to no explanations. "It's got a trunk," I says. – "My trunk," you says: "I'm fond of travellin', and a change does me good." – "But the blasted thing's got tusks," I says. – "Don't look a gift 'orse in the mouth," you says, "but thank the goodness and the graice that on your birth 'as smiled." – "But it's nearly as big as the 'ouse," I says. – "That's the bloomin' perspective," you says, "and the sacred magic of distance." – "Why, the elephant's trumpetin' like the Day of Judgement," I says. – "That's your own conscience a-talking to you, Moses Gould," you says in a grive and tender voice. Well, I 'ave got a conscience as much as you. I don't believe most of the things they tell you in church on Sundays; and I don't believe these 'ere things any more because you goes on about 'em as if you was in church. I believe an elephant's a great big ugly dingerous beast – and I believe Smith's another.'

'Do you mean to say,' asked Inglewood, 'that you still doubt the evidence of exculpation we have brought forward?'

'Yes, I do still doubt it,' said Gould warmly. 'It's all a bit too far-fetched, and some of it a bit too far off. 'Ow can we test all those tales? 'Ow can we drop in and buy the "Pink 'Un" at the railway station at Kosky Wosky or whatever it was? 'Ow can we go and do a gargle at the saloon-bar on top of the Sierra Mountains? But anybody can go and see Bunting's boarding-house at Worthing.'

Moon regarded him with an expression of real or assumed surprise.

'Anyone,' continued Gould, 'can call on Mr Trip.'

'It is a comforting thought,' replied Michael with restraint; 'but why should anyone call on Mr Trip?'

'For just exactly the sime reason,' cried the excited Moses, hammering on the table with both hands, 'for just exactly the sime reason that he should communicate with Messrs 'Anbury and Bootle of Paternoster Row and with Miss Gridley's 'igh-class Academy at 'Endon, and with old Lady Bullingdon who lives at Penge.'

'Again, to go at once to the moral roots of life,' said Michael, 'why is it among the duties of man to communicate with old Lady Bullingdon who lives at Penge?'

'It ain't one of the duties of man,' said Gould, 'nor one of his pleasures, either, I can tell you. She takes the crumpet, does Lady Bullingdon at Penge. But it's one of the duties of a prosecutor pursuin' the innocent, blameless butterfly career of your friend Smith, and it's the sime with all the others I mentioned.'

'But why do you bring in these people here?' asked Inglewood.

'Why! Because we've got proof enough to sink a steamboat,' roared Moses; 'because I've got the papers in my very 'and; because your precious Innocent is a blackguard and 'ome smasher, and these are the 'omes he's smashed. I don't set up for a 'oly man; but I wouldn't 'ave all those poor girls on my conscience for something. And I think a chap that's capable of deserting and perhaps killing 'em all is about capable of cracking a crib or shootin' an old schoolmaster – so I don't care much about the other yarns one way or another.'

'I think,' said Dr Cyrus Pym with a refined cough, 'that we are approaching this matter rather irregularly. This is really the fourth charge on the charge sheet, and perhaps I had better put it before you in an ordered and scientific manner.'

Nothing but a faint groan from Michael broke the silence of the darkening room.

CHAPTER 4

The Wild Weddings; or, the Polygamy Charge

'A modern man,' said Dr Cyrus Pym, 'must, if he be thoughtful, approach the problem of marriage with some caution. Marriage is a stage – doubtless a suitable stage – in the long advance of mankind towards a goal which we cannot as yet conceive; which we are not, perhaps, as yet fitted even to desire. What, gentlemen, is now the ethical position of marriage? Have we outived it?'

'Outlived it?' broke out Moon; 'why, nobody's ever survived it! Look at all the people married since Adam and Eve – and all as dead as mutton.'

'This is no doubt an inter-pellation joc'lar in its character,' said Dr Pym frigidly. 'I cannot tell what may be Mr Moon's matured and ethical view of marriage – '

'I can tell,' said Michael savagely, out of the gloom. 'Marriage is a duel to the death, which no man of honour should decline.'

'Michael,' said Arthur Inglewood in a low voice, 'you *must* keep quiet.'

'Mr Moon,' said Pym with exquisite good temper, 'probably regards the institution in a more antiquated manner. Probably he would make it stringent and uniform. He would treat divorce in some great soul of steel – the divorce of a Julius Caesar or of a Salt Ring Robinson – exactly as he would treat some no-account tramp or labourer who scoots from his wife. Science has views broader and more humane. Just as murder for the scientist is a thirst for absolute destruction, just as theft for the scientist is a hunger for monotonous acquisition, so polygamy for the scientist is an extreme development of the instinct for variety. A man thus afflicted is incapable of constancy. Doubtless there is a physical cause for this flitting from flower to flower – as there is, doubtless, for the intermittent groaning which appears to afflict Mr Moon at the present moment. Our own world-scorning Winterbottom has even dared to say, "For a certain rare and fine physical type polygamy is but the realisation of the variety of females, as comradeship is the realisation of the variety of males." In any case, the type that tends to variety is recognised by all authoritative enquirers. Such a type, if the widower of a negress, does in many ascertained cases espouse *en secondes noces* an albino; such a type, when freed from the gigantic embraces of a female Patagonian, will often evolve from its own imaginative instinct the consoling figure of an Eskimo. To such a type there can be no doubt that the prisoner belongs. If blind doom and unbearable temptation constitute any slight excuse for a man, there is no doubt that he has these excuses.

'Earlier in the enquiry the defence showed real chivalric ideality in admitting half of our story without further dispute. We should like to acknowledge and imitate so eminently large-hearted a style by conceding also that the story told by Curate Percy about the canoe, the weir, and the young wife seems to be substantially true. Apparently Smith did marry a young woman he had nearly run down in a boat; it only remains to be considered whether it would not have been kinder of him to have murdered her instead of marrying her. In confirmation of this fact I can now concede to the defence an unquestionable record of such a marriage.'

So saying, he handed across to Michael a cutting from the *Maidenhead Gazette* which distinctly recorded the marriage of the daughter of a 'coach', a tutor well known in the place, to Mr Innocent Smith, late of Brakespeare College, Cambridge.

When Dr Pym resumed it was realised that his face had grown at once both tragic and triumphant.

'I pause upon this pre-liminary fact,' he said seriously, 'because this fact alone would give us the victory, were we aspiring after victory and not after truth. As far as the personal and domestic problem holds us, that problem is solved. Dr Warner and I entered this house at an instant of highly emotional diff'culty. England's Warner has entered many houses to save human kind from sickness; this time he entered to save an innocent lady from a walking pestilence. Smith was just about to carry away a young girl from this house; his cab and bag were at the very door. He had told her she was going to await the marriage licence at the house of his aunt. That aunt,' continued Cyrus Pym, his face darkening grandly – 'that visionary aunt had been the dancing will-o'-the-wisp who had led many a high-souled maiden to her doom. Into how many virginal ears has he whispered that holy word? When he said "aunt" there glowed about her all the merriment and high morality of the Anglo-Saxon home. Kettles began to hum, pussy cats to purr, in that very wild cab that was being driven to destruction.'

Inglewood looked up, to find, to his astonishment (as many another denizen of the eastern hemisphere has found), that the American was not only perfectly serious, but was really eloquent and affecting – when the difference of the hemispheres was adjusted.

'It is therefore atrociously evident that the man Smith has at least represented himself to one innocent female of this house as an eligible bachelor, being, in fact, a married man. I agree with my colleague, Mr Gould, that no other crime could approximate to this. As to whether what our ancestors called purity has any ultimate ethical value indeed, science hesitates with a high, proud hesitation. But what hesitation can there be about the baseness of a citizen who ventures, by brutal experiments upon living females, to anticipate the verdict of science on such a point?

'The woman mentioned by Curate Percy as living with Smith in Highbury may or may not be the same as the lady he married in Maidenhead. If one short sweet spell of constancy and heart repose interrupted the plunging torrent of his profligate life, we will not deprive him of that long past possibility. After that conjectural date, alas, he seems to have plunged deeper and deeper into the shaking quagmires of infidelity and shame.'

Dr Pym closed his eyes, but the unfortunate fact that there was no more light left this familiar signal without its full and proper moral effect. After a pause, which almost partook of the character of prayer, he continued.

'The first instance of the accused's repeated and irregular nuptials,' he exclaimed, 'comes from Lady Bullingdon, who expresses herself with the high haughtiness which must be excused in those who look out upon all mankind from the turrets of a Norman and ancestral keep. The communication she has sent to us runs as follows:

'Lady Bullingdon recalls the painful incident to which reference is made, and has no desire to deal with it in detail. The girl Polly Green was a perfectly adequate dressmaker, and lived in the village for about two years. Her unattached condition was bad for her as well as for the general morality of the village. Lady Bullingdon, therefore, allowed it to be understood that she favoured the marriage of the young woman. The villagers, naturally wishing to oblige Lady Bullingdon, came forward in several cases; and all would have been well had it not been for the deplorable eccentricity or depravity of the girl Green herself. Lady Bullingdon supposes that where there is a village there must be a village idiot, and in her village, it seems, there was one of these wretched creatures. Lady Bullingdon only saw him once, and she is quite aware that it is really difficult to distinguish between actual idiots and the ordinary heavy type of the rural lower classes. She noticed, however, the startling smallness of his head in comparison to the rest of his body; and, indeed, the fact of his having appeared upon election day wearing the rosette of both the two opposing parties appears to Lady Bullingdon to put the matter quite beyond doubt. Lady Bullingdon was astounded to learn that this afflicted being had put himself forward as one of the suitors of the girl in question. Lady Bullingdon's nephew interviewed the wretch upon the point, telling him that he was a "donkey" to dream of such a thing, and actually received, along with an imbecile grin, the answer that donkeys generally go after carrots. But Lady Bullingdon was yet further amazed to find the unhappy girl inclined to accept this monstrous proposal, though she was actually asked in marriage by Garth, the undertaker, a man in a far superior position to her own. Lady Bullingdon could not, of course, countenance such an arrangement for a moment, and the two unhappy persons escaped for a clandestine marriage. Lady Bullingdon cannot exactly recall the man's name, but thinks it was Smith. He was always called in the village the Innocent. Later, Lady Bullingdon believes he murdered Green in a mental outbreak.'

'The next communication,' proceeded Pym, 'is more conspicuous for brevity, but I am of the opinion that it will adequately convey its upshot. It is dated from the offices of Messrs Hanbury and Bootle, publishers, and is as follows:

'Sir – Yrs. rcd. and conts. noted. Rumour *re* typewriter possibly refers to a Miss Blake or similar name, left here nine years ago to marry an organ-grinder. Case was undoubtedly curious, and attracted police attention. Girl worked excellently till about Oct. 1907, when apparently went mad. Record was written at the time, part of which I enclose.

'Yrs., etc.,

'W. Trip.'

'The fuller statement runs as follows:

'On October 12 a letter was sent from this office to Messrs Bernard and Juke, bookbinders. Opened by Mr Juke, it was found to contain the following: "Sir, our Mr Trip will call at 3, as we wish to know whether it is really decided 00000073*bb* !!!!! *xy*." To this Mr Juke, a person of a playful mind, returned the answer: "Sir, I am in a position to give it as my most decided opinion that it is not really decided that 00000073*bb* !!!!! *xy*.

' "Yrs., etc.,

' "J. Juke."

'On receiving this extraordinary reply, our Mr Trip asked for the original letter sent from him, and found that the typewriter had indeed substituted these demented hieroglyphics for the sentences really dictated to her. Our Mr Trip interviewed the girl, fearing that she was in an unbalanced state, and was not much reassured when she merely remarked that she always went like that when she heard the barrel organ. Becoming yet more hysterical and extravagant, she made a series of most improbable statements – as, that she was engaged to the barrel-organ man, that he was in the habit of serenading her on that instrument, that she was in the habit of playing back to him upon the typewriter (in the style of King Richard and Blondel), and that the organ man's musical ear was so exquisite and his adoration of herself so ardent that he could detect the note of the different letters on the machine, and was enraptured by them as by a melody. To all these statements of course our Mr Trip and the rest of us only paid that sort of assent that is paid to persons who must as quickly as possible be put in the charge of their relations. But on our conducting the lady downstairs, her story received the most startling and even exasperating confirmation; for the organ-grinder, an enormous man with a small head and manifestly a fellow-lunatic, had pushed his barrel organ in at the office doors like a battering-ram, and was boisterously demanding his alleged fiancée. When I myself came on the scene he was flinging his great, apelike arms about and reciting a poem to her. But we were used to lunatics coming and reciting poems in our office, and we were not quite prepared for what followed. The actual verse he uttered began, I think,

' "O vivid, inviolate head,
Ringed – "

but he never got any further. Mr Trip made a sharp movement towards him, and the next moment the giant picked up the poor lady typewriter like a doll, sat her on top of the organ, ran it with a crash out of the office doors, and raced away down the street like a flying wheelbarrow. I put the police upon the matter; but no trace of the amazing pair could be found. I was sorry myself; for the lady was not only pleasant but unusually cultivated for her position. As I am leaving the service of Messrs Hanbury and Bootle, I put these things in a record and leave it with them.

'(*Signed*) AUBREY CLARKE, *Publishers' Reader*.

'And the last document,' said Dr Pym complacently, 'is from one of those high-souled women who have in this age introduced your English girlhood to hockey, the higher mathematics, and every form of ideality.

'DEAR SIR [she writes] – I have no objection to telling you the facts about the absurd incident you mention; though I would ask you to communicate them with some caution, for such things, however entertaining in the abstract, are not always auxiliary to the success of a girls' school. The truth is this: I wanted someone to deliver a lecture on a philological or historical question – a lecture which, while containing solid educational matter, should be a little more popular and entertaining than usual, as it was the last lecture of the term. I remembered that a Mr Smith of Cambridge had written somewhere or other an amusing essay about his own somewhat ubiquitous name – an essay which showed considerable knowledge of genealogy and topography. I wrote to him, asking if he would come and give us a bright address upon English surnames; and he did. It was very bright, almost too bright. To put the matter otherwise, by the time that he was halfway through it became apparent to the other mistresses and myself that the man was totally and entirely off his head. He began rationally enough by dealing with the two departments of place names and trade names, and he said (quite rightly, I dare say) that the loss of all significance in names was an instance of the deadening of civilisation. But then he went on calmly to maintain that every man who had a place name ought to go to live in that place, and that every man who had a trade name ought instantly to adopt that trade; that people named after colours should always dress in those colours, and that people named after trees or plants (such as Beech or Rose) ought to surround and decorate themselves with these vegetables. In a slight discussion that arose afterwards among the elder girls the difficulties of the proposal were clearly, and even eagerly, pointed out. It was urged, for instance, by Miss Younghusband that it was substantially impossible for her to play the part assigned to her; Miss Mann was in a similar dilemma, from which no modern views on the sexes could apparently extricate her; and some young ladies, whose surnames happened to be Low, Coward, and Craven, were quite enthusiastic against the idea. But all this happened afterwards. What happened at the crucial moment was that the lecturer produced several horseshoes and a large iron hammer from his bag, announced his immediate intention of setting up a smithy in the neighbourhood, and called on everyone to rise in the same cause as for a heroic revolution. The other mistresses and I attempted to stop the wretched man, but I must confess that by an accident this very intercession produced the worst explosion of his insanity. He was waving the hammer, and wildly demanding the names of everybody; and it so happened that Miss Brown, one of the younger teachers, was wearing a brown dress – a reddish-brown dress that went quietly enough with the warmer colour of her hair, as well she knew. She was a nice girl, and nice girls do know about those things. But when our maniac discovered that we really had a Miss Brown who *was* brown, his *idée fixe* blew up like a powder magazine, and there, in the presence of all the mistresses and girls, he publicly proposed to the lady in the red-brown dress. You can imagine the effect of such a scene at a girls' school. At least, if you fail to imagine it, I certainly fail to describe it.

'Of course, the anarchy died down in a week or two, and I can think of it now as a joke. There was only one curious detail, which I will tell you, as you say your enquiry is vital; but I should desire you to consider it a little more confidential than the rest. Miss Brown, who was an excellent girl in every way, did quite suddenly and surreptitiously leave us only a day or two afterwards. I should never have thought that her head would be the one to be really turned by so absurd an excitement.

'Believe me, yours faithfully,

'Ada Gridley.

'I think,' said Pym, with a really convincing simplicity and seriousness, 'that these letters speak for themselves.'

Mr Moon rose for the last time in a darkness that gave no hint of whether his native gravity was mixed with his native irony.

'Throughout this enquiry,' he said, 'but especially in this its closing phase, the prosecution has perpetually relied upon one argument; I mean the fact that no one knows what has become of all the unhappy women apparently seduced by Smith. There is no sort of proof that they were murdered, but that implication is perpetually made when the question is asked as to how they died. Now I am not interested in how they died, or when they died, or whether they died. But I am interested in another analogous question – that of how they were born, and when they were born, and whether they were born. Do not misunderstand me. I do not dispute the existence of these women, or the veracity of those who have witnessed to them. I merely remark on the notable fact that only one of these victims, the Maidenhead girl, is described as having any home or parents. All the rest are boarders or birds of passage – a guest, a solitary dressmaker, a bachelor-girl doing typewriting. Lady Bullingdon, looking from her turrets, which she bought from the Whartons with the old soap-boiler's money when she jumped at marrying an unsuccessful gentleman from Ulster – Lady Bullingdon, looking out from those turrets, did really see an object which she describes as Green. Mr Trip, of Hanbury and Bootle, really did have a typewriter betrothed to Smith. Miss Gridley, though idealistic, is absolutely honest. She did house, feed, and teach a young woman whom Smith succeeded in decoying away. We admit that all these women really lived. But we still ask whether they were ever born?'

'Oh, crikey!' said Moses Gould, stifled with amusement.

'There could hardly,' interposed Pym with a quiet smile, 'be a better instance of the neglect of true scientific process. The scientist, when once convinced of the fact of vitality and consciousness, would infer from these the previous process of generation.'

'If these gals,' said Gould impatiently – 'if these gals were all alive (all alive O!) I'd chance a fiver they were all born.'

'You'd lose your fiver,' said Michael, speaking gravely out of the gloom. 'All those admirable ladies were alive. They were more alive for having come into contact with Smith. They were all quite definitely alive, but only one of them was ever born.'

'Are you asking us to believe – ' began Dr Pym.

'I am asking you a second question,' said Moon sternly. 'Can the court now sitting throw any light on a truly singular circumstance? Dr Pym, in his interesting lecture on what are called, I believe, the relations of the sexes, said that Smith was the slave of a lust for variety which would lead a man first to a negress and then to an albino, first to a Patagonian giantess and then to a tiny Eskimo. But is there any evidence of such variety here? Is there any trace of a gigantic Patagonian in the story? Was the typewriter an Eskimo? So picturesque a circumstance would not surely have escaped remark. Was Lady Bullingdon's dressmaker a negress? A voice in my bosom answers, "No!" Lady Bullingdon, I am sure, would think a negress so conspicuous as to be almost Socialistic, and would feel something a little rakish even about an albino.

'But was there in Smith's taste any such variety as the learned doctor describes? So far as our slight materials go, the very opposite seems to be the case. We have only one actual description of any of the prisoner's wives – the short but highly poetic account by the aesthetic curate. "Her dress was the colour of spring, and her hair of autumn leaves." Autumn leaves, of course, are of various colours, some of which would be rather startling in hair (green, for instance); but I think such an expression would be most naturally used of the shades from red-brown to red, especially as ladies with their coppery-coloured hair do frequently wear light artistic greens. Now when we come to the next wife, we find the eccentric lover, when told he is a donkey, answering that donkeys always go after carrots; a remark which Lady Bullingdon evidently regarded as pointless and part of the natural table-talk of a village idiot, but which has an obvious meaning if we suppose that Polly's hair was red. Passing to the next wife, the one he took from the girls' school, we find Miss Gridley noticing that the schoolgirl in question wore "a reddish-brown dress, that went quietly enough with the warmer colour of her hair." In other words, the colour of the girl's hair was something redder than red-brown. Lastly, the romantic organ-grinder declaimed in the office some poetry that only got as far as the words,

' "O vivid, inviolate head,
Ringed – "

But I think that a wide study of the worst modern poets will enable us to guess that "ringed with a glory of red", or "ringed with its passionate red", was the line that rhymed to "head". In this case once more, therefore, there is good reason to suppose that Smith fell in love with a girl with some sort of auburn or darkish-red hair – rather,' he said, looking down at the table, 'rather like Miss Gray's hair.'

Cyrus Pym was leaning forward with lowered eyelids, ready with one of his more pedantic interpellations; but Moses Gould suddenly struck his forefinger on his nose, with an expression of extreme astonishment and intelligence in his brilliant eyes.

'Mr Moon's contention at present,' interposed Pym, 'is not, even if veracious, inconsistent with the lunatico-criminal view of I. Smith, which we have nailed to the mast. Science has long anticipated such a complication. An incurable attraction to a particular type of physical woman is one of the commonest of criminal perversities, and when not considered narrowly, but in the light of induction and evolution – '

'At this late stage,' said Michael Moon very quietly, 'I may perhaps relieve myself of a simple emotion that has been pressing me throughout the proceedings, by saying that induction and evolution may go and boil themselves. The Missing Link and all that is well enough for kids, but I'm talking about things we know. All we know of the Missing Link is that he is missing – and he won't be missed either. I know all about his human head and his horrid tail; they belong to a very old game called "Heads I win, tails you lose". If you do find a fellow's bones, it proves he lived a long while ago; if you don't find his bones, it proves how long ago he lived. That is the game you've been playing with this Smith affair. Because Smith's head is small for his shoulders you call him microcephalous; if it had been large, you'd have called it water-on-the-brain. As long as poor old Smith's seraglio seemed pretty various, variety was the sign of madness: now, because it's turning out to be a bit monochrome – now monotony is the sign of madness. I suffer from all the disadvantages of being a grown-up person, and I'm jolly well going to get some of the advantages too; and with all politeness I propose not to be bullied with long words instead of short reasons, or consider your business a triumphant progress merely because you're always finding out that you were wrong. Having relieved myself of these feelings, I have merely to add that I regard Dr Pym as an ornament to the world far more beautiful than the Parthenon, or the monument on Bunker's Hill, and that I propose to resume and conclude my remarks on the many marriages of Mr Innocent Smith.

'Besides this red hair, there is another unifying thread that runs through these scattered incidents. There is something very peculiar and suggestive about the names of these women. Mr Trip, you will remember, said he thought the typewriter's name was Blake, but could not remember exactly. I suggest that it might have been Black, and in that case we have a curious series: Miss Green in Lady Bullingdon's village; Miss Brown at the Hendon School; Miss Black at the publishers. A chord of colours, as it were, which ends up with Miss Gray at Beacon House, West Hampstead.'

Amid a dead silence Moon continued his exposition. 'What is the meaning of this queer coincidence about colours? Personally I cannot doubt for a moment that these names are purely arbitrary names, assumed as part of some general scheme or joke. I think it very probable that they were taken from a series of costumes – that Polly Green only meant Polly (or Mary) when in green, and that Mary Gray only means Mary (or Polly) when in grey. This would explain – '

Cyrus Pym was standing up rigid and almost pallid. 'Do you actually mean to suggest – ' he cried.

'Yes,' said Michael; 'I do mean to suggest that. Innocent Smith has had many wooings, and many weddings for all I know; but he has had only one wife. She was sitting on that chair an hour ago, and is now talking to Miss Duke in the garden.

'Yes, Innocent Smith has behaved here, as he has on hundreds of other occasions, upon a plain and perfectly blameless principle. It is odd and extravagant in the modern world, but not more than any other principle plainly applied in the modern world would be. His principle can be quite simply stated: he refuses to die while he is still alive. He seeks to remind himself, by every electric shock to the intellect, that he is still a man alive, walking on two legs about the world. For this reason he fires bullets at his best friends; for this reason he arranges ladders and collapsible chimneys to steal his own property; for this reason he goes plodding around a whole planet to get back to his own home; and for this reason he has been in the habit of taking the woman whom he loved with a permanent loyalty, and leaving her about (so to speak) at schools, boarding-houses, and places of business, so that he might recover her again and again with a raid and a romantic elopement. He seriously sought by a perpetual recapture of his bride to keep alive the sense of her perpetual value, and the perils that should be run for her sake.

'So far his motives are clear enough; but perhaps his convictions are not quite so clear. I think Innocent Smith has an idea at the bottom of all this. I am by no means sure that I believe it myself, but I am quite sure that it is worth a man's uttering and defending.

'The idea that Smith is attacking is this. Living in an entangled civilisation, we have come to think certain things wrong which are not wrong at all. We have come to think outbreak and exuberance, banging and barging, rotting and wrecking, wrong. In themselves they are not merely pardonable; they are unimpeachable. There is nothing wicked about firing a pistol off even at a friend, so long as you do not mean to hit him and know you won't. It is no more wrong than throwing a pebble at the sea – less, for you do occasionally hit the sea. There is nothing wrong in bashing down a chimney-pot and breaking through a roof, so long as you are not injuring the life or property of other men. It is no more wrong to choose to enter a house from the top than to choose to open a packing-case from the bottom. There is nothing wicked about walking round the world and coming back to your own house; it is no more wicked than walking round the garden and coming back to your own house. And there is nothing wicked about picking up your wife here, there, and everywhere, if, forsaking all others, you keep only to her so long as you both shall live. It is as innocent as playing a game of hide-and-seek in the garden. You associate such acts with blackguardism by a mere snobbish association, as you think there is something vaguely vile about going (or being seen going) into a pawnbroker's or a public-house. You think there is something squalid and commonplace about such a connection. You are mistaken.

'This man's spiritual power has been precisely this, that he has distinguished between custom and creed. He has broken the conventions, but he has kept the commandments. It is as if a man were found gambling wildly in a gambling hell, and you found that he only played for trouser buttons. It is as if you found a man making a clandestine appointment with a lady at a Covent Garden ball, and then you found it was his grandmother. Everything is ugly and discreditable, except the facts; everything is wrong about him, except that he has done no wrong.

'It will then be asked, "Why does Innocent Smith continue far into his middle age a farcical existence, that exposes him to so many false charges?" To this I merely answer that he does it because he really is happy, because he really is hilarious, because he really is a man and alive. He is so young that climbing garden trees and playing silly practical jokes are still to him what they once were to us all. And if you ask me yet again why he alone among men should be fed with such inexhaustible follies, I have a very simple answer to that, though it is one that will not be approved.

'There is but one answer, and I am sorry if you don't like it. If Innocent is happy, it is because he *is* innocent. If he can defy the conventions, it is just because he can keep the commandments. It is just because he does not want to kill but to excite to life that a pistol is still as exciting to him as it is to a schoolboy. It is just because he does not want to steal, because he does not covet his neighbour's goods, that he has captured the trick (oh, how we all long for it!), the trick of coveting his own goods. It is just because he does not want to commit adultery that he achieves the romance of sex; it is just because he loves one wife that he has a hundred honeymoons. If he had really murdered a man, if he had really deserted a woman, he would not be able to feel that a pistol or a love-letter was like a song – at least, not a comic song.

'Do not imagine, please, that any such attitude is easy to me or appeals in any particular way to my sympathies. I am an Irishman, and a certain sorrow is in my bones, bred either of the persecutions of my creed, or of my creed itself. Speaking singly, I feel as if man was tied to tragedy, and there was no way out of the trap of old age and doubt. But if there is a way out, then, by Christ and St Patrick, this is the way out. If one could keep as happy as a child or a dog, it would be by being as innocent as a child, or as sinless as a dog. Barely and brutally to be good – that may be the road, and he may have found it. Well, well, well, I see a look of scepticism on the face of my old friend

Moses. Mr Gould does not believe that being perfectly good in all respects would make a man merry.'

'No,' said Gould, with an unusual and convincing gravity; 'I do not believe that being perfectly good in all respects would make a man merry.'

'Well,' said Michael quietly, 'will you tell me one thing? Which of us has ever tried it?'

A silence ensued, rather like the silence of some long geological epoch which awaits the emergence of some unexpected type; for there rose at last in the stillness a massive figure that the other men had almost completely forgotten.

'Well, gentlemen,' said Dr Warner cheerfully, 'I've been pretty well entertained with all this pointless and incompetent tomfoolery for a couple of days; but it seems to be wearing rather thin, and I'm engaged for a city dinner. Among the hundred flowers of futility on both sides I was unable to detect any sort of reason why a lunatic should be allowed to shoot me in the back garden.'

He had settled his silk hat on his head and gone out sailing placidly to the garden gate, while the almost wailing voice of Pym still followed him: 'But really the bullet missed you by several feet.' And another voice added: 'The bullet missed him by several years.'

There was a long and mainly unmeaning silence, and then Moon said suddenly, 'We have been sitting with a ghost. Dr Herbert Warner died years ago.'

CHAPTER 5

How the Great Wind Went from Beacon House

Mary was walking between Diana and Rosamund slowly up and down the garden; they were silent, and the sun had set. Such spaces of daylight as remained open in the west were of a warm-tinted white, which can be compared to nothing but a cream cheese; and the lines of plumy cloud that ran across them had a soft but vivid violet bloom, like a violet smoke. All the rest of the scene swept and faded away into a dovelike grey, and seemed to melt and mount into Mary's dark-grey figure until she seemed clothed with the garden and the skies. There was something in these last quiet colours that gave her a setting and a supremacy; and the twilight, which concealed Diana's statelier figure and Rosamund's braver array, exhibited and emphasised her, leaving her the lady of the garden, and alone.

When they spoke at last it was evident that a conversation long fallen silent was being suddenly revived.

'But where is your husband taking you?' asked Diana in her practical voice.

'To an aunt,' said Mary; 'that's just the joke. There really is an aunt, and we left the children with her when I arranged to be turned out of the other boarding-house down the road. We never take more than a week of this kind of holiday, but sometimes we take two of them together.'

'Does the aunt mind much?' asked Rosamund innocently. 'Of course, I dare say it's very narrow-minded and – what's that other word? – you know, what Goliath was – but I've known many aunts who would think it – well, silly.'

'Silly?' cried Mary with great heartiness. 'Oh, my Sunday hat! I should think it was silly! But what do you expect? He really is a good man, and it might have been snakes or something.'

'Snakes?' enquired Rosamund, with a slightly puzzled interest.

'Uncle Harry kept snakes, and said they loved him,' replied Mary with perfect simplicity. 'Auntie let him have them in his pockets, but not in the bedroom.'

'And you – ' began Diana, knitting her dark brows a little.

'Oh, I do as auntie did,' said Mary; 'as long as we're not away from the children more than a fortnight together I play the game. He calls me "Manalive"; and you must write it all in one word, or he's quite flustered.'

'But if men want things like that – ' began Diana.

'Oh, what's the good of talking about men?' cried Mary impatiently; 'why, one might as well be a lady novelist or some horrid thing. There aren't any men. There are no such people. There's a man; and whoever he is he's quite different.'

'So there's no safety,' said Diana in a low voice.

'Oh, I don't know,' answered Mary, lightly enough; 'there's only two things generally true of them. At certain curious times they're just fit to take care of us, and they're never fit to take care of themselves.'

'There is a gale getting up,' said Rosamund suddenly. 'Look at those trees over there, a long way off, and the clouds going quicker.'

'I know what you're thinking about,' said Mary; 'and don't you be silly fools. Don't you listen to the lady novelists. You go down the king's highway; for God's truth, it is God's. Yes, my dear Michael will often be extremely untidy. Arthur Inglewood will be worse – he'll be tidy. But what else are all the trees and clouds for, you silly kittens?'

'The clouds and trees are all waving about,' said Rosamund. 'There is a storm coming, and it makes me feel quite excited, somehow. Michael is really rather like a storm: he frightens me and makes me happy.'

'Don't you be frightened,' said Mary. 'All over, these men have one advantage: they are the sort that go out.'

A sudden thrust of wind through the trees drifted the dying leaves along the path, and they could hear the far-off trees roaring faintly.

'I mean,' said Mary, 'they are the kind that look outwards and get interested in the world. It doesn't matter a bit whether it's arguing, or bicycling, or breaking down the ends of the earth as poor old Innocent does. Stick to the man who looks out of the window and tries to understand the world. Keep clear of the man who looks in at the window and tries to understand you. When poor old Adam had gone out gardening (Arthur will go out gardening), the other sort came along and wormed himself in, nasty old snake.'

'You agree with your aunt,' said Rosamund, smiling: 'no snakes in the bedroom.'

'I didn't agree with my aunt very much,' replied Mary simply, 'but I think she was right to let Uncle Harry collect dragons and griffins, so long as it got him out of the house.'

Almost at the same moment lights sprang up inside the darkened house, turning the two glass doors into the garden into gates of beaten gold. The golden gates were burst open, and the enormous Smith, who had sat like a clumsy statue for so many hours, came flying and turning cart-wheels down the lawn and shouting, 'Acquitted! acquitted!' Echoing the cry, Michael scampered across the lawn to Rosamund and wildly swung her into a few steps of what was supposed to be a waltz. But the company knew Innocent and Michael by this time, and their extravagances were gaily taken for granted; it was far more extraordinary that Arthur Inglewood walked straight up to Diana and kissed her as if it had been his sister's birthday. Even Dr Pym, though he refrained from dancing, looked on with real benevolence; for indeed the whole of the absurd revelation had disturbed him less than the others; he half supposed that such irresponsible tribunals and insane discussions were part of the mediaeval mummeries of the Old Land.

While the tempest tore the sky as with trumpets, window after window was lighted up in the house within; and before the company, broken with laughter and the buffeting of the wind, had groped their way to the house again, they saw that the great apish figure of Innocent Smith had clambered out of his own attic window, and roaring again and again, 'Beacon House!' whirled round his head a huge log or trunk from the wood fire below, of which the river of crimson flame and purple smoke drove out on the deafening air.

He was evident enough to have been seen from three counties; but when the wind died down, and the party, at the top of their evening's merriment, looked again for Mary and for him, they were not to be found.

[illegible] the path, and they could [illegible] the [illegible] [illegible] [illegible].

[illegible] in the world [illegible] [illegible] of the [illegible] [illegible] the man who [illegible] [illegible] [illegible] the [illegible] the other [illegible] [illegible] [illegible].

[illegible]

[illegible] she was [illegible] Uncle [illegible] [illegible] [illegible] [illegible].

[illegible] the garden [illegible] [illegible] gold. The garden gates were [illegible] open [illegible] [illegible] the lawn [illegible] [illegible] [illegible] and [illegible] [illegible] birthday [illegible] for indeed the whole of [illegible] [illegible] him less than the others [illegible] [illegible] [illegible] of the Old Land.

[illegible] the [illegible] [illegible] [illegible] the world [illegible] [illegible] [illegible].

[illegible] [illegible] the [illegible] [illegible] [illegible].

THE WISDOM OF FATHER BROWN

The Wisdom of Father Brown

Contents

The Absence of Mr Glass

The consulting-rooms of Dr Orion Hood, the eminent criminologist and specialist in certain moral disorders, lay along the sea-front at Scarborough, in a series of very large and well-lighted french windows, which showed the North Sea like one endless outer wall of blue-green marble. In such a place the sea had something of the monotony of a blue-green dado: for the chambers themselves were ruled throughout by a terrible tidiness not unlike the terrible tidiness of the sea. It must not be supposed that Dr Hood's apartments excluded luxury, or even poetry. These things were there, in their place; but one felt that they were never allowed out of their place. Luxury was there: there stood upon a special table eight or ten boxes of the best cigars; but they were built upon a plan so that the strongest were always nearest the wall and the mildest nearest the window. A tantalus containing three kinds of spirit, all of a liqueur excellence, stood always on this table of luxury; but the fanciful have asserted that the whisky, brandy, and rum seemed always to stand at the same level. Poetry was there: the left-hand corner of the room was lined with as complete a set of English classics as the right hand could show of English and foreign physiologists. But if one took a volume of Chaucer or Shelley from that rank, its absence irritated the mind like a gap in a man's front teeth. One could not say the books were never read; probably they were, but there was a sense of their being chained to their places, like the Bibles in the old churches. Dr Hood treated his private bookshelf as if it were a public library. And if this strict scientific intangibility steeped even the shelves laden with lyrics and ballads and the tables laden with drink and tobacco, it goes without saying that yet more of such heathen holiness protected the other shelves that held the specialist's library, and the other tables that sustained the frail and even fairylike instruments of chemistry or mechanics.

Dr Hood paced the length of his string of apartments, bounded – as the boys' geographies say – on the east by the North Sea and on the west by the serried ranks of his sociological and criminologist library. He was clad in an artist's velvet, but with none of an artist's negligence; his hair was heavily shot with grey, but growing thick and healthy; his face was lean, but sanguine and expectant. Everything about him and his room indicated something at once rigid and restless, like that great northern sea by which (on pure principles of hygiene) he had built his home.

Fate, being in a funny mood, pushed the door open and introduced into those long, strict, sea-flanked apartments one who was perhaps the most startling opposite of them and their master. In answer to a curt but civil summons, the door opened inwards and there shambled into the room a shapeless little figure, which seemed to find its own hat and umbrella as unmanageable as a mass of luggage. The umbrella was a black and prosaic bundle long past repair; the hat was a broad-curved black hat, clerical but not common in England; the man was the very embodiment of all that is homely and helpless.

The doctor regarded the newcomer with a restrained astonishment, not unlike that he would have shown if some huge but obviously harmless sea-beast had crawled into his room. The newcomer regarded the doctor with that beaming but breathless geniality which characterises a corpulent char-woman who has just managed to stuff herself into an omnibus. It is a rich confusion of social self-congratulation and bodily disarray. His hat tumbled to the carpet, his heavy umbrella slipped between his knees with a thud; he reached after the one and ducked after the other, but with an unimpaired smile on his round face spoke simultaneously as follows: 'My name is Brown. Pray excuse me. I've come about that business of the MacNabs. I have heard you often help people out of such troubles. Pray excuse me if I am wrong.'

By this time he had sprawlingly recovered the hat, and made an odd little bobbing bow over it, as if setting everything quite right.

'I hardly understand you,' replied the scientist, with a cold intensity of manner. 'I fear you have mistaken the chambers. I am Dr Hood, and my work is almost entirely literary and educational. It is true that I have sometimes been consulted by the police in cases of peculiar difficulty and importance, but – '

'Oh, this is of the greatest importance,' broke in the little man called Brown. 'Why, her mother won't let them get engaged.' And he leaned back in his chair in radiant rationality.

The brows of Dr Hood were drawn down darkly, but the eyes under them were bright with something that might be anger or might be amusement. 'And still,' he said, 'I do not quite understand.'

'You see, they want to get married,' said the man with the clerical hat. 'Maggie MacNab and young Todhunter want to get *married*. Now, what can be more important than that?'

The great Orion Hood's scientific triumphs had deprived him of many things – some said of his health, others of his God; but they had not wholly despoiled him of his sense of the absurd. At the last plea of the ingenuous priest a chuckle broke out of him from inside, and he threw himself into an armchair in an ironical attitude of the consulting physician.

'Mr Brown,' he said gravely, 'it is quite fourteen and a half years since I was personally asked to test a personal problem: then it was the case of an attempt to poison the French President at a Lord Mayor's Banquet. It is now, I understand, a question of whether some friend of yours called Maggie is a suitable fiancée for some friend of hers called Todhunter. Well, Mr Brown, I am a sportsman. I will take it on. I will give the MacNab family my best advice, as good as I gave the French Republic and the King of England – no, better: fourteen years better. I have nothing else to do this afternoon. Tell me your story.'

The little clergyman called Brown thanked him with unquestionable warmth, but still with a queer kind of simplicity. It was rather as if he were thanking a stranger in a smoking-room for some trouble in passing the matches, than as if he were (as he was) practically thanking the Curator of Kew Gardens for coming with him into a field to find a four-leaved clover. With scarcely a semicolon after his hearty thanks, the little man began his recital: 'I told you my name was Brown; well, that's the fact, and I'm the priest of the little Catholic Church I dare say you've seen beyond those straggly streets, where the town ends towards the north. In the last and straggliest of those streets which runs along the sea like a sea wall there is a very honest but rather sharp-tempered member of my flock, a widow called MacNab. She has one daughter, and she lets lodgings, and between her and the daughter, and between her and the lodgers – well, I dare say there is a great deal to be said on both sides. At present she has only one lodger, the young man called Todhunter; but he has given more trouble than all the rest, for he wants to marry the young woman of the house.'

'And the young woman of the house,' asked Dr Hood, with huge and silent amusement, 'what does she want?'

'Why, she wants to marry him,' cried Father Brown, sitting up eagerly. 'That is just the awful complication.'

'It is indeed a hideous enigma,' said Dr Hood.

'This young James Todhunter,' continued the cleric, 'is a very decent man so far as I know; but then nobody knows very much. He is a bright, brownish little fellow, agile like a monkey, clean-shaven like an actor, and obliging like a born courtier. He seems to have quite a pocketful of money, but nobody knows what his trade is. Mrs MacNab, therefore (being of a pessimistic turn), is quite sure it is something dreadful, and probably connected with dynamite. The dynamite must be of a shy and noiseless sort, for the poor fellow only shuts himself up for several hours of the day and studies something behind a locked door. He declares his privacy is temporary and justified, and promises to explain before the wedding. That is all that anyone knows for certain, but Mrs MacNab will tell you a great deal more than even she is certain of. You know how the tales grow like grass on such a patch of ignorance as that. There are tales of two voices heard talking in the room; though, when the door is opened, Todhunter is always found alone. There are tales of a mysterious tall man in a silk hat, who once came out of the sea-mists and apparently out of the sea, stepping softly across the sandy fields and through the small back garden at twilight, till he was heard talking to the lodger at his open window. The colloquy seemed to end in a quarrel. Todhunter dashed down his window with violence, and the man in the high hat melted into the sea-fog again. This story is told by the family with the fiercest mystification; but I really think Mrs MacNab prefers her own original tale: that the Other Man (or whatever it is) crawls out every night from the big box in the corner, which is kept locked all day. You see, therefore, how this sealed door of Todhunter's is treated as the gate of all the fancies and monstrosities of the *Thousand and One Nights*. And yet there is the little fellow in his respectable black jacket, as punctual and innocent as a parlour clock. He pays his rent to the tick; he is practically a teetotaller; he is tirelessly kind with the younger children, and can keep them amused for a day on end; and, last and most urgent of all, he has made himself equally popular with the eldest daughter, who is ready to go to church with him tomorrow.'

A man warmly concerned with any large theories has always a relish for applying them to any triviality. The great specialist having condescended to the priest's simplicity, condescended expansively. He settled himself with comfort in his armchair and began to talk in the tone of a somewhat absent-minded lecturer: 'Even in a minute instance, it is best to look first to the main tendencies of Nature. A particular flower may not be dead in early winter, but the flowers are dying; a particular pebble may never be wetted with the tide, but the tide is coming in. To the scientific eye all human history is a series of collective movements, destructions or migrations, like the massacre of flies in winter or the return of birds in spring. Now the root fact in all history is Race. Race produces religion; Race produces legal and ethical wars. There is no stronger case than that of the wild, unworldly and perishing stock which we commonly call the Celts, of whom your friends the MacNabs are specimens. Small, swarthy, and of this dreamy and drifting blood, they accept easily the superstitious explanation of any incidents, just as they still accept (you will excuse me for saying) that superstitious explanation of all incidents which you and your Church represent. It is not remarkable that such people, with the sea moaning behind them and the Church (excuse me again) droning in front of them, should put fantastic features into what are probably plain events. You, with your small parochial responsibilities, see only this particular Mrs MacNab, terrified with this particular tale of two voices and a tall man out of the sea. But the man with the scientific imagination sees, as it were, the whole clans of MacNab scattered over the whole world, in its ultimate average as uniform as a tribe of birds. He sees thousands of Mrs MacNabs, in thousands of houses, dropping their little drop of morbidity in the teacups of their friends; he sees – '

Before the scientist could conclude his sentence, another and more impatient summons sounded from without; someone with swishing skirts was marshalled hurriedly down the corridor, and the door opened on a young girl, decently dressed but disordered and red-hot with haste. She had sea-blown blonde hair, and would have been entirely beautiful if her cheekbones had not been, in the Scotch manner, a little high in relief as well as in colour. Her apology was almost as abrupt as a command.

'I'm sorry to interrupt you, sir,' she said, 'but I had to follow Father Brown at once; it's nothing less than life or death.'

Father Brown began to get to his feet in some disorder. 'Why, what has happened, Maggie?' he said.

'James has been murdered, for all I can make out,' answered the girl, still breathing hard from her rush. 'That man Glass has been with him again; I heard them talking through the door quite plain. Two separate voices: for James speaks low, with a burr, and the other voice was high and quavery.'

'That man Glass?' repeated the priest in some perplexity.

'I know his name is Glass,' answered the girl, in great impatience. 'I heard it through the door. They were quarrelling – about money, I think – for I heard James say again and again, "That's right, Mr Glass," or "No, Mr Glass," and then, "Two or three, Mr Glass." But we're talking too much; you must come at once, and there may be time yet.'

'But time for what?' asked Dr Hood, who had been studying the young lady with marked interest. 'What is there about Mr Glass and his money troubles that should impel such urgency?'

'I tried to break down the door and couldn't,' answered the girl shortly. 'Then I ran to the backyard, and managed to climb on to the window-sill that looks into the room. It was all dim, and seemed to be empty, but I swear I saw James lying huddled up in a corner, as if he were drugged or strangled.'

'This is very serious,' said Father Brown, gathering his errant hat and umbrella and standing up; 'in point of fact I was just putting your case before this gentleman, and his view – '

'Has been largely altered,' said the scientist gravely. 'I do not think this young lady is so Celtic as I had supposed. As I have nothing else to do, I will put on my hat and stroll down the town with you.'

In a few minutes all three were approaching the dreary tail of the MacNabs' street: the girl with the stern and breathless stride of the mountaineer, the criminologist with a lounging grace (which was not without a certain leopard-like swiftness), and the priest at an energetic trot entirely devoid of distinction. The aspect of this edge of the town was not entirely without justification for the doctor's hints about desolate moods and environments. The scattered houses stood farther and farther apart in a broken string along the seashore; the afternoon was closing with a premature and partly lurid twilight; the sea was of an inky purple and murmuring ominously. In the scrappy back garden of the MacNabs which ran down towards the sand, two black, barren-looking trees stood up like demon hands held up in astonishment, and as Mrs MacNab ran down the street to meet them with lean hands similarly spread, and her fierce face in shadow, she was a little like a demon herself. The doctor and the priest made scant reply to her shrill reiterations of her daughter's story, with more disturbing details of her own, to the divided vows of vengeance against Mr Glass for murdering, and against Mr Todhunter for being murdered, or against the latter for having dared to want to marry her daughter, and for not having lived to do it. They passed through the narrow passage in the front of the house until they came to the lodger's door at the back, and there Dr Hood, with the trick of an old detective, put his shoulder sharply to the panel and burst in the door.

It opened on a scene of silent catastrophe. No one seeing it, even for a flash, could doubt that the room had been the theatre of some thrilling collision between two, or perhaps more, persons. Playing-cards lay littered across the table or fluttered about the floor as if a game had been interrupted. Two wine glasses stood ready for wine on a side-table, but a third lay smashed in a star of crystal upon the carpet. A few feet from it lay what looked like a long knife or short sword, straight, but with an ornamental and pictured handle; its dull blade just caught a grey glint from the dreary window behind, which showed the black trees against the leaden level of the sea. Towards the opposite corner of the room was rolled a gentleman's silk top hat, as if it had just been knocked off his head; so much so, indeed, that one almost looked to see it still rolling. And in the corner behind it, thrown like a sack of potatoes, but corded like a railway trunk, lay Mr James Todhunter, with a scarf across his mouth, and six or seven ropes knotted round his elbows and ankles. His brown eyes were alive and shifted alertly.

Dr Orion Hood paused for one instant on the doormat and drank in the whole scene of voiceless violence. Then he stepped swiftly across the carpet, picked up the tall silk hat, and gravely put it upon the head of the yet pinioned Todhunter. It was so much too large for him that it almost slipped down on to his shoulders.

'Mr Glass's hat,' said the doctor, returning with it and peering into the inside with a pocket lens. 'How to explain the absence of Mr Glass and the presence of Mr Glass's hat? For Mr Glass is not a careless man with his clothes. That hat is of a stylish shape and systematically brushed and burnished, though not very new. An old dandy, I should think.'

'But, good heavens!' called out Miss MacNab, 'aren't you going to untie the man first?'

'I say "old" with intention, though not with certainty,' continued the expositor; 'my reason for it might seem a little far-fetched. The hair of human beings falls out in very varying degrees, but almost always falls out slightly, and with the lens I should see the tiny hairs in a hat recently worn. It has none, which leads me to guess that Mr Glass is bald. Now when this i s taken with the high-pitched and querulous voice which Miss MacNab described so vividly (patience, my dear lady, patience), when we take the hairless head together with the tone common in senile anger, I should think we may deduce some advance in years. Nevertheless, he was probably vigorous, and he was almost certainly tall. I might rely in some degree on the story of his previous appearance at the window, as a tall man in a silk hat, but I think I have more exact indication. This wine glass has been smashed all over the place, but one of its splinters lies on the high bracket beside the mantelpiece. No such fragment could have fallen there if the vessel had been smashed in the hand of a comparatively short man like Mr Todhunter.'

'By the way,' said Father Brown, 'might it not be as well to untie Mr Todhunter?'

'Our lesson from the drinking-vessels does not end here,' proceeded the specialist. 'I may say at once that it is possible that the man Glass was bald or nervous through dissipation rather than age. Mr Todhunter, as has been remarked, is a quiet thrifty gentleman, essentially an abstainer. These cards and wine cups are no part of his normal habit; they have been produced for a particular companion. But, as it happens, we may go farther. Mr Todhunter may or may not possess this wine service, but there is no appearance of his possessing any wine. What, then, were these vessels to contain? I would at once suggest some brandy or whisky, perhaps of a luxurious sort, from a flask in the pocket of Mr Glass. We have thus something like a picture of the man, or at least of the type: tall, elderly, fashionable, but somewhat frayed, certainly fond of play and strong waters, perhaps rather too fond of them. Mr Glass is a gentleman not unknown on the fringes of society.'

'Look here,' cried the young woman, 'if you don't let me pass to untie him I'll run outside and scream for the police.'

'I should not advise *you*, Miss MacNab,' said Dr Hood gravely, 'to be in any hurry to fetch the police. Father Brown, I seriously ask you to compose your flock, for their sakes, not for mine. Well, we have seen something of the figure and quality of Mr Glass; what are the chief facts known of Mr Todhunter? They are substantially three: that he is economical, that he is more or less wealthy, and that he has a secret. Now, surely it is obvious that there are the three chief marks of the kind of man who is blackmailed. And surely it is equally obvious that the faded finery, the profligate habits, and the shrill irritation of Mr Glass are the unmistakable marks of the kind of man who blackmails him. We have the two typical figures of a tragedy of hush money: on the one hand, the respectable man with a mystery; on the other, the West-end vulture with a scent for a mystery. These two men have met here today and have quarrelled, using blows and a bare weapon.'

'Are you going to take those ropes off?' asked the girl stubbornly.

Dr Hood replaced the silk hat carefully on the side-table, and went across to the captive. He studied him intently, even moving him a little and half-turning him round by the shoulders, but he only answered: 'No; I think these ropes will do very well till your friends the police bring the handcuffs.'

Father Brown, who had been looking dully at the carpet, lifted his round face and said: 'What do you mean?'

The man of science had picked up the peculiar dagger-sword from the carpet and was examining it intently as he answered: 'Because you find Mr Todhunter tied up,' he said, 'you all jump to the conclusion that Mr Glass had tied him up; and then, I suppose, escaped. There are four objections to this. First, why should a gentleman so dressy as our friend Glass leave his hat behind him, if he left of his own free will? Second,' he continued, moving towards the window, 'this is the only exit, and it is locked on the inside. Third, this blade here has a tiny touch of blood at the point, but there is no wound on Mr Todhunter. Mr Glass took that wound away with him, dead or alive. Add to all this primary probability. It is much more likely that the blackmailed person would try to kill his incubus, rather than that the blackmailer would try to kill the goose that lays his golden egg. There, I think, we have a pretty complete story.'

'But the ropes?' enquired the priest, whose eyes had remained open with a rather vacant admiration.

'Ah, the ropes,' said the expert with a singular intonation. 'Miss MacNab very much wanted to know why I did not set Mr Todhunter free from his ropes. Well, I will tell her. I did not do it because Mr Todhunter can set himself free from them at any minute he chooses.'

'What?' cried the audience on quite different notes of astonishment.

'I have looked at all the knots on Mr Todhunter,' reiterated Hood quietly. 'I happen to know something about knots; they are quite a branch of criminal science. Every one of those knots he has made himself and could loosen himself; not one of them would have been made by an enemy really trying to pinion him. The whole of this affair of the ropes is a clever fake, to make us think him the victim of the struggle instead of the wretched Glass, whose corpse may be hidden in the garden or stuffed up the chimney.'

There was a rather depressed silence; the room was darkening, the sea-blighted boughs of the garden trees looked leaner and blacker than ever, yet they seemed to have come nearer to the window. One could almost fancy they were sea-monsters like krakens or cuttlefish, writhing polypi who had crawled up from the sea to see the end of this tragedy, even as he, the villain and victim of it, the terrible man in the tall hat, had once crawled up from the sea. For the whole air was dense with the morbidity of blackmail, which is the most morbid of human things, because it is a crime concealing a crime; a black plaster on a blacker wound.

The face of the little Catholic priest, which was commonly complacent and even comic, had suddenly become knotted with a curious frown. It was not the blank curiosity of his first innocence. It was rather that creative curiosity which comes when a man has the beginnings of an idea. 'Say it again, please,' he said in a simple, bothered manner; 'do you mean that Todhunter can tie himself up all alone and untie himself all alone?'

'That is what I mean,' said the doctor.

'Jerusalem!' ejaculated Brown suddenly, 'I wonder if it could possibly be that!'

He scuttled across the room rather like a rabbit, and peered with quite a new impulsiveness into the partially covered face of the captive. Then he turned his own rather fatuous face to the company. 'Yes, that's it!' he cried in a certain excitement. 'Can't you see it in the man's face? Why, look at his eyes!'

Both the Professor and the girl followed the direction of his glance. And though the broad black scarf completely masked the lower half of Todhunter's visage, they did grow conscious of something struggling and intense about the upper part of it.

'His eyes do look queer,' cried the young woman, strongly moved. 'You brutes; I believe it's hurting him!'

'Not that, I think,' said Dr Hood; 'the eyes have certainly a singular expression. But I should interpret those transverse wrinkles as expressing rather such slight psychological abnormality – '

'Oh, bosh!' cried Father Brown: 'can't you see he's laughing?'

'Laughing!' repeated the doctor, with a start; 'but what on earth can he be laughing at?'

'Well,' replied the Revd Brown apologetically, 'not to put too fine a point on it, I think he is laughing at you. And indeed, I'm a little inclined to laugh at myself, now I know about it.'

'Now you know about what?' asked Hood, in some exasperation.

'Now I know,' replied the priest, 'the profession of Mr Todhunter.'

He shuffled about the room, looking at one object after another with what seemed to be a vacant stare, and then invariably bursting into an equally vacant laugh, a highly irritating process for those who had to watch it. He laughed very much over the hat, still more uproariously over the broken glass, but the blood on the sword point sent him into mortal convulsions of amusement. Then he turned to the fuming specialist.

'Dr Hood,' he cried enthusiastically, 'you are a great poet! You have called an uncreated being out of the void. How much more godlike that is than if you had only ferreted out the mere facts! Indeed, the mere facts are rather commonplace and comic by comparison.'

'I have no notion what you are talking about,' said Dr Hood rather haughtily; 'my facts are all inevitable, though necessarily incomplete. A place may be permitted to intuition, perhaps (or poetry if you prefer the term), but only because the corresponding details cannot as yet be ascertained. In the absence of Mr Glass –'

'That's it, that's it,' said the little priest, nodding quite eagerly, 'that's the first idea to get fixed; the absence of Mr Glass. He is so extremely absent. I suppose,' he added reflectively, 'that there was never anybody so absent as Mr Glass.'

'Do you mean he is absent from the town?' demanded the doctor.

'I mean he is absent from everywhere,' answered Father Brown; 'he is absent from the Nature of Things, so to speak.'

'Do you seriously mean,' said the specialist with a smile, 'that there is no such person?'

The priest made a sign of assent. 'It does seem a pity,' he said.

Orion Hood broke into a contemptuous laugh. 'Well,' he said, 'before we go on to the hundred and one other evidences, let us take the first proof we found; the first fact we fell over when we fell into this room. If there is no Mr Glass, whose hat is this?'

'It is Mr Todhunter's,' replied Father Brown.

'But it doesn't fit him,' cried Hood impatiently. 'He couldn't possibly wear it!'

Father Brown shook his head with ineffable mildness. 'I never said he could wear it,' he answered. 'I said it was his hat. Or, if you insist on a shade of difference, a hat that is his.'

'And what is the shade of difference?' asked the criminologist with a slight sneer.

'My good sir,' cried the mild little man, with his first movement akin to impatience, 'if you will walk down the street to the nearest hatter's shop, you will see that there is, in common speech, a difference between a man's hat and the hats that are his.'

'But a hatter,' protested Hood, 'can get money out of his stock of new hats. What could Todhunter get out of this one old hat?'

'Rabbits,' replied Father Brown promptly.

'What?' cried Dr Hood.

'Rabbits, ribbons, sweetmeats, goldfish, rolls of coloured paper,' said the reverend gentleman with rapidity. 'Didn't you see it all when you found out the faked ropes? It's just the same with the sword. Mr Todhunter hasn't got a scratch on him, as you say; but he's got a scratch in him, if you follow me.'

'Do you mean inside Mr Todhunter's clothes?' enquired Mrs MacNab sternly.

'I do not mean inside Mr Todhunter's clothes,' said Father Brown. 'I mean inside Mr Todhunter.'

'Well, what in the name of Bedlam do you mean?'

'Mr Todhunter,' explained Father Brown placidly, 'is learning to be a professional conjurer, as well as juggler, ventriloquist, and expert in the rope trick. The conjuring explains the hat. It is without traces of hair, not because it is worn by the prematurely bald Mr Glass, but because it has never been worn by anybody. The juggling explains the three glasses, which Todhunter was teaching himself to throw up and catch in rotation. But, being only at the stage of practice, he smashed one glass against the ceiling. And the juggling also explains the sword, which it was Mr Todhunter's professional pride and duty to swallow. But, again, being at the stage of practice, he very slightly grazed the inside of his throat with the weapon. Hence he has a wound inside him, which I am sure (from the expression on his face) is not a serious one. He was also practising the trick of a release from ropes, like the Davenport Brothers, and he was just about to free himself when we all burst into the room. The cards, of course, are for card tricks, and they are scattered on the floor because he had just been practising one of those dodges of sending them flying through the air. He merely kept his trade secret, because he had to keep his tricks secret, like any other conjurer. But the mere fact of an idler in a top hat having once looked in at his back window, and been driven away by him with great indignation, was enough to set us all on a wrong track of romance, and make us imagine his whole life overshadowed by the silk-hatted spectre of Mr Glass.'

'But what about the two voices?' asked Maggie, staring.

'Have you never heard a ventriloquist?' asked Father Brown. 'Don't you know they speak first in their natural voice, and then answer themselves in just that shrill, squeaky, unnatural voice that you heard?'

There was a long silence, and Dr Hood regarded the little man who had spoken with a dark and attentive smile. 'You are certainly a very ingenious person,' he said; 'it could not have been done better in a book. But there is just one part of Mr Glass you have not succeeded in explaining away, and that is his name. Miss MacNab distinctly heard him so addressed by Mr Todhunter.'

The Revd Mr Brown broke into a rather childish giggle. 'Well, that,' he said, 'that's the silliest part of the whole silly story. When our juggling friend here threw up the three glasses in turn, he counted them aloud as he caught them, and also commented aloud when he failed to catch them. What he really said was: "One, two and three – missed a glass one, two – missed a glass." And so on.'

There was a second of stillness in the room, and then everyone with one accord burst out laughing. As they did so the figure in the corner complacently uncoiled all the ropes and let them fall with a flourish. Then, advancing into the middle of the room with a bow, he produced from his pocket a big bill printed in blue and red, which announced that ZALADIN, the World's Greatest Conjurer, Contortionist, Ventriloquist and Human Kangaroo would be ready with an entirely new series of tricks at the Empire Pavilion, Scarborough, on Monday next at eight o'clock precisely.

The Paradise of Thieves

The great Muscari, most original of the young Tuscan poets, walked swiftly into his favourite restaurant, which overlooked the Mediterranean, was covered by an awning and fenced by little lemon and orange trees. Waiters in white aprons were already laying out on white tables the insignia of an early and elegant lunch; and this seemed to increase a satisfaction that already touched the top of swagger. Muscari had an eagle nose like Dante; his hair and neckerchief were dark and flowing; he carried a black cloak, and might almost have carried a black mask, so much did he bear with him a sort of Venetian melodrama. He acted as if a troubadour had still a definite social office, like a bishop. He went as near as his century permitted to walking the world literally like Don Juan, with rapier and guitar.

For he never travelled without a case of swords, with which he had fought many brilliant duels, or without a corresponding case for his mandolin, with which he had actually serenaded Miss Ethel Harrogate, the highly conventional daughter of a Yorkshire banker on a holiday. Yet he was neither a charlatan nor a child; but a hot, logical Latin who liked a certain thing and was it. His poetry was as straightforward as anyone else's prose. He desired fame or wine or the beauty of women with a torrid directness inconceivable among the cloudy ideals or cloudy compromises of the north; to vaguer races his intensity smelt of danger or even crime. Like fire or the sea, he was too simple to be trusted.

The banker and his beautiful English daughter were staying at the hotel attached to Muscari's restaurant; that was why it was his favourite restaurant. A glance flashed around the room told him at once, however, that the English party had not descended. The restaurant was glittering, but still comparatively empty. Two priests were talking at a table in a corner, but Muscari (an ardent Catholic) took no more notice of them than of a couple of crows. But from a yet farther seat, partly concealed behind a dwarf tree golden with oranges, there rose and advanced towards the poet a person whose costume was the most aggressively opposite to his own.

This figure was clad in tweeds of a piebald check, with a pink tie, a sharp collar and protuberant yellow boots. He contrived, in the true tradition of 'Arry at Margate, to look at once startling and commonplace. But as the Cockney apparition drew nearer, Muscari was astounded to observe that the head was distinctly different from the body. It was an Italian head: fuzzy, swarthy and very vivacious, that rose abruptly out of the standing collar like cardboard and the comic pink tie. In fact it was a head he knew. He recognised it, above all the dire erection of English holiday array, as the face of an old but forgotten friend named Ezza. This youth had been a prodigy at college, and European fame was promised him when he was barely fifteen; but when he appeared in the world he failed, first publicly as a dramatist and a demagogue, and then privately for years on end as an actor, a traveller, a commission agent or a journalist. Muscari had known him last behind the footlights; he was but too well attuned to the excitements of that profession, and it was believed that some moral calamity had swallowed him up.

'Ezza!' cried the poet, rising and shaking hands in a pleasant astonishment. 'Well, I've seen you in many costumes in the green room; but I never expected to see you dressed up as an Englishman.'

'This,' answered Ezza gravely, 'is not the costume of an Englishman, but of the Italian of the future.'

'In that case,' remarked Muscari, 'I confess I prefer the Italian of the past.'

'That is your old mistake, Muscari,' said the man in tweeds, shaking his head; 'and the mistake of Italy. In the sixteenth century we Tuscans made the morning: we had the newest steel, the newest carving, the newest chemistry. Why should we not now have the newest factories, the newest motors, the newest finance – the newest clothes?'

'Because they are not worth having,' answered Muscari. 'You cannot make Italians really progressive; they are too intelligent. Men who see the short cut to good living will never go by the new elaborate roads.'

'Well, to me Marconi, or D'Annunzio, is the star of Italy,' said the other. 'That is why I have become a Futurist – and a courier.'

'A courier!' cried Muscari, laughing. 'Is that the last of your list of trades? And whom are you conducting?'

'Oh, a man of the name of Harrogate, and his family, I believe.'

'Not the banker in this hotel?' enquired the poet, with some eagerness.

'That's the man,' answered the courier.

'Does it pay well?' asked the troubadour innocently.

'It will pay me,' said Ezza, with a very enigmatic smile. 'But I am a rather curious sort of courier.' Then, as if changing the subject, he said abruptly: 'He has a daughter – and a son.'

'The daughter is divine,' affirmed Muscari, 'the father and son are, I suppose, human. But granted his harmless qualities doesn't that banker strike you as a splendid instance of my argument? Harrogate has millions in his safes, and I have – the hole in my pocket. But you daren't say – you can't say – that he's cleverer than I, or bolder than I, or even more energetic. He's not clever, he's got eyes like blue buttons; he's not energetic, he moves from chair to chair like a paralytic. He's a conscientious, kindly old blockhead; but he's got money simply because he collects money, as a boy collects stamps. You're too strong-minded for business, Ezza. You won't get on. To be clever enough to get all that money, one must be stupid enough to want it.'

'I'm stupid enough for that,' said Ezza gloomily. 'But I should suggest a suspension of your critique of the banker, for here he comes.'

Mr Harrogate, the great financier, did indeed enter the room, but nobody looked at him. He was a massive elderly man with a boiled blue eye and faded grey-sandy moustaches; but for his heavy stoop he might have been a colonel. He carried several unopened letters in his hand. His son Frank was a really fine lad, curly-haired, sunburnt and strenuous; but nobody looked at him either. All eyes, as usual, were riveted, for the moment at least, upon Ethel Harrogate, whose golden Greek head and colour of the dawn seemed set purposely above that sapphire sea, like a goddess's. The poet Muscari drew a deep breath as if he were drinking something, as indeed he was. He was drinking the Classic; which his fathers made. Ezza studied her with a gaze equally intense and far more baffling.

Miss Harrogate was specially radiant and ready for conversation on this occasion; and her family had fallen into the easier Continental habit, allowing the stranger Muscari and even the courier Ezza to share their table and their talk. In Ethel Harrogate conventionality crowned itself with a perfection and splendour of its own. Proud of her father's prosperity, fond of fashionable pleasures, a fond daughter but an arrant flirt, she was all these things with a sort of golden good-nature that made her very pride pleasing and her worldly respectability a fresh and hearty thing.

They were in an eddy of excitement about some alleged peril in the mountain path they were to attempt that week. The danger was not from rock and avalanche, but from something yet more romantic. Ethel had been earnestly assured that brigands, the true cut-throats of the modern legend, still haunted that ridge and held that pass of the Apennines.

'They say,' she cried, with the awful relish of a schoolgirl, 'that all that country isn't ruled by the King of Italy, but by the King of Thieves. Who is the King of Thieves?'

'A great man,' replied Muscari, 'worthy to rank with your own Robin Hood, signorina. Montano, the King of Thieves, was first heard of in the mountains some ten years ago, when people said brigands were extinct. But his wild authority spread with the swiftness of a silent revolution. Men found his fierce proclamations nailed in every mountain village; his sentinels, gun in hand, in every mountain ravine. Six times the Italian Government tried to dislodge him, and was defeated in six pitched battles as if by Napoleon.'

'Now that sort of thing,' observed the banker weightily, 'would never be allowed in England; perhaps, after all, we had better choose another route. But the courier thought it perfectly safe.'

'It is perfectly safe,' said the courier contemptuously. 'I have been over it twenty times. There may have been some old jailbird called a King in the time of our grandmothers; but he belongs to history if not to fable. Brigandage is utterly stamped out.'

'It can never be utterly stamped out,' Muscari answered; 'because armed revolt is a recreation natural to southerners. Our peasants are like their mountains, rich in grace and green gaiety, but with the fires beneath. There is a point of human despair where the northern poor take to drink – and our own poor take to daggers.'

'A poet is privileged,' replied Ezza, with a sneer. 'If Signor Muscari were English he would still be looking for highwaymen in Wandsworth. Believe me, there is no more danger of being captured in Italy than of being scalped in Boston.'

'Then you propose to attempt it?' asked Mr Harrogate, frowning.

'Oh, it sounds rather dreadful,' cried the girl, turning her glorious eyes on Muscari. 'Do you really think the pass is dangerous?'

Muscari threw back his black mane. 'I know it is dangerous,' he said. 'I am crossing it tomorrow.'

The young Harrogate was left behind for a moment emptying a glass of white wine and lighting a cigarette, as the beauty retired with the banker, the courier and the poet, distributing peals of silvery satire. At about the same instant the two priests in the corner rose; the taller, a white-haired Italian, taking his leave. The shorter priest turned and walked towards the banker's son, and the latter was astonished to realise that though a Roman priest the man was an Englishman. He vaguely remembered meeting him at the social crushes of some of his Catholic friends. But the man spoke before his memories could collect themselves.

'Mr Frank Harrogate, I think,' he said. 'I have had an introduction, but I do not mean to presume on it. The odd thing I have to say will come far better from a stranger. Mr Harrogate, I say one word and go: take care of your sister in her great sorrow.'

Even for Frank's truly fraternal indifference the radiance and derision of his sister still seemed to sparkle and ring; he could hear her laughter still from the garden of the hotel, and he stared at his sombre adviser in puzzledom.

'Do you mean the brigands?' he asked; and then, remembering a vague fear of his own, 'or can you be thinking of Muscari?'

'One is never thinking of the real sorrow,' said the strange priest. 'One can only be kind when it comes.'

And he passed promptly from the room, leaving the other almost with his mouth open.

* * *

A day or two afterwards a coach containing the company was really crawling and staggering up the spurs of the menacing mountain range. Between Ezza's cheery denial of the danger and Muscari's boisterous defiance of it, the financial family were firm in their original purpose; and Muscari made his mountain journey coincide with theirs. A more surprising feature was the appearance at the coast-town station of the little priest of the restaurant; he alleged merely that business led him also to cross the mountains of the midland. But young Harrogate could not but connect his presence with the mystical fears and warnings of yesterday.

The coach was a kind of commodious wagonette, invented by the modernist talent of the courier, who dominated the expedition with his scientific activity and breezy wit. The theory of danger from thieves was banished from thought and speech; though so far conceded in formal act that some slight protection was employed. The courier and the young banker carried loaded revolvers, and Muscari (with much boyish gratification) buckled on a kind of cutlass under his black cloak.

He had planted his person at a flying leap next to the lovely Englishwoman; on the other side of her sat the priest, whose name was Brown and who was fortunately a silent individual; the courier and the father and son were on the *banc* behind. Muscari was in towering spirits, seriously believing in the peril, and his talk to Ethel might well have made her think him a maniac. But there was something in the crazy and gorgeous ascent, amid crags like peaks loaded with woods like orchards, that dragged her spirit up alone with his into purple preposterous heavens with wheeling suns. The white road climbed like a white cat; it spanned sunless chasms like a tight-rope; it was flung round far-off headlands like a lasso.

And yet, however high they went, the desert still blossomed like the rose. The fields were burnished in sun and wind with the colour of kingfisher and parrot and humming-bird, the hues of a hundred flowering flowers. There are no lovelier meadows and woodlands than the English, no nobler crests or chasms than those of Snowdon and Glencoe. But Ethel Harrogate had never before seen the southern parks tilted on the splintered northern peaks; the gorge of Glencoe laden with the fruits of Kent. There was nothing here of that chill and desolation that in Britain one associates with high and wild scenery. It was rather like a mosaic palace, rent with earthquakes; or like a Dutch tulip garden blown to the stars with dynamite.

'It's like Kew Gardens on Beachy Head,' said Ethel.

'It is our secret,' answered he, 'the secret of the volcano; that is also the secret of the revolution – that a thing can be violent and yet fruitful.'

'You are rather violent yourself,' and she smiled at him.

'And yet rather fruitless,' he admitted; 'if I die tonight I die unmarried and a fool.'

'It is not my fault if you have come,' she said after a difficult silence.

'It is never your fault,' answered Muscari; 'it was not your fault that Troy fell.'

As they spoke they came under overwhelming cliffs that spread almost like wings above a corner of peculiar peril. Shocked by the big shadow on the narrow ledge, the horses stirred doubtfully. The driver leapt to the earth to hold their heads, and they became ungovernable. One horse reared up to his full height – the titanic and terrifying height of a horse when he becomes a biped. It was just enough to alter the equilibrium; the whole coach heeled over like a ship and crashed through the fringe of bushes over the cliff. Muscari threw an arm round Ethel, who clung to him, and shouted aloud. It was for such moments that he lived.

At the moment when the gorgeous mountain walls went round the poet's head like a purple windmill a thing happened which was superficially even more startling. The elderly and lethargic banker sprang erect in the coach and leapt over the precipice before the tilted vehicle could take him there. In the first flash it looked as wild as suicide; but in the second it was as sensible as a safe investment. The Yorkshireman had evidently more promptitude, as well as more sagacity, than Muscari had given him credit for; for he landed in a lap of land which might have been specially padded with turf and clover to receive him. As it happened, indeed, the whole company were equally lucky, if less dignified in their form of ejection. Immediately under this abrupt turn of the road was a grassy and flowery hollow like a sunken meadow; a sort of green velvet pocket in the long, green, trailing garments of the hills. Into this they were all tipped or tumbled with little damage, save that their smallest baggage and even the contents of their pockets were scattered in the grass around them. The wrecked coach still hung above, entangled in the tough hedge, and the horses plunged painfully down the slope. The first to sit up was the little priest, who scratched his head with a face of foolish wonder. Frank Harrogate heard him say to himself: 'Now why on earth have we fallen just here?'

He blinked at the litter around him, and recovered his own very clumsy umbrella. Beyond it lay the broad sombrero fallen from the head of Muscari, and beside it a sealed business letter which, after a glance at the address, he returned to the elder Harrogate. On the other side of him the grass partly hid Miss Ethel's sunshade, and just beyond it lay a curious little glass bottle hardly two inches long. The priest picked it up; in a quick, unobtrusive manner he uncorked and sniffed it, and his heavy face turned the colour of clay.

'Heaven deliver us!' he muttered; 'it can't be hers! Has her sorrow come on her already?' He slipped it into his own waistcoat pocket. 'I think I'm justified,' he said, 'till I know a little more.'

He gazed painfully at the girl, at that moment being raised out of the flowers by Muscari, who was saying: 'We have fallen into heaven; it is a sign. Mortals climb up and they fall down; but it is only gods and goddesses who can fall upwards.'

And indeed she rose out of the sea of colours so beautiful and happy a vision that the priest felt his suspicion shaken and shifted. 'After all,' he thought, 'perhaps the poison isn't hers; perhaps it's one of Muscari's melodramatic tricks.'

Muscari set the lady lightly on her feet, made her an absurdly theatrical bow, and then, drawing his cutlass, hacked hard at the taut reins of the horses, so that they scrambled to their feet and stood in the grass trembling. When he had done so, a most remarkable thing occurred. A very quiet man, very poorly dressed and extremely sunburnt, came out of the bushes and took hold of the horses' heads. He had a queer-shaped knife, very broad and crooked, buckled on his belt; there was nothing else remarkable about him, except his sudden and silent appearance. The poet asked him who he was, and he did not answer.

Looking around him at the confused and startled group in the hollow, Muscari then perceived that another tanned and tattered man, with a short gun under his arm, was looking at them from the ledge just below, leaning his elbows on the edge of the turf. Then he looked up at the road from which they had fallen and saw, looking down on them, the muzzles of four other carbines and four other brown faces with bright but quite motionless eyes.

'The brigands!' cried Muscari, with a kind of monstrous gaiety. 'This was a trap. Ezza, if you will oblige me by shooting the coachman first, we can cut our way out yet. There are only six of them.'

'The coachman,' said Ezza, who was standing grimly with his hands in his pockets, 'happens to be a servant of Mr Harrogate's.'

'Then shoot him all the more,' cried the poet impatiently; 'he was bribed to upset his master. Then put the lady in the middle, and we will break the line up there – with a rush.'

And, wading in wild grass and flowers, he advanced fearlessly on the four carbines; but finding that no one followed except young Harrogate, he turned, brandishing his cutlass to wave the others on. He beheld the courier still standing slightly astride in the centre of the grassy ring, his hands in his pockets; and his lean, ironical Italian face seemed to grow longer and longer in the evening light.

'You thought, Muscari, I was the failure among our schoolfellows,' he said, 'and you thought you were the success. But I have succeeded more than you and fill a bigger place in history. I have been acting epics while you have been writing them.'

'Come on, I tell you!' thundered Muscari from above. 'Will you stand there talking nonsense about yourself with a woman to save and three strong men to help you? What do you call yourself?'

'I call myself Montano,' cried the strange courier in a voice equally loud and full. 'I am the King of Thieves, and I welcome you all to my summer palace.'

And even as he spoke five more silent men with weapons ready came out of the bushes, and looked towards him for their orders. One of them held a large paper in his hand.

'This pretty little nest where we are all picnicking,' went on the courier-brigand, with the same easy yet sinister smile, 'is, together with some caves underneath it, known by the name of the Paradise of Thieves. It is my principal stronghold on these hills; for (as you have doubtless noticed) the eyrie is invisible both from the road above and from the valley below. It is something better than impregnable; it is unnoticeable. Here I mostly live, and here I shall certainly die, if the gendarmes ever track me here. I am not the kind of criminal that "reserves his defence", but the better kind that reserves his last bullet.'

All were staring at him thunderstruck and still, except Father Brown, who heaved a huge sigh as of relief and fingered the little phial in his pocket. 'Thank God!' he muttered; 'that's much more probable. The poison belongs to this robber-chief, of course. He carries it so that he may never be captured, like Cato.'

The King of Thieves was, however, continuing his address with the same kind of dangerous politeness. 'It only remains for me,' he said, 'to explain to my guests the social conditions upon which I have the pleasure of entertaining them. I need not expound the quaint old ritual of ransom, which it is incumbent upon me to keep up; and even this only applies to a part of the company. The Revd Father Brown and the celebrated Signor Muscari I shall release tomorrow at dawn and escort to my outposts. Poets and priests, if you will pardon my simplicity of speech, never have any money. And so (since it is impossible to get anything out of them), let us seize the opportunity to show our admiration for classic literature and our reverence for Holy Church.'

He paused with an unpleasing smile; and Father Brown blinked repeatedly at him, and seemed suddenly to be listening with great attention. The brigand captain took the large paper from the attendant brigand and, glancing over it, continued: 'My other intentions are clearly set forth in this public document, which I will hand round in a moment; and which after that will be posted on a tree by every village in the valley, and every cross-road in the hills. I will not weary you with the verbalism, since you will be able to check it; the substance of my proclamation is this: I announce first that I have captured the English millionaire, the colossus of finance, Mr

Samuel Harrogate. I next announce that I have found on his person notes and bonds for two thousand pounds, which he has given up to me. Now since it would be really immoral to announce such a thing to a credulous public if it had not occurred, I suggest it should occur without further delay. I suggest that Mr Harrogate senior should now give me the two thousand pounds in his pocket.'

The banker looked at him under lowering brows, red-faced and sulky, but seemingly cowed. That leap from the failing carriage seemed to have used up his last virility. He had held back in a hangdog style when his son and Muscari had made a bold movement to break out of the brigand trap. And now his red and trembling hand went reluctantly to his breast-pocket, and passed a bundle of papers and envelopes to the brigand.

'Excellent!' cried that outlaw gaily; 'so far we are all cosy. I resume the points of my proclamation, so soon to be published to all Italy. The third item is that of ransom. I am asking from the friends of the Harrogate family a ransom of three thousand pounds, which I am sure is almost insulting to that family in its moderate estimate of their importance. Who would not pay triple this sum for another day's association with such a domestic circle? I will not conceal from you that the document ends with certain legal phrases about the unpleasant things that may happen if the money is not paid; but meanwhile, ladies and gentlemen, let me assure you that I am comfortably off here for accommodation, wine and cigars, and bid you for the present a sportsman-like welcome to the luxuries of the Paradise of Thieves.'

All the time that he had been speaking, the dubious-looking men with carbines and dirty slouch hats had been gathering silently in such preponderating numbers that even Muscari was compelled to recognise his sally with the sword as hopeless. He glanced around him; but the girl had already gone over to soothe and comfort her father, for her natural affection for his person was as strong or stronger than her somewhat snobbish pride in his success. Muscari, with the illogicality of a lover, admired this filial devotion, and yet was irritated by it. He slapped his sword back in the scabbard and went and flung himself somewhat sulkily on one of the green banks. The priest sat down within a yard or two, and Muscari turned his aquiline nose on him in an instantaneous irritation.

'Well,' said the poet tartly, 'do people still think me too romantic? Are there, I wonder, any brigands left in the mountains?'

'There may be,' said Father Brown agnostically.

'What do you mean?' asked the other sharply.

'I mean I am puzzled,' replied the priest. 'I am puzzled about Ezza or Montano, or whatever his name is. He seems to me much more inexplicable as a brigand even than he was as a courier.'

'But in what way?' persisted his companion. 'Santa Maria! I should have thought the brigand was plain enough.'

'I find three curious difficulties,' said the priest in a quiet voice. 'I should like to have your opinion on them. First of all I must tell you I was lunching in that restaurant at the seaside. As four of you left the room, you and Miss Harrogate went ahead, talking and laughing; the banker and the courier came behind, speaking sparely and rather low. But I could not help hearing Ezza say these words – "Well, let her have a little fun; you know the blow may smash her any minute." Mr Harrogate answered nothing; so the words must have had some meaning. On the impulse of the moment I warned her brother that she might be in peril; I said nothing of its nature, for I did not know. But if it meant this capture in the hills, the thing is nonsense. Why should the brigand-courier warn his patron, even by a hint, when it was his whole purpose to lure him into the mountain-mousetrap? It could not have meant that. But if not, what is this disaster, known both to courier and banker, which hangs over Miss Harrogate's head?'

'Disaster to Miss Harrogate!' ejaculated the poet, sitting up with some ferocity. 'Explain yourself; go on.'

'All my riddles, however, revolve round our bandit chief,' resumed the priest reflectively. 'And here is the second of them. Why did he put so prominently in his demand for ransom the fact that he had taken two thousand pounds from his victim on the spot? It had no faintest tendency to evoke the ransom. Quite the other way, in fact. Harrogate's friends would be far likelier to fear for his fate if they thought the thieves were poor and desperate. Yet the spoliation on the spot was emphasised and even put first in the demand. Why should Ezza Montano want so specially to tell all Europe that he had picked the pocket before he levied the blackmail?'

'I cannot imagine,' said Muscari, rubbing up his black hair for once with an unaffected gesture. 'You may think you enlighten me, but you are leading me deeper in the dark. What may be the third objection to the King of the Thieves?'

'The third objection,' said Father Brown, still in meditation, 'is this bank we are sitting on. Why does our brigand-courier call this his chief fortress and the Paradise of Thieves? It is certainly a soft spot to fall on and a sweet spot to look at. It is also quite true, as he says, that it is invisible from valley and peak, and is therefore a hiding-place. But it is not a fortress. It never could be a fortress. I think it would be the worst fortress in the world. For it is actually commanded from above by the common highroad across the mountains – the very place where the police would most probably pass. Why, five shabby short guns held us helpless here about half an hour ago. The quarter of a company of any kind of soldiers could have blown us over the precipice. Whatever is the meaning of this odd little nook of grass and flowers, it is not an entrenched position. It is something else; it has some other strange sort of importance; some value that I do not understand. It is more like an accidental theatre or a natural green-room; it is like the scene for some romantic comedy; it is like. . .'

As the little priest's words lengthened and lost themselves in a dull and dreamy sincerity, Muscari, whose animal senses were alert and impatient, heard a new noise in the mountains. Even for him the sound was as yet very small and faint; but he could have sworn the evening breeze bore with it something like the pulsation of horses' hoofs and a distant hallooing.

At the same moment, and long before the vibration had touched the less-experienced English ears, Montano the brigand ran up the bank above them and stood in the broken hedge, steadying himself against a tree and peering down the road. He was a strange figure as he stood there, for he had assumed a flapped fantastic hat and swinging baldric and cutlass in his capacity of bandit king, but the bright prosaic tweed of the courier showed through in patches all over him.

The next moment he turned his olive, sneering face and made a movement with his hand. The brigands scattered at the signal, not in confusion, but in what was evidently a kind of guerrilla discipline. Instead of occupying the road along the ridge, they sprinkled themselves along the side of it behind the trees and the hedge, as if watching unseen for an enemy. The noise beyond grew stronger, beginning to shake the mountain road, and a voice could be clearly heard calling out orders. The brigands swayed and huddled, cursing and whispering, and the evening air was full of little metallic noises as they cocked their pistols, or loosened their knives, or trailed their scabbards over the stones. Then the noises from both quarters seemed to meet on the road above; branches broke, horses neighed, men cried out.

'A rescue!' cried Muscari, springing to his feet and waving his hat; 'the gendarmes are on them! Now for freedom and a blow for it! Now to be rebels against robbers! Come, don't let us leave everything to the police; that is so dreadfully modern. Fall on the rear of these ruffians. The gendarmes are rescuing us; come, friends, let us rescue the gendarmes!'

And throwing his hat over the trees, he drew his cutlass once more and began to escalade the slope up to the road. Frank Harrogate jumped up and ran across to help him, revolver in hand, but was astounded to hear himself imperatively recalled by the raucous voice of his father, who seemed to be in great agitation.

'I won't have it,' said the banker in a choking voice; 'I command you not to interfere.'

'But, father,' said Frank very warmly, 'an Italian gentleman has led the way. You wouldn't have it said that the English hung back.'

'It is useless,' said the older man, who was trembling violently, 'it is useless. We must submit to our lot.'

Father Brown looked at the banker; then he put his hand instinctively as if on his heart, but really on the little bottle of poison; and a great light came into his face like the light of the revelation of death.

Muscari meanwhile, without waiting for support, had crested the bank up to the road, and struck the brigand king heavily on the shoulder, causing him to stagger and swing round. Montano also had his cutlass unsheathed, and Muscari, without further speech, sent a slash at his head which he was compelled to catch and parry. But even as the two short blades crossed and clashed the King of Thieves deliberately dropped his point and laughed.

'What's the good, old man?' he said in spirited Italian slang; 'this damned farce will soon be over.'

'What do you mean, you shuffler?' panted the fire-eating poet. 'Is your courage a sham as well as your honesty?'

'Everything about me is a sham,' responded the ex-courier in complete good-humour. 'I am an actor; and if I ever had a private character, I have forgotten it. I am no more a genuine brigand than I am a genuine courier. I am only a bundle of masks, and you can't fight a duel with that.' And he laughed with boyish pleasure and fell into his old straddling attitude, with his back to the skirmish up the road.

Darkness was deepening under the mountain walls, and it was not easy to discern much of the progress of the struggle, save that tall men were pushing their horses' muzzles through a clinging crowd of brigands, who seemed more inclined to harass and hustle the invaders than to kill them. It was more like a town crowd preventing the passage of the police than anything the poet had ever pictured as the last stand of doomed and outlawed men of blood. Just as he was rolling his eyes in bewilderment he felt a touch on his elbow, and found the odd little priest standing there like a small Noah with a large hat, and requesting the favour of a word or two.

'Signor Muscari,' said the cleric, 'in this queer crisis personalities may be pardoned. I may tell you without offence of a way in which you will do more good than by helping the gendarmes, who are bound to break through in any case. You will permit me the impertinent intimacy, but do you care about that girl? Care enough to marry her and make her a good husband, I mean?'

'Yes,' said the poet quite simply.

'Does she care about you?'

'I think so,' was the equally grave reply.

'Then go over there and offer yourself,' said the priest: 'offer her everything you can; offer her heaven and earth if you've got them. The time is short.'

'Why?' asked the astonished man of letters.

'Because,' said Father Brown, 'her Doom is coming up the road.'

'Nothing is coming up the road,' argued Muscari, 'except the rescue.'

'Well, you go over there,' said his adviser, 'and be ready to rescue her from the rescue.'

Almost as he spoke the hedges were broken all along the ridge by a rush of the escaping brigands. They dived into bushes and thick grass like defeated men pursued; and the great cocked hats of the mounted gendarmerie were seen passing along above the broken hedge. Another order was given; there was a noise of dismounting, and a tall officer with cocked hat, a grey imperial, and a paper in his hand appeared in the gap that was the gate of the Paradise of Thieves. There was a momentary silence, broken in an extraordinary way by the banker, who cried out in a hoarse and strangled voice: 'Robbed! I've been robbed!'

'Why, that was hours ago,' cried his son in astonishment: 'when you were robbed of two thousand pounds.'

'Not of two thousand pounds,' said the financier, with an abrupt and terrible composure, 'only of a small bottle.'

The policeman with the grey imperial was striding across the green hollow. Encountering the King of the Thieves in his path, he clapped him on the shoulder with something between a caress and a buffet and gave him a push that sent him staggering away. 'You'll get into trouble, too,' he said, 'if you play these tricks.'

Again to Muscari's artistic eye it seemed scarcely like the capture of a great outlaw at bay. Passing on, the policeman halted before the Harrogate group and said: 'Samuel Harrogate, I arrest you in the name of the law for embezzlement of the funds of the Hull and Huddersfield Bank.'

The great banker nodded with an odd air of business assent, seemed to reflect a moment, and before they could interpose took a half turn and a step that brought him to the edge of the outer mountain wall. Then, flinging up his hands, he leapt exactly as he leapt out of the coach. But this time he did not fall into a little meadow just beneath; he fell a thousand feet below, to become a wreck of bones in the valley.

The anger of the Italian policeman, which he expressed volubly to Father Brown, was largely mixed with admiration. 'It was like him to escape us at last,' he said. 'He was a great brigand if you like. This last trick of his I believe to be absolutely unprecedented. He fled with the company's money to Italy, and actually got himself captured by sham brigands in his own pay, so as to explain both the disappearance of the money and the disappearance of himself. That demand for ransom was really taken seriously by most of the police. But for years he's been doing things as good as that, quite as good as that. He will be a serious loss to his family.'

Muscari was leading away the unhappy daughter, who held hard to him, as she did for many a year after. But even in that tragic wreck he could not help having a smile and a hand of half-mocking friendship for the indefensible Ezza Montano. 'And where are you going next?' he asked him over his shoulder.

'Birmingham,' answered the actor, puffing a cigarette. 'Didn't I tell you I was a Futurist? I really do believe in those things if I believe in anything. Change, bustle and new things every morning. I am going to Manchester, Liverpool, Leeds, Hull, Huddersfield, Glasgow, Chicago – in short, to enlightened, energetic, civilised society!'

'In short,' said Muscari, 'to the real Paradise of Thieves.'

The Duel of Dr Hirsch

M. Maurice Brun and M. Armand Armagnac were crossing the sunlit Champs-Elysées with a kind of vivacious respectability. They were both short, brisk and bold. They both had black beards that did not seem to belong to their faces, after the strange French fashion which makes real hair look like artificial. M. Brun had a dark wedge of beard apparently affixed under his lower lip. M. Armagnac, by way of a change, had two beards; one sticking out from each corner of his emphatic chin. They were both young. They were both atheists, with a depressing fixity of outlook but great mobility of exposition. They were both pupils of the great Dr Hirsch, scientist, publicist and moralist.

M. Brun had become prominent by his proposal that the common expression 'Adieu' should be obliterated from all the French classics, and a slight fine imposed for its use in private life. 'Then,' he said, 'the very name of your imagined God will have echoed for the last time in the ear of man.' M. Armagnac specialised rather in a resistance to militarism, and wished the chorus of the Marseillaise altered from 'Aux armes, citoyens' to 'Aux grèves, citoyens'. But his anti-militarism was of a peculiar and Gallic sort. An eminent and very wealthy English Quaker, who had come to see him to arrange for the disarmament of the whole planet, was rather distressed by Armagnac's proposal that (by way of beginning) the soldiers should shoot their officers.

And indeed it was in this regard that the two men differed most from their leader and father in philosophy. Dr Hirsch, though born in France and covered with the most triumphant favours of French education, was temperamentally of another type – mild, dreamy, humane; and, despite his sceptical system, not devoid of transcendentalism. He was, in short, more like a German than a Frenchman; and much as they admired him, something in the subconsciousness of these Gauls was irritated at his pleading for peace in so peaceful a manner. To their party throughout Europe, however, Paul Hirsch was a saint of science. His large and daring cosmic theories advertised his austere life and innocent, if somewhat frigid, morality; he held something of the position of Darwin doubled with the position of Tolstoy. But he was neither an anarchist nor an anti-patriot; his views on disarmament were moderate and evolutionary – the Republican Government put considerable confidence in him as to various chemical improvements. He had lately even discovered a noiseless explosive, the secret of which the Government was carefully guarding.

His house stood in a handsome street near the Elysée – a street which in that strong summer seemed almost as full of foliage as the park itself; a row of chestnuts shattered the sunshine, interrupted only in one place where a large café ran out into the street. Almost opposite to this were the white and green blinds of the great scientist's house, an iron balcony, also painted green, running along in front of the first-floor windows. Beneath this was the entrance into a kind of court, gay with shrubs and tiles, into which the two Frenchmen passed in animated talk.

The door was opened to them by the doctor's old servant, Simon, who might very well have passed for a doctor himself, having a strict suit of black, spectacles, grey hair, and a confidential manner. In fact, he was a far more presentable man of science than his master, Dr Hirsch, who was a forked radish of a fellow, with just enough bulb of a head to make his body insignificant. With all the gravity of a great physician handling a prescription, Simon handed a letter to M. Armagnac. That gentleman ripped it up with a racial impatience, and rapidly read the following:

I cannot come down to speak to you. There is a man in this house whom I refuse to meet. He is a Chauvinist officer, Dubosc. He is sitting on the stairs. He has been kicking the furniture about in all the other rooms; I have locked myself in my study, opposite that café. If you love me, go over to the café and wait at one of the tables outside. I will try to send him over to you. I want you to answer him and deal with him. I cannot meet him myself. I cannot: I will not.

There is going to be another Dreyfus case.

P. Hirsch

M. Armagnac looked at M. Brun. M. Brun borrowed the letter, read it, and looked at M. Armagnac. Then both betook themselves briskly to one of the little tables under the chestnuts opposite, where they procured two tall glasses of horrible green absinthe, which they could drink apparently in any weather and at any time. Otherwise the café seemed empty, except for one soldier drinking coffee at one table, and at another a large man drinking a small syrup and a priest drinking nothing.

Maurice Brun cleared his throat and said: 'Of course we must help the master in every way, but –'

There was an abrupt silence, and Armagnac said: 'He may have excellent reasons for not meeting the man himself, but –'

Before either could complete a sentence, it was evident that the invader had been expelled from the house opposite. The shrubs under the archway swayed and burst apart, as that unwelcome guest was shot out of them like a cannonball.

He was a sturdy figure in a small and tilted Tyrolean felt hat, a figure that had indeed something generally Tyrolean about it. The man's shoulders were big and broad, but his legs were neat and active in knee-breeches and knitted stockings. His face was brown like a nut; he had very bright and restless brown eyes; his dark hair was brushed back stiffly in front and cropped close behind, outlining a square and powerful skull; and he had a huge black moustache like the horns of a bison. Such a substantial head is generally based on a bull neck; but this was hidden by a big coloured scarf, swathed round up the man's ears and falling in front inside his jacket like a sort of fancy waistcoat. It was a scarf of strong dead colours, dark red and old gold and purple, probably of Oriental fabrication. Altogether the man had something a shade barbaric about him; more like a Hungarian squire than an ordinary French officer. His French, however, was obviously that of a native; and his French patriotism was so impulsive as to be slightly absurd. His first act when he burst out of the archway was to call in a clarion voice down the street: 'Are there any Frenchmen here?' as if he were calling for Christians in Mecca.

Armagnac and Brun instantly stood up; but they were too late. Men were already running from the street corners; there was a small but ever-clustering crowd. With the prompt French instinct for the politics of the street, the man with the black moustache had already run across to a corner of the café, sprung on one of the tables, and seizing a branch of chestnut to steady himself, shouted as Camille Desmoulins once shouted when he scattered the oak-leaves among the populace.

'Frenchmen!' he volleyed; 'I cannot speak! God help me, that is why I am speaking! The fellows in their filthy parliaments who learn to speak also learn to be silent – silent as that spy cowering in the house opposite! Silent as he is when I beat on his bedroom door! Silent as he is now, though he hears my voice across this street and shakes where he sits! Oh, they can be silent eloquently – the politicians! But the time has come when we that cannot speak must speak. You are betrayed to the Prussians. Betrayed at this moment. Betrayed by that man. I am Jules Dubosc, Colonel of Artillery, Belfort. We caught a German spy in the Vosges yesterday, and a paper was found on him – a paper I hold in my hand. Oh, they tried to hush it up; but I took it direct to the man who wrote it – the man in that house! It is in his hand. It is signed with his initials. It is a direction for finding the secret of this new Noiseless Powder. Hirsch invented it; Hirsch wrote this note about it. This note is in German, and was found in a German's pocket. "Tell the man the formula for powder is in grey envelope in first drawer to the left of Secretary's desk, War Office, in red ink. He must be careful. P.H." '

He rattled short sentences like a quick-firing gun, but he was plainly the sort of man who is either mad or right. The mass of the crowd was

Nationalist, and already in threatening uproar; and a minority of equally angry Intellectuals, led by Armagnac and Brun, only made the majority more militant.

'If this is a military secret,' shouted Brun, 'why do you yell about it in the street?'

'I will tell you why I do!' roared Dubosc above the roaring crowd. 'I went to this man in straight and civil style. If he had any explanation it could have been given in complete confidence. He refuses to explain. He refers me to two strangers in a café as to two flunkeys. He has thrown me out of the house, but I am going back into it, with the people of Paris behind me!'

A shout seemed to shake the very façade of mansions and two stones flew, one breaking a window above the balcony. The indignant Colonel plunged once more under the archway and was heard crying and thundering inside. Every instant the human sea grew wider and wider; it surged up against the rails and steps of the traitor's house; it was already certain that the place would be burst into like the Bastille, when the broken french window opened and Dr Hirsch came out on the balcony. For an instant the fury half turned to laughter; for he was an absurd figure in such a scene. His long bare neck and sloping shoulders were the shape of a champagne bottle, but that was the only festive thing about him. His coat hung on him as on a peg; he wore his carrot-coloured hair long and weedy; his cheeks and chin were fully fringed with one of those irritating beards that begin far from the mouth. He was very pale, and he wore blue spectacles.

Livid as he was, he spoke with a sort of prim decision, so that the mob fell silent in the middle of his third sentence.

'. . . only two things to say to you now. The first is to my foes, the second to my friends. To my foes I say: it is true I will not meet M. Dubosc, though he is storming outside this very room. It is true I have asked two other men to confront him for me. And I will tell you why! Because I will not and must not see him – because it would be against all rules of dignity and honour to see him. Before I am triumphantly cleared before a court, there is another arbitration this gentleman owes me as a gentleman, and in referring him to my seconds I am strictly –'

Armagnac and Brun were waving their hats wildly, and even the Doctor's enemies roared applause at this unexpected defiance. Once more a few sentences were inaudible, but they could hear him say: 'To my friends – I myself should always prefer weapons purely intellectual, and to these an evolved humanity will certainly confine itself. But our own most precious truth is the fundamental force of matter and heredity. My books are successful; my theories are unrefuted; but I suffer in politics from a prejudice almost physical in the French. I cannot speak like Clemenceau and Déroulède, for their words are like echoes of their pistols. The French ask for a duellist as the English ask for a sportsman. Well, I give my proofs: I will pay this barbaric bribe, and then go back to reason for the rest of my life.'

Two men were instantly found in the crowd itself to offer their services to Colonel Dubosc, who came out presently, satisfied. One was the common soldier with the coffee, who said simply: 'I will act for you, sir. I am the Duc de Valognes.' The other was the big man, whom his friend the priest sought at first to dissuade; and then walked away alone.

In the early evening a light dinner was spread at the back of the Café Charlemagne. Though unroofed by any glass or gilt plaster, the guests were nearly all under a delicate and irregular roof of leaves; for the ornamental trees stood so thick around and among the tables as to give something of the dimness and the dazzle of a small orchard. At one of the central tables a very stumpy little priest sat in complete solitude, and applied himself to a pile of whitebait with the gravest sort of enjoyment. His daily living being very plain, he had a peculiar taste for sudden and isolated luxuries; he was an abstemious epicure. He did not lift his eyes from his plate, round which red pepper, lemons, brown bread and butter, etc., were rigidly ranked, until a tall shadow fell across the table, and his friend Flambeau sat down opposite. Flambeau was gloomy.

'I'm afraid I must chuck this business,' said he heavily. 'I'm all on the side of the French soldiers like Dubosc, and I'm all against the French atheists like Hirsch; but it seems to me in this case we've made a mistake. The Duke and I thought it as well to investigate the charge, and I must say I'm glad we did.'

'Is the paper a forgery, then?' asked the priest

'That's just the odd thing,' replied Flambeau. 'It's exactly like Hirsch's writing, and nobody can point out any mistake in it. But it wasn't written by Hirsch. If he's a French patriot he didn't write it, because it gives information to Germany. And if he's a German spy he didn't write it, well – because it doesn't give information to Germany.'

'You mean the information is wrong?' asked Father Brown.

'Wrong,' replied the other, 'and wrong exactly where Dr Hirsch would have been right – about the hiding-place of his own secret formula in his own official department. By favour of Hirsch and the authorities, the Duke and I have actually been allowed to inspect the secret drawer at the War Office where the Hirsch formula is kept. We are the only people who have ever known it, except the inventor himself and the Minister for War; but the Minister permitted it to save Hirsch from fighting. After that we really can't support Dubosc if his revelation is a mare's nest.'

'And it is?' asked Father Brown.

'It is,' said his friend gloomily. 'It is a clumsy forgery by somebody who knew nothing of the real hiding-place. It says the paper is in the cupboard on the right of the Secretary's desk. As a fact the cupboard with the secret drawer is some way to the left of the desk. It says the grey envelope contains a long document written in red ink. It isn't written in red ink, but in ordinary black ink. It's manifestly absurd to say that Hirsch can have made a mistake about a paper that nobody knew of but himself; or can have tried to help a foreign thief by telling him to fumble in the wrong drawer. I think we must chuck it up and apologise to old Carrots.'

Father Brown seemed to cogitate; he lifted a little whitebait on his fork. 'You are sure the grey envelope was in the left cupboard?' he asked.

'Positive,' replied Flambeau. 'The grey envelope – it was a white envelope really – was – '

Father Brown put down the small silver fish and the fork and stared across at his companion. 'What?' he asked, in an altered voice.

'Well, what?' repeated Flambeau, eating heartily.

'It was not grey,' said the priest. 'Flambeau, you frighten me.'

'What the deuce are you frightened of?'

'I'm frightened of a white envelope,' said the other seriously. 'If it had only just been grey! Hang it all, it might as well have been grey. But if it was white, the whole business is black. The Doctor has been dabbling in some of the old brimstone after all.'

'But I tell you he couldn't have written such a note!' cried Flambeau. 'The note is utterly wrong about the facts. And innocent or guilty, Dr Hirsch knew all about the facts.'

'The man who wrote that note knew all about the facts,' said his clerical companion soberly. 'He could never have got 'em so wrong with-out knowing about 'em. You have to know an awful lot to be wrong on every subject – like the devil.'

'Do you mean – ?'

'I mean a man telling lies on chance would have told some of the truth,' said his friend firmly. 'Suppose someone sent you to find a house with a green door and a blue blind, with a front garden but no back garden, with a dog but no cat, and where they drank coffee but not tea. You would say if you found no such house that it was all made up. But I say no. I say if you found a house where the door was blue and the blind green, where there was a back garden and no front garden, where cats were common and dogs instantly shot, where tea was drunk in quarts and coffee forbidden – then you would know you had found the house. The man must have known that particular house to be so accurately inaccurate.'

'But what could it mean?' demanded the diner opposite.

'I can't conceive,' said Brown; 'I don't understand this Hirsch affair at all. As long as it was only the left drawer instead of the right, and red ink instead of black, I thought it must be the chance blunders of a forger, as you say. But three is a mystical number; it finishes things. It finishes this. That the direction about the drawer, the colour of ink, the colour of envelope, should none of them be right by accident, that can't be a coincidence. It wasn't.'

'What was it, then? Treason?' asked Flambeau, resuming his dinner.

'I don't know that either,' answered Brown, with a face of blank bewilderment. 'The only thing I can think of . . . Well, I never understood that Dreyfus case. I can always grasp moral evidence easier than the other sorts. I go by a man's eyes and voice, don't you know, and whether his family seems happy, and by what subjects he chooses – and avoids. Well, I was puzzled in the Dreyfus case. Not by the horrible things imputed both ways; I know (though it's not modern to say so) that human nature in the highest places is still capable of being Cenci or Borgia. No, what puzzled me was the *sincerity* of both parties. I don't mean the political parties; the rank and file are always roughly honest, and often duped. I mean the persons of the play. I mean the conspirators, if they were conspirators. I mean the traitor, if he was a traitor. I mean the men who *must* have known the truth. Now Dreyfus went on like a man who *knew* he was a wronged man. And yet the French statesmen and soldiers went on as if they *knew* he wasn't a wronged man but simply a wrong 'un. I don't mean they behaved well; I mean they behaved as if they were sure. I can't describe these things; I know what I mean.'

'I wish I did,' said his friend. 'And what has it to do with old Hirsch?'

'Suppose a person in a position of trust,' went on the priest, 'began to give the enemy information because it was false information. Suppose he even thought he was saving his country by misleading the foreigner. Suppose this brought him into spy circles, and little loans were made to him, and little ties tied on to him. Suppose he kept up his contradictory position in a confused way by never telling the foreign spies the truth, but letting it more and more be guessed. The better part of him (what was left of it) would still say: "I have not helped the enemy; I said it was the left drawer." The meaner part of him would already be saying: "But they may have the sense to see that means the right." I think it is psychologically possible – in an enlightened age, you know.'

'It may be psychologically possible,' answered Flambeau, 'and it certainly would explain Dreyfus being certain he was wronged and his judges being sure he was guilty. But it won't wash historically, because Dreyfus's document (if it was his document) was literally correct.'

'I wasn't thinking of Dreyfus,' said Father Brown.

Silence had sunk around them with the emptying of the tables; it was already late, though the sunlight still clung to everything, as if accidentally entangled in the trees. In the stillness Flambeau shifted his seat sharply – making an isolated and echoing noise – and threw his elbow over the angle of it. 'Well,' he said, rather harshly, 'if Hirsch is not better than a timid treason-monger . . . '

'You mustn't be too hard on them,' said Father Brown gently. 'It's not entirely their fault; but they have no instincts. I mean those things that make a woman refuse to dance with a man or a man to touch an investment. They've been taught that it's all a matter of degree.'

'Anyhow,' cried Flambeau impatiently, 'he's not a patch on my principal; and I shall go through with it. Old Dubosc may be a bit mad, but he's a sort of patriot after all.'

Father Brown continued to consume whitebait.

Something in the stolid way he did so caused Flambeau's fierce black eyes to ramble over his companion afresh. 'What's the matter with you?' Flambeau demanded. 'Dubosc's all right in that way. You don't doubt him?'

'My friend,' said the small priest, laying down his knife and fork in a kind of cold despair, 'I doubt everything. Everything, I mean, that has happened today. I doubt the whole story, though it has been acted before my face. I doubt every sight that my eyes have seen since morning. There is something in this business quite different from the ordinary police mystery where one man is more or less lying and the other man more or less telling the truth. Here both men . . . Well! I've told you the only theory I can think of that could satisfy anybody. It doesn't satisfy me.'

'Nor me either,' replied Flambeau frowning, while the other went on eating fish with an air of entire resignation. 'If all you can suggest is that notion of a message conveyed by contraries, I call it uncommonly clever, but . . . well, what would you call it?'

'I should call it thin,' said the priest promptly. 'I should call it uncommonly thin. But that's the queer thing about the whole business. The lie is like a schoolboy's. There are only three versions, Dubosc's and Hirsch's and that fancy of mine. Either that note was written by a French officer to ruin a French official; or it was written by the French official to help German officers; or it was written by the French official to mislead German officers. Very well. You'd expect a secret paper passing between such people, officials or officers, to look quite different from that. You'd expect, probably a cipher, certainly abbreviations; most certainly scientific and strictly professional terms. But this thing's elaborately simple, like a penny dreadful: "In the purple grotto you will find the golden casket." It looks as if . . . as if it were meant to be seen through at once.'

Almost before they could take it in a short figure in French uniform had walked up to their table like the wind, and sat down with a sort of thump.

'I have extraordinary news,' said the Duc de Valognes. 'I have just come from this Colonel of ours. He is packing up to leave the country, and he asks us to make his excuses *sur le terrain*.'

'What?' cried Flambeau, with an incredulity quite frightful – '*apologise*?'

'Yes,' said the Duke gruffly; 'then and there – before everybody – when the swords are drawn. And you and I have to do it while he is leaving the country.'

'But what can this mean?' cried Flambeau. 'He can't be afraid of that little Hirsch! Confound it!' he cried, in a kind of rational rage; 'nobody could be afraid of Hirsch!'

'I believe it's some plot!' snapped Valognes – 'some plot of the Jews and Freemasons. It's meant to work up glory for Hirsch . . .'

The face of Father Brown was commonplace, but curiously contented; it could shine with ignorance as well as with knowledge. But there was always one flash when the foolish mask fell, and the wise mask fitted itself in its place; and Flambeau, who knew his friend, knew that his friend had suddenly understood. Brown said nothing, but finished his plate of fish.

'Where did you last see our precious Colonel?' asked Flambeau, irritably.

'He's round at the Hotel Saint Louis by the Elysée, where we drove with him. He's packing up, I tell you.'

'Will he be there still, do you think?' asked Flambeau, frowning at the table.

'I don't think he can get away yet,' replied the Duke; 'he's packing to go a long journey . . .'

'No,' said Father Brown, quite simply, but suddenly standing up, 'for a very short journey. For one of the shortest, in fact. But we may still be in time to catch him if we go there in a motor-cab.'

Nothing more could be got out of him until the cab swept round the corner by the Hotel Saint Louis, where they got out, and he led the party up a side lane already in deep shadow with the growing dusk. Once, when the Duke impatiently asked whether Hirsch was guilty of treason or not, he answered rather absently: 'No; only of ambition – like Caesar.' Then he somewhat inconsequently added: 'He lives a very lonely life; he has had to do everything for himself.'

'Well, if he's ambitious, he ought to be satisfied now,' said Flambeau rather bitterly. 'All Paris will cheer him now our cursed Colonel has turned tail.'

'Don't talk so loud,' said Father Brown, lowering his voice, 'your cursed Colonel is just in front.'

The other two started and shrank farther back into the shadow of the wall, for the sturdy figure of their runaway principal could indeed be seen shuffling along in the twilight in front, a bag in each hand. He looked much the same as when they first saw him, except that he had changed his picturesque mountaineering knickers for a conventional pair of trousers. It was clear he was already escaping from the hotel.

The lane down which they followed him was one of those that seem to be at the back of things, and look like the wrong side of the stage scenery. A colourless, continuous wall ran down one flank of it, interrupted at intervals by dull-hued and dirt-stained doors, all shut fast and featureless save for the chalk scribbles of some passing *gamin*. The tops of trees, mostly rather depressing evergreens, showed at intervals over the top of the wall, and beyond them in the grey and purple gloaming could be seen the back of some long terrace of tall Parisian houses, really comparatively close, but somehow looking as inaccessible as a range of marble mountains. On the other side of the lane ran the high gilt railings of a gloomy park.

Flambeau was looking round him in rather a weird way. 'Do you know,' he said, 'there is something about this place that – '

'Hullo!' called out the Duke sharply; 'that fellow's disappeared. Vanished, like a blasted fairy!'

'He has a key,' explained their clerical friend. 'He's only gone into one of these garden doors,' and as he spoke they heard one of the dull wooden doors close again with a click in front of them.

Flambeau strode up to the door thus shut almost in his face, and stood in front of it for a moment, biting his black moustache in a fury of curiosity. Then he threw up his long arms and swung himself aloft like a monkey and stood on the top of the wall, his enormous figure dark against the purple sky, like the dark tree-tops.

The Duke looked at the priest. 'Dubosc's escape is more elaborate than we thought,' he said; 'but I suppose he is escaping from France.'

'He is escaping from everywhere,' answered Father Brown.

Valognes's eyes brightened, but his voice sank. 'Do you mean suicide?' he asked.

'You will not find his body,' replied the other.

A kind of cry came from Flambeau on the wall above. 'My God,' he exclaimed in French, 'I know what this place is now! Why, it's the back of the street where old Hirsch lives. I thought I could recognise the back of a house as well as the back of a man.'

'And Dubosc's gone in there!' cried the Duke, smiting his hip. 'Why, they'll meet after all!' And with sudden Gallic vivacity he hopped up on the wall beside Flambeau and sat there positively kicking his legs with excitement. The priest alone remained below, leaning against the wall, with his back to the whole theatre of events, and looking wistfully across to the park palings and the twinkling, twilit trees.

The Duke, however stimulated, had the instincts of an aristocrat, and desired rather to stare at the house than to spy on it; but Flambeau, who had the instincts of a burglar (and a detective), had already swung himself from the wall into the fork of a straggling tree from which he could crawl quite close to the only illuminated window in the back of the high dark house. A red blind had been pulled down over the light, but pulled crookedly, so that it gaped on one side, and by risking his neck along a branch that looked as treacherous as a twig, Flambeau could just see Colonel Dubosc walking about in a brilliantly-lighted and luxurious bedroom. But close as Flambeau was to the house, he heard the words of his colleagues by the wall, and repeated them in a low voice.

'Yes, they will meet now after all!'

'They will never meet,' said Father Brown. 'Hirsch was right when he said that in such an affair the principals must not meet. Have you read a queer psychological story by Henry James, of two persons who so perpetually missed meeting each other by accident that they began to feel quite frightened of each other, and to think it was fate? This is something of the kind, but more curious.'

'There are people in Paris who will cure them of such morbid fancies,' said Valognes vindictively. 'They will jolly well have to meet if we capture them and force them to fight.'

'They will not meet on the Day of Judgement,' said the priest. 'If God Almighty held the truncheon of the lists, if St Michael blew the trumpet for the swords to cross – even then, if one of them stood ready, the other would not come.'

'Oh, what does all this mysticism mean?' cried the Duc de Valognes, impatiently; 'why on earth shouldn't they meet like other people?'

'They are the opposite of each other,' said Father Brown, with a queer kind of smile. 'They contradict each other. They cancel out, so to speak.'

He continued to gaze at the darkening trees opposite, but Valognes turned his head sharply at a suppressed exclamation from Flambeau. That investigator, peering into the lighted room, had just seen the Colonel, after a pace or two, proceed to take his coat off. Flambeau's first thought was that this really looked like a fight; but he soon dropped the thought for another. The solidity and squareness of Dubosc's chest and shoulders was all a powerful piece of padding and came off with his coat. In his shirt and trousers he was a comparatively slim gentleman, who walked across the bedroom to the bathroom with no more pugnacious purpose than that of washing himself. He bent over a basin, dried his dripping hands and face on a towel, and turned again so that the strong light fell on his face. His brown complexion had gone, his big black moustache had gone; he was clean-shaven and very pale. Nothing remained of the Colonel but his bright, hawklike, brown eyes. Under the wall Father Brown was going on in heavy meditation, as if to himself.

'It is all just like what I was saying to Flambeau. These opposites won't do. They don't work. They don't fight. If it's white instead of black, and solid instead of liquid, and so on all along the line – then there's something wrong, Monsieur, there's something wrong. One of these men is fair and the other dark, one stout and the other slim, one strong and the other weak. One has a moustache and no beard, so you can't see his mouth; the other has a beard and no moustache, so you can't see his chin. One has hair cropped to his skull, but a scarf to hide his neck; the other has low shirt-collars, but long hair to hide his skull. It's all too neat and correct, Monsieur, and there's something wrong. Things made so opposite are things that cannot quarrel. Wherever the one sticks out the other sinks in. Like a face and a mask, like a lock and a key . . .'

Flambeau was peering into the house with a visage as white as a sheet. The occupant of the room was standing with his back to him, but in front of a looking-glass, and had already fitted round his face a sort of framework of rank red hair, hanging disordered from the head and clinging round the jaws and chin while leaving the mocking mouth uncovered. Seen thus in the glass the white face looked like the face of Judas laughing horribly and surrounded by capering flames of hell. For a spasm Flambeau saw the fierce, red-brown eyes dancing, then they were covered with a pair of blue spectacles. Slipping on a loose black coat, the figure vanished towards the front of the house. A few moments later a roar of popular applause from the street beyond announced that Dr Hirsch had once more appeared upon the balcony.

The Man in the Passage

Two men appeared simultaneously at the two ends of a sort of passage running along the side of the Apollo Theatre in the Adelphi. The evening daylight in the streets was large and luminous, opalescent and empty. The passage was comparatively long and dark, so each man could see the other as a mere black silhouette at the other end. Nevertheless, each man knew the other, even in that inky outline; for they were both men of striking appearance and they hated each other.

The covered passage opened at one end on one of the steep streets of the Adelphi, and at the other on a terrace overlooking the sunset-coloured river. One side of the passage was a blank wall, for the building it supported was an old unsuccessful theatre restaurant, now shut up. The other side of the passage contained two doors, one at each end. Neither was what was commonly called the stage door; they were a sort of special and private stage doors used by very special performers, and in this case by the star actor and actress in the Shakespearean performance of the day. Persons of that eminence often like to have such private exits and entrances, for meeting friends or avoiding them.

The two men in question were certainly two such friends, men who evidently knew the doors and counted on their opening, for each approached the door at the upper end with equal coolness and confidence. Not, however, with equal speed; but the man who walked fast was the man from the other end of the tunnel, so they both arrived before the secret stage door almost at the same instant. They saluted each other with civility, and waited a moment before one of them, the sharper walker who seemed to have the shorter patience, knocked at the door.

In this and everything else each man was opposite and neither could be called inferior. As private persons both were handsome, capable and popular. As public persons, both were in the first public rank. But everything about them, from their glory to their good looks, was of a diverse and incomparable kind. Sir Wilson Seymour was the kind of man whose importance is known to everybody who knows. The more you mixed with the innermost ring in every polity or profession, the more often you met Sir Wilson Seymour. He was the one intelligent man on twenty unintelligent committees – on every sort of subject, from the reform of the Royal Academy to the project of bimetallism for Greater Britain. In the Arts especially he was omnipotent. He was so unique that nobody could quite decide whether he was a great aristocrat who had taken up Art, or a great artist whom the aristocrats had taken up. But you could not meet him for five minutes without realising that you had really been ruled by him all your life.

His appearance was 'distinguished' in exactly the same sense; it was at once conventional and unique. Fashion could have found no fault with his high silk hat, yet it was unlike anyone else's hat – a little higher, perhaps, and adding something to his natural height. His tall, slender figure had a slight stoop yet it looked the reverse of feeble. His hair was silver-grey, but he did not look old; it was worn longer than the common yet he did not look effeminate; it was curly but it did not look curled. His carefully pointed beard made him look more manly and militant than otherwise, as it does in those old admirals of Velazquez with whose dark portraits his house was hung. His grey gloves were a shade bluer, his silver-knobbed cane a shade longer than scores of such gloves and canes flapped and flourished about the theatres and the restaurants.

The other man was not so tall, yet would have struck nobody as short, but merely as strong and handsome. His hair also was curly, but fair and cropped close to a strong, massive head – the sort of head you break a door with, as Chaucer said of the Miller's. His military moustache and the carriage of his shoulders showed him a soldier, but he had a pair of those peculiar frank and piercing blue eyes which are more common in sailors. His face was somewhat square, his jaw was square, his shoulders were square, even his jacket was square. Indeed, in the wild school of caricature then current, Mr Max Beerbohm had represented him as a proposition in the fourth book of Euclid.

For he also was a public man, though with quite another sort of success. You did not have to be in the best society to have heard of Captain Cutler, of the siege of Hong Kong, and the great march across China. You could not get away from hearing of him wherever you were; his portrait was on every other postcard; his maps and battles in every other illustrated paper; songs in his honour in every other music-hall turn or on every other barrel-organ. His fame, though probably more temporary, was ten times more wide, popular and spontaneous than the other man's. In thousands of English homes he appeared enormous above England, like Nelson. Yet he had infinitely less power in England than Sir Wilson Seymour.

The door was opened to them by an aged servant or 'dresser', whose broken-down face and figure and black shabby coat and trousers contrasted queerly with the glittering interior of the great actress's dressing-room. It was fitted and filled with looking-glasses at every angle of refraction, so that they looked like the hundred facets of one huge diamond – if one could get inside a diamond. The other features of luxury, a few flowers, a few coloured cushions, a few scraps of stage costume, were multiplied by all the mirrors into the madness of the Arabian Nights, and danced and changed places perpetually as the shuffling attendant shifted a mirror outwards or shot one back against the wall.

They both spoke to the dingy dresser by name, calling him Parkinson, and asking for the lady as Miss Aurora Rome. Parkinson said she was in the other room, but he would go and tell her. A shade crossed the brow of both visitors; for the other room was the private room of the great actor with whom Miss Aurora was performing, and she was of the kind that does not inflame admiration without inflaming jealousy. In about half a minute, however, the inner door opened, and she entered as she always did, even in private life, so that the very silence seemed to be a roar of applause, and one well-deserved. She was clad in a somewhat strange garb of peacock green and peacock blue satins, that gleamed like blue and green metals, such as delight children and aesthetes, and her heavy, hot brown hair framed one of those magic faces which are dangerous to all men, but especially to boys and to men growing grey. In company with her male colleague, the great American actor, Isidore Bruno, she was producing a particularly poetical and fantastic interpretation of *Midsummer Night's Dream*: in which the artistic prominence was given to Oberon and Titania, or in other words to Bruno and herself. Set in dreamy and exquisite scenery, and moving in mystical dances, the green costume, like burnished beetle-wings, expressed all the elusive individuality of an elfin queen. But when personally confronted in what was still broad daylight, a man looked only at the woman's face.

She greeted both men with the beaming and baffling smile which kept so many males at the same just dangerous distance from her. She accepted some flowers from Cutler, which were as tropical and expensive as his victories; and another sort of present from Sir Wilson Seymour, offered later on and more nonchalantly by that gentleman. For it was against his breeding to show eagerness, and against his conventional unconventionality to give anything so obvious as flowers. He had picked up a trifle, he said, which was rather a curiosity; it was an ancient Greek dagger of the Mycenaean Epoch, and might well have been worn in the time of Theseus and Hippolyta. It was made of brass like all the Heroic weapons, but, oddly enough, sharp enough to prick anyone still. He had really been attracted to it by the leaflike shape; it was as perfect as a Greek vase. If it was of any interest to Miss Rome or could come in anywhere in the play, he hoped she would –

The inner door burst open and a big figure appeared, who was more of a contrast to the explanatory Seymour than even Captain Cutler. Nearly six-foot-six, and of more than theatrical thews and muscles, Isidore Bruno, in the gorgeous leopard skin and golden-brown garments of Oberon, looked like a barbaric god. He leaned on a sort of hunting-spear, which across a theatre looked a slight, silvery wand, but which in the small and comparatively crowded room looked as plain as a pikestaff – and as menacing.

His vivid black eyes rolled volcanically, his bronzed face, handsome as it was, showed at that moment a combination of high cheekbones with set white teeth, which recalled certain American conjectures about his origin in the Southern plantations.

'Aurora,' he began, in that deep voice like a drum of passion that had moved so many audiences, 'will you – '

He stopped indecisively because a sixth figure had suddenly presented itself just inside the doorway – a figure so incongruous in the scene as to be almost comic. It was a very short man in the black uniform of the Roman secular clergy, and looking (especially in such a presence as Bruno's and Aurora's) rather like the wooden Noah out of an ark. He did not, however, seem conscious of any contrast, but said with dull civility: 'I believe Miss Rome sent for me.'

A shrewd observer might have remarked that the emotional temperature rather rose at so unemotional an interruption. The detachment of a professional celibate seemed to reveal to the others that they stood round the woman as a ring of amorous rivals; just as a stranger coming in with frost on his coat will reveal that a room is like a furnace. The presence of the one man who did not care about her increased Miss Rome's sense that everybody else was in love with her, and each in a somewhat dangerous way: the actor with all the appetite of a savage and a spoilt child; the soldier with all the simple selfishness of a man of will rather than mind; Sir Wilson with that daily hardening concentration with which old Hedonists take to a hobby; nay, even the abject Parkinson, who had known her before her triumphs, and who followed her about the room with eyes or feet, with the dumb fascination of a dog.

A shrewd person might also have noted a yet odder thing. The man like a black wooden Noah (who was not wholly without shrewdness) noted it with a considerable but contained amusement. It was evident that the great Aurora, though by no means indifferent to the admiration of the other sex, wanted at this moment to get rid of all the men who admired her and be left alone with the man who did not – did not admire her in that sense at least; for the little priest did admire and even enjoy the firm feminine diplomacy with which she set about her task. There was, perhaps, only one thing that Aurora Rome was clever about, and that was one half of humanity – the other half. The little priest watched, like a Napoleonic campaign, the swift precision of her policy for expelling all while banishing none. Bruno, the big actor, was so babyish that it was easy to send him off in brute sulks, banging the door. Cutler, the British officer, was pachydermatous to ideas, but punctilious about behaviour. He would ignore all hints, but he would die rather than ignore a definite commission from a lady. As to old Seymour, he had to be treated differently; he had to be left to the last. The only way to move him was to appeal to him in confidence as an old friend, to let him into the secret of the clearance. The priest did really admire Miss Rome as she achieved all these three objects in one selected action.

She went across to Captain Cutler and said in her sweetest manner: 'I shall value all these flowers, because they must be your favourite flowers. But they won't be complete, you know, without *my* favourite flower. Do go over to that shop round the corner and get me some lilies-of-the-valley, and then it will be *quite lovely*.'

The first object of her diplomacy, the exit of the enraged Bruno, was at once achieved. He had already handed his spear in a lordly style, like a sceptre, to the piteous Parkinson, and was about to assume one of the cushioned seats like a throne. But at this open appeal to his rival there glowed in his opal eyeballs all the sensitive insolence of the slave; he knotted his enormous brown fists for an instant, and then, dashing open the door, disappeared into his own apartments beyond. But meanwhile Miss Rome's experiment in mobilising the British Army had not succeeded so simply as seemed probable. Cutler had indeed risen stiffly and suddenly, and walked towards the door, hatless, as if at a word of command. But perhaps there was something ostentatiously elegant about the languid figure of Seymour leaning against one of the looking-glasses that brought him up short at the entrance, turning his head this way and that like a bewildered bulldog.

'I must show this stupid man where to go,' said Aurora in a whisper to Seymour, and ran out to the threshold to speed the parting guest.

Seymour seemed to be listening, elegant and unconscious as was his posture, and he seemed relieved when he heard the lady call out some last instructions to the Captain, and then turn sharply and run laughing down the passage towards the other end, the end on the terrace above the Thames. Yet a second or two after Seymour's brow darkened again. A man in his position has so many rivals, and he remembered that at the other end of the passage was the corresponding entrance to Bruno's private room. He did not lose his dignity; he said some civil words to Father Brown about the revival of Byzantine architecture in the Westminster Cathedral, and then, quite naturally, strolled out himself into the upper end of the passage. Father Brown and Parkinson were left alone, and they were neither of them men with a taste for superfluous conversation. The dresser went round the room, pulling out looking-glasses and pushing them in again, his dingy dark coat and trousers looking all the more dismal since he was still holding the festive fairy spear of King Oberon. Every time he pulled out the frame of a new glass, a new black figure of Father Brown appeared; the absurd glass chamber was full of Father Browns, upside down in the air like angels, turning somersaults like acrobats, turning their backs to everybody like very rude persons.

Father Brown seemed quite unconscious of this cloud of witnesses, but followed Parkinson with an idly attentive eye till he took himself and his absurd spear into the farther room of Bruno. Then he abandoned himself to such abstract meditations as always amused him – calculating the angles of the mirrors, the angles of each refraction, the angle at which each must fit into the wall . . . when he heard a strong but strangled cry.

He sprang to his feet and stood rigidly listening. At the same instant Sir Wilson Seymour burst back into the room, white as ivory. 'Who's that man in the passage?' he cried. 'Where's that dagger of mine?'

Before Father Brown could turn in his heavy boots Seymour was plunging about the room looking for the weapon. And before he could possibly find that weapon or any other, a brisk running of feet broke upon the pavement outside, and the square face of Cutler was thrust into the same doorway. He was still grotesquely grasping a bunch of lilies-of-the-valley. 'What's this?' he cried. 'What's that creature down the passage? Is this some of your tricks?'

'My tricks!' hissed his pale rival, and made a stride towards him.

In the instant of time in which all this happened Father Brown stepped out into the top of the passage, looked down it, and at once walked briskly towards what he saw.

At this the other two men dropped their quarrel and darted after him, Cutler calling out: 'What are you doing? Who are you?'

'My name is Brown,' said the priest sadly, as he bent over something and straightened himself again. 'Miss Rome sent for me, and I came as quickly as I could. I have come too late.'

The three men looked down, and in one of them at least the life died in that late light of afternoon. It ran along the passage like a path of gold, and in the midst of it Aurora Rome lay lustrous in her robes of green and gold, with her dead face turned upwards. Her dress was torn away as in a struggle, leaving the right shoulder bare, but the wound from which the blood was welling was on the other side. The brass dagger lay flat and gleaming a yard or so away.

There was a blank stillness for a measurable time, so that they could hear far off a flower-girl's laugh outside Charing Cross, and someone whistling furiously for a taxicab in one of the streets off the Strand. Then the Captain, with a movement so sudden that it might have been passion or play-acting, took Sir Wilson Seymour by the throat.

Seymour looked at him steadily without either fight or fear. 'You need not kill me,' he said in a voice quite cold; 'I shall do that on my own account.'

The Captain's hand hesitated and dropped; and the other added with the same icy candour: 'If I find I haven't the nerve to do it with that dagger I can do it in a month with drink.'

'Drink isn't good enough for me,' replied Cutler, 'but I'll have blood for this before I die. Not yours – but I think I know whose.'

And before the others could appreciate his intention he snatched up the dagger, sprang at the other door at the lower end of the passage, burst it open, bolt and all, and confronted Bruno in his dressing-room. As he did so, old Parkinson tottered in his wavering way out of the door and caught sight of the corpse lying in the passage. He moved shakily towards it; looked at it weakly with a working face; then moved shakily back into the dressing-room again, and sat down suddenly on one of the richly cushioned chairs. Father Brown instantly ran across to him, taking no notice of Cutler and the colossal actor, though the room already rang with their blows and they began to struggle for the dagger. Seymour, who retained some practical sense, was whistling for the police at the end of the passage.

When the police arrived it was to tear the two men from an almost apelike grapple; and, after a few formal enquiries, to arrest Isidore Bruno upon a charge of murder, brought against him by his furious opponent. The idea that the great national hero of the hour had arrested a wrongdoer with his own hand doubtless had its weight with the police, who are not without elements of the journalist. They treated Cutler with a certain solemn attention, and pointed out that he had got a slight slash on the hand. Even as Cutler bore him back across tilted chair and table, Bruno had twisted the dagger out of his grasp and disabled him just below the wrist. The injury was really slight, but till he was removed from the room the half-savage prisoner stared at the running blood with a steady smile.

'Looks a cannibal sort of chap, don't he?' said the constable confidentially to Cutler.

Cutler made no answer, but said sharply a moment after: 'We must attend to the . . . the death . . . ' and his voice escaped from articulation.

'The two deaths,' came in the voice of the priest from the farther side of the room. 'This poor fellow was gone when I got across to him.' And he stood looking down at old Parkinson, who sat in a black huddle on the gorgeous chair. He also had paid his tribute, not without eloquence, to the woman who had died.

The silence was first broken by Cutler, who seemed not untouched by a rough tenderness. 'I wish I was him,' he said huskily. 'I remember he used to watch her wherever she walked more than – anybody. She was his air, and he's dried up. He's just dead.'

'We are all dead,' said Seymour in a strange voice, looking down the road.

They took leave of Father Brown at the corner of the road, with some random apologies for any rudeness they might have shown. Both their faces were tragic, but also cryptic.

The mind of the little priest was always a rabbit-warren of wild thoughts that jumped too quickly for him to catch them. Like the white tail of a rabbit he had the vanishing thought that he was certain of their grief, but not so certain of their innocence.

'We had better all be going,' said Seymour heavily; 'we have done all we can to help.'

'Will you understand my motives,' asked Father Brown quietly, 'if I say you have done all you can to hurt?'

They both started as if guiltily, and Cutler said sharply: 'To hurt whom?'

'To hurt yourselves,' answered the priest. 'I would not add to your troubles if it weren't common justice to warn you. You've done nearly everything you could do to hang yourselves, if this actor should be acquitted. They'll be sure to subpoena me; I shall be bound to say that after the cry was heard each of you rushed into the room in a wild state and began quarrelling about a dagger. As far as my words on oath can go, you might either of you have done it. You hurt yourselves with that; and then Captain Cutler must have hurt himself with the dagger.'

'Hurt myself!' exclaimed the Captain, with contempt. 'A silly little scratch.'

'Which drew blood,' replied the priest, nodding. 'We know there's blood on the brass now. And so we shall never know whether there was blood on it before.'

There was a silence; and then Seymour said, with an emphasis quite alien to his daily accent: 'But I saw a man in the passage.'

'I know you did,' answered the cleric Brown with a face of wood, 'so did Captain Cutler. That's what seems so improbable.'

Before either could make sufficient sense of it even to answer, Father Brown had politely excused himself and gone stumping up the road with his stumpy old umbrella.

As modern newspapers are conducted, the most honest and most important news is the police news. If it be true that in the twentieth century more space is given to murder than to politics, it is for the excellent reason that murder is a more serious subject. But even this would hardly explain the enormous omnipresence and widely distributed detail of 'The Bruno Case', or 'The Passage Mystery', in the Press of London and the provinces. So vast was the excitement that for some weeks the Press really told the truth; and the reports of examination and cross-examination, if interminable, even if intolerable are at least reliable. The true reason, of course, was the coincidence of persons. The victim was a popular actress; the accused was a popular actor; and the accused had been caught red-handed, as it were, by the most popular soldier of the patriotic season. In those extraordinary circumstances the Press was paralysed into probity and accuracy; and the rest of this somewhat singular business can practically be recorded from reports of Bruno's trial.

The trial was presided over by Mr Justice Monkhouse, one of those who are jeered at as humorous judges, but who are generally much more serious than the serious judges, for their levity comes from a living impatience of professional solemnity; while the serious judge is really filled with frivolity, because he is filled with vanity. All the chief actors being of a worldly importance, the barristers were well balanced; the prosecutor for the Crown was Sir Walter Cowdray, a heavy, but weighty advocate of the sort that knows how to seem English and trustworthy, and how to be rhetorical with reluctance. The prisoner was defended by Mr Patrick Butler, K.C., who was mistaken for a mere *flâneur* by those who misunderstood the Irish character – and those who had not been examined by him. The medical evidence involved no contradictions, the doctor, whom Seymour had summoned on the spot, agreeing with the eminent surgeon who had later examined the body. Aurora Rome had been stabbed with some sharp instrument such as a knife or dagger; some instrument, at least, of which the blade was short. The wound was just over the heart, and she had died instantly. When the doctor first saw her she could hardly have been dead for twenty minutes. Therefore when Father Brown found her she could hardly have been dead for three.

Some official detective evidence followed, chiefly concerned with the presence or absence of any proof of a struggle; the only suggestion of this was the tearing of the dress at the shoulder, and this did not seem to fit in particularly well with the direction and finality of the blow. When these details had been supplied, though not explained, the first of the important witnesses was called.

Sir Wilson Seymour gave evidence as he did everything else that he did at all – not only well, but perfectly. Though himself much more of a public man than the judge, he conveyed exactly the fine shade of self-effacement before the King's justice; and though everyone looked at him as they would at the Prime Minister or the Archbishop of Canterbury, they could have said nothing of his part in it but that it was that of a private gentleman, with an accent on the noun. He was also refreshingly lucid, as he was on the committees. He had been calling on Miss Rome at the theatre; he had met Captain Cutler there; they had been joined for a short time by the accused, who had then returned to his own dressing-room; they had then been joined by a Roman Catholic priest, who asked for the deceased lady and said his name was Brown. Miss Rome had then gone just outside the theatre to the entrance of the passage, in order to point out to Captain Cutler a flower-shop at which he was to buy her some more flowers; and the witness had remained in the room, exchanging a few words with the priest. He had then distinctly heard the deceased, having sent the Captain on his errand, turn round laughing and run down the passage towards its other end, where was the prisoner's dressing-room. In idle curiosity as to the rapid movement of his friends, he had strolled out to the head of the passage himself and looked down it towards the prisoner's door. Did he see anything in the passage? Yes; he saw something in the passage.

Sir Walter Cowdray allowed an impressive interval, during which the witness looked down, and for all his usual composure seemed to have more than his usual pallor. Then the barrister said in a lower voice, which seemed at once sympathetic and creepy: 'Did you see it distinctly?'

Sir Wilson Seymour, however moved, had his excellent brains in full working-order. 'Very distinctly as regards its outline, but quite indistinctly, indeed not at all, as regards the details inside the outline. The passage is of such length that anyone in the middle of it appears quite black against the light at the other end.' The witness lowered his steady eyes once more and added: 'I had noticed the fact before, when Captain Cutler first entered it.' There was another silence, and the judge leaned forward and made a note.

'Well,' said Sir Walter patiently, 'what was the outline like? Was it, for instance, like the figure of the murdered woman?'

'Not in the least,' answered Seymour quietly.

'What did it look like to you?'

'It looked to me,' replied the witness, 'like a tall man.'

Everyone in court kept his eyes riveted on his pen, or his umbrella-handle, or his book, or his boots or whatever he happened to be looking at. They seemed to be holding their eyes away from the prisoner by main force; but they felt his figure in the dock, and they felt it as gigantic. Tall as Bruno was to the eye, he seemed to swell taller and taller when all eyes had been torn away from him.

Cowdray was resuming his seat with his solemn face, smoothing his black silk robes, and white silk whiskers. Sir Wilson was leaving the witness-box, after a few final particulars to which there were many other witnesses, when the counsel for the defence sprang up and stopped him.

'I shall only detain you a moment,' said Mr Butler, who was a rustic-looking person with red eyebrows and an expression of partial slumber. 'Will you tell his lordship how you knew it was a man?'

A faint, refined smile seemed to pass over Seymour's features. 'I'm afraid it is the vulgar test of trousers,' he said. 'When I saw daylight between the long legs I was sure it was a man, after all.'

Butler's sleepy eyes opened as suddenly as some silent explosion. 'After all!' he repeated slowly. 'So you did think at first it was a woman?'

Seymour looked troubled for the first time. 'It is hardly a point of fact,' he said, 'but if his lordship would like me to answer for my impression, of course I shall do so. There was something about the thing that was not exactly a woman and yet was not quite a man; somehow the curves were different. And it had something that looked like long hair.'

'Thank you,' said Mr Butler, K.C., and sat down suddenly, as if he had got what he wanted.

Captain Cutler was a far less plausible and composed witness than Sir Wilson, but his account of the opening incidents was solidly the same. He described the return of Bruno to his dressing-room, the dispatching of himself to buy a bunch of lilies-of-the-valley, his return to the upper end of the passage, the thing he saw in the passage, his suspicion of Seymour, and his struggle with Bruno. But he could give little artistic assistance about the black figure that he and Seymour had seen. Asked about its outline, he said he was no art critic – with a somewhat too obvious sneer at Seymour. Asked if it was a man or a woman, he said it looked more like a beast – with a too obvious snarl at the prisoner. But the man was plainly shaken with sorrow and sincere anger, and Cowdray quickly excused him from confirming facts that were already fairly clear.

The defending counsel also was again brief in his cross-examination; although (as was his custom) even in being brief, he seemed to take a long time about it. 'You used a rather remarkable expression,' he said, looking at Cutler sleepily. 'What do you mean by saying that it looked more like a beast than a man or a woman?'

Cutler seemed seriously agitated. 'Perhaps I oughtn't to have said that,' he said; 'but when the brute has huge humped shoulders like a chimpanzee, and bristles sticking out of its head like a pig – '

Mr Butler cut short his curious impatience in the middle. 'Never mind whether its hair was like a pig's,' he said, 'was it like a woman's?'

'A woman's!' cried the soldier. 'Great Scott, no!'

'The last witness said it was,' commented the counsel, with unscrupulous swiftness. 'And did the figure have any of those serpentine and semi-feminine curves to which eloquent allusion has been made? No? No feminine curves? The figure, if I understand you, was rather heavy and square than otherwise?'

'He may have been bending forward,' said Cutler, in a hoarse and rather faint voice.

'Or again, he may not,' said Mr Butler, and sat down suddenly for the second time.

The third witness called by Sir Walter Cowdray was the little Catholic clergyman, so little, compared with the others, that his head seemed hardly to come above the box, so that it was like cross-examining a child. But unfortunately Sir Walter had somehow got it into his head (mostly by some ramifications of his family's religion) that Father Brown was on the side of the prisoner, because the prisoner was wicked and foreign and even partly black. Therefore he took Father Brown up sharply whenever that proud pontiff tried to explain anything; and told him to answer yes or no, and tell the plain facts without any jesuitry. When Father Brown began, in his simplicity, to say who he thought the man in the passage was, the barrister told him that he did not want his theories.

'A black shape was seen in the passage. And you say you saw the black shape. Well, what shape was it?'

Father Brown blinked as under rebuke; but he had long known the literal nature of obedience. 'The shape,' he said, 'was short and thick, but had two sharp, black projections curved upwards on each side of the head or top, rather like horns, and – '

'Oh! the devil with horns, no doubt,' ejaculated Cowdray, sitting down in triumphant jocularity. 'It was the devil come to eat Protestants.'

'No,' said the priest dispassionately; 'I know who it was.'

Those in court had been wrought up to an irrational, but real sense of some monstrosity. They had forgotten the figure in the dock and thought only of the figure in the passage. And the figure in the passage, described by three capable and respectable men who had all seen it, was a shifting nightmare: one called it a woman, and the other a beast, and the other a devil . . .

The judge was looking at Father Brown with level and piercing eyes. 'You are a most extraordinary witness,' he said; 'but there is something about you that makes me think you are trying to tell the truth. Well, who was the man you saw in the passage?'

'He was myself,' said Father Brown.

Butler, K.C., sprang to his feet in an extraordinary stillness, and said quite calmly: 'Your lordship will allow me to cross-examine?' And then, without stopping, he shot at Brown the apparently disconnected question: 'You have heard about this dagger; you know the experts say the crime was committed with a short blade?'

'A short blade,' assented Brown, nodding solemnly like an owl, 'but a very long hilt.'

Before the audience could quite dismiss the idea that the priest had really seen himself doing murder with a short dagger with a long hilt (which seemed somehow to make it more horrible), he had himself hurried on to explain.

'I mean daggers aren't the only things with short blades. Spears have short blades. And spears catch at the end of the steel just like daggers, if they're that sort of fancy spear they had in theatres; like the spear poor old Parkinson killed his wife with, just when she'd sent for me to settle their family troubles – and I came just too late, God forgive me! But he died penitent – he just died of being penitent. He couldn't bear what he'd done.'

The general impression in court was that the little priest, who was gabbling away, had literally gone mad in the box. But the judge still looked at him with bright and steady eyes of interest; and the counsel for the defence went on with his questions unperturbed.

'If Parkinson did it with that pantomime spear,' said Butler, 'he must have thrust from four yards away. How do you account for signs of struggle, like the dress dragged off the shoulder?' He had slipped into treating his mere witness as an expert; but no one noticed it now.

'The poor lady's dress was torn,' said the witness, 'because it was caught in a panel that slid to just behind her. She struggled to free herself, and as she did so Parkinson came out of the prisoner's room and lunged with the spear.'

'A panel?' repeated the barrister in a curious voice.

'It was a looking-glass on the other side,' explained Father Brown. 'When I was in the dressing-room I noticed that some of them could probably be slid out into the passage.'

There was another vast and unnatural silence, and this time it was the judge who spoke. 'So you really mean that when you looked down that passage, the man you saw was yourself – in a mirror?'

'Yes, my lord; that was what I was trying to say,' said Brown, 'but they asked me for the shape; and our hats have corners just like horns, and so I – '

The judge leaned forward, his old eyes yet more brilliant, and said in specially distinct tones: 'Do you really mean to say that when Sir Wilson Seymour saw that wild what-you-call-him with curves and a woman's hair and a man's trousers, what he saw was Sir Wilson Seymour?'

'Yes, my lord,' said Father Brown.

'And you mean to say that when Captain Cutler saw that chimpanzee with humped shoulders and hog's bristles, he simply saw himself?'

'Yes, my lord.'

The judge leaned back in his chair with a luxuriance in which it was hard to separate the cynicism and the admiration. 'And can you tell us why,' he asked, 'you should know your own figure in a looking-glass, when two such distinguished men don't?'

Father Brown blinked even more painfully than before; then he stammered: 'Really, my lord, I don't know . . . unless it's because I don't look at it so often.'

The Mistake of the Machine

Flambeau and his friend the priest were sitting in the Temple Gardens about sunset; and their neighbourhood or some such accidental influence had turned their talk to matters of legal process. From the problem of the licence in cross-examination, their talk strayed to Roman and mediaeval torture, to the examining magistrate in France and the Third Degree in America.

'I've been reading,' said Flambeau, 'of this new psychometric method they talk about so much, especially in America. You know what I mean; they put a pulsometer on a man's wrist and judge by how his heart goes at the pronunciation of certain words. What do you think of it?'

'I think it very interesting,' replied Father Brown; 'it reminds me of that interesting idea in the Dark Ages that blood would flow from a corpse if the murderer touched it.'

'Do you really mean,' demanded his friend, 'that you think the two methods equally valuable?'

'I think them equally valueless,' replied Brown. 'Blood flows, fast or slow, in dead folk or living, for so many more million reasons than we can ever know. Blood will have to flow very funnily; blood will have to flow up the Matterhorn, before I will take it as a sign that I am to shed it.'

'The method,' remarked the other, 'has been guaranteed by some of the greatest American men of science.'

'What sentimentalists men of science are!' exclaimed Father Brown, 'and how much more sentimental must American men of science be! Who but a Yankee would think of proving anything from heart-throbs? Why, they must be as sentimental as a man who thinks a woman is in love with him if she blushes. That's a test from the circulation of the blood, discovered by the immortal Harvey; and a jolly rotten test, too.'

'But surely,' insisted Flambeau, 'it might point pretty straight at something or other.'

'There's a disadvantage in a stick pointing straight,' answered the other. 'What is it? Why, the other end of the stick always points the opposite way. It depends whether you get hold of the stick by the right end. I saw the thing done once and I've never believed in it since.' And he proceeded to tell the story of his disillusionment.

* * *

It happened nearly twenty years before, when he was chaplain to his co-religionists in a prison in Chicago – where the Irish population displayed a capacity both for crime and penitence which kept him tolerably busy. The official second-in-command under the Governor was an ex-detective named Greywood Usher, a cadaverous, careful-spoken Yankee philosopher, occasionally varying a very rigid visage with an odd apologetic grimace. He liked Father Brown in a slightly patronising way; and Father Brown liked him, though he heartily disliked his theories. His theories were extremely complicated and were held with extreme simplicity.

One evening he had sent for the priest, who, according to his custom, took a seat in silence at a table piled and littered with papers, and waited. The official selected from the papers a scrap of newspaper cutting, which he handed across to the cleric, who read it gravely. It appeared to be an extract from one of the pinkest of American Society papers, and ran as follows: 'Society's brightest widower is once more on the Freak Dinner stunt. All our exclusive citizens will recall the Perambulator Parade Dinner, in which Last-Trick Todd, at his palatial home at Pilgrim's Pond, caused so many of our prominent *débutantes* to look even younger than their years. Equally elegant and more miscellaneous and large-hearted in social outlook was Last-Trick's show the year previous, the popular Cannibal Crush Lunch, at which the confections handed round were sarcastically moulded in the forms of human arms and legs, and during which more than one of our gayest mental gymnasts was heard offering to eat his partner. The witticism which will inspire this evening is as yet in Mr Todd's pretty reticent intellect, or locked in the jewelled bosoms of our city's gayest leaders; but there is talk of a pretty parody of the simple manners and customs at the other end of Society's scale. This would be all the more telling, as hospitable Todd is entertaining in Lord Falconroy, the famous traveller, a true-blooded aristocrat fresh from England's oak-groves. Lord Falconroy's travels began before his ancient feudal title was resurrected; he was in the Republic in his youth, and fashion murmurs a sly reason for his return. Miss Etta Todd is one of our deep-souled New Yorkers, and comes into an income of nearly twelve hundred million dollars.'

'Well,' asked Usher, 'does that interest you?'

'Why, words rather fail me,' answered Father Brown. 'I cannot think at this moment of anything in this world that would interest me less. And, unless the just anger of the Republic is at last going to electrocute journalists for writing like that, I don't quite see why it should interest you either.'

'Ah!' said Mr Usher dryly, and handing across another scrap of newspaper. 'Well, does that interest you?'

The paragraph was headed 'Savage Murder of a Warder. Convict Escapes', and ran: 'Just before dawn this morning a shout for help was heard in the

Convict Settlement at Sequah in this State. The authorities, hurrying in the direction of the cry, found the corpse of the warder who patrols the top of the north wall of the prison, the steepest and most difficult exit, for which one man has always been found sufficient. The unfortunate officer had, however, been hurled from the high wall, his brains beaten out as with a club, and his gun was missing. Further enquiries showed that one of the cells was empty; it had been occupied by a rather sullen ruffian giving his name as Oscar Rian. He was only temporarily detained for some comparatively trivial assault; but he gave everyone the impression of a man with a black past and a dangerous future. Finally, when daylight had fully revealed the scene of murder, it was found that he had written on the wall above the body a fragmentary sentence, apparently with a finger dipped in blood: "This was self-defence and he had the gun. I meant no harm to him or any man but one. I am keeping the bullet for Pilgrim's Pond – O.R." A man must have used most fiendish treachery or most savage and amazing bodily daring to have stormed such a wall in spite of an armed man.'

'Well, the literary style is somewhat improved,' admitted the priest cheerfully, 'but still I don't see what I can do for you. I should cut a poor figure, with my short legs, running about this State after an athletic assassin of that sort. I doubt whether anybody could find him. The convict settlement at Sequah is thirty miles from here; the country between is wild and tangled enough, and the country beyond, where he will surely have the sense to go, is a perfect no-man's land tumbling away to the prairies. He may be in any hole or up any tree.'

'He isn't in any hole,' said the governor; 'he isn't up any tree.'

'Why, how do you know?' asked Father Brown, blinking.

'Would you like to speak to him?' enquired Usher.

Father Brown opened his innocent eyes wide. 'He is here?' he exclaimed. 'Why, how did your men get hold of him?'

'I got hold of him myself,' drawled the American, rising and lazily stretching his lanky legs before the fire. 'I got hold of him with the crooked end of a walking-stick. Don't look so surprised. I really did. You know I sometimes take a turn in the country lanes outside this dismal place; well, I was walking early this evening up a steep lane with dark hedges and grey-looking ploughed fields on both sides; and a young moon was up and silvering the road. By the light of it I saw a man running across the field towards the road; running with his body bent and at a good mile-race trot. He appeared to be much exhausted; but when he came to the thick black hedge he went through it as if it were made of spiders' webs; – or rather (for I heard the strong branches breaking and snapping like bayonets) as if he himself were made of stone. In the instant in which he appeared up against the moon, crossing the road, I slung my hooked cane at his legs, tripping him and bringing him down. Then I blew my whistle long and loud, and our fellows came running up to secure him.'

'It would have been rather awkward,' remarked Brown, 'if you had found he was a popular athlete practising a mile race.'

'He was not,' said Usher grimly. 'We soon found out who he was; but I had guessed it with the first glint of the moon on him.'

'You thought it was the runaway convict,' observed the priest simply, 'because you had read in the newspaper cutting that morning that a convict had run away.'

'I had somewhat better grounds,' replied the governor coolly. 'I pass over the first as too simple to be emphasised – I mean that fashionable athletes do not run across ploughed fields or scratch their eyes out in bramble hedges. Nor do they run all doubled up like a crouching dog. There were more decisive details to a fairly well-trained eye. The man was clad in coarse and ragged clothes, but they were something more than merely coarse and ragged. They were so ill-fitting as to be quite grotesque; even as he appeared in black outline against the moonrise, the coat-collar in which his head was buried made him look like a hunchback, and the long loose sleeves looked as if he had no hands. It at once occurred to me that he had somehow managed to change his convict clothes for some confederate's clothes which did not fit him. Second, there was a pretty stiff wind against which he was running; so that I must have seen the streaky look of blowing hair, if the hair had not been very short. Then I remembered that beyond these ploughed fields he was crossing lay Pilgrim's Pond, for which (you will remember) the convict was keeping his bullet; and I sent my walking-stick flying.'

'A brilliant piece of rapid deduction,' said Father Brown; 'but had he got a gun?'

As Usher stopped abruptly in his walk the priest added apologetically: 'I've been told a bullet is not half so useful without it.'

'He had no gun,' said the other gravely; 'but that was doubtless due to some very natural mischance or change of plans. Probably the same policy that made him change the clothes made him drop the gun; he began to repent the coat he had left behind him in the blood of his victim.'

'Well, that is possible enough,' answered the priest.

'And it's hardly worth speculating on,' said Usher, turning to some other papers, 'for we know it's the man by this time.'

His clerical friend asked faintly: 'But how?' And Greywood Usher threw down the newspapers and took up the two press-cuttings again.

'Well, since you are so obstinate,' he said, 'let's begin at the beginning. You will notice that these two cuttings have only one thing in common, which is the mention of Pilgrim's Pond, the estate, as you know, of the millionaire Ireton Todd. You also know that he is a remarkable character; one of those that rose on stepping-stones – '

'Of our dead selves to higher things,' assented his companion. 'Yes; I know that. Petroleum, I think.'

'Anyhow,' said Usher, 'Last-Trick Todd counts for a great deal in this rum affair.'

He stretched himself once more before the fire and continued talking in his expansive, radiantly explanatory style.

'To begin with, on the face of it, there is no mystery here at all. It is not mysterious, it is not even odd, that a jailbird should take his gun to Pilgrim's Pond. Our people aren't like the English, who will forgive a man for being rich if he throws away money on hospitals or horses. Last-Trick Todd has made himself big by his own considerable abilities; and there's no doubt that many of those on whom he has shown his abilities would like to show theirs on him with a shotgun. Todd might easily get dropped by some man he'd never even heard of; some labourer he'd locked out, or some clerk in a business he'd busted. Last-Trick is a man of mental endowments and a high public character; but in this country the relations of employers and employed are considerably strained.

'That's how the whole thing looks supposing this Rian made for Pilgrim's Pond to kill Todd. So it looked to me, till another little discovery woke up what I have of the detective in me. When I had my prisoner safe, I picked up my cane again and strolled down the two or three turns of country road that brought me to one of the side entrances of Todd's grounds, the one nearest to the pool or lake after which the place is named. It was some two hours ago, about seven by this time; the moonlight was more luminous, and I could see the long white streaks of it lying on the mysterious mere with its grey, greasy, half-liquid shores in which they say our fathers used to make witches walk until they sank. I'd forgotten the exact tale; but you know the place I mean; it lies north of Todd's house towards the wilderness, and has two queer wrinkled trees, so dismal that they look more like huge fungoids than decent foliage. As I stood peering at this misty pool, I fancied I saw the faint figure of a man moving from the house towards it, but it was all too dim and distant for one to be certain of the fact, and still less of the details. Besides, my attention was very sharply arrested by something much closer. I crouched behind the fence which ran not more than two hundred yards from one wing of the great mansion, and which was fortunately split in places, as if specially for the application of a cautious eye. A door had opened in the dark bulk of the left wing, and a figure appeared black against the illuminated interior – a muffled figure bending forward, evidently peering out into the night. It closed the door behind it, and I saw it was carrying a lantern, which threw a patch of imperfect light on the dress and figure of the wearer. It seemed to be the figure of a woman, wrapped up in a ragged cloak and evidently disguised to avoid notice; there was something very strange both about the rags and the furtiveness in a person coming out of those rooms lined with gold. She took cautiously the curved garden path which brought her within half a hundred yards of me, then she stood up for an instant on the terrace of turf that looks towards the slimy lake, and holding her flaming lantern above her head she deliberately swung it three times to and fro as for a signal. As she swung it the second time a flicker of its light fell for a moment on her own face, a face that I knew. She was unnaturally pale, and her head was bundled in her borrowed plebeian shawl; but I am certain it was Etta Todd, the millionaire's daughter.

'She retraced her steps in equal secrecy and the door closed behind her again. I was about to climb the fence and follow, when I realised that the detective fever that had lured me into the adventure was rather undignified; and that in a more authoritative capacity I already held all the cards in my hand. I was just turning away when a new noise broke on the night. A window was thrown up in one of the upper floors, but just round the corner of the house so that I could not see it; and a voice of terrible distinctness was heard shouting across the dark garden to know where Lord Falconroy was, for he was missing from every room in the house. There was no mistaking that voice. I have heard it on many a political platform or meeting of directors; it was Ireton Todd himself. Some of the others seemed to have gone to the lower windows or on to the steps, and were calling up to him that Falconroy had gone for a stroll down to the Pilgrim's Pond an hour before, and could not be traced since. Then Todd cried "Mighty Murder!" and shut down the window violently; and I could hear him plunging down the stairs inside. Repossessing myself of my former and wiser purpose, I whipped out of the way of the general search that must follow; and returned here not later than eight o'clock.

'I now ask you to recall that little Society paragraph which seemed to you so painfully lacking in interest. If the convict was not keeping the shot for Todd, as he evidently wasn't, it is most likely that he was keeping it for Lord Falconroy; and it looks as if he had delivered the goods. No more handy place to shoot a man than in the curious geological surroundings of that pool, where a body thrown down would sink through thick slime to a depth practically unknown. Let us suppose, then, that our friend with the cropped hair came to kill Falconroy and not Todd. But, as I have pointed out, there are many reasons why people in America might want to kill Todd. There is no reason why anybody in America should want to kill an English lord newly landed, except for the one reason mentioned in the pink paper – that the lord is paying his attentions to the millionaire's daughter. Our crop-haired friend, despite his ill-fitting clothes, must be an aspiring lover.

'I know the notion will seem to you jarring and even comic; but that's because you are English. It sounds to you like saying the Archbishop of Canterbury's daughter will be married in St George's, Hanover Square, to a crossing-sweeper on ticket-of-leave. You don't do justice to the climbing and aspiring power of our more remarkable citizens. You see a good-looking grey-haired man in evening dress with a sort of authority about him, you know he is a pillar of the State, and you fancy he had a father. You are in error. You do not realise that a comparatively few years ago he may have been in a tenement or (quite likely) in a jail. You don't allow for our national buoyancy and uplift. Many of our most influential citizens have not only risen recently, but risen comparatively late in life. Todd's daughter was fully eighteen when her father first made his pile; so there isn't really anything impossible in her having a hanger-on in low life; or even in her hanging on to him, as I think she must be doing, to judge by the lantern business. If so, the hand that held the lantern may not be unconnected with the hand that held the gun. This case, sir, will make a noise.'

'Well,' said the priest patiently, 'and what did you do next?'

'I reckon you'll be shocked,' replied Greywood Usher, 'as I know you don't cotton to the march of science in these matters. I am given a good deal of discretion here, and perhaps take a little more than I'm given; and I thought it was an excellent opportunity to test that Psychometric Machine I told you about. Now, in my opinion, that machine can't lie.'

'No machine can lie,' said Father Brown; 'nor can it tell the truth.'

'It did in this case, as I'll show you,' went on Usher positively. 'I sat the man in the ill-fitting clothes in a comfortable chair, and simply wrote words on a blackboard; and the machine simply recorded the variations of his pulse; and I simply observed his manner. The trick is to introduce some word connected with the supposed crime in a list of words connected with something quite different, yet a list in which it occurs quite naturally. Thus I wrote "heron" and "eagle" and "owl", and when I wrote "falcon" he was tremendously agitated; and when I began to make an "r" at the end of the word, that machine just bounded. Who else in this republic has any reason to jump at the name of a newly-arrived Englishman like Falconroy except the man who's shot him? Isn't that better evidence than a lot of gabble from witnesses – if the evidence of a reliable machine?'

'You always forget,' observed his companion, 'that the reliable machine always has to be worked by an unreliable machine.'

'Why, what do you mean?' asked the detective.

'I mean Man,' said Father Brown, 'the most unreliable machine I know of. I don't want to be rude; and I don't think you will consider Man to be an offensive or inaccurate description of yourself. You say you observed his manner; but how do you know you observed it right? You say the words have to come in a natural way; but how do you know that you did it naturally? How do you know, if you come to that, that he did not observe your manner? Who is to prove that you were not tremendously agitated? There was no machine tied on to your pulse.'

'I tell you,' cried the American in the utmost excitement, 'I was as cool as a cucumber.'

'Criminals also can be as cool as cucumbers,' said Brown with a smile. 'And almost as cool as you.'

'Well, this one wasn't,' said Usher, throwing the papers about. 'Oh, you make me tired!'

'I'm sorry,' said the other. 'I only point out what seems a reasonable possibility. If you could tell by his manner when the word that might hang him had come, why shouldn't he tell from your manner that the word that might hang him was coming? I should ask for more than words myself before I hanged anybody.'

Usher smote the table and rose in a sort of angry triumph.

'And that,' he cried, 'is just what I'm going to give you. I tried the machine first just in order to test the thing in other ways afterwards and the machine, sir, is right.'

He paused a moment and resumed with less excitement. 'I rather want to insist, if it comes to that, that so far I had very little to go on except the scientific experiment. There was really nothing against the man at all. His clothes were ill-fitting, as I've said, but they were rather better, if anything, than those of the submerged class to which he evidently belonged. Moreover, under all the stains of his plunging through ploughed fields or bursting through dusty hedges, the man was comparatively clean. This might mean, of course, that he had only just broken prison; but it reminded me more of the desperate decency of the comparatively respectable poor. His demeanour was, I am bound to confess, quite in accordance with theirs. He was silent and dignified as they are; he seemed to have a big, but buried, grievance, as they do. He professed total ignorance of the crime and the whole question; and showed nothing but a sullen impatience for something sensible that might come to take him out of his meaningless scrape. He asked me more than once if he could telephone for a lawyer who had helped him a long time ago in a trade dispute, and in every sense acted as you would expect an innocent man to act. There was nothing against him in the world except that little finger on the dial that pointed to the change of his pulse.

'Then, sir, the machine was on its trial; and the machine was right. By the time I came with him out of the private room into the vestibule where all sorts of other people were awaiting examination, I think he had already more or less made up his mind to clear things up by something like a confession. He turned to me and began to say in a low voice: "Oh, I can't stick this any more. If you must know all about me – "

'At the same instant one of the poor women sitting on the long bench stood up, screaming aloud and pointing at him with her finger. I have never in my life heard anything more demoniacally distinct. Her lean finger seemed to pick him out as if it were a pea-shooter. Though the word was a mere howl, every syllable was as clear as a separate stroke on the clock.

' "Drugger Davis!" she shouted. "They've got Drugger Davis!" '

'Among the wretched women, mostly thieves and streetwalkers, twenty faces were turned, gaping with glee and hate. If I had never heard the words, I should have known by the very shock upon his features that the so-called Oscar Rian had heard his real name. But I'm not quite so ignorant, you may be surprised to hear. Drugger Davis was one of the most terrible and depraved criminals that ever baffled our police. It is certain he had done murder more than once long before his last exploit with the warder. But he was never entirely fixed for it, curiously enough because he did it in the same manner as those milder – or meaner – crimes for which he was fixed pretty often. He was a handsome, well-bred-looking brute, as he still is, to some extent; and he used mostly to go about with barmaids or shop-girls and do them out of their money. Very often, though, he went a good deal farther; and they were found drugged with cigarettes or chocolates and their whole property missing. Then came one case where the girl was found dead; but deliberation could not quite be proved, and, what was more practical still, the criminal could not be found. I heard a rumour of his having reappeared somewhere in the opposite character this time, lending money instead of borrowing it; but still to such poor widows as he might personally fascinate, but still with the same bad result for them. Well, there is your innocent man, and there is his innocent record. Even, since then, four criminals and three warders have identified him and confirmed the story. Now what have you got to say to my poor little machine after that? Hasn't the machine done for him? Or do you prefer to say that the woman and I have done for him?'

'As to what you've done for him,' replied Father Brown, rising and shaking himself in a floppy way, 'you've saved him from the electrical chair. I don't think they can kill Drugger Davis on that old vague story of the poison; and as for the convict who killed the warder, I suppose it's obvious that you haven't got him. Mr Davis is innocent of that crime, at any rate.'

'What do you mean?' demanded the other. 'Why should he be innocent of that crime?'

'Why, bless us all!' cried the small man in one of his rare moments of animation, 'why, because he's guilty of the other crimes! I don't know what you people are made of. You seem to think that all sins are kept together in a bag. You talk as if a miser on Monday were always a spendthrift on Tuesday.

You tell me this man you have here spent weeks and months wheedling needy women out of small sums of money; that he used a drug at the best, and a poison at the worst; that he turned up afterwards as the lowest kind of moneylender, and cheated most poor people in the same patient and pacific style. Let it be granted – let us admit, for the sake of argument, that he did all this. If that is so, I will tell you what he didn't do. He didn't storm a spiked wall against a man with a loaded gun. He didn't write on the wall with his own hand, to say he had done it. He didn't stop to state that his justification was self-defence. He didn't explain that he had no quarrel with the poor warder. He didn't name the house of the rich man to which he was going with the gun. He didn't write his own initials in a man's blood. Saints alive! Can't you see the whole character is different, in good and evil? Why, you don't seem to be like I am a bit. One would think you'd never had any vices of your own.'

The amazed American had already parted his lips in protest when the door of his private and official room was hammered and rattled in an unceremonious way to which he was totally unaccustomed.

The door flew open. The moment before Greywood Usher had been coming to the conclusion that Father Brown might possibly be mad. The moment after he began to think he was mad himself. There burst and fell into his private room a man in the filthiest rags, with a greasy squash hat still askew on his head, and a shabby green shade shoved up from one of his eyes, both of which were glaring like a tiger's. The rest of his face was almost undiscoverable, being masked with a matted beard and whiskers through which the nose could barely thrust itself, and further buried in a squalid red scarf or handkerchief. Mr Usher prided himself on having seen most of the roughest specimens in the State, but he thought he had never seen such a baboon dressed as a scarecrow as this. But, above all, he had never in all his placid scientific existence heard a man like that speak to him first.

'See here, old man Usher,' shouted the being in the red handkerchief, 'I'm getting tired. Don't you try any of your hide-and-seek on me; I don't get fooled any. Leave go of my guests, and I'll let up on the fancy clockwork. Keep him here for a split instant and you'll feel pretty mean. I reckon I'm not a man with no pull.'

The eminent Usher was regarding the bellowing monster with an amazement which had dried up all other sentiments. The mere shock to his eyes had rendered his ears almost useless. At last he rang a bell with a hand of violence. While the bell was still strong and pealing, the voice of Father Brown fell soft but distinct.

'I have a suggestion to make,' he said, 'but it seems a little confusing. I don't know this gentleman – but – but I think I know him. Now, you know him – you know him quite well – but you don't know him – naturally. Sounds paradoxical, I know.'

'I reckon the Cosmos is cracked,' said Usher, and fell asprawl in his round office chair.

'Now, see here,' vociferated the stranger, striking the table, but speaking in a voice that was all the more mysterious because it was comparatively mild and rational though still resounding. 'I won't let you in. I want – '

'Who in hell are you?' yelled Usher, suddenly sitting up straight.

'I think the gentleman's name is Todd,' said the priest.

Then he picked up the pink slip of newspaper.

'I fear you don't read the Society papers properly,' he said, and began to read out in a monotonous voice, ' "Or locked in the jewelled bosoms of our city's gayest leaders; but there is talk of a pretty parody of the manners and customs of the other end of Society's scale." There's been a big Slum Dinner up at Pilgrim's Pond tonight; and a man, one of the guests, disappeared. Mr Ireton Todd is a good host, and has tracked him here, without even waiting to take off his fancy-dress.'

'What man do you mean?'

'I mean the man with comically ill-fitting clothes you saw running across the ploughed field. Hadn't you better go and investigate him? He will be rather impatient to get back to his champagne, from which he ran away in such a hurry, when the convict with the gun hove in sight.'

'Do you seriously mean – ' began the official.

'Why, look here, Mr Usher,' said Father Brown quietly, 'you said the machine couldn't make a mistake; and in one sense it didn't. But the other machine did; the machine that worked it. You assumed that the man in rags jumped at the name of Lord Falconroy, because he was Lord Falconroy's murderer. He jumped at the name of Lord Falconroy because he is Lord Falconroy.'

'Then why the blazes didn't he say so?' demanded the staring Usher.

'He felt his plight and recent panic were hardly patrician,' replied the priest, 'so he tried to keep the name back at first. But he was just going to tell it you, when' – and Father Brown looked down at his boots – 'when a woman found another name for him.'

'But you can't be so mad as to say,' said Greywood Usher, very white, 'that Lord Falconroy was Drugger Davis.'

The priest looked at him very earnestly, but with a baffling and undecipherable face.

'I am not saying anything about it,' he said. 'I leave all the rest to you. Your pink paper says that the title was recently revived for him; but those papers are very unreliable. It says he was in the States in youth; but the whole story seems very strange. Davis and Falconroy are both pretty considerable cowards, but so are lots of other men. I would not hang a dog on my own opinion about this. But I think,' he went on softly and reflectively, 'I think you Americans are too modest. I think you idealise the English aristocracy – even in assuming it to be so aristocratic. You see a good-looking Englishman in evening dress; you know he's in the House of Lords; and you fancy he has a father. You don't allow for our national buoyancy and uplift. Many of our most influential noblemen have not only risen recently, but – '

'Oh, stop it!' cried Greywood Usher, wringing one lean hand in impatience against a shade of irony in the other's face.

'Don't stay talking to this lunatic!' cried Todd brutally. 'Take me to my friend.'

Next morning Father Brown appeared with the same demure expression, carrying yet another piece of pink newspaper.

'I'm afraid you neglect the fashionable press rather,' he said, 'but this cutting may interest you.'

Usher read the headlines, 'Last-Trick's Strayed Revellers: Mirthful Incident near Pilgrim's Pond'. The paragraph went on: 'A laughable occurrence took place outside Wilkinson's Motor Garage last night. A policeman on duty had his attention drawn by larrikins to a man in prison dress who was stepping with considerable coolness into the steering-seat of a pretty high-toned Panhard; he was accompanied by a girl wrapped in a ragged shawl. On the police interfering, the young woman threw back the shawl, and all recognised Millionaire Todd's daughter, who had just come from the Slum Freak Dinner at the Pond, where all the choicest guests were in a similar *déshabille*. She and the gentleman who had donned prison uniform were going for the customary joy-ride.'

Under the pink slip Mr Usher found a strip of a later paper, headed, 'Astounding Escape of Millionaire's Daughter with Convict. She had Arranged Freak Dinner. Now Safe in – '

Mr Greenwood Usher lifted his eyes, but Father Brown was gone.

The Head of Caesar

There is somewhere in Brompton or Kensington an interminable avenue of tall houses, rich but largely empty, that looks like a terrace of tombs. The very steps up to the dark front doors seem as steep as the side of pyramids; one would hesitate to knock at the door, lest it should be opened by a mummy. But a yet more depressing feature in the grey façade is its telescopic length and changeless continuity. The pilgrim walking down it begins to think he will never come to a break or a corner; but there is one exception – a very small one, but hailed by the pilgrim almost with a shout. There is a sort of mews between two of the tall mansions, a mere slit like the crack of a door by comparison with the street, but just large enough to permit a pigmy alehouse or eating-house, still allowed by the rich to their stable-servants, to stand in the angle. There is something cheery in its very dinginess, and something free and elfin in its very insignificance. At the feet of those grey stone giants it looks like a lighted house of dwarfs.

Anyone passing the place during a certain autumn evening, itself almost fairylike, might have seen a hand pull aside the red half-blind which (along with some large white lettering) half hid the interior from the street, and a face peer out not unlike a rather innocent goblin's. It was, in fact, the face of one with the harmless human name of Brown, formerly priest of Cobhole in Essex, and now working in London. His friend, Flambeau, a semi-official investigator, was sitting opposite him, making his last notes of a case he had cleared up in the neighbourhood. They were sitting at a small table, close up to the window, when the priest pulled the curtain back and looked out. He waited till a stranger in the street had passed the window, to let the curtain fall into its place again. Then his round eyes rolled to the large white lettering on the window above his head, and then strayed to the next table, at which sat only a navvy with beer and cheese, and a young girl with red hair and a glass of milk. Then (seeing his friend put away the pocketbook), he said softly: 'If you've got ten minutes, I wish you'd follow that man with the false nose.'

Flambeau looked up in surprise; but the girl with the red hair also looked up, and with something that was stronger than astonishment. She was simply and even loosely dressed in light brown sacking stuff; but she was a lady, and even, on a second glance, a rather needlessly haughty one. 'The man with the false nose!' repeated Flambeau. 'Who's he?'

'I haven't a notion,' answered Father Brown. 'I want you to find out; I ask it as a favour. He went down there' – and he jerked his thumb over his shoulder in one of his undistinguished gestures – 'and can't have passed three lamp posts yet. I only want to know the direction.'

Flambeau gazed at his friend for some time, with an expression between perplexity and amusement; and then, rising from the table; squeezed his huge form out of the little door of the dwarf tavern, and melted into the twilight.

Father Brown took a small book out of his pocket and began to read steadily; he betrayed no consciousness of the fact that the red-haired lady had left her own table and sat down opposite him. At last she leaned over and said in a low, strong voice: 'Why do you say that? How do you know it's false?'

He lifted his rather heavy eyelids, which fluttered in considerable embarrassment. Then his dubious eye roamed again to the white lettering on the glass front of the public-house. The young woman's eyes followed his, and rested there also, but in pure puzzledom.

'No,' said Father Brown, answering her thoughts. 'It doesn't say "Sela", like the thing in the Psalms; I read it like that myself when I was woolgathering just now; it says "Ales".'

'Well?' enquired the staring young lady. 'What does it matter what it says?'

His ruminating eye roved to the girl's light canvas sleeve, round the wrist of which ran a very slight thread of artistic pattern, just enough to distinguish it from a working-dress of a common woman and make it more like the working-dress of a lady art-student. He seemed to find much food for thought in this; but his reply was very slow and hesitant. 'You see, madam,' he said, 'from outside the place looks – well, it is a perfectly decent place – but ladies like you don't – don't generally think so. They never go into such places from choice, except –'

'Well?' she repeated.

'Except an unfortunate few who don't go in to drink milk.'

'You are a most singular person,' said the young lady. 'What is your object in all this?'

'Not to trouble you about it,' he replied, very gently. 'Only to arm myself with knowledge enough to help you, if ever you freely ask my help.'

'But why should I need help?'

He continued his dreamy monologue. 'You couldn't have come in to see *protégées*, humble friends, that sort of thing, or you'd have gone through into the parlour . . . and you couldn't have come in because you were ill, or you'd have spoken to the woman of the place, who's obviously respectable . . . besides, you don't look ill in that way, but only unhappy . . . This street is the only original long lane that has no turning; and the houses on both sides are shut up . . . I could only suppose that you'd seen somebody coming whom you didn't want to meet; and found the public-house was the only shelter in this wilderness of stone . . . I don't think I went beyond the licence of a stranger in glancing at the only man who passed immediately after . . . And as I thought he looked like the wrong sort . . . and you looked like the right sort . . . I held myself ready to help if he annoyed you; that is all. As for my friend, he'll be back soon; and he certainly can't find out anything by stumping down a road like this . . . I didn't think he could.'

'Then why did you send him out?' she cried, leaning forward with yet warmer curiosity. She had the proud, impetuous face that goes with reddish colouring, and a Roman nose, as it did in Marie Antoinette.

He looked at her steadily for the first time, and said: 'Because I hoped you would speak to me.'

She looked back at him for some time with a heated face, in which there hung a red shadow of anger; then, despite her anxieties, humour broke out of her eyes and the corners of her mouth, and she answered almost grimly: 'Well, if you're so keen on my conversation, perhaps you'll answer my question.' After a pause she added: 'I had the honour to ask you why you thought the man's nose was false.'

'The wax always spots like that just a little in this weather,' answered Father Brown with entire simplicity,

'But it's such a *crooked* nose,' remonstrated the red-haired girl.

The priest smiled in his turn. 'I don't say it's the sort of nose one would wear out of mere foppery,' he admitted. 'This man, I think, wears it because his real nose is so much nicer.'

'But why?' she insisted.

'What is the nursery-rhyme?' observed Brown absent-mindedly. 'There was a crooked man and he went a crooked mile . . . That man, I fancy, has gone a very crooked road – by following his nose.'

'Why, what's he done?' she demanded, rather shakily.

'I don't want to force your confidence by a hair,' said Father Brown, very quietly. 'But I think you could tell me more about that than I can tell you.'

The girl sprang to her feet and stood quite quietly, but with clenched hands, like one about to stride away; then her hands loosened slowly, and she sat down again. 'You are more of a mystery than all the others,' she said desperately, 'but I feel there might be a heart in your mystery.'

'What we all dread most,' said the priest in a low voice, 'is a maze with *no* centre. That is why atheism is only a nightmare.'

'I will tell you everything,' said the red-haired girl doggedly, 'except why I am telling you; and that I don't know.'

She picked at the darned tablecloth and went on: 'You look as if you knew what isn't snobbery as well as what is; and when I say that ours is a good old family, you'll understand it is a necessary part of the story; indeed, my chief danger is in my brother's high-and-dry notions, *noblesse oblige* and all that. Well, my name is Christabel Carstairs; and my father was that Colonel Carstairs you've probably heard of, who made the famous Carstairs Collection of Roman coins. I could never describe my father to you; the nearest I can say is that he was very like a Roman coin himself. He was as handsome and as genuine and as valuable and as metallic and as out-of-date. He was prouder of his Collection than of his coat-of-arms – nobody could say more than that. His extraordinary character came out most in his will. He had two sons and one daughter. He quarrelled with one son, my brother Giles, and sent him to Australia on a small allowance. He then made a will leaving the Carstairs Collection, actually with a yet smaller allowance, to my brother Arthur. He meant it as a reward, as the highest honour he could offer, in acknowledgement of Arthur's loyalty and rectitude and the distinctions he had already gained in mathematics and economics at Cambridge. He left me practically all his pretty large fortune; and I am sure he meant it in contempt.

'Arthur, you may say, might well complain of this; but Arthur is my father over again. Though he had some differences with my father in early youth, no sooner had he taken over the Collection than he became like a pagan priest dedicated to a temple. He mixed up these Roman halfpence with the honour of the Carstairs family in the same stiff, idolatrous way as his father before him. He acted as if Roman money must be guarded by all the Roman virtues. He took no pleasures; he spent nothing on himself; he lived for the Collection. Often he would not trouble to dress for his simple meals; but pattered about among the corded brown-paper parcels (which no one else was allowed to touch) in an old brown dressing-gown. With its rope and tassel and his pale, thin, refined face, it made him look like an old ascetic monk. Every now and then, though, he would appear dressed like a decidedly fashionable gentleman; but that was only when he went up to the London sales or shops to make an addition to the Carstairs Collection.

'Now, if you've known any young people, you won't be shocked if I say that I got into rather a low frame of mind with all this; the frame of mind in which one begins to say that the Ancient Romans were all very well in their way. I'm not like my brother Arthur; I can't help enjoying enjoyment. I got a lot of romance and rubbish where I got my red hair, from the other side of the family. Poor Giles was the same; and I think the atmosphere of coins might count in excuse for him; though he really did wrong and nearly went to prison. But he didn't behave any worse than I did; as you shall hear.

'I come now to the silly part of the story. I think a man as clever as you can guess the sort of thing that would begin to relieve the monotony for an unruly girl of seventeen placed in such a position. But I am so rattled with more dreadful things that I can hardly read my own feeling; and don't know whether I despise it now as a flirtation or bear it as a broken heart. We lived then at a little seaside watering-place in South Wales, and a retired sea-captain living a few doors off had a son about five years older than myself, who had been a friend of Giles before he went to the Colonies. His name does not affect my tale; but I tell you it was Philip Hawker, because I am telling you everything. We used to go shrimping together, and said and thought we were in love with each other; at least he certainly said he was, and I certainly thought I was. If I tell you he had bronzed curly hair and a falconish sort of face, bronzed by the sea also, it's not for his sake, I assure you, but for the story; for it was the cause of a very curious coincidence.

'One summer afternoon, when I had promised to go shrimping along the sands with Philip, I was waiting rather impatiently in the front drawing-room, watching Arthur handle some packets of coins he had just purchased and slowly shunt them, one or two at a time, into his own dark study and museum which was at the back of the house. As soon as I heard the heavy door close on him finally, I made a bolt for my shrimping-net and tam-o'-shanter and was just going to slip out, when I saw that my brother had left behind him one coin that lay gleaming on the long bench by the window. It was a bronze coin, and the colour, combined with the exact curve of the Roman nose and something in the very lift of the long, wiry neck, made the head of Caesar on it the almost precise portrait of Philip Hawker. Then I suddenly remembered Giles telling Philip of a coin that was like him, and Philip wishing he had it. Perhaps you can fancy the wild, foolish thoughts with which my head went round; I felt as if I had had a gift from the fairies. It seemed to me that if I could only run away with this, and give it to Philip like a wild sort of wedding-ring, it would be a bond between us for ever; I felt a thousand such things at once. Then there yawned under me, like the pit, the enormous, awful notion of what I was doing; above all, the unbearable thought, which was like touching hot iron, of what Arthur would think of it. A Carstairs a thief; and a thief of the Carstairs treasure! I believe my brother could see me burned like a witch for such a thing. But then, the very thought of such fanatical cruelty heightened my old hatred of his dingy old antiquarian fussiness and my longing for the youth and liberty that called to me from the sea. Outside was strong sunlight with a wind; and a yellow head of some broom or gorse in the garden rapped against the glass of the window. I thought of that living and growing gold calling to me from all the heaths of the world – and then of that dead, dull gold and bronze and brass of my brother's growing dustier and dustier as life went by. Nature and the Carstairs Collection had come to grips at last.

'Nature is older than the Carstairs Collection. As I ran down the streets to the sea, the coin clenched tight in my fist, I felt all the Roman Empire on my back as well as the Carstairs pedigree. It was not only the old lion argent that was roaring in my ear, but all the eagles of the Caesars seemed flapping and screaming in pursuit of me. And yet my heart rose higher and higher like a child's kite, until I came over the loose, dry sand-hills and to the flat, wet sands, where Philip stood already up to his ankles in the shallow shining water, some hundred yards out to sea. There was a great red sunset; and the long stretch of low water, hardly rising over the ankle for half a mile, was like a lake of ruby flame. It was not till I had torn off my shoes and stockings and waded to where he stood, which was well away from the dry land, that I turned and looked round. We were quite alone in a circle of sea-water and wet sand, and I gave him the head of Caesar.

'At the very instant I had a shock of fancy: that a man far away on the sand-hills was looking at me intently. I must have felt immediately after that it was a mere leap of unreasonable nerves; for the man was only a dark dot in the distance, and I could only just see that he was standing quite still and gazing, with his head a little on one side. There was no earthly logical evidence that he was looking at me; he might have been looking at a ship, or the sunset, or the sea-gulls, or at any of the people who still strayed here and there on the shore between us. Nevertheless, whatever my start sprang from was prophetic; for, as I gazed, he started walking briskly in a bee-line towards us across the wide wet sands. As he drew nearer and nearer I saw that he was dark and bearded, and that his eyes were marked with dark spectacles. He was dressed poorly but respectably in black, from the old black top hat on his head to the solid black boots on his feet. In spite of these he walked straight into the sea without a flash of hesitation, and came on at me with the steadiness of a travelling bullet.

'I can't tell you the sense of monstrosity and miracle I had when he thus silently burst the barrier between land and water. It was as if he had walked straight off a cliff and still marched steadily in mid-air. It was as if a house had flown up into the sky or a man's head had fallen off. He was only wetting his boots; but he seemed to be a demon disregarding a law of Nature. If he had hesitated an instant at the water's edge it would have been nothing. As it was, he seemed to look so much at me alone as not to notice the ocean. Philip was some yards away with his back to me, bending over his net. The stranger came on till he stood within two yards of me, the water washing halfway up to his knees. Then he said, with a clearly modulated and rather mincing articulation: "Would it discommode you to contribute elsewhere a coin with a somewhat different superscription?"

'With one exception there was nothing definably abnormal about him. His tinted glasses were not really opaque, but of a blue kind common enough, nor were the eyes behind them shifty, but regarded me steadily. His dark beard was not really long or wild, but he looked rather hairy, because the beard began very high up in his face, just under the cheekbones. His complexion was neither sallow nor livid, but on the contrary rather clear and youthful; yet this gave a pink-and-white wax look which somehow (I don't know why) rather increased the horror. The only oddity one could fix was that his nose, which was otherwise of a good shape, was just slightly turned sideways at the tip; as if, when it was soft, it had been tapped on one side with a toy hammer. The thing was hardly a deformity; yet I cannot tell you what a living nightmare it was to me. As he stood there in the sunset-stained water he affected me as some hellish sea-monster just risen roaring out of a sea like blood. I don't know why a touch on the nose should affect my imagination so much. I think it seemed as if he could move his nose like a finger. And as if he had just that moment moved it.

' "Any little assistance," he continued with the same queer, priggish accent, "that may obviate the necessity of my communicating with the family."

'Then it rushed over me that I was being blackmailed for the theft of the bronze piece; and all my merely superstitious fears and doubts were swallowed up in one overpowering, practical question. How could he have found out? I had stolen the thing suddenly and on impulse; I was certainly alone; for I always made sure of being unobserved when I slipped out to see Philip in this way. I had not, to all appearance, been followed in the street; and if I had, they could not "X-ray" the coin in my closed hand. The man standing on the sand-hills could no more have seen what I gave Philip than shoot a fly in one eye, like the man in the fairy tale.

' "Philip," I cried helplessly, "ask this man what he wants."

'When Philip lifted his head at last from mending his net he looked rather red, as if sulky or ashamed; but it may have been only the exertion of stooping and the red evening light; I may have only had another of the morbid fancies that seemed to be dancing about me. He merely said gruffly to the man: "You clear out of this." And, motioning me to follow, set off wading shoreward without paying further attention to him. He stepped on to a stone breakwater that ran out from among the roots of the sand-hills, and so struck homeward, perhaps thinking our incubus would find it less easy to walk on such rough stones, green and slippery with seaweed, than we, who were young and used to it. But my persecutor walked as daintily as he talked; and he still followed me, picking his way and picking his phrases. I heard his delicate, detestable voice appealing to me over my shoulder, until at last, when we had crested the sand-hills, Philip's patience (which was by no means so conspicuous on most occasions) seemed to snap. He turned suddenly, saying, "Go back. I can't talk to you now." And as the man hovered and opened his mouth, Philip struck him a buffet on it that sent him flying from the top of the tallest sand-hill to the bottom. I saw him crawling out below, covered with sand.

'This stroke comforted me somehow, though it might well increase my peril; but Philip showed none of his usual elation at his own prowess. Though as affectionate as ever, he still seemed cast down; and before I could ask him anything fully, he parted with me at his own gate, with two remarks that struck me as strange. He said that, all things considered, I ought to put the coin back in the Collection; but that he himself would keep it "for the present". And then he added quite suddenly and irrelevantly: "You know Giles is back from Australia?" '

The door of the tavern opened and the gigantic shadow of the investigator Flambeau fell across the table. Father Brown presented him to the lady in his own slight, persuasive style of speech, mentioning his knowledge and sympathy in such cases; and almost without knowing, the girl was soon reiterating her story to two listeners. But Flambeau, as he bowed and sat down, handed the priest a small slip of paper. Brown accepted it with some surprise and read on it: 'Cab to Wagga Wagga, 379 Mafeking Avenue, Putney'. The girl was going on with her story.

'I went up the steep street to my own house with my head in a whirl; it had not begun to clear when I came to the doorstep, on which I found a milk-can – and the man with the twisted nose. The milk-can told me the servants were all out; for, of course, Arthur, browsing about in his brown dressing-gown in a brown study, would not hear or answer a bell. Thus there was no one to help me in the house, except my brother, whose help must be my ruin. In desperation I thrust two shillings into the horrid thing's hand, and told him to call again in a few days, when I had thought it out. He went off sulking, but more sheepishly than I had expected – perhaps he had been shaken by his fall – and I watched the star of sand splashed on his back receding down the road with a horrid vindictive pleasure. He turned a corner some six houses down.

'Then I let myself in, made myself some tea, and tried to think it out. I sat at the drawing-room window looking on to the garden, which still glowed with the last full evening light. But I was too distracted and dreamy to look at the lawns and flowerpots and flowerbeds with any concentration. So I took the shock the more sharply because I'd seen it so slowly.

'The man or monster I'd sent away was standing quite still in the middle of the garden. Oh, we've all read a lot about pale-faced phantoms in the dark; but this was more dreadful than anything of that kind could ever be. Because, though he cast a long evening shadow, he still stood in warm sunlight. And because his face was not pale, but had that waxen bloom still upon it that belongs to a barber's dummy. He stood quite still, with his face towards me; and I can't tell you how horrid he looked among the tulips and all those tall, gaudy, almost hothouse-looking flowers. It looked as if we'd stuck up a waxwork instead of a statue in the centre of our garden.

'Yet almost the instant he saw me move in the window he turned and ran out of the garden by the back gate, which stood open and by which he had undoubtedly entered. This renewed timidity on his part was so different from the impudence with which he had walked into the sea, that I felt vaguely comforted. I fancied, perhaps, that he feared confronting Arthur more than I knew. Anyhow, I settled down at last, and had a quiet dinner alone (for it was against the rules to disturb Arthur when he was rearranging the museum), and, my thoughts, a little released, fled to Philip and lost themselves, I suppose. Anyhow, I was looking blankly, but rather pleasantly than otherwise, at another window, uncurtained, but by this time black as a slate with the final nightfall. It seemed to me that something like a snail was on the outside of the window-pane. But when I stared harder, it was more like a man's thumb pressed on the pane; it had that curled look that a thumb has. With my fear and courage reawakened together, I rushed at the window and then recoiled with a strangled scream that any man but Arthur must have heard.

'For it was not a thumb, any more than it was a snail. It was the tip of a crooked nose, crushed against the glass; it looked white with the pressure; and the staring face and eyes behind it were at first invisible and afterwards grey like a ghost. I slammed the shutters together somehow, rushed up to my room and locked myself in. But, even as I passed, I could swear I saw a second black window with something on it that was like a snail.

'It might be best to go to Arthur after all. If the thing was crawling close all around the house like a cat, it might have purposes worse even than blackmail. My brother might cast me out and curse me for ever, but he was a gentleman, and would defend me on the spot. After ten minutes' curious thinking, I went down, knocked on the door and then went in: to see the last and worst sight.

'My brother's chair was empty, and he was obviously out. But the man with the crooked nose was sitting waiting for his return, with his hat still insolently on his head, and actually reading one of my brother's books under my brother's lamp. His face was composed and occupied, but his nose-tip still had the air of being the most mobile part of his face, as if it had just turned from left to right like an elephant's proboscis. I had thought him poisonous enough while he was pursuing and watching me; but I think his unconsciousness of my presence was more frightful still.

'I think I screamed loud and long; but that doesn't matter. What I did next does matter: I gave him all the money I had, including a good deal in paper which, though it was mine, I dare say I had no right to touch. He went off at last, with hateful, tactful regrets all in long words; and I sat down, feeling ruined in every sense. And yet I was saved that very night by a pure accident. Arthur had gone off suddenly to London, as he so often did, for bargains; and returned, late but radiant, having nearly secured a treasure that was an added splendour even to the family Collection. He was so resplendent that I was almost emboldened to confess the abstraction of the lesser gem, but he bore down all other topics with his overpowering projects. Because the bargain might still misfire any moment, he insisted on my packing at once and going up with him to lodgings he had already taken in Fulham, to be near the curio-shop in question. Thus in spite of myself, I fled from my foe almost in the dead of night – but from Philip also . . . My brother was often at the South Kensington Museum, and, in order to make some sort of secondary life for myself, I paid for a few lessons at the Art Schools. I was coming back from them this evening, when I saw the abomination of desolation walking alive down the long straight street and the rest is as this gentleman has said.

'I've got only one thing to say. I don't deserve to be helped; and I don't question or complain of my punishment; it is just, it ought to have happened. But I still question, with bursting brains, how it can have happened. Am I punished by miracle? or how *can* anyone but Philip and myself know I gave him a tiny coin in the middle of the sea?'

'It is an extraordinary problem,' admitted Flambeau.

'Not so extraordinary as the answer,' remarked Father Brown rather gloomily. 'Miss Carstairs, will you be at home if we call at your Fulham place in an hour and a half hence?'

The girl looked at him, and then rose and put her gloves on. 'Yes,' she said, 'I'll be there'; and almost instantly left the place.

That night the detective and the priest were still talking of the matter as they drew near the Fulham house, a tenement strangely mean even for a temporary residence of the Carstairs family.

'Of course the superficial, on reflection,' said Flambeau, 'would think first of this Australian brother who's been in trouble before, who's come back so suddenly and who's just the man to have shabby confederates. But I can't see how he can come into the thing by any process of thought, unless . . .'

'Well?' asked his companion patiently.

Flambeau lowered his voice. 'Unless the girl's lover comes in, too, and he would be the blacker villain. The Australian chap did know that Hawker wanted the coin. But I can't see how on earth he could know that Hawker had got it, unless Hawker signalled to him or his representative across the shore.'

'That is true,' assented the priest, with respect.

'Have you noted another thing?' went on Flambeau eagerly; 'this Hawker hears his love insulted, but doesn't strike till *he's got to the soft sand-hills*, where he can be victor in a mere sham-fight. If he'd struck amid rocks and sea, he might have hurt his ally.'

'That is true again,' said Father Brown, nodding.

'And now, take it from the start. It lies between few people, but at least three. You want one person for suicide; two people for murder; but at least three people for blackmail.'

'Why?' asked the priest softly.

'Well, obviously,' cried his friend, 'there must be one to be exposed; one to threaten exposure; and one at least whom exposure would horrify.'

After a long ruminant pause, the priest said: 'You miss a logical step. Three persons are needed as ideas. Only two are needed as agents.'

'What can you mean?' asked the other.

'Why shouldn't a blackmailer,' asked Brown, in a low voice, 'threaten his victim with himself? Suppose a wife became a rigid teetotaller *in order* to frighten her husband into concealing *his* pub-frequenting, and then wrote him blackmailing letters in another hand, threatening to tell his wife! Why shouldn't it work? Suppose a father forbade a son to gamble and then, following him in a good disguise, threatened the boy with his own sham paternal strictness! Suppose – but, here we are, my friend.'

'My God!' cried Flambeau; 'you don't mean – '

An active figure ran down the steps of the house and showed under the golden lamplight the unmistakable head that resembled the Roman coin. 'Miss Carstairs,' said Hawker without ceremony, 'wouldn't go in till you came.'

'Well,' observed Brown confidently, 'don't you think it's the best thing she can do to stop outside – with you to look after her? You see, I rather guess you have guessed it all yourself.'

'Yes,' said the young man, in an undertone, 'I guessed on the sands and now I know; that was why I let him fall soft.'

Taking a latchkey from the girl and the coin from Hawker, Flambeau let himself and his friend into the empty house and passed into the outer parlour. It was empty of all occupants but one. The man whom Father Brown had seen pass the tavern was standing against the wall as if at bay; unchanged, save that he had taken off his black coat and was wearing a brown dressing-gown.

'We have come,' said Father Brown politely, 'to give back this coin to its owner.' And he handed it to the man with the nose.

Flambeau's eyes rolled. 'Is this man a coin-collector?' he asked.

'This man is Mr Arthur Carstairs,' said the priest positively, 'and he is a coin-collector of a somewhat singular kind.'

The man changed colour so horribly that the crooked nose stood out on his face like a separate and comic thing. He spoke, nevertheless, with a sort of despairing dignity. 'You shall see, then,' he said, 'that I have not lost all the family qualities.' And he turned suddenly and strode into an inner room, slamming the door.

'Stop him!' shouted Father Brown, bounding and half falling over a chair; and, after a wrench or two, Flambeau had the door open. But it was too late. In dead silence Flambeau strode across and telephoned for doctor and police.

An empty medicine bottle lay on the floor. Across the table the body of the man in the brown dressing-gown lay amid his burst and gaping brown-paper parcels; out of which poured and rolled, not Roman, but very modern English coins.

The priest held up the bronze head of Caesar. 'This,' he said, 'was all that was left of the Carstairs Collection.'

After a silence he went on, with more than common gentleness: 'It was a cruel will his wicked father made, and you see he did resent it a little. He hated the Roman money he had, and grew fonder of the real money denied him. He not only sold the Collection bit by bit, but sank bit by bit to the basest ways of making money – even to blackmailing his own family in a disguise. He blackmailed his brother from Australia for his little forgotten crime (that is why he took the cab to Wagga Wagga in Putney), he blackmailed his sister for the theft he alone could have noticed. And that, by the way, is why she had that supernatural guess when he was away on the sand-dunes. Mere figure and gait, however distant, are more likely to remind us of somebody than a well-made-up face quite close.'

There was another silence. 'Well,' growled the detective, 'and so this great numismatist and coin-collector was nothing but a vulgar miser.'

'Is there so great a difference?' asked Father Brown, in the same strange, indulgent tone. 'What is there wrong about a miser that is not often as wrong about a collector? What is wrong, except . . . thou shalt not make to thyself any graven image; thou shalt not bow down to them nor serve them, for I . . . but we must go and see how the poor young people are getting on.'

'I think,' said Flambeau, 'that in spite of everything, they are probably getting on very well.'

The Purple Wig

Mr Edward Nutt, the industrious editor of the *Daily Reformer*, sat at his desk, opening letters and marking proofs to the merry tune of a typewriter, worked by a vigorous young lady.

He was a stoutish, fair man, in his shirt-sleeves; his movements were resolute, his mouth firm and his tones final; but his round, rather babyish blue eyes had a bewildered and even wistful look that rather contradicted all this. Nor indeed was the expression altogether misleading. It might truly be said of him, as for many journalists in authority, that his most familiar emotion was one of continuous fear; fear of libel actions, fear of lost advertisements, fear of misprints, fear of the sack.

His life was a series of distracted compromises between the proprietor of the paper (and of him), who was a senile soap-boiler with three ineradicable mistakes in his mind, and the very able staff he had collected to run the paper; some of whom were brilliant and experienced men and (what was even worse) sincere enthusiasts for the political policy of the paper.

A letter from one of these lay immediately before him, and rapid and resolute as he was, he seemed almost to hesitate before opening it. He took up a strip of proof instead, ran down it with a blue eye, and a blue pencil, altered the word 'adultery' to the word 'impropriety', and the word 'Jew' to the word 'Alien', rang a bell and sent it flying upstairs.

Then, with a more thoughtful eye, he ripped open the letter from his more distinguished contributor, which bore a postmark of Devonshire, and read as follows:

> Dear Nutt – As I see you're working Spooks and Dooks at the same time, what about an article on that rum business of the Eyres of Exmoor; or as the old women call it down here, the Devil's Ear of Eyre? The head of the family, you know, is the Duke of Exmoor; he is one of the few really stiff old Tory aristocrats left, a sound old crusted tyrant it is quite in our line to make trouble about. And I think I'm on the track of a story that will make trouble.
>
> Of course I don't believe in the old legend about James I; and as for you, you don't believe in anything, not even in journalism. The legend, you'll probably remember, was about the blackest business in English history – the poisoning of Overbury by that witch's cat Frances Howard, and the quite mysterious terror which forced the King to pardon the murderers. There was a lot of alleged witchcraft mixed up with it; and the story goes

that a manservant listening at the keyhole heard the truth in a talk between the King and Carr; and the bodily ear with which he heard grew large and monstrous as by magic, so awful was the secret. And though he had to be loaded with lands and gold and made an ancestor of dukes, the elf-shaped ear is still recurrent in the family. Well, you don't believe in black magic; and if you did, you couldn't use it for copy. If a miracle happened in your office, you'd have to hush it up, now so many bishops are agnostics. But that is not the point. The point is that there really is something queer about Exmoor and his family; something quite natural, I dare say, but quite abnormal. And the Ear is in it somehow, I fancy; either a symbol or a delusion or disease or something. Another tradition says that Cavaliers just after James I began to wear their hair long only to cover the ear of the first Lord Exmoor. This also is no doubt fanciful.

The reason I point it out to you is this: it seems to me that we make a mistake in attacking aristocracy entirely for its champagne and diamonds. Most men rather admire the nobs for having a good time, but I think we surrender too much when we admit that aristocracy has made even the aristocrats happy. I suggest a series of articles pointing out how dreary, how inhuman, how downright diabolist, is the very smell and atmosphere of some of these great houses. There are plenty of instances; but you couldn't begin with a better one than the Ear of the Eyres. By the end of the week I think I can get you the truth about it.

Yours ever,

FRANCIS FINN

Mr Nutt reflected a moment, staring at his left boot; then he called out in a strong, loud and entirely lifeless voice, in which every syllable sounded alike: 'Miss Barlow, take down a letter to Mr Finn, please. Dear Finn, I think it would do; copy should reach us second post Saturday. Yours, E. Nutt.'

This elaborate epistle he articulated as if it were all one word; and Miss Barlow rattled it down as if it were all one word. Then he took up another strip of proof and a blue pencil, and altered the word 'supernatural' to the word 'marvellous', and the expression 'shoot down' to the expression 'repress'.

In such happy, healthful activities did Mr Nutt disport himself, until the ensuing Saturday found him at the same desk, dictating to the same typist, and using the same blue pencil on the first instalment of Mr Finn's revelations. The opening was a sound piece of slashing invective about the evil secrets of princes, and despair in the high places of the earth. Though written violently, it was in excellent English; but the editor, as usual, had given to somebody else the task of breaking it up into subheadings, which were of a spicier sort, as 'Peeress and Poisons', and 'The Eerie Ear', 'The Eyres in their Eyrie', and so on through a hundred happy changes. Then followed the legend of the Ear, amplified from Finn's first letter, and then the substance of his later discoveries.

* * *

I know it is the practice of journalists to put the end of the story at the beginning and call it a headline. I know that journalism largely consists in saying 'Lord Jones Dead' to people who never knew that Lord Jones was alive. Your present correspondent thinks that this, like many other journalistic customs, is bad journalism; and that the *Daily Reformer* has to set a better example in such things. He proposes to tell his story as it occurred, step by step. He will use the real names of the parties, who in most cases are ready to confirm his testimony. As for the headlines, the sensational proclamations – they will come at the end.

I was walking along a public path that threads through a private Devonshire orchard and seems to point towards Devonshire cider, when I came suddenly upon just such a place as the path suggested. It was a long, low inn, consisting really of a cottage and two barns; thatched all over with the thatch that looks like brown and grey hair grown before history. But outside the door was a sign which called it the Blue Dragon; and under the sign was one of those long rustic tables that used to stand outside most of the free English inns, before teetotallers and brewers between them destroyed freedom. And at this table sat three gentlemen, who might have lived a hundred years ago.

Now that I know them all better, there is no difficulty about disentangling the impressions; but just then they looked like three very solid ghosts. The dominant figure, both because he was bigger in all three dimensions, and because he sat centrally in the length of the table, facing me, was a tall, fat man dressed completely in black, with a rubicund, even apoplectic visage, but a rather bald and rather bothered brow. Looking at him again, more strictly, I could not exactly say what it was that gave me the sense of antiquity, except the antique cut of his white clerical necktie and the barred wrinkles across his brow.

It was even less easy to fix the impression in the case of the man at the right end of the table, who, to say truth, was as commonplace a person as could be seen anywhere, with a round, brown-haired head and a round snub nose, but also clad in clerical black, of a stricter cut. It was only when I saw his broad curved hat lying on the table beside him that I realised why I connected him with anything ancient. He was a Roman Catholic priest.

Perhaps the third man, at the other end of the table, had really more to do with it than the rest, though he was both slighter in physical presence and more inconsiderate in his dress. His lank limbs were clad, I might also say clutched, in very tight grey sleeves and pantaloons; he had a long, sallow, aquiline face which seemed somehow all the more saturnine because his lantern jaws were imprisoned in his collar and neck-cloth more in the style of the old stock; and his hair (which ought to have been dark brown) was of an odd dim, russet colour which, in conjunction with his yellow face, looked rather purple than red. The unobtrusive yet unusual colour was all the more notable because his hair was almost unnaturally healthy and curling, and he wore it full. But, after all analysis, I incline to think that what gave me my first old-fashioned impression was simply a set of tall, old-fashioned wine glasses, one or two lemons and two churchwarden pipes. And also, perhaps, the old-world errand on which I had come.

Being a hardened reporter, and it being apparently a public inn, I did not need to summon much of my impudence to sit down at the long table and order some cider. The big man in black seemed very learned, especially about local antiquities; the small man in black, though he talked much less, surprised me with a yet wider culture. So we got on very well together; but the third man, the old gentleman in the tight pantaloons, seemed rather distant and haughty, until I slid into the subject of the Duke of Exmoor and his ancestry.

I thought the subject seemed to embarrass the other two a little; but it broke the spell of the third man's silence most successfully. Speaking with restraint and with the accent of a highly educated gentleman, and puffing at intervals at his long churchwarden pipe, he proceeded to tell me some of the most horrible stories I have ever heard in my life: how one of the Eyres in the former ages had hanged his own father; and another had his wife scourged at the cart tail through the village; and another had set fire to a church full of children, and so on.

Some of the tales, indeed, are not fit for public print, such as the story of the Scarlet Nuns, the abominable story of the Spotted Dog, or the thing that was done in the quarry. And all this red roll of impieties came from his thin, genteel lips rather primly than otherwise, as he sat sipping the wine out of his tall, thin glass.

I could see that the big man opposite me was trying, if anything, to stop him; but he evidently held the old gentleman in considerable respect, and could not venture to do so at all abruptly. And the little priest at the other end of the table, though free from any such air of embarrassment, looked steadily at the table, and seemed to listen to the recital with great pain – as well as he might.

'You don't seem,' I said to the narrator, 'to be very fond of the Exmoor pedigree.'

He looked at me a moment, his lips still prim, but whitening and tightening; then he deliberately broke his long pipe and glass on the table and stood up, the very picture of a perfect gentleman with the framing temper of a fiend.

'These gentlemen,' he said, 'will tell you whether I have cause to like it. The curse of the Eyres of old has lain heavy on this country, and many have suffered from it. They know there are none who have suffered from it as I have.' And with that he crushed a piece of the fallen glass under his heel, and strode away among the green twilight of the twinkling apple trees.

'That is an extraordinary old gentleman,' I said to the other two; 'do you happen to know what the Exmoor family has done to him? Who is he?'

The big man in black was staring at me with the wild air of a baffled bull; he did not at first seem to take it in. Then he said at last, 'Don't you know who he is?'

I reaffirmed my ignorance, and there was another silence; then the little priest said, still looking at the table, 'That is the Duke of Exmoor.'

Then, before I could collect my scattered senses, he added equally quietly, but with an air of regularising things: 'My friend here is Doctor Mull, the Duke's librarian. My name is Brown.'

'But,' I stammered, 'if that is the Duke, why does he damn all the old dukes like that?'

'He seems really to believe,' answered the priest called Brown, 'that they have left a curse on him.' Then he added, with some irrelevance, 'That's why he wears a wig.'

It was a few moments before his meaning dawned on me. 'You don't mean that fable about the fantastic ear?' I demanded. 'I've heard of it, of course, but surely it must be a superstitious yarn spun out of something much simpler. I've sometimes thought it was a wild version of one of those mutilation stories. They used to crop criminals' ears in the sixteenth century.'

'I hardly think it was that,' answered the little man thoughtfully, 'but it is not outside ordinary science or natural law for a family to have some deformity frequently reappearing – such as one ear bigger than the other.'

The big librarian had buried his big bald brow in his big red hands, like a man trying to think out his duty. 'No,' he groaned. 'You do the man a wrong after all. Understand, I've no reason to defend him, or even keep faith with him. He has been a tyrant to me as to everybody else. Don't fancy because you see him sitting here that he isn't a great lord in the worst sense of the word. He would fetch a man a mile to ring a bell a yard off – if it would summon another man three miles to fetch a matchbox three yards off. He must have a footman to carry his walking-stick; a body servant to hold up his opera-glasses – '

'But not a valet to brush his clothes,' cut in the priest, with a curious dryness, 'for the valet would want to brush his wig, too.'

The librarian turned to him and seemed to forget my presence; he was strongly moved and, I think, a little heated with wine. 'I don't know how you know it, Father Brown,' he said, 'but you are right. He lets the whole world do everything for him – except dress him. And that he insists on doing in a literal solitude like a desert. Anybody is kicked out of the house without a character who is so much as found near his dressing-room door.'

'He seems a pleasant old party,' I remarked.

'No,' replied Dr Mull quite simply; 'and yet that is just what I mean by saying you are unjust to him after all. Gentlemen, the Duke does really feel the bitterness about the curse that he uttered just now. He does, with sincere shame and terror, hide under that purple wig something he thinks it would blast the sons of man to see. I know it is so; and I know it is not a mere natural disfigurement, like a criminal mutilation, or a hereditary disproportion in the features. I know it is worse than that; because a man told me who was present at a scene that no man could invent, where a stronger man than any of us tried to defy the secret, and was scared away from it.'

I opened my mouth to speak, but Mull went on in oblivion of me, speaking out of the cavern of his hands. 'I don't mind telling you, Father, because it's really more defending the poor Duke than giving him away. Didn't you ever hear of the time when he very nearly lost all the estates?'

The priest shook his head; and the librarian proceeded to tell the tale as he had heard it from his predecessor in the same post, who had been his patron and instructor, and whom he seemed to trust implicitly. Up to a certain point it was a common enough tale of the decline of a great family's fortunes – the tale of a family lawyer. His lawyer, however, had the sense to cheat honestly, if the expression explains itself. Instead of using funds he held in trust, he took advantage of the Duke's carelessness to put the family in a financial hole, in which it might be necessary for the Duke to let him hold them in reality.

The lawyer's name was Isaac Green, but the Duke always called him Elisha; presumably in reference to the fact that he was quite bald, though certainly not more than thirty. He had risen very rapidly, but from very dirty beginnings; being first a 'nark' or informer, and then a money-lender: but as solicitor to the Eyres he had the sense, as I say, to keep technically straight until he was ready to deal the final blow. The blow fell at dinner; and the old librarian said he should never forget the very look of the lampshades and the decanters, as the little lawyer, with a steady smile, proposed to the great landlord that they should halve the estates between them. The sequel certainly could not be overlooked; for the Duke, in dead silence, smashed a decanter on the man's bald head as suddenly as I had seen him smash the glass that day in the orchard. It left a red triangular scar on the scalp, and the lawyer's eyes altered, but not his smile.

He rose tottering to his feet, and struck back as such men do strike. 'I am glad of that,' he said, 'for now I can take the whole estate. The law will give it to me.'

Exmoor, it seems, was white as ashes, but his eyes still blazed. 'The law will give it you,' he said; 'but you will not take it . . . Why not? Why? because it would mean the crack of doom for me, and if you take it I shall take off my wig . . . Why, you pitiful plucked fowl, anyone can see your bare head. But no man shall see mine and live.'

Well, you may say what you like and make it mean what you like. But Mull swears it is the solemn fact that the lawyer, after shaking his knotted fists in the air for an instant, simply ran from the room and never reappeared in the countryside; and since then Exmoor has been feared more for a warlock than even for a landlord and a magistrate.

Now Dr Mull told his story with rather wild theatrical gestures, and with a passion I think at least partisan. I was quite conscious of the possibility that the whole was the extravagance of an old braggart and gossip. But before I end this half of my discoveries, I think it due to Dr Mull to record that my two first enquiries have confirmed his story. I learned from an old apothecary in the village that there was a bald man in evening dress, giving the name of Green, who came to him one night to have a three-cornered cut on his forehead plastered. And I learnt from the legal records and old newspapers that there was a lawsuit threatened, and at least begun, by one Green against the Duke of Exmoor.

* * *

Mr Nutt, of the *Daily Reformer*, wrote some highly incongruous words across the top of the copy, made some highly mysterious marks down the side of it, and called to Miss Barlow in the same loud, monotonous voice: 'Take down a letter to Mr Finn. Dear Finn, your copy will do, but I have had to headline it a bit; and our public would never stand a Romanist priest in the story – you must keep your eye on the suburbs. I've altered him to Mr Brown, a Spiritualist. Yours, E. Nutt.'

A day or two afterwards found the active and judicious editor examining, with blue eyes that seemed to grow rounder and rounder, the second instalment of Mr Finn's tale of mysteries in high life.

* * *

I have made an astounding discovery. I freely confess it is quite different from anything I expected to discover, and will give a much more practical shock to the public. I venture to say, without any vanity, that the words I now write will be read all over Europe, and certainly all over America and the Colonies. And yet I heard all I have to tell before I left this same little wooden table in this same little wood of apple trees.

I owe it all to the small priest Brown; he is an extraordinary man. The big librarian had left the table, perhaps ashamed of his long tongue, perhaps anxious about the storm in which his mysterious master had vanished: anyway, he betook himself heavily in the Duke's tracks through the trees. Father Brown had picked up one of the lemons and was eyeing it with an odd pleasure.

'What a lovely colour a lemon is!' he said. 'There's one thing I don't like about the Duke's wig – the colour.'

'I don't think I understand,' I answered.

'I dare say he's got good reason to cover his ears, like King Midas,' went on the priest, with a cheerful simplicity which somehow seemed rather flippant under the circumstances. 'I can quite understand that it's nicer to cover them with hair than with brass plates or leather flaps. But if he wants to use hair, why doesn't he make it look like hair? There never was hair of that colour in this world. It looks more like a sunset-cloud coming through the wood. Why doesn't he conceal the family curse better, if he's really so ashamed of it? Shall I tell you? It's because he isn't ashamed of it. He's proud of it.'

'It's an ugly wig to be proud of – and an ugly story,' I said.

'Consider,' replied this curious little man, 'how you yourself really feel about such things. I don't suggest you're either more snobbish or more morbid than the rest of us: but don't you feel in a vague way that a genuine old family curse is rather a fine thing to have? Would you be ashamed, wouldn't you be a little proud, if the heir of the Glamis horror called you his friend? or if Byron's family had confided, to you only, the evil adventures of their race? Don't be too hard on the aristocrats themselves if their heads are as weak as ours would be, and they are snobs about their own sorrows.'

'By Jove!' I cried; 'and that's true enough. My own mother's family had a banshee; and, now I come to think of it, it has comforted me in many a cold hour.'

'And think,' he went on, 'of that stream of blood and poison that spurted from his thin lips the instant you so much as mentioned his ancestors. Why should he show every stranger over such a Chamber of Horrors unless he is proud of it? He doesn't conceal his wig, he doesn't conceal his blood, he doesn't conceal his family curse, he doesn't conceal the family crimes – but – '

The little man's voice changed so suddenly, he shut his hand so sharply, and his eyes so rapidly grew rounder and brighter like a waking owl's, that it had all the abruptness of a small explosion on the table.

'But,' he ended, 'he does really conceal his toilet.'

It somehow completed the thrill of my fanciful nerves that at that instant the Duke appeared again silently among the glimmering trees, with his soft foot and sunset-hued hair, coming round the corner of the house in company with his librarian. Before he came within earshot, Father Brown had added quite composedly, 'Why does he really hide the secret of what he does with the purple wig? Because it isn't the sort of secret we suppose.'

The Duke came round the corner and resumed his seat at the head of the table with all his native dignity. The embarrassment of the librarian left him hovering on his hind legs, like a huge bear. The Duke addressed the priest with great seriousness. 'Father Brown,' he said, 'Doctor Mull informs me that you have come here to make a request. I no longer profess an observance of the religion of my fathers; but for their sakes, and for the sake of the days when we met before, I am very willing to hear you. But I presume you would rather be heard in private.'

Whatever I retain of the gentleman made me stand up. Whatever I have attained of the journalist made me stand still. Before this paralysis could pass, the priest had made a momentarily detaining motion. 'If,' he said, 'your Grace will permit me my real petition, or if I retain any right to advise you, I would urge that as many people as possible should be present. All over this country I have found hundreds, even of my own faith and flock, whose imaginations are poisoned by the spell which I implore you to break. I wish we could have all Devonshire here to see you do it.'

'To see me do what?' asked the Duke, arching his eyebrows.

'To see you take off your wig,' said Father Brown.

The Duke's face did not move; but he looked at his petitioner with a glassy stare which was the most awful expression I have ever seen on a human face. I could see the librarian's great legs wavering under him like the shadows of stems in a pool; and I could not banish from my own brain the fancy that the trees all around us were filling softly in the silence with devils instead of birds.

'I spare you,' said the Duke in a voice of inhuman pity. 'I refuse. If I gave you the faintest hint of the load of horror I have to bear alone, you would lie shrieking at these feet of mine and begging to know no more. I will spare you the hint. You shall not spell the first letter of what is written on the altar of the Unknown God.'

'I know the Unknown God,' said the little priest, with an unconscious grandeur of certitude that stood up like a granite tower. 'I know his name; it is Satan. The true God was made flesh and dwelt among us. And I say to you, wherever you find men ruled merely by mystery, it is the mystery of iniquity. If the devil tells you something is too fearful to look at, look at it. If he says something is too terrible to hear, hear it. If you think some truth unbearable, bear it. I entreat your Grace to end this nightmare now and here at this table.'

'If I did,' said the Duke in a low voice, 'you and all you believe, and all by which alone you live, would be the first to shrivel and perish. You would have an instant to know the great Nothing before you died.'

'The Cross of Christ be between me and harm,' said Father Brown. 'Take off your wig.'

I was leaning over the table in ungovernable excitement; in listening to this extraordinary duel half a thought had come into my head. 'Your Grace,' I cried, 'I call your bluff. Take off that wig or I will knock it off.'

I suppose I can be prosecuted for assault, but I am very glad I did it. When he said, in the same voice of stone, 'I refuse,' I simply sprang on him. For three long instants he strained against me as if he had all hell to help him; but I forced his head until the hairy cap fell off it. I admit that, whilst wrestling, I shut my eyes as it fell.

I was awakened by a cry from Mull, who was also by this time at the Duke's side. His head and mine were both bending over the bald head of the wigless Duke. Then the silence was snapped by the librarian exclaiming: 'What can it mean? Why, the man had nothing to hide. His ears are just like everybody else's.'

'Yes,' said Father Brown, 'that is what he had to hide.'

The priest walked straight up to him, but strangely enough did not even glance at his ears. He stared with an almost comical seriousness at his bald forehead, and pointed to a three-cornered cicatrice, long healed, but still discernible. 'Mr Green, I think,' he said politely, 'and he did get the whole estate after all.'

And now let me tell the readers of the *Daily Reformer* what I think the most remarkable thing in the whole affair. This transformation scene, which will seem to you as wild and purple as a Persian fairy tale, has been (except for my technical assault) strictly legal and constitutional from its first beginnings. This man with the odd scar and the ordinary ears is not an impostor. Though (in one sense) he wears another man's wig and claims another man's ear, he has not stolen another man's coronet. He really is the one and only Duke of Exmoor. What happened was this. The old Duke really had a slight malformation of the ear, which really was more or less hereditary. He really was morbid about it; and it is likely enough that he did invoke it as a kind of curse in the violent scene (which undoubtedly happened) in which he struck Green with the decanter. But the contest ended very differently. Green pressed his claim and got the estates; the dispossessed nobleman shot himself and died without issue. After a decent interval the beautiful English Government revived the 'extinct' peerage of Exmoor, and bestowed it, as is usual, on the most important person, the person who had got the property.

This man used the old feudal fables – properly, in his snobbish soul, really envied and admired them. So that thousands of poor English people trembled before a mysterious chieftain with an ancient destiny and a diadem of evil stars – when they are really trembling before a guttersnipe who was a pettifogger and a pawnbroker not twelve years ago. I think it very typical of the real case against our aristocracy as it is, and as it will be till God sends us braver men.

* * *

Mr Nutt put down the manuscript and called out with unusual sharpness: 'Miss Barlow, please take down a letter to Mr Finn. Dear Finn. You must be mad; we can't touch this. I wanted vampires and the bad old days and aristocracy hand-in-hand with superstition. They like that. But you must know the Exmoors would never forgive this. And what would our people say then, I should like to know! Why, Sir Simon is one of Exmoor's greatest pals; and it would ruin that cousin of the Eyres that's standing for us at Bradford. Besides, old Soap-Suds was sick enough at not getting his peerage last year; he'd sack me by wire if I lost him it with such lunacy as this. And what about Duffey? He's doing us some rattling articles on 'The Heel of the Norman'. And how can he write about Normans if the man's only a solicitor? Do be reasonable. Yours, E. Nutt

As Miss Barlow rattled away cheerfully, he crumpled up the copy and tossed it into the waste-paper basket; but not before he had, automatically and by force of habit, altered the word 'God' to the word 'circumstances'.

The Perishing of the Pendragons

Father Brown was in no mood for adventures. He had lately fallen ill with over-work, and when he began to recover, his friend Flambeau had taken him on a cruise in a small yacht with Sir Cecil Fanshaw, a young Cornish squire and an enthusiast for Cornish coast scenery. But Brown was still rather weak; he was no very happy sailor; and though he was never of the sort that either grumbles or breaks down, his spirits did not rise above patience and civility. When the other two men praised the ragged violet sunset or the ragged volcanic crags, he agreed with them. When Flambeau pointed out a rock shaped like a dragon, he looked at it and thought it very like a dragon. When Fanshaw more excitedly indicated a rock that was like Merlin, he looked at it, and signified assent. When Flambeau asked whether this rocky gate of the twisted river was not the gate of Fairyland, he said 'Yes.' He heard the most important things and the most trivial with the same tasteless absorption. He heard that the coast was death to all but careful seamen; he also heard that the ship's cat was asleep. He heard that Fanshaw couldn't find his cigar-holder anywhere; he also heard the pilot deliver the oracle 'Both eyes bright, she's all right; one eye winks, down she sinks.' He heard Flambeau say to Fanshaw that no doubt this meant the pilot must keep both eyes open and be spry. And he heard Fanshaw say to Flambeau that, oddly enough, it didn't mean this: it meant that while they saw two of the coast lights, one near and the other distant, exactly side by side, they were in the right river-channel; but that if one light was hidden behind the other, they were going on the rocks. He heard Fanshaw add that his country was full of such quaint fables and idioms; it was the very home of romance; he even pitted this part of Cornwall against Devonshire, as a claimant to the laurels of Elizabethan seamanship. According to him there had been captains among these coves and islets compared with whom Drake was practically a landsman. He heard Flambeau laugh, and ask if, perhaps, the adventurous title of 'Westward Ho!' only meant that all Devonshire men wished they were living in Cornwall. He heard Fanshaw say there was no need to be silly; that not only had Cornish captains been heroes, but that they were heroes still: that near that very spot there was an old admiral, now retired, who was scarred by thrilling voyages full of adventures; and who had in his youth found the last group of eight Pacific Islands that was added to the chart of the world. This Cecil Fanshaw was, in person, of the kind that commonly urges such crude but pleasing enthusiasms; a very young man, light-haired, high-coloured, with an eager profile; with a boyish bravado of spirits, but an almost girlish delicacy of tint and type. The big shoulders, black brows and black mousquetaire swagger of Flambeau were a great contrast.

All these trivialities Brown heard and saw; but heard them as a tired man hears a tune in the railway wheels, or saw them as a sick man sees the pattern of his wallpaper. No one can calculate the turns of mood in convalescence: but Father Brown's depression must have had a great deal to do with his mere unfamiliarity with the sea. For as the river mouth narrowed like the neck of a bottle, and the water grew calmer and the air warmer and more earthly, he seemed to wake up and take notice like a baby. They had reached that phase just after sunset when air and water both look bright, but earth and all its growing things look almost black by comparison. About this particular evening, however, there was something exceptional. It was one of those rare atmospheres in which a smoked-glass slide seems to have been slid away from between us and Nature; so that even dark colours on that day look more gorgeous than bright colours on cloudier days. The trampled earth of the river-banks and the peaty stain in the pools did not look drab but glowing umber, and the dark woods astir in the breeze did not look, as usual, dim blue with mere depth of distance, but more like wind-tumbled masses of some vivid violet blossom. This magic clearness and intensity in the colours was further forced on Brown's slowly reviving senses by something romantic and even secret in the very form of the landscape.

The river was still well wide and deep enough for a pleasure boat so small as theirs; but the curves of the countryside suggested that it was closing in on either hand; the woods seemed to be making broken and flying attempts at bridge-building – as if the boat were passing from the romance of a valley to the romance of a hollow and so to the supreme romance of a tunnel. Beyond this mere look of things there was little for Brown's freshening fancy to feed on; he saw no human beings, except some gypsies trailing along the river-bank, with faggots and osiers cut in the forest; and one sight no longer unconventional, but in such remote parts still uncommon: a dark-haired lady, bare-headed, and paddling her own canoe. If Father Brown ever attached any importance to either of these, he certainly forgot them at the next turn of the river which brought in sight a singular object.

The water seemed to widen and split, being cloven by the dark wedge of a fish-shaped and wooded islet. With the rate at which they went, the islet seemed to swim towards them like a ship; a ship with a very high prow – or, to speak more strictly, a very high funnel. For at the extreme point nearest them stood up an odd-looking building, unlike anything they could remember or connect with any purpose. It was not specially high, but it was too high for its breadth to be called anything but a tower. Yet it appeared to be built entirely of wood, and that in a most unequal and eccentric way. Some of the planks and beams were of good, seasoned oak; some of such wood cut raw and recent; some again of white pinewood, and a great deal more of the same sort of wood painted black with tar. These black beams were set crooked or crisscross at all kinds of angles, giving the whole a most patchy and puzzling appearance. There were one or two windows, which appeared to be coloured and leaded in an old-fashioned but more elaborate style. The travellers looked at it with that paradoxical feeling we have when something reminds us of something, and yet we are certain it is something very different.

Father Brown, even when he was mystified, was clever in analysing his own mystification. And he found himself reflecting that the oddity seemed to consist in a particular shape cut out in an incongruous material; as if one saw a top hat made of tin, or a frock-coat cut out of tartan. He was sure he had seen timbers of different tints arranged like that somewhere, but never in such architectural proportions. The next moment a glimpse through the dark trees told him all he wanted to know and he laughed. Through a gap in the foliage there appeared for a moment one of those old wooden houses, faced with black beams, which are still to be found here and there in England, but which most of us see imitated in some show called 'Old London' or 'Shakespeare's England'. It was in view only long enough for the priest to see that, however old-fashioned, it was a comfortable and well-kept country-house, with flowerbeds in front of it. It had none of the piebald and crazy look of the tower that seemed made out of its refuse.

'What on earth's this?' said Flambeau, who was still staring at the tower.

Fanshaw's eyes were shining, and he spoke triumphantly. 'Aha! you've not seen a place quite like this before, I fancy; that's why I've brought you here, my friend. Now you shall see whether I exaggerate about the mariners of Cornwall. This place belongs to Old Pendragon, whom we call the Admiral; though he retired before getting the rank. The spirit of Raleigh and Hawkins is a memory with the Devon folk; it's a modern fact with the Pendragons. If Queen Elizabeth were to rise from the grave and come up this river in a gilded barge, she would be received by the Admiral in a house exactly such as she was accustomed to, in every corner and casement, in every panel on the wall or plate on the table. And she would find an English Captain still talking fiercely of fresh lands to be found in little ships, as much as if she had dined with Drake.'

'She'd find a rum sort of thing in the garden,' said Father Brown, 'which would not please her Renaissance eye. That Elizabethan domestic architecture is charming in its way; but it's against the very nature of it to break out into turrets.'

'And yet,' answered Fanshaw, 'that's the most romantic and Elizabethan part of the business. It was built by the Pendragons in the very days of the Spanish wars; and though it's needed patching and even rebuilding for another reason, it's always been rebuilt in the old way. The story goes that the lady of Sir Peter Pendragon built it in this place and to this height, because from the top you can just see the corner where vessels turn into the river mouth; and she wished to be the first to see her husband's ship, as he sailed home from the Spanish Main.'

'For what other reason,' asked Father Brown, 'do you mean that it has been rebuilt?'

'Oh, there's a strange story about that, too,' said the young squire with relish. 'You are really in a land of strange stories. King Arthur was here and Merlin and the fairies before him. The story goes that Sir Peter Pendragon, who (I fear) had some of the faults of the pirates as well as the virtues of the sailor, was bringing home three Spanish gentlemen in honourable captivity, intending to escort them to Elizabeth's court. But he was a man of flaming and tigerish temper, and coming to high words with one of them, he caught him by the throat and flung him, by accident or design, into the sea. A second Spaniard, who was the brother of the first, instantly drew his sword and flew at Pendragon, and after a short but furious combat in which both got three wounds in as many minutes, Pendragon drove his blade through the other's body and the second Spaniard was accounted for. As it happened the ship had already turned into the river mouth and was close to comparatively shallow water. The third Spaniard sprang over the side of the ship, struck out for the shore, and was soon near enough to it to stand up to his waist in water. And turning again to face the ship, and holding up both arms to Heaven – like a prophet calling plagues upon a wicked city – he called out to Pendragon in a piercing and terrible voice, that he at least was yet living, that he would go on living, that he would live for ever; and that generation after generation the house of Pendragon should never see him or his, but should know by very certain signs that he and his vengeance were alive. With that he dived under the wave, and was either drowned or swam so long under water that no hair of his head was seen afterwards.'

'There's that girl in the canoe again,' said Flambeau irrelevantly, for good-looking young women would call him off any topic. 'She seems bothered by the queer tower just as we were.'

Indeed, the black-haired young lady was letting her canoe float slowly and silently past the strange islet; and was looking intently up at the strange tower, with a strong glow of curiosity on her oval and olive face.

'Never mind girls,' said Fanshaw impatiently, 'there are plenty of them in the world, but not many things like the Pendragon Tower. As you may easily suppose, plenty of superstitions and scandals have followed in the track of the Spaniard's curse; and no doubt, as you would put it, any accident happening to this Cornish family would be connected with it by rural credulity. But it is perfectly true that this tower has been burnt down two or three times; and the family can't be called lucky, for more than two, I think, of the Admiral's near kin have perished by shipwreck; and one at least, to my own knowledge, on practically the same spot where Sir Peter threw the Spaniard overboard.'

'What a pity!' exclaimed Flambeau. 'She's going.'

'When did your friend the Admiral tell you this family history?' asked Father Brown, as the girl in the canoe paddled off, without showing the least intention of extending her interest from the tower to the yacht, which Fanshaw had already caused to lie alongside the island.

'Many years ago,' replied Fanshaw; 'he hasn't been to sea for some time now, though he is as keen on it as ever. I believe there's a family compact or something. Well, here's the landing-stage; let's come ashore and see the old boy.'

They followed him on to the island, just under the tower, and Father Brown, whether from the mere touch of dry land, or the interest of something on the other bank of the river (which he stared at very hard for some seconds), seemed singularly improved in briskness. They entered a wooded avenue between two fences of thin greyish wood, such as often enclose parks or gardens, and over the top of which the dark trees tossed to and fro like black and purple plumes upon the hearse of a giant. The tower, as they left it behind, looked all the quainter, because such entrances are usually flanked by two towers; and this one looked lopsided. But for this, the avenue had the usual appearance of the entrance to a gentleman's grounds; and, being so curved that the house was now out of sight, somehow looked a much larger park than any plantation on such an island could really be. Father Brown was, perhaps, a little fanciful in his fatigue, but he almost thought the whole place must be growing larger, as things do in a nightmare. Anyhow, a mystical monotony was the only character of their march, until Fanshaw suddenly stopped, and pointed to something sticking out through the grey fence – something that looked at first rather like the imprisoned horn of some beast. Closer observation showed that it was a slightly curved blade of metal that shone faintly in the fading light.

Flambeau, who like all Frenchmen had been a soldier, bent over it and said in a startled voice: 'Why, it's a sabre! I believe I know the sort, heavy and curved, but shorter than the cavalry; they used to have them in artillery and the –'

As he spoke the blade plucked itself out of the crack it had made and came down again with a more ponderous slash, splitting the fissiparous fence to the bottom with a rending noise. Then it was pulled out again, flashed above the fence some feet further along, and again split it halfway down with the first stroke; and after waggling a little to extricate itself (accompanied with curses in the darkness) split it down to the ground with a second. Then a kick of devilish energy sent the whole loosened square of thin wood flying into the pathway, and a great gap of dark coppice gaped in the paling.

Fanshaw peered into the dark opening and uttered an exclamation of astonishment. 'My dear Admiral!' he exclaimed, 'do you – er – do you generally cut out a new front door whenever you want to go for a walk?'

The voice in the gloom swore again, and then broke into a jolly laugh. 'No,' it said; 'I've really got to cut down this fence somehow; it's spoiling all the plants, and no one else here can do it. But I'll only carve another bit off the front door, and then come out and welcome you.'

And sure enough, he heaved up his weapon once more, and, hacking twice, brought down another and similar strip of fence, making the opening about fourteen feet wide in all. Then through this larger forest gateway he came out into the evening light, with a chip of grey wood sticking to his sword-blade.

He momentarily fulfilled all Fanshaw's fable of an old piratical Admiral; though the details seemed afterwards to decompose into accidents. For instance, he wore a broad-brimmed hat as protection against the sun; but the front flap of it was turned up straight to the sky, and the two corners pulled down lower than the ears, so that it stood across his forehead in a crescent like the old cocked hat worn by Nelson. He wore an ordinary dark-blue jacket, with nothing special about the buttons, but the combination of it with white linen trousers somehow had a sailorish look. He was tall and loose, and walked with a sort of swagger, which was not a sailor's roll, and yet somehow suggested it; and he held in his hand a short sabre which was like a navy cutlass, but about twice as big. Under the bridge of the hat his eagle face looked eager, all the more because it was not only clean-shaven, but without eyebrows. It seemed almost as if all the hair had come off his face from his thrusting it through a throng of elements. His eyes were prominent and piercing. His colour was curiously attractive, while partly tropical; it reminded one vaguely of a blood-orange. That is, that while it was ruddy and sanguine, there was a yellow in it that was in no way sickly, but seemed rather to glow like gold apples of the Hesperides – Father Brown thought he had never seen a figure so expressive of all the romances about the countries of the Sun.

When Fanshaw had presented his two friends to their host he fell again into a tone of rallying the latter about his wreckage of the fence and his apparent rage of profanity. The Admiral pooh-poohed it at first as a piece of necessary but annoying garden work; but at length the ring of real energy came back into his laughter, and he cried with a mixture of impatience and good humour: 'Well, perhaps I do go at it a bit rabidly, and feel a kind of pleasure in smashing anything. So would you if your only pleasure was in cruising about to find some new Cannibal Islands, and you had to stick on this muddy little rockery in a sort of rustic pond. When I remember how I've cut down a mile and a half of green poisonous jungle with an old cutlass half as sharp as this; and then remember I must stop here and chop this matchwood, because of some confounded old bargain scribbled in a family Bible, why, I – '

He swung up the heavy steel again; and this time sundered the wall of wood from top to bottom at one stroke.

'I feel like that,' he said laughing, but furiously flinging the sword some yards down the path, 'and now let's go up to the house; you must have some dinner.'

The semicircle of lawn in front of the house was varied by three circular garden beds, one of red tulips, a second of yellow tulips, and the third of some white, waxen-looking blossoms that the visitors did not know and presumed to be exotic. A heavy, hairy and rather sullen-looking gardener was hanging up a heavy coil of garden hose. The corners of the expiring sunset which seemed to cling about the corners of the house gave glimpses here and there of the colours of remoter flowerbeds; and in a treeless space on one side of the house opening upon the river stood a tall brass tripod on which was tilted a big brass telescope. Just outside the steps of the porch stood a little painted green garden table, as if someone had just had tea there. The entrance was flanked with two of those half-featured lumps of stone with holes for eyes that are said to be South Sea idols; and on the brown oak beam across the doorway were some confused carvings that looked almost as barbaric.

As they passed indoors, the little cleric hopped suddenly on to the table, and standing on it peered unaffectedly through his spectacles at the mouldings in the oak. Admiral Pendragon looked very much astonished, though not particularly annoyed; while Fanshaw was so amused with what looked like a performing pigmy on his little stand, that he could not control his laughter. But Father Brown was not likely to notice either the laughter or the astonishment.

He was gazing at three carved symbols, which, though very worn and obscure, seemed still to convey some sense to him. The first seemed to be the outline of some tower or other building, crowned with what looked like curly-pointed ribbons. The second was clearer: an old Elizabethan galley with decorative waves beneath it, but interrupted in the middle by a curious jagged rock, which was either a fault in the wood or some conventional representation of the water coming in. The third represented the upper half of a human figure, ending in an escalloped line like the waves; the face was rubbed and featureless, and both arms were held very stiffly up in the air.

'Well,' muttered Father Brown, blinking, 'here is the legend of the Spaniard plain enough. Here he is holding up his arms and cursing in the sea; and here are the two curses: the wrecked ship and the burning of Pendragon Tower.'

Pendragon shook his head with a kind of venerable amusement. 'And how many other things might it not be?' he said. 'Don't you know that that sort of half-man, like a half-lion or half-stag, is quite common in heraldry? Might not that line through the ship be one of those *parti-per-pale* lines, *indented*, I think they call it? And though the third thing isn't so very heraldic, it would be more heraldic to suppose it a tower crowned with laurel than with fire; and it looks just as like it.'

'But it seems rather odd,' said Flambeau, 'that it should exactly confirm the old legend.'

'Ah,' replied the sceptical traveller, 'but you don't know how much of the old legend may have been made up from the old figures. Besides, it isn't the only old legend. Fanshaw, here, who is fond of such things, will tell you there are other versions of the tale, and much more horrible ones. One story credits my unfortunate ancestor with having had the Spaniard cut in two; and that will fit the pretty picture also. Another obligingly credits our family with the possession of a tower full of snakes and explains those little, wriggly things in that way. And a third theory supposes the crooked line on the ship to be a conventionalised thunderbolt; but that alone, if seriously examined, would show what a very little way these unhappy coincidences really go.'

'Why, how do you mean?' asked Fanshaw.

'It so happens,' replied his host coolly, 'that there was no thunder and lightning at all in the two or three shipwrecks I know of in our family.'

'Oh!' said Father Brown, and jumped down from the little table.

There was another silence in which they heard the continuous murmur of the river; then Fanshaw said, in a doubtful and perhaps disappointed tone: 'Then you don't think there is anything in the tales of the tower in flames?'

'There are the tales, of course,' said the Admiral, shrugging his shoulders; 'and some of them, I don't deny, on evidence as decent as one ever gets for such things. Someone saw a blaze hereabout, don't you know, as he walked home through a wood; someone keeping sheep on the uplands inland thought he saw a flame hovering over Pendragon Tower. Well, a damp dab of mud like this confounded island seems the last place where one would think of fires.'

'What is that fire over there?' asked Father Brown with a gentle suddenness, pointing to the woods on the left river-bank. They were all thrown a little off their balance, and the more fanciful Fanshaw had even some difficulty in recovering his, as they saw a long, thin stream of blue smoke ascending silently into the end of the evening light.

Then Pendragon broke into a scornful laugh again. 'Gypsies!' he said;

'they've been camping about here for about a week. Gentlemen, you want your dinner,' and he turned as if to enter the house.

But the antiquarian superstition in Fanshaw was still quivering, and he said hastily: 'But, Admiral, what's that hissing noise quite near the island? It's very like fire.'

'It's more like what it is,' said the Admiral, laughing as he led the way; 'it's only some canoe going by.'

Almost as he spoke, the butler, a lean man in black, with very black hair and a very long, yellow face, appeared in the doorway and told him that dinner was served.

The dining-room was as nautical as the cabin of a ship; but its note was rather that of the modern than the Elizabethan captain. There were, indeed, three antiquated cutlasses in a trophy over the fireplace, and one brown sixteenth-century map with Tritons and little ships dotted about a curly sea. But such things were less prominent on the white panelling than some cases of quaint-coloured South American birds, very scientifically stuffed, fantastic shells from the Pacific, and several instruments so rude and queer in shape that savages might have used them either to kill their enemies or to cook them. But the alien colour culminated in the fact that, besides the butler, the Admiral's only servants were two Negroes, somewhat quaintly clad in tight uniforms of yellow. The priest's instinctive trick of analysing his own impressions told him that the colour and the little neat coat-tails of these bipeds had suggested the word 'Canary', and so by a mere pun connected them with southward travel. Towards the end of the dinner they took their yellow clothes and black faces out of the room, leaving only the black clothes and yellow face of the butler.

'I'm rather sorry you take this so lightly,' said Fanshaw to the host; 'for the truth is, I've brought these friends of mine with the idea of their helping you, as they know a good deal of these things. Don't you really believe in the family story at all?'

'I don't believe in anything,' answered Pendragon very briskly, with a bright eye cocked at a red tropical bird. 'I'm a man of science.'

Rather to Flambeau's surprise, his clerical friend, who seemed to have entirely woken up, took up the digression and talked natural history with his host with a flow of words and much unexpected information, until the dessert and decanters were set down and the last of the servants vanished. Then he said, without altering his tone, 'Please don't think me impertinent, Admiral Pendragon. I don't ask for curiosity, but really for my guidance and your convenience. Have I made a bad shot if I guess you don't want these old things talked of before your butler?'

The Admiral lifted the hairless arches over his eyes and exclaimed: 'Well, I don't know where you got it, but the truth is I can't stand the fellow, though I've no excuse for discharging a family servant. Fanshaw, with his fairy tales, would say my blood moved against men with that black, Spanish-looking hair.'

Flambeau struck the table with his heavy fist. 'By Jove!' he cried; 'and so had that girl!'

'I hope it'll all end tonight,' continued the Admiral, 'when my nephew comes back safe from his ship. You looked surprised. You won't understand, I suppose, unless I tell you the story. You see, my father had two sons; I remained a bachelor, but my elder brother married, and had a son who became a sailor like all the rest of us, and will inherit the proper estate. Well, my father was a strange man; he somehow combined Fanshaw's superstition with a good deal of my scepticism – they were always fighting in him; and after my first voyages, he developed a notion which he thought somehow would settle finally whether the curse was truth or trash. If all the Pendragons sailed about anyhow, he thought there would be too much chance of natural catastrophes to prove anything. But if we went to sea one at a time in strict order of succession to the property, he thought it might show whether any connected fate followed the family as a family. It was a silly notion, I think, and I quarrelled with my father pretty heartily; for I was an ambitious man and was left to the last, coming, by succession, after my own nephew.'

'And your father and brother,' said the priest, very gently, 'died at sea, I fear.'

'Yes,' groaned the Admiral; 'by one of those brutal accidents on which are built all the lying mythologies of mankind, they were both shipwrecked. My father, coming up this coast out of the Atlantic, was washed up on these Cornish rocks. My brother's ship was sunk, no one knows where, on the voyage home from Tasmania. His body was never found. I tell you it was from perfectly natural mishap; lots of other people besides Pendragons were drowned; and both disasters are discussed in a normal way by navigators. But, of course, it set this forest of superstition on fire; and men saw the flaming tower everywhere. That's why I say it will be all right when Walter returns. The girl he's engaged to was coming today; but I was so afraid of some chance delay frightening her that I wired her not to come till she heard from me. But he's practically sure to be here sometime tonight, and then it'll all end in smoke – tobacco smoke. We'll crack that old lie when we crack a bottle of this wine.'

'Very good wine,' said Father Brown, gravely lifting his glass, 'but, as you see, a very bad wine-bibber. I most sincerely beg your pardon': for he had spilt a small spot of wine on the tablecloth. He drank and put down the glass with a composed face; but his hand had started at the exact moment when he became conscious of a face looking in through the garden window just behind the Admiral – the face of a woman, swarthy, with southern hair and eyes, and young, but like a mask of tragedy.

After a pause the priest spoke again in his mild manner. 'Admiral,' he said, 'will you do me a favour? Let me, and my friends if they like, stop in that tower of yours just for tonight? Do you know that in my business you're an exorcist almost before anything else?'

Pendragon sprang to his feet and paced swiftly to and fro across the window, from which the face had instantly vanished. 'I tell you there is nothing in it,' he cried, with ringing violence. 'There is one thing I know about this matter. You may call me an atheist. I am an atheist.' Here he swung round and fixed Father Brown with a face of frightful concentration. 'This business is perfectly natural. There is no curse in it at all.'

Father Brown smiled. 'In that case,' he said, 'there can't be any objection to my sleeping in your delightful summerhouse.'

'The idea is utterly ridiculous,' replied the Admiral, beating a tattoo on the back of his chair.

'Please forgive me for everything,' said Brown in his most sympathetic tone, 'including spilling the wine. But it seems to me you are not quite so easy about the flaming tower as you try to be.'

Admiral Pendragon sat down again as abruptly as he had risen; but he sat quite still, and when he spoke again it was in a lower voice. 'You do it at your own peril,' he said; 'but wouldn't you be an atheist to keep sane in all this devilry?'

Some three hours afterwards Fanshaw, Flambeau and the priest were still dawdling about the garden in the dark; and it began to dawn on the other two that Father Brown had no intention of going to bed either in the tower or the house.

'I think the lawn wants weeding,' said he dreamily. 'If I could find a spud or something I'd do it myself.'

They followed him, laughing and half remonstrating; but he replied with the utmost solemnity, explaining to them, in a maddening little sermon, that one can always find some small occupation that is helpful to others. He did not find a spud; but he found an old broom made of twigs, with which he began energetically to brush the fallen leaves off the grass.

'Always some little thing to be done,' he said with idiotic cheerfulness; 'as George Herbert says: "Who sweeps an Admiral's garden in Cornwall as for Thy laws makes that and the action fine." And now,' he added, suddenly slinging the broom away, 'let's go and water the flowers.'

With the same mixed emotions they watched him uncoil some considerable lengths of the large garden hose, saying with an air of wistful discrimination: 'The red tulips before the yellow, I think. Look a bit dry, don't you think?'

He turned the little tap on the instrument, and the water shot out straight and solid as a long rod of steel.

'Look out, Samson,' cried Flambeau; 'why, you've cut off the tulip's head.'

Father Brown stood ruefully contemplating the decapitated plant.

'Mine does seem to be a rather kill or cure sort of watering,' he admitted, scratching his head. 'I suppose it's a pity I didn't find the spud. You should have seen me with the spud! Talking of tools, you've got that sword stick, Flambeau, you always carry? That's right; and Sir Cecil could have that sword the Admiral threw away by the fence here. How grey everything looks!'

'The mist's rising from the river,' said the staring Flambeau.

Almost as he spoke the huge figure of the hairy gardener appeared on a higher ridge of the trenched and terraced lawn, hailing them with a brandished rake and a horribly bellowing voice. 'Put down that hose,' he shouted; 'put down that hose and go to your – '

'I am fearfully clumsy,' replied the reverend gentleman weakly; 'do you know, I upset some wine at dinner.' He made a wavering half-turn of apology towards the gardener, with the hose still spouting in his hand. The gardener caught the cold crash of the water full in his face like the crash of a cannonball; staggered, slipped and went sprawling with his boots in the air.

'How very dreadful!' said Father Brown, looking round in a sort of wonder. 'Why, I've hit a man!'

He stood with his head forward for a moment as if looking or listening; and then set off at a trot towards the tower, still trailing the hose behind him. The tower was quite close, but its outline was curiously dim.

'Your river mist,' he said, 'has a rum smell.'

'By the Lord it has,' cried Fanshaw, who was very white. 'But you can't mean – '

'I mean,' said Father Brown, 'that one of the Admiral's scientific predictions is coming true tonight. This story is going to end in smoke.'

As he spoke a most beautiful rose-red light seemed to burst into blossom like a gigantic rose; but accompanied with a crackling and rattling noise that was like the laughter of devils.

'My God! what is this?' cried Sir Cecil Fanshaw.

'The sign of the flaming tower,' said Father Brown, and sent the driving water from his hose into the heart of the red patch.

'Lucky we hadn't gone to bed!' ejaculated Fanshaw. 'I suppose it can't spread to the house.'

'You may remember,' said the priest quietly, 'that the wooden fence that might have carried it was cut away.'

Flambeau turned electrified eyes upon his friend, but Fanshaw only said rather absently: 'Well, nobody can be killed, anyhow.'

'This is rather a curious kind of tower,' observed Father Brown, 'when it takes to killing people, it always kills people who are somewhere else.'

At the same instant the monstrous figure of the gardener with the streaming beard stood again on the green ridge against the sky, waving others to come on; but now waving not a rake but a cutlass. Behind him came the two Negroes, also with the old crooked cutlasses out of the trophy. But in the blood-red glare, with their black faces and yellow figures, they looked like devils carrying instruments of torture. In the dim garden behind them a distant voice was heard calling out brief directions. When the priest heard the voice, a terrible change came over his countenance.

But he remained composed; and never took his eye off the patch of flame which had begun by spreading, but now seemed to shrink a little as it hissed under the torch of the long silver spear of water. He kept his finger along the nozzle of the pipe to ensure the aim, and attended to no other business, knowing only by the noise and that semi-conscious corner of the eye, the exciting incidents that began to tumble themselves about the island garden. He gave two brief directions to his friends. One was: 'Knock these fellows down somehow and tie them up, whoever they are; there's rope down by those faggots. They want to take away my nice hose.' The other was: 'As soon as you get a chance, call out to that canoeing girl; she's over on the bank with the gypsies. Ask her if they could get some buckets across and fill them from the river.' Then he closed his mouth and continued to water the new red flower as ruthlessly as he had watered the red tulip.

He never turned his head to look at the strange fight that followed between the foes and friends of the mysterious fire. He almost felt the island shake when Flambeau collided with the huge gardener; he merely imagined how it would whirl round them as they wrestled. He heard the crashing fall; and his friend's gasp of triumph as he dashed on to the first Negro; and the cries of both the blacks as Flambeau and Fanshaw bound them. Flambeau's enormous strength more than redressed the odds in the fight, especially as the fourth man still hovered near the house, only a shadow and a voice. He heard also the water broken by the paddles of a canoe; the girl's voice giving orders, the voices of gypsies answering and coming nearer, the plumping and sucking noise of empty buckets plunged into a full stream; and finally the sound of many feet around the fire. But all this was less to him than the fact that the red rent, which had lately once more increased, had once more slightly diminished.

Then came a cry that very nearly made him turn his head. Flambeau and Fanshaw, now reinforced by some of the gypsies, had rushed after the mysterious man by the house; and he heard from the other end of the garden the Frenchman's cry of horror and astonishment. It was echoed by a howl not to be called human, as the being broke from their hold and ran along the garden. Three times at least it raced round the whole island, in a way that was as horrible as the chase of a lunatic, both in the cries of the pursued and the ropes carried by the pursuers; but was more horrible still, because it somehow suggested one of the chasing games of children in a garden. Then, finding them closing in on every side, the figure sprang upon one of the higher river-banks and disappeared with a splash into the dark and driving river.

'You can do no more, I fear,' said Brown in a voice cold with pain. 'He has been washed down to the rocks by now, where he has sent so many others. He knew the use of a family legend.'

'Oh, don't talk in these parables,' cried Flambeau impatiently. 'Can't you put it simply in words of one syllable?'

'Yes,' answered Brown, with his eye on the hose. ' "Both eyes bright, she's all right; one eye blinks, down she sinks." '

The fire hissed and shrieked more and more, like a strangled thing, as it grew narrower and narrower under the flood from the pipe and buckets, but Father Brown still kept his eye on it as he went on speaking: 'I thought of asking this young lady, if it were morning yet, to look through that telescope at the river mouth and the river. She might have seen something to interest her: the sign of the ship, or Mr Walter Pendragon coming home, and perhaps even the sign of the half-man, for though he is certainly safe by now, he may very well have waded ashore. He has been within a shave of another shipwreck; and would never have escaped it, if the lady hadn't had the sense to suspect the old Admiral's telegram and come down to watch him. Don't let's talk about the old Admiral. Don't let's talk about anything. It's enough to say that whenever this tower, with its pitch and resin-wood, really caught fire, the spark on the horizon always looked like the twin light to the coast lighthouse.'

'And that,' said Flambeau, 'is how the father and brother died. The wicked uncle of the legends very nearly got his estate after all.'

Father Brown did not answer; indeed, he did not speak again, save for civilities, till they were all safe round a cigar-box in the cabin of the yacht. He saw that the frustrated fire was extinguished; and then refused to linger, though he actually heard young Pendragon, escorted by an enthusiastic crowd, come tramping up the river-bank; and might (had he been moved by romantic curiosities) have received the combined thanks of the man from the ship and the girl from the canoe. But his fatigue had fallen on him once more, and he only started once, when Flambeau abruptly told him he had dropped cigar-ash on his trousers.

'That's no cigar-ash,' he said rather wearily. 'That's from the fire, but you don't think so because you're all smoking cigars. That's just the way I got my first faint suspicion about the chart.'

'Do you mean Pendragon's chart of his Pacific Islands?' asked Fanshaw.

'You thought it was a chart of the Pacific Islands,' answered Brown. 'Put a feather with a fossil and a bit of coral and everyone will think it's a specimen. Put the same feather with a ribbon and an artificial flower and everyone will think it's for a lady's hat. Put the same feather with an ink-bottle, a book and a stack of writing-paper, and most men will swear they've seen a quill pen. So you saw that map among tropic birds and shells and thought it was a map of Pacific Islands. It was the map of this river.'

'But how do you know?' asked Fanshaw.

'I saw the rock you thought was like a dragon, and the one like Merlin, and – '

'You seem to have noticed a lot as we came in,' cried Fanshaw. 'We thought you were rather abstracted.'

'I was seasick,' said Father Brown simply. 'I felt simply horrible. But feeling horrible has nothing to do with not seeing things.' And he closed his eyes.

'Do you think most men would have seen that?' asked Flambeau. He received no answer: Father Brown was asleep.

The God of the Gongs

It was one of those chilly and empty afternoons in early winter, when the daylight is silver rather than gold and pewter rather than silver. If it was dreary in a hundred bleak offices and yawning drawing-rooms, it was drearier still along the edges of the flat Essex coast, where the monotony was the more inhuman for being broken at very long intervals by a lamp post that looked less civilised than a tree, or a tree that looked more ugly than a lamp post. A light fall of snow had half-melted into a few strips, also looking leaden rather than silver, when it had been fixed again by the seal of frost; no fresh snow had fallen, but a ribbon of the old snow ran along the very margin of the coast, so as to parallel the pale ribbon of the foam.

The line of the sea looked frozen in the very vividness of its violet-blue, like the vein of a frozen finger. For miles and miles, forward and back, there was no breathing soul, save two pedestrians, walking at a brisk pace, though one had much longer legs and took much longer strides than the other.

It did not seem a very appropriate place or time for a holiday, but Father Brown had few holidays, and had to take them when he could, and he always preferred, if possible, to take them in company with his old friend Flambeau, ex-criminal and ex-detective. The priest had had a fancy for visiting his old parish at Cobhole, and was going north-eastward along the coast.

After walking a mile or two farther, they found that the shore was beginning to be formally embanked, so as to form something like a parade; the ugly lamp posts became less few and far between and more ornamental, though quite equally ugly. Half a mile farther on Father Brown was puzzled first by little labyrinths of flowerless flowerpots, covered with the low, flat, quiet-coloured plants that look less like a garden than a tessellated pavement, between weak curly paths studded with seats with curly backs. He faintly sniffed the atmosphere of a certain sort of seaside town that he did not specially care about, and, looking ahead along the parade by the sea, he saw something that put the matter beyond a doubt. In the grey distance the big bandstand of a watering-place stood up like a giant mushroom with six legs.

'I suppose,' said Father Brown, turning up his coat-collar and drawing a woollen scarf rather closer round his neck, 'that we are approaching a pleasure resort.'

'I fear,' answered Flambeau, 'a pleasure resort to which few people just now have the pleasure of resorting. They try to revive these places in the winter, but it never succeeds except with Brighton and the old ones. This must be Seawood, I think – Lord Pooley's experiment; he had the Sicilian Singers down at Christmas, and there's talk about holding one of the great glove-fights here. But they'll have to chuck the rotten place into the sea; it's as dreary as a lost railway-carriage.'

They had come under the big bandstand, and the priest was looking up at it with a curiosity that had something rather odd about it, his head a little on one side, like a bird's. It was the conventional, rather tawdry kind of erection for its purpose: a flattened dome or canopy, gilt here and there, and lifted on six slender pillars of painted wood, the whole being raised about five feet above the parade on a round wooden platform like a drum. But there was something fantastic about the snow combined with something artificial about the gold that haunted Flambeau as well as his friend with some association he could not capture, but which he knew was at once artistic and alien.

'I've got it,' he said at last. 'It's Japanese. It's like those fanciful Japanese prints, where the snow on the mountain looks like sugar, and the gilt on the pagodas is like gilt on gingerbread. It looks just like a little pagan temple.'

'Yes,' said Father Brown. 'Let's have a look at the god.' And with an agility hardly to be expected of him, he hopped up on to the raised platform.

'Oh, very well,' said Flambeau, laughing; and the next instant his own towering figure was visible on that quaint elevation.

Slight as was the difference of height, it gave in those level wastes a sense of seeing yet farther and farther across land and sea. Inland the little wintry gardens faded into a confused grey copse; beyond that, in the distance, were long low barns of a lonely farmhouse, and beyond that nothing but the long East Anglian plains. Seawards there was no sail or sign of life save a few seagulls: and even they looked like the last snowflakes, and seemed to float rather than fly.

Flambeau turned abruptly at an exclamation behind him. It seemed to come from lower down than might have been expected, and to be addressed to his heels rather than his head. He instantly held out his hand, but he could hardly help laughing at what he saw. For some reason or other the platform had given way under Father Brown, and the unfortunate little man had dropped through to the level of the parade. He was just tall enough, or short enough, for his head alone to stick out of the hole in the broken wood, looking like St John the Baptist's head on a charger. The face wore a disconcerted expression, as did, perhaps, that of St John the Baptist.

In a moment he began to laugh a little. 'This wood must be rotten,' said Flambeau. 'Though it seems odd it should bear me, and you go through the weak place. Let me help you out.'

But the little priest was looking rather curiously at the corners and edges of the wood alleged to be rotten, and there was a sort of trouble on his brow.

'Come along,' cried Flambeau impatiently, still with his big brown hand extended. 'Don't you want to get out?'

The priest was holding a splinter of the broken wood between his finger and thumb, and did not immediately reply. At last he said thoughtfully: 'Want to get out? Why, no. I rather think I want to get in.' And he dived into the darkness under the wooden floor so abruptly as to knock off his big curved clerical hat and leave it lying on the boards above, without any clerical head in it.

Flambeau looked once more inland and out to sea, and once more could see nothing but seas as wintry as the snow, and snows as level as the sea.

There came a scurrying noise behind him, and the little priest came scrambling out of the hole faster than he had fallen in. His face was no longer disconcerted, but rather resolute, and, perhaps only through the reflections of the snow, a trifle paler than usual.

'Well?' asked his tall friend. 'Have you found the god of the temple?'

'No,' answered Father Brown. 'I have found what was sometimes more important. The Sacrifice.'

'What the devil do you mean?' cried Flambeau, quite alarmed.

Father Brown did not answer. He was staring, with a knot in his forehead, at the landscape; and he suddenly pointed at it. 'What's that house over there?' he asked.

Following his finger, Flambeau saw for the first time the corners of a building nearer than the farmhouse, but screened for the most part with a fringe of trees. It was not a large building, and stood well back from the shore, but a glint of ornament on it suggested that it was part of the same watering-place scheme of decoration as the bandstand, the little gardens and the curly-backed iron seats.

Father Brown jumped off the bandstand, his friend following; and as they walked in the direction indicated the trees fell away to right and left, and they saw a small, rather flashy hotel, such as is common in resorts – the hotel of the Saloon Bar rather than the Bar Parlour. Almost the whole frontage was of gilt plaster and figured glass, and between that grey seascape and the grey, witchlike trees, its gimcrack quality had something spectral in its melancholy. They both felt vaguely that if any food or drink were offered at such a hostelry, it would be the pasteboard ham and empty mug of the pantomime.

In this, however, they were not altogether confirmed. As they drew nearer and nearer to the place they saw in front of the buffet, which was apparently closed, one of the iron garden-seats with curly backs that had adorned the gardens, but much longer, running almost the whole length of the frontage. Presumably, it was placed so that visitors might sit there and look at the sea, but one hardly expected to find anyone doing it in such weather.

Nevertheless, just in front of the extreme end of the iron seat stood a small round restaurant table, and on this stood a small bottle of Chablis and a plate of almonds and raisins. Behind the table and on the seat sat a dark-haired young man, bare-headed, and gazing at the sea in a state of almost astonishing immobility.

But though he might have been a waxwork when they were within four yards of him, he jumped up like a jack-in-the-box when they came within three, and said in a deferential, though not undignified, manner: 'Will you step inside, gentlemen? I have no staff at present, but I can get you anything simple myself.'

'Much obliged,' said Flambeau. 'So you are the proprietor?'

'Yes,' said the dark man, dropping back a little into his motionless manner. 'My waiters are all Italians, you see, and I thought it only fair they should see their countryman beat the black, if he really can do it. You know the great fight between Malvoli and Nigger Ned is coming off after all?'

'I'm afraid we can't wait to trouble your hospitality seriously,' said Father Brown. 'But my friend would be glad of a glass of sherry, I'm sure, to keep out the cold and drink success to the Latin champion.'

Flambeau did not understand the sherry, but he did not object to it in the least. He could only say amiably: 'Oh, thank you very much.'

'Sherry, sir – certainly,' said their host, turning to his hostel. 'Excuse me if I detain you a few minutes. As I told you, I have no staff – ' And he went towards the black windows of his shuttered and unlighted inn.

'Oh, it doesn't really matter,' began Flambeau, but the man turned to reassure him.

'I have the keys,' he said. 'I could find my way in the dark.'

'I didn't mean – ' began Father Brown.

He was interrupted by a bellowing human voice that came out of the bowels of the uninhabited hotel. It thundered some foreign name loudly but inaudibly, and the hotel proprietor moved more sharply towards it than he had done for Flambeau's sherry. As instant evidence proved, the proprietor had told, then and after, nothing but the literal truth. But both Flambeau and Father Brown have often confessed that, in all their (often outrageous) adventures, nothing had so chilled their blood as that voice of an ogre, sounding suddenly out of a silent and empty inn.

'My cook!' cried the proprietor hastily. 'I had forgotten my cook. He will be starting presently. Sherry, sir?'

And, sure enough, there appeared in the doorway a big white bulk with white cap and white apron, as befits a cook, but with the needless emphasis of a black face. Flambeau had often heard that Negroes made good cooks. But somehow something in the contrast of colour and caste increased his surprise that the hotel proprietor should answer the call of the cook, and not the cook the call of the proprietor. But he reflected that head cooks are proverbially arrogant; and, besides, the host had come back with the sherry, and that was the great thing.

'I rather wonder,' said Father Brown, 'that there are so few people about the beach, when this big fight is coming on after all. We only met one man for miles.'

The hotel proprietor shrugged his shoulders. 'They come from the other end of the town, you see – from the station, three miles from here. They are only interested in the sport, and will stop in hotels for the night only. After all, it is hardly weather for basking on the shore.'

'Or on the seat,' said Flambeau, and pointed to the little table.

'I have to keep a look-out,' said the man with the motionless face. He was a quiet, well-featured fellow, rather sallow; his dark clothes had nothing distinctive about them, except that his black necktie was worn rather high, like a stock, and secured by a gold pin with some grotesque head to it. Nor was there anything notable in the face, except something that was probably a mere nervous trick – a habit of opening one eye more narrowly than the other, giving the impression that the other was larger, or was, perhaps, artificial.

The silence that ensued was broken by their host saying quietly: 'Whereabouts did you meet the one man on your march?'

'Curiously enough,' answered the priest, 'close by here – just by that bandstand.'

Flambeau, who had sat on the long iron seat to finish his sherry, put it down and rose to his feet, staring at his friend in amazement. He opened his mouth to speak, and then shut it again.

'Curious,' said the dark-haired man thoughtfully. 'What was he like?'

'It was rather dark when I saw him,' began Father Brown, 'but he was – '

As has been said, the hotel-keeper can be proved to have told the precise truth. His phrase that the cook was starting presently was fulfilled to the letter, for the cook came out, pulling his gloves on, even as they spoke.

But he was a very different figure from the confused mass of white and black that had appeared for an instant in the doorway. He was buttoned and buckled up to his bursting eyeballs in the most brilliant fashion. A tall black hat was tilted on his broad black head – a hat of the sort that the French wit has compared to eight mirrors. But somehow the black man was like the black hat. He also was black, and yet his glossy skin flung back the light at eight angles or more. It is needless to say that he wore white spats and a white slip inside his waistcoat. The red flower stood up in his buttonhole aggressively, as if it had suddenly grown there. And in the way he carried his cane in one hand and his cigar in the other there was a certain attitude – an attitude we must always remember when we talk of racial prejudices: something innocent and insolent – the cake walk.

'Sometimes,' said Flambeau, looking after him, 'I'm not surprised that they lynch them.'

'I am never surprised,' said Father Brown, 'at any work of hell. But as I was saying,' he resumed, as the Negro, still ostentatiously pulling on his yellow gloves, betook himself briskly towards the watering-place, a queer music-hall figure against that grey and frosty scene – 'as I was saying, I couldn't describe the man very minutely, but he had a flourish and old-fashioned whiskers and moustachios, dark or dyed, as in the pictures of foreign financiers, round his neck was wrapped a long purple scarf that thrashed out in the wind as he walked. It was fixed at the throat rather in the way that nurses fix children's comforters with a safety-pin. Only this,' added the priest, gazing placidly out to sea, 'was not a safety-pin.'

The man sitting on the long iron bench was also gazing placidly out to sea. Now he was once more in repose. Flambeau felt quite certain that one of his eyes was naturally larger than the other. Both were now well opened, and he could almost fancy the left eye grew larger as he gazed.

'It was a very long gold pin, and had the carved head of a monkey or some such thing,' continued the cleric; 'and it was fixed in a rather odd way – he wore pince-nez and a broad black – '

The motionless man continued to gaze at the sea, and the eyes in his head might have belonged to two different men. Then he made a movement of blinding swiftness.

Father Brown had his back to him, and in that flash might have fallen dead on his face. Flambeau had no weapon, but his large brown hands were resting on the end of the long iron seat. His shoulders abruptly altered their shape, and he heaved the whole huge thing high over his head, like a headsman's axe about to fall. The mere height of the thing, as he held it vertical, looked like a long iron ladder by which he was inviting men to climb towards the stars. But the long shadow, in the level evening light, looked like a giant brandishing the Eiffel Tower. It was the shock of that shadow, before the shock of the iron crash, that made the stranger quail and dodge, and then dart into his inn, leaving the flat and shining dagger he had dropped exactly where it had fallen.

'We must get away from here instantly,' cried Flambeau, flinging the huge seat away with furious indifference on the beach. He caught the little priest by the elbow and ran him down a grey perspective of barren back garden, at the end of which there was a closed back garden door. Flambeau bent over it an instant in violent silence, and then said: 'The door is locked.'

As he spoke a black feather from one of the ornamental firs fell, brushing the brim of his hat. It startled him more than the small and distant detonation that had come just before. Then came another distant detonation, and the door he was trying to open shook under the bullet buried in it. Flambeau's shoulders again filled out and altered suddenly. Three hinges and a lock burst at the same instant, and he went out into the empty path behind, carrying the great garden door with him, as Samson carried the gates of Gaza.

Then he flung the garden door over the garden wall, just as a third shot picked up a spurt of snow and dust behind his heel. Without ceremony he snatched up the little priest, slung him astraddle on his shoulders, and went racing towards Seawood as fast as his long legs could carry him. It was not until nearly two miles farther on that he set his small companion down. It had hardly been a dignified escape, in spite of the classic model of Anchises, but Father Brown's face only wore a broad grin.

'Well,' said Flambeau, after an impatient silence, as they resumed their more conventional tramp through the streets on the edge of the town, where no outrage need be feared, 'I don't know what all this means, but I take it I may trust my own eyes that you never met the man you have so accurately described.'

'I did meet him in a way,' Brown said, biting his finger rather nervously – 'I did really. And it was too dark to see him properly, because it was under that bandstand affair. But I'm afraid I didn't describe him so very accurately after all, for his pince-nez was broken under him, and the long gold pin wasn't stuck through his purple scarf but through his heart.'

'And I suppose,' said the other in a lower voice, 'that glass-eyed guy had something to do with it.'

'I had hoped he had only a little,' answered Brown in a rather troubled voice, 'and I may have been wrong in what I did. I acted on impulse. But I fear this business has deep roots and dark.'

They walked on through some streets in silence. The yellow lamps were beginning to be lit in the cold blue twilight, and they were evidently approaching the more central parts of the town. Highly coloured bills announcing the glove-fight between Nigger Ned and Malvoli were slapped about the walls.

'Well,' said Flambeau, 'I never murdered anyone, even in my criminal days, but I can almost sympathise with anyone doing it in such a dreary place. Of all Godforsaken dustbins of Nature, I think the most heart-breaking are places like that bandstand, that were meant to be festive and are forlorn. I can fancy a morbid man feeling he must kill his rival in the solitude and irony of such a scene. I remember once taking a tramp in your glorious Surrey hills, thinking of nothing but gorse and skylarks, when I came out on a vast circle of land, and over me lifted a vast, voiceless structure, tier above tier of seats, as huge as a Roman amphitheatre and as empty as a new letter-rack. A bird sailed in heaven over it. It was the Grand Stand at Epsom. And I felt that no one would ever be happy there again.'

'It's odd you should mention Epsom,' said the priest. 'Do you remember what was called the Sutton Mystery, because two suspected men – ice-cream men, I think – happened to live at Sutton? They were eventually released. A man was found strangled, it was said, on the Downs round that part. As a fact, I know (from an Irish policeman who is a friend of mine) that he was found close up to the Epsom Grand Stand – in fact, only hidden by one of the lower doors being pushed back.'

'That is queer,' assented Flambeau. 'But it rather confirms my view that such pleasure places look awfully lonely out of season, or the man wouldn't have been murdered there.'

'I'm not so sure he – ' began Brown, and stopped.

'Not so sure he was murdered?' queried his companion.

'Not so sure he was murdered out of the season,' answered the little priest, with simplicity. 'Don't you think there's something rather tricky about this solitude, Flambeau? Do you feel sure a wise murderer would always want the spot to be lonely? It's very, very seldom a man is quite alone. And, short of that, the more alone he is, the more certain he is to be seen. No; I think there must be some other – Why, here we are at the Pavilion or Palace, or whatever they call it.'

They had emerged on a small square, brilliantly lighted, of which the principal building was gay with gilding, gaudy with posters, and flanked with two giant photographs of Malvoli and Nigger Ned.

'Hallo!' cried Flambeau in great surprise, as his clerical friend stumped straight up the broad steps. 'I didn't know pugilism was your latest hobby. Are you going to see the fight?'

'I don't think there will be any fight,' replied Father Brown.

They passed rapidly through ante-rooms and inner rooms; they passed through the hall of combat itself, raised, roped, and padded with innumerable seats and boxes, and still the cleric did not look round or pause till he came to a clerk at a desk outside a door marked 'Committee'. There he stopped and asked to see Lord Pooley.

The attendant observed that his lordship was very busy, as the fight was coming on soon, but Father Brown had a good-tempered tedium of reiteration for which the official mind is generally not prepared. In a few moments the rather baffled Flambeau found himself in the presence of a man who was still shouting directions to another man going out of the room. 'Be careful, you know, about the ropes after the fourth – Well, and what do you want, I wonder!'

Lord Pooley was a gentleman, and, like most of the few remaining to our race, was worried – especially about money. He was half grey and half flaxen, and he had the eyes of fever and a high-bridged, frostbitten nose.

'Only a word,' said Father Brown. 'I have come to prevent a man being killed.'

Lord Pooley bounded off his chair as if a spring had flung him from it. 'I'm damned if I'll stand any more of this!' he cried. 'You and your committees and parsons and petitions! Weren't there parsons in the old days, when they fought without gloves? Now they're fighting with the regulation gloves, and there's not the rag of a possibility of either of the boxers being killed.'

'I didn't mean either of the boxers,' said the little priest.

'Well, well, well!' said the nobleman, with a touch of frosty humour. 'Who's going to be killed? The referee?'

'I don't know who's going to be killed,' replied Father Brown, with a reflective stare. 'If I did I shouldn't have to spoil your pleasure. I could simply get him to escape. I never could see anything wrong about prize-fights. As it is, I must ask you to announce that the fight is off for the present.'

'Anything else?' jeered the gentleman with feverish eyes. 'And what do you say to the two thousand people who have come to see it?'

'I say there will be one thousand nine-hundred and ninety-nine of them left alive when they have seen it,' said Father Brown.

Lord Pooley looked at Flambeau. 'Is your friend mad?' he asked.

'Far from it,' was the reply.

'And look here,' resumed Pooley in his restless way, 'it's worse than that. A whole pack of Italians have turned up to back Malvoli – swarthy, savage fellows of some country, anyhow. You know what these Mediterranean races are like. If I send out word that it's off we shall have Malvoli storming in here at the head of a whole Corsican clan.'

'My lord, it is a matter of life and death,' said the priest. 'Ring your bell. Give your message. And see whether it is Malvoli who answers.'

The nobleman struck the bell on the table with an odd air of new curiosity. He said to the clerk who appeared almost instantly in the doorway: 'I have a serious announcement to make to the audience shortly. Meanwhile, would you kindly tell the two champions that the fight will have to be put off.'

The clerk stared for some seconds as if at a demon and vanished.

'What authority have you for what you say?' asked Lord Pooley abruptly. 'Whom did you consult?'

'I consulted a bandstand,' said Father Brown, scratching his head. 'But, no, I'm wrong; I consulted a book, too. I picked it up on a bookstall in London – very cheap, too.'

He had taken out of his pocket a small, stout, leather-bound volume, and Flambeau, looking over his shoulder, could see that it was some book of old travels, and had a leaf turned down for reference.

' "The only form in which Voodoo – " ' began Father Brown, reading aloud.

'In which what?' enquired his lordship.

' "In which Voodoo," ' repeated the reader, almost with relish, ' "is widely organised outside Jamaica itself is in the form known as the Monkey, or the God of the Gongs, which is powerful in many parts of the two American continents, especially among half-breeds, many of whom look exactly like white men. It differs from most other forms of devil-worship and human sacrifice in the fact that the blood is not shed formally on the altar, but by a sort of assassination among the crowd. The gongs beat with a deafening din as the doors of the shrine open and the monkey-god is revealed; almost the whole congregation rivet ecstatic eyes on him. But after – " '

The door of the room was flung open, and the fashionable Negro stood framed in it, his eyeballs rolling, his silk hat still insolently tilted on his head. 'Huh!' he cried, showing his apish teeth. 'What this? Huh! Huh! You steal a coloured gentleman's prize – prize his already – yo' think yo' jes' save that white 'Talian trash – '

'The matter is only deferred,' said the nobleman quietly. 'I will be with you to explain in a minute or two.'

'Who you to – ' shouted Nigger Ned, beginning to storm.

'My name is Pooley,' replied the other, with a creditable coolness. 'I am the organising secretary, and I advise you just now to leave the room.'

'Who this fellow?' demanded the dark champion, pointing to the priest disdainfully.

'My name is Brown,' was the reply. 'And I advise you just now to leave the country.'

The prize-fighter stood glaring for a few seconds, and then, rather to the surprise of Flambeau and the others, strode out, sending the door to with a crash behind him.

'Well,' asked Father Brown rubbing his dusty hair up, 'what do you think of Leonardo da Vinci? A beautiful Italian head.'

'Look here,' said Lord Pooley, 'I've taken a considerable responsibility, on your bare word. I think you ought to tell me more about this.'

'You are quite right, my lord,' answered Brown. 'And it won't take long to tell.' He put the little leather book in his overcoat pocket. 'I think we know all that this can tell us, but you shall look at it to see if I'm right. That Negro who has just swaggered out is one of the most dangerous men on earth, for he has the brains of a European, with the instincts of a cannibal. He has turned what was clean, common-sense butchery among his fellow-barbarians into a very modern and scientific secret society of assassins. He doesn't know I know it, nor, for the matter of that, that I can't prove it.'

There was a silence, and the little man went on.

'But if I want to murder somebody, will it really be the best plan to make sure I'm alone with him?'

Lord Pooley's eyes recovered their frosty twinkle as he looked at the little clergyman. He only said: 'If you want to murder somebody, I should advise it.'

Father Brown shook his head, like a murderer of much riper experience. 'So Flambeau said,' he replied, with a sigh. 'But consider. The more a man feels lonely the less he can be sure he is alone. It must mean empty spaces round him, and they are just what make him obvious. Have you never seen one ploughman from the heights, or one shepherd from the valleys? Have you never walked along a cliff, and seen one man walking along the sands? Didn't you know when he's killed a crab, and wouldn't you have known if it had been a creditor? No! No! No! For an intelligent murderer, such as you or I might be, it is an impossible plan to make sure that nobody is looking at you.'

'But what other plan is there?'

'There is only one,' said the priest. 'To make sure that everybody is looking at something else. A man is throttled close by the big stand at Epsom. Anybody might have seen it done while the stand stood empty – any tramp under the hedges or motorist among the hills. But nobody would have seen it when the stand was crowded and the whole ring roaring, when the favourite was coming in first – or wasn't. The twisting of a neck-cloth, the thrusting of a body behind a door could be done in an instant – so long as it was that instant. It was the same, of course,' he continued turning to Flambeau, 'with that poor fellow under the bandstand. He was dropped through the hole (it wasn't an accidental hole) just at some very dramatic moment of the entertainment, when the bow of some great violinist or the voice of some great singer opened or came to its climax. And here, of course, when the knock-out blow came – it would not be the only one. That is the little trick Nigger Ned has adopted from his old God of Gongs.'

'By the way, Malvoli – ' Pooley began.

'Malvoli,' said the priest, 'has nothing to do with it. I dare say he has some Italians with him, but our amiable friends are not Italians. They are octoroons and African half-bloods of various shades, but I fear we English think all foreigners are much the same so long as they are dark and dirty. Also,' he added, with a smile, 'I fear the English decline to draw any fine distinction between the moral character produced by my religion and that which blooms out of Voodoo.'

* * *

The blaze of the spring season had burst upon Seawood, littering its foreshore with famines and bathing-machines, with nomadic preachers and nigger minstrels, before the two friends saw it again, and long before the storm of pursuit after the strange secret society had died away. Almost on every hand the secret of their purpose perished with them. The man of the hotel was found drifting dead on the sea like so much seaweed; his right eye was closed in peace, but his left eye was wide open, and glistened like glass in the moon. Nigger Ned had been overtaken a mile or two away, and murdered three policemen with his closed left hand. The remaining officer was surprised – nay, pained – and the Negro got away. But this was enough to set all the English papers in a flame, and for a month or two the main purpose of the British Empire was to prevent the buck nigger (who was so in both senses) escaping by any English port. Persons of a figure remotely reconcilable with his were subjected to quite extraordinary inquisitions, made to scrub their faces before going on board ship, as if each white complexion were made up like a mask, of greasepaint. Every Negro in England was put under special regulations and made to report himself; the outgoing ships would no more have taken a nigger than a basilisk. For people had found out how fearful and vast and silent was the force of the savage secret society, and by the time Flambeau and Father Brown were leaning on the parade parapet in April, the Black Man meant in England almost what he once meant in Scotland.

'He must be still in England,' observed Flambeau, 'and horridly well hidden, too. They must have found him at the ports if he had only whitened his face.'

'You see, he is really a clever man,' said Father Brown apologetically. 'And I'm sure he wouldn't whiten his face.'

'Well, but what would he do?'

'I think,' said Father Brown, 'he would blacken his face.'

Flambeau, leaning motionless on the parapet, laughed and said: 'My dear fellow!'

Father Brown, also leaning motionless on the parapet, moved one finger for an instant into the direction of the soot-masked niggers singing on the sands.

The Salad of Colonel Cray

Father Brown was walking home from Mass on a white weird morning when the mists were slowly lifting – one of those mornings when the very element of light appears as something mysterious and new. The scattered trees outlined themselves more and more out of the vapour, as if they were first drawn in grey chalk and then in charcoal. At yet more distant intervals appeared the houses upon the broken fringe of the suburb; their outlines became clearer and clearer until he recognised many in which he had chance acquaintances, and many more the names of whose owners he knew. But all the windows and doors were sealed; none of the people were of the sort that would be up at such a time, or still less on such an errand. But as he passed under the shadow of one handsome villa with verandas and wide ornate gardens, he heard a noise that made him almost involuntarily stop. It was the unmistakable noise of a pistol or carbine or some light firearm discharged; but it was not this that puzzled him most. The first full noise was immediately followed by a series of fainter noises – as he counted them, about six. He supposed it must be the echo; but the odd thing was that the echo was not in the least like the original sound. It was not like anything else that he could think of; the three things nearest to it seemed to be the noise made by siphons of soda-water, one of the many noises made by an animal, and the noise made by a person attempting to conceal laughter. None of which seemed to make much sense.

Father Brown was made of two men. There was a man of action, who was as modest as a primrose and as punctual as a clock; who went his small round of duties and never dreamed of altering it. There was also a man of reflection, who was much simpler but much stronger, who could not easily be stopped; whose thought was always (in the only intelligent sense of the words) free thought. He could not help, even unconsciously, asking himself all the questions that there were to be asked, and answering as many of them as he could; all that went on like his breathing or circulation. But he never consciously carried his actions outside the sphere of his own duty; and in this case the two attitudes were aptly tested. He was just about to resume his trudge in the twilight, telling himself it was no affair of his, but instinctively twisting and untwisting twenty theories about what the odd noises might mean. Then the grey skyline brightened into silver, and in the broadening light he realised that he had been to the house which belonged to an Anglo-Indian Major named Putnam; and that the Major had a native cook from Malta who was of his communion. He also began to remember that pistol-shots are sometimes serious things; accompanied with consequences with which he was legitimately concerned. He turned back and went in at the garden gate, making for the front door.

Halfway down one side of the house stood out a projection like a very low shed; it was, as he afterwards discovered, a large dustbin. Round the corner of this came a figure, at first a mere shadow in the haze, apparently bending and peering about. Then, coming nearer, it solidified into a figure that was, indeed, rather unusually solid. Major Putnam was a bald-headed, bull-necked man, short and very broad, with one of those rather apoplectic faces that are produced by a prolonged attempt to combine the oriental climate with the occidental luxuries. But the face was a good-humoured one, and even now, though evidently puzzled and inquisitive, wore a kind of innocent grin. He had a large palm-leaf hat on the back of his head (suggesting a halo that was by no means appropriate to the face), but otherwise he was clad only in a very vivid suit of striped scarlet and yellow pyjamas; which, though glowing enough to behold, must have been, on a fresh morning, pretty chilly to wear. He had evidently come out of his house in a hurry, and the priest was not surprised when he called out without further ceremony: 'Did you hear that noise?'

'Yes,' answered Father Brown; 'I thought I had better look in, in case anything was the matter.'

The Major looked at him rather queerly with his good-humoured gooseberry eyes. 'What do you think the noise was?' he asked.

'It sounded like a gun or something,' replied the other, with some hesitation; 'but it seemed to have a singular sort of echo.'

The Major was still looking at him quietly, but with protruding eyes, when the front door was flung open, releasing a flood of gaslight on the face of the fading mist; and another figure in pyjamas sprang or tumbled out into the garden. The figure was much longer, leaner, and more athletic; the pyjamas, though equally tropical, were comparatively tasteful, being of white with a light lemon-yellow stripe. The man was haggard, but handsome, more sunburned than the other; he had an aquiline profile and rather deep-sunken eyes, and a slight air of oddity arising from the combination of coal-black hair with a much lighter moustache. All this Father Brown absorbed in detail more at leisure. For the moment he only saw one thing about the man; which was the revolver in his hand.

'Cray!' exclaimed the Major, staring at him; 'did you fire that shot?'

'Yes, I did,' retorted the black-haired gentleman hotly; 'and so would you in my place. If you were chased everywhere by devils and nearly – '

The Major seemed to intervene rather hurriedly. 'This is my friend Father Brown,' he said. And then to Brown: 'I don't know whether you've met Colonel Cray of the Royal Artillery.'

'I have heard of him, of course,' said the priest innocently. 'Did you – did you hit anything?'

'I thought so,' answered Cray with gravity.

'Did he – ' asked Major Putnam in a lowered voice, 'did he fall or cry out, or anything?'

Colonel Cray was regarding his host with a strange and steady stare. 'I'll tell you exactly what he did,' he said. 'He sneezed.'

Father Brown's hand went halfway to his head, with the gesture of a man remembering somebody's name. He knew now what it was that was neither soda-water nor the snorting of a dog.

'Well,' ejaculated the staring Major, 'I never heard before that a service revolver was a thing to be sneezed at.'

'Nor I,' said Father Brown faintly. 'It's lucky you didn't turn your artillery on him or you might have given him quite a bad cold.' Then, after a bewildered pause, he said: 'Was it a burglar?'

'Let us go inside,' said Major Putnam, rather sharply, and led the way into his house.

The interior exhibited a paradox often to be marked in such morning hours: that the rooms seemed brighter than the sky outside; even after the Major had turned out the one gaslight in the front hall. Father Brown was surprised to see the whole dining-table set out as for a festive meal, with napkins in their rings, and wine glasses of some six unnecessary shapes set beside every plate. It was common enough, at that time of the morning, to find the remains of a banquet overnight; but to find it freshly spread so early was unusual.

While he stood wavering in the hall Major Putnam rushed past him and sent a raging eye over the whole oblong of the tablecloth. At last he spoke, spluttering: 'All the silver gone!' he gasped. 'Fish-knives and forks gone. Old cruet-stand gone. Even the old silver cream-jug gone. And now, Father Brown, I am ready to answer your question of whether it was a burglar.'

'They're simply a blind,' said Cray stubbornly. 'I know better than you why people persecute this house; I know better than you why – '

The Major patted him on the shoulder with a gesture almost peculiar to the soothing of a sick child, and said: 'It was a burglar. Obviously it was a burglar.'

'A burglar with a bad cold,' observed Father Brown, 'that might assist you to trace him in the neighbourhood.'

The Major shook his head in a sombre manner. 'He must be far beyond trace now, I fear,' he said.

Then, as the restless man with the revolver turned again towards the door in the garden, he added in a husky, confidential voice: 'I doubt whether I should send for the police, for fear my friend here has been a little too free with his bullets, and got on the wrong side of the law. He's lived in very wild places; and, to be frank with you, I think he sometimes fancies things.'

'I think you once told me,' said Brown, 'that he believes some Indian secret society is pursuing him.'

Major Putnam nodded, but at the same time shrugged his shoulders. 'I suppose we'd better follow him outside,' he said. 'I don't want any more – shall we say, sneezing?'

They passed out into the morning light, which was now even tinged with sunshine, and saw Colonel Cray's tall figure bent almost double, minutely examining the condition of gravel and grass. While the Major strolled unobtrusively towards him, the priest took an equally indolent turn, which took him round the next corner of the house to within a yard or two of the projecting dustbin.

He stood regarding this dismal object for some minute and a half, then he stepped towards it, lifted the lid and put his head inside. Dust and other discolouring matter shook upwards as he did so; but Father Brown never observed his own appearance, whatever else he observed. He remained thus for a measurable period, as if engaged in some mysterious prayers. Then he came out again, with some ashes on his hair, and walked unconcernedly away.

By the time he came round to the garden door again he found a group there which seemed to roll away morbidities as the sunlight had already rolled away the mists. It was in no way rationally reassuring; it was simply broadly comic, like a cluster of Dickens's characters. Major Putnam had managed to slip inside and plunge into a proper shirt and trousers, with a crimson cummerbund, and a light square jacket over all; thus normally set off, his red festive face seemed bursting with a commonplace cordiality. He was indeed emphatic, but then he was talking to his cook – the swarthy son of Malta, whose lean, yellow and rather careworn face contrasted quaintly with his snow-white cap and costume. The cook might well be careworn, for cookery was the Major's hobby. He was one of those amateurs who always know more than the professional. The only other person he even admitted to be a judge of an omelette was his friend Cray – and as Brown remembered this, he turned to look for the other officer. In the new presence of daylight and people clothed and in their right mind, the sight of him was rather a shock. The taller and more elegant man was still in his night-garb, with tousled black hair, and now crawling about the garden on his hands and knees, still looking for traces of the burglar; and now and again, to all appearance, striking the ground with his hand in anger at not finding him. Seeing him thus quadrupedal in the grass, the priest raised his eyebrows rather sadly; and for the first time guessed that 'fancies things' might be an euphemism.

The third item in the group of the cook and the epicure was also known to Father Brown; it was Audrey Watson, the Major's ward and housekeeper; and at this moment, to judge by her apron, tucked-up sleeves and resolute manner, much more the housekeeper than the ward.

'It serves you right,' she was saying: 'I always told you not to have that old-fashioned cruet-stand.'

'I prefer it,' said Putnam, placably. 'I'm old-fashioned myself; and the things keep together.'

'And vanish together, as you see,' she retorted. 'Well, if you are not going to bother about the burglar, I shouldn't bother about the lunch. It's Sunday, and we can't send for vinegar and all that in the town; and you Indian gentlemen can't enjoy what you call a dinner without a lot of hot things. I wish to goodness now you hadn't asked Cousin Oliver to take me to the musical service. It isn't over till half-past twelve, and the Colonel has to leave by then. I don't believe you men can manage alone.'

'Oh yes, we can, my dear,' said the Major, looking at her very amiably. 'Marco has all the sauces, and we've often done ourselves well in very rough places, as you might know by now. And it's time you had a treat, Audrey; you mustn't be a housekeeper every hour of the day; and I know you want to hear the music.'

'I want to go to church,' she said, with rather severe eyes.

She was one of those handsome women who will always be handsome, because the beauty is not in an air or a tint, but in the very structure of the head and features. But though she was not yet middle-aged and her auburn hair was of a Titianesque fullness in form and colour, there was a look in her mouth and around her eyes which suggested that some sorrows wasted her, as winds waste at last the edges of a Greek temple. For indeed the little domestic difficulty of which she was now speaking so decisively was rather comic than tragic. Father Brown gathered, from the course of the conversation, that Cray, the other gourmet, had to leave before the usual lunchtime; but that Putnam, his host, not to be done out of a final feast with an old crony, had arranged for a special *déjeuner* to be set out and consumed in the course of the morning, while Audrey and other graver persons were at morning service. She was going there under the escort of a relative and old friend of hers, Dr Oliver Oman, who, though a scientific man of a somewhat bitter type, was enthusiastic for music, and would go even to church to get it. There was nothing in all this that could conceivably concern the tragedy in Miss Watson's face; and by a half conscious instinct, Father Brown turned again to the seeming lunatic grubbing about in the grass.

When he strolled across to him, the black, unbrushed head was lifted abruptly, as if in some surprise at his continued presence. And indeed, Father Brown, for reasons best known to himself, had lingered much longer than politeness required; or even, in the ordinary sense, permitted.

'Well!' cried Cray, with wild eyes. 'I suppose you think I'm mad, like the rest?'

'I have considered the thesis,' answered the little man, composedly. 'And I incline to think you are not.'

'What do you mean?' snapped Cray quite savagely.

'Real madmen,' explained Father Brown, 'always encourage their own morbidity. They never strive against it. But you are trying to find traces of the burglar; even when there aren't any. You are struggling against it. You want what no madman ever wants.'

'And what is that?'

'You want to be proved wrong,' said Brown.

During the last words Cray had sprung or staggered to his feet and was regarding the cleric with agitated eyes. 'By hell, but that is a true word!' he cried. 'They are all at me here that the fellow was only after the silver – as if I shouldn't be only too pleased to think so! She's been at me,' and he tossed his tousled black head towards Audrey, but the other had no need of the direction, 'she's been at me today about how cruel I was to shoot a poor harmless housebreaker, and how I have the devil in me against poor harmless natives. But I was a good-natured man once – as good-natured as Putnam.'

After a pause he said: 'Look here, I've never seen you before; but you shall judge of the whole story. Old Putnam and I were friends in the same mess; but, owing to some accidents on the Afghan border, I got my command much sooner than most men; only we were both invalided home for a bit. I was engaged to Audrey out there; and we all travelled back together. But on the journey back things happened. Curious things. The result of them was that Putnam wants it broken off, and even Audrey keeps it hanging on – and I know what they mean. I know what they think I am. So do you.

'Well, these are the facts. The last day we were in an Indian city I asked Putnam if I could get some Trichinopoli cigars; he directed me to a little place opposite his lodgings. I have since found he was quite right; but "opposite" is a dangerous word when one decent house stands opposite five or six squalid ones; and I must have mistaken the door. It opened with difficulty, and then only on darkness; but as I turned back, the door behind me sank back and settled into its place with a noise as of innumerable bolts. There was nothing to do but to walk forward; which I did through passage after passage, pitch-dark. Then I came to a flight of steps, and then to a blind door, secured by a latch of elaborate Eastern ironwork, which I could only trace by touch, but which I loosened at last. I came out again upon gloom, which was half turned into a greenish twilight by a multitude of small but steady lamps below. They showed merely the feet or fringes of some huge and empty architecture. Just in front of me was something that looked like a mountain. I confess I nearly fell on the great stone platform on which I had emerged, to realise that it was an idol. And worst of all, an idol with its back to me.

'It was hardly half human, I guessed; to judge by the small squat head, and still more by a thing like a tail or extra limb turned up behind and pointing, like a loathsome large finger, at some symbol graven in the centre of the vast stone back. I had begun, in the dim light, to guess at the hieroglyphic, not without horror, when a more horrible thing happened. A door opened silently in the temple wall behind me and a man came out, with a brown face and a black coat. He had a carved smile on his face, of copper flesh and ivory teeth; but I think the most hateful thing about him was that he was in European dress. I was prepared, I think, for shrouded priests or naked fakirs. But this seemed to say that the devilry was over all the earth. As indeed I found it to be.

' "If you had only seen the Monkey's Feet," he said, smiling steadily, and without other preface, "we should have been very gentle – you would only be tortured and die. If you had seen the Monkey's Face, still we should be very moderate, very tolerant – you would only be tortured and live. But as you have seen the Monkey's Tail, we must pronounce the worst sentence, which is – Go Free."

'When he said the words I heard the elaborate iron latch with which I had struggled, automatically unlock itself: and then, far down the dark passages I had passed, I heard the heavy street-door shifting its own bolts backwards.

' "It is vain to ask for mercy; you must go free," said the smiling man. "Henceforth a hair shall slay you like a sword, and a breath shall bite you like an adder; weapons shall come against you out of nowhere; and you shall die many times." And with that he was swallowed once more in the wall behind; and I went out into the street.'

Cray paused; and Father Brown unaffectedly sat down on the lawn and began to pick daisies.

Then the soldier continued: 'Putnam, of course, with his jolly common sense, pooh-poohed all my fears; and from that time dates his doubt of my mental balance. Well, I'll simply tell you, in the fewest words, the three things that have happened since; and you shall judge which of us is right.

'The first happened in an Indian village on the edge of the jungle, but hundreds of miles from the temple, or town, or type of tribes and customs where the curse had been put on me. I woke in black midnight, and lay thinking of nothing in particular, when I felt a faint tickling thing, like a thread or a hair, trailed across my throat. I shrank back out of its way, and could not help thinking of the words in the temple. But when I got up and sought lights and a mirror, the line across my neck was a line of blood.

'The second happened in a lodging in Port Said, later, on our journey home together. It was a jumble of tavern and curiosity-shop; and though there was nothing there remotely suggesting the cult of the Monkey, it is, of course, possible that some of its images or talismans were in such a place. Its curse was there, anyhow. I woke again in the dark with a sensation that could not be put in colder or more literal words than that a breath bit like an adder. Existence was an agony of extinction; I dashed my head against walls until I dashed it against a window; and fell rather than jumped into the garden below. Putnam, poor fellow, who had called the other thing a chance scratch, was bound to take seriously the fact of finding me half insensible on the grass at dawn. But I fear it was my mental state he took seriously; and not my story.

'The third happened in Malta. We were in a fortress there; and as it happened our bedrooms overlooked the open sea, which almost came up to our window-sills, save for a flat white outer wall as bare as the sea. I woke up again; but it was not dark. There was a full moon, as I walked to the window; I could have seen a bird on the bare battlement, or a sail on the horizon. What I did see was a sort of stick or branch circling, self-supported, in the empty sky. It flew straight in at my window and smashed the lamp beside the pillow I had just quitted. It was one of those queer-shaped war-clubs some Eastern tribes use. But it had come from no human hand.'

Father Brown threw away a daisy-chain he was making, and rose with a wistful look. 'Has Major Putnam,' he asked, 'got any Eastern curios, idols, weapons and so on, from which one might get a hint?'

'Plenty of those, though not much use, I fear,' replied Cray; 'but by all means come into his study.'

As they entered they passed Miss Watson buttoning her gloves for church, and heard the voice of Putnam downstairs still giving a lecture on cookery to the cook. In the Major's study and den of curios they came suddenly on a third party, silk-hatted and dressed for the street, who was poring over an open book on the smoking-table – a book which he dropped rather guiltily, and turned.

Cray introduced him civilly enough, as Dr Oman, but he showed such disfavour in his very face that Brown guessed the two men, whether Audrey knew it or not, were rivals. Nor was the priest wholly unsympathetic with the prejudice. Dr Oman was a very well-dressed gentleman indeed; well-featured, though almost dark enough for an Asiatic. But Father Brown had to tell himself sharply that one should be in charity even with those who wax their pointed beards, who have small gloved hands, and who speak with perfectly modulated voices.

Cray seemed to find something specially irritating in the small prayer-book in Oman's dark-gloved hand. 'I didn't know that was in your line,' he said rather rudely.

Oman laughed mildly, but without offence. 'This is more so, I know,' he said, laying his hand on the big book he had dropped, 'a dictionary of drugs and such things. But it's rather too large to take to church.' Then he closed the larger book, and there seemed again the faintest touch of hurry and embarrassment.

'I suppose,' said the priest, who seemed anxious to change the subject, 'all these spears and things are from India?'

'From everywhere,' answered the doctor. 'Putnam is an old soldier, and has been in Mexico and Australia, and the Cannibal Islands for all I know.'

'I hope it was not in the Cannibal Islands,' said Brown, 'that he learnt the art of cookery.' And he ran his eyes over the stew-pots or other strange utensils on the wall.

At this moment the jolly subject of their conversation thrust his laughing, lobsterish face into the room. 'Come along, Cray,' he cried. 'Your lunch is just coming in. And the bells are ringing for those who want to go to church.'

Cray slipped upstairs to change; Dr Oman and Miss Watson betook themselves solemnly down the street, with a string of other churchgoers; but Father Brown noticed that the doctor twice looked back and scrutinised the house; and even came back to the corner of the street to look at it again.

The priest looked puzzled. 'He can't have been at the dustbin,' he muttered. 'Not in those clothes. Or was he there earlier today?'

Father Brown, touching other people, was as sensitive as a barometer; but today he seemed about as sensitive as a rhinoceros. By no social law, rigid or implied, could he be supposed to linger round the lunch of the Anglo-Indian friends; but he lingered, covering his position with torrents of amusing but quite needless conversation. He was the more puzzling because he did not seem to want any lunch. As one after another of the most exquisitely balanced kedgerees of curries, accompanied with their appropriate vintages, were laid before the other two, he only repeated that it was one of his fast-days, and munched a piece of bread and sipped and then left untasted a tumbler of cold water. His talk, however, was exuberant.

'I'll tell you what I'll do for you,' he cried, 'I'll mix you a salad! I can't eat it, but I'll mix it like an angel! You've got a lettuce there.'

'Unfortunately it's the only thing we have got,' answered the good-humoured Major. 'You must remember that mustard, vinegar, oil and so on vanished with the cruet and the burglar.'

'I know,' replied Brown, rather vaguely. 'That's what I've always been afraid would happen. That's why I always carry a cruet-stand about with me. I'm so fond of salads.'

And to the amazement of the two men he took a pepper-pot out of his waistcoat pocket and put it on the table.

'I wonder why the burglar wanted mustard, too,' he went on, taking a mustard-pot from another pocket. 'A mustard plaster, I suppose. And vinegar' – and producing that condiment – 'haven't I heard something about vinegar and brown paper? As for oil, which I think I put in my left – '

His garrulity was an instant arrested; for lifting his eyes, he saw what no one else saw – the black figure of Dr Oman standing on the sunlit lawn and looking steadily into the room. Before he could quite recover himself Cray had cloven in.

'You're an astounding card,' he said, staring. 'I shall come and hear your sermons, if they're as amusing as your manners.' His voice changed a little, and he leaned back in his chair.

'Oh, there are sermons in a cruet-stand, too,' said Father Brown, quite gravely. 'Have you heard of faith like a grain of mustard-seed; or charity that anoints with oil? And as for vinegar, can any soldiers forget that solitary soldier, who, when the sun was darkened – '

Colonel Cray leaned forward a little and clutched the tablecloth.

Father Brown, who was making the salad, tipped two spoonfuls of the mustard into the tumbler of water beside him; stood up and said in a new, loud and sudden voice – 'Drink that!'

At the same moment the motionless doctor in the garden came running, and bursting open a window cried: 'Am I wanted? Has he been poisoned?'

'Pretty near,' said Brown, with the shadow of a smile; for the emetic had very suddenly taken effect. And Cray lay in a deck-chair, gasping as for life, but alive.

Major Putnam had sprung up, his purple face mottled. 'A crime!' he cried hoarsely. 'I will go for the police!'

The priest could hear him dragging down his palm-leaf hat from the peg and tumbling out of the front door; he heard the garden gate slam. But he only stood looking at Cray; and after a silence said quietly: 'I shall not talk to you much; but I will tell you what you want to know. There is no curse on you. The Temple of the Monkey was either a coincidence or a part of the trick; the trick was the trick of a white man. There is only one weapon that will bring blood with that mere feathery touch: a razor held by a white man. There is one way of making a common room full of invisible, overpowering poison: turning on the gas – the crime of a white man. And there is only one kind of club that can be thrown out of a window, turn in mid-air and come back to the window next to it: the Australian boomerang. You'll see some of them in the Major's study.'

With that he went outside and spoke for a moment to the doctor. The moment after, Audrey Watson came rushing into the house and fell on her knees beside Cray's chair. He could not hear what they said to each other; but their faces moved with amazement, not unhappiness. The doctor and the priest walked slowly towards the garden gate.

'I suppose the Major was in love with her, too,' he said with a sigh; and when the other nodded, observed: 'You were very generous, doctor. You did a fine thing. But what made you suspect?'

'A very small thing,' said Oman; 'but it kept me restless in church till I came back to see that all was well. That book on his table was a work on poisons; and was put down open at the place where it stated that a certain Indian poison, though deadly and difficult to trace, was particularly easily reversible by the use of the commonest emetics. I suppose he read that at the last moment – '

'And remembered that there were emetics in the cruet-stand,' said Father Brown. 'Exactly. He threw the cruet in the dustbin – where I found it, along with other silver – for the sake of a burglary blind. But if you look at that pepper-pot I put on the table, you'll see a small hole. That's where Cray's bullet struck, shaking up the pepper and making the criminal sneeze.'

There was a silence. Then Dr Oman said grimly: 'The Major is a long time looking for the police.'

'Or the police in looking for the Major?' said the priest. 'Well, goodbye.'

The Strange Crime of John Boulnois

Mr Calhoun Kidd was a very young gentleman with a very old face, a face dried up with its own eagerness, framed in blue-black hair and a black butterfly tie. He was the emissary in England of the colossal American daily called the *Western Sun* – also humorously described as the 'Rising Sunset'. This was in allusion to a great journalistic declaration (attributed to Mr Kidd himself) that 'he guessed the sun would rise in the west yet, if American citizens did a bit more hustling'. Those, however, who mock American journalism from the standpoint of somewhat mellower traditions forget a certain paradox which partly redeems it. For while the journalism of the States permits a pantomimic vulgarity long past anything English, it also shows a real excitement about the most earnest mental problems, of which English papers are innocent, or rather incapable. The *Sun* was full of the most solemn matters treated in the most farcical way. William James figured there as well as 'Weary Willie', and pragmatists alternated with pugilists in the long procession of its portraits.

Thus, when a very unobtrusive Oxford man named John Boulnois wrote in a very unreadable review called the *Natural Philosophy Quarterly* a series of articles on alleged weak points in Darwinian evolution, it fluttered no corner of the English papers; though Boulnois's theory (which was that of a comparatively stationary universe visited occasionally by convulsions of change) had some rather faddy fashionableness at Oxford, and got so far as to be named 'Catastrophism'. But many American papers seized on the challenge as a great event; and the *Sun* threw the shadow of Mr Boulnois quite gigantically across its pages. By the paradox already noted, articles of valuable intelligence and enthusiasm were presented with headlines apparently written by an illiterate maniac, headlines such as 'Darwin Chews Dirt; Critic Boulnois says He Jumps the Shocks' – or 'Keep Catastrophic, says Thinker Boulnois'. And Mr Calhoun Kidd, of the *Western Sun*, was bidden to take his butterfly tie and lugubrious visage down to the little house outside Oxford where Thinker Boulnois lived in happy ignorance of such a title.

That fated philosopher had consented, in a somewhat dazed manner, to receive the interviewer, and had named the hour of nine that evening. The last of a summer sunset clung about Cumnor and the low wooded hills; the romantic Yankee was both doubtful of his road and inquisitive about his surroundings; and seeing the door of a genuine feudal old-country inn, the Champion Arms, standing open, he went in to make enquiries.

In the bar parlour he rang the bell, and had to wait some little time for a reply to it. The only other person present was a lean man with close red hair and loose, horsey-looking clothes, who was drinking very bad whisky, but smoking a very good cigar. The whisky, of course, was the choice brand of the Champion Arms; the cigar he had probably brought with him from London. Nothing could be more different than his cynical negligence from the dapper dryness of the young American; but something in his pencil and open notebook, and perhaps in the expression of his alert blue eye, caused Kidd to guess, correctly, that he was a brother journalist.

'Could you do me the favour,' asked Kidd, with the courtesy of his nation, 'of directing me to the Grey Cottage, where Mr Boulnois lives, as I understand?'

'It's a few yards down the road,' said the red-haired man, removing his cigar; 'I shall be passing it myself in a minute, but I'm going on to Pendragon Park to try and see the fun.'

'What is Pendragon Park?' asked Calhoun Kidd.

'Sir Claude Champion's place – haven't you come down for that, too?' asked the other pressman, looking up. 'You're a journalist, aren't you?'

'I have come to see Mr Boulnois,' said Kidd.

'I've come to see Mrs Boulnois,' replied the other. 'But I shan't catch her at home.' And he laughed rather unpleasantly.

'Are you interested in Catastrophism?' asked the wondering Yankee.

'I'm interested in catastrophes; and there are going to be some,' replied his companion gloomily. 'Mine's a filthy trade, and I never pretend it isn't.'

With that he spat on the floor; yet somehow in the very act and instant one could realise that the man had been brought up as a gentleman.

The American pressman considered him with more attention. His face was pale and dissipated, with the promise of formidable passions yet to be loosed; but it was a clever and sensitive face; his clothes were coarse and careless, but he had a good seal ring on one of his long, thin fingers. His name, which came out in the course of talk, was James Dalroy; he was the son of a bankrupt Irish landlord, and attached to a pink paper which he heartily despised, called *Smart Society*, in the capacity of reporter and of something painfully like a spy.

Smart Society, I regret to say, felt none of that interest in Boulnois on Darwin which was such a credit to the head and hearts of the *Western Sun*. Dalroy had come down, it seemed, to snuff up the scent of a scandal which might very well end in the Divorce Court, but which was at present hovering between Grey Cottage and Pendragon Park.

Sir Claude Champion was known to the readers of the *Western Sun* as well as Mr Boulnois. So were the Pope and the Derby Winner; but the idea of their intimate acquaintanceship would have struck Kidd as equally incongruous. He had heard of (and written about, nay, falsely pretended to know) Sir Claude Champion, as 'one of the brightest and wealthiest of England's Upper Ten'; as the great sportsman who raced yachts round the world; as the great traveller who wrote books about the Himalayas, as the politician who swept constituencies with a startling sort of Tory Democracy, and as the great dabbler in art, music, literature, and, above all, acting. Sir Claude was really rather magnificent in other than American eyes. There was something of the Renascence Prince about his omnivorous culture and restless publicity; he was not only a great amateur, but an ardent one. There was in him none of that antiquarian frivolity that we convey by the word 'dilettante'.

That faultless falcon profile with purple-black Italian eye, which had been snap-shotted so often both for *Smart Society* and the *Western Sun*, gave everyone the impression of a man eaten by ambition as by a fire, or even a disease. But though Kidd knew a great deal about Sir Claude – a great deal more, in fact, than there was to know – it would never have crossed his wildest dreams to connect so showy an aristocrat with the newly unearthed founder of Catastrophism, or to guess that Sir Claude Champion and John Boulnois could be intimate friends. Such, according to Dalroy's account, was nevertheless the fact. The two had hunted in couples at school and college, and, though their social destinies had been very different (for Champion was a great landlord and almost a millionaire, while Boulnois was a poor scholar and, until just lately, an unknown one), they still kept in very close touch with each other. Indeed, Boulnois's cottage stood just outside the gates of Pendragon Park.

But whether the two men could be friends much longer was becoming a dark and ugly question. A year or two before, Boulnois had married a beautiful and not unsuccessful actress, to whom he was devoted in his own shy and ponderous style; and the proximity of the household to Champion's had given that flighty celebrity opportunities for behaving in a way that could not but cause painful and rather base excitement. Sir Claude had carried the arts of publicity to perfection; and he seemed to take a crazy pleasure in being equally ostentatious in an intrigue that could do him no sort of honour. Footmen from Pendragon were perpetually leaving bouquets for Mrs Boulnois; carriages and motor cars were perpetually calling at the cottage for Mrs Boulnois; balls and masquerades perpetually filled the grounds in which the baronet paraded Mrs Boulnois, like the Queen of Love and Beauty at a tournament. That very evening, marked by Mr Kidd for the exposition of Catastrophism, had been marked by Sir Claude Champion for an open-air rendering of *Romeo and Juliet*, in which he was to play Romeo to a Juliet it was needless to name.

'I don't think it can go on without a smash,' said the young man with red hair, getting up and shaking himself. 'Old Boulnois may be squared – or he may be square. But if he's square he's thick – what you might call cubic. But I don't believe it's possible.'

'He is a man of grand intellectual powers,' said Calhoun Kidd in a deep voice.

'Yes,' answered Dalroy; 'but even a man of grand intellectual powers can't be such a blighted fool as all that. Must you be going on? I shall be following myself in a minute or two.'

But Calhoun Kidd, having finished a milk and soda, betook himself smartly up the road towards the Grey Cottage, leaving his cynical informant to his whisky and tobacco. The last of the daylight had faded; the skies were of a dark, green-grey, like slate, studded here and there with a star, but lighter on the left side of the sky, with the promise of a rising moon.

The Grey Cottage, which stood entrenched, as it were, in a square of stiff, high thorn-hedges, was so close under the pines and palisades of the Park that Kidd at first mistook it for the Park Lodge. Finding the name on the narrow wooden gate, however, and seeing by his watch that the hour of the 'Thinker's' appointment had just struck, he went in and knocked at the front door. Inside the garden hedge, he could see that the house, though unpretentious enough, was larger and more luxurious than it looked at first, and was quite a different kind of place from a porter's lodge. A dog-kennel and a beehive stood outside, like symbols of old English country-life; the moon was rising behind a plantation of prosperous pear trees, the dog that came out of the kennel was reverend-looking and reluctant to bark; and the plain, elderly manservant who opened the door was brief but dignified.

'Mr Boulnois asked me to offer his apologies, sir,' he said, 'but he has been obliged to go out suddenly.'

'But see here, I had an appointment,' said the interviewer, with a rising voice. 'Do you know where he went to?'

'To Pendragon Park, sir,' said the servant, rather sombrely, and began to close the door.

Kidd started a little.

'Did he go with Mrs – with the rest of the party?' he asked rather vaguely.

'No, sir,' said the man shortly; 'he stayed behind, and then went out alone.' And he shut the door, brutally, but with an air of duty not done.

The American, that curious compound of impudence and sensitiveness, was annoyed. He felt a strong desire to hustle them all along a bit and teach them business habits; the hoary old dog and the grizzled, heavy-faced old butler with his prehistoric shirt-front, and the drowsy old moon, and above all the scatterbrained old philosopher who couldn't keep an appointment.

'If that's the way he goes on he deserves to lose his wife's purest devotion,' said Mr Calhoun Kidd. 'But perhaps he's gone over to make a row. In that case I reckon a man from the *Western Sun* will be on the spot.'

And turning the corner by the open lodge-gates, he set off, stumping up the long avenue of black pine woods that pointed in abrupt perspective towards the inner gardens of Pendragon Park. The trees were as black and orderly as plumes upon a hearse; there were still a few stars. He was a man with more literary than direct natural associations; the word 'Ravenswood' came into his head repeatedly. It was partly the raven colour of the pine woods; but partly also an indescribable atmosphere almost described in Scott's great tragedy; the smell of something that died in the eighteenth century; the smell of dank gardens and broken urns, of wrongs that will never now be righted; of something that is none the less incurably sad because it is strangely unreal.

More than once, as he went up that strange, black road of tragic artifice, he stopped, startled, thinking he heard steps in front of him. He could see nothing in front but the twin sombre walls of pine and the wedge of starlit sky above them. At first he thought he must have fancied it or been mocked by a mere echo of his own tramp. But as he went on he was more and more inclined to conclude, with the remains of his reason, that there really were other feet upon the road. He thought hazily of ghosts; and was surprised how swiftly he could see the image of an appropriate and local ghost, one with a face as white as Pierrot's, but patched with black. The apex of the triangle of dark-blue sky was growing brighter and bluer, but he did not realise as yet that this was because he was coming nearer to the lights of the great house and garden. He only felt that the atmosphere was growing more intense, there was in the sadness more violence and secrecy – more – he hesitated for the word, and then said it with a jerk of laughter – Catastrophism.

More pines, more pathway slid past him, and then he stood rooted as by a blast of magic. It is vain to say that he felt as if he had got into a dream; but this time he felt quite certain that he had got into a book. For we human beings are used to inappropriate things; we are accustomed to the clatter of the incongruous; it is a tune to which we can go to sleep. If one appropriate thing happens, it wakes us up like the pang of a perfect chord. Something happened such as would have happened in such a place in a forgotten tale.

Over the black pine wood came flying and flashing in the moon a naked sword – such a slender and sparkling rapier as may have fought many an unjust duel in that ancient park. It fell on the pathway far in front of him and lay there glistening like a large needle. He ran like a hare and bent to look at it. Seen at close quarters it had rather a showy look: the big red jewels in the hilt and guard were a little dubious. But there were other red drops upon the blade which were not dubious.

He looked round wildly in the direction from which the dazzling missile had come, and saw that at this point the sable façade of fir and pine was interrupted by a smaller road at right angles; which, when he turned it, brought him in full view of the long, lighted house, with a lake and fountains in front of it. Nevertheless, he did not look at this, having something more interesting to look at.

Above him, at the angle of the steep green bank of the terraced garden, was one of those small picturesque surprises common in the old landscape gardening; a kind of small round hill or dome of grass, like a giant molehill, ringed and crowned with three concentric fences of roses, and having a sundial in the highest point in the centre. Kidd could see the finger of the dial stand up dark against the sky like the dorsal fin of a shark and the vain moonlight clinging to that idle clock. But he saw something else clinging to it also, for one wild moment – the figure of a man.

Though he saw it there only for a moment, though it was outlandish and incredible in costume, being clad from neck to heel in tight crimson, with glints of gold, yet he knew in one flash of moonlight who it was. That white face flung up to heaven, clean-shaven and so unnaturally young, like Byron with a Roman nose, those black curls already grizzled – he had seen the thousand public portraits of Sir Claude Champion. The wild red figure reeled an instant against the sundial; the next it had rolled down the steep bank and lay at the American's feet, faintly moving one arm. A gaudy, unnatural gold ornament on the arm suddenly reminded Kidd of *Romeo and Juliet*; of course the tight crimson suit was part of the play. But there was a long red stain down the bank from which the man had rolled – that was no part of the play. He had been run through the body.

Mr Calhoun Kidd shouted and shouted again. Once more he seemed to hear phantasmal footsteps, and started to find another figure already near him. He knew the figure, and yet it terrified him. The dissipated youth who had called himself Dalroy had a horribly quiet way with him; if Boulnois failed to keep appointments that had been made, Dalroy had a sinister air of keeping appointments that hadn't. The moonlight discoloured everything; against Dalroy's red hair his wan face looked not so much white as pale green.

All this morbid impressionism must be Kidd's excuse for having cried out, brutally and beyond all reason: 'Did you do this, you devil?'

James Dalroy smiled his unpleasing smile; but before he could speak, the fallen figure made another movement of the arm, waving vaguely towards the place where the sword fell; then came a moan, and then it managed to speak.

'Boulnois . . . Boulnois, I say . . . Boulnois did it . . . jealous of me . . . he was jealous, he was, he was . . .'

Kidd bent his head down to hear more, and just managed to catch the words: 'Boulnois . . . with my own sword . . . he threw it . . .'

Again the failing hand waved towards the sword, and then fell rigid with a thud. In Kidd rose from its depth all that acrid humour that is the strange salt of the seriousness of his race.

'See here,' he said sharply and with command, 'you must fetch a doctor. This man's dead.'

'And a priest, too, I suppose,' said Dalroy in an undecipherable manner. 'All these Champions are papists.'

The American knelt down by the body, felt the heart, propped up the head and used some last efforts at restoration; but before the other journalist reappeared, followed by a doctor and a priest, he was already prepared to assert they were too late.

'Were you too late also?' asked the doctor, a solid prosperous-looking man, with conventional moustache and whiskers, but a lively eye, which darted over Kidd dubiously.

'In one sense,' drawled the representative of the *Sun*. 'I was too late to save the man, but I guess I was in time to hear something of importance. I heard the dead man denounce his assassin.'

'And who was the assassin?' asked the doctor, drawing his eyebrows together.

'Boulnois,' said Calhoun Kidd, and whistled softly.

The doctor stared at him gloomily with a reddening brow, but he did not contradict. Then the priest, a shorter figure in the background, said mildly: 'I understood that Mr Boulnois was not coming to Pendragon Park this evening.'

'There again,' said the Yankee grimly, 'I may be in a position to give the old country a fact or two. Yes, sir, John Boulnois was going to stay in all this evening; he fixed up a real good appointment there with me. But John Boulnois changed his mind; John Boulnois left his home abruptly and all alone, and came over to this darned Park an hour or so ago. His butler told me so. I think we hold what the all-wise police call a clue – have you sent for them?'

'Yes,' said the doctor, 'but we haven't alarmed anyone else yet.'

'Does Mrs Boulnois know?' asked James Dalroy, and again Kidd was conscious of an irrational desire to hit him on his curling mouth.

'I have not told her,' said the doctor gruffly, 'but here come the police.'

The little priest had stepped out into the main avenue, and now returned with the fallen sword, which looked ludicrously large and theatrical when attached to his dumpy figure, at once clerical and commonplace. 'Just before the police come,' he said apologetically, 'has anyone got a light?'

The Yankee journalist took an electric torch from his pocket, and the priest held it close to the middle part of the blade, which he examined with blinking care. Then, without glancing at the point or pommel, he handed the long weapon to the doctor.

'I fear I'm no use here,' he said, with a brief sigh. 'I'll say good-night to you, gentlemen.' And he walked away up the dark avenue towards the house, his hands clasped behind him and his big head bent in cogitation.

The rest of the group made increased haste towards the lodge-gates, where an inspector and two constables could already be seen in consultation with the lodge-keeper. But the little priest only walked slower and slower in the dim cloister of pine, and at last stopped dead, on the steps of the house. It was his silent way of acknowledging an equally silent approach; for there came towards him a presence that might have satisfied even Calhoun Kidd's demands for a lovely and aristocratic ghost. It was a young woman in silvery satins of a Renascence design; she had golden hair in two long shining ropes, and a face so startingly pale between them that she might have been chryselephantine – made, that is, like some old Greek statues, out of ivory and gold. But her eyes were very bright, and her voice, though low, was confident.

'Father Brown?' she said.

'Mrs Boulnois?' he replied gravely. Then he looked at her and immediately said: 'I see you know about Sir Claude.'

'How do you know I know?' she asked steadily.

He did not answer the question, but asked another: 'Have you seen your husband?'

'My husband is at home,' she said. 'He has nothing to do with this.'

Again he did not answer; and the woman drew nearer to him, with a curiously intense expression on her face.

'Shall I tell you something more?' she said, with a rather fearful smile. 'I don't think he did it, and *you* don't either.'

Father Brown returned her gaze with a long, grave stare, and then nodded, yet more gravely.

'Father Brown,' said the lady, 'I am going to tell you all I know, but I want you to do me a favour first. Will you tell me why you haven't jumped to the conclusion of poor John's guilt, as all the rest have done? Don't mind what you say: I – I know about the gossip and the appearances that are against me.'

Father Brown looked honestly embarrassed, and passed his hand across his forehead. 'Two very little things,' he said. 'At least, one's very trivial and the other very vague. But such as they are, they don't fit in with Mr Boulnois being the murderer.'

He turned his blank, round face up to the stars and continued absent-mindedly: 'To take the vague idea first. I attach a good deal of importance to vague ideas. All those things that "aren't evidence" are what convince me. I think a moral impossibility the biggest of all impossibilities. I know your husband only slightly, but I think this crime of his, as generally conceived, something very like a moral impossibility. Please do not think I mean that

Boulnois could not be so wicked. Anybody can be wicked – as wicked as he chooses. We can direct our moral wills; but we can't generally change our instinctive tastes and ways of doing things. Boulnois might commit a murder, but not this murder. He would not snatch Romeo's sword from its romantic scabbard; or slay his foe on the sundial as on a kind of altar; or leave his body among the roses, or fling the sword away among the pines. If Boulnois killed anyone he'd do it quietly and heavily, as he'd do any other doubtful thing – take a tenth glass of port, or read a loose Greek poet. No, the romantic setting is not like Boulnois. It's more like Champion.'

'Ah!' she said, and looked at him with eyes like diamonds.

'And the trivial thing was this,' said Brown. 'There were fingerprints on that sword; fingerprints can be detected quite a time after they are made if they're on some polished surface like glass or steel. These were on a polished surface. They were halfway down the blade of the sword. Whose prints they were I have no earthly clue; but why should anybody hold a sword halfway down? It was a long sword, but length is an advantage in lunging at an enemy. At least, at most enemies. At all enemies except one.'

'Except one,' she repeated.

'There is only one enemy,' said Father Brown, 'whom it is easier to kill with a dagger than a sword.'

'I know,' said the woman. 'Oneself.'

There was a long silence, and then the priest said quietly but abruptly: 'Am I right, then? Did Sir Claude kill himself?'

'Yes,' she said, with a face like marble. 'I saw him do it.'

'He died,' said Father Brown, 'for love of you?'

An extraordinary expression flashed across her face, very different from pity, modesty, remorse, or anything her companion had expected: her voice became suddenly strong and full. 'I don't believe,' she said, 'he ever cared about me a rap. He hated my husband.'

'Why?' asked the other, and turned his round face from the sky to the lady.

'He hated my husband because . . . it is so strange I hardly know how to say it . . . because . . .'

'Yes?' said Brown patiently.

'Because my husband wouldn't hate him.'

Father Brown only nodded, and seemed still to be listening; he differed from most detectives in fact and fiction in a small point – he never pretended not to understand when he understood perfectly well.

Mrs Boulnois drew near once more with the same contained glow of certainty. 'My husband,' she said, 'is a great man. Sir Claude Champion was not a great man: he was a celebrated and successful man. My husband has never been celebrated or successful; and it is the solemn truth that he has never dreamed of being so. He no more expects to be famous for thinking than for smoking cigars. On all that side he has a sort of splendid stupidity. He has never grown up. He still liked Champion exactly as he liked him at school; he admired him as he would admire a conjuring trick done at the dinner-table. But he couldn't be got to conceive the notion of *envying* Champion. *And Champion wanted to be envied.* He went mad and killed himself for that.'

'Yes,' said Father Brown; 'I think I begin to understand.'

'Oh, don't you see?' she cried; 'the whole picture is made for that – the place is planned for it. Champion put John in a little house at his very door, like a dependant – to make him *feel* a failure. He never felt it. He thinks no more about such things than – than an absent-minded lion. Champion would burst in on John's shabbiest hours or homeliest meals with some dazzling present or announcement or expedition that made it like the visit of Haroun Alraschid, and John would accept or refuse amiably with one eye off, so to speak, like one lazy schoolboy agreeing or disagreeing with another. After five years of it John had not turned a hair; and Sir Claude Champion was a monomaniac.'

'And Haman began to tell them,' said Father Brown, 'of all the things wherein the king had honoured him; and he said: "All these things profit me nothing while I see Mordecai the Jew sitting in the gate." '

'The crisis came,' Mrs Boulnois continued, 'when I persuaded John to let me take down some of his speculations and send them to a magazine. They began to attract attention, especially in America, and one paper wanted to interview him. When Champion (who was interviewed nearly every day) heard of this late little crumb of success falling to his unconscious rival, the last link snapped that held back his devilish hatred. Then he began to lay that insane siege to my own love and honour which has been the talk of the shire. You will ask me why I allowed such atrocious attentions. I answer that I could not have declined them except by explaining to my husband, and there are some things the soul cannot do, as the body cannot fly. Nobody could have explained to my husband. Nobody could do it now. If you said to him in so many words, "Champion is stealing your wife," he would think the joke a little vulgar: that it could be anything but a joke – that notion could find no crack in his great skull to get in by. Well, John was to come and see us act this evening, but just as we were starting he said he wouldn't; he had got an interesting book and a cigar. I told this to Sir Claude, and it was his death-blow. The monomaniac suddenly saw despair. He stabbed himself, crying out like a devil that Boulnois was slaying him; he lies there in the garden dead of his own jealousy to produce jealousy; and John is sitting in the dining-room reading a book.'

There was another silence, and then the little priest said: 'There is only one weak point, Mrs Boulnois, in all your very vivid account. Your husband is not sitting in the dining-room reading a book. That American reporter told me he had been to your house, and your butler told him Mr Boulnois had gone to Pendragon Park after all.'

Her bright eyes widened to an almost electric glare; and yet it seemed rather bewilderment than confusion or fear. 'Why, what can you mean?' she cried. 'All the servants were out of the house, seeing the theatricals. And we don't keep a butler, thank goodness!'

Father Brown started and spun half round like an absurd teetotum. 'What, what?' he cried, seeming galvanised into sudden life. 'Look here – I say – can I make your husband hear if I go to the house?'

'Oh, the servants will be back by now,' she said, wondering.

'Right, right!' rejoined the cleric energetically, and set off scuttling up the path towards the Park gates. He turned once to say: 'Better get hold of that Yankee, or "Crime of John Boulnois" will be all over the Republic in large letters.'

'You don't understand,' said Mrs Boulnois. 'He wouldn't mind. I don't think he imagines that America really is a place.'

When Father Brown reached the house with the beehive and the drowsy dog, a small and neat maidservant showed him into the dining-room, where Boulnois sat reading by a shaded lamp, exactly as his wife described him. A decanter of port and a wine glass were at his elbow; and the instant the priest entered he noted the long ash stand out unbroken on his cigar.

'He has been here for half an hour at least,' thought Father Brown. In fact, he had the air of sitting where he had sat when his dinner was cleared away.

'Don't get up, Mr Boulnois,' said the priest in his pleasant, prosaic way. 'I shan't interrupt you a moment. I fear I break in on some of your scientific studies.'

'No,' said Boulnois; 'I was reading *The Bloody Thumb.*' He said it with neither frown nor smile, and his visitor was conscious of a certain deep and virile indifference in the man which his wife had called greatness. He laid down a gory yellow 'shocker' without even feeling its incongruity enough to comment on it humorously. John Boulnois was a big, slow-moving man with a massive head, partly grey and partly bald, and blunt, burly features. He was in shabby and very old-fashioned evening dress, with a narrow triangular opening of shirt-front: he had assumed it that evening in his original purpose of going to see his wife act Juliet.

'I won't keep you long from "The Bloody Thumb" or any other catastrophic affairs,' said Father Brown, smiling. 'I only came to ask you about the crime you committed this evening.'

Boulnois looked at him steadily, but a red bar began to show across his broad brow; and he seemed like one discovering embarrassment for the first time.

'I know it was a strange crime,' assented Brown in a low voice. 'Stranger than murder perhaps – to you. The little sins are sometimes harder to confess than the big ones – but that's why it's so important to confess them. Your crime is committed by every fashionable hostess six times a week: and yet you find it sticks to your tongue like a nameless atrocity.'

'It makes one feel,' said the philosopher slowly, 'such a damned fool.'

'I know,' assented the other, 'but one often has to choose between feeling a damned fool and being one.'

'I can't analyse myself well,' went on Boulnois; 'but sitting in that chair with that story I was as happy as a schoolboy on a half-holiday. It was security, eternity – I can't convey it . . . the cigars were within reach . . . the matches were within reach . . . the *Thumb* had four more appearances to . . . it was not only a peace, but a plenitude. Then that bell rang, and I thought for one long, mortal minute that I couldn't get out of that chair – literally, physically, muscularly couldn't. Then I did it like a man lifting the world, because I knew all the servants were out. I opened the front door, and there was a little man with his mouth open to speak and his notebook open to write in. I remembered the Yankee interviewer I had forgotten. His hair was parted in the middle, and I tell you that murder – '

'I understand,' said Father Brown. 'I've seen him.'

'I didn't commit murder,' continued the Catastrophist mildly, 'but only perjury. I said I had gone across to Pendragon Park and shut the door in his face. That is my crime, Father Brown, and I don't know what penance you would inflict for it.'

'I shan't inflict any penance,' said the clerical gentleman, collecting his heavy hat and umbrella with an air of some amusement; 'quite the contrary. I came here specially to let you off the little penance which would otherwise have followed your little offence.'

'And what,' asked Boulnois, smiling, 'is the little penance I have so luckily been let off?'

'Being hanged,' said Father Brown.

The Fairy Tale of Father Brown

The picturesque city and state of Heiligwaldenstein was one of those toy kingdoms of which certain parts of the German Empire still consist. It had come under the Prussian hegemony quite late in history – hardly fifty years before the fine summer day when Flambeau and Father Brown found themselves sitting in its gardens and drinking its beer. There had been not a little of war and wild justice there within living memory, as soon will be shown. But in merely looking at it one could not dismiss that impression of childishness which is the most charming side of Germany – those little pantomime, paternal monarchies in which a king seems as domestic as a cook. The German soldiers by the innumerable sentry-boxes looked strangely like German toys, and the clean-cut battlements of the castle, gilded by the sunshine, looked the more like the gilt gingerbread. For it was brilliant weather. The sky was as Prussian a blue as Potsdam itself could require, but it was yet more like that lavish and glowing use of the colour which a child extracts from a shilling paintbox. Even the grey-ribbed trees looked young, for the pointed buds on them were still pink, and in a pattern against the strong blue looked like innumerable childish figures.

Despite his prosaic appearance and generally practical walk of life, Father Brown was not without a certain streak of romance in his composition, though he generally kept his daydreams to himself, as many children do. Amid the brisk, bright colours of such a day, and in the heraldic framework of such a town, he did feel rather as if he had entered a fairy tale. He took a childish pleasure, as a younger brother might, in the formidable sword-stick which Flambeau always flung as he walked, and which now stood upright beside his tall mug of Münich. Nay, in his sleepy irresponsibility, he even found himself eyeing the knobbed and clumsy head of his own shabby umbrella, with some faint memories of the ogre's club in a coloured toy-book. But he never composed anything in the form of fiction, unless it be the tale that follows: 'I wonder,' he said, 'whether one would have real adventures in a place like this, if one put oneself in the way? It's a splendid back-scene for them, but I always have a kind of feeling that they would fight you with pasteboard sabres more than real, horrible swords.'

'You are mistaken,' said his friend. 'In this place they not only fight with swords, but kill without swords. And there's worse than that.'

'Why, what do you mean?' asked Father Brown.

'Why,' replied the other, 'I should say this was the only place in Europe where a man was ever shot without firearms.'

'Do you mean a bow and arrow?' asked Brown in some wonder.

'I mean a bullet in the brain,' replied Flambeau. 'Don't you know the story of the late Prince of this place? It was one of the great police mysteries about twenty years ago. You remember, of course, that this place was forcibly annexed at the time of Bismarck's very earliest schemes of consolidation – forcibly, that is, but not at all easily. The empire (or what wanted to be one) sent Prince Otto of Grossenmark to rule the place in the Imperial interests. We saw his portrait in the gallery there – a handsome old gentleman if he'd had any hair or eyebrows, and hadn't been wrinkled all over like a vulture; but he had things to harass him, as I'll explain in a minute. He was a soldier of distinguished skill and success, but he didn't have altogether an easy job with this little place. He was defeated in several battles by the celebrated Arnhold brothers – the three guerrilla patriots to whom Swinburne wrote a poem, you remember:

> Wolves with the hair of the ermine,
> Crows that are crowned and kings –
> These things be many as vermin,
> Yet Three shall abide these things.

Or something of that kind. Indeed, it is by no means certain that the occupation would ever have been successful had not one of the three brothers, Paul, despicably, but very decisively declined to abide these things any longer, and, by surrendering all the secrets of the insurrection, ensured its overthrow and his own ultimate promotion to the post of chamberlain to Prince Otto. After this, Ludwig, the one genuine hero among Mr Swinburne's heroes, was killed, sword in hand, in the capture of the city; and the third, Heinrich, who, though not a traitor, had always been tame and even timid compared with his active brothers, retired into something like a hermitage, became converted to a Christian quietism which was almost Quakerish, and never mixed with men except to give nearly all he had to the poor. They tell me that not long ago he could still be seen about the neighbourhood occasionally, a man in a black cloak, nearly blind, with very wild, white hair, but a face of astonishing softness.'

'I know,' said Father Brown. 'I saw him once.'

His friend looked at him in some surprise. 'I didn't know you'd been here before,' he said. 'Perhaps you know as much about it as I do. Anyhow, that's the story of the Arnholds, and he was the last survivor of them. Yes, and of all the men who played parts in that drama.'

'You mean that the Prince, too, died long before?'

'Died,' repeated Flambeau, 'and that's about as much as we can say. You must understand that towards the end of his life he began to have those tricks of the nerves not uncommon with tyrants. He multiplied the ordinary daily and nightly guard round his castle till there seemed to be more sentry-boxes than houses in the town, and doubtful characters were shot without mercy. He lived almost entirely in a little room that was in the very centre of the enormous labyrinth of all the other rooms, and even in this he erected another sort of central cabin or cupboard, lined with steel, like a safe or a battleship. Some say that under the floor of this again was a secret hole in the earth, no more than large enough to hold him, so that, in his anxiety to avoid the grave, he was willing to go into a place pretty much like it. But he went further yet. The populace had been supposed to be disarmed ever since the suppression of the revolt, but Otto now insisted, as governments very seldom insist, on an absolute and literal disarmament. It was carried out, with extraordinary thoroughness and severity, by very well-organised officials over a small and familiar area, and, so far as human strength and science can be absolutely certain of anything, Prince Otto was absolutely certain that nobody could introduce so much as a toy pistol into Heiligwaldenstein.'

'Human science can never be quite certain of things like that,' said Father Brown, still looking at the red budding of the branches over his head, 'if only because of the difficulty about definition and connotation. What is a weapon? People have been murdered with the mildest domestic comforts; certainly with tea-kettles, probably with tea-cosies. On the other hand, if you showed an Ancient Briton a revolver, I doubt if he would know it was a weapon – until it was fired into him, of course. Perhaps somebody introduced a firearm so new that it didn't even look like a firearm. Perhaps it looked like a thimble or something. Was the bullet at all peculiar?'

'Not that I ever heard of,' answered Flambeau; 'but my information is fragmentary, and only comes from my old friend Grimm. He was a very able detective in the German service, and he tried to arrest me; I arrested him instead, and we had many interesting chats. He was in charge here of the enquiry about Prince Otto, but I forgot to ask him anything about the bullet. According to Grimm, what happened was this.' He paused a moment to drain the greater part of his dark lager at a draught, and then resumed: 'On the evening in question, it seems, the Prince was expected to appear in one of the outer rooms, because he had to receive certain visitors whom he really wished to meet. They were geological experts sent to investigate the old question of the alleged supply of gold from the rocks round here, upon which (as it was said) the small city-state had so long maintained its credit and been able to negotiate with its neighbours even under the ceaseless bombardment of bigger armies. Hitherto it had never been found by the most exacting enquiry which could – '

'Which could be quite certain of discovering a toy pistol,' said Father Brown with a smile. 'But what about the brother who ratted? Hadn't he anything to tell the Prince?'

'He always asseverated that he did not know,' replied Flambeau; 'that this was the one secret his brothers had not told him. It is only right to say that it received some support from fragmentary words – spoken by the great Ludwig in the hour of death, when he looked at Heinrich but pointed at Paul, and said, "You have not told *him* . . . " and was soon afterwards incapable of speech. Anyhow, the deputation of distinguished geologists and mineralogists from Paris and Berlin were there in the most magnificent and appropriate dress, for there are no men who like wearing their decorations so much as the men of science – as anybody knows who has ever been to a soirée of the Royal Society. It was a brilliant gathering, but very late, and gradually the Chamberlain – you saw his portrait, too: a man with black eyebrows, serious eyes, and a meaningless sort of smile underneath – the Chamberlain, I say, discovered there was everything there except the Prince himself. He searched all the outer salons; then, remembering the man's mad fits of fear, hurried to the inmost chamber. That also was empty, but the steel turret or cabin erected in the middle of it took some time to open. When it did open it was empty, too. He went and looked into the hole in the ground, which seemed deeper and somehow all the more like a grave – that is his account, of course. And even as he did so he heard a burst of cries and tumult in the long rooms and corridors without.

'First it was a distant din and thrill of something unthinkable on the horizon of the crowd, even beyond the castle. Next it was a wordless clamour startlingly close, and loud enough to be distinct if each word had not killed the other. Next came words of a terrible clearness, coming nearer, and next one man, rushing into the room and telling the news as briefly as such news is told.

'Otto, Prince of Heiligwaldenstein and Grossenmark, was lying in the dews of the darkening twilight in the woods beyond the castle, with his arms flung out and his face flung up to the moon. The blood still pulsed from his shattered temple and jaw, but it was the only part of him that moved like a living thing. He was clad in his full white and yellow uniform, as to receive his guests within, except that the sash or scarf had been unbound and lay rather crumpled by his side. Before he could be lifted he was dead. But, dead or alive, he was a riddle – he who had always hidden in the inmost chamber out there in the wet woods, unarmed and alone.'

'Who found his body?' asked Father Brown.

'Some girl attached to the Court named Hedwig von something or other,' replied his friend, 'who had been out in the wood picking wild flowers.'

'Had she picked any?' asked the priest, staring rather vacantly at the veil of the branches above him.

'Yes,' replied Flambeau. 'I particularly remember that the Chamberlain, or old Grimm or somebody, said how horrible it was, when they came up at her call, to see a girl holding spring flowers and bending over that – that bloody collapse. However, the main point is that before help arrived he was dead, and the news, of course, had to be carried back to the castle. The consternation it created was something beyond even that natural in a Court at the fall of a potentate. The foreign visitors, especially the mining experts, were in the wildest doubt and excitement, as well as many important Prussian officials, and it soon began to be clear that the scheme for finding the treasure bulked much bigger in the business than people had supposed. Experts and officials had been promised great prizes or international advantages, and some even said that the Prince's secret apartments and strong military protection were due less to fear of the populace than to the pursuit of some private investigation of – '

'Had the flowers got long stalks?' asked Father Brown.

Flambeau stared at him. 'What an odd person you are!' he said. 'That's exactly what old Grimm said. He said the ugliest part of it, he thought – uglier than the blood and bullet – was that the flowers were quite short, plucked close under the head.'

'Of course,' said the priest, 'when a grown-up girl is really picking flowers, she picks them with plenty of stalk. If she just pulled their heads off, as a child does, it looks as if – ' And he hesitated.

'Well?' enquired the other.

'Well, it looks rather as if she had snatched them nervously, to make an excuse for being there after – well, after she was there.'

'I know what you're driving at,' said Flambeau rather gloomily. 'But that and every other suspicion breaks down on the one point – the want of a weapon. He could have been killed, as you say, with lots of other things – even with his own military sash; but we have to explain not how he was killed, but how he was shot. And the fact is we can't. They had the girl most ruthlessly searched; for, to tell the truth, she was a little suspect, though the niece and ward of the wicked old Chamberlain, Paul Arnhold. But she was very romantic, and was suspected of sympathy with the old revolutionary enthusiasm in her family. All the same, however romantic you are, you can't imagine a big bullet into a man's jaw or brain without using a gun or pistol. And there was no pistol, though there were two pistol shots. I leave it to you, my friend.'

'How do you know there were two shots?' asked the little priest.

'There was only one in his head,' said his companion, 'but there was another bullet-hole in the sash.'

Father Brown's smooth brow became suddenly constricted. 'Was the other bullet found?' he demanded.

Flambeau started a little. 'I don't think I remember,' he said.

'Hold on! Hold on! Hold on!' cried Brown, frowning more and more, with a quite unusual concentration of curiosity. 'Don't think me rude. Let me think this out for a moment.'

'All right,' said Flambeau, laughing, and finished his beer. A slight breeze stirred the budding trees and blew up into the sky cloudlets of white and pink that seemed to make the sky bluer and the whole coloured scene more quaint. They might have been cherubs flying home to the casements of a sort of celestial nursery. The oldest tower of the castle, the Dragon Tower, stood up as grotesque as the ale-mug, but as homely. Only beyond the tower glimmered the wood in which the man had lain dead.

'What became of this Hedwig eventually?' asked the priest at last.

'She is married to General Schwartz,' said Flambeau. 'No doubt you've heard of his career, which was rather romantic. He had distinguished himself even before his exploits at Sadowa and Gravelotte; in fact, he rose from the ranks, which is very unusual even in the smallest of the German . . .'

Father Brown sat up suddenly.

'Rose from the ranks!' he cried, and made a mouth as if to whistle. 'Well, well, what a queer story! What a queer way of killing a man; but I suppose it was the only one possible. But to think of hate so patient –'

'What do you mean?' demanded the other. 'In what way did they kill him?'

'They killed him with the sash,' said Brown carefully; and then, as Flambeau protested: 'Yes, yes, I know about the bullet. Perhaps I ought to say he died of having a sash. I know it doesn't sound like having a disease.'

'I suppose,' said Flambeau, 'that you've got some notion in your head, but it won't easily get the bullet out of his. As I explained before, he might easily have been strangled. But he was shot. By whom? By what?'

'He was shot by his own orders,' said the priest.

'You mean he committed suicide?'

'I didn't say by his own wish,' replied Father Brown. 'I said by his own orders.'

'Well, anyhow, what is your theory?'

Father Brown laughed. 'I am only on my holiday,' he said. 'I haven't got any theories. Only this place reminds me of fairy stories, and, if you like, I'll tell you a story.'

The little pink clouds, that looked rather like sweet-stuff, had floated up to crown the turrets of the gilt gingerbread castle, and the pink baby fingers of the budding trees seemed spreading and stretching to reach them; the blue sky began to take a bright violet of evening, when Father Brown suddenly spoke again: 'It was on a dismal night, with rain still dropping from the trees and dew already clustering, that Prince Otto of Grossenmark stepped hurriedly out of a side door of the castle and walked swiftly into the wood. One of the innumerable sentries saluted him, but he did not notice it. He had no wish to be specially noticed himself. He was glad when the great trees, grey and already greasy with rain, swallowed him up like a swamp. He had deliberately chosen the least frequented side of his palace, but even that was more frequented than he liked. But there was no particular chance of officious or diplomatic pursuit, for his exit had been a sudden impulse. All the full-dressed diplomatists he left behind were unimportant. He had realised suddenly that he could do without them.

'His great passion was not the much nobler dread of death, but the strange desire of gold. For this legend of the gold he had left Grossenmark and invaded Heiligwaldenstein. For this and only this he had bought the traitor and butchered the hero, for this he had long questioned and cross-questioned the false Chamberlain, until he had come to the conclusion that, touching his ignorance, the renegade really told the truth. For this he had, somewhat reluctantly, paid and promised money on the chance of gaining the larger amount; and for this he had stolen out of his palace like a thief in the rain, for he had thought of another way to get the desire of his eyes, and to get it cheap.

'Away at the upper end of a rambling mountain path to which he was making his way, among the pillared rocks along the ridge that hangs above the town, stood the hermitage, hardly more than a cavern fenced with thorn, in which the third of the great brethren had long hidden himself from the world. He, thought Prince Otto, could have no real reason for refusing to give up the gold. He had known its place for years, and made no effort to find it, even before his new ascetic creed had cut him off from property or pleasures. True, he had been an enemy, but he now professed a duty of having no enemies. Some concession to his cause, some appeal to his principles, would probably get the mere money secret out of him. Otto was no coward, in spite of his network of military precautions, and, in any case, his avarice was stronger than his fears. Nor was there much cause for fear. Since he was certain there were no private arms in the whole principality, he was a hundred times more certain there were none in the Quaker's little hermitage on the hill, where he lived on herbs, with two old rustic servants, and with no other voice of man for year after year. Prince Otto looked down with something of a grim smile at the bright, square labyrinths of the lamp-lit city below him. For as far as the eye could see there ran the rifles of his friends, and not one pinch of powder for his enemies. Rifles ranked so close even to that mountain path that a cry from him would bring the soldiers rushing up the hill, to say nothing of the fact that the wood and ridge were patrolled at regular intervals; rifles so far away, in the dim woods, dwarfed by distance, beyond the river, that an enemy could not slink into the town by any detour. And round the palace rifles at the west door and the east door, at the north door and the south, and all along the four façades linking them. He was safe.

'It was all the more clear when he had crested the ridge and found how naked was the nest of his old enemy. He found himself on a small platform of rock, broken abruptly by the three corners of precipice. Behind was the black cave, masked with green thorn, so low that it was hard to believe that a man could enter it. In front was the fall of the cliffs and the vast but cloudy vision of the valley. On the small rock platform stood an old bronze lectern or reading-stand, groaning under a great German Bible. The bronze or copper of it had grown green with the eating airs of that exalted place, and Otto had instantly the thought, "Even if they had arms, they must be rusted by now." Moonrise had already made a deathly dawn behind the crests and crags, and the rain had ceased.

'Behind the lectern, and looking across the valley, stood a very old man in a black robe that fell as straight as the cliffs around him, but whose white hair and weak voice seemed alike to waver in the wind. He was evidently reading some daily lesson as part of his religious exercises. "They trust in their horses . . . "

' "Sir," said the Prince of Heiligwaldenstein, with quite unusual courtesy, "I should like only one word with you."

' ". . . and in their chariots," went on the old man weakly, "but we will trust in the name of the Lord of Hosts . . . " His last words were inaudible, but he closed the book reverently and, being nearly blind, made a groping movement and gripped the reading-stand. Instantly his two servants slipped out of the low-browed cavern and supported him. They wore dull-black gowns like his own, but they had not the frosty silver on the hair, nor the frostbitten refinement of the features. They were peasants, Croat or Magyar, with broad, blunt visages and blinking eyes. For the first time something troubled the Prince, but his courage and diplomatic sense stood firm.

' "I fear we have not met," he said, "since that awful cannonade in which your poor brother died."

' "All my brothers died," said the old man, still looking across the valley. Then, for one instant turning on Otto his drooping, delicate features, and the wintry hair that seemed to drip over his eyebrows like icicles, he added: "You see, I am dead, too."

' "I hope you'll understand," said the Prince, controlling himself almost to a point of conciliation, "that I do not come here to haunt you, as a mere ghost of those great quarrels. We will not talk about who was right or wrong in that, but at least there was one point on which we were never wrong, because you were always right. Whatever is to be said of the policy of your family, no one for one moment imagines that you were moved by the mere gold; you have proved yourself above the suspicion that . . . "

'The old man in the black gown had hitherto continued to gaze at him with watery blue eyes and a sort of weak wisdom in his face. But when the word "gold" was said he held out his hand as if in arrest of something, and turned away his face to the mountains.

' "He has spoken of gold," he said. "He has spoken of things not lawful. Let him cease to speak."

'Otto had the vice of his Prussian type and tradition, which is to regard success not as an incident but as a quality. He conceived himself and his like as perpetually conquering peoples who were perpetually being conquered. Consequently, he was ill acquainted with the emotion of surprise, and ill prepared for the next movement, which startled and stiffened him. He had opened his mouth to answer the hermit, when the mouth was stopped and the voice strangled by a soft gag suddenly twisted round his head like a tourniquet. It was fully forty seconds before he realised that the two Hungarian servants had done it, and that they had done it with his own military scarf.

'The old man went again weakly to his great brazen-supported Bible, turned over the leaves, with a patience that had something horrible about it, till he came to the Epistle of St James, and then began to read: "The tongue is a little member, but – "

'Something in the very voice made the Prince turn suddenly and plunge down the mountain path he had climbed. He was halfway towards the gardens of the palace before he even tried to tear the strangling scarf from his neck and jaws. He tried again and again, and it was impossible; the men who had knotted that gag knew the difference between what a man can do with his hands in front of him and what he can do with his hands behind his head. His legs were free to leap like an antelope on the mountains, his arms were free to use any gesture or wave any signal, but he could not speak.

'He had come close to the woods that walled in the castle before he had quite realised what his wordless state meant and was meant to mean. Once more he looked down grimly at the bright, square labyrinths of the lamp-lit city below him, and he smiled no more. He felt himself repeating the phrases of his former mood with a murderous irony. Far as the eye could see ran the rifles of his friends, every one of whom would shoot him dead if he could not answer the challenge. Rifles were so near that the wood and ridge could be patrolled at regular intervals; therefore it was useless to hide in the wood till morning. Rifles were ranked so far away that an enemy could not slink into the town by any detour; therefore it was vain to return to the city by any remote course. A cry from him would bring his soldiers rushing up the hill. But from him no cry would come.

'The moon had risen in strengthening silver, and the sky showed in stripes of bright, nocturnal blue between the black stripes of the pines about the castle. Flowers of some wide and feathery sort – for he had never noticed such things before – were at once luminous and discoloured by the moonshine, and seemed indescribably fantastic as they clustered, as if crawling about the roots of the trees. Perhaps his reason had been suddenly unseated by the unnatural captivity he carried with him, but in that wood he felt something unfathomably German – the fairy tale. He knew with half his mind that he was drawing near to the castle of an ogre – he had forgotten that he was the ogre. He remembered asking his mother if bears lived in the old park at home. He stooped to pick a flower, as if it were a charm against enchantment. The stalk was stronger than he expected, and broke with a slight snap. Carefully trying to place it in his scarf, he heard the halloo, "Who goes there?" Then he remembered the scarf was not in its usual place.

'He tried to scream and was silent. The second challenge came; and then a shot that shrieked as it came and then was stilled suddenly by impact. Otto of Grossenmark lay very peacefully among the fairy trees, and would do no more harm either with gold or steel; only the silver pencil of the moon would pick out and trace here and there the intricate ornament of his uniform, or the old wrinkles on his brow. May God have mercy on his soul.

'The sentry who had fired, according to the strict orders of the garrison, naturally ran forward to find some trace of his quarry. He was a private named Schwartz, since not unknown in his profession, and what he found was a bald man in uniform, but with his face so bandaged by a kind of mask made of his own military scarf that nothing but open, dead eyes could be seen, glittering stonily in the moonlight. The bullet had gone through the gag into the jaw; that is why there was a shot-hole in the scarf, but only one shot. Naturally, if not correctly, young Schwartz tore off the mysterious silken mask and cast it on the grass; and then he saw whom he had slain.

'We cannot be certain of the next phase. But I incline to believe that there was a fairy tale, after all, in that little wood, horrible as was its occasion. Whether the young lady named Hedwig had any previous knowledge of the soldier she saved and eventually married, or whether she came accidentally upon the accident and their intimacy began that night, we shall probably never know. But we can know, I fancy, that this Hedwig was a heroine, and deserved to marry a man who became something of a hero. She did the bold and the wise thing. She persuaded the sentry to go back to his post, in which place there was nothing to connect him with the disaster; he was but one of the most loyal and orderly of fifty such sentries within call. She remained by the body and gave the alarm; and there was nothing to connect her with the disaster either, since she had not got, and could not have, any firearms.

'Well,' said Father Brown rising cheerfully. 'I hope they're happy.'

'Where are you going?' asked his friend.

'I'm going to have another look at that portrait of the Chamberlain, the Arnhold who betrayed his brethren,' answered the priest. 'I wonder what part – I wonder if a man is less a traitor when he is twice a traitor?'

And he ruminated long before the portrait of a white-haired man with black eyebrows and a pink, painted sort of smile that seemed to contradict the black warning in his eyes.

THE MAN WHO KNEW TOO MUCH

The Man Who Knew Too Much

Contents

I

The Face in the Target

Harold March, the rising reviewer and social critic, was walking vigorously across a great tableland of moors and commons, the horizon of which was fringed with the far-off woods of the famous estate of Torwood Park. He was a good-looking young man in tweeds, with very pale curly hair and pale clear eyes. Walking in wind and sun in the very landscape of liberty, he was still young enough to remember his politics and not merely try to forget them. For his errand at Torwood Park was a political one; it was the place of appointment named by no less a person than the Chancellor of the Exchequer, Sir Howard Horne, then introducing his so-called Socialist Budget, and prepared to expound it in an interview with so promising a penman. Harold March was the sort of man who knows everything about politics, and nothing about politicians. He also knew a great deal about art, letters, philosophy, and general culture; about almost everything, indeed, except the world he was living in.

Abruptly, in the middle of those sunny and windy flats, he came upon a sort of cleft almost narrow enough to be called a crack in the land. It was just large enough to be the watercourse for a small stream which vanished at intervals under green tunnels of undergrowth, as if in a dwarfish forest. Indeed, he had an odd feeling as if he were a giant looking over the valley of the pygmies. When he dropped into the hollow, however, the impression was lost; the rocky banks, though hardly above the height of a cottage, hung over and had the profile of a precipice. As he began to wander down the course of the stream, in idle but romantic curiosity, and saw the water shining in short strips between the great grey boulders and bushes as soft as great green mosses, he fell into quite an opposite vein of fantasy. It was rather as if the earth had opened and swallowed him into a sort of underworld of dreams. And when he became conscious of a human figure dark against the silver stream, sitting on a large boulder and looking rather like a large bird, it was perhaps with some of the premonitions proper to a man who meets the strangest friendship of his life.

The man was apparently fishing; or, at least, was fixed in a fisherman's attitude with more than a fisherman's immobility. March was able to examine the man almost as if he had been a statue for some minutes before the statue spoke. He was a tall, fair man, cadaverous and a little lackadaisical, with heavy eyelids and a high-bridged nose. When his face was shaded with his wide white hat, his light moustache and lithe figure gave him a look of youth. But the Panama lay on the moss beside him; and the spectator could see that his brow was prematurely bald; and this, combined with a certain hollowness about the eyes, had an air of head work and even headache. But the most curious thing about him, realised after a short scrutiny, was that, though he looked like a fisherman, he was not fishing.

He was holding, instead of a rod, something that might have been a landing-net which some fishermen use, but which was much more like the ordinary toy net which children carry, and which they generally use indifferently for shrimps or butterflies. He was dipping this into the water at intervals, gravely regarding its harvest of weed or mud, and emptying it out again.

'No, I haven't caught anything,' he remarked, calmly, as if answering an unspoken query. 'When I do I have to throw it back again; especially the big fish. But some of the little beasts interest me when I get 'em.'

'A scientific interest, I suppose?' observed March.

'Of a rather amateurish sort, I fear,' answered the strange fisherman. 'I have a sort of hobby about what they call "phenomena of phosphorescence". But it would be rather awkward to go about in society carrying stinking fish.'

'I suppose it would,' said March, with a smile.

'Rather odd to enter a drawing-room carrying a large luminous cod,' continued the stranger, in his listless way. 'How quaint it would be if one could carry it about like a lantern, or have little sprats for candles. Some of the sea beasts would really be very pretty like lampshades; the blue sea-snail that glitters all over like starlight; and some of the red starfish really shine like red stars. But, naturally, I'm not looking for them here.'

March thought of asking him what he was looking for; but, feeling unequal to a technical discussion at least as deep as the deep-sea fishes, he returned to more ordinary topics.

'Delightful sort of hole this is,' he said. 'This little dell and river here. It's like those places Stevenson talks about, where something ought to happen.'

'I know,' answered the other. 'I think it's because the place itself, so to speak, seems to happen and not merely to exist. Perhaps that's what old Picasso and some of the Cubists are trying to express by angles and jagged lines. Look at that wall like low cliffs that juts forward just at right angles to the slope of turf sweeping up to it. That's like a silent collision. It's like a breaker and the backwash of a wave.'

March looked at the low-browed crag overhanging the green slope and nodded. He was interested in a man who turned so easily from the technicalities of science to those of art; and asked him if he admired the new angular artists.

'As I feel it, the Cubists are not Cubist enough,' replied the stranger. 'I mean they're not thick enough. By making things mathematical they make them thin. Take the living lines out of that landscape, simplify it to a right angle, and you flatten it out to a mere diagram on paper. Diagrams have their own beauty; but it is of just the other sort. They stand for the unalterable things; the calm, eternal, mathematical sort of truths; what somebody calls the "white radiance of" –'

He stopped, and before the next word came something had happened almost too quickly and completely to be realised. From behind the overhanging rock came a noise and rush like that of a railway train; and a great motor car appeared. It topped the crest of cliff, black against the sun, like a battle-chariot rushing to destruction in some wild epic. March automatically put out his hand in one futile gesture, as if to catch a falling teacup in a drawing-room.

For the fraction of a flash it seemed to leave the ledge of rock like a flying ship; then the very sky seemed to turn over like a wheel, and it lay a ruin amid the tall grasses below, a line of grey smoke going up slowly from it into the silent air. A little lower the figure of a man with grey hair lay tumbled down the steep green slope, his limbs lying all at random, and his face turned away.

The eccentric fisherman dropped his net and walked swiftly towards the spot, his new acquaintance following him. As they drew near there seemed a sort of monstrous irony in the fact that the dead machine was still throbbing and thundering as busily as a factory, while the man lay so still.

He was unquestionably dead. The blood flowed in the grass from a hopelessly fatal fracture at the back of the skull; but the face, which was turned to the sun, was uninjured and strangely arresting in itself. It was one of those cases of a strange face so unmistakable as to feel familiar. We feel, somehow, that we ought to recognise it, even though we do not. It was of the broad, square sort with great jaws, almost like that of a highly intellectual ape; the wide mouth shut so tight as to be traced by a mere line; the nose short with the sort of nostrils that seem to gape with an appetite for the air. The oddest thing about the face was that one of the eyebrows was cocked up at a much sharper angle than the other. March thought he had never seen a face so naturally alive as that dead one. And its ugly energy seemed all the stranger for its halo of hoary hair. Some papers lay half fallen out of the pocket, and from among them March extracted a card-case. He read the name on the card aloud.

'Sir Humphrey Turnbull. I'm sure I've heard that name somewhere.'

His companion only gave a sort of a little sigh and was silent for a moment, as if ruminating, then he merely said, 'The poor fellow is quite gone,' and added some scientific terms in which his auditor once more found himself out of his depth.

'As things are,' continued the same curiously well-informed person, 'it will be more legal for us to leave the body as it is until the police are informed. In fact, I think it will be well if nobody except the police is informed. Don't be surprised if I seem to be keeping it dark from some of our neighbours round here.' Then, as if prompted to regularise his rather abrupt confidence, he said: 'I've come down to see my cousin at Torwood; my name is Horne Fisher. Might be a pun on my pottering about here, mightn't it?'

'Is Sir Howard Horne your cousin?' asked March. 'I'm going to Torwood Park to see him myself; only about his public work, of course, and the wonderful stand he is making for his principles. I think this Budget is the greatest thing in English history. If it fails, it will be the most heroic failure in English history. Are you an admirer of your great kinsman, Mr Fisher?'

'Rather,' said Mr Fisher. 'He's the best shot I know.'

Then, as if sincerely repentant of his nonchalance, he added, with a sort of enthusiasm: 'No, but really, he's a *beautiful* shot.'

As if fired by his own words, he took a sort of leap at the ledges of the rock above him, and scaled them with a sudden agility in startling contrast to his general lassitude. He had stood for some seconds on the headland above, with his aquiline profile under the Panama hat relieved against the sky and peering over the countryside, before his companion had collected himself sufficiently to scramble up after him.

The level above was a stretch of common turf on which the tracks of the fated car were ploughed plainly enough, but the brink of it was broken as with rocky teeth; broken boulders of all shapes and sizes lay near the edge; it was almost incredible that anyone could have deliberately driven into such a death trap, especially in broad daylight.

'I can't make head or tail of it,' said March. 'Was he blind? Or blind drunk?'

'Neither, by the look of him,' replied the other.

'Then it was suicide.'

'It doesn't seem a cosy way of doing it,' remarked the man called Fisher. 'Besides, I don't fancy poor old Puggy would commit suicide, somehow.'

'Poor old who?' enquired the wondering journalist. 'Did you know this unfortunate man?'

'Nobody knew him exactly,' replied Fisher, with some vagueness. 'But one *knew* him, of course. He'd been a terror in his time, in Parliament and the courts, and so on; especially in that row about the aliens who were deported as undesirables, when he wanted one of 'em hanged for murder. He was so sick about it that he retired from the bench. Since then he mostly motored about by himself; but he was coming to Torwood, too, for the weekend; and I don't see why he should deliberately break his neck almost at the very door. I believe Hoggs – I mean my cousin Howard – was coming down specially to meet him.'

'Torwood Park doesn't belong to your cousin?' enquired March.

'No; it used to belong to the Winthrops, you know,' replied the other. 'Now a new man's got it; a man from Montreal named Jenkins. Hoggs comes for the shooting; I told you he was a lovely shot.'

This repeated eulogy on the great social statesman affected Harold March as if somebody had defined Napoleon as a distinguished player of nap. But he had another half-formed impression struggling in this flood of unfamiliar things, and he brought it to the surface before it could vanish.

'Jenkins,' he repeated. 'Surely you don't mean Jefferson Jenkins, the social reformer? I mean the man who's fighting for the new cottage-estate scheme. It would be as interesting to meet him as any Cabinet Minister in the world, if you'll excuse my saying so.'

'Yes; Hoggs told him it would have to be cottages,' said Fisher. 'He said the breed of cattle had improved too often, and people were beginning to laugh. And, of course, you must hang a peerage on to something; though the poor chap hasn't got it yet. Hullo, here's somebody else.'

They had started walking in the tracks of the car, leaving it behind them in the hollow, still humming horribly like a huge insect that had killed a man. The tracks took them to the corner of the road, one arm of which went on in the same line towards the distant gates of the park. It was clear that the car had been driven down the long straight road, and then, instead of turning with the road to the left, had gone straight on over the turf to its doom. But it was not this discovery that had riveted Fisher's eye, but something even more solid. At the angle of the white road a dark and solitary figure was standing almost as still as a finger post. It was that of a big man in rough shooting-clothes, bareheaded, and with tousled curly hair that gave him a rather wild look. On a nearer approach this first more fantastic impression faded; in a full light the figure took on more conventional colours, as of an ordinary gentleman who happened to have come out without a hat and without very studiously brushing his hair. But the massive stature remained, and something deep and even cavernous about the setting of the eyes redeemed his animal good looks from the commonplace. But March had no time to study the man more closely, for, much to his astonishment, his guide merely observed, 'Hullo, Jack!' and walked past him as if he had indeed been a signpost, and without attempting to inform him of the catastrophe beyond the rocks. It was relatively a small thing, but it was only the first in a string of singular antics on which his new and eccentric friend was leading him.

The man they had passed looked after them in rather a suspicious fashion, but Fisher continued serenely on his way along the straight road that ran past the gates of the great estate.

'That's John Burke, the traveller,' he condescended to explain. 'I expect you've heard of him; shoots big game and all that. Sorry I couldn't stop to introduce you, but I dare say you'll meet him later on.'

'I know his book, of course,' said March, with renewed interest. 'That is certainly a fine piece of description, about their being only conscious of the closeness of the elephant when the colossal head blocked out the moon.'

'Yes, young Halkett writes jolly well, I think. What? Didn't you know Halkett wrote Burke's book for him? Burke can't use anything except a gun; and you can't write with that. Oh, he's genuine enough in his way, you know, as brave as a lion, or a good deal braver by all accounts.'

'You seem to know all about him,' observed March, with a rather bewildered laugh, 'and about a good many other people.'

Fisher's bald brow became abruptly corrugated, and a curious expression came into his eyes.

'I know too much,' he said. 'That's what's the matter with me. That's what's the matter with all of us, and the whole show; we know too much. Too much about one another; too much about ourselves. That's why I'm really interested, just now, about one thing that I don't know.'

'And that is?' enquired the other.

'Why that poor fellow is dead.'

They had walked along the straight road for nearly a mile, conversing at intervals in this fashion; and March had a singular sense of the whole world being turned inside out. Mr Horne Fisher did not especially abuse his friends and relatives in fashionable society; of some of them he spoke with affection. But they seemed to be an entirely new set of men and women, who happened to have the same names as the men and women mentioned most often in the newspapers. Yet no fury of revolt could have seemed to him more utterly revolutionary than this cold familiarity. It was like daylight on the other side of stage scenery.

They reached the great lodge gates of the park, and, to March's surprise, passed them and continued along the interminable white, straight road. But he was himself too early for his appointment with Sir Howard, and was not disinclined to see the end of his new friend's experiment, whatever it might be. They had long left the moorland behind them, and half the white road was grey in the great shadow of the Torwood pine forests, themselves like grey bars shuttered against the sunshine and within, amid that clear noon, manufacturing their own midnight. Soon, however, rifts began to appear in them like gleams of coloured windows; the trees thinned and fell away as the road went forward, showing the wild, irregular copses in which, as Fisher said, the house-party had been blazing away all day. And about two hundred yards farther on they came to the first turn of the road.

At the corner stood a sort of decayed inn with the dingy sign of the

Grapes. The signboard was dark and indecipherable by now, and hung black against the sky and the grey moorland beyond, about as inviting as a gallows. March remarked that it looked like a tavern for vinegar instead of wine.

'A good phrase,' said Fisher, 'and so it would be if you were silly enough to drink wine in it. But the beer is very good, and so is the brandy.'

March followed him to the bar parlour with some wonder, and his dim sense of repugnance was not dismissed by the first sight of the innkeeper, who was widely different from the genial innkeepers of romance, a bony man, very silent behind a black moustache, but with black, restless eyes. Taciturn as he was, the investigator succeeded at last in extracting a scrap of information from him, by dint of ordering beer and talking to him persistently and minutely on the subject of motor cars. He evidently regarded the innkeeper as in some singular way an authority on motor cars; as being deep in the secrets of the mechanism, management, and mismanagement of motor cars; holding the man all the time with a glittering eye like the Ancient Mariner. Out of all this rather mysterious conversation there did emerge at last a sort of admission that one particular motor car, of a given description, had stopped before the inn about an hour before, and that an elderly man had alighted, requiring some mechanical assistance. Asked if the visitor required any other assistance, the innkeeper said shortly that the old gentleman had filled his flask and taken a packet of sandwiches. And with these words the somewhat inhospitable host had walked hastily out of the bar, and they heard him banging doors in the dark interior.

Fisher's weary eye wandered round the dusty and dreary inn parlour and rested dreamily on a glass case containing a stuffed bird, with a gun hung on hooks above it, which seemed to be its only ornament.

'Puggy was a humorist,' he observed, 'at least in his own rather grim style. But it seems rather too grim a joke for a man to buy a packet of sandwiches when he is just going to commit suicide.'

'If you come to that,' answered March, 'it isn't very usual for a man to buy a packet of sandwiches when he's just outside the door of a grand house he's going to stop at.'

'No . . . no,' repeated Fisher, almost mechanically; and then suddenly cocked his eye at his interlocutor with a much livelier expression.

'By Jove! that's an idea. You're perfectly right. And that suggests a very queer idea, doesn't it?'

There was a silence, and then March started with irrational nervousness as the door of the inn was flung open and another man walked rapidly to the counter. He had struck it with a coin and called out for brandy before he saw the other two guests, who were sitting at a bare wooden table under the window. When he turned about with a rather wild stare, March had yet another unexpected emotion, for his guide hailed the man as Hoggs and introduced him as Sir Howard Horne.

He looked rather older than his boyish portraits in the illustrated papers, as is the way of politicians; his flat, fair hair was touched with grey, but his face was almost comically round, with a Roman nose which, when combined with his quick, bright eyes, raised a vague reminiscence of a parrot. He had a cap rather at the back of his head and a gun under his arm. Harold March had imagined many things about his meeting with the great political reformer, but he had never pictured him with a gun under his arm, drinking brandy in a public house.

'So you're stopping at Jink's, too,' said Fisher. 'Everybody seems to be at Jink's.'

'Yes,' replied the Chancellor of the Exchequer. 'Jolly good shooting. At least all of it that isn't Jink's shooting. I never knew a chap with such good shooting that was such a bad shot. Mind you, he's a jolly good fellow and all that; I don't say a word against him. But he never learned to hold a gun when he was packing pork or whatever he did. They say he shot the cockade off his own servant's hat; just like him to have cockades, of course. He shot the weathercock off his own ridiculous gilded summerhouse. It's the only cock he'll ever kill, I should think. Are you coming up there now?'

Fisher said, rather vaguely, that he was following soon, when he had fixed something up; and the Chancellor of the Exchequer left the inn. March fancied he had been a little upset or impatient when he called for the brandy; but he had talked himself back into a satisfactory state, if the talk had not been quite what his literary visitor had expected. Fisher, a few minutes afterwards, slowly led the way out of the tavern and stood in the middle of the road, looking down in the direction from which they had travelled. Then he walked back about two hundred yards in that direction and stood still again.

'I should think this is about the place,' he said.

'What place?' asked his companion.

'The place where the poor fellow was killed,' said Fisher, sadly.

'What do you mean?' demanded March. 'He was smashed up on the rocks a mile and a half from here.'

'No, he wasn't,' replied Fisher. 'He didn't fall on the rocks at all. Didn't you notice that he only fell on the slope of soft grass underneath? But I saw that he had a bullet in him already.'

Then after a pause he added: 'He was alive at the inn, but he was dead long before he came to the rocks. So he was shot as he drove his car down this strip of straight road, and I should think somewhere about here. After that, of course, the car went straight on with nobody to stop or turn it. It's really a very cunning dodge in its way; for the body would be found far away, and most people would say, as you do, that it was an accident to a motorist. The murderer must have been a clever brute.'

'But wouldn't the shot be heard at the inn or somewhere?' asked March.

'It would be heard. But it would not be noticed. That,' continued the investigator, 'is where he was clever again. Shooting was going on all over the place all day; very likely he timed his shot so as to drown it in a number of others. Certainly he was a first-class criminal. And he was something else as well.'

'What do you mean?' asked his companion, with a creepy premonition of something coming, he knew not why.

'He was a first-class shot,' said Fisher.

He had turned his back abruptly and was walking down a narrow, grassy lane, little more than a cart track, which lay opposite the inn and marked the end of the great estate and the beginning of the open moors. March plodded after him with the same idle perseverance, and found him staring through a gap in giant weeds and thorns at the flat face of a painted paling. From behind the paling rose the great grey columns of a row of poplars, which filled the heavens above them with dark-green shadow and shook faintly in a wind which had sunk slowly into a breeze. The afternoon was already deepening into evening, and the titanic shadows of the poplars lengthened over a third of the landscape.

'Are you a first-class criminal?' asked Fisher, in a friendly tone. 'I'm afraid I'm not. But I think I can manage to be a sort of fourth-rate burglar.'

And before his companion could reply he had managed to swing himself up and over the fence; March followed without much bodily effort, but with considerable mental disturbance. The poplars grew so close against the fence that they had some difficulty in slipping past them, and beyond the poplars they could see only a high hedge of laurel, green and lustrous in the level sun. Something in this limitation by a series of living walls made him feel as if he were really entering a shattered house instead of an open field. It was as if he came in by a disused door or window and found the way blocked by furniture. When they had circumvented the laurel hedge, they came out on a sort of terrace of turf, which fell by one green step to an oblong lawn like a bowling green. Beyond this was the only building in sight, a low conservatory, which seemed far away from anywhere, like a glass cottage standing in its own fields in fairyland. Fisher knew that lonely look of the outlying parts of a great house well enough. He realised that it is more of a satire on aristocracy than if it were choked with weeds and littered with ruins. For it is not neglected and yet it is deserted; at any rate, it is disused. It is regularly swept and garnished for a master who never comes.

Looking over the lawn, however, he saw one object which he had not apparently expected. It was a sort of tripod supporting a large disc like the round top of a table tipped sideways, and it was not until they had dropped on to the lawn and walked across to look at it that March realised that it was a target. It was worn and weather-stained; the gay colours of its concentric rings were faded; possibly it had been set up in those far-off Victorian days when there was a fashion of archery. March had one of his vague visions of ladies in cloudy crinolines and gentlemen in outlandish hats and whiskers revisiting that lost garden like ghosts.

Fisher, who was peering more closely at the target, startled him by an exclamation.

'Hullo!' he said. 'Somebody has been peppering this thing with shot, after all, and quite lately, too. Why, I believe old Jink's been trying to improve his bad shooting here.'

'Yes, and it looks as if it still wanted improving,' answered March, laughing. 'Not one of these shots is anywhere near the bull's-eye; they seem just scattered about in the wildest way.'

'In the wildest way,' repeated Fisher, still peering intently at the target. He seemed merely to assent, but March fancied his eye was shining under its sleepy lid and that he straightened his stooping figure with a strange effort.

'Excuse me a moment,' he said, feeling in his pockets. 'I think I've got some of my chemicals; and after that we'll go up to the house.'

And he stooped again over the target, putting something with his finger over each of the shot-holes, so far as March could see merely a dull-grey smear. Then they went through the gathering twilight up the long green avenues to the great house.

Here again, however, the eccentric investigator did not enter by the front door. He walked round the house until he found a window open, and, leaping into it, introduced his friend to what appeared to be the gunroom. Rows of the regular instruments for bringing down birds stood against the walls; but across a table in the window lay one or two weapons of a heavier and more formidable pattern.

'Hullo! these are Burke's big-game rifles,' said Fisher. 'I never knew he kept them here.'

He lifted one of them, examined it briefly, and put it down again, frowning heavily. Almost as he did so a strange young man came hurriedly into the room. He was dark and sturdy, with a bumpy forehead and a bulldog jaw, and he spoke with a curt apology.

'I left Major Burke's guns here,' he said, 'and he wants them packed up. He's going away tonight.'

And he carried off the two rifles without casting a glance at the stranger; through the open window they could see his short, dark figure walking away across the glimmering garden. Fisher got out of the window again and stood looking after him.

'That's Halkett, whom I told you about,' he said. 'I knew he was a sort of secretary and had to do with Burke's papers; but I never knew he had anything to do with his guns. But he's just the sort of silent, sensible little devil who might be very good at anything; the sort of man you know for years before you find he's a chess champion.'

He had begun to walk in the direction of the disappearing secretary, and they soon came within sight of the rest of the house-party talking and laughing on the lawn. They could see the tall figure and loose mane of the lion-hunter dominating the little group.

'By the way,' observed Fisher, 'when we were talking about Burke and Halkett, I said that a man couldn't very well write with a gun. Well, I'm not so sure now. Did you ever hear of an artist so clever that he could draw with a gun? There's a wonderful chap loose about here.'

Sir Howard hailed Fisher and his friend the journalist with almost boisterous amiability. The latter was presented to Major Burke and Mr Halkett and also (by way of a parenthesis) to his host, Mr Jenkins, a commonplace little man in loud tweeds, whom everybody else seemed to treat with a sort of affection, as if he were a baby.

The irrepressible Chancellor of the Exchequer was still talking about the birds he had brought down, the birds that Burke and Halkett had brought down, and the birds that Jenkins, their host, had failed to bring down. It seemed to be a sort of sociable monomania.

'You and your big game,' he ejaculated, aggressively, to Burke. 'Why, anybody could shoot big game. You want to be a shot to shoot small game.'

'Quite so,' interposed Horne Fisher. 'Now if only a hippopotamus could fly up in the air out of that bush, or you preserved flying elephants on the estate, why, then – '

'Why even Jink might hit that sort of bird,' cried Sir Howard, hilariously slapping his host on the back. 'Even he might hit a haystack or a hippo.'

'Look here, you fellows,' said Fisher. 'I want you to come along with me for a minute and shoot at something else. Not a hippopotamus. Another kind of queer animal I've found on the estate. It's an animal with three legs and one eye, and it's all the colours of the rainbow.'

'What the deuce are you talking about?' asked Burke.

'You come along and see,' replied Fisher, cheerfully.

Such people seldom reject anything nonsensical, for they are always seeking for something new. They gravely rearmed themselves from the gunroom and trooped along at the tail of their guide, Sir Howard only pausing, in a sort of ecstasy, to point out the celebrated gilt summerhouse on which the gilt weathercock still stood crooked. It was dusk turning to dark by the time they reached the remote green by the poplars and accepted the new and aimless game of shooting at the old mark.

The last light seemed to fade from the lawn, and the poplars against the sunset were like great plumes upon a purple hearse, when the futile procession finally curved round, and came out in front of the target. Sir Howard again slapped his host on the shoulder, shoving him playfully forward to take the first shot. The shoulder and arm he touched seemed unnaturally stiff and angular. Mr Jenkins was holding his gun in an attitude more awkward than any that his satiric friends had seen or expected.

At the same instant a horrible scream seemed to come from nowhere. It was so unnatural and so unsuited to the scene that it might have been made by some inhuman thing flying on wings above them or eavesdropping in the dark woods beyond. But Fisher knew that it had started and stopped on the pale lips of Jefferson Jenkins, of Montreal, and no one at that moment catching sight of Jefferson Jenkins's face would have complained that it was commonplace. The next moment a torrent of guttural but good-humoured oaths came from Major Burke as he and the two other men saw what was in front of them. The target stood up in the dim grass like a dark goblin grinning at them, and it was literally grinning. It had two eyes like stars, and in similar livid points of light were picked out the two upturned and open nostrils and the two ends of the wide and tight mouth. A few white dots above each eye indicated the hoary eyebrows, and one of them ran upwards almost erect. It was a brilliant caricature done in bright dotted lines; and March knew of whom. It shone in the shadowy grass, smeared with sea fire as if one of the submarine monsters had crawled into the twilight garden; but it had the head of a dead man.

'It's only luminous paint,' said Burke. 'Old Fisher's been having a joke with that phosphorescent stuff of his.'

'Seems to be meant for old Puggy,' observed Sir Howard. 'Hits him off very well.'

With that they all laughed, except Jenkins. When they had all done, he made a noise like the first effort of an animal to laugh, and Horne Fisher suddenly strode across to him and said: 'Mr Jenkins, I must speak to you at once in private.'

* * *

It was by the little watercourse in the moors, on the slope under the hanging rock, that March met his new friend Fisher, by appointment, shortly after the ugly and almost grotesque scene that had broken up the group in the garden.

'It was a monkey-trick of mine,' observed Fisher, gloomily, 'putting phosphorus on the target; but the only chance to make him jump was to give him the horrors suddenly. And when he saw the face he'd shot at shining on the target he practised on, all lit up with an infernal light, he did jump. Quite enough for my own intellectual satisfaction.'

'I'm afraid I don't quite understand even now,' said March, 'exactly what he did or why he did it.'

'You ought to,' replied Fisher, with his rather dreary smile, 'for you gave me the first suggestion yourself. Oh yes, you did; and it was a very shrewd one. You said a man wouldn't take sandwiches with him to dine at a great house. It was quite true; and the inference was that, though he was going there, he didn't mean to dine there. Or, at any rate, that he might not be dining there. It occurred to me at once that he probably expected the visit to be unpleasant, or the reception doubtful, or something that would prevent his accepting hospitality. Then it struck me that Turnbull was a terror to certain shady characters in the past, and that he had come down to identify and denounce one of them. The chances at the start pointed to the host – that is, Jenkins. I'm morally certain now that Jenkins was the undesirable alien Turnbull wanted to convict in another shooting affair, but you see the shooting gentleman had another shot in his locker.'

'But you said he would have to be a very good shot,' protested March.

'Jenkins is a very good shot,' said Fisher. 'A very good shot who can pretend to be a very bad shot. Shall I tell you the second hint I hit on, after yours, to make me think it was Jenkins? It was my cousin's account of his bad shooting. He'd shot a cockade off a hat and a weathercock off a building. Now, in fact, a man must shoot very well indeed to shoot so badly as that. He must shoot very neatly to hit the cockade and not the head, or even the hat. If the shots had really gone at random, the chances are a thousand to one that they would not have hit such prominent and picturesque objects. They were chosen because they were prominent and picturesque objects. They make a story to go the round of society. He keeps the crooked weathercock in the summerhouse to perpetuate the story of a legend. And then he lay in wait with his evil eye and wicked gun, safely ambushed behind the legend of his own incompetence.

'But there is more than that. There is the summerhouse itself. I mean there is the whole thing. There's all that Jenkins gets chaffed about, the gilding and the gaudy colours and all the vulgarity that's supposed to stamp him as an upstart. Now, as a matter of fact, upstarts generally don't do this. God knows there's enough of 'em in society; and one knows 'em well enough. And this is the very last thing they do. They're generally only too keen to know the right thing and do it; and they instantly put themselves body and soul into the hands of art decorators and art experts, who do the whole thing for them. There's hardly another millionaire alive who has the moral courage to have a gilt monogram on a chair like that one in the gunroom. For that matter, there's the name as well as the monogram. Names like Tompkins and Jenkins and Jinks are funny without being vulgar; I mean they are vulgar without being common. If you prefer it, they are commonplace without being common. They are just the names to be chosen to *look* ordinary, but they're really rather extraordinary. Do you know many people called Tompkins? It's a good deal rarer than Talbot. It's pretty much the same with the comic clothes of the parvenu. Jenkins dresses like a character in *Punch*. But that's because he is a character in *Punch*. I mean he's a fictitious character. He's a fabulous animal. He doesn't exist.

'Have you ever considered what it must be like to be a man who doesn't exist? I mean to be a man with a fictitious character that he has to keep up at the expense not merely of personal talents. To be a new kind of hypocrite hiding a talent in a new kind of napkin. This man has chosen his hypocrisy very ingeniously; it was really a new one. A subtle villain has dressed up as a dashing gentleman and a worthy business man and a philanthropist and a saint; but the loud checks of a comical little cad were really rather a new disguise. But the disguise must be very irksome to a man who can really do things. This is a dexterous little cosmopolitan guttersnipe who can do scores of things, not only shoot, but draw and paint, and probably play the fiddle. Now a man like that may find the hiding of his talents useful; but he could never help wanting to use them where they were useless. If he can draw, he will draw absent-mindedly on blotting paper. I suspect this rascal has often drawn poor old Puggy's face on blotting paper. Probably he began doing it in blots as he afterwards did it in dots, or rather shots. It was the same sort of thing; he found a disused target in a deserted yard and couldn't resist indulging in a little secret shooting, like secret drinking. You thought the shots all scattered and irregular, and so they were; but not accidental. No two distances were alike; but the different points were exactly where he wanted to put them. There's nothing needs such mathematical precision as a wild caricature. I've dabbled a little in drawing myself, and I assure you that to put one dot where you want it is a marvel with a pen close to a piece of paper. It was a miracle to do it across a garden with a gun. But a man who can work those miracles will always itch to work them, if it's only in the dark.'

After a pause March observed, thoughtfully, 'But he couldn't have brought him down like a bird with one of those little guns.'

'No; that was why I went into the gunroom,' replied Fisher. 'He did it with one of Burke's rifles, and Burke thought he knew the sound of it. That's why he rushed out without a hat, looking so wild. He saw nothing but a car passing quickly, which he followed for a little way, and then concluded he'd made a mistake.'

There was another silence, during which Fisher sat on a great stone as motionless as on their first meeting, and watched the grey and silver river eddying past under the bushes. Then March said, abruptly, 'Of course he knows the truth now.'

'Nobody knows the truth but you and I,' answered Fisher, with a certain softening in his voice. 'And I don't think you and I will ever quarrel.'

'What do you mean?' asked March, in an altered accent. 'What have you done about it?'

Horne Fisher continued to gaze steadily at the eddying stream. At last he said, 'The police have proved it was a motor accident.'

'But you know it was not.'

'I told you that I know too much,' replied Fisher, with his eye on the river. 'I know that, and I know a great many other things. I know the atmosphere and the way the whole thing works. I know this fellow has succeeded in making himself something incurably commonplace and comic. I know you can't get up a persecution of old Toole or Little Tich. If I were to tell Hoggs or Halkett that old Jink was an assassin, they would almost die of laughter before my eyes. Oh, I don't say their laughter's quite innocent, though it's genuine in its way. They want old Jink, and they couldn't do without him. I don't say I'm quite innocent. I like Hoggs; I don't want him to be down and out; and he'd be done for if Jink can't pay up for his coronet. They were devilish near the line at the last election, *I* can tell you. But the only real objection to it is that it's impossible. Nobody would believe it; it's not in the picture. The crooked weathercock would always turn it into a joke.'

'Don't you think this is infamous?' asked March, quietly.

'I think a good many things,' replied the other. 'If you people ever happen to blow the whole tangle of society to hell with dynamite, I don't know that the human race will be much the worse. But don't be too hard on me merely because I know what society is. That's why I moon away my time over things like stinking fish.'

There was a pause as he settled himself down again by the stream; and then he added: 'I told you before I had to throw back the big fish.'

2

The Vanishing Prince

This tale begins among a tangle of tales round a name that is at once recent and legendary. The name is that of Michael O'Neill, popularly called Prince Michael, partly because he claimed descent from ancient Fenian princes, and partly because he was credited with a plan to make himself prince president of Ireland, as the last Napoleon did of France. He was undoubtedly a gentleman of honourable pedigree and of many accomplishments, but two of his accomplishments emerged from all the rest. He had a talent for appearing when he was not wanted and a talent for disappearing when he was wanted, especially when he was wanted by the police. It may be added that his disappearances were more dangerous than his appearances. In the latter he seldom went beyond the sensational – pasting up seditious placards, tearing down official placards, making flamboyant speeches, or unfurling forbidden flags. But in order to effect the former he would sometimes fight for his freedom with startling energy, from which men were sometimes lucky to escape with a broken head instead of a broken neck. His most famous feats of escape, however, were due to dexterity and not to violence. On a cloudless summer morning he had come down a country road white with dust, and, pausing outside a farmhouse, had told the farmer's daughter, with elegant indifference, that the local police were in pursuit of him. The girl's name was Bridget Royce, a sombre and even sullen type of beauty, and she looked at him darkly, as if in doubt, and said, 'Do you want me to hide you?' Upon which he only laughed, leaped lightly over the stone wall, and strode toward the farm, merely throwing over his shoulder the remark, 'Thank you, I have generally been quite capable of hiding myself.' In which proceeding he acted with a tragic ignorance of the nature of women; and there fell on his path in that sunshine a shadow of doom.

While he disappeared through the farmhouse the girl remained for a few moments looking up the road, and two perspiring policemen came ploughing up to the door where she stood. Though still angry, she was still silent, and a quarter of an hour later the officers had searched the house and were already inspecting the kitchen garden and cornfield behind it. In the ugly reaction of her mood she might have been tempted even to point out the fugitive, but for a small difficulty that she had no more notion than the policemen had of where he could possibly have gone. The kitchen garden was enclosed by a very low wall, and the cornfield beyond lay aslant like a square patch on a great green hill on which he could still have been seen even as a dot in the distance. Everything stood solid in its familiar place; the apple tree was too small to support or hide a climber; the only shed stood open and obviously empty; there was no sound save the droning of summer flies and the occasional flutter of a bird unfamiliar enough to be surprised by the scarecrow in the field; there was scarcely a shadow save a few blue lines that fell from the thin tree; every detail was picked out by the brilliant daylight as if in a microscope. The girl described the scene later, with all the passionate realism of her race, and, whether or no the policemen had a similar eye for the picturesque, they had at least an eye for the facts of the case, and were compelled to give up the chase and retire from the scene. Bridget Royce remained as if in a trance, staring at the sunlit garden in which a man had just vanished like a fairy. She was still in a sinister mood, and the miracle took in her mind a character of unfriendliness and fear, as if the fairy were decidedly a bad fairy. The sun upon the glittering garden depressed her more than the darkness, but she continued to stare at it. Then the world itself went half-witted and she screamed. The scarecrow moved in the sunlight. It had stood with its back to her in a battered old black hat and a tattered garment, and with all its tatters flying, it strode away across the hill.

She did not analyse the audacious trick by which the man had turned to his advantage the subtle effects of the expected and the obvious; she was still under the cloud of more individual complexities, and she noticed most of all that the vanishing scarecrow did not even turn to look at the farm. And the fates that were running so adverse to his fantastic career of freedom ruled that his next adventure, though it had the same success in another quarter, should increase the danger in this quarter. Among the many similar adventures related of him in this manner it is also said that some days afterwards another girl, named Mary Cregan, found him concealed on the farm where she worked; and if the story is true, she must also have had the shock of an uncanny experience, for when she was busy at some lonely task in the yard she heard a voice speaking out of the well, and found that the eccentric had managed to drop himself into the bucket which was some little way below, the well only partly full of water. In this case, however, he had to appeal to the woman to wind up the rope. And men say it was when this news was told to the other woman that her soul walked over the border line of treason.

Such, at least, were the stories told of him in the countryside, and there were many more – as that he had stood insolently in a splendid green dressing gown on the steps of a great hotel, and then led the police a chase through a long suite of grand apartments, and finally through his own bedroom on to a balcony that overhung the river. The moment the pursuers stepped on to the balcony it broke under them, and they dropped pell-mell into the eddying waters, while Michael, who had thrown off his gown and dived, was able to swim away. It was said that he had carefully cut away the props so that they would not support anything so heavy as a policeman. But here again he was immediately fortunate, yet ultimately unfortunate, for it is said that one of the men was drowned, leaving a family feud which made a little rift in his popularity. These stories can now be told in some detail, not because they are the most marvellous of his many adventures, but because these alone were not covered with silence by the loyalty of the peasantry. These alone found their way into official reports, and it is these which three of the chief officials of the country were reading and discussing when the more remarkable part of this story begins.

Night was far advanced and the lights shone in the cottage that served for a temporary police station near the coast. On one side of it were the last houses of the straggling village, and on the other nothing but a waste moorland stretching away towards the sea, the line of which was broken by no landmark except a solitary tower of the prehistoric pattern still found in Ireland, standing up as slender as a column, but pointed like a pyramid. At a wooden table in front of the window, which normally looked out on this landscape, sat two men in plain clothes, but with something of a military bearing, for indeed they were the two chiefs of the detective service of that district. The senior of the two, both in age and rank, was a sturdy man with a short white beard, and frosty eyebrows fixed in a frown which suggested rather worry than severity.

His name was Morton, and he was a Liverpool man long pickled in the Irish quarrels, and doing his duty among them in a sour fashion not altogether unsympathetic. He had spoken a few sentences to his companion, Nolan, a tall, dark man with a cadaverous equine Irish face, when he seemed to remember something and touched a bell which rang in another room. The subordinate he had summoned immediately appeared with a sheaf of papers in his hand.

'Sit down, Wilson,' he said. 'Those are the depositions, I suppose.'

'Yes,' replied the third officer. 'I think I've got all there is to be got out of them, so I sent the people away.'

'Did Mary Cregan give evidence?' asked Morton, with a frown that looked a little heavier than usual.

'No, but her master did,' answered the man called Wilson, who had flat, red hair and a plain, pale face, not without sharpness. 'I think he's hanging round the girl himself and is out against a rival. There's always some reason of that sort when we are told the truth about anything. And you bet the other girl told right enough.'

'Well, let's hope they'll be some sort of use,' remarked Nolan, in a somewhat hopeless manner, gazing out into the darkness.

'Anything is to the good,' said Morton, 'that lets us know anything about him.'

'Do we know anything about him?' asked the melancholy Irishman.

'We know one thing about him,' said Wilson, 'and it's the one thing that nobody ever knew before. We know where he is.'

'Are you sure?' enquired Morton, looking at him sharply.

'Quite sure,' replied his assistant. 'At this very minute he is in that tower over there by the shore. If you go near enough you'll see the candle burning in the window.'

As he spoke the noise of a horn sounded on the road outside, and a moment after they heard the throbbing of a motor car brought to a standstill before the door. Morton instantly sprang to his feet.

'Thank the Lord, that's the car from Dublin,' he said. 'I can't do anything without special authority, not if he were sitting on the top of the tower and putting out his tongue at us. But the Chief can do what he thinks best.'

He hurried out to the entrance and was soon exchanging greetings with a big handsome man in a fur coat, who brought into the dingy little station the indescribable glow of the great cities and the luxuries of the great world.

For this was Sir Walter Carey, an official of such eminence in Dublin Castle that nothing short of the case of Prince Michael would have brought him on such a journey in the middle of the night. But the case of Prince Michael, as it happened, was complicated by legalism as well as lawlessness. On the last occasion he had escaped by a forensic quibble and not, as usual, by a private escapade; and it was a question whether at the moment he was amenable to the law or not. It might be necessary to stretch a point, but a man like Sir Walter could probably stretch it as far as he liked.

Whether he intended to do so was a question to be considered. Despite the almost aggressive touch of luxury in the fur coat, it soon became apparent that Sir Walter's large leonine head was for use as well as ornament, and he considered the matter soberly and sanely enough. Five chairs were set round the plain deal table, for who should Sir Walter bring with him but his young relative and secretary, Horne Fisher. Sir Walter listened with grave attention, and his secretary with polite boredom, to the string of episodes by which the police had traced the flying rebel from the steps of the hotel to the solitary tower beside the sea. There at least he was cornered between the moors and the breakers; and the scout sent by Wilson reported him as writing under a solitary candle, perhaps composing another of his tremendous proclamations. Indeed, it would have been typical of him to choose it as the place in which finally to turn to bay. He had some remote claim on it, as on a family castle; and those who knew him thought him capable of imitating the primitive Irish chieftains who fell fighting against the sea.

'I saw some queer-looking people leaving as I came in,' said Sir Walter

Carey. 'I suppose they were your witnesses. But why do they turn up here at this time of night?'

Morton smiled grimly. 'They come here by night because they would be dead men if they came here by day. They are criminals committing a crime that is more horrible here than theft or murder.'

'What crime do you mean?' asked the other, with some curiosity.

'They are helping the law,' said Morton.

There was a silence, and Sir Walter considered the papers before him with an abstracted eye. At last he spoke.

'Quite so; but look here, if the local feeling is as lively as that there are a good many points to consider. I believe the new Act will enable me to collar him now if I think it best. But is it best? A serious rising would do us no good in Parliament, and the government has enemies in England as well as Ireland. It won't do if I have done what looks a little like sharp practice, and then only raised a revolution.'

'It's all the other way,' said the man called Wilson, rather quickly. 'There won't be half so much of a revolution if you arrest him as there will if you leave him loose for three days longer. But, anyhow, there can't be anything nowadays that the proper police can't manage.'

'Mr Wilson is a Londoner,' said the Irish detective, with a smile.

'Yes, I'm a cockney, all right,' replied Wilson, 'and I think I'm all the better for that. Especially at this job, oddly enough.'

Sir Walter seemed slightly amused at the pertinacity of the third officer, and perhaps even more amused at the slight accent with which he spoke, which rendered rather needless his boast about his origin.

'Do you mean to say,' he asked, 'that you know more about the business here because you have come from London?'

'Sounds funny, I know, but I do believe it,' answered Wilson. 'I believe these affairs want fresh methods. But most of all I believe they want a fresh eye.'

The superior officers laughed, and the red-haired man went on with a slight touch of temper: 'Well, look at the facts. See how the fellow got away every time, and you'll understand what I mean. Why was he able to stand in the place of the scarecrow, hidden by nothing but an old hat? Because it was a village policeman who knew the scarecrow was there, was expecting it, and therefore took no notice of it. Now I never expect a scarecrow. I've never seen one in the street, and I stare at one when I see it in the field. It's a new thing to me and worth noticing. And it was just the same when he hid in the well. You are ready to find a well in a place like that; you look for a well, and so you don't see it. I don't look for it, and therefore I do look at it.'

'It is certainly an idea,' said Sir Walter, smiling, 'but what about the balcony? Balconies are occasionally seen in London.'

'But not rivers right under them, as if it was in Venice,' replied Wilson.

'It is certainly a new idea,' repeated Sir Walter, with something like respect. He had all the love of the luxurious classes for new ideas. But he also had a critical faculty, and was inclined to think, after due reflection, that it was a true idea as well.

Growing dawn had already turned the window panes from black to grey when Sir Walter got abruptly to his feet. The others rose also, taking this for a signal that the arrest was to be undertaken. But their leader stood for a moment in deep thought, as if conscious that he had come to a parting of the ways.

Suddenly the silence was pierced by a long, wailing cry from the dark moors outside. The silence that followed it seemed more startling than the shriek itself, and it lasted until Nolan said, heavily: ' 'Tis the banshee. Somebody is marked for the grave.'

His long, large-featured face was as pale as a moon, and it was easy to remember that he was the only Irishman in the room.

'Well, I know that banshee,' said Wilson, cheerfully, 'ignorant as you think I am of these things. I talked to that banshee myself an hour ago, and I sent that banshee up to the tower and told her to sing out like that if she could get a glimpse of our friend writing his proclamation.'

'Do you mean that girl Bridget Royce?' asked Morton, drawing his frosty brows together. 'Has she turned king's evidence to that extent?'

'Yes,' answered Wilson. 'I know very little of these local things, you tell me, but I reckon an angry woman is much the same in all countries.'

Nolan, however, seemed still moody and unlike himself. 'It's an ugly noise and an ugly business altogether,' he said. 'If it's really the end of Prince Michael it may well be the end of other things as well. When the spirit is on him he would escape by a ladder of dead men, and wade through that sea if it were made of blood.'

'Is that the real reason of your pious alarms?' asked Wilson, with a slight sneer.

The Irishman's pale face blackened with a new passion.

'I have faced as many murderers in County Clare as you ever fought with in Clapham Junction, Mr Cockney,' he said.

'Hush, please,' said Morton, sharply. 'Wilson, you have no kind of right to imply doubt of your superior's conduct. I hope you will prove yourself as courageous and trustworthy as he has always been.'

The pale face of the red-haired man seemed a shade paler, but he was silent and composed, and Sir Walter went up to Nolan with marked courtesy, saying, 'Shall we go outside now, and get this business done?'

Dawn had lifted, leaving a wide chasm of white between a great grey cloud and the great grey moorland, beyond which the tower was outlined against the daybreak and the sea.

Something in its plain and primitive shape vaguely suggested the dawn in the first days of the earth, in some prehistoric time when even the colours were hardly created, when there was only blank daylight between cloud and clay. These dead hues were relieved only by one spot of gold – the spark of the candle alight in the window of the lonely tower, and burning on into the broadening daylight. As the group of detectives, followed by a cordon of policemen, spread out into a crescent to cut off all escape, the light in the tower flashed as if it were moved for a moment, and then went out. They knew the man inside had realised the daylight and blown out his candle.

'There are other windows, aren't there?' asked Morton, 'and a door, of course, somewhere round the corner? Only a round tower has no corners.'

'Another example of my small suggestion,' observed Wilson, quietly. 'That queer tower was the first thing I saw when I came to these parts; and I can tell you a little more about it – or, at any rate, the outside of it. There are four windows altogether, one a little way from this one, but just out of sight. Those are both on the ground floor, and so is the third on the other side, making a sort of triangle. But the fourth is just above the third, and I suppose it looks on an upper floor.'

'It's only a sort of loft, reached by a ladder,' said Nolan. 'I've played in the place when I was a child. It's no more than an empty shell.' And his sad face grew sadder, thinking perhaps of the tragedy of his country and the part that he played in it.

'The man must have got a table and chair, at any rate,' said Wilson, 'but no doubt he could have got those from some cottage. If I might make a suggestion, sir, I think we ought to approach all the five entrances at once, so to speak. One of us should go to the door and one to each window; Macbride here has a ladder for the upper window.'

Mr Horne Fisher, the languid secretary, turned to his distinguished relative and spoke for the first time.

'I am rather a convert to the cockney school of psychology,' he said in an almost inaudible voice.

The others seemed to feel the same influence in different ways, for the group began to break up in the manner indicated. Morton moved towards the window immediately in front of them, where the hidden outlaw had just snuffed the candle; Nolan, a little farther westward to the next window; while Wilson, followed by Macbride with the ladder, went round to the two windows at the back. Sir Walter Carey himself, followed by his secretary, began to walk round towards the only door, to demand admittance in a more regular fashion.

'He will be armed, of course,' remarked Sir Walter, casually.

'By all accounts,' replied Horne Fisher, 'he can do more with a candlestick than most men with a pistol. But he is pretty sure to have the pistol, too.'

Even as he spoke the question was answered with a tongue of thunder. Morton had just placed himself in front of the nearest window, his broad shoulders blocking the aperture. For an instant it was lit from within as with red fire, followed by a thundering throng of echoes. The square shoulders seemed to alter in shape, and the sturdy figure collapsed among the tall, rank grasses at the foot of the tower. A puff of smoke floated from the window like a little cloud. The two men behind rushed to the spot and raised him, but he was dead.

Sir Walter straightened himself and called out something that was lost in another noise of firing; it was possible that the police were already avenging their comrade from the other side. Fisher had already raced round to the next window, and a new cry of astonishment from him brought his patron to the same spot. Nolan, the Irish policeman, had also fallen, sprawling all his great length in the grass, and it was red with his blood. He was still alive when they reached him, but there was death on his face, and he was only able to make a final gesture telling them that all was over; and, with a broken word and a heroic effort, motioning them on to where his other comrades were besieging the back of the tower. Stunned by these rapid and repeated shocks, the two men could only vaguely obey the gesture, and, finding their way to the other windows at the back, they discovered a scene equally startling, if less final and tragic. The other two officers were not dead or mortally wounded, but Macbride lay with a broken leg and his ladder on top of him, evidently thrown down from the top window of the tower; while Wilson lay on his face, quite still as if stunned, with his red head among the grey and silver of the sea holly. In him, however, the impotence was but momentary, for he began to move and rise as the others came round the tower.

'My God! it's like an explosion!' cried Sir Walter; and indeed it was the only word for this unearthly energy, by which one man had been able to deal death or destruction on three sides of the same small triangle at the same instant.

Wilson had already scrambled to his feet and with splendid energy flew again at the window, revolver in hand. He fired twice into the opening and then disappeared in his own smoke; but the thud of his feet and the shock of a falling chair told them that the intrepid Londoner had managed at last to leap into the room. Then followed a curious silence; and Sir Walter, walking to the window through the thinning smoke, looked into the hollow shell of the ancient tower. Except for Wilson, staring around him, there was nobody there.

The inside of the tower was a single empty room, with nothing but a plain wooden chair and a table on which were pens, ink and paper, and the candlestick. Halfway up the high wall there was a rude timber platform under the upper window, a small loft which was more like a large shelf. It was reached only by a ladder, and it seemed to be as bare as the bare walls. Wilson completed his survey of the place and then went and stared at the things on the table. Then he silently pointed with his lean forefinger at the open page of the large notebook. The writer had suddenly stopped writing, even in the middle of a word.

'I said it was like an explosion,' said Sir Walter Carey at last. 'And really the man himself seems to have suddenly exploded. But he has blown himself up somehow without touching the tower. He's burst more like a bubble than a bomb.'

'He has touched more valuable things than the tower,' said Wilson, gloomily.

There was a long silence, and then Sir Walter said, seriously: 'Well, Mr Wilson, I am not a detective, and these unhappy happenings have left you in charge of that branch of the business. We all lament the cause of this, but I should like to say that I myself have the strongest confidence in your capacity for carrying on the work. What do you think we should do next?'

Wilson seemed to rouse himself from his depression and acknowledged the speaker's words with a warmer civility than he had hitherto shown to anybody. He called in a few of the police to assist in routing out the interior, leaving the rest to spread themselves in a search party outside.

'I think,' he said, 'the first thing is to make quite sure about the inside of this place, as it was hardly physically possible for him to have got outside. I suppose poor Nolan would have brought in his banshee and said it was supernaturally possible. But I've got no use for disembodied spirits when I'm dealing with facts. And the facts before me are an empty tower with a ladder, a chair, and a table.'

'The spiritualists,' said Sir Walter, with a smile, 'would say that spirits could find a great deal of use for a table.'

'I dare say they could if the spirits were on the table – in a bottle,' replied Wilson, with a curl of his pale lip. 'The people round here, when they're all sodden up with Irish whiskey, may believe in such things. I think they want a little education in this country.'

Horne Fisher's heavy eyelids fluttered in a faint attempt to rise, as if he were tempted to a lazy protest against the contemptuous tone of the investigator.

'The Irish believe far too much in spirits to believe in spiritualism,' he murmured. 'They know too much about 'em. If you want a simple and childlike faith in any spirit that comes along you can get it in your favourite London.'

'I don't want to get it anywhere,' said Wilson, shortly. 'I say I'm dealing with much simpler things than your simple faith, with a table and a chair and a ladder. Now what I want to say about them at the start is this. They are all three made roughly enough of plain wood. But the table and the chair are fairly new and comparatively clean. The ladder is covered with dust and there is a cobweb under the top rung of it. That means that he borrowed the first two quite recently from some cottage, as we supposed, but the ladder has been a long time in this rotten old dustbin. Probably it was part of the original furniture, an heirloom in this magnificent palace of the Irish kings.'

Again Fisher looked at him under his eyelids, but seemed too sleepy to speak, and Wilson went on with his argument.

'Now it's quite clear that something very odd has just happened in this place. The chances are ten to one, it seems to me, that it had something specially to do with this place. Probably he came here because he could do it only here; it doesn't seem very inviting otherwise. But the man knew it of old; they say it belonged to his family, so that altogether, I think, everything points to something in the construction of the tower itself.'

'Your reasoning seems to me excellent,' said Sir Walter, who was listening attentively. 'But what could it be?'

'You see now what I mean about the ladder,' went on the detective; 'it's the only old piece of furniture here and the first thing that caught that cockney eye of mine. But there is something else. That loft up there is a sort of lumber room without any lumber. So far as I can see, it's as empty as everything else; and, as things are, I don't see the use of the ladder leading to it. It seems to me, as I can't find anything unusual down here, that it might pay us to look up there.'

He got briskly off the table on which he was sitting (for the only chair was allotted to Sir Walter) and ran rapidly up the ladder to the platform above. He was soon followed by the others, Mr Fisher going last, however, with an appearance of considerable nonchalance.

At this stage, however, they were destined to disappointment; Wilson nosed in every corner like a terrier and examined the roof almost in the posture of a fly, but half an hour afterwards they had to confess that they were still without a clue. Sir Walter's private secretary seemed more and more threatened with inappropriate slumber, and, having been the last to climb up the ladder, seemed now to lack the energy even to climb down again.

'Come along, Fisher,' called out Sir Walter from below, when the others had regained the floor. 'We must consider whether we'll pull the whole place to pieces to see what it's made of.'

'I'm coming in a minute,' said the voice from the ledge above their heads, a voice somewhat suggestive of an articulate yawn.

'What are you waiting for?' asked Sir Walter, impatiently. 'Can you see anything there?'

'Well, yes, in a way,' replied the voice, vaguely. 'In fact, I see it quite plain now.'

'What is it?' asked Wilson, sharply, from the table on which he sat kicking his heels restlessly.

'Well, it's a man,' said Horne Fisher.

Wilson bounded off the table as if he had been kicked off it. 'What do you mean?' he cried. 'How can you possibly see a man?'

'I can see him through the window,' replied the secretary, mildly. 'I see him coming across the moor. He's making a bee line across the open country towards this tower. He evidently means to pay us a visit. And, considering who it seems to be, perhaps it would be more polite if we were all at the door to receive him.' And in a leisurely manner the secretary came down the ladder.

'Who it seems to be!' repeated Sir Walter in astonishment.

'Well, I think it's the man you call Prince Michael,' observed Mr Fisher, airily. 'In fact, I'm sure it is. I've seen the police portraits of him.'

There was a dead silence, and Sir Walter's usually steady brain seemed to go round like a windmill.

'But, hang it all!' he said at last, 'even supposing his own explosion could have thrown him half a mile away, without passing through any of the windows, and left him alive enough for a country walk – even then, why the devil should he walk in this direction? The murderer does not generally revisit the scene of his crime so rapidly as all that.'

'He doesn't know yet that it is the scene of his crime,' answered Horne Fisher.

'What on earth do you mean? You credit him with rather singular absence of mind.'

'Well, the truth is, it isn't the scene of his crime,' said Fisher, and went and looked out of the window.

There was another silence, and then Sir Walter said, quietly: 'What sort of notion have you really got in your head, Fisher? Have you developed a new theory about how this fellow escaped out of the ring round him?'

'He never escaped at all,' answered the man at the window, without turning round. 'He never escaped out of the ring because he was never inside the ring. He was not in this tower at all, at least not when we were surrounding it.'

He turned and leaned back against the window, but, in spite of his usual listless manner, they almost fancied that the face in shadow was a little pale.

'I began to guess something of the sort when we were some way from the tower,' he said. 'Did you notice that sort of flash or flicker the candle gave before it was extinguished? I was almost certain it was only the last leap the flame gives when a candle burns itself out. And then I came into this room and I saw that.'

He pointed at the table, and Sir Walter caught his breath with a sort of curse at his own blindness. For the candle in the candlestick had obviously burned itself away to nothing and left him, mentally, at least, very completely in the dark.

'Then there is a sort of mathematical question,' went on Fisher, leaning back in his limp way and looking up at the bare walls, as if tracing imaginary diagrams there. 'It's not so easy for a man in the third angle to face the other two at the same moment, especially if they are at the base of an isosceles. I am sorry if it sounds like a lecture on geometry, but – '

'I'm afraid we have no time for it,' said Wilson, coldly. 'If this man is really coming back, I must give my orders at once.'

'I think I'll go on with it, though,' observed Fisher, staring at the roof with insolent serenity.

'I must ask you, Mr Fisher, to let me conduct my enquiry on my own lines,' said Wilson, firmly. 'I am the officer in charge now.'

'Yes,' remarked Horne Fisher, softly, but with an accent that somehow chilled the hearer. 'Yes. But why?'

Sir Walter was staring, for he had never seen his rather lackadaisical young friend look like that before. Fisher was looking at Wilson with lifted lids, and the eyes under them seemed to have shed or shifted a film, as do the eyes of an eagle.

'Why are you the officer in charge now?' he asked. 'Why can you conduct the enquiry on your own lines now? How did it come about, I wonder, that the elder officers are not here to interfere with anything you do?'

Nobody spoke, and nobody can say how soon anyone would have collected his wits to speak when a noise came from without. It was the heavy and hollow sound of a blow upon the door of the tower, and to their shaken spirits it sounded strangely like the hammer of doom.

The wooden door of the tower moved on its rusty hinges under the hand that struck it and Prince Michael came into the room. Nobody had the smallest doubt about his identity. His light clothes, though frayed with his adventures, were of fine and almost foppish cut, and he wore a pointed beard, or imperial, perhaps as a further reminiscence of Louis Napoleon; but he was a much taller and more graceful man that his prototype. Before anyone could speak he had silenced everyone for an instant with a slight but splendid gesture of hospitality.

'Gentlemen,' he said, 'this is a poor place now, but you are heartily welcome.'

Wilson was the first to recover, and he took a stride towards the newcomer.

'Michael O'Neill, I arrest you in the King's name for the murder of Francis Morton and James Nolan. It is my duty to warn you – '

'No, no, Mr Wilson,' cried Fisher, suddenly. 'You shall not commit a third murder.'

Sir Walter Carey rose from his chair, which fell over with a crash behind him. 'What does all this mean?' he called out in an authoritative manner.

'It means,' said Fisher, 'that this man, Hooker Wilson, as soon as he had put his head in at that window, killed his two comrades who had put their heads in at the other windows, by firing across the empty room. That is what it means. And if you want to know, count how many times he is supposed to have fired and then count the charges left in his revolver.'

Wilson, who was still sitting on the table, abruptly put a hand out for the weapon that lay beside him. But the next movement was the most unexpected of all, for the prince standing in the doorway passed suddenly from the dignity of a statue to the swiftness of an acrobat and rent the revolver out of the detective's hand.

'You dog!' he cried. 'So you are the type of English truth, as I am of Irish tragedy – you who come to kill me, wading through the blood of your brethren. If they had fallen in a feud on the hillside, it would be called murder, and yet your sin might be forgiven you. But I, who am innocent, I was to be slain with ceremony. There would be long speeches and patient judges listening to my vain plea of innocence, noting down my despair and disregarding it. Yes, that is what I call assassination. But killing may be no murder; there is one shot left in this little gun, and I know where it should go.'

Wilson turned quickly on the table, and even as he turned he twisted in agony, for Michael shot him through the body where he sat, so that he tumbled off the table like lumber.

The police rushed to lift him; Sir Walter stood speechless; and then, with a strange and weary gesture, Horne Fisher spoke.

'You are indeed a type of the Irish tragedy,' he said. 'You were entirely in the right, and you have put yourself in the wrong.'

The prince's face was like marble for a space; then there dawned in his eyes a light not unlike that of despair. He laughed suddenly and flung the smoking pistol on the ground.

'I am indeed in the wrong,' he said. 'I have committed a crime that may justly bring a curse on me and my children.'

Horne Fisher did not seem entirely satisfied with this very sudden repentance; he kept his eyes on the man and only said, in a low voice, 'What crime do you mean?'

'I have helped English justice,' replied Prince Michael. 'I have avenged your King's officers; I have done the work of his hangman. For that truly I deserve to be hanged.'

And he turned to the police with a gesture that did not so much surrender to them, but rather command them to arrest him.

* * *

This was the story that Horne Fisher told to Harold March, the journalist, many years after, in a little, but luxurious, restaurant near Piccadilly. He had invited March to dinner some time after the affair he called 'The Face in the Target', and the conversation had naturally turned on that mystery and afterwards on earlier memories of Fisher's life and the way in which he was led to study such problems as those of Prince Michael. Horne Fisher was fifteen years older; his thin hair had faded to frontal baldness, and his long, thin hands dropped less with affectation and more with fatigue. And he told the story of the Irish adventure of his youth, because it recorded the first occasion on which he had ever come in contact with crime, or discovered how darkly and how terribly crime can be entangled with law.

'Hooker Wilson was the first criminal I ever knew, and he was a policeman,' explained Fisher, twirling his wine glass. 'And all my life has been a mixed-up business of the sort. He was a man of very real talent, and perhaps genius, and well worth studying, both as a detective and a criminal. His white face and red hair were typical of him, for he was one of those who are cold and yet on fire for fame; and he could control anger, but not ambition. He swallowed the snubs of his superiors in that first quarrel, though he boiled with resentment; but when he suddenly saw the two heads dark against the dawn and framed in the two windows, he could not miss the chance, not only of revenge, but of the removal of the two obstacles to his promotion. He was a dead shot and counted on silencing both, though proof against him would have been hard in any case. But, as a matter of fact, he had a narrow escape, in the case of Nolan, who lived just long enough to say "Wilson" and point. We thought he was summoning help for his comrade, but he was really denouncing his murderer. After that it was easy to throw down the ladder above him (for a man up a ladder cannot see clearly what is below and behind) and to throw himself on the ground as another victim of the catastrophe.

'But there was mixed up with his murderous ambition a real belief, not only in his own talents, but in his own theories. He did believe in what he called a fresh eye, and he did want scope for fresh methods. There was something in his view, but it failed where such things commonly fail, because the fresh eye cannot see the unseen. It is true about the ladder and the scarecrow, but not about the life and the soul; and he made a bad mistake about what a man like Michael would do when he heard a woman scream. All Michael's very vanity and vainglory made him rush out at once; he would have walked into Dublin Castle for a lady's glove. Call it his pose or what you will, but he would have done it. What happened when he met her is another story, and one we may never know, but from tales I've heard since, they must have been reconciled. Wilson was wrong there; but there was something, for all that, in his notion that the newcomer sees most, and that the man on the spot may know too much to know anything. He was right about some things. He was right about me.'

'About you?' asked Harold March in some wonder.

'I am the man who knows too much to know anything, or, at any rate, to do anything,' said Horne Fisher. 'I don't mean especially about Ireland. I mean about England. I mean about the whole way we are governed, and perhaps the only way we can be governed. You asked me just now what became of the survivors of that tragedy. Well, Wilson recovered and we managed to persuade him to retire. But we had to pension that damnable murderer more magnificently than any hero who ever fought for England. I managed to save Michael from the worst, but we had to send that perfectly innocent man to penal servitude for a crime we know he never committed, and it was only afterwards that we could connive in a sneakish way at his escape. And Sir Walter Carey is Prime Minister of this country, which he would probably never have been if the truth had been told of such a horrible scandal in his department. It might have done for us altogether in Ireland; it would certainly have done for him. And he is my father's old friend, and has always smothered me with kindness. I am too tangled up with the whole thing, you see, and I was certainly never born to set it right. You look distressed, not to say shocked, and I'm not at all offended at it. Let us change the subject by all means, if you like. What do you think of this Burgundy? It's rather a discovery of mine, like the restaurant itself.'

And he proceeded to talk learnedly and luxuriantly on all the wines of the world; on which subject, also, some moralists would consider that he knew too much.

3
The Soul of the Schoolboy

A large map of London would be needed to display the wild and zigzag course of one day's journey undertaken by an uncle and his nephew; or, to speak more truly, of a nephew and his uncle. For the nephew, a schoolboy on a holiday, was in theory the god in the car, or in the cab, tram, tube, and so on, while his uncle was at most a priest dancing before him and offering sacrifices. To put it more soberly, the schoolboy had something of the stolid air of a young duke doing the grand tour, while his elderly relative was reduced to the position of a courier, who nevertheless had to pay for everything like a patron. The schoolboy was officially known as Summers Minor, and in a more social manner as Stinks, the only public tribute to his career as an amateur photographer and electrician. The uncle was the Revd Thomas Twyford, a lean and lively old gentleman with a red, eager face and white hair. He was in the ordinary way a country clergyman, but he was one of those who achieve the paradox of being famous in an obscure way, because they are famous in an obscure world. In a small circle of ecclesiastical archaeologists, who were the only people who could even understand one another's discoveries, he occupied a recognised and respectable place. And a critic might have found even in that day's journey at least as much of the uncle's hobby as of the nephew's holiday.

His original purpose had been wholly paternal and festive. But, like many other intelligent people, he was not above the weakness of playing with a toy to amuse himself, on the theory that it would amuse a child. His toys were crowns and mitres and croziers and swords of state; and he had lingered over them, telling himself that the boy ought to see all the sights of London. And at the end of the day, after a tremendous tea, he rather gave the game away by winding up with a visit in which hardly any human boy could be conceived as taking an interest – an underground chamber supposed to have been a chapel, recently excavated on the north bank of the Thames, and containing literally nothing whatever but one old silver coin. But the coin, to those who knew, was more solitary and splendid than the Koh-i-noor. It was Roman, and was said to bear the head of St Paul; and round it raged the most vital controversies about the ancient British Church. It could hardly be denied, however, that the controversies left Summers Minor comparatively cold.

Indeed, the things that interested Summers Minor, and the things that did not interest him, had mystified and amused his uncle for several hours. He exhibited the English schoolboy's startling ignorance and startling knowledge – knowledge of some special classification in which he can generally correct and confound his elders. He considered himself entitled, at Hampton Court on a holiday, to forget the very names of Cardinal Wolsey or William of Orange; but he could hardly be dragged from some details about the arrangement of the electric bells in the neighbouring hotel. He was solidly dazed by Westminster Abbey, which is not so unnatural since that church became the lumber room of the larger and less successful statuary of the eighteenth century. But he had a magic and minute knowledge of the Westminster omnibuses, and indeed of the whole omnibus system of London, the colours and numbers of which he knew as a herald knows heraldry. He would cry out against a momentary confusion between a light-green Paddington and a dark-green Bayswater vehicle, as his uncle would at the identification of a Greek ikon and a Roman image.

'Do you collect omnibuses like stamps?' asked his uncle. 'They must need a rather large album. Or do you keep them in your locker?'

'I keep them in my head,' replied the nephew, with legitimate firmness.

'It does you credit, I admit,' replied the clergyman. 'I suppose it were vain to ask for what purpose you have learned that out of a thousand things. There hardly seems to be a career in it, unless you could be permanently on the pavement to prevent old ladies getting into the wrong bus. Well, we must get out of this one, for this is our place. I want to show you what they call St Paul's Penny.'

'Is it like St Paul's Cathedral?' asked the youth with resignation, as they alighted.

At the entrance their eyes were arrested by a singular figure evidently hovering there with a similar anxiety to enter. It was that of a dark, thin man in a long black robe rather like a cassock; but the black cap on his head was of too strange a shape to be a biretta. It suggested, rather, some archaic headdress of Persia or Babylon. He had a curious black beard appearing only at the corners of his chin, and his large eyes were oddly set in his face like the flat decorative eyes painted in old Egyptian profiles. Before they had gathered more than a general impression of him, he had dived into the doorway that was their own destination.

Nothing could be seen above ground of the sunken sanctuary except a strong wooden hut, of the sort recently run up for many military and official purposes, the wooden floor of which was indeed a mere platform over the excavated cavity below. A soldier stood as a sentry outside, and a superior soldier, an Anglo-Indian officer of distinction, sat writing at the desk inside. Indeed, the sightseers soon found that this particular sight was surrounded with the most extraordinary precautions. I have compared the silver coin to the Koh-i-noor, and in one sense it was even conventionally comparable, since by a historical accident it was at one time almost counted among the Crown jewels, or at least the Crown relics, until one of the royal princes publicly restored it to the shrine to which it was supposed to belong. Other causes combined to concentrate official vigilance upon it; there had been a scare about spies carrying explosives in small objects, and one of those experimental orders which pass like waves over bureaucracy had decreed first that all visitors should change their clothes for a sort of official sack-cloth, and then (when this method caused some murmurs) that they should at least turn out their pockets. Colonel Morris, the officer in charge, was a short, active man with a grim and leathery face, but a lively and humorous eye – a contradiction borne out by his conduct, for he at once derided the safeguards and yet insisted on them.

'I don't care a button myself for Paul's Penny, or such things,' he admitted in answer to some antiquarian openings from the clergyman who was slightly acquainted with him, 'but I wear the King's coat, you know, and it's a serious thing when the King's uncle leaves a thing here with his own hands under my charge. But as for saints and relics and things, I fear I'm a bit of a Voltairian; what you would call a sceptic.'

'I'm not sure it's even sceptical to believe in the royal family and not in the "Holy" Family,' replied Mr Twyford. 'But, of course, I can easily empty my pockets, to show I don't carry a bomb.'

The little heap of the parson's possessions which he left on the table consisted chiefly of papers, over and above a pipe and a tobacco pouch and some Roman and Saxon coins. The rest were catalogues of old books, and pamphlets, like one entitled 'The Use of Sarum', one glance at which was sufficient both for the colonel and the schoolboy. They could not see the use of Sarum at all. The contents of the boy's pockets naturally made a larger heap, and included marbles, a ball of string, an electric torch, a magnet, a small catapult, and, of course, a large pocketknife, almost to be described as a small tool box, a complex apparatus on which he seemed disposed to linger, pointing out that it included a pair of nippers, a tool for punching holes in wood, and, above all, an instrument for taking stones out of a horse's hoof. The comparative absence of any horse he appeared to regard as irrelevant, as if it were a mere appendage easily supplied. But when the turn came of the gentleman in the black gown, he did not turn out his pockets, but merely spread out his hands.

'I have no possessions,' he said.

'I'm afraid I must ask you to empty your pockets and make sure,' observed the colonel, gruffly.

'I have no pockets,' said the stranger.

Mr Twyford was looking at the long black gown with a learned eye.

'Are you a monk?' he asked, in a puzzled fashion.

'I am a magus,' replied the stranger. 'You have heard of the magi, perhaps? I am a magician.'

'Oh, I say!' exclaimed Summers Minor, with prominent eyes.

'But I was once a monk,' went on the other. 'I am what you would call an escaped monk. Yes, I have escaped into eternity. But the monks held one truth at least, that the highest life should be without possessions. I have no pocket money and no pockets, and all the stars are my trinkets.'

'They are out of reach, anyhow,' observed Colonel Morris, in a tone which suggested that it was well for them. 'I've known a good many magicians myself in India – mango plant and all. But the Indian ones are all frauds, I'll swear. In fact, I had a good deal of fun showing them up. More fun than I have over this dreary job, anyhow. But here comes Mr Symon, who will show you over the old cellar downstairs.'

Mr Symon, the official guardian and guide, was a young man, prematurely grey, with a grave mouth which contrasted curiously with a very small, dark moustache with waxed points, that seemed somehow separate from it, as if a black fly had settled on his face. He spoke with the accent of Oxford and the permanent official, but in as dead a fashion as the most indifferent hired guide. They descended a dark stone staircase, at the floor of which Symon pressed a button and a door opened on a dark room, or, rather, a room which had an instant before been dark. For almost as the heavy iron door swung open an almost blinding blaze of electric lights filled the whole interior. The fitful enthusiasm of Stinks at once caught fire, and he eagerly asked if the lights and the door worked together.

'Yes, it's all one system,' replied Symon. 'It was all fitted up for the day His Royal Highness deposited the thing here. You see, it's locked up behind a glass case exactly as he left it.'

A glance showed that the arrangements for guarding the treasure were indeed as strong as they were simple. A single pane of glass cut off one corner of the room, in an iron framework let into the rock walls and the wooden roof above; there was now no possibility of reopening the case without elaborate labour, except by breaking the glass, which would probably arouse the night watchman who was always within a few feet of it, even if he had fallen asleep. A close examination would have showed many more ingenious safeguards; but the eye of the Revd Thomas Twyford, at least, was already riveted on what interested him much more – the dull silver disc which shone in the white light against a plain background of black velvet.

'St Paul's Penny, said to commemorate the visit of St Paul to Britain, was probably preserved in this chapel until the eighth century,' Symon was saying in his clear but colourless voice. 'In the ninth century it is supposed to have been carried away by the barbarians, and it reappears, after the conversion of the northern Goths, in the possession of the royal family of Gothland. His Royal Highness, the Duke of Gothland, retained it always in his own private custody, and when he decided to exhibit it to the public, placed it here with his own hand. It was immediately sealed up in such a manner – '

Unluckily at this point Summers Minor, whose attention had somewhat strayed from the religious wars of the ninth century, caught sight of a short length of wire appearing in a broken patch in the wall. He precipitated himself at it, calling out, 'I say, does that connect?'

It was evident that it did connect, for no sooner had the boy given it a twitch than the whole room went black, as if they had all been struck blind, and an instant afterward they heard the dull crash of the closing door.

'Well, you've done it now,' said Symon, in his tranquil fashion. Then after a pause he added, 'I suppose they'll miss us sooner or later, and no doubt they can get it open; but it may take some little time.'

There was a silence, and then the unconquerable Stinks observed: 'Rotten that I had to leave my electric torch.'

'I think,' said his uncle, with restraint, 'that we are sufficiently convinced of your interest in electricity.'

Then after a pause he remarked, more amiably: 'I suppose if I regretted any of my own *impedimenta*, it would be the pipe. Though, as a matter of fact, it's not much fun smoking in the dark. Everything seems different in the dark.'

'Everything is different in the dark,' said a third voice, that of the man who called himself a magician. It was a very musical voice, and rather in contrast with his sinister and swarthy visage, which was now invisible. 'Perhaps you don't know how terrible a truth that is. All you see are pictures made by the sun, faces and furniture and flowers and trees. The things themselves may be quite strange to you. Something else may be standing now where you saw a table or a chair. The face of your friend may be quite different in the dark.'

A short, indescribable noise broke the stillness. Twyford started for a second, and then said, sharply: 'Really, I don't think it's a suitable occasion for trying to frighten a child.'

'Who's a child?' cried the indignant Summers, with a voice that had a crow, but also something of a crack in it. 'And who's a funk, either? Not me.'

'I will be silent, then,' said the other voice out of the darkness. 'But silence also makes and unmakes.'

The required silence remained unbroken for a long time until at last the clergyman said to Symon in a low voice: 'I suppose it's all right about air?'

'Oh, yes,' replied the other aloud; 'there's a fireplace and a chimney in the office just by the door.'

A bound and the noise of a falling chair told them that the irrepressible rising generation had once more thrown itself across the room. They heard the ejaculation: 'A chimney! Why, I'll be – ' and the rest was lost in muffled, but exultant, cries.

The uncle called repeatedly and vainly, groped his way at last to the opening, and, peering up it, caught a glimpse of a disc of daylight, which seemed to suggest that the fugitive had vanished in safety. Making his way back to the group by the glass case, he fell over the fallen chair and took a moment to collect himself again. He had opened his mouth to speak to Symon, when he stopped, and suddenly found himself blinking in the full shock of the white light, and looking over the other man's shoulder, he saw that the door was standing open.

'So they've got at us at last,' he observed to Symon.

The man in the black robe was leaning against the wall some yards away, with a smile carved on his face.

'Here comes Colonel Morris,' went on Twyford, still speaking to Symon. 'One of us will have to tell him how the light went out. Will you?'

But Symon still said nothing. He was standing as still as a statue, and looking steadily at the black velvet behind the glass screen. He was looking at the black velvet because there was nothing else to look at. St Paul's Penny was gone.

Colonel Morris entered the room with two new visitors, presumably two new sightseers delayed by the accident. The foremost was a tall, fair, rather languid-looking man with a bald brow and a high-bridged nose; his companion was a younger man with light, curly hair and frank, and even innocent, eyes. Symon scarcely seemed to hear the newcomers; it seemed almost as if he had not realised that the return of the light revealed his brooding attitude. Then he started in a guilty fashion, and when he saw the elder of the two strangers, his pale face seemed to turn a shade paler.

'Why it's Horne Fisher!' and then after a pause he said in a low voice, 'I'm in the devil of a hole, Fisher.'

'There does seem a bit of a mystery to be cleared up,' observed the gentleman so addressed.

'It will never be cleared up,' said the pale Symon. 'If anybody could clear it up, you could. But nobody could.'

'I rather think I could,' said another voice from outside the group, and they turned in surprise to realise that the man in the black robe had spoken again.

'You!' said the colonel, sharply. 'And how do you propose to play the detective?'

'I do not propose to play the detective,' answered the other, in a clear voice like a bell. 'I propose to play the magician. One of the magicians you show up in India, Colonel.'

No one spoke for a moment, and then Horne Fisher surprised everybody by saying, 'Well, let's go upstairs, and this gentleman can have a try.'

He stopped Symon, who had an automatic finger on the button, saying: 'No, leave all the lights on. It's a sort of safeguard.'

'The thing can't be taken away now,' said Symon, bitterly.

'It can be put back,' replied Fisher.

Twyford had already run upstairs for news of his vanishing nephew, and he received news of him in a way that at once puzzled and reassured him. On the floor above lay one of those large paper darts which boys throw at each other when the schoolmaster is out of the room. It had evidently been thrown in at the window, and on being unfolded displayed a scrawl of bad handwriting which ran: 'Dear Uncle; I am all right. Meet you at the hotel later on,' and then the signature.

Insensibly comforted by this, the clergyman found his thoughts reverting voluntarily to his favourite relic, which came a good second in his sympathies to his favourite nephew, and before he knew where he was he found himself encircled by the group discussing its loss, and more or less carried away on the current of their excitement. But an undercurrent of query continued to run in his mind, as to what had really happened to the boy, and what was the boy's exact definition of being all right.

Meanwhile Horne Fisher had considerably puzzled everybody with his new tone and attitude. He had talked to the colonel about the military and mechanical arrangements, and displayed a remarkable knowledge both of the details of discipline and the technicalities of electricity. He had talked to the clergyman, and shown an equally surprising knowledge of the religious and historical interests involved in the relic. He had talked to the man who called himself a magician, and not only surprised but scandalised the company by an equally sympathetic familiarity with the most fantastic forms of Oriental occultism and psychic experiment. And in this last and least respectable line of enquiry he was evidently prepared to go farthest; he openly encouraged the magician, and was plainly prepared to follow the wildest ways of investigation in which that magus might lead him.

'How would you begin now?' he enquired, with an anxious politeness that reduced the colonel to a congestion of rage.

'It is all a question of a force, of establishing communications for a force,' replied that adept, affably, ignoring some military mutterings about the police force. 'It is what you in the West used to call animal magnetism, but it is much more than that. I had better not say how much more. As to setting about it, the usual method is to throw some susceptible person into a trance, which serves as a sort of bridge or cord of communication, by which the force beyond can give him, as it were, an electric shock, and awaken his higher senses. It opens the sleeping eye of the mind.'

'I'm susceptible,' said Fisher, either with simplicity or with a baffling irony. 'Why not open my mind's eye for me? My friend Harold March here will tell you I sometimes see things, even in the dark.'

'Nobody sees anything except in the dark,' said the magician.

Heavy clouds of sunset were closing round the wooden hut, enormous clouds, of which only the corners could be seen in the little window, like purple horns and tails, almost as if some huge monsters were prowling round the place. But the purple was already deepening to dark grey; it would soon be night.

'Do not light the lamp,' said the magus with quiet authority, arresting a movement in that direction. 'I told you before that things happen only in the dark.'

How such a topsy-turvy scene ever came to be tolerated in the colonel's office, of all places, was afterwards a puzzle in the memory of many, including the colonel. They recalled it like a sort of nightmare, like something they could not control. Perhaps there was really a magnetism about the mesmerist; perhaps there was even more magnetism about the man mesmerised. Anyhow, the man was being mesmerised, for Horne Fisher had collapsed into a chair with his long limbs loose and sprawling and his eyes staring at vacancy; and the other man was mesmerising him, making sweeping movements with his darkly draped arms as if with black wings. The colonel had passed the point of explosion, and he dimly realised that eccentric aristocrats are allowed their fling. He comforted himself with the knowledge that he had already sent for the police, who would break up any such masquerade, and with lighting a cigar, the red end of which, in the gathering darkness, glowed with protest.

'Yes, I see pockets,' the man in the trance was saying. 'I see many pockets, but they are all empty. No; I see one pocket that is not empty.'

There was a faint stir in the stillness, and the magician said, 'Can you see what is in the pocket?'

'Yes,' answered the other; 'there are two bright things. I think they are two bits of steel. One of the pieces of steel is bent or crooked.'

'Have they been used in the removal of the relic from downstairs?'

'Yes.'

There was another pause and the enquirer added, 'Do you see anything of the relic itself?'

'I see something shining on the floor, like the shadow or the ghost of it. It is over there in the corner beyond the desk.'

There was a movement of men turning and then a sudden stillness, as of their stiffening, for over in the corner on the wooden floor there was really a round spot of pale light. It was the only spot of light in the room. The cigar had gone out.

'It points the way,' came the voice of the oracle. 'The spirits are pointing the way to penitence, and urging the thief to restitution. I can see nothing more.' His voice trailed off into a silence that lasted solidly for many minutes, like the long silence below when the theft had been committed. Then it was broken by the ring of metal on the floor, and the sound of something spinning and falling like a tossed halfpenny.

'Light the lamp!' cried Fisher in a loud and even jovial voice, leaping to his feet with far less languor than usual. 'I must be going now, but I should like to see it before I go. Why, I came on purpose to see it.'

The lamp was lit, and he did see it, for St Paul's Penny was lying on the floor at his feet.

* * *

'Oh, as for that,' explained Fisher, when he was entertaining March and Twyford at lunch about a month later, 'I merely wanted to play with the magician at his own game.'

'I thought you meant to catch him in his own trap,' said Twyford. 'I can't make head or tail of anything yet, but to my mind he was always the suspect. I don't think he was necessarily a thief in the vulgar sense. The police always seem to think that silver is stolen for the sake of silver, but a thing like that might well be stolen out of some religious mania. A runaway monk turned mystic might well want it for some mystical purpose.'

'No,' replied Fisher, 'the runaway monk is not a thief. At any rate he is not the thief. And he's not altogether a liar, either. He said one true thing at least that night.'

'And what was that?' enquired March.

'He said it was all magnetism. As a matter of fact, it was done by means of a magnet.' Then, seeing they still looked puzzled, he added, 'It was that toy magnet belonging to your nephew, Mr Twyford.'

'But I don't understand,' objected March. 'If it was done with the schoolboy's magnet, I suppose it was done by the schoolboy.'

'Well,' replied Fisher, reflectively, 'it rather depends which schoolboy.'

'What on earth do you mean?'

'The soul of a schoolboy is a curious thing,' Fisher continued, in a meditative manner. 'It can survive a great many things besides climbing out of a chimney. A man can grow grey in great campaigns, and still have the soul of a schoolboy. A man can return with a great reputation from India and be put in charge of a great public treasure, and still have the soul of a schoolboy, waiting to be awakened by an accident. And it is ten times more so when to the schoolboy you add the sceptic, who is generally a sort of stunted schoolboy. You said just now that things might be done by religious mania. Have you ever heard of irreligious mania? I assure you it exists very violently, especially in men who like showing up magicians in

India. But here the sceptic had the temptation of showing up a much more tremendous sham nearer home.'

A light came into Harold March's eyes as he suddenly saw, as if afar off, the wider implication of the suggestion. But Twyford was still wrestling with one problem at a time.

'Do you really mean,' he said, 'that Colonel Morris took the relic?'

'He was the only person who could use the magnet,' replied Fisher. 'In fact, your obliging nephew left him a number of things he could use. He had a ball of string, and an instrument for making a hole in the wooden floor – I made a little play with that hole in the floor in my trance, by the way; with the lights left on below, it shone like a new shilling.' Twyford suddenly bounded on his chair. 'But in that case,' he cried, in a new and altered voice, 'why then of course – you said a piece of steel – ?'

'I said there were two pieces of steel,' said Fisher. 'The bent piece of steel was the boy's magnet. The other was the relic in the glass case.'

'But that is silver,' answered the archaeologist, in a voice now almost unrecognisable.

'Oh,' replied Fisher, soothingly, 'I dare say it was painted with silver a little.'

There was a heavy silence, and at last Harold March said, 'But where is the real relic?'

'Where it has been for five years,' replied Horne Fisher, 'in the possession of a mad millionaire named Vandam, in Nebraska. There was a playful little photograph about him in a society paper the other day, mentioning his delusion, and saying he was always being taken in about relics.'

Harold March frowned at the tablecloth; then, after an interval, he said: 'I think I understand your notion of how the thing was actually done; according to that, Morris just made a hole and fished it up with a magnet at the end of a string. Such a monkey trick looks like mere madness, but I suppose he was mad, partly with the boredom of watching over what he felt was a fraud, though he couldn't prove it. Then came a chance to prove it, to himself at least, and he had what he called "fun" with it. Yes, I think I see a lot of details now. But it's just the whole thing that knocks me. How did it all come to be like that?'

Fisher was looking at him with level lids and an immovable manner.

'Every precaution was taken,' he said. 'The Duke carried the relic on his own person, and locked it up in the case with his own hands.'

March was silent; but Twyford stammered: 'I don't understand you. You give me the creeps. Why don't you speak plainer?'

'If I spoke plainer you would understand me less,' said Horne Fisher.

'All the same I should try,' said March, still without lifting his head.

'Oh, very well,' replied Fisher, with a sigh; 'the plain truth is, of course, that it's a bad business. Everybody knows it's a bad business who knows anything about it. But it's always happening, and in one way one can hardly blame them. They get stuck on to a foreign princess that's as stiff as a Dutch doll, and they have their fling. In this case it was a pretty big fling.'

The face of the Revd Thomas Twyford certainly suggested that he was a little out of his depth in the seas of truth, but as the other went on speaking vaguely the old gentleman's features sharpened and set.

'If it were some decent morganatic affair I wouldn't say; but he must have been a fool to throw away thousands on a woman like that. At the end it was sheer blackmail; but it's something that the old ass didn't get it out of the taxpayers. He could only get it out of the Yank, and there you are.'

The Revd Thomas Twyford had risen to his feet.

'Well, I'm glad my nephew had nothing to do with it,' he said. 'And if that's what the world is like, I hope he will never have anything to do with it.'

'I hope not,' answered Horne Fisher. 'No one knows so well as I do that one can have far too much to do with it.'

* * *

For Summers Minor had indeed nothing to do with it; and it is part of his higher significance that he has really nothing to do with the story, or with any such stories. The boy went like a bullet through the tangle of this tale of crooked politics and crazy mockery and came out on the other side, pursuing his own unspoiled purposes. From the top of the chimney he climbed he had caught sight of a new omnibus, whose colour and name he had never known, as a naturalist might see a new bird or a botanist a new flower. And he had been sufficiently enraptured in rushing after it, and riding away upon that fairy ship.

4

The Bottomless Well

In an oasis, or green island, in the red and yellow seas of sand that stretch beyond Europe towards the sunrise, there can be found a rather fantastic contrast, which is none the less typical of such a place, since international treaties have made it an outpost of the British occupation. The site is famous among archaeologists for something that is hardly a monument, but merely a hole in the ground. But it is a round shaft, like that of a well, and probably a part of some great irrigation works of remote and disputed date, perhaps more ancient than anything in that ancient land. There is a green fringe of palm and prickly pear round the black mouth of the well; but nothing of the upper masonry remains except two bulky and battered stones standing like the pillars of a gateway of nowhere, in which some of the more transcendental archaeologists, in certain moods at moonrise or sunset, think they can trace the faint lines of figures or features of more than Babylonian monstrosity; while the more rationalistic archaeologists, in the more rational hours of daylight, see nothing but two shapeless rocks. It may have been noticed, however, that all Englishmen are not archaeologists. Many of those assembled in such a place for official and military purposes have hobbies other than archaeology. And it is a solemn fact that the English in this Eastern exile have contrived to make a small golf links out of the green scrub and sand; with a comfortable clubhouse at one end of it and this primeval monument at the other. They did not actually use this archaic abyss as a bunker, because it was by tradition unfathomable, and even for practical purposes unfathomed. Any sporting projectile sent into it might be counted most literally as a lost ball. But they often sauntered round it in their interludes of talking and smoking cigarettes, and one of them had just come down from the clubhouse to find another gazing somewhat moodily into the well.

Both the Englishmen wore light clothes and white pith helmets and puggrees, but there, for the most part, their resemblance ended. And they both almost simultaneously said the same word, but they said it on two totally different notes of the voice.

'Have you heard the news?' asked the man from the club. 'Splendid.'

'Splendid,' replied the man by the well. But the first man pronounced the word as a young man might say it about a woman, and the second as an old man might say it about the weather, not without sincerity, but certainly without fervour.

And in this the tone of the two men was sufficiently typical of them. The first, who was a certain Captain Boyle, was of a bold and boyish type, dark, and with a sort of native heat in his face that did not belong to the atmosphere of the East, but rather to the ardours and ambitions of the West. The other was an older man and certainly an older resident, a civilian official – Horne Fisher; and his drooping eyelids and drooping light moustache expressed all the paradox of the Englishman in the East. He was much too hot to be anything but cool.

Neither of them thought it necessary to mention what it was that was splendid. That would indeed have been superfluous conversation about something that everybody knew. The striking victory over a menacing combination of Turks and Arabs in the north, won by troops under the command of Lord Hastings, the veteran of so many striking victories, was already spread by the newspapers all over the Empire, let alone to this small garrison so near to the battlefield.

'Now, no other nation in the world could have done a thing like that,' cried Captain Boyle, emphatically.

Horne Fisher was still looking silently into the well; a moment later he answered: 'We certainly have the art of unmaking mistakes. That's where the poor old Prussians went wrong. They could only make mistakes and stick to them. There is really a certain talent in unmaking a mistake.'

'What do you mean,' asked Boyle, 'what mistakes?'

'Well, everybody knows it looked like biting off more than we could chew,' replied Horne Fisher. It was a peculiarity of Mr Fisher that he always said that everybody knew things which about one person in two million was ever allowed to hear of. 'And it was certainly jolly lucky that Travers turned up so well in the nick of time. Odd how often the right thing's been done for us by the second in command, even when a great man was first in command. Like Colborne at Waterloo.'

'It ought to add a whole province to the Empire,' observed the other.

'Well, I suppose the Zimmernes would have insisted on it as far as the canal,' observed Fisher, thoughtfully, 'though everybody knows adding provinces doesn't always pay much nowadays.'

Captain Boyle frowned in a slightly puzzled fashion. Being cloudily conscious of never having heard of the Zimmernes in his life, he could only remark, stolidly: 'Well, one can't be a Little Englander.'

Horne Fisher smiled, and he had a pleasant smile.

'Every man out here is a Little Englander,' he said. 'He wishes he were back in Little England.'

'I don't know what you're talking about, I'm afraid,' said the younger man, rather suspiciously. 'One would think you didn't really admire Hastings or – or – anything.'

'I admire him no end,' replied Fisher. 'He's by far the best man for this post; he understands the Moslems and can do anything with them. That's why I'm all against pushing Travers against him, merely because of this last affair.'

'I really don't understand what you're driving at,' said the other, frankly.

'Perhaps it isn't worth understanding,' answered Fisher, lightly, 'and, anyhow, we needn't talk politics. Do you know the Arab legend about that well?'

'I'm afraid I don't know much about Arab legends,' said Boyle, rather stiffly.

'That's rather a mistake,' replied Fisher, 'especially from your point of view. Lord Hastings himself is an Arab legend. That is perhaps the very greatest thing he really is. If his reputation went it would weaken us all over Asia and Africa. Well, the story about that hole in the ground, that goes down nobody knows where, has always fascinated me, rather. It's Mohammedan in form now, but I shouldn't wonder if the tale is a long way older than Mohammed. It's all about somebody they call the Sultan Aladdin, not our friend of the lamp, of course, but rather like him in having to do with genii or giants or something of that sort. They say he commanded the giants to build him a sort of pagoda, rising higher and higher above all the stars. The Utmost for the Highest, as the people said when they built the Tower of Babel. But the builders of the Tower of Babel were quite modest and domestic people, like mice, compared with old Aladdin. They only wanted a tower that would reach heaven – a mere trifle. He wanted a tower that would pass heaven and rise above it, and go on rising for ever and ever. And Allah cast him down to earth with a thunderbolt, which sank into the earth, boring a hole deeper and deeper, till it made a well that was without a bottom as the tower was to have been without a top. And down that inverted tower of darkness the soul of the proud Sultan is falling for ever and ever.'

'What a queer chap you are,' said Boyle. 'You talk as if a fellow could believe those fables.'

'Perhaps I believe the moral and not the fable,' answered Fisher. 'But here comes Lady Hastings. You know her, I think.'

The clubhouse on the golf links was used, of course, for many other purposes besides that of golf. It was the only social centre of the garrison beside the strictly military headquarters; it had a billiard room and a bar, and even an excellent reference library for those officers who were so perverse as to take their profession seriously. Among these was the great general himself, whose head of silver and face of bronze, like that of a brazen eagle, were often to be found bent over the charts and folios of the library. The great Lord Hastings believed in science and study, as in other severe ideals of life, and had given much paternal advice on the point to young Boyle, whose appearances in that place of research were rather more intermittent. It was from one of these snatches of study that the young man had just come out through the glass doors of the library on to the golf links. But, above all, the club was so appointed as to serve the social conveniences of ladies at least as much as gentlemen, and Lady Hastings was able to play the queen in such a society almost as much as in her own ballroom. She was eminently calculated and, as some said, eminently inclined to play such a part. She was much younger than her husband, an attractive and sometimes dangerously attractive lady; and Mr Horne Fisher looked after her a little sardonically as she swept away with the young soldier. Then his rather dreary eye strayed to the green and prickly growths round the well, growths of that curious cactus formation in which one thick leaf grows directly out of the other without stalk or twig. It gave his fanciful mind a sinister feeling of a blind growth without shape or purpose. A flower or shrub in the West grows to the blossom which is its crown, and is content. But this was as if hands could grow out of hands or legs grow out of legs in a nightmare. 'Always adding a province to the Empire,' he said, with a smile, and then added, more sadly, 'but I doubt if I was right, after all!'

A strong but genial voice broke in on his meditations and he looked up and smiled, seeing the face of an old friend. The voice was, indeed, rather more genial than the face, which was at the first glance decidedly grim. It was a typically legal face, with angular jaws and heavy, grizzled eyebrows; and it belonged to an eminently legal character, though he was now attached in a semi-military capacity to the police of that wild district. Cuthbert Grayne was perhaps more of a criminologist than either a lawyer or a policeman, but in his more barbarous surroundings he had proved successful in turning himself into a practical combination of all three. The discovery of a whole series of strange Oriental crimes stood to his credit. But as few people were acquainted with, or attracted to, such a hobby or branch of knowledge, his intellectual life was somewhat solitary. Among the few exceptions was Horne Fisher, who had a curious capacity for talking to almost anybody about almost anything.

'Studying botany, or is it archaeology?' enquired Grayne. 'I shall never come to the end of your interests, Fisher. I should say that what you don't know isn't worth knowing.'

'You are wrong,' replied Fisher, with a very unusual abruptness, and even bitterness. 'It's what I do know that isn't worth knowing. All the seamy side of things, all the secret reasons and rotten motives and bribery and blackmail they call politics. I needn't be so proud of having been down all these sewers that I should brag about it to the little boys in the street.'

'What do you mean? What's the matter with you?' asked his friend. 'I never knew you taken like this before.'

'I'm ashamed of myself,' replied Fisher. 'I've just been throwing cold water on the enthusiasms of a boy.'

'Even that explanation is hardly exhaustive,' observed the criminal expert.

'Damned newspaper nonsense the enthusiasms were, of course,' continued Fisher, 'but I ought to know that at that age illusions can be ideals. And they're better than the reality, anyhow. But there is one very ugly responsibility about jolting a young man out of the rut of the most rotten ideal.'

'And what may that be?' enquired his friend.

'It's very apt to set him off with the same energy in a much worse direction,' answered Fisher; 'a pretty endless sort of direction, a bottomless pit as deep as the bottomless well.'

Fisher did not see his friend until a fortnight later, when he found himself in the garden at the back of the clubhouse on the opposite side from the links, a garden heavily coloured and scented with sweet semitropical plants in the glow of a desert sunset. Two other men were with him, the third being the now celebrated second in command, familiar to everybody as Tom Travers, a lean, dark man, who looked older than his years, with a furrow in his brow and something morose about the very shape of his black moustache. They had just been served with black coffee by the Arab now officiating as the temporary servant of the club, though he was a figure already familiar, and even famous, as the old servant of the general. He went by the name of Said, and was notable among other Semites for that unnatural length of his yellow face and height of his narrow forehead which is sometimes seen among them, and gave an irrational impression of something sinister, in spite of his agreeable smile.

'I never feel as if I could quite trust that fellow,' said Grayne, when the man had gone away. 'It's very unjust, I take it, for he was certainly devoted to Hastings, and saved his life, they say. But Arabs are often like that, loyal to one man. I can't help feeling he might cut anybody else's throat, and even do it treacherously.'

'Well,' said Travers, with a rather sour smile, 'so long as he leaves Hastings alone the world won't mind much.'

There was a rather embarrassing silence, full of memories of the great battle, and then Horne Fisher said, quietly: 'The newspapers aren't the world, Tom. Don't you worry about them. Everybody in your world knows the truth well enough.'

'I think we'd better not talk about the general just now,' remarked Grayne, 'for he's just coming out of the club.'

'He's not coming here,' said Fisher. 'He's only seeing his wife to the car.'

As he spoke, indeed, the lady came out on the steps of the club, followed by her husband, who then went swiftly in front of her to open the garden gate. As he did so she turned back and spoke for a moment to a solitary man still sitting in a cane chair in the shadow of the doorway, the only man left in the deserted club save for the three that lingered in the garden. Fisher peered for a moment into the shadow, and saw that it was Captain Boyle.

The next moment, rather to their surprise, the general reappeared and, remounting the steps, spoke a word or two to Boyle in his turn. Then he signalled to Said, who hurried up with two cups of coffee, and the two men re-entered the club, each carrying his cup in his hand. The next moment a gleam of white light in the growing darkness showed that the electric lamps had been turned on in the library beyond.

'Coffee and scientific researches,' said Travers, grimly. 'All the luxuries of learning and theoretical research. Well, I must be going, for I have my work to do as well.' And he got up rather stiffly, saluted his companions, and strode away into the dusk.

'I only hope Boyle is sticking to scientific researches,' said Horne Fisher. 'I'm not very comfortable about him myself. But let's talk about something else.'

They talked about something else longer than they probably imagined, until the tropical night had come and a splendid moon painted the whole scene with silver; but before it was bright enough to see by Fisher had already noted that the lights in the library had been abruptly extinguished. He waited for the two men to come out by the garden entrance, but nobody came.

'They must have gone for a stroll on the links,' he said.

'Very possibly,' replied Grayne. 'It's going to be a beautiful night.'

A moment or two after he had spoken they heard a voice hailing them out of the shadow of the clubhouse, and were astonished to perceive Travers hurrying towards them, calling out as he came: 'I shall want your help, you fellows,' he cried. 'There's something pretty bad out on the links.'

They found themselves plunging through the club smoking room and the library beyond, in complete darkness, mental as well as material. But Horne Fisher, in spite of his affectation of indifference, was a person of a curious and almost transcendental sensibility to atmospheres, and he already felt the presence of something more than an accident. He collided with a piece of furniture in the library, and almost shuddered with the shock, for the thing moved as he could never have fancied a piece of furniture moving. It seemed to move like a living thing, yielding and yet striking back. The next moment Grayne had turned on the lights, and he saw he had only stumbled against one of the revolving bookstands that had swung round and struck him; but his involuntary recoil had revealed to him his own subconscious sense of something mysterious and monstrous. There were several of these revolving bookcases standing here and there about the library; on one of them stood the two cups of coffee, and on another a large open book. It was Budge's book on Egyptian hieroglyphics, with coloured plates of strange birds and gods, and even as he rushed past, he was conscious of something odd about the fact that this, and not any work of military science, should be open in that place at that moment. He was even conscious of the gap in the well-lined bookshelf from which it had been taken, and it seemed almost to gape at him in an ugly fashion, like a gap in the teeth of some sinister face.

A run brought them in a few minutes to the other side of the ground in front of the bottomless well, and a few yards from it, in a moonlight almost as broad as daylight, they saw what they had come to see.

The great Lord Hastings lay prone on his face, in a posture in which there was a touch of something strange and stiff, with one elbow erect above his body, the arm being doubled, and his big, bony hand clutching the rank and ragged grass. A few feet away was Boyle, almost as motionless, but supported on his hands and knees, and staring at the body. It might have been no more than shock and accident; but there was something ungainly and unnatural about the quadrupedal posture and the gaping face. It was as if his reason had fled from him. Behind, there was nothing but the clear blue southern sky, and the beginning of the desert, except for the two great broken stones in front of the well. And it was in such a light and atmosphere that men could fancy they traced in them enormous and evil faces, looking down.

Horne Fisher stooped and touched the strong hand that was still clutching the grass, and it was as cold as a stone. He knelt by the body and was busy for a moment applying other tests; then he rose again, and said, with a sort of confident despair: 'Lord Hastings is dead.'

There was a stony silence, and then Travers remarked, gruffly: 'This is your department, Grayne; I will leave you to question Captain Boyle. I can make no sense of what he says.'

Boyle had pulled himself together and risen to his feet, but his face still wore an awful expression, making it like a new mask or the face of another man.

'I was looking at the well,' he said, 'and when I turned he had fallen down.'

Grayne's face was very dark. 'As you say, this is my affair,' he said. 'I must first ask you to help me carry him to the library and let me examine things thoroughly.'

When they had deposited the body in the library, Grayne turned to Fisher and said, in a voice that had recovered its fullness and confidence, 'I am going to lock myself in and make a thorough examination first. I look to you to keep in touch with the others and make a preliminary examination of Boyle. I will talk to him later. And just telephone to headquarters for a policeman, and let him come here at once and stand by till I want him.'

Without more words the great criminal investigator went into the lighted library, shutting the door behind him, and Fisher, without replying, turned and began to talk quietly to Travers. 'It is curious,' he said, 'that the thing should happen just in front of that place.'

'It would certainly be very curious,' replied Travers, 'if the place played any part in it.'

'I think,' replied Fisher, 'that the part it didn't play is more curious still.'

And with these apparently meaningless words he turned to the shaken Boyle and, taking his arm, began to walk him up and down in the moonlight, talking in low tones.

Dawn had begun to break abrupt and white when Cuthbert Grayne turned out the lights in the library and came out on to the links. Fisher was lounging about alone, in his listless fashion; but the police messenger for whom he had sent was standing at attention in the background.

'I sent Boyle off with Travers,' observed Fisher, carelessly; 'he'll look after him, and he'd better have some sleep, anyhow.'

'Did you get anything out of him?' asked Grayne. 'Did he tell you what he and Hastings were doing?'

'Yes,' answered Fisher, 'he gave me a pretty clear account, after all. He said that after Lady Hastings went off in the car the general asked him to take coffee with him in the library and look up a point about local antiquities. He himself was beginning to look for Budge's book in one of the revolving bookstands when the general found it in one of the bookshelves on the wall. After looking at some of the plates they went out, it would seem, rather abruptly, on to the links, and walked towards the old well; and while Boyle was looking into it he heard a thud behind him, and turned round to find the general lying as we found him. He himself dropped on his knees to examine the body, and then was paralysed with a sort of terror and could not come nearer to it or touch it. But I think very little of that; people caught in a real shock of surprise are sometimes found in the queerest postures.'

Grayne wore a grim smile of attention, and said, after a short silence: 'Well, he hasn't told you many lies. It's really a creditably clear and consistent account of what happened, with everything of importance left out.'

'Have you discovered anything in there?' asked Fisher.

'I have discovered everything,' answered Grayne.

Fisher maintained a somewhat gloomy silence, as the other resumed his explanation in quiet and assured tones.

'You were quite right, Fisher, when you said that young fellow was in danger of going down dark ways towards the pit. Whether or no, as you fancied, the jolt you gave to his view of the general had anything to do with it, he has not been treating the general well for some time. It's an unpleasant business, and I don't want to dwell on it; but it's pretty plain that his wife was not treating him well, either. I don't know how far it went, but it went as far as concealment, anyhow; for when Lady Hastings spoke to Boyle it was to tell him she had hidden a note in the Budge book in the library. The general overheard, or came somehow to know, and he went straight to the book and found it. He confronted Boyle with it, and they had a scene, of course. And Boyle was confronted with something else; he was confronted with an awful alternative, in which the life of one old man meant ruin and his death meant triumph and even happiness.'

'Well,' observed Fisher, at last, 'I don't blame him for not telling you the woman's part of the story. But how do you know about the letter?'

'I found it on the general's body,' answered Grayne, 'but I found worse things than that. The body had stiffened in the way rather peculiar to poisons of a certain Asiatic sort. Then I examined the coffee cups, and I knew enough chemistry to find poison in the dregs of one of them. Now, the general went straight to the bookcase, leaving his cup of coffee on the bookstand in the middle of the room. While his back was turned, and Boyle was pretending to examine the bookstand, he was left alone with the coffee cup. The poison takes about ten minutes to act, and ten minutes' walk would bring them to the bottomless well.'

'Yes,' remarked Fisher, 'and what about the bottomless well?'

'What has the bottomless well got to do with it?' asked his friend.

'It has nothing to do with it,' replied Fisher. 'That is what I find utterly confounding and incredible.'

'And why should that particular hole in the ground have anything to do with it?'

'It is a particular hole in your case,' said Fisher. 'But I won't insist on that just now. By the way, there is another thing I ought to tell you. I said I sent Boyle away in charge of Travers. It would be just as true to say I sent Travers in charge of Boyle.'

'You don't mean to say you suspect Tom Travers?' cried the other.

'He was a deal bitterer against the general than Boyle ever was,' observed Horne Fisher, with a curious indifference.

'Man, you're not saying what you mean,' cried Grayne. 'I tell you I found the poison in one of the coffee cups.'

'There was always Said, of course,' added Fisher, 'either for hatred or hire. We agreed he was capable of almost anything.'

'And we agreed he was incapable of hurting his master,' retorted Grayne.

'Well, well,' said Fisher, amiably, 'I dare say you are right; but I should just like to have a look at the library and the coffee cups.'

He passed inside, while Grayne turned to the policeman in attendance and handed him a scribbled note, to be telegraphed from headquarters. The man saluted and hurried off; and Grayne, following his friend into the library, found him beside the bookstand in the middle of the room, on which were the empty cups.

'This is where Boyle looked for Budge, or pretended to look for him, according to your account,' he said.

As Fisher spoke he bent down in a half-crouching attitude, to look at the volumes in the low, revolving shelf, for the whole bookstand was not much higher than an ordinary table. The next moment he sprang up as if he had been stung.

'Oh, my God!' he cried.

Very few people, if any, had ever seen Mr Horne Fisher behave as he behaved just then. He flashed a glance at the door, saw that the open window was nearer, went out of it with a flying leap, as if over a hurdle, and went racing across the turf, in the track of the disappearing policeman. Grayne, who stood staring after him, soon saw his tall, loose figure returning, restored to all its normal limpness and air of leisure. He was fanning himself slowly with a piece of paper, the telegram he had so violently intercepted.

'Lucky I stopped that,' he observed. 'We must keep this affair as quiet as death. Hastings must die of apoplexy or heart disease.'

'What on earth is the trouble?' demanded the other investigator.

'The trouble is,' said Fisher, 'that in a few days we should have had a very agreeable alternative – of hanging an innocent man or knocking the British Empire to hell.'

'Do you mean to say,' asked Grayne, 'that this infernal crime is not to be punished?'

Fisher looked at him steadily.

'It is already punished,' he said.

After a moment's pause he went on. 'You reconstructed the crime with admirable skill, old chap, and nearly all you said was true. Two men with two coffee cups did go into the library and did put their cups on the bookstand and did go together to the well, and one of them was a murderer and had put poison in the other's cup. But it was not done while Boyle was looking at the revolving bookcase. He did look at it, though, searching for the Budge book with the note in it, but I fancy that Hastings had already moved it to the shelves on the wall. It was part of that grim game that he should find it first.

'Now, how does a man search a revolving bookcase? He does not generally hop all round it in a squatting attitude, like a frog. He simply gives it a touch and makes it revolve.'

He was frowning at the floor as he spoke, and there was a light under his heavy lids that was not often seen there. The mysticism that was buried deep under all the cynicism of his experience was awake and moving in the depths. His voice took unexpected turns and inflections, almost as if two men were speaking.

'That was what Boyle did; he barely touched the thing, and it went round as easily as the world goes round. Yes, very much as the world goes round, for the hand that turned it was not his. God, who turns the wheel of all the stars, touched that wheel and brought it full circle, that His dreadful justice might return.'

'I am beginning,' said Grayne, slowly, 'to have some hazy and horrible idea of what you mean.'

'It is very simple,' said Fisher. 'When Boyle straightened himself from his stooping posture, something had happened which he had not noticed, which his enemy had not noticed, which nobody had noticed. The two coffee cups had exactly changed places.'

The rocky face of Grayne seemed to have sustained a shock in silence; not a line of it altered, but his voice when it came was unexpectedly weakened.

'I see what you mean,' he said, 'and, as you say, the less said about it the better. It was not the lover who tried to get rid of the husband, but – the other thing. And a tale like that about a man like that would ruin us here. Had you any guess of this at the start?'

'The bottomless well, as I told you,' answered Fisher, quietly; 'that was what stumped me from the start. Not because it had anything to do with it, because it had nothing to do with it.'

He paused a moment, as if choosing an approach, and then went on: 'When a man knows his enemy will be dead in ten minutes, and takes him to the edge of an unfathomable pit, he means to throw his body into it. What else should he do? A born fool would have the sense to do it, and Boyle is not a born fool. Well, why did not Boyle do it? The more I thought of it the more I suspected there was some mistake in the murder, so to speak. Somebody had taken somebody there to throw him in, and yet he was not thrown in. I had already an ugly, unformed idea of some substitution or reversal of parts; then I stooped to turn the bookstand myself, by accident, and I instantly knew everything, for I saw the two cups revolve once more, like moons in the sky.'

After a pause, Cuthbert Grayne said, 'And what are we to say to the newspapers?'

'My friend, Harold March, is coming along from Cairo today,' said Fisher. 'He is a very brilliant and successful journalist. But for all that he's a thoroughly honourable man, so you must not tell him the truth.'

Half an hour later Fisher was again walking to and fro in front of the clubhouse, with Captain Boyle, the latter by this time with a very buffeted and bewildered air; perhaps a sadder and a wiser man.

'What about me, then?' he was saying. 'Am I cleared? Am I not going to be cleared?'

'I believe and hope,' answered Fisher, 'that you are not going to be suspected. But you are certainly not going to be cleared. There must be no suspicion against him, and therefore no suspicion against you. Any suspicion against him, let alone such a story against him, would knock us endways from Malta to Mandalay. He was a hero as well as a holy terror among the Moslems. Indeed, you might almost call him a Moslem hero in the English service. Of course he got on with them partly because of his own little dose of Eastern blood; he got it from his mother, the dancer from Damascus; everybody knows that.'

'Oh,' repeated Boyle, mechanically, staring at him with round eyes, 'everybody knows that.'

'I dare say there was a touch of it in his jealousy and ferocious vengeance,' went on Fisher. 'But, for all that, the crime would ruin us among the Arabs, all the more because it was something like a crime against hospitality. It's been hateful for you and it's pretty horrid for me. But there are some things that damned well can't be done, and while I'm alive that's one of them.'

'What do you mean?' asked Boyle, glancing at him curiously. 'Why should you, of all people, be so passionate about it?'

Horne Fisher looked at the young man with a baffling expression.

'I suppose,' he said, 'it's because I'm a Little Englander.'

'I can never make out what you mean by that sort of thing,' answered Boyle, doubtfully.

'Do you think England is so little as all that,' said Fisher, with a warmth in his cold voice, 'that it can't hold a man across a few thousand miles? You lectured me with a lot of ideal patriotism, my young friend; but it's practical patriotism now for you and me, and with no lies to help it. You talked as if everything always went right with us all over the world, in a triumphant crescendo culminating in Hastings. I tell you everything has gone wrong with us here, except Hastings. He was the one name we had left to conjure with, and that mustn't go as well, no, by God! It's bad enough that some gang should plant us here, where there's no earthly English interest to serve, and all hell beating up against us, simply because Nosey Zimmerne has lent money to half the Cabinet. It's bad enough that an old pawnbroker from Baghdad should make us fight his battles; we can't fight with our right hand cut off. Our one score was Hastings and his victory, which was really somebody else's victory. Tom Travers has to suffer, and so have you.'

Then, after a moment's silence, he pointed towards the bottomless well and said, in a quieter tone: 'I told you that I didn't believe in the philosophy of the Tower of Aladdin. I don't believe in the Empire growing until it reaches the sky; I don't believe in the Union Jack going up and up eternally like the Tower. But if you think I am going to let the Union Jack go down and down eternally, like the bottomless well, down into the blackness of the bottomless pit, down in defeat and derision – no I won't, and that's flat; not if the Chancellor were blackmailed by twenty millionaires with their gutter rags, not if the Prime Minister married twenty Yankee heiresses, not if

Woodville and Carstairs had shares in twenty swindling mines. If the thing is really tottering, God help it, it mustn't be we who tip it over.'

Boyle was regarding him with a bewilderment that was almost fear, and had even a touch of distaste.

'Somehow,' he said, 'there seems to be something rather horrid about the things you know.'

'There is,' replied Horne Fisher. 'I am not at all pleased with my small stock of knowledge and reflection. But as it is partly responsible for your not being hanged, I don't know that you need complain of it.'

And, as if a little ashamed of his first boast, he turned and strolled away towards the bottomless well.

5

The Fad of the Fisherman

A thing can sometimes be too extraordinary to be remembered. If it is clean out of the course of things, and has apparently no causes and no consequences, subsequent events do not recall it, and it remains only a subconscious thing, to be stirred by some accident long after. It drifts apart like a forgotten dream; and it was in the hour of many dreams, at daybreak and very soon after the end of dark, that such a strange sight was given to a man sculling a boat down a river in the West Country. The man was awake; indeed, he considered himself rather wide awake, being the political journalist, Harold March, on his way to interview various political celebrities in their country seats. But the thing he saw was so inconsequent that it might have been imaginary. It simply slipped past his mind and was lost in later and utterly different events; nor did he even recover the memory till he had long afterwards discovered the meaning.

Pale mists of morning lay on the fields and the rushes along one margin of the river; along the other side ran a wall of tawny brick almost overhanging the water. He had shipped his oars and was drifting for a moment with the stream, when he turned his head and saw that the monotony of the long brick wall was broken by a bridge; rather an elegant eighteenth-century sort of bridge with little columns of white stone turning grey. There had been floods and the river still stood very high, with dwarfish trees waist deep in it, and rather a narrow arc of white dawn gleamed under the curve of the bridge.

As his own boat went under the dark archway he saw another boat coming towards him, rowed by a man as solitary as himself. His posture prevented much being seen of him, but as he neared the bridge he stood up in the boat and turned round. He was already so close to the dark entry, however, that his whole figure was black against the morning light, and March could see nothing of his face except the end of two long whiskers or moustaches that gave something sinister to the silhouette, like horns in the wrong place. Even these details March would never have noticed but for what happened in the same instant. As the man came under the low bridge he made a leap at it and hung, with his legs dangling, letting the boat float away from under him. March had a momentary vision of two black kicking legs; then of one black kicking leg; and then of nothing except the eddying stream and the long perspective of the wall. But whenever he thought of it again, long afterwards, when he understood the story in which it figured, it was always fixed in that one fantastic shape – as if those wild legs were a grotesque graven ornament of the bridge itself, in the manner of a gargoyle. At the moment he merely passed, staring, down the stream. He could see no flying figure on the bridge, so it must have already fled; but he was half conscious of some faint significance in the fact that among the trees round the bridge-head opposite the wall he saw a lamppost; and, beside the lamppost, the broad blue back of an unconscious policeman.

Even before reaching the shrine of his political pilgrimage he had many other things to think of besides the odd incident of the bridge; for the management of a boat by a solitary man was not always easy even on such a solitary stream. And indeed it was only by an unforeseen accident that he was solitary. The boat had been purchased and the whole expedition planned in conjunction with a friend, who had at the last moment been forced to alter all his arrangements. Harold March was to have travelled with his friend Horne Fisher on that inland voyage to Willowood Place, where the Prime Minister was a guest at the moment. More and more people were hearing of Harold March, for his striking political articles were opening to him the doors of larger and larger salons; but he had never met the Prime Minister yet. Scarcely anybody among the general public had ever heard of Horne Fisher; but he had known the Prime Minister all his life. For these reasons, had the two taken the projected journey together, March might have been slightly disposed to hasten it and Fisher vaguely content to lengthen it out. For Fisher was one of those people who are born knowing the Prime Minister. The knowledge seemed to have no very exhilarant effect, and in his case bore some resemblance to being born tired. But he was distinctly annoyed to receive, just as he was doing a little light packing of fishing tackle and cigars for the journey, a telegram from Willowood asking him to come down at once by train, as the Prime Minister had to leave that night. Fisher knew that his friend the journalist could not possibly start till the next day, and he liked his friend the journalist, and had looked forward to a few days on the river. He did not particularly like or dislike the Prime Minister, but he intensely disliked the alternative of a few hours in the train. Nevertheless, he accepted Prime Ministers as he accepted railway trains – as part of a system which he, at least, was not the revolutionist sent on earth to destroy. So he telephoned to March, asking him, with many apologetic curses and faint damns, to take the boat down the river as arranged, that they might meet at Willowood by the time settled; then he went outside and hailed a taxicab to take him to the railway station. There he paused at the bookstall to add to his light luggage a number of cheap murder stories, which he read with great pleasure, and without any premonition that he was about to walk into as strange a story in real life.

A little before sunset he arrived, with his light suitcase in hand, before the gate of the long riverside gardens of Willowood Place, one of the smaller seats of Sir Isaac Hook, the master of much shipping and many newspapers. He entered by the gate giving on the road, at the opposite side to the river, but there was a mixed quality in all that watery landscape which perpetually reminded a traveller that the river was near. White gleams of water would shine suddenly like swords or spears in the green thickets. And even in the garden itself, divided into courts and curtained with hedges and high garden trees, there hung everywhere in the air the music of water. The first of the green courts which he entered appeared to be a somewhat neglected croquet lawn, in which was a solitary young man playing croquet against himself. Yet he was not an enthusiast for the game, or even for the garden; and his sallow but well-featured face looked rather sullen than otherwise. He was only one of those young men who cannot support the burden of consciousness unless they are doing something, and whose conceptions of doing something are limited to a game of some kind. He was dark and well dressed in a light holiday fashion, and Fisher recognised him at once as a young man named James Bullen, called, for some unknown reason, Bunker. He was the nephew of Sir Isaac; but, what was much more important at the moment, he was also the private secretary of the Prime Minister.

'Hullo, Bunker!' observed Horne Fisher. 'You're the sort of man I wanted to see. Has your chief come down yet?'

'He's only staying for dinner,' replied Bullen, with his eye on the yellow ball. 'He's got a great speech tomorrow at Birmingham and he's going straight through tonight. He's motoring himself there; driving the car, I mean. It's the one thing he's really proud of.'

'You mean you're staying here with your uncle, like a good boy?' replied Fisher. 'But what will the chief do at Birmingham without the epigrams whispered to him by his brilliant secretary?'

'Don't you start ragging me,' said the young man called Bunker. 'I'm only too glad not to go trailing after him. He doesn't know a thing about maps or money or hotels or anything, and I have to dance about like a courier. As for my uncle, as I'm supposed to come into the estate, it's only decent to be here sometimes.'

'Very proper,' replied the other. 'Well, I shall see you later on,' and, crossing the lawn, he passed out through a gap in the hedge.

He was walking across the lawn towards the landing stage on the river, and still felt all around him, under the dome of golden evening, an Old World savour and reverberation in that river-haunted garden. The next square of turf which he crossed seemed at first sight quite deserted, till he saw in the twilight of trees in one corner of it a hammock and in the hammock a man, reading a newspaper and swinging one leg over the edge of the net.

Him also he hailed by name, and the man slipped to the ground and strolled forward. It seemed fated that he should feel something of the past in the accidents of that place, for the figure might well have been an early-Victorian ghost revisiting the ghosts of the croquet hoops and mallets. It was the figure of an elderly man with long whiskers that looked almost fantastic, and a quaint and careful cut of collar and cravat. Having been a fashionable dandy forty years ago, he had managed to preserve the dandyism while ignoring the fashions. A white top-hat lay beside the *Morning Post* in the hammock behind him. This was the Duke of Westmoreland, the relic of a family really some centuries old; and the antiquity was not heraldry but history. Nobody knew better than Fisher how rare such noblemen are in fact, and how numerous in fiction. But whether the duke owed the general respect he enjoyed to the genuineness of his pedigree or to the fact that he owned a vast amount of very valuable property was a point about which Mr Fisher's opinion might have been more interesting to discover.

'You were looking so comfortable,' said Fisher, 'that I thought you must be one of the servants. I'm looking for somebody to take this bag of mine; I haven't brought a man down, as I came away in a hurry.'

'Nor have I, for that matter,' replied the duke, with some pride. 'I never do. If there's one animal alive I loathe it's a valet. I learned to dress myself at an early age and was supposed to do it decently. I may be in my second childhood, but I've not go so far as being dressed like a child.'

'The Prime Minister hasn't brought a valet; he's brought a secretary instead,' observed Fisher. 'Devilish inferior job. Didn't I hear that Harker was down here?'

'He's over there on the landing stage,' replied the duke, indifferently, and resumed the study of the *Morning Post*.

Fisher made his way beyond the last green wall of the garden on to a sort of towing path looking on the river and a wooden island opposite. There, indeed, he saw a lean, dark figure with a stoop almost like that of a vulture, a posture well known in the law courts as that of Sir John Harker, the Attorney-General. His face was lined with head work, for alone among the three idlers in the garden he was a man who had made his own way; and round his bald brow and hollow temples clung dull red hair, quite flat, like plates of copper.

'I haven't seen my host yet,' said Horne Fisher, in a slightly more serious tone than he had used to the others, 'but I suppose I shall meet him at dinner.'

'You can see him now; but you can't meet him,' answered Harker.

He nodded his head towards one end of the island opposite, and, looking steadily in the same direction, the other guest could see the dome of a bald head and the top of a fishing rod, both equally motionless, rising out of the tall undergrowth against the background of the stream beyond. The fisherman seemed to be seated against the stump of a tree and facing towards the other bank, so that his face could not be seen, but the shape of his head was unmistakable.

'He doesn't like to be disturbed when he's fishing,' continued Harker. 'It's a sort of fad of his to eat nothing but fish, and he's very proud of catching his own. Of course he's all for simplicity, like so many of these millionaires. He likes to come in saying he's worked for his daily bread like a labourer.'

'Does he explain how he blows all the glass and stuffs all the upholstery,' asked Fisher, 'and makes all the silver forks, and grows all the grapes and peaches, and designs all the patterns on the carpets? I've always heard he was a busy man.'

'I don't think he mentioned it,' answered the lawyer. 'What is the meaning of this social satire?'

'Well, I am a trifle tired,' said Fisher, 'of the Simple Life and the Strenuous Life as lived by our little set. We're all really dependent in nearly everything, and we all make a fuss about being independent in something. The Prime Minister prides himself on doing without a chauffeur, but he can't do without a factotum and Jack-of-all-trades; and poor old Bunker has to play the part of a universal genius, which God knows he was never meant for. The duke prides himself on doing without a valet, but, for all that, he must give a lot of people an infernal lot of trouble to collect such extraordinary old clothes as he wears. He must have them looked up in the British Museum or excavated out of the tombs. That white hat alone must require a sort of expedition fitted out to find it, like the North Pole. And here we have old Hook pretending to produce his own fish when he couldn't produce his own fish knives or fish forks to eat it with. He may be simple about simple things like food, but you bet he's luxurious about luxurious things, especially little things. I don't include you; you've worked too hard to enjoy playing at work.'

'I sometimes think,' said Harker, 'that you conceal a horrid secret of being useful sometimes. Haven't you come down here to see Number One before he goes on to Birmingham?'

Horne Fisher answered, in a lower voice: 'Yes; and I hope to be lucky enough to catch him before dinner. He's got to see Sir Isaac about something just afterwards.'

'Hullo!' exclaimed Harker. 'Sir Isaac's finished his fishing. I know he prides himself on getting up at sunrise and going in at sunset.'

The old man on the island had indeed risen to his feet, facing round and showing a bush of grey beard with rather small, sunken features, but fierce eyebrows and keen, choleric eyes. Carefully carrying his fishing tackle, he was already making his way back to the mainland across a bridge of flat stepping-stones a little way down the shallow stream; then he veered round, coming towards his guests and civilly saluting them. There were several fish in his basket and he was in a good temper.

'Yes,' he said, acknowledging Fisher's polite expression of surprise, 'I get up before anybody else in the house, I think. The early bird catches the worm.'

'Unfortunately,' said Harker, 'it is the early fish that catches the worm.'

'But the early man catches the fish,' replied the old man, gruffly.

'But from what I hear, Sir Isaac, you are the late man, too,' interposed Fisher. 'You must do with very little sleep.'

'I never had much time for sleeping,' answered Hook, 'and I shall have to be the late man tonight, anyhow. The Prime Minister wants to have a talk, he tells me, and, all things considered, I think we'd better be dressing for dinner.'

Dinner passed off that evening without a word of politics and little enough but ceremonial trifles. The Prime Minister, Lord Merivale, who was a long, slim man with curly grey hair, was gravely complimentary to his host about his success as a fisherman and the skill and patience he displayed; the conversation flowed like the shallow stream through the stepping-stones.

'It wants patience to wait for them, no doubt,' said Sir Isaac, 'and skill to play them, but I'm generally pretty lucky at it.'

'Does a big fish ever break the line and get away?' enquired the politician, with respectful interest.

'Not the sort of line I use,' answered Hook, with satisfaction. 'I rather specialise in tackle, as a matter of fact. If he were strong enough to do that, he'd be strong enough to pull me into the river.'

'A great loss to the community,' said the Prime Minister, bowing.

Fisher had listened to all these futilities with inward impatience, waiting for his own opportunity, and when the host rose he sprang to his feet with an alertness he rarely showed. He managed to catch Lord Merivale before Sir Isaac bore him off for the final interview. He had only a few words to say, but he wanted to get them said.

He said, in a low voice as he opened the door for the Premier, 'I have seen Montmirail; he says that unless we protest immediately on behalf of Denmark, Sweden will certainly seize the ports.'

Lord Merivale nodded. 'I'm just going to hear what Hook has to say about it,' he said.

'I imagine,' said Fisher, with a faint smile, 'that there is very little doubt what he will say about it.'

Merivale did not answer, but lounged gracefully towards the library, whither his host had already preceded him. The rest drifted towards the billiard room, Fisher merely remarking to the lawyer: 'They won't be long. We know they're practically in agreement.'

'Hook entirely supports the Prime Minister,' assented Harker.

'Or the Prime Minister entirely supports Hook,' said Horne Fisher, and began idly to knock the balls about on the billiard table.

Horne Fisher came down next morning in a late and leisurely fashion, as was his reprehensible habit; he had evidently no appetite for catching worms. But the other guests seemed to have felt a similar indifference, and they helped themselves to breakfast from the sideboard at intervals during the hours verging upon lunch. So that it was not many hours later when the first sensation of that strange day came upon them. It came in the form of a young man with light hair and a candid expression, who came sculling down the river and disembarked at the landing stage. It was, in fact, no other than Mr Harold March, whose journey had begun far away up the river in the earliest hours of that day. He arrived late in the afternoon, having stopped for tea in a large riverside town, and he had a pink evening paper sticking out of his pocket. He fell on the riverside garden like a quiet and well-behaved thunderbolt, but he was a thunderbolt without knowing it.

The first exchange of salutations and introductions was commonplace enough, and consisted, indeed, of the inevitable repetition of excuses for the eccentric seclusion of the host. He had gone fishing again, of course, and must not be disturbed till the appointed hour, though he sat within a stone's throw of where they stood.

'You see it's his only hobby,' observed Harker, apologetically, 'and, after all, it's his own house; and he's very hospitable in other ways.'

'I'm rather afraid,' said Fisher, in a lower voice, 'that it's becoming more of a mania than a hobby. I know how it is when a man of that age begins to collect things, if it's only collecting those rotten little river fish. You remember Talbot's uncle with his toothpicks, and poor old Buzzy and the waste of cigar ashes. Hook has done a lot of big things in his time – the great deal in the Swedish timber trade and the Peace Conference at Chicago – but I doubt whether he cares now for any of those big things as he cares for those little fish.'

'Oh, come, come,' protested the Attorney-General. 'You'll make Mr March think he has come to call on a lunatic. Believe me, Hook only does it for fun, like any other sport, only he's of the kind that takes his fun sadly. But I bet if there were big news about timber or shipping, he would drop his fun and his fish all right.'

'Well, I wonder,' said Horne Fisher, looking sleepily at the island in the river.

'By the way, is there any news of anything?' asked Harker of Harold March. 'I see you've got an evening paper; one of those enterprising evening papers that come out in the morning.'

'The beginning of Lord Merivale's Birmingham speech,' replied March, handing him the paper. 'It's only a paragraph, but it seems to me rather good.'

Harker took the paper, flapped and refolded it, and looked at the 'Stop Press' news. It was, as March had said, only a paragraph. But it was a paragraph that had a peculiar effect on Sir John Harker. His lowering brows lifted with a flicker and his eyes blinked, and for a moment his leathery jaw was loosened. He looked in some odd fashion like a very old man. Then, hardening his voice and handing the paper to Fisher without a tremor, he simply said: 'Well, here's a chance for the bet. You've got your big news to disturb the old man's fishing.'

Horne Fisher was looking at the paper, and over his more languid and less expressive features a change also seemed to pass. Even that little paragraph had two or three large headlines, and his eye encountered, 'Sensational Warning to Sweden', and, 'We Shall Protest'.

'What the devil – ' he said, and his words softened first to a whisper and then a whistle.

'We must tell old Hook at once, or he'll never forgive us,' said Harker. 'He'll probably want to see Number One instantly, though it may be too late now. I'm going across to him at once. I bet I'll make him forget his fish, anyhow.' And, turning his back, he made his way hurriedly along the riverside to the causeway of flat stones.

March was staring at Fisher, in amazement at the effect his pink paper had produced.

'What does it all mean?' he cried. 'I always supposed we should protest in defence of the Danish ports, for their sakes and our own. What is all this botheration about Sir Isaac and the rest of you? Do you think it bad news?'

'Bad news!' repeated Fisher, with a sort of soft emphasis beyond expression.

'Is it as bad as all that?' asked his friend, at last.

'As bad as all that?' repeated Fisher. 'Why of course it's as good as it can be. It's great news. It's glorious news! That's where the devil of it comes in, to knock us all silly. It's admirable. It's inestimable. It is also quite incredible.'

He gazed again at the grey and green colours of the island and the river, and his rather dreary eye travelled slowly round to the hedges and the lawns.

'I felt this garden was a sort of dream,' he said, 'and I suppose I must be dreaming. But there is grass growing and water moving; and something impossible has happened.'

Even as he spoke the dark figure with a stoop like a vulture appeared in the gap of the hedge just above him.

'You have won your bet,' said Harker, in a harsh and almost croaking voice. 'The old fool cares for nothing but fishing. He cursed me and told me he would talk no politics.'

'I thought it might be so,' said Fisher, modestly. 'What are you going to do next?'

'I shall use the old idiot's telephone, anyhow,' replied the lawyer. 'I must find out exactly what has happened. I've got to speak for the Government myself tomorrow.' And he hurried away towards the house.

In the silence that followed, a very bewildering silence so far as March was concerned, they saw the quaint figure of the Duke of Westmoreland, with his white hat and whiskers, approaching them across the garden. Fisher instantly stepped towards him with the pink paper in his hand, and, with a few words, pointed out the apocalyptic paragraph. The duke, who had been walking slowly, stood quite still, and for some seconds he looked like a tailor's dummy standing and staring outside some antiquated shop. Then March heard his voice, and it was high and almost hysterical: 'But he must see it; he must be made to understand. It cannot have been put to him properly.' Then, with a certain recovery of fullness and even pomposity in the voice, 'I shall go and tell him myself.'

Among the queer incidents of that afternoon, March always remembered something almost comical about the clear picture of the old gentleman in his wonderful white hat carefully stepping from stone to stone across the river, like a figure crossing the traffic in Piccadilly. Then he disappeared behind the trees of the island, and March and Fisher turned to meet the Attorney-General, who was coming out of the house with a visage of grim assurance.

'Everybody is saying,' he said, 'that the Prime Minister has made the greatest speech of his life. Peroration and loud and prolonged cheers. Corrupt financiers and heroic peasants. We will not desert Denmark again.'

Fisher nodded and turned away towards the towing path, where he saw the duke returning with a rather dazed expression. In answer to questions he said, in a husky and confidential voice: 'I really think our poor friend cannot be himself. He refused to listen; he – ah – suggested that I might frighten the fish.'

A keen ear might have detected a murmur from Mr Fisher on the subject of a white hat, but Sir John Harker struck it more decisively: 'Fisher was quite right. I didn't believe it myself, but it's quite clear that the old fellow is fixed on this fishing notion by now. If the house caught fire behind him he would hardly move till sunset.'

Fisher had continued his stroll towards the higher embanked ground of the towing path, and he now swept a long and searching gaze, not towards the island, but towards the distant wooded heights that were the walls of the valley. An evening sky as clear as that of the previous day was settling down all over the dim landscape, but towards the west it was now red rather than gold; there was scarcely any sound but the monotonous music of the river. Then came the sound of a half-stifled exclamation from Horne Fisher, and Harold March looked up at him in wonder.

'You spoke of bad news,' said Fisher. 'Well, there is really bad news now. I am afraid this is a bad business.'

'What bad news do you mean?' asked his friend, conscious of something strange and sinister in his voice.

'The sun has set,' answered Fisher.

He went on with the air of one conscious of having said something fatal. 'We must get somebody to go across whom he will really listen to. He may be mad, but there's method in his madness. There nearly always is method in madness. It's what drives men mad, being methodical. And he never goes on sitting there after sunset, with the whole place getting dark. Where's his nephew? I believe he's really fond of his nephew.'

'Look!' cried March, abruptly. 'Why, he's been across already. There he is coming back.'

And, looking up the river once more, they saw, dark against the sunset reflections, the figure of James Bullen stepping hastily and rather clumsily from stone to stone. Once he slipped on a stone with a slight splash. When he rejoined the group on the bank his olive face was unnaturally pale.

The other four men had already gathered on the same spot and almost simultaneously were calling out to him, 'What does he say now?'

'Nothing. He says – nothing.'

Fisher looked at the young man steadily for a moment; then he started from his immobility and, making a motion to March to follow him, himself strode down to the river crossing. In a few moments they were on the little beaten track that ran round the wooded island, to the other side of it where the fisherman sat. Then they stood and looked at him, without a word.

Sir Isaac Hook was still sitting propped up against the stump of the tree, and that for the best of reasons. A length of his own infallible fishing line was twisted and tightened twice round his throat and then twice round the wooden prop behind him. The leading investigator ran forward and touched the fisherman's hand, and it was as cold as a fish.

'The sun has set,' said Horne Fisher, in the same terrible tones, 'and he will never see it rise again.'

Ten minutes afterwards the five men, shaken by such a shock, were again together in the garden, looking at one another with white but watchful faces. The lawyer seemed the most alert of the group; he was articulate if somewhat abrupt.

'We must leave the body as it is and telephone for the police,' he said. 'I think my own authority will stretch to examining the servants and the poor fellow's papers, to see if there is anything that concerns them. Of course, none of you gentlemen must leave this place.'

Perhaps there was something in his rapid and rigorous legality that suggested the closing of a net or trap. Anyhow, young Bullen suddenly broke down, or perhaps blew up, for his voice was like an explosion in the silent garden.

'I never touched him,' he cried. 'I swear I had nothing to do with it!'

'Who said you had?' demanded Harker, with a hard eye. 'Why do you cry out before you're hurt?'

'Because you all look at me like that,' cried the young man, angrily. 'Do you think I don't know you're always talking about my damned debts and expectations?'

Rather to March's surprise, Fisher had drawn away from this first collision, leading the duke with him to another part of the garden. When he was out of earshot of the others he said, with a curious simplicity of manner: 'Westmoreland, I am going straight to the point.'

'Well?' said the other, staring at him stolidly.

'You have a motive for killing him,' said Fisher.

The duke continued to stare, but he seemed unable to speak.

'I hope you had a motive for killing him,' continued Fisher, mildly. 'You see, it's rather a curious situation. If you have a motive for murdering, you probably didn't murder. But if you hadn't any motive, why, then perhaps you did.'

'What on earth are you talking about?' demanded the duke, violently.

'It's quite simple,' said Fisher. 'When you went across he was either alive or dead. If he was alive, it might be you who killed him, or why should you have held your tongue about his death? But if he was dead, and you had a reason for killing him, you might have held your tongue for fear of being accused.' Then after a silence he added, abstractedly: 'Cyprus is a beautiful place, I believe. Romantic scenery and romantic people. Very intoxicating for a young man.'

The duke suddenly clenched his hands and said, thickly, 'Well, I had a motive.'

'Then you're all right,' said Fisher, holding out his hand with an air of huge relief. 'I was pretty sure you wouldn't really do it; you had a fright when you saw it done, as was only natural. Like a bad dream come true, wasn't it?'

While this curious conversation was passing, Harker had gone into the house, disregarding the demonstrations of the sulky nephew, and came back presently with a new air of animation and a sheaf of papers in his hand.

'I've telephoned for the police,' he said, stopping to speak to Fisher, 'but I think I've done most of their work for them. I believe I've found out the truth. There's a paper here – ' He stopped, for Fisher was looking at him with a singular expression; and it was Fisher who spoke next: 'Are there any papers that are not there, I wonder? I mean that are not there now?' After a pause he added: 'Let us have the cards on the table. When you went through his papers in such a hurry, Harker, weren't you looking for something to – to make sure it shouldn't be found?'

Harker did not turn a red hair on his hard head, but he looked at the other out of the corners of his eyes.

'And I suppose,' went on Fisher, smoothly, 'that is why you, too, told us lies about having found Hook alive. You knew there was something to show that you might have killed him, and you didn't dare tell us he was killed. But, believe me, it's much better to be honest now.'

Harker's haggard face suddenly lit up as if with infernal flames.

'Honest!' he cried, 'it's not so damned fine of you fellows to be honest! You're all born with silver spoons in your mouths, and then you swagger about with everlasting virtue because you haven't got other people's spoons in your pockets. But I was born in a Pimlico lodging house and I had to make my spoon, and there'd be plenty to say I only spoiled a horn or an honest man. And if a struggling man staggers a bit over the line in his youth, in the lower parts of the law which are pretty dingy, anyhow, there's always some old vampire to hang on to him all his life for it.'

'Guatemalan Golcondas, wasn't it?' said Fisher, sympathetically.

Harker suddenly shuddered. Then he said, 'I believe you must know everything, like God Almighty.'

'I know too much,' said Horne Fisher, 'and all the wrong things.'

The other three men were drawing nearer to them, but before they came too near, Harker said, in a voice that had recovered all its firmness: 'Yes, I did destroy a paper, but I really did find a paper, too; and I believe that it clears us all.'

'Very well,' said Fisher, in a louder and more cheerful tone; 'let us all have the benefit of it.'

'On the very top of Sir Isaac's papers,' explained Harker, 'there was a threatening letter from a man named Hugo. It threatens to kill our unfortunate friend very much in the way that he was actually killed. It is a wild letter, full of taunts; you can see it for yourselves; but it makes a particular point of poor Hook's habit of fishing from the island. Above all, the man professes to be writing from a boat. And, since we alone went across to him,' and he smiled in a rather ugly fashion, 'the crime must have been committed by a man passing in a boat.'

'Why, dear me!' cried the duke, with something almost amounting to animation. 'Why, I remember the man called Hugo quite well! He was a sort of body servant and bodyguard of Sir Isaac. You see, Sir Isaac was in some fear of assault. He was – he was not very popular with several people. Hugo was discharged after some row or other; but I remember him well. He was a great big Hungarian fellow with great moustaches that stood out on each side of his face.'

A door opened in the darkness of Harold March's memory, or, rather, oblivion, and showed a shining landscape, like that of a lost dream. It was rather a waterscape than a landscape, a thing of flooded meadows and low trees and the dark archway of a bridge. And for one instant he saw again the man with moustaches like dark horns leap up on to the bridge and disappear.

'Good heavens!' he cried. 'Why, I met the murderer this morning!'

* * *

Horne Fisher and Harold March had their day on the river, after all, for the little group broke up when the police arrived. They declared that the coincidence of March's evidence had cleared the whole company, and clinched the case against the flying Hugo. Whether that Hungarian fugitive would ever be caught appeared to Horne Fisher to be highly doubtful; nor can it be pretended that he displayed any very demoniac detective energy in the matter as he leaned back in the boat cushions, smoking, and watching the swaying reeds slide past.

'It was a very good notion to hop up on to the bridge,' he said. 'An empty boat means very little; he hasn't been seen to land on either bank, and he's walked off the bridge without walking on to it, so to speak. He's got twenty-four hours' start; his moustaches will disappear, and then he will disappear. I think there is every hope of his escape.'

'Hope?' repeated March, and stopped sculling for an instant.

'Yes, hope,' repeated the other. 'To begin with, I'm not going to be exactly consumed with Corsican revenge because somebody has killed Hook. Perhaps you may guess by this time what Hook was. A damned blood-sucking blackmailer was that simple, strenuous, self-made captain of industry. He had secrets against nearly everybody; one against poor old Westmoreland about an early marriage in Cyprus that might have put the duchess in a queer position; and one against Harker about some flutter with his client's money when he was a young solicitor. That's why they went to pieces when they found him murdered, of course. They felt as if they'd done it in a dream. But I admit I have another reason for not wanting our Hungarian friend actually hanged for the murder.'

'And what is that?' asked his friend.

'Only that he didn't commit the murder,' answered Fisher.

Harold March laid down the oars and let the boat drift for a moment.

'Do you know, I was half expecting something like that,' he said. 'It was quite irrational, but it was hanging about in the atmosphere, like thunder in the air.'

'On the contrary, it's finding Hugo guilty that's irrational,' replied Fisher. 'Don't you see that they're condemning him for the very reason for which they acquit everybody else? Harker and Westmoreland were silent because they found him murdered, and knew there were papers that made them look like the murderers. Well, so did Hugo find him murdered, and so did Hugo know there was a paper that would make him look like the murderer. He had written it himself the day before.'

'But in that case,' said March, frowning, 'at what sort of unearthly hour in the morning was the murder really committed? It was barely daylight when I met him at the bridge, and that's some way above the island.'

'The answer is very simple,' replied Fisher. 'The crime was not committed in the morning. The crime was not committed on the island.'

March stared at the shining water without replying, but Fisher resumed like one who had been asked a question: 'Every intelligent murder involves taking advantage of some one uncommon feature in a common situation. The feature here was the fancy of old Hook for being the first man up every morning, his fixed routine as an angler, and his annoyance at being disturbed. The murderer strangled him in his own house after dinner on the night before, carried his corpse, with all his fishing tackle, across the stream in the dead of night, tied him to the tree, and left him there under the stars. It was a dead man who sat fishing there all day. Then the murderer went back to the house, or, rather, to the garage, and went off in his motor car. The murderer drove his own motor car.'

Fisher glanced at his friend's face and went on. 'You look horrified, and the thing is horrible. But other things are horrible, too. If some obscure man had been hag-ridden by a blackmailer and had his family life ruined, you wouldn't think the murder of his persecutor the most inexcusable of murders. Is it any worse when a whole great nation is set free as well as a family? By this warning to Sweden we shall probably prevent war and not precipitate it, and save many thousand lives rather more valuable than the life of that viper. Oh, I'm not talking sophistry or seriously justifying the thing, but the slavery that held him and his country was a thousand times less justifiable. If I'd really been sharp I should have guessed it from his smooth, deadly smiling at dinner that night. Do you remember that silly talk about how old Isaac could always play his fish? In a pretty hellish sense he was a fisher of men.'

Harold March took the oars and began to row again.

'I remember,' he said, 'and about how a big fish might break the line and get away.'

6

The Hole in the Wall

Two men, the one an architect and the other an archaeologist, met on the steps of the great house at Prior's Park; and their host, Lord Bulmer, in his breezy way, thought it natural to introduce them. It must be confessed that he was hazy as well as breezy, and had no very clear connection in his mind, beyond the sense that an architect and an archaeologist begin with the same series of letters. The world must remain in a reverent doubt as to whether he would, on the same principles, have presented a diplomatist to a dipsomaniac or a ratiocinator to a rat catcher. He was a big, fair, bull-necked young man, abounding in outward gestures, unconsciously flapping his gloves and flourishing his stick.

'You two ought to have something to talk about,' he said, cheerfully. 'Old buildings and all that sort of thing; this is rather an old building, by the way, though I say it who shouldn't. I must ask you to excuse me a moment; I've got to go and see about the cards for this Christmas romp my sister's arranging. We hope to see you all there, of course. Juliet wants it to be a fancy-dress affair – abbots and crusaders and all that. My ancestors, I suppose, after all.'

'I trust the abbot was not an ancestor,' said the archaeological gentleman, with a smile.

'Only a sort of great-uncle, I imagine,' answered the other, laughing. Then his rather rambling eye rolled round the ordered landscape in front of the house; an artificial sheet of water ornamented with an antiquated nymph in the centre and surrounded by a park of tall trees now grey and black and frosty, for it was in the depth of a severe winter.

'It's getting jolly cold,' his lordship continued. 'My sister hopes we shall have some skating as well as dancing.'

'If the crusaders come in full armour,' said the other, 'you must be careful not to drown your ancestors.'

'Oh, there's no fear of that,' answered Bulmer; 'this precious lake of ours is not two feet deep anywhere.' And with one of his flourishing gestures he stuck his stick into the water to demonstrate its shallowness. They could see the short end bent in the water, so that he seemed for a moment to lean his large weight on a breaking staff.

'The worst you can expect is to see an abbot sit down rather suddenly,' he added, turning away. 'Well, au revoir; I'll let you know about it later.'

The archaeologist and the architect were left on the great stone steps smiling at each other; but whatever their common interests, they presented a considerable personal contrast, and the fanciful might even have found some contradiction in each considered individually. The former, a Mr James Haddow, came from a drowsy den in the Inns of Court, full of leather and parchment, for the law was his profession and history only his hobby; he was indeed, among other things, the solicitor and agent of the Prior's Park estate. But he himself was far from drowsy and seemed remarkably wide awake, with shrewd and prominent blue eyes, and red hair brushed as neatly as his very neat costume. The latter, whose name was Leonard Crane, came straight from a crude and almost cockney office of builders and house agents in the neighbouring suburb, sunning itself at the end of a new row of jerry-built houses with plans in very bright colours and notices in very large letters. But a serious observer, at a second glance, might have seen in his eyes something of that shining sleep that is called vision; and his yellow hair, while not affectedly long, was unaffectedly untidy. It was a manifest if melancholy truth that the architect was an artist. But the artistic temperament was far from explaining him; there was something else about him that was not definable, but which some even felt to be dangerous. Despite his dreaminess, he would sometimes surprise his friends with arts and even sport apart from his ordinary life, like memories of some previous existence. On this occasion, nevertheless, he hastened to disclaim any authority on the other man's hobby.

'I mustn't appear on false pretences,' he said, with a smile. 'I hardly even know what an archaeologist is, except that a rather rusty remnant of Greek suggests that he is a man who studies old things.'

'Yes,' replied Haddow, grimly. 'An archaeologist is a man who studies old things and finds they are new.'

Crane looked at him steadily for a moment and then smiled again.

'Dare one suggest,' he said, 'that some of the things we have been talking about are among the old things that turn out not to be old?'

His companion also was silent for a moment, and the smile on his rugged face was fainter as he replied, quietly: 'The wall round the park is really old. The one gate in it is Gothic, and I cannot find any trace of destruction or restoration. But the house and the estate generally – well, the romantic ideas read into these things are often rather recent romances, things almost like fashionable novels. For instance, the very name of this place, Prior's Park, makes everybody think of it as a moonlit mediaeval abbey; I dare say the spiritualists by this time have discovered the ghost of a monk there. But, according to the only authoritative study of the matter I can find, the place was simply called Prior's as any rural place is called Podger's. It was the house of a Mr Prior, a farmhouse, probably, that stood here at some time or other and was a local landmark. Oh, there are a great many examples of the same thing, here and everywhere else. This suburb of ours used to be a village, and because some of the people slurred the name and pronounced it Holliwell, many a minor poet indulged in fancies about a Holy Well, with spells and fairies and all the rest of it, filling the suburban drawing-rooms with the Celtic twilight. Whereas anyone acquainted with the facts knows that "Hollinwall" simply means "the hole in the wall", and probably referred to some quite trivial accident. That's what I mean when I say that we don't so much find old things as we find new ones.'

Crane seemed to have grown somewhat inattentive to the little lecture on antiquities and novelties, and the cause of his restlessness was soon apparent, and indeed approaching. Lord Bulmer's sister, Juliet Bray, was coming slowly across the lawn, accompanied by one gentleman and followed by two others. The young architect was in the illogical condition of mind in which he preferred three to one.

The man walking with the lady was no other than the eminent Prince Borodino, who was at least as famous as a distinguished diplomatist ought to be, in the interests of what is called secret diplomacy. He had been paying a round of visits at various English country houses, and exactly what he was doing for diplomacy at Prior's Park was as much a secret as any diplomatist could desire. The obvious thing to say of his appearance was that he would have been extremely handsome if he had not been entirely bald. But, indeed, that would itself be a rather bald way of putting it. Fantastic as it sounds, it would fit the case better to say that people would have been surprised to see hair growing on him; as surprised as if they had found hair growing on the bust of a Roman emperor. His tall figure was buttoned up in a tight-waisted fashion that rather accentuated his potential bulk, and he wore a red flower in his buttonhole. Of the two men walking behind one was also bald, but in a more partial and also a more premature fashion, for his drooping moustache was still yellow, and if his eyes were somewhat heavy it was with languor and not with age. It was Horne Fisher, and he was talking as easily and idly about everything as he always did. His companion was a more striking, and even more sinister, figure, and he had the added importance of being Lord Bulmer's oldest and most intimate friend. He was generally known with a severe simplicity as Mr Brain; but it was understood that he had been a judge and police official in India, and that he had enemies, who had represented his measures against crime as themselves almost criminal. He was a brown skeleton of a man with dark, deep, sunken eyes and a black moustache that hid the meaning of his mouth. Though he had the look of one wasted by some tropical disease, his movements were much more alert than those of his lounging companion.

'It's all settled,' announced the lady, with great animation, when they came within hailing distance. 'You've all got to put on masquerade things and very likely skates as well, though the prince says they don't go with it; but we don't care about that. It's freezing already, and we don't often get such a chance in England.'

'Even in India we don't exactly skate all the year round,' observed Mr Brain.

'And even Italy is not primarily associated with ice,' said the Italian.

'Italy is primarily associated with ices,' remarked Mr Horne Fisher. 'I mean with ice cream men. Most people in this country imagine that Italy is entirely populated with ice cream men and organ grinders. There certainly are a lot of them; perhaps they're an invading army in disguise.'

'How do you know they are not the secret emissaries of our diplomacy?' asked the prince, with a slightly scornful smile. 'An army of organ grinders might pick up hints, and their monkeys might pick up all sort of things.'

'The organs are organised, in fact,' said the flippant Mr Fisher. 'Well, I've known it pretty cold before now in Italy and even in India, up on the Himalayan slopes. The ice on our own little round pond will be quite cosy by comparison.'

Juliet Bray was an attractive lady with dark hair and eyebrows and dancing eyes, and there was a geniality and even generosity in her rather imperious ways. In most matters she could command her brother, though that nobleman, like many other men of vague ideas, was not without a touch of the bully when he was at bay. She could certainly command her guests, even to the extent of decking out the most respectable and reluctant of them with her mediaeval masquerade. And it really seemed as if she could command the elements also, like a witch. For the weather steadily hardened and sharpened; that night the ice of the lake, glimmering in the moonlight, was like a marble floor, and they had begun to dance and skate on it before it was dark.

Prior's Park, or, more properly, the surrounding district of Holinwall, was a country seat that had become a suburb; having once had only a dependent village at its doors, it now found outside all its doors the signals of the expansion of London. Mr Haddow, who was engaged in historical researches both in the library and the locality, could find little assistance in the latter. He had already realised, from the documents, that Prior's Park had originally been something like Prior's Farm, named after some local figure, but the new social conditions were all against his tracing the story by its traditions. Had any of the real rustics remained, he would probably have found some lingering legend of Mr Prior, however remote he might be. But the new nomadic population of clerks and artisans, constantly shifting their homes from one suburb to another, or their children from one school to another, could have no corporate continuity. They had all that forgetfulness of history that goes everywhere with the extension of education.

Nevertheless, when he came out of the library next morning and saw the wintry trees standing round the frozen pond like a black forest, he felt he might well have been far in the depths of the country. The old wall running round the park kept that enclosure itself still entirely rural and romantic, and one could easily imagine that the depths of that dark forest faded away indefinitely into distant vales and hills. The grey and black and silver of the wintry wood were all the more severe or sombre as a contrast to the coloured carnival groups that already stood on and around the frozen pool. For the house party had already flung themselves impatiently into fancy dress, and the lawyer, with his neat black suit and red hair, was the only modern figure left among them.

'Aren't you going to dress up?' asked Juliet, indignantly shaking at him a horned and towering blue headdress of the fourteenth century which framed her face very becomingly, fantastic as it was. 'Everybody here has to be in the Middle Ages. Even Mr Brain has put on a sort of brown dressing gown and says he's a monk; and Mr Fisher got hold of some old potato sacks in the kitchen and sewed them together; he's supposed to be a monk, too. As to the prince, he's perfectly glorious, in great crimson robes as a cardinal. He looks as if he could poison everybody. You simply must be something.'

'I will be something later in the day,' he replied. 'At present I am nothing but an antiquary and an attorney. I have to see your brother presently, about some legal business and also some local investigations he asked me to make. I must look a little like a steward when I give an account of my stewardship.'

'Oh, but my brother has dressed up!' cried the girl. 'Very much so. No end, if I may say so. Why, he's bearing down on you now in all his glory.'

The noble lord was indeed marching towards them in a magnificent sixteenth-century costume of purple and gold, with a gold-hilted sword and a plumed cap, and manners to match. Indeed, there was something more than his usual expansiveness of bodily action in his appearance at that moment. It almost seemed, so to speak, that the plumes on his hat had gone to his head. He flapped his great, gold-lined cloak like the wings of a fairy king in a pantomime; he even drew his sword with a flourish and waved it about as he did his walking stick. In the light of after events there seemed to be something monstrous and ominous about that exuberance, something of the spirit that is called *fey*. At the time it merely crossed a few people's minds that he might possibly be drunk.

As he strode towards his sister the first figure he passed was that of Leonard Crane, clad in Lincoln green, with the horn and baldrick and sword appropriate to Robin Hood; for he was standing nearest to the lady, where, indeed, he might have been found during a disproportionate part of the time. He had displayed one of his buried talents in the matter of skating, and now that the skating was over seemed disposed to prolong the partnership. The boisterous Bulmer playfully made a pass at him with his drawn sword, going forward with the lunge in the proper fencing fashion, and making a somewhat too familiar Shakespearean quotation about a rodent and a Venetian coin.

Probably in Crane also there was a subdued excitement just then; anyhow, in one flash he had drawn his own sword and parried; and then suddenly, to the surprise of everyone, Bulmer's weapon seemed to spring out of his hand into the air and rolled away on the ringing ice.

'Well, I never!' said the lady, as if with justifiable indignation. 'You never told me you could fence, too.'

Bulmer put up his sword with an air rather bewildered than annoyed, which increased the impression of something irresponsible in his mood at the moment; then he turned rather abruptly to his lawyer, saying: 'We can settle up about the estate after dinner; I've missed nearly all the skating as it is, and I doubt if the ice will hold till tomorrow night. I think I shall get up early and have a spin by myself.'

'You won't be disturbed with my company,' said Horne Fisher, in his weary fashion. 'If I have to begin the day with ice, in the American fashion, I prefer it in smaller quantities. But no early hours for me in December. The early bird catches the cold.'

'Oh, I shan't die of catching a cold,' answered Bulmer, and laughed.

* * *

A considerable group of the skating party had consisted of the guests staying at the house, and the rest had tailed off in twos and threes some time before most of the guests began to retire for the night. Neighbours, always invited to Prior's Park on such occasions, went back to their own houses in motors or on foot; the legal and archaeological gentleman had returned to the Inns of Court by a late train, to get a paper called for during his consultation with his client; and most of the other guests were drifting and lingering at various stages on their way up to bed. Horne Fisher, as if to deprive himself of any excuse for his refusal of early rising, had been the first to retire to his room; but, sleepy as he looked, he could not sleep. He had picked up from a table the book of antiquarian topography, in which Haddow had found his first hints about the origin of the local name, and, being a man with a quiet and quaint capacity for being interested in anything, he began to read it steadily, making notes now and then of details on which his previous reading left him with a certain doubt about his present conclusions. His room was the one nearest to the lake in the centre of the woods, and was therefore the quietest, and none of the last echoes of the evening's festivity could reach him. He had followed carefully the argument which established the derivation from Mr Prior's farm and the hole in the wall, and disposed of any fashionable fancy about monks and magic wells, when he began to be conscious of a noise audible in the frozen silence of the night. It was not a particularly loud noise, but it seemed to consist of a series of thuds or heavy blows, such as might be struck on a wooden door by a man seeking to enter. They were followed by something like a faint creak or crack, as if the obstacle had either been opened or had given way. He opened his own bedroom door and listened, but as he heard talk and laughter all over the lower floors, he had no reason to fear that a summons would be neglected or the house left without protection. He went to his open window, looking out over the frozen pond and the moonlit statue in the middle of their circle of darkling woods, and listened again. But silence had returned to that silent place, and, after straining his ears for a considerable time, he could hear nothing but the solitary hoot of a distant departing train. Then he reminded himself how many nameless noises can be heard by the wakeful during the most ordinary night, and shrugging his shoulders, went wearily to bed.

He awoke suddenly and sat up in bed with his ears filled, as with thunder, with the throbbing echoes of a rending cry. He remained rigid for a moment, and then sprang out of bed, throwing on the loose gown of sacking he had worn all day. He went first to the window, which was open, but covered with a thick curtain, so that his room was still completely dark; but when he tossed the curtain aside and put his head out, he saw that a grey and silver daybreak had already appeared behind the black woods that surrounded the little lake, and that was all that he did see. Though the sound had certainly come in through the open window from this direction, the whole scene was still and empty under the morning light as under the moonlight. Then the long, rather lackadaisical hand he had laid on a window sill gripped it tighter, as if to master a tremor, and his peering blue eyes grew bleak with fear. It may seem that his emotion was exaggerated and needless, considering the effort of common sense by which he had conquered his nervousness about the noise on the previous night. But that had been a very different sort of noise. It might have been made by half a hundred things, from the chopping of wood to the breaking of bottles. There was only one thing in nature from which could come the sound that echoed through the dark house at daybreak. It was the awful articulate voice of man; and it was something worse, for he knew what man.

He knew also that it had been a shout for help. It seemed to him that he had heard the very word; but the word, short as it was, had been swallowed up, as if the man had been stifled or snatched away even as he spoke. Only the mocking reverberations of it remained even in his memory, but he had no doubt of the original voice. He had no doubt that the great bull's voice of Francis Bray, Baron Bulmer, had been heard for the last time between the darkness and the lifting dawn.

How long he stood there he never knew, but he was startled into life by the first living thing that he saw stirring in that half-frozen landscape. Along the path beside the lake, and immediately under his window, a figure was walking slowly and softly, but with great composure – a stately figure in robes of a splendid scarlet; it was the Italian prince, still in his cardinal's costume. Most of the company had indeed lived in their costumes for the last day or two, and Fisher himself had assumed his frock of sacking as a convenient dressing gown; but there seemed, nevertheless, something unusually finished and formal, in the way of an early bird, about this magnificent red cockatoo. It was as if the early bird had been up all night.

'What is the matter?' he called, sharply, leaning out of the window; and the Italian turned up his great yellow face like a mask of brass.

'We had better discuss it downstairs,' said Prince Borodino.

Fisher ran downstairs, and encountered the great, red-robed figure entering the doorway and blocking the entrance with his bulk.

'Did you hear that cry?' demanded Fisher.

'I heard a noise and I came out,' answered the diplomatist, and his face was too dark in the shadow for its expression to be read.

'It was Bulmer's voice,' insisted Fisher. 'I'll swear it was Bulmer's voice.'

'Did you know him well?' asked the other.

The question seemed irrelevant, though it was not illogical, and Fisher could only answer in a random fashion that he knew Lord Bulmer only slightly.

'Nobody seems to have known him well,' continued the Italian, in level tones. 'Nobody except that man Brain. Brain is rather older than Bulmer, but I fancy they shared a good many secrets.'

Fisher moved abruptly, as if waking from a momentary trance, and said, in a new and more vigorous voice, 'But look here, hadn't we better get outside and see if anything has happened.'

'The ice seems to be thawing,' said the other, almost with indifference.

When they emerged from the house, dark stains and stars in the grey field of ice did indeed indicate that the frost was breaking up, as their host had prophesied the day before, and the very memory of yesterday brought back the mystery of today.

'He knew there would be a thaw,' observed the prince. 'He went out skating quite early on purpose. Did he call out because he landed in the water, do you think?'

Fisher looked puzzled. 'Bulmer was the last man to bellow like that because he got his boots wet. And that's all he could do here; the water would hardly come up to the calf of a man of his size. You can see the flat weeds on the floor of the lake, as if it were through a thin pane of glass. No, if Bulmer had only broken the ice he wouldn't have said much at the moment, though possibly a good deal afterwards. We should have found him stamping and damning up and down this path, and calling for clean boots.'

'Let us hope we shall find him as happily employed,' remarked the diplomatist. 'In that case the voice must have come out of the wood.'

'I'll swear it didn't come out of the house,' said Fisher; and the two disappeared together into the twilight of wintry trees.

The plantation stood dark against the fiery colours of sunrise, a black fringe having that feathery appearance which makes trees when they are bare the very reverse of rugged. Hours and hours afterwards, when the same dense, but delicate, margin was dark against the greenish colours opposite the sunset, the search thus begun at sunrise had not come to an end. By successive stages, and to slowly gathering groups of the company, it became apparent that the most extraordinary of all gaps had appeared in the party; the guests could find no trace of their host anywhere. The servants reported that his bed had been slept in and his skates and his fancy costume were gone, as if he had risen early for the purpose he had himself avowed. But from the top of the house to the bottom, from the walls round the park to the pond in the centre, there was no trace of Lord Bulmer, dead or alive. Horne Fisher realised that a chilling premonition had already prevented him from expecting to find the man alive. But his bald brow was wrinkled over an entirely new and unnatural problem, in not finding the man at all.

He considered the possibility of Bulmer having gone off of his own accord, for some reason; but after fully weighing it he finally dismissed it. It was inconsistent with the unmistakable voice heard at daybreak, and with many other practical obstacles. There was only one gateway in the ancient and lofty wall round the small park; the lodge keeper kept it locked till late in the morning, and the lodge keeper had seen no one pass. Fisher was fairly sure that he had before him a mathematical problem in an enclosed space. His instinct had been from the first so attuned to the tragedy that it would have been almost a relief to him to find the corpse. He would have been grieved, but not horrified, to come on the nobleman's body dangling from one of his own trees as from a gibbet, or floating in his own pool like a pallid weed. What horrified him was to find nothing.

He soon become conscious that he was not alone even in his most individual and isolated experiments. He often found a figure following him like his shadow, in silent and almost secret clearings in the plantation or outlying nooks and corners of the old wall. The dark-moustached mouth was as mute as the deep eyes were mobile, darting incessantly hither and thither, but it was clear that Brain of the Indian police had taken up the trail like an old hunter after a tiger. Seeing that he was the only personal friend of the vanished man, this seemed natural enough, and Fisher resolved to deal frankly with him.

'This silence is rather a social strain,' he said. 'May I break the ice by talking about the weather? – which, by the way, has already broken the ice. I know that breaking the ice might be a rather melancholy metaphor in this case.'

'I don't think so,' replied Brain, shortly. 'I don't fancy the ice had much to do with it. I don't see how it could.'

'What would you propose doing?' asked Fisher.

'Well, we've sent for the authorities, of course, but I hope to find something out before they come,' replied the Anglo-Indian. 'I can't say I have much hope from police methods in this country. Too much red tape, habeas corpus and that sort of thing. What we want is to see that nobody bolts; the nearest we could get to it would be to collect the company and count them, so to speak. Nobody's left lately, except that lawyer who was poking about for antiquities.'

'Oh, he's out of it; he left last night,' answered the other. 'Eight hours after Bulmer's chauffeur saw his lawyer off by the train I heard Bulmer's own voice as plain as I hear yours now.'

'I suppose you don't believe in spirits?' said the man from India. After a pause he added: 'There's somebody else I should like to find, before we go after a fellow with an alibi in the Inner Temple. What's become of that fellow in green – the architect dressed up as a forester? I haven't seen him about.'

Mr Brain managed to secure his assembly of all the distracted company before the arrival of the police. But when he first began to comment once more on the young architect's delay in putting in an appearance, he found himself in the presence of a minor mystery, and a psychological development of an entirely unexpected kind.

Juliet Bray had confronted the catastrophe of her brother's disappearance with a sombre stoicism in which there was, perhaps, more paralysis than pain; but when the other question came to the surface she was both agitated and angry.

'We don't want to jump to any conclusions about anybody,' Brain was saying in his staccato style. 'But we should like to know a little more about Mr Crane. Nobody seems to know much about him, or where he comes from. And it seems a sort of coincidence that yesterday he actually crossed swords with poor Bulmer, and could have stuck him, too, since he showed himself the better swordsman. Of course, that may be an accident and couldn't possibly be called a case against anybody; but then we haven't the means to make a real case against anybody. Till the police come we are only a pack of very amateur sleuth-hounds.'

'And I think you're a pack of snobs,' said Juliet. 'Because Mr Crane is a genius who's made his own way, you try to suggest he's a murderer without daring to say so. Because he wore a toy sword and happened to know how to use it, you want us to believe he used it like a bloodthirsty maniac for no reason in the world. And because he could have hit my brother and didn't, you deduce that he did. That's the sort of way you argue. And as for his having disappeared, you're wrong in that as you are in everything else, for here he comes.'

And, indeed, the green figure of the fictitious Robin Hood slowly detached itself from the grey background of the trees, and came towards them as she spoke.

He approached the group slowly, but with composure; but he was decidedly pale, and the eyes of Brain and Fisher had already taken in one detail of the green-clad figure more clearly than all the rest. The horn still swung from his baldrick, but the sword was gone.

Rather to the surprise of the company, Brain did not follow up the question thus suggested; but, while retaining an air of leading the enquiry, had also an appearance of changing the subject.

'Now we're all assembled,' he observed, quietly, 'there is a question I want to ask to begin with. Did anybody here actually see Lord Bulmer this morning?'

Leonard Crane turned his pale face round the circle of faces till he came to Juliet's; then he compressed his lips a little and said: 'Yes, I saw him.'

'Was he alive and well?' asked Brain, quickly. 'How was he dressed?'

'He appeared exceedingly well,' replied Crane, with a curious intonation. 'He was dressed as he was yesterday, in that purple costume copied from the portrait of his ancestor in the sixteenth century. He had his skates in his hand.'

'And his sword at his side, I suppose,' added the questioner. 'Where is your own sword, Mr Crane?'

'I threw it away.'

In the singular silence that ensued, the train of thought in many minds became involuntarily a series of coloured pictures.

They had grown used to their fanciful garments looking more gay and gorgeous against the dark grey and streaky silver of the forest, so that the moving figures glowed like stained-glass saints walking. The effect had been more fitting because so many of them had idly parodied pontifical or monastic dress. But the most arresting attitude that remained in their memories had been anything but merely monastic; that of the moment when the figure in bright green and the other in vivid violet had for a moment made a silver cross of their crossing swords. Even when it was a jest it had been something of a drama; and it was a strange and sinister thought that in the grey daybreak the same figures in the same posture might have been repeated as a tragedy.

'Did you quarrel with him?' asked Brain, suddenly.

'Yes,' replied the immovable man in green. 'Or he quarrelled with me.'

'Why did he quarrel with you?' asked the investigator; and Leonard Crane made no reply.

Horne Fisher, curiously enough, had only given half his attention to this crucial cross-examination. His heavy-lidded eyes had languidly followed the figure of Prince Borodino, who at this stage had strolled away towards the fringe of the wood; and, after a pause, as of meditation, had disappeared into the darkness of the trees.

He was recalled from his irrelevance by the voice of Juliet Bray, which rang out with an altogether new note of decision: 'If that is the difficulty, it had best be cleared up. I am engaged to Mr Crane, and when we told my brother he did not approve of it; that is all.'

Neither Brain nor Fisher exhibited any surprise, but the former added, quietly: 'Except, I suppose, that he and your brother went off into the wood to discuss it, where Mr Crane mislaid his sword, not to mention his companion.'

'And may I ask,' enquired Crane, with a certain flicker of mockery passing over his pallid features, 'what I am supposed to have done with either of them? Let us adopt the cheerful thesis that I am a murderer; it has yet to be shown that I am a magician. If I ran your unfortunate friend through the body, what did I do with the body? Did I have it carried away by seven flying dragons, or was it merely a trifling matter of turning it into a milk-white hind?'

'It is no occasion for sneering,' said the Anglo-Indian judge, with abrupt authority. 'It doesn't make it look better for you that you can joke about the loss.'

Fisher's dreamy, and even dreary eye was still on the edge of the wood behind, and he became conscious of masses of dark red, like a stormy sunset cloud, glowing through the grey network of the thin trees, and the prince in his cardinal's robes re-emerged on to the pathway. Brain had had half a notion that the prince might have gone to look for the lost rapier. But when he reappeared he was carrying in his hand, not a sword, but an axe.

The incongruity between the masquerade and the mystery had created a curious psychological atmosphere. At first they had all felt horribly ashamed at being caught in the foolish disguises of a festival, by an event that had only too much the character of a funeral. Many of them would have already gone back and dressed in clothes that were more funereal or at least more formal. But somehow at the moment this seemed like a second masquerade, more artificial and frivolous than the first. And as they reconciled themselves to their ridiculous trappings, a curious sensation had come over some of them, notably over the more sensitive, like Crane and Fisher and Juliet, but in some degree over everybody except the practical Mr Brain. It was almost as if they were the ghosts of their own ancestors haunting that dark wood and dismal lake, and playing some old part that they only half remembered. The movements of those coloured figures seemed to mean something that had been settled long before, like a silent heraldry. Acts, attitudes, external objects, were accepted as an allegory even without the key; and they knew when a crisis had come, when they did not know what it was. And somehow they knew subconsciously that the whole tale had taken a new and terrible turn, when they saw the prince stand in the gap of the gaunt trees, in his robes of angry crimson and with his lowering face of bronze, bearing in his hand a new shape of death. They could not have named a reason, but the two swords seemed indeed to have become toy swords and the whole tale of them broken and tossed away like a toy. Borodino looked like the Old World headsman, clad in terrible red, and carrying the axe for the execution of the criminal. And the criminal was not Crane.

Mr Brain of the Indian police was glaring at the new object, and it was a moment or two before he spoke, harshly and almost hoarsely.

'What are you doing with that?' he asked. 'Seems to be a woodsman's chopper.'

'A natural association of ideas,' observed Horne Fisher. 'If you meet a cat in a wood you think it's a wildcat, though it may have just strolled from the drawing-room sofa. As a matter of fact, I happen to know that is not the woodsman's chopper. It's the kitchen chopper, or meat axe, or something like that, that somebody has thrown away in the wood. I saw it in the kitchen myself when I was getting the potato sacks with which I reconstructed a mediaeval hermit.'

'All the same, it is not without interest,' remarked the prince, holding out the instrument to Fisher, who took it and examined it carefully. 'A butcher's cleaver that has done butcher's work.'

'It was certainly the instrument of the crime,' assented Fisher, in a low voice.

Brain was staring at the dull blue gleam of the axe head with fierce and fascinated eyes. 'I don't understand you,' he said. 'There is no – there are no marks on it.'

'It has shed no blood,' answered Fisher, 'but for all that it has committed a crime. This is as near as the criminal came to the crime when he committed it.'

'What do you mean?'

'He was not there when he did it,' explained Fisher. 'It's a poor sort of murderer who can't murder people when he isn't there.'

'You seem to be talking merely for the sake of mystification,' said Brain. 'If you have any practical advice to give you might as well make it intelligible.'

'The only practical advice I can suggest,' said Fisher, thoughtfully, 'is a little research into local topography and nomenclature. They say there used to be a Mr Prior, who had a farm in this neighbourhood. I think some details about the domestic life of the late Mr Prior would throw a light on this terrible business.'

'And you have nothing more immediate than your topography to offer,' said Brain, with a sneer, 'to help me avenge my friend?'

'Well,' said Fisher, 'I should find out the truth about the Hole in the Wall.'

* * *

That night, at the close of a stormy twilight and under a strong west wind that followed the breaking of the frost, Leonard Crane was wending his way in a wild rotatory walk round and round the high, continuous wall that enclosed the little wood. He was driven by a desperate idea of solving for himself the riddle that had clouded his reputation and already even threatened his liberty. The police authorities, now in charge of the enquiry, had not arrested him, but he knew well enough that if he tried to move far afield he would be instantly arrested. Horne Fisher's fragmentary hints, though he had refused to expand them as yet, had stirred the artistic temperament of the architect to a sort of wild analysis, and he was resolved to read the hieroglyph upside down and every way until it made sense. If it was something connected with a hole in the wall he would find the hole in the wall; but, as a matter of fact, he was unable to find the faintest crack in the wall. His professional knowledge told him that the masonry was all of one workmanship and one date, and, except for the regular entrance, which threw no light on the mystery, he found nothing suggesting any sort of hiding place or means of escape. Walking a narrow path between the winding wall and the wild eastward bend and sweep of the grey and feathery trees, seeing shifting gleams of a lost sunset winking almost like lightning as the clouds of tempest scudded across the sky and mingling with the first faint blue light from a slowly strengthened moon behind him, he began to feel his head going round as his heels were going round and round the blind recurrent barrier. He had thoughts on the border of thought; fancies about a fourth dimension which was itself a hole to hide anything, of seeing everything from a new angle out of a new window in the senses; or of some mystical light and transparency, like the new rays of chemistry, in which he could see Bulmer's body, horrible and glaring, floating in a lurid halo over the woods and the wall. He was haunted also with the hint, which somehow seemed to be equally horrifying, that it all had something to do with Mr Prior. There seemed even to be something creepy in the fact that he was always respectfully referred to as Mr Prior, and that it was in the domestic life of the dead farmer that he had been bidden to seek the seed of these dreadful things. As a matter of fact, he had found that no local enquiries had revealed anything at all about the Prior family. He dimly imagined Mr prior in an old top-hat, perhaps with a chin-beard or whiskers. But he had no face.

The moonlight had broadened and brightened, the wind had driven off the clouds and itself died fitfully away, when he came round again to the artificial lake in front of the house. For some reason it looked a very artificial lake; indeed, the whole scene was like a classical landscape with a touch of Watteau; the Palladian façade of the house pale in the moon, and the same silver touching the very pagan and naked marble nymph in the middle of the pond. Rather to his surprise, he found another figure there beside the statue, sitting almost equally motionless; and the same silver pencil traced the wrinkled brow and patient face of Horne Fisher, still dressed as a hermit and apparently practising something of the solitude of a hermit. Nevertheless, he looked up at Leonard Crane and smiled, almost as if he had expected him.

'Look here,' said Crane, planting himself in front of him, 'can you tell me anything about this business?'

'I shall soon have to tell everybody everything about it,' replied Fisher, 'but I've no objection to telling you something first. But, to begin with, will you tell me something? What really happened when you met Bulmer this morning? You did throw away your sword, but you didn't kill him.'

'I didn't kill him because I threw away my sword,' said the other. 'I did it on purpose – or I'm not sure what might have happened.'

After a pause he went on, quietly: 'The late Lord Bulmer was a very breezy gentleman, extremely breezy. He was very genial with his inferiors, and would have his lawyer and his architect staying in his house for all sorts of holidays and amusements. But there was another side to him, which they found out when they tried to be his equals. When I told him that his sister and I were engaged, something happened which I simply can't and won't describe. It seemed to me like some monstrous upheaval of madness. But I suppose the truth is painfully simple. There is such a thing as the coarseness of a gentleman. And it is the most horrible thing in humanity.'

'I know,' said Fisher. 'The Renaissance nobles of the Tudor time were like that.'

'It is odd that you should say that,' Crane went on. 'For while we were talking there came on me a curious feeling that we were repeating some scene of the past, and that I was really some outlaw, found in the woods like Robin Hood, and that he had really stepped in all his plumes and purple out of the picture frame of the ancestral portrait. Anyhow, he was the man in possession, and he neither feared God nor regarded man. I defied him, of course, and walked away. I might really have killed him if I had not walked away.'

'Yes,' said Fisher, nodding, 'his ancestor was in possession and he was in possession, and this is the end of the story. It all fits in.'

'Fits in with what?' cried his companion, with sudden impatience. 'I can't make head or tail of it. You tell me to look for the secret in the hole in the wall, but I can't find any hole in the wall.'

'There isn't any,' said Fisher. 'That's the secret.' After reflecting a moment, he added: 'Unless you call it a hole in the wall of the world. Look here; I'll tell you if you like, but I'm afraid it involves an introduction. You've got to understand one of the tricks of the modern mind, a tendency that most people obey without noticing it. In the village or suburb outside there's an inn with the sign of St George and the Dragon. Now suppose I went about telling everybody that this was only a corruption of King George and the Dragoon. Scores of people would believe it, without any enquiry, from a vague feeling that it's probable because it's prosaic. It turns something romantic and legendary into something recent and ordinary. And that somehow makes it sound rational, though it is unsupported by reason. Of course some people would have the sense to remember having seen St George in old Italian pictures and French romances, but a good many wouldn't think about it at all. They would just swallow the scepticism because it was scepticism. Modern intelligence won't accept anything on authority. But it will accept anything without authority. That's exactly what has happened here.

'When some critic or other chose to say that Prior's Park was not a priory, but was named after some quite modern man named Prior, nobody really tested the theory at all. It never occurred to anybody repeating the story to ask if there *was* any Mr Prior, if anybody had ever seen him or heard of him. As a matter of fact, it was a priory, and shared the fate of most priories – that is, the Tudor gentleman with the plumes simply stole it by brute force and turned it into his own private house; he did worse things, as you shall hear. But the point here is that this is how the trick works, and the trick works in the same way in the other part of the tale. The name of this district is printed Holinwall in all the best maps produced by the scholars; and they allude lightly, not without a smile, to the fact that it was pronounced Holiwell by the most ignorant and old-fashioned of the poor. But it is spelled wrong and pronounced right.'

'Do you mean to say,' asked Crane, quickly, 'that there really was a well?'

'There is a well,' said Fisher, 'and the truth lies at the bottom of it.'

As he spoke he stretched out his hand and pointed towards the sheet of water in front of him.

'The well is under that water somewhere,' he said, 'and this is not the first tragedy connected with it. The founder of this house did something which his fellow ruffians very seldom did; something that had to be hushed up even in the anarchy of the pillage of the monasteries. The well was connected with the miracles of some saint, and the last prior that guarded it was something like a saint himself; certainly he was something very like a martyr. He defied the new owner and dared him to pollute the place, till the noble, in a fury, stabbed him and flung his body into the well, whither, after four hundred years, it has been followed by an heir of the usurper, clad in the same purple and walking the world with the same pride.'

'But how did it happen,' demanded Crane, 'that for the first time Bulmer fell in at that particular spot?'

'Because the ice was only loosened at that particular spot, by the only man who knew it,' answered Horne Fisher. 'It was cracked deliberately, with the kitchen chopper, at that special place; and I myself heard the hammering and did not understand it. The place had been covered with an artificial lake, if only because the whole truth had to be covered with an artificial legend. But don't you see that it is exactly what those pagan nobles would have done, to desecrate it with a sort of heathen goddess, as the Roman Emperor built a temple to Venus on the Holy Sepulchre? But the truth could still be traced out, by any scholarly man determined to trace it. And this man was determined to trace it.'

'What man?' asked the other, with a shadow of the answer in his mind.

'The only man who has an alibi,' replied Fisher. 'James Haddow, the antiquarian lawyer, left the night before the fatality, but he left that black star of death on the ice. He left abruptly, having previously proposed to stay; probably, I think, after an ugly scene with Bulmer, at their legal interview. As you know yourself, Bulmer could make a man feel pretty murderous, and I rather fancy the lawyer had himself irregularities to confess, and was in danger of exposure by his client. But it's my reading of human nature that a man will cheat in his trade, but not in his hobby. Haddow may have been a dishonest lawyer, but he couldn't help being an honest antiquary. When he got on the track of the truth about the Holy Well he had to follow it up; he was not to be bamboozled with newspaper anecdotes about Mr Prior and a hole in the wall; he found out everything, even to the exact location of the well, and he was rewarded, if being a successful assassin can be regarded as a reward.'

'And how did you get on the track of all this hidden history?' asked the young architect.

A cloud came across the brow of Horne Fisher. 'I knew only too much about it already,' he said, 'and, after all, it's shameful for me to be speaking lightly of poor Bulmer, who has paid his penalty; but the rest of us haven't. I dare say every cigar I smoke and every liqueur I drink comes directly or indirectly from the harrying of the holy places and the persecution of the poor. After all, it needs very little poking about in the past to find that hole in the wall, that great breach in the defences of English history. It lies just under the surface of a thin sheet of sham information and instruction, just as the black and blood-stained well lies just under that floor of shallow water and flat weeds. Oh, the ice is thin, but it bears; it is strong enough to support us when we dress up as monks and dance on it, in mockery of the dear, quaint old Middle Ages. They told me I must put on fancy dress; so I did put on fancy dress, according to my own taste and fancy. I put on the only costume I think fit for a man who has inherited the position of a gentleman, and yet has not entirely lost the feelings of one.'

In answer to a look of enquiry, he rose with a sweeping and downward gesture.

'Sackcloth,' he said; 'and I would wear the ashes as well if they would stay on my bald head when I put them there.'

7
The Fool of the Family

Harold March and the few who cultivated the friendship of Horne Fisher, especially if they saw something of him in his own social setting, were conscious of a certain solitude in his very sociability. They seemed to be always meeting his relations and never meeting his family. Perhaps it would be truer to say that they saw much of his family and nothing of his home. His cousins and connections ramified like a labyrinth all over the governing class of Great Britain, and he seemed to be on good, or at least on good-humoured, terms with most of them. For Horne Fisher was remarkable for a curious impersonal information and interest touching all sorts of topics, so that one could sometimes fancy that his culture, like his colourless, fair moustache and pale, drooping features, had the neutral nature of a chameleon. Anyhow, he could always get on with viceroys and Cabinet Ministers and all the great men responsible for great departments, and talk to each of them on his own subject, on the branch of study with which he was most seriously concerned. Thus he could converse with the Minister for War about silkworms, with the Minister of Education about detective stories, with the Minister of Labour about Limoges enamel, and with the Minister of Missions and Moral Progress (if that be his correct title) about the pantomime boys of the last four decades. And as the first was his first cousin, the second his second cousin, the third his brother-in-law, and the fourth his uncle by marriage, this conversational versatility certainly served in one sense to create a happy family. But March never seemed to get a glimpse of that domestic interior to which men of the middle classes are accustomed in their friendships, and which is indeed the foundation of friendship and love and everything else in any sane and stable society. He wondered whether Horne Fisher was both an orphan and an only child.

It was, therefore, with something like a start that he found that Fisher had a brother, much more prosperous and powerful than himself, though hardly, March thought, so entertaining. Sir Henry Harland Fisher, with half the alphabet after his name, was something at the Foreign Office far more tremendous than the Foreign Secretary. Apparently, it ran in the family, after all; for it seemed there was another brother, Ashton Fisher, in India, rather more tremendous than the Viceroy. Sir Henry Fisher was a heavier, but handsomer edition of his brother, with a brow equally bald, but much more smooth. He was very courteous, but a shade patronising, not only to

March, but even, as March fancied, to Horne Fisher as well. The latter gentleman, who had many intuitions about the half-formed thoughts of others, glanced at the topic himself as they came away from the great house in Berkeley Square.

'Why, don't you know,' he observed quietly, 'that I am the fool of the family?'

'It must be a clever family,' said Harold March, with a smile.

'Very gracefully expressed,' replied Fisher; 'that is the best of having a literary training. Well, perhaps it is an exaggeration to say I am the fool of the family. It's enough to say I am the failure of the family.'

'It seems queer to me that you should fail especially,' remarked the journalist. 'As they say in the examinations, what did you fail in?'

'Politics,' replied his friend. 'I stood for Parliament when I was quite a young man and got in by an enormous majority, with loud cheers and chairing round the town. Since then, of course, I've been rather under a cloud.'

'I'm afraid I don't quite understand the "of course",' answered March, laughing.

'That part of it isn't worth understanding,' said Fisher. 'But as a matter of fact, old chap, the other part of it was rather odd and interesting. Quite a detective story in its way, as well as the first lesson I had in what modern politics are made of. If you like, I'll tell you all about it.' And the following, recast in a less allusive and conversational manner, is the story that he told.

* * *

Nobody privileged of late years to meet Sir Henry Harland Fisher would believe that he had ever been called Harry. But, indeed, he had been boyish enough when a boy, and that serenity which shone on him through life, and which now took the form of gravity, had once taken the form of gaiety. His friends would have said that he was all the more ripe in his maturity for having been young in his youth. His enemies would have said that he was still light-minded, but no longer light-hearted. But in any case, the whole of the story Horne Fisher had to tell arose out of the accident which had made young Harry Fisher private secretary to Lord Saltoun. Hence his later connection with the Foreign Office, which had, indeed, come to him as a sort of legacy from his lordship when that great man was the power behind the throne. This is not the place to say much about Saltoun, little as was known of him and much as there was worth knowing. England has had at least three or four such secret statesmen. An aristocratic polity produces every now and then an aristocrat who is also an accident, a man of intellectual independence and insight, a Napoleon born in the purple. His vast work was mostly invisible, and very little could be got out of him in private life except a crusty and rather cynical sense of humour. But it was certainly the accident of his presence at a family dinner of the Fishers, and the unexpected opinion he expressed, which turned what might have been a dinner-table joke into a sort of small sensational novel.

Save for Lord Saltoun, it was a family party of Fishers, for the only other distinguished stranger had just departed after dinner, leaving the rest to their coffee and cigars. This had been a figure of some interest – a young Cambridge man named Eric Hughes, who was the rising hope of the party of Reform to which the Fisher family, along with their friend Saltoun, had long been at least formally attached. The personality of Hughes was substantially summed up in the fact that he talked eloquently and earnestly through the whole dinner, but left immediately after to be in time for an appointment. All his actions had something at once ambitious and conscientious; he drank no wine, but was slightly intoxicated with words. And his face and phrases were on the front page of all the newspapers just then, because he was contesting the safe seat of Sir Francis Verner in the great by-election in the west. Everybody was talking about the powerful speech against squirearchy which he had just delivered; even in the Fisher circle everybody talked about it except Horne Fisher himself, who sat in a corner, lowering over the fire. In his early manhood the manner which afterwards became languid had rather the air of being sullen; he drifted about and dipped into odd books on odd subjects; in contrast with his political family, his future seemed featureless and undetermined.

'We jolly well have to thank him for putting some new life into the old party,' Ashton Fisher was saying. 'This campaign against the old squires just hits the degree of democracy there is in this county. This act for extending county council control is practically his bill; so you may say he's in the government even before he's in the House.'

'One's easier than the other,' said Harry, carelessly. 'I bet the squire's a bigger pot than the county council in that country. Verner is pretty well rooted; all these rural places are what you call reactionary. Damning aristocrats won't alter it.'

'He damns them rather well,' observed Ashton. 'We never had a better meeting than the one in Barkington, which generally goes Constitutional. And when he said, "Sir Francis may boast of blue blood; let us show we have red blood," and went on to talk about manhood and liberty, the room simply rose at him.'

'Speaks very well,' said Lord Saltoun, gruffly, making his only contribution to the conversation so far.

Then the almost equally silent Horne Fisher suddenly spoke, without taking his brooding eyes off the fire.

'What I can't understand,' he said, 'is why nobody is ever slanged for the real reason.'

'Hullo!' remarked Harry, humorously, 'you beginning to take notice?'

'Well, take Verner,' continued Horne Fisher. 'If we want to attack Verner, why not attack him? Why compliment him on being a romantic reactionary aristocrat? Who is Verner? Where does he come from? His name sounds old, but I never heard of it before, as the man said of the Crucifixion. Why talk about his blue blood? His blood may be gamboge yellow with green spots, for all anybody knows. All we know is that the old squire, Hawker, somehow ran through his money (and his second wife's, I suppose, for she was rich enough), and sold the estate to a man named Verner. What did he make his money in? Oil? Army contracts?'

'I don't know,' said Saltoun, looking at him thoughtfully.

'First thing I ever knew you didn't know,' cried the exuberant Harry.

'And there's more, besides,' went on Horne Fisher, who seemed to have suddenly found his tongue. 'If we want country people to vote for us, why don't we get somebody with some notion about the country? We don't talk to people in Threadneedle Street about nothing but turnips and pigsties. Why do we talk to people in Somerset about nothing but slums and socialism? Why don't we give the squire's land to the squire's tenants, instead of dragging in the county council?'

'Three acres and a cow,' cried Harry, emitting what the Parliamentary reports call an ironical cheer.

'Yes,' replied his brother, stubbornly. 'Don't you think agricultural labourers would rather have three acres and a cow than three acres of printed forms and a committee? Why doesn't somebody start a yeoman party in politics, appealing to the old traditions of the small landowner? And why don't they attack men like Verner for what they are, which is something about as old and traditional as an American oil trust?'

'You'd better lead the yeoman party yourself,' laughed Harry. 'Don't you think it would be a joke, Lord Saltoun, to see my brother and his merry men, with their bows and bills, marching down to Somerset all in Lincoln green instead of Lincoln and Bennet hats?'

'No,' answered Old Saltoun, 'I don't think it would be a joke. I think it would be an exceedingly serious and sensible idea.'

'Well, I'm jiggered!' cried Harry Fisher, staring at him. 'I said just now it was the first fact you didn't know, and I should say this is the first joke you didn't see.'

'I've seen a good many things in my time,' said the old man, in his rather sour fashion. 'I've told a good many lies in my time, too, and perhaps I've got rather sick of them. But there are lies and lies, for all that. Gentlemen used to lie just as schoolboys lie, because they hung together and partly to help one another out. But I'm damned if I can see why we should lie for these cosmopolitan cads who only help themselves. They're not backing us up any more; they're simply crowding us out. If a man like your brother likes to go into Parliament as a yeoman or a gentleman or a Jacobite or an Ancient Briton, I should say it would be a jolly good thing.'

In the rather startled silence that followed Horne Fisher sprang to his feet and all his dreary manner dropped off him.

'I'm ready to do it tomorrow,' he cried. 'I suppose none of you fellows would back me up.'

Then Harry Fisher showed the finer side of his impetuosity. He made a sudden movement as if to shake hands.

'You're a sport,' he said, 'and I'll back you up, if nobody else will. But we can all back you up, can't we? I see what Lord Saltoun means, and, of course, he's right. He's always right.'

'So I will go down to Somerset,' said Horne Fisher.

'Yes, it is on the way to Westminster,' said Lord Saltoun, with a smile.

And so it happened that Horne Fisher arrived some days later at the little station of a rather remote market town in the west, accompanied by a light suitcase and a lively brother. It must not be supposed, however, that the brother's cheerful tone consisted entirely of chaff. He supported the new candidate with hope as well as hilarity; and at the back of his boisterous partnership there was an increasing sympathy and encouragement. Harry Fisher had always had an affection for his more quiet and eccentric brother, and was now coming more and more to have a respect for him. As the campaign proceeded the respect increased to ardent admiration. For Harry was still young, and could feel the sort of enthusiasm for his captain in electioneering that a schoolboy can feel for his captain in cricket.

Nor was the admiration undeserved. As the new three-cornered contest developed it became apparent to others besides his devoted kinsman that there was more in Horne Fisher than had ever met the eye. It was clear that his outbreak by the family fireside had been but the culmination of a long course of brooding and studying on the question. The talent he retained through life for studying his subject, and even somebody else's subject, had long been concentrated on this idea of championing a new peasantry against a new plutocracy. He spoke to a crowd with eloquence and replied to an individual with humour, two political arts that seemed to come to him naturally. He certainly knew much more about rural problems than either Hughes, the Reform candidate, or Verner, the Constitutional candidate. And he probed those problems with a human curiosity, and went below the surface in a way that neither of them dreamed of doing. He soon became the voice of popular feelings that are never found in the popular press. New angles of criticism, arguments that had never before been uttered by an educated voice, tests and comparisons that had been made only in dialect by men drinking in the little local public houses, crafts half forgotten that had come down by sign of hand and tongue from remote ages when their fathers were free – all this created a curious and double excitement. It startled the well informed by being a new and fantastic idea they had never encountered. It startled the ignorant by being an old and familiar idea they never thought to have seen revived. Men saw things in a new light, and knew not even whether it was the sunset or the dawn.

Practical grievances were there to make the movement formidable. As Fisher went to and fro among the cottages and country inns, it was borne in on him without difficulty that Sir Francis Verner was a very bad landlord. Nor was the story of his acquisition of the land any more ancient and dignified than he had supposed; the story was well known in the county and in most respects was obvious enough. Hawker, the old squire, had been a loose, unsatisfactory sort of person, had been on bad terms with his first wife (who died, as some said, of neglect), and had then married a flashy South American heiress with a fortune. But he must have worked his way through this fortune also with marvellous rapidity, for he had been compelled to sell the estate to Verner and had gone to live in South America, possibly on his wife's estates. But Fisher noticed that the laxity of the old squire was far less hated than the efficiency of the new squire. Verner's history seemed to be full of smart bargains and financial flutters that left other people short of money and temper. But though he heard a great deal about Verner, there was one thing that continually eluded him; something that nobody knew, that even Saltoun had not known. He could not find out how Verner had originally made his money.

'He must have kept it specially dark,' said Horne Fisher to himself. 'It must be something he's really ashamed of. Hang it all! what *is* a man ashamed of nowadays?'

And as he pondered on the possibilities they grew darker and more distorted in his mind; he thought vaguely of things remote and repulsive, strange forms of slavery or sorcery, and then of ugly things yet more unnatural but nearer home. The figure of Verner seemed to be blackened and transfigured in his imagination, and to stand against varied backgrounds and strange skies.

As he strode up a village street, brooding thus, his eyes encountered a complete contrast in the face of his other rival, the Reform candidate. Eric Hughes, with his blown blond hair and eager undergraduate face, was just getting into his motor car and saying a few final words to his agent, a sturdy, grizzled man named Gryce. Eric Hughes waved his hand in a friendly fashion; but Gryce eyed him with some hostility. Eric Hughes was a young man with genuine political enthusiasms, but he knew that political opponents are people with whom one may have to dine any day. But Mr Gryce was a grim little local Radical, a champion of the chapel, and one of those happy people whose work is also their hobby. He turned his back as the motor car drove away, and walked briskly up the sunlit high street of the little town, whistling, with political papers sticking out of his pocket.

Fisher looked pensively after the resolute figure for a moment, and then, as if by an impulse, began to follow it. Through the busy marketplace, amid the baskets and barrows of market day, under the painted wooden sign of the Green Dragon, up a dark side entry, under an arch, and through a tangle of crooked cobbled streets the two threaded their way, the square, strutting figure in front and the lean, lounging figure behind him, like his shadow in the sunshine. At length they came to a brown brick house with a brass plate, on which was Mr Gryce's name, and that individual turned and beheld his pursuer with a stare.

'Could I have a word with you, sir?' asked Horne Fisher, politely. The agent stared still more, but assented civilly, and led the other into an office littered with leaflets and hung all round with highly coloured posters which linked the name of Hughes with all the higher interests of humanity.

'Mr Horne Fisher, I believe,' said Mr Gryce. 'Much honoured by the call, of course. Can't pretend to congratulate you on entering the contest, I'm afraid; you won't expect that. Here we've been keeping the old flag flying for freedom and reform, and you come in and break the battle line.'

For Mr Elijah Gryce abounded in military metaphors and in denunciations of militarism. He was a square-jawed, blunt-featured man with a pugnacious cock of the eyebrow. He had been pickled in the politics of that countryside from boyhood, he knew everybody's secrets, and electioneering was the romance of his life.

'I suppose you think I'm devoured with ambition,' said Horne Fisher, in his rather listless voice, 'aiming at a dictatorship and all that. Well, I think I can clear myself of the charge of mere selfish ambition. I only want certain things done. I don't want to do them. I very seldom want to do anything. And I've come here to say that I'm quite willing to retire from the contest if you can convince me that we really want to do the same thing.'

The agent of the Reform party looked at him with an odd and slightly puzzled expression, and before he could reply, Fisher went on in the same level tones: 'You'd hardly believe it, but I keep a conscience concealed about me; and I am in doubt about several things. For instance, we both want to turn Verner out of Parliament, but what weapon are we to use? I've heard a lot of gossip against him, but is it right to act on mere gossip? Just as I want to be fair to you, so I want to be fair to him. If some of the things I've heard are true he ought to be turned out of Parliament and every other club in London. But I don't want to turn him out of Parliament if they aren't true.'

At this point the light of battle sprang into Mr Gryce's eyes and he became voluble, not to say violent. He, at any rate, had no doubt that the stories were true; he could testify, to his own knowledge, that they were true. Verner was not only a hard landlord, but a mean landlord, a robber as well as a rack-renter; any gentleman would be justified in hounding him out. He had cheated old Wilkins out of his freehold by a trick fit for a pickpocket; he had driven old Mother Biddle to the workhouse; he had stretched the law against Long Adam, the poacher, till all the magistrates were ashamed of him.

'So if you'll serve under the old banner,' concluded Mr Gryce, more genially, 'and turn out a swindling tyrant like that, I'm sure you'll never regret it.'

'And if that is the truth,' said Horne Fisher, 'are you going to tell it?'

'What do you mean? Tell the truth?' demanded Gryce.

'I mean you are going to tell the truth as you have just told it,' replied Fisher. 'You are going to placard this town with the wickedness done to old Wilkins. You are going to fill the newspapers with the infamous story of Mrs Biddle. You are going to denounce Verner from a public platform, naming him for what he did and naming the poacher he did it to. And you're going to find out by what trade this man made the money with which he bought the estate; and when you know the truth, as I said before, of course you are going to tell it. Upon those terms I come under the old flag, as you call it, and haul down my little pennon.'

The agent was eying him with a curious expression, surly but not entirely unsympathetic. 'Well,' he said, slowly, 'you have to do these things in a regular way, you know, or people don't understand. I've had a lot of experience, and I'm afraid what you say wouldn't do. People understand slanging squires in a general way, but those personalities aren't considered fair play. Looks like hitting below the belt.'

'Old Wilkins hasn't got a belt, I suppose,' replied Horne Fisher. 'Verner can hit him anyhow, and nobody must say a word. It's evidently very important to have a belt. But apparently you have to be rather high up in society to have one. Possibly,' he added, thoughtfully – 'possibly the explanation of the phrase "a belted earl", the meaning of which has always eluded me.'

'I mean those personalities won't do,' returned Gryce, frowning at the table.

'And Mother Biddle and Long Adam, the poacher, are not personalities,' said Fisher, 'and I suppose we mustn't ask how Verner made all the money that enabled him to become – a personality.'

Gryce was still looking at him under lowering brows, but the singular light in his eyes had brightened. At last he said, in another and much quieter voice: 'Look here, sir. I like you, if you don't mind my saying so. I think you are really on the side of the people and I'm sure you're a brave man. A lot braver than you know, perhaps. We daren't touch what you propose with a barge pole; and so far from wanting you in the old party, we'd rather you ran your own risk by yourself. But because I like you and respect your pluck, I'll do you a good turn before we part. I don't want you to waste time barking up the wrong tree. You talk about how the new squire got the money to buy, and the ruin of the old squire, and all the rest of it. Well, I'll give you a hint about that, a hint about something precious few people know.'

'I am very grateful,' said Fisher, gravely. 'What is it?'

'It's in two words,' said the other. 'The new squire was quite poor when he bought. The old squire was quite rich when he sold.'

Horne Fisher looked at him thoughtfully as he turned away abruptly and busied himself with the papers on his desk. Then Fisher uttered a short phrase of thanks and farewell, and went out into the street, still very thoughtful.

His reflection seemed to end in resolution, and, falling into a more rapid stride, he passed out of the little town along a road leading towards the gate of the great park, the country seat of Sir Francis Verner. A glitter of sunlight made the early winter more like a late autumn, and the dark woods were touched here and there with red and golden leaves, like the last rays of a lost sunset. From a higher part of the road he had seen the long, classical façade of the great house with its many windows, almost immediately beneath him, but when the road ran down under the wall of the estate, topped with towering trees behind, he realised that it was half a mile round to the lodge gates. After walking for a few minutes along the lane, however, he came to a place where the wall had cracked and was in process of repair. As it was, there was a great gap in the grey masonry that looked at first as black as a cavern and only showed at a second glance the twilight of the twinkling trees. There was something fascinating about that unexpected gate, like the opening of a fairy tale.

Horne Fisher had in him something of the aristocrat, which is very near to the anarchist. It was characteristic of him that he turned into this dark and irregular entry as casually as into his own front door, merely thinking that it would be a short cut to the house. He made his way through the dim wood for some distance and with some difficulty, until there began to shine through the trees a level light, in lines of silver, which he did not at first understand. The next moment he had come out into the daylight at the top of a steep bank, at the bottom of which a path ran round the rim of a large ornamental lake. The sheet of water which he had seen shimmering through the trees was of considerable extent, but was walled in on every side with woods which were not only dark, but decidedly dismal. At one end of the path was a classical statue of some nameless nymph, and at the other end it was flanked by two classical urns; but the marble was weather-stained and streaked with green and grey. A hundred other signs, smaller but more significant, told him that he had come on some outlying corner of the grounds neglected and seldom visited. In the middle of the lake was what appeared to be an island, and on the island what appeared to be meant for a classical temple, not open like a temple of the winds, but with a blank wall between its Doric pillars. We may say it only seemed like an island, because a second glance revealed a low causeway of flat stones running up to it from the shore and turning it into a peninsula. And certainly it only seemed like a temple, for nobody knew better than Horne Fisher that no god had ever dwelt in that shrine.

'That's what makes all this classical landscape gardening so desolate,' he said to himself. 'More desolate than Stonehenge or the Pyramids. We don't believe in Egyptian mythology, but the Egyptians did; and I suppose even the Druids believed in Druidism. But the eighteenth-century gentleman who built these temples didn't believe in Venus or Mercury any more than we do; that's why the reflection of those pale pillars in the lake is truly only the shadow of a shade. They were men of the age of Reason; they, who filled their gardens with these stone nymphs, had less hope than any men in all history of really meeting a nymph in the forest.'

His monologue stopped abruptly with a sharp noise like a thunder crack that rolled in dreary echoes round the dismal mere. He knew at once what it was – somebody had fired off a gun. But as to the meaning of it he was momentarily staggered, and strange thoughts thronged into his mind. The next moment he laughed; for he saw lying a little way along the path below him the dead bird that the shot had brought down.

At the same moment, however, he saw something else, which interested him more. A ring of dense trees ran round the back of the island temple, framing the façade of it in dark foliage, and he could have sworn he saw a stir as of something moving among the leaves. The next moment his suspicion was confirmed, for a rather ragged figure came from under the shadow of the temple and began to move along the causeway that led to the bank. Even at that distance the figure was conspicuous by its great height and Fisher could see that the man carried a gun under his arm. There came back into his memory at once the name of Long Adam, the poacher.

With a rapid sense of strategy he sometimes showed, Fisher sprang from the bank and raced round the lake to the head of the little pier of stones. If once a man reached the mainland he could easily vanish into the woods. But when Fisher began to advance along the stones towards the island, the man was cornered in a blind alley and could only back towards the temple. Putting his broad shoulders against it, he stood as if at bay; he was a comparatively young man, with fine lines in his lean face and figure and a mop of ragged red hair. The look in his eyes might well have been disquieting to anyone left alone with him on an island in the middle of a lake.

'Good-morning,' said Horne Fisher, pleasantly. 'I thought at first you were a murderer. But it seems unlikely, somehow, that the partridge rushed between us and died for love of me, like the heroines in the romances; so I suppose you are a poacher.'

'I suppose you would call me a poacher,' answered the man; and his voice was something of a surprise coming from such a scarecrow; it had that hard fastidiousness to be found in those who have made a fight for their own refinement among rough surroundings. 'I consider I have a perfect right to shoot game in this place. But I am well aware that people of your sort take me for a thief, and I suppose you will try to land me in jail.'

'There are preliminary difficulties,' replied Fisher. 'To begin with, the mistake is flattering, but I am not a gamekeeper. Still less am I three gamekeepers, who would be, I imagine, about your fighting weight. But I confess I have another reason for not wanting to jail you.'

'And what is that?' asked the other.

'Only that I quite agree with you,' answered Fisher. 'I don't exactly say you have a right to poach, but I never could see that it was as wrong as being a thief. It seems to me against the whole normal notion of property that a man should own something because it flies across his garden. He might as well own the wind, or think he could write his name on a morning cloud. Besides, if we want poor people to respect property we must give them some property to respect. You ought to have land of your own; and I'm going to give you some if I can.'

'Going to give me some land!' repeated Long Adam.

'I apologise for addressing you as if you were a public meeting,' said Fisher, 'but I am an entirely new kind of public man who says the same thing in public and in private. I've said this to a hundred huge meetings throughout the county, and I say it to you on this queer little island in this dismal pond. I would cut up a big estate like this into small estates for everybody, even for poachers. I would do in England as they did in Ireland – buy the big men out, if possible; get them out, anyhow. A man like you ought to have a little place of his own. I don't say you could keep pheasants, but you might keep chickens.'

The man stiffened suddenly and he seemed at once to blanch and flame at the promise as if it were a threat.

'Chickens!' he repeated, with a passion of contempt.

'Why do you object?' asked the placid candidate. 'Because keeping hens is rather a mild amusement for a poacher? What about poaching eggs?'

'Because I am not a poacher,' cried Adam, in a rending voice that rang round the hollow shrines and urns like the echoes of his gun. 'Because the partridge lying dead over there is my partridge. Because the land you are standing on is my land. Because my own land was only taken from me by a crime, and a worse crime than poaching. This has been a single estate for hundreds and hundreds of years, and if you or any meddlesome mountebank comes here and talks of cutting it up like a cake, if I ever hear a word more of you and your levelling lies – '

'You seem to be a rather turbulent public,' observed Horne Fisher, 'but do go on. What will happen if I try to divide this estate decently among decent people?'

The poacher had recovered a grim composure as he replied. 'There will be no partridge to rush in between.'

With that he turned his back, evidently resolved to say no more, and walked past the temple to the extreme end of the islet, where he stood staring into the water. Fisher followed him, but, when his repeated questions evoked no answer, turned back towards the shore. In doing so he took a second and closer look at the artificial temple, and noted some curious things about it. Most of these theatrical things were as thin as theatrical scenery, and he expected the classic shrine to be a shallow thing, a mere shell or mask. But there was some substantial bulk of it behind, buried in the trees, which had a grey, labyrinthian look, like serpents of stone, and lifted a load of leafy towers to the sky. But what arrested Fisher's eye was that in this bulk of grey-white stone behind there was a single door with great, rusty bolts outside; the bolts, however, were not shot across so as to secure it. Then he walked round the small building, and found no other opening except one small grating like a ventilator, high up in the wall. He retraced his steps thoughtfully along the causeway to the banks of the lake, and sat down on the stone steps between the two sculptured funereal urns. Then he lit a cigarette and smoked it in ruminant manner; eventually he took out a note-book and wrote down various phrases, numbering and renumbering them till they stood in the following order:

(1) Squire Hawker disliked his first wife.
(2) He married his second wife for her money.
(3) Long Adam says the estate is really his.
(4) Long Adam hangs round the island temple, which looks like a prison.
(5) Squire Hawker was not poor when he gave up the estate.
(6) Verner was poor when he got the estate.

He gazed at these notes with a gravity which gradually turned to a hard smile, threw away his cigarette, and resumed his search for a short cut to the great house. He soon picked up the path which, winding among clipped hedges and flower beds, brought him in front of its long Palladian façade. It had the usual appearance of being, not a private house, but a sort of public building sent into exile in the provinces.

He first found himself in the presence of the butler, who really looked much older than the building, for the architecture was dated as Georgian;

but the man's face, under a highly unnatural brown wig, was wrinkled with what might have been centuries. Only his prominent eyes were alive and alert, as if with protest. Fisher glanced at him, and then stopped and said: 'Excuse me. Weren't you with the late squire, Mr Hawker?'

'Yes, sir,' said the man, gravely. 'Usher is my name. What can I do for you?'

'Only take me into Sir Francis Verner,' replied the visitor.

Sir Francis Verner was sitting in an easy chair beside a small table in a large room hung with tapestries. On the table were a small flask and glass, with the green glimmer of a liqueur and a cup of black coffee. He was clad in a quiet grey suit with a moderately harmonious purple tie; but Fisher saw something about the turn of his fair moustache and the lie of his flat hair – it suddenly revealed that his name was Franz Werner.

'You are Mr Horne Fisher,' he said. 'Won't you sit down?'

'No, thank you,' replied Fisher. 'I fear this is not a friendly occasion, and I shall remain standing. Possibly you know that I am already standing – standing for Parliament, in fact – '

'I am aware we are political opponents,' replied Verner, raising his eyebrows. 'But I think it would be better if we fought in a sporting spirit; in a spirit of English fair play.'

'Much better,' assented Fisher. 'It would be much better if you were English and very much better if you had ever played fair. But what I've come to say can be said very shortly. I don't quite know how we stand with the law about that old Hawker story, but my chief object is to prevent England being entirely ruled by people like you. So whatever the law would say, I will say no more if you will retire from the election at once.'

'You are evidently a lunatic,' said Verner.

'My psychology may be a little abnormal,' replied Horne Fisher, in a rather hazy manner. 'I am subject to dreams, especially day-dreams. Sometimes what is happening to me grows vivid in a curious double way, as if it had happened before. Have you ever had that mystical feeling that things have happened before?'

'I hope you are a harmless lunatic,' said Verner.

But Fisher was still staring in an absent fashion at the golden gigantic figures and traceries of brown and red in the tapestries on the walls; then he looked again at Verner and resumed: 'I have a feeling that this interview has happened before, here in this tapestried room, and we are two ghosts revisiting a haunted chamber. But it was Squire Hawker who sat where you sit and it was you who stood where I stand.' He paused a moment and then added, with simplicity, 'I suppose I am a blackmailer, too.'

'If you are,' said Sir Francis, 'I promise you you shall go to jail.' But his face had a shade on it that looked like the reflection of the green wine gleaming on the table.

Horne Fisher regarded him steadily and answered, quietly enough: 'Blackmailers do not always go to jail. Sometimes they go to Parliament. But, though Parliament is rotten enough already, you shall not go there if I can help it. I am not so criminal as you were in bargaining with crime. You made a squire give up his country seat. I only ask you to give up your Parliamentary seat.'

Sir Francis Verner sprang to his feet and looked about for one of the bell ropes of the old-fashioned, curtained room.

'Where is Usher?' he cried, with a livid face.

'And who is Usher?' said Fisher, softly. 'I wonder how much Usher knows of the truth.'

Verner's hand fell from the bell rope and, after standing for a moment with rolling eyes, he strode abruptly from the room. Fisher went out by the other door, by which he had entered, and, seeing no sign of Usher, let himself out and betook himself again towards the town.

That night he put an electric torch in his pocket and set out alone in the darkness to add the last links to his argument. There was much that he did not know yet; but he thought he knew where he could find the knowledge. The night closed dark and stormy and the black gap in the wall looked blacker than ever; the wood seemed to have grown thicker and darker in a day. If the deserted lake with its black woods and grey urns and images looked desolate even by daylight, under the night and the growing storm it seemed still more like the pool of Acheron in the land of lost souls. As he stepped carefully along the jetty of stones he seemed to be travelling farther and farther into the abyss of night, and to have left behind him the last points from which it would be possible to signal to the land of the living. The lake seemed to have grown larger than a sea, but a sea of black and slimy waters that slept with abominable serenity, as if they had washed out the world. There was so much of this nightmare sense of extension and expansion that he was strangely surprised to come to his desert island so soon. But he knew it for a place of inhuman silence and solitude; and he felt as if he had been walking for years.

Nerving himself to a more normal mood, he paused under one of the dark dragon trees that branched out above him, and, taking out his torch, turned in the direction of the door at the back of the temple. It was unbolted as before, and the thought stirred faintly in him that it was slightly open, though only by a crack. The more he thought of it, however, the more certain he grew that this was but one of the common illusions of light coming from a different angle. He studied in a more scientific spirit the details of the door, with its rusty bolts and hinges, when he became conscious of something very near him – indeed, nearly above his head. Something was dangling from the tree that was not a broken branch. For some seconds he stood as still as a stone, and as cold. What he saw above him were the legs of a man hanging, presumably a dead man hanged. But the next moment he knew better. The man was literally alive and kicking; and an instant after he had dropped to the ground and turned on the intruder. Simultaneously three or four other trees seemed to come to life in the same fashion. Five or six other figures had fallen on their feet from these unnatural nests. It was as if the place were an island of monkeys. But a moment after they had made a stampede towards him, and when they laid their hands on him he knew that they were men.

With the electric torch in his hand he struck the foremost of them so furiously in the face that the man stumbled and rolled over on the slimy grass; but the torch was broken and extinguished, leaving everything in a denser obscurity. He flung another man flat against the temple wall, so that he slid to the ground; but a third and fourth carried Fisher off his feet and began to bear him, struggling, towards the doorway. Even in the bewilderment of the battle he was conscious that the door was standing open. Somebody was summoning the roughs from inside.

The moment they were within they hurled him upon a sort of bench or bed with violence, but no damage; for the settee, or whatever it was, seemed to be comfortably cushioned for his reception. Their violence had in it a great element of haste, and before he could rise they had all rushed for the door to escape. Whatever bandits they were that infested this desert island, they were obviously uneasy about their job and very anxious to be quit of it. He had the flying fancy that regular criminals would hardly be in such a panic. The next moment the great door crashed to and he could hear the bolts shriek as they shot into their place, and the feet of the retreating men scampering and stumbling along the causeway. But rapidly as it happened, it did not happen before Fisher had done something that he wanted to do. Unable to rise from his sprawling attitude in that flash of time, he had shot out one of his long legs and hooked it round the ankle of the last man disappearing through the door. The man swayed and toppled over inside the prison chamber, and the door closed between him and his fleeing companions. Clearly they were in too much haste to realise that they had left one of their company behind.

The man sprang to his feet again and hammered and kicked furiously at the door. Fisher's sense of humour began to recover from the struggle and he sat up on his sofa with something of his native nonchalance. But as he listened to the captive captor beating on the door of the prison, a new and curious reflection came to him.

The natural course for a man thus wishing to attract his friends' attention would be to call out, to shout as well as kick. This man was making as much noise as he could with his feet and hands, but not a sound came from his throat. Why couldn't he speak? At first he thought the man might be gagged, which was manifestly absurd. Then his fancy fell back on the ugly idea that the man was dumb. He hardly knew why it was so ugly an idea, but it affected his imagination in a dark and disproportionate fashion. There seemed to be something creepy about the idea of being left in a dark room with a deaf mute. It was almost as if such a defect were a deformity. It was almost as if it went with other and worse deformities. It was as if the shape he could not trace in the darkness were some shape that should not see the sun.

Then he had a flash of sanity and also of insight. The explanation was very simple, but rather interesting. Obviously the man did not use his voice because he did not wish his voice to be recognised. He hoped to escape from that dark place before Fisher found out who he was. And who was he? One thing at least was clear. He was one or other of the four or five men with whom Fisher had already talked in these parts, and in the development of that strange story.

'Now I wonder who you are,' he said, aloud, with all his old lazy urbanity. 'I suppose it's no use trying to throttle you in order to find out; it would be displeasing to pass the night with a corpse. Besides, I might be the corpse. I've got no matches and I've smashed my torch, so I can only speculate. Who could you be, now? Let us think.'

The man thus genially addressed had desisted from drumming on the door and retreated sullenly into a corner as Fisher continued to address him in a flowing monologue.

'Probably you are the poacher who says he isn't a poacher. He says he's a landed proprietor; but he will permit me to inform him that, whatever he is, he's a fool. What hope can there ever be of a free peasantry in England if the peasants themselves are such snobs as to want to be gentlemen? How can we make a democracy with no democrats? As it is, you want to be a landlord and so you consent to be a criminal. And in that, you know, you are rather like somebody else. And, now I think of it, perhaps you are somebody else.'

There was a silence broken by breathing from the corner and the murmur of the rising storm, that came in through the small grating above the man's head. Horne Fisher continued: 'Are you only a servant, perhaps, that rather sinister old servant who was butler to Hawker and Verner? If so, you are certainly the only link between the two periods. But if so, why do you degrade yourself to serve this dirty foreigner, when you at least saw the last of a genuine national gentry? People like you are generally at least patriotic. Doesn't England mean anything to you, Mr Usher? All of which eloquence is possibly wasted, as perhaps you are not Mr Usher.

'More likely you are Verner himself; and it's no good wasting eloquence to make you ashamed of yourself. Nor is it any good to curse you for corrupting England; nor are you the right person to curse. It is the English who deserve to be cursed, and are cursed, because they allowed such vermin to crawl into the high places of their heroes and their kings. I won't dwell on the idea that you're Verner, or the throttling might begin, after all. Is there anyone else you could be? Surely you're not some servant of the other rival organisation. I can't believe you're Gryce, the agent; and yet Gryce had a spark of the fanatic in his eye, too; and men will do extraordinary things in these paltry feuds of politics. Or if not the servant, is it the . . . No, I can't believe it . . . not the red blood of manhood and liberty . . . not the democratic ideal . . .'

He sprang up in excitement, and at the same moment a growl of thunder came through the grating beyond. The storm had broken, and with it a new light broke on his mind. There was something else that might happen in a moment.

'Do you know what that means?' he cried. 'It means that God himself may hold a candle to show me your infernal face.'

Then next moment came a crash of thunder; but before the thunder a white light had filled the whole room for a single split second.

Fisher had seen two things in front of him. One was the black-and-white pattern of the iron grating against the sky; the other was the face in the corner. It was the face of his brother. Nothing came from Horne Fisher's lips except a Christian name, which was followed by a silence more dreadful than the dark. At last the other figure stirred and sprang up, and the voice of Harry Fisher was heard for the first time in that horrible room.

'You've seen me, I suppose,' he said, 'and we may as well have a light now. You could have turned it on at any time, if you'd found the switch.'

He pressed a button in the wall and all the details of that room sprang into something stronger than daylight. Indeed, the details were so unexpected that for a moment they turned the captive's rocking mind from the last personal revelation. The room, so far from being a dungeon cell, was more like a drawing-room, even a lady's drawing-room, except for some boxes of cigars and bottles of wine that were stacked with books and magazines on a side table. A second glance showed him that the more masculine fittings were quite recent, and that the more feminine background was quite old. His eye caught a strip of faded tapestry, which startled him into speech, to the momentary oblivion of bigger matters.

'This place was furnished from the great house,' he said.

'Yes,' replied the other, 'and I think you know why.'

'I think I do,' said Horne Fisher, 'and before I go on to more extraordinary things, I will say what I think. Squire Hawker played both the bigamist and the bandit. His first wife was not dead when he married the heiress; she was imprisoned on this island. She bore him a child here, who now haunts his birthplace under the name of Long Adam. A bankrupt company promoter named Werner discovered the secret and blackmailed the squire into surrendering the estate. That's all quite clear and very easy. And now let me go on to something more difficult. And that is for you to explain what the devil you are doing kidnapping your born brother.'

After a pause Henry Fisher answered: 'I suppose you didn't expect to see me,' he said. 'But, after all, what could you expect?'

'I'm afraid I don't follow,' said Horne Fisher.

'I mean what else could you expect, after making such a muck of it?' said his brother, sulkily. 'We all thought you were so clever. How could we know you were going to be – well, really, such a rotten failure?'

'This is rather curious,' said the candidate, frowning. 'Without vanity, I was not under the impression that my candidature was a failure. All the big meetings were successful and crowds of people have promised me votes.'

'I should jolly well think they had,' said Henry, grimly. 'You've made a landslide with your confounded acres and a cow, and Verner can hardly get a vote anywhere. Oh, it's too rotten for anything!'

'What on earth do you mean?'

'Why, you lunatic,' cried Henry, in tones of ringing sincerity, 'you don't suppose you were meant to *win* the seat, did you? Oh, it's too childish! I tell you Verner's *got* to get in. Of course he's got to get in. He's to have the Exchequer next session, and there's the Egyptian loan and Lord knows what else. We only wanted you to split the Reform vote because accidents might happen after Hughes had made a score at Barkington.'

'I see,' said Fisher, 'and you, I think, are a pillar and ornament of the Reform party. As you say, I am not clever.'

The appeal to party loyalty fell on deaf ears; for the pillar of Reform was brooding on other things. At last he said, in a more troubled voice: 'I didn't want you to catch me; I knew it would be a shock. But I tell you what, you never would have caught me if I hadn't come here myself, to see they didn't ill treat you and to make sure everything was as comfortable as it could be.' There was even a sort of break in his voice as he added, 'I got those cigars because I knew you liked them.'

Emotions are queer things, and the idiocy of this concession suddenly softened Horne Fisher like an unfathomable pathos.

'Never mind, old chap,' he said; 'we'll say no more about it. I'll admit that you're really as kind-hearted and affectionate a scoundrel and hypocrite as ever sold himself to ruin his country. There, I can't say handsomer than that. Thank you for the cigars, old man. I'll have one if you don't mind.'

By the time that Horne Fisher had ended his telling of this story to Harold March they had come out into one of the public parks and taken a seat on a rise of ground overlooking wide green spaces under a blue and empty sky; and there was something incongruous in the words with which the narration ended.

'I have been in that room ever since,' said Horne Fisher. 'I am in it now. I won the election, but I never went to the House. My life has been a life in that little room on that lonely island. Plenty of books and cigars and luxuries, plenty of knowledge and interest and information, but never a voice out of that tomb to reach the world outside. I shall probably die there.' And he smiled as he looked across the vast green park to the grey horizon.

8

The Vengeance of the Statue

It was on the sunny veranda of a seaside hotel, overlooking a pattern of flower beds and a strip of blue sea, that Horne Fisher and Harold March had their final explanation, which might be called an explosion.

Harold March had come to the little table and sat down at it with a subdued excitement smouldering in his somewhat cloudy and dreamy blue eyes. In the newspapers which he tossed from him on to the table there was enough to explain some if not all of his emotion. Public affairs in every department had reached a crisis. The government which had stood so long that men were used to it, as they are used to a hereditary despotism, had begun to be accused of blunders and even of financial abuses. Some said that the experiment of attempting to establish a peasantry in the west of England, on the lines of an early fancy of Horne Fisher's, had resulted in nothing but dangerous quarrels with more industrial neighbours. There had been particular complaints of the ill treatment of harmless foreigners, chiefly Asiatics, who happened to be employed in the new scientific works constructed on the coast. Indeed, the new Power which had arisen in Siberia, backed by Japan and other powerful allies, was inclined to take the matter up in the interests of its exiled subjects; and there had been wild talk about ambassadors and ultimatums. But something much more serious, in its personal interest for March himself, seemed to fill his meeting with his friend with a mixture of embarrassment and indignation.

Perhaps it increased his annoyance that there was a certain unusual liveliness about the usually languid figure of Fisher. The ordinary image of him in March's mind was that of a pallid and bald-browed gentleman, who seemed to be prematurely old as well as prematurely bald. He was remembered as a man who expressed the opinions of a pessimist in the language of a lounger. Even now March could not be certain whether the change was merely a sort of masquerade of sunshine, or that effect of clear colours and clean-cut outlines that is always visible on the parade of a marine resort, relieved against the blue dado of the sea. But Fisher had a flower in his buttonhole, and his friend could have sworn he carried his cane with something almost like the swagger of a fighter. With such clouds gathering over England, the pessimist seemed to be the only man who carried his own sunshine.

'Look here,' said Harold March, abruptly, 'you've been no end of a friend to me, and I never was so proud of a friendship before; but there's something I must get off my chest. The more I found out, the less I understood how you could stand it. And I tell you I'm going to stand it no longer.'

Horne Fisher gazed across at him gravely and attentively, but rather as if he were a long way off.

'You know I always liked you,' said Fisher, quietly, 'but I also respect you, which is not always the same thing. You may possibly guess that I like a good many people I don't respect. Perhaps it is my tragedy, perhaps it is my fault. But you are very different, and I promise you this: that I will never try to keep you as somebody to be liked, at the price of your not being respected.'

'I know you are magnanimous,' said March after a silence, 'and yet you tolerate and perpetuate everything that is mean.' Then after another silence he added: 'Do you remember when we first met, when you were fishing in that brook in the affair of the target? And do you remember you said that, after all, it might do no harm if I could blow the whole tangle of this society to hell with dynamite?'

'Yes, and what of that?' asked Fisher.

'Only that I'm going to blow it to hell with dynamite,' said Harold March, 'and I think it right to give you fair warning. For a long time I didn't believe things were as bad as you said they were. But I never felt as if I could have bottled up what you knew, supposing you really knew it. Well, the long and the short of it is that I've got a conscience; and now, at last, I've also got a chance. I've been put in charge of a big independent paper, with a free hand, and we're going to open a cannonade on corruption.'

'That will be – Attwood, I suppose,' said Fisher, reflectively. 'Timber merchant. Knows a lot about China.'

'He knows a lot about England,' said March, doggedly, 'and now I know it, too, we're not going to hush it up any longer. The people of this country have a right to know how they're ruled – or, rather, ruined. The Chancellor is in the pocket of the money lenders and has to do as he is told; otherwise he's bankrupt, and a bad sort of bankruptcy, too, with nothing but cards and actresses behind it. The Prime Minister was in the petrol-contract business; and deep in it, too. The Foreign Minister is a wreck of drink and drugs. When you say that plainly about a man who may send thousands of Englishmen to die for nothing, you're called personal. If a poor engine driver gets drunk and sends thirty or forty people to death, nobody complains of the exposure being personal. The engine driver is not a person.'

'I quite agree with you,' said Fisher, calmly. 'You are perfectly right.'

'If you agree with us, why the devil don't you act with us?' demanded his friend. 'If you think it's right, why don't you do what's right? It's awful to think of a man of your abilities simply blocking the road to reform.'

'We have often talked about that,' replied Fisher, with the same cool composure. 'The Prime Minister is my father's friend. The Foreign Minister married my sister. The Chancellor of the Exchequer is my first cousin. I mention the genealogy in some detail just now for a particular reason. The truth is I have a curious kind of cheerfulness at the moment. It isn't altogether the sun and the sea, sir. I am enjoying an emotion that is entirely new to me; a happy sensation I never remember having had before.'

'What the devil do you mean?'

'I am feeling proud of my family,' said Horne Fisher.

Harold March stared at him with round blue eyes, and seemed too much mystified even to ask a question. Fisher leaned back in his chair in his lazy fashion, and smiled as he continued.

'Look here, my dear fellow. Let me ask a question in turn. You imply that I have always known these things about my unfortunate kinsmen. So I have. Do you suppose that Attwood hasn't always known them? Do you suppose he hasn't always known you as an honest man who would say these things when he got a chance? Why does Attwood unmuzzle you like a dog at this moment, after all these years? I know why he does; I know a good many things, far too many things. And therefore, as I have the honour to remark, I am proud of my family at last.'

'But why?' repeated March, rather feebly.

'I am proud of the Chancellor because he gambled and the Foreign Minister because he drank and the Prime Minister because he took a commission on a contract,' said Fisher, firmly. 'I am proud of them because they did these things, and can be denounced for them, and know they can be denounced for them, and are *standing firm for all that.* I take off my hat to them because they are defying blackmail, and refusing to smash their country to save themselves. I salute them as if they were going to die on the battlefield.'

After a pause he continued: 'And it will be a battlefield, too, and not a metaphorical one. We have yielded to foreign financiers so long that now it is war or ruin. Even the people, even the country people, are beginning to suspect that they are being ruined. That is the meaning of the regrettable incidents in the newspapers.'

'The meaning of the outrages on Orientals?' asked March.

'The meaning of the outrages on Orientals,' replied Fisher, 'is that the financiers have introduced Chinese labour into this country with the deliberate intention of reducing workmen and peasants to starvation. Our unhappy politicians have made concession after concession; and now they are asking concessions which amount to our ordering a massacre of our own poor. If we do not fight now we shall never fight again. They will have put England in an economic position of starving in a week. But we are going to fight now; I shouldn't wonder if there were an ultimatum in a week and an invasion in a fortnight. All the past corruption and cowardice is hampering us, of course; the West Country is pretty stormy and doubtful even in a military sense; and the Irish regiments there, that are supposed to support us by the new treaty, are pretty well in mutiny; for, of course, this infernal coolie capitalism is being pushed in Ireland, too. But it's to stop now; and if the government message of reassurance gets through to them in time, they may turn up after all by the time the enemy lands. For my poor old gang is going to stand to its guns at last. Of course it's only natural that when they have been whitewashed for half a century as paragons, their sins should come back on them at the very moment when they are behaving like men for the first time in their lives. Well, I tell you, March, I know them inside out; and I know they are behaving like heroes. Every man of them ought to have a statue, and on the pedestal words like those of the noblest ruffian of the Revolution: "*Que mon nom soit flétri; que la France soit libre*".'

'Good God!' cried March, 'shall we never get to the bottom of your mines and countermines?'

After a silence Fisher answered in a lower voice, looking his friend in the eyes.

'Did you think there was nothing but evil at the bottom of them?' he asked, gently. 'Did you think I had found nothing but filth in the deep seas into which fate has thrown me? Believe me, you never know the best about men till you know the worst about them. It does not dispose of their strange human souls to know that they were exhibited to the world as impossibly impeccable wax works, who never looked after a woman or knew the meaning of a bribe. Even in a palace, life can be lived well; and even in a Parliament, life can be lived with occasional efforts to live it well. I tell you it is as true of these rich fools and rascals as it is true of every poor footpad and pickpocket; that only God knows how good they have tried to be. God alone knows what the conscience can survive, or how a man who has lost his honour will still try to save his soul.'

There was another silence, and March sat staring at the table and Fisher at the sea. Then Fisher suddenly sprang to his feet and caught up his hat and stick with all his new alertness and even pugnacity.

'Look here, old fellow,' he cried, 'let us make a bargain. Before you open your campaign for Attwood come down and stay with us for one week, to hear what we're really doing. I mean with the Faithful Few, formerly known as the Old Gang, occasionally to be described as the Low Lot. There are really only five of us that are quite fixed, and organising the national defence; and we're living like a garrison in a sort of broken-down hotel in Kent. Come and see what we're really doing and what there is to be done, and do us justice. And after that, with unalterable love and affection for you, publish and be damned.'

Thus it came about that in the last week before war, when events moved most rapidly, Harold March found himself one of a sort of small house party of the people he was proposing to denounce. They were living simply enough, for people with their tastes, in an old brown-brick inn faced with ivy and surrounded by rather dismal gardens. At the back of the building the garden ran up very steeply to a road along the ridge above; and a zigzag path scaled the slope in sharp angles, turning to and fro amid evergreens so sombre that they might rather be called everblack. Here and there up the slope were statues having all the cold monstrosity of such minor ornaments of the eighteenth century; and a whole row of them ran as on a terrace along the last bank at the bottom, opposite the back door. This detail fixed itself first in March's mind merely because it figured in the first conversation he had with one of the cabinet ministers.

The cabinet ministers were rather older than he had expected to find them. The Prime Minister no longer looked like a boy, though he still looked a little like a baby. But it was one of those old and venerable babies, and the baby had soft grey hair. Everything about him was soft, to his speech and his way of walking; but over and above that his chief function seemed to be sleep. People left alone with him got so used to his eyes being closed that they were almost startled when they realised in the stillness that the eyes were wide open, and even watching. One thing at least would always make the old gentleman open his eyes. The one thing he really cared for in this world was his hobby of armoured weapons, especially Eastern weapons, and he would talk for hours about Damascus blades and Arab swordsmanship. Lord James Herries, the Chancellor of the Exchequer, was a short, dark, sturdy man with a very sallow face and a very sullen manner, which contrasted with the gorgeous flower in his buttonhole and his festive trick of being always slightly overdressed. It was something of a euphemism to call him a well-known man about town. There was perhaps more mystery in the question of how a man who lived for pleasure seemed to get so little pleasure out of it. Sir David Archer, the Foreign Secretary, was the only one of them who was a self-made man, and the only one of them who looked like an aristocrat. He was tall and thin and very handsome, with a grizzled beard; his grey hair was very curly, and even rose in front in two rebellious ringlets that seemed to the fanciful to tremble like the antennae of some giant insect, or to stir sympathetically with the restless tufted eyebrows over his rather haggard eyes. For the Foreign Secretary made no secret of his somewhat nervous condition, whatever might be the cause of it.

'Do you know that mood when one could scream because a mat is crooked?' he said to March, as they walked up and down in the back garden below the line of dingy statues. 'Women get into it when they've worked too hard; and I've been working pretty hard lately, of course. It drives me mad when Herries will wear his hat a little crooked – habit of looking like a gay dog. Sometime I swear I'll knock it off. That statue of Britannia over there isn't quite straight; it sticks forward a bit as if the lady were going to topple over. The damned thing is that it doesn't topple over and be done with it. See, it's clamped with an iron prop. Don't be surprised if I get up in the middle of the night to hike it down.'

They paced the path for a few moments in silence and then he continued: 'It's odd those little things seem specially big when there are bigger things to worry about. We'd better go in and do some work.'

Horne Fisher evidently allowed for all the neurotic possibilities of Archer and the dissipated habits of Herries; and whatever his faith in their present firmness, did not unduly tax their time and attention, even in the case of the Prime Minister. He had got the consent of the latter finally to the committing of the important documents, with the orders to the Western armies, to the care of a less conspicuous and more solid person – an uncle of his named Horne Hewitt, a rather colourless country squire who had been a good soldier, and was the military adviser of the committee. He was charged with expediting the government pledge, along with the concerted military plans, to the half-mutinous command in the west; and the still more urgent task of seeing that it did not fall into the hands of the enemy, who might appear at any moment from the east. Over and above this military official, the only other person present was a police official, a certain Dr Prince, originally a police surgeon and now a distinguished detective, sent to be a bodyguard to the group. He was a square-faced man with big spectacles and a grimace that expressed the intention of keeping his mouth shut. Nobody else shared their captivity except the hotel proprietor, a crusty Kentish man with a crab-apple face, one or two of his servants, and another servant privately attached to Lord James Herries. He was a young Scotchman named Campbell, who looked much more distinguished than his bilious-looking master, having chestnut hair and a long saturnine face with large but fine features. He was probably the one really efficient person in the house.

After about four days of the informal council, March had come to feel a sort of grotesque sublimity about these dubious figures, defiant in the twilight of danger, as if they were hunchbacks and cripples left alone to defend a town. All were working hard; and he himself looked up from writing a page of memoranda in a private room to see Horne Fisher standing in the doorway, accoutred as if for travel. He fancied that Fisher looked a little pale; and after a moment that gentleman shut the door behind him and said, quietly: 'Well, the worst has happened. Or nearly the worst.'

'The enemy has landed,' cried March, and sprang erect out of his chair.

'Oh, I knew the enemy would land,' said Fisher, with composure. 'Yes, he's landed; but that's not the worst that could happen. The worst is that there's a leak of some sort, even from this fortress of ours. It's been a bit of a shock to me, I can tell you; though I suppose it's illogical. After all, I was full of admiration at finding three honest men in politics. I ought not to be full of astonishment if I find only two.'

He ruminated a moment and then said, in such a fashion that March could hardly tell if he were changing the subject or no: 'It's hard at first to believe that a fellow like Herries, who had pickled himself in vice like vinegar, can have any scruple left. But about that I've noticed a curious thing. Patriotism is not the first virtue. Patriotism rots into Prussianism when you pretend it is the first virtue. But patriotism is sometimes the last virtue. A man will swindle or seduce who will not sell his country. But who knows?'

'But what is to be done?' cried March, indignantly.

'My uncle has the papers safe enough,' replied Fisher, 'and is sending them west tonight; but somebody is trying to get at them from outside, I fear with the assistance of somebody inside. All I can do at present is to try to head off the man outside; and I must get away now and do it. I shall be back in about twenty-four hours. While I'm away I want you to keep an eye on these people and find out what you can. Au revoir.' He vanished down the stairs; and from the window March could see him mount a motor cycle and trail away towards the neighbouring town.

On the following morning, March was sitting in the window seat of the old inn parlour, which was oak-panelled and ordinarily rather dark; but on that occasion it was full of the white light of a curiously clear morning – the moon had shone brilliantly for the last two or three nights. He was himself somewhat in shadow in the corner of the window seat; and Lord James Herries, coming in hastily from the garden behind, did not see him. Lord James clutched the back of a chair, as if to steady himself, and, sitting down abruptly at the table, littered with the last meal, poured himself out a tumbler of brandy and drank it. He sat with his back to March, but his yellow face appeared in a round mirror beyond and the tinge of it was like that of some horrible malady. As March moved he started violently and faced round.

'My God!' he cried, 'have you seen what's outside?'

'Outside?' repeated the other, glancing over his shoulder at the garden.

'Oh, go and look for yourself,' cried Herries in a sort of fury. 'Hewitt's murdered and his papers stolen, that's all.'

He turned his back again and sat down with a thud; his square shoulders were shaking. Harold March darted out of the doorway into the back garden with its steep slope of statues.

The first thing he saw was Dr Prince, the detective, peering through his spectacles at something on the ground; the second was the thing he was peering at. Even after the sensational news he had heard inside, the sight was something of a sensation.

The monstrous stone image of Britannia was lying prone and face downwards on the garden path; and there stuck out at random from underneath it, like the legs of a smashed fly, an arm clad in a white shirt sleeve and a leg clad in a khaki trouser, and hair of the unmistakable sandy grey that belonged to Horne Fisher's unfortunate uncle. There were pools of blood and the limbs were quite stiff in death.

'Couldn't this have been an accident?' said March, finding words at last.

'Look for yourself, I say,' repeated the harsh voice of Herries, who had followed him with restless movements out of the door. 'The papers are gone, I tell you. The fellow tore the coat off the corpse and cut the papers out of the inner pocket. There's the coat over there on the bank, with the great slash in it.'

'But wait a minute,' said the detective, Prince, quietly. 'In that case there seems to be something of a mystery. A murderer might somehow have managed to throw the statue down on him, as he seems to have done. But I bet he couldn't easily have lifted it up again. I've tried; and I'm sure it would want three men at least. Yet we must suppose, on that theory, that the murderer first knocked him down as he walked past, using the statue as a stone club, then lifted it up again, took him out and deprived him of his coat, then put him back again in the posture of death and neatly replaced the statue. I tell you it's physically impossible. And how else could he have unclothed a man covered with that stone monument? It's worse than the conjurer's trick, when a man shuffles a coat off with his wrists tied.'

'Could he have thrown down the statue after he'd stripped the corpse?' asked March.

'And why?' asked Prince, sharply. 'If he'd killed his man and got his papers, he'd be away like the wind. He wouldn't potter about in a garden excavating the pedestals of statues. Besides – Hullo, who's that up there?'

High on the ridge above them, drawn in dark thin lines against the sky, was a figure looking so long and lean as to be almost spidery. The dark silhouette of the head showed two small tufts like horns; and they could almost have sworn that the horns moved.

'Archer!' shouted Herries, with sudden passion, and called to him with curses to come down. The figure drew back at the first cry, with an agitated movement so abrupt as almost to be called an antic. The next moment the man seemed to reconsider and collect himself, and began to come down the zigzag garden path, but with obvious reluctance, his feet falling in slower and slower rhythm. Through March's mind were throbbing the phrases that this man himself had used, about going mad in the middle of the night and wrecking the stone figure. Just so, he could fancy, the maniac who had done such a thing might climb the crest of the hill, in that feverish dancing fashion, and look down on the wreck he had made. But the wreck he had made here was not only a wreck of stone.

When the man emerged at last on to the garden path, with the full light on his face and figure, he was walking slowly indeed, but easily, and with no appearance of fear.

'This is a terrible thing,' he said. 'I saw it from above; I was taking a stroll along the ridge.'

'Do you mean that you saw the murder?' demanded March, 'or the accident? I mean did you see the statue fall?'

'No,' said Archer, 'I mean I saw the statue fallen.'

Prince seemed to be paying but little attention; his eye was riveted on an object lying on the path a yard or two from the corpse. It seemed to be a rusty iron bar bent crooked at one end.

'One thing I don't understand,' he said, 'is all this blood. The poor fellow's skull isn't smashed; most likely his neck is broken; but blood seems to have spouted as if all his arteries were severed. I was wondering if some other instrument . . . that iron thing, for instance; but I don't see that even that is sharp enough. I suppose nobody knows what it is.'

'I know what it is,' said Archer in his deep but somewhat shaky voice. 'I've seen it in my nightmares. It was the iron clamp or prop on the pedestal, stuck on to keep the wretched image upright when it began to wobble, I suppose. Anyhow, it was always stuck in the stonework there; and I suppose it came out when the thing collapsed.'

Dr Prince nodded, but he continued to look down at the pools of blood and the bar of iron.

'I'm certain there's something more underneath all this,' he said at last. 'Perhaps something more underneath the statue. I have a huge sort of hunch that there is. We are four men now and between us we can lift that great tombstone there.'

They all bent their strength to the business; there was a silence save for heavy breathing; and then, after an instant of the tottering and staggering of eight legs, the great carven column of rock was rolled away, and the body lying in its shirt and trousers was fully revealed. The spectacles of Dr Prince seemed almost to enlarge with a restrained radiance like great eyes; for other things were revealed also. One was that the unfortunate Hewitt had a deep gash across the jugular, which the triumphant doctor instantly identified as having been made with a sharp steel edge like a razor. The other was that immediately under the bank lay littered three shining scraps of steel, each nearly a foot long, one pointed and another fitted into a gorgeously jewelled hilt or handle. It was evidently a sort of long Oriental knife, long enough to be called a sword, but with a curious wavy edge; and there was a touch or two of blood on the point.

'I should have expected more blood, hardly on the point,' observed Dr Prince, thoughtfully, 'but this is certainly the instrument. The slash was certainly made with a weapon shaped like this, and probably the slashing of the pocket as well. I suppose the brute threw in the statue, by way of giving him a public funeral.'

March did not answer; he was mesmerised by the strange stones that glittered on the strange sword hilt; and their possible significance was broadening upon him like a dreadful dawn. It was a curious Asiatic weapon. He knew what name was connected in his memory with curious Asiatic weapons. Lord James spoke his secret thought for him, and yet it startled him like an irrelevance.

'Where is the Prime Minister?' Herries had cried, suddenly, and somehow like the bark of a dog at some discovery.

Dr Prince turned on him his goggles and his grim face; and it was grimmer than ever.

'I cannot find him anywhere,' he said. 'I looked for him at once, as soon as I found the papers were gone. That servant of yours, Campbell, made a most efficient search, but there are no traces.'

There was a long silence, at the end of which Herries uttered another cry, but upon an entirely new note.

'Well, you needn't look for him any longer,' he said, 'for here he comes, along with your friend Fisher. They look as if they'd been for a little walking tour.'

The two figures approaching up the path were indeed those of Fisher, splashed with the mire of travel and carrying a scratch like that of a bramble across one side of his bald forehead, and of the great and grey-haired statesman who looked like a baby and was interested in Eastern swords and swordsmanship. But beyond this bodily recognition, March could make neither head nor tail of their presence or demeanour, which seemed to give a final touch of nonsense to the whole nightmare. The more closely he watched them, as they stood listening to the revelations of the detective, the more puzzled he was by their attitude – Fisher seemed grieved by the death of his uncle, but hardly shocked at it; the older man seemed almost openly thinking about something else, and neither had anything to suggest about a further pursuit of the fugitive spy and murderer, in spite of the prodigious importance of the documents he had stolen. When the detective had gone off to busy himself with that department of the business, to telephone and write his report, when Herries had gone back, probably to the brandy bottle, and the Prime Minister had blandly sauntered away towards a comfortable armchair in another part of the garden, Horne Fisher spoke directly to Harold March.

'My friend,' he said, 'I want you to come with me at once; there is no one else I can trust so much as that. The journey will take us most of the day, and the chief business cannot be done till nightfall. So we can talk things over thoroughly on the way. But I want you to be with me; for I rather think it is my hour.'

March and Fisher both had motor bicycles; and the first half of their day's journey consisted in coasting eastwards amid the unconversational noise of those uncomfortable engines. But when they came out beyond Canterbury into the flats of eastern Kent, Fisher stopped at a pleasant little public house beside a sleepy stream; and they sat down to eat and to drink and to speak almost for the first time. It was a brilliant afternoon, birds were singing in the wood behind, and the sun shone full on their ale bench and table; but the face of Fisher in the strong sunlight had a gravity never seen on it before.

'Before we go any farther,' he said, 'there is something you ought to know. You and I have seen some mysterious things and got to the bottom of them before now; and it's only right that you should get to the bottom of this one. But in dealing with the death of my uncle I must begin at the other end from where our old detective yarns began. I will give you the steps of deduction presently, if you want to listen to them; but I did not reach the truth of this by steps of deduction. I will first of all tell you the truth itself, because I knew the truth from the first. The other cases I approached from the outside, but in this case I was inside. I myself was the very core and centre of everything.'

Something in the speaker's pendent eyelids and grave grey eyes suddenly shook March to his foundations; and he cried, distractedly, 'I don't understand!' as men do when they fear that they do understand. There was no sound for a space but the happy chatter of the birds, and then Horne Fisher said, calmly: 'It was I who killed my uncle. If you particularly want more, it was I who stole the state papers from him.'

'Fisher!' cried his friend in a strangled voice.

'Let me tell you the whole thing before we part,' continued the other, 'and let me put it, for the sake of clearness, as we used to put our old problems. Now there are two things that are puzzling people about that problem, aren't there? The first is how the murderer managed to slip off the dead man's coat, when he was already pinned to the ground with that stone incubus. The other, which is much smaller and less puzzling, is the fact of the sword that cut his throat being slightly stained at the point, instead of a good deal more stained at the edge. Well, I can dispose of the first question easily. Horne Hewitt took off his own coat before he was killed. I might say he took off his coat to be killed.'

'Do you call that an explanation?' exclaimed March. 'The words seem more meaningless than the facts.'

'Well, let us go on to the other facts,' continued Fisher, equably. 'The reason that particular sword is not stained at the edge with Hewitt's blood is that it was not used to kill Hewitt.'

'But the doctor,' protested March, 'declared distinctly that the wound was made by that particular sword.'

'I beg your pardon,' replied Fisher. 'He did not declare that it was made by that particular sword. He declared it was made by a sword of that particular pattern.'

'But it was quite a queer and exceptional pattern,' argued March; 'surely it is far too fantastic a coincidence to imagine – '

'It was a fantastic coincidence,' reflected Horne Fisher. 'It's extraordinary what coincidences do sometimes occur. By the oddest chance in the world, by one chance in a million, it so happened that another sword of exactly the same shape was in the same garden at the same time. It may be partly explained by the fact that I brought them both into the garden myself . . . come, my dear fellow; surely you can see now what it means. Put those two things together; there were two duplicate swords and he took off his coat for himself. It may assist your speculations to recall the fact that I am not exactly an assassin.'

'A duel!' exclaimed March, recovering himself. 'Of course, I ought to have thought of that. But who was the spy who stole the papers?'

'My uncle was the spy who stole the papers,' replied Fisher, 'or who tried to steal the papers when I stopped him – in the only way I could. The papers, that should have gone west to reassure our friends and give them the plans for repelling the invasion, would in a few hours have been in the hands of the invader. What could I do? To have denounced one of our friends at this moment would have been to play into the hands of your friend Attwood, and all the party of panic and slavery. Besides, it may be that a man over forty has a subconscious desire to die as he has lived, and that I wanted, in a sense, to carry my secrets to the grave. Perhaps a hobby hardens with age; and my hobby has been silence. Perhaps I feel that I have killed my mother's brother, but I have saved my mother's name. Anyhow, I chose a time when I knew you were all asleep, and he was walking alone in the garden. I saw all the stone statues standing in the moonlight; and I myself was like one of those stone statues walking. In a voice that was not my own, I told him of his treason and demanded the papers; and when he refused, I forced him to take one of the two swords. The swords were among some specimens sent down here for the Prime Minister's inspection; he is a collector, you know; they were the only equal weapons I could find. To cut an ugly tale short, we fought there on the path in front of the Britannia statue; he was a man of great strength, but I had somewhat the advantage in skill. His sword grazed my forehead almost at the moment when mine sank into the joint in his neck. He fell against the statue, like Caesar against Pompey's, hanging on to the iron rail; his sword was already broken. When I saw the blood from that deadly wound, everything else went from me; I dropped my sword and ran as if to lift him up. As I bent towards him something happened too quick for me to follow. I do not know whether the iron bar was rotted with rust and came away in his hand, or whether he rent it out of the rock with his apelike strength; but the thing was in his hand, and with his dying energies he swung it over my head, as I knelt there unarmed beside him. I looked up wildly to avoid the blow, and saw above us the great bulk of Britannia leaning outwards like the figurehead of a ship. The next instant I saw it was leaning an inch or two more than usual, and all the skies with their outstanding stars seemed to be leaning with it. For the third second it was as if the skies fell; and in the fourth I was standing in the quiet garden, looking down on that flat ruin of stone and bone at which you were looking today. He had plucked out the last prop that held up the British goddess, and she had fallen and crushed the traitor in her fall. I turned and darted for the coat which I knew to contain the package, ripped it up with my sword, and raced away up the garden path to where my motor bike was waiting on the road above. I had every reason for haste; but I fled without looking back at the statue and the body; and I think the thing I fled from was the sight of that appalling allegory.

'Then I did the rest of what I had to do. All through the night and into the daybreak and the daylight I went humming through the villages and markets of South England like a travelling bullet, till I came to the headquarters in the west where the trouble was. I was just in time. I was able to placard the place, so to speak, with the news that the government had not betrayed them, and that they would find supports if they would push eastwards against the enemy. There's no time to tell you all that happened; but I tell you it was the day of my life. A triumph like a torchlight procession, with torchlights that might have been firebrands. The mutinies simmered down; the men of Somerset and the western counties came pouring into the marketplaces; the men who died with Arthur and stood firm with Alfred. The Irish regiments rallied to them, after a scene like a riot, and marched eastwards out of the town singing Fenian songs. There was all that is not understood about the dark laughter of that people, in the delight with which, even when marching with the English to the defence of England, they shouted at the top of their voices, "High upon the gallows tree stood the noble-hearted three . . . With England's cruel cord about them cast." However, the chorus was "God save Ireland," and we could all have sung that just then, in one sense or another.

'But there was another side to my mission. I carried the plans of the defence; and to a great extent, luckily, the plans of the invasion also. I won't worry you with strategies; but we knew where the enemy had pushed forward the great battery that covered all his movements; and though our friends from the west could hardly arrive in time to intercept the main movement, they might get within long artillery range of the battery and shell it, if they only knew exactly where it was. They could hardly tell that unless somebody round about here sent up some sort of signal. But, somehow, I rather fancy that somebody will.'

With that he got up from the table, and they remounted their machines and went eastwards into the advancing twilight of evening. The levels of the landscape were repeated in flat strips of floating cloud and the last colours of day clung to the circle of the horizon. Receding farther and farther behind them was the semicircle of the last hills; and it was quite suddenly that they saw afar off the dim line of the sea. It was not a strip of bright blue as they had seen it from the sunny veranda, but of a sinister and smoky violet, a tint that seemed ominous and dark. Here Horne Fisher dismounted once more.

'We must walk the rest of the way,' he said, 'and the last bit of all I must walk alone.'

He bent down and began to unstrap something from his bicycle. It was something that had puzzled his companion all the way in spite of what held him to more interesting riddles; it appeared to be several lengths of pole strapped together and wrapped up in paper. Fisher took it under his arm and began to pick his way across the turf. The ground was growing more tumbled and irregular and he was walking towards a mass of thickets and small woods; night grew darker every moment. 'We must not talk any more,' said Fisher. 'I shall whisper to you when you are to halt. Don't try to follow me then, for it will only spoil the show; one man can barely crawl safely to the spot, and two would certainly be caught.'

'I would follow you anywhere,' replied March, 'but I would halt, too, if that is better.'

'I know you would,' said his friend in a low voice. 'Perhaps you're the only man I ever quite trusted in this world.'

A few paces farther on they came to the end of a great ridge or mound looking monstrous against the dim sky; and Fisher stopped with a gesture. He caught his companion's hand and wrung it with a violent tenderness, and then darted forward into the darkness. March could faintly see his figure crawling along under the shadow of the ridge, then he lost sight of it, and then he saw it again standing on another mound two hundred yards away. Beside him stood a singular erection made apparently of two rods. He bent over it and there was the flare of a light; all March's schoolboy memories woke in him, and he knew what it was. It was the stand of a rocket. The confused, incongruous memories still possessed him up to the very moment of a fierce but familiar sound; and an instant after the rocket left its perch and went up into endless space like a starry arrow aimed at the stars. March thought suddenly of the signs of the last days and knew he was looking at the apocalyptic meteor of something like a Day of Judgement.

Far up in the infinite heavens the rocket drooped and sprang into scarlet stars. For a moment the whole landscape out to the sea and back to the crescent of the wooded hills was like a lake of ruby light, of a red strangely rich and glorious, as if the world were steeped in wine rather than blood, or the earth were an earthly paradise, over which paused for ever the sanguine moment of morning.

'God save England!' cried Fisher, with a tongue like the peal of a trumpet. 'And now it is for God to save.'

As darkness sank again over land and sea, there came another sound; far away in the passes of the hills behind them the guns spoke like the baying of great hounds. Something that was not a rocket, that came not hissing but screaming, went over Harold March's head and expanded beyond the mound into light and deafening din, staggering the brain with unbearable brutalities of noise. Another came, and then another, and the world was full of uproar and volcanic vapour and chaotic light. The artillery of the West Country and the Irish had located the great enemy battery, and were pounding it to pieces.

In the mad excitement of that moment March peered through the storm, looking again for the long lean figure that stood beside the stand of the rocket. Then another flash lit up the whole ridge. The figure was not there.

Before the fires of the rocket had faded from the sky, long before the first gun had sounded from the distant hills, a splutter of rifle fire had flashed and flickered all around from the hidden trenches of the enemy. Something lay in the shadow at the foot of the ridge, as stiff as the stick of the fallen rocket; and the man who knew too much knew what is worth knowing.

THE INCREDULITY OF FATHER BROWN

The Incredulity of Father Brown

Contents

The Resurrection of Father Brown

There was a brief period during which Father Brown enjoyed, or rather did not enjoy, something like fame. He was a nine days' wonder in the newspapers; he was even a common topic of controversy in the weekly reviews; his exploits were narrated eagerly and inaccurately in any number of clubs and drawing-rooms, especially in America. Incongruous and indeed incredible as it may seem to anyone who knew him, his adventures as a detective were even made the subject of short stories appearing in magazines.

Strangely enough, this wandering limelight struck him in the most obscure, or at least the most remote, of his many places of residence. He had been sent out to officiate, as something between a missionary and a parish priest, in one of those sections of the northern coast of South America, where strips of country still cling insecurely to European powers, or are continually threatening to become independent republics, under the gigantic shadow of President Monroe. The population was red and brown with pink spots; that is, it was Spanish-American, and largely Spanish-American-Indian, but there was a considerable and increasing infiltration of Americans of the northern sort – Englishmen, Germans, and the rest. And the trouble seems to have begun when one of these visitors, very recently landed and very much annoyed at having lost one of his bags, approached the first building of which he came in sight – which happened to be the mission-house and chapel attached to it, in front of which ran a long veranda and a long row of stakes, up which were trained the black twisted vines, their square leaves red with autumn. Behind them, also in a row, a number of human beings sat almost as rigid as the stakes, and coloured in some fashion like the vines. For while their broad-brimmed hats were as black as their unblinking eyes, the complexions of many of them might have been made out of the dark red timber of those transatlantic forests. Many of them were smoking very long, thin black cigars; and in all that group the smoke was almost the only moving thing. The visitor would probably have described them as natives, though some of them were very proud of Spanish blood. But he was not one to draw any fine distinction between Spaniards and Red Indians, being rather disposed to dismiss people from the scene when once he had convicted them of being native to it.

He was a newspaper man from Kansas City, a lean, light-haired man with what Meredith called an adventurous nose; one could almost fancy it found its way by feeling its way and moved like the proboscis of an ant-eater. His name was Snaith, and his parents, after some obscure meditation, had called him Saul, a fact which he had the good feeling to conceal as far as possible. Indeed, he had ultimately compromised by calling himself Paul, though by no means for the same reason that had affected the Apostle of the Gentiles. On the contrary, so far as he had any views on such things, the name of the persecutor would have been more appropriate; for he regarded organised religion with the conventional contempt which can be learnt more easily from Ingersoll than from Voltaire. And this was, as it happened, the not very important side of his character which he turned towards the mission-station and the groups in front of the veranda. Something in their shameless repose and indifference inflamed his own fury of efficiency; and, as he could get no particular answer to his first questions, he began to do all the talking himself.

Standing out there in the strong sunshine, a spick-and-span figure in his Panama hat and neat clothes, his grip-sack held in a steely grip, he began to shout at the people in the shadow. He began to explain to them very loudly why they were lazy and filthy, and bestially ignorant and lower than the beasts that perish, in case this problem should have previously exercised their minds. In his opinion it was the deleterious influence of priests that had made them so miserably poor and so hopelessly oppressed that they were able to sit in the shade and smoke and do nothing.

'And a mighty soft crowd you must be at that,' he said, 'to be bullied by these stuck-up josses because they walk about in their mitres and their tiaras and their gold copes and other glad rags, looking down on everybody else like dirt – being bamboozled by crowns and canopies and sacred umbrellas like a kid at a pantomime; just because a pompous old High Priest of Mumbo-Jumbo looks as if he was the lord of the earth. What about you? What do you look like, you poor simps? I tell you, that's why you're way-back in barbarism and can't read or write and – '

At this point the High Priest of Mumbo-Jumbo came in an undignified hurry out of the door of the mission-house, not looking very like a lord of the earth, but rather like a bundle of black second-hand clothes buttoned round a short bolster in the semblance of a guy. He was not wearing his tiara, supposing him to possess one, but a shabby broad hat not very dissimilar from those of the Spanish Indians, and it was thrust to the back of his head with a gesture of botheration. He seemed just about to speak to the motionless natives when he caught sight of the stranger and said quickly: 'Oh, can I be of any assistance? Would you like to come inside?'

Mr Paul Snaith came inside; and it was the beginning of a considerable increase of that journalist's information on many things. Presumably his journalistic instinct was stronger than his prejudices, as, indeed, it often is in clever journalists; and he asked a good many questions, the answers to which interested and surprised him. He discovered that the Indians could read and write, for the simple reason that the priest had taught them; but that they did not read or write any more than they could help, from a natural preference for more direct communications. He learned that these strange people, who sat about in heaps on the veranda without stirring a hair, could work quite hard on their own patches of land; especially those of them who were more than half Spanish; and he learned with still more astonishment that they all had patches of land that were really their own. That much was part of a stubborn tradition that seemed quite native to natives. But in that also the priest had played a certain part, and by doing so had taken perhaps what was his first and last part in politics, if it was only local politics.

There had recently swept through that region one of those fevers of atheist and almost anarchist Radicalism which break out periodically in countries of the Latin culture, generally beginning in a secret society and generally ending in a civil war and in very little else. The local leader of the iconoclastic party was a certain Alvarez, a rather picturesque adventurer of Portuguese nationality but, as his enemies said, of partly Negro origin, the head of any number of lodges and temples of initiation of the sort that in such places clothe even atheism with something mystical. The leader on the more conservative side was a much more commonplace person, a very wealthy man named Mendoza, the owner of many factories and quite respectable, but not very exciting. It was the general opinion that the cause of law and order would have been entirely lost if it had not adopted a more popular policy of its own, in the form of securing land for the peasants; and this movement had mainly originated from the little mission-station of Father Brown.

While he was talking to the journalist, Mendoza, the Conservative leader, came in. He was a stout, dark man, with a bald head like a pear and a round body also like a pear; he was smoking a very fragrant cigar, but he threw it away, perhaps a little theatrically, when he came into the presence of the priest, as if he had been entering church; and bowed with a curve that in so corpulent a gentleman seemed quite improbable. He was always exceedingly serious in his social gestures, especially towards religious institutions. He was one of those laymen who are much more ecclesiastical than ecclesiastics. It embarrassed Father Brown a good deal, especially when carried thus into private life.

'I think I am an anti-clerical,' Father Brown would say with a faint smile; 'but there wouldn't be half so much clericalism if they would only leave things to the clerics.'

'Why Mr Mendoza,' exclaimed the journalist with a new animation, 'I think we have met before. Weren't you at the Trade Congress in Mexico last year?'

The heavy eyelids of Mr Mendoza showed a flutter of recognition, and he smiled in his slow way. 'I remember.'

'Pretty big business done there in an hour or two,' said Snaith with relish. 'Made a good deal of difference to you, too, I guess.'

'I have been very fortunate,' said Mendoza modestly.

'Don't you believe it!' cried the enthusiastic Snaith. 'Good fortune comes to the people who know when to catch hold; and you caught hold good and sure. But I hope I'm not interrupting your business?'

'Not at all,' said the other. 'I often have the honour of calling on the padre for a little talk. Merely for a little talk.'

It seemed as if this familiarity between Father Brown and a successful and even famous man of business completed the reconciliation between the priest and the practical Mr Snaith. He felt, it might be supposed, a new respectability clothe the station and the mission, and was ready to overlook such occasional reminders of the existence of religion as a chapel and a presbytery can seldom wholly avoid. He became quite enthusiastic about the priest's programme – at least on its secular and social side – and announced himself ready at any moment to act in the capacity of a live wire for its communication to the world at large. And it was at this point that Father Brown began to find the journalist rather more troublesome in his sympathy than in his hostility.

Mr Paul Snaith set out vigorously to feature Father Brown. He sent long and loud eulogies on him across the continent to his newspaper in the Middle West. He took snapshots of the unfortunate cleric in the most commonplace occupations, and exhibited them in gigantic photographs in the gigantic Sunday papers of the United States. He turned his sayings into slogans, and was continually presenting the world with 'A message' from the reverend gentleman in South America. Any stock less strong and strenuously receptive than the American race would have become very much bored with Father Brown. As it was, he received handsome and eager offers to go on a lecturing tour in the States; and when he declined, the terms were raised with expressions of respectful wonder. A series of stories about him, like the stories of Sherlock Holmes, were, by the instrumentality of Mr Snaith, planned out and put before the hero with requests for his assistance and encouragement. As the priest found they had started, he could offer no suggestion except that they should stop. And this in turn was taken by Mr Snaith as the text for a discussion on whether Father Brown should disappear temporarily over a cliff, in the manner of Dr Watson's hero. To all these demands the priest had patiently to reply in writing, saying that he would consent on such terms to the temporary cessation of the stories and begging that a considerable interval might occur before they began again. The notes he wrote grew shorter and shorter; and as he wrote the last of them, he sighed.

Needless to say, this strange boom in the North reacted on the little outpost in the South where he had expected to live in so lonely an exile. The considerable English and American population already on the spot began to be proud of possessing so widely advertised a person. American tourists, of the sort who land with a loud demand for Westminster Abbey, landed on that distant coast with a loud demand for Father Brown. They were within measurable distance of running excursion trains named after him, and bringing crowds to see him as if he were a public monument. He was especially troubled by the active and ambitious new traders and shopkeepers of the place, who were perpetually pestering him to try their wares and to give them testimonials. Even if the testimonials were not forthcoming, they would prolong the correspondence for the purpose of collecting autographs. As he was a good-natured person they got a good deal of what they wanted out of him; and it was in answer to a particular request from a Frankfurt wine-merchant named Eckstein that he wrote hastily a few words on a card, which were to prove a terrible turning-point in his life.

Eckstein was a fussy little man with fuzzy hair and pince-nez, who was wildly anxious that the priest should not only try some of his celebrated medicinal port, but should let him know where and when he would drink it, in acknowledging its receipt. The priest was not particularly surprised at the request, for he was long past surprise at the lunacies of advertisement. So he scribbled something down and turned to other business which seemed a little more sensible. He was again interrupted, by a note from no less a person than his political enemy Alvarez, asking him to come to a conference at which it was hoped that a compromise on an outstanding question might be reached; and suggesting an appointment that evening at a café just outside the walls of the little town. To this also he sent a message of acceptance by the rather florid and military messenger who was waiting for it; and then, having an hour or two before him, sat down to attempt to get through a little of his own legitimate business. At the end of the time he poured himself out a glass of Mr Eckstein's remarkable wine and, glancing at the clock with a humorous expression, drank it and went out into the night.

Strong moonlight lay on the little Spanish town, so that when he came to the picturesque gateway, with its rather rococo arch and the fantastic fringe of palms beyond it, it looked rather like a scene in a Spanish opera. One long leaf of palm with jagged edges, black against the moon, hung down on the other side of the arch, visible through the archway, and had something of the look of the jaw of a black crocodile. The fancy would not have lingered in his imagination but for something else that caught his naturally alert eye. The air was deathly still, and there was not a stir of wind; but he distinctly saw the pendent palm-leaf move.

He looked around him and realised that he was alone. He had left behind the last houses, which were mostly closed and shuttered, and was walking between two long blank walls built of large and shapeless but flattened stones, tufted here and there with the queer prickly weeds of that region – walls which ran parallel all the way to the gateway. He could not see the lights of the café outside the gate; probably it was too far away. Nothing could be seen under the arch but a wider expanse of large-flagged pavement, pale in the moon, with the straggling prickly pear here and there. He had a strong sense of the smell of evil; he felt queer physical oppression; but he did not think of stopping. His courage, which was considerable, was perhaps even less strong a part of him than his curiosity. All his life he had been led by an intellectual hunger for the truth, even of trifles. He often controlled it in the name of proportion; but it was always there. He walked straight through the gateway, and on the other side a man sprang like a monkey out of the tree-top and struck at him with a knife. At the same moment another man came crawling swiftly along the wall and, whirling a cudgel round his head, brought it down. Father Brown turned, staggered, and sank in a heap, but as he sank there dawned on his round face an expression of mild and immense surprise.

There was living in the same little town at this time another young American, particularly different from Mr Paul Snaith. His name was John Adams Race, and he was an electrical engineer, employed by Mendoza to fit out the old town with all the new conveniences. He was a figure far less familiar in satire and international gossip than that of the American journalist. Yet, as a matter of fact, America contains a million men of the moral type of Race to one of the moral type of Snaith. He was exceptional in being exceptionally good at his job, but in every other way he was very simple. He had begun life as a druggist's assistant in a Western village, and risen by sheer work and merit; but he still regarded his home town as the natural heart of the habitable world. He had been taught a very Puritan, or purely Evangelical, sort of Christianity from the Family Bible at his mother's knee; and in so far as he had time to have any religion, that was still his religion. Amid all the dazzling lights of the latest and even wildest discoveries, when he was at the very edge and extreme of experiment, working miracles of light and sound like a god creating new stars and solar systems, he never for a moment doubted that the things 'back home' were the best things in the world; his mother and the Family Bible and the quiet and quaint morality of his village. He had as serious and noble a sense of the sacredness of his mother as if he had been a frivolous Frenchman. He was quite sure the Bible religion was really the right thing; only he vaguely missed it wherever he went in the modern world. He could hardly be expected to sympathise with the religious externals of Catholic countries; and in a dislike of mitres and croziers he sympathised with Mr Snaith, though not in so cocksure a fashion. He had no liking for the public bowings and scrapings of Mendoza and certainly no temptation to the masonic mysticism of the atheist Alvarez. Perhaps all that semi-tropical life was too coloured for him, shot with Indian red and Spanish gold. Anyhow, when he said there was nothing to touch his home town, he was not boasting. He really meant that there was somewhere something plain and unpretentious and touching, which he really respected more than anything else in the world. Such being the mental attitude of John Adams Race in a South American station, there had been growing on him for some time a curious feeling, which contradicted all his prejudices and for which he could not account. For the truth was this: that the only thing he had ever met in his travels that in the least reminded him of the old wood-pile and the provincial proprieties and the Bible on his mother's knee was (for some inscrutable reason) the round face and black clumsy umbrella of Father Brown.

He found himself insensibly watching that commonplace and even comic black figure as it went bustling about; watching it with an almost morbid fascination, as if it were a walking riddle or contradiction. He had found something he could not help liking in the heart of everything he hated; it was as if he had been horribly tormented by lesser demons and then found that the Devil was quite an ordinary person.

Thus it happened that, looking out of his window on that moonlit night, he saw the Devil go by, the demon of unaccountable blamelessness, in his broad black hat and long black coat, shuffling along the street towards the gateway, and saw it with an interest which he could not himself understand. He wondered where the priest was going, and what he was really up to; and remained gazing out into the moonlit street long after the little black figure had passed. And then he saw something else that intrigued him further. Two other men whom he recognised passed across his window as across a lighted stage. A sort of blue limelight of the moon ran in a spectral halo round the big bush of hair that stood erect on the head of little Eckstein, the wine-seller, and it outlined a taller and darker figure with an eagle profile and a queer old-fashioned and very top-heavy black hat, which seemed to make the whole outline still more bizarre, like a shape in a shadow pantomime. Race rebuked himself for allowing the moon to play such tricks with his fancy; for on a second glance he recognised the black Spanish sidewhiskers and high-featured face of Dr Calderon, a worthy medical man of the town, whom he had once found attending professionally on Mendoza. Still, there was something in the way the men were whispering to each other and peering up the street that struck him as peculiar. On a sudden impulse he leapt over the low window-sill and himself went bare-headed up the road, following their trail. He saw them disappear under the dark archway, and a moment after there came a dreadful cry from beyond; curiously loud and piercing, and all the more blood-curdling to Race because it said something very distinctly in some tongue that he did not know.

The next moment there was a rushing of feet, more cries, and then a confused roar of rage or grief that shook the turrets and tall palm trees of the place; there was a movement in the mob that had gathered, as if they were sweeping backwards through the gateway. And then the dark archway resounded with a new voice, this time intelligible to him and falling with the note of doom, as someone shouted through the gateway: 'Father Brown is dead!'

He never knew what prop gave way in his mind, or why something on which he had been counting suddenly failed him; but he ran towards the gateway and was just in time to meet his countryman, the journalist Snaith, coming out of the dark entrance, deadly pale and snapping his fingers nervously.

'It's quite true,' said Snaith, with something which for him approached to reverence. 'He's a goner. The doctor's been looking at him, and there's no hope. Some of these damned Dagos clubbed him as he came through the gate – God knows why. It'll be a great loss to the place.'

Race did not or perhaps could not reply, but ran on under the arch to the scene beyond. The small black figure lay where it had fallen on the wilderness of wide stones starred here and there with green thorn; and the great crowd was being kept back, chiefly by the mere gestures of one gigantic figure in the foreground. For there were many there who swayed hither and thither at the mere movement of his hand, as if he had been a magician.

Alvarez, the dictator and demagogue, was a tall, swaggering figure, always rather flamboyantly clad, and on this occasion he wore a green uniform with embroideries like silver snakes crawling all over it, with an order round his neck hung on a very vivid maroon ribbon. His close curling hair was already grey, and in contrast his complexion, which his friends called olive and his foes octoroon, looked almost literally golden, as if it were a mask moulded in gold. But his large-featured face, which was powerful and humorous, was at this moment properly grave and grim. He had been waiting, he explained, for Father Brown at the café when he had heard a rustle and a fall and, coming out, had found the corpse lying on the flagstones.

'I know what some of you are thinking,' he said, looking round proudly, 'and if you are afraid of me – as you are – I will say it for you. I am an atheist; I have no god to call on for those who will not take my word. But I tell you in the name of every root of honour that may be left to a soldier and a man, that I had no part in this. If I had the men here that did it, I would rejoice to hang them on that tree.'

'Naturally we are glad to hear you say so,' said old Mendoza stiffly and solemnly, standing by the body of his fallen coadjutor. 'This blow has been too appalling for us to say what else we feel at present. I suggest that it will be more decent and proper if we remove my friend's body and break up this irregular meeting. I understand,' he added gravely to the doctor, 'that there is unfortunately no doubt.'

'There is no doubt,' said Dr Calderon.

John Race went back to his lodgings sad and with a singular sense of emptiness. It seemed impossible that he should miss a man whom he never knew. He learned that the funeral was to take place next day; for all felt that the crisis should be past as quickly as possible, for fear of riots that were hourly growing more probable. When Snaith had seen the row of Red Indians sitting on the veranda, they might have been a row of ancient Aztec images carved in red wood. But he had not seen them as they were when they heard that the priest was dead.

Indeed they would certainly have risen in revolution and lynched the republican leader, if they had not been immediately blocked by the direct necessity of behaving respectfully to the coffin of their own religious leader. The actual assassins, whom it would have been most natural to lynch, seemed to have vanished into thin air. Nobody knew their names; and nobody would ever know whether the dying man had even seen their faces. That strange look of surprise that was apparently his last look on earth might have been the recognition of their faces. Alvarez repeated violently that it was no work of his, and attended the funeral, walking behind the coffin in his splendid silver and green uniform with a sort of bravado of reverence.

Behind the veranda a flight of stone steps scaled a very steep green bank, fenced by a cactus-hedge, and up this the coffin was laboriously lifted to the ground above, and placed temporarily at the foot of the great gaunt crucifix that dominated the road and guarded the consecrated ground. Below in the road were great seas of people lamenting and telling their beads – an orphan population that had lost a father. Despite all these symbols that were provocative enough to him, Alvarez behaved with restraint and respect; and all would have gone well – as Race told himself – had the others only let him alone.

Race told himself bitterly that old Mendoza had always looked like an old fool and had now very conspicuously and completely behaved like an old fool. By a custom common in simpler societies, the coffin was left open and the face uncovered, bringing the pathos to the point of agony for all those simple people. This, being consonant to tradition, need have done no harm; but some officious person had added to it the custom of the French free-thinkers, of having speeches by the graveside. Mendoza proceeded to make a speech – a rather long speech, and the longer it was, the longer and lower sank John Race's spirits and sympathies with the religious ritual involved. A list of saintly attributes, apparently of the most antiquated sort, was rolled out with the dilatory dullness of an after-dinner speaker who does not know how to sit down. That was bad enough; but Mendoza had also the ineffable stupidity to start reproaching and even taunting his political opponents. In three minutes he had succeeded in making a scene, and a very extraordinary scene it was.

'We may well ask,' he said, looking around him pompously; 'we may well ask where such virtues can be found among those who have madly abandoned the creed of their fathers. It is when we have atheists among us, atheist leaders, nay sometimes even atheist rulers, that we find their infamous philosophy bearing fruit in crimes like this. If we ask who murdered this holy man, we shall assuredly find – '

Africa of the forests looked out of the eyes of Alvarez the hybrid adventurer; and Race fancied he could see suddenly that the man was after all a barbarian, who could not control himself to the end; one might guess that all his 'illuminated' transcendentalism had a touch of Voodoo. Anyhow, Mendoza could not continue, for Alvarez had sprung up and was shouting back at him and shouting him down, with infinitely superior lungs.

'Who murdered him?' he roared. 'Your God murdered him! His own God murdered him! According to you, he murders all his faithful and foolish servants – as he murdered *that* one,' and he made a violent gesture, not towards the coffin but the crucifix. Seeming to control himself a little, he went on in a tone still angry but more argumentative: 'I don't believe it, but you do. Isn't it better to have no God than one that robs you in this fashion? I, at least, am not afraid to say that there is none. There is no power in all this blind and brainless universe that can hear your prayer or return your friend. Though you beg Heaven to raise him, he will not rise. Though I dare Heaven to raise him, he will not rise. Here and now I will put it to the test – I defy the God who is not there to waken the man who sleeps for ever.'

There was a shock of silence, and the demagogue had made his sensation.

'We might have known,' cried Mendoza in a thick gobbling voice, 'when we allowed such men as you – '

A new voice cut into his speech; a high and shrill voice with a Yankee accent.

'Stop! Stop!' cried Snaith the journalist; 'something's up! I swear I saw him move.'

He went racing up the steps and rushed to the coffin, while the mob below swayed with indescribable frenzies. The next moment he had turned a face of amazement over his shoulder and made a signal with his finger to Dr Calderon, who hastened forward to confer with him. When the two men stepped away again from the coffin, all could see that the position of the head had altered. A roar of excitement rose from the crowd and seemed to stop suddenly, as if cut off in mid-air; for the priest in the coffin gave a groan and raised himself on one elbow, looking with bleared and blinking eyes at the crowd.

John Adams Race, who had hitherto known only miracles of science, never found himself able in after years to describe the topsy-turvydom of the next few days. He seemed to have burst out of the world of time and space, and to be living in the impossible. In half an hour the whole of that town and district had been transformed into something never known for a thousand years; a medieval people turned to a mob of monks by a staggering miracle; a Greek city where the god had descended among men. Thousands prostrated themselves in the road; hundreds took vows on the spot; and even the outsiders, like the two Americans, were able to think and speak of nothing but the prodigy. Alvarez himself was shaken, as well he might be; and sat down, with his head upon his hands.

And in the midst of all this tornado of beatitude was a little man struggling to be heard. His voice was small and faint, and the noise was deafening. He made weak little gestures that seemed more those of irritation than anything else. He came to the edge of the parapet above the crowd, waving it to be quiet, with movements rather like the flap of the short wings of a penguin. There was something a little more like a lull in the noise; and then Father Brown for the first time reached the utmost stretch of the indignation that he could launch against his children.

'Oh, you *silly* people,' he said in a high and quavering voice. 'Oh, you silly, *silly* people.'

Then he suddenly seemed to pull himself together, made a bolt for the steps with his more normal gait, and began hurriedly to descend.

'Where are you going, Father?' said Mendoza, with more than his usual veneration.

'To the telegraph office,' said Father Brown hastily. 'What? No; of course it's not a miracle. Why should there be a miracle? Miracles are not so cheap as all that.'

And he came tumbling down the steps, the people flinging themselves before him to implore his blessing.

'Bless you, bless you,' said Father Brown hastily. 'God bless you all and give you more sense.'

And he scuttled away with extraordinary rapidity to the telegraph office, where he wired to his Bishop's secretary: 'There is some mad story about a miracle here; hope his lordship not give authority. Nothing in it.'

As he turned away from his effort, he tottered a little with the reaction, and John Race caught him by the arm.

'Let me see you home,' he said; 'you deserve more than these people are giving you.'

* * *

John Race and the priest were seated in the presbytery; the table was still piled up with the papers with which the latter had been wrestling the day before; the bottle of wine and the emptied wine glass still stood where he had left them.

'And now,' said Father Brown almost grimly, 'I can begin to think.'

'I shouldn't think too hard just yet,' said the American. 'You must be wanting a rest. Besides, what are you going to think about?'

'I have pretty often had the task of investigating murders, as it happens,' said Father Brown. 'Now I have got to investigate my own murder.'

'If I were you,' said Race, 'I should take a little wine first.'

Father Brown stood up and filled himself another glass, lifted it, looked thoughtfully into vacancy, and put it down again. Then he sat down once more and said: 'Do you know what I felt like when I died? You may not believe it, but my feeling was one of overwhelming astonishment.'

'Well,' answered Race, 'I suppose you were astonished at being knocked on the head.'

Father Brown leaned over to him and said in a low voice, 'I was astonished at not being knocked on the head.'

Race looked at him for a moment as if he thought the knock on the head had been only too effective; but he only said: 'What do you mean?'

'I mean that when that man brought his bludgeon down with a great swipe, it stopped at my head and did not even touch it. In the same way, the other fellow made as if to strike me with a knife, but he never gave me a scratch. It was just like play-acting. I think it was. But then followed the extraordinary thing.'

He looked thoughtfully at the papers on the table for a moment and then went on: 'Though I had not even been touched with knife or stick, I began to feel my legs doubling up under me and my very life failing. I knew I was being struck down by something, but it was not by those weapons. Do you know what I think it was?' And he pointed to the wine on the table.

Race picked up the wine glass and looked at it and smelt it.

'I think you are right,' he said. 'I began as a druggist and studied chemistry. I couldn't say for certain without an analysis; but I think there's something very unusual in this stuff. There are drugs by which the Asiatics produce a temporary sleep that looks like death.'

'Quite so,' said the priest calmly. 'The whole of this miracle was faked, for some reason or other. That funeral scene was staged – and timed. I think it is part of that raving madness of publicity that has got hold of Snaith; but I can hardly believe he would go quite so far, merely for that. After all, it's one thing to make copy out of me and run me as a sort of sham Sherlock Holmes, and – '

Even as the priest spoke his face altered. His blinking eyelids shut suddenly and he stood up as if he were choking. Then he put one wavering hand as if groping his way towards the door.

'Where are you going?' asked the other in some wonder.

'If you ask me,' said Father Brown, who was quite white, 'I was going to pray. Or rather, to praise.'

'I'm not sure I understand. What is the matter with you?'

'I was going to praise God for having so strangely and so incredibly saved me – saved me by an inch.'

'Of course,' said Race, 'I am not of your religion; but believe me, I have religion enough to understand that. Of course, you would thank God for saving you from death.'

'No,' said the priest. 'Not from death. From disgrace.'

The other sat staring; and the priest's next words broke out of him with a sort of cry. 'And if it had only been my disgrace! But it was the disgrace of all I stand for; the disgrace of the Faith that they went about to encompass. What it might have been! The most huge and horrible scandal ever launched against us since the last lie was choked in the throat of Titus Oates.'

'What on earth are you talking about?' demanded his companion.

'Well, I had better tell you at once,' said the priest; and sitting down, he went on more composedly: 'It came to me in a flash when I happened to mention Snaith and Sherlock Holmes. Now I happen to remember what I wrote about his absurd scheme; it was the natural thing to write, and yet I think they had ingeniously manoeuvred me into writing just those words. They were something like "I am ready to die and come to life again like Sherlock Holmes, if that is the best way." And the moment I thought of that, I realised that I had been made to write all sorts of things of that kind, all pointing to the same idea. I wrote, as if to an accomplice, saying that I would drink the drugged wine at a particular time. Now, don't you see?'

Race sprang to his feet still staring: 'Yes,' he said, 'I think I begin to see.'

'*They* would have boomed the miracle. Then *they* would have bust up the miracle. And what is the worst, they would have proved that I was in the conspiracy. It would have been *our* sham miracle. That's all there is to it; and about as near hell as you and I will ever be, I hope.'

Then he said, after a pause, in quite a mild voice: 'They certainly would have got quite a lot of good copy out of me.'

Race looked at the table and said darkly: 'How many of these brutes were in it?'

Father Brown shook his head. 'More than I like to think of,' he said; 'but I hope some of them were only tools. Alvarez might think that all's fair in war, perhaps; he has a queer mind. I'm very much afraid that Mendoza is an old hypocrite; I never trusted him, and he hated my action in an industrial matter. But all that will wait; I have only got to thank God for the escape. And especially that I wired at once to the Bishop.'

John Race appeared to be very thoughtful. 'You've told me a lot I didn't know,' he said at last, 'and I feel inclined to tell you the only thing you don't know. I can imagine how those fellows calculated well enough. They thought any man alive, waking up in a coffin to find himself canonised like a saint, and made into a walking miracle for everyone to admire, would be swept along with his worshippers and accept the crown of glory that fell on him out the sky. And I reckon their calculation was pretty practical psychology, as men go. I've seen all sorts of men in all sorts of places; and I tell you frankly I don't believe there's one man in a thousand who could wake up like that with all his wits about him; and while he was still almost talking in his sleep, would have the sanity and the simplicity and the humility to – ' He was much surprised to find himself moved, and his level voice wavering.

Father Brown was gazing abstractedly, and in a rather cock-eyed fashion, at the bottle on the table. 'Look here,' he said, 'what about a bottle of real wine?'

The Arrow of Heaven

It is to be feared that about a hundred detective stories have begun with the discovery that an American millionaire has been murdered; an event which is, for some reason, treated as a sort of calamity. This story, I am happy to say, has to begin with a murdered millionaire; in one sense, indeed, it has to begin with three murdered millionaires, which some may regard as an *embarras de richesse*. But it was chiefly this coincidence or continuity of criminal policy that took the whole affair out of the ordinary run of criminal cases and made it the extraordinary problem that it was.

It was very generally said that they had all fallen victims to some vendetta or curse attaching to the possession of a relic of great value both intrinsically and historically: a sort of chalice inlaid with precious stones and commonly called the Coptic Cup. Its origin was obscure, but its use was conjectured to be religious; and some attributed the fate that followed its possessors to the fanaticism of some Oriental Christian horrified at its passing through such materialistic hands. But the mysterious slayer, whether or no he was such a fanatic, was already a figure of lurid and sensational interest in the world of journalism and gossip. The nameless being was provided with a name, or a nickname. But it is only with the story of the third victim that we are now concerned; for it was only in this case that a certain Father Brown, who is the subject of these sketches, had an opportunity of making his presence felt.

When Father Brown first stepped off an Atlantic liner on to American soil, he discovered, as many another Englishman has done, that he was a much more important person than he had ever supposed. His short figure, his short-sighted and undistinguished countenance, his rather rusty-black clerical clothes, could pass through any crowd in his own country without being noticed as anything unusual, except perhaps unusually insignificant. But America has a genius for the encouragement of fame; and his appearance in one or two curious criminal problems, together with his long association with Flambeau, the ex-criminal and detective, had consolidated a reputation in America out of what was little more than a rumour in England. His round face was blank with surprise when he found himself held up on the quay by a group of journalists, as by a gang of brigands, who asked him questions about all the subjects on which he was least likely to regard himself as an authority, such as the details of female dress and the criminal statistics of the country that he had only that moment clapped his eyes on. Perhaps it was the contrast with the black embattled solidarity of this group that made more vivid another figure that stood apart from it, equally black against the burning white daylight of that brilliant place and season, but entirely solitary; a tall, rather yellow-faced man in great goggles, who arrested him with a gesture when the journalists had finished and said: 'Excuse me, but maybe you are looking for Captain Wain.'

Some apology may be made for Father Brown; for he himself would have been sincerely apologetic. It must be remembered that he had never seen America before, and more especially that he had never seen that sort of tortoiseshell spectacles before; for the fashion at this time had not spread to England. His first sensation was that of gazing at some goggling sea-monster with a faint suggestion of a diver's helmet. Otherwise the man was exquisitely dressed; and to Brown, in his innocence, the spectacles seemed the queerest disfigurement for a dandy. It was as if a dandy had adorned himself with a wooden leg as an extra touch of elegance. The question also embarrassed him. An American aviator of the name of Wain, a friend of some friends of his own in France, was indeed one of a long list of people he had some hope of seeing during his American visit; but he had never expected to hear of him so soon.

'I beg your pardon,' he said doubtfully, 'are you Captain Wain? Do you – do you know him?'

'Well, I'm pretty confident I'm not Captain Wain,' said the man in goggles, with a face of wood. 'I was pretty clear about that when I saw him waiting for you over there in the car. But the other question's a bit more problematical. I reckon I know Wain and his uncle, and old man Merton, too. I know old man Merton, but old man Merton don't know me. And he thinks he has the advantage, and I think I have the advantage. See?'

Father Brown did not quite see. He blinked at the glittering seascape and the pinnacles of the city, and then at the man in goggles. It was not only the masking of the man's eyes that produced the impression of something impenetrable. Something in his yellow face was almost Asiatic, even Chinese; and his conversation seemed to consist of stratified layers of irony. He was a type to be found here and there in that hearty and sociable population; he was the inscrutable American.

'My name's Drage,' he said, 'Norman Drage, and I'm an American citizen, which explains everything. At least I imagine your friend Wain would like to explain the rest; so we'll postpone the Fourth of July till another date.'

Father Brown was dragged in a somewhat dazed condition towards a car at some little distance, in which a young man with tufts of untidy yellow hair and a rather harassed and haggard expression, hailed him from afar, and presented himself as Peter Wain. Before he knew where he was he was stowed in the car and travelling with considerable speed through and beyond the city. He was unused to the impetuous practicality of such

American action, and felt about as bewildered as if a chariot drawn by dragons had carried him away into fairyland. It was under these disconcerting conditions that he heard for the first time, in long monologues from Wain, and short sentences from Drage, the story of the Coptic Cup and the two crimes already connected with it.

It seemed that Wain had an uncle named Crake who had a partner named Merton, who was number three in the series of rich business men to whom the cup had belonged. The first of them, Titus P. Trant, the Copper King, had received threatening letters from somebody signing himself Daniel Doom. The name was presumably a pseudonym, but it had come to stand for a very public if not a very popular character; for somebody as well known as Robin Hood and Jack the Ripper combined. For it soon became clear that the writer of the threatening letter did not confine himself to threatening. Anyhow, the upshot was that old Trant was found one morning with his head in his own lily-pond, and there was not the shadow of a clue. The cup was, fortunately, safe in the bank; and it passed with the rest of Trant's property to his cousin, Brian Horder, who was also a man of great wealth and who was also threatened by the nameless enemy. Brian Horder was picked up dead at the foot of a cliff outside his seaside residence, at which there was a burglary, this time on a large scale. For though the cup apparently again escaped, enough bonds and securities were stolen to leave Horder's financial affairs in confusion.

'Brian Horder's widow,' explained Wain, 'had to sell most of his valuables, I believe, and Brander Merton must have purchased the cup at that time, for he had it when I first knew him. But you can guess for yourself that it's not a very comfortable thing to have.'

'Has Mr Merton ever had any of the threatening letters?' asked Father Brown, after a pause.

'I imagine he has,' said Mr Drage; and something in his voice made the priest look at him curiously, until he realised that the man in goggles was laughing silently, in a fashion that gave the newcomer something of a chill.

'I'm pretty sure he has,' said Peter Wain, frowning. 'I've not seen the letters, only his secretary sees any of his letters, for he is pretty reticent about business matters, as big business men have to be. But I've seen him real upset and annoyed with letters; and letters that he tore up, too, before even his secretary saw them. The secretary himself is getting nervous and says he is sure somebody is laying for the old man; and the long and the short of it is, that we'd be very grateful for a little advice in the matter. Everybody knows your great reputation, Father Brown, and the secretary asked me to see if you'd mind coming straight out to the Merton house at once.'

'Oh, I see,' said Father Brown, on whom the meaning of this apparent kidnapping began to dawn at last. 'But, really, I don't see that I can do any more than you can. You're on the spot, and must have a hundred times more data for a scientific conclusion than a chance visitor.'

'Yes,' said Mr Drage dryly; 'our conclusions are much too scientific to be true. I reckon if anything hit a man like Titus P. Trant, it just came out of the sky without waiting for any scientific explanation. What they call a bolt from the blue.'

'You can't possibly mean,' cried Wain, 'that it was supernatural!'

But it was by no means easy at any time to discover what Mr Drage could possibly mean; except that if he said somebody was a real smart man, he very probably meant he was a fool. Mr Drage maintained an Oriental immobility until the car stopped, a little while after, at what was obviously their destination. It was rather a singular place. They had been driving through a thinly wooded country that opened into a wide plain, and just in front of them was a building consisting of a single wall or very high fence, round, like a Roman camp, and having rather the appearance of an aerodrome. The barrier did not look like wood or stone, and closer inspection proved it to be of metal.

They all alighted from the car, and one small door in the wall was slid open with considerable caution, after manipulations resembling the opening of a safe. But, much to Father Brown's surprise, the man called Norman Drage showed no disposition to enter, but took leave of them with sinister gaiety.

'I won't come in,' he said. 'It 'ud be too much pleasurable excitement for old man Merton, I reckon. He loves the sight of me so much that he'd die of joy.'

And he strode away, while Father Brown, with increasing wonder, was admitted through the steel door which instantly clicked behind him. Inside was a large and elaborate garden of gay and varied colours, but entirely without any trees or tall shrubs or flowers. In the centre of it rose a house of handsome and even striking architecture, but so high and narrow as rather to resemble a tower. The burning sunlight gleamed on glass roofing here and there at the top, but there seemed to be no windows at all in the lower part of it. Over everything was that spotless and sparkling cleanliness that seemed so native to the clear American air. When they came inside the portal, they stood amid resplendent marble and metals and enamels of brilliant colours, but there was no staircase. Nothing but a single shaft for a lift went up the centre between the solid walls, and the approach to it was guarded by heavy, powerful men like plain-clothes policemen.

'Pretty elaborate protection, I know,' said Wain. 'Maybe it makes you smile a little, Father Brown, to find Merton has to live in a fortress like this without even a tree in the garden for anyone to hide behind. But you don't know what sort of proposition we're up against in this country. And perhaps you don't know just what the name of Brander Merton means. He's a quiet-looking man enough, and anybody might pass him in the street; not that they get much chance nowadays, for he can only go out now and then in a closed car. But if anything happened to Brander Merton there'd be earthquakes from Alaska to the Cannibal Islands. I fancy there was never a king or emperor who had such power over the nations as he has. After all, I suppose if you'd been asked to visit the tsar, or the king of England, you'd have had the curiosity to go. You mayn't care much for tsars or millionaires; but it just means that power like that is always interesting. And I hope it's not against your principles to visit a modern sort of emperor like Merton.'

'Not at all,' said Father Brown, quietly. 'It is my duty to visit prisoners and all miserable men in captivity.'

There was a silence, and the young man frowned with a strange and almost shifty look on his lean face. Then he said, abruptly: 'Well, you've got to remember it isn't only common crooks or the Black Hand that's against him. This Daniel Doom is pretty much like the devil. Look how he dropped Trant in his own gardens and Horder outside his house, and got away with it.'

The top floor of the mansion, inside the enormously thick walls, consisted of two rooms; an outer room which they entered, and an inner room that was the great millionaire's sanctum. They entered the outer room just as two other visitors were coming out of the inner one. One was hailed by Peter Wain as his uncle – a small but very stalwart and active man with a shaven head that looked bald, and a brown face that looked almost too brown to have ever been white. This was old Crake, commonly called Hickory Crake in reminiscence of the more famous Old Hickory, because of his fame in the last Red Indian wars. His companion was a singular contrast – a very dapper gentleman with dark hair like a black varnish and a broad, black ribbon to his monocle: Barnard Blake, who was old Merton's lawyer and had been discussing with the partners the business of the firm. The four men met in the middle of the outer room and paused for a little polite conversation, in the act of respectively going and coming. And through all goings and comings another figure sat at the back of the room near the inner door, massive and motionless in the half-light from the inner window; a man with a Negro face and enormous shoulders. This was what the humorous self-criticism of America playfully calls the Bad Man; whom his friends might call a bodyguard and his enemies a bravo.

This man never moved or stirred to greet anybody; but the sight of him in the outer room seemed to move Peter Wain to his first nervous query.

'Is anybody with the chief?' he asked.

'Don't get rattled, Peter,' chuckled his uncle. 'Wilton the secretary is with him, and I hope that's enough for anybody. I don't believe Wilton ever sleeps for watching Merton. He is better than twenty bodyguards. And he's quick and quiet as an Indian.'

'Well, you ought to know,' said his nephew, laughing. 'I remember the Red Indian tricks you used to teach me when I was a boy and liked to read Red Indian stories. But in my Red Indian stories Red Indians seemed always to have the worst of it.'

'They didn't in real life,' said the old frontiersman grimly.

'Indeed?' enquired the bland Mr Blake. 'I should have thought they could do very little against our firearms.'

'I've seen an Indian stand under a hundred guns with nothing but a little scalping-knife and kill a white man standing on the top of a fort,' said Crake.

'Why, what did he do with it?' asked the other.

'Threw it,' replied Crake, 'threw it in a flash before a shot could be fired. I don't know where he learnt the trick.'

'Well, I hope you didn't learn it,' said his nephew, laughing.

'It seems to me,' said Father Brown, thoughtfully, 'that the story might have a moral.'

While they were speaking Mr Wilton, the secretary, had come out of the inner room and stood waiting; a pale, fair-haired man with a square chin and steady eyes with a look like a dog's; it was not difficult to believe that he had the single-eye of a watchdog.

He only said, 'Mr Merton can see you in about ten minutes,' but it served for a signal to break up the gossiping group. Old Crake said he must be off, and his nephew went out with him and his legal companion, leaving Father Brown for the moment alone with his secretary; for the Negroid giant at the other end of the room could hardly be felt as if he were human or alive; he sat so motionless with his broad back to them, staring towards the inner room.

'Arrangements rather elaborate here, I'm afraid,' said the secretary. 'You've probably heard all about this Daniel Doom, and why it isn't safe to leave the boss very much alone.'

'But he is alone just now, isn't he?' said Father Brown.

The secretary looked at him with grave, grey eyes. 'For fifteen minutes,' he said. 'For fifteen minutes out of the twenty-four hours. That is all the real solitude he has; and that he insists on, for a pretty remarkable reason.'

'And what is the reason?' enquired the visitor. Wilton, the secretary, continued his steady gaze, but his mouth, that had been merely grave, became grim.

'The Coptic Cup,' he said. 'Perhaps you've forgotten the Coptic Cup; but he hasn't forgotten that or anything else. He doesn't trust any of us about the Coptic Cup. It's locked up somewhere and somehow in that room so that only he can find it; and he won't take it out till we're all out of the way.

So we have to risk that quarter of an hour while he sits and worships it; I reckon it's the only worshipping he does. Not that there's any risk really; for I've turned all this place into a trap I don't believe the devil himself could get into – or at any rate, get out of. If this infernal Daniel Doom pays us a visit, he'll stay to dinner and a good bit later, by God! I sit here on hot bricks for the fifteen minutes, and the instant I heard a shot or a sound of struggle I'd press this button and an electrocuting current would run in a ring round that garden wall, so that it 'ud be death to cross or climb it. Of course, there couldn't be a shot, for this is the only way in; and the only window he sits at is away up on the top of a tower as smooth as a greasy pole. But, anyhow, we're all armed here, of course; and if Doom did get into that room he'd be dead before he got out.'

Father Brown was blinking at the carpet in a brown study. Then he said suddenly, with something like a jerk: 'I hope you won't mind my mentioning it, but a kind of a notion came into my head just this minute. It's about you.'

'Indeed,' remarked Wilton, 'and what about me?'

'I think you are a man of one idea,' said Father Brown, 'and you will forgive me for saying that it seems to be even more the idea of catching Daniel Doom than of defending Brander Merton.'

Wilton started a little and continued to stare at his companion; then very slowly his grim mouth took on a rather curious smile. 'How did you – what makes you think that?' he asked.

'You said that if you heard a shot you could instantly electrocute the escaping enemy,' remarked the priest. 'I suppose it occurred to you that the shot might be fatal to your employer before the shock was fatal to his foe. I don't mean that you wouldn't protect Mr Merton if you could, but it seems to come rather second in your thoughts. The arrangements are very elaborate, as you say, and you seem to have elaborated them. But they seem even more designed to catch a murderer than to save a man.'

'Father Brown,' said the secretary, who had recovered his quiet tone, 'you're very smart, but there's something more to you than smartness. Somehow you're the sort of man to whom one wants to tell the truth; and besides, you'll probably hear it, anyhow, for in one way it's a joke against me already. They all say I'm a monomaniac about running down this big crook, and perhaps I am. But I'll tell you one thing that none of them know. My full name is John Wilton Border.' Father Brown nodded as if he were completely enlightened, but the other went on.

'This fellow who calls himself Doom killed my father and uncle and ruined my mother. When Merton wanted a secretary I took the job, because I thought that where the cup was the criminal might sooner or later be. But I didn't know who the criminal was and could only wait for him; and I meant to serve Merton faithfully.'

'I understand,' said Father Brown gently; 'and, by the way, isn't it time that we attended on him?'

'Why, yes,' answered Wilton, again starting a little out of his brooding so that the priest concluded that his vindictive mania had again absorbed him for a moment. 'Go in now by all means.'

Father Brown walked straight into the inner room. No sound of greetings followed, but only a dead silence; and a moment after the priest reappeared in the doorway.

At the same moment the silent bodyguard sitting near the door moved suddenly; and it was as if a huge piece of furniture had come to life. It seemed as though something in the very attitude of the priest had been a signal; for his head was against the light from the inner window and his face was in shadow.

'I suppose you will press that button,' he said with a sort of sigh.

Wilton seemed to awake from his savage brooding with a bound and leapt up with a catch in his voice.

'There was no shot,' he cried.

'Well,' said Father Brown, 'it depends what you mean by a shot.'

Wilton rushed forward, and they plunged into the inner room together. It was a comparatively small room and simply though elegantly furnished. Opposite to them one wide window stood open, overlooking the garden and the wooded plain. Close up against the window stood a chair and a small table, as if the captive desired as much air and light as was allowed him during his brief luxury of loneliness.

On the little table under the window stood the Coptic Cup; its owner had evidently been looking at it in the best light. It was well worth looking at, for that white and brilliant daylight turned its precious stones to many-coloured flames so that it might have been a model of the Holy Grail. It was well worth looking at; but Brander Merton was not looking at it. For his head had fallen back over his chair, his mane of white hair hanging towards the floor, and his spike of grizzled beard thrust up towards the ceiling, and out of his throat stood a long, brown-painted arrow with red feathers at the other end.

'A silent shot,' said Father Brown, in a low voice; 'I was just wondering about those new inventions for silencing firearms. But this is a very old invention, and quite as silent.'

Then, after a moment, he added: 'I'm afraid he is dead. What are you going to do?'

The pale secretary roused himself with abrupt resolution. 'I'm going to press that button, of course,' he said, 'and if that doesn't do for Daniel Doom, I'm going to hunt him through the world till I find him.'

'Take care it doesn't do for any of our friends,' observed Father Brown; 'they can hardly be far off; we'd better call them.'

'That lot know all about the wall,' answered Wilton. 'None of them will try to climb it, unless one of them . . . is in a great hurry.'

Father Brown went to the window by which the arrow had evidently entered and looked out. The garden, with its flat flowerbeds, lay far below like a delicately coloured map of the world. The whole vista seemed so vast and empty, the tower seemed set so far up in the sky that as he stared out a strange phrase came back to his memory.

'A bolt from the blue,' he said. 'What was that somebody said about a bolt from the blue and death coming out of the sky? Look how far away everything looks; it seems extraordinary that an arrow could come so far, unless it were an arrow from heaven.'

Wilton had returned, but did not reply, and the priest went on as in soliloquy. 'One thinks of aviation. We must ask young Wain . . . about aviation.'

'There's a lot of it round here,' said the secretary.

'Case of very old or very new weapons,' observed Father Brown. 'Some would be quite familiar to his old uncle, I suppose; we must ask him about arrows. This looks rather like a Red Indian arrow. I don't know where the Red Indian shot it from; but you remember the story the old man told. I said it had a moral.'

'If it had a moral,' said Wilton warmly, 'it was only that a real Red Indian might shoot a thing farther than you'd fancy. It's nonsense your suggesting a parallel.'

'I don't think you've got the moral quite right,' said Father Brown.

Although the little priest appeared to melt into the millions of New York next day, without any apparent attempt to be anything but a number in a numbered street, he was, in fact, unobtrusively busy for the next fortnight with the commission that had been given him, for he was filled with profound fear about a possible miscarriage of justice. Without having any particular air of singling them out from his other new acquaintances, he found it easy to fall into talk with the two or three men recently involved in the mystery; and with old Hickory Crake especially he had a curious and interesting conversation. It took place on a seat in Central Park, where the veteran sat with his bony hands and hatchet face resting on the oddly shaped head of a walking-stick of dark red wood, possibly modelled on a tomahawk.

'Well, it may be a long shot,' he said, wagging his head, 'but I wouldn't advise you to be too positive about how far an Indian arrow could go. I've known some bow-shots that seemed to go straighter than any bullets, and hit the mark to amazement, considering how long they had been travelling. Of course, you practically never hear now of a Red Indian with a bow and arrows, still less of a Red Indian hanging about here. But if by any chance there were one of the old Indian marksmen, with one of the old Indian bows, hiding in those trees hundreds of yards beyond the Merton outer wall – why, then I wouldn't put it past the noble savage to be able to send an arrow over the wall and into the top window of Merton's house; no, nor into Merton, either. I've seen things quite as wonderful as that done in the old days.'

'No doubt,' said the priest, 'you have done things quite as wonderful, as well as seen them.'

Old Crake chuckled, and then said gruffly: 'Oh, that's all ancient history.'

'Some people have a way of studying ancient history,' the priest said. 'I suppose we may take it there is nothing in your old record to make people talk unpleasantly about this affair.'

'What do you mean?' demanded Crake, his eyes shifting sharply for the first time, in his red, wooden face, that was rather like the head of a tomahawk.

'Well, since you were so well acquainted with all the arts and crafts of the Redskin – ' began Father Brown slowly.

Crake had had a hunched and almost shrunken appearance as he sat with his chin propped on its queer-shaped crutch. But the next instant he stood erect in the path like a fighting bravo with the crutch clutched like a cudgel.

'What?' he cried – in something like a raucous screech – 'what the hell! Are you standing up to me to tell me I might happen to have murdered my own brother-in-law?'

From a dozen seats dotted about the path people looked towards the disputants, as they stood facing each other in the middle of the path, the bald-headed energetic little man brandishing his outlandish stick like a club, and the black, dumpy figure of the little cleric looking at him without moving a muscle, save for his blinking eyelids. For a moment it looked as if the black, dumpy figure would be knocked on the head, and laid out with true Red Indian promptitude and dispatch; and the large form of an Irish policeman could be seen heaving up in the distance and bearing down on the group. But the priest only said, quite placidly, like one answering an ordinary query: 'I have formed certain conclusions about it, but I do not think I will mention them till I make my report.'

Whether under the influence of the footsteps of the policeman or of the eyes of the priest, old Hickory tucked his stick under his arm and put his hat on again, grunting. The priest bade him a placid good-morning, and passed in an unhurried fashion out of the park, making his way to the lounge of the hotel where he knew that young Wain was to be found. The young man sprang up with a greeting; he looked even more haggard and harassed than before, as if some worry were eating him away; and the priest had a suspicion that his young friend had recently been engaged, with only too conspicuous success, in evading the last Amendment to the American Constitution. But at the first word about his hobby or favourite science he was vigilant and concentrated enough. For Father Brown had asked, in an idle and conversational fashion, whether much flying was done in that district, and had told how he had at first mistaken Mr Merton's circular wall for an aerodrome.

'It's a wonder you didn't see any while we were there,' answered Captain Wain. 'Sometimes they're as thick as flies; that open plain is a great place for them, and I shouldn't wonder if it were the chief breeding-ground, so to speak, for my sort of birds in the future. I've flown a good deal there myself, of course, and I know most of the fellows about here who flew in the war; but there are a whole lot of people taking to it out there now whom I never heard of in my life. I suppose it will be like motoring soon, and every man in the States will have one.'

'Being endowed by his Creator,' said Father Brown with a smile, 'with the right to life, liberty, and the pursuit of motoring – not to mention aviation. So I suppose we may take it that one strange aeroplane passing over that house, at certain times, wouldn't be noticed much.'

'No,' replied the young man; 'I don't suppose it would.'

'Or even if the man were known,' went on the other, 'I suppose he might get hold of a machine that wouldn't be recognised as his. If you, for instance, flew in the ordinary way, Mr Merton and his friends might recognise the rig-out, perhaps; but you might pass pretty near that window on a different pattern of plane, or whatever you call it; near enough for practical purposes.'

'Well, yes,' began the young man, almost automatically, and then ceased, and remained staring at the cleric with an open mouth and eyes standing out of his head.

'My God!' he said, in a low voice; 'my God!'

Then he rose from the lounge seat, pale and shaking from head to foot and still staring at the priest.

'Are you mad?' he said; 'are you raving mad?'

There was a silence and then he spoke again in a swift hissing fashion. 'You positively come here to suggest – '

'No; only to collect suggestions,' said Father Brown, rising. 'I may have formed some conclusions provisionally, but I had better reserve them for the present.'

And then saluting the other with the same stiff civility, he passed out of the hotel to continue his curious peregrinations.

By the dusk of that day they had led him down the dingy streets and steps that straggled and tumbled towards the river in the oldest and most irregular part of the city. Immediately under the coloured lantern that marked the entrance to a rather low Chinese restaurant he encountered a figure he had seen before, though by no means presenting itself to the eye as he had seen it.

Mr Norman Drage still confronted the world grimly behind his great goggles, which seemed somehow to cover his face like a dark mask of glass. But except for the goggles, his appearance had undergone a strange transformation in the month that had elapsed since the murder. He had then, as Father Brown had noted, been dressed up to the nines – up to that point, indeed, where there begins to be too fine a distinction between the dandy and the dummy outside a tailor's shop. But now all those externals were mysteriously altered for the worse; as if the tailor's dummy had been turned into a scarecrow. His top hat still existed, but it was battered and shabby; his clothes were dilapidated; his watch-chain and minor ornaments were gone. Father Brown, however, addressed him as if they had met yesterday, and made no demur to sitting down with him on a bench in the cheap eating-house whither he was bound. It was not he, however, who began the conversation.

'Well?' growled Drage, 'and have you succeeded in avenging your holy and sainted millionaire? We know all millionaires are holy and sainted; you can find it all in the papers next day, about how they lived by the light of the Family Bible they read at their mother's knee. Gee! if they'd only read out some of the things there are in the Family Bible, the mother might have been startled some. And the millionaire, too, I reckon. The old Book's full of a lot of grand fierce old notions they don't grow nowadays; sort of wisdom of the Stone Age and buried under the Pyramids. Suppose somebody had flung old man Merton from the top of that tower of his, and let him be eaten by dogs at the bottom, it would be no worse than what happened to Jezebel. Wasn't Agag hacked into little pieces, for all he went walking delicately? Merton walked delicately all his life, damn him – until he got too delicate to walk at all. But the shaft of the Lord found him out, as it might have done in the old Book, and struck him dead on the top of his tower to be a spectacle to the people.'

'The shaft was material, at least,' said his companion.

'The Pyramids are mighty material, and they hold down the dead kings all right,' grinned the man in the goggles. 'I think there's a lot to be said for these old material religions. There's old carvings that have lasted for thousands of years, showing their gods and emperors with bended bows; with hands that look as if they could really bend bows of stone. Material, perhaps – but what materials! Don't you sometimes stand staring at those old Eastern patterns and things, till you have a hunch that old Lord God is still driving like a dark Apollo, and shooting black rays of death?'

'If he is,' replied Father Brown, 'I might call him by another name. But I doubt whether Merton died by a dark ray or even a stone arrow.'

'I guess you think he's St Sebastian,' sneered Drage, 'killed with an arrow. A millionaire must be a martyr. How do you know he didn't deserve it? You don't know much about your millionaire, I fancy. Well, let me tell you he deserved it a hundred times over.'

'Well,' asked Father Brown gently, 'why didn't you murder him?'

'You want to know why I didn't?' said the other, staring. 'Well, you're a nice sort of clergyman.'

'Not at all,' said the other, as if waving away a compliment.

'I suppose it's your way of saying I did,' snarled Drage. 'Well, prove it, that's all. As for him, I reckon he was no loss.'

'Yes, he was,' said Father Brown, sharply. 'He was a loss to you. That's why you didn't kill him.'

And he walked out of the room, leaving the man in goggles gaping after him.

It was nearly a month later that Father Brown revisited the house where the third millionaire had suffered from the vendetta of Daniel Doom. A sort of council was held of the persons most interested. Old Crake sat at the head of the table with his nephew at his right hand, the lawyer on his left; the big man with the African features, whose name appeared to be Harris, was ponderously present, if only as a material witness; a red-haired, sharp-nosed individual addressed as Dixon seemed to be the representative of Pinkerton's or some such private agency; and Father Brown slipped unobtrusively into an empty seat beside him.

Every newspaper in the world was full of the catastrophe of the colossus of finance, of the great organiser of the Big Business that bestrides the modern world; but from the tiny group that had been nearest to him at the very instant of his death very little could be learned. The uncle, nephew, and attendant solicitor declared they were well outside the outer wall before the alarm was raised; and enquiries of the official guardians at both barriers brought answers that were rather confused, but on the whole confirmatory. Only one other complication seemed to call for consideration. It seemed that round about the time of the death, before or after, a stranger had been found hanging mysteriously round the entrance and asking to see Mr Merton. The servants had some difficulty in understanding what he meant, for his language was very obscure; but it was afterwards considered to be also very suspicious, since he had said something about a wicked man being destroyed by a word out of the sky.

Peter Wain leaned forward, the eyes bright in his haggard face, and said: 'I'll bet on that, anyhow. Norman Drage.'

'And who in the world is Norman Drage?' asked his uncle.

'That's what I want to know,' replied the young man. 'I practically asked him, but he has got a wonderful trick of twisting every straight question crooked; it's like lunging at a fencer. He hooked on to me with hints about the flying-ship of the future; but I never trusted him much.'

'But what sort of a man is he?' asked Crake.

'He's a mystagogue,' said Father Brown, with innocent promptitude.

'There are quite a lot of them about; the sort of men about town who hint to you in Paris cafés and cabarets that they've lifted the veil of Isis or know the secret of Stonehenge. In a case like this they're sure to have some sort of mystical explanations.'

The smooth, dark head of Mr Barnard Blake, the lawyer, was inclined politely towards the speaker, but his smile was faintly hostile.

'I should hardly have thought, sir,' he said, 'that you had any quarrel with mystical explanations.'

'On the contrary,' replied Father Brown, blinking amiably at him. 'That's just why I can quarrel with 'em. Any sham lawyer could bamboozle me, but he couldn't bamboozle you; because you're a lawyer yourself. Any fool could dress up as a Red Indian and I'd swallow him whole as the only original Hiawatha; but Mr Crake would see through him at once. A swindler could pretend to me that he knew all about aeroplanes, but not to Captain Wain. And it's just the same with the other, don't you see? It's just because I have picked up a little about mystics that I have no use for mystagogues. Real mystics don't hide mysteries, they reveal them. They set a thing up in broad daylight, and when you've seen it it's still a mystery. But the mystagogues hide a thing in darkness and secrecy, and when you find it, it's a platitude. But in the case of Drage, I admit he had also another and more practical notion in talking about fire from heaven or bolts from the blue.'

'And what was his notion?' asked Wain. 'I think it wants watching whatever it is.'

'Well,' replied the priest, slowly, 'he wanted us to think the murders were miracles because . . . well, because he knew they weren't.'

'Ah,' said Wain, with a sort of hiss, 'I was waiting for that. In plain words, he is the criminal.'

'In plain words, he is the criminal who didn't commit the crime,' answered Father Brown calmly.

'Is that your conception of plain words?' enquired Blake politely.

'You'll be saying I'm the mystagogue now,' said Father Brown somewhat abashed, but with a broad smile, 'but it was really quite accidental. Drage didn't commit the crime – I mean this crime. His only crime was blackmailing somebody, and he hung about here to do it; but he wasn't likely to want the secret to be public property or the whole business to be cut short by death. We can talk about him afterwards. Just at the moment, I only want him cleared out of the way.'

'Out of the way of what?' asked the other.

'Out of the way of the truth,' replied the priest, looking at him tranquilly, with level eyelids.

'Do you mean,' faltered the other, 'that you know the truth?'

'I rather think so,' said Father Brown modestly.

There was an abrupt silence, after which Crake cried out suddenly and irrelevantly in a rasping voice: 'Why, where is that secretary fellow? Wilton! He ought to be here.'

'I am in communication with Mr Wilton,' said Father Brown gravely; 'in fact, I asked him to ring me up here in a few minutes from now. I may say that we've worked the thing out together, in a manner of speaking.'

'If you're working together, I suppose it's all right,' grumbled Crake. 'I know he was always a sort of bloodhound on the trail of his vanishing crook, so perhaps it was well to hunt in couples with him. But if you know the truth about this, where the devil did you get it from?'

'I got it from you,' answered the priest, quietly, and continued to gaze mildly at the glaring veteran. 'I mean I made the first guess from a hint in a story of yours about an Indian who threw a knife and hit a man on the top of a fortress.'

'You've said that several times,' said Wain, with a puzzled air; 'but I can't see any inference, except that this murderer threw an arrow and hit a man on the top of a house very like a fortress. But of course the arrow wasn't thrown but shot, and would go much further. Certainly it went uncommonly far; but I don't see how it brings us any farther.'

'I'm afraid you missed the point of the story,' said Father Brown. 'It isn't that if one thing can go far another can go farther. It is that the wrong use of a tool can cut both ways. The men on Crake's fort thought of a knife as a thing for a hand-to-hand fight and forgot that it could be a missile like a javelin. Some other people I know thought of a thing as a missile like a javelin and forgot that, after all, it could be used hand-to-hand as a spear. In short, the moral of the story is that since a dagger can be turned into an arrow, so can an arrow be turned into a dagger.'

They were all looking at him now; but he continued in the same casual and unconscious tone: 'Naturally we wondered and worried a good deal about who shot that arrow through the window and whether it came from far away, and so on. But the truth is that nobody shot the arrow at all. It never came in at the window at all.'

'Then how did it come there?' asked the swarthy lawyer, with a rather lowering face.

'Somebody brought it with him, I suppose,' said Father Brown; 'it wouldn't be hard to carry or conceal. Somebody had it in his hand as he stood with Merton in Merton's own room. Somebody thrust it into Merton's throat like a poignard, and then had the highly intelligent idea of placing the whole thing at such a place and angle that we all assumed in a flash that it had flown in at the window like a bird.'

'Somebody,' said old Crake, in a voice as heavy as stone.

The telephone bell rang with a strident and horrible clamour of insistence.

It was in the adjoining room, and Father Brown had darted there before anybody else could move.

'What the devil is it all about?' cried Peter Wain, who seemed all shaken and distracted.

'He said he expected to be rung up by Wilton, the secretary,' replied his uncle in the same dead voice.

'I suppose it is Wilton?' observed the lawyer, like one speaking to fill up a silence. But nobody answered the question until Father Brown reappeared suddenly and silently in the room, bringing the answer.

'Gentlemen,' he said, when he had resumed his seat, 'it was you who asked me to look into the truth about this puzzle; and having found the truth, I must tell it, without any pretence of softening the shock. I'm afraid anybody who pokes his nose into things like this can't afford to be a respecter of persons.'

'I suppose,' said Crake, breaking the silence that followed, 'that means that some of us are accused, or suspected.'

'All of us are suspected,' answered Father Brown. 'I may be suspected myself, for I found the body.'

'Of course we're suspected,' snapped Wain. 'Father Brown kindly explained to me how I could have besieged the tower in a flying-machine.'

'No,' replied the priest, with a smile; 'you described to me how you could have done it. That was just the interesting part of it.'

'He seemed to think it likely,' growled Crake, 'that I killed him myself with a Red Indian arrow.'

'I thought it most unlikely,' said Father Brown, making rather a wry face. 'I'm sorry if I did wrong, but I couldn't think of any other way of testing the matter. I can hardly think of anything more improbable than the notion that Captain Wain went careering in a huge machine past the window, at the very moment of the murder, and nobody noticed it; unless, perhaps, it were the notion that a respectable old gentleman should play at Red Indians with a bow and arrow behind the bushes, to kill somebody he could have killed in twenty much simpler ways. But I had to find out if they had had anything to do with it; and so I had to accuse them in order to prove their innocence.'

'And how have you proved their innocence?' asked Blake the lawyer, leaning forward eagerly.

'Only by the agitation they showed when they were accused,' answered the other.

'What do you mean, exactly?'

'If you will permit me to say so,' remarked Father Brown, composedly enough, 'I did undoubtedly think it my duty to suspect them and everybody else. I did suspect Mr Crake and I did suspect Captain Wain, in the sense that I considered the possibility or probability of their guilt. I told them I had formed conclusions about it; and I will now tell them what those conclusions were. I was sure they were innocent, because of the manner and the moment in which they passed from unconsciousness to indignation. So long as they never thought they were accused, they went on giving me materials to support the accusation. They practically explained to me how they might have committed the crime. Then they suddenly realised with a shock and a shout of rage that they were accused; they realised it long after they might well have expected to be accused, but long before I had accused them. Now no guilty person could possibly do that. He might be snappy and suspicious from the first; or he might simulate unconsciousness and innocence up to the end. But he wouldn't begin by making things worse for himself and then give a great jump and begin furiously denying the notion he had himself helped to suggest. That could only come by his having really failed to realise what he was suggesting. The self-consciousness of a murderer would always be at least morbidly vivid enough to prevent him first forgetting his relation with the thing and then remembering to deny it. So I ruled you both out and others for other reasons I needn't discuss now. For instance, there was the secretary –

'But I'm not talking about that just now. Look here, I've just heard from Wilton on the phone, and he's given me permission to tell you some rather serious news. Now I suppose you all know by this time who Wilton was, and what he was after.'

'I know he was after Daniel Doom and wouldn't be happy till he got him,' answered Peter Wain; 'and I've heard the story that he's the son of old Horder, and that's why he's the avenger of blood. Anyhow, he's certainly looking for the man called Doom.'

'Well,' said Father Brown, 'he has found him.'

Peter Wain sprang to his feet in excitement.

'The murderer!' he cried. 'Is the murderer in the lock-up already?'

'No,' said Father Brown, gravely; 'I said the news was serious, and it's more serious than that. I'm afraid poor Wilton has taken a terrible responsibility. I'm afraid he's going to put a terrible responsibility on us. He hunted the criminal down, and just when he had him cornered at last – well, he has taken the law into his own hands.'

'You mean that Daniel Doom – ' began the lawyer.

'I mean that Daniel Doom is dead,' said the priest. 'There was some sort of wild struggle, and Wilton killed him.'

'Serve him right,' growled Mr Hickory Crake.

'Can't blame Wilton for downing a crook like that, especially considering the feud,' assented Wain; 'it was like stepping on a viper.'

'I don't agree with you,' said Father Brown. 'I suppose we all talk romantic stuff at random in defence of lynching and lawlessness; but I have a suspicion that if we lose our laws and liberties we shall regret it. Besides, it seems to me illogical to say there is something to be said for Wilton committing murder, without even enquiring whether there was anything to be said for Doom committing it. I rather doubt whether Doom was merely a vulgar assassin; he may have been a sort of outlaw with a mania about the cup, demanding it with threats and only killing after a struggle; both victims were thrown down just outside their houses. The objection to Wilton's way of doing it is that we shall never hear Doom's side of the case.'

'Oh, I've no patience with all this sentimental whitewashing of worthless, murderous blackguards,' cried Wain, heatedly. 'If Wilton croaked the criminal he did a jolly good day's work, and there's an end of it.'

'Quite so, quite so,' said his uncle, nodding vigorously.

Father Brown's face had a yet heavier gravity as he looked slowly round the semicircle of faces. 'Is that really what you all think?' he asked. Even as he did so he realised that he was an Englishman and an exile. He realised that he was among foreigners, even if he was among friends. Around that ring of foreigners ran a restless fire that was not native to his own breed; the fiercer spirit of the western nation that can rebel and lynch, and above all, combine. He knew that they had already combined.

'Well,' said Father Brown, with a sigh, 'I am to understand, then, that you do definitely condone this unfortunate man's crime, or act of private justice, or whatever you call it. In that case it will not hurt him if I tell you a little more about it.'

He rose suddenly to his feet; and though they saw no meaning in his movement, it seemed in some way to change or chill the very air in the room.

'Wilton killed Doom in a rather curious way,' he began.

'How did Wilton kill him?' asked Crake, abruptly.

'With an arrow,' said Father Brown.

Twilight was gathering in the long room, and daylight dwindling to a gleam from the great window in the inner room, where the great millionaire had died. Almost automatically the eyes of the group turned slowly towards it, but as yet there was no sound. Then the voice of Crake came cracked and high and senile in a sort of crowing gabble.

'What you mean? What you mean? Brander Merton killed by an arrow. This crook killed by an arrow –'

'By the same arrow,' said the priest, 'and at the same moment.'

Again there was a sort of strangled and yet swollen and bursting silence, and young Wain began: 'You mean –'

'I mean that your friend Merton was Daniel Doom,' said Father Brown firmly; 'and the only Daniel Doom you'll ever find. Your friend Merton was always crazy after that Coptic Cup that he used to worship like an idol every day; and in his wild youth he had really killed two men to get it, though I still think the deaths may have been in a sense accidents of the robbery. Anyhow, he had it; and that man Drage knew the story and was blackmailing him. But Wilton was after him for a very different purpose; I fancy he only discovered the truth when he'd got into this house. But anyhow, it was in this house, and in that room, that this hunt ended, and he slew the slayer of his father.'

For a long time nobody answered. Then old Crake could be heard drumming with his fingers on the table and muttering: 'Brander must have been mad. He must have been mad.'

'But, good Lord!' burst out Peter Wain; 'what are we to do? What are we to say? Oh, it's all quite different! What about the papers and the big business people? Brander Merton is a thing like the President or the Pope of Rome.'

'I certainly think it is rather different,' began Barnard Blake, the lawyer, in a low voice. 'The difference involves a whole – '

Father Brown struck the table so that the glasses on it rang; and they could almost fancy a ghostly echo from the mysterious chalice that still stood in the room beyond.

'No!' he cried, in a voice like a pistol-shot. 'There shall be no difference. I gave you your chance of pitying the poor devil when you thought he was a common criminal. You wouldn't listen then; you were all for private vengeance then. You were all for letting him be butchered like a wild beast without a hearing or a public trial, and said he had only got his deserts. Very well then, if Daniel Doom has got his deserts, Brander Merton has got his deserts. If that was good enough for Doom, by all that is holy it is good enough for Merton. Take your wild justice or our dull legality; but in the name of Almighty God, let there be an equal lawlessness or an equal law.'

Nobody answered except the lawyer, and he answered with something like a snarl: 'What will the police say if we tell them we mean to condone a crime?'

'What will they say if I tell them you did condone it?' replied Father Brown. 'Your respect for the law comes rather late, Mr Barnard Blake.'

After a pause he resumed in a milder tone: 'I, for one, am ready to tell the truth if the proper authorities ask me; and the rest of you can do as you like. But as a fact, it will make very little difference. Wilton only rang me up to tell me that I was now free to lay his confession before you; for when you heard it, he would be beyond pursuit.'

He walked slowly into the inner room and stood there by the little table beside which the millionaire had died. The Coptic Cup still stood in the same place, and he remained there for a space staring at its cluster of all the colours of the rainbow, and beyond it into a blue abyss of sky.

The Oracle of the Dog

'Yes,' said Father Brown, 'I always like a dog, so long as he isn't spelt backwards.'

Those who are quick in talking are not always quick in listening. Sometimes even their brilliancy produces a sort of stupidity. Father Brown's friend and companion was a young man with a stream of ideas and stories, an enthusiastic young man named Fiennes, with eager blue eyes and blond hair that seemed to be brushed back, not merely with a hairbrush but with the wind of the world as be rushed through it. But he stopped in the torrent of his talk in a momentary bewilderment before he saw the priest's very simple meaning.

'You mean that people make too much of them?' he said. 'Well, I don't know. They're marvellous creatures. Sometimes I think they know a lot more than we do.'

Father Brown said nothing, but continued to stroke the head of the big retriever in a half-abstracted but apparently soothing fashion.

'Why,' said Fiennes, warming again to his monologue, 'there was a dog in the case I've come to see you about: what they call the "Invisible Murder Case", you know. It's a strange story, but from my point of view the dog is about the strangest thing in it. Of course, there's the mystery of the crime itself, and how old Druce can have been killed by somebody else when he was all alone in the summer-house – '

The hand stroking the dog stopped for a moment in its rhythmic movement, and Father Brown said calmly: 'Oh, it was a summer-house, was it?'

'I thought you'd read all about it in the papers,' answered Fiennes. 'Stop a minute; I believe I've got a cutting that will give you all the particulars.' He produced a strip of newspaper from his pocket and handed it to the priest, who began to read it, holding it close to his blinking eyes with one hand while the other continued its half-conscious caresses of the dog. It looked like the parable of a man not letting his right hand know what his left hand did.

* * *

Many mystery stories, about men murdered behind locked doors and windows, and murderers escaping without means of entrance and exit, have come true in the course of the extraordinary events at Cranston on the coast of Yorkshire, where Colonel Druce was found stabbed from behind by a dagger that has entirely disappeared from the scene, and apparently even from the neighbourhood.

The summer-house in which he died was indeed accessible at one entrance, the ordinary doorway which looked down the central walk of the garden towards the house. But, by a combination of events almost to be called a coincidence, it appears that both the path and the entrance were watched during the crucial time, and there is a chain of witnesses who confirm each other. The summer-house stands at the extreme end of the garden, where there is no exit or entrance of any kind. The central garden path is a lane between two ranks of tall delphiniums, planted so close that any stray step off the path would leave its traces; and both path and plants run right up to the very mouth of the summer-house, so that no straying from that straight path could fail to be observed, and no other mode of entrance can be imagined.

Patrick Floyd, secretary of the murdered man, testified that he had been in a position to overlook the whole garden from the time when Colonel Druce last appeared alive in the doorway to the time when he was found dead; as he, Floyd, had been on the top of a step-ladder clipping the garden hedge. Janet Druce, the dead man's daughter, confirmed this, saying that she had sat on the terrace of the house throughout that time and had seen Floyd at his work. Touching some part of the time, this is again supported by Donald Druce, her brother – who overlooked the garden – standing at his bedroom window in his dressing-gown, for he had risen late. Lastly, the account is consistent with that given by Dr Valentine, a neighbour, who called for a time to talk with Miss Druce on the terrace, and by the Colonel's solicitor, Mr Aubrey Traill, who was apparently the last to see the murdered man alive – presumably with the exception of the murderer.

All are agreed that the course of events was as follows: about half-past three in the afternoon, Miss Druce went down the path to ask her father when he would like tea; but he said he did not want any and was waiting to see Traill, his lawyer, who was to be sent to him in the summer-house. The girl then came away and met Traill coming down the path; she directed him to her father and he went in as directed. About half an hour afterwards he came out again, the Colonel coming with him to the door and showing himself to all appearance in health and even high spirits. He had been somewhat annoyed earlier in the day by his son's irregular hours, but seemed to recover his temper in a perfectly normal fashion, and had been rather markedly genial in receiving other visitors, including two of his nephews, who came over for the day. But as these were out walking during the whole period of the tragedy, they had no evidence to give. It is said, indeed, that the Colonel was not on very good terms with Dr Valentine, but that gentleman only had a brief interview with the daughter of the house, to whom he is supposed to be paying serious attentions.

Trall, the solicitor, says he left the Colonel entirely alone in the summer-house, and this is confirmed by Floyd's bird's-eye view of the garden, which showed nobody else passing the only entrance. Ten minutes later, Miss Druce again went down the garden and had not reached the end of the path when she saw her father, who was conspicuous by his white linen coat, lying in a heap on the floor. She uttered a scream which brought others to the spot, and on entering the place they found the Colonel lying dead beside his basket-chair, which was also upset. Dr Valentine, who was still in the immediate neighbourhood, testified that the wound was made by some sort of stiletto, entering under the shoulder-blade and piercing the heart. The police have searched the neighbourhood for such a weapon, but no trace of it can be found.

* * *

'So Colonel Druce wore a white coat, did he?' said Father Brown as he put down the paper.

'Trick he learnt in the tropics,' replied Fiennes, with some wonder. 'He'd had some queer adventures there, by his own account; and I fancy his dislike of Valentine was connected with the doctor coming from the tropics, too. But it's all an infernal puzzle. The account there is pretty accurate. I didn't see the tragedy, in the sense of the discovery; I was out walking with the young nephews and the dog – the dog I wanted to tell you about. But I saw the stage set for it as described; the straight lane between the blue flowers right up to the dark entrance, and the lawyer going down it in his blacks and his silk hat, and the red head of the secretary showing high above the green hedge as he worked on it with his shears. Nobody could have mistaken that red head at any distance; and if people say they saw it there all the time, you may be sure they did. This red-haired secretary, Floyd, is quite a character; a breathless bounding sort of fellow, always doing everybody's work as he was doing the gardener's. I think he is an American; he's certainly got the American view of life – what they call the viewpoint, bless 'em.'

'What about the lawyer?' asked Father Brown.

There was a silence and then Fiennes spoke quite slowly for him. 'Traill struck me as a singular man. In his fine black clothes he was almost foppish, yet you can hardly call him fashionable. For he wore a pair of long, luxuriant black whiskers such as haven't been seen since Victorian times. He had rather a fine grave face and a fine grave manner, but every now and then he seemed to remember to smile. And when he showed his white teeth he seemed to lose a little of his dignity, and there was something faintly fawning about him. It may have been only embarrassment, for he would also fidget with his cravat and his tie-pin, which were at once handsome and unusual, like himself. If I could think of anybody – but what's the good, when the whole thing's impossible? Nobody knows who did it. Nobody knows how it could be done. At least there's only one exception I'd make, and that's why I really mentioned the whole thing. The dog knows.'

Father Brown sighed and then said absently: 'You were there as a friend of young Donald, weren't you? He didn't go on your walk with you?'

'No,' replied Fiennes smiling. 'The young scoundrel had gone to bed that morning and got up that afternoon. I went with his cousins, two young officers from India, and our conversation was trivial enough. I remember the elder, whose name I think is Herbert Druce and who is an authority on horse-breeding, talked about nothing but a mare he had bought and the moral character of the man who sold her; while his brother Harry seemed to be brooding on his bad luck at Monte Carlo. I only mention it to show you, in the light of what happened on our walk, that there was nothing psychic about us. The dog was the only mystic in our company.'

'What sort of a dog was he?' asked the priest.

'Same breed as that one,' answered Fiennes. 'That's what started me off on the story, your saying you didn't believe in believing in a dog. He's a big black retriever, named Nox, and a suggestive name, too; for I think what he did a darker mystery than the murder. You know Druce's house and garden are by the sea; we walked about a mile from it along the sands and then turned back, going the other way. We passed a rather curious rock called the Rock of Fortune, famous in the neighbourhood because it's one of those examples of one stone barely balanced on another, so that a touch would knock it over. It is not really very high but the hanging outline of it makes it look a little wild and sinister; at least it made it look so to me, for I don't imagine my jolly young companions were afflicted with the picturesque. But it may be that I was beginning to feel an atmosphere; for just then the question arose of whether it was time to go back to tea, and even then I think I had a premonition that time counted for a good deal in the business. Neither Herbert Druce nor I had a watch, so we called out to his brother, who was some paces behind, having stopped to light his pipe under the hedge. Hence it happened that he shouted out the hour, which was twenty past four, in his big voice through the growing twilight; and somehow the loudness of it made it sound like the proclamation of something tremendous. His unconsciousness seemed to make it all the more so; but that was always the way with omens; and particular ticks of the clock were really very ominous things that afternoon. According to Dr Valentine's testimony, poor Druce had actually died just about half-past four.

'Well, they said we needn't go home for ten minutes, and we walked a little farther along the sands, doing nothing in particular – throwing stones for the dog and throwing sticks into the sea for him to swim after. But to me the twilight seemed to grow oddly oppressive, and the very shadow of the top-heavy Rock of Fortune lay on me like a load. And then the curious thing happened. Nox had just brought back Herbert's walking-stick out of the sea and his brother had thrown his in also. The dog swam out again, but just about what must have been the stroke of the half-hour, he stopped swimming. He came back again on to the shore and stood in front of us. Then he suddenly threw up his head and sent up a howl or wail of woe – if ever I heard one in the world.

' "What the devil's the matter with the dog?" asked Herbert; but none of us could answer. There was a long silence after the brute's wailing and whining died away on the desolate shore; and then the silence was broken. As I live, it was broken by a faint and far-off shriek, like the shriek of a woman from beyond the hedges inland. We didn't know what it was then; but we knew afterwards. It was the cry the girl gave when she first saw the body of her father.'

'You went back, I suppose,' said Father Brown patiently. 'What happened then?'

'I'll tell you what happened then,' said Fiennes with a grim emphasis. 'When we got back into that garden the first thing we saw was Traill, the lawyer; I can see him now with his black hat and black whiskers relieved against the perspective of the blue flowers stretching down to the summer-house, with the sunset and the strange outline of the Rock of Fortune in the distance. His face and figure were in shadow against the sunset; but I swear the white teeth were showing in his head and he was smiling. The moment Nox saw that man the dog dashed forward and stood in the middle of the path barking at him madly, murderously, volleying out curses that were almost verbal in their dreadful distinctness of hatred. And the man doubled up and fled, along the path between the flowers.'

Father Brown sprang to his feet with a startling impatience. 'So the dog denounced him, did he?' he cried. 'The oracle of the dog condemned him. Did you see what birds were flying, and are you sure whether they were on the right hand or the left? Did you consult the augurs about the sacrifices? Surely you didn't omit to cut open the dog and examine his entrails. That is the sort of scientific test you heathen humanitarians seem to trust when you are thinking of taking away the life and honour of a man.'

Fiennes sat gaping for an instant before he found breath to say: 'Why, what's the matter with you? What have I done now?'

A sort of anxiety came back into the priest's eyes – the anxiety of a man who has run against a post in the dark and wonders for a moment whether he has hurt it.

'I'm most awfully sorry,' he said with sincere distress. 'I beg your pardon for being so rude; pray forgive me.'

Fiennes looked at him curiously. 'I sometimes think you are more of a mystery than any of the mysteries,' he said. 'But anyhow, if you don't believe in the mystery of the dog, at least you can't get over the mystery of the man. You can't deny that at the very moment when the beast came back from the sea and bellowed, his master's soul was driven out of his body by the blow of some unseen power that no mortal man can trace or even imagine. And as for the lawyer – I don't go only by the dog – there are other curious details, too. He struck me as a smooth, smiling, equivocal sort of person; and one of his tricks seemed like a sort of hint. You know the doctor and the police were on the spot very quickly; Valentine was brought back when walking away from the house, and he telephoned instantly. That, with the secluded house, small numbers, and enclosed space, made it pretty possible to search everybody who could have been near; and everybody was thoroughly searched – for a weapon. The whole house, garden, and shore were combed for a weapon. The disappearance of the dagger is almost as crazy as the disappearance of the man.'

'The disappearance of the dagger,' said Father Brown, nodding. He seemed to have become suddenly attentive.

'Well,' continued Fiennes, 'I told you that man Traill had a trick of fidgeting with his tie and tie-pin – especially his tie-pin. His pin, like himself, was at once showy and old-fashioned. It had one of those stones with concentric coloured rings that look like an eye; and his own concentration on it got on my nerves, as if he had been a Cyclops with one eye in the middle of his body. But the pin was not only large but long; and it occurred to me that his anxiety about its adjustment was because it was even longer than it looked; as long as a stiletto in fact.'

Father Brown nodded thoughtfully. 'Was any other instrument ever suggested?' he asked.

'There was another suggestion,' answered Fiennes, 'from one of the young Druces – the cousins, I mean. Neither Herbert nor Harry Druce would have struck one at first as likely to be of assistance in scientific detection; but while Herbert was really the traditional type of heavy Dragoon, caring for nothing but horses and being an ornament to the Horse Guards, his younger brother Harry had been in the Indian Police and knew something about such things. Indeed, in his own way he was quite clever; and I rather fancy he had been too clever; I mean he had left the police through breaking some red-tape regulations and taking some sort of risk and responsibility of his own. Anyhow, he was in some sense a detective out of work, and threw himself into this business with more than the ardour of an amateur. And it was with him that I had an argument about the weapon – an argument that led to something new. It began by his countering my description of the dog barking at Traill; and he said that a dog at his worst didn't bark, but growled.'

'He was quite right there,' observed the priest.

'This young fellow went on to say that, if it came to that, he'd heard Nox growling at other people before then; and among others at Floyd, the secretary. I retorted that his own argument answered itself; for the crime couldn't be brought home to two or three people, and least of all to Floyd, who was as innocent as a harum-scarum schoolboy, and had been seen by everybody all the time perched above the garden hedge with his fan of red hair as conspicuous as a scarlet cockatoo.

' "I know there's difficulties anyhow," said my colleague, "but I wish you'd come with me down the garden a minute. I want to show you something I don't think anyone else has seen." This was on the very day of the discovery, and the garden was just as it had been. The step-ladder was still standing by the hedge, and just under the hedge my guide stopped and disentangled something from the deep grass. It was the shears used for clipping the hedge, and on the point of one of them was a smear of blood.'

There was a short silence, and then Father Brown said suddenly; 'What was the lawyer there for?'

'He told us the Colonel sent for him to alter his will,' answered Fiennes. 'And, by the way, there was another thing about the business of the will that I ought to mention. You see, the will wasn't actually signed in the summer-house that afternoon.'

'I suppose not,' said Father Brown; 'there would have to be two witnesses.'

'The lawyer actually came down the day before and it was signed then; but he was sent for again next day because the old man had a doubt about one of the witnesses and had to be reassured.'

'Who were the witnesses?' asked Father Brown.

'That's just the point,' replied his informant eagerly, 'the witnesses were Floyd, the secretary, and this Dr Valentine, the foreign sort of surgeon or whatever he is; and the two had a quarrel. Now I'm bound to say that the secretary is something of a busybody. He's one of those hot and headlong people whose warmth of temperament has unfortunately turned mostly to pugnacity and bristling suspicion; to distrusting people instead of to trusting them. That sort of red-haired red-hot fellow is always either universally credulous or universally incredulous; and sometimes both. He was not only a Jack-of-all-trades, but he knew better than all tradesmen. He not only knew everything, but he warned everybody against everybody. All that must be taken into account in his suspicions about Valentine; but in that particular case there seems to have been something behind it. He said the name of Valentine was not really Valentine. He said he had seen him elsewhere known by the name of De Villon. He said it would invalidate the will; of course he was kind enough to explain to the lawyer what the law was on that point. They were both in a frightful wax.'

Father Brown laughed. 'People often are when they are to witness a will,' he said; 'for one thing, it means that they can't have any legacy under it. But what did Dr Valentine say? No doubt the universal secretary knew more about the doctor's name than the doctor did. But even the doctor might have some information about his own name.'

Fiennes paused a moment before he replied. 'Dr Valentine took it in a curious way. Dr Valentine is a curious man. His appearance is rather striking but very foreign. He is young but wears a beard cut square; and his face is very pale, dreadfully pale – and dreadfully serious. His eyes have a sort of ache in them, as if he ought to wear glasses, or had given himself a headache with thinking; but he is quite handsome and always very formally dressed, with a top hat and a dark coat and a little red rosette. His manner is rather cold and haughty, and he has a way of staring at you which is very disconcerting. When thus charged with having changed his name, he merely stared like a sphinx and then said with a little laugh that he supposed Americans had no names to change. At that I think the Colonel also got into a fuss and said all sorts of angry things to the doctor; all the more angry because of the doctor's pretensions to a future place in his family. But I shouldn't have thought much of that but for a few words that I happened to hear later, early in the afternoon of the tragedy. I don't want to make a lot of them, for they weren't the sort of words on which one would like, in the ordinary way, to play the eavesdropper. As I was passing out towards the front gate with my two companions and the dog, I heard voices which told me that Dr Valentine and Miss Druce had withdrawn for a moment in the shadow of the house, in an angle behind a row of flowering plants, and were talking to each other in passionate whisperings – sometimes almost like hissings; for it was something of a lovers' quarrel as well as a lovers' tryst. Nobody repeats the sort of things they said for the most part; but in an unfortunate business like this I'm bound to say that there was repeated more than once a phrase about killing somebody. In fact, the girl seemed to be begging him not to kill somebody, or saying that no provocation could justify killing anybody; which seems an unusual sort of talk to address to a gentleman who has dropped in to tea.'

'Do you know,' asked the priest, 'whether Dr Valentine seemed to be very angry after the scene with the secretary and the Colonel – I mean about witnessing the will?'

'By all accounts,' replied the other, 'he wasn't half so angry as the secretary was. It was the secretary who went away raging after witnessing the will.'

'And now,' said Father Brown, 'what about the will itself?'

'The Colonel was a very wealthy man, and his will was important. Traill wouldn't tell us the alteration at that stage, but I have since heard – only this morning in fact – that most of the money was transferred from the son to the daughter. I told you that Druce was wild with my friend Donald over his dissipated hours.'

'The question of motive has been rather overshadowed by the question of method,' observed Father Brown thoughtfully. 'At that moment, apparently, Miss Druce was the immediate gainer by the death.'

'Good God! What a cold-blooded way of talking,' cried Fiennes, staring at him. 'You don't really mean to hint that she – '

'Is she going to marry that Dr Valentine?' asked the other.

'Some people are against it,' answered his friend. 'But he is liked and respected in the place and is a skilled and devoted surgeon.'

'So devoted a surgeon,' said Father Brown, 'that he had surgical instruments with him when he went to call on the young lady at teatime. For he must have used a lancet or something, and he never seems to have gone home.'

Fiennes sprang to his feet and looked at him in a heat of enquiry. 'You suggest he might have used the very same lancet – '

Father Brown shook his head. 'All these suggestions are fancies just now,' he said. 'The problem is not who did it or what did it, but how it was done. We might find many men and even many tools – pins and shears and lancets. But how did a man get into the room? How did even a pin get into it?'

He was staring reflectively at the ceiling as he spoke, but as he said the last words his eye cocked in an alert fashion as if he had suddenly seen a curious fly on the ceiling.

'Well, what would you do about it?' asked the young man. 'You have a lot of experience; what would you advise now?'

'I'm afraid I'm not much use,' said Father Brown with a sigh. 'I can't suggest very much without having ever been near the place or the people. For the moment you can only go on with local enquiries. I gather that your friend from the Indian Police is more or less in charge of your enquiry down there. I should run down and see how he is getting on. See what he's been doing in the way of amateur detection. There may be news already.'

As his guests, the biped and the quadruped, disappeared, Father Brown took up his pen and went back to his interrupted occupation of planning a course of lectures on the Encyclical *Rerum Novarum*. The subject was a large one and he had to recast it more than once, so that he was somewhat similarly employed some two days later when the big black dog again came bounding into the room and sprawled all over him with enthusiasm and excitement. The master who followed the dog shared the excitement if not the enthusiasm. He had been excited in a less pleasant fashion, for his blue eyes seemed to start from his head and his eager face was even a little pale.

'You told me,' he said abruptly and without preface, 'to find out what Harry Druce was doing. Do you know what he's done?' The priest did not reply, and the young man went on in jerky tones: 'I'll tell you what he's done. He's killed himself.'

Father Brown's lips moved only faintly, and there was nothing practical about what he was saying – nothing that has anything to do with this story or this world.

'You give me the creeps sometimes,' said Fiennes. 'Did you – did you expect this?'

'I thought it possible,' said Father Brown; 'that was why I asked you to go and see what he was doing. I hoped you might not be too late.'

'It was I who found him,' said Fiennes rather huskily. 'It was the ugliest and most uncanny thing I ever knew. I went down that old garden again, and I knew there was something new and unnatural about it besides the murder. The flowers still tossed about in blue masses on each side of the black entrance into the old grey summerhouse; but to me the blue flowers looked like blue devils dancing before some dark cavern of the underworld. I looked all round; everything seemed to be in its ordinary place. But the queer notion grew on me that there was something wrong with the very shape of the sky. And then I saw what it was. The Rock of Fortune always rose in the background beyond the garden hedge and against the sea. The Rock of Fortune was gone.'

Father Brown had lifted his head and was listening intently.

'It was as if a mountain had walked away out of a landscape or a moon fallen from the sky; though I knew, of course, that a touch at any time would have tipped the thing over. Something possessed me and I rushed down that garden path like the wind and went crashing through that hedge as if it were a spider's web. It was a thin hedge really, though its undisturbed trimness had made it serve all the purposes of a wall. On the shore I found the loose rock fallen from its pedestal; and poor Harry Druce lay like a wreck underneath it. One arm was thrown round it in a sort of embrace as if he had pulled it down on himself; and on the broad brown sands beside it, in large crazy lettering, he had scrawled the words: "The Rock of Fortune falls on the Fool".'

'It was the Colonel's will that did that,' observed Father Brown. 'The young man had staked everything on profiting himself by Donald's disgrace, especially when his uncle sent for him on the same day as the lawyer, and welcomed him with so much warmth. Otherwise he was done; he'd lost his police job; he was beggared at Monte Carlo. And he killed himself when he found he'd killed his kinsman for nothing.'

'Here, stop a minute!' cried the staring Fiennes. 'You're going too fast for me.'

'Talking about the will, by the way,' continued Father Brown calmly, 'before I forget it, or we go on to bigger things, there was a simple explanation, I think, of all that business about the doctor's name. I rather fancy I have heard both names before somewhere. The doctor is really a French nobleman with the title of the Marquis de Villon. But he is also an ardent Republican and has abandoned his title and fallen back on the forgotten family surname. "With your Citizen Riquetti you have puzzled Europe for ten days." '

'What is that?' asked the young man blankly.

'Never mind,' said the priest. 'Nine times out of ten it is a rascally thing to change one's name; but this was a piece of fine fanaticism. That's the point of his sarcasm about Americans having no names – that is, no titles. Now in England the Marquis of Hartington is never called Mr Hartington; but in France the Marquis de Villon is called M. de Villon. So it might well look like a change of name. As for the talk about killing, I fancy that also was a point of French etiquette. The doctor was talking about challenging Floyd to a duel, and the girl was trying to dissuade him.'

'Oh, I see,' cried Fiennes slowly. 'Now I understand what she meant.'

'And what is that about?' asked his companion, smiling.

'Well,' said the young man, 'it was something that happened to me just before I found that poor fellow's body; only the catastrophe drove it out of my head. I suppose it's hard to remember a little romantic idyll when you've just come on top of a tragedy. But as I went down the lanes leading to the Colonel's old place I met his daughter walking with Dr Valentine. She was in mourning, of course, and he always wore black as if he were going to a funeral; but I can't say that their faces were very funereal. Never have I seen two people looking in their own way more respectably radiant and cheerful. They stopped and saluted me, and then she told me they were married and living in a little house on the outskirts of the town, where the doctor was continuing his practice. This rather surprised me, because I knew that her old father's will had left her his property; and I hinted at it delicately by saying I was going along to her father's old place and had half expected to meet her there. But she only laughed and said: "Oh, we've given up all that. My husband doesn't like heiresses." And I discovered with some astonishment they really had insisted on restoring the property to poor Donald; so I hope he's had a healthy shock and will treat it sensibly. There was never much really the matter with him; he was very young and his father was not very wise. But it was in connection with that that she said something I didn't understand at the time; but now I'm sure it must be as you say. She said with a sort of sudden and splendid arrogance that was entirely altruistic: "I hope it'll stop that red-haired fool from fussing any more about the will. Does he think my husband, who has given up a crest and a coronet as old as the Crusades for his principles, would kill an old man in a summer-house for a legacy like that?" Then she laughed again and said, "My husband isn't killing anybody except in the way of business. Why, he didn't even ask his friends to call on the secretary." Now, of course, I see what she meant.'

'I see part of what she meant, of course,' said Father Brown. 'What did she mean exactly by the secretary fussing about the will?'

Fiennes smiled as he answered, 'I wish you knew the secretary, Father Brown. It would be a joy to you to watch him make things hum, as he calls it. He made the house of mourning hum. He filled the funeral with all the snap and zip of the brightest sporting event. There was no holding him, after something had really happened. I've told you how he used to oversee the gardener as he did the garden, and how he instructed the lawyer in the law. Needless to say, he also instructed the surgeon in the practice of surgery; and as the surgeon was Dr Valentine, you may be sure it ended in accusing him of something worse than bad surgery. The secretary got it fixed in his red head that the doctor had committed the crime, and when the police arrived he was perfectly sublime. Need I say that he became, on the spot, the greatest of all amateur detectives? Sherlock Holmes never towered over Scotland Yard with more Titanic intellectual pride and scorn than Colonel Druce's private secretary over the police investigating Colonel Druce's death. I tell you it was a joy to see him. He strode about with an abstracted air, tossing his scarlet crest of hair and giving curt impatient replies. Of course it was his demeanour during these days that made Druce's daughter so wild with him. Of course he had a theory. It's just the sort of theory a man would have in a book; and Floyd is the sort of man who ought to be in a book. He'd be better fun and less bother in a book.'

'What was his theory?' asked the other.

'Oh, it was full of pep,' replied Fiennes gloomily. 'It would have been glorious copy if it could have held together for ten minutes longer. He said the Colonel was still alive when they found him in the summer-house, and the doctor killed him with the surgical instrument on pretence of cutting the clothes.'

'I see,' said the priest. 'I suppose he was lying flat on his face on the mud floor as a form of siesta.'

'It's wonderful what hustle will do,' continued his informant. 'I believe Floyd would have got his great theory into the papers at any rate, and perhaps had the doctor arrested, when all these things were blown sky high as if by dynamite by the discovery of that dead body lying under the Rock of Fortune. And that's what we come back to after all. I suppose the suicide is almost a confession. But nobody will ever know the whole story.'

There was a silence, and then the priest said modestly: 'I rather think I know the whole story.'

Fiennes stared. 'But look here,' he cried; 'how do you come to know the whole story, or to be sure it's the true story? You've been sitting here a hundred miles away writing a sermon; do you mean to tell me you really know what happened already? If you've really come to the end, where in the world do you begin? What started you off with your own story?'

Father Brown jumped up with a very unusual excitement and his first exclamation was like an explosion.

'The dog!' he cried. 'The dog, of course! You had the whole story in your hands in the business of the dog on the beach, if you'd only noticed the dog properly.'

Fiennes stared still more. 'But you told me before that my feelings about the dog were all nonsense, and the dog had nothing to do with it.'

'The dog had everything to do with it,' said Father Brown, 'as you'd have found out if you'd only treated the dog as a dog, and not as God Almighty judging the souls of men.'

He paused in an embarrassed way for a moment, and then said, with a rather pathetic air of apology: 'The truth is, I happen to be awfully fond of dogs. And it seemed to me that in all this lurid halo of dog superstitions nobody was really thinking about the poor dog at all. To begin with a small point, about his barking at the lawyer or growling at the secretary. You asked how I could guess things a hundred miles away; but honestly it's mostly to your credit, for you described people so well that I know the types. A man like Traill, who frowns usually and smiles suddenly, a man who fiddles with things, especially at his throat, is a nervous, easily embarrassed man. I shouldn't wonder if Floyd, the efficient secretary, is nervy and jumpy, too; those Yankee hustlers often are. Otherwise he wouldn't have cut his fingers on the shears and dropped them when he heard Janet Druce scream.

'Now dogs hate nervous people. I don't know whether they make the dog nervous, too; or whether, being after all a brute, he is a bit of a bully; or whether his canine vanity (which is colossal) is simply offended at not being liked. But anyhow there was nothing in poor Nox protesting against those people, except that he disliked them for being afraid of him. Now I know you're awfully clever, and nobody of sense sneers at cleverness. But I sometimes fancy, for instance, that you are too clever to understand animals. Sometimes you are too clever to understand men, especially when they act almost as simply as animals. Animals are very literal; they live in a world of truisms. Take this case: a dog barks at a man and a man runs away from a dog. Now you do not seem to be quite simple enough to see the fact: that the dog barked because he disliked the man and the man fled because he was frightened of the dog. They had no other motives and they needed none; but you must read psychological mysteries into it and suppose the dog had super-normal vision, and was a mysterious mouthpiece of doom. You must suppose the man was running away, not from the dog but from the hangman. And yet, if you come to think if it, all this deeper psychology is exceedingly improbable. If the dog really could completely and consciously realise the murderer of his master he wouldn't stand yapping as he might at a curate at a tea-party; he's much more likely to fly at his throat. And on the other hand, do you really think a man who had hardened his heart to murder an old friend and then walk about smiling at the old friend's family, under the eyes of his old friend's daughter and post-mortem doctor – do you think a man like that would be doubled up by mere remorse because a dog barked? He might feel the tragic irony of it; it might shake his soul, like any other tragic trifle. But he wouldn't rush madly the length of a garden to escape from the only witness whom he knew to be unable to talk. People have a panic like that when they are frightened, not of tragic ironies, but of teeth. The whole thing is simpler than you can understand.

'But when we come to that business by the seashore, things are much more interesting. As you stated them, they were much more puzzling. I didn't understand that tale of the dog going in and out of the water; it didn't seem to me a doggy thing to do. If Nox had been very much upset about something else, he might possibly have refused to go after the stick at all. He'd probably go off nosing in whatever direction he suspected the mischief. But when once a dog is actually chasing a thing, a stone or a stick or a rabbit, my experience is that he won't stop for anything but the most peremptory command, and not always for that. That he should turn round because his mood changed seems to me unthinkable.'

'But he did turn round,' insisted Fiennes; 'and came back without the stick.'

'He came back without the stick for the best reason in the world,' replied the priest. 'He came back because he couldn't find it. He whined because he couldn't find it. That's the sort of thing a dog really does whine about. A dog is a devil of a ritualist. He is as particular about the precise routine of a game as a child about the precise repetition of a fairy tale. In this case something had gone wrong with the game. He came back to complain seriously of the conduct of the stick. Never had such a thing happened before. Never had an eminent and distinguished dog been so treated by a rotten old walking-stick.'

'Why, what had the walking-stick done?' enquired the young man.

'It had sunk,' said Father Brown.

Fiennes said nothing, but continued to stare; and it was the priest who continued: 'It had sunk because it was not really a stick, but a rod of steel with a very thin shell of cane and a sharp point. In other words, it was a sword stick. I suppose a murderer never gets rid of a bloody weapon so oddly and yet so naturally as by throwing it into the sea for a retriever.'

'I begin to see what you mean,' admitted Fiennes; 'but even if a sword-stick was used, I have no guess of how it was used.'

'I had a sort of guess,' said Father Brown, 'right at the beginning when you said the word summer-house. And another when you said that Druce wore a white coat. As long as everybody was looking for a short dagger, nobody thought of it; but if we admit a rather long blade like a rapier, it's not so impossible.'

He was leaning back, looking at the ceiling, and began like one going back to his own first thoughts and fundamentals.

'All that discussion about detective stories like the Yellow Room, about a man found dead in sealed chambers which no one could enter, does not apply to the present case, because it is a summerhouse. When we talk of a Yellow Room, or any room, we imply walls that are really homogeneous and impenetrable. But a summerhouse is not made like that; it is often made, as it was in this case, of closely interlaced but separate boughs and strips of wood, in which there are chinks here and there. There was one of them just behind Druce's back as he sat in his chair up against the wall. But just as the room was a summer-house, so the chair was a basket-chair. That also was a lattice of loopholes. Lastly, the summer-house was close up under the hedge; and you have just told me that it was really a thin hedge. A man standing outside it could easily see, amid a network of twigs and branches and canes, one white spot of the Colonel's coat as plain as the white of a target.

'Now, you left the geography a little vague; but it was possible to put two and two together. You said the Rock of Fortune was not really high; but you also said it could be seen dominating the garden like a mountain-peak. In other words, it was very near the end of the garden, though your walk had taken you a long way round to it. Also, it isn't likely the young lady really howled so as to be heard half a mile. She gave an ordinary involuntary cry, and yet you heard it on the shore. And among other interesting things that you told me, may I remind you that you said Harry Druce had fallen behind to light his pipe under a hedge.'

Fiennes shuddered slightly. 'You mean he drew his blade there and sent it through the hedge at the white spot. But surely it was a very odd chance and a very sudden choice. Besides, he couldn't be certain the old man's money had passed to him, and as a fact it hadn't.'

Father Brown's face became animated. 'You misunderstand the man's character,' he said, as if he himself had known the man all his life. 'A curious but not unknown type of character. If he had really known the money would come to him, I seriously believe he wouldn't have done it. He would have seen it as the dirty thing it was.'

'Isn't that rather paradoxical?' asked the other.

'This man was a gambler,' said the priest, 'and a man in disgrace for having taken risks and anticipated orders. It was probably for something pretty unscrupulous, for every imperial police is more like a Russian secret police than we like to think. But he had gone beyond the line and failed. Now, the temptation of that type of man is to do a mad thing precisely because the risk will be wonderful in retrospect. He wants to say, "Nobody but I could have seized that chance or seen that it was then or never. What a wild and wonderful guess it was, when I put all those things together; Donald in disgrace; and the lawyer being sent for; and Herbert and I sent for at the same time – and then nothing more but the way the old man grinned at me and shook hands. Anybody would say I was mad to risk it; but that is how fortunes are made, by the man mad enough to have a little foresight." In short, it is the vanity of guessing. It is the megalomania of the gambler. The more incongruous the coincidence, the more instantaneous the decision, the more likely he is to snatch the chance. The accident, the very triviality of the white speck and the hole in the hedge intoxicated him like a vision of the world's desire. Nobody clever enough to see such a combination of accidents could be cowardly enough not to use them! That is how the devil talks to the gambler. But the devil himself would hardly have induced that unhappy man to go down in a dull, deliberate way and kill an old uncle from whom he'd always had expectations. It would be too respectable.'

He paused a moment, and then went on with a certain quiet emphasis.

'And now try to call up the scene, even as you saw it yourself. As he stood there, dizzy with his diabolical opportunity, he looked up and saw that strange outline that might have been the image of his own tottering soul; the one great crag poised perilously on the other like a pyramid on its point, and remembered that it was called the Rock of Fortune. Can you guess how such a man at such a moment would read such a signal? I think it strung him up to action and even to vigilance. He who would be a tower must not fear to be a toppling tower. Anyhow, he acted; his next difficulty was to cover his tracks. To be found with a sword-stick, let alone a blood-stained sword-stick, would be fatal in the search that was certain to follow. If he left it anywhere, it would be found and probably traced. Even if he threw it into the sea the action might be noticed, and thought noticeable – unless indeed he could think of some more natural way of covering the action. As you know, he did think of one, and a very good one. Being the only one of you with a watch, he told you it was not yet time to return, strolled a little farther, and started the game of throwing in sticks for the retriever. But how his eyes must have rolled darkly over all that desolate sea-shore before they alighted on the dog!'

Fiennes nodded, gazing thoughtfully into space. His mind seemed to have drifted back to a less practical part of the narrative.

'It's queer,' he said, 'that the dog really was in the story after all.'

'The dog could almost have told you the story, if he could talk,' said the priest. 'All I complain of is that because he couldn't talk you made up his story for him, and made him talk with the tongues of men and angels. It's part of something I've noticed more and more in the modern world, appearing in all sorts of newspaper rumours and conversational catchwords; something that's arbitrary without being authoritative. People readily swallow the untested claims of this, that, or the other. It's drowning all your old rationalism and scepticism, it's coming in like a sea; and the name of it is superstition.' He stood up abruptly, his face heavy with a sort of frown, and went on talking almost as if he were alone. 'It's the first effect of not believing in God that you lose your common sense and can't see things as they are. Anything that anybody talks about, and says there's a good deal in it, extends itself indefinitely like a vista in a nightmare. And a dog is an omen, and a cat is a mystery, and a pig is a mascot, and a beetle is a scarab, calling up all the menagerie of polytheism from Egypt and old India; Dog Anubis and great green-eyed Pasht and all the holy howling Bulls of Bashan; reeling back to the bestial gods of the beginning, escaping into elephants and snakes and crocodiles; and all because you are frightened of four words: "He was made Man".'

The young man got up with a little embarrassment, almost as if he had overheard a soliloquy. He called to the dog and left the room with vague but breezy farewells. But he had to call the dog twice, for the dog had remained behind quite motionless for a moment, looking up steadily at Father Brown as the wolf looked at St Francis.

The Miracle of Moon Crescent

Moon Crescent was meant in a sense to be as romantic as its name; and the things that happened there were romantic enough in their way. At least it had been an expression of that genuine element of sentiment – historic and almost heroic – which manages to remain side by side with commercialism in the elder cities on the eastern coast of America. It was originally a curve of classical architecture really recalling that eighteenth-century atmosphere in which men like Washington and Jefferson had seemed to be all the more republicans for being aristocrats. Travellers faced with the recurrent query of what they thought of our city were understood to be specially answerable for what they thought of our Moon Crescent. The very contrasts that confuse its original harmony were characteristic of its survival. At one extremity or horn of the crescent its last windows looked over an enclosure like a strip of a gentleman's park, with trees and hedges as formal as a Queen Anne garden. But immediately round the corner, the other windows, even of the same rooms, or rather 'apartments', looked out on the blank, unsightly wall of a huge warehouse attached to some ugly industry. The apartments of Moon Crescent itself were at that end remodelled on the monotonous pattern of an American hotel, and rose to a height, which, though lower than the colossal warehouse, would have been called a skyscraper in London. But the colonnade that ran round the whole frontage upon the street had a grey and weather-stained stateliness suggesting that the ghosts of the Fathers of the Republic might still be walking to and fro in it. The insides of the rooms, however, were as neat and new as the last New York fittings could make them, especially at the northern end between the neat garden and the blank warehouse wall. They were a system of very small flats, as we should say in England, each consisting of a sitting-room, bedroom, and bathroom, as identical as the hundred cells of a hive. In one of these the celebrated Warren Wynd sat at his desk sorting letters and scattering orders with wonderful rapidity and exactitude. He could only be compared to a tidy whirlwind.

Warren Wynd was a very little man with loose grey hair and a pointed beard, seemingly frail but fierily active. He had very wonderful eyes, brighter than stars and stronger than magnets, which nobody who had ever seen them could easily forget. And indeed in his work as a reformer and regulator of many good works he had shown at least that he had a pair of eyes in his head. All sorts of stories and even legends were told of the miraculous rapidity with which he could form a sound judgement, especially of human character. It was said that he selected the wife who worked with him so long in so charitable a fashion, by picking her out of a whole regiment of women in uniform marching past at some official celebration, some said of the Girl Guides and some of the Women Police. Another story was told of how three tramps, indistinguishable from each other in their community of filth and rags, had presented themselves before him asking for charity. Without a moment's hesitation he had sent one of them to a particular hospital devoted to a certain nervous disorder, had recommended the second to an inebriates' home, and had engaged the third at a handsome salary as his own private servant, a position which he filled successfully for years afterwards. There were, of course, the inevitable anecdotes of his prompt criticisms and curt repartees when brought in contact with Roosevelt, with Henry Ford, and with Mrs Asquith and all other persons with whom an American public man ought to have a historic interview, if only in the newspapers. Certainly he was not likely to be overawed by such personages; and at the moment here in question he continued very calmly his centrifugal whirl of papers, though the man confronting him was a personage of almost equal importance.

Silas T. Vandam, the millionaire and oil magnate, was a lean man with a long, yellow face and blue-black hair, colours which were the less conspicuous yet somehow the more sinister because his face and figure showed dark against the window and the white warehouse wall outside it; he was buttoned up tight in an elegant overcoat with strips of astrakhan. The eager face and brilliant eyes of Wynd, on the other hand, were in the full light from the other window overlooking the little garden, for his chair and desk stood facing it; and though the face was preoccupied, it did not seem unduly preoccupied about the millionaire. Wynd's valet or personal servant, a big, powerful man with flat fair hair, was standing behind his master's desk holding a sheaf of letters; and Wynd's private secretary, a neat, red-haired youth with a sharp face, had his hand already on the door handle, as if guessing some purpose or obeying some gesture of his employer. The room was not only neat, but austere to the point of emptiness; for Wynd, with characteristic thoroughness, had rented the whole floor above, and turned it into a loft or storeroom, where all his other papers and possessions were stacked in boxes and corded bales.

'Give these to the floor-clerk, Wilson,' said Wynd to the servant holding the letters, 'and then get me the pamphlet on the Minneapolis Night Clubs; you'll find it in the bundle marked "G". I shall want it in half an hour, but don't disturb me till then. Well, Mr Vandam, I think your proposition sounds very promising; but I can't give a final answer till I've seen the report. It ought to reach me tomorrow afternoon, and I'll phone you at once. I'm sorry I can't say anything more definite just now.'

Mr Vandam seemed to feel that this was something like a polite dismissal;

and his sallow, saturnine face suggested that he found a certain irony in the fact.

'Well, I suppose I must be going,' he said.

'Very good of you to call, Mr Vandam,' said Wynd, politely; 'you will excuse my not coming out, as I've something here I must fix at once. Fenner,' he added to the secretary, 'show Mr Vandam to his car, and don't come back again for half an hour. I've something here I want to work out by myself; after that I shall want you.'

The three men went out into the hallway together, closing the door behind them. The big servant, Wilson, was turning down the hallway in the direction of the floor-clerk, and the other two moving in the opposite direction towards the lift; for Wynd's apartment was high up on the fourteenth floor. They had hardly gone a yard from the closed door when they became conscious that the corridor was filled with a marching and even magnificent figure. The man was very tall and broad-shouldered, his bulk being the more conspicuous for being clad in white, or a light grey that looked like it, with a very wide white Panama hat and an almost equally wide fringe or halo of almost equally white hair. Set in this aureole his face was strong and handsome, like that of a Roman emperor, save that there was something more than boyish, something a little childish, about the brightness of his eyes and the beatitude of his smile. 'Mr Warren Wynd in?' he asked, in hearty tones.

'Mr Warren Wynd is engaged,' said Fenner; 'he must not be disturbed on any account. I may say I am his secretary and can take any message.'

'Mr Warren Wynd is not at home to the Pope or the Crowned Heads,' said Vandam, the oil magnate, with sour satire. 'Mr Warren Wynd is mighty particular. I went in there to hand him over a trifle of twenty thousand dollars on certain conditions, and he told me to call again like as if I was a call-boy.'

'It's a fine thing to be a boy,' said the stranger, 'and a finer to have a call; and I've got a call he's just got to listen to. It's a call of the great good country out West, where the real American is being made while you're all snoring. Just tell him that Art Alboin of Oklahoma City has come to convert him.'

'I tell you nobody can see him,' said the red-haired secretary sharply. 'He has given orders that he is not to be disturbed for half an hour.'

'You folks down East are all against being disturbed,' said the breezy Mr Alboin, 'but I calculate there's a big breeze getting up in the West that will have to disturb you. He's been figuring out how much money must go to this and that stuffy old religion; but I tell you any scheme that leaves out the new Great Spirit movement in Texas and Oklahoma, is leaving out the religion of the future.'

'Oh; I've sized up those religions of the future,' said the millionaire, contemptuously. 'I've been through them with a tooth-comb; and they're as mangy as yellow dogs. There was that woman called herself Sophia: ought to have called herself Sapphira, I reckon. Just a plum fraud. Strings tied to all the tables and tambourines. Then there were the Invisible Life bunch; said they could vanish when they liked, and they did vanish, too, and a hundred thousand of my dollars vanished with them. I knew Jupiter Jesus out in Denver; saw him for weeks on end; and he was just a common crook. So was the Patagonian Prophet; you bet he's made a bolt for Patagonia. No, I'm through with all that; from now on I only believe what I see. I believe they call it being an atheist.'

'I guess you got me wrong,' said the man from Oklahoma, almost eagerly. 'I guess I'm as much of an atheist as you are. No supernatural or superstitious stuff in our movement; just plain science. The only real right science is just health, and the only real right health is just breathing. Fill your lungs with the wide air of the prairie and you could blow all your old eastern cities into the sea. You could just puff away their biggest men like thistledown. That's what we do in the new movement out home: we breathe. We don't pray; we breathe.'

'Well, I suppose you do,' said the secretary, wearily. He had a keen, intelligent face which could hardly conceal the weariness; but he had listened to the two monologues with the admirable patience and politeness (so much in contrast with the legends of impatience and insolence) with which such monologues are listened to in America.

'Nothing supernatural,' continued Alboin, 'just the great natural fact behind all the supernatural fancies. What did the Jews want with a God except to breathe into man's nostrils the breath of life? We do the breathing into our own nostrils out in Oklahoma. What's the meaning of the very word Spirit? It's just the Greek for breathing exercises. Life, progress, prophecy; it's all breath.'

'Some would allow it's all wind,' said Vandam; 'but I'm glad you've got rid of the divinity stunt, anyhow.'

The keen face of the secretary, rather pale against his red hair, showed a flicker of some odd feeling suggestive of a secret bitterness.

'I'm not glad,' he said, 'I'm just sure. You seem to like being atheists; so you may be just believing what you like to believe. But I wish to God there were a God; and there ain't. It's just my luck.'

Without a sound or stir they all became almost creepily conscious at this moment that the group, halted outside Wynd's door, had silently grown from three figures to four. How long the fourth figure had stood there none of the earnest disputants could tell, but he had every appearance of waiting respectfully and even timidly for the opportunity to say something urgent. But to their nervous sensibility he seemed to have sprung up suddenly and silently like a mushroom. And indeed, he looked rather like a big, black mushroom, for he was quite short and his small, stumpy figure was eclipsed by his big, black clerical hat; the resemblance might have been more complete if mushrooms were in the habit of carrying umbrellas, even of a shabby and shapeless sort.

Fenner, the secretary, was conscious of a curious additional surprise at recognising the figure of a priest; but when the priest turned up a round face under the round hat and innocently asked for Mr Warren Wynd, he gave the regular negative answer rather more curtly than before. But the priest stood his ground.

'I do really want to see Mr Wynd,' he said. 'It seems odd, but that's exactly what I do want to do. I don't want to speak to him. I just want to see him. I just want to see if he's there to be seen.'

'Well, I tell you he's there and can't be seen,' said Fenner, with increasing annoyance. 'What do you mean by saying you want to see if he's there to be seen? Of course he's there. We all left him there five minutes ago, and we've stood outside this door ever since.'

'Well, I want to see if he's all right,' said the priest.

'Why?' demanded the secretary, in exasperation.

'Because I have a serious, I might say solemn, reason,' said the cleric, gravely, 'for doubting whether he is all right.'

'Oh, Lord!' cried Vandam, in a sort of fury; 'not more superstitions.'

'I see I shall have to give my reasons,' observed the little cleric, gravely. 'I suppose I can't expect you even to let me look through the crack of a door till I tell you the whole story.' He was silent a moment as in reflection, and then went on without noticing the wondering faces around him. 'I was walking outside along the front of the colonnade when I saw a very ragged man running hard round the corner at the end of the crescent. He came pounding along the pavement towards me, revealing a great raw-boned figure and a face I knew. It was the face of a wild Irish fellow I once helped a little; I will not tell you his name. When he saw me he staggered, calling me by mine and saying, "Saints alive, it's Father Brown; you're the only man whose face could frighten me today."

'I knew he meant he'd been doing some wild thing or other, and I don't think my face frightened him much, for he was soon telling me about it. And a very strange thing it was. He asked me if I knew Warren Wynd, and I said no, though I knew he lived near the top of these flats. He said, "That's a man who thinks he's a saint of God; but if he knew what I was saying of him he should be ready to hang himself." And he repeated hysterically more than once, "Yes, ready to hang himself." I asked him if he'd done any harm to Wynd, and his answer was rather a queer one. He said: "I took a pistol and I loaded it with neither shot nor slug, but only with a curse." As far as I could make out, all he had done was to go down that little alley between this building and the big warehouse, with an old pistol loaded with a blank charge, and merely fire it against the wall, as if that would bring down the building. "But as I did it," he said, "I cursed him with the great curse, that the justice of God should take him by the hair and the vengeance of hell by the heels, and he should be torn asunder like Judas and the world know him no more."

'Well, it doesn't matter now what else I said to the poor, crazy fellow; he went away quieted down a little, and I went round to the back of the building to inspect. And sure enough, in the little alley at the foot of this wall there lay a rusty antiquated pistol; I know enough about pistols to know it had been loaded only with a little powder; there were the black marks of powder and smoke on the wall, and even the mark of the muzzle, but not even a dent of any bullet. He had left no trace of destruction; he had left no trace of anything, except those black marks and that black curse he had hurled into heaven. So I came back here to ask for this Warren Wynd and find out if he's all right.'

Fenner the secretary laughed. 'I can soon settle that difficulty for you. I assure you he's quite all right; we left him writing at his desk only a few minutes ago. He was alone in his flat; it's a hundred feet up from the street, and so placed that no shot could have reached him, even if your friend hadn't fired blank. There's no other entrance to this place but this door, and we've been standing outside it ever since.'

'All the same,' said Father Brown, gravely, 'I should like to look in and see.'

'Well, you can't,' retorted the other. 'Good Lord, you don't tell me you think anything of the curse.'

'You forget,' said the millionaire, with a slight sneer, 'the reverend gentleman's whole business is blessings and cursings. Come, sir, if he's been cursed to hell, why don't you bless him back again? What's the good of your blessings if they can't beat an Irish larrykin's curse?'

'Does anybody believe such things now?' protested the Westerner.

'Father Brown believes a good number of things, I take it,' said Vandam, whose temper was suffering from the past snub and the present bickering. 'Father Brown believes a hermit crossed a river on a crocodile conjured out of nowhere, and then he told the crocodile to die, and it sure did. Father Brown believes that some blessed saint or other died, and had his dead body turned into three dead bodies, to be served out to three parishes that were all bent on figuring as his home-town. Father Brown believes that a saint hung his cloak on a sunbeam, and another used his for a boat to cross the Atlantic. Father Brown believes the holy donkey had six legs and the house of Loretto flew through the air. He believes in hundreds of stone virgins winking and weeping all day long. It's nothing to him to believe that a man might escape through the keyhole or vanish out of a locked room. I reckon he doesn't take much stock of the laws of nature.'

'Anyhow, I have to take stock in the laws of Warren Wynd,' said the secretary, wearily, 'and it's his rule that he's to be left alone when he says so. Wilson will tell you just the same,' for the large servant who had been sent for the pamphlet, passed placidly down the corridor even as he spoke, carrying the pamphlet, but serenely passing the door. 'He'll go and sit on the bench by the floor-clerk and twiddle his thumbs till he's wanted; but he won't go in before then; and nor will I. I reckon we both know which side our bread is buttered, and it'd take a good many of Father Brown's saints and angels to make us forget it.'

'As for saints and angels – ' began the priest.

'It's all nonsense,' repeated Fenner. 'I don't want to say anything offensive, but that sort of thing may be very well for crypts and cloisters and all sorts of moonshiny places. But ghosts can't get through a closed door in an American hotel.'

'But men can open a door, even in an American hotel,' replied Father Brown, patiently. 'And it seems to me the simplest thing would be to open it.'

'It would be simple enough to lose me my job,' answered the secretary, 'and Warren Wynd doesn't like his secretaries so simple as that. Not simple enough to believe in the sort of fairy tales you seem to believe in.'

'Well,' said the priest gravely, 'it is true enough that I believe in a good many things that you probably don't. But it would take a considerable time to explain all the things I believe in, and all the reasons I have for thinking I'm right. It would take about two seconds to open that door and prove I am wrong.'

Something in the phrase seemed to please the more wild and restless spirit of the man from the West.

'I'll allow I'd love to prove you wrong,' said Alboin, striding suddenly past them, 'and I will.'

He threw open the door of the flat and looked in. The first glimpse showed that Warren Wynd's chair was empty. The second glance showed that his room was empty also.

Fenner, electrified with energy in his turn, dashed past the other into the apartment.

'He's in his bedroom,' he said curtly, 'he must be.'

As he disappeared into the inner chamber the other men stood in the empty outer room staring about them. The severity and simplicity of its fittings, which had already been noted, returned on them with a rigid challenge. Certainly in this room there was no question of hiding a mouse, let alone a man. There were no curtains and, what is rare in American arrangements, no cupboards. Even the desk was no more than a plain table with a shallow drawer and a tilted lid. The chairs were hard and high-backed skeletons. A moment after the secretary reappeared at the inner door, having searched the two inner rooms. A staring negation stood in his eyes, and his mouth seemed to move in a mechanical detachment from it as he said sharply: 'He didn't come out through here?'

Somehow the others did not even think it necessary to answer that negation in the negative. Their minds had come up against something like the blank wall of the warehouse that stared in at the opposite window, gradually turning from white to grey as dusk slowly descended with the advancing afternoon. Vandam walked over to the window-sill against which he had leant half an hour before and looked out of the open window. There was no pipe or fire-escape, no shelf or foothold of any kind on the sheer fall to the little by-street below, there was nothing on the similar expanse of wall that rose many stories above. There was even less variation on the other side of the street; there was nothing whatever but the wearisome expanse of whitewashed wall. He peered downwards, as if expecting to see the vanished philanthropist lying in a suicidal wreck on the path. He could see nothing but one small dark object which, though diminished by distance, might well be the pistol that the priest had found lying there. Meanwhile, Fenner had walked to the other window, which looked out from a wall equally blank and inaccessible, but looking out over a small ornamental park instead of a side street. Here a clump of trees interrupted the actual view of the ground; but they reached but a little way up the huge human cliff. Both turned back into the room and faced each other in the gathering twilight where the last silver gleams of daylight on the shiny tops of desks and tables were rapidly turning grey. As if the twilight itself irritated him, Fenner touched the switch and the scene sprang into the startling distinctness of electric light.

'As you said just now,' said Vandam grimly, 'there's no shot from down there could hit him, even if there was a shot in the gun. But even if he was hit with a bullet he wouldn't have just burst like a bubble.'

The secretary, who was paler than ever, glanced irritably at the bilious visage of the millionaire. 'What's got you started on those morbid notions? Who's talking about bullets and bubbles? Why shouldn't he be alive?'

'Why not indeed?' replied Vandam smoothly. 'If you'll tell me where he is, I'll tell you how he got there.'

After a pause the secretary muttered, rather sulkily: 'I suppose you're right. We're right up against the very thing we were talking about. It'd be a queer thing if you or I ever came to think there was anything in cursing. But who could have harmed Wynd shut up in here?'

Mr Alboin, of Oklahoma, had been standing rather astraddle in the middle of the room, his white, hairy halo as well as his round eyes seeming to radiate astonishment. At this point he said, abstractedly, with something of the irrelevant impudence of an *enfant terrible*: 'You didn't cotton to him much, did you, Mr Vandam?'

Mr Vandam's long yellow face seemed to grow longer as it grew more sinister, while he smiled and answered quietly: 'If it comes to these coincidences, it was you, I think, who said that a wind from the West would blow away our big men like thistledown.'

'I know I said it would,' said the Westerner, with candour; 'but all the same, how the devil could it?'

The silence was broken by Fenner saying with an abruptness amounting to violence: 'There's only one thing to say about this affair. It simply hasn't happened. It can't have happened.'

'Oh, yes,' said Father Brown out of the corner; 'it has happened all right.'

They all jumped; for the truth was they had all forgotten the insignificant little man who had originally induced them to open the door. And the recovery of memory went with a sharp reversal of mood; it came back to them with a rush that they had all dismissed him as a superstitious dreamer for even hinting at the very thing that had since happened before their eyes.

'Snakes!' cried the impetuous Westerner, like one speaking before he could stop himself; 'suppose there were something in it, after all!'

'I must confess,' said Fenner, frowning at the table, 'that his reverence's anticipations were apparently well founded. I don't know whether he has anything else to tell us.'

'He might possibly tell us,' said Vandam, sardonically, 'what the devil we are to do now.'

The little priest seemed to accept the position in a modest, but matter-of-fact manner. 'The only thing I can think of,' he said, 'is first to tell the authorities of this place, and then to see if there were any more traces of my man who let off the pistol. He vanished round the other end of the crescent where the little garden is. There are seats there, and it's a favourite place for tramps.'

Direct consultations with the headquarters of the hotel, leading to indirect consultations with the authorities of the police, occupied them for a considerable time; and it was already nightfall when they went out under the long, classical curve of the colonnade. The crescent looked as cold and hollow as the moon after which it was named, and the moon itself was rising luminous but spectral behind the black tree-tops when they turned the corner by the little public garden. Night veiled much of what was merely urban and artificial about the place, and as they melted into the shadows of the trees they had a strange feeling of having suddenly travelled many hundred miles from their homes. When they had walked in silence for a little, Alboin, who had something elemental about him, suddenly exploded.

'I give up,' he cried; 'I hand in my checks. I never thought I should come to such things; but what happens when the things come to you? I beg your pardon, Father Brown; I reckon I'll just come across, so far as you and your fairy tales are concerned. After this, it's me for the fairy tales. Why, you said yourself, Mr Vandam, that you're an atheist and only believe what you see. Well, what was it you did see? Or rather, what was it you didn't see?'

'I know,' said Vandam and nodded in a gloomy fashion.

'Oh, it's partly all this moon and trees that get on one's nerves,' said Fenner obstinately. 'Trees always look queer by moonlight, with their branches crawling about. Look at that – '

'Yes,' said Father Brown, standing still and peering at the moon through a tangle of trees. 'That's a very queer branch up there.'

When he spoke again he only said: 'I thought it was a broken branch.'

But this time there was a catch in his voice that unaccountably turned his hearers cold. Something that looked rather like a dead branch was certainly dependent in a limp fashion from the tree that showed dark against the moon; but it was not a dead branch. When they came close to it to see what it was Fenner sprang away again with a ringing oath. Then he ran in again and loosened a rope from the neck of the dingy little body dangling with drooping plumes of grey hair. Somehow he knew that the body was a dead body before he managed to take it down from the tree. A very long coil of rope was wrapped round and round the branches, and a comparatively short length of it hung from the fork of the branch to the body. A long garden tub was rolled a yard or so from under the feet, like the stool kicked away from the feet of a suicide.

'Oh, my God!' said Alboin, so that it seemed as much a prayer as an oath. 'What was it that man said about him? – "If he knew, he would be ready to hang himself." Wasn't that what he said, Father Brown?'

'Yes,' said Father Brown.

'Well,' said Vandam in a hollow voice, 'I never thought to see or say such a thing. But what can one say except that the curse has worked?'

Fenner was standing with hands covering his face; and the priest laid a hand on his arm and said, gently, 'Were you very fond of him?'

The secretary dropped his hands and his white face was ghastly under the moon.

'I hated him like hell,' he said; 'and if he died by a curse it might have been mine.'

The pressure of the priest's hand on his arm tightened; and the priest said, with an earnestness he had hardly yet shown: 'It wasn't your curse; pray be comforted.'

The police of the district had considerable difficulty in dealing with the four witnesses who were involved in the case. All of them were reputable, and even reliable people in the ordinary sense; and one of them was a person of considerable power and importance: Silas Vandam of the Oil Trust. The first police-officer who tried to express scepticism about his story struck sparks from the steel of that magnate's mind very rapidly indeed.

'Don't you talk to me about sticking to the facts,' said the millionaire with asperity. 'I've stuck to a good many facts before you were born and a few of the facts have stuck to me. I'll give you the facts all right if you've got the sense to take 'em down correctly.'

The policeman in question was youthful and subordinate, and had a hazy idea that the millionaire was too political to be treated as an ordinary citizen; so he passed him and his companions on to a more stolid superior, one Inspector Collins, a grizzled man with a grimly comfortable way of talking; as one who was genial but would stand no nonsense.

'Well, well,' he said, looking at the three figures before him with twinkling eyes, 'this seems to be a funny sort of a tale.'

Father Brown had already gone about his daily business; but Silas Vandam had suspended even the gigantic business of the markets for an hour or so to testify to his remarkable experience. Fenner's business as secretary had ceased in a sense with his employer's life; and the great Art Alboin, having no business in New York or anywhere else, except the spreading of the Breath of Life religion or the Great Spirit, had nothing to draw him away at the moment from the immediate affair. So they stood in a row in the inspector's office, prepared to corroborate each other.

'Now I'd better tell you to start with,' said the inspector cheerfully, 'that it's no good for anybody to come to me with any miraculous stuff. I'm a practical man and a policeman, and that sort of thing is all very well for priests and parsons. This priest of yours seems to have got you all worked up about some story of a dreadful death and judgement; but I'm going to leave him and his religion out of it altogether. If Wynd came out of that room, somebody let him out. And if Wynd was found hanging on that tree, somebody hung him there.'

'Quite so,' said Fenner; 'but as our evidence is that nobody let him out, the question is how could anybody have hung him there?'

'How could anybody have a nose on his face?' asked the inspector. 'He had a nose on his face, and he had a noose round his neck. Those are facts; and, as I say, I'm a practical man and go by the facts. It can't have been done by a miracle, so it must have been done by a man.'

Alboin had been standing rather in the background; and indeed his broad figure seemed to form a natural background to the leaner and more vivacious men in front of him. His white head was bowed with a certain abstraction; but as the inspector said the last sentence, he lifted it, shaking his hoary mane in a leonine fashion, and looking dazed but awakened. He moved forward into the centre of the group, and they had a vague feeling that he was even vaster than before. They had been only too prone to take him for a fool or a mountebank; but he was not altogether wrong when he said that there was in him a certain depth of lungs and life, like a west wind stored up in its strength, which might someday puff lighter things away.

'So you're a practical man, Mr Collins,' he said, in a voice at once soft and heavy. 'It must be the second or third time you've mentioned in this little conversation that you are a practical man; so I can't be mistaken about that. And a very interesting little fact it is for anybody engaged in writing your life, letters, and table-talk, with portrait at the age of five, daguerreotype of your grandmother and views of the old home-town; and I'm sure your biographer won't forget to mention it along with the fact that you had a pug nose with a pimple on it, and were nearly too fat to walk. And as you're a practical man, perhaps you would just go on practising till you've brought Warren Wynd to life again, and found out exactly how a practical man gets through a deal door. But I think you've got it wrong. You're not a practical man. You're a practical joke; that's what you are. The Almighty was having a bit of fun with us when he thought of you.'

With a characteristic sense of drama he went sailing towards the door before the astonished inspector could reply; and no after-recriminations could rob him of a certain appearance of triumph.

'I think you were perfectly right,' said Fenner. 'If those are practical men, give me priests.'

Another attempt was made to reach an official version of the event when the authorities fully realised who were the backers of the story, and what were the implications of it. Already it had broken out in the Press in its most sensationally and even shamelessly psychic form. Interviews with Vandam on his marvellous adventure, articles about Father Brown and his mystical intuitions, soon led those who feel responsible for guiding the public to wish to guide it into a wiser channel. Next time the inconvenient witnesses were approached in a more indirect and tactful manner. They were told, almost in an airy fashion, that Professor Vair was very much interested in such abnormal experiences; was especially interested in their own astonishing case. Professor Vair was a psychologist of great distinction; he had been known to take a detached interest in criminology; it was only some little time afterwards that they discovered that he was in any way connected with the police.

Professor Vair was a courteous gentleman, quietly dressed in pale grey clothes, with an artistic tie and a fair, pointed beard; he looked more like a landscape painter to anyone not acquainted with a certain special type of don. He had an air not only of courtesy, but of frankness.

'Yes, yes, I know,' he said smiling; 'I can guess what you must have gone through. The police do not shine in enquiries of a psychic sort, do they? Of course, dear old Collins said he only wanted the facts. What an absurd blunder! In a case of this kind we emphatically do not only want the facts. It is even more essential to have the fancies.'

'Do you mean,' asked Vandam gravely, 'that all that we thought facts were merely fancies?'

'Not at all,' said the professor; 'I only mean that the police are stupid in thinking they can leave out the psychological element in these things. Well, of course, the psychological element is everything in everything, though it is only just beginning to be understood. To begin with, take the element called personality. Now I have heard of this priest, Father Brown, before; and he is one of the most remarkable men of our time. Men of that sort carry a sort of atmosphere with them; and nobody knows how much his nerves and even his very senses are affected by it for the time being. People are hypnotised – yes, hypnotised; for hypnotism, like everything else, is a matter of degree; it enters slightly into all daily conversation: it is not necessarily conducted by a man in evening dress on a platform in a public hall. Father Brown's religion has always understood the psychology of atmospheres, and knows how to appeal to everything simultaneously; even, for instance, to the sense of smell. It understands those curious effects produced by music on animals and human beings; it can –'

'Hang it,' protested Fenner, 'you don't think he walked down the corridor carrying a church organ?'

'He knows better than to do that,' said Professor Vair laughing. 'He knows how to concentrate the essence of all these spiritual sounds and sights, and even smells, in a few restrained gestures; in an art or school of manners. He could contrive so to concentrate your minds on the supernatural by his mere presence, that natural things slipped off your minds to left and right unnoticed. Now you know,' he proceeded with a return to cheerful good sense, 'that the more we study it the more queer the whole question of human evidence becomes. There is not one man in twenty who really observes things at all. There is not one man in a hundred who observes them with real precision; certainly not one in a hundred who can first observe, then remember, and finally describe. Scientific experiments have been made again and again showing that men under strain have thought a door was shut when it was open, or open when it was shut. Men have differed about the number of doors or windows in a wall just in front of them. They have suffered optical illusions in broad daylight. They have done this even without the hypnotic effect of personality; but here we have a very powerful and persuasive personality bent upon fixing only one picture on your minds; the picture of the wild Irish rebel shaking his pistol at the sky and firing that vain volley, whose echoes were the thunders of heaven.'

'Professor,' cried Fenner, 'I'd swear on my deathbed that door never opened.'

'Recent experiments,' went on the professor, quietly, 'have suggested that our consciousness is not continuous, but is a succession of very rapid impressions like a cinema; it is possible that somebody or something may, so to speak, slip in or out between the scenes. It acts only in the instant while the curtain is down. Probably the patter of conjurors and all forms of sleight of hand depend on what we may call these black flashes of blindness between the flashes of sight. Now this priest and preacher of transcendental notions had filled you with a transcendental imagery; the image of the Celt like a Titan shaking the tower with his curse. Probably he accompanied it with some slight but compelling gesture, pointing your eyes and minds in the direction of the unknown destroyer below. Or perhaps something else happened, or somebody else passed by.'

'Wilson, the servant,' grunted Alboin, 'went down the hallway to wait on the bench, but I guess he didn't distract us much.'

'You never know how much,' replied Vair; 'it might have been that or more likely your eyes following some gesture of the priest as he told his tale of magic. It was in one of those black flashes that Mr Warren Wynd slipped out of his door and went to his death. That is the most probable explanation. It is an illustration of the new discovery. The mind is not a continuous line, but rather a dotted line.'

'Very dotted,' said Fenner feebly. 'Not to say dotty.'

'You don't really believe,' asked Vair, 'that your employer was shut up in a room like a box?'

'It's better than believing that I ought to be shut up in a room like a padded cell,' answered Fenner. 'That's what I complain of in your suggestions, professor. I'd as soon believe in a priest who believes in a miracle, as disbelieve in any man having any right to believe in a fact. The priest tells me that a man can appeal to a God I know nothing about to avenge him by the laws of some higher justice that I know nothing about. There's nothing for me to say except that I know nothing about it. But, at least, if the poor Paddy's prayer and pistol could be heard in a higher world, that higher world might act in some way that seems odd to us. But you ask me to disbelieve the facts of this world as they appear to my own five wits. According to you, a whole procession of Irishmen carrying blunderbusses may have walked through this room while we were talking, so long as they took care to tread on the blind spots in our minds. Miracles of the monkish sort, like materialising a crocodile or hanging a cloak on a sunbeam, seem quite sane compared to you.'

'Oh, well,' said Professor Vair, rather curtly, 'if you are resolved to believe in your priest and his miraculous Irishman I can say no more. I'm afraid you have not had an opportunity of studying psychology.'

'No,' said Fenner dryly; 'but I've had an opportunity to study psychologists.'

And, bowing politely, he led his deputation out of the room and did not speak till he got into the street; then he addressed them rather explosively.

'Raving lunatics!' cried Fenner in a fume. 'What the devil do they think is to happen to the world if nobody knows whether he's seen anything or not? I wish I'd blown his silly head off with a blank charge, and then explained that I did it in a blind flash. Father Brown's miracle may be miraculous or no, but he said it would happen and it did happen. All these blasted cranks can do is to see a thing happen and then say it didn't. Look here, I think we owe it to the padre to testify to his little demonstration. We're all sane, solid men who never believed in anything. We weren't drunk. We weren't devout. It simply happened just as he said it would.'

'I quite agree,' said the millionaire. 'It may be the beginning of mighty big things in the spiritual line; but anyhow, the man who's in the spiritual line himself, Father Brown, has certainly scored over this business.'

A few days afterwards Father Brown received a very polite note signed Silas T. Vandam, and asking him if he would attend at a stated hour at the apartment which was the scene of the disappearance, in order to take steps for the establishment of that marvellous occurrence. The occurrence itself had already begun to break out in the newspapers, and was being taken up everywhere by the enthusiasts of occultism. Father Brown saw the flaring posters inscribed 'Suicide of Vanishing Man', and 'Man's Curse Hangs Philanthropist', as he passed towards Moon Crescent and mounted the steps on the way to the elevator. He found the little group much as he left it, Vandam, Alboin, and the secretary; but there was an entirely new respectfulness and even reverence in their tone towards himself. They were standing by Wynd's desk, on which lay a large paper and writing materials; they turned to greet him.

'Father Brown,' said the spokesman, who was the white-haired Westerner, somewhat sobered with his responsibility, 'we asked you here in the first place to offer our apologies and our thanks. We recognise that it was you that spotted the spiritual manifestation from the first. We were hard-shell sceptics, all of us; but we realise now that a man must break that shell to get at the great things behind the world. You stand for those things; you stand for the super-normal explanation of things; and we have to hand it to you. And in the second place, we feel that this document would not be complete without your signature. We are notifying the exact facts to the Psychical Research Society, because the newspaper accounts are not what you might call exact. We've stated how the curse was spoken out in the street; how the man was sealed up here in a room like a box; how the curse dissolved him straight into thin air, and in some unthinkable way materialised him as a suicide hoisted on a gallows. That's all we can say about it; but all that we know, and have seen with our own eyes. And as you were the first to believe in the miracle, we all feel that you ought to be the first to sign.'

'No, really,' said Father Brown, in embarrassment. 'I don't think I should like to do that.'

'You mean you'd rather not sign first?'

'I mean I'd rather not sign at all,' said Father Brown, modestly. 'You see, it doesn't quite do for a man in my position to joke about miracles.'

'But it was you who said it was a miracle,' said Alboin, staring.

'I'm so sorry,' said Father Brown; 'I'm afraid there's some mistake. I don't think I ever said it was a miracle. All I said was that it might happen. What you said was that it couldn't happen, because it would be a miracle if it did. And then it did. And so you said it was a miracle. But I never said a word about miracles or magic, or anything of the sort from beginning to end.'

'But I thought you believed in miracles,' broke out the secretary.

'Yes,' answered Father Brown, 'I believe in miracles. I believe in man-eating tigers, but I don't see them running about everywhere. If I want any miracles, I know where to get them.'

'I can't understand your taking this line, Father Brown,' said Vandam, earnestly. 'It seems so narrow; and you don't look narrow to me, though you are a parson. Don't you see, a miracle like this will knock all materialism endways? It will just tell the whole world in big print that spiritual powers can work and do work. You'll be serving religion as no parson ever served it yet.'

The priest had stiffened a little and seemed in some strange way clothed with unconscious and impersonal dignity, for all his stumpy figure. 'Well,' he said, 'you wouldn't suggest I should serve religion by what I know to be a lie? I don't know precisely what you mean by the phrase; and, to be quite candid, I'm not sure you do. Lying may be serving religion; I'm sure it's not serving God. And since you are harping so insistently on what I believe, wouldn't it be as well if you had some sort of notion of what it is?'

'I don't think I quite understand,' observed the millionaire, curiously.

'I don't think you do,' said Father Brown, with simplicity. 'You say this thing was done by spiritual powers. What spiritual powers? You don't think the holy angels took him and hung him on a garden tree, do you? And as for the unholy angels – no, no, no. The men who did this did a wicked thing, but they went no further than their own wickedness; they weren't wicked enough to be dealing with spiritual powers. I know something about Satanism, for my sins; I've been forced to know. I know what it is, what it practically always is. It's proud and it's sly. It likes to be superior; it loves to horrify the innocent with things half understood, to make children's flesh creep. That's why it's so fond of mysteries and initiations and secret societies and all the rest of it. Its eyes are turned inwards, and however grand and grave it may look, it's always hiding a small, mad smile.' He shuddered suddenly, as if caught in an icy draught of air. 'Never mind about them; they've got nothing to do with this, believe me. Do you think that poor, wild Irishman of mine, who ran raving down the street, who blurted out half of it when he first saw my face, and ran away for fear he should blurt out more, do you think Satan confides any secrets to him? I admit he joined in a plot, probably in a plot with two other men worse than himself; but for all that, he was just in an everlasting rage when he rushed down the lane and let off his pistol and his curse.'

'But what on earth does all this mean?' demanded Vandam. 'Letting off a toy pistol and a twopenny curse wouldn't do what was done, except by a miracle. It wouldn't make Wynd disappear like a fairy. It wouldn't make him reappear a quarter of a mile away with a rope round his neck.'

'No,' said Father Brown sharply; 'but what would it do?'

'And still I don't follow you,' said the millionaire gravely.

'I say, what would it do?' repeated the priest; showing, for the first time, a sort of animation verging on annoyance. 'You keep on repeating that a blank pistol-shot wouldn't do this and wouldn't do that; that if that was all, the murder wouldn't happen or the miracle wouldn't happen. It doesn't seem to occur to you to ask what would happen. What would happen to you if a lunatic let off a firearm without rhyme or reason right under your window? What's the very first thing that would happen?'

Vandam looked thoughtful. 'I guess I should look out of the window,' he said.

'Yes,' said Father Brown, 'you'd look out of the window. That's the whole story. It's a sad story, but it's finished now; and there were extenuating circumstances.'

'Why should looking out of the window hurt him?' asked Alboin. 'He didn't fall out, or he'd have been found in the lane.'

'No,' said Father Brown, in a low voice. 'He didn't fall. He rose.'

There was something in his voice like the groan of a gong, a note of doom, but otherwise he went on steadily: 'He rose, but not on wings; not on the wings of any holy or unholy angels. He rose at the end of a rope, exactly as you saw him in the garden; a noose dropped over his head the moment it was poked out of the window. Don't you remember Wilson, that big servant of his, a man of huge strength, while Wynd was the lightest of little shrimps? Didn't Wilson go to the floor above to get a pamphlet, to a room full of luggage corded in coils and coils of rope? Has Wilson been seen since that day? I fancy not.'

'Do you mean,' asked the secretary, 'that Wilson whisked him clean out of his own window like a trout on a line?'

'Yes,' said the other, 'and let him down again out of the other window into the park, where the third accomplice hooked him on to a tree. Remember the lane was always empty; remember the wall opposite was quite blank; remember it was all over in five minutes after the Irishman gave the signal with the pistol. There were three of them in it of course; and I wonder whether you can all guess who they were.'

They were all three staring at the plain, square window and the blank, white wall beyond; and nobody answered.

'By the way,' went on Father Brown, 'don't think I blame you for jumping to preternatural conclusions. The reason's very simple, really. You all swore you were hard-shelled materialists; and as a matter of fact you were all balanced on the very edge of belief – of belief in almost anything. There are thousands balanced on it today; but it's a sharp, uncomfortable edge to sit on. You won't rest till you believe something; that's why Mr Vandam went through new religions with a tooth-comb, and Mr Alboin quotes Scripture for his religion of breathing exercises, and Mr Fenner grumbles at the very God he denies. That's where you all split; it's natural to believe in the supernatural. It never feels natural to accept only natural things. But though it wanted only a touch to tip you into preternaturalism about these things, these things really were only natural things. They were not only natural, they were almost unnaturally simple. I suppose there never was quite so simple a story as this.'

Fenner laughed and then looked puzzled. 'I don't understand one thing,' he said. 'If it was Wilson, how did Wynd come to have a man like that on such intimate terms? How did he come to be killed by a man he'd seen every day for years? He was famous as being a judge of men.'

Father Brown thumped his umbrella on the ground with an emphasis he rarely showed.

'Yes,' he said, almost fiercely; 'that was how he came to be killed. He was killed for just that. He was killed for being a judge of men.'

They all stared at him, but he went on, almost as if they were not there.

'What is any man that he should be a judge of men?' he demanded. 'These three were the tramps that once stood before him and were dismissed rapidly right and left to one place or another; as if for them there were no cloak of courtesy, no stages of intimacy, no free-will in friendship. And twenty years has not exhausted the indignation born of that unfathomable insult in that moment when he dared to know them at a glance.'

'Yes,' said the secretary; 'I understand . . . and I understand how it is that you understand – all sorts of things.'

'Well, I'm blamed if I understand,' cried the breezy Western gentleman boisterously. 'Your Wilson and your Irishman seem to be just a couple of cut-throat murderers who killed their benefactor. I've no use for a black and bloody assassin of that sort, in my morality, whether it's religion or not.'

'He was a black and bloody assassin, no doubt,' said Fenner quietly. 'I'm not defending him; but I suppose it's Father Brown's business to pray for all men, even for a man like – '

'Yes,' assented Father Brown, 'it's my business to pray for all men, even for a man like Warren Wynd.'

The Curse of the Golden Cross

Six people sat around a small table, seeming almost as incongruous and accidental as if they had been shipwrecked separately on the same small desert island. At least the sea surrounded them; for in one sense their island was enclosed in another island, a large and flying island like Laputa. For the little table was one of many little tables dotted about in the dining-saloon of that monstrous ship the *Moravia*, speeding through the night and the everlasting emptiness of the Atlantic. The little company had nothing in common except that all were travelling from America to England. Two of them at least might be called celebrities; others might be called obscure, and in one or two cases even dubious.

The first was the famous Professor Smaill, an authority on certain archaeological studies touching the later Byzantine Empire. His lectures, delivered in an American University, were accepted as of the first authority even in the most authoritative seats of learning in Europe. His literary works were so steeped in a mellow and imaginative sympathy with the European past, that it often gave strangers a start to hear him speak with an American accent. Yet he was, in his way, very American; he had long fair hair brushed back from a big square forehead, long straight features and a curious mixture of preoccupation with a poise of potential swiftness, like a lion pondering absent-mindedly on his next leap.

There was only one lady in the group; and she was (as the journalists often said of her) a host in herself; being quite prepared to play hostess, not to say empress, at that or any other table. She was Lady Diana Wales, the celebrated lady traveller in tropical and other countries; but there was nothing rugged or masculine about her appearance at dinner. She was herself handsome in an almost tropical fashion, with a mass of hot and heavy red hair; she was dressed in what the journalists call a daring fashion, but her face was intelligent and her eyes had that bright and rather prominent appearance which belongs to the eyes of ladies who ask questions at political meetings.

The other four figures seemed at first like shadows in this shining presence; but they showed differences on a close view. One of them was a young man entered on the ship's register as Paul T. Tarrant. He was an American type which might be more truly called an American anti-type. Every nation probably has an anti-type; a sort of extreme exception that proves the national rule. Americans really respect work, rather as Europeans respect war. There is a halo of heroism about it; and he who shrinks from it is less than a man. The anti-type is evident through being exceedingly rare. He is the dandy or dude: the wealthy waster who makes a weak villain for so many American novels. Paul Tarrant seemed to have nothing whatever to do but change his clothes, which he did about six times a day; passing into paler or richer shades of his suit of exquisite light grey, like the delicate silver changes of the twilight. Unlike most Americans, he cultivated very carefully a short, curly beard; and unlike most dandies, even of his own type, he seemed rather sulky than showy. Perhaps there was something almost Byronic about his silence and his gloom.

The next two travellers were naturally classed together; merely because they were both English lecturers returning from an American tour. One of them was described as Leonard Smyth, apparently a minor poet, but something of a major journalist; long-headed, light-haired, perfectly dressed, and perfectly capable of looking after himself. The other was a rather comic contrast, being short and broad, with a black, walrus moustache, and as taciturn as the other was talkative. But as he had been both charged with robbing and praised for rescuing a Romanian Princess threatened by a jaguar in his travelling menagerie, and had thus figured in a fashionable case, it was naturally felt that his views on God, progress, his own early life, and the future of Anglo-American relations would be of great interest and value to the inhabitants of Minneapolis and Omaha. The sixth and most insignificant figure was that of a little English priest going by the name of Brown. He listened to the conversation with respectful attention, and he was at that moment forming the impression that there was one rather curious thing about it.

'I suppose those Byzantine studies of yours, Professor,' Leonard Smyth was saying, 'would throw some light on this story of a tomb found somewhere on the south coast; near Brighton, isn't it? Brighton's a long way from Byzantium, of course. But I read something about the style of burying or embalming or something being supposed to be Byzantine.'

'Byzantine studies certainly have to reach a long way,' replied the Professor dryly. 'They talk about specialists; but I think the hardest thing on earth is to specialise. In this case, for instance: how can a man know anything about Byzantium till he knows everything about Rome before it and about Islam after it? Most Arab arts were old Byzantine arts. Why, take algebra – '

'But I won't take algebra,' cried the lady decisively. 'I never did, and I never do. But I'm awfully interested in embalming. I was with Gatton, you know, when he opened the Babylonian tombs. Ever since then I found mummies and preserved bodies and all that perfectly thrilling. Do tell us about this one.'

'Gatton was an interesting man,' said the Professor. 'They were an interesting family. That brother of his who went into Parliament was much more than an ordinary politician. I never understood the Fascisti till he made that speech about Italy.'

'Well, we're not going to Italy on this trip,' said Lady Diana persistently, 'and I believe you're going to that little place where they've found the tomb. In Sussex, isn't it?'

'Sussex is pretty large, as these little English sections go,' replied the Professor. 'One might wander about in it for a goodish time; and it's a good place to wander in. It's wonderful how large those low hills seem when you're on them.'

There was an abrupt accidental silence; and then the lady said, 'Oh, I'm going on deck,' and rose, the men rising with her. But the Professor lingered and the little priest was the last to leave the table, carefully folding up his napkin. And as they were thus left alone together the Professor said suddenly to his companion: 'What would you say was the point of that little talk?'

'Well,' said Father Brown, smiling, 'since you ask me, there was something that amused me a little. I may be wrong; but it seemed to me that the company made three attempts to get you to talk about an embalmed body said to be found in Sussex. And you, on your side, very courteously offered to talk – first about algebra, and then about the Fascisti, and then about the landscape of the Downs.'

'In short,' replied the Professor, 'you thought I was ready to talk about any subject but that one. You were quite right.'

The Professor was silent for a little time, looking down at the tablecloth; then he looked up and spoke with that swift impulsiveness that suggested the lion's leap.

'See here, Father Brown,' he said, 'I consider you about wisest and whitest man I ever met.'

Father Brown was very English. He had all the normal nation helplessness about what to do with a serious and sincere compliment suddenly handed to him to his face in the American manner. His reply was a meaningless murmur; and it was the Professor who proceeded, with the same staccato earnestness: 'You see, up to a point it's all simple enough. A Christian tomb of the Dark Ages, apparently that of a bishop, has been found under a little church at Dulham on the Sussex coast. The Vicar happens to be a good bit of an archaeologist himself and has been able to find a good deal more than I know yet. There was a rumour of the corpse being embalmed in a way peculiar to Greeks and Egyptians but unknown in the West, especially at that date. So Mr Walters (that is the Vicar) naturally wonders about Byzantine influences. But he also mentions something else, that is of even more personal interest to me.'

His long grave face seemed to grow even longer and graver as he frowned down at the tablecloth. His long finger seemed to be tracing patterns on it like the plans of dead cities and their temples and tombs.

'So I'm going to tell you, and nobody else, why it is I have to be careful about mentioning that matter in mixed company; and why, the more eager they are to talk about it, the more cautious I have to be. It is also stated that in the coffin is a chain with a cross, common enough to look at, but with a certain secret symbol on the back found on only one other cross in the world. It is from the arcana of the very earliest Church, and is supposed to indicate St Peter setting up his See at Antioch before he came to Rome. Anyhow, I believe there is but one other like it, and it belongs to me. I hear there is some story about a curse on it; but I take no notice of that. But whether or no there is a curse, there really is, in one sense, a conspiracy; though the conspiracy should only consist of one man.'

'Of one man?' repeated Father Brown almost mechanically.

'Of one madman, for all I know,' said Professor Smaill. 'It's a long story and in some ways a silly one.'

He paused again, tracing plans like architectural drawings with his finger on the cloth, and then resumed: 'Perhaps I had better tell you about it from the beginning, in case you see some little point in the story that is meaningless to me. It began years and years ago, when I was conducting some investigations on my own account in the antiquities of Crete and the Greek islands. I did a great deal of it practically single-handed; sometimes with the most rude and temporary help from the inhabitants of the place, and sometimes literally alone. It was under the latter circumstances that I found a maze of subterranean passages which led at last to a heap of rich refuse, broken ornaments and scattered gems which I took to be the ruins of some sunken altar, and in which I found the curious gold cross. I turned it over, and on the back of it I saw the Ichthus or fish, which was an early Christian symbol, but of a shape and pattern rather different from that commonly found; and, as it seemed to me, more realistic – more as if the archaic designer had meant it to be not merely a conventional enclosure or nimbus, but to look a little more like a real fish. It seemed to me that there was a flattening towards one end of it that was not like mere mathematical decoration, but rather like a sort of rude or even savage zoology.

'In order to explain very briefly why I thought this find important, I must tell you the point of the excavation. For one thing, it had something of the nature of an excavation of an excavation. We were on the track not only of antiquities, but of the antiquarians of antiquity. We had reason to believe, or some of us thought we had reason to believe, that these underground passages, mostly of the Minoan period, like that famous one which is actually identified with the labyrinth of the Minotaur, had not really been lost and left undisturbed for all the ages between the Minotaur and the modern explorer. We believed that these underground places, I might almost say these underground towns and villages, had already been penetrated during the intervening period by some persons prompted by some motive. About the motive there were different schools of thought: some holding that the Emperors had ordered an official exploration out of mere scientific curiosity; others that the furious fashion in the later Roman Empire for all sorts of lurid Asiatic superstitions had started some nameless Manichaean sect or other rioting in the caverns in orgies that had to be hidden from the face of the sun. I belong to the group which believed that these caverns had been used in the same way as the catacombs. That is, we believed that, during some of the persecutions which spread like a fire over the whole Empire, the Christians had concealed themselves in these ancient pagan labyrinths of stone. It was therefore with a thrill as sharp as a thunderclap that I found and picked up the fallen golden cross and saw the design upon it; and it was with still more of a shock of felicity that, on turning to make my way once more outwards and upwards into the light of day, I looked up at the walls of bare rock that extended endlessly along the low passages, and saw scratched in yet ruder outline, but if possible more unmistakable, the shape of the Fish.

'Something about it made it seem as if it might be a fossil fish or some rudimentary organism fixed for ever in a frozen sea. I could not analyse this analogy, otherwise unconnected with a mere drawing scratched upon the stone, till I realised that I was saying in my subconscious mind that the first Christians must have seemed something like fish, dumb and dwelling in a fallen world of twilight and silence, dropped far below the feet of men and moving in dark and twilight and a soundless world.

'Everyone walking along stone passages knows what it is to be followed by phantom feet. The echo follows flapping or clapping behind or in front, so that it is almost impossible for the man who is really lonely to believe in his loneliness. I had got used to the effects of this echo and had not noticed it much for some time past, when I caught sight of the symbolical shape scrawled on the wall of rock. I stopped, and at the same instant it seemed as if my heart stopped, too; for my own feet had halted, but the echo went marching on.

'I ran forward, and it seemed as if the ghostly footsteps ran also, but not with that exact imitation which marks the material reverberation of a sound. I stopped again, and the steps stopped also; but I could have sworn they stopped an instant too late; I called out a question; and my cry was answered; but the voice was not my own.

'It came round the corner of a rock just in front of me; and throughout that uncanny chase I noticed that it was always at some such angle of the crooked path that it paused and spoke. The little space in front of me that could be illuminated by my small electric torch was always as empty as an empty room. Under these conditions I had a conversation with I know not whom, which lasted all the way to the first white gleam of daylight, and even there I could not see in what fashion he vanished into the light of day. But the mouth of the labyrinth was full of many openings and cracks and chasms, and it would not have been difficult for him to have somehow darted back and disappeared again into the underworld of the caves. I only know that I came out on the lonely steps of a great mountain like a marble terrace, varied only with a green vegetation that seemed somehow more tropical than the purity of the rock, like the Oriental invasion that has spread sporadically over the fall of classic Hellas. I looked out on a sea of stainless blue, and the sun shone steadily on utter loneliness and silence; and there was not a blade of grass stirred with a whisper of flight nor the shadow of a shadow of man.

'It had been a terrible conversation; so intimate and so individual and in a sense so casual. This being, bodiless, faceless, nameless and yet calling me by my name, had talked to me in those crypts and cracks where we were buried alive with no more passion or melodrama than if we had been sitting in two armchairs at a club. But he had told me also that he would unquestionably kill me or any other man who came into the possession of the cross with the mark of the fish. He told me frankly he was not fool enough to attack me there in the labyrinth, knowing I had a loaded revolver, and that he ran as much risk as I. But he told me, equally calmly, that he would plan my murder with the certainty of success, with every detail developed and every danger warded off, with the sort of artistic perfection that a Chinese craftsman or an Indian embroiderer gives to the artistic work of a lifetime. Yet he was no Oriental; I am certain he was a white man. I suspect that he was a countryman of my own.

'Since then I have received from time to time signs and symbols and queer impersonal messages that have made me certain, at least, that if the man is a maniac he is a monomaniac. He is always telling me, in this airy and detached way, that the preparations for my death and burial are proceeding satisfactorily; and that the only way in which I can prevent their being crowned with a comfortable success is to give up the relic in my possession – the unique cross that I found in the cavern. He does not seem to have any religious sentiment or fanaticism on the point; he seems to have no passion but the passion of a collector of curiosities. That is one of the things that makes me feel sure he is a man of the West and not of the East. But this particular curiosity seems to have driven him quite crazy.

'And then came this report, as yet unsubstantiated, about the duplicate relic found on an embalmed body in a Sussex tomb. If he had been a maniac before, this news turned him into a demoniac possessed of seven devils. That there should be one of them belonging to another man was bad enough, but that there should be two of them and neither belonging to him was a torture not to be borne. His mad messages began to come thick and fast like showers of poisoned arrows, and each cried out more confidently than the last that death would strike me at the moment when I stretched out my unworthy hand towards the cross in the tomb.

' "You will never know me," he wrote, "you will never say my name; you will never see my face; you will die, and never know who has killed you. I may be in any form among those about you; but I shall be in that alone at which you have forgotten to look."

'From those threats I deduce that he is quite likely to shadow me on this expedition; and try to steal the relic or do me some mischief for possessing it. But as I never saw the man in my life, he may be almost any man I meet. Logically speaking, he may be any of the waiters who wait on me at table. He may be any of the passengers who sit with me at table.'

'He may be me,' said Father Brown, with cheerful contempt for grammar.

'He may be anybody else,' answered Smaill seriously. 'That is what I meant by what I said just now. You are the only man I feel sure is not the enemy.'

Father Brown again looked embarrassed; then he smiled and said: 'Well, oddly enough, I'm not. What we have to consider is any chance of finding out if he really is here before he – before he makes himself unpleasant.'

'There is one chance of finding out, I think,' remarked the Professor rather grimly. 'When we get to Southampton I shall take a car at once along the coast; I should be glad if you would come with me, but in the ordinary sense, of course, our little party will break up. If any one of them turns up again in that little churchyard on the Sussex coast, we shall know who he really is.'

The Professor's programme was duly carried out, at least to the extent of the car and its cargo in the form of Father Brown. They coasted along the road with the sea on one side and the hills of Hampshire and Sussex on the other; nor was there visible to the eye any shadow of pursuit. As they approached the village of Dulham only one man crossed their path who had any connection with the matter in hand; a journalist who had just visited the church and been courteously escorted by the vicar through the new excavated chapel; but his remarks and notes seemed to be of the ordinary newspaper sort. But Professor Smaill was perhaps a little fanciful, and could not dismiss the sense of something odd and discouraging in the attitude and appearance of the man, who was tall and shabby, hook-nosed and hollow-eyed, with moustaches that drooped with depression. He seemed anything but enlivened by his late experiment as a sightseer; indeed, he seemed to be striding as fast as possible from the sight, when they stopped him with a question.

'It's all about a curse,' he said; 'a curse on the place, according to the guidebook or the parson, or the oldest inhabitant or whoever is the authority; and really, it feels jolly like it. Curse or no curse, I'm glad to have got out of it.'

'Do you believe in curses?' asked Smaill curiously.

'I don't believe in anything; I'm a journalist,' answered the melancholy being – 'Boon, of the *Daily Wire*. But there's a something creepy about that crypt; and I'll never deny I felt a chill.' And he strode on towards the railway station with a further accelerated pace.

'Looks like a raven or a crow, that fellow,' observed Smaill as they turned towards the churchyard. 'What is it they say about a bird of ill omen?'

They entered the churchyard slowly, the eyes of the American antiquary lingering luxuriantly over the isolated roof of the lych-gate and the large unfathomable black growth of the yew looking like night itself defying the broad daylight. The path climbed up amid heaving levels of turf in which the gravestones were tilted at all angles like stone rafts tossed on a green sea, till it came to the ridge beyond which the great sea itself ran like an iron bar, with pale lights in it like steel. Almost at their feet the tough rank grass turned into a tuft of sea-holly and ended in grey and yellow sand; and a foot or two from the holly, and outlined darkly against the steely sea, stood a motionless figure. But for its dark-grey clothing it might almost have been the statue on some sepulchral monument. But Father Brown instantly recognised something in the elegant stoop of the shoulders and the rather sullen outward thrust of the short beard.

'Gee!' exclaimed the professor of archaeology; 'it's that man Tarrant, if you call him a man. Did you think, when I spoke on the boat, that I should ever get so quick an answer to my question?'

'I thought you might get too many answers to it,' answered Father Brown.

'Why, how do you mean?' enquired the Professor, darting a look at him over his shoulder.

'I mean,' answered the other mildly, 'that I thought I heard voices behind the yew tree. I don't think Mr Tarrant is so solitary as he looks; I might even venture to say, so solitary as he likes to look.'

Even as Tarrant turned slowly round in his moody manner, the confirmation came. Another voice, high and rather hard, but none the less feminine, was saying with experienced raillery: 'And how was I to know he would be here?' It was borne in upon Professor Smaill that this gay observation was not addressed to him; so he was forced to conclude in some bewilderment, that yet a third person was present. As Lady Diana Wales came out, radiant and resolute as ever, from the shadow of the yew, he noted grimly that she had a living shadow of her own. The lean dapper figure of Leonard Smyth, that insinuating man of letters, appeared immediately behind her own flamboyant form, smiling, his head a little on one side like a dog's.

'Snakes!' muttered Smaill; 'why, they're all here! Or all except that little showman with the walrus whiskers.'

He heard Father Brown laughing softly beside him; and indeed the situation was becoming something more than laughable. It seemed to be turning topsy-turvy and tumbling about their ears like a pantomime trick; for even while the Professor had been speaking, his words had received the most comical contradiction. The round head with the grotesque black crescent of moustache had appeared suddenly and seemingly out of a hole in the ground. An instant afterwards they realised that the hole was in fact a very large hole, leading to a ladder which descended into the bowels of the earth; that it was in fact the entrance to the subterranean scene they had come to visit. The little man had been the first to find the entrance and had already descended a rung or two of the ladder before he put his head out again to address his fellow-travellers. He looked like some particularly preposterous Grave-digger in a burlesque of *Hamlet*. He only said thickly behind his thick moustaches, 'It is down here.' But it came to the rest of the company with a start of realisation that, though they had sat opposite him at meal-times for a week, they had hardly ever heard him speak before; and that though he was supposed to be an English lecturer, he spoke with a rather occult foreign accent.

'You see, my dear Professor,' cried Lady Diana with trenchant cheerfulness, 'your Byzantine mummy was simply too exciting to be missed. I simply had to come along and see it; and I'm sure the gentlemen felt just the same. Now you must tell us all about it.'

'I do not know all about it,' said the Professor gravely, not to say grimly. 'In some respects I don't even know what it's all about. It certainly seems odd that we should have all met again so soon, but I suppose there are no limits to the modern thirst for information. But if we are all to visit the place it must be done in a responsible way and, if you will forgive me, under responsible leadership. We must notify whoever is in charge of the excavations; we shall probably at least have to put our names in a book.'

Something rather like a wrangle followed on this collision between the impatience of the lady and the suspicions of the archaeologist; but the latter's insistence on the official rights of the Vicar and the local investigation ultimately prevailed; the little man with the moustaches came reluctantly out of his grave again and silently acquiesced in a less impetuous descent. Fortunately, the clergyman himself appeared at this stage – a grey-haired, good-looking gentleman with a droop accentuated by double eyeglasses; and while rapidly establishing sympathetic relations with the Professor as a fellow-antiquarian, he did not seem to regard his rather motley group of companions with anything more hostile than amusement.

'I hope you are none of you superstitious,' he said pleasantly. 'I ought to tell you, to start with, that there are supposed to be all sorts of bad omens and curses hanging over our devoted heads in this business. I have just been deciphering a Latin inscription which was found over the entrance to the chapel; and it would seem that there are no less than three curses involved; a curse for entering the sealed chamber, a double curse for opening the coffin, and a triple and most terrible curse for touching the gold relic found inside it. The two first maledictions I have already incurred myself,' he added with a smile; 'but I fear that even you will have to incur the first and mildest of them if you are to see anything at all. According to the story, the curses descend in a rather lingering fashion, at long intervals and on later occasions. I don't know whether that is any comfort to you.' And the Revd Mr Walters smiled once more in his drooping and benevolent manner.

'Story,' repeated Professor Smaill, 'why, what story is that?'

'It is rather a long story and varies, like other local legends,' answered the Vicar. 'But it is undoubtedly contemporary with the time of the tomb; and the substance of it is embodied in the inscription and is roughly this: Guy de Gisors, a lord of the manor here early in the thirteenth century, had set his heart on a beautiful black horse in the possession of an envoy from Genoa, which that practical merchant prince would not sell except for a huge price. Guy was driven by avarice to the crime of pillaging the shrine and, according to one story, even killing the bishop, who was then resident there. Anyhow, the bishop uttered a curse which was to fall on anybody who should continue to withhold the gold cross from its resting-place in his tomb, or should take steps to disturb it when it had returned there. The feudal lord raised the money for the horse by selling the gold relic to a goldsmith in the town; but on the first day he mounted the horse the animal reared and threw him in front of the church porch, breaking his neck. Meanwhile the goldsmith, hitherto wealthy and prosperous, was ruined by a series of inexplicable accidents, and fell into the power of a Jew money-lender living in the manor. Eventually the unfortunate goldsmith, faced with nothing but starvation, hanged himself on an apple tree. The gold cross with all his other goods, his house, shop, and tools, had long ago passed into the possession of the money-lender. Meanwhile, the son and heir of the feudal lord, shocked by the judgement on his blasphemous sire, had become a religious devotee in the dark and stern spirit of those times, and conceived it his duty to persecute all heresy and unbelief among his vassals. Thus the Jew, in his turn, who had been cynically tolerated by the father, was ruthlessly burnt by order of the son; so that he, in his turn, suffered for the possession of the relic; and after these three judgements, it was returned to the bishop's tomb; since when no eye has seen and no hand has touched it.'

Lady Diana Wales seemed to be more impressed than might have been expected. 'It really gives one rather a shiver,' she said, 'to think that we are going to be the first, except the vicar.'

The pioneer with the big moustaches and the broken English did not descend after all by his favourite ladder, which indeed had only been used by some of the workmen conducting the excavation; for the clergyman led them round to a larger and more convenient entrance about a hundred yards away, out of which he himself had just emerged from his investigations underground. Here the descent was by a fairly gradual slope with no difficulties save the increasing darkness; for they soon found themselves moving in single file down a tunnel as black as pitch, and it was some little time before they saw a glimmer of light ahead of them. Once during that silent march there was a sound like a catch in somebody's breath, it was impossible to say whose; and once there was an oath like a dull explosion, and it was in an unknown tongue.

They came out in a circular chamber like a basilica in a ring of round arches; for that chapel had been built before the first pointed arch of the Gothic had pierced our civilisation like a spear. A glimmer of greenish light between some of the pillars marked the place of the other opening into the world above, and gave a vague sense of being under the sea, which was intensified by one or two other incidental and perhaps fanciful resemblances. For the dog-tooth pattern of the Norman was faintly traceable round all the arches, giving them, above the cavernous darkness, something of the look of the mouths of monstrous sharks. And in the centre the dark bulk of the tomb itself, with its lifted lid of stone, might almost have been the jaws of some such leviathan.

Whether out of the sense of fitness or from the lack of more modern appliances, the clerical antiquary had arranged for the illumination of the chapel only by four tall candles in big wooden candlesticks standing on the floor. Of these only one was alight when they entered, casting a faint glimmer over the mighty architectural forms. When they had all assembled, the clergyman proceeded to light the three others, and the appearance and contents of the great sarcophagus came more clearly into view.

All eyes went first to the face of the dead, preserved across all those ages in the lines of life by some secret Eastern process, it was said, inherited from heathen antiquity and unknown to the simple graveyards of our own island. The Professor could hardly repress an exclamation of wonder; for, though the face was as pale as a mask of wax, it looked otherwise like a sleeping man, who had but that moment closed his eyes. The face was of the ascetic, perhaps even the fanatical type, with a high framework of bones; the figure was clad in a golden cope and gorgeous vestments, and high up on the breast, at the base of the throat, glittered the famous gold cross upon a short gold chain, or rather necklace. The stone coffin had been opened by lifting the lid of it at the head and propping it aloft upon two strong wooden shafts or poles, hitched above under the edge of the upper slab and wedged below into the corners of the coffin behind the head of the corpse. Less could therefore be seen of the feet or the lower part of the figure, but the candle-light shone full on the face; and in contrast with its tones of dead ivory the cross of gold seemed to stir and sparkle like a fire.

Professor Smaill's big forehead had carried a big furrow of reflection, or possibly of worry, ever since the clergyman had told the story of the curse. But feminine intuition, not untouched by feminine hysteria, understood the meaning of his brooding immobility better than did the men around him. In the silence of that candle-lit cavern Lady Diana cried out suddenly: 'Don't touch it, I tell you!'

But the man had already made one of his swift leonine movements, leaning forward over the body. The next instant they all darted, some forward and some backward, but all with a dreadful ducking motion as if the sky were falling.

As the Professor laid a finger on the gold cross, the wooden props, that bent very slightly in supporting the lifted lid of stone, seemed to jump and straighten themselves with a jerk. The lip of the stone slab slipped from its wooden perch; and in all their souls and stomachs came a sickening sense of down-rushing ruin, as if they had all been flung off a precipice. Smaill had withdrawn his head swiftly, but not in time; and he lay senseless beside the coffin, in a red puddle of blood from scalp or skull. And the old stone coffin was once more closed as it had been for centuries; save that one or two sticks or splinters stuck in the crevice, horribly suggestive of bones crunched by an ogre. The leviathan had snapped its jaws of stone.

Lady Diana was looking at the wreck with eyes that had an electric glare as of lunacy; her red hair looked scarlet against the pallor of her face in the greenish twilight. Smyth was looking at her, still with something dog-like in the turn of his head; but it was the expression of a god who looks at a master whose catastrophe he can only partly understand. Tarrant and the foreigner had stiffened in their usual sullen attitudes, but their faces had turned the colour of clay. The Vicar seemed to have fainted. Father Brown was kneeling beside the fallen figure, trying to test its condition.

Rather to the general surprise, the Byronic lounger, Paul Tarrant, came forward to help him.

'He'd better be carried up into the air,' he said. 'I suppose there's just a chance for him.'

'He isn't dead,' said Father Brown in a low voice, 'but I think it's pretty bad; you aren't a doctor by any chance?'

'No; but I've had to pick up a good many things in my time,' said the other. 'But never mind about me just now. My real profession would probably surprise you.'

'I don't think so,' replied Father Brown, with a slight smile. 'I thought of it about halfway through the voyage. You are a detective shadowing somebody. Well, the cross is safe from thieves now, anyhow.'

While they were speaking Tarrant had lifted the frail figure of the fallen man with easy strength and dexterity, and was carefully carrying him towards the exit. He answered over his shoulder: 'Yes, the cross is safe enough.'

'You mean that nobody else is,' replied Brown. 'Are you thinking of the curse, too?'

Father Brown went about for the next hour or two under a burden of frowning perplexity that was something beyond the shock of the tragic accident. He assisted in carrying the victim to the little inn opposite the church, interviewed the doctor, who reported the injury as serious and threatening, though not certainly fatal, and carried the news to the little group of travellers who had gathered round the table in the inn parlour. But wherever he went the cloud of mystification rested on him and seemed to grow darker the more deeply he pondered. For the central mystery was growing more and more mysterious, actually in proportion as many of the minor mysteries began to clear themselves up in his mind. Exactly in proportion as the meaning of individual figures in that motley group began to explain itself, the thing that had happened grew more and more difficult to explain. Leonard Smyth had come merely because Lady Diana had come; and Lady Diana had come merely because she chose. They were engaged in one of those floating Society flirtations that are all the more silly for being semi-intellectual. But the lady's romanticism had a superstitious side to it; and she was pretty well prostrated by the terrible end of her adventure. Paul Tarrant was a private detective, possibly watching the flirtation, for some wife or husband; possibly shadowing the foreign lecturer with the moustaches, who had much the air of an undesirable alien. But if he or anybody else had intended to steal the relic, the intention had been finally frustrated. And to all mortal appearance, what had frustrated it was either an incredible coincidence or the intervention of the ancient curse.

As he stood in unusual perplexity in the middle of the village street, between the inn and the church, he felt a mild shock of surprise at seeing a recently familiar but rather unexpected figure advancing up the street. Mr Boon, the journalist, looking very haggard in the sunshine, which showed up his shabby raiment like that of a scarecrow, had his dark and deep-set eyes (rather close together on either side of the long drooping nose) fixed on the priest. The latter looked twice before he realised that the heavy dark moustache hid something like a grin or at least a grim smile.

'I thought you were going away,' said Father Brown a little sharply. 'I thought you left by that train two hours ago.'

'Well, you see I didn't,' said Boon.

'Why have you come back?' asked the priest almost sternly.

'This is not the sort of little rural paradise for a journalist to leave in a hurry,' replied the other. 'Things happen too fast here to make it worth while to go back to a dull place like London. Besides, they can't keep me out of the affair – I mean this second affair. It was I that found the body, or at any rate the clothes. Quite suspicious conduct on my part, wasn't it? Perhaps you think I wanted to dress up in his clothes. Shouldn't I make a lovely parson?'

And the lean and long-nosed mountebank suddenly made an extravagant gesture in the middle of the market-place, stretching out his arms and spreading out his dark-gloved hands in a sort of burlesque benediction and saying: 'Oh, my dear brethren and sisters, for I would embrace you all . . . '

'What on earth are you talking about?' cried Father Brown, and rapped the stones slightly with his stumpy umbrella, for he was a little less patient than usual.

'Oh, you'll find out all about it if you ask that picnic party of yours at the inn,' replied Boon scornfully. 'That man Tarrant seems to suspect me merely because I found the clothes; though he only came up a minute too late to find them himself. But there are all sorts of mysteries in this business. The little man with the big moustaches may have more in him than meets the eye. For that matter I don't see why you shouldn't have killed the poor fellow yourself.'

Father Brown did not seem in the least annoyed at the suggestion, but he seemed exceedingly bothered and bewildered by the remark. 'Do you mean,' he asked with simplicity, 'that it was I who tried to kill Professor Smaill?'

'Not at all,' said the other, waving his hand with the air of one making a handsome concession. 'Plenty of dead people for you to choose among. Not limited to Professor Smaill. Why, didn't you know somebody else had turned up, a good deal deader than Professor Smaill? And I don't see why you shouldn't have done him in, in a quiet way. Religious differences, you know . . . lamentable disunion of Christendom . . . I suppose you've always wanted to get the English parishes back.'

'I'm going back to the inn,' said the priest quietly; 'you say the people there know what you mean, and perhaps *they* may be able to say it.'

In truth, just afterwards his private perplexities suffered a momentary dispersal at the news of a new calamity. The moment he entered the little parlour where the rest of the company were collected, something in their pale faces told him they were shaken by something yet more recent than the accident at the tomb. Even as he entered, Leonard Smyth was saying: 'Where is all this going to end?'

'It will never end, I tell you,' repeated Lady Diana, gazing into vacancy with glassy eyes; 'it will never end till we all end. One after another the curse will take us; perhaps slowly, as the poor vicar said; but it will take us all as it has taken him.'

'What in the world has happened now?' asked Father Brown.

There was a silence, and then Tarrant said in a voice that sounded a little hollow: 'Mr Walters, the Vicar, has committed suicide. I suppose it was the shock unhinged him. But I fear there can be no doubt about it. We've just found his black hat and clothes on a rock jutting out from the shore. He seems to have jumped into the sea. I thought he looked as if it had knocked him half-witted, and perhaps we ought to have looked after him; but there was so much to look after.'

'You could have done nothing,' said the lady. 'Don't you see the thing is dealing doom in a sort of dreadful order? The Professor touched the cross, and he went first; the Vicar had opened the tomb, and he went second; we only entered the chapel, and we –'

'Hold on,' said Father Brown, in a sharp voice he very seldom used; 'this has got to stop.'

He still wore a heavy though unconscious frown, but in his eyes was no longer the cloud of mystification, but a light of almost terrible understanding. 'What a fool I am!' he muttered. 'I ought to have seen it long ago. The tale of the curse ought to have told me.'

'Do you mean to say,' demanded Tarrant, 'that we can really be killed now by something that happened in the thirteenth century?'

Father Brown shook his head and answered with quiet emphasis: 'I won't discuss whether we can be killed by something that happened in the thirteenth century; but I'm jolly certain that we can't be killed by something that never happened in the thirteenth century, something that never happened at all.'

'Well,' said Tarrant, 'it's refreshing to find a priest so sceptical of the supernatural as all that.'

'Not at all,' replied the priest calmly; 'it's not the supernatural part I doubt. It's the natural part. I'm exactly in the position of the man who said, "I can believe the impossible, but not the improbable." '

'That's what you call a paradox, isn't it?' asked the other.

'It's what I call common sense, properly understood,' replied Father Brown. 'It really is more natural to believe a preternatural story, that deals with things we don't understand, than a natural story that contradicts things we do understand. Tell me that the great Mr Gladstone, in his last hours, was haunted by the ghost of Parnell, and I will be agnostic about it. But tell me that Mr Gladstone, when first presented to Queen Victoria, wore his hat in her drawing-room and slapped her on the back and offered her a cigar, and I am not agnostic at all. That is not impossible; it's only incredible. But I'm much more certain it didn't happen than that Parnell's ghost didn't appear; because it violates the laws of the world I do understand. So it is with that tale of the curse. It isn't the legend that I disbelieve – it's the history.'

Lady Diana had recovered a little from her trance of Cassandra, and her perennial curiosity about new things began to peer once more out of her bright and prominent eyes.

'What a curious man you are!' she said. 'Why should you disbelieve the history?'

'I disbelieve the history because it isn't history,' answered Father Brown. 'To anybody who happens to know a little about the Middle Ages, the whole story was about as probable as Gladstone offering Queen Victoria a cigar. But does anybody know anything about the Middle Ages? Do you know what a Guild was? Have you ever heard of *salvo managio suo*? Do you know what sort of people were *Servi Regis*?'

'No, of course I don't,' said the lady, rather crossly. 'What a lot of Latin words!'

'No, of course,' said Father Brown. 'If it had been Tutankhamen and a set of dried-up Africans preserved, Heaven knows why, at the other end of the world; if it had been Babylonia or China; if it had been some race as remote and mysterious as the Man in the Moon, your newspapers would have told you all about it, down to the last discovery of a toothbrush or a collar-stud. But the men who built your own parish churches, and gave the names to your own towns and trades, and the very roads you walk on – it has never occurred to you to know anything about them. I don't claim to know a lot myself; but I know enough to see that story is stuff and nonsense from beginning to end. It was illegal for a money-lender to distrain on a man's shop and tools. It's exceedingly unlikely that the Guild would not have saved a man from such utter ruin, especially if he were ruined by a Jew. Those people had vices and tragedies of their own; they sometimes tortured and burned people. But that idea of a man, without God or hope in the world, crawling away to die because nobody cared whether he lived – that isn't a medieval idea. That's a product of our economic science and progress. The Jew wouldn't have been a vassal of the feudal lord. The Jews normally had a special position as servants of the King. Above all, the Jew couldn't possibly have been burned for his religion.'

'The paradoxes are multiplying,' observed Tarrant; 'but surely, you won't deny that Jews were persecuted in the Middle Ages?'

'It would be nearer the truth,' said Father Brown, 'to say they were the only people who weren't persecuted in the Middle Ages. If you want to satirise medievalism, you could make a good case by saying that some poor Christian might be burned alive for making a mistake about the Homoousion, while a rich Jew might walk down the street openly sneering at Christ and the Mother of God. Well, that's what the story is like. It was never a story of the Middle Ages; it was never even a legend about the Middle Ages. It was made up by somebody whose notions came from novels and newspapers, and probably made up on the spur of the moment.'

The others seemed a little dazed by the historical digression, and seemed to wonder vaguely why the priest emphasised it and made it so important a part of the puzzle. But Tarrant, whose trade it was to pick the practical detail out of many tangles of digression, had suddenly become alert. His bearded chin was thrust forward farther than ever, but his sullen eyes were wide awake. 'Ah,' he said; 'made up on the spur of the moment!'

'Perhaps that is an exaggeration,' admitted Father Brown calmly. 'I should rather say made up more casually and carelessly than the rest of an uncommonly careful plot. But the plotter did not think the details of medieval history would matter much to anybody. And his calculation in a general way was pretty nearly right, like most of his other calculations.'

'Whose calculations? Who was right?' demanded the lady with a sudden passion of impatience. 'Who is this person you are talking about? Haven't we gone through enough, without your making our flesh creep with your he's and him's?'

'I am talking about the murderer,' said Father Brown.

'What murderer?' she asked sharply. 'Do you mean that the poor Professor was murdered?'

'Well,' said the staring Tarrant gruffly into his beard, 'we can't say "murdered", for we don't know he's killed.'

'The murderer killed somebody else, who was not Professor Smaill,' said the priest gravely.

'Why, whom else could he kill?' asked the other.

'He killed the Revd John Walters, the Vicar of Dulham,' replied Father Brown with precision. 'He only wanted to kill those two, because they both had got hold of relics of one rare pattern. The murderer was a sort of monomaniac on the point.'

'It all sounds very strange,' muttered Tarrant. 'Of course we can't swear that the Vicar's really dead either. We haven't seen his body.'

'Oh yes, you have,' said Father Brown.

There was a silence as sudden as the stroke of a gong; a silence in which that subconscious guesswork that was so active and accurate in the woman moved her almost to a shriek.

'That is exactly what you have seen,' went on the priest. 'You have seen his body. You haven't seen him – the real living man; but you have seen his body all right. You have stared at it hard by the light of four great candles; and it was not tossing suicidally in the sea but lying in state like a Prince of the Church in a shrine built before the Crusade.'

'In plain words,' said Tarrant, 'you actually ask us to believe that the embalmed body was really the corpse of a murdered man.'

Father Brown was silent for a moment; then he said almost with an air of irrelevance: 'The first thing I noticed about it was the cross; or rather the string suspending the cross. Naturally, for most of you, it was only a string of beads and nothing else in particular; but, naturally also, it was rather more in my line than yours. You remember it lay close up to the chin, with only a few beads showing, as if the whole necklet were quite short. But the beads that showed were arranged in a special way, first one and then three, and so on; in fact, I knew at a glance that it was a rosary, an ordinary rosary with a cross at the end of it. But a rosary has at least five decades and additional beads as well; and I naturally wondered where all the rest of it was. It would go much more than once round the old man's neck. I couldn't understand it at the time; and it was only afterwards I guessed where the extra length had gone to. It was coiled round and round the foot of the wooden prop that was fixed in the corner of the coffin, holding up the lid. So that when poor Smaill merely plucked at the cross it jerked the prop out of its place and the lid fell on his skull like a club of stone.'

'By George!' said Tarrant; 'I'm beginning to think there's something in what you say. This is a queer story if it's true.'

'When I realised that,' went on Father Brown, 'I could manage more or less to guess the rest. Remember, first of all, that there never was any responsible archaeological authority for anything more than investigation. Poor old Walters was an honest antiquary, who was engaged in opening the tomb to find out if there was any truth in the legend about embalmed bodies. The rest was all rumour, of the sort that often anticipates or exaggerates such finds. As a fact, he found the body had not been embalmed, but had fallen into dust long ago. Only while he was working there by the light of his lonely candle in that sunken chapel, the candle-light threw another shadow that was not his own.'

'Ah!' cried Lady Diana with a catch in her breath; 'and I know what you mean now. You mean to tell us we have met the murderer, talked and joked with the murderer, let him tell us a romantic tale, and let him depart untouched.'

'Leaving his clerical disguise on a rock,' assented Brown. 'It is all dreadfully simple. This man got ahead of the Professor in the race to the churchyard and chapel, possibly while the Professor was talking to that lugubrious journalist. He came on the old clergyman beside the empty coffin and killed him. Then he dressed himself in the black clothes from the corpse, wrapped it in an old cope which had been among the real finds of the exploration, and put it in the coffin, arranging the rosary and the wooden support as I have described. Then, having thus set the trap for his second enemy, he went up into the daylight and greeted us all with the most amiable politeness of a country clergyman.'

'He ran a considerable risk,' objected Tarrant, 'of somebody knowing Walters by sight.'

'I admit he was half-mad,' agreed Father Brown; 'and I think you will admit that the risk was worth taking, for he has got off, after all.'

'I'll admit he was very lucky,' growled Tarrant. 'And who the devil was he?'

'As you say, he was very lucky,' answered Father Brown, 'and not least in that respect. For that is the one thing we may never know.' He frowned at the table for a moment and then went on: 'This fellow has been hovering round and threatening for years, but the one thing he was careful of was to keep the secret of who he was; and he has kept it still. But if poor Smaill recovers, as I think he will, it is pretty safe to say that you will hear more of it.'

'Why, what will Professor Smaill do, do you think?' asked Lady Diana.

'I should think the first thing he would do,' said Tarrant, 'would be to put the detectives on like dogs after this murdering devil. I should like to have a go at him myself.'

'Well,' said Father Brown, smiling suddenly after his long fit of frowning perplexity, 'I think I know the very first thing he ought to do.'

'And what is that?' asked Lady Diana with graceful eagerness.

'He ought to apologise to all of you,' said Father Brown.

It was not upon this point, however, that Father Brown found himself talking to Professor Smaill as he sat by the bedside during the slow convalescence of that eminent archaeologist. Nor, indeed, was it chiefly Father Brown who did the talking; for though the Professor was limited to small doses of the stimulant of conversation, he concentrated most of it upon these interviews with his clerical friend. Father Brown had a talent for being silent in an encouraging way and Smaill was encouraged by it to talk about many strange things not always easy to talk about; such as the morbid phases of recovery and the monstrous dreams that often accompany delirium. It is often rather an unbalancing business to recover slowly from a bad knock on the head; and when the head is as interesting a head as that of Professor Smaill even its disturbances and distortions are apt to be original and curious. His dreams were like bold and big designs rather out of drawing, as they can be seen in the strong but stiff archaic arts that he had studied; they were full of strange saints with square and triangular haloes, of golden outstanding crowns and glories round dark and flattened faces, of eagles out of the east and the high head-dresses of bearded men with their hair bound like women. Only, as he told his friend, there was one much simpler and less entangled type, that continually recurred to his imaginative memory. Again and again all these Byzantine patterns would fade away like the fading gold on which they were traced as upon fire; and nothing remained but the dark bare wall of rock on which the shining shape of the fish was traced as with a finger dipped in the phosphorescence of fishes. For that was the sign which he once looked up and saw, in the moment when he first heard round the corner of the dark passage the voice of his enemy.

'And at last,' he said, 'I think I have seen a meaning in the picture and the voice; and one that I never understood before. Why should I worry because one madman among a million of sane men, leagued in a great society against him, chooses to brag of persecuting me or pursuing me to death? The man who drew in the dark catacomb the secret symbol of Christ was persecuted in a very different fashion. He was the solitary madman; the whole sane society was leagued together not to save but to slay him. I have sometimes fussed and fidgeted and wondered whether this or that man was my persecutor; whether it was Tarrant; whether it was Leonard Smyth; whether it was any one of them. Suppose it had been all of them? Suppose it had been all the men on the boat and the men on the train and the men in the village. Suppose, so far as I was concerned, they were all murderers. I thought I had a right to be alarmed because I was creeping through the bowels of the earth in the dark and there was a man who would destroy me. What would it have been like, if the destroyer had been up in the daylight and had owned all the earth and commanded all the armies and the crowds? How if he had been able to stop all the earths or smoke me out of my hole, or kill me the moment I put my nose out in the daylight? What was it like to deal with murder on that scale? The world has forgotten these things, as until a little while ago it had forgotten war.'

'Yes,' said Father Brown, 'but the war came. The fish may be driven underground again, but it will come up into the daylight once more. As St Antony of Padua humorously remarked, "It is only fishes who survive the Deluge." '

The Dagger with Wings

Father Brown, at one period of his life, found it difficult to hang his hat on a hat-peg without repressing a slight shudder. The origin of this idiosyncrasy was indeed a mere detail in much more complicated events; but it was perhaps the only detail that remained to him in his busy life to remind him of the whole business. Its remote origin was to be found in the facts which led Dr Boyne, the medical officer attached to the police force, to send for the priest on a particular frosty morning in December.

Dr Boyne was a big dark Irishman, one of those rather baffling Irishmen to be found all over the world, who will talk scientific scepticism, materialism, and cynicism at length and at large, but who never dream of referring anything touching the ritual of religion to anything except the traditional religion of their native land. It would be hard to say whether their creed is a very superficial varnish or a very fundamental substratum; but most probably it is both, with a mass of materialism in between. Anyhow, when he thought that matters of that sort might be involved, he asked Father Brown to call, though he made no pretence of preference for that aspect of them.

'I'm not sure I want you, you know,' was his greeting. 'I'm not sure about anything yet. I'm hanged if I can make out whether it's a case for a doctor, or a policeman, or a priest.'

'Well,' said Father Brown with a smile, 'as I suppose you're both a policeman and a doctor, I seem to be rather in a minority.'

'I admit you're what politicians call an instructed minority,' replied the doctor. 'I mean, I know you've had to do a little in our line as well as your own. But it's precious hard to say whether this business is in your line or ours, or merely in the line of the Commissioners in Lunacy. We've just had a message from a man living near here, in that white house on the hill, asking for protection against a murderous persecution. We've gone into the facts as far as we could, and perhaps I'd better tell you the story as it is supposed to have happened, from the beginning.

'It seems that a man named Aylmer, who was a wealthy landowner in the West Country, married rather late in life and had three sons, Philip, Stephen, and Arnold. But in his bachelor days, when he thought he would have no heir, he had adopted a boy whom he thought very brilliant and promising, who went by the name of John Strake. His origin seems to be vague; they say he was a foundling; some say he was a gypsy. I think the last notion is mixed up with the fact that Aylmer in his old age dabbled in all sorts of dingy occultism, including palmistry and astrology, and his three sons say that

Strake encouraged him in it. But they said a great many other things besides that. They said Strake was an amazing scoundrel, and especially an amazing liar; a genius in inventing lies on the spur of the moment, and telling them so as to deceive a detective. But that might very well be a natural prejudice, in the light of what happened. Perhaps you can more or less imagine what happened. The old man left practically everything to the adopted son; and when he died the three real sons disputed the will. They said their father had been frightened into surrender and, not to put too fine a point on it, into gibbering idiocy. They said Strake had the strangest and most cunning ways of getting at him, in spite of the nurses and the family, and terrorising him on his deathbed. Anyhow, they seemed to have proved something about the dead man's mental condition, for the courts set aside the will and the sons inherited. Strake is said to have broken out in the most dreadful fashion, and sworn he would kill all three of them, one after another, and that nothing could hide them from his vengeance. It is the third or last of the brothers, Arnold Aylmer, who is asking for police protection.'

'Third and last,' said the priest, looking at him gravely.

'Yes,' said Boyne. 'The other two are dead.'

There was a silence before he continued. 'That is where the doubt comes in. There is no proof they were murdered, but they might possibly have been. The eldest, who took up his position as squire, was supposed to have committed suicide in his garden. The second, who went into trade as a manufacturer, was knocked on the head by the machinery in his factory; he might very well have taken a false step and fallen. But if Strake did kill them, he is certainly very cunning in his way of getting to work and getting away. On the other hand, it's more than likely that the whole thing is a mania of conspiracy founded on a coincidence. Look here, what I want is this. I want somebody of sense, who isn't an official, to go up and have a talk with this Mr Arnold Aylmer and form an impression of him. You know what a man with a delusion is like, and how a man looks when he is telling the truth. I want you to be the advance guard, before we take the matter up.'

'It seems rather odd,' said Father Brown, 'that you haven't had to take it up before. If there is anything in this business, it seems to have been going on for a good time. Is there any particular reason why he should send for you just now, any more than any other time?'

'That had occurred to me, as you may imagine,' answered Dr Boyne. 'He does give a reason, but I confess it is one of the things that make me wonder whether the whole thing isn't only the whim of some half-witted crank. He declared that all his servants have suddenly gone on strike and left him, so that he is obliged to call on the police to look after his house. And on making enquiries, I certainly do find that there has been a general exodus of servants from that house on the hill; and of course the town is full of tales, very one-sided tales I dare say. Their account of it seems to be that their employer had become quite impossible in his fidgets and fears and exactions; that he wanted them to guard the house like sentries, or sit up like night nurses in a hospital; that they could never be left alone because he must never be left alone. So they all announced in a loud voice that he was a lunatic, and left. Of course that does not prove he is a lunatic; but it seems rather rum nowadays for a man to expect his valet or his parlourmaid to act as an armed guard.'

'And so,' said the priest with a smile, 'he wants a policeman to act as his parlourmaid because his parlourmaid won't act as a policeman.'

'I thought that rather thick, too,' agreed the doctor; 'but I can't take the responsibility of a flat refusal till I've tried a compromise. You are the compromise.'

'Very well,' said Father Brown simply. 'I'll go and call on him now if you like.'

The rolling country round the little town was sealed and bound with frost, and the sky was as clear and cold as steel, except in the north-east where clouds with lurid haloes were beginning to climb up the sky. It was against these darker and more sinister colours that the house on the hill gleamed with a row of pale pillars, forming a short colonnade of the classical sort. A winding road led up to it across the curve of the down, and plunged into a mass of dark bushes. Just before it reached the bushes the air seemed to grow colder and colder, as if he were approaching an icehouse or the North Pole. But he was a highly practical person, never entertaining such fancies except as fancies. And he merely cocked his eye at the great livid cloud crawling up over the house, and remarked cheerfully: 'It's going to snow.'

Through a low ornamental iron gateway of the Italianate pattern he entered a garden having something of that desolation which only belongs to the disorder of orderly things. Deep-green growths were grey with the faint powder of the frost, large weeds had fringed the fading pattern of the flowerbeds as if in a ragged frame; and the house stood as if waist-high in a stunted forest of shrubs and bushes. The vegetation consisted largely of evergreens or very hardy plants; and though it was thus thick and heavy, it was too northern to be called luxuriant. It might be described as an Arctic jungle. So it was in some sense with the house itself, which had a row of columns and a classical façade, which might have looked out on the Mediterranean; but which seemed now to be withering in the wind of the North Sea. Classical ornament here and there accentuated the contrast; caryatides and carved masks of comedy or tragedy looked down from corners of the building upon the grey confusion of the garden paths; but the faces seemed to be frostbitten. The very volutes of the capitals might have curled up with the cold.

Father Brown went up the grassy steps to a square porch flanked by big pillars and knocked at the door. About four minutes afterwards he knocked again. Then he stood still patiently waiting with his back to the door and looked out on the slowly darkening landscape. It was darkening under the shadow of that one great continent of cloud that had come flying out of the north; and even as he looked out beyond the pillars of the porch, which seemed huge and black above him in the twilight, he saw the opalescent crawling rim of the great cloud as it sailed over the roof and bowed over the porch like a canopy. The great canopy with its faintly coloured fringes seemed to sink lower and lower upon the garden beyond, until what had recently been a clear and pale-hued winter sky was left in a few silver ribbons and rags like a sickly sunset. Father Brown waited, and there was no sound within.

Then he betook himself briskly down the steps and round the house to look for another entrance. He eventually found one, a side door in the flat wall, and on this also he hammered and outside this also he waited. Then he tried the handle and found the door apparently bolted or fastened in some fashion; and then he moved along that side of the house, musing on the possibilities of the position, and wondering whether the eccentric Mr Aylmer had barricaded himself too deep in the house to hear any kind of summons; or whether perhaps he would barricade himself all the more, on the assumption that any summons must be the challenge of the avenging Strake. It might be that the decamping servants had only unlocked one door when they left in the morning, and that their master had locked that; but whatever he might have done it was unlikely that they, in the mood of that moment, had looked so carefully to the defences. He continued his prowl round the place: it was not really a large place, though perhaps a little pretentious; and in a few moments he found he had made the complete circuit. A moment after he found what he suspected and sought. The french window of one room, curtained and shadowed with creeper, stood open by a crack, doubtless accidentally left ajar, and he found himself in a central room, comfortably upholstered in a rather old-fashioned way, with a staircase leading up from it on one side and a door leading out of it on the other. Immediately opposite him was another door with red glass let into it, a little gaudily for later tastes; something that looked like a red-robed figure in cheap stained glass. On a round table to the right stood a sort of aquarium – a great bowl full of greenish water, in which fishes and similar things moved about as in a tank; and just opposite it a plant of the palm variety with very large green leaves. All this looked so very dusty and Early Victorian that the telephone, visible in the curtained alcove, was almost a surprise.

'Who is that?' a voice called out sharply and rather suspiciously from behind the stained-glass door.

'Could I see Mr Aylmer?' asked the priest apologetically.

The door opened and a gentleman in a peacock-green dressing-gown came out with an enquiring look. His hair was rather rough and untidy, as if he had been in bed or lived in a state of slowly getting up, but his eyes were not only awake but alert, and some would have said alarmed. Father Brown knew that the contradiction was likely enough in a man who had rather run to seed under the shadow either of a delusion or a danger. He had a fine aquiline face when seen in profile, but when seen full face the first impression was that of the untidiness and even the wilderness of his loose brown beard.

'I am Mr Aylmer,' he said, 'but I've got out of the way of expecting visitors.'

Something about Mr Aylmer's unrestful eye prompted the priest to go straight to the point. If the man's persecution was only a monomania, he would be the less likely to resent it.

'I was wondering,' said Father Brown softly, 'whether it is quite true that you never expect visitors.'

'You are right,' replied his host steadily. 'I always expect one visitor. And he may be the last.'

'I hope not,' said Father Brown, 'but at least I am relieved to infer that I do not look very like him.'

Mr Aylmer shook himself with a sort of savage laugh. 'You certainly do not,' he said.

'Mr Aylmer,' said Father Brown frankly, 'I apologise for the liberty, but some friends of mine have told me about your trouble, and asked me to see if I could do anything for you. The truth is, I have some little experience in affairs like this.'

'There are no affairs like this,' said Aylmer.

'You mean,' observed Father Brown, 'that the tragedies in your unfortunate family were not normal deaths?'

'I mean they were not even normal murders,' answered the other. 'The man who is hounding us all to death is a hell-hound, and his power is from hell.'

'All evil has one origin,' said the priest gravely. 'But how do you know they were not normal murders?'

Aylmer answered with a gesture which offered his guest a chair; then he seated himself slowly in another, frowning, with his hands on his knees; but when he looked up his expression had grown milder and more thoughtful, and his voice was quite cordial and composed.

'Sir,' he said, 'I don't want you to imagine that I'm in the least an unreasonable person. I have come to these conclusions by reason, because unfortunately reason really leads there. I have read a great deal on these subjects; for I was the only one who inherited my father's scholarship in somewhat obscure matters, and I have since inherited his library. But what I tell you does not rest on what I have read but on what I have seen.'

Father Brown nodded, and the other proceeded, as if picking his words: 'In my elder brother's case I was not certain at first. There were no marks or footprints where he was found shot, and the pistol was left beside him. But he had just received a threatening letter, certainly from our enemy, for it was marked with a sign like a winged dagger, which was one of his infernal cabalistic tricks. And a servant said she had seen something moving along the garden wall in the twilight that was much too large to be a cat. I leave it there; all I can say is that if the murderer came, he managed to leave no traces of his coming. But when my brother Stephen died it was different; and since then I have known. A machine was working in an open scaffolding under the factory tower; I scaled the platform a moment after he had fallen under the iron hammer that struck him; I did not see anything else strike him, but I saw what I saw.

'A great drift of factory smoke was rolling between me and the factory tower; but through a rift of it I saw on the top of it a dark human figure wrapped in what looked like a black cloak. Then the sulphurous smoke drove between us again; and when it cleared I looked up at the distant chimney – there was nobody there. I am a rational man, and I will ask all rational men how he had reached that dizzy unapproachable turret, and how he left it.'

He stared across at the priest with a sphinx-like challenge; then after a silence he said abruptly: 'My brother's brains were knocked out, but his body was not much damaged. And in his pocket we found one of those warning messages dated the day before and stamped with the flying dagger.

'I am sure,' he went on gravely, 'that the symbol of the winged dagger is not merely arbitrary or accidental. Nothing about that abominable man is accidental. He is all design; though it is indeed a most dark and intricate design. His mind is woven not only out of elaborate schemes but out of all sorts of secret languages and signs, and dumb signals and wordless pictures which are the names of nameless things. He is the worst sort of man that the world knows: he is the wicked mystic. Now, I don't pretend to penetrate all that is conveyed by this symbol; but it seems surely that it must have a relation to all that was most remarkable, or even incredible, in his movements as he had hovered round my unfortunate family. Is there no connection between the idea of a winged weapon and the mystery by which Philip was struck dead on his own lawn without the lightest touch of any footprint having disturbed the dust or grass? Is there no connection between the plumed poignard flying like a feathered arrow and that figure which hung on the far top of the toppling chimney, clad in a cloak for pinions?'

'You mean,' said Father Brown thoughtfully, 'that he is in a perpetual state of levitation.'

'Simon Magus did it,' replied Aylmer, 'and it was one of the commonest predictions of the Dark Ages that Antichrist would be able to fly. Anyhow, there was the flying dagger on the document; and whether or no it could fly, it could certainly strike.'

'Did you notice what sort of paper it was on?' asked Father Brown. 'Common paper?'

The sphinx-like face broke abruptly into a harsh laugh.

'You can see what they're like,' said Aylmer grimly, 'for I got one myself this morning.'

He was leaning back in his chair now, with his long legs thrust out from under the green dressing-gown, which was a little short for him, and his bearded chin pillowed on his chest. Without moving otherwise, he thrust his hand deep in the dressing-gown pocket and held out a fluttering scrap of paper at the end of a rigid arm. His whole attitude was suggestive of a sort of paralysis, that was both rigidity and collapse. But the next remark of the priest had a curious effect of rousing him.

Father Brown was blinking in his short-sighted way at the paper presented to him. It was a singular sort of paper, rough without being common, as from an artist's sketchbook; and on it was drawn boldly in red ink a dagger decorated with wings like the rod of Hermes, with the written words, 'Death comes the day after this, as it came to your brothers.'

Father Brown tossed the paper on the floor and sat bolt upright in his chair.

'You mustn't let that sort of stuff stupefy you,' he said sharply. 'These devils always try to make us helpless by making us hopeless.'

Rather to his surprise, an awakening wave went over the prostrate figure, which sprang from its chair as if startled out of a dream.

'You're right, you're right!' cried Aylmer with a rather uncanny animation; 'and the devils shall find that I'm not so hopeless after all, nor so helpless either. Perhaps I have more hope and better help than you fancy.'

He stood with his hands in his pockets, frowning down at the priest, who had a momentary doubt, during that strained silence, about whether the man's long peril had not touched his brain. But when he spoke it was quite soberly.

'I believe my unfortunate brothers failed because they used the wrong weapons. Philip carried a revolver, and that was how his death came to be called suicide. Stephen had police protection, but he also had a sense of what made him ridiculous; and he could not allow a policeman to climb up a ladder after him to a scaffolding where he stood only a moment. They were both scoffers, reacting into scepticism from the strange mysticism of my father's last days. But I always knew there was more in my father than they understood. It is true that by studying magic he fell at last under the blight of black magic; the black magic of this scoundrel Strake. But my brothers were wrong about the antidote. The antidote to black magic is not brute materialism or worldly wisdom. The antidote to black magic is white magic.'

'It rather depends,' said Father Brown, 'what you mean by white magic.'

'I mean silver magic,' said the other, in a low voice, like one speaking of a secret revelation. Then after a silence he said: 'Do you know what I mean by silver magic? Excuse me a moment.'

He turned and opened the central door with the red glass and went into a passage beyond it. The house had less depth than Brown had supposed; instead of the door opening into interior rooms, the corridor it revealed ended in another door on the garden. The door of one room was on one side of the passage; doubtless, the priest told himself, the proprietor's bedroom whence he had rushed out in his dressing-gown. There was nothing else on that side but an ordinary hat-stand with the ordinary dingy cluster of old hats and overcoats; but on the other side was something more interesting: a very dark old oak sideboard laid out with some old silver, and overhung by a trophy or ornament of old weapons. It was by that that Arnold Aylmer halted, looking up at a long antiquated pistol with a bell-shaped mouth.

The door at the end of the passage was barely open, and through the crack came a streak of white daylight. The priest had very quick instincts about natural things, and something in the unusual brilliancy of that white line told him what had happened outside. It was indeed what he had prophesied when he was approaching the house. He ran past his rather startled host and opened the door, to face something that was at once a blank and a blaze. What he had seen shining through the crack was not only the most negative whiteness of daylight but the positive whiteness of snow. All round, the sweeping fall of the country was covered with that shining pallor that seems at once hoary and innocent.

'Here is white magic anyhow,' said Father Brown in his cheerful voice. Then, as he turned back into the hall, he murmured, 'And silver magic too, I suppose,' for the white lustre touched the silver with splendour and lit up the old steel here and there in the darkling armoury. The shaggy head of the brooding Aylmer seemed to have a halo of silver fire, as he turned with his face in shadow and the outlandish pistol in his hand.

'Do you know why I chose this sort of old blunderbuss?' he asked. 'Because I can load it with this sort of bullet.'

He had picked up a small apostle spoon from the sideboard and by sheer violence broke off the small figure at the top. 'Let us go back into the other room,' he added.

'Did you ever read about the death of Dundee?' he asked when they had reseated themselves. He had recovered from his momentary annoyance at the priest's restlessness. 'Graham of Claverhouse, you know, who persecuted the Covenanters and had a black horse that could ride straight up a precipice. Don't you know he could only be shot with a silver bullet, because he had sold himself to the Devil? That's one comfort about you; at least you know enough to believe in the Devil.'

'Oh, yes,' replied Father Brown, 'I believe in the Devil. What I don't believe in is the Dundee. I mean the Dundee of Covenanting legends, with his nightmare of a horse. John Graham was simply a seventeenth-century professional soldier, rather better than most. If he dragooned them it was because he was a dragoon, but not a dragon. Now my experience is that it's not that sort of swaggering blade who sells himself to the Devil. The devil-worshippers I've known were quite different. Not to mention names, which might cause a social flutter, I'll take a man in Dundee's own day. Have you ever heard of Dalrymple of Stair?'

'No,' replied the other gruffly.

'You've heard of what he did,' said Father Brown, 'and it was worse than anything Dundee ever did; yet he escapes the infamy by oblivion. He was the man who made the Massacre of Glencoe. He was a very learned man and lucid lawyer, a statesman with very serious and enlarged ideas of statesmanship, a quiet man with a very refined and intellectual face. That's the sort of man who sells himself to the Devil.'

Aylmer half started from his chair with an enthusiasm of eager assent.

'By God! you are right,' he cried. 'A refined intellectual face! That is the face of John Strake.'

Then he raised himself and stood looking at the priest with a curious concentration. 'If you will wait here a little while,' he said, 'I will show you something.'

He went back through the central door, closing it after him; going, the priest presumed, to the old sideboard or possibly to his bedroom. Father Brown remained seated, gazing abstractedly at the carpet, where a faint red glimmer shone from the glass in the doorway. Once it seemed to brighten like a ruby and then darkened again, as if the sun of that stormy day had passed from cloud to cloud. Nothing moved except the aquatic creatures which floated to and fro in the dim green bowl. Father Brown was thinking hard.

A minute or two afterwards he got up and slipped quietly to the alcove of the telephone, where he rang up his friend Dr Boyne, at the official headquarters. 'I wanted to tell you about Aylmer and his affairs,' he said quietly. 'It's a queer story, but I rather think there's something in it. If I were you I'd send some men up here straight away; four or five men, I think, and surround the house. If anything does happen there'll probably be something startling in the way of an escape.'

Then he went back and sat down again, staring at the dark carpet, which again glowed blood-red with the light from the glass door. Something in the filtered light set his mind drifting on certain borderlands of thought, with the first white daybreak before the coming of colour, and all that mystery which is alternately veiled and revealed in the symbol of windows and of doors.

An inhuman howl in a human voice came from beyond the closed doors, almost simultaneously with the noise of firing. Before the echoes of the shot had died away the door was violently flung open and his host staggered into the room, the dressing-gown half torn from his shoulder and the long pistol smoking in his hand. He seemed to be shaking in every limb, yet he was shaken in part with an unnatural laughter.

'Glory be to the White Magic!' he cried. 'Glory be to the silver bullet! The hell-hound had hunted once too often, and my brothers are avenged at last.'

He sank into a chair and the pistol slid from his hand and fell on the floor. Father Brown darted past him, slipped through the glass door and went down the passage. As he did so he put his hand on the handle of the bedroom door, as if half intending to enter; then he stooped a moment, as if examining something – and then he ran to the outer door and opened it.

On the field of snow, which had been so blank a little while before, lay one black object. At the first glance it looked a little like an enormous bat. A second glance showed that it was, after all, a human figure; fallen on its face, the whole head covered by a broad black hat having something of a Latin-American look; while the appearance of black wings came from the two flaps or loose sleeves of a very vast black cloak spread out, perhaps by accident, to their utmost length on either side. Both the hands were hidden, though Father Brown thought he could detect the position of one of them, and saw close to it, under the edge of the cloak, the glimmer of some metallic weapon. The main effect, however, was curiously like that of the simple extravagances of heraldry; like a black eagle displayed on a white ground. But by walking round it and peering under the hat the priest got a glimpse of the face, which was indeed what his host had called refined and intellectual; even sceptical and austere: the face of John Strake.

'Well, I'm jiggered,' muttered Father Brown. 'It really does look like some vast vampire that has swooped down like a bird.'

'How else could he have come?' came a voice from the doorway, and Father Brown looked up to see Aylmer once more standing there.

'Couldn't he have walked?' replied Father Brown evasively.

Aylmer stretched out his arm and swept the white landscape with a gesture.

'Look at the snow,' he said in a deep voice that had a sort of roll and thrill in it. 'Is not the snow unspotted – pure as the white magic you yourself called it? Is there a speck on it for miles, save that one foul black blot that has fallen there? There are no footprints, but a few of yours and mine; there are none approaching the house from anywhere.'

Then he looked at the little priest for a moment with a concentrated and curious expression, and said: 'I will tell you something else. That cloak he flies with is too long to walk with. He was not a very tall man, and it would trail behind him like a royal train. Stretch it out over his body, if you like, and see.'

'What happened to you both?' asked Father Brown abruptly.

'It was too swift to describe,' answered Aylmer. 'I had looked out of the door and was turning back when there came a kind of rushing of wind all around me, as if I were being buffeted by a wheel revolving in mid-air. I spun round somehow and fired blindly; and then I saw nothing but what you see now. But I am morally certain that you wouldn't see it if I had not had a silver shot in my gun. It would have been a different body lying there in the snow.'

'By the way,' remarked Father Brown, 'shall we leave it lying there in the snow? Or would you like it taken into your room – I suppose that's your bedroom in the passage?'

'No, no,' replied Aylmer hastily, 'we must leave it here till the police have seen it. Besides, I've had as much of such things as I can stand for the moment. Whatever else happens, I'm going to have a drink. After that, they can hang me if they like.'

Inside the central apartment, between the palm plant and the bowl of fishes, Aylmer tumbled into a chair. He had nearly knocked the bowl over as he lurched into the room, but he had managed to find the decanter of brandy after plunging his hand rather blindly into several cupboards and corners. He did not at any time look like a methodical person, but at this moment his distraction must have been extreme. He drank with a long gulp and began to talk rather feverishly, as if to fill up a silence.

'I see you are still doubtful,' he said, 'though you have seen the thing with your own eyes. Believe me, there was something more behind the quarrel between the spirit of Strake and the spirit of the house of Aylmer. Besides, you have no business to be an unbeliever. You ought to stand for all the things these stupid people call superstitions. Come now, don't you think there's a lot in those old wives' tales about luck and charms and so on, silver bullets included? What do you say about them as a Catholic?'

'I say I'm an agnostic,' replied Father Brown, smiling.

'Nonsense,' said Aylmer impatiently. 'It's your business to believe things.'

'Well, I do believe some things, of course,' conceded Father Brown; 'and therefore, of course, I don't believe other things.'

Aylmer was leaning forward, and looking at him with a strange intensity that was almost like that of a mesmerist.

'You do believe it,' he said. 'You do believe everything. We all believe everything, even when we deny everything. The deniers believe. The unbelievers believe. Don't you feel in your heart that these contradictions do not really contradict: that there is a cosmos that contains them all? The soul goes round upon a wheel of stars and all things return; perhaps Strake and I have striven in many shapes, beast against beast and bird against bird, and perhaps we shall strive for ever. But since we seek and need each other, even that eternal hatred is an eternal love. Good and evil go round in a wheel that is one thing and not many. Do you not realise in your heart, do you not believe behind all your beliefs, that there is but one reality and we are its shadows; and that all things are but aspects of one thing: a centre where men melt into Man and Man into God?'

'No,' said Father Brown.

Outside, twilight had begun to fall, in that phase of such a snow-laden evening when the land looks brighter than the sky. In the porch of the main entrance, visible through a half-curtained window, Father Brown could dimly see a bulky figure standing. He glanced casually at the french windows through which he had originally entered, and saw they were darkened with two equally motionless figures. The inner door with the coloured glass stood slightly ajar; and he could see in the short corridor beyond, the ends of two long shadows, exaggerated and distorted by the level light of evening, but still like grey caricatures of the figures of men. Dr Boyne had already obeyed the telephone message. The house was surrounded.

'What is the good of saying no?' insisted his host, still with the same hypnotic stare. 'You have seen part of that eternal drama with your own eyes. You have seen the threat of John Strake to slay Arnold Aylmer by black magic. You have seen Arnold Aylmer slay John Strake by white magic. You see Arnold Aylmer alive and talking to you now. And yet you don't believe it.'

'No, I do not believe it,' said Father Brown, and rose from his chair like one terminating a visit.

'Why not?' asked the other.

The priest only lifted his voice a little, but it sounded in every corner of the room like a bell. 'Because you are not Arnold Aylmer,' he said. 'I know who you are. Your name is John Strake; and you have murdered the last of the brothers, who is lying outside in the snow.'

A ring of white showed round the iris of the other man's eyes; he seemed to be making, with bursting eyeballs, a last effort to mesmerise and master his companion. Then he made a sudden movement sideways; and even as he did so the door behind him opened and a big detective in plain clothes put one hand quietly on his shoulder. The other hand hung down, but it held a revolver. The man looked wildly round, and saw plain-clothes men in all corners of the quiet room.

That evening Father Brown had another and longer conversation with Dr Boyne about the tragedy of the Aylmer family. By that time there was no longer any doubt of the central fact of the case, for John Strake had confessed his identity and even confessed his crimes; only it would be truer to say that he boasted of his victories. Compared to the fact that he had rounded off his life's work with the last Aylmer lying dead, everything else, including existence itself, seemed to be indifferent to him.

'The man is a sort of monomaniac,' said Father Brown. 'He is not interested in any other matter; not even in any other murder. I owe him something for that; for I had to comfort myself with the reflection a good many times this afternoon. As has doubtless occurred to you, instead of weaving all that wild but ingenious romance about winged vampires and silver bullets, he might have put an ordinary leaden bullet into me, and walked out of the house. I assure you it occurred quite frequently to me.'

'I wonder why he didn't,' observed Boyne. 'I don't understand it; but I don't understand anything yet. How on earth did you discover it, and what in the world did you discover?'

'Oh, you provided me with very valuable information,' replied Father Brown modestly, 'especially the one piece of information that really counted. I mean the statement that Strake was a very inventive and imaginative liar, with great presence of mind in producing his lies. This afternoon he needed it; but he rose to the occasion. Perhaps his only mistake was in choosing a preternatural story; he had the notion that because I am a clergyman I should believe anything. Many people have little notions of that kind.'

'But I can't make head or tail of it,' said the doctor. 'You must really begin at the beginning.'

'The beginning of it was a dressing-gown,' said Father Brown simply. 'It was the one really good disguise I've ever known. When you meet a man in a house with a dressing-gown on, you assume quite automatically that he's in his own house. I assumed it myself; but afterwards queer little things began to happen. When he took the pistol down he clicked it at arm's length, as a man does to make sure a strange weapon isn't loaded; of course he would know whether the pistols in his own hall were loaded or not. I didn't like the way he looked for the brandy, or the way he nearly barged into the bowl of fishes. For a man who has a fragile thing of that sort as a fixture in his rooms gets a quite mechanical habit of avoiding it. But these things might possibly have been fancies; the first real point was this. He came out from the little passage between the two doors; and in that passage there's only one other door leading to a room; so I assumed it was the bedroom he had just come from. I tried the handle; but it was locked. I thought this odd; and looked through the keyhole. It was an utterly bare room, obviously deserted; no bed, no anything. Therefore he had not come from inside any room, but from outside the house. And when I saw that, I think I saw the whole picture.

'Poor Arnold Aylmer doubtless slept and perhaps lived upstairs, and came down in his dressing-gown and passed through the red glass door. At the end of the passage, black against the winter daylight, he saw the enemy of his house. He saw a tall bearded man in a broad-brimmed black hat and a large flapping black cloak. He did not see much more in this world. Strake sprang at him, throttling or stabbing him; we cannot be sure till the inquest. Then Strake, standing in the narrow passage between the hat-stand and the old sideboard, and looking down in triumph on the last of his foes, heard something he had not expected. He heard footsteps in the parlour beyond. It was myself entering by the french windows.

'His masquerade was a miracle of promptitude. It involved not only a disguise but a romance – an impromptu romance. He took off his big black hat and cloak and put on the dead man's dressing-gown. Then he did a rather grisly thing; at least a thing that affects my fancy as more grisly than the rest. He hung the corpse like a coat on one of the hat pegs. He draped it in his own long cloak, and found it hung well below the heels; he covered the head entirely with his own wide hat. It was the only possible way of hiding it in that little passage with the locked door; but it was really a very clever one. I myself walked past the hat-stand once without knowing it was anything but a hat-stand. I think that unconsciousness of mine will always give me a shiver.

'He might perhaps have left it at that; but I might have discovered the corpse at any minute; and, hung where it was, it was a corpse calling for what you might call an explanation. He adopted the bolder stroke of discovering it himself and explaining it himself.

'Then there dawned on this strange and frightfully fertile mind the conception of a story of substitution; the reversal of the parts. He had already assumed the part of Arnold Aylmer. Why should not his dead enemy assume the part of John Strake? There must have been something in that topsy-turvydom to take the fancy of that darkly fanciful man. It was like some frightful fancy-dress ball to which the two mortal enemies were to go dressed up as each other. Only, the fancy-dress ball was to be a dance of death: and one of the dancers would be dead. That is why I can imagine that man putting it in his own mind, and I can imagine him smiling.'

Father Brown was gazing into vacancy with his large grey eyes, which, when not blurred by his trick of blinking, were the one notable thing in his face. He went on speaking simply and seriously: 'All things are from God; and above all, reason and imagination and the great gifts of the mind. They are good in themselves; and we must not altogether forget their origin even in their perversion. Now this man had in him a very noble power to be perverted; the power of telling stories. He was a great novelist; only he had twisted his fictive power to practical and to evil ends; to deceiving men with false fact instead of with true fiction. It began with his deceiving old Aylmer with elaborate excuses and ingeniously detailed lies; but even that may have been, at the beginning, little more than the tall stories and tarradiddles of the child who may say equally he has seen the King of England or the King of the Fairies. It grew strong in him through the vice that perpetuates all vices, pride; he grew more and more vain of his promptitude in producing stories of his originality, and subtlety in developing them. That is what the young Aylmers meant by saying that he could always cast a spell over their father; and it was true. It was the sort of spell that the storyteller cast over the tyrant in the Arabian Nights. And to the last he walked the world with the pride of a poet, and with the false yet unfathomable courage of a great liar. He could always produce more Arabian Nights if ever his neck was in danger. And today his neck was in danger.

'But I am sure, as I say, that he enjoyed it as a fantasy as well as a conspiracy. He set about the task of telling the true story the wrong way round: of treating the dead man as living and the live man as dead. He had already got into Aylmer's dressing-gown; he proceeded to get into Aylmer's body and soul. He looked at the corpse as if it were his own corpse lying cold in the snow. Then he spreadeagled it in that strange fashion to suggest the sweeping descent of a bird of prey, and decked it out not only in his own dark and flying garments but in a whole dark fairy tale about the black bird that could only fall by the silver bullet. I do not know whether it was the silver glittering on the sideboard or the snow shining beyond the door that suggested to his intensely artistic temperament the theme of white magic and the white metal used against magicians. But whatever its origin, he made it his own like a poet; and did it very promptly, like a practical man. He completed the exchange and reversal of parts by flinging the corpse out on to the snow as the corpse of Strake. He did his best to work up a creepy conception of Strake as something hovering in the air everywhere, a harpy with wings of speed and claws of death; to explain the absence of footprints and other things. For one piece of artistic impudence I hugely admire him. He actually turned one of the contradictions in his case into an argument for it; and said that the man's cloak being too long for him proved that he never walked on the ground like an ordinary mortal. But he looked at me very hard while he said that; and something told me that he was at that moment trying a very big bluff.'

Dr Boyne looked thoughtful. 'Had you discovered the truth by then?' he asked. 'There is something very queer and close to the nerves, I think, about notions affecting identity. I don't know whether it would be more weird to get a guess like that swiftly or slowly. I wonder when you suspected and when you were sure.'

'I think I really suspected when I telephoned to you,' replied his friend. 'And it was nothing more than the red light from the closed door brightening and darkening on the carpet. It looked like a splash of blood that grew vivid as it cried for vengeance. Why should it change like that? I knew the sun had not come out; it could only be because the second door behind it had been opened and shut on the garden. But if he had gone out and seen his enemy then, he would have raised the alarm then; and it was some time afterwards that the fracas occurred. I began to feel he had gone out to do something . . . to prepare something . . . but as to when I was certain, that is a different matter. I knew that right at the end he was trying to hypnotise me, to master me by the black art of eyes like talismans and a voice like an incantation. That's what he used to do with old Aylmer, no doubt. But it wasn't only the way he said it, it was what he said. It was the religion and philosophy of it.'

'I'm afraid I'm a practical man,' said the doctor with gruff humour, 'and I don't bother much about religion and philosophy.'

'You'll never be a practical man till you do,' said Father Brown. 'Look here, doctor; you know me pretty well; I think you know I'm not a bigot. You know I know there are all sorts in all religions; good men in bad ones and bad men in good ones. But there's just one little fact I've learned simply as a practical man, an entirely practical point, that I've picked up by experience, like the tricks of an animal or the trademark of a good wine. I've scarcely ever met a criminal who philosophised at all, who didn't philosophise along those lines of orientalism and recurrence and reincarnation, and the wheel of destiny and the serpent biting its own tail. I have found merely in practice that there is a curse on the servants of that serpent; on their belly shall they go and the dust shall they eat; and there was never a blackguard or a profligate born who could not talk that sort of spirituality. It may not be like that in its real religious origins; but here in our working world it is the religion of rascals; and I knew it was a rascal who was speaking.'

'Why,' said Boyne, 'I should have thought that a rascal could pretty well profess any religion he chose.'

'Yes,' assented the other; 'he could profess any religion; that is he could pretend to any religion, if it was all a pretence. If it was mere mechanical hypocrisy and nothing else, no doubt it could be done by a mere mechanical hypocrite. Any sort of mask can be put on any sort of face. Anybody can learn certain phrases or state verbally that he holds certain views. I can go out into the street and state that I am a Wesleyan Methodist or a Sandemanian, though I fear in no very convincing accent. But we are talking about an artist; and for the enjoyment of the artist the mask must be to some extent moulded on the face. What he makes outside him must correspond to something inside him; he can only make his effects out of some of the materials of his soul. I suppose he could have said he was a Wesleyan Methodist; but he could never be an eloquent Methodist as he can be an eloquent mystic and fatalist. I am talking of the sort of ideal such a man thinks of if he really tries to be idealistic. It was his whole game with me to be as idealistic as possible; and whenever that is attempted by that sort of man, you will generally find it is that sort of ideal. That sort of man may be dripping with gore; but he will always be able to tell you quite sincerely that Buddhism is better than Christianity. Nay, he will tell you quite sincerely that Buddhism is more Christian than Christianity. That alone is enough to throw a hideous and ghastly ray of light on his notion of Christianity.'

'Upon my soul,' said the doctor, laughing, 'I can't make out whether you're denouncing or defending him.'

'It isn't defending a man to say he is a genius,' said Father Brown. 'Far from it. And it is simply a psychological fact that an artist will betray himself by some sort of sincerity. Leonardo da Vinci cannot draw as if he couldn't draw. Even if he tried, it will always be a strong parody of a weak thing. This man would have made something much too fearful and wonderful out of the Wesleyan Methodist.'

When the priest went forth again and set his face homeward, the cold had grown more intense and yet was somehow intoxicating. The trees stood up like silver candelabra of some incredible cold candlemas of purification. It was a piercing cold, like that silver sword of pure pain that once pierced the very heart of purity. But it was not a killing cold, save in the sense of seeming to kill all the mortal obstructions to our immortal and immeasurable vitality. The pale green sky of twilight, with one star like the star of Bethlehem, seemed by some strange contradiction to be a cavern of clarity. It was as if there could be a green furnace of cold which wakened all things to life like warmth, and that the deeper they went into those cold crystalline colours the more were they light like winged creatures and clear like coloured glass! It tingled with truth and it divided truth from error with a blade like ice; but all that was left had never felt so much alive. It was as if all joy were a jewel in the heart of an iceberg. The priest hardly understood his own mood as he advanced deeper and deeper into the green gloaming, drinking deeper and deeper draughts of that virginal vivacity of the air. Some forgotten muddle and morbidity seemed to be left behind, or wiped out as the snow had painted out the footprints of the man of blood. As he shuffled homewards through the snow, he muttered to himself: 'And yet he is right enough about there being a white magic, if he only knows where to look for it.'

The Doom of the Darnaways

Two landscape-painters stood looking at one landscape, which was also a seascape, and both were curiously impressed by it, though their impressions were not exactly the same. To one of them, who was a rising artist from London, it was new as well as strange. To the other, who was a local artist but with something more than a local celebrity, it was better known; but perhaps all the more strange for what he knew of it.

In terms of tone and form, as these men saw it, it was a stretch of sands against a stretch of sunset, the whole scene lying in strips of sombre colour, dead green and bronze and brown and a drab that was not merely dull but in that gloaming in some way more mysterious than gold. All that broke these level lines was a long building which ran out from the fields into the sands of the sea, so that its fringe of dreary weeds and rushes seemed almost to meet the seaweed. But its most singular feature was that the upper part of it had the ragged outlines of a ruin, pierced by so many wide windows and large rents as to be a mere dark skeleton against the dying light; while the lower bulk of the building had hardly any windows at all, most of them being blind and bricked up and their outlines only faintly traceable in the twilight. But one window at least was still a window; and it seemed strangest of all that it showed a light.

'Who on earth can live in that old shell?' exclaimed the Londoner, who was a big, bohemian-looking man, young but with a shaggy red beard that made him look older; Chelsea knew him familiarly as Harry Payne.

'Ghosts, you might suppose,' replied his friend Martin Wood. 'Well, the people who live there really are rather like ghosts.'

It was perhaps rather a paradox that the London artist seemed almost bucolic in his boisterous freshness and wonder, while the local artist seemed a more shrewd and experienced person, regarding him with mature and amiable amusement; indeed, the latter was altogether a quieter and more conventional figure, wearing darker clothes and with his square and stolid face clean shaven.

'It is only a sign of the times, of course,' he went on, 'or of the passing of old times and old families with them. The last of the great Darnaways live in that house, and not many of the new poor are as poor as they are. They can't even afford to make their own top-storey habitable; but have to live in the lower rooms of a ruin, like bats and owls. Yet they have family portraits that go back to the Wars of the Roses and the first portrait-painting in England, and very fine some of them are; I happen to know, because they asked for my professional advice in overhauling them. There's one of them especially, and one of the earliest, but it's so good that it gives you the creeps.'

'The whole place gives you the creeps, I should think by the look of it,' replied Payne.

'Well,' said his friend, 'to tell you the truth, it does.'

The silence that followed was stirred by a faint rustle among the rushes by the moat; and it gave them, rationally enough, a slight nervous start when a dark figure brushed along the bank, moving rapidly and almost like a startled bird. But it was only a man walking briskly with a black bag in his hand: a man with a long sallow face and sharp eyes that glanced at the London stranger in a slightly darkling and suspicious manner.

'It's only Dr Barnet,' said Wood with a sort of relief. 'Good-evening, Doctor. Are you going up to the house? I hope nobody's ill.'

'Everybody's always ill in a place like that,' growled the doctor; 'only sometimes they're too ill to know it. The very air of the place is a blight and a pestilence. I don't envy the young man from Australia.'

'And who,' asked Payne abruptly and rather absently, 'may the young man from Australia be?'

'Ah!' snorted the doctor; 'hasn't your friend told you about him? As a matter of fact I believe he is arriving today. Quite a romance in the old style of melodrama: the heir back from the colonies to his ruined castle, all complete even down to an old family compact for his marrying the lady watching in the ivied tower. Queer old stuff, isn't it? but it really happens sometimes. He's even got a little money, which is the only bright spot there ever was in this business.'

'What does Miss Darnaway herself, in her ivied tower, think of the business?' asked Martin Wood dryly.

'What she thinks of everything else by this time,' replied the doctor. 'They don't think in this weedy old den of superstitions, they only dream and drift. I think she accepts the family contract and the colonial husband as part of the Doom of the Darnaways, don't you know. I really think that if he turned out to be a hump-backed Negro with one eye and a homicidal mania, she would only think it added a finishing touch and fitted in with the twilight scenery.'

'You're not giving my friend from London a very lively picture of my friends in the country,' said Wood, laughing. 'I had intended taking him there to call; no artist ought to miss those Darnaway portraits if he gets the chance. But perhaps I'd better postpone it if they're in the middle of the Australian invasion.'

'Oh, do go in and see them, for the Lord's sake,' said Dr Barnet warmly. 'Anything that will brighten their blighted lives will make my task easier. It will need a good many colonial cousins to cheer things up, I should think; and the more the merrier. Come, I'll take you in myself.'

As they drew nearer to the house it was seen to be isolated like an island in a moat of brackish water which they crossed by a bridge. On the other side spread a fairly wide stony floor or embankment with great cracks across it, in which little tufts of weed and thorn sprouted here and there. This rock platform looked large and bare in the grey twilight, and Payne could hardly have believed that such a corner of space could have contained so much of the soul of a wilderness. This platform only jutted out on one side, like a giant doorstep and beyond it was the door; a very low-browed Tudor archway standing open, but dark like a cave.

When the brisk doctor led them inside without ceremony, Payne had, as it were, another shock of depression. He could have expected to find himself mounting to a very ruinous tower, by very narrow winding staircases; but in this case the first steps into the house were actually steps downwards. They went down several short and broken stairways into large twilit rooms which, but for their lines of dark pictures and dusty bookshelves, might have been the traditional dungeons beneath the castle moat. Here and there a candle in an old candlestick lit up some dusty accidental detail of a dead elegance; but the visitor was not so much impressed or depressed by this artificial light as by the one pale gleam of natural light. As he passed down the long room he saw the only window in that wall – a curious low oval window of a late seventeenth-century fashion. But the strange thing about it was that it did not look out directly on any space of sky but only on a reflection of sky; a pale strip of daylight merely mirrored in the moat, under the hanging shadow of the bank. Payne had a memory of the Lady of Shallot who never saw the world outside except in a mirror. The lady of this Shallot not only in some sense saw the world in a mirror, but even saw the world upside-down.

'It's as if the house of Darnaway were falling literally as well as metaphorically,' said Wood in a low voice; 'as if it were sinking slowly into a swamp or a quicksand, until the sea goes over it like a green roof.'

Even the sturdy Dr Barnet started a little at the silent approach of the figure that came to receive them. Indeed, the room was so silent that they were all startled to realise that it was not empty. There were three people in it when they entered: three dim figures motionless in the dim room; all three dressed in black and looking like dark shadows. As the foremost figure drew nearer the grey light from the window, he showed a face that looked almost as grey as its frame of hair. This was old Vine, the steward, long left *in loco parentis* since the death of that eccentric parent, the last Lord Darnaway. He would have been a handsome old man if he had had no teeth. As it was, he had one which showed every now and then and gave him a rather sinister appearance. He received the doctor and his friends with a fine courtesy and escorted them to where the other two figures in black were seated. One of them seemed to Payne to give another appropriate touch of gloomy antiquity to the castle by the mere fact of being a Roman Catholic priest, who might have come out of a priest's hole in the dark old days. Payne could imagine him muttering prayers or telling beads, or tolling bells or doing a number of indistinct and melancholy things in that melancholy place. Just then he might be supposed to have been giving religious consolation to the lady; but it could hardly be supposed that the consolation was very consoling, or at any rate that it was very cheering. For the rest, the priest was personally insignificant enough, with plain and rather expressionless features; but the lady was a very different matter. Her face was very far from being plain or insignificant; it stood out from the darkness of her dress and hair and background with a pallor that was almost awful, but a beauty that was almost awfully alive. Payne looked at it as long as he dared; and he was to look at it a good deal longer before he died.

Wood merely exchanged with his friends such pleasant and polite phrases as would lead up to his purpose of revisiting the portraits. He apologised for calling on the day which he heard was to be one of family welcome; but he was soon convinced that the family was rather mildly relieved to have visitors to distract them or break the shock. He did not hesitate, therefore, to lead Payne through the central reception room into the library beyond, where hung the portrait, for there was one which he was especially bent on showing, not only as a picture but almost as a puzzle. The little priest trudged along with them; he seemed to know something about old pictures as well as about old prayers.

'I'm rather proud of having spotted this,' said Wood. 'I believe it's a Holbein. If it isn't, there was somebody living in Holbein's time who was as great as Holbein.'

It was a portrait in the hard but sincere and living fashion of the period, representing a man clad in black trimmed with gold and fur, with a heavy, full, rather pale face but watchful eyes.

'What a pity art couldn't have stopped for ever at just that transition stage,' cried Wood, 'and never transitioned any more. Don't you see it's just realistic enough to be real? Don't you see the face speaks all the more because it stands out from a rather stiffer framework of less essential things? And the eyes are even more real than the face. On my soul, I think the eyes are too real for the face! It's just as if those sly, quick eyeballs were protruding out of a great pale mask.'

'The stiffness extends to the figure a little, I think,' said Payne. 'They hadn't quite mastered anatomy when medievalism ended, at least in the north. That left leg looks to me a good deal out of drawing.'

'I'm not so sure,' replied Wood quietly. 'Those fellows who painted just when realism began to be done, and before it began to be overdone, were often more realistic than we think. They put real details of portraiture into things that are thought merely conventional. You might say this fellow's eyebrows or eye-sockets are a little lopsided; but I bet if you knew him you'd find that one of his eyebrows did really stick up more than the other. And I shouldn't wonder if he was lame or something, and that black leg was meant to be crooked.'

'What an old devil he looks!' burst out Payne suddenly. 'I trust his reverence will excuse my language.'

'I believe in the devil, thank you,' said the priest with an inscrutable face. 'Curiously enough there was a legend that the devil was lame.'

'I say,' protested Payne, 'you can't really mean that he was the devil; but who the devil was he?'

'He was the Lord Darnaway under Henry VII and Henry VIII,' replied his companion. 'But there are curious legends about him, too; one of them is referred to in that inscription round the frame, and further developed in some notes left by somebody in a book I found here. They are both rather curious reading.'

Payne leaned forward, craning his head so as to follow the archaic inscription round the frame. Leaving out the antiquated lettering and spelling, it seemed to be a sort of rhyme running somewhat thus: In the seventh heir I shall return: In the seventh hour I shall depart: None in that hour shall hold my hand: And woe to her that holds my heart.

'It sounds creepy somehow,' said Payne, 'but that may be partly because I don't understand a word of it.'

'It's pretty creepy even when you do,' said Wood in a low voice. 'The record made at a later date, in the old book I found, is all about how this beauty deliberately killed himself in such a way that his wife was executed for his murder. Another note commemorates a later tragedy, seven successions later – under the Georges – in which another Darnaway committed suicide, having first thoughtfully left poison in his wife's wine. It's said that both suicides took place at seven in the evening. I suppose the inference is that he does really return with every seventh inheritor and makes things unpleasant, as the rhyme suggests, for any lady unwise enough to marry him.'

'On that argument,' replied Payne, 'it would be a trifle uncomfortable for the next seventh gentleman.'

Wood's voice was lower still as he said: 'The new heir will be the seventh.'

Harry Payne suddenly heaved up his great chest and shoulders like a man flinging off a burden.

'What crazy stuff are we all talking?' he cried. 'We're all educated men in an enlightened age, I suppose. Before I came into this damned dank atmosphere I'd never have believed I should be talking of such things, except to laugh at them.'

'You are right,' said Wood. 'If you lived long enough in this underground palace you'd begin to feel differently about things. I've begun to feel very curiously about that picture, having had so much to do with handling and hanging it. It sometimes seems to me that the painted face is more alive than the dead faces of the people living here; that it is a sort of talisman or magnet: that it commands the elements and draws out the destinies of men and things. I suppose you would call it very fanciful.'

'What is that noise?' cried Payne suddenly.

They all listened, and there seemed to be no noise except the dull boom of the distant sea; then they began to have the sense of something mingling with it; something like a voice calling through the sound of the surf, dulled by it at first, but coming nearer and nearer. The next moment they were certain: someone was shouting outside in the dusk.

Payne turned to the low window behind him and bent to look out. It was the window from which nothing could be seen except the moat with its reflection of bank and sky. But that inverted vision was not the same that he had seen before. From the hanging shadow of the bank in the water depended two dark shadows reflected from the feet and legs of a figure standing above upon the bank. Through that limited aperture they could see nothing but the two legs black against the reflection of a pale and livid sunset. But somehow that very fact of the head being invisible, as if in the clouds, gave something dreadful to the sound that followed; the voice of a man crying aloud what they could not properly hear or understand. Payne especially was peering out of the little window with an altered face, and he spoke with an altered voice: 'How queerly he's standing!'

'No, no,' said Wood, in a sort of soothing whisper. 'Things often look like that in reflection. It's the wavering of the water that makes you think that.'

'Think what?' asked the priest shortly.

'That his left leg is crooked,' said Wood.

Payne had thought of the oval window as a sort of mystical mirror; and it seemed to him that there were in it other inscrutable images of doom. There was something else beside the figure that he did not understand; three thinner legs showing in dark lines against the light, as if some monstrous three-legged spider or bird were standing beside the stranger. Then he had the less crazy thought of a tripod like that of the heathen oracles; and the next moment the thing had vanished and the legs of the human figure passed out of the picture.

He turned to meet the pale face of old Vine, the steward, with his mouth open, eager to speak, and his single tooth showing. 'He has come,' he said. 'The boat arrived from Australia this morning.'

Even as they went back out of the library into the central salon they heard the footsteps of the newcomer clattering down the entrance steps, with various items of light luggage trailed behind him. When Payne saw one of them, he laughed with a reaction of relief. His tripod was nothing but the telescopic legs of a portable camera, easily packed and unpacked; and the man who was carrying it seemed so far to take on equally solid and normal qualities. He was dressed in dark clothes, but of a careless and holiday sort; his shirt was of grey flannel, and his boots echoed uncompromisingly enough in those still chambers. As he strode forward to greet his new circle his stride had scarcely more than the suggestion of a limp. But Payne and his companions were looking at his face, and could scarcely take their eyes from it.

He evidently felt there was something curious and uncomfortable about his reception; but they could have sworn that he did not himself know the cause of it. The lady, supposed to be in some sense already betrothed to him, was certainly beautiful enough to attract him; but she evidently also frightened him. The old steward brought him a sort of feudal homage, yet treated him as if he were the family ghost. The priest still looked at him with a face which was quite indecipherable, and therefore perhaps all the more unnerving. A new sort of irony, more like the Greek irony, began to pass over Payne's mind. He had dreamed of the stranger as a devil, but it seemed almost worse that he was an unconscious destiny. He seemed to march towards crime with the monstrous innocence of Oedipus. He had approached the family mansion in so blindly buoyant a spirit as to have set up his camera to photograph his first sight of it; and even the camera had taken on the semblance of the tripod of a tragic pythoness.

Payne was surprised, when taking his leave a little while after, at something which showed that the Australian was already less unconscious of his surroundings. He said in a low voice: 'Don't go . . . or come again soon. You look like a human being. This place fairly gives me the jumps.'

When Payne emerged out of those almost subterranean halls and came into the night air and the smell of the sea, he felt as if he had come out of that underworld of dreams in which events jumble on top of each other in a way at once unrestful and unreal. The arrival of the strange relative had been somehow unsatisfying and, as it were, unconvincing. The doubling of the same face in the old portrait and the new arrival troubled him like a two-headed monster. And yet it was not altogether a nightmare; nor was it that face, perhaps, that he saw most vividly.

'Did you say?' he asked of the doctor, as they strode together across the striped dark sands by the darkening sea; 'did you say that young man was betrothed to Miss Darnaway by a family compact or something? Sounds rather like a novel.'

'But an historical novel,' answered Dr Barnet. 'The Darnaways all went to sleep a few centuries ago, when things were really done that we only read of in romances. Yes; I believe there's some family tradition by which second or third cousins always marry when they stand in a certain relation of age, in order to unite the property. A damned silly tradition, I should say; and if they often married in and in, in that fashion, it may account on principles of heredity for their having gone so rotten.'

'I should hardly say,' answered Payne a little stiffly, 'that they had all gone rotten.'

'Well,' replied the doctor, 'the young man doesn't *look* rotten, of course, though he's certainly lame.'

'The young man!' cried Payne, who was suddenly and unreasonably angry. 'Well, if you think the young lady looks rotten, I think it's you who have rotten taste.'

The doctor's face grew dark and bitter. 'I fancy I know more about it than you do,' he snapped.

They completed the walk in silence, each feeling that he had been irrationally rude and had suffered equally irrational rudeness; and Payne was left to brood alone on the matter, for his friend Wood had remained behind to attend to some of his business in connection with the pictures.

Payne took very full advantage of the invitation extended by the colonial cousin, who wanted somebody to cheer him up. During the next few weeks he saw a good deal of the dark interior of the Darnaway home; though it might be said that he did not confine himself entirely to cheering up the colonial cousin. The lady's melancholy was of longer standing and perhaps needed more lifting; anyhow, he showed a laborious readiness to lift it. He was not without a conscience, however, and the situation made him doubtful and uncomfortable. Weeks went by and nobody could discover from the demeanour of the new Darnaway whether he considered himself engaged according to the old compact or no. He went mooning about the dark galleries and stood staring vacantly at the dark and sinister picture. The shades of that prison-house were certainly beginning to close on him, and there was little of his Australian assurance left. But Payne could discover nothing upon the point that concerned him most. Once he attempted to confide in his friend Martin Wood, as he was pottering about in his capacity of picture-hanger; but even out of him he got very little satisfaction.

'It seems to me you can't butt in,' said Wood shortly, 'because of the engagement.'

'Of course I shan't butt in if there is an engagement,' retorted his friend; 'but is there? I haven't said a word to her of course; but I've seen enough of her to be pretty certain she doesn't think there is, even if she thinks there may be. He doesn't say there is, or even hint that there ought to be. It seems to me this shilly-shallying is rather unfair on everybody.'

'Especially on you, I suppose,' said Wood a little harshly. 'But if you ask me, I'll tell you what I think – I think he's afraid.'

'Afraid of being refused?' asked Payne.

'No; afraid of being accepted,' answered the other. 'Don't bite my head off – I don't mean afraid of the lady. I mean afraid of the picture.'

'Afraid of the picture!' repeated Payne.

'I mean afraid of the curse,' said Wood. 'Don't you remember the rhyme about the Darnaway doom falling on him and her?'

'Yes, but look here,' cried Payne; 'even the Darnaway doom can't have it both ways. You tell me first that I mustn't have my own way because of the compact, and then that the compact mustn't have its own way because of the curse. But if the curse can destroy the compact, why should she be tied to the compact? If they're frightened of marrying each other, they're free to marry anybody else, and there's an end of it. Why should I suffer for the observance of something they don't propose to observe? It seems to me your position is very unreasonable.'

'Of course it's all a tangle,' said Wood rather crossly, and went on hammering at the frame of a canvas.

Suddenly, one morning, the new heir broke his long and baffling silence. He did it in a curious fashion, a little crude, as was his way, but with an obvious anxiety to do the right thing. He asked frankly for advice, not of this or that individual as Payne had done, but collectively as of a crowd. When he did speak he threw himself on the whole company like a statesman going to the country. He called it 'a showdown'. Fortunately the lady was not included in this large gesture; and Payne shuddered when he thought of her feelings. But the Australian was quite honest; he thought the natural thing was to ask for help and for information, calling a sort of family council at which he put his cards on the table. It might be said that he flung down his cards on the table, for he did it with a rather desperate air, like one who had been harassed for days and nights by the increasing pressure of a problem. In that short time the shadows of that place of low windows and sinking pavements had curiously changed him, and increased a certain resemblance that crept through all their memories.

The five men, including the doctor, were sitting round a table; and Payne was idly reflecting that his own light tweeds and red hair must be the only colours in the room, for the priest and the steward were in black, and Wood and Darnaway habitually wore dark grey suits that looked almost like black. Perhaps this incongruity had been what the young man had meant by calling him a human being. At that moment the young man himself turned abruptly in his chair and began to talk. A moment after the dazed artist knew that he was talking about the most tremendous thing in the world.

'Is there anything in it?' he was saying. 'That is what I've come to asking myself till I'm nearly crazy. I'd never have believed I should come to thinking of such things; but I think of the portrait and the rhyme and the coincidences or whatever you call them, and I go cold. Is there anything in it? Is there any Doom of the Darnaways or only a damned queer accident? Have I got a right to marry, or shall I bring something big and black out of the sky, that I know nothing about, on myself and somebody else?'

His rolling eye had roamed round the table and rested on the plain face of the priest, to whom he now seemed to be speaking. Payne's submerged practicality rose in protest against the problem of superstition being brought before that supremely superstitious tribunal. He was sitting next to Darnaway and struck in before the priest could answer.

'Well, the coincidences are curious, I admit,' he said, rather forcing a note of cheerfulness; 'but surely we – ' and then he stopped as if he had been struck by lightning. For Darnaway had turned his head sharply over his shoulder at the interruption, and with the movement, his left eyebrow jerked up far above its fellow and for an instant the face of the portrait glared at him with a ghastly exaggeration of exactitude. The rest saw it; and all had the air of having been dazzled by an instant of light. The old steward gave a hollow groan.

'It is no good,' he said hoarsely; 'we are dealing with something too terrible.'

'Yes,' assented the priest in a low voice, 'we are dealing with something terrible; with the most terrible thing I know, and the name of it is nonsense.'

'What did you say?' said Darnaway, still looking towards him.

'I said nonsense,' repeated the priest. 'I have not said anything in particular up to now, for it was none of my business; I was only taking temporary duty in the neighbourhood and Miss Darnaway wanted to see me. But since you're asking me personally and point-blank, why, it's easy enough to answer. Of course there's no Doom of the Darnaways to prevent your marrying anybody you have any decent reason for marrying. A man isn't fated to fall into the smallest venial sin, let alone into crimes like suicide and murder. You can't be made to do wicked things against your will because your name is Darnaway, any more than I can because my name is Brown. The Doom of the Browns,' he added with relish – 'the Weird of the Browns would sound even better.'

'And you of all people,' repeated the Australian, staring, 'tell me to think like that about it.'

'I tell you to think about something else,' replied the priest cheerfully. 'What has become of the rising art of photography? How is the camera getting on? I know it's rather dark downstairs, but those hollow arches on the floor above could easily be turned into a first-rate photographic studio. A few workmen could fit it out with a glass roof in no time.'

'Really,' protested Martin Wood, 'I do think you should be the last man in the world to tinker about with those beautiful Gothic arches, which are about the best work your own religion has ever done in the world. I should have thought you'd have had some feeling for that sort of art; but I can't see why you should be so uncommonly keen on photography.'

'I'm uncommonly keen on daylight,' answered Father Brown, 'especially in this dingy business; and photography has the virtue of depending on daylight. And if you don't know that I would grind all the Gothic arches in the world to powder to save the sanity of a single human soul, you don't know so much about my religion as you think you do.'

The young Australian had sprung to his feet like a man rejuvenated. 'By George! that's the talk,' he cried; 'though I never thought to hear it from that quarter. I'll tell you what, reverend sir, I'll do something that will show I haven't lost my courage after all.'

The old steward was still looking at him with quaking watchfulness, as if he felt something fey about the young man's defiance. 'Oh,' he cried, 'what are you going to do now?'

'I am going to photograph the portrait,' replied Darnaway.

Yet it was barely a week afterwards that the storm of the catastrophe seemed to stoop out of the sky, darkening that sun of sanity to which the priest had appealed in vain, and plunging the mansion once more in the darkness of the Darnaway doom. It had been easy enough to fit up the new studio; and seen from inside it looked very like any other such studio, empty except for the fullness of the white light. A man coming from the gloomy rooms below had more than normally the sense of stepping into a more than modern brilliancy, as blank as the future. At the suggestion of Wood, who knew the castle well and had got over his first aesthetic grumblings, a small room remaining intact in the upper ruins was easily turned into a dark room, into which Darnaway went out of the white daylight to grope by the crimson gleams of a red lamp. Wood said, laughing, that the red lamp had reconciled him to the vandalism; as that bloodshot darkness was as romantic as an alchemist's cave.

Darnaway had risen at daybreak on the day that he meant to photograph the mysterious portrait, and had it carried up from the library by the single corkscrew staircase that connected the two floors. There he had set it up in the wide white daylight on a sort of easel and planted his photographic tripod in front of it. He said he was anxious to send a reproduction of it to a great antiquary who had written on the antiquities of the house; but the others knew that this was an excuse covering much deeper things. It was, if not exactly a spiritual duel between Darnaway and the demoniac picture, at least a duel between Darnaway and his own doubts. He wanted to bring the daylight of photography face to face with that dark masterpiece of painting; and to see whether the sunshine of the new art would not drive out the shadows of the old.

Perhaps this was why he preferred to do it by himself, even if some of the details seemed to take longer and involve more than normal delay. Anyhow, he rather discouraged the few who visited his studio during the day of the experiment, and who found him focusing and fussing about in a very isolated and impenetrable fashion. The steward had left a meal for him, as he refused to come down; the old gentleman also returned some hours afterwards and found the meal more or less normally disposed of; but when he brought it he got no more gratitude than a grunt. Payne went up once to see how he was getting on, but finding the photographer disinclined for conversation came down again. Father Brown had wandered that way in an unobtrusive style to take Darnaway a letter from the expert to whom the photograph was to be sent. But he left the letter on a tray, and whatever he thought of that great glasshouse full of daylight and devotion to a hobby, a world he had himself in some sense created, he kept it to himself and came down. He had reason to remember very soon that he was the last to come down the solitary staircase connecting the floors, leaving a lonely man and an empty room behind him. The others were standing in the salon that led into the library, just under the great black ebony clock that looked like a titanic coffin.

'How was Darnaway getting on,' asked Payne, a little later, 'when you last went up?'

The priest passed a hand over his forehead. 'Don't tell me I'm getting psychic,' he said with a sad smile. 'I believe I'm quite dazzled with daylight up in that room and couldn't see things straight. Honestly, I felt for a flash as if there were something uncanny about Darnaway's figure standing before that portrait.'

'Oh, that's the lame leg,' said Barnet promptly. 'We know all about that.'

'Do you know,' said Payne abruptly, but lowering his voice, 'I don't think we do know all about it or anything about it. What's the matter with his leg? What was the matter with his ancestor's leg?'

'Oh, there's something about that in the book I was reading in there, in the family archives,' said Wood; 'I'll fetch it for you.' And he stepped into the library just beyond.

'I think,' said Father Brown quietly, 'Mr Payne must have some particular reason for asking that.'

'I may as well blurt it out once and for all,' said Payne, but in a yet lower voice. 'After all, there is a rational explanation. A man from anywhere might have made up to look like the portrait. What do we know about Darnaway? He is behaving rather oddly – '

The others were staring at him in a rather startled fashion; but the priest seemed to take it very calmly.

'I don't think the old portrait's ever been photographed,' he said. 'That's why he wants to do it. I don't think there's anything odd about that.'

'Quite an ordinary state of things, in fact,' said Wood with a smile; he had just returned with the book in his hand. And even as he spoke there was a stir in the clockwork of the great dark clock behind him and successive strokes thrilled through the room up to the number of seven. With the last stroke there came a crash from the floor above that shook the house like a thunderbolt; and Father Brown was already two steps up the winding staircase before the sound had ceased.

'My God!' cried Payne involuntarily; 'he is alone up there.'

'Yes,' said Father Brown without turning, as he vanished up the stairway. 'We shall find him alone.'

When the rest recovered from their first paralysis and ran helter-skelter up the stone steps and found their way to the new studio, it was true in that sense that they found him alone. They found him lying in a wreck of his tall camera, with its long splintered legs standing out grotesquely at three different angles; and Darnaway had fallen on top of it with one black crooked leg lying at a fourth angle along the floor. For the moment the dark heap looked as if he were entangled with some huge and horrible spider. Little more than a glance and a touch were needed to tell them that he was dead. Only the portrait stood untouched upon the easel, and one could fancy the smiling eyes shone.

An hour afterwards Father Brown, in helping to calm the confusion of the stricken household, came upon the old steward muttering almost as mechanically as the clock had ticked and struck the terrible hour. Almost without hearing them, he knew what the muttered words must be.

'In the seventh heir I shall return. In the seventh hour I shall depart.'

As he was about to say something soothing, the old man seemed suddenly to start awake and stiffen into anger; his mutterings changed to a fierce cry.

'You!' he cried; 'you and your daylight! Even you won't say now there is no Doom for the Darnaways.'

'My opinion about that is unchanged,' said Father Brown mildly. Then after a pause he added: 'I hope you will observe poor Darnaway's last wish, and see the photograph is sent off.'

'The photograph!' cried the doctor sharply. 'What's the good of that? As a matter of fact, it's rather curious; but there isn't any photograph. It seems he never took it after all, after pottering about all day.'

Father Brown swung round sharply. 'Then take it yourselves,' he said. 'Poor Darnaway was perfectly right. It's most important that the photograph should be taken.'

As all the visitors, the doctor, the priest, and the two artists trailed away in a black and dismal procession across the brown and yellow sands, they were at first more or less silent, rather as if they had been stunned. And certainly there had been something like a crack of thunder in a clear sky about the fulfilment of that forgotten superstition at the very time when they had most forgotten it; when the doctor and the priest had both filled their minds with rationalism as the photographer had filled his rooms with daylight. They might be as rationalistic as they liked; but in broad daylight the seventh heir had returned, and in broad daylight at the seventh hour he had perished.

'I'm afraid everybody will always believe in the Darnaway superstition now,' said Martin Wood.

'I know one who won't,' said the doctor sharply. 'Why should I indulge in superstition because somebody else indulges in suicide?'

'You think poor Mr Darnaway committed suicide?' asked the priest.

'I'm sure he committed suicide,' replied the doctor.

'It is possible,' agreed the other.

'He was quite alone up there, and he had a whole drug-store of poisons in the dark room. Besides, it's just the sort of thing that Darnaways do.'

'You don't think there's anything in the fulfilment of the family curse?'

'Yes,' said the doctor; 'I believe in one family curse, and that is the family constitution. I told you it was heredity, and they are all half mad. If you stagnate and breed in and brood in your own swamp like that, you're bound to degenerate whether you like it or not. The laws of heredity can't be dodged; the truths of science can't be denied. The minds of the Darnaways are falling to pieces, as their blighted old sticks and stones are falling to pieces, eaten away by the sea and the salt air. Suicide – of course he committed suicide; I dare say all the rest will commit suicide. Perhaps the best thing they could do.'

As the man of science spoke there sprang suddenly and with startling clearness into Payne's memory the face of the daughter of the Darnaways, a tragic mask pale against an unfathomable blackness, but itself of a blinding and more than mortal beauty. He opened his mouth to speak and found himself speechless.

'I see,' said Father Brown to the doctor; 'so you do believe in the superstition after all?'

'What do you mean – believe in the superstition? I believe in the suicide as a matter of scientific necessity.'

'Well,' replied the priest, 'I don't see a pin to choose between your scientific superstition and the other magical superstition. They both seem to end in turning people into paralytics, who can't move their own legs or arms or save their own lives or souls. The rhyme said it was the Doom of the Darnaways to be killed, and the scientific textbook says it is the Doom of the Darnaways to kill themselves. Both ways they seem to be slaves.'

'But I thought you said you believed in rational views of these things,' said Dr Barnet. 'Don't you believe in heredity?'

'I said I believed in daylight,' replied the priest in a loud and clear voice, 'and I won't choose between two tunnels of subterranean superstition that both end in the dark. And the proof of it is this: that you are all entirely in the dark about what really happened in that house.'

'Do you mean about the suicide?' asked Payne.

'I mean about the murder,' said Father Brown; and his voice, though only slightly lifted to a louder note, seemed somehow to resound over the whole shore. 'It was murder; but murder is of the will, which God made free.'

What the other said at the moment in answer to it Payne never knew. For the word had a rather curious effect on him; stirring him like the blast of a trumpet and yet bringing him to a halt. He stood still in the middle of the sandy waste and let the others go on in front of him; he felt the blood crawling through all his veins and the sensation that is called the hair standing on end; and yet he felt a new and unnatural happiness. A psychological process too quick and too complicated for himself to follow had already reached a conclusion that he could not analyse; but the conclusion was one of relief. After standing still for a moment he turned and went back slowly across the sands to the house of the Darnaways.

He crossed the moat with a stride that shook the bridge, descended the stairs and traversed the long rooms with a resounding tread, till he came to the place where Adelaide Darnaway sat haloed with the low light of the oval window, almost like some forgotten saint left behind in the land of death. She looked up, and an expression of wonder made her face yet more wonderful.

'What is it?' she said. 'Why have you come back?'

'I have come for the Sleeping Beauty,' he said in a tone that had the resonance of a laugh. 'This old house went to sleep long ago, as the doctor said; but it is silly for you to pretend to be old. Come up into the daylight and hear the truth. I have brought you a word; it is a terrible word, but it breaks the spell of your captivity.'

She did not understand a word he said, but something made her rise and let him lead her down the long hall and up the stairs and out under the evening sky. The ruins of a dead garden stretched towards the sea, and an old fountain with the figure of a triton, green with rust, remained poised there, pouring nothing out of a dried horn into an empty basin. He had often seen that desolate outline against the evening sky as he passed, and it had seemed to him a type of fallen fortunes in more ways than one. Before long, doubtless, those hollow fonts would be filled, but it would be with the pale green bitter waters of the sea and the flowers would be drowned and strangled in seaweed. So, he had told himself, the daughter of the Darnaways might indeed be wedded; but she would be wedded to death and a doom as deaf and ruthless as the sea. But now he laid a hand on the bronze triton that was like the hand of a giant, and shook it as if he meant to hurl it over like an idol or an evil god of the garden.

'What do you mean?' she asked steadily. 'What is this word that will set us free?'

'The word is murder,' he said, 'and the freedom it brings is as fresh as the flowers of spring. No; I do not mean I have murdered anybody. But the fact that anybody can be murdered is itself good news, after the evil dreams you have been living in. Don't you understand? In that dream of yours everything that happened to you came from inside you; the Doom of the Darnaways was stored up in the Darnaways; it unfolded itself like a horrible flower. There was no escape even by happy accident; it was all inevitable; whether it was Vine and his old-wives' tales, or Barnet and his newfangled heredity. But this man who died was not the victim of a magic curse or an inherited madness. He was murdered; and for us that murder is simply an accident; yes, *requiescat in pace*: but a happy accident. It is a ray of daylight, because it comes from outside.'

She suddenly smiled. 'Yes, I believe I understand. I suppose you are talking like a lunatic, but I understand. But who murdered him?'

'I do not know,' he answered calmly, 'but Father Brown knows. And as Father Brown says, murder is at least done by the will, free as that wind from the sea.'

'Father Brown is a wonderful person,' she said after a pause; 'he was the only person who ever brightened my existence in any way at all until – '

'Until what?' asked Payne, and made a movement almost impetuous, leaning towards her and thrusting away the bronze monster so that it seemed to rock on its pedestal.

'Well, until you did,' she said and smiled again.

So was the sleeping palace awakened, and it is no part of this story to describe the stages of its awakening, though much of it had come to pass before the dark of that evening had fallen upon the shore. As Harry Payne strode homewards once more, across those dark sands that he had crossed in so many moods, he was at the highest turn of happiness that is given in this mortal life, and the whole red sea within him was at the top of its tide. He would have had no difficulty in picturing all that place again in flower, and the bronze triton bright as a golden god and the fountain flowing with water or with wine. But all this brightness and blossoming had been unfolded for him by the one word 'murder', and it was still a word that he did not understand. He had taken it on trust, and he was not unwise; for he was one of those who have a sense of the sound of truth.

It was more than a month later that Payne returned to his London house to keep an appointment with Father Brown, taking the required photograph with him. His personal romance had prospered as well as was fitting under the shadow of such a tragedy, and the shadow itself therefore lay rather more lightly on him; but it was hard to view it as anything but the shadow of a family fatality. In many ways he had been much occupied; and it was not until the Darnaway household had resumed its somewhat stern routine, and the portrait had long been restored to its place in the library, that he had managed to photograph it with a magnesium flare. Before sending it to the antiquary, as originally arranged, he brought it to the priest who had so pressingly demanded it.

'I can't understand your attitude about all this, Father Brown,' he said. 'You act as if you had already solved the problem in some way of your own.'

The priest shook his head mournfully. 'Not a bit of it,' he answered. 'I must be very stupid, but I'm quite stuck; stuck about the most practical point of all. It's a queer business; so simple up to a point and then – Let me have a look at that photograph, will you?'

He held it close to his screwed, short-sighted eyes for a moment, and then said: 'Have you got a magnifying glass?'

Payne produced one, and the priest looked through it intently for some time and then said: 'Look at the title of that book at the edge of the bookshelf beside the frame; it's "The History of Pope Joan". Now, I wonder . . . yes, by George; and the one above is something or other of Iceland. Lord! what a queer way to find it out! What a dolt and donkey I was not to notice it when I was there!'

'But what have you found out?' asked Payne impatiently.

'The last link,' said Father Brown, 'and I'm not stuck any longer. Yes; I think I know how that unhappy story went from first to last now.'

'But why?' insisted the other.

'Why, because,' said the priest with a smile, 'the Darnaway library contained books about Pope Joan and Iceland, not to mention another I see with the title beginning "The Religion of Frederick", which is not so very hard to fill up.' Then, seeing the other's annoyance, his smile faded and he said more earnestly: 'As a matter of fact, this last point, though it is the last link, is not the main business. There were much more curious things in the case than that. One of them is rather a curiosity of evidence. Let me begin by saying something that may surprise you. Darnaway did not die at seven o'clock that evening. He had been already dead for a whole day.'

'Surprise is rather a mild word,' said Payne grimly, 'since you and I both saw him walking about afterwards.'

'No, we did not,' replied Father Brown quietly. 'I think we both saw him, or thought we saw him, fussing about with the focusing of his camera. Wasn't his head under that black cloak when you passed through the room? It was when I did. And that's why I felt there was something queer about the room and the figure. It wasn't that the leg was crooked, but rather that it wasn't crooked. It was dressed in the same sort of dark clothes; but if you see what you believe to be one man standing in the way that another man stands, you will think he's in a strange and strained attitude.'

'Do you really mean,' cried Payne with something like a shudder, 'that it was some unknown man?'

'It was the murderer,' said Father Brown. 'He had already killed Darnaway at daybreak and hid the corpse and himself in the dark room – an excellent hiding-place, because nobody normally goes into it or can see much if he does. But he let it fall out on the floor at seven o'clock, of course, that the whole thing might be explained by the curse.'

'But I don't understand,' observed Payne. 'Why didn't he kill him at seven o'clock then, instead of loading himself with a corpse for fourteen hours?'

'Let me ask you another question,' said the priest. 'Why was there no photograph taken? Because the murderer made sure of killing him when he first got up, and before he could take it. It was essential to the murderer to prevent that photograph reaching the expert on the Darnaway antiquities.'

There was a sudden silence for a moment, and then the priest went on in a lower tone: 'Don't you see how simple it is? Why, you yourself saw one side of the possibility; but it's simpler even than you thought. You said a man might be faked to resemble an old picture. Surely it's simpler that a picture should be faked to resemble a man. In plain words, it's true in a rather special way that there was no Doom of the Darnaways. There was no old picture; there was no old rhyme; there was no legend of a man who caused his wife's death. But there was a very wicked and a very clever man who was willing to cause another man's death in order to rob him of his promised wife.'

The priest suddenly gave Payne a sad smile, as if in reassurance. 'For the moment I believe you thought I meant you,' he said, 'but you were not the only person who haunted that house for sentimental reasons. You know the man, or rather you think you do. But there were depths in the man called Martin Wood, artist and antiquary, which none of his mere artistic acquaintances were likely to guess. Remember that he was called in to criticise and catalogue the pictures; in an aristocratic dustbin of that sort that practically means simply to tell the Darnaways what art treasures they had got. They would not be surprised at things turning up they had never noticed before. It had to be done well, and it was; perhaps he was right when he said that if it wasn't Holbein it was somebody of the same genius.'

'I feel rather stunned,' said Payne; 'and there are twenty things I don't see yet. How did he know what Darnaway looked like? How did he actually kill him? The doctors seem rather puzzled at present.'

'I saw a photograph the lady had which the Australian sent on before him,' said the priest, 'and there are several ways in which he could have learned things when the new heir was once recognised. We may not know these details; but they are not difficulties. You remember he used to help in the dark room; it seems to me an ideal place, say, to prick a man with a poisoned pin, with the poisons all handy. No; I say these were not difficulties. The difficulty that stumped me was how Wood could be in two places at once. How could he take the corpse from the dark room and prop it against the camera so that it would fall in a few seconds, without coming downstairs, when he was in the library looking out a book? And I was such a fool that I never looked at the books in the library; and it was only in this photograph, by very undeserved good luck, that I saw the simple fact of a book about Pope Joan.'

'You've kept your best riddle for the end,' said Payne grimly. 'What on earth can Pope Joan have to do with it?'

'Don't forget the book about the Something of Iceland,' advised the priest, 'or the religion of somebody called Frederick. It only remains to ask what sort of man was the late Lord Darnaway.'

'Oh, does it?' observed Payne heavily.

'He was a cultivated, humorous sort of eccentric, I believe,' went on Father Brown. 'Being cultivated, he knew there was no such person as Pope Joan. Being humorous, he was very likely to have thought of the title of "The Snakes of Iceland" or something else that didn't exist. I venture to reconstruct the third title as "The Religion of Frederick the Great" – which also doesn't exist. Now, doesn't it strike you that those would be just the titles to put on the backs of books that didn't exist; or in other words on a bookcase that wasn't a bookcase?'

'Ah!' cried Payne; 'I see what you mean now. There was some hidden staircase – '

'Up to the room Wood himself selected as a dark room,' said the priest nodding. 'I'm sorry. It couldn't be helped. It's dreadfully banal and stupid, as stupid as I have been on this pretty banal case. But we were mixed up in a real musty old romance of decayed gentility and a fallen family mansion; and it was too much to hope that we could escape having a secret passage. It was a priest's hole; and I deserve to be put in it.'

The Ghost of Gideon Wise

Father Brown always regarded the case as the queerest example of the theory of an alibi: the theory by which it is maintained, in defiance of the mythological Irish bird, that it is impossible for anybody to be in two places at once. To begin with, James Byrne, being an Irish journalist, was perhaps the nearest approximation to the Irish bird. He came as near as anybody could to being in two places at once: for he was in two places at the opposite extremes of the social and political world within the space of twenty minutes. The first was in the Babylonian halls of the big hotel, which was the meeting place of the three commercial magnates concerned with arranging for a coal lock-out and denouncing it as a coal-strike, the second was in a curious tavern, having the façade of a grocery store, where met the more subterranean triumvirate of those who would have been very glad to turn the lock-out into a strike – and the strike into a revolution. The reporter passed to and fro between the three millionaires and the three Bolshevist leaders with the immunity of the modern herald or the new ambassador.

He found the three mining magnates hidden in a jungle of flowering plants and a forest of fluted and florid columns of gilded plaster; gilded birdcages hung high under the painted domes amid the highest leaves of the palms; and in them were birds of motley colours and varied cries. No bird in the wilderness ever sang more unheeded, and no flower ever wasted its sweetness on the desert air more completely than the blossoms of those tall plants wasted theirs upon the brisk and breathless business men, mostly American, who talked and ran to and fro in that place. And there, amid a riot of rococo ornament that nobody ever looked at, and a chatter of expensive foreign birds that nobody ever heard, and a mass of gorgeous upholstery and a labyrinth of luxurious architecture, the three men sat and talked of how success was founded on thought and thrift and a vigilance of economy and self-control.

One of them indeed did not talk so much as the others; but he watched with very bright and motionless eyes, which seemed to be pinched together by his pince-nez, and the permanent smile under his small black moustache was rather like a permanent sneer. This was the famous Jacob P. Stein, and he did not speak till he had something to say. But his companion, old Gallup the Pennsylvanian, a huge fat fellow with reverend grey hair but a face like a pugilist, talked a great deal. He was in a jovial mood and was half rallying, half bullying the third millionaire, Gideon Wise – a hard, dried, angular old bird of the type that his countrymen compare to hickory, with a stiff grey chin-beard and the manners and clothes of any old farmer from the central plains. There was an old argument between Wise and Gallup about combination and competition. For old Wise still retained, with the manners of the old backwoodsman, something of his opinions of the old individualist; he belonged, as we should say in England, to the Manchester School; and Gallup was always trying to persuade him to cut out competition and pool the resources of the world.

'You'll have to come in, old fellow, sooner or later,' Gallup was saying genially as Byrne entered. 'It's the way the world is going, and we can't go back to the one-man business now. We've all got to stand together.'

'If I might say a word,' said Stein, in his tranquil way, 'I would say there is something a little more urgent even than standing together commercially. Anyhow, we must stand together politically; and that's why I've asked Mr Byrne to meet us here today. On the political issue we must combine; for the simple reason that all our most dangerous enemies are already combined.'

'Oh, I quite agree about political combination,' grumbled Gideon Wise.

'See here,' said Stein to the journalist; 'I know you have the run of these queer places, Mr Byrne, and I want you to do something for us unofficially. You know where these men meet; there are only two or three of them that count, John Elias and Jake Halket, who does all the spouting, and perhaps that poet fellow, Horne.'

'Why, Horne used to be a friend of Gideon,' said the jeering Mr Gallup; 'used to be in his Sunday School class or something.'

'He was a Christian, then,' said old Gideon solemnly; 'but when a man takes up with atheists you never know. I still meet him now and then. I was quite ready to back him against war and conscription and all that, of course, but when it comes to all the goddam bolshies in creation – '

'Excuse me,' interposed Stein, 'the matter is rather urgent, so I hope you will excuse me putting it before Mr Byrne at once. Mr Byrne, I may tell you in confidence that I hold information, or rather evidence that would land at least two of those men in prison for long terms, in connection with conspiracies during the late war. I don't want to use that evidence. But I want you to go to them quietly and tell them that I shall use it, and use it tomorrow, unless they alter their attitude.'

'Well,' replied Byrne, 'what you propose would certainly be called compounding a felony and might be called blackmail. Don't you think it is rather dangerous?'

'I think it is rather dangerous for them,' said Stein with a snap; 'and I want you to go and tell them so.'

'Oh, very well,' said Byrne standing up, with a half humorous sigh. 'It's all in the day's work; but if I get into trouble, I warn you I shall try to drag you into it.'

'You will try, boy,' said old Gallup with a hearty laugh.

For so much still lingers of that great dream of Jefferson and the thing that men have called Democracy that in his country, while the rich rule like tyrants, the poor do not talk like slaves; but there is candour between the oppressor and the oppressed.

The meeting-place of the revolutionists was a queer, bare, whitewashed place, on the walls of which were one or two distorted uncouth sketches in black and white, in the style of something that was supposed to be Proletarian Art, of which not one proletarian in a million could have made head or tail. Perhaps the one point in common to the two council chambers was that both violated the American Constitution by the display of strong drink. Cocktails of various colours had stood before the three millionaires. Halket, the most violent of the Bolshevists, thought it only appropriate to drink vodka. He was a long, hulking fellow with a menacing stoop, and his very profile was aggressive like a dog's, the nose and lips thrust out together, the latter carrying a ragged red moustache and the whole curling outwards with perpetual scorn. John Elias was a dark watchful man in spectacles, with a black pointed beard; and he had learnt in many European cafés a taste for absinthe. The journalist's first and last feeling was how very like each other, after all, were John Elias and Jacob P. Stein. They were so like in face and mind and manner, that the millionaire might have disappeared down a trapdoor in the Babylon Hotel and come up again in the stronghold of the Bolshevists.

The third man also had a curious taste in drinks, and his drink was symbolic of him. For what stood in front of the poet Horne was a glass of milk, and its very mildness seemed in that setting to have something sinister about it, as if its opaque and colourless colour were of some leprous paste more poisonous than the dead sick green of absinthe. Yet in truth the mildness was so far genuine enough; for Henry Horne came to the camp of revolution along a very different road and from very different origins from those of Jake, the common tub-thumper, and Elias, the cosmopolitan wire-puller. He had had what is called a careful upbringing, had gone to chapel in his childhood, and carried through life a teetotalism which he could not shake off when he cast away such trifles as Christianity and marriage. He had fair hair and a fine face that might have looked like Shelley, if he had not weakened the chin with a little foreign fringe of beard. Somehow the beard made him look more like a woman; it was as if those few golden hairs were all he could do.

When the journalist entered, the notorious Jake was talking, as he generally was. Horne had uttered some casual and conventional phrase about 'Heaven forbid' something or other, and this was quite enough to set Jake off with a torrent of profanity.

'Heaven forbid! and that's about all it bally well does do,' he said. 'Heaven never does anything but forbid this, that and the other; forbids us to strike, and forbids us to fight, and forbids us to shoot the damned usurers and bloodsuckers where they sit. Why doesn't Heaven forbid them something for a bit? Why don't the damned priests and parsons stand up and tell the truth about those brutes for a change? Why doesn't their precious God – '

Elias allowed a gentle sigh, as of faint fatigue, to escape him.

'Priests,' he said, 'belonged, as Marx has shown, to the feudal stage of economic development and are therefore no longer really any part of the problem. The part once played by the priest is now played by the capitalist expert and – '

'Yes,' interrupted the journalist, with his grim and ironic implacability, 'and it's about time you knew that some of them are jolly expert in playing it.' And without moving his own eyes from the bright but dead eyes of Elias, he told him of the threat of Stein.

'I was prepared for something of that sort,' said the smiling Elias without moving; 'I may say quite prepared.'

'Dirty dogs!' exploded Jake. 'If a poor man said a thing like that he'd go to penal servitude. But I reckon they'll go somewhere worse before they guess. If they don't go to hell, I don't know where the hell they'll go to – '

Horne made a movement of protest, perhaps not so much at what the man was saying as at what he was going to say, and Elias cut the speech short with cold exactitude.

'It is quite unnecessary for us,' he said, looking at Byrne steadily through his spectacles, 'to bandy threats with the other side. It is quite sufficient that their threats are quite ineffective so far as we are concerned. We also have made all our own arrangements, and some of them will not appear until they appear in motion. So far as we are concerned, an immediate rupture and an extreme trial of strength will be quite according to plan.'

As he spoke in a quite quiet and dignified fashion, something in his motionless yellow face and his great goggles started a faint fear creeping up the journalist's spine. Halket's savage face might seem to have a snarl in its very silhouette when seen sideways; but when seen face to face, the smouldering rage in his eyes had also something of anxiety, as if the ethical and economic riddle were after all a little too much for him; and Horne seemed even more hanging on wires of worry and self-criticism. But about this third man with the goggles, who spoke so sensibly and simply, there was something uncanny; it was like a dead man talking at the table.

As Byrne went out with his message of defiance, and passed along the very narrow passage beside the grocery store, he found the end of it blocked by a strange though strangely familiar figure: short and sturdy, and looking rather quaint when seen in dark outline with its round head and wide hat.

'Father Brown!' cried the astonished journalist. 'I think you must have come into the wrong door. You're not likely to be in this little conspiracy.'

'Mine is a rather older conspiracy,' replied Father Brown smiling, 'but it is quite a widespread conspiracy.'

'Well,' replied Byrne,'you can't imagine any of the people here being within a thousand miles of your concern.'

'It is not always easy to tell,' replied the priest equably; 'but as a matter of fact, there is one person here who's within an inch of it.'

He disappeared into the dark entrance and the journalist went on his way very much puzzled. He was still more puzzled by a small incident that happened to him as he turned into the hotel to make his report to his capitalist clients. The bower of blossoms and birdcages in which those crabbed old gentlemen were embosomed was approached by a flight of marble steps, flanked by gilded nymphs and tritons. Down these steps ran an active young man with black hair, a snub nose, and a flower in his buttonhole, who seized him and drew him aside before he could ascend the stair.

'I say,' whispered the young man, 'I'm Potter – old Gid's secretary, you know: now, between ourselves, there is a sort of a thunderbolt being forged, isn't there, now?'

'I came to the conclusion,' replied Byrne cautiously, 'that the Cyclops had something on the anvil. But always remember that the Cyclops is a giant, but he has only one eye. I think Bolshevism is –'

While he was speaking the secretary listened with a face that had a certain almost Mongolian immobility, despite the liveliness of his legs and his attire. But when Byrne said the word 'Bolshevism', the young man's sharp eyes shifted and he said quickly: 'What has that – oh yes, that sort of thunderbolt; so sorry, my mistake. So easy to say anvil when you mean icebox.'

With which the extraordinary young man disappeared down the steps and Byrne continued to mount them, more and more mystification clouding his mind.

He found the group of three augmented to four by the presence of a hatchet-faced person with very thin straw-coloured hair and a monocle, who appeared to be a sort of adviser to old Gallup, possibly his solicitor, though he was not definitely so called. His name was Nares, and the questions which he directed towards Byrne referred chiefly, for some reason or other, to the number of those probably enrolled in the revolutionary organisation. Of this, as Byrne knew little, he said less; and the four men eventually rose from their seats, the last word being with the man who had been most silent.

'Thank you, Mr Byrne,' said Stein, folding up his eyeglasses. 'It only remains to say that everything is ready; on that point I quite agree with Mr Elias. Tomorrow, before noon, the police will have arrested Mr Elias, on evidence I shall by then have put before them, and those three at least will be in jail before night. As you know, I attempted to avoid this course. I think that is all, gentlemen.'

But Mr Jacob P. Stein did not lay his formal information next day, for a reason that has often interrupted the activities of such industrious characters. He did not do it because he happened to be dead; and none of the rest of the programme was carried out, for a reason which Byrne found displayed in gigantic letters when he opened his morning paper: 'Terrific Triple Murder: Three Millionaires Slain in One Night'. Other exclamatory phrases followed in smaller letters, only about four times the size of normal type, which insisted on the special feature of the mystery: the fact that the three men had been killed not only simultaneously but in three widely separated places – Stein in his artistic and luxurious country seat a hundred miles inland, Wise outside the little bungalow on the coast where he lived on sea breezes and the simple life, and old Gallup in a thicket just outside the lodge-gates of his great house at the other end of the county. In all three cases there could be no doubt about the scenes of violence that had preceded death, though the actual body of Gallup was not found till the second day, where it hung, huge and horrible, amid the broken forks and branches of the little wood into which its weight had crashed, like a bison rushing on the spears: while Wise had clearly been flung over the cliff into the sea, not without a struggle, for his scraping and slipping footprints could still be traced upon the very brink. But the first signal of the tragedy had been the sight of his large limp straw hat, floating far out upon the waves and conspicuous from the cliffs above. Stein's body also had at first eluded search, till a faint trail of blood led the investigators to a bath on the ancient Roman model he had been constructing in his garden; for he had been a man of an experimental turn of mind with a taste for antiquities.

Whatever he might think, Byrne was bound to admit that there was no legal evidence against anybody as things stood. A motive for murder was not enough. Even a moral aptitude for murder was not enough. And he could not conceive that pale young pacifist, Henry Horne, butchering another man by brutal violence, though he might imagine the blaspheming Jake and even the sneering Jew as capable of anything. The police, and the man who appeared to be assisting them (who was no other than the rather mysterious man with the monocle, who had been introduced as Mr Nares), realised the position quite as clearly as the journalist. They knew that at the moment the Bolshevist conspirators could not be prosecuted and convicted, and that it would be a highly sensational failure if they were prosecuted and acquitted. Nares started with an artful candour by calling them in some sense to the council, inviting them to a private conclave and asking them to give their opinions freely in the interests of humanity. He had started his investigations at the nearest scene of tragedy, the bungalow by the sea; and Byrne was permitted to be present at a curious scene, which was at once a peaceful parley of diplomatists and a veiled inquisition or putting of suspects to the question. Rather to Byrne's surprise the incongruous company, seated round the table in the seaside bungalow, included the dumpy figure and owlish head of Father Brown, though his connection with the affair did not appear until some time afterwards. The presence of young Potter, the dead man's secretary, was more natural; yet somehow his demeanour was not quite so natural. He alone was quite familiar with their meeting-place, and was even in some grim sense their host; yet he offered little assistance or information. His round snub-nosed face wore an expression more like sulks than sorrow.

Jake Halket as usual talked most; and a man of his type could not be expected to keep up the polite fiction that he and his friends were not accused. Young Horne, in his more refined way, tried to restrain him when he began to abuse the men who had been murdered; but Jake was always quite as ready to roar down his friends as his foes. In a spout of blasphemies he relieved his soul of a very unofficial obituary notice of the late Gideon Wise. Elias sat quite still and apparently indifferent behind those spectacles that masked his eyes.

'It would be useless, I suppose,' said Nares coldly, 'to tell you that your remarks are indecent. It may affect you more if I tell you they are imprudent. You practically admit that you hated the dead man.'

'Going to put me in quod for that, are you?' jeered the demagogue. 'All right. Only you'll have to build a prison for a million men if you're going to jail all the poor people who had reason to hate Gid Wise. And you know it's God truth as well as I do.'

Nares was silent; and nobody spoke until Elias interposed with his clear though faintly lisping drawl.

'This appears to me to be a highly unprofitable discussion on both sides,' he said. 'You have summoned us here either to ask us for information or to subject us to cross-examination. If you trust us, we tell you we have no information. If you distrust us, you must tell us of what we are accused, or have the politeness to keep the fact to yourselves. Nobody has been able to suggest the faintest trace of evidence connecting any one of us with these tragedies any more than with the murder of Julius Caesar. You dare not arrest us, and you will not believe us. What is the good of our remaining here?'

And he rose, calmly buttoning his coat, his friends following his example. As they went towards the door, young Horne turned back and faced the investigators for a moment with his pale fanatical face.

'I wish to say,' he said, 'that I went to a filthy jail during the whole war because I would not consent to kill a man.'

With that they passed out, and the members of the group remaining looked grimly at each other.

'I hardly think,' said Father Brown, 'that we remain entirely victorious, in spite of the retreat.'

'I don't mind anything,' said Nares, 'except being bullyragged by that blasphemous blackguard Halket. Horne is a gentleman, anyhow. But whatever they say, I am dead certain they know; they are in it, or most of them are. They almost admitted it. They taunted us with not being able to prove we're right, much more than with being wrong. What do you think, Father Brown?'

The person addressed looked across at Nares with a gaze almost disconcertingly mild and meditative.

'It is quite true,' he said, 'that I have formed an idea that one particular person knows more than he has told us. But I think it would be well if I did not mention his name just yet.'

Nares's eyeglass dropped from his eye, and he looked up sharply. 'This is unofficial so far,' he said. 'I suppose you know that at a later stage if you withhold information, your position may be serious.'

'My position is simple,' replied the priest. 'I am here to look after the legitimate interests of my friend Halket. I think it will be in his interest, under the circumstances, if I tell you I think he will before long sever his connection with this organisation, and cease to be a Socialist in that sense. I have every reason to believe he will probably end as a Catholic.'

'Halket!' exploded the other incredulously. 'Why, he curses priests from morning till night!'

'I don't think you quite understand that kind of man,' said Father Brown mildly. 'He curses priests for failing (in his opinion) to defy the whole world for justice. Why should he expect them to defy the whole world for justice, unless he had already begun to assume they were – what they are? But we haven't met here to discuss the psychology of conversion. I only mention this because it may simplify your task – perhaps narrow your search.'

'If it is true, it would jolly well narrow it to that narrow-faced rascal Elias – and I shouldn't wonder, for a more creepy, cold-blooded, sneering devil I never saw.'

Father Brown sighed. 'He always reminded me of poor Stein,' he said, 'in fact I think he was some relation.'

'Oh, I say,' began Nares, when his protest was cut short by the door being flung open, revealing once more the long loose figure and pale face of young Horne; but it seemed as if he had not merely his natural, but a new and unnatural pallor.

'Hullo,' cried Nares, putting up his single eyeglass, 'why have you come back again?'

Horne crossed the room rather shakily without a word and sat down heavily in a chair. Then he said, as in a sort of daze: 'I missed the others . . . I lost my way. I thought I'd better come back.'

The remains of evening refreshments were on the table, and Henry Horne, that lifelong Prohibitionist, poured himself out a wine-glassful of liqueur brandy and drank it at a gulp.

'You seem upset,' said Father Brown.

Horne had put his hands to his forehead and spoke as from under the shadow of it: he seemed to be speaking to the priest only, in a low voice.

'I may as well tell you. I have seen a ghost.'

'A ghost!' repeated Nares in astonishment. 'Whose ghost?'

'The ghost of Gideon Wise, the master of this house,' answered Horne more firmly, 'standing over the abyss into which he fell.'

'Oh, nonsense!' said Nares; 'no sensible person believes in ghosts.'

'That is hardly exact,' said Father Brown, smiling a little. 'There is really quite as good evidence for many ghosts as there is for most crimes.'

'Well, it's my business to run after the criminals,' said Nares rather roughly, 'and I will leave other people to run away from the ghosts. If anybody at this time of day chooses to be frightened of ghosts it's his affair.'

'I didn't say I was frightened of them, though I dare say I might be,' said Father Brown. 'Nobody knows till he tries. I said I believed in them, at any rate, enough to want to hear more about this one. What, exactly, did you see, Mr Horne?'

'It was over there on the brink of those crumbling cliffs; you know there is a sort of gap or crevice just about the spot where he was thrown over. The others had gone on ahead, and I was crossing the moor towards the path along the cliff. I often went that way, for I liked seeing the high seas dash up against the crags. I thought little of it tonight, beyond wondering that the sea should be so rough on this sort of clear moonlight night. I could see the pale crests of spray appear and disappear as the great waves leapt up at the headland. Thrice I saw the momentary flash of foam in the moonlight and then I saw something inscrutable. The fourth flash of the silver foam seemed to be fixed in the sky. It did not fall; I waited with insane intensity for it to fall. I fancied I was mad, and that time had been for me mysteriously arrested or prolonged. Then I drew nearer, and then I think I screamed aloud. For that suspended spray, like unfallen snowflakes, had fitted together into a face and a figure, white as the shining leper in a legend, and terrible as the fixed lightning.'

'And it was Gideon Wise, you say?'

Horne nodded without speech. There was a silence broken abruptly by Nares rising to his feet; so abruptly indeed that he knocked a chair over.

'Oh, this is all nonsense,' he said, 'but we'd better go out and see.'

'I won't go,' said Horne with sudden violence. 'I'll never walk by that path again.'

'I think we must all walk by that path tonight,' said the priest gravely; 'though I will never deny it has been a perilous path . . . to more people than one.'

'I will not . . . God, how you all goad me,' cried Horne, and his eyes began to roll in a strange fashion. He had risen with the rest, but he made no motion towards the door.

'Mr Horne,' said Nares firmly, 'I am a police-officer, and this house, though you may not know it, is surrounded by the police. I have tried to investigate in a friendly fashion, but I must investigate everything, even anything so silly as a ghost. I must ask you to take me to the spot you speak of.'

There was another silence while Horne stood heaving and panting as with indescribable fears. Then he suddenly sat down on his chair again and said with an entirely new and much more composed voice: 'I can't do it. You may just as well know why. You will know it sooner or later. I killed him.'

For an instant there was the stillness of a house struck by a thunderbolt and full of corpses. Then the voice of Father Brown sounded in that enormous silence strangely small like the squeak of a mouse.

'Did you kill him deliberately?' he asked.

'How can one answer such a question?' answered the man in the chair, moodily gnawing his finger. 'I was mad, I suppose. He was intolerable and insolent, I know. I was on his land and I believe he struck me; anyhow, we came to a grapple and he went over the cliff. When I was well away from the scene it burst upon me that I had done a crime that cut me off from men; the brand of Cain throbbed on my brow and my very brain; I realised for the first time that I had indeed killed a man. I knew I should have to confess it sooner or later.' He sat suddenly erect in his chair. 'But I will say nothing against anybody else. It is no use asking me about plots or accomplices – I will say nothing.'

'In the light of the other murders,' said Nares, 'it is difficult to believe that the quarrel was quite so unpremeditated. Surely somebody sent you there?'

'I will say nothing against anybody I worked with,' said Horne proudly. 'I am a murderer, but I will not be a traitor.'

Nares stepped between the man and the door and called out in an official fashion to someone outside.

'We will all go to the place, anyhow,' he said in a low voice to the secretary; 'but this man must go in custody.'

The company generally felt that to go spook-hunting on a sea-cliff was a very silly anti-climax after the confession of the murderer. But Nares, though the most sceptical and scornful of all, thought it his duty to leave no stone unturned; as one might say, no gravestone unturned. For, after all, that crumbling cliff was the only gravestone over the watery grave of poor Gideon Wise. Nares locked the door, being the last out of the house, and followed the rest across the moor to the cliff, when he was astonished to see young Potter, the secretary, coming back quickly towards them, his face in the moonlight looking white as a moon.

'By God, sir,' he said, speaking for the first time that night, 'there really is something there. It – it's just like him.'

'Why, you're raving,' gasped the detective. 'Everybody's raving.'

'Do you think I don't know him when I see him?' cried the secretary with singular bitterness. 'I have reason to.'

'Perhaps,' said the detective sharply, 'you are one of those who had reason to hate him, as Halket said.'

'Perhaps,' said the secretary; 'anyhow, I know him, and I tell you I can see him standing there stark and staring under this hellish moon.'

And he pointed towards the crack in the cliffs, where they could already see something that might have been a moonbeam or a streak of foam, but which was already beginning to look a little more solid. They had crept a hundred yards nearer, and it was still motionless; but it looked like a statue in silver.

Nares himself looked a little pale and seemed to stand debating what to do. Potter was frankly as much frightened as Horne himself; and even Byrne, who was a hardened reporter, was rather reluctant to go any nearer if he could help it. He could not help considering it a little quaint, therefore, that the only man who did not seem to be frightened of a ghost was the man who had said openly that he might be. For Father Brown was advancing as steadily, at his stumping pace, as if he were going to consult a notice-board.

'It don't seem to bother you much,' said Byrne to the priest; 'and yet I thought you were the only one who believed in spooks.'

'If it comes to that,' replied Father Brown, 'I thought you were one who didn't believe in them. But believing in ghosts is one thing, and believing in a ghost is quite another.'

Byrne looked rather ashamed of himself, and glanced almost covertly at the crumbling headlands in the cold moonlight which were the haunts of the vision or delusion. 'I didn't believe in it till I saw it,' he said.

'And I did believe in it till I saw it,' said Father Brown. The journalist stared after him as he went stumping across the great waste ground that rose towards the cloven headland like the sloping side of a hill cut in two. Under the discolouring moon the grass looked like long grey hair all combed one way by the wind, and seeming to point towards the place where the breaking cliff showed pale gleams of chalk in the grey-green turf, and where stood the pale figure or shining shade that none could yet understand. As yet that pale figure dominated a desolate landscape that was empty except for the black square back and businesslike figure of the priest advancing alone towards it. Then the prisoner Horne broke suddenly from his captors with a piercing cry and ran ahead of the priest, falling on his knees before the spectre.

'I have confessed,' they heard him crying. 'Why have you come to tell them I killed you?'

'I have come to tell them you did not,' said the ghost, and stretched forth a hand to him. Then the kneeling man sprang up with quite a new kind of scream; and they knew it was the hand of flesh.

It was the most remarkable escape from death in recent records, said the experienced detective and the no less experienced journalist. Yet, in a sense, it had been very simple after all. Flakes and shards of the cliff were continually falling away, and some had caught in the gigantic crevice, so as to form what was really a ledge or pocket in what was supposed to be a sheer drop through darkness to the sea. The old man, who was a very tough and wiry old man, had fallen on this lower shoulder of rock and had passed a pretty terrible twenty-four hours in trying to climb back by crags that constantly collapsed under him, but at length formed by their very ruins a sort of stairway of escape. This might be the explanation of Horne's optical illusion about a white wave that appeared and disappeared, and finally came to stay. But anyhow there was Gideon Wise, solid in bone and sinew, with his white hair and white dusty country clothes and harsh country features, which were, however, a great deal less harsh than usual. Perhaps it is good for millionaires to spend twenty-four hours on a ledge of rock within a foot of eternity. Anyhow, he not only disclaimed all malice against the criminal, but gave an account of the matter which considerably modified the crime. He declared that Horne had not thrown him over at all; that the continually breaking ground had given way under him, and that Horne had even made some movement as of attempted rescue.

'On that providential bit of rock down there,' he said solemnly, 'I promised the Lord to forgive my enemies; and the Lord would think it mighty mean if I didn't forgive a little accident like that.'

Horne had to depart under police supervision, of course, but the detective did not disguise from himself that the prisoner's detention would probably be short, and his punishment, if any, trifling. It is not every murderer who can put the murdered man in the witness-box to give him a testimonial.

'It's a strange case,' said Byrne, as the detective and the others hastened along the cliff path towards the town.

'It is,' said Father Brown. 'It's no business of ours; but I wish you'd stop with me and talk it over.'

There was a silence and then Byrne complied by saying suddenly: 'I suppose you were thinking of Horne already, when you said somebody wasn't telling all he knew.'

'When I said that,' replied his friend, 'I was thinking of the exceedingly silent Mr Potter, the secretary of the no longer late or (shall we say) lamented Mr Gideon Wise.'

'Well, the only time Potter ever spoke to me I thought he was a lunatic,' said Byrne, staring, 'but I never thought of his being a criminal. He said something about it all having to do with an icebox.'

'Yes, I thought he knew something about it,' said Father Brown reflectively. 'I never said he had anything to do with it . . . I suppose old Wise really is strong enough to have climbed out of that chasm.'

'What do you mean?' asked the astonished reporter. 'Why, of course he got out of that chasm; for there he is.'

The priest did not answer the question but asked abruptly: 'What do you think of Horne?'

'Well, one can't call him a criminal exactly,' answered Byrne. 'He never was at all like any criminal I ever knew, and I've had some experience; and, of course, Nares has had much more. I don't think we ever quite believed him a criminal.'

'And I never believed in him in another capacity,' said the priest quietly. 'You may know more about criminals. But there's one class of people I probably do know more about than you do, or even Nares for that matter. I've known quite a lot of them, and I know their little ways.'

'Another class of people,' repeated Byrne, mystified. 'Why, what class do you know about?'

'Penitents,' said Father Brown.

'I don't quite understand,' objected Byrne. 'Do you mean you don't believe in his crime?'

'I don't believe in his confession,' said Father Brown. 'I've heard a good many confessions, and there was never a genuine one like that. It was romantic; it was all out of books. Look how he talked about having the brand of Cain. That's out of books. It's not what anyone would feel who had in his own person done a thing hitherto horrible to him. Suppose you were an honest clerk or shop-boy shocked to feel that for the first time you'd stolen money. Would you immediately reflect that your action was the same as that of Barabbas? Suppose you'd killed a child in some ghastly anger. Would you go back through history, till you could identify your action with that of an Idumean potentate named Herod? Believe me, our own crimes are far too hideously private and prosaic to make our first thoughts turn towards historical parallels, however apt. And why did he go out of his way to say he would not give his colleagues away? Even in saying so, he was giving them away. Nobody had asked him so far to give away anything or anybody. No; I don't think he was genuine, and I wouldn't give him absolution. A nice state of things, if people started getting absolved for what they hadn't done.' And Father Brown, his head turned away, looked steadily out to sea.

'But I don't understand what you're driving at,' cried Byrne. 'What's the good of buzzing round him with suspicions when he's pardoned? He's out of it anyhow. He's quite safe.'

Father Brown spun round like a teetotum and caught his friend by the coat with unexpected and inexplicable excitement.

'That's it,' he cried emphatically. 'Freeze on to that! He's quite safe. He's out of it. That's why he's the key of the whole puzzle.'

'Oh, help,' said Byrne feebly.

'I mean,' persisted the little priest, 'he's in it because he's out of it. That's the whole explanation.'

'And a very lucid explanation too,' said the journalist with feeling.

They stood looking out to sea for a time in silence, and then Father Brown said cheerfully: 'And so we come back to the icebox. Where you have all gone wrong from the first in this business is where a good many of the papers and the public men do go wrong. It's because you assumed that there is nothing whatever in the modern world to fight about except Bolshevism. This story has nothing whatever to do with Bolshevism; except perhaps as a blind.'

'I don't see how that can be,' remonstrated Byrne. 'Here you have the three millionaires in that one business murdered –'

'No!' said the priest in a sharp ringing voice. 'You do not. That is just the point. You do not have three millionaires murdered. You have two millionaires murdered; and you have the third millionaire very much alive and kicking and quite ready to kick. And you have that third millionaire freed for ever from the threat that was thrown at his head before your very face, in playfully polite terms, and in that conversation you described as taking place in the hotel. Gallup and Stein threatened the more old-fashioned and independent old huckster that if he would not come into their combine they would freeze him out. Hence the icebox, of course.'

After a pause he went on. 'There is undoubtedly a Bolshevist movement in the modern world, and it must undoubtedly be resisted, though I do not believe very much in your way of resisting it. But what nobody notices is that there is another movement equally modern and equally moving: the great movement towards monopoly or the turning of all trades into trusts. That also is a revolution. That also produces what all revolutions produce. Men will kill for that and against that, as they do for and against Bolshevism. It has its ultimatums and its invasions and its executions. These trust magnates have their courts like kings; they have their bodyguard and bravos; they have their spies in the enemy camp. Horne was one of old Gideon's spies in one of the enemy camps; but he was used here against another enemy: the rivals who were ruining him for standing out.'

'I still don't quite see how he was used,' said Byrne, 'or what was the good of it.'

'Don't you see,' cried Father Brown sharply, 'that they gave each other an alibi?'

Byrne still looked at him a little doubtfully, though understanding was dawning on his face.

'That's what I mean,' continued the other, 'when I say they were in it because they were out of it. Most people would say they must be out of the other two crimes, because they were in this one. As a fact, they were in the other two because they were out of this one; because this one never happened at all. A very queer, improbable sort of alibi, of course; improbable and therefore impenetrable. Most people would say a man who confesses a murder must be sincere; a man who forgives his murderer must be sincere. Nobody would think of the notion that the thing never happened, so that one man had nothing to forgive and the other nothing to fear. They were fixed here for that night by a story against themselves. But they were not here that night; for Horne was murdering old Gallup in the wood, while Wise was strangling that little Jew in his Roman bath. That's why I ask whether Wise was really strong enough for the climbing adventure.'

'It was quite a good adventure,' said Byrne regretfully. 'It fitted into the landscape, and was really very convincing.'

'Too convincing to convince,' said Father Brown, shaking his head. 'How very vivid was that moonlit foam flung up and turning to a ghost. And how very literary! Horne is a sneak and a skunk, but do not forget that, like many other sneaks and skunks in history, he is also a poet.'

THE SECRET OF FATHER BROWN

The Secret of Father Brown

TO

Father John O'Connor

of St Cuthbert's Bradford

whose truth is stranger than fiction,

with a gratitude greater than the world

Contents

large enough to give [illegible]

The Secret of Father Brown

Flambeau, once the most famous criminal in France and later a very private detective in England, had long retired from both professions. Some say a career of crime had left him with too many scruples for a career of detection. Anyhow, after a life of romantic escapes and tricks of evasion, he had ended at what some might consider an appropriate address: in a castle in Spain. The castle, however, was solid though relatively small; and the black vineyard and green stripes of kitchen garden covered a respectable square on the brown hillside. For Flambeau, after all his violent adventures, still possessed what is possessed by so many Latins, what is absent (for instance) in so many Americans, the energy to retire. It can be seen in many a large hotel-proprietor whose one ambition is to be a small peasant. It can be seen in many a French provincial shopkeeper, who pauses at the moment when he might develop into a detestable millionaire and buy a street of shops, to fall back quietly and comfortably on domesticity and dominoes. Flambeau had casually and almost abruptly fallen in love with a Spanish Lady, married and brought up a large family on a Spanish estate, without displaying any apparent desire to stray again beyond its borders. But on one particular morning he was observed by his family to be unusually restless and excited; and he outran the little boys and descended the greater part of the long mountain slope to meet the visitor who was coming across the valley; even when the visitor was still a black dot in the distance.

The black dot gradually increased in size without very much altering in the shape; for it continued, roughly speaking, to be both round and black. The black clothes of clerics were not unknown upon those hills; but these clothes, however clerical, had about them something at once commonplace and yet almost jaunty in comparison with the cassock or soutane, and marked the wearer as a man from the north-western islands, as clearly as if he had been labelled Clapham Junction. He carried a short thick umbrella with a knob like a club, at the sight of which his Latin friend almost shed tears of sentiment; for it had figured in many adventures that they shared long ago. For this was the Frenchman's English friend, Father Brown, paying a long-desired but long-delayed visit. They had corresponded constantly, but they had not met for years.

Father Brown was soon established in the family circle, which was quite large enough to give the general sense of company or a community. He was introduced to the big wooden images of the Three Kings, of painted and gilded wood, who bring the gifts to the children at Christmas; for Spain is a country where the affairs of the children bulk large in the life of the home. He was introduced to the dog and the cat and the livestock on the farm. But he was also, as it happened, introduced to one neighbour who, like himself, had brought into that valley the garb and manners of distant lands.

It was on the third night of the priest's stay at the little château that he beheld a stately stranger who paid his respects to the Spanish household with bows that no Spanish grandee could emulate. He was a tall, thin grey-haired and very handsome gentleman, and his hands, cuffs and cuff-links had something overpowering in their polish. But his long face had nothing of that languor which is associated with long cuffs and manicuring in the caricatures of our own country. It was rather arrestingly alert and keen; and the eyes had an innocent intensity of enquiry that does not go often with grey hairs. That alone might have marked the man's nationality, as well the nasal note in his refined voice and his rather too ready assumption of the vast antiquity of all the European things around him. This was, indeed, no less a person than Mr Grandison Chace, of Boston, an American traveller who had halted for a time in his American travels by taking a lease of the adjoining estate; a somewhat similar castle on a somewhat similar hill. He delighted in his old castle, and he regarded his friendly neighbour as a local antiquity of the same type. For Flambeau managed, as we have said, really to look retired in the sense of rooted. He might have grown there with his own vine and fig tree for ages. He had resumed his real family name of Duroc; for the other title of 'The Torch' had only been a *nom de guerre*, like that under which such a man will often wage war on society. He was fond of his wife and family; he never went farther afield than was needed for a little shooting; and he seemed, to the American globe-trotter, the embodiment of that cult of a sunny respectability and a temperate luxury, which the American was wise enough to see and admire in the Mediterranean peoples. The rolling stone from the West was glad to rest for a moment on this rock in the South that had gathered so very much moss. But Mr Chace had heard of Father Brown, and his tone faintly changed, as towards a celebrity. The interviewing instinct awoke, tactful but tense. If he did try to draw Father Brown, as if he were a tooth, it was done with the most dexterous and painless American dentistry.

They were sitting in a sort of partly unroofed outer court of the house, such as often forms the entrance to Spanish houses. It was dusk turning to dark; and as all that mountain air sharpens suddenly after sunset, a small stove stood on the flagstones, glowing with red eyes like a goblin, and painting a red pattern on the pavement; but scarcely a ray of it reached the lower bricks of the great bare, brown brick wall that went soaring up above them into the deep blue night. Flambeau's big broad-shouldered figure and great moustaches, like sabres, could be traced dimly in the twilight, as he moved about, drawing dark wine from a great cask and handing it round. In his shadow, the priest looked very shrunken and small, as if huddled over the stove; but the American visitor leaned forward elegantly with his elbow on his knee and his fine pointed features in the full light; his eyes shone with inquisitive intelligence.

'I can assure you, sir,' he was saying, 'we consider your achievement in the matter of the Moonshine Murder the most remarkable triumph in the history of detective science.'

Father Brown murmured something; some might have imagined that the murmur was a little like a moan.

'We are well acquainted,' went on the stranger firmly, 'with the alleged achievements of Dupin and others; and with those of Lecocq, Sherlock Holmes, Nicholas Carter, and other imaginative incarnations of the craft. But we observe there is in many ways, a marked difference between your own method of approach and that of these other thinkers, whether fictitious or actual. Some have spec'lated, sir, as to whether the difference of method may perhaps involve rather the absence of method.'

Father Brown was silent; then he started a little, almost as if he had been nodding over the stove, and said: 'I beg your pardon. Yes . . . Absence of method . . . Absence of mind, too, I'm afraid.'

'I should say of strictly tabulated scientific method,' went on the enquirer. 'Edgar Poe throws off several little essays in a conversational form, explaining Dupin's method, with its fine links of logic. Dr Watson had to listen to some pretty exact expositions of Holmes's method with its observation of material details. But nobody seems to have got on to any full account of your method, Father Brown, and I was informed you declined the offer to give a series of lectures in the States on the matter.'

'Yes,' said the priest, frowning at the stove; 'I declined.'

'Your refusal gave rise to a remarkable lot of interesting talk,' remarked Chace. 'I may say that some of our people are saying your science can't be expounded, because it's something more than just natural science. They say your secret's not to be divulged, as being occult in its character.'

'Being what?' asked Father Brown, rather sharply.

'Why, kind of esoteric,' replied the other. 'I can tell you, people got considerably worked up about Gallup's murder, and Stein's murder, and then old man Merton's murder, and now Judge Gwynne's murder, and a double murder by Dalmon, who was well known in the States. And there were you, on the spot every time, slap in the middle of it; telling everybody how it was done and never telling anybody how you knew. So some people got to think you knew without looking, so to speak. And Carlotta Brownson gave a lecture on Thought-Forms with illustrations from these cases of yours. The Second Sight Sisterhood of Indianapolis –'

Father Brown was still staring at the stove; then he said quite loud yet as if hardly aware that anyone heard him: 'Oh, I say. This will never do.'

'I don't exactly know how it's to be helped,' said Mr Chace humorously. 'The Second Sight Sisterhood want a lot of holding down. The only way I can think of stopping it is for you to tell us the secret after all.'

Father Brown groaned. He put his head on his hands and remained a moment, as if full of a silent convulsion of thought. Then he lifted his head and said in a dull voice: 'Very well. I must tell the secret.'

His eyes rolled darkly over the whole darkling scene, from the red eyes of the little stove to the stark expanse of the ancient wall, over which were standing out, more and more brightly, the strong stars of the south.

'The secret is,' he said; and then stopped as if unable to go on. Then he began again and said: 'You see, it was I who killed all those people.'

'What?' repeated the other, in a small voice out of a vast silence.

'You see, I had murdered them all myself,' explained Father Brown patiently. 'So, of course, I knew how it was done.'

Grandison Chace had risen to his great height like a man lifted to the ceiling by a sort of slow explosion. Staring down at the other he repeated his incredulous question.

'I had planned out each of the crimes very carefully,' went on Father Brown, 'I had thought out exactly how a thing like that could be done, and in what style or state of mind a man could really do it. And when I was quite sure that I felt exactly like the murderer myself, of course I knew who he was.'

Chace gradually released a sort of broken sigh.

'You frightened me all right,' he said. 'For the minute I really did think you meant you were the murderer. Just for the minute I kind of saw it splashed over all the papers in the States: "Saintly Sleuth Exposed as Killer: Hundred Crimes of Father Brown". Why, of course, if it's just a figure of speech and means you tried to reconstruct the psychology – '

Father Brown rapped sharply on the stove with the short pipe he was about to fill; one of his very rare spasms of annoyance contracted his face.

'No, no, no,' he said, almost angrily; 'I don't mean just a figure of speech. This is what comes of trying to talk about deep things . . . What's the good of words . . .? If you try to talk about a truth that's merely moral, people always think it's merely metaphorical. A real live man with two legs once said to me: "I only believe in the Holy Ghost in a spiritual sense." Naturally, I said: "In what other sense could you believe it?" And *then* he thought I meant he needn't believe in anything except evolution, or ethical fellowship, or some bilge . . . I mean that I really did see myself, and my real self, committing the murders. I didn't actually kill the men by material means; but that's not the point. Any brick or bit of machinery might have killed them by material means. I mean that I thought and thought about how a man might come to be like that, until I realised that I really *was* like that, in everything except actual final consent to the action. It was once suggested to me by a friend of mine, as a sort of religious exercise. I believe he got it from Pope Leo XIII, who was always rather a hero of mine.'

'I'm afraid,' said the American, in tones that were still doubtful, and keeping his eye on the priest rather as if he were a wild animal, 'that you'd have to explain a lot to me before I knew what you were talking about. The science of detection – '

Father Brown snapped his fingers with the same animated annoyance. 'That's it,' he cried; 'that's just where we part company. Science is a grand thing when you can get it; in its real sense one of the grandest words in the world. But what do these men mean, nine times out of ten, when they use it nowadays? When they say detection is a science? When they say criminology is a science? They mean getting *outside* a man and studying him as if he were a gigantic insect: in what they would call a dry impartial light, in what I should call a dead and dehumanised light. They mean getting a long way off him, as if he were a distant prehistoric monster; staring at the shape of his "criminal skull" as if it were a sort of eerie growth, like the horn on a rhinoceros's nose. When the scientist talks about a type, he never means himself, but always his neighbour; probably his poorer neighbour. I don't deny the dry light may sometimes do good; though in one sense it's the very reverse of science. So far from being knowledge, it's actually suppression of what we know. It's treating a friend as a stranger, and pretending that something familiar is really remote and mysterious. It's like saying that a man has a proboscis between the eyes, or that he falls down in a fit of insensibility once every twenty-four hours. Well, what you call "the secret" is exactly the opposite. I don't try to get outside the man. I try to get inside the murderer . . . Indeed it's much more than that, don't you see? I am inside a man. I am always inside a man, moving his arms and legs; but I wait till I know I am inside a murderer, thinking his thoughts, wrestling with his passions; till I have bent myself into the posture of his hunched and peering hatred; till I see the world with his bloodshot and squinting eyes, looking between the blinkers of his half-witted concentration; looking up the short and sharp perspective of a straight road to a pool of blood. Till I am really a murderer.'

'Oh,' said Mr Chace, regarding him with a long, grim face, and added: 'And that is what you call a religious exercise.'

'Yes,' said Father Brown; 'that is what I call a religious exercise.'

After an instant's silence he resumed: 'It's so real a religious exercise that I'd rather not have said anything about it. But I simply couldn't have you going off and telling all your countrymen that I had a secret magic connected with Thought-Forms, could I? I've put it badly, but it's true. No man's really any good till he knows how bad he is, or might be; till he's realised exactly how much right he has to all this snobbery, and sneering, and talking about "criminals," as if they were apes in a forest ten thousand miles away; till he's got rid of all the dirty self-deception of talking about low types and deficient skulls; till he's squeezed out of his soul the last drop of the oil of the Pharisees; till his only hope is somehow or other to have captured one criminal, and kept him safe and sane under his own hat.'

Flambeau came forward and filled a great goblet with Spanish wine and set it before his friend, as he had already set one before his fellow guest. Then he himself spoke for the first time: 'I believe Father Brown has had a new batch of mysteries. We were talking about them the other day, I fancy. He has been dealing with some queer people since we last met.'

'Yes; I know the stories more or less – but not the application,' said Chace, lifting his glass thoughtfully. 'Can you give me any examples, I wonder . . . I mean, did you deal with this last batch in that introspective style?'

Father Brown also lifted his glass, and the glow of the fire turned the red wine transparent, like the glorious blood-red glass of a martyr's window. The red flame seemed to hold his eyes and absorb his gaze that sank deeper and deeper into it, as if that single cup held a red sea of the blood of all men, and his soul were a diver, ever plunging in dark humility and inverted imagination, lower than its lowest monsters and its most ancient slime. In that cup, as in a red mirror, he saw many things; the doings of his last days moved in crimson shadows; the examples that his companions demanded danced in symbolic shapes; and there passed before him all the stories that are told here. Now, the luminous wine was like a vast red sunset upon dark red sands, where stood dark figures of men; one was fallen and another running towards him. Then the sunset seemed to break up into patches: red lanterns swinging from garden trees and a pond gleaming red with reflection; and then all the colour seemed to cluster again into a great rose of red crystal, a jewel that irradiated the world like a red sun, save for the shadow of a tall figure with a high head-dress as of some prehistoric priest; and then faded again till nothing was left but a flame of wild red beard blowing in the wind upon a wild grey moor. All these things, which may be seen later from other angles and in other moods than his own, rose up in his memory at the challenge and began to form themselves into anecdotes and arguments.

'Yes,' he said, as he raised the wine cup slowly to his lips, 'I can remember pretty well – '

The Mirror of the Magistrate

James Bagshaw and Wilfred Underhill were old friends, and were fond of rambling through the streets at night, talking interminably as they turned corner after corner in the silent and seemingly lifeless labyrinth of the large suburb in which they lived. The former, a big, dark, good-humoured man with a strip of black moustache, was a professional police detective; the latter, a sharp-faced, sensitive-looking gentleman with light hair, was an amateur interested in detection. It will come as a shock to the readers of the best scientific romance to learn that it was the policeman who was talking and the amateur who was listening, even with a certain respect.

'Ours is the only trade,' said Bagshaw, 'in which the professional is always supposed to be wrong. After all, people don't write stories in which hairdressers can't cut hair and have to be helped by a customer; or in which a cabman can't drive a cab until his fare explains to him the philosophy of cab-driving. For all that, I'd never deny that we often tend to get into a rut: or, in other words, have the disadvantages of going by a rule. Where the romancers are wrong is, that they don't allow us even the advantages of going by a rule.'

'Surely,' said Underhill, 'Sherlock Holmes would say that he went by a logical rule.'

'He may be right,' answered the other; 'but I mean a collective rule. It's like the staff work of an army. We pool our information.'

'And you don't think detective stories allow for that?' asked his friend.

'Well, let's take any imaginary case of Sherlock Holmes, and Lestrade, the official detective. Sherlock Holmes, let us say, can guess that a total stranger crossing the street is a foreigner, merely because he seems to look for the traffic to go to the right instead of the left. I'm quite ready to admit Holmes might guess that. I'm quite sure Lestrade wouldn't guess anything of the kind. But what they leave out is the fact that the policeman, who couldn't guess, might very probably know. Lestrade might know the man was a foreigner merely because his department has to keep an eye on all foreigners; some would say on all natives, too. As a policeman I'm glad the police know so much; for every man wants to do his own job well. But as a citizen, I sometimes wonder whether they don't know too much.'

'You don't seriously mean to say,' cried Underhill incredulously, 'that you know anything about strange people in a strange street. That if a man walked out of that house over there, you would know anything about him?'

'I should if he was the householder,' answered Bagshaw. 'That house is rented by a literary man of Anglo-Romanian extraction, who generally lives in Paris, but is over here in connection with some poetical play of his. His name's Osric Orm, one of the new poets, and pretty steep to read, I believe.'

'But I mean all the people down the road,' said his companion. 'I was thinking how strange and new and nameless everything looks, with these high blank walls and these houses lost in large gardens. You can't know all of them.'

'I know a few,' answered Bagshaw. 'This garden wall we're walking under is at the end of the grounds of Sir Humphrey Gwynne, better known as Mr Justice Gwynne, the old judge who made such a row about spying during the war. The house next door to it belongs to a wealthy cigar merchant. He comes from Spanish-America and looks very swarthy and Spanish himself; but he bears the very English name of Buller. The house beyond that – did you hear that noise?'

'I heard something,' said Underhill, 'but I really don't know what it was.'

'I know what it was,' replied the detective, 'it was a rather heavy revolver, fired twice, followed by a cry for help. And it came straight out of the back garden of Mr Justice Gwynne, that paradise of peace and legality.'

He looked up and down the street sharply and then added: 'And the only gate of the back garden is half a mile round on the other side. I wish this wall were a little lower, or I were a little lighter; but it's got to be tried.'

'It is lower a little farther on,' said Underhill, 'and there seems to be a tree that looks helpful.'

They moved hastily along and found a place where the wall seemed to stoop abruptly, almost as if it had half-sunk into the earth; and a garden tree, flamboyant with the gayest garden blossom, straggled out of the dark enclosure and was gilded by the gleam of a solitary street-lamp. Bagshaw caught the crooked branch and threw one leg over the low wall; and the next moment they stood knee-deep amid the snapping plants of a garden border.

The garden of Mr Justice Gwynne by night was rather a singular spectacle. It was large and lay on the empty edge of the suburb, in the shadow of a tall, dark house that was the last in its line of houses. The house was literally dark, being shuttered and unlighted, at least on the side overlooking the garden. But the garden itself, which lay in its shadow and should have been a tract of absolute darkness, showed a random glitter, like that of fading fireworks; as if a giant rocket had fallen in fire among the trees. As they advanced they were able to locate it as the light of several coloured lamps, entangled in the trees like the jewel fruits of Aladdin, and especially as the light from a small, round lake or pond, which gleamed with pale colours as if a lamp were kindled under it.

'Is he having a party?' asked Underhill. 'The garden seems to be illuminated.'

'No,' answered Bagshaw. 'It's a hobby of his, and I believe he prefers to do it when he's alone. He likes playing with a little plant of electricity that he works from that bungalow or hut over there, where he does his work and keeps his papers. Buller, who knows him very well, says the coloured lamps are rather more often a sign he's not to be disturbed.'

'Sort of red danger signals,' suggested the other.

'Good Lord! I'm afraid they are danger signals!' and he began suddenly to run.

A moment after Underhill saw what he had seen. The opalescent ring of light, like the halo of the moon, round the sloping sides of the pond, was broken by two black stripes or streaks which soon proved themselves to be the long, black legs of a figure fallen head downwards into the hollow, with the head in the pond.

'Come on,' cried the detective sharply, 'that looks to me like – '

His voice was lost, as he ran on across the wide lawn, faintly luminous in the artificial light, making a bee-line across the big garden for the pool and the fallen figure. Underhill was trotting steadily in that straight track, when something happened that startled him for the moment. Bagshaw, who was travelling as steadily as a bullet towards the black figure by the luminous pool, suddenly turned at a sharp angle and began to run even more rapidly towards the shadow of the house. Underhill could not imagine what he meant by the altered direction. The next moment, when the detective had vanished into the shadow of the house, there came out of that obscurity the sound of a scuffle and a curse; and Bagshaw returned lugging with him a little struggling man with red hair. The captive had evidently been escaping under the shelter of the building, when the quicker ears of the detective had heard him rustling like a bird among the bushes.

'Underhill,' said the detective, 'I wish you'd run on and see what's up by the pool. And now, who are you?' he asked, coming to a halt. 'What's your name?'

'Michael Flood,' said the stranger in a snappy fashion. He was an unnaturally lean little man, with a hooked nose too large for his face, which was colourless, like parchment, in contrast with the ginger colour of his hair. 'I've got nothing to do with this. I found him lying dead and I was scared; but I only came to interview him for a paper.'

'When you interview celebrities for the Press,' said Bagshaw, 'do you generally climb over the garden wall?'

And he pointed grimly to a trail of footprints coming and going along the path towards the flower bed.

The man calling himself Flood wore an expression equally grim.

'An interviewer might very well get over the wall,' he said, 'for I couldn't make anybody hear at the front door. The servant had gone out.'

'How do you know he'd gone out?' asked the detective suspiciously.

'Because,' said Flood, with an almost unnatural calm, 'I'm not the only person who gets over garden walls. It seems just possible that you did it yourself. But, anyhow, the servant did; for I've just this moment seen him drop over the wall, away on the other side of the garden, just by the garden door.'

'Then why didn't he use the garden door?' demanded the cross-examiner.

'How should I know?' retorted Flood. 'Because it was shut, I suppose. But you'd better ask him, not me; he's coming towards the house at this minute.'

There was, indeed, another shadowy figure beginning to be visible through the fire-shot gloaming, a squat, square-headed figure, wearing a red waistcoat as the most conspicuous part of a rather shabby livery. He appeared to be making with unobtrusive haste towards a side-door in the house, until Bagshaw halloed to him to halt. He drew nearer to them very reluctantly, revealing a heavy, yellow face, with a touch of something Asiatic which was consonant with his flat, blue-black hair.

Bagshaw turned abruptly to the man called Flood. 'Is there anybody in this place,' he said, 'who can testify to your identity?'

'Not many, even in this country,' growled Flood. 'I've only just come from Ireland; the only man I know round here is the priest at St Dominic's Church – Father Brown.'

'Neither of you must leave this place,' said Bagshaw, and then added to the servant: 'But you can go into the house and ring up St Dominic's Presbytery and ask Father Brown if he would mind coming round here at once. No tricks, mind.'

While the energetic detective was securing the potential fugitives, his companion, at his direction, had hastened on to the actual scene of the tragedy. It was a strange enough scene; and, indeed, if the tragedy had not been tragic it would have been highly fantastic. The dead man (for the briefest examination proved him to be dead) lay with his head in the pond, where the glow of the artificial illumination encircled the head with something of the appearance of an unholy halo. The face was gaunt and rather sinister, the brow bald, and the scanty curls dark grey, like iron rings; and, despite the damage done by the bullet wound in the temple, Underhill had no difficulty in recognising the features he had seen in the many portraits of Sir Humphrey Gwynne. The dead man was in evening dress, and his long, black legs, so thin as to be almost spidery, were sprawling at different angles up the steep bank from which he had fallen. As by some weird whim of diabolical arabesque, blood was eddying out, very slowly, into the luminous water in snaky rings, like the transparent crimson of sunset clouds.

Underhill did not know how long he stood staring down at this macabre figure, when he looked up and saw a group of four figures standing above him on the bank. He was prepared for Bagshaw and his Irish captive, and he had no difficulty in guessing the status of the servant in the red waistcoat. But the fourth figure had a sort of grotesque solemnity that seemed strangely congruous to that incongruity. It was a stumpy figure with a round face and a hat like a black halo. He realised that it was, in fact, a priest; but there was something about it that reminded him of some quaint old black woodcut at the end of a Dance of Death.

Then he heard Bagshaw saying to the priest: 'I'm glad you can identify this man; but you must realise that he's to some extent under suspicion. Of course, he may be innocent; but he did enter the garden in an irregular fashion.'

'Well, I think he's innocent myself,' said the little priest in a colourless voice. 'But, of course, I may be wrong.'

'Why do you think he is innocent?'

'Because he entered the garden in an irregular fashion,' answered the cleric. 'You see, I entered it in a regular fashion myself. But I seem to be almost the only person who did. All the best people seem to get over garden walls nowadays.'

'What do you mean by a regular fashion?' asked the detective.

'Well,' said Father Brown, looking at him with limpid gravity, 'I came in by the front door. I often come into houses that way.'

'Excuse me,' said Bagshaw, 'but does it matter very much how you came in, unless you propose to confess to the murder?'

'Yes, I think it does,' said the priest mildly. 'The truth is, that when I came in at the front door I saw something I don't think any of the rest of you have seen. It seems to me it might have something to do with it.'

'What did you see?'

'I saw a sort of general smash-up,' said Father Brown in his mild voice. 'A big looking-glass broken, and a small palm tree knocked over, and the pot smashed all over the floor. Somehow, it looked to me as if something had happened.'

'You are right,' said Bagshaw after a pause. 'If you saw that, it certainly looks as if it had something to do with it.'

'And if it had anything to do with it,' said the priest very gently, 'it looks as if there was one person who had nothing to do with it; and that is Mr Michael Flood, who entered the garden over the wall in an irregular fashion, and then tried to leave it in the same irregular fashion. It is his irregularity that makes me believe in his innocence.'

'Let us go into the house,' said Bagshaw abruptly.

As they passed in at the side-door, the servant leading the way, Bagshaw fell back a pace or two and spoke to his friend.

'Something odd about that servant,' he said. 'Says his name is Green, though he doesn't look it; but there seems no doubt he's really Gwynne's servant, apparently the only regular servant he had. But the queer thing is, that he flatly denied that his master was in the garden at all, dead or alive. Said the old judge had gone out to a grand legal dinner and couldn't be home for hours, and gave that as his excuse for slipping out.'

'Did he,' asked Underhill, 'give any excuse for his curious way of slipping in?'

'No, none that I can make sense of,' answered the detective. 'I can't make him out. He seems to be scared of something.'

Entering by the side-door, they found themselves at the inner end of the entrance hall, which ran along the side of the house and ended with the front door, surmounted by a dreary fanlight of the old-fashioned pattern. A faint, grey light was beginning to outline its radiation upon the darkness, like some dismal and discoloured sunrise; but what light there was in the hall came from a single, shaded lamp, also of an antiquated sort, that stood on a bracket in a corner. By the light of this Bagshaw could distinguish the debris of which Brown had spoken. A tall palm, with long sweeping leaves, had fallen full length, and its dark red pot was shattered into shards. They lay littered on the carpet, along with pale and gleaming fragments of a broken mirror, of which the almost empty frame hung behind them on the wall at the end of the vestibule. At right angles to this entrance, and directly opposite the side-door as they entered, was another and similar passage leading into the rest of the house. At the other end of it could be seen the telephone which the servant had used to summon the priest; and a half-open door, showing, even through the crack, the serried ranks of great leather-bound books, marked the entrance to the judge's study.

Bagshaw stood looking down at the fallen pot and the mingled fragments at his feet.

'You're quite right,' he said to the priest; 'there's been a struggle here. And it must have been a struggle between Gwynne and his murderer.'

'It seemed to me,' said Father Brown modestly, 'that something had happened here.'

'Yes; it's pretty clear what happened,' assented the detective. 'The murderer entered by the front door and found Gwynne; probably Gwynne let him in. There was a death grapple, possibly a chance shot, that hit the glass, though they might have broken it with a stray kick or anything. Gwynne managed to free himself and fled into the garden, where he was pursued and shot finally by the pond. I fancy that's the whole story of the crime itself; but, of course, I must look round the other rooms.'

The other rooms, however, revealed very little, though Bagshaw pointed significantly to the loaded automatic pistol that he found in a drawer of the library desk.

'Looks as if he was expecting this,' he said; 'yet it seems queer he didn't take it with him when he went out into the hall.'

Eventually they returned to the hall, making their way towards the front door, Father Brown letting his eye rove around in a rather absent-minded fashion. The two corridors, monotonously papered in the same grey and faded pattern, seemed to emphasise the dust and dingy floridity of the few early Victorian ornaments, the green rust that devoured the bronze of the lamp, the dull gold that glimmered in the frame of the broken mirror.

'They say it's bad luck to break a looking-glass,' he said. 'This looks like the very house of ill-luck. There's something about the very furniture –'

'That's rather odd,' said Bagshaw sharply. 'I thought the front door would be shut, but it's left on the latch.'

There was no reply; and they passed out of the front door into the front garden, a narrower and more formal plot of flowers, having at one end a curiously clipped hedge with a hole in it, like a green cave, under the shadow of which some broken steps peeped out.

Father Brown strolled up to the hole and ducked his head under it. A few moments after he had disappeared they were astonished to hear his quiet voice in conversation above their heads, as if he were talking to somebody at the top of a tree. The detective followed, and found that the curious covered stairway led to what looked like a broken bridge, over-hanging the darker and emptier spaces of the garden. It just curled round the corner of the house, bringing in sight the field of coloured lights beyond and beneath. Probably it was the relic of some abandoned architectural fancy of building a sort of terrace on arches across the lawn. Bagshaw thought it a curious cul-de-sac in which to find anybody in the small hours between night and morning; but he was not looking at the details of it just then. He was looking at the man who was found.

As the man stood with his back turned – a small man in light grey clothes – the one outstanding feature about him was a wonderful head of hair, as yellow and radiant as the head of a huge dandelion. It was literally outstanding like a halo, and something in that association made the face, when it was slowly and sulkily turned on them, rather a shock of contrast. That halo should have enclosed an oval face of the mildly angelic sort; but the face was crabbed and elderly with a powerful jowl and a short nose that somehow suggested the broken nose of a pugilist.

'This is Mr Orm, the celebrated poet, I understand,' said Father Brown, as calmly as if he were introducing two people in a drawing-room.

'Whoever he is,' said Bagshaw, 'I must trouble him to come with me and answer a few questions.'

Mr Osric Orm, the poet, was not a model of self-expression when it came to the answering of questions. There, in that corner of the old garden, as the grey twilight before dawn began to creep over the heavy hedges and the broken bridge, and afterwards in a succession of circumstances and stages of legal inquiry that grew more and more ominous, he refused to say anything except that he had intended to call on Sir Humphrey Gwynne, but had not done so because he could not get anyone to answer the bell. When it was pointed out that the door was practically open, he snorted. When it was hinted that the hour was somewhat late, he snarled. The little that he said was obscure, either because he really knew hardly any English, or because he knew better than to know any. His opinions seemed to be of a nihilistic and destructive sort, as was indeed the tendency of his poetry for those who could follow it; and it seemed possible that his business with the judge, and perhaps his quarrel with the judge, had been something in the anarchist line. Gwynne was known to have had something of a mania about Bolshevist spies, as he had about German spies. Anyhow, one coincidence, only a few moments after his capture, confirmed Bagshaw in the impression that the case must be taken seriously. As they went out of the front gate into the street, they so happened to encounter yet another neighbour, Buller, the cigar merchant from next door, conspicuous by his brown, shrewd face and the unique orchid in his buttonhole; for he had a name in that branch of horticulture. Rather to the surprise of the rest, he hailed his neighbour, the poet, in a matter-of-fact manner, almost as if he had expected to see him.

'Hallo, here we are again,' he said. 'Had a long talk with old Gwynne, I suppose?'

'Sir Humphrey Gwynne is dead,' said Bagshaw. 'I am investigating the case and I must ask you to explain.'

Buller stood as still as the lamp-post beside him, possibly stiffened with surprise. The red end of his cigar brightened and darkened rhythmically, but his brown face was in shadow; when he spoke it was with quite a new voice.

'I only mean,' he said, 'that when I passed two hours ago Mr Orm was going in at this gate to see Sir Humphrey.'

'He says he hasn't seen him yet,' observed Bagshaw, 'or even been into the house.'

'It's a long time to stand on the doorstep,' observed Buller.

'Yes,' said Father Brown; 'it's rather a long time to stand in the street.'

'I've been home since then,' said the cigar merchant. 'Been writing letters and came out again to post them.'

'You'll have to tell all that later,' said Bagshaw. 'Good-night – or good-morning.'

The trial of Osric Orm for the murder of Sir Humphrey Gwynne, which filled the newspapers for so many weeks, really turned entirely on the same crux as that little talk under the lamp-post, when the grey-green dawn was breaking about the dark streets and gardens. Everything came back to the enigma of those two empty hours between the time when Buller saw Orm going in at the garden gate, and the time when Father Brown found him apparently still lingering in the garden. He had certainly had the time to commit six murders, and might almost have committed them for want of something to do; for he could give no coherent account of what he was doing. It was argued by the prosecution that he had also the opportunity, as the front door was unlatched, and the side-door into the larger garden left standing open. The court followed, with considerable interest, Bagshaw's clear reconstruction of the struggle in the passage, of which the traces were so evident; indeed, the police had since found the shot that had shattered the glass. Finally, the hole in the hedge to which he had been tracked, had very much the appearance of a hiding-place. On the other hand, Sir Matthew Blake, the very able counsel for the defence, turned this last argument the other way: asking why any man should entrap himself in a place without possible exit, when it would obviously be much more sensible to slip out into the street. Sir Matthew Blake also made effective use of the mystery that still rested upon the motive for the murder. Indeed, upon this point, the passages between Sir Matthew Blake and Sir Arthur Travers, the equally brilliant advocate for the prosecution, turned rather to the advantage of the prisoner. Sir Arthur could only throw out suggestions about a Bolshevist conspiracy which sounded a little thin. But when it came to investigating the facts of Orm's mysterious behaviour that night he was considerably more effective.

The prisoner went into the witness-box, chiefly because his astute counsel calculated that it would create a bad impression if he did not. But he was almost as uncommunicative to his own counsel as to the prosecuting counsel. Sir Arthur Travers made all possible capital out of his stubborn silence, but did not succeed in breaking it. Sir Arthur was a long, gaunt man, with a long, cadaverous face, in striking contrast to the sturdy figure and bright, bird-like eye of Sir Matthew Blake. But if Sir Matthew suggested a very cocksure sort of cock-sparrow, Sir Arthur might more truly have been compared to a crane or stork; as he leaned forward, prodding the poet with questions, his long nose might have been a long beak.

'Do you mean to tell the jury,' he asked, in tones of grating incredulity, 'that you never went in to see the deceased gentleman at all?'

'No!' replied Orm shortly.

'You wanted to see him, I suppose. You must have been very anxious to see him. Didn't you wait two whole hours in front of his front door?'

'Yes,' replied the other.

'And yet you never even noticed the door was open?'

'No,' said Orm.

'What in the world were you doing for two hours in somebody's else's front garden?' insisted the barrister. 'You were doing something, I suppose?'

'Yes.'

'Is it a secret?' asked Sir Arthur, with adamantine jocularity.

'It's a secret from you,' answered the poet.

It was upon this suggestion of a secret that Sir Arthur seized in developing his line of accusation. With a boldness which some thought unscrupulous, he turned the very mystery of the motive, which was the strongest part of his opponent's case, into an argument for his own. He gave it as the first fragmentary hint of some far-flung and elaborate conspiracy, in which a patriot had perished like one caught in the coils of an octopus.

'Yes,' he cried in a vibrating voice, 'my learned friend is perfectly right! We do not know the exact reason why this honourable public servant was murdered. We shall not know the reason why the next public servant is murdered. If my learned friend himself falls a victim to his eminence, and the hatred which the hellish powers of destruction feel for the guardians of law, he will be murdered, and he will not know the reason. Half the decent people in this court will be butchered in their beds, and we shall not know the reason. And we shall never know the reason and never arrest the massacre, until it has depopulated our country, so long as the defence is permitted to stop all proceedings with this stale tag about "motive", when every other fact in the case, every glaring incongruity, every gaping silence, tells us that we stand in the presence of Cain.'

'I never knew Sir Arthur so excited,' said Bagshaw to his group of companions afterwards. 'Some people are saying he went beyond the usual limit and that the prosecutor in a murder case oughtn't to be so vindictive. But I must say there was something downright creepy about that little goblin with the yellow hair, that seemed to play up to the impression. I was vaguely recalling, all the time, something that De Quincey says about Mr Williams, that ghastly criminal who slaughtered two whole families almost in silence. I think he says that Williams had hair of a vivid unnatural yellow; and that he thought it had been dyed by a trick learned in India, where they dye horses green or blue. Then there was his queer, stony silence, like a troglodyte's; I'll never deny that it all worked me up until I felt there was a sort of monster in the dock. If that was only Sir Arthur's eloquence, then he certainly took a heavy responsibility in putting so much passion into it.'

'He was a friend of poor Gwynne's, as a matter of fact,' said Underhill, more gently; 'a man I know saw them hobnobbing together after a great legal dinner lately. I dare say that's why he feels so strongly in this case. I suppose it's doubtful whether a man ought to act in such a case on mere personal feeling.'

'He wouldn't,' said Bagshaw. 'I bet Sir Arthur Travers wouldn't act only on feeling, however strongly he felt. He's got a very stiff sense of his own professional position. He's one of those men who are ambitious even when they've satisfied their ambition. I know nobody who'd take more trouble to keep his position in the world. No; you've got hold of the wrong moral to his rather thundering sermon. If he lets himself go like that, it's because he thinks he can get a conviction, anyhow, and wants to put himself at the head of some political movement against the conspiracy he talks about. He must have some very good reason for wanting to convict Orm and some very good reason for thinking he can do it. That means that the facts will support him. His confidence doesn't look well for the prisoner.' He became conscious of an insignificant figure in the group.

'Well, Father Brown,' he said with a smile; 'what do you think of our judicial procedure?'

'Well,' replied the priest rather absently, 'I think the thing that struck me most was how different men look in their wigs. You talk about the prosecuting barrister being so tremendous. But I happened to see him take his wig off for a minute, and he really looks quite a different man. He's quite bald, for one thing.'

'I'm afraid that won't prevent his being tremendous,' answered Bagshaw. 'You don't propose to found the defence on the fact that the prosecuting counsel is bald, do you?'

'Not exactly,' said Father Brown good-humouredly. 'To tell the truth, I was thinking how little some kinds of people know about other kinds of people. Suppose I went among some remote people who had never even heard of England. Suppose I told them that there is a man in my country who won't ask a question of life and death, until he has put an erection made of horsehair on the top of his head, with little tails behind, and grey corkscrew curls at the side, like an Early Victorian old woman. They would think he must be rather eccentric; but he isn't at all eccentric, he's only conventional. They would think so, because they don't know anything about English barristers; because they don't know what a barrister is. Well, that barrister doesn't know what a poet is. He doesn't understand that a poet's eccentricities wouldn't seem eccentric to other poets. He thinks it odd that Orm should walk about in a beautiful garden for two hours, with nothing to do. God bless my soul! a poet would think nothing of walking about in the same backyard for ten hours if he had a poem to do. Orm's own counsel was quite as stupid. It never occurred to him to ask Orm the obvious question.'

'What question do you mean?' asked the other.

'Why, what poem he was making up, of course,' said Father Brown rather impatiently. 'What line he was stuck at, what epithet he was looking for, what climax he was trying to work up to. If there were any educated people in court, who know what literature is, they would have known well enough whether he had had anything genuine to do. You'd have asked a manufacturer about the conditions of his factory; but nobody seems to consider the conditions under which poetry is manufactured. It's done by doing nothing.'

'That's all very well,' replied the detective; 'but why did he hide? Why did he climb up that crooked little stairway and stop there; it led nowhere.'

'Why, because it led nowhere, of course,' cried Father Brown explosively. 'Anybody who clapped eyes on that blind alley ending in mid-air might have known an artist would want to go there, just as a child would.'

He stood blinking for a moment, and then said apologetically: 'I beg your pardon; but it seems odd that none of them understand these things. And then there was another thing. Don't you know that everything has, for an artist, one aspect or angle that is exactly *right*? A tree, a cow, and a cloud, in a certain relation only, mean something; as three letters, in one order only, mean a word. Well, the view of that illuminated garden from that unfinished bridge was the right view of it. It was as unique as the fourth dimension. It was a sort of fairy foreshortening; it was like looking *down* at heaven and seeing all the stars growing on trees and that luminous pond like a moon fallen flat on the fields in some happy nursery talc. He could have looked at it for ever. If you told him the path led nowhere, he would tell you it had led him to the country at the end of the world. But do you expect him to tell you that in the witness-box? What would you say to him if he did? You talk about a man having a jury of his peers. Why don't you have a jury of poets?'

'You talk as if you were a poet yourself,' said Bagshaw.

'Thank your stars I'm not,' said Father Brown. 'Thank your lucky stars a priest has to be more charitable than a poet. Lord have mercy on us, if you knew what a crushing, what a cruel contempt he feels for the lot of you, you'd feel as if you were under Niagara.'

'You may know more about the artistic temperament than I do,' said Bagshaw after a pause; 'but, after all, the answer is simple. You can only show that he might have done what he did, without committing the crime. But it's equally true that he might have committed the crime. And who else could have committed it?'

'Have you thought about the servant, Green?' asked Father Brown, reflectively. 'He told a rather queer story.'

'Ah,' cried Bagshaw quickly, 'you think Green did it, after all.'

'I'm quite sure he didn't,' replied the other. 'I only asked if you'd thought about his queer story. He only went out for some trifle, a drink or an assignation or what not. But he went out by the garden door and came back over the garden wall. In other words, he left the door open, but he came back to find it shut. Why? Because Somebody Else had already passed out that way.'

'The murderer,' muttered the detective doubtfully. 'Do you know who he was?'

'I know what he looked like,' answered Father Brown quietly. 'That's the only thing I do know. I can almost see him as he came in at the front door, in the gleam of the hall lamp; his figure, his clothes, even his face!'

'What's all this?'

'He looked like Sir Humphrey Gwynne,' said the priest.

'What the devil do you mean?' demanded Bagshaw. 'Gwynne was lying dead with his head in the pond.'

'Oh, yes,' said Father Brown.

After a moment he went on: 'Let's go back to that theory of yours, which was a very good one, though I don't quite agree with it. You suppose the murderer came in at the front door, met the judge in the front hall, struggling with him and breaking the mirror; that the judge then retreated into the garden, where he was finally shot. Somehow, it doesn't sound natural to me. Granted he retreated down the hall, there are two exits at the end, one into the garden and one into the house. Surely, he would be more likely to retreat into the house? His gun was there; his telephone was there; his servant, so far as he knew, was there. Even the nearest neighbours were in that direction. Why should he stop to open the garden door and go out alone on the deserted side of the house?'

'But we know he did go out of the house,' replied his companion, puzzled. 'We know he went out of the house, because he was found in the garden.'

'He never went out of the house, because he never was in the house,' said Father Brown. 'Not that evening, I mean. He was sitting in that bungalow. I read *that* lesson in the dark, at the beginning, in red and golden stars across the garden. They were worked from the hut; they wouldn't have been burning at all if he hadn't been in the hut. He was trying to run across to the house and the telephone, when the murderer shot him beside the pond.'

'But what about the pot and the palm and the broken mirror?' cried Bagshaw. 'Why, it was you who found them! It was you yourself who said there must have been a struggle in the hall.'

The priest blinked rather painfully. 'Did I?' he muttered. 'Surely, I didn't say that. I never thought that. What I think I said, was that something had happened in the hall. And something did happen; but it wasn't a struggle.'

'Then what broke the mirror?' asked Bagshaw shortly.

'A bullet broke the mirror,' answered Father Brown gravely; 'a bullet fired by the criminal. The big fragments of falling glass were quite enough to knock over the pot and the palm.'

'Well, what else could he have been firing at except Gwynne?' asked the detective.

'It's rather a fine metaphysical point,' answered his clerical companion almost dreamily. 'In one sense, of course, he was firing at Gwynne. But Gwynne wasn't there to be fired at. The criminal was alone in the hall.'

He was silent for a moment, and then went on quietly. 'Imagine the looking-glass at the end of the passage, before it was broken, and the tall palm arching over it. In the half-light, reflecting these monochrome walls, it would look like the end of the passage. A man reflected in it would look like a man coming from inside the house. It would look like the master of the house – if only the reflection were a little like him.'

'Stop a minute,' cried Bagshaw. 'I believe I begin –'

'You begin to see,' said Father Brown. 'You begin to see why all the suspects in this case must be innocent. Not one of them could possibly have mistaken his own reflection for old Gwynne. Orm would have known at once that his bush of yellow hair was not a bald head. Flood would have seen his own red head, and Green his own red waistcoat. Besides, they're all short and shabby; none of them could have thought his own image was a tall, thin, old gentleman in evening dress. We want another, equally tall and thin, to match him. That's what I meant by saying that I knew what the murderer looked like.'

'And what do you argue from that?' asked Bagshaw, looking at him steadily.

The priest uttered a sort of sharp, crisp laugh, oddly different from his ordinary mild manner of speech.

'I am going to argue,' he said, 'the very thing that you said was so ludicrous and impossible.'

'What do you mean?'

'I'm going to base the defence,' said Father Brown, 'on the fact that the prosecuting counsel has a bald head.'

'Oh, my God!' said the detective quietly, and got to his feet, staring.

Father Brown had resumed his monologue in an unruffled manner.

'You've been following the movements of a good many people in this business; you policemen were prodigiously interested in the movements of the poet, and the servant, and the Irishman. The man whose movements seem to have been rather forgotten is the dead man himself. His servant was quite honestly astonished at finding his master had returned. His master had gone to a great dinner of all the leaders of the legal profession, but had left it abruptly and come home. He was not ill, for he summoned no assistance; he had almost certainly quarrelled with some leader of the legal profession. It's among the leaders of that profession that we should have looked first for his enemy. He returned, and shut himself up in the bungalow, where he kept all his private documents about treasonable practices. But the leader of the legal profession, who knew there was something against him in those documents, was thoughtful enough to follow his accuser home; he also being in evening dress, but with a pistol in his pocket. That is all; and nobody could ever have guessed it except for the mirror.'

He seemed to be gazing into vacancy for a moment, and then added: 'A queer thing is a mirror; a picture frame that holds hundreds of different pictures, all vivid and all vanished for ever. Yet, there was something specially strange about the glass that hung at the end of that grey corridor under that green palm. It is as if it was a magic glass and had a different fate from others, as if its picture could somehow survive it, hanging in the air of that twilight house like a spectre; or at least like an abstract diagram, the skeleton of an argument. We could, at least, conjure out of the void the thing that Sir Arthur Travers saw. And by the way, there was one very true thing that you said about him.'

'I'm glad to hear it,' said Bagshaw with grim good-nature. 'And what was it?'

'You said,' observed the priest, 'that Sir Arthur must have some good reason for wanting to get Orm hanged.'

A week later the priest met the police detective once more, and learned that the authorities had already been moving on the new lines of enquiry when they were interrupted by a sensational event.

'Sir Arthur Travers,' began Father Brown.

'Sir Arthur Travers is dead,' said Bagshaw, briefly.

'Ah!' said the other, with a little catch in his voice; 'you mean that he – '

'Yes,' said Bagshaw, 'he shot at the same man again, but not in a mirror.'

The Man with Two Beards

This tale was told by Father Brown to Professor Crake, the celebrated criminologist, after dinner at a club, where the two were introduced to each other as sharing a harmless hobby of murder and robbery. But, as Father Brown's version rather minimised his own part in the matter, it is here retold in a more impartial style. It arose out of a playful passage of arms, in which the professor was very scientific and the priest rather sceptical.

'My good sir,' said the professor in remonstrance, 'don't you believe that criminology is a science?'

'I'm not sure,' replied Father Brown. 'Do you believe that hagiology is a science?'

'What's that?' asked the specialist sharply.

'No; it's not the study of hags, and has nothing to do with burning witches,' said the priest, smiling. 'It's the study of holy things, saints and so on. You see, the Dark Ages tried to make a science about good people. But our own humane and enlightened age is only interested in a science about bad ones. Yet I think our general experience is that every conceivable sort of man has been a saint. And I suspect you will find, too, that every conceivable sort of man has been a murderer.'

'Well, we believe murderers can be pretty well classified,' observed Crake. 'The list sounds rather long and dull; but I think it's exhaustive. First, all killing can be divided into rational and irrational, and we'll take the last first, because they are much fewer. There is such a thing as homicidal mania, or love of butchery in the abstract. There is such a thing as irrational antipathy, though it's very seldom homicidal. Then we come to the true motives: of these, some are less rational in the sense of being merely romantic and retrospective. Acts of pure revenge are acts of hopeless revenge. Thus a lover will sometimes kill a rival he could never supplant, or a rebel assassinate a tyrant after the conquest is complete. But, more often, even these acts have a rational explanation. They are hopeful murders. They fall into the larger section of the second division, of what we may call prudential crimes. These, again, fall chiefly under two descriptions. A man kills either in order to obtain what the other man possesses, either by theft or inheritance, or to stop the other man from acting in some way: as in the case of killing a blackmailer or a political opponent; or, in the case of a rather more passive obstacle, a husband or wife whose continued functioning, as such, interferes with other things. We believe that classification is pretty thoroughly thought out and, properly applied, covers the whole ground. But I'm afraid that it perhaps sounds rather dull; I hope I'm not boring you.'

'Not at all,' said Father Brown. 'If I seemed a little absent-minded I must apologise; the truth is, I was thinking of a man I once knew. He was a murderer; but I can't see where he fits into your museum of murderers. He was not mad, nor did he like killing. He did not hate the man he killed; he hardly knew him, and certainly had nothing to avenge on him. The other man did not possess anything that he could possibly want. The other man was not behaving in any way which the murderer wanted to stop. The murdered man was not in a position to hurt, or hinder, or even affect the murderer in any way. There was no woman in the case. There were no politics in the case. This man killed a fellow-creature who was practically a stranger, and that for a very strange reason; which is possibly unique in human history.'

And so, in his own more conversational fashion, he told the story. The story may well begin in a sufficiently respectable setting, at the breakfast table of a worthy though wealthy suburban family named Bankes, where the normal discussion of the newspaper had, for once, been silenced by the discussion about a mystery nearer home. Such people are sometimes accused of gossip about their neighbours, but they are in that matter almost inhumanly innocent. Rustic villagers tell tales about their neighbours, true and false; but the curious culture of the modern suburb will believe anything it is told in the papers about the wickedness of the Pope, or the martyrdom of the King of the Cannibal Islands, and, in the excitement of these topics, never knows what is happening next door. In this case, however, the two forms of interest actually coincided in a coincidence of thrilling intensity. Their own suburb had actually been mentioned in their favourite newspaper. It seemed to them like a new proof of their own existence when they saw the name in print. It was almost as if they had been unconscious and invisible before; and now they were as real as the King of the Cannibal Islands.

It was stated in the paper that a once famous criminal, known as Michael Moonshine, and many other names that were presumably not his own, had recently been released after a long term of imprisonment for his numerous burglaries; that his whereabouts was being kept quiet, but that he was believed to have settled down in the suburb in question, which we will call for convenience Chisham. A résumé of some of his famous and daring exploits and escapes was given in the same issue. For it is a character of that kind of press, intended for that kind of public, that it assumes that its reader have no memories. While the peasant will remember an outlaw like Robin Hood or Rob Roy for centuries, the clerk will hardly remember the name of the criminal about whom he argued in trams and tubes two years before. Yet, Michael Moonshine had really shown some of the heroic rascality of

Rob Roy or Robin Hood. He was worthy to be turned into legend and not merely into news. He was far too capable a burglar to be a murderer. But his terrific strength and the ease with which he knocked policemen over like ninepins, stunned people, and bound and gagged them, gave something almost like a final touch of fear or mystery to the fact that he never killed them. People almost felt that he would have been more human if he had.

Mr Simon Bankes, the father of the family, was at once better read and more old-fashioned than the rest. He was a sturdy man, with a short grey beard and a brow barred with wrinkles. He had a turn for anecdotes and reminiscence, and he distinctly remembered the days when Londoners had lain awake listening for Mike Moonshine as they did for Spring-heeled Jack. Then there was his wife, a thin, dark lady. There was a sort of acid elegance about her, for her family had much more money than her husband's, if rather less education; and she even possessed a very valuable emerald necklace upstairs, that gave her a right to prominence in a discussion about thieves. There was his daughter, Opal, who was also thin and dark and supposed to be psychic – at any rate, by herself; for she had little domestic encouragement. Spirits of an ardently astral turn will be well advised not to materialise as members of a large family. There was her brother John, a burly youth, particularly boisterous in his indifference to her spiritual development; and otherwise distinguishable only by his interest in motor cars. He seemed to be always in the act of selling one car and buying another; and by some process, hard for the economic theorist to follow, it was always possible to buy a much better article by selling the one that was damaged or discredited. There was his brother Philip, a young man with dark curly hair, distinguished by his attention to dress; which is doubtless part of the duty of a stockbroker's clerk, but, as the stockbroker was prone to hint, hardly the whole of it. Finally, there was present at this family scene his friend, Daniel Devine, who was also dark and exquisitely dressed, but bearded in a fashion that was somewhat foreign, and therefore, for many, slightly menacing.

It was Devine who had introduced the topic of the newspaper paragraph, tactfully insinuating so effective an instrument of distraction at what looked like the beginning of a small family quarrel; for the psychic lady had begun the description of a vision she had had of pale faces floating in empty night outside her window, and John Bankes was trying to roar down this revelation of a higher state with more than his usual heartiness.

But the newspaper reference to their new and possibly alarming neighbour soon put both controversialists out of court.

'How frightful,' cried Mrs Bankes. 'He must be quite a newcomer; but who can he possibly be?'

'I don't know any particularly newcomers,' said her husband, 'except Sir Leopold Pulman, at Beechwood House.'

'My dear,' said the lady, 'how absurd you are – Sir Leopold!' Then, after a pause, she added: 'If anybody suggested his secretary now – that man with the whiskers; I've always said, ever since he got the place Philip ought to have had – '

'Nothing doing,' said Philip languidly, making his sole contribution to the conversation. 'Not good enough.'

'The only one I know,' observed Devine, 'is that man called Carver, who is stopping at Smith's Farm. He lives a very quiet life, but he's quite interesting to talk to. I think John has had some business with him.'

'Knows a bit about cars,' conceded the monomaniac John. 'He'll know a bit more when he's been in my new car.'

Devine smiled slightly; everybody had been threatened with the hospitality of John's new car. Then he added reflectively: 'That's a little what I feel about him. He knows a lot about motoring and travelling, and the active ways of the world, and yet he always stays at home pottering about round old Smith's beehives. Says he's only interested in bee culture, and that's why he's staying with Smith. It seems a very quiet hobby for a man of his sort. However, I've no doubt John's car will shake him up a bit.'

As Devine walked away from the house that evening his dark face wore an expression of concentrated thought. His thoughts would, perhaps, have been worthy of our attention, even at this stage; but it is enough to say that their practical upshot was a resolution to pay an immediate visit to Mr Carver at the house of Mr Smith. As he was making his way thither he encountered Barnard, the secretary at Beechwood House, conspicuous by his lanky figure and the large side whiskers which Mrs Bankes counted among her private wrongs. Their acquaintance was slight, and their conversation brief and casual; but Devine seemed to find in it food for further cogitation.

'Look here,' he said abruptly, 'excuse my asking, but is it true that Lady Pulman has some very famous jewellery up at the House? I'm not a professional thief, but I've just heard there's one hanging about.'

'I'll get her to give an eye to them,' answered the secretary. 'To tell the truth, I've ventured to warn her about them already myself. I hope she has attended to it.'

As they spoke, there came the hideous cry of a motor-horn just behind, and John Bankes came to a stop beside them, radiant at his own steering-wheel. When he heard of Devine's destination he claimed it as his own, though his tone suggested rather an abstract relish for offering people a ride. The ride was consumed in continuous praises of the car, now mostly in the matter of its adaptability to weather.

'Shuts up as tight as a box,' he said, 'and opens as easy – as easy as opening your mouth.'

Devine's mouth, at the moment, did not seem so easy to open, and they arrived at Smith's farm to the sound of a soliloquy. Passing the outer gate, Devine found the man he was looking for without going into the house. The man was walking about in the garden, with his hands in his pockets, wearing a large, limp straw hat; a man with a long face and a large chin. The wide brim cut off the upper part of his face with a shadow that looked a little like a mask. In the background was a row of sunny beehives, along which an elderly man, presumably Mr Smith, was moving accompanied by a short, commonplace-looking companion in black clerical costume.

'I say,' burst in the irrepressible John, before Devine could offer any polite greeting, 'I've brought her round to give you a little run. You see if she isn't better than a "Thunderbolt". '

Mr Carver's mouth set into a smile that may have been meant to be gracious, but looked rather grim. 'I'm afraid I shall be too busy for pleasure this evening,' he said.

'How doth the little busy bee,' observed Devine, equally enigmatically. 'Your bees must be very busy if they keep you at it all night. I was wondering if – '

'Well,' demanded Carver, with a certain cool defiance.

'Well, they say we should make hay while the sun shines,' said Devine. 'Perhaps you make honey while the moon shines.'

There came a flash from the shadow of the broad-brimmed hat, as the whites of the man's eyes shifted and shone.

'Perhaps there is a good deal of moonshine in the business,' he said: 'but I warn you my bees do not only make honey. They sting.'

'Are you coming along in the car?' insisted the staring John. But Carver, though he threw off the momentary air of sinister significance with which he had been answering Devine, was still positive in his polite refusal.

'I can't possibly go,' he said. 'Got a lot of writing to do. Perhaps you'd be kind enough to give some of my friends a run, if you want a companion. This is my friend, Mr Smith, Father Brown – '

'Of course,' cried Bankes; 'let 'em all come.'

'Thank you very much,' said Father Brown. 'I'm afraid I shall have to decline; I've got to go on to Benediction in a few minutes.'

'Mr Smith is your man, then,' said Carver, with something almost like impatience. 'I'm sure Smith is longing for a motor ride.'

Smith, who wore a broad grin, bore no appearance of longing for anything. He was an active little old man with a very honest wig; one of those wigs that look no more natural than a hat. Its tinge of yellow was out of keeping with his colourless complexion. He shook his head and answered with amiable obstinacy: 'I remember I went over this road ten years ago – in one of those contraptions. Came over in it from my sister's place at

Holmgate, and never been over that road in a car since. It was rough going I can tell you.'

'Ten years ago!' scoffed John Bankes. 'Two thousand years ago you went in an ox wagon. Do you think cars haven't changed in ten years – and roads, too, for that matter? In my little bus you don't know the wheels are going round. You think you're just flying.'

'I'm sure Smith wants to go flying,' urged Carver. 'It's the dream of his life. Come, Smith, go over to Holmgate and see your sister. You know you ought to go and see your sister. Go over and stay the night if you like.'

'Well, I generally walk over, so I generally do stay the night,' said old Smith. 'No need to trouble the gentleman today, particularly.'

'But think what fun it will be for your sister to see you arrive in a car!' cried Carver. 'You really ought to go. Don't be so selfish.'

'That's it,' assented Bankes, with buoyant benevolence. 'Don't you be selfish. It won't hurt you. You aren't afraid of it, are you?'

'Well,' said Mr Smith, blinking thoughtfully, 'I don't want to be selfish, and I don't think I'm afraid – I'll come with you if you put it that way.'

The pair drove off, amid waving salutations that seemed somehow to give the little group the appearance of a cheering crowd. Yet Devine and the priest only joined in out of courtesy, and they both felt it was the dominating gesture of their host that gave it its final air of farewell. The detail gave them a curious sense of the pervasive force of his personality.

The moment the car was out of sight he turned to them with a sort of boisterous apology and said: 'Well!'

He said it with that curious heartiness which is the reverse of hospitality. That extreme geniality is the same as a dismissal.

'I must be going,' said Devine. 'We must not interrupt the busy bee. I'm afraid I know very little about bees; sometimes I can hardly tell a bee from a wasp.'

'I've kept wasps, too,' answered the mysterious Mr Carver. When his guests were a few yards down the street, Devine said rather impulsively to his companion: 'Rather an odd scene that, don't you think?'

'Yes,' replied Father Brown. 'And what do you think about it?'

Devine looked at the little man in black, and something in the gaze of his great, grey eyes seemed to renew his impulse.

'I think,' he said, 'that Carver was very anxious to have the house to himself tonight. I don't know whether you had any such suspicions?'

'I may have my suspicions,' replied the priest, 'but I'm not sure whether they're the same as yours.'

That evening, when the last dusk was turning into dark in the gardens round the family mansion, Opal Bankes was moving through some of the dim and empty rooms with even more than her usual abstraction; and anyone who had looked at her closely would have noted that her pale face had more than its usual pallor. Despite its bourgeois luxury, the house as a whole had a rather unique shade of melancholy. It was the sort of immediate sadness that belongs to things that are old rather than ancient. It was full of faded fashions, rather than historic customs; of the order and ornament that is just recent enough to be recognised as dead. Here and there, Early Victorian coloured glass tinted the twilight; the high ceilings made the long rooms look narrow; and at the end of the long room down which she was walking was one of those round windows, to be found in the buildings of its period. As she came to about the middle of the room, she stopped, and then suddenly swayed a little, as if some invisible hand had struck her on the face.

An instant after there was the noise of knocking on the front door, dulled by the closed doors between. She knew that the rest of the household were in the upper parts of the house, but she could not have analysed the motive that made her go to the front door herself. On the doorstep stood a dumpy and dingy figure in black, which she recognised as the Roman Catholic priest, whose name was Brown. She knew him only slightly; but she liked him. He did not encourage her psychic views; quite the contrary; but he discouraged them as if they mattered and not as if they did not matter. It was not so much that he did not sympathise with her opinions, as that he did sympathise but did not agree. All this was in some sort of chaos in her mind as she found herself saying, without greeting, or waiting to hear his business: 'I'm so glad you've come. I've seen a ghost.'

'There's no need to be distressed about that,' he said. 'It often happens. Most of the ghosts aren't ghosts, and the few that may be won't do you any harm. Was it any ghost in particular?'

'No,' she admitted, with a vague feeling of relief, 'it wasn't so much the thing itself as an atmosphere of awful decay, a sort of luminous ruin. It was a face. A face at the window. But it was pale and goggling, and looked like the picture of Judas.'

'Well, some people do look like that,' reflected the priest, 'and I dare say they look in at windows, sometimes. May I come in and see where it happened?'

When she returned to the room with the visitor, however, other members of the family had assembled, and those of a less psychic habit had thought it convenient to light the lamps. In the presence of Mrs Bankes, Father Brown assumed a more conventional civility, and apologised for his intrusion.

'I'm afraid it is taking a liberty with your house, Mrs Bankes,' he said. 'But I think I can explain how the business happens to concern you. I was up at the Pulmans' place just now, when I was rung up and asked to come round here to meet a man who is coming to communicate something that may be of some moment to you. I should not have added myself to the party, only I am wanted, apparently, because I am a witness to what has happened up at Beechwood. In fact, it was I who had to give the alarm.'

'What has happened?' repeated the lady.

'There has been a robbery up at Beechwood House,' said Father Brown, gravely; 'a robbery, and what I fear is worse, Lady Pulman's jewels have gone; and her unfortunate secretary, Mr Barnard, was picked up in the garden, having evidently been shot by the escaping burglar.'

'That man,' ejaculated the lady of the house. 'I believe he was – '

She encountered the grave gaze of the priest, and her words suddenly went from her; she never knew why.

'I communicated with the police,' he went on, 'and with another authority interested in this case; and they say that even a superficial examination has revealed footprints and fingerprints and other indications of a well-known criminal.'

At this point, the conference was for a moment disturbed, by the return of John Bankes, from what appeared to be an abortive expedition in the car. Old Smith seemed to have been a disappointing passenger, after all.

'Funked it, after all, at the last minute,' he announced with noisy disgust. 'Bolted off while I was looking at what I thought was a puncture. Last time I'll take one of these yokels – '

But his complaints received small attention in the general excitement that gathered round Father Brown and his news.

'Somebody will arrive in a moment,' went on the priest, with the same air of weighty reserve, 'who will relieve me of this responsibility. When I have confronted you with him I shall have done my duty as a witness in a serious business. It only remains for me to say that a servant up at Beechwood House told me that she had seen a face at one of the windows – '

'I saw a face,' said Opal, 'at one of our windows.'

'Oh, you are always seeing faces,' said her brother John roughly.

'It is as well to see facts even if they are faces,' said Father Brown equably, 'and I think the face you saw – '

Another knock at the front door sounded through the house, and a minute afterwards the door of the room opened and another figure appeared. Devine half-rose from his chair at the sight of it.

It was a tall, erect figure, with a long, rather cadaverous face, ending in a formidable chin. The brow was rather bald, and the eyes bright and blue, which Devine had last seen obscured with a broad straw hat.

'Pray don't let anybody move,' said the man called Carver, in clear and courteous tones. But to Devine's disturbed mind the courtesy had an ominous resemblance to that of a brigand who holds a company motionless with a pistol.

'Please sit down, Mr Devine,' said Carver; 'and, with Mrs Bankes's permission, I will follow your example. My presence here necessitates an explanation. I rather fancy you suspected me of being an eminent and distinguished burglar.'

'I did,' said Devine grimly.

'As you remarked,' said Carver, 'it is not always easy to know a wasp from a bee.'

After a pause, he continued: 'I can claim to be one of the more useful, though equally annoying, insects. I am a detective, and I have come down to investigate an alleged renewal of the activities of the criminal calling himself Michael Moonshine. Jewel robberies were his speciality; and there has just been one of them at Beechwood House, which, by all the technical tests, is obviously his work. Not only do the prints correspond, but you may possibly know that when he was last arrested, and it is believed on other occasions also, he wore a simple but effective disguise of a red beard and a pair of large horn-rimmed spectacles.'

Opal Bankes leaned forward fiercely.

'That was it,' she cried in excitement, 'that was the face I saw, with great goggles and a red, ragged beard like Judas. I thought it was a ghost.'

'That was also the ghost the servant at Beechwood saw,' said Carver dryly.

He laid some papers and packages on the table, and began carefully to unfold them. 'As I say,' he continued, 'I was sent down here to make enquiries about the criminal plans of this man, Moonshine. That is why I interested myself in bee-keeping and went to stay with Mr Smith.'

There was a silence, and then Devine started and spoke: 'You don't seriously mean to say that nice old man – '

'Come, Mr Devine,' said Carver, with a smile, 'you believed a beehive was only a hiding-place for me. Why shouldn't it be a hiding-place for him?'

Devine nodded gloomily, and the detective turned back to his papers. 'Suspecting Smith, I wanted to get him out of the way and go through his belongings; so I took advantage of Mr Bankes's kindness in giving him a joy ride. Searching his house, I found some curious things to be owned by an innocent old rustic interested only in bees. This is one of them.'

From the unfolded paper he lifted a long, hairy object almost scarlet in colour – the sort of sham beard that is worn in theatricals.

Beside it lay an old pair of heavy horn-rimmed spectacles.

'But I also found something,' continued Carver, 'that more directly concerns this house, and must be my excuse for intruding tonight. I found a memorandum, with notes of the names and conjectural value of various pieces of jewellery in the neighbourhood. Immediately after the note of Lady Pulman's tiara was the mention of an emerald necklace belonging to Mrs Bankes.'

Mrs Bankes, who had hitherto regarded the invasion of her house with an air of supercilious bewilderment, suddenly grew attentive. Her face suddenly looked ten years older and much more intelligent. But before she could speak the impetuous John had risen to his full height like a trumpeting elephant.

'And the tiara's gone already,' he roared; 'and the necklace – I'm going to see about that necklace!'

'Not a bad idea,' said Carver, as the young man rushed from the room; 'though, of course, we've been keeping our eyes open since we've been here. Well, it took me a little time to make out the memorandum, which was in cipher, and Father Brown's telephone message from the House came as I was near the end. I asked him to run round here first with the news, and I would follow; and so – '

His speech was sundered by a scream. Opal was standing up and pointing rigidly at the round window.

'There it is again!' she cried.

For a moment they all saw something – something that cleared the lady of the charges of lying and hysteria not uncommonly brought against her. Thrust out of the slate-blue darkness without, the face was pale, or, perhaps, blanched by pressure against the glass; and the great, glaring eyes, encircled as with rings, gave it rather the look of a great fish out of the dark-blue sea nosing at the port-hole of a ship. But the gills or fins of the fish were a coppery red; they were, in truth, fierce red whiskers and the upper part of a red beard. The next moment it had vanished.

Devine had taken a single stride towards the window when a shout resounded through the house, a shout that seemed to shake it. It seemed almost too deafening to be distinguishable as words; yet it was enough to stop Devine in his stride, and he knew what had happened.

'Necklace gone!' shouted John Bankes, appearing huge and heaving in the doorway, and almost instantly vanishing again with the plunge of a pursuing hound.

'Thief was at the window just now!' cried the detective, who had already darted to the door, following the headlong John, who was already in the garden.

'Be careful,' wailed the lady, 'they have pistols and things.'

'So have I,' boomed the distant voice of the dauntless John out of the dark garden.

Devine had, indeed, noticed as the young man plunged past him that he was defiantly brandishing a revolver, and hoped there would be no need for him to so defend himself. But even as he had the thought, came the shock of two shots, as if one answered the other, and awakened a wild flock of echoes in that still suburban garden. They flapped into silence.

'Is John dead?' asked Opal in a low, shuddering voice.

Father Brown had already advanced deeper into the darkness, and stood with his back to them, looking down at something. It was he who answered her.

'No,' he said; 'it is the other.'

Carver had joined him, and for a moment the two figures, the tall and the short, blocked out what view the fitful and stormy moonlight would allow. Then they moved to one side and the others saw the small, wiry figure lying slightly twisted, as if with its last struggle. The false red beard was thrust upwards, as if scornfully at the sky, and the moon shone on the great sham spectacles of the man who had been called Moonshine.

'What an end,' muttered the detective, Carver. 'After all his adventures, to be shot almost by accident by a stockbroker in a suburban garden.'

The stockbroker himself naturally regarded his own triumph with more solemnity, though not without nervousness.

'I had to do it,' he gasped, still panting with exertion. 'I'm sorry, he fired at me.'

'There will have to be an inquest, of course,' said Carver, gravely. 'But I think there will be nothing for you to worry about. There's a revolver fallen from his hand with one shot discharged; and he certainly didn't fire after he'd got yours.'

By this time they had assembled again in the room, and the detective was getting his papers together for departure. Father Brown was standing opposite to him, looking down at the table, as if in a brown study. Then he spoke abruptly: 'Mr Carver, you have certainly worked out a very complete case in a very masterly way. I rather suspected your professional business; but I never guessed you would link everything up together so quickly – the bees and the beard and the spectacles and the cipher and the necklace and everything.'

'Always satisfactory to get a case really rounded off,' said Carver.

'Yes,' said Father Brown, still looking at the table. 'I admire it very much.' Then he added with a modesty verging on nervousness: 'It's only fair to you to say that I don't believe a word of it.'

Devine leaned forward with sudden interest. 'Do you mean you don't believe he is Moonshine, the burglar?'

'I know he is the burglar, but he didn't burgle,' answered Father Brown. 'I know he didn't come here, or to the great house, to steal jewels, or get shot getting away with them. Where are the jewels?'

'Where they generally are in such cases,' said Carver. 'He's either hidden them or passed them on to a confederate. This was not a one-man job. Of course, my people are searching the garden and warning the district.'

'Perhaps,' suggested Mrs Bankes, 'the confederate stole the necklace while Moonshine was looking in at the window.'

'Why was Moonshine looking in at the window?' asked Father Brown quietly. 'Why should he want to look in at the window?'

'Well, what do you think?' cried the cheery John.

'I think,' said Father Brown, 'that he never did want to look in at the window.'

'Then why did he do it?' demanded Carver. 'What's the good of talking in the air like that? We've seen the whole thing acted before our very eyes.'

'I've seen a good many things acted before my eyes that I didn't believe in,' replied the priest. 'So have you, on the stage and off.'

'Father Brown,' said Devine, with a certain respect in his tones, 'will you tell us why you can't believe your eyes?'

'Yes, I will try to tell you,' answered the priest. Then he said gently: 'You know what I am and what we are. We don't bother you much. We try to be friends with all our neighbours. But you can't think we do nothing. You can't think we know nothing. We mind our own business; but we know our own people. I knew this dead man very well indeed; I was his confessor, and his friend. So far as a man can, I knew his mind when he left that garden today; and his mind was like a glass hive full of golden bees. It's an understatement to say his reformation was sincere. He was one of those great penitents who manage to make more out of penitence than others can make out of virtue. I say I was his confessor; but, indeed, it was I who went to him for comfort. It did me good to be near so good a man. And when I saw him lying there dead in the garden, it seemed to me as if certain strange words that were said of old were spoken over him aloud in my ear. They might well be; for if ever a man went straight to heaven, it might be he.'

'Hang it all,' said John Bankes restlessly, 'after all, he was a convicted thief.'

'Yes,' said Father Brown; 'and only a convicted thief has ever in this world heard that assurance: "This night shalt thou be with Me in Paradise." '

Nobody seemed to know what to do with the silence that followed, until Devine said, abruptly, at last: 'Then how in the world would you explain it all?'

The priest shook his head. 'I can't explain it at all, just yet,' he said, simply. 'I can see one or two odd things, but I don't understand them. As yet I've nothing to go on to prove the man's innocence, except the man. But I'm quite sure I'm right.'

He sighed, and put out his hand for his big, black hat. As he removed it he remained gazing at the table with rather a new expression, his round, straight-haired head cocked at a new angle. It was rather as if some curious animal had come out of his hat, as out of the hat of a conjurer. But the others, looking at the table, could see nothing there but the detective's documents and the tawdry old property beard and spectacles.

'Lord bless us,' muttered Father Brown, 'and he's lying outside dead, in a beard and spectacles.' He swung round suddenly upon Devine. 'Here's something to follow up, if you want to know. *Why did he have two beards*?'

With that he bustled in his undignified way out of the room; but Devine was now devoured with curiosity, and pursued him into the front garden.

'I can't tell you now,' said Father Brown. 'I'm not sure, and I'm bothered about what to do. Come round and see me tomorrow, and I may be able to tell you the whole thing. It may already be settled for me, and – did you hear that noise?'

'A motor car starting,' remarked Devine.

'Mr John Bankes's motor car,' said the priest. 'I believe it goes very fast.'

'He certainly is of that opinion.' said Devine, with a smile.

'It will go far, as well as fast, tonight,' said Father Brown.

'And what do you mean by that?' demanded the other.

'I mean it will not return,' replied the priest. 'John Bankes suspected something of what I knew from what I said. John Bankes has gone and the emeralds and all the other jewels with him.'

Next day, Devine found Father Brown moving to and fro in front of the row of beehives, sadly, but with a certain serenity.

'I've been telling the bees,' he said. 'You know one has to tell the bees! "Those singing masons building roofs of gold." What a line!' Then more abruptly, 'He would like the bees looked after.'

'I hope he doesn't want the human beings neglected, when the whole swarm is buzzing with curiosity,' observed the young man. 'You were quite right when you said that Bankes was gone with the jewels; but I don't know how you knew, or even what there was to be known.'

Father Brown blinked benevolently at the beehives and said: 'One sort of stumbles on things, and there was one stumbling-block at the start. I was puzzled by poor Barnard being shot up at Beechwood House. Now, even when Michael was a master criminal, he made it a point of honour, even a point of vanity, to succeed without any killing. It seemed extraordinary that when he had become a sort of saint he should go out of his way to commit the sin he had despised when he was a sinner. The rest of the business puzzled me to the last; I could make nothing out of it, except that it wasn't true. Then I had a belated gleam of sense when I saw the beard and goggles and remembered the thief had come in another beard with other goggles. Now, of course, it was just possible that he had duplicates; but it was at least a coincidence that he used neither the old glasses nor the old beard, both in good repair. Again, it was just possible that he went out without them and had to procure new ones; but it was unlikely. There was nothing to make him go motoring with Bankes at all; if he was really going burgling, he could have taken his outfit easily in his pocket. Besides, beards don't grow on bushes. He would have found it hard to get such things anywhere in the time.

'No, the more I thought of it the more I felt there was something funny about his having a completely new outfit. And then the truth began to dawn on me by reason, which I knew already by instinct. He never did go out with Bankes with any intention of putting on the disguise. He never did put on the disguise. Somebody else manufactured the disguise at leisure, and then put it on him.'

'Put it on him!' repeated Devine. 'How the devil could they?'

'Let us go back,' said Father Brown, 'and look at the thing through another window – the window through which the young lady saw the ghost.'

'The ghost!' repeated the other, with a slight start.

'She called it the ghost,' said the little man, with composure, 'and perhaps she was not so far wrong. It's quite true that she is what they call psychic. Her only mistake is in thinking that being psychic is being spiritual. Some animals are psychic; anyhow, she is a sensitive, and she was right when she felt that the face at the window had a sort of horrible halo of deathly things.'

'You mean –' began Devine.

'I mean it was a dead man who looked in at the window,' said Father Brown. 'It was a dead man who crawled round more than one house, looking in at more than one window. Creepy, wasn't it? But in one way it was the reverse of a ghost; for it was not the antic of the soul freed from the body. It was the antic of the body freed from the soul.'

He blinked again at the beehive and continued: 'But, I suppose, the shortest explanation is to take it from the standpoint of the man who did it. You know the man who did it. John Bankes.'

'The very last man I should have thought of,' said Devine.

'The very first man I thought of,' said Father Brown; 'in so far as I had any right to think of anybody. My friend, there are no good or bad social types or trades. Any man can be a murderer like poor John; any man, even the same man, can be a saint like poor Michael. But if there is one type that tends at times to be more utterly godless than another, it is that rather brutal sort of business man. He has no social ideal, let alone religion; he has neither the gentleman's traditions nor the trade unionist's class loyalty. All his boasts about getting good bargains were practically boasts of having cheated people. His snubbing of his sister's poor little attempts at mysticism was detestable. Her mysticism was all nonsense; but he only hated spiritualism because it was spirituality. Anyhow, there's no doubt he was the villain of the piece; the only interest is in a rather original piece of villainy. It was really a new and unique motive for murder. It was the motive of using the corpse as a stage property – a sort of hideous doll or dummy. At the start he conceived a plan of killing Michael in the motor, merely to take him home and pretend to have killed him in the garden. But all sorts of fantastic finishing touches followed quite naturally from the primary fact; that he had at his disposal in a closed car at night the dead body of a recognised and recognisable burglar. He could leave his fingerprints and footprints; he could lean the familiar face against windows and take it away. You will notice that Moonshine ostensibly appeared and vanished while Bankes was ostensibly out of the room looking for the emerald necklace.

'Finally, he had only to tumble the corpse on to the lawn, fire a shot from each pistol, and there he was. It might never have been found out but for a guess about the two beards.'

'Why had your friend Michael kept the old beard?' Devine said thoughtfully. 'That seems to me questionable.'

'To me, who knew him, it seems quite inevitable,' replied Father Brown. 'His whole attitude was like that wig that he wore. There was no disguise about his disguises. He didn't want the old disguise any more, but he wasn't frightened of it; he would have felt it false to destroy the false beard. It would have been like hiding; and he was not hiding. He was not hiding from God; he was not hiding from himself. He was in the broad daylight. If they'd taken him back to prison, he'd still have been quite happy. He was not whitewashed, but washed white. There was something very strange about him; almost as strange as the grotesque dance of death through which he was dragged after he was dead. When he moved to and fro smiling among these beehives, even then, in a most radiant and shining sense, he was dead. He was out of the judgement of this world.'

There was a short pause, and then Devine shrugged his shoulders and said: 'It all comes back to bees and wasps looking very much alike in this world, doesn't it?'

The Song of the Flying Fish

The soul of Mr Peregrine Smart hovered like a fly round one possession and one joke. It might be considered a mild joke, for it consisted merely of asking people if they had seen his goldfish. It might also be considered an expensive joke; but it is doubtful whether he was not secretly more attached to the joke than to the evidence of expenditure. In talking to his neighbours in the little group of new houses that had grown up round the old village green, he lost no time in turning the conversation in the direction of his hobby. To Dr Burdock, a rising biologist with a resolute chin and hair brushed back like a German's, Mr Smart made the easy transition. 'You are interested in natural history; have you seen my goldfish?' To so orthodox an evolutionist as Dr Burdock doubtless all nature was one; but at first sight the link was not close, as he was a specialist who had concentrated entirely upon the primitive ancestry of the giraffe. To Father Brown, from a church in the neighbouring provincial town, he traced a rapid train of thought which touched on the topics of 'Rome – St Peter – fisherman – fish – goldfish'. In talking to Mr Imlack Smith, the bank manager, a slim and sallow gentleman of dressy appearance but quiet demeanour, he violently wrenched the conversation to the subject of the gold standard, from which it was merely a step to goldfish. In talking to that brilliant Oriental traveller and scholar, Count Yvon de Lara (whose title was French and his face rather Russian, not to say Tartar), the versatile conversationalist showed an intense and intelligent interest in the Ganges and the Indian Ocean, leading naturally to the possible presence of goldfish in those waters. From Mr Harry Hartopp, the very rich but very shy and silent young gentleman who had recently come down from London, he had at last extorted the information that the embarrassed youth in question was not interested in fishing, and had then added: 'Talking about fishing, have you seen my goldfish?'

The peculiar thing about the goldfish was that they were made of gold. They were part of an eccentric but expensive toy, said to have been made by the freak of some rich Eastern prince, and Mr Smart had picked it up at some sale or in some curiosity shop, such as he frequented for the purpose of lumbering up his house with unique and useless things. From the other end of the room it looked like a rather unusually large bowl containing rather unusually large living fish; a closer inspection showed it to be a huge bubble of beautifully blown Venetian glass, very thin and delicately clouded with faintly iridescent colour, in the tinted twilight of which hung grotesque golden fishes with great rubies for eyes. The whole thing was undoubtedly worth a great deal in solid material; how much more would depend upon the waves of lunacy passing over the world of collectors. Mr Smart's new secretary, a young man named Francis Boyle, though an Irishman and not credited with caution, was mildly surprised at his talking so freely of the gems of his collection to the group of comparative strangers who happened to have alighted in a rather nomadic fashion in the neighbourhood; for collectors are commonly vigilant and sometimes secretive. In the course of settling down to his new duties, Mr Boyle found he was not alone in this sentiment, and that in others, it passed from a mild wonder to a grave disapproval.

'It's a wonder his throat isn't cut,' said Mr Smart's valet, Harris, not without a hypothetical relish, almost as if he had said, in a purely artistic sense: 'It's a pity.'

'It's extraordinary how he leaves things about,' said Mr Smart's head clerk, Jameson, who had come up from the office to assist the new secretary, 'and he won't even put up those ramshackle old bars across his ramshackle old door.'

'It's all very well with Father Brown and the doctor,' said Mr Smart's housekeeper, with a certain vigorous vagueness that marked her opinions, 'but when it comes to foreigners, I call it tempting providence. It isn't only the Count, either; that man at the bank looks to me much too yellow to be English.'

'Well, that young Hartopp is English enough,' said Boyle good-humouredly, 'to the extent of not having a word to say for himself.'

'He thinks the more,' said the housekeeper. 'He may not be exactly a foreigner, but he is not such a fool as he looks. Foreign is as foreign does, I say,' she added darkly.

Her disapproval would probably have deepened if she had heard the conversation in her master's drawing-room that afternoon, a conversation of which the goldfish were the text, though the offensive foreigner tended more and more to be the central figure. It was not that he spoke so very much; but even his silences had something positive about them. He looked the more massive for sitting in a sort of heap on a heap of cushions, and in the deepening twilight his wide Mongolian face seemed faintly luminous, like a moon. Perhaps his background brought out something atmospherically Asiatic about his face and figure, for the room was a chaos of more or less costly curiosities, amid which could be seen the crooked curves and burning colours of countless Eastern weapons, Eastern pipes and vessels, Eastern musical instruments and illuminated manuscripts. Anyhow, as the conversation proceeded, Boyle felt more and more that the figure seated on the cushions and dark against the twilight had the exact outline of a huge image of Buddha.

The conversation was general enough, for all the little local group were present. They were, indeed, often in the habit of dropping in at each other's houses, and by this time constituted a sort of club, of people coming from the four or five houses standing round the green. Of these houses Peregrine Smart's was the oldest, largest, and most picturesque; it straggled down almost the whole of one side of the square, leaving only room for a small villa, inhabited by a retired colonel named Varney, who was reported to be an invalid, and certainly was never seen to go abroad. At right angles to these stood two or three shops that served the simpler needs of the hamlet, and at the corner the inn of the Blue Dragon, at which Mr Hartopp, the stranger from London, was staying. On the opposite side were three houses, one rented by the Count de Lara, one by Dr Burdock, and the third still standing empty. On the fourth side was the bank, with an adjoining house for the bank manager, and a line of fence enclosing some land that was let for building. It was thus a very self-contained group, and the comparative emptiness of the open ground for miles round it threw the members more and more on each other's society. That afternoon, one stranger had indeed broken into the magic circle: a hatchet-faced fellow with fierce tufts of eyebrows and moustache, and so shabbily dressed that he must have been a millionaire or a duke if he had really (as was alleged) come down to do business with the old collector. But he was known, at the Blue Dragon at least, as Mr Harmer.

To him had been recounted anew the glories of the gilded fish and the criticisms regarding their custody.

'People are always telling me I ought to lock them up more carefully,' observed Mr Smart, cocking an eyebrow over his shoulder at the dependant who stood there holding some papers from the office. Smart was a round-faced, round-bodied little old man rather like a bald parrot. 'Jameson and Harris and the rest are always at me to bar the doors as if it were a medieval fortress, though really these rotten old rusty bars are too medieval to keep anybody out, I should think. I prefer to trust to luck and the local police.'

'It is not always the best bars that keep people out,' said the Count. 'It all depends on who's trying to get in. There was an ancient Hindu hermit who lived naked in a cave and passed through the three armies that encircled the Mogul and took the great ruby out of the tyrant's turban, and went back unscathed like a shadow. For he wished to teach the great how small are the laws of space and time.'

'When we really study the small laws of space and time,' said Dr Burdock dryly, 'we generally find out how those tricks are done. Western science has let in daylight on a good deal of Eastern magic. Doubtless a great deal can be done with hypnotism and suggestion, to say nothing of sleight-of-hand.'

'The ruby was not in the royal tent,' observed the Count in his dream fashion; 'but he found it among a hundred tents.'

'Can't all that be explained by telepathy?' asked the doctor sharply. The question sounded the sharper because it was followed by a heavy silence, almost as if the distinguished Oriental traveller had, with imperfect politeness, gone to sleep.

'I beg your pardon,' he said rousing himself with a sudden smile. 'I had forgotten we were talking with words. In the east we talk with thoughts, and so we never misunderstand each other. It is strange how you people worship words and are satisfied with words. What difference does it make to a thing that you now call it telepathy, as you once called it tomfoolery? If a man climbs into the sky on a mango tree, how is it altered by saying it is only levitation, instead of saying it is only lies. If a medieval witch waved a wand and turned me into a blue baboon, you would say it was only atavism.'

The doctor looked for a moment as if he might say that it would not be so great a change after all. But before his irritation could find that or any other vent, the man called Harmer interrupted gruffly: 'It's true enough those Indian conjurers can do queer things, but I notice they generally do them in India. Confederates, perhaps, or merely mass psychology. I don't think those tricks have ever been played in an English village, and I should say our friend's goldfish were quite safe.'

'I will tell you a story,' said de Lara, in his motionless way, 'which happened not in India, but outside an English barrack in the most modernised part of Cairo. A sentinel was standing inside the grating of an iron gateway looking out between the bars on to the street. There appeared outside the gate a beggar, barefoot and in native rags, who asked him, in English that was startlingly distinct and refined, for a certain official document kept in the building for safety. The soldier told the man, of course, that he could not come inside; and the man answered, smiling: "What is inside and what is outside?" The soldier was still staring scornfully through the iron grating when he gradually realised that, though neither he nor the gate had moved, he was actually standing in the street and looking in at the barrack yard, where the beggar stood still and smiling and equally motionless. Then, when the beggar turned towards the building, the sentry awoke to such sense as he had left, and shouted a warning to all the soldiers within the gated enclosure to hold the prisoner fast. "You won't get out of there anyhow," he said vindictively. Then the beggar said in his silvery voice: "What is outside and what is inside?" And the soldier, still glaring through the same bars, saw that they were once more between him and the street, where the beggar stood free and smiling with a paper in his hand.'

Mr Imlack Smith, the bank manager, was looking at the carpet with his dark sleek head bowed, and he spoke for the first time.

'Did anything happen about the paper?' he asked.

'Your professional instincts are correct, sir,' said the Count with grim affability. 'It was a paper of considerable financial importance. Its consequences were international.'

'I hope they don't occur often,' said young Hartopp gloomily.

'I do not touch the political side,' said the Count serenely, 'but only the philosophical. It illustrates how the wise man can get behind time and space and turn the levers of them, so to speak, so that the whole world turns round before our eyes. But is it so hard for you people to believe that spiritual powers are really more powerful than material ones.'

'Well,' said old Smart cheerfully, 'I don't profess to be an authority on spiritual powers. What do you say, Father Brown?'

'The only thing that strikes me,' answered the little priest, 'is that all the supernatural acts we have yet heard of seem to be thefts. And stealing by spiritual methods seems to me much the same as stealing by material ones.'

'Father Brown is a Philistine,' said the smiling Smith.

'I have a sympathy with the tribe,' said Father Brown. 'A Philistine is only a man who is right without knowing why.'

'All this is too clever for me,' said Hartopp heartily.

'Perhaps,' said Father Brown with a smile, 'you would like to speak without words, as the Count suggests. He would begin by saying nothing in a pointed fashion, and you would retort with a burst of taciturnity.'

'Something might be done with music,' murmured the Count dreamily. 'It would be better than all these words.'

'Yes, I might understand that better,' said the young man in a low voice.

Boyle had followed the conversation with curious attention, for there was something in the demeanour of more than one of the talkers that seemed to him significant or even odd. As the talk drifted to music, with an appeal to the dapper bank manager (who was an amateur musician of some merit), the young secretary awoke with a start to his secretarial duties, and reminded his employer that the head clerk was still standing patiently with the papers in his hand.

'Oh, never mind about those just now, Jameson,' said Smart rather hurriedly. 'Only something about my account; I'll see Mr Smith about it later. You were saying that the 'cello, Mr Smith – '

But the cold breath of business had sufficed to disperse the fumes of transcendental talk, and the guests began one after another to say farewell. Only Mr Imlack Smith, bank manager and musician, remained to the last; and when the rest were gone he and his host went into the inner room, where the goldfish were kept, and closed the door.

The house was long and narrow, with a covered balcony running along the first floor, which consisted mostly of a sort of suite of rooms used by the householder himself, his bedroom and dressing-room, and an inner room in which his very valuable treasures were sometimes stored for the night instead of being left in the rooms below. This balcony, like the insufficiently barred door below it, was a matter of concern to the housekeeper and the head clerk and the others who lamented the carelessness of the collector; but, in truth, that cunning old gentleman was more careful than he seemed. He professed no great belief in the antiquated fastenings of the old house, which the housekeeper lamented to see rusting in idleness, but he had an eye to the more important point of strategy. He always put his favourite goldfish in the room at the back of his bedroom for the night, and slept in front of it, as it were, with a pistol under his pillow. And when Boyle and Jameson, awaiting his return from the tête-à-tête, at length saw the door open and their employer reappear, he was carrying the great glass bowl as reverently as if it had been the relic of a saint.

Outside, the last edges of the sunset still clung to the corners of the green square; but inside, a lamp had already been kindled; and in the mingling of the two lights the coloured globe glowed like some monstrous jewel, and the fantastic outlines of the fiery fishes seemed to give it, indeed, something of the mystery of a talisman, like strange shapes seen by a seer in the crystal of doom. Over the old man's shoulder the olive face of Imlack Smith stared like a sphinx.

'I am going up to London tonight, Mr Boyle,' said old Smart, with more gravity than he commonly showed. 'Mr Smith and I are catching the six-forty-five. I should prefer you, Jameson, to sleep upstairs in my room tonight; if you put the bowl in the back room as usual, it will be quite safe then. Not that I suppose anything could possibly happen.'

'Anything may happen anywhere,' said the smiling Mr Smith. 'I think you generally take a gun to bed with you. Perhaps you had better leave it behind in this case.'

Peregrine Smart did not reply, and they passed out of the house on to the road round the village green.

The secretary and the head clerk slept that night as directed in their employer's bedroom. To speak more strictly, Jameson, the head clerk, slept in a bed in the dressing-room, but the door stood open between, and the two rooms running along the front were practically one. Only the bedroom had a long french window giving on the balcony, and an entrance at the back into the inner apartment where the goldfish bowl had been placed for safety. Boyle dragged his bed right across so as to bar this entrance, put the revolver under his pillow, and then undressed and went to bed, feeling that he had taken all possible precautions against an impossible or improbable event. He did not see why there should be any particular danger of normal burglary; and as for the spiritual burglary that figured in the traveller's tales of the Count de Lara, if his thoughts ran on them so near to sleep it was because they were such stuff as dreams are made of. They soon turned into dreams with intervals of dreamless slumber. The old clerk was a little more restless as usual; but after fussing about a little longer and repeating some of his favourite regrets and warnings, he also retired to his bed in the same manner and slept. The moon brightened and grew dim again above the green square and the grey blocks of houses in a solitude and silence that seemed to have no human witness; and it was when the white cracks of daybreak had already appeared in the corners of the grey sky that the thing happened.

Boyle, being young, was naturally both the healthier and the heavier sleeper of the two. Though active enough when he was once awake, he always had a load to lift in waking. Moreover, he had dreams of the sort that cling to the emerging mind like the dim tentacles of an octopus. They were a medley of many things, including his last look from the balcony across the four grey roads and the green square. But the pattern of them changed and shifted and turned dizzily, to the accompaniment of a low grinding noise, which sounded somehow like a subterranean river, and may have been no more than old Mr Jameson snoring in the dressing-room. But in the dreamer's mind all that murmur and motion was vaguely connected with the words of the Count de Lara, about a wisdom that could hold the levers of time and space and turn the world. In the dream it seemed as if a vast murmuring machinery under the world were really moving whole landscapes hither and thither, so that the ends of the earth might appear in a man's front garden, or his own front garden be exiled beyond the sea.

The first complete impressions he had were the words of a song, with a rather thin metallic accompaniment; they were sung in a foreign accent and a voice that was still strange and yet faintly familiar. And yet he could hardly feel sure that he was not making up poetry in his sleep.

> Over the land and over the sea
> My flying fishes will come to me,
> For the note is not of the world that wakes them,
> But in –

He struggled to his feet and saw that his fellow-guardian was already out of bed; Jameson was peering out of the long window on to the balcony and calling out sharply to someone in the street below.

'Who's that?' he called out sharply. 'What do you want?'

He turned to Boyle in agitation, saying: 'There's somebody prowling about just outside. I knew it wasn't safe. I'm going down to bar that front door, whatever they say.'

He ran downstairs in a flutter and Boyle could hear the clattering of the bars upon the front door; but Boyle himself stepped out upon the balcony and looked out on the long grey road that led up to the house, and he thought he was still dreaming.

Upon that grey road leading across that empty moor and through that little English hamlet, there had appeared a figure that might have stepped straight out of the jungle or the bazaar – a figure out of one of the Count's fantastic stories; a figure out of the *Arabian Nights*. The rather ghostly grey twilight which begins to define and yet to discolour everything when the light in the east has ceased to be localised, lifted slowly like a veil of grey gauze and showed him a figure wrapped in outlandish raiment. A scarf of a strange sea-blue, vast and voluminous, went round the head like a turban, and then again round the chin, giving rather the general character of a hood; so far as the face was concerned it had all the effects of a mask. For the raiment round the head was drawn close as a veil; and the head itself was bowed over a queer-looking musical instrument made of silver or steel, and shaped like a deformed or crooked violin. It was played with something like a silver comb, and the notes were curiously thin and keen. Before Boyle could open his mouth, the same haunting alien accent came from under the shadow of the burnous, singing words of the same sort:

As the golden birds go back to the tree
My golden fishes return to me.
Return –

'You've no right here,' called out Boyle in exasperation, hardly knowing what he said.

'I have a right to the goldfish,' said the stranger, speaking more like King Solomon than an unsandalled Bedouin in a ragged blue cloak. 'And they will come to me. Come!'

He struck his strange fiddle as his voice rose sharply on the word. There was a pang of sound that seemed to pierce the mind, and then there came a fainter sound, like an answer: a vibrant whisper. It came from the dark room behind where the bowl of goldfish was standing.

Boyle turned towards it; and even as he turned the echo in the inner room changed to a long tingling sound like an electric bell, and then to a faint crash. It was still a matter of seconds since he had challenged the man from the balcony; but the old clerk had already regained the top of the stairs, panting a little, for he was an elderly gentleman.

'I've locked up the door, anyhow,' he said.

'The stable door,' said Boyle out of the darkness of the inner room.

Jameson followed him into that apartment and found him staring down at the floor, which was covered with a litter of coloured glass like the curved bits of a broken rainbow.

'What do you mean by the stable door?' began Jameson.

'I mean that the steed is stolen,' answered Boyle. 'The flying steeds. The flying fishes our Arab friend outside has just whistled to like so many performing puppies.'

'But how could he?' exploded the old clerk, as if such events were hardly respectable.

'Well, they're gone,' said Boyle shortly. 'The broken bowl is here, which would have taken a long time to open properly, but only a second to smash. But the fish are gone, God knows how, though I think our friend ought to be asked.'

'We are wasting time,' said the distracted Jameson. 'We ought to be after him at once.'

'Much better be telephoning the police at once,' answered Boyle. 'They ought to outstrip him in a flash with motors and telephones that go a good deal farther than we should ever get, running through the village in our nightgowns. But it may be there are things even the police cars and wires won't outstrip.'

While Jameson was talking to the police-station through the telephone in an agitated voice, Boyle went out again on to the balcony and hastily scanned that grey landscape of daybreak. There was no trace of the man in the turban, and no other sign of life, except some faint stirrings an expert might have recognised in the hotel of the Blue Dragon. Only Boyle, for the first time, noted consciously something that he had all along been noting unconsciously. It was like a fact struggling in the submerged mind and demanding its own meaning. It was simply the fact that the grey landscape had never been entirely grey; there was one gold spot amid its stripes of colourless colour, a lamp lighted in one of the houses on the other side of the green. Something, perhaps irrational, told him that it had been burning through all the hours of the darkness and was only fading with the dawn. He counted the houses, and his calculation brought out a result which seemed to fit in with something, he knew not what. Anyhow, it was apparently the house of the Count Yvon de Lara.

Inspector Pinner had arrived with several policemen, and done several things of a rapid and resolute sort, being conscious that the very absurdity of the costly trinkets might give the case considerable prominence in the newspapers. He had examined everything, measured everything, taken down everybody's deposition, taken everybody's fingerprints, put everybody's back up, and found himself at the end left facing a fact which he could not believe. An Arab from the desert had walked up the public road and stopped in front of the house of Mr Peregrine Smart, where a bowl of artificial goldfish was kept in an inner room; he had then sung or recited a little poem, and the bowl had exploded like a bomb and the fishes vanished into thin air. Nor did it soothe the inspector to be told by a foreign Count – in a soft, purring voice – that the bounds of experience were being enlarged.

Indeed, the attitude of each member of the little group was characteristic enough. Peregrine Smart himself had come back from London the next morning to hear the news of his loss. Naturally he admitted a shock; but it was typical of something sporting and spirited in the little old gentleman, something that always made his small strutting figure look like a cock-sparrow's, that he showed more vivacity in the search than depression at the loss. The man named Harmer, who had come to the village on purpose to buy the goldfish, might be excused for being a little testy on learning they were not there to be bought. But, in truth, his rather aggressive moustache and eyebrows seemed to bristle with something more definite than disappointment, and the eyes that darted over the company were bright with a vigilance that might well be suspicion. The sallow face of the bank manager, who had also returned from London though by a later train, seemed again and again to attract those shining and shifting eyes like a magnet. Of the two remaining figures of the original circle, Father Brown was generally silent when he was not spoken to, and the dazed Hartopp was often silent even when he was.

But the Count was not a man to let anything pass that gave an apparent advantage to his views. He smiled at his rationalistic rival, the doctor, in the manner of one who knows how it is possible to be irritating by being ingratiating.

'You will admit, doctor,' he said, 'that at least some of the stories you thought so improbable look a little more realistic today than they did yesterday. When a man as ragged as those I described is able, by speaking a word, to dissolve a solid vessel inside the four walls of the house he stands outside, it might perhaps be called an example of what I said about spiritual powers and material barriers.'

'And it might be called an example of what I said,' said the doctor sharply, 'about a little scientific knowledge being enough to show how the tricks are done.'

'Do you really mean, doctor,' asked Smart in some excitement, 'that you can throw any scientific light on this mystery?'

'I can throw light on what the Count calls a mystery,' said the doctor, 'because it is not a mystery at all. That part of it is plain enough. A sound is only a wave of vibration, and certain vibrations can break glass, if the sound is of a certain kind and the glass of a certain kind. The man did not stand in the road and think, which the Count tells us is the ideal method when Orientals want a little chat. He sang out what he wanted, quite loud, and struck a shrill note on an instrument. It is similar to many experiments by which glass of special composition has been cracked.'

'Such as the experiment,' said the Count lightly, 'by which several lumps of solid gold have suddenly ceased to exist.'

'Here comes Inspector Pinner,' said Boyle. 'Between ourselves, I think he would regard the doctor's natural explanation as quite as much of a fairy tale as the Count's preternatural one. A very sceptical intellect, Mr Pinner's, especially about me. I rather think I am under suspicion.'

'I think we are all under suspicion,' said the Count.

It was the presence of this suspicion in his own case that led Boyle to seek the personal advice of Father Brown. They were walking round the village green together, some hours later in the day, when the priest, who was frowning thoughtfully at the ground as he listened, suddenly stopped.

'Do you see that?' he asked. 'Somebody's been washing the pavement here – just this little strip of pavement outside Colonel Varney's house. I wonder whether that was done yesterday.'

Father Brown looked rather earnestly at the house, which was high and narrow, and carried rows of striped sun-blinds of gay but already faded colours. The chinks or crannies that gave glimpses of the interior looked all the darker; indeed, they looked almost black in contrast with the façade thus golden in the morning light.

'That is Colonel Varney's house, isn't it?' he asked. 'He comes from the East, too, I fancy. What sort of man is he?'

'I've never even seen him,' answered Boyle. 'I don't think anybody's seen him, except Dr Burdock, and I rather fancy the doctor doesn't see him more than he need.'

'Well, I'm going to see him for a minute,' said Father Brown.

The big front door opened and swallowed the small priest, and his friend stood staring at it in a dazed and irrational manner, as if wondering whether it would ever open again. It opened in a few minutes, and Father Brown emerged, still smiling, and continued his slow and pottering progress round the square of roads. Sometimes he seemed to have forgotten the matter in hand altogether, for he would make passing remarks on historical and social questions, or on the prospects of development in the district. He remarked on the soil used for the beginning of a new road by the bank; he looked across the old village green with a vague expression.

'Common land. I suppose people ought to feed their pigs and geese on it, if they had any pigs or geese; as it is, it seems to feed nothing but nettles and thistles. What a pity that what was supposed to be a sort of large meadow has been turned into a small and petty wilderness. That's Dr Burdock's house opposite, isn't it?'

'Yes,' answered Boyle, almost jumping at this abrupt postscript.

'Very well,' answered Father Brown, 'then I think we'll go indoors again.'

As they opened the front door of Smart's house and mounted the stairs, Boyle repeated to his companion many details of the drama enacted there at daybreak.

'I suppose you didn't doze off again?' asked Father Brown, 'giving time for somebody to scale the balcony while Jameson ran down to secure the door.'

'No,' answered Boyle; 'I am sure of that. I woke up to hear Jameson challenging the stranger from the balcony; then I heard him running downstairs and putting up the bars, and then in two strides I was on the balcony myself.'

'Or could he have slipped in between you from another angle? Are there any other entrances besides the front entrance?'

'Apparently there are not,' said Boyle gravely.

'I had better make sure, don't you think?' asked Father Brown apologetically, and scuttled softly downstairs again. Boyle remained in the front bedroom gazing rather doubtfully after him. After a comparatively brief interval the round and rather rustic visage appeared again at the head of the stairs, looking rather like a turnip ghost with a broad grin.

'No; I think that settles the matter of entrances,' said the turnip ghost, cheerfully. 'And now, I think, having got everything in a tight box, so to speak, we can take stock of what we've got. It's rather a curious business.'

'Do you think,' asked Boyle, 'that the Count or the colonel, or any of these Eastern travellers have anything to do with it? Do you think it is – preternatural?'

'I will grant you this,' said the priest gravely, 'if the Count, or the colonel, or any of your neighbours did dress up in Arab masquerade and creep up to this house in the dark – then it was preternatural.'

'What do you mean? Why?'

'Because the Arab left no footprints,' answered Father Brown. 'The colonel on the one side and the banker on the other are the nearest of your neighbours. That loose red soil is between you and the bank, it would print off bare feet like a plaster cast and probably leave red marks everywhere. I braved the colonel's curry-seasoned temper to verify the fact that the front pavement was washed yesterday and not today; it was wet enough to make wet footprints all along the road. Now, if the visitor were the Count or the doctor in the houses opposite, he might possibly, of course, have come across the common. But he must have found it exceedingly uncomfortable with bare feet, for it is, as I remarked, one mass of thorns and thistles and stinging nettles. He would surely have pricked himself and probably left traces of it. Unless, as you say, he was a preternatural being.'

Boyle looked steadily at the grave and indecipherable face of his clerical friend.

'Do you mean that he was?' he asked, at length.

'There is one general truth to remember,' said Father Brown, after a pause. 'A thing can sometimes be too close to be seen, as, for instance, a man cannot see himself. There was a man who had a fly in his eye when he looked through the telescope, and he discovered that there was a most incredible dragon in the moon. And I am told that if a man hears the exact reproduction of his own voice it sounds like the voice of a stranger. In the same way, if anything is right in the foreground of our life we hardly see it, and if we did we might think it quite odd. If the thing in the foreground got into the middle distance, we should probably think it had come from the remote distance. Just come outside the house again for a moment. I want to show you how it looks from another standpoint.'

He had already risen, and as they descended the stairs he continued his remarks in a rather groping fashion as if he were thinking aloud.

'The Count and the Asiatic atmosphere all come in, because, in a case like this, everything depends on the preparation of the mind. A man can reach a condition in which a brick, falling on his head, will seem to be a Babylonian brick carved with cuneiform, and dropped from the Hanging Gardens of Babylon, so that he will never even look at the brick and see it is of one pattern with the bricks or his own house. So in your case – '

'What does this mean?' interrupted Boyle, staring and pointing at the entrance. 'What in the name of wonder does it mean? The door is barred again.'

He was staring at the front door by which they had entered but a little while before, and across which stood, once more, the great dark bands of rusty iron which had once, as he had said, locked the stable door too late. There was something darkly and dumbly ironic in those old fastenings closing behind them and imprisoning them as if of their own motion.

'Oh those!' said Father Brown casually. 'I put up those bars myself, just now. Didn't you hear me?'

'No,' answered Boyle, staring. 'I heard nothing.'

'Well, I rather thought you wouldn't,' said the other equably. 'There's really no reason why anybody upstairs should hear those bars being put up. A sort of hook fits easily into a sort of hole. When you're quite close you hear a dull click; but that's all. The only thing that makes any noise a man could hear upstairs, is this.'

And he lifted the bar out of its socket and let it fall with a clang at the side of the door.

'It does make a noise if you *unbar* the door,' said Father Brown gravely, 'even if you do it pretty carefully.'

'You mean – '

'I mean,' said Father Brown, 'that what you heard upstairs was Jameson opening the door and not shutting it. And now let's open the door ourselves and go outside.'

When they stood outside in the street, under the balcony, the little priest resumed his previous explanation as coolly as if it had been a chemical lecture.

'I was saying that a man may be in the mood to look for something very distant, and not realise that it is something very close, something very close to himself, perhaps something very like himself. It was a strange and outlandish thing that you saw when you looked down at this road. I suppose it never occurred to you to consider what he saw when he looked up at that balcony?'

Boyle was staring at the balcony and did not answer, and the other added: 'You thought it very wild and wonderful that an Arab should come through civilised England with bare feet. You did not remember that at the same moment you had bare feet yourself.'

Boyle at last found words, and it was to repeat words already spoken.

'Jameson opened the door,' he said mechanically.

'Yes,' assented his friend. 'Jameson opened the door and came out into the road in his nightclothes, just as you came out on the balcony. He caught up two things that you had seen a hundred times: the length of old blue curtain that he wrapped round his head, and the Oriental musical instrument you must have often seen in that heap of Oriental curiosities. The rest was atmosphere and acting, very fine acting, for he is a very fine artist in crime.'

'Jameson!' exclaimed Boyle incredulously. 'He was such a dull old stick that I never even noticed him.'

'Precisely,' said the priest, 'he was an artist. If he could act a wizard or a troubadour for six minutes, do you think he could not act a clerk for six weeks?'

'I am still not quite sure of his object,' said Boyle.

'His object has been achieved,' replied Father Brown, 'or very nearly achieved. He had taken the goldfish already, of course, as he had twenty chances of doing. But if he had simply taken them, everybody would have realised that he had twenty chances of doing it. By creating a mysterious magician from the end of the earth, he set everybody's thoughts wandering far afield to Arabia and India, so that you yourself can hardly believe that the whole thing was so near home. It was too close to you to be seen.'

'If this is true,' said Boyle, 'it was an extraordinary risk to run, and he had to cut it very fine. It's true I never heard the man in the street say anything while Jameson was talking from the balcony, so I suppose that was all a fake. And I suppose it's true that there was time for him to get outside before I had fully woken up and got out on to the balcony.'

'Every crime depends on somebody not waking up too soon,' replied Father Brown; 'and in every sense most of us wake up too late. I, for one, have woken up much too late. For I imagine he's bolted long ago, just before or just after they took his fingerprints.'

'You woke up before anybody else, anyhow,' said Boyle, 'and I should never have woken up in that sense. Jameson was so correct and colourless that I forgot all about him.'

'Beware of the man you forget,' replied his friend; 'he is the one man who has you entirely at a disadvantage. But I did not suspect him, either, until you told me how you had heard him barring the door.'

'Anyhow, we owe it all to you,' said Boyle warmly.

'You owe it all to Mrs Robinson,' said Father Brown with a smile.

'Mrs Robinson?' questioned the wondering secretary. 'You don't mean the housekeeper?'

'Beware of the woman you forget, and even more,' answered the other. 'This man was a very high-class criminal; he had been an excellent actor, and therefore he was a good psychologist. A man like the Count never hears any voice but his own; but this man could listen, when you had all forgotten he was there, and gather exactly the right materials for his romance and know exactly the right note to strike to lead you all astray. But he made one bad mistake in the psychology of Mrs Robinson, the housekeeper.'

'I don't understand,' answered Boyle, 'what she can have to do with it.'

'Jameson did not expect the doors to be barred,' said Father Brown. 'He knew that a lot of men, especially careless men like you and your employer, could go on saying for days that something ought to be done, or might as well be done. But if you convey to a woman that something ought to be done, there is always a dreadful danger that she will suddenly do it.'

The Actor and the Alibi

Mr Mundon Mandeville, the theatrical manager, walked briskly through the passages behind the scenes, or rather below the scenes. His attire was smart and festive, perhaps a little too festive; the flower in his buttonhole was festive; the very varnish on his boots was festive; but his face was not at all festive. He was a big, bull-necked, black-browed man, and at the moment his brow was blacker than usual. He had in any case, of course, the hundred botherations that besiege a man in such a position; and they ranged from large to small and from new to old. It annoyed him to pass through the passages where the old pantomime scenery was stacked; because he had successfully begun, his career at that theatre with very popular pantomimes, and had since been induced to gamble in more serious and classical drama over which he had dropped a good deal of money. Hence, to see the sapphire Gates of Bluebeard's Blue Palace, or portions of the Enchanted Grove of Golden Orange Trees, leaning up against the wall to be festooned with cobwebs or nibbled by mice, did not give him that soothing sense of a return to simplicity which we all ought to have when given a glimpse of that wonderland of our childhood. Nor had he any time to drop a tear where he had dropped the money, or to dream of this Paradise of Peter Pan; for he had been summoned hurriedly to settle a practical problem, not of the past but of the moment. It was the sort of thing that does sometimes happen in that strange world behind the scenes; but it was big enough to be serious. Miss Maroni, the talented young actress of Italian parentage, who had undertaken to act an important part in the play that was to be rehearsed that afternoon and performed that evening, had abruptly and even violently refused at the last moment to do anything of the kind. He had not even seen the exasperating lady yet; and as she had locked herself up in her dressing-room and defied the world through the door, it seemed unlikely, for the present, that he would. Mr Mundon Mandeville was sufficiently British to explain it by murmuring that all foreigners were mad; but the thought of his good fortune in inhabiting the only sane island of the planet did not suffice to soothe him any more than the memory of the Enchanted Grove. All these things, and many more, were annoying; and yet a very intimate observer might have suspected that something was wrong with Mr Mandeville that went beyond annoyance.

If it be possible for a heavy and healthy man to look haggard, he looked haggard. His face was full, but his eye-sockets were hollow; his mouth twitched as if it were always trying to bite the black strip of moustache that was just too short to be bitten. He might have been a man who had begun to take drugs; but even on that assumption there was something that suggested that he had a reason for doing it; that the drug was not the cause of the tragedy, but the tragedy the cause of the drug. Whatever was his deeper secret, it seemed to inhabit that dark end of the long passage where was the entrance to his own little study; and as he went along the empty corridor, he threw back a nervous glance now and then.

However, business is business; and he made his way to the opposite end of the passage where the blank green door of Miss Maroni defied the world. A group of actors and other people involved were already standing in front of it, conferring and considering, one might almost fancy, the advisability of a battering-ram. The group contained one figure, at least, who was already well enough known; whose photograph was on many mantelpieces and his autograph in many albums. For though Norman Knight was playing the hero in a theatre that was still a little provincial and old-fashioned and capable of calling him the first walking gentleman, he, at least, was certainly on the way to wider triumphs. He was a good-looking man with a long cleft chin and fair hair low on his forehead, giving him a rather Neronian look that did not altogether correspond to his impulsive and plunging movements. The group also contained Ralph Randall, who generally acted elderly character parts, and had a humorous hatchet face, blue with shaving, and discoloured with grease paint. It contained Mandeville's second walking gentleman, carrying on the not yet wholly vanished tradition of Charles's Friend, a dark, curly-haired youth of somewhat Semitic profile bearing the name of Aubrey Vernon.

It included Mr Mundon Mandeville's wife's maid or dresser, a very powerful-looking person with tight red hair and a hard wooden face. It also, incidentally, included Mandeville's wife, a quiet woman in the background, with a pale, patient face, the lines of which had not lost a classical symmetry and severity, but which looked all the paler because her very eyes were pale, and her pale yellow hair lay in two plain bands like some very archaic Madonna. Not everybody knew that she had once been a serious and successful actress in Ibsen and the intellectual drama. But her husband did not think much of problem plays; and certainly at the moment was more interested in the problem of getting a foreign actress out of a locked room; a new version of the conjuring trick of the Vanishing Lady.

'Hasn't she come out yet?' he demanded, speaking to his wife's businesslike attendant rather than to his wife.

'No, sir,' answered the woman – who was known as Mrs Sands – in a sombre manner.

'We are beginning to get a little alarmed,' said old Randall. 'She seemed quite unbalanced, and we're afraid she might even do herself some mischief.'

'Hell!' said Mandeville in his simple and artless way. 'Advertisement's very good, but we don't want that sort of advertisement. Hasn't she any friends here? Has nobody any influence with her?'

'Jarvis thinks the only man who might manage her is her own priest round the corner,' said Randall; 'and in case she does start hanging herself on a hat peg, I really thought perhaps he'd better be here. Jarvis has gone to fetch him – and, as a matter of fact, here he comes.'

Two more figures appeared in that subterranean passage under the stage: the first was Ashton Jarvis, a jolly fellow who generally acted villains, but who had surrendered that high vocation for the moment to the curly-headed youth with the nose. The other figure was short and square and clad all in black; it was Father Brown from the church round the corner.

Father Brown seemed to take it quite naturally and even casually, that he should be called in to consider the queer conduct of one of his flock, whether she was to be regarded as a black sheep or only as a lost lamb. But he did not seem to think much of the suggestion of suicide.

'I suppose there was some reason for her flying off the handle like that,' he said. 'Does anybody know what it was?'

'Dissatisfied with her part, I believe,' said the older actor.

'They always are,' growled Mr Mundon Mandeville. 'And I thought my wife would look after those arrangements.'

'I can only say,' said Mrs Mundon Mandeville rather wearily, 'that I gave her what ought to be the best part. It's supposed to be what stage-struck young women want, isn't it – to act the beautiful young heroine and marry the beautiful young hero in a shower of bouquets and cheers from the gallery? Women of my age naturally have to fall back on acting respectable matrons, and I was careful to confine myself to that.'

'It would be devilish awkward to alter the parts now, anyhow,' said Randall.

'It's not to be thought of,' declared Norman Knight firmly. 'Why, I could hardly act – but anyhow it's much too late.'

Father Brown had slipped forward and was standing outside the locked door listening.

'Is there no sound?' asked the manager anxiously; and then added in a lower voice: 'Do you think she can have done herself in?'

'There is a certain sound,' replied Father Brown calmly. 'I should be inclined to deduce from the sound that she is engaged in breaking windows or looking-glasses, probably with her feet. No; I do not think there is much danger of her going on to destroy herself. Breaking looking-glasses with your feet is a very unusual prelude to suicide. If she had been a German, gone away to think quietly about metaphysics and *weltschmerz*, I should be all for breaking the door down. These Italians don't really die so easily; and are not liable to kill themselves in a rage. Somebody else, perhaps – yes, possibly – it might be well to take ordinary precautions if she comes out with a leap.'

'So you're not in favour of forcing the door?' asked Mandeville.

'Not if you want her to act in your play,' replied Father Brown. 'If you do that, she'll raise the roof and refuse to stay in the place; if you leave her alone she'll probably come out from mere curiosity. If I were you, I should just leave somebody to guard the door, more or less, and trust to time for an hour or two.'

'In that case,' said Mandeville, 'we can only get on with rehearsing the scenes where she doesn't appear. My wife will arrange all that is necessary for scenery just now. After all, the fourth act is the main business. You had better get on with that.'

'Not a dress rehearsal,' said Mandeville's wife to the others.

'Very well,' said Knight, 'not a dress rehearsal, of course. I wish the dresses of the infernal period weren't so elaborate.'

'What is the play?' asked the priest with a touch of curiosity.

'*The School for Scandal*,' said Mandeville. 'It may be literature, but I want plays. My wife likes what she calls classical comedies. A long sight more classic than comic.'

At this moment, the old doorkeeper known as Sam, and the solitary inhabitant of the theatre during off-hours, came waddling up to the manager with a card, to say that Lady Miriam Marden wished to see him. He turned away, but Father Brown continued to blink steadily for a few seconds in the direction of the manager's wife, and saw that her wan face wore a faint smile; not altogether a cheerful smile.

Father Brown moved off in company with the man who had brought him in, who happened, indeed, to be a friend and person of a similar persuasion, which is not uncommon among actors. As he moved off, however, he heard Mrs Mandeville give quiet directions to Mrs Sands that she should take up the post of watcher beside the closed door.

'Mrs Mandeville seems to be an intelligent woman,' said the priest to his companion, 'though she keeps so much in the background.'

'She was once a highly intellectual woman,' said Jarvis sadly; 'rather washed-out and wasted, some would say, by marrying a bounder like Mandeville. She has the very highest ideals of the drama, you know; but, of course, it isn't often she can get her lord and master to look at anything in that light. Do you know, he actually wanted a woman like that to act as a pantomime boy? Admitted that she was a fine actress, but said pantomimes paid better. That will give you about a measure of his psychological insight and sensibility. But she never complained. As she said to me once: "Complaint always comes back in an echo from the ends of the world; but silence strengthens us." If only she were married to somebody who understood her ideas she might have been one of the great actresses of the age; indeed, the highbrow critics still think a lot of her. As it is, she is married to that.'

And he pointed to where the big black bulk of Mandeville stood with his back to them, talking to the ladies who had summoned him forth into the vestibule. Lady Miriam was a very long and languid and elegant lady, handsome in a recent fashion largely modelled on Egyptian mummies; her dark hair cut low and square, like a sort of helmet, and her lips very painted and prominent and giving her a permanent expression of contempt. Her companion was a very vivacious lady with an ugly attractive face and hair powdered with grey. She was a Miss Theresa Talbot and she talked a great deal, while her companion seemed too tired to talk at all. Only, just as the two men passed, Lady Miriam summoned up the energy to say: 'Plays are a bore; but I've never seen a rehearsal in ordinary clothes. Might be a bit funny. Somehow, nowadays, one can never find a thing one's never seen.'

'Now, Mr Mandeville,' said Miss Talbot, tapping him on the arm with animated persistence, 'you simply must let us see that rehearsal. We can't come tonight, and we don't want to. We want to see all the funny people in the wrong clothes.'

'Of course I can give you a box if you wish it,' said Mandeville hastily. 'Perhaps your ladyship would come this way.' And he led them off down another corridor.

'I wonder,' said Jarvis in a meditative manner, 'whether even Mandeville prefers that sort of woman.'

'Well,' asked his clerical companion, 'have you any reason to suppose that Mandeville does prefer her?'

Jarvis looked at him steadily for an instant before answering.

'Mandeville is a mystery,' he said gravely. 'Oh, yes, I know that he looks about as commonplace a cad as ever walked down Piccadilly. But he really is a mystery for all that. There's something on his conscience. There's a shadow in his life. And I doubt whether it has anything more to do with a few fashionable flirtations than it has with his poor neglected wife. If it has, there's something more in them than meets the eye. As a matter of fact, I happen to know rather more about it than anyone else does, merely by accident. But even I can't make anything of what I know, except a mystery.'

He looked around him in the vestibule to see that they were alone and then added, lowering his voice: 'I don't mind telling you, because I know you are a tower of silence where secrets are concerned. But I had a curious shock the other day; and it has been repeated several times since. You know that Mandeville always works in that little room at the end of the passage, just under the stage. Well, twice over I happened to pass by there when everyone thought he was alone; and what's more, when I myself happened to be able to account for all the women in the company, and all the women likely to have to do with him, being absent or at their usual posts.'

'All the women?' remarked Father Brown enquiringly.

'There was a woman with him,' said Jarvis almost in a whisper. 'There is some woman who is always visiting him; somebody that none of us knows. I don't even know how she comes there, since it isn't down the passage to the door; but I think I once saw a veiled or cloaked figure passing out into the twilight at the back of the theatre, like a ghost. But she can't be a ghost. And I don't believe she's even an ordinary "affair". I don't think it's love-making. I think it's blackmail.'

'What makes you think that?' asked the other.

'Because,' said Jarvis, his face turning from grave to grim, 'I once heard sounds like a quarrel; and then the strange woman said in a metallic, menacing voice, four words: "I am your wife." '

'You think he's a bigamist,' said Father Brown reflectively. 'Well, bigamy and blackmail often go together, of course. But she may be bluffing as well as blackmailing. She may be mad. These theatrical people often have monomaniacs running after them. You may be right, but I shouldn't jump to conclusions . . . And talking about theatrical people, isn't the rehearsal going to begin, and aren't you a theatrical person?'

'I'm not on in this scene,' said Jarvis with a smile. 'They're only doing one act, you know, until your Italian friend comes to her senses.'

'Talking about my Italian friend,' observed the priest, 'I should rather like to know whether she has come to her senses.'

'We can go back and see, if you like,' said Jarvis; and they descended again to the basement and the long passage, at one end of which was Mandeville's study and at the other the closed door of Signora Maroni. The door seemed to be still closed; and Mrs Sands sat grimly outside it, as motionless as a wooden idol.

Near the other end of the passage they caught a glimpse of some of the other actors in the scene mounting the stairs to the stage just above. Vernon and old Randall went ahead, running rapidly up the stairs; but Mrs Mandeville went more slowly, in her quietly dignified fashion, and Norman Knight seemed to linger a little to speak to her. A few words fell on the ears of the unintentional eavesdroppers as they passed.

'I tell you a woman visits him,' Knight was saying violently.

'Hush!' said the lady in her voice of silver that still had in it something of steel. 'You must not talk like this. Remember, he is my husband.'

'I wish to God I could forget it,' said Knight, and rushed up the stairs to the stage.

The lady followed him, still pale and calm, to take up her own position there.

'Somebody else knows it,' said the priest quietly; 'but I doubt whether it is any business of ours.'

'Yes,' muttered Jarvis; 'it seems as if everybody knows it and nobody knows anything about it.'

They proceeded along the passage to the other end, where the rigid attendant sat outside the Italian's door.

'No; she ain't come out yet,' said the woman in her sullen way; 'and she ain't dead, for I heard her moving about now and then. I dunno what tricks she's up to.'

'Do you happen to know, ma'am,' said Father Brown with abrupt politeness, 'where Mr Mandeville is just now?'

'Yes,' she replied promptly. 'Saw him go into his little room at the end of the passage a minute or two ago; just before the prompter called and the curtain went up. Must be there still, for I ain't seen him come out.'

'There's no other door to his office, you mean,' said Father Brown in an offhand way. 'Well, I suppose the rehearsal's going in full swing now, for all the Signora's sulking.'

'Yes,' said Jarvis after a moment's silence; 'I can just hear the voices on the stage from here. Old Randall has a splendid carrying voice.'

They both remained for an instant in a listening attitude, so that the booming voice of the actor on the stage could indeed be heard rolling faintly down the stairs and along the passage. Before they had spoken again or resumed their normal poise, their ears were filled with another sound. It was a dull but heavy crash and it came from behind the closed door of Mundon Mandeville's private room.

Father Brown went racing along the passage like an arrow from the bow and was struggling with the door-handle before Jarvis had wakened with a start and begun to follow him.

'The door is locked,' said the priest, turning a face that was a little pale. 'And I am all in favour of breaking down *this* door.'

'Do you mean,' asked Jarvis with a rather ghastly look, 'that the unknown visitor has got in here again? Do you think it's anything serious?' After a moment he added: 'I may be able to push back the bolt; I know the fastening on these doors.'

He knelt down and pulled out a pocket-knife with a long steel implement, manipulated it for a moment, and the door swung open on the manager's study. Almost the first thing they noticed was that there was no other door and even no window, but a great electric lamp stood on the table. But it was not quite the first thing that they noticed; for even before that they had seen that Mandeville was lying flat on his face in the middle of the room and the blood was crawling out from under his fallen face like a pattern of scarlet snakes that glittered evilly in that unnatural subterranean light.

They did not know how long they had been staring at each other when Jarvis said, like one letting loose something that he had held back with his breath: 'If the stranger got in somehow, she has gone somehow.'

'Perhaps we think too much about the stranger,' said Father Brown. 'There are so many strange things in this strange theatre that you rather tend to forget some of them.'

'Why, which things do you mean?' asked his friend quickly.

'There are many,' said the priest. 'There is the other locked door, for instance.'

'But the other door *is* locked,' cried Jarvis staring.

'But you forgot it all the same,' said Father Brown. A few moments afterwards he said thoughtfully: 'That Mrs Sands is a grumpy and gloomy sort of card.'

'Do you mean,' asked the other in a lowered voice, 'that she's lying and the Italian did come out?'

'No,' said the priest calmly; 'I think I meant it more or less as a detached study of character.'

'You can't mean,' cried the actor, 'that Mrs Sands did it herself?'

'I didn't mean a study of *her* character,' said Father Brown.

While they had been exchanging these abrupt reflections, Father Brown had knelt down by the body and ascertained that it was beyond any hope or question a dead body. Lying beside it, though not immediately visible from the doorway, was a dagger of the theatrical sort; lying as if it had fallen from the wound or from the hand of the assassin. According to Jarvis, who recognised the instrument, there was not very much to be learned from it, unless the experts could find some fingerprints. It was a property dagger; that is, it was nobody's property; it had been kicking about the theatre for a long time, and anybody might have picked it up. Then the priest rose and looked gravely round the room.

'We must send for the police,' he said; 'and for a doctor, though the doctor comes too late. Looking at this room, by the way, I don't see how our Italian friend could manage it.'

'The Italian!' cried his friend; 'I should think not. I should have thought she had an alibi, if anybody had. Two separate rooms, both locked, at opposite ends of a long passage, with a fixed witness watching it.'

'No,' said Father Brown. 'Not quite. The difficulty is how she could have got in this end. I think she might have got out the other end.'

'And why?' asked the other.

'I told you,' said Father Brown, 'that it sounded as if she was breaking glass – mirrors or windows. Stupidly enough I forgot something I knew quite well; that she is pretty superstitious. She wouldn't be likely to break a mirror; so I suspect she broke a window. It's true that all this is under the ground floor; but it might be a skylight or a window opening on an area. But there don't seem to be any skylights or areas here.' And he stared at the ceiling very intently for a considerable time.

Suddenly he came back to conscious life again with a start. 'We must go upstairs and telephone and tell everybody. It is pretty painful . . . My God, can you hear those actors still shouting and ranting upstairs? The play is still going on. I suppose that's what they mean by tragic irony.'

* * *

When it was fated that the theatre should be turned into a house of mourning, an opportunity was given to the actors to show many of the real virtues of their type and trade. They did, as the phrase goes, behave like gentlemen; and not only like first walking gentlemen. They had not all of them liked or trusted Mandeville, but they knew exactly the right things to say about him; they showed not only sympathy but delicacy in their attitude to his widow. She had become, in a new and very different sense, a tragedy queen – her lightest word was law and while she moved about slowly and sadly, they ran her many errands.

'She was always a strong character,' said old Randall rather huskily; 'and had the best brains of any of us. Of course poor Mandeville was never on her level in education and so on; but she always did her duty splendidly. It was quite pathetic the way she would sometimes say she wished she had more intellectual life; but Mandeville – well, *nil nisi bonum*, as they say.' And the old gentleman went away wagging his head sadly.

'*Nil nisi bonum* indeed,' said Jarvis grimly. 'I don't think Randall at any rate has heard of the story of the strange lady visitor. By the way, don't you think it probably was the strange woman?'

'It depends,' said the priest, 'whom you mean by the strange woman.'

'Oh! I don't mean the Italian woman,' said Jarvis hastily. 'Though, as a matter of fact, you were quite right about her, too. When they went in the skylight was smashed and the room was empty; but so far as the police can discover, she simply went home in the most harmless fashion. No, I mean the woman who was heard threatening him at that secret meeting; the woman who said she was his wife. Do you think she really was his wife?'

'It is possible,' said Father Brown, staring blankly into the void, 'that she really was his wife.'

'That would give us the motive of jealousy over his bigamous remarriage,' reflected Jarvis, 'for the body was not robbed in any way. No need to poke about for thieving servants or even impecunious actors. But as for that, of course, you've noticed the outstanding and peculiar thing about the case?'

'I have noticed several peculiar things,' said Father Brown. 'Which one do you mean?'

'I mean the corporate alibi,' said Jarvis gravely. 'It's not often that practically a whole company has a public alibi like that; an alibi on a lighted stage and all witnessing to each other. As it turns out it is jolly lucky for our friends here that poor Mandeville did put those two silly society women in the box to watch the rehearsal. They can bear witness that the whole act was performed without a hitch, with the characters on the stage all the time. They began long before Mandeville was last seen going into his room. They went on at least five or ten minutes after you and I found his dead body. And, by a lucky coincidence, the moment we actually heard him fall was during the time when all the characters were on the stage together.'

'Yes, that is certainly very important and simplifies everything,' agreed Father Brown. 'Let us count the people covered by the alibi. There was Randall: I rather fancy Randall practically hated the manager, though he is very properly covering his feelings just now. But he is ruled out; it was his voice we heard thundering over our heads from the stage. There is our *jeune premier*, Mr Knight: I have rather good reason to suppose he was in love with Mandeville's wife and not concealing that sentiment so much as he might; but he is out of it, for he was on the stage at the same time, being thundered at. There was that amiable Jew who calls himself Aubrey Vernon, he's out of it; and there's Mrs Mandeville, she's out of it. Their corporate alibi, as you say, depends chiefly on Lady Miriam and her friend in the box; though there is the general common-sense corroboration that the act had to be gone through and the routine of the theatre seems to have suffered no interruption. The legal witnesses, however, are Lady Miriam and her friend, Miss Talbot. I suppose you feel sure *they* are all right?'

'Lady Miriam?' said Jarvis in surprise. 'Oh, yes . . . I suppose you mean that she looks a queer sort of vamp. But you've no notion what even the ladies of the best families are looking like nowadays. Besides, is there any particular reason for doubting their evidence?'

'Only that it brings us up against a blank wall,' said Father Brown. 'Don't you see that this collective alibi practically covers everybody? Those four were the only performers in the theatre at the time; and there were scarcely any servants in the theatre; none indeed, except old Sam, who guards the only regular entrance, and the woman who guarded Miss Maroni's door. There is nobody else left available but you and me. We certainly might be accused of the crime, especially as we found the body. There seems nobody else who can be accused. You didn't happen to kill him when I wasn't looking, I suppose?'

Jarvis looked up with a slight start and stared a moment, then the broad grin returned to his swarthy face. He shook his head.

'You didn't do it,' said Father Brown; 'and we will assume for the moment, merely for the sake of argument, that I didn't do it. The people on the stage being out of it, it really leaves the Signora behind her locked door, the sentinel in front of her door, and old Sam. Or are you thinking of the two ladies in the box? Of course they might have slipped out of the box.'

'No,' said Jarvis; 'I am thinking of the unknown woman who came and told Mandeville she was his wife.'

'Perhaps she was,' said the priest; and this time there was a note in his steady voice that made his companion start to his feet once more and lean across the table.

'We said,' he observed in a low, eager voice, 'that this first wife might have been jealous of the other wife.'

'No,' said Father Brown; 'she might have been jealous of the Italian girl, perhaps, or of Lady Miriam Marden. But she was not jealous of the other wife.'

'And why not?'

'Because there was no other wife,' said Father Brown. 'So far from being a bigamist, Mr Mandeville seems to me to have been a highly monogamous person. His wife was almost too much with him; so much with him that you all charitably suppose that she must be somebody else. But I don't see how she could have been with him when he was killed, for we agree that she was acting all the time in front of the footlights. Acting an important part, too . . .'

'Do you really mean,' cried Jarvis, 'that the strange woman who haunted him like a ghost was only the Mrs Mandeville we know?' But he received no answer; for Father Brown was staring into vacancy with a blank expression almost like an idiot's. He always did look most idiotic at the instant when he was most intelligent.

The next moment he scrambled to his feet, looking very harassed and distressed. 'This is awful,' he said. 'I'm not sure it isn't the worst business I ever had; but I've got to go through with it. Would you go and ask Mrs Mandeville if I may speak to her in private?'

'Oh, certainly,' said Jarvis, as he turned towards the door. 'But what's the matter with you?'

'Only being a born fool,' said Father Brown; 'a very common complaint in this vale of tears. I was fool enough to forget altogether that the play was *The School for Scandal*.'

He walked restlessly up and down the room until Jarvis reappeared at the door with an altered and even alarmed face.

'I can't find her anywhere,' he said. 'Nobody seems to have seen her.'

'They haven't seen Norman Knight either, have they?' asked Father Brown dryly. 'Well, it saves me the most painful interview of my life. Saving the grace of God, I was very nearly frightened of that woman. But she was frightened of me, too; frightened of something I'd seen or said. Knight was always begging her to bolt with him. Now she's done it; and I'm devilish sorry for him.'

'For him?' enquired Jarvis.

'Well, it can't be very nice to elope with a murderess,' said the other dispassionately. 'But as a matter of fact she was something very much worse than a murderess.'

'And what is that?'

'An egoist,' said Father Brown. 'She was the sort of person who had looked in the mirror before looking out of the window, and it is the worst calamity of mortal life. The looking-glass was unlucky for her, all right; but rather because it wasn't broken.'

'I can't understand what all this means,' said Jarvis. 'Everybody regarded her as a person of the most exalted ideals, almost moving on a higher spiritual plane than the rest of us . . .'

'She regarded herself in that light,' said the other; 'and she knew how to hypnotise everybody else into it. Perhaps I hadn't known her long enough to be wrong about her. But I knew the sort of person she was five minutes after I clapped eyes on her.'

'Oh, come!' cried Jarvis; 'I'm sure her behaviour about the Italian was beautiful.'

'Her behaviour always was beautiful,' said the other. 'I've heard from everybody here all about her refinements and subtleties and spiritual soarings above poor Mandeville's head. But all these spiritualities and subtleties seem to me to boil themselves down to the simple fact that she certainly was a lady and he most certainly was not a gentleman. But, do you know, I have never felt quite sure that St Peter will make that the only test at the gate of heaven.

'As for the rest,' he went on with increasing animation, 'I knew from the very first words she said that she was not really being fair to the poor Italian, with all her fine airs of frigid magnanimity. And again, I realised it when I knew that the play was *The School for Scandal*.'

'You are going rather too fast for me,' said Jarvis in some bewilderment. 'What does it matter what the play was?'

'Well,' said the priest, 'she said she had given the girl the part of the beautiful heroine and had retired into the background herself with the older part of a matron. Now that might have applied to almost any play; but it falsifies the facts about that particular play. She can only have meant that she gave the other actress the part of Maria, which is hardly a part at all. And the part of the obscure and self-effacing married woman, if you please, must have been the part of Lady Teazle, which is the only part any actress wants to act. If the Italian was a first-rate actress who had been promised a first-rate part, there was really some excuse, or at least some cause, for her mad Italian rage. There generally is for mad Italian rages: Latins are logical and have a reason for going mad. But that one little thing let in daylight for me on the meaning of her magnanimity. And there was another thing, even then. You laughed when I said that the sulky look of Mrs Sands was a study in character; but not in the character of Mrs Sands. But it was true. If you want to know what a lady is really like, don't look at her; for she may be too clever for you. Don't look at the men round her, for they may be too silly about her. But look at some other woman who is always near to her, and especially one who is under her. You will see in that mirror her real face, and the face mirrored in Mrs Sands was very ugly.

'And as for all the other impressions, what were they? I heard a lot about the unworthiness of poor old Mandeville; but it was all about his being unworthy of her, and I am pretty certain it came indirectly from her. And, even so, it betrayed itself. Obviously, from what every man said, she had confided in every man about her confounded intellectual loneliness. You yourself said she never complained; and then quoted her about how her uncomplaining silence strengthened her soul. And that is just the note; that's the unmistakable style. People who complain are just jolly, human Christian nuisances; I don't mind them. But people who complain that they never complain are the devil. They are really the devil; isn't that swagger of stoicism the whole point of the Byronic cult of Satan? I heard all this; but for the life of me I couldn't hear of anything tangible she had to complain of. Nobody pretended that her husband drank, or beat her, or left her without money, or even was unfaithful, until the rumour about the secret meetings, which were simply her own melodramatic habit of pestering him with curtain-lectures in his own business office. And when one looked at the facts, apart from the atmospheric impression of martyrdom she contrived to spread, the facts were really quite the other way. Mandeville left off making money on pantomimes to please her; he started losing money on classical drama to please her. She arranged the scenery and furniture as she liked. She wanted Sheridan's play and she had it; she wanted the part of Lady Teazle and she had it; she wanted a rehearsal without costume at that particular hour and she had it. It may be worth remarking on the curious fact that she wanted that.'

'But what is the use of all this tirade?' asked the actor, who had hardly ever heard his clerical friend make so long a speech before. 'We seem to have got a long way from the murder in all this psychological business. She may have eloped with Knight; she may have bamboozled Randall; she may have bamboozled me. But she can't have murdered her husband – for everyone agrees she was on the stage through the whole scene. She may be wicked; but she isn't a witch.'

'Well, I wouldn't be so sure,' said Father Brown, with a smile. 'But she didn't need to use any witchcraft in this case. I know now that she did it, and very simply indeed.'

'Why are you so sure of that?' asked Jarvis, looking at him in a puzzled way.

'Because the play was *The School for Scandal*,' replied Father Brown, 'and that particular act of *The School for Scandal*. I should like to remind you, as I said just now, that she always arranged the furniture how she liked. I should also like to remind you that this stage was built and used for pantomimes; it would naturally have trapdoors and trick exits of that sort. And when you say that witnesses could attest to having seen all the performers on the stage, I should like to remind you that in the principal scene of *The School for Scandal* one of the principal performers remains for a considerable time on the stage, but is not seen. She is technically "on", but she might practically be very much "off". That is the Screen of Lady Teazle and the Alibi of Mrs Mandeville.'

There was a silence and then the actor said: 'You think she slipped through a trapdoor behind a screen down to the floor below, where the manager's room was?'

'She certainly slipped away in some fashion; and that is the most probable fashion,' said the other. 'I think it all the more probable because she took the opportunity of an undress rehearsal, and even indeed arranged for one. It is a guess; but I fancy if it had been a dress rehearsal it might have been more difficult to get through a trapdoor in the hoops of the eighteenth century. There are many little difficulties, of course, but I think they could all be met in time and in turn.'

'What I can't meet is the big difficulty,' said Jarvis, putting his head on his hand with a sort of groan. 'I simply can't bring myself to believe that a radiant and serene creature like that could so lose, so to speak, her bodily balance, to say nothing of her moral balance. Was any motive strong enough? Was she very much in love with Knight?'

'I hope so,' replied his companion; 'for really it would be the most human excuse. But I'm sorry to say that I have my doubts. She wanted to get rid of her husband, who was an old-fashioned, provincial hack, not even making much money. She wanted to have a career as the brilliant wife of a brilliant and rapidly rising actor. But she didn't want in that sense to act in *The School for Scandal*. She wouldn't have run away with a man except in the last resort. It wasn't a human passion with her, but a sort of hellish respectability. She was always dogging her husband in secret and badgering him to divorce himself or otherwise get out of the way; and as he refused he paid at last for his refusal. There's another thing you've got to remember. You talk about these highbrows having a higher art and a more philosophical drama. But remember what a lot of the philosophy is! Remember what sort of conduct those highbrows often present to the highest! All about the Will to Power and the Right to Live and the Right to Experience – damned nonsense and more than damned nonsense – nonsense that can damn.'

Father Brown frowned, which he did very rarely; and there was still a cloud on his brow as he put on his hat and went out into the night.

The Vanishing of Vaudrey

Sir Arthur Vaudrey, in his light grey summer suit, and wearing on his grey head the white hat which he so boldly affected, went walking briskly up the road by the river from his own house to the little group of houses that were almost like outhouses to his own, entered that little hamlet, and then vanished completely as if he had been carried away by the fairies.

The disappearance seemed the more absolute and abrupt because of the familiarity of the scene and the extreme simplicity of the conditions of the problem. The hamlet could not be called a village; indeed, it was little more than a small and strangely isolated street. It stood in the middle of wide and open fields and plains, a mere string of the four or five shops absolutely needed by the neighbours; that is, by a few farmers and the family at the great house. There was a butcher's at the corner, at which, it appeared, Sir Arthur had last been seen. He was seen by two young men staying at his house: Evan Smith, who was acting as his secretary, and John Dalmon, who was generally supposed to be engaged to his ward. There was next to the butcher's a small shop combining a large number of functions, such as is found in villages, in which a little old woman sold sweets, walking-sticks, golfballs, gum, balls of string and a very faded sort of stationery. Beyond this was the tobacconist, to which the two young men were betaking themselves when they last caught a glimpse of their host standing in front of the butcher's shop; and beyond that was a dingy little dressmaker's, kept by two ladies. A pale and shiny shop, offering to the passerby great goblets of very wan, green lemonade, completed the block of buildings; for the only real and Christian inn in the neighbourhood stood by itself some way down the main road. Between the inn and the hamlet was a crossroads, at which stood a policeman and a uniformed official of a motoring club; and both agreed that Sir Arthur had never passed that point on the road.

It had been at an early hour of a very brilliant summer day that the old gentleman had gone gaily striding up the road, swinging his walking-stick and flapping his yellow gloves. He was a good deal of a dandy, but one of a vigorous and virile sort, especially for his age. His bodily strength and activity were still very remarkable, and his curly hair might have been a yellow so pale as to look white instead of a white that was a faded yellow. His clean-shaven face was handsome, with a high-bridged nose like the Duke of Wellington's; but the most outstanding features were his eyes. They were not merely metaphorically outstanding; something prominent and almost bulging about them was perhaps the only disproportion in his features; but his lips were sensitive and set a little tightly, as if by an act of will. He was the squire of all that country and the owner of the little hamlet. In that sort of place everybody not only knows everybody else, but generally knows where anybody is at any given moment. The normal course would have been for Sir Arthur to walk to the village, to say whatever he wanted to say to the butcher or anybody else, and then walk back to his house again, all in the course of about half an hour: as the two young men did when they had bought their cigarettes. But they saw nobody on the road returning; indeed, there was nobody in sight except the one other guest at the house, a certain Dr Abbott, who was sitting with his broad back to them on the river-bank, very patiently fishing.

When all the three guests returned to breakfast, they seemed to think little or nothing of the continued absence of the squire; but when the day wore on and he missed one meal after another, they naturally began to be puzzled, and Sybil Rye, the lady of the household, began to be seriously alarmed. Expeditions of discovery were dispatched to the village again and again without finding any trace; and eventually, when darkness fell, the house was full of a definite fear. Sybil had sent for Father Brown, who was a friend of hers and had helped her out of a difficulty in the past; and under the pressure of the apparent peril he had consented to remain at the house and see it through.

Thus it happened that when the new day's dawn broke without news, Father Brown was early afoot and on the lookout for anything; his black, stumpy figure could be seen pacing the garden path where the garden was embanked along the river, as he scanned the landscape up and down with his short-sighted and rather misty gaze.

He realised that another figure was moving even more restlessly along the embankment, and saluted Evan Smith, the secretary, by name.

Evan Smith was a tall, fair-haired young man, looking rather harassed, as was perhaps natural in that hour of distraction. But something of the sort hung about him at all times. Perhaps it was more marked because he had the sort of athletic reach and poise and the sort of leonine yellow hair and moustache which accompany (always in fiction and sometimes in fact) a frank and cheerful demeanour of 'English youth'. As in his case they accompanied deep and cavernous eyes and a rather haggard look, the contrast with the conventional tall figure and fair hair of romance may have had a touch of something sinister. But Father Brown smiled at him amiably enough and then said more seriously: 'This is a trying business.'

'It's a very trying business for Miss Rye,' answered the young man gloomily; 'and I don't see why I should disguise what's the worst part of it for me, even if she is engaged to Dalmon. Shocked, I suppose?'

Father Brown did not look very much shocked, but his face was often rather expressionless; he merely said, mildly: 'Naturally, we all sympathise with her anxiety. I suppose you haven't any news or views in the matter?'

'I haven't any news exactly,' answered Smith; 'no news from outside at least. As for views . . . ' And he relapsed into moody silence.

'I should be very glad to hear your views,' said the little priest pleasantly. 'I hope you don't mind my saying that you seem to have something on your mind.'

The young man stirred rather than started and looked at the priest steadily, with a frown that threw his hollow eyes into dense shadow.

'Well, you're right enough,' he said at last. 'I suppose I shall have to tell somebody. And you seem a safe sort of person to tell.'

'Do you know what has happened to Sir Arthur?' asked Father Brown calmly, as if it were the most casual matter in the world.

'Yes,' said the secretary harshly, 'I think I know what has happened to Sir Arthur.'

'A beautiful morning,' said a bland voice in his ear; 'a beautiful morning for a rather melancholy meeting.'

This time the secretary jumped as if he had been shot, as the large shadow of Dr Abbott fell across his path in the already strong sunshine. Dr Abbott was still in his dressing-gown – a sumptuous oriental dressing-gown covered with coloured flowers and dragons, looking rather like one of the most brilliant flowerbeds that were growing under the glowing sun. He also wore large, flat slippers, which was doubtless why he had come so close to the others without being heard. He would normally have seemed the last person for such a light and airy approach, for he was a very big, broad and heavy man, with a powerful benevolent face very much sunburnt, in a frame of old-fashioned grey whiskers and chin beard, which hung about him luxuriantly, like the long, grey curls of his venerable head. His long slits of eyes were rather sleepy and, indeed, he was an elderly gentleman to be up so early; but he had a look at once robust and weatherbeaten, as of an old farmer or sea captain who had once been out in all weathers. He was the only old comrade and contemporary of the squire in the company that met at the house.

'It seems truly extraordinary,' he said, shaking his head. 'Those little houses are like dolls' houses, always open front and back, and there's hardly room to hide anybody, even if they wanted to hide him. And I'm sure they don't. Dalmon and I cross-examined them all yesterday; they're mostly little old women that couldn't hurt a fly. The men are nearly all away harvesting, except the butcher; and Arthur was seen coining out of the butcher's. And nothing could have happened along that stretch by the river, for I was fishing there all day.'

Then he looked at Smith and the look in his long eyes seemed for the moment not only sleepy, but a little sly.

'I think you and Dalmon can testify,' he said, 'that you saw me sitting there through your whole journey there and back.'

'Yes,' said Evan Smith shortly, and seemed rather impatient at the long interruption.

'The only thing I can think of,' went on Dr Abbott slowly; and then the interruption was itself interrupted. A figure at once light and sturdy strode very rapidly across the green lawn between the gay flowerbeds, and John Dalmon appeared among them, holding a paper in his hand. He was neatly dressed and rather swarthy, with a very fine square Napoleonic face and very sad eyes – eyes so sad that they looked almost dead. He seemed to be still young, but his black hair had gone prematurely grey about the temples.

'I've just had this telegram from the police,' he said. 'I wired to them last night and they say they're sending down a man at once. Do you know, Dr Abbott, of anybody else we ought to send for? Relations, I mean, and that sort of thing.'

'There is his nephew, Vernon Vaudrey, of course,' said the old man. 'If you will come with me, I think I can give you his address and – and tell you something rather special about him.'

Dr Abbott and Dalmon moved away in the direction of the house and, when they had gone a certain distance, Father Brown said simply, as if there had been no interruption: 'You were saying?'

'You're a cool hand,' said the secretary. 'I suppose it comes of hearing confessions. I feel rather as if I were going to make a confession. Some people would feel a bit jolted out of the mood of confidence by that queer old elephant creeping up like a snake. But I suppose I'd better stick to it, though it really isn't my confession, but somebody else's.' He stopped a moment, frowning and pulling his moustache; then he said, abruptly: 'I believe Sir Arthur has bolted, and I believe I know why.'

There was a silence and then he exploded again.

'I'm in a damnable position, and most people would say I was doing a damnable thing. I am now going to appear in the character of a sneak and a skunk and I believe I am doing my duty.'

'You must be the judge,' said Father Brown gravely. 'What is the matter with your duty?'

'I'm in the perfectly foul position of telling tales against a rival, and a successful rival, too,' said the young man bitterly; 'and I don't know what else in the world I can do. You were asking what was the explanation of Vaudrey's disappearance. I am absolutely convinced that Dalmon is the explanation.'

'You mean,' said the priest, with composure, 'that Dalmon has killed Sir Arthur?'

'No!' exploded Smith, with startling violence. 'No, a hundred times! He hasn't done that, whatever else he's done. He isn't a murderer, whatever else he is. He has the best of all alibis; the evidence of a man who hates him. I'm not likely to perjure myself for love of Dalmon; and I could swear in any court he did nothing to the old man yesterday. Dalmon and I were together all day, or all that part of the day, and he did nothing in the village except buy cigarettes, and nothing here except smoke them and read in the library. No; I believe he is a criminal, but he did not kill Vaudrey. I might even say more; because he is a criminal he did not kill Vaudrey.'

'Yes,' said the other patiently, 'and what does that mean?'

'It means,' replied the secretary, 'that he is a criminal committing another crime: and his crime depends on keeping Vaudrey alive.'

'Oh, I see,' said Father Brown.

'I know Sybil Rye pretty well, and her character is a great part of this story. It is a very fine character in both senses: that is, it is of a noble quality and only too delicate a texture. She is one of those people who are terribly conscientious, without any of that armour of habit and hard common sense that many conscientious people get. She is almost insanely sensitive and at the same time quite unselfish. Her history is curious: she was left literally penniless like a foundling and Sir Arthur took her into his house and treated her with consideration, which puzzled many; for, without being hard on the old man, it was not much in his line. But, when she was about seventeen, the explanation came to her with a shock; for her guardian asked her to marry him. Now I come to the curious part of the story. Somehow or other, Sybil had heard from somebody (I rather suspect from old Abbott) that Sir Arthur Vaudrey, in his wilder youth, had committed some crime or, at least, done some great wrong to somebody, which had got him into serious trouble. I don't know what it was. But it was a sort of nightmare to the girl at her crude sentimental age, and made him seem like a monster, at least too much so for the close relation of marriage. What she did was incredibly typical of her. With helpless terror and with heroic courage she told him the truth with her own trembling lips. She admitted that her repulsion might be morbid; she confessed it like a secret madness. To her relief and surprise he took it quietly and courteously, and apparently said no more on the subject; and her sense of his generosity was greatly increased by the next stage of the story. There came into her lonely life the influence of an equally lonely man. He was camping-out like a sort of hermit on one of the islands in the river; and I suppose the mystery made him attractive, though I admit he is attractive enough; a gentleman, and quite witty, though very melancholy – which, I suppose, increased the romance. It was this man, Dalmon, of course; and to this day I'm not sure how far she really accepted him; but it got as far as his getting permission to see her guardian. I can fancy her awaiting that interview in an agony of terror and wondering how the old beau would take the appearance of a rival. But here, again, she found she had apparently done him an injustice. He received the younger man with hearty hospitality and seemed to be delighted with the prospects of the young couple. He and Dalmon went shooting and fishing together and were the best of friends, when one day she had another shock. Dalmon let slip in conversation some chance phrase that the old man "had not changed much in thirty years", and the truth about the odd intimacy burst upon her. All that introduction and hospitality had been a masquerade; the men had obviously known each other before. That was why the younger man had come down rather covertly to that district. That was why the elder man was lending himself so readily to promote the match. I wonder what you are thinking?'

'I know what you are thinking,' said Father Brown, with a smile, 'and it seems entirely logical. Here we have Vaudrey, with some ugly story in his past – a mysterious stranger come to haunt him, and getting whatever he wants out of him. In plain words, you think Dalmon is a blackmailer.'

'I do,' said the other; 'and a rotten thing to think, too.'

Father Brown reflected for a moment and then said: 'I think I should like to go up to the house now and have a talk to Dr Abbott.'

When he came out of the house again an hour or two afterwards, he may have been talking to Dr Abbott, but he emerged in company with Sybil Rye, a pale girl with reddish hair and a profile delicate and almost tremulous; at the sight of her, one could instantly understand all the secretary's story of her shuddering candour. It recalled Godiva and certain tales of virgin martyrs; only the shy can be so shameless for conscience's sake. Smith came forward to meet them, and for a moment they stood talking on the lawn. The day which had been brilliant from daybreak was now glowing and even glaring; but Father Brown carried his black bundle of an umbrella as well as wearing his black umbrella of a hat; and seemed, in a general way, buttoned up to breast the storm. But perhaps it was only an unconscious effect of attitude; and perhaps the storm was not a material storm.

'What I hate about it all,' Sybil was saying in a low voice, 'is the talk that's beginning already; suspicions against everybody. John and Evan can answer for each other, I suppose; but Dr Abbott has had an awful scene with the butcher, who thinks he is accused and is throwing accusations about in consequence.'

Evan Smith looked very uncomfortable; then blurted out: 'Look here, Sybil, I can't say much, but we don't believe there's any need for all that. It's all very beastly, but we don't think there's been – any violence.'

'Have you got a theory, then?' said the girl, looking instantly at the priest.

'I have heard a theory,' he replied, 'which seems to me very convincing.'

He stood looking rather dreamily towards the river; and Smith and Sybil began to talk to each other swiftly, in lowered tones. The priest drifted along the river-bank, ruminating, and plunged into a plantation of thin trees on an almost overhanging bank. The strong sun beat on the thin veil of little dancing leaves like small green flames, and all the birds were singing as if the tree had a hundred tongues. A minute or two later, Evan Smith heard his own name called cautiously and yet clearly from the green depths of the thicket. He stepped rapidly in that direction and met Father Brown returning. The priest said to him, in a very low voice: 'Don't let the lady come down here. Can't you get rid of her? Ask her to telephone or something; and then come back here again.'

Evan Smith turned with a rather desperate appearance of carelessness and approached the girl; but she was not the sort of person whom it is hard to make busy with small jobs for others. In a very short time she had vanished into the house and Smith turned to find that Father Brown had once more vanished into the thicket. Just beyond the clump of trees was a sort of small chasm where the turf had subsided to the level of the sand by the river. Father Brown was standing on the brink of this cleft, looking down; but, either by accident or design, he was holding his hat in his hand, in spite of the strong sun pouring on his head.

'You had better see this yourself,' he said, heavily, 'as a matter of evidence. But I warn you to be prepared.'

'Prepared for what?' asked the other.

'Only for the most horrible thing I ever saw in my life,' said Father Brown.

Even Smith stepped to the brink of the bank of turf and with difficulty repressed a cry rather like a scream.

Sir Arthur Vaudrey was glaring and grinning up at him; the face was turned up so that he could have put his foot on it; the head was thrown back, with its wig of whitish yellow hair towards him, so that he saw the face upside down. This made it seem all the more like a part of a nightmare; as if a man were walking about with his head stuck on the wrong way. What was he doing? Was it possible that Vaudrey was really creeping about, hiding in the cracks of field and bank, and peering out at them in this unnatural posture? The rest of the figure seemed hunched and almost crooked, as if it had been crippled or deformed, but on looking more closely, this seemed only the foreshortening of limbs fallen in a heap. Was he mad? Was he? The more Smith looked at him the stiffer the posture seemed.

'You can't see it from here properly,' said Father Brown, 'but his throat is cut.'

Smith shuddered suddenly. 'I can well believe it's the most horrible thing you've seen,' he said. 'I think it's seeing the face upside down. I've seen that face at breakfast, or dinner, every day for ten years; and it always looked quite pleasant and polite. You turn it upside down and it looks like the face of a fiend.'

'The face really is smiling,' said Father Brown, soberly; 'which is perhaps not the least part of the riddle. Not many men smile while their throats are being cut, even if they do it themselves. That smile, combined with those gooseberry eyes of his that always seemed standing out of his head, is enough, no doubt, to explain the expression. But it's true, things look different upside down. Artists often turn their drawings upside down to test their correctness. Sometimes, when it's difficult to turn the object itself upside down (as in the case of the Matterhorn, let us say), they have been known to stand on their heads, or at least look between their legs.'

The priest, who was talking thus flippantly to steady the other man's nerves, concluded by saying, in a more serious tone: 'I quite understand how it must have upset you. Unfortunately, it also upset something else.'

'What do you mean?'

'It has upset the whole of our very complete theory,' replied the other; and he began clambering down the bank on to the little strip of sand by the river.

'Perhaps he did it himself,' said Smith abruptly. 'After all, that's the most obvious sort of escape, and fits in with our theory very well. He wanted a quiet place and he came here and cut his throat.'

'He didn't come here at all,' said Father Brown. 'At least, not alive, and not by land. He wasn't killed here; there's not enough blood. This sun has dried his hair and clothes pretty well by now; but there are the traces of two trickles of water in the sand. Just about here the tide comes up from the sea and makes an eddy that washed the body into the creek and left it when the tide retired. But the body must first have been washed down the river, presumably from the village, for the river runs just behind the row of little houses and shops. Poor Vaudrey died up in the hamlet, somehow; after all, I don't think he committed suicide; but the trouble is who would, or could, have killed him up in that potty little place?'

He began to draw rough designs with the point of his stumpy umbrella on the strip of sand.

'Let's see; how does the row of shops run? First, the butcher's; well, of course, a butcher would be an ideal performer with a large carving-knife. But you saw Vaudrey come out, and it isn't very probable that he stood in the outer shop while the butcher said: "Good-morning. Allow me to cut your throat! Thank you. And the next article, please?" Sir Arthur doesn't strike me as the sort of man who'd have stood there with a pleasant smile while this happened. He was a very strong and vigorous man, with rather a violent temper. And who else, except the butcher, could have stood up to him? The next shop is kept by an old woman. Then comes the tobacconist, who is certainly a man, but I am told quite a small and timid one. Then there is the dressmaker's, run by two maiden ladies, and then a refreshment shop run by a man who happens to be in hospital and who has left his wife in charge. There are two or three village lads, assistants and errand boys, but they were away on a special job. The refreshment shop ends the street; there is nothing beyond that but the inn, with the policeman between.'

He made a punch with the ferrule of his umbrella to represent the policeman, and remained moodily staring up the river. Then he made a slight movement with his hand and, stepping quickly across, stooped over the corpse.

'Ah,' he said, straightening himself and letting out a great breath. 'The tobacconist! Why in the world didn't I remember that about the tobacconist?'

'What is the matter with you?' demanded Smith in some exasperation; for Father Brown was rolling his eyes and muttering, and he had uttered the word 'tobacconist' as if it were a terrible word of doom.

'Did you notice,' said the priest, after a pause, 'something rather curious about his face?'

'Curious, my God!' said Evan, with a retrospective shudder. 'Anyhow, his throat was cut . . . '

'I said his face,' said the cleric quietly. 'Besides, don't you notice he has hurt his hand and there's a small bandage round it?'

'Oh, that has nothing to do with it,' said Evan hastily. 'That happened before and was quite an accident. He cut his hand with a broken ink bottle while we were working together.'

'It has something to do with it, for all that,' replied Father Brown.

There was a long silence, and the priest walked moodily along the sand, trailing his umbrella and sometimes muttering the word 'tobacconist', till the very word chilled his friend with fear. Then he suddenly lifted the umbrella and pointed to a boathouse among the rushes.

'Is that the family boat?' he asked. 'I wish you'd just scull me up the river; I want to look at those houses from the back. There's no time to lose. They may find the body; but we must risk that.'

Smith was already pulling the little boat upstream towards the hamlet before Father Brown spoke again. Then he said: 'By the way, I found out from old Abbott what was the real story about poor Vaudrey's misdemeanour. It was a rather curious story about an Egyptian official who had insulted him by saying that a good Muslim would avoid swine and Englishmen, but preferred swine; or some such tactful remark. Whatever happened at the time, the quarrel was apparently renewed some years after, when the official visited England; and Vaudrey, in his violent passion, dragged the man to a pigsty on the farm attached to the country house and threw him in, breaking his arm and leg and leaving him there till next morning. There was rather a row about it, of course, but many people thought Vaudrey had acted in a pardonable passion of patriotism. Anyhow, it seems not quite the thing that would have kept a man silent under deadly blackmail for decades.'

'Then you don't think it had anything to do with the story we are considering?' asked the secretary, thoughtfully.

'I think it had a thundering lot to do with the story I am considering now,' said Father Brown.

They were now floating past the low wall and the steep strips of back garden running down from the back doors to the river. Father Brown counted them carefully, pointing with his umbrella, and when he came to the third he said again: 'Tobacconist! Is the tobacconist by any chance . . . ? But I think I'll act on my guess till I know. Only, I'll tell you what it was I thought odd about Sir Arthur's face.'

'And what was that?' asked his companion, pausing and resting on his oars for an instant.

'He was a great dandy,' said Father Brown, 'and the face was only half-shaved . . . Could you stop here a moment? We could tie up the boat to that post.'

A minute or two afterwards they had clambered over the little wall and were mounting the steep cobbled paths of the little garden, with its rectangular beds of vegetables and flowers.

'You see, the tobacconist does grow potatoes,' said Father Brown. 'Associations with Sir Walter Raleigh, no doubt. Plenty of potatoes and plenty of potato sacks. These little country people have not lost all the habits of peasants; they still run two or three jobs at once. But country tobacconists very often do one odd job extra, that I never thought of till I saw Vaudrey's chin. Nine times out of ten you call the shop the tobacconist's, but it is also the barber's. He'd cut his hand and couldn't shave himself; so he came up here. Does that suggest anything else to you?'

'It suggests a good deal,' replied Smith; 'but I expect it will suggest a good deal more to you.'

'Does it suggest, for instance,' observed Father Brown, 'the only conditions in which a vigorous and rather violent gentleman might be smiling pleasantly when his throat was cut?'

The next moment they had passed through a dark passage or two at the back of the house, and came into the back room of the shop, dimly lit by filtered light from beyond and a dingy and cracked looking-glass. It seemed, somehow, like the green twilight of a tank; but there was light enough to see the rough apparatus of a barber's shop and the pale and even panic-sticken face of a barber.

Father Brown's eye roamed round the room, which seemed to have been just recently cleaned and tidied, till his gaze found something in a dusty corner just behind the door. It was a hat hanging on a hat-peg. It was a white hat, and one very well known to all that village. And yet, conspicuous as it had always seemed in the street, it seemed only an example of the sort of little thing a certain sort of man often entirely forgets, when he has most carefully washed floors or destroyed stained rags.

'Sir Arthur Vaudrey was shaved here yesterday morning, I think,' said Father Brown in a level voice.

To the barber, a small, bald-headed, spectacled man whose name was Wicks, the sudden appearance of these two figures out of his own back premises was like the appearance of two ghosts risen out of a grave under the floor. But it was at once apparent that he had more to frighten him than any fancy of superstition. He shrank, we might almost say that he shrivelled, into a corner of the dark room; and everything about him seemed to dwindle, except his great goblin spectacles.

'Tell me one thing,' continued the priest, quietly. 'You had a reason for hating the squire?'

The man in the corner babbled something that Smith could not hear; but the priest nodded.

'I know you had,' he said. 'You hated him; and that's how I know you didn't kill him. Will you tell us what happened, or shall I?'

There was a silence filled with the faint ticking of a clock in the back kitchen; and then Father Brown went on.

'What happened was this. When Mr Dalmon stepped inside your outer shop, he asked for some cigarettes that were in the window. You stepped outside for a moment, as shopmen often do, to make sure of what he meant; and in that moment of time he perceived in the inner room the razor you had just laid down, and the yellow-white head of Sir Arthur in the barber's chair; probably both glimmering in the light of that little window beyond. It took but an instant for him to pick up the razor and cut the throat and come back to the counter. The victim would not even be alarmed at the razor and the hand. He died smiling at his own thoughts. And what thoughts! Nor, I think, was Dalmon alarmed. He had done it so quickly and quietly that Mr Smith here could have sworn in court that the two were together all the time. But there was somebody who was alarmed, very legitimately, and that was you. You had quarrelled with your landlord about arrears of rent and so on; you came back into your own shop and found your enemy murdered in your own chair, with your own razor. It was not altogether unnatural that you despaired of clearing yourself, and preferred to clear up the mess; to clean the floor and throw the corpse into the river at night, in a potato sack rather loosely tied. It was rather lucky that there were fixed hours after which your barber's shop was shut; so you had plenty of time. You seem to have remembered everything but the hat . . . Oh, don't be frightened; I shall forget everything, including the hat.'

And he passed placidly through the outer shop into the street beyond, followed by the wondering Smith, and leaving behind the barber stunned and staring.

'You see,' said Father Brown to his companion, 'it was one of those cases where a motive really is too weak to convict a man and yet strong enough to acquit him. A little nervous fellow like that would be the last man really to kill a big strong man for a tiff about money. But he would be the first man to fear that he would be accused of having done it. . . Ah, there was a thundering difference in the motive of the man who did do it.' And he relapsed into reflection, staring and almost glaring at vacancy.

'It is simply awful,' groaned Evan Smith. 'I was abusing Dalmon as a blackmailer and a blackguard an hour or two ago, and yet it breaks me all up to hear he really did this, after all.'

The priest still seemed to be in a sort of trance, like a man staring down into an abyss. At last his lips moved and he murmured, more as if it were a prayer than an oath: 'Merciful God, what a horrible revenge!'

His friend questioned him, but he continued as if talking to himself.

'What a horrible tale of hatred! What a vengeance for one mortal worm to take on another! Shall we ever get to the bottom of this bottomless human heart, where such abominable imaginations can abide? God save us all from pride; but I cannot yet make any picture in my mind of hate and vengeance like that.'

'Yes,' said Smith; 'and I can't quite picture why he should kill Vaudrey at all. If Dalmon was a blackmailer, it would seem more natural for Vaudrey to kill him. As you say, the throat-cutting was a horrid business, but – '

Father Brown started, and blinked like a man awakened from sleep.

'Oh, that!' he corrected hastily. 'I wasn't thinking about that. I didn't mean the murder in the barber's shop, when – when I said a horrible tale of vengeance. I was thinking of a much more horrible tale than that; though, of course, that was horrible enough, in its way. But that was much more comprehensible; almost anybody might have done it. In fact, it was very nearly an act of self-defence.'

'What?' exclaimed the secretary incredulously. 'A man creeps up behind another man and cuts his throat, while he is smiling pleasantly at the ceiling in a barber's chair, and you say it was self-defence!'

'I do not say it was justifiable self-defence,' replied the other. 'I only say that many a man would have been driven to it, to defend himself against an appalling calamity – which was also an appalling crime. It was that other crime that I was thinking about. To begin with, about that question you asked just now: why should the blackmailer be the murderer? Well, there are a good many conventional confusions and errors on a point like that.' He paused, as if collecting his thoughts after his recent trance of horror, and went on in ordinary tones.

'You observe that two men, an older and a younger, go about together and agree on a matrimonial project; but the origin of their intimacy is old and concealed. One is rich and the other poor; and you guess at blackmail. You are quite right, at least to that extent. Where you are quite wrong is in guessing which is which. You assume that the poor man was blackmailing the rich man. As a matter of fact, the rich man was blackmailing the poor man.'

'But that seems nonsense,' objected the secretary.

'It is much worse than nonsense; but it is not at all uncommon,' replied the other. 'Half modern politics consists of rich men blackmailing people. Your notion that it's nonsense rests on two illusions which are both nonsensical. One is, that rich men never want to be richer; the other is, that a man can only be blackmailed for money. It's the last that is in question here. Sir Arthur Vaudrey was acting not for avarice, but for vengeance. And he planned the most hideous vengeance I ever heard of.'

'But why should he plan vengeance on John Dalmon?' enquired Smith.

'It wasn't on John Dalmon that he planned vengeance,' replied the priest, gravely.

There was a silence; and he resumed, almost as if changing the subject. 'When we found the body, you remember, we saw the face upside down; and you said it looked like the face of a fiend. Has it occurred to you that the murderer also saw the face upside down, coming behind the barber's chair?'

'But that's all morbid extravagance,' remonstrated his companion. 'I was quite used to the face when it was the right way up.'

'Perhaps you have never seen it the right way up,' said Father Brown. 'I told you that artists turn a picture the wrong way up when they want to see it the right way up. Perhaps, over all those breakfasts and tea-tables, you had got used to the face of a fiend.'

'What on earth are you driving at?' demanded Smith, impatiently.

'I speak in parables,' replied the other in a rather sombre tone. 'Of course, Sir Arthur was not actually a fiend; he was a man with a character which he had made out of a temperament that might also have been turned to good. But those goggling, suspicious eyes; that tight, yet quivering mouth, might have told you something if you had not been so used to them. You know, there are physical bodies on which a wound will not heal. Sir Arthur had a mind of that sort. It was as if it lacked a skin; he had a feverish vigilance of vanity; those strained eyes were open with an insomnia of egoism. Sensibility need not be selfishness. Sybil Rye, for instance, has the same thin skin and manages to be a sort of saint. But Vaudrey had turned it all to poisonous pride; a pride that was not even secure and self-satisfied. Every scratch on the surface of his soul festered. And that is the meaning of that old story about throwing the man into the pigsty. If he'd thrown him then and there, after being called a pig, it might have been a pardonable burst of passion. But there was no pigsty; and that is just the point. Vaudrey remembered the silly insult for years and years, till he could get the Oriental into the improbable neighbourhood of a pigsty; and then he took what he considered the only appropriate and artistic revenge . . . Oh, my God! he liked his revenges to be appropriate and artistic.'

Smith looked at him curiously. 'You are not thinking of the pigsty story,' he said.

'No,' said Father Brown; 'of the other story.' He controlled the shudder in his voice, and went on: 'Remembering that story of a fantastic and yet patient plot to make the vengeance fit the crime, consider the other story before us. Had anybody else, to your knowledge, ever insulted Vaudrey, or offered him what he thought a mortal insult? Yes; a woman insulted him.'

A sort of vague horror began to dawn in Evan's eyes; he was listening intently.

'A girl, little more than a child, refused to marry him, because he had once been a sort of criminal; had, indeed, been in prison for a short time for the outrage on the Egyptian. And that madman said, in the hell of his heart: "She shall marry a murderer." '

They took the road towards the great house and went along by the river for some time in silence, before he resumed: 'Vaudrey was in a position to blackmail Dalmon, who had committed a murder long ago; probably he knew of several crimes among the wild comrades of his youth. Probably it was a wild crime with some redeeming features; for the wildest murders are never the worst. And Dalmon looks to me like a man who knows remorse, even for killing Vaudrey. But he was in Vaudrey's power and, between them, they entrapped the girl very cleverly into an engagement; letting the lover try his luck first, for instance, and the other only encouraging magnificently. But Dalmon himself did not know, nobody but the Devil himself did know, what was really in that old man's mind.

'Then, a few days ago, Dalmon made a dreadful discovery. He had obeyed, not altogether unwillingly; he had been a tool; and he suddenly found how the tool was to be broken and thrown away. He came upon certain notes of Vaudrey's in the library which, disguised as they were, told of preparations for giving information to the police. He understood the whole plot and stood stunned as I did when I first understood it. The moment the bride and bridegroom were married, the bridegroom would be arrested and hanged. The fastidious lady, who objected to a husband who had been in prison, should have no husband except a husband on the gallows. That is what Sir Arthur Vaudrey considered an artistic rounding off of the story.'

Evan Smith, deadly pale, was silent; and, far away, down the perspective of the road, they saw the large figure and wide hat of Dr Abbott advancing towards them; even in the outline there was a certain agitation. But they were still shaken with their own private apocalypse.

'As you say, hate is a hateful thing,' said Evan at last; 'and, do you know, one thing gives me a sort of relief. All my hatred of poor Dalmon is gone out of me – now I know how he was twice a murderer.'

It was in silence that they covered the rest of the distance and met the big doctor coming towards them, with his large gloved hands thrown out in a sort of despairing gesture and his grey beard tossing in the wind.

'There is dreadful news,' he said. 'Arthur's body has been found. He seems to have died in his garden.'

'Dear me,' said Father Brown, rather mechanically. 'How dreadful!'

'And there is more,' cried the doctor breathlessly. 'John Dalmon went off to see Vernon Vaudrey, the nephew; but Vernon Vaudrey hasn't heard of him and Dalmon seems to have disappeared entirely.'

'Dear me,' said Father Brown. 'How strange!'

The Worst Crime in the World

Father Brown was wandering through a picture gallery with an expression that suggested that he had not come there to look at the pictures. Indeed, he did not want to look at the pictures, though he liked pictures well enough. Not that there was anything immoral or improper about those highly modern pictorial designs. He would indeed be of an inflammable temperament who was stirred to any of the more pagan passions by the display of interrupted spirals, inverted cones and broken cylinders with which the art of the future inspired or menaced mankind. The truth is that Father Brown was looking for a young friend who had appointed that somewhat incongruous meeting-place, being herself of a more futuristic turn. The young friend was also a young relative; one of the few relatives that he had. Her name was Elizabeth Fane, simplified into Betty, and she was the child of a sister who had married into a race of refined but impoverished squires. As the squire was dead as well as impoverished, Father Brown stood in the relation of a protector as well as a priest, and in some sense a guardian as well as an uncle. At the moment, however, he was blinking about at the groups in the gallery without catching sight of the familiar brown hair and bright face of his niece. Nevertheless, he saw some people he knew and a number of people he did not know, including some that, as a mere matter of taste, he did not much want to know.

Among the people the priest did not know and who yet aroused his interest was a lithe and alert young man, very beautifully dressed and looking rather like a foreigner, because, while his beard was cut in a spade shape like an old Spaniard's, his dark hair was cropped so close as to look like a tight black skull-cap. Among the people the priest did not particularly want to know was a very dominant-looking lady, sensationally clad in scarlet, with a mane of yellow hair too long to be called bobbed, but too loose to be called anything else. She had a powerful and rather heavy face of a pale and rather unwholesome complexion, and when she looked at anybody she cultivated the fascinations of a basilisk. She towed in attendance behind her a short man with a big beard and a very broad face, with long sleepy slits of eyes. The expression of his face was beaming and benevolent, if only partially awake; but his bull neck, when seen from behind, looked a little brutal.

Father Brown gazed at the lady, feeling that the appearance and approach of his niece would be an agreeable contrast. Yet he continued to gaze, for some reason, until he reached the point of feeling that the appearance of anybody would be an agreeable contrast. It was therefore with a certain relief, though with a slight start as of awakening, that he turned at the sound of his name and saw another face that he knew.

It was the sharp but not unfriendly face of a lawyer named Granby, whose patches of grey hair might almost have been the powder from a wig, so incongruous were they with his youthful energy of movement. He was one of those men in the City who run about like schoolboys in and out of their offices. He could not run round the fashionable picture gallery quite in that fashion; but he looked as if he wanted to, and fretted as he glanced to left and right, seeking somebody he knew.

'I didn't know,' said Father Brown, smiling, 'that you were a patron of the New Art.'

'I didn't know that you were,' retorted the other. 'I came here to catch a man.'

'I hope you will have good sport,' answered the priest. 'I'm doing much the same.'

'Said he was passing through to the Continent,' snorted the solicitor, 'and could I meet him in this cranky place.' He ruminated a moment, and said abruptly: 'Look here, I know you can keep a secret. Do you know Sir John Musgrave?'

'No,' answered the priest; 'but I should hardly have thought he was a secret, though they say he does hide himself in a castle. Isn't he the old man they tell all those tales about – how he lives in a tower with a real portcullis and drawbridge, and generally refuses to emerge from the Dark Ages? Is he one of your clients?'

'No,' replied Granby shortly: 'it's his son, Captain Musgrave, who has come to us. But the old man counts for a good deal in the affair, and I don't know him; that's the point. Look here, this is confidential, as I say, but I can confide in you.' He dropped his voice and drew his friend apart into a side gallery containing representations of various real objects, which was comparatively empty.

'This young Musgrave,' he said, 'wants to raise a big sum from us on a *post obit* on his old father in Northumberland. The old man's long past seventy and presumably will *obit* sometime or other; but what about the *post*, so to speak? What will happen afterwards to his cash and castles and portcullises and all the rest? It's a very fine old estate, and still worth a lot, but strangely enough it isn't entailed. So you see how we stand. The question is, as the man said in Dickens, is the old man friendly?'

'If he's friendly to his son you'll feel all the friendlier,' observed Father Brown. 'No, I'm afraid I can't help you. I never met Sir John Musgrave, and I understand very few people do meet him nowadays. But it seems obvious you have a right to an answer on that point before you lend the young gentleman your firm's money. Is he the sort that people cut off with a shilling?'

'Well, I'm doubtful,' answered the other. 'He's very popular and brilliant and a great figure in society; but he's a great deal abroad, and he's been a journalist.'

'Well,' said Father Brown, 'that's not a crime. At least not always.'

'Nonsense!' said Granby curtly. 'You know what I mean – he's rather a rolling stone, who's been a journalist and a lecturer and an actor, and all sorts of things. I've got to know where I stand . . . Why, there he is.'

And the solicitor, who had been stamping impatiently about the emptier gallery, turned suddenly and darted into the more crowded room at a run. He was running towards the tall and well-dressed young man with the short hair and the foreign-looking beard.

The two walked away together talking, and for some moments afterwards Father Brown followed them with his screwed, short-sighted eyes. His gaze was shifted and recalled, however, by the breathless and even boisterous arrival of his niece, Betty. Rather to the surprise of her uncle, she led him back into the emptier room and planted him on a seat that was like an island in that sea of floor.

'I've got something I must tell you,' she said. 'It's so silly that nobody else will understand it.'

'You overwhelm me,' said Father Brown. 'Is it about this business your mother started telling me about? Engagements and all that; not what the military historians call a general engagement.'

'You know,' she said, 'that she wants me to be engaged to Captain Musgrave.'

'I didn't,' said Father Brown with resignation; 'but Captain Musgrave seems to be quite a fashionable topic.'

'Of course we're very poor,' she said, 'and it's no good saying it makes no difference.'

'Do you want to marry him?' asked Father Brown, looking at her through his half-closed eyes.

She frowned at the floor, and answered in a lower tone: 'I thought I did. At least I think I thought I did. But I've just had rather a shock.'

'Then tell us all about it.'

'I heard him laugh,' she said.

'It is an excellent social accomplishment,' he replied.

'You don't understand,' said the girl. 'It wasn't social at all. That was just the point of it – that it wasn't social.'

She paused a moment, and then went on firmly: 'I came here quite early, and saw him sitting quite alone in the middle of that gallery with the new pictures, that was quite empty then. He had no idea I or anybody was near; he was sitting quite alone, and he laughed.'

'Well, no wonder,' said Father Brown. 'I'm not an art critic myself, but as a general view of the pictures taken as a whole – '

'Oh, you won't understand,' she said almost angrily. 'It wasn't a bit like that. He wasn't looking at the pictures. He was staring right up at the ceiling; but his eyes seemed to be turned inwards, and he laughed so that my blood ran cold.'

The priest had risen and was pacing the room with his hands behind him. 'You mustn't be hasty in a case of this sort,' he began. 'There are two kinds of men – but we can hardly discuss him just now, for here he is.'

Captain Musgrave entered the room swiftly and swept it with a smile. Granby, the lawyer, was just behind him, and his legal face bore a new expression of relief and satisfaction.

'I must apologise for everything I said about the Captain,' he said to the priest as they drifted together towards the door. 'He's a thoroughly sensible fellow and quite sees my point. He asked me himself why I didn't go north and see his old father; I could hear from the old man's own lips how it stood about the inheritance. Well, he couldn't say fairer than that, could he? But he's so anxious to get the thing settled that he offered to take me up in his own car to Musgrave Moss. That's the name of the estate. I suggested that, if he was so kind, we might go together; and we're starting tomorrow morning.'

As they spoke Betty and the Captain came through the doorway together, making in that framework at least a sort of picture that some would be sentimental enough to prefer to cones and cylinders. Whatever their other affinities, they were both very good-looking; and the lawyer was moved to a remark on the fact, when the picture abruptly altered.

Captain James Musgrave looked out into the main gallery, and his laughing and triumphant eyes were riveted on something that seemed to change him from head to foot. Father Brown looked round as under an advancing shadow of premonition; and he saw the lowering, almost livid face of the large woman in scarlet under its leonine yellow hair. She always stood with a slight stoop, like a bull lowering its horns, and the expression of her pale pasty face was so oppressive and hypnotic that they hardly saw the little man with the large beard standing beside her.

Musgrave advanced into the centre of the room towards her, almost like a beautifully dressed waxwork wound up to walk. He said a few words to her that could not be heard. She did not answer; but they turned away together, walking down the long gallery as if in debate, the short, bull-necked man with the beard bringing up the rear like some grotesque goblin page.

'Heaven help us!' muttered Father Brown, frowning after them. 'Who in the world is that woman?'

'No pal of mine, I'm happy to say,' replied Granby with grim flippancy. 'Looks as if a little flirtation with her might end fatally, doesn't it?'

'I don't think he's flirting with her,' said Father Brown.

Even as he spoke the group in question turned at the end of the gallery and broke up, and Captain Musgrave came back to them in hasty strides.

'Look here,' he cried, speaking naturally enough, though they fancied his colour was changed. 'I'm awfully sorry, Mr Granby, but I find I can't come north with you tomorrow. Of course, you will take the car all the same. Please do; I shan't want it. I – I have to be in London for some days. Take a friend with you if you like.'

'My friend, Father Brown – ' began the lawyer.

'If Captain Musgrave is really so kind,' said Father Brown gravely, 'I may explain that I have some status in Mr Granby's enquiry, and it would be a great relief to my mind if I could go.'

Which was how it came about that a very elegant car, with an equally elegant chauffeur, shot north the next day over the Yorkshire moors, bearing the incongruous burden of a priest who looked rather like a black bundle, and a lawyer who had the habit of running about on his feet instead of racing on somebody else's wheels.

They broke their journey very agreeably in one of the great dales of the West Riding, dining and sleeping at a comfortable inn, and starting early next day, began to run along the Northumbrian coast till they reached a country that was a maze of sand dunes and rank sea meadows, somewhere in the heart of which lay the old Border castle which had remained so unique and yet so secretive a monument of the old Border wars. They found it at last, by following a path running beside a long arm of the sea that ran inland, and turned eventually into a sort of rude canal ending in the moat of the castle. The castle really was a castle, of the square, embattled plan that the Normans built everywhere from Galilee to the Grampians. It did really and truly have a portcullis and a drawbridge, and they were very realistically reminded of the fact by an accident that delayed their entrance.

They waded amid long coarse grass and thistle to the bank of the moat which ran in a ribbon of black with dead leaves and scum upon it, like ebony inlaid with a pattern of gold. Barely a yard or two beyond the black ribbon was the other green bank and the big stone pillars of the gateway. But so little, it would seem, had this lonely fastness been approached from outside that when the impatient Granby halloed across to the dim figures behind the portcullis, they seemed to have considerable difficulty even in lowering the great rusty drawbridge. It started on its way, turning over like a great falling tower above them, and then stuck, sticking out in mid-air at a threatening angle.

The impatient Granby, dancing upon the bank, called out to his companion: 'Oh, I can't stand these stick-in-the-mud ways! Why, it'd be less trouble to jump.'

And with characteristic impetuosity he did jump, landing with a slight stagger in safety on the inner shore. Father Brown's short legs were not adapted to jumping. But his temper was more adapted than most people's to falling with a splash into very muddy water. By the promptitude of his companion he escaped falling in very far. But as he was being hauled up the green, slimy bank, he stopped with bent head, peering at a particular point upon the grassy slope.

'Are you botanising?' asked Granby irritably. 'We've got no time for you to collect rare plants after your last attempt as a diver among the wonders of the deep. Come on, muddy or no, we've got to present ourselves before the baronet.'

When they had penetrated into the castle, they were received courteously enough by an old servant, the only one in sight, and after indicating their business were shown into a long oak-panelled room with latticed windows of antiquated pattern. Weapons of many different centuries hung in balanced patterns on the dark walls, and a complete suit of fourteenth-century armour stood like a sentinel beside the large fireplace. In another long room beyond could be seen, through the half-open door, the dark colours of the rows of family portraits.

'I feel as if I'd got into a novel instead of a house,' said the lawyer. 'I'd no idea anybody did really keep up the "Mysteries of Udolpho" in this fashion.'

'Yes; the old gentleman certainly carries out his historical craze consistently,' answered the priest; 'and these things are not fakes, either. It's not done by somebody who thinks all medieval people lived at the same time. Sometimes they make up suits of armour out of different bits; but that suit all covered one man, and covered him very completely. You see it's the late sort of tilting-armour.'

'I think he's a late sort of host, if it comes to that,' grumbled Granby. 'He's keeping us waiting the devil of a time.'

'You must expect everything to go slowly in a place like this,' said Father Brown. 'I think it's very decent of him to see us at all: two total strangers come to ask him highly personal questions.'

And, indeed, when the master of the house appeared they had no reason to complain of their reception; but rather became conscious of something genuine in the traditions of breeding and behaviour that could retain their native dignity without difficulty in that barbarous solitude, and after those long years of rustication and moping. The baronet did not seem either surprised or embarrassed at the rare visitation; though they suspected that he had not had a stranger in his house for a quarter of a lifetime, he behaved as if he had been bowing out duchesses a moment before. He showed neither shyness nor impatience when they touched on the very private matter of their errand; after a little leisurely reflection he seemed to recognise their curiosity as justified under the circumstances. He was a thin, keen-looking old gentleman, with black eyebrows and a long chin, and though the carefully curled hair he wore was undoubtedly a wig, he had the wisdom to wear the grey wig of an elderly man.

'As regards the question that immediately concerns you,' he said, 'the answer is very simple indeed. I do most certainly propose to hand on the whole of my property to my son, as my father handed it on to me; and nothing – I say advisedly, nothing – would induce me to take any other course.'

'I am most profoundly grateful for the information,' answered the lawyer. 'But your kindness encourages me to say that you are putting it very strongly. I would not suggest that it is in the least likely that your son would do anything to make you doubt his fitness for the charge. Still, he might – '

'Exactly,' said Sir John Musgrave dryly, 'he might. It is rather an understatement to say that he might. Will you be good enough to step into the next room with me for a moment.'

He led them into the further gallery, of which they had already caught a glimpse, and gravely paused before a row of the blackened and lowering portraits.

'This is Sir Roger Musgrave,' he said, pointing to a long-faced person in a black periwig. 'He was one of the lowest liars and rascals in the rascally time of William of Orange, a traitor to two kings and something like the murderer of two wives. That is his father, Sir Robert, a perfectly honest old cavalier. That is his son, Sir James, one of the noblest of the Jacobite martyrs and one of the first men to attempt some reparation to the Church and the poor. Does it matter that the House of Musgrave, the power, the honour, the authority, descended from one good man to another good man through the interval of a bad one? Edward I governed England well. Edward III covered England with glory. And yet the second glory came from the first glory through the infamy and imbecility of Edward II, who fawned upon Gaveston and ran away from Bruce. Believe me, Mr Granby, the greatness of a great house and history is something more than these accidental individuals who carry it on, even though they do not grace it. From father to son our heritage has come down, and from father to son it shall continue. You may assure yourselves, gentlemen, and you may assure my son, that I shall not leave my money to a home for lost cats. Musgrave shall leave it to Musgrave till the heavens fall.'

'Yes,' said Father Brown thoughtfully; 'I see what you mean.'

'And we shall be only too glad,' said the solicitor, 'to convey such a happy assurance to your son.'

'You may convey the assurance,' said their host gravely. 'He is secure in any event of having the castle, the title, the land and the money. There is only a small and merely private addition to that arrangement. Under no circumstances whatever will I ever speak to him as long as I live.'

The lawyer remained in the same respectful attitude, but he was now respectfully staring.

'Why, what on earth has he – '

'I am a private gentleman,' said Musgrave, 'as well as the custodian of a great inheritance. And my son did something so horrible that he has ceased to be – I will not say a gentleman – but even a human being. It is the worst crime in the world. Do you remember what Douglas said when Marmion, his guest, offered to shake hands with him?'

'Yes,' said Father Brown.

' "My castles are my king's alone, from turret to foundation stone",' said Musgrave. ' "The hand of Douglas is his own".'

He turned towards the other room and showed his rather dazed visitors back into it.

'I hope you will take some refreshment,' he said, in the same equable fashion. 'If you have any doubt about your movements, I should be delighted to offer you the hospitality of the castle for the night.'

'Thank you, Sir John,' said the priest in a dull voice, 'but I think we had better go.'

'I will have the bridge lowered at once,' said their host; and in a few moments the creaking of that huge and absurdly antiquated apparatus filled the castle like the grinding of a mill. Rusty as it was, however, it worked successfully this time, and they found themselves standing once more on the grassy bank beyond the moat.

Granby was suddenly shaken by a shudder.

'What in hell was it that his son did?' he cried.

Father Brown made no answer. But when they had driven off again in their car and pursued their journey to a village not far off, called Graystones, where they alighted at the inn of the Seven Stars, the lawyer learned with a little mild surprise that the priest did not propose to travel much farther; in other words, that he had apparently every intention of remaining in the neighbourhood.

'I cannot bring myself to leave it like this,' he said gravely. 'I will send back the car, and you, of course, may very naturally want to go with it. Your question is answered; it is simply whether your firm can afford to lend money on young Musgrave's prospects. But my question isn't answered; it is whether he is a fit husband for Betty. I must try to discover whether he's really done something dreadful, or whether it's the delusion of an old lunatic.'

'But,' objected the lawyer, 'if you want to find out about him, why don't you go after him? Why should you hang about in this desolate hole where he hardly ever comes?'

'What would be the use of my going after him?' asked the other. 'There's no sense in going up to a fashionable young man in Bond Street and saying: "Excuse me, but have you committed a crime too horrible for a human being?" If he's bad enough to do it, he's certainly bad enough to deny it. And we don't even know what it is. No, there's only one man that knows, and *may* tell, in some further outburst of dignified eccentricity. I'm going to keep near him for the present.'

And in truth Father Brown did keep near the eccentric baronet, and did actually meet him on more than one occasion, with the utmost politeness on both sides. For the baronet, in spite of his years, was very vigorous and a great walker, and could often be seen stumping through the village, and along the country lanes. Only the day after their arrival, Father Brown, coming out of the inn on to the cobbled market-place, saw the dark and distinguished figure stride past in the direction of the post office. He was very quietly dressed in black, but his strong face was even more arresting in the strong sunlight; with his silvery hair, swarthy eyebrows and long chin, he had something of a reminiscence of Henry Irving, or some other famous actor. In spite of his hoary hair, his figure as well as his face suggested strength, and he carried his stick more like a cudgel than a crutch. He saluted the priest, and spoke with the same air of coming fearlessly to the point which had marked his revelations of yesterday.

'If you are still interested in my son,' he said, using the term with an icy indifference, 'you will not see very much of him. He has just left the country. Between ourselves, I might say fled the country.'

'Indeed,' said Father Brown with a grave stare.

'Some people I never heard of, called Grunov, have been pestering me, of all people, about his whereabouts,' said Sir John; 'and I've just come in to send off a wire to tell them that, so far as I know, he's living in the Poste Restante, Riga. Even that has been a nuisance. I came in yesterday to do it, but was five minutes too late for the post office. Are you staying long? I hope you will pay me another visit.'

When the priest recounted to the lawyer his little interview with old Musgrave in the village, the lawyer was both puzzled and interested. 'Why has the Captain bolted?' he asked. 'Who are the other people who want him? Who on earth are the Grunovs?'

'For the first, I don't know,' replied Father Brown. 'Possibly his mysterious sin has come to light. I should rather guess that the other people are blackmailing him about it. For the third, I think I do know. That horrible fat woman with yellow hair is called Madame Grunov, and that little man passes as her husband.'

The next day Father Brown came in rather wearily, and threw down his black bundle of an umbrella with the air of a pilgrim laying down his staff.

He had an air of some depression. But it was as it was so often in his criminal investigations. It was not the depression of failure, but the depression of success.

'It's rather a shock,' he said in a dull voice; 'but I ought to have guessed it. I ought to have guessed it when I first went in and saw the thing standing there.'

'When you saw what?' asked Granby impatiently.

'When I saw there was only one suit of armour,' answered Father Brown. There was a silence during which the lawyer only stared at his friend, and then the friend resumed.

'Only the other day I was just going to tell my niece that there are two types of men who can laugh when they are alone. One might almost say the man who does it is either very good or very bad. You see, he is either confiding the joke to God or confiding it to the Devil. But anyhow he has an inner life. Well, there really is a kind of man who confides the joke to the Devil. He does not mind if nobody sees the joke; if nobody can safely be allowed even to know the joke. The joke is enough in itself, if it is sufficiently sinister and malignant.'

'But what are you talking about?' demanded Granby. '*Whom* are you talking about? Which of them, I mean? *Who* is this person who is having a sinister joke with his Satanic Majesty?'

Father Brown looked across at him with a ghastly smile.

'Ah,' he said, 'that's the joke.'

There was another silence, but this time the silence seemed to be rather full and oppressive than merely empty; it seemed to settle down on them like the twilight that was gradually turning from dusk to dark. Father Brown went on speaking in a level voice, sitting stolidly with his elbows on the table.

'I've been looking up the Musgrave family,' he said. 'They are vigorous and long-lived stock, and even in the ordinary way I should think you would wait a good time for your money.'

'We're quite prepared for that,' answered the solicitor; 'but anyhow it can't last indefinitely. The old man is nearly eighty, though he still walks about, and the people at the inn here laugh and say they don't believe he will ever die.'

Father Brown jumped up with one of his rare but rapid movements, but remained with his hands on the table, leaning forward and looking his friend in the face.

'That's it,' he cried in a low but excited voice. 'That's the only problem. That's the only real difficulty. How will he die? How on earth is he to die?'

'What on earth do you mean?' asked Granby.

'I mean,' came the voice of the priest out of the darkening room, 'that I know the crime that James Musgrave committed.'

His tones had such a chill in them that Granby could hardly repress a shiver; he murmured a further question.

'It was really the worst crime in the world,' said Father Brown. 'At least, many communities and civilisations have accounted it so. It was always from the earliest times marked out in tribe and village for tremendous punishment. But anyhow, I know now what young Musgrave really did and why he did it.'

'And what did he do?' asked the lawyer.

'He killed his father,' answered the priest.

The lawyer in his turn rose from his seat and gazed across the table with wrinkled brows.

'But his father is at the castle,' he cried in sharp tones.

'His father is in the moat,' said the priest, 'and I was a fool not to have known it from the first when something bothered me about that suit of armour. Don't you remember the look of that room? How very carefully it was arranged and decorated? There were two crossed battle-axes hung on one side of the fireplace, two crossed battle-axes on the other. There was a round Scottish shield on one wall, a round Scottish shield on the other. And there was a stand of armour guarding one side of the hearth, and an empty space on the other. Nothing will make me believe that a man who arranged all the rest of that room with that exaggerated symmetry left that one feature of it lopsided. There was almost certainly another man in armour. And what has become of him?'

He paused a moment, and then went on in a more matter-of-fact tone: 'When you come to think of it, it's a very good plan for a murder, and meets the permanent problem of the disposal of the body. The body could stand inside that complete tilting-armour for hours, or even days, while servants came and went, until the murderer could simply drag it out in the dead of night and lower it into the moat, without even crossing the bridge. And then what a good chance he ran! As soon as the body was at all decayed in the stagnant water there would sooner or later be nothing but a skeleton in fourteenth-century armour, a thing very likely to be found in the moat of an old Border castle. It was unlikely that anybody would look for anything there, but if they did, that would soon be all they would find. And I got some confirmation of that. That was when you said I was looking for a rare plant; it was a plant in a good many senses, if you'll excuse the jest. I saw the marks of two feet sunk so deep into the solid bank I was sure that the man was either very heavy or was carrying something very heavy. Also, by the way, there's another moral from that little incident when I made my celebrated graceful and cat-like leap.'

'My brain is rather reeling,' said Granby, 'but I begin to have some notion of what all this nightmare is about. What about you and your cat-like leap?'

'At the post office today,' said Father Brown, 'I casually confirmed the statement the baronet made to me yesterday, that he had been there just after closing-time on the day previous – that is, not only on the very day we arrived, but at the very time we arrived. Don't you see what that means? It means that he was actually out when we called, and came back while we were waiting; and that was why we had to wait so long. And when I saw that, I suddenly saw a picture that told the whole story.'

'Well,' asked the other impatiently, 'and what about it?'

'An old man of eighty can walk,' said Father Brown. 'An old man can even walk a good deal, pottering about in country lanes. But an old man can't *jump*. He would be an even less graceful jumper than I was. Yet, if the baronet came back while we were waiting, he must have come in as we came in – by jumping the moat – for the bridge wasn't lowered till later. I rather guess he had hampered it himself to delay inconvenient visitors, to judge by the rapidity with which it was repaired. But that doesn't matter. When I saw that fancy picture of the black figure with the grey hair taking a flying leap across the moat I knew instantly that it was a young man dressed up as an old man. And there you have the whole story.'

'You mean,' said Granby slowly, 'that this pleasing youth killed his father, hid the corpse first in the armour and then in the moat, disguised himself and so on?'

'They happened to be almost exactly alike,' said the priest. 'You could see from the family portraits how strong the likeness ran. And then you talk of his disguising himself. But in a sense everybody's dress is a disguise. The old man disguised himself in a wig, and the young man in a foreign beard. When he shaved and put the wig on his cropped head he was exactly like his father, with a little make-up. Of course, you understand now why he was so very polite about getting you to come up next day here by car. It was because he himself was coming up that night by train. He got in front of you, committed his crime, assumed his disguise, and was ready for the legal negotiations.'

'Ah,' said Granby thoughtfully, 'the legal negotiations! You mean, of course, that the real old baronet would have negotiated very differently.'

'He would have told you plainly that the Captain would never get a penny,' said Father Brown. 'The plot, queer as it sounds, was really the only way of preventing his telling you so. But I want you to appreciate the cunning of what the fellow did tell you. His plan answered several purposes at once. He was being blackmailed by these Russians for some villainy; I suspect for treason during the war. He escaped from them at a stroke, and probably sent them chasing off to Riga after him. But the most beautiful refinement of all was that theory he enunciated about recognising his son as an heir, but not as a human being. Don't you see that while it secured the *post obit*, it also provided some sort of answer to what would soon be the greatest difficulty of all?'

'I see several difficulties,' said Granby; 'which one do you mean?'

'I mean that if the son was not even disinherited, it would look rather odd that the father and son never met. The theory of a private repudiation answered that. So there only remained one difficulty, as I say, which is probably perplexing the gentleman now. How on earth is the old man to die?'

'I know how he ought to die,' said Granby.

Father Brown seemed to be a little bemused, and went on in a more abstracted fashion.

'And yet there is something more in it than that,' he said. 'There was something about that theory that he liked in a way that is more – well, more theoretical. It gave him an insane intellectual pleasure to tell you in one character that he had committed a crime in another character – when he really had. That is what I mean by the infernal irony; by the joke shared with the Devil. Shall I tell you something that sounds like what they call a paradox? Sometimes it is a joy in the very heart of hell to tell the truth. And above all, to tell it so that everybody misunderstands it. That is why he liked that antic of pretending to be somebody else, and then painting himself as black – as he was. And that was why my niece heard him laughing to himself all alone in the picture gallery.'

Granby gave a slight start, like a person brought back to common things with a bump.

'Your niece,' he cried. 'Didn't her mother want her to marry Musgrave? A question of wealth and position, I suppose.'

'Yes,' said Father Brown dryly; 'her mother was all in favour of a prudent marriage.'

The Red Moon of Meru

Everyone agreed that the bazaar at Mallowood Abbey (by kind permission of Lady Mounteagle) was a great success; there were roundabouts and swings and side-shows, which the people greatly enjoyed; I would also mention the Charity, which was the excellent object of the proceedings, if any of them could tell me what it was. However, it is only with a few of them that we are here concerned; and especially with three of them, a lady and two gentlemen, who passed between two of the principal tents or pavilions, their voices high in argument. On their right was the tent of the Master of the Mountain, that world-famous fortune-teller by crystals and chiromancy; a rich purple tent, all over which were traced, in black and gold, the sprawling outlines of Asiatic gods waving any number of arms like octopods. Perhaps they symbolised the readiness of divine help to be had within; perhaps they merely implied that the ideal being of a pious palmist would have as many hands as possible. On the other side stood the plainer tent of Phroso the Phrenologist; more austerely decorated with diagrams of the heads of Socrates and Shakespeare, which were apparently of a lumpy sort. But these were presented merely in black and white, with numbers and notes, as became the rigid dignity of a purely rationalistic science. The purple tent had an opening like a black cavern, and all was fittingly silent within. But Phroso the Phrenologist, a lean, shabby, sunburnt person, with an almost improbably fierce black moustache and whiskers, was standing outside his own temple, and talking, at the top of his voice, to nobody in particular, explaining that the head of any passerby would doubtless prove, on examination, to be every bit as knobbly as Shakespeare's. Indeed, the moment the lady appeared between the tents, the vigilant Phroso leapt on her and offered, with a pantomime of old-world courtesy, to feel her bumps.

She refused with civility that was rather like rudeness; but she must be excused, because she was in the middle of an argument. She also had to be excused, or at any rate was excused, because she was Lady Mounteagle. She was not a nonentity, however, in any sense; she was at once handsome and haggard, with a hungry look in her deep, dark eyes and something eager and almost fierce about her smile. Her dress was bizarre for the period; for it was before the Great War had left us in our present mood of gravity and recollection. Indeed, the dress was rather like the purple tent; being of a semi-oriental sort, covered with exotic and esoteric emblems. But everyone knew that the Mounteagles were mad; which was the popular way of saying that she and her husband were interested in the creeds and culture of the East.

The eccentricity of the lady was a great contrast to the conventionality of the two gentlemen, who were braced and buttoned up in all the stiffer fashion of that far-off day, from the tips of their gloves to their bright top hats. Yet even here there was a difference; for James Hardcastle managed at once to look correct and distinguished, while Tommy Hunter only looked correct and commonplace. Hardcastle was a promising politician; who seemed in society to be interested in everything except politics. It may be answered gloomily that every politician is emphatically a promising politician. But to do him justice, he had often exhibited himself as a performing politician. No purple tent in the bazaar, however, had been provided for him to perform in.

'For my part,' he said, screwing in the monocle that was the only gleam in his hard, legal face, 'I think we must exhaust the possibilities of mesmerism before we talk about magic. Remarkable psychological powers undoubtedly exist, even in apparently backward peoples. Marvellous things have been done by fakirs.'

'Did you say done by fakers?' asked the other young man, with doubtful innocence.

'Tommy, you are simply silly,' said the lady. 'Why will you keep barging in on things you don't understand? You're like a schoolboy screaming out that he knows how a conjuring trick is done. It's all so Early Victorian – that schoolboy scepticism. As for mesmerism, I doubt whether you can stretch it to – '

At this point Lady Mounteagle seemed to catch sight of somebody she wanted; a black stumpy figure standing at a booth where children were throwing hoops at hideous table ornaments. She darted across and cried: 'Father Brown, I've been looking for you. I want to ask you something. Do you believe in fortune-telling?'

The person addressed looked rather helplessly at the little hoop in his hand and said at last: 'I wonder in which sense you're using the word "believe". Of course, if it's all a fraud – '

'Oh, but the Master of the Mountain isn't a bit of a fraud,' she cried. 'He isn't a common conjurer or a fortune-teller at all. It's really a great honour for him to condescend to tell fortunes at my parties; he's a great religious leader in his own country; a Prophet and a Seer. And even his fortune-telling isn't vulgar stuff about coming into a fortune. He tells you great spiritual truths about yourself, about your ideals.'

'Quite so,' said Father Brown. 'That's what I object to. I was just going to say that if it's all a fraud, I don't mind it so much. It can't be much more of a fraud than most things at fancy bazaars; and there, in a way, it's a sort of practical joke. But if it's a religion and reveals spiritual truths – then it's all as false as hell and I wouldn't touch it with a bargepole.'

'That is something of a paradox,' said Hardcastle, with a smile.

'I wonder what a paradox is,' remarked the priest in a ruminant manner. 'It seems to me obvious enough. I suppose it wouldn't do very much harm if somebody dressed up as a German spy and pretended to have told all sorts of lies to the Germans. But if a man is trading in the truth with the Germans – well! So I think if a fortune-teller is trading in truth like that – '

'You really think,' began Hardcastle grimly.

'Yes,' said the other; 'I think he is trading with the enemy.'

Tommy Hunter broke into a chuckle. 'Well,' he said, 'if Father Brown thinks they're good so long as they're frauds, I should think he'd consider this copper-coloured prophet a sort of saint.'

'My cousin Tom is incorrigible,' said Lady Mounteagle. 'He's always going about showing up adepts, as he calls it. He only came down here in a hurry when he heard the Master was to be here, I believe. He'd have tried to show up Buddha or Moses.'

'Thought you wanted looking after a bit,' said the young man, with a grin on his round face. 'So I toddled down. Don't like this brown monkey crawling about.'

'There you go again!' said Lady Mounteagle. 'Years ago, when I was in India, I suppose we all had that sort of prejudice against brown people. But now I know something about their wonderful spiritual powers, I'm glad to say I know better.'

'Our prejudices seem to cut opposite ways,' said Father Brown. 'You excuse his being brown because he is brahminical; and I excuse his being brahminical because he is brown. Frankly, I don't care for spiritual powers much myself. I've got much more sympathy with spiritual weaknesses. But I can't see why anybody should dislike him merely because he is the same beautiful colour as copper, or coffee, or nut-brown ale, or those jolly peat-streams in the North. But then,' he added, looking across at the lady and screwing up his eyes, 'I suppose I'm prejudiced in favour of anything that's called brown.'

'There now!' cried Lady Mounteagle with a sort of triumph. 'I knew you were only talking nonsense!'

'Well,' grumbled the aggrieved youth with the round face. 'When anybody talks sense you call it schoolboy scepticism. When's the crystal-gazing going to begin?'

'Any time you like, I believe,' replied the lady. 'It isn't crystal-gazing, as a matter of fact, but palmistry; I suppose you would say it was all the same sort of nonsense.'

'I think there is a *via media* between sense and nonsense,' said Hardcastle, smiling. 'There are explanations that are natural and not at all nonsensical; and yet the results are very amazing. Are you coming in to be operated on? I confess I am full of curiosity.'

'Oh, I've no patience with such nonsense,' spluttered the sceptic, whose round face had become rather a red face with the heat of his contempt and incredulity. 'I'll let you waste your time on your mahogany mountebank; I'd rather go and throw at coconuts.'

The Phrenologist, still hovering near, darted at the opening.

'Heads, my dear sir,' he said, 'human skulls are of a contour far more subtle than that of coconuts. No coconut can compare with your own most – '

Hardcastle had already dived into the dark entry of the purple tent; and they heard a low murmur of voices within. As Tom Hunter turned on the Phrenologist with an impatient answer, in which he showed a regrettable indifference to the line between natural and preternatural sciences, the lady was just about to continue her little argument with the little priest, when she stopped in some surprise. James Hardcastle had come out of the tent again, and in his grim face and glaring monocle, surprise was even more vividly depicted. 'He's not there,' remarked the politician abruptly. 'He's gone. Some aged nigger, who seems to constitute his suite, jabbered something to me to the effect that the Master had gone forth rather than sell sacred secrets for gold.'

Lady Mounteagle turned radiantly to the rest. 'There now,' she cried. 'I told you he was a cut above anything you fancied! He hates being here in a crowd; he's gone back to his solitude.'

'I am sorry,' said Father Brown gravely. 'I may have done him an injustice. Do you know where he has gone?'

'I think so,' said his hostess equally gravely. 'When he wants to be alone, he always goes to the cloisters, just at the end of the left wing, beyond my husband's study and private museum, you know. Perhaps you know this house was once an abbey.'

'I have heard something about it,' answered the priest, with a faint smile.

'We'll go there, if you like,' said the lady, briskly. 'You really ought to see my husband's collection; or the Red Moon at any rate. Haven't you ever heard of the Red Moon of Meru? Yes, it's a ruby.'

'I should be delighted to see the collection,' said Hardcastle quietly, 'including the Master of the Mountain, if that prophet is one exhibit in the museum.' And they all turned towards the path leading to the house.

'All the same,' muttered the sceptical Thomas, as he brought up the rear, 'I should very much like to know what the brown beast did come here for, if he didn't come to tell fortunes.'

As he disappeared, the indomitable Phroso made one more dart after him, almost snatching at his coat-tails. 'The bump – ' he began.

'No bump,' said the youth, 'only a hump. Hump I always have when I come down to see Mounteagle.' And he took to his heels to escape the embrace of the man of science.

On their way to the cloisters the visitors had to pass through the long room that was devoted by Lord Mounteagle to his remarkable private museum of Asiatic charms and mascots. Through one open door, in the length of the wall opposite, they could see the Gothic arches and the glimmer of daylight between them, marking the square open space, round the roofed border of which the monks had walked in older days. But they had to pass something that seemed at first sight rather more extraordinary than the ghost of a monk.

It was an elderly gentleman, robed from head to foot in white, with a pale green turban, but a very pink and white English complexion and the smooth white moustaches of some amiable Anglo-Indian colonel. This was Lord Mounteagle, who had taken his Oriental pleasures more sadly, or at least more seriously than his wife. He could talk of nothing whatever, except Oriental religion and philosophy; and had thought it necessary even to dress in the manner of an Oriental hermit. While he was delighted to show his treasures, he seemed to treasure them much more for the truths supposed to be symbolised in them than for their value in collections, let alone cash. Even when he brought out the great ruby, perhaps the only thing of great value in the museum, in a merely monetary sense, he seemed to be much more interested in its name than in its size, let alone its price.

The others were all staring at what seemed a stupendously large red stone, burning like a bonfire seen through a rain of blood. But Lord Mounteagle rolled it loosely in his palm without looking at it; and staring at the ceiling, told them a long tale about the legendary character of Mount Meru, and how, in the Gnostic mythology, it had been the place of the wrestling of nameless primeval powers.

Towards the end of the lecture on the Demiurge of the Gnostics (not forgetting its connection with the parallel concept of Manichaeus), even the tactful Mr Hardcastle thought it time to create a diversion. He asked to be allowed to look at the stone; and as evening was closing in, and the long room with its single door was steadily darkening, he stepped out in the cloister beyond, to examine the jewel by a better light. It was then that they first became conscious, slowly and almost creepily conscious, of the living presence of the Master of the Mountain.

The cloister was on the usual plan, as regards its original structure; but the line of Gothic pillars and pointed arches that formed the inner square was linked together all along by a low wall, about waist high, turning the Gothic doors into Gothic windows and giving each a sort of flat window-sill of stone. This alteration was probably of ancient date; but there were other alterations of a quainter sort, which witnessed to the rather unusual individual ideas of Lord and Lady Mounteagle. Between the pillars hung thin curtains, or rather veils, made of beads or light canes, in a continental or southern manner; and on these again could be traced the lines and colours of Asiatic dragons or idols, that contrasted with the grey Gothic framework in which they were suspended. But this, while it further troubled the dying light of the place, was the least of the incongruities of which the company, with very varying feelings, became aware.

In the open space surrounded by the cloisters, there ran, like a circle in a square, a circular path paved with pale stones and edged with some sort of green enamel like an imitation lawn. Inside that, in the very centre, rose the basin of a dark-green fountain, or raised pond, in which water-lilies floated and goldfish flashed to and fro; and high above these, its outline dark against the dying light, was a great green image. Its back was turned to them and its face so completely invisible in the hunched posture that the statue might almost have been headless. But in that mere dark outline, in the dim twilight, some of them could see instantly that it was the shape of no Christian thing.

A few yards away, on the circular path, and looking towards the great green god, stood the man called the Master of the Mountain. His pointed and finely finished features seemed moulded by some skilful craftsman as a mask of copper. In contrast with this, his dark-grey beard looked almost blue like indigo; it began in a narrow tuft on his chin, and then spread outwards like a great fan or the tail of a bird. He was robed in peacock green and wore on his bald head a high cap of uncommon outline: a head-dress none of them had ever seen before; but it looked rather Egyptian than Indian. The man was standing with staring eyes; wide open, fish-shaped eyes, so motionless that they looked like the eyes painted on a mummy-case. But though the figure of the Master of the Mountain was singular enough, some of the company, including Father Brown, did not look at him; they still looked at the dark-green idol at which he himself was looking.

'This seems a queer thing,' said Hardcastle, frowning a little, 'to set up in the middle of an old abbey cloister.'

'Now, don't tell me you're going to be silly,' said Lady Mounteagle. 'That's just what we meant; to link up the great religions of East and West; Buddha and Christ. Surely you must understand that all religions are really the same.'

'If they are,' said Father Brown mildly, 'it seems rather unnecessary to go into the middle of Asia to get one.'

'Lady Mounteagle means that they are different aspects or facets, as there are of this stone,' began Hardcastle; and becoming interested in the new topic, laid the great ruby down on the stone sill or ledge under the Gothic arch. 'But it does not follow that we can mix the aspects in one artistic style. You may mix Christianity and Islam, but you can't mix Gothic and Saracenic, let alone real Indian.'

As he spoke, the Master of the Mountain seemed to come to life like a cataleptic, and moved gravely round another quarter segment of the circle, and took up his position outside their own row of arches, standing with his back to them and looking now towards the idol's back. It was obvious that he was moving by stages round the whole circle, like a hand round a clock; but pausing for prayer or contemplation.

'What is his religion?' asked Hardcastle, with a faint touch of impatience.

'He says,' replied Lord Mounteagle, reverently, 'that it is older than Brahminism and purer than Buddhism.'

'Oh,' said Hardcastle, and continued to stare through his single eyeglass, standing with both his hands in his pockets.

'They say,' observed the nobleman in his gentle but didactic voice, 'that the deity called the God of Gods is carved in a colossal form in the cavern of Mount Meru – '

Even his lordship's lecturing serenity was broken abruptly by the voice that came over his shoulder. It came out of the darkness of the museum they had just left, when they stepped out into the cloister. At the sound of it the two younger men looked first incredulous, then furious, and then almost collapsed into laughter.

'I hope I do not intrude,' said the urbane and seductive voice of Professor Phroso, that unconquerable wrestler of the truth, 'but it occurred to me that some of you might spare a little time for that much despised science of Bumps, which – '

'Look here,' cried the impetuous Tommy Hunter, 'I haven't got any bumps; but you'll jolly well have some soon, you – '

Hardcastle mildly restrained him as he plunged back through the door; and for the moment all the group had turned again and were looking back into the inner room.

It was at that moment that the thing happened. It was the impetuous Tommy, once more, who was the first to move, and this time to better effect. Before anyone else had seen anything, when Hardcastle had barely remembered with a jump that he had left the gem on the stone sill, Tommy was across the cloister with the leap of a cat and, leaning with his head and shoulders out of the aperture between two columns, had cried out in a voice that rang down all the arches: 'I've got him!'

In that instant of time, just after they turned, and just before they heard his triumphant cry, they had all seen it happen. Round the corner of one of the two columns, there had darted in and out again a brown or rather bronze-coloured hand, the colour of dead gold; such as they had seen elsewhere. The hand had struck as straight as a striking snake; as instantaneous as the flick of the long tongue of an ant-eater. But it had licked up the jewel. The stone slab of the window-sill shone bare in the pale and fading light.

'I've got him,' gasped Tommy Hunter; 'but he's wriggling pretty hard. You fellows run round him in front – he can't have got rid of it, anyhow.'

The others obeyed, some racing down the corridor and some leaping over the low wall, with the result that a little crowd, consisting of Hardcastle, Lord Mounteagle, Father Brown, and even the undetachable Mr Phroso of the bumps, had soon surrounded the captive Master of the Mountain, whom Hunter was hanging on to desperately by the collar with one hand, and shaking every now and then in a manner highly insensible to the dignity of Prophets as a class.

'Now we've got him, anyhow,' said Hunter, letting go with a sigh. 'We've only got to search him. The thing must be here.'

Three-quarters of an hour later, Hunter and Hardcastle, their top hats, ties, gloves, slips and spats somewhat the worse for their recent activities, came face to face in the cloister and gazed at each other.

'Well,' asked Hardcastle with restraint, 'have you any views on the mystery?'

'Hang it all,' replied Hunter; 'you can't call it a mystery. Why, we all saw him take it ourselves.'

'Yes,' replied the other, 'but we didn't all see him lose it ourselves. And the mystery is, where has he lost it so that we can't find it?'

'It must be somewhere,' said Hunter. 'Have you searched the fountain and all round that rotten old god there?'

'I haven't dissected the little fishes,' said Hardcastle, lifting his eyeglass and surveying the other. 'Are you thinking of the ring of Polycrates?'

Apparently the survey, through the eyeglass, of the round face before him, convinced him that it covered no such meditation on Greek legend.

'It's not on him, I admit,' repeated Hunter, suddenly, 'unless he's swallowed it.'

'Are we to dissect the Prophet, too?' asked the other smiling. 'But here comes our host.'

'This is a most distressing matter,' said Lord Mounteagle, twisting his white moustache with a nervous and even tremulous hand. 'Horrible thing to have a theft in one's house, let alone connecting it with a man like the Master. But, I confess, I can't quite make head or tail of the way in which he is talking about it. I wish you'd come inside and see what you think.'

They went in together, Hunter falling behind and dropping into conversation with Father Brown, who was kicking his heels round the cloister.

'You must be very strong,' said the priest pleasantly. 'You held him with one hand; and he seemed pretty vigorous, even when we had eight hands to hold him, like one of those Indian gods.'

They took a turn or two round the cloister, talking; and then they also went into the inner room, where the Master of the Mountain was seated on a bench, in the capacity of a captive, but with more of the air of a king.

It was true, as Lord Mounteagle said, that his air and tone were not very easy to understand. He spoke with a serene, and yet secretive sense of power. He seemed rather amused at their suggestions about trivial hiding-places for the gem; and certainly he showed no resentment whatever. He seemed to be laughing, in a still unfathomable fashion, at their efforts to trace what they had all seen him take.

'You are learning a little,' he said, with insolent benevolence, 'of the laws of time and space; about which your latest science is a thousand years behind our oldest religion. You do not even know what is really meant by hiding a thing. Nay, my poor little friends, you do not even know what is meant by seeing a thing; or perhaps you would see this as plainly as I do.'

'Do you mean it is here?' demanded Hardcastle harshly.

'Here is a word of many meanings, also,' replied the mystic. 'But I did not say it was here. I only said I could see it.'

There was an irritated silence, and he went on sleepily.

'If you were to be utterly, unfathomably, silent, do you think you might hear a cry from the other end of the world? The cry of a worshipper alone in those mountains, where the original image sits, itself like a mountain. Some say that even Jews and Muslims might worship that image; because it was never made by man. Hark! Do you hear the cry with which he lifts his head and sees in that socket of stone, that has been hollow for ages, the one red and angry moon that is the eye of the mountain?'

'Do you really mean,' cried Lord Mounteagle, a little shaken, 'that you could make it pass from here to Mount Meru? I used to believe you had great spiritual powers, but – '

'Perhaps,' said the Master, 'I have more than you will ever believe.'

Hardcastle rose impatiently and began to pace the room with his hands in his pockets.

'I never believed so much as you did; but I admit that powers of a certain type may . . . Good God!'

His high, hard voice had been cut off in mid-air, and he stopped staring; the eyeglass fell out of his eye. They all turned their faces in the same direction; and on every face there seemed to be the same suspended animation.

The Red Moon of Meru lay on the stone window-sill, exactly as they had last seen it. It might have been a red spark blown there from a bonfire, or a red rose-petal tossed from a broken rose; but it had fallen in precisely the same spot where Hardcastle had thoughtlessly laid it down.

This time Hardcastle did not attempt to pick it up again; but his demeanour was somewhat notable. He turned slowly and began to stride about the room again; but there was in his movements something masterful, where before it had been only restless. Finally, he brought himself to a standstill in front of the seated Master, and bowed with a somewhat sardonic smile.

'Master,' he said, 'we all owe you an apology and, what is more important, you have taught us all a lesson. Believe me, it will serve as a lesson as well as a joke. I shall always remember the very remarkable powers you really possess, and how harmlessly you use them. Lady Mounteagle,' he went on, turning towards her, 'you will forgive me for having addressed the Master first; but it was to you I had the honour of offering this explanation some time ago. I may say that I explained it before it had happened. I told you that most of these things could be interpreted by some kind of hypnotism. Many believe that this is the explanation of all those Indian stories about the mango plant and the boy who climbs a rope thrown into the air. It does not really happen; but the spectators are mesmerised into imagining that it happened. So we were all mesmerised into imagining this theft had happened. That brown hand coming in at the window, and whisking away the gem, was a momentary delusion; a hand in a dream. Only, having seen the stone vanish, we never looked for it where it was before. We plunged into the pond and turned every leaf of the water lilies; we were almost giving emetics to the goldfish. But the ruby has been here all the time.'

And he glanced across at the opalescent eyes and smiling bearded mouth of the Master, and saw that the smile was just a shade broader. There was something in it that made the others jump to their feet with an air of sudden relaxation and general, gasping relief.

'This is a very fortunate escape for us all,' said Lord Mounteagle, smiling rather nervously. 'There cannot be the least doubt it is as you say. It has been a most painful episode and I really don't know what apologies – '

'I have no complaints,' said the Master of the Mountain, still smiling. 'You have never touched Me at all.'

While the rest went off rejoicing, with Hardcastle for the hero of the hour, the little Phrenologist with the whiskers sauntered back towards his preposterous tent. Looking over his shoulder he was surprised to find Father Brown following him.

'Can I feel your bumps?' asked the expert, in his mildly sarcastic tone.

'I don't think you want to feel any more, do you?' said the priest goodhumouredly. 'You're a detective, aren't you?'

'Yep,' replied the other. 'Lady Mounteagle asked me to keep an eye on the Master, being no fool, for all her mysticism; and when he left his tent, I could only follow by behaving like a nuisance and a monomaniac. If anybody had come into my tent, I'd have had to look up Bumps in an encyclopaedia.'

'Bumps, What Ho She; see Folk-Lore,' observed Father Brown, dreamily. 'Well, you were quite in the part in pestering people – at a bazaar.'

'Rum case, wasn't it?' remarked the fallacious Phrenologist. 'Queer to think the thing was there all the time.'

'Very queer,' said the priest.

Something in his voice made the other man stop and stare.

'Look here!' he cried; 'what's the matter with you? What are you looking like that for! Don't you *believe* that it was there all the time?'

Father Brown blinked rather as if he had received a buffet; then he said slowly and with hesitation: 'No, the fact is . . . I can't – I can't quite bring myself to believe it.'

'You're not the sort of chap,' said the other shrewdly, 'who'd say that without reason. Why don't you think the ruby had been there all the time?'

'Only because I put it back myself,' said Father Brown.

The other man stood rooted to the spot, like one whose hair was standing on end. He opened his mouth without speech.

'Or rather,' went on the priest, 'I persuaded the thief to let me put it back. I told him what I'd guessed and showed him there was still time for repentance. I don't mind telling you in professional confidence; besides, I don't think the Mounteagles would prosecute, now they've got the thing back, especially considering who stole it.'

'Do you mean the Master?' asked the late Phroso.

'No,' said Father Brown, 'the Master didn't steal it.'

'But I don't understand,' objected the other. 'Nobody was outside the window except the Master; and a hand certainly came from outside.'

'The hand came from outside, but the thief came from the inside,' said Father Brown.

'We seem to be back among the mystics again. Look here, I'm a practical man; I only wanted to know if it is all right with the ruby – '

'I knew it was all wrong,' said Father Brown, 'before I even knew there was a ruby.'

After a pause he went on thoughtfully, 'Right away back in that argument of theirs, by the tents, I knew things were going wrong. People will tell you that theories don't matter and that logic and philosophy aren't practical. Don't you believe them. Reason is from God, and when things are unreasonable there is something the matter. Now, that quite abstract argument ended with something funny. Consider what the theories were. Hardcastle was a trifle superior and said that all things were perfectly possible; but they were mostly done merely by mesmerism, or clairvoyance; scientific names for philosophical puzzles, in the usual style. But Hunter thought it all sheer fraud and wanted to show it up. By Lady Mounteagle's testimony, he not only went about showing up fortune-tellers and suchlike, but he had actually come down specially to confront this one. He didn't often come; he didn't get on with Mounteagle, from whom, being a spendthrift, he always tried to borrow; but when he heard the Master was coming, he came hurrying down. Very well. In spite of that, it was Hardcastle who went to consult the wizard and Hunter who refused. He said he'd waste no time on such nonsense; having apparently wasted a lot of his life on proving it to be nonsense. That seems inconsistent. He thought in this case it was crystal-gazing; but he found it was palmistry.'

'Do you mean he made that an excuse?' asked his companion, puzzled.

'I thought so at first,' replied the priest; 'but I know now it was not an excuse, but a reason. He really was put off by finding it was a palmist, because – '

'Well,' demanded the other impatiently.

'Because he didn't want to take his glove off,' said Father Brown.

'Take his glove off?' repeated the enquirer.

'If he had,' said Father Brown mildly, 'we should all have seen that his hand was painted pale brown already . . . Oh, yes, he did come down specially because the Master was here. He came down very fully prepared.'

'You mean,' cried Phroso, 'that it was Hunter's hand, painted brown, that came in at the window? Why, he was with us all the time!'

'Go and try it on the spot and you'll find it's quite possible,' said the priest. 'Hunter leapt forward and leaned out of the window; in a flash he could tear off his glove, tuck up his sleeve, and thrust his hand back round the other side of the pillar, while he gripped the Indian with the other hand and halloed out that he'd caught the thief. I remarked at the time that he held the thief with one hand, where any sane man would have used two. But the other hand was slipping the jewel into his trouser pocket.'

There was a long pause and then the ex-Phrenologist said slowly. 'Well, that's a staggerer. But the thing stumps me still. For one thing, it doesn't explain the queer behaviour of the old magician himself. If he was entirely innocent, why the devil didn't he say so? Why wasn't he indignant at being accused and searched? Why did he only sit smiling and hinting in a sly way what wild and wonderful things he could do?'

'Ah!' cried Father Brown, with a sharp note in his voice: 'there you come up against it! Against everything these people don't and won't understand. All religions are the same, says Lady Mounteagle. Are they, by George! I tell you some of them are so different that the best man of one creed will be callous, where the worst man of another will be sensitive. I told you I didn't like spiritual power, because the accent is on the word power. I don't say the Master would steal a ruby, very likely he wouldn't; very likely he wouldn't think it worth stealing. It wouldn't be specially his temptation to take jewels; but it would be his temptation to take credit for miracles that didn't belong to him any more than the jewels. It was to *that* sort of temptation, to *that* sort of stealing that he yielded today. He liked us to think that he had marvellous mental powers that could make a material object fly through space; and even when he hadn't done it, he allowed us to think he had. The point about private property wouldn't occur primarily to him at all. The question wouldn't present itself in the form: "Shall I *steal* this pebble?" but only in the form: "Could I make a pebble vanish and reappear on a distant mountain?" The question of *whose* pebble would strike him as irrelevant. That is what I mean by religions being different. He is very proud of having what he calls spiritual powers. But what he calls spiritual doesn't mean what we call moral. It means rather mental; the power of the mind over matter; the magician controlling the elements. Now we are not like that, even when we are no better; even when we are worse. We, whose fathers at least were Christians, who have grown up under those medieval arches even if we bedizen them with all the demons in Asia – we have the very opposite ambition and the very opposite shame. We should all be anxious that nobody should think we had done it. He was actually anxious that everybody should think he had – even when he hadn't. He actually stole the credit of stealing. While we were all casting the crime from us like a snake, he was actually luring it to him like a snake-charmer. But snakes are not pets in this country! Here the traditions of Christendom tell at once under a test like this. Look at old Mounteagle himself, for instance! Ah, you may be as Eastern and esoteric as you like, and weal a turban and a long robe and live on messages from Mahatmas; but if a bit of stone is stolen in your house, and your friends are suspected, you will jolly soon find out that you're an ordinary English gentleman in a fuss. The man who really did it would never want us to think he did it, for he also was an English gentleman. He was also something very much better; he was a Christian thief. I hope and believe he was a penitent thief.'

'By your account,' said his companion laughing, 'the Christian thief and the heathen fraud went by contraries. One was sorry he'd done it and the other was sorry he hadn't.'

'We mustn't be too hard on either of them,' said Father Brown. 'Other English gentlemen have stolen before now, and been covered by legal and political protection; and the West also has its own way of covering theft with sophistry. After all, the ruby is not the only kind of valuable stone in the world that has changed owners; it is true of other precious stones; often carved like cameos and coloured like flowers.'

The other looked at him enquiringly; and the priest's finger was pointed to the Gothic outline of the great Abbey. 'A great graven stone,' he said, 'and that was also stolen.'

The Chief Mourner of Marne

A blaze of lightning blanched the grey woods tracing all the wrinkled foliage down to the last curled leaf, as if every detail were drawn in silverpoint or graven in silver. The same strange trick of lightning by which it seems to record millions of minute things in an instant of time, picked out everything, from the elegant litter of the picnic spread under the spreading tree to the pale lengths of winding road, at the end of which a white car was waiting. In the distance a melancholy mansion with four towers like a castle, which in the grey evening had been but a dim and distant huddle of walls like a crumbling cloud, seemed to spring into the foreground, and stood up with all its embattled roofs and blank and staring windows. And in this, at least, the light had something in it of revelation. For to some of those grouped under the tree that castle was, indeed, a thing faded and almost forgotten, which was to prove its power to spring up again in the foreground of their lives.

The light also clothed for an instant, in the same silver splendour, at least one human figure that stood up as motionless as one of the towers. It was that of a tall man standing on a rise of ground above the rest, who were mostly sitting on the grass or stooping to gather up the hamper and crockery. He wore a picturesque short cloak or cape clasped with a silver clasp and chain, which blazed like a star when the flash touched it; and something metallic in his motionless figure was emphasised by the fact that his closely curled hair was of the burnished yellow that can be really called gold; and had the look of being younger than his face, which was handsome in a hard aquiline fashion, but looked, under the strong light, a little wrinkled and withered. Possibly it had suffered from wearing a mask of make-up, for Hugo Romaine was the greatest actor of his day. For that instant of illumination the golden curls and ivory mask and silver ornament made his figure gleam like that of a man in armour; the next instant his figure was a dark and even black silhouette against the sickly grey of the rainy evening sky.

But there was something about its stillness, like that of a statue, that distinguished it from the group at his feet. All the other figures around him had made the ordinary involuntary movement at the unexpected shock of light; for though the skies were rainy it was the first flash of the storm. The only lady present, whose air of carrying grey hair gracefully, as if she were really proud of it, marked her a matron of the United States, unaffectedly shut her eyes and uttered a sharp cry. Her English husband, General

Outram, a very stolid Anglo-Indian, with a bald head and black moustache and whiskers of antiquated pattern, looked up with one stiff movement and then resumed his occupation of tidying up. A young man of the name of Mallow, very big and shy, with brown eyes like a dog's, dropped a cup and apologised awkwardly. A third man, much more dressy, with a resolute head, like an inquisitive terrier's, and grey hair brushed stiffly back, was no other than the great newspaper proprietor, Sir John Cockspur; he cursed freely, but not in an English idiom or accent, for he came from Toronto. But the tall man in the short cloak stood up literally like a statue in the twilight; his eagle face under the full glare had been like the bust of a Roman Emperor, and the carved eyelids had not moved.

A moment after, the dark dome cracked across with thunder, and the statue seemed to come to life. He turned his head over his shoulder and said casually, 'About a minute and a half between the flash and the bang, but I think the storm's coming nearer. A tree is not supposed to be a good umbrella for the lightning, but we shall want it soon for the rain. I think it will be a deluge.'

The young man glanced at the lady a little anxiously and said: 'Can't we get shelter anywhere? There seems to be a house over there.'

'There is a house over there,' remarked the general, rather grimly; 'but not quite what you'd call a hospitable hotel.'

'It's curious,' said his wife sadly, 'that we should be caught in a storm with no house near but that one, of all others.'

Something in her tone seemed to check the younger man, who was both sensitive and comprehending; but nothing of that sort daunted the man from Toronto.

'What's the matter with it?' he asked. 'Looks rather like a ruin.'

'That place,' said the general dryly, 'belongs to the Marquis of Marne.'

'Gee!' said Sir John Cockspur. 'I've heard all about that bird, anyhow; and a queer bird, too. Ran him as a front-page mystery in the *Comet* last year. "The Nobleman Nobody Knows". '

'Yes, I've heard of him, too,' said young Mallow in a low voice. 'There seem to be all sorts of weird stories about why he hides himself like that. I've heard that he wears a mask because he's a leper. But somebody else told me quite seriously that there's a curse on the family; a child born with some frightful deformity that's kept in a dark room.'

'The Marquis of Marne has three heads,' remarked Romaine quite gravely. 'Once in every three hundred years a three-headed nobleman adorns the family tree. No human being dares approach the accursed house except a silent procession of hatters, sent to provide an abnormal number of hats. But' – and his voice took one of those deep and terrible turns, that could cause such a thrill in the theatre – 'my friends, *those hats are of no human shape*.'

The American lady looked at him with a frown and a slight air of distrust, as if that trick of voice had moved her in spite of herself.

'I don't like your ghoulish jokes,' she said; 'and I'd rather you didn't joke about this, anyhow.'

'I hear and obey,' replied the actor; 'but am I, like the Light Brigade, forbidden even to reason why?'

'The reason,' she replied, 'is that he isn't the Nobleman Nobody Knows. I know him myself, or, at least, I knew him very well when he was an attaché at Washington thirty years ago, when we were all young. And he didn't wear a mask, at least, he didn't wear it with me. He wasn't a leper, though he may be almost as lonely. And he had only one head and only one heart, and that was broken.'

'Unfortunate love affair, of course,' said Cockspur. 'I should like that for the *Comet*.'

'I suppose it's a compliment to us,' she replied thoughtfully, 'that you always assume a man's heart is broken by a woman. But there are other kinds of love and bereavement. Have you never read "In Memoriam"? Have you never heard of David and Jonathan? What broke poor Marne up was the death of his brother; at least, he was really a first cousin, but had been brought up with him like a brother, and was much nearer than most brothers. James Mair, as the marquis was called when I knew him, was the elder of the two, but he always played the part of worshipper, with Maurice Mair as a god. And, by his account, Maurice Mair was certainly a wonder. James was no fool, and very good at his own political job; but it seems that Maurice could do that and everything else; that he was a brilliant artist and amateur actor and musician, and all the rest of it. James was very good-looking himself, long and strong and strenuous, with a high-bridged nose; though I suppose the young people would think he looked very quaint with his beard divided into two bushy whiskers in the fashion of those Victorian times. But Maurice was clean-shaven, and, by the portraits shown to me, certainly quite beautiful; though he looked a little more like a tenor than a gentleman ought to look. James was always asking me again and again whether his friend was not a marvel, whether any woman wouldn't fall in love with him, and so on, until it became rather a bore, except that it turned so suddenly into a tragedy. His whole life seemed to be in that idolatry, and one day the idol tumbled down, and was broken like any china doll. A chill caught at the seaside, and it was all over.'

'And after that,' asked the young man, 'did he shut himself up like this?'

'He went abroad at first,' she answered; 'away to Asia and the Cannibal Islands and Lord knows where. These deadly strokes take different people in different ways. It took him in the way of an utter sundering or severance from everything, even from tradition and as far as possible from memory.

He could not bear a reference to the old tie; a portrait or an anecdote or even an association. He couldn't bear the business of a great public funeral. He longed to get away. He stayed away for ten years. I heard some rumour that he had begun to revive a little at the end of the exile; but when he came back to his own home he relapsed completely. He settled down into religious melancholia, and that's practically madness.'

'The priests got hold of him, they say,' grumbled the old general. 'I know he gave thousands to found a monastery, and lives himself rather like a monk – or, at any rate, a hermit. Can't understand what good they think that will do.'

'Goddarned superstition,' snorted Cockspur; 'that sort of thing ought to be shown up. Here's a man that might have been useful to the Empire and the world, and these vampires get hold of him and suck him dry. I bet with their unnatural notions they haven't even let him marry.'

'No, he has never married,' said the lady. 'He was engaged when I knew him, as a matter of fact, but I don't think it ever came first with him, and I think it went with the rest when everything else went. Like Hamlet and Ophelia – he lost hold of love because he lost hold of life. But I knew the girl; indeed, I know her still. Between ourselves, it was Viola Grayson, daughter of the old admiral. She's never married either.'

'It's infamous! It's infernal!' cried Sir John, bounding up. 'It's not only a tragedy, but a crime. I've got a duty to the public, and I mean to see all this nonsensical nightmare . . . in the twentieth century – '

He was almost choked with his own protest, and then, after a silence, the old soldier said: 'Well, I don't profess to know much about those things, but I think these religious people need to study a text which says: "Let the dead bury their dead." '

'Only, unfortunately, that's just what it looks like,' said his wife with a sigh. 'It's just like some creepy story of a dead man burying another dead man, over and over again for ever.'

'The storm has passed over us,' said Romaine, with a rather inscrutable smile. 'You will not have to visit the inhospitable house after all.'

She suddenly shuddered.

'Oh, I'll never do that again!' she exclaimed.

Mallow was staring at her.

'Again! Have you tried it before?' he cried.

'Well, I did once,' she said, with a lightness not without a touch of pride; 'but we needn't go back on all that. It's not raining now, but I think we'd better be moving back to the car.'

As they moved off in procession, Mallow and the general brought up the rear; and the latter said abruptly, lowering his voice: 'I don't want that little cad Cockspur to hear but as you've asked you'd better know. It's the one thing I can't forgive Marne; but I suppose these monks have drilled him that way. My wife, who had been the best friend he ever had in America, actually came to that house when he was walking in the garden. He was looking at the ground like a monk, and hidden in a black hood that was really as ridiculous as any mask. She had sent her card in, and stood there in his very path. And he walked past her without a word or a glance, as if she had been a stone. He wasn't human; he was like some horrible automaton. She may well call him a dead man.'

'It's all very strange,' said the young man rather vaguely. 'It isn't like – like what I should have expected.'

Young Mr Mallow, when he left that rather dismal picnic, took himself thoughtfully in search of a friend. He did not know any monks, but he knew one priest, whom he was very much concerned to confront with the curious revelations he had heard that afternoon. He felt he would very much like to know the truth about the cruel superstition that hung over the house of Marne, like the black thundercloud he had seen hovering over it.

After being referred from one place to another, he finally ran his friend Father Brown to earth in the house of another friend, a Roman Catholic friend, with a large family. He entered somewhat abruptly to find Father Brown sitting on the floor with a serious expression, and attempting to pin the somewhat florid hat belonging to a wax doll on to the head of a teddy bear.

Mallow felt a faint sense of incongruity; but he was far too full of his problem to put off the conversation if he could help it. He was staggering from a sort of setback in a subconscious process that had been going on for some time. He poured out the whole tragedy of the house of Marne as he had heard it from the general's wife, along with most of the comments of the general and the newspaper proprietor. A new atmosphere of attention seemed to be created with the mention of the newspaper proprietor.

Father Brown neither knew nor cared that his attitudes were comic or commonplace. He continued to sit on the floor, where his large head and short legs made him look very like a baby playing with toys. But there came into his great grey eyes a certain expression that has been seen in the eyes of many men in many centuries through the story of nineteen hundred years; only the men were not generally sitting on floors, but at council tables, or on the seats of chapters, or the thrones of bishops and cardinals; a far-off, watchful look, heavy with the humility of a charge too great for men. Something of that anxious and far-reaching look is found in the eyes of sailors and of those who have steered through so many storms the ship of St Peter.

'It's very good of you to tell me this,' he said. 'I'm really awfully grateful, for we may have to do something about it. If it were only people like you and the general, it might be only a private matter; but if Sir John Cockspur is going to spread some sort of scare in his papers – well, he's a Toronto Orangeman, and we can hardly keep out of it.'

'But what will you say about it?' asked Mallow anxiously.

'The first thing I should say about it,' said Father Brown, 'is that, as you tell it, it doesn't sound like life. Suppose, for the sake of argument, that we are all pessimistic vampires blighting all human happiness. Suppose I'm a pessimistic vampire.' He scratched his nose with the teddy bear, became faintly conscious of the incongruity, and put it down. 'Suppose we do destroy all human and family ties. Why should we entangle a man again in an old family tie just when he showed signs of getting loose from it? Surely it's a little unfair to charge us both with crushing such affection and encouraging such infatuation. I don't see why even a religious maniac should be that particular sort of monomaniac, or how religion could increase that mania, except by brightening it with a little hope.'

Then he said, after a pause: 'I should like to talk to that general of yours.'

'It was his wife who told me,' said Mallow.

'Yes,' replied the other; 'but I'm more interested in what he didn't tell you than in what she did.'

'You think he knows more than she does?'

'I think he knows more than she says,' answered Father Brown. 'You tell me he used a phrase about forgiving everything except the rudeness to his wife. After all, what else was there to forgive?'

Father Brown had risen and shaken his shapeless clothes, and stood looking at the young man with screwed-up eyes and slightly quizzical expression. The next moment he had turned, and picking up his equally shapeless umbrella and large shabby hat, went stumping down the street.

He plodded through a variety of wide streets and squares till he came to a handsome old-fashioned house in the West End, where he asked the servant if he could see General Outram. After some little palaver he was shown into a study, fitted out less with books than with maps and globes, where the bald-headed, black-whiskered Anglo-Indian sat smoking a long, thin, black cigar and playing with pins on a chart.

'I am sorry to intrude,' said the priest, 'and all the more because I can't help the intrusion looking like interference. I want to speak to you about a private matter, but only in the hope of keeping it private. Unfortunately, some people are likely to make it public. I think, general, that you know Sir John Cockspur.'

The mass of black moustache and whisker served as a sort of mask for the lower half of the old general's face; it was always hard to see whether he smiled, but his brown eyes often had a certain twinkle.

'Everybody knows him, I suppose,' he said. 'I don't know him very well.'

'Well, you know everybody knows whatever he knows,' said Father Brown, smiling, 'when he thinks it convenient to print it. And I understand from my friend Mr Mallow, whom, I think, you know, that Sir John is going to print some scorching anti-clerical articles founded on what he would call the Marne Mystery. "Monks Drive Marquis Mad", etc.'

'If he is,' replied the general, 'I don't see why you should come to me about it. I ought to tell you I'm a strong Protestant.'

'I'm very fond of strong Protestants,' said Father Brown. 'I came to you because I was sure you would tell the truth. I hope it is not uncharitable to feel less sure of Sir John Cockspur.'

The brown eyes twinkled again, but the general said nothing.

'General,' said Father Brown, 'suppose Cockspur or his sort were going to make the world ring with tales against your country and your flag. Suppose he said your regiment ran away in battle, or your staff were in the pay of the enemy. Would you let anything stand between you and the facts that would refute him? Wouldn't you get on the track of the truth at all costs to anybody? Well, I have a regiment, and I belong to an army. It is being discredited by what I am certain is a fictitious story; but I don't know the true story. Can you blame me for trying to find it out?'

The soldier was silent, and the priest continued: 'I have heard the story Mallow was told yesterday, about Marne retiring with a broken heart through the death of his more than brother. I am sure there was more in it than that. I came to ask you if you know any more.'

'No,' said the general shortly; 'I cannot tell you any more.'

'General,' said Father Brown with a broad grin, 'you would have called me a Jesuit if I had used that equivocation.'

The soldier laughed gruffly, and then growled with much greater hostility.

'Well, I won't tell you, then,' he said. 'What do you say to that?'

'I only say,' said the priest mildly, 'that in that case I shall have to tell you.'

The brown eyes stared at him; but there was no twinkle in them now. He went on: 'You compel me to state, less sympathetically perhaps than you could, why it is obvious that there is more behind. I am quite sure the marquis has better cause for his brooding and secretiveness than merely having lost an old friend. I doubt whether priests have anything to do with it; I don't even know if he's a convert or merely a man comforting his conscience with charities; but I'm sure he's something more than a chief mourner. Since you insist, I will tell you one or two of the things that made me think so.

'First, it was stated that James Mair was engaged to be married, but somehow became unattached again after the death of Maurice Mair. Why should an honourable man break off his engagement merely because he was depressed by the death of a third party? He's much more likely to have turned for consolation to it; but, anyhow, he was bound in decency to go through with it.'

The general was biting his black moustache, and his brown eyes had become very watchful and even anxious, but he did not answer.

'A second point,' said Father Brown, frowning at the table. 'James Mair was always asking his lady friend whether his cousin Maurice was not very fascinating, and whether women would not admire him. I don't know if it occurred to the lady that there might be another meaning to that enquiry.'

The general got to his feet and began to walk or stamp about the room.

'Oh, damn it all,' he said, but without any air of animosity.

'The third point,' went on Father Brown, 'is James Mair's curious manner of mourning – destroying all relics, veiling all portraits, and so on. It does sometimes happen, I admit; it might mean mere affectionate bereavement. But it might mean something else.'

'Confound you,' said the other. 'How long are you going on piling this up?'

'The fourth and fifth points are pretty conclusive,' said the priest calmly, 'especially if you take them together. The first is that Maurice Mair seems to have had no funeral in particular, considering he was a cadet of a great family. He must have been buried hurriedly; perhaps secretly. And the last point is, that James Mair instantly disappeared to foreign parts; fled, in fact, to the ends of the earth.

'And so,' he went on, still in the same soft voice, 'when you would blacken my religion to brighten the story of the pure and perfect affection of two brothers, it seems – '

'Stop!' cried Outram in a tone like a pistol shot. 'I must tell you more, or you will fancy worse. Let me tell you one thing to start with. It was a fair fight.'

'Ah,' said Father Brown, and seemed to exhale a huge breath.

'It was a duel,' said the other. 'It was probably the last duel fought in England, and it is long ago now.'

'That's better,' said Father Brown. 'Thank God; that's a great deal better.'

'Better than the ugly things you thought of, I suppose?' said the general gruffly. 'Well, it's all very well for you to sneer at the pure and perfect affection; but it was true for all that. James Mair really was devoted to his cousin, who'd grown up with him like a younger brother. Elder brothers and sisters do sometimes devote themselves to a child like that, especially when he's a sort of infant phenomenon. But James Mair was the sort of simple character in whom even hate is in a sense unselfish. I mean that even when his tenderness turns to rage it is still objective, directed outwards to its object; he isn't conscious of himself. Now poor Maurice Mair was just the opposite. He was far more friendly and popular; but his success had made him live in a house of mirrors. He was first in every sort of sport and art and accomplishment; he nearly always won and took his winning amiably. But if ever, by any chance, he lost, there was just a glimpse of something not so amiable; he was a little jealous. I needn't tell you the whole miserable story of how he was a little jealous of his cousin's engagement; how he couldn't keep his restless vanity from interfering. It's enough to say that one of the few things in which James Mair was admittedly ahead of him was marksmanship with a pistol; and with that the tragedy ended.'

'You mean the tragedy began,' replied the priest. 'The tragedy of the survivor. I thought he did not need any monkish vampires to make him miserable.'

'To my mind he's more miserable than he need be,' said the general. 'After all, as I say, it was a ghastly tragedy, but it was a fair fight. And Jim had great provocation.'

'How do you know all this?' asked the priest.

'I know it because I saw it,' answered Outram stolidly. 'I was James Mair's second, and I saw Maurice Mair shot dead on the sands before my very eyes.'

'I wish you would tell me more about it,' said Father Brown reflectively. 'Who was Maurice Mair's second?'

'He had a more distinguished backing,' replied the general grimly. 'Hugo Romaine was his second; the great actor, you know. Maurice was mad on acting and had taken up Romaine (who was then a rising but still a struggling man), and financed the fellow and his ventures in return for taking lessons from the professional in his own hobby of amateur acting. But Romaine was then, I suppose, practically dependent on his rich friend; though he's richer now than any aristocrat. So his serving as second proves very little about what he thought of the quarrel. They fought in the English fashion, with only one second apiece; I wanted at least to have a surgeon, but Maurice boisterously refused it, saying the fewer people who knew, the better; and at the worst we could immediately get help. "There's a doctor in the village not half a mile away," he said; "I know him and he's got the fastest horse in the country. He could be brought here in no time; but there's no need to bring him here till we know." Well, we all knew that Maurice ran most risk, as the pistol was not his weapon; so when he refused aid nobody liked to ask for it. The duel was fought on a flat stretch of sand on the east coast of Scotland; and both the sight and sound of it were masked from the hamlets inland by a long rampart of sandhills patched with rank grass; probably part of the links, though in those days no Englishman had heard of golf. There was one deep, crooked cranny in the sandhills through which we came out on the sands. I can see them now; first a wide strip of dead yellow, and beyond, a narrower strip of dark red; a dark red that seemed already like the long shadow of a deed of blood.

'The thing itself seemed to happen with horrible speed; as if a whirlwind had struck the sand. With the very crack of sound Maurice Mair seemed to spin like a teetotum and pitch upon his face like a ninepin. And queerly enough, while I'd been worrying about him up to that moment, the instant he was dead all my pity was for the man who killed him; as it is to this day and hour. I knew that with that, the whole huge terrible pendulum of my friend's life-long love would swing back; and that whatever cause others might find to pardon him, he would never pardon himself for ever and ever. And so, somehow, the really vivid thing, the picture that burns in my memory so that I can't forget it, is not that of the catastrophe, the smoke and the flash and the falling figure. That seemed to be all over, like the noise that wakes a man up. What I saw, what I shall always see, is poor Jim hurrying across towards his fallen friend and foe; his brown beard looking black against the ghastly pallor of his face, with its high features cut out against the sea; and the frantic gestures with which he waved me to run for the surgeon in the hamlet behind the sandhills. He had dropped his pistol as he ran; he had a glove in one hand and the loose and fluttering fingers of it seemed to elongate and emphasise his wild pantomime of pointing or hailing for help. That is the picture that really remains with me; and there is nothing else in that picture, except the striped background of sands and sea and the dark, dead body lying still as a stone, and the dark figure of the dead man's second standing grim and motionless against the horizon.'

'Did Romaine stand motionless?' asked the priest. 'I should have thought he would have run even quicker towards the corpse.'

'Perhaps he did when I had left,' replied the general. 'I took in that undying picture in an instant and the next instant I had dived among the sandhills, and was far out of sight of the others. Well, poor Maurice had made a good choice in the matter of doctors; though the doctor came too late, he came quicker than I should have thought possible. This village surgeon was a very remarkable man, red-haired, irascible, but extraordinarily strong in promptitude and presence of mind. I saw him but for a flash as he leapt on his horse and went thundering away to the scene of death, leaving me far behind. But in that flash I had so strong a sense of his personality that I wished to God he had really been called in before the duel began; for I believe on my soul he would have prevented it somehow. As it was, he cleaned up the mess with marvellous swiftness; long before I could trail back to the sea-shore on my two feet his impetuous practicality had managed everything; the corpse was temporarily buried in the sandhills and the unhappy homicide had been persuaded to do the only thing he could do – to flee for his life. He slipped along the coast till he came to a port and managed to get out of the country. You know the rest; poor Jim remained abroad for many years; later, when the whole thing had been hushed up or forgotten, he returned to his dismal castle and automatically inherited the title. I have never seen him from that day to this, and yet I know what is written in red letters in the inmost darkness of his brain.'

'I understand,' said Father Brown, 'that some of you have made efforts to see him?'

'My wife never relaxed her efforts,' said the general. 'She refuses to admit that such a crime ought to cut a man off for ever; and I confess I am inclined to agree with her. Eighty years before it would have been thought quite normal; and really it was manslaughter rather than murder. My wife is a great friend of the unfortunate lady who was the occasion of the quarrel and she has an idea that if Jim would consent to see Viola Grayson once again, and receive her assurance that old quarrels are buried, it might restore his sanity. My wife is calling a sort of council of old friends tomorrow, I believe. She is very energetic.'

Father Brown was playing with the pins that lay beside the general's map; he seemed to listen rather absent-mindedly. He had the sort of mind that sees things in pictures; and the picture which had coloured even the prosaic mind of the practical soldier took on tints yet more significant and sinister in the more mystical mind of the priest. He saw the dark-red desolation of sand, the very hue of Aceldama, and the dead man lying in a dark heap, and the slayer, stooping as he ran, gesticulating with a glove in demented remorse, and always his imagination came back to the third thing that he could not yet fit into any human picture: the second of the slain man standing motionless and mysterious, like a dark statue on the edge of the sea. It might seem to some a detail; but for him it was that stiff figure that stood up like a standing note of interrogation.

Why had not Romaine moved instantly? It was the natural thing for a second to do, in common humanity, let alone friendship. Even if there were some double-dealing or darker motive not yet understood, one would think it would be done for the sake of appearances. Anyhow, when the thing was all over, it would be natural for the second to stir long before the other second had vanished beyond the sandhills.

'Does this man Romaine move very slowly?' he asked.

'It's queer you should ask that,' answered Outram, with a sharp glance. 'No, as a matter of fact he moves very quickly when he moves at all. But, curiously enough, I was just thinking that only this afternoon I saw him stand exactly like that, during the thunderstorm. He stood in that silver-clasped cape of his, and with one hand on his hip, exactly and in every line as he stood on those bloody sands long ago. The lightning blinded us all, but he did not blink. When it was dark again he was standing there still.'

'I suppose he isn't standing there now?' enquired Father Brown. 'I mean, I suppose he moved sometime?'

'No, he moved quite sharply when the thunder came,' replied the other. 'He seemed to have been waiting for it, for he told us the exact time of the interval. Is anything the matter?'

'I've pricked myself with one of your pins,' said Father Brown. 'I hope I haven't damaged it.' But his eyes had snapped and his mouth abruptly shut.

'Are you ill?' enquired the general, staring at him.

'No,' answered the priest; 'I'm only not quite so stoical as your friend Romaine. I can't help blinking when I see light.'

He turned to gather up his hat and umbrella; but when he had got to the door he seemed to remember something and turned back. Coming up close to Outram, he gazed up into his face with a rather helpless expression, as of a dying fish, and made a motion as if to hold him by the waistcoat.

'General,' he almost whispered, 'for God's sake don't let your wife and that other woman insist on seeing Marne again. Let sleeping dogs lie, or you'll unleash all the hounds of hell.'

The general was left alone with a look of bewilderment in his brown eyes, as he sat down again to play with his pins.

Even greater, however, was the bewilderment which attended the successive stages of the benevolent conspiracy of the general's wife, who had assembled her little group of sympathisers to storm the castle of the misanthrope. The first surprise she encountered was the unexplained absence of one of the actors in the ancient tragedy. When they assembled by agreement at a quiet hotel quite near the castle, there was no sign of Hugo Romaine, until a belated telegram from a lawyer told them that the great actor had suddenly left the country. The second surprise, when they began the bombardment by sending up word to the castle with an urgent request for an interview, was the figure which came forth from those gloomy gates to receive the deputation in the name of the noble owner. It was no such figure as they would have conceived suitable to those sombre avenues or those almost feudal formalities. It was not some stately steward or major-domo, nor even a dignified butler or tall and ornamental footman. The only figure that came out of the cavernous castle doorway was the short and shabby figure of Father Brown.

'Look here,' he said, in his simple, bothered fashion. 'I told you you'd much better leave him alone. He knows what he's doing and it'll only make everybody unhappy.'

Lady Outram, who was accompanied by a tall and quietly dressed lady, still very handsome, presumably the original Miss Grayson, looked at the little priest with cold contempt.

'Really, sir,' she said; 'this is a very private occasion, and I don't understand what you have to do with it.'

'Trust a priest to have to do with a private occasion,' snarled Sir John

Cockspur. 'Don't you know they live behind the scenes like rats behind a wainscot burrowing their way into everybody's private rooms. See how he's already in possession of poor Marne.' Sir John was slightly sulky, as his aristocratic friends had persuaded him to give up the great scoop of publicity in return for the privilege of being really inside a Society secret. It never occurred to him to ask himself whether he was at all like a rat in a wainscot.

'Oh, that's all right,' said Father Brown, with the impatience of anxiety. 'I've talked it over with the marquis and the only priest he's ever had anything to do with; his clerical tastes have been much exaggerated. I tell you he knows what he's about; and I do implore you all to leave him alone.'

'You mean to leave him to this living death of moping and going mad in a ruin!' cried Lady Outram, in a voice that shook a little. 'And all because he had the bad luck to shoot a man in a duel more than a quarter of a century ago. Is that what you call Christian charity?'

'Yes,' answered the priest stolidly; 'that is what I call Christian charity.'

'It's about all the Christian charity you'll ever get out of these priests,' cried Cockspur bitterly. 'That's their only idea of pardoning a poor fellow for a piece of folly; to wall him up alive and starve him to death with fasts and penances and pictures of hell-fire. And all because a bullet went wrong.'

'Really, Father Brown,' said General Outram, 'do you honestly think he deserves this? Is that your Christianity?'

'Surely the true Christianity,' pleaded his wife more gently, 'is that which knows all and pardons all; the love that can remember – and forget.'

'Father Brown,' said young Mallow, very earnestly, 'I generally agree with what you say; but I'm hanged if I can follow you here. A shot in a duel, followed instantly by remorse, is not such an awful offence.'

'I admit,' said Father Brown dully, 'that I take a more serious view of his offence.'

'God soften your hard heart,' said the strange lady, speaking for the first time. 'I am going to speak to my old friend.'

Almost as if her voice had raised a ghost in that great grey house, something stirred within and a figure stood in the dark doorway at the top of the great stone flight of steps. It was clad in dead black, but there was something wild about the blanched hair and something in the pale features that was like the wreck of a marble statue.

Viola Grayson began calmly to move up the great flight of steps; and Outram muttered in his thick black moustache: 'He won't cut her dead as he did my wife, I fancy.'

Father Brown, who seemed in a collapse of resignation, looked up at him for a moment.

'Poor Marne has enough on his conscience,' he said. 'Let us acquit him of what we can. At least he never cut your wife.'

'What do you mean by that?'

'He never knew her,' said Father Brown.

As they spoke, the tall lady proudly mounted the last step and came face to face with the Marquis of Marne. His lips moved, but something happened before he could speak.

A scream rang across the open space and went wailing away in echoes along those hollow walls. By the abruptness and agony with which it broke from the woman's lips it might have been a mere inarticulate cry. But it was an articulated word; and they all heard it with a horrible distinctness.

'Maurice!'

'What is it, dear?' cried Lady Outram, and began to run up the steps; for the other woman was swaying as if she might fall down the whole stone flight. Then she faced about and began to descend, all bowed and shrunken and shuddering. 'Oh, my God,' she was saying. 'Oh, my God, it isn't Jim at all. It's Maurice!'

'I think, Lady Outram,' said the priest gravely, 'you had better go with your friend.'

As they turned, a voice fell on them like a stone from the top of the stone stair, a voice that might have come out of an open grave. It was hoarse and unnatural, like the voices of men who are left alone with wild birds on desert islands. It was the voice of the Marquis of Marne, and it said: 'Stop!'

'Father Brown,' he said, 'before your friends disperse I authorise you to tell them all I have told you. Whatever follows, I will hide from it no longer.'

'You are right,' said the priest, 'and it shall be counted to you.'

'Yes,' said Father Brown quietly to the questioning company afterwards. 'He has given me the right to speak; but I will not tell it as he told me, but as I found it out for myself. Well, I knew from the first that the blighting monkish influence was all nonsense out of novels. Our people might possibly, in certain cases, encourage a man to go regularly into a monastery, but certainly not to hang about in a medieval castle. In the same way, they certainly wouldn't want him to dress up as a monk when he wasn't a monk. But it struck me that he might himself want to wear a monk's hood or even a mask. I had heard of him as a mourner, and then as a murderer; but already I had hazy suspicions that his reason for hiding might not only be concerned with what he was, but with who he was.

'Then came the general's vivid description of the duel; and the most vivid thing in it to me was the figure of Mr Romaine in the background; it was vivid because it was in the background. Why did the general leave behind him on the sand a dead man, whose friend stood yards away from him like a stock or a stone? Then I heard something, a mere trifle, about a trick habit that Romaine has of standing quite still when he is waiting for something to happen; as he waited for the thunder to follow the lightning. Well, that automatic trick in this case betrayed everything. Hugo Romaine on that old occasion, also, was waiting for something.'

'But it was all over,' said the general. 'What could he have been waiting for?'

'He was waiting for the duel,' said Father Brown.

'But I tell you I saw the duel!' cried the general.

'And I tell you you didn't see the duel,' said the priest.

'Are you mad?' demanded the other. 'Or why should you think I am blind?'

'Because you were blinded – that you might not see,' said the priest. 'Because you are a good man and God had mercy on your innocence, and he turned your face away from that unnatural strife. He set a wall of sand and silence between you and what really happened on that horrible red shore, abandoned to the raging spirits of Judas and of Cain.'

'Tell us what happened!' gasped the lady impatiently.

'I will tell it as I found it,' proceeded the priest. 'The next thing I found was that Romaine the actor had been training Maurice Mair in all the tricks of the trade of acting. I once had a friend who went in for acting. He gave me a very amusing account of how his first week's training consisted entirely of falling down; of learning how to fall flat without a stagger, as if he were stone dead.'

'God have mercy on us!' cried the general, and gripped the arms of his chair as if to rise.

'Amen,' said Father Brown. 'You told me how quickly it seemed to come; in fact, Maurice fell before the bullet flew, and lay perfectly still, waiting. And his wicked friend and teacher stood also in the background, waiting.'

'We are waiting,' said Cockspur, 'and I feel as if I couldn't wait.'

'James Mair, already broken with remorse, rushed across to the fallen man and bent over to lift him up. He had thrown away his pistol like an unclean thing; but Maurice's pistol still lay under his hand and it was undischarged. Then as the elder man bent over the younger, the younger lifted himself on his left arm and shot the elder through the body. He knew he was not so good a shot, but there was no question of missing the heart at that distance.'

The rest of the company had risen and stood staring down at the narrator with pale faces. 'Are you sure of this?' asked Sir John at last, in a thick voice.

'I am sure of it,' said Father Brown, 'and now I leave Maurice Mair, the present Marquis of Marne, to your Christian charity. You have told me something today about Christian charity. You seemed to me to give it almost too large a place; but how fortunate it is for poor sinners like this man that you err so much on the side of mercy, and are ready to be reconciled to all mankind.'

'Hang it all,' exploded the general; 'if you think I'm going to be reconciled to a filthy viper like that, I tell you I wouldn't say a word to save him from hell. I said I could pardon a regular decent duel, but of all the treacherous assassins – '

'He ought to be lynched,' cried Cockspur excitedly. 'He ought to burn alive like a nigger in the States. And if there is such a thing as burning for ever, he jolly well – '

'I wouldn't touch him with a barge-pole myself,' said Mallow.

'There is a limit to human charity,' said Lady Outram, trembling all over.

'There is,' said Father Brown dryly; 'and that is the real difference between human charity and Christian charity. You must forgive me if I was not altogether crushed by your contempt for my uncharitableness today; or by the lectures you read me about pardon for every sinner. For it seems to me that you only pardon the sins that you don't really think sinful. You only forgive criminals when they commit what you don't regard as crimes, but rather as conventions. So you tolerate a conventional duel, just as you tolerate a conventional divorce. You forgive because there isn't anything to be forgiven.'

'But, hang it all,' cried Mallow, 'you don't expect us to be able to pardon a vile thing like this?'

'No,' said the priest; 'but *we* have to be able to pardon it.'

He stood up abruptly and looked round at them.

'We have to touch such men, not with a bargepole, but with a benediction,' he said. 'We have to say the word that will save them from hell. We alone are left to deliver them from despair when your human charity deserts them. Go on your own primrose path pardoning all your favourite vices and being generous to your fashionable crimes; and leave us in the darkness, vampires of the night, to console those who really need consolation; who do things really indefensible, things that neither the world nor they themselves can defend; and none but a priest will pardon. Leave us with the men who commit the mean and revolting and real crimes; mean as St Peter when the cock crew, and yet the dawn came.'

'The dawn,' repeated Mallow doubtfully. 'You mean hope – for him?'

'Yes,' replied the other. 'Let me ask you one question. You are great ladies and men of honour and secure of yourselves; you would never, you can tell yourselves, stoop to such squalid reason as that. But tell me this. If any of you had so stooped, which of you, years afterwards, when you were old and rich and safe, would have been driven by conscience or confessor to tell such a story of yourself? You say you could not commit so base a crime. Could you confess so base a crime?'

The others gathered their possessions together and drifted by twos and threes out of the room in silence. And Father Brown, also in silence, went back to the melancholy castle of Marne.

The Secret of Flambeau

' – The sort of murders in which I played the part of the murderer,' said Father Brown, putting down the wine glass. The row of red pictures of crime had passed before him in that moment.

'It is true,' he resumed, after a momentary pause, 'that somebody else had played the part of the murderer before me and done me out of the actual experience. I was a sort of understudy; always in a state of being ready to act the assassin. I always made it my business, at least, to know the part thoroughly. What I mean is that, when I tried to imagine the state of mind in which such a thing would be done, I always realised that I might have done it myself under certain mental conditions, but not under others; and not generally under the obvious ones. And then, of course, I knew who really had done it; and he was not generally the obvious person.

'For instance, it seemed obvious to say that the revolutionary poet had killed the old judge who saw red about red revolutionaries. But that isn't really a reason for the revolutionary poet *killing* him. It isn't, if you think what it would really be like to be a revolutionary poet. Now I set myself conscientiously down to *be* a revolutionary poet. I mean that particular sort of pessimistic anarchical lover of revolt, not as reform, but rather as destruction. I tried to clear my mind of such elements of sanity and constructive common sense as I have had the luck to learn or inherit. I shut down and darkened all the skylights through which comes the good daylight out of heaven; I imagined a mind lit only by a red light from below; a fire rending rocks and cleaving abysses *upwards*. And even with the vision at its wildest and worst, I could not see why such a visionary should cut short his own career by colliding with a common policeman, for killing one out of a million conventional old fools, as he would have called them. He wouldn't do it; however much he wrote songs of violence. He wouldn't do it, *because* he wrote songs of violence. A man who can express himself in song need not express himself in suicide. A poem was an event to him; and he would want to have more of them. Then I thought of another sort of heathen; the sort that is not destroying the world but entirely depending on the world. I thought that, save for the grace of God, I might have been a man for whom the world was a blaze of electric lights, with nothing but utter darkness beyond and around it. The worldly man, who really lives only for this world and believes in no other, whose worldly success and pleasure are all he can ever snatch out of nothingness – *that* is the man who will really do anything, when he is in danger of losing the whole world and saving nothing. It is not the revolutionary man but the respectable man who would commit any crime – to save his respectability. Think what exposure would mean to a man like that fashionable barrister; and exposure of the one crime still really hated by his fashionable world – treason against patriotism. If I had been in his position, and had nothing better than his philosophy, heaven alone knows what I might have done. That is just where this little religious exercise is so wholesome.'

'Some people would think it was rather morbid,' said Grandison Chace dubiously.

'Some people,' said Father Brown gravely, 'undoubtedly *do* think that charity and humility are morbid. Our friend the poet probably would. But I'm not arguing those questions; I'm only trying to answer your question about how I generally go to work. Some of your countrymen have apparently done me the honour to ask how I managed to frustrate a few miscarriages of justice. Well, you can go back and tell them that I do it by morbidity. But I most certainly don't want them to think I do it by magic.'

Chace continued to look at him with a reflective frown; he was too intelligent not to understand the idea; he would also have said that he was too healthy-minded to like it. He felt as if he were talking to one man and yet to a hundred murderers. There was something uncanny about that very small figure, perched like a goblin beside the goblin stove; and the sense that its round head had held such a universe of wild unreason and imaginative injustice. It was as if the vast void of dark behind it were a throng of dark gigantic figures, the ghosts of great criminals held at bay by the magic circle of the red stove, but ready to tear their master in pieces.

'Well, I'm afraid I do think it's morbid,' he said frankly. 'And I'm not sure it isn't almost as morbid as magic. But morbidity or no, there's one thing to be said; it must be an interesting experience.' Then he added, after reflection: 'I don't know whether you would make a really good criminal. But you ought to make a rattling good novelist.'

'I only have to deal with real events,' said Father Brown. 'But it's sometimes harder to imagine real things than unreal ones.'

'Especially,' said the other, 'when they are the great crimes of the world.'

'It's not the great crimes but the small crimes that are really hard to imagine,' replied the priest.

'I don't quite know what you mean by that,' said Chace.

'I mean commonplace crimes like stealing jewels,' said Father Brown; 'like that affair of the emerald necklace or the Ruby of Meru or the artificial goldfish. The difficulty in those cases is that you've got to make your mind small. High and mighty humbugs, who deal in big ideas, don't do those obvious things. I was sure the Prophet hadn't taken the ruby; or the Count the goldfish; though a man like Bankes might easily take the emeralds. For them, a jewel is a piece of glass: and they can see through the glass. But the little, literal people take it at its market value.

'For that you've got to have a small mind. It's awfully hard to get; like focusing smaller and sharper in a wobbling camera. But some things helped; and they threw a lot of light on the mystery, too. For instance, the sort of man who brags about having "shown up" sham magicians or poor quacks of any sort – he's *always* got a small mind. He is the sort of man who "sees through" tramps and trips them up in telling lies. I dare say it might sometimes be a painful duty. It's an uncommonly base pleasure. The moment I realised what a small mind meant, I knew where to look for it – in the man who wanted to expose the Prophet – and it was he that sneaked the ruby; in the man who jeered at his sister's psychic fancies – and it was he who nabbed the emeralds. Men like that always have their eye on jewels; they never could rise, with the higher humbugs, to *despising* jewels. Those criminals with small minds are always quite conventional. They become criminals out of sheer conventionality.

'It takes you quite a long time to feel so crudely as that, though. It's quite a wild effort of imagination to be so conventional. To want one potty little object as seriously as all that. But you can do it . . . You can get nearer to it. Begin by thinking of being a greedy child; of how you might have stolen a sweet in a shop; of how there was one particular sweet you wanted – then you must subtract the childish poetry; shut off the fairy light that shone on the sweet-stuff shop; imagine you really think you know the world and the market value of sweets – you contract your mind like the camera focus – the thing shapes and then sharpens . . . and then, suddenly, it comes!'

He spoke like a man who had once captured a divine vision. Grandison Chace was still looking at him with a frown of mingled mystification and interest. It must be confessed that there did flash once beneath his heavy frown a look of something almost like alarm. It was as if the shock of the first strange confession of the priest still thrilled faintly through him like the last vibration of a thunderclap in the room. Under the surface he was saying to himself that the mistake had only been a temporary madness; that, of course, Father Brown could not really be the monster and murderer he had beheld for that blinding and bewildering instant. But was there not *something* wrong with the man who talked in that calm way about being a murderer? Was it possible that the priest was a little mad?

'Don't you think,' he said, abruptly; 'that this notion of yours, of a man trying to feel like a criminal, might make him a little too tolerant of crime?'

Father Brown sat up and spoke in a more staccato style.

'I know it does just the opposite. It solves the whole problem of time and sin. It gives a man his remorse beforehand.'

There was a silence; the American looked at the high and steep roof that stretched half across the enclosure; his host gazed into the fire without moving; and then the priest's voice came on a different note, as if from lower down.

'There are two ways of renouncing the devil,' he said; 'and the difference is perhaps the deepest chasm in modern religion. One is to have a horror of him because he is so far off; and the other to have it because he is so near. And no virtue and vice are so much divided as those two virtues.'

They did not answer and he went on in the same heavy tone, as if he were dropping words like molten lead.

'You may think a crime horrible because you could never commit it. I think it horrible because I could commit it. You think of it as something like an eruption of Vesuvius; but that would not really be so terrible as this house catching fire. If a criminal suddenly appeared in this room – '

'If a criminal appeared in this room,' said Chace, smiling, 'I think you would be a good deal too favourable to him. Apparently you would start by telling him that you were a criminal yourself and explaining how perfectly natural it was that he should have picked his father's pocket or cut his mother's throat. Frankly, I don't think it's practical. I think that the practical effect would be that no criminal would ever reform. It's easy enough to theorise and take hypothetical cases; but we all know we're only talking in the air. Sitting here in M. Duroc's nice, comfortable house, conscious of our respectability and all the rest of it, it just gives us a theatrical thrill to talk about thieves and murderers and the mysteries of their souls. But the people who really have to deal with thieves and murderers have to deal with them differently. We are safe by the fireside; and we know the house is not on fire. We know there is not a criminal in the room.'

The M. Duroc to whom allusion had been made rose slowly from what had been called his fireside, and his huge shadow flung from the fire seemed to cover everything and darken even the very night above him.

'There *is* a criminal in this room,' he said. 'I am one. I am Flambeau, and the police of two hemispheres are still hunting for me.'

The American remained gazing at him with eyes of a stony brightness; he seemed unable to speak or move.

'There is nothing mystical, or metaphorical, or vicarious about my confession,' said Flambeau. 'I stole for twenty years with these two hands; I fled from the police on these two feet. I hope you will admit that my activities were practical. I hope you will admit that my judges and pursuers really had to deal with crime. Do you think I do not know all about their way of reprehending it? Have I not heard the sermons of the righteous and seen the cold stare of the respectable; have I not been lectured in the lofty and distant style, asked how it was possible for anyone to fall so low, told that no decent person could ever have dreamed of such depravity? Do you think all that ever did anything but make me laugh? Only my friend told me that he knew exactly why I stole; and I have never stolen since.'

Father Brown made a gesture as of deprecation; and Grandison Chace at last let out a long breath like a whistle.

'I have told you the exact truth,' said Flambeau; 'and it is open to you to hand me over to the police.'

There was an instant of profound stillness, in which could be faintly heard the belated laughter of Flambeau's children in the high, dark house above them, and the crunching and snorting of the great, grey pigs in the twilight. And then it was cloven by a high voice, vibrant and with a touch of offence, almost surprising for those who do not understand the sensitive American spirit, and how near, in spite of commonplace contrasts, it can sometimes come to the chivalry of Spain.

'Monsieur Duroc,' he said rather stiffly. 'We have been friends, I hope, for some considerable period; and I should be pretty much pained to suppose you thought me capable of playing you such a trick while I was enjoying your hospitality and the society of your family, merely because you chose to tell me a little of your own autobiography of your own free will. And when you spoke merely in defence of your friend – no, sir, I can't imagine any gentleman double-crossing another under such circumstances; it would be a damned sight better to be a dirty informer and sell men's blood for money. But in a case like this – ! Could you conceive any man being such a Judas?'

'I could try,' said Father Brown.

THE POET AND THE LUNATICS

The Poet and the Lunatics

EPISODES IN THE LIFE OF GABRIEL GALE

Contents

[illegible] have [illegible] with [illegible]
or a rope or anythin[illegible]

The melanchol[illegible] [illegible] [illegible]
on [illegible] [illegible] [illegible]
[illegible] all.

I

The Fantastic Friends

The inn called the Rising Sun had an exterior rather suggesting the title of the Setting Sun. It stood in a narrow triangle of garden, more grey than green, with broken-down hedges mingling with the melancholy reeds of a river; with a few dark and dank arbours, of which the roofs and the seats had alike collapsed; and a dingy dried-up fountain, with a weather-stained water-nymph and no water. The house itself seemed rather devoured by ivy than decorated with it; as if its old bones of brown brick were slowly broken by the dragon coils of that gigantic parasite. On the other side it looked on a lonely road leading across the hills down to a ford across the river; now largely disused since the building of a bridge lower down. Outside the door was a wooden bench and table, and above it a wooden sign, much darkened, with the gold of the sun's disc faded to a brown; and under the sign stood the innkeeper, gazing gloomily up the road. His hair was black and flat, and his face, of a congested purple, had all the sombreness, if not all the beauty, of sunset.

The only person in the place who exhibited any liveliness was the person who was leaving it. He was the first and last customer for many months; a solitary swallow who had conspicuously failed to make a summer; and the swallow was now flitting. He was a medical man on a holiday; young, and of an agreeable ugliness, with a humorous hatchet face and red hair; and the cat-like activity of his movements contrasted with the stagnant inertia of the inn by the ford. He was strapping up his own bag on the table under the sign; and neither his host, who stood a yard off, nor the single servant, who moved heavily and obscurely within, offered to help him; possibly through sulkiness, possibly merely through dreaminess and disuse.

The long silence, idle or busy, was broken for the first time by two sharp and explosive sounds. The first was the abrupt bursting of the strap which the doctor was tightening round the bag on the table; and the second was the loud and cheerful 'Damn!' which was his comment upon it.

'Here's a pretty go,' observed the medical gentleman, who went by the name of Garth; 'I shall have to tie it up with something. Have you got a cord or a rope or anything?'

The melancholy innkeeper turned very slowly and went indoors, coming out presently with a length of dusty rope in a loop like a halter, probably for tethering a donkey or a calf.

'That's all I've got,' he said; 'I'm pretty well at the end of my own tether anyhow.'

'You seem a bit depressed,' observed Dr Garth; 'you probably want a tonic. Perhaps this medicine chest burst open to give you one.'

'Prussic acid is the kind of tonic I feel inclined for,' answered the landlord of the Rising Sun.

'I never recommend it,' observed the doctor cheerfully. 'It's very pleasant at the moment, no doubt; but I never feel I can guarantee a complete recovery afterwards. But you certainly seem down in the mouth; you didn't even brighten up when I indulged in such an eccentricity as paying my bill.'

'Much obliged to you, sir,' observed the other gruffly, 'but it would want a lot more bills to keep this rotten old show from going to pot. It was a good business once, when the right-of-way was open beyond the river, and everybody used this ford. But the last squire shut up the path somehow; and now everything goes by the new bridge a mile away. Nobody comes this way; and, saving your presence, I don't know why anybody should.'

'Well, they say the new squire is nearly bankrupt himself,' observed Dr Garth. 'So history brings its revenges. Westermaine's his name, isn't it? I'm told there's a brother and sister living in the big house over there, with precious little to live on. I suppose the whole countryside's rather gone downhill. But you're wrong about nobody coming here,' he added suddenly, 'for there are two men coming over the hill now.'

The road ran across the valley at right angles to the river; beyond the ford the forgotten right-of-way could be traced more faintly up the slope to where the ruined gate that marked Westermaine Abbey stood dark against clouds of a pallor that was faintly lurid, as with a hint of storm. But on the other side of the valley the sky was clear; and the early afternoon seemed as bright and brisk as morning. And on this side, where the white road curved over the hill, two figures were advancing, which seemed, even when they were hardly more than dots in the distance, to be markedly dissimilar.

As they came nearer to the inn, the contrast increased, and was accentuated by the very fact of their air of mutual familiarity; as if they were almost walking arm in arm. One was comparatively short and very sturdy; the other unusually tall and slender. They were both fair; but the blond hair of the shorter man was neatly parted and smoothly plastered down; while that of the other stood up in erratic wisps and tufts that looked fantastic. The shorter man had a full square face sharpened by a very pointed nose, and a pair of bright, birdlike eyes, that made it look like a small beak. There was something of the cock sparrow about him; and, indeed, he seemed more of a town bird than a country bird. His clothes were as neat and commonplace as a clerk's; and he carried a businesslike little bag as if he was going up to the City; while his tall companion had bundled on his back a loose knapsack, and what was evidently the paraphernalia of a painter. He had a long, slightly cadaverous face, with absent-minded eyes; but the chin beneath jutted forward, almost as if it had formed an unconscious resolution of its own, of which the blank blue eyes were still unaware. They were both young; and they both walked without hats, probably through the heat of walking; for the one held a hard straw hat in his hand, and the other had a loose grey felt stuffed anyhow into his knapsack.

They came to a halt before the inn; and the shorter man said jovially to his companion, 'Here's a field for your efforts, anyhow.'

Then he called out with breezy civility to the innkeeper, asking him to bring out two pots of ale; and when that gloomy character had disappeared into his gloomy place of entertainment, he turned to the doctor with the same radiant loquacity: 'My friend's a painter,' he explained, 'but rather a special sort of painter. You might call him a house-painter; but he's not quite what most people mean by one. It may surprise you, sir, but he's an R.A., and not the stuffy sort that sometimes suggests, either. One of the first among the young geniuses, and exhibits at all their cranky galleries. But his whole aim and glory in life is to go about repainting inn-signs. There; you don't meet a genius with that little fancy every day. What's the name of this pub?'

And he stood on tiptoe, craning and peering at the blackened sign with an extraordinary contained vivacity in his curiosity.

'The Rising Sun,' he commented, turning eagerly again to his silent friend. 'That's what you would call an omen, after what you were saying this morning about reviving the real inns. My friend is very poetical; and he said it would make a sunrise all over England.'

'Well, they say the sun never sets on the British Empire,' observed the doctor, with a laugh.

'I don't feel it about the Empire so much,' said the painter simply, breaking his silence like one spontaneously thinking aloud. 'After all, one doesn't fancy an English inn on the top of Mount Everest, or somewhere on the Suez Canal. But one's life would be well spent in waking up the dead inns of England and making them English and Christian again. If I could do it, I would do nothing else till I die.'

'Of course you can do it,' replied his travelling companion. 'A picture by an artist like you, and hung outside a public-house, makes it fashionable for miles round.'

'Is it really true, then,' enquired Dr Garth, 'that you employ all your serious powers on subjects like public-house signs?'

'What finer subjects are there, even as subjects?' asked the painter; he was now evidently full of his favourite subject and he was one of those who are either abstractedly silent or ardently argumentative. 'Is it more dignified to paint an Academy portrait of some snobbish mayor in a gold chain, or some swindling millionaire's wife in a diamond tiara, than to paint the heads of great English admirals, to be toasted in good ale? Is it better to paint some nepotistical old noodle wearing his George and Garter than to paint St George himself in the very act of killing the Dragon? I've repainted six old signs of St George and the Dragon, or even the Dragon without St George; a sign called the Green Dragon is usually very suggestive to anybody with a little imagination; you can make him a sort of spirit and terror of tropical forests. Even a Blue Boar is suggestive; something nocturnal with stars like the Great Bear; like that dim monstrous boar that stood for chaos and old night in the Celtic mythology.'

And he reached for his pewter pot, and applied himself to it with absorption.

'He's a poet as well as a painter, you know,' explained the smaller man, still regarding his companion with an absurd air of proprietorship, as if he himself were the keeper and showman of some singular wild animal; 'You've probably heard of the poems of Gabriel Gale, illustrated by himself? I can get you a copy if you are interested in these things. I'm his agent and business man; my name's Hurrel . . . James Hurrel. People laugh at us and call us the Heavenly Twins, because we're inseparable, and I never let him out of my sight. Have to look after him . . . eccentricities of genius, you know.'

The painter took his face off the pewter pot, a face fiery with controversy.

'Genius oughtn't to be eccentric!' he cried in some excitement. 'Genius ought to be centric. It ought to be in the core of the cosmos, not on the revolving edges. People seem to think it a compliment to accuse one of being an outsider, and to talk about the eccentricities of genius. What would they think, if I said I only wish to God I had the centricities of genius?'

'I fear they would think it was the beer,' replied Dr Garth, 'that had slightly confused your polysyllables. Well, it may be a romantic idea to revive the old signs, as you say. Romance is not much in my line.'

Mr Hurrel, the agent, cut in sharply, and even eagerly. 'But it isn't only a romantic idea,' he explained; 'it's a real, practical idea, too. I'm a business man, and you may believe me it's really a business proposition. Not only for us, but for the other people too . . . for the innkeepers and the villagers and the squires, and everybody. Why, look at this broken-down alehouse they call the Rising Sun. If everyone would work together, they could have this empty hole humming like a hive in a year. If the squire would open the old road and let people visit the ruins, if he'd build a bridge here by the inn and hang out a sign painted by Gabriel Gale, you'd have all the cultivated sightseers in Europe stopping here for lunch.'

'Hullo!' cried the doctor. 'It looks as if they were coming to lunch already. Really, our pessimistic friend inside talked as if this were a ruin in the desert; but I begin to believe it does a trade like the Savoy.'

They had all been standing with their backs to the road, looking at the dark tavern under discussion; but even before the doctor began to speak, Gabriel Gale, the painter and poet, had become in some odd fashion conscious of an addition to the company. Perhaps it was because the elongated shadows of a horse and two human figures had for some little time rested on the sunny road beside him. He turned his head over his shoulder, and remained staring at what he saw.

A high dog-cart had drawn up on the other side of the road. The reins were in the gloved hands of a tall, dark young lady, clad in dark blue of the tailor-made type, neat but not particularly new. By her side was a man, perhaps ten years older than herself, but seeming in many ways much more, for his high-featured face was wasted as with sickness, and there was a great anxiety in his large grey eyes.

In the momentary silence the clear voice of the girl came like an echo of the doctor's phrase, saying: 'I am sure we can get some lunch here.' She slipped lightly to the ground and stood by the horse's head, while her companion descended with a little more hesitation. He was dressed in light tweeds, which seemed somehow slightly incongruous with his invalid air, and he addressed Hurrel with a rather nervous smile.

'I hope you won't regard me as an eavesdropper, sir; but you were not exactly speaking as if you were talking secrets.'

Hurrel, indeed, had been talking as if he were a cheap-jack dominating the noise of the fair; and he smiled and answered quite pleasantly: 'I was only saying what anybody might about what a squire might do with a property like this. I don't in the least mind anybody listening who happens to be interested.'

'I happen to be a little interested,' answered the man in tweeds, 'because, as it happens, I am the squire if there are any squires nowadays.'

'I sincerely apologise,' answered the agent, still smiling; 'but, if you will play Haroun Alraschid . . . '

'Oh, I'm not at all offended,' answered the other. 'To tell the truth, I'm rather wondering whether you aren't quite right.'

Gabriel Gale had been looking at the girl in dark blue rather longer than was quite polite; but painters and absent-minded persons may sometimes be excused in such cases. His friend would probably have infuriated him by calling it one of the eccentricities of genius, but it might have been disputed whether his admiration was entirely eccentric. Lady Diana Westermaine would have made a most satisfactory sign for an inn – a bush worthy of the best wine – or might even have uplifted the lowly estate of an Academy picture, though it was long since her unfortunate family could have easily afforded one. She had hair of a curious dark brown, which in ordinary shades looked black, while the lights in it looked almost red; her dark eyebrows had a touch of temper both in the good and the bad sense; her eyes were even larger and greyer than her brother's, but less filled with mere worry and more with a more spiritual weariness. Gale had the sense that her soul was more hungry than her body. But he had also the thought that people are only hungry because they are healthy. He thought all this in the brief moments before he remembered his manners, and turned to consider the other group.

When he had left off looking at her, she began looking at him, but with a somewhat cooler curiosity.

Meanwhile, Mr James Hurrel had been working wonders, not to say miracles. With something more than the tenacity of a tout, with something of the eloquence of the born diplomatist, he had already wound round the squire a web of suggestions and proposals and possibilities. There was really something about him of that imaginative business man of whom we hear so much and see so little. Affairs which a man like Westermaine could never normally have conceived as being settled except by long lawyers' letters extending over several months, seemed to be arranging themselves before him in several minutes. A new bridge of the most artistic woodwork seemed already to point across the river to the open road; a new and higher class of rents seemed already to be dotting the valley with artistic villages; and a new golden sign of the Rising Sun, with the signature of Gabriel Gale, already blazed above them, a symbol that the sun had risen indeed.

Before they knew where they were the whole company had been bustled in the most friendly fashion through the inn, and set down to a luncheon that was really a committee round the table in the dreary garden beside the river. Hurrel was drawing plans on the wooden table and making calculations on pieces of paper, and reeling off figures and answering objections and growing every moment more restless and radiant. He had one piece of magic for making others believe – the fact that he evidently believed himself; and the squire, who had never met such a person before, had no weapons with which to fight him, even if it had been his interest to do so. Amid all this whirl Lady Diana looked across at Gale, who sat at the opposite corner of the table, somewhat detached and dreamy.

'What do you think of it, Mr Gale?' she said; but Mr Gale's business adviser answered for him, as he answered for everybody and answered for everything.

'Oh, it's no good asking him about business,' he cried boisterously. 'He's only one of the assets; he brings in all the artistic people. He's a great painter; but we only want a painter to paint. Lord bless you, he won't mind my saying that; he never minds what I say, or what anybody says, for that matter. He doesn't answer a question for about half an hour, as a rule.'

Nevertheless, the painter answered the lady's question under the time specified; but all he said was, 'I think we ought to consult the innkeeper.'

'Oh, very well,' cried the resilient Hurrel, leaping up. 'I'll do that now, if you like. Back in a minute.' And he disappeared again through the dark interior of the inn.

'Our friend is very eager,' said the squire, smiling; 'but, after all, those are the sort of people who get things done. I mean practical things.'

The lady was again looking at the painter with a slightly constricted brow; she seemed to be almost sorry for him in his comparative eclipse; but he only smiled and said: 'No, I'm no good at practical things.'

Almost as he spoke a noise like a sort of cry came through the inn from the road beyond, and Dr Garth sprang to his feet and stood peering in at the door. The next moment Gale also seemed to rouse himself with a sort of sudden agitation; and the moment after that the others were all following the doctor, who had already started through the house. But when he came to the front door Gale turned for a moment, barring the exit with his tall figure, and said: 'Don't let the lady come out.'

The squire had already seen over the painter's shoulder a horrible instantaneous image. It was the black figure of a man hanging from the signboard of the Rising Sun.

It was only instantaneous; for the next moment Dr Garth had cut him down, with the assistance of Hurrel, who had presumably uttered the first cry of alarm. The man over whom the doctor was bending was the unfortunate innkeeper; and this was apparently the form in which he took his prussic acid.

After being busy in silence for a few moments, the doctor gave a grunt of relief and said: 'He's not dead; in fact he'll be all right presently.' Then he said, with a sort of disgust: 'Why the devil did I leave that rope there instead of tying up my bag like a tidy professional man? I forgot all about it in all this fuss. Well, Mr Hurrel, the sun nearly rose too late for somebody.'

Hurrel and the doctor carried the unfortunate innkeeper into his inn, the latter declaring that the would-be suicide would soon be in a position to be questioned, if questioning was necessary. Gale paced up and down outside in his aimless fashion, frequently frowning at the sign that had served as a gallows (and the table that had probably served as the proverbial stool kicked away) with a frown that seemed not only pained but puzzled.

'This is a most distressing business,' said the squire. 'Of course I am a magistrate and all that, but I should hate to have to trouble the poor fellow with the police.' At the sound of the word, Gabriel Gale swung round and said in a loud harsh voice: 'Oh, I forgot the police. Of course, he must be locked up in a cell to show him that life is worth living after all, and the world a bright, happy place to live in.'

He laughed shortly and frowned heavily, and then after ruminating a moment, said with a certain abruptness: 'Look here, I want to ask you a favour, which may seem an odd one. I want you to let me question this poor chap when he comes to. Give me ten minutes alone with him, and I will promise to cure him of suicidal mania better than a policeman could.'

'But why you especially?' asked the doctor, in some natural annoyance.

'Because I am no good at practical things,' answered Gale, 'and you have got beyond practical things.'

There was another silence, and he spoke again with the same strange air of authority.

'What you want is an unpractical man. That is what people always want in the last resort and the worst conditions. What can practical men do here? Waste their practical time in running after the poor fellow and cutting him down from one pub sign after another? Waste their practical lives watching him day and night, to see he doesn't get hold of a rope or a razor? Do you call that practical? You can only forbid him to die. Can you persuade him to live? Believe me, that is where we come in. A man must have his head in the clouds and his wits wool gathering in fairyland, before he can do anything so practical as that.'

The group felt a growing bewilderment at his new attitude; it seemed to fill the stage in a strange fashion; nor was it lessened when he actually or apparently fulfilled his undertaking, coming out of the inn twenty minutes afterwards, and cheerfully announcing that the innkeeper would not hang himself again. The next moment he had jumped on to the table under the sign with a large piece of chalk in his hand, and was making sketchy and slashing strokes of design on the brown face of the Rising Sun.

Lady Diana was looking on at the operation with a dark and watchful face. She was of a type more intellectual than the others, and she recognised a real thread of thought running through all that seemed to them transcendental tomfoolery. She had understood the implied irony of his first reference to their host; the moral that had come before the frightful fable. After all, they had certainly been thinking of everything about the inn except the innkeeper. She could see there was an intelligent case, and a practical example, of the occasions when the poet can be more useful than the policeman. But she was conscious also of something baffling about him above and beyond all this; of a disquiet in him with some deeper cause, and something in his eye that belied the new levity of his manner. His draughtsmanship, however, was proceeding in the most dashing and even dazzling fashion, when Lady Diana spoke: 'I can't think how you can do it,' she said, 'on the very place where a man has hung himself like Judas.'

'It was the treason, not the despair of Judas, that was really bad,' he answered. 'I was just thinking of something like that for the picture. I prefer it to Apollo and all that, for a treatment of the sunrise. Look here, you have a big head blocked in with some shadows, in the centre,' and he made some bold markings on the sun's disc. 'His dark face hidden in his hands like that, but a burst of golden dawn behind like a glory. Red bars of level cloud and a red cock, just there. The greatest of sinners and of saints; his reproach the cock, and his halo the Rising Sun.'

The nameless shadow seemed to have fallen from him as he talked and worked; and by an almost symbolic coincidence the strong afternoon sun fell with a strange fullness and splendour upon him and his work, which shone out against a blackening background of clouds continually gathering and darkening on the stormy side of the valley, beyond the ford. Against those masses of sinister purple and indigo, his figure looked like that of some legendary craftsman clad in gold and painting the frescoes of a golden chapel. The impression increased as the head and halo of St Peter grew under his hand; and the lady was of the sort not disinclined to dream herself back in some distant period, about which she did not know too much. She felt herself back among the sacred arts and crafts of the medieval world; which were all she knew of the medieval world.

Unfortunately, a shadow came between her and the sun in a shape that did not remind her of the medieval world. Mr James Hurrel, the agent, his stiff hat a little on one side, jumped on to the same table on which the artist stood, and sat within two yards of him, with dangling legs, and somewhat aggressive cigar. 'Always have to keep an eye on him, your ladyship, or he'd be giving 'em away,' he called out, and somehow his voice and figure failed to fit in with the picture of pious and primitive craftsmanship.

Diana Westermaine explained to herself lucidly that she had no sort of reason to be angry; but she was exceedingly angry. The conversation of the two had been of no particular intimacy; but its increase to three had a very practical and painful effect of intrusion. She could not imagine why the artist, who was a gentleman, should go about with such a little bounder as his business adviser; and she wanted to hear more about the picture of St Peter, or something interesting. As the agent sat down he had audibly observed something about making room for a little one. If he, at that moment, had been suddenly suspended from the sign, it is doubtful if the lady would have cut him down.

At this moment a much quieter voice said in her ear: 'Excuse me, but might I have one word with you?'

She turned and found Dr Garth, with his bag in his hand, evidently about to resume his journey at last.

'I'm going,' he said, 'and I feel I really ought to tell you something before I go.'

He drew her a little way up the road of his departure, and then turned with an abrupt and hurried air of farewell.

'Doctors are often in delicate situations,' he said, 'and a troublesome sense of duty drives me to saying a rather delicate thing. I tell it to you and not your brother, because I think you have a long way the better nerve of the two. There is something I suspect about those two men who go about painting signs.'

From where they stood on the higher ground she could still see the sign itself shining with its new accretion of colours, and the tall, actively moving figure, shining also with sunlight, and from that distance altogether dwarfing the small and dingy figure near his feet. There returned on her still more strongly the vision of a true creator, making pure colours in the innocent morning of the world.

'They are called the Heavenly Twins,' went on the doctor, 'because they are inseparable. Well, there are many kinds of couples that are inseparable, and many causes for their never separating. But there is one sort that specially concerns me, and I should be sorry to see mixed up with you.'

'I haven't the least idea what you mean,' replied Lady Diana.

'What about a lunatic and his keeper?' said the doctor, and walked on rapidly along the road, leaving her behind him.

She had the sensation of furiously flinging a suggestion from her, from the top of a high tower to the bottom of an abyss, combined with the sensation that the tower was not high enough nor the abyss deep enough; she even had the novel sensation that there was something weak about her throwing. While the tower of her mind was still rocking with the effort, she was interrupted by her brother, who came hastily, and even excitedly, towards her.

'I've just asked these gentlemen across to our place,' he said, 'to fix up this business better. And we'd better be starting, for there's a storm beating up, and even the ford sometimes gets pretty dicky. As it is, we shall have to cross two at a time in our own rotten old cart.'

It was in a sort of dream that she found herself again untethering the horse and again taking the reins. It was in a dream that she heard the voice that irritated her so much saying, 'Heavenly Twins, you know, Heavenly Twins; we mustn't be parted'; and then the voice of the squire replying, 'Oh, it'll only be for a minute, anyhow; she'll send Wilson back with the dog-cart at once. There's only room for two at a time, I'm afraid.' They stood a little way back in the doorway of the inn as they talked, and Gabriel Gale had just stepped from the table and was standing nearer to the dog-cart.

Then there surged up in her suddenly she knew not what movement of impatience or defiance; and she said in a matter-of-fact tone: 'Are you coming first, Mr Gale?'

The face of the artist blanched as if he were blasted with white lightning in the sunlight. He gave one look over his shoulder and then leapt into the seat beside her, and the horse threw up his head and began to move towards the ford. The rain must have already fallen further upstream, for there was already the sensation of water flowing more deeply about the horse's legs; and, though they were only fording a river, she had a hazy sensation of crossing a Rubicon.

Enoch Wilson, the groom, one of the small group left at Westermaine Abbey, died and was gathered to his fathers without having the faintest notion of the determining part which he played in the dark events of that night. And his private life, though, like that of other immortal spirits, of an intense interest, does not in any other point affect this story. It is enough to say that he was rather deaf, and, like many grooms, more sympathetic with the moods of horses than of men. Lady Diana sought him out in the stable, which stood far from the house and near the river, and told him to take the dog-cart back for the rest of the party. She spoke hurriedly and told him to hurry, because the rain would soon make the ford difficult; and her phrases, combined with his own bias, turned his mind chiefly to a consideration of the horse. He drove across under the gathering storm, and as he drew near the dark inn he heard high and excited voices. Mr Hurrel was evidently hot upon his hobby or campaign. The groom got the impression that there was a quarrel; and took a few testy words from his master as meaning that he was not to be disturbed. So the careful Wilson took the horse back across the ford and back into the stable, congratulating himself on having saved the valuable quadruped from the worst inconveniences of what threatened to be a flood. Then he betook himself to his own occupations, leaving a trail of destiny behind him.

Meanwhile Diana Westermaine had left the stable and made her way across the grounds to rejoin the guest who had gone in front of her. As she went up through a lane of hollyhocks and tall plants, she saw the vast flying island or continent of rain cloud, with its volcanic hues and outline, come sailing slowly over the dark, wooded ridge that was the wall of the valley. There was already something faintly lurid about the twilight with which it covered the rich colours of the garden; but higher up the climbing path a strip of lawn was golden in a chance gleam of sunlight, and against it she saw the figure she had come to seek. She recognised it by the light-brown clothes that had looked like gold in the evening light, but there was something very extraordinary about the shape as distinct from the colour. He seemed to be waving his arms slowly like branches in a breeze, and she fancied the arms were unnaturally long. For an instant she had the ugly fancy that the figure was deformed; and yet the more unearthly fancy that it had no head. Then the nightmare turned into ordinary nonsense, for the man threw a sort of cartwheel and alighted on his feet laughing. He had actually been standing on his head, or rather on his hands.

'Excuse me,' he said, 'I often do that. It's a very good thing for a landscape-painter to see the landscape upside down. He sees things then as they really are; yes, and that's true in philosophy as well as art.' He brooded and then explained explosively.

'It's all very well to talk about being topsy-turvy. But when the angels hang head downwards, we know they come from above. It's only those that come from below that always have their noses in the air.'

Despite his hilarious manner, she approached him with a certain subconscious fear; which was not lessened when he lowered his voice and added: 'Shall I tell you a secret?'

At the same moment were heard overhead the first heavy movements of the thunder, through which his voice came, perhaps, with an accidental air as of loud whispering.

'The world is upside down. We're all upside down. We're all flies crawling on a ceiling, and it's an everlasting mercy that we don't drop off.'

At that instant the twilight turned to a white blaze of lightning; and she was shocked to see that his face was quite serious.

She said with a sort of irritation, 'You do say such crazy things,' and the next moment her voice was lost in the thronging echoes of the thunder, which seemed to shake everything, shouting the same word again and again . . . crazy, crazy, crazy. She had unconsciously given a word for the worst thought in her mind.

As yet no rain had fallen on the garden slopes, though the noise of it was already troubling the river beyond. But even had it done so, she herself doubted if the man would have noticed it. Even in more normal moments he seemed to be one who singly pursued a solitary train of thought, and he was still talking, like a man talking to himself, about the rationality of topsy-turvydom.

'We were talking about St Peter,' he said; 'you remember that he was crucified upside down. I've often fancied his humility was rewarded by seeing in death the beautiful vision of his boyhood. He also saw the landscape as it really is: with the stars like flowers, and the clouds like hills, and all men hanging on the mercy of God.'

Then a heavy drop of rain fell on him; and the effect of it was indescribable. It seemed to sting him like a wasp and wake him out of a trance. He started and stared round; and then said in a new and more natural voice: 'My God, where is Hurrel? What are the others doing? Aren't they here yet?'

With an impulse not to be analysed, Diana dashed through the swaying plants to the top of a neighbouring hillock, and looked across the valley to the inn of the Rising Sun. And she saw flowing between them and that place a heavier and wider flood, which in that wild moment looked impassable, like the river of death.

In a strange way it seemed to her a symbol of something greater than the mere grim realism that would have told her, now only too plainly, that she was left alone with a lunatic. Somehow it seemed that the lunacy itself was only a sort of abominable accident and obstacle between her and something that might have been beautiful and a satisfaction of the soul. Another dark river was flowing between her and her own fairyland.

At the same moment Gabriel Gale gave a terrible cry; he also had seen afar off the sundering flood.

'You were right, after all,' he said. 'You spoke of Judas, when I dared to speak of Peter. I have blasphemed and done the unpardonable sin. I am the traitor now.' Then he added in lower and heavier tones: 'Yes, I am the man who sold God.'

The girl's mind was growing clearer with the cold pain of reality. She had heard that maniacs sometimes accused themselves of the unpardonable sin. Something of her natural courage returned also, and she was ready to do anything, though she did not yet see very clearly what to do. As she was fighting for a solution, the question was settled for her in some degree by her companion himself, who started running down the slope.

'I must get across again if I swim the river,' he said. 'I ought never to be away from Hurrel like this. I can never tell what will happen next.'

She followed his descent, and was rather surprised to see him deflect it to dart towards the stable. Before she knew where she was, he was struggling with the horse and dragging it out into the shafts; and she felt an irrational pleasure in the fact that he had the strength of a man, if it was the strength of a madman. But her own high spirit and self-respect had returned to her, and there rose in her a furious refusal to be a passive spectator of what might well be merely a suicide. After all, however mad he might be, the man was doing the right thing in trying to rejoin his medical attendant; and she would not have the last effort of his sanity frustrated by the antics of his disease.

'I'll drive if we must,' she said in a ringing tone. 'He'll go better with me.'

The sun had set behind the hills opposite, and night was already deepening the darkness of the storm. As the rocking vehicle splashed up to the hub of its wheel in the eddying water, she could only faintly see the long water-rushes streaming with the stream, as if they were indeed the shades of the underworld hovering without hope beside the Styx. But she had no longer need to call it, merely in metaphor, a river of death. Death was driving hard against horse and cart, staggering the insecure foothold of the one, and swaying the human burden of the other; the thunder was about their ears, and on their dreadful path scarce any light but the lightning; and her human companion was a man uttering a monologue, of which she heard snatches, more shocking than the thunder. All the reason and realism in her told her that he might at any moment tear her in pieces. But underneath all such things there was something else contrary and incredible; something in the need and the companionship, and the courage and heroism she was showing; and it was too deep in her dizzy soul for her to know that it was exultation.

The horse almost fell just as they came to the end of the ford, but Gale sprang from the cart and held it, standing knee-deep in water.

In a lull in the noise of the storm she heard for the first time voices from the inn beside the river . . . voices high, and even shrill, as if the altercation that the groom had heard had risen steadily like the rise of the storm. Then there came what sounded like the crash of a falling chair. Gale dragged the horse to land with the energy of a demon, then dropped the bridle, and set off running towards the inn.

Even as he did so a piercing shriek rose into the night from the doors of that solitary and sinister tavern by the river. It died away in a wailing echo along the reedy banks of the river itself, as if the reeds were indeed the lost spirits by the river of Hades; and the very thunder seemed to have stopped and held its breath to hear it. Then before the thunder moved again came one wide flash of lightning, as wide as an instantaneous daylight, picking out the most minute details of the distance, of the branches and twigs upon the wooded heights, and the clover in the flat fields beside the river. And with the same clarity she saw for an instant something incredible and abominable, and yet not wholly new or unfamiliar . . . something that returned in the waking world as a detested nightmare will return in sleep. It was the black figure of a man dangling from the painted gallows of the Rising Sun. But it was not the same man.

Diana was convinced for the moment that she herself had gone mad. She could only imagine dully that her own mind had snapped under the strain, and that the dark objects she saw were but dancing dots upon a void. But one of those black dots had certainly seemed to be the figure of her own brother thus lassoed to the beam; and the other black dot, literally a dancing dot, had been the figure of that energetic business man, Mr James Hurrel. For just then his energy was taking the form of dancing; he was hopping and capering with excitement in front of that frightful signboard.

Darkness followed the flash, and a moment after she heard the great voice of Gale himself, a larger and louder voice than she had imagined him to possess, bellowing through the darkness and the stress of wind. 'It's all right . . . he's quite safe now.' Little as she understood of anything yet, she understood with a cold thrill that they had come just in time.

She was still dazed when she staggered somehow through the din and distraction of the tempest into the inn parlour, with a smoky lamp on the table, and the three figures of that frustrated tragedy around it. The squire, her brother, in a sort of collapse of convalescence, sat or lay in an armchair with a stiff dose of brandy in front of him. Gabriel Gale was standing up, like one who had taken command, with a face as white but as hard as marble. He was speaking to the man named Hurrel in low level, and quiet tones, but with one finger pointed, as when a man speaks to a dog.

'Go over there and sit by the window,' he said. 'You must keep quite quiet.'

The man obeyed, taking a seat at the other end of the room, and looked out of the window at the storm, without hearing or seeking to hear the talk of the others.

'What does it all mean?' asked Diana at last. 'I thought you . . . the truth is Dr Garth gave me a hint that you were only a lunatic and his keeper.'

'And so we are, as you see,' answered Gale; 'but the keeper has behaved far worse than the lunatic.'

'But I thought you were the lunatic,' she said with simplicity.

'No,' he replied; 'I am the criminal.'

They had drawn nearer to the doorway, and their voices also were covered by the noise of the elements, so that they were almost as much alone as when they stood beyond the river. She remembered the earlier dialogue, and the violent and mysterious language he had used in it; and she said doubtfully: 'You said things like that and worse over the other side, and that's what made me think so. I couldn't understand why you should say such wild things against yourself.'

'I suppose I do talk rather wildly,' he said. 'Perhaps you were not so wrong, after all, and I have a streak of sympathy with lunatics . . . and that's why I can manage them. Anyhow, I happen to be the only person who can manage this particular lunatic. It's a long story, and perhaps I shall tell it someday. This poor fellow once did me a great service, and I feel I can only repay it by looking after him and saving him from the infernal brutality of officials. You see, the truth is they say I have a talent for it . . . a sort of psychological imagination. I generally know what they're going to do or fancy next. I've known a lot of them, one way or another . . . religious maniacs who thought they were divine or damned, or what not, and revolutionary maniacs, who believed in dynamite or doing without clothes; or philosophical lunatics, of whom I could tell you some tall stories, too . . . men who behaved as if they lived in another world and under different stars, as I suppose they did. But of all the maniacs I have tried to manage, the maddest of all maniacs was the man of business.'

He smiled rather sourly, and then the tragedy returned to his face as he went on: 'As for your other question, I may have talked wildly against myself, but I didn't talk worse than I deserve. Hadn't I deserted my post, like a traitor? Didn't I leave my wretched friend in the lurch, like a Judas? It's true he'd never broken out like this before; but I was sure in my heart there was one of his antics mixed up with that first affair of the innkeeper. But the innkeeper really was suicidal, and I fancy Hurrel only helped him, so to speak; but it was that that put the damnable notion in his head. I never dreamed he would break out against your brother, or I would . . . but why do I try to make excuses when there is no excuse? I followed my own will till it went within an inch of murder; and it's I who ought to be hanging from the wooden sign, if hanging weren't too good for me.'

'But why . . . ' she began automatically, and then stopped dead, with the sense of a whole new world surging up against her.

'Ah, why,' he repeated with a changed voice; 'but I think you know why. It is not your fault, but you know why. You know what has often made a sentinel leave his post. You know what brought Troilus out of Troy and perhaps Adam out of Eden. And I have neither the need nor the right to tell you.'

She stood looking out into the darkness, and her face wore a singular smile.

'Well, there's the other story you promised to tell someday,' she said. 'Perhaps you will tell it me if we meet again.' And she held out her hand in farewell.

The sinister and fantastic partners had set off again next morning when the sun first shone upon the road; the storm had rolled away along the valley and the birds were singing after the rain. Stranger things yet were to happen before he and she should meet again; but for the moment she had a curious relapse into repose and contemplation. She reminded herself of the words about the world being upside down; and thought it had indeed turned upside down many times in that single night. And she could not analyse the sensation that, in spite of everything, it had come the right side up.

2

The Yellow Bird

Five men had halted at the top of a hill overlooking a valley beautiful enough to be called a vision, but too neglected ever to have been vulgarised by being called a view. They were a sketching club on a walking tour; but when they had come to that place they did no more walking, and, strangely enough, very little sketching. It was as if they had come to some quiet end of the world; that corner of the earth seemed to have a curious effect on them, varying with their various personalities, but acting on all as something arresting and vaguely final. Yet the quality was as nameless as it was unique; there was nothing definably different from twenty other wooded valleys in those western shires upon the marches of Wales. Green slopes dived into a fringe of dark forests that looked black by comparison, but the grey columns of which were mirrored in the curving river like a long winding colonnade. Only a little way along, on one side of the river, the bank was cleared of timber, and formed a platform for old gardens and orchards, in the midst of which stood an old tall house, of a rich brown brick with blue shutters, and rather neglected creepers clinging to it, more like moss to a stone than like flowers to a flower-bed. The roof was flat, with a chimney near the centre of it, from which a thin thread of smoke was drawn up into the sky; the only sign that the house was not wholly deserted. Of the five men who looked down at the landscape, only one had any special reason for looking at the house.

The eldest of the artists, a dark, active, ambitious man in spectacles, destined to be famous afterwards under the name of Luke Walton, was affected by the place in a curious fashion. It seemed to tease him like a fly or something elusive; he could not please himself with a point of view, but was perpetually shifting his camp-stool from place to place, crossing and recrossing the theatre of these events amid the jeers of his companions. The second, a heavy, fair-haired man named Hutton, stared at the scene in a somewhat bovine fashion, made a few lines on a sketching block, and then announced in a loud voice that it was a good place for a picnic, and that he was going to have his lunch. The third painter agreed with him; but as he was said to be a poet as well as a painter, he was expected to show a certain fervour for any opportunities of avoiding work. Indeed, this particular artist, whose name was Gabriel Gale, did not seem disposed even to look at the landscape, far less to paint it; but after taking a bite out of a ham sandwich, and a swig at somebody else's flask of claret, incontinently lay down on his back under a tree and stared up at the twilight of twinkling leaves; some believing him to be asleep, while others more generously supposed him to be composing poetry. The fourth, a smaller and more alert man named Garth, could only be regarded as an honorary member of the artistic group; for he was more interested in science than in art, and carried not a paintbox but a camera. Nevertheless, he was not without an intelligent appreciation of scenery, and he was in the act of fixing up his photographic apparatus so that it covered the angle of the river where stood the neglected garden and the distant house. And at that moment the fifth man, who had not yet moved or spoken, made so abrupt and arresting a gesture that one might say that he struck up the camera, like a gun pointed to kill.

'Don't,' he said; 'it's bad enough when they try to paint it.'

'What's the matter?' asked Garth. 'Don't you like that house?'

'I like it too much,' said the other, 'or rather, I love it too much to like it at all.'

The fifth man who spoke was the youngest of the party, but he had already at least some local success and celebrity; partly because he had devoted his talent to the landscape and legends of that countryside, and partly because he came of a family of small squires whose name was historic in those hills. He was tall, with dark-brown hair and a long brown face, with a high-bridged nose that looked rather distinguished than handsome; and there was a permanent cloud of consideration on his brow that made him seem much older than his years. He alone of all these men had made no gesture, either of labour or relaxation, on coming to the crest of the hill. While Walton went to and fro, and Hutton started cheerfully on his meal, and Gale flung himself on the couch of leaves to look up into the tree-tops, this man had stood like a statue looking across the valley to the house, and it was only when Garth pointed his camera that he had even lifted a hand.

Garth turned on him a humorous face, in spite of its hard angular features; for the little scientist was a man of admirable good temper.

'I suppose there's a story about it,' he said; 'you look as if you were in quite a confidential mood. If you like to tell me, I assure you I can keep a secret. I'm a medical man and have to keep secrets, especially those of the insane. That ought to encourage you.'

The younger man, whose name was John Mallow, continued to gaze moodily across the valley, but there was something about him that suggested that the other had guessed right, and he was about to speak.

'Don't bother about the others,' said Garth, 'they can't hear; they're too busy doing nothing. Hutton,' he called out in much more strident tones, 'Gale, are you fellows listening?'

'Yes; I'm listening to the birds,' came the half-buried voice of Gale out of his leafy lair.

'Hutton's asleep,' observed Garth with satisfaction. 'No wonder, after all that lunch. Are you asleep, Gale?'

'Not asleep, but dreaming,' answered the other. 'If you look up long enough, there isn't any more up or down, but a sort of green, dizzy dream; with birds that might as well be fishes. They're just odd shapes of different colours against the green, brown and grey, and one of them looks quite yellow.'

'A yellowhammer, I suppose,' remarked Garth.

'It doesn't look like a hammer,' said Gale, sleepily; 'not such an odd shape as all that.'

'Ass!' said Garth briefly. 'Did you expect it to look like an auctioneer's hammer? You poets who are so strong about Nature are generally weak in natural history. Well, Mallow,' he added, turning to his companion, 'you've nothing to fear from them, if you like to talk in an ordinary voice. What about this house of yours?'

'It's not mine,' said Mallow. 'As a matter of fact, it belongs to an old friend of my mother's, a Mrs Verney, a widow. The place has very much run to seed now, as you see, for the Verneys have got poorer and poorer, and don't know what to do next, which is the beginning of the trouble. But I have passed happier times there than I shall probably ever have again.'

'Was Mrs Verney so enchanting a character?' asked his friend softly; 'or may I take the liberty of supposing there was a rising generation?'

'Unfortunately for me, it is a very rising generation,' replied Mallow. 'It rises in a sort of small revolution; and it rises rather above my head.' Then, after a silence, he said somewhat abruptly, 'Do you believe in lady doctors?'

'I don't believe in any doctors,' answered Garth. 'I'm one myself.'

'Well, it isn't exactly lady doctors, I believe, but it's something of that sort,' went on Mallow; 'study of psychological science, and so on. Laura has got it very badly, and is helping some Russian psychologist or other.'

'Your narrative style is a little sketchy,' remarked Dr Garth, 'but I suppose I may infer that Laura is a daughter of Mrs Verney, and also that Laura has some logical connection with the happy days that will not return.'

'Suppose it all, and have done with it,' replied the young man. 'You know what I mean; but the real point is this. Laura has all the new ideas, and has persuaded her mother to come down off the high horse of genteel poverty in all sorts of ways. I don't say she's not right in that; but as it works out there are some curious complications. For one thing, Laura not only earns her own living but earns it in the laboratory of this mysterious Muscovite; and for another, she has bounced her mother into taking a paying guest. And the paying guest is the mysterious Muscovite again, who wants a quiet rest in the country.'

'And I suppose, I may take it,' said the doctor, 'that you feel there is a little too much of the Muscovite in your young life?'

'As a matter of fact, he moved into the house late last night,' continued Mallow, 'and I suppose that's really why I drifted in this direction this morning, trailing you all at my heels. I said it was a beautiful place, and so it is; but I don't want to paint it, and I don't even want to visit it; but all the same, I had a vague sort of feeling I should like to be somewhere near.'

'And, as you couldn't get rid of us, you brought us along,' said Garth with a smile. 'Well, I think I can understand all that. Do you know anything about this Russian professor?'

'I know nothing whatever against him,' answered the other. 'He is a very famous man both in science and politics. He escaped from a Siberian prison in the old days, by blowing up the wall with a bomb of his own construction; it's quite an exciting story, and he must at least be a man of courage. He has written a great book called *The Psychology of Liberty*, I believe; and Laura is very keen on his views. It's rather an indescribable thing altogether; she and I are very fond of each other, and I don't think she mistakes me for a fool, and I don't think I am a fool. But whenever we have met lately it has been literally like a meeting on a high road, when two people are going opposite ways. And I think I know what it is; she is always going outwards, and I am always going inwards. The more I see of the world, and the more men I meet or books I read or questions I answer, the more I come back with increased conviction to those places where I was born or played as a boy, narrowing my circles like a bird going back to a nest. That seems to me the end of all travel, and especially of the widest travel – to get home. But she has another idea in her mind. It's not only that she says that old brown brick house is like a prison, or that the hills are like walls shutting her in; I dare say things do get pretty dull in such a place. There's a theory in it, too, which I suppose she's got from her psychological friend. She says that even in her own valley, and in her own garden, the trees only grow because they radiate outwards, which is only the Latin for branching. She says the very word "radiant" shows it is the secret of happiness. There is something in it, I suppose; but I radiate inwards, so to speak; that is why I paint all my pictures of this little corner of the world. If I could only paint this valley, I might go on to paint that garden; and, if only I could paint that garden, I might be worthy to paint the creeper under her window.'

The sleeping Hutton awoke with an uproarious yawn, and lifting himself from his bed of leaves, wandered away to where the more industrious Walton had at last settled down to work on the other side of the hill. But the poet Gale still lay gazing at his topsy-turvydom of tree-tops. And the only reply he would make to a further challenge from Garth was to say heavily. 'They've driven the yellow one away.'

'Who have driven what away?' demanded Mallow, rather irritably.

'The other birds attacked the yellow one and drove it away,' said the poet.

'Regarded it as an undesirable alien, no doubt,' said Garth.

'The Yellow Peril,' said Gale, and relapsed into his dreams.

Mallow had already resumed his monologue: 'The name of this psychologist is Ivanhov, and he's said to be writing another great book in his country retreat; I believe she is acting as his secretary. It is to embody some mathematical theory about the elimination of limits and – '

'Hullo!' cried Garth. 'This moated grange of yours is actually coming to life. Somebody is actually beginning to open a window.'

'You haven't been looking at it as I have,' answered Mallow quietly. 'Just round the angle on the left there's a little window that's been open all the time. That belongs to the little sitting-room out of the spare bedroom. It used to be Laura's room, and still has a lot of her things in it; but I think they give it now to their guests.'

'Including, doubtless, their paying guest,' observed Garth.

'He's a queer sort of guest. I only hope he's a paying one,' returned the other. 'That big window where they just opened the shutters is at the end of the long library; all these windows belong to it. I expect they'll stick the philosopher in there if he wants to philosophise.'

'The philosopher seems to be philosophical about draughts,' observed Dr Garth; 'he or somebody else has opened three more windows, and seems to be struggling with another.'

Even as he spoke the fifth window burst open, and even from where they stood they could see a creeper that had strayed across it snap and drop with the gesture. It had the look of the snapping of some green chain securing the house like a prison. It had almost the look of the breaking of the seal of a tomb.

For Mallow, against all his prejudices, felt the presence and pressure of that revolutionary ideal which he recognised as his rival. All along the shattered façade of the old brown house the windows were opening one after another like the eyes of an Argus waking from his giant sleep. He was forced to admit to himself that he had never seen the place thus coming to life from within, as a plant unfolds itself. The last three windows were now open to the morning; the long room must already be full of light, to say nothing of air. Garth had spoken of a philosopher enduring draughts; but it seemed more as if a pagan priest had been turned into a temple of the winds. But there was more in that morning vision than the mere accident of a row of windows open when they were commonly closed. The same fancy about unfolding life seemed to fill the whole scene like a new atmosphere. It was as if a fresh air had streamed out of the windows instead of into them. The sun was already fairly high, but it came out of the morning mists above the house with something of the silent explosion of daybreak. The very shapes of the forest trees, spreading themselves like fans, seemed to repeat the original word 'radiant', which he had thought of almost as a Latin pun. Sailing over his head, as if sent flying by a sort of centrifugal force, the clouds still carried into the height of noon the colours of sunrise. He felt all the fresh things that he feared coming at him by an irrepressible expansion. Everything seemed to enlarge itself. Even when his eye fell on a stunted gatepost standing alone in the old garden, he could fancy that it swelled as he stared at it.

A sharp exclamation from his friend woke him from his unnatural day-dream, which might rather be called, by a contradiction, a white nightmare of light.

'By blazes! he's found another window,' cried the doctor; 'a window in the roof.'

There was, indeed, the gleam of a skylight which caught the sun at an angle as it was forced upwards, and out of the opening emerged the moving figure of a man. Little could be seen of him at that distance, except that he was tall and slim and had yellow hair which looked like gold in the strong sun. He was dressed in some long, light-coloured garment, probably a dressing-gown, and he stretched his long limbs as if with the sleepy exultation of one arisen from sleep.

'Look here!' said Mallow suddenly, an indescribable expression flashing across his face and vanishing; 'I'm going to pay a call.'

'I rather thought you might,' answered Garth. 'Do you want to go alone?'

As he spoke he looked round for the rest of the company, but Walton and Hutton were still chatting some distance away on the other side of the hill, and only Gale still lay in the shadow of the thick trees staring up at the birds, as if he had never stirred. Garth called to him by name, but it was only after a silence that Gale spoke. What he said was: 'Were you ever an isosceles triangle?'

'Very seldom,' replied Garth with restraint. 'May I ask what the devil you are talking about?'

'Only something I was thinking about,' answered the poet, lifting himself on to one elbow. 'I wondered whether it would be a cramping sort of thing to be surrounded by straight lines, and whether being in a circle would be any better. Did anybody ever live in a round prison?'

'Where do you get these cracked notions?' enquired the doctor.

'A little bird told me,' Gale said gravely. 'Oh, it's quite true.'

He had risen to his feet by this time, and came slowly forward to the brow of the hill, looking across at the house by the river. As he looked his dreamy blue eyes seemed to wake up, like the windows opening in the house he gazed at.

'Another bird,' he said softly, 'like a sparrow on the house-tops. And that fits in with it exactly.'

There was some suggestion of truth in the phrase, for the strange figure was standing on the very edge of the roof, with space below him and his hands spread out almost as if he wished to fly. But the last sentence, and still more the strange manner in which it was spoken, puzzled the doctor completely.

'Fits in with what?' he asked, rather sharply.

'He's like that yellow bird,' said Gale vaguely. 'In fact, he is a yellow bird, with that hair and the sun on him. What did you say you thought it was . . . a yellowhammer?'

'Yellowhammer yourself,' retorted Garth; 'you're quite as yellow as he is. In fact, with your long legs and straw-coloured hair, you're really rather like him.'

Mallow, in his more mystical mood, looked strangely from one to the other, for indeed there was a certain vague similarity between the two tall, fair-haired figures, the one on the house and the other on the hill.

'Perhaps I am rather like him,' said Gale quietly. 'Perhaps I'm just sufficiently like him to learn not to be like him, so to speak. We may both be birds of a feather, the yellow feather; but we don't flock together, because he likes to flock by himself. And as to being a hammer, yellow or otherwise, well, that also is an allegory.'

'I decline to make head or tail of your allegories,' said Dr Garth shortly.

'I used to want a hammer to smash things with,' continued Gale; 'but I've learnt to do something else with a hammer, which is what a hammer is meant for; and every now and then I manage to do it.'

'What do you mean by that?' enquired the doctor.

'I can hit the right nail on the head,' answered the poet.

It was not, in fact, until later in the day that Mallow paid his call at Mrs Verney's house. Mrs Verney was going up to the neighbouring village for the afternoon; and Mallow had more than one motive for making his attack when the stranger was alone with his secretary. He had a general idea of using his friends to detach or detain the stranger while he himself sought for explanation from the secretary; so he dragged Garth and Gale along with him to Mrs Verney's drawing-room; or rather he would have done so if Gale had been an easy person to drag successfully anywhere. But Gale had a tendency to get detached from any such group, and was always being left behind. Large as he was, he had a way of getting mislaid. His friends forgot him, as they had almost forgotten him when he was lying under the tree. It was not that he was unsociable; on the contrary, he was very fond of his friends and very fond of his opinions, and always delighted to detail the latter to the former. Strangers would have said that he was very fond of the sound of his own voice, but friends who were fond of him knew better. They knew that he had hardly ever heard his own voice, in the sense of listening to it. What made his movements incalculable was that his thinking or talking would start from any small thing that seemed to him a large thing. What are to most men impressions, or half impressions, were to him incidents; and the chief incidents of the day. Many imaginative people know what is meant by saying that certain empty rooms or open doors are suggestive; but he always acted on the suggestion. Most of them understand that there can be something vaguely inviting about a gap in a garden hedge, or the abrupt angle of a path; but he always accepted the invitation. The shape of a hill, or the corner of a house, checked him like a challenge. He wrestled with it seriously till it had given up something of its secret, till he could put something like a name to his nameless fancy; and these things were the active adventures of his life. Hence it was that he would sometimes follow one train of thought for hours, as steadily as a bird winging its way homewards. But it might start anywhere; and hence, in his actual movements, he looked more like a floating tuft of thistledown caught upon any thorn.

On this occasion his friends lost him, or left him behind, as they turned the corner of the house just after passing an old-fashioned bow-window looking out on the garden. Inside the window stood a small round table on which was a bowl of goldfish; and Gale stopped abruptly and stared at it as if he had never seen such a thing before. He had often maintained that the main object of a man's life was to see a thing as if he had never seen it before. But in this case the twilight of the little empty room, touched here and there with the late afternoon sunlight, seemed somehow a subtle but suitable background for the thing that he saw. The heart of a dark green sphere was alive with little living flames.

'Why the devil do they call them goldfish?' he asked almost irritably. 'They're a much more gorgeous colour than gold; I've never seen it anywhere except in very rare red clouds in a sunset. Gold suggests yellow, and not the best yellow either; not half so good as the clear lemon yellow of that bird I saw today. They're more like copper than gold. And copper is twenty times finer than gold. Why isn't copper the most precious metal, I wonder?'

He paused a moment and then said reflectively: 'Would it do, I wonder, when one changed a cheque into gold, to give a man coppers instead, and explain that they have more of the rich tones of sunset?'

His enquiry remained unanswered, for he made it to the empty air. His companions were deficient in his sense of the importance of goldfish, and had gone on impatiently to the main entrance of the house, leaving him lingering by the bowl near the bow-window. He continued to look at it for a considerable time, and when at last he turned away, it was not to follow his friends, but to pace the paths of the garden in the deepening and darkening twilight, revolving in his mind some occult romance beginning with a bowl of fish.

Meanwhile, his more practical friends, pursuing the main purpose of the story, had penetrated into the house and found at least some members of the household. There had been many things in the garden or the gateway over which Mallow also might have been disposed to linger if his mood had been merely sentimental; an old swing standing by the corner of the orchard, the angle of a faded tennis lawn, the fork of a pear tree, all of which had stories attached to them. But he was possessed of a passionate curiosity far too practical for sentiment of the merely reminiscent sort; he was resolved to run to earth the mystery of the new man in the old house. He felt that a change had come over everything with the man's mere presence; and wished to know how far that change had gone. He half expected to see those familiar rooms swept bare, or filled with strange furniture where the stranger had passed.

Accident, indeed, gave to their passage through those empty rooms an air of pursuit, as if something were escaping. For, as they passed from an outer room into the long library, the stranger, who was at the other end by the window, emphasised his restless love of the open air by putting one long leg over the low window-sill and stepping out on to the lawn. He had evidently, however, no real desire to avoid them, for he stood there smiling in the sunlight, and uttered some greeting very pleasantly with a slight foreign accent. He was still wearing the long lemon-coloured dressing-gown which, along with his yellow hair, had suggested the comparison of a yellow bird. Under the yellow hair his brow was broad but not high, and the nose was not only long and straight, but came down in a single line from the forehead in the manner that may be seen on many Greek coins and carvings, but which has an unnatural and even sinister symmetry when seen in real life. There was nothing else eccentric or exuberant about him; his manners were casual, but not ungraceful; and nothing contradicted the sunny ease of his situation and demeanour except, perhaps, a slightly strained look in the eyes, which were eager and prominent. Until his acquaintances grew accustomed to it, as a fixed involuntary feature of his face, they occasionally had a sort of shock when catching his quiet face in shadow and realising that the round eyes were standing out of his head.

The first thing the eyes seemed to encounter was Dr Garth's hand-camera; and, as soon as introductions and salutations had passed, he plunged into talk about photography. He prophesied its extension at the expense of painting, and brushed aside the objection, which even the doctor offered, that painting had the superiority in colour.

'Colour-photography will soon be completed,' he said hastily; 'or rather, it will never be completed, but will always be improved. That is the point of science. You know more or less finally what can be done, well or ill, with a draughtsman's chalk or a sculptor's chisel. But with us the instruments themselves are always changing. That's the real triumph of a telescope . . . that it is telescopic.'

'Well,' said Mallow grimly, 'I shall wait for one more change in the camera as a scientific instrument before I cut up my old easel for firewood.'

'What change is that?' asked the Russian with a kind of eagerness.

'I shall wait till one of those tall cameras walks on its own three legs along a country lane to pick out the view it likes best.'

'Even something like that may be more possible than you think,' replied the other. 'In these days when a man has his eyes and ears at the end of long wires; his own nerves, so to speak, spread over a city in the form of telephones and telegraphs. A great modern city will become a great machine with its handle in the human hand. Thus only can a man become a giant.'

John Mallow looked at the man rather darkly for a moment, and then said: 'If you are so very fond of a big modern city,' he said, 'why do you hide yourself in such a quiet little hole in the country?'

For a flash the stranger's face seemed to wince and alter in the white sunlight; but the next instant he was still smiling, though he spoke a little more apologetically.

'There is certainly more space,' he answered. 'I confess I like a lot of space. But even there the science of the city will ultimately provide its own remedy. The answer is in one word – aviation.'

Before the other could reply the speaker went on, his prominent eye kindling and his whole figure filling out with animation. He made a movement with his hand like a man throwing a stone into the air.

'It's upwards the new extension will be,' he cried. 'That road is wide enough, and that window is always open. The new roads will stand up like towers. The new harbours will stand far out in that sea above our heads . . . a sea you can never find the end of. It would only be a beginning to conquer the planets and colonise the fixed stars.'

'I think,' said Mallow, 'that you will have conquered the remotest star before you really conquer this one old corner of the earth. It has a magic of its own which I think will outlast all such conjuring tricks. This was the house of Merlin; and, though they say Merlin himself fell under a spell, it was not that of Marconi.'

'No,' answered the stranger, still smiling. 'We all know the spell under which Merlin fell.'

Mallow knew enough about Russian intellectuals not to be surprised at the wide knowledge of the poetry and culture of the West; but here it seemed the almost satiric symbol of a deeper familiarity, and a mocking whisper told him what might have chained this magician in that western valley.

Laura Verney was coming across the garden towards them with some papers in her hand. She was of a red-haired, full-blooded type, handsome in a fashion which seemed to have a certain pagan exuberance till she came near enough to show the concentrated seriousness of her clear eyes; she might be called a pagan with the eyes of a puritan. She saluted her guests without any change of countenance, and handed the papers to the professor without any word of comment. Something in her automatic manner seemed to sting Mallow to a final impatience; and, picking up his hat from the window-sill, he called out in a loud and careless voice: 'Laura, will you show me the way out of this garden? I've forgotten the way.'

It was some time afterwards, however, that he said any sort of final farewell to her, under the shadow of the outer wall, and near the ultimate gate of the garden. In the somewhat bitter intensity of his mood, he seemed rather to be exaggerating the finality of the farewell; not only touching herself, but all the things which he had always felt to be full of her presence.

'You will pull down that old swing, I suppose?' he had said as they went through the garden, 'and put up an electric steel swing that will take anybody in ten seconds to the moon.'

'I can't pull down the moon, anyhow,' replied the girl, with a smile, 'and I don't know that I want to.'

'That's rather reactionary of you,' remarked Mallow. 'The moon is a very extinct volcano, valuable only to old-fashioned romanticists. And I suppose you'll turn our old lawn-tennis lawn into a place where tennis can be played by machinery, by pressing buttons a hundred miles away. I'm not sure whether they've yet finished the plans for a pear tree that grows pears by electricity.'

'But surely,' she replied, looking a little troubled, 'the world can go on without losing the things it seems to leave behind. And, after all, surely the world must go on; at least, it must go on growing. I think that's where you misunderstand. It isn't only going on; it's more like growing outwards.

'It's expansion, that's the word; growing broader, always describing wider and wider circles; but that only means more self-fulfilment, and therefore serenity and peace; it means . . .'

She stopped short, as if at a spoken answer, but it was only because the moon had flung a new shadow across her. It was from a figure standing on the wall. The moonshine made a halo of pale yellow round the head; and for a moment they thought it was the Russian, standing on the wall as he had stood on the roof. Then Mallow looked more closely at the face in shadow, and uttered, with some astonishment, the name of Gale.

'You must get away from here at once,' said the poet sharply; 'everybody who can must get away from this house. There's no time to explain.'

As he spoke, he sprang from the wall and alighted beside them, and his friend, catching his face in a new light, saw that it was quite pale.

'What's the matter with you?' he demanded. 'Have you seen a ghost?'

'The ghost of a fish,' answered the poet; 'three little grey ghosts of three little fishes. We must get away at once.'

Without turning his head again, he led the way up the rising ground beyond the garden towards the clump of trees where the party had first encamped. Both Mallow and the girl pursued him with questions; but to only one of them did he give any answer. When Laura insisted on knowing whether her mother had come home yet, he answered shortly, 'No; thank God! I sent Garth off to stop her on the road from the village. She's all right, anyhow.'

But Laura Verney was a lady who could not be indefinitely dragged at the tail of a total stranger talking in a tone of authority; and by the time they came to the top of a hill, and the trees in whose shadow the poet had indulged in his meditations on birds, she halted and resolutely demanded his reasons.

'I won't go a step farther,' she said firmly, 'till you've given me some sort of proofs.'

He turned with passion in his pale face.

'Oh, proofs!' he cried; 'I know the sort of proofs you want. The footprints of the remarkable boots. The bloody fingerprint carefully compared with the one at Scotland Yard. The conveniently mislaid matchbox, and the ashes of the unique tobacco. Do you suppose I've never read any detective stories? Well, I haven't got any proofs . . . of that sort. I haven't got any proofs at all, in that sense. If I told you my reasons, you'd think them the most rambling nonsense in the world. You must either do as I tell you and thank me afterwards; or you must let me talk as I like, and as long as I like, and thank your God you've come as far as this towards safety.'

Mallow was looking at the poet in his quiet and intense fashion; and after a moment's pause, he said: 'You'd better tell us your own reasons in your own way. I know you generally have pretty good ones, really.'

Gale's eyes wandered from the staring face of the girl to that of his friend, and then to the drift of dead leaves under the tree where he had once rested.

'I was lying there looking up at the sky, or, rather, the tree-tops,' he said slowly. 'I didn't hear what the others were talking about, because I was listening to the birds and looking at them. You know what happens when you go on staring at something like that; it turns into a sort of pattern like a wallpaper; and this was a quiet pattern of green and grey and brown. It seemed as if the whole world was that pattern; as if God had never made anything except a world of birds; of tree-tops hung in space.'

Laura made a half-protest that sounded like a laugh, but Mallow said steadily: 'Go on!'

'And then I slowly became conscious that there was a spot of yellow in the pattern. I slowly realised that it was another bird, and then what sort of bird. Somebody said it must be a yellowhammer; but, little as I knew about it, I knew better than that. It was a canary.'

The girl, who had already turned away, looked back at him with her first flash of interest.

'I wondered vaguely how a canary would get on in the world of birds, and how it had got there. I didn't think of any human being in particular. Only I saw in a sort of vision, somewhere against the morning sky, a window standing open, and the door of a cage standing open. Then I saw that all the brown birds were trying to kill the yellow one, and that started my thoughts off as it might anybody's. Is it always kind to set a bird at liberty? What exactly is liberty? First and foremost, surely, it is the power of a thing to be itself. In some ways the yellow bird was free in the cage. It was free to be alone. It was free to sing. In the forest its feathers would be torn to pieces and its voice choked for ever. Then I began to think that being oneself, which is liberty, is itself limitation. We are limited by our brains and bodies; and if we break out, we cease to be ourselves, and, perhaps, to be anything. That was when I asked you whether an isosceles triangle felt itself in prison, and if there were such a thing as a round prison. We shall hear more of the round prison before this story is over.

'Then I saw the man on the roof, with his hands spread like wings to the sky. I knew nothing of him; but I knew on the instant that he was the man who had given a bird its freedom at any risk. As we went down the hill I heard a little more about him; how he had escaped by blowing up his prison; and I felt that one fact had filled all his life with a philosophy of emancipation and escape. Always at the back of his mind, I was certain, was that one bursting moment when he saw white daylight shining through the shattered wall. I knew why he let birds out of cages and why he had written a book on the psychology of liberty. Then I stopped outside a window to stare at those gorgeous goldfish, merely because I had a fancy for such things; they coloured my thoughts, so to speak, with a sort of orange or scarlet, for long afterwards. And long afterwards I was again passing that window; and I found their colours were faded and their positions changed. At that time it was already dark, with a rising moon; and what forms I could see scattered in the shadow seemed almost grey, and even outlined in lines of grey light, which might have been moonlight, but I think was the corpse-light of phosphorescence. They lay scattered at random on the round table; and I saw by the faint glimmer that the glass bowl was broken. So I found my romance when I returned to it; for those fantastic fishes had been to me like the hieroglyphics of a message, which the fiery finger of God had thus written in red-hot gold. But when I looked again, the finger had written another lesson in letters of an awful and ashen silver. And what the new message said was: "The man is mad."

'Perhaps you think I am as mad as he; and I have told you that I am at once like him and unlike him. I am like him because I also can go on the wild journeys of such wild minds, and have a sympathy with his love of liberty. I am unlike him because, thank God, I can generally find my way home again.

The lunatic is he who loses his way and cannot return. Now, almost before my eyes, this man had made the great stride from liberty to lunacy. The man who opened the birdcage loved freedom; possibly too much; certainly very much. But the man who broke the bowl merely because he thought it a prison for the fish, when it was their only possible house of life . . . that man was already outside the world of reason, raging with a desire to be outside everything. In a most literal and living sense, he was out of his wits. And there was another thing revealed to me by the grey ghosts of the fishes. The rise of the insanity had been very rapid and steep. To send the bird into danger was only a disputable kindness, to fling the fish to death was a dance of raving destruction. What would he do next?

'I have spoken of a round prison. After all, to any mind that can move parallel to a mood like this, there really is a round prison. The sky itself, studded with stars, the serene arch of what we call infinity . . .'

As he spoke he staggered, clutched at the air, and fell all his great length on the grass. At the same moment Mallow was hurled against a tree, and the girl collapsed against him, clinging to him in a way which even in that blinding whirl, was an answer to many of his questionings. It was only when they had picked themselves up and pulled themselves together that they were fully conscious that the valley was still resounding with echoes of one hideous and rending uproar; or that the darkness had just shut down upon a blaze that blinded them like red lightning. For the instant that it lasted it was a standing glory, like a great sunrise. There rose to the surface of Mallow's memory only one word for it; the word radiant.

Mallow found himself reflecting in a dull fashion that it was lighter than it might have been at that hour, because of a friendly flame that was licking itself in a lively fashion a few yards away. Then he saw that it was the smouldering ruin of the blue wooden gatepost at which he had gazed that morning, flung all the way through the air like a flaming thunderbolt. They had come just far enough from the house to be out of danger. Then he looked again at the blue-painted wood curling with golden flames, and for the first time began to tremble.

The next moment he caught sight of the faces of his other friends, Walton and Hutton, pale in the flame as they hurried up the road from the remoter inn to which they had retired for the evening.

'What was it?' Walton was calling out.

'An explosion,' said Hutton rather hazily.

'An expansion,' replied Mallow, and mastered himself with the effort of a grim smile.

By this time, more people were running out from remote cottages, and Gabriel Gale turned his face to something like a small crowd.

'It was only the prison gun,' he said, 'the signal that a prisoner has escaped.'

3

The Shadow of the Shark

It is notable that the late Mr Sherlock Holmes, in the course of those inspiring investigations for which we can never be sufficiently grateful to their ingenious author, seems only twice to have ruled out an explanation as intrinsically impossible. And it is curious to notice that in both cases the distinguished author himself has since come to regard that impossible thing as possible, and even as positively true. In the first case the great detective declared that he never knew a crime committed by a flying creature. Since the development of aviation, and especially the development of German aviation, Sir Arthur Conan Doyle, patriot and war historian, has seen a good many crimes committed by flying creatures. And in the other case the detective implied that no deed need be attributed to spirits or supernatural beings; in short, to any of the agencies to which Sir Arthur is now the most positive and even passionate witness. Presumably, in his present mood and philosophy, the Hound of the Baskervilles might well have been a really ghostly hound; at least, if the optimism which seems to go with spiritualism would permit him to believe in such a thing as a hell-hound. It may be worth while to note this coincidence, however, in telling a tale in which both these explanations necessarily played a part. The scientists were anxious to attribute it to aviation, and the spiritualists to attribute it to spirits; though it might be questioned whether either the spirit or the flying-man should be congratulated on his utility as an assassin.

A mystery which may yet linger as a memory, but which was in its time a sensation, revolved round the death of a certain Sir Owen Cram, a wealthy eccentric, chiefly known as a patron of learning and the arts. And the peculiarity of the case was that he was found stabbed in the middle of a great stretch of yielding sand by the seashore, on which there was absolutely no trace of any footprints but his own. It was admitted that the wound could not have been self-inflicted; and it grew more and more difficult even to suggest how it could have been inflicted at all. Many theories were suggested, ranging, as we have said, from that of the enthusiasts for aviation to that of the enthusiasts for psychical research; it being evidently regarded as a feather in the cap either of science or spiritualism to have effected so neat an operation. The true story of this strange business has never been told; it certainly contained elements which, if not supernatural, were at least supernormal. But to make it clear, we must go back to the scene with which it began; the scene on the lawn of Sir Owen's seaside residence, where the old gentleman acted as a sort of affable umpire in the disputes of the young students who were his favourite company; the scene which led up to the singular silence and isolation, and ultimately to the rather eccentric exit of Mr Amos Boon.

* * *

Mr Amos Boon had been a missionary, and still dressed like one; at any rate, he dressed like nothing else. His sturdy, full-bearded figure carried a broad-brimmed hat combined with a frock-coat; which gave him an air at once outlandish and dowdy. Though he was no longer a missionary, he was still a traveller. His face was brown and his long beard was black; there was a furrow of thought in his brow and a rather strained look in his eyes, one of which sometimes looked a little larger than the other, giving a sinister touch to what was in some ways so commonplace. He had ceased to be a missionary through what he himself would have called the broadening of his mind. Some said there had been a broadening of his morals as well as of his mind; and that the South Sea Islands, where he had lived, had seen not a little of such ethical emancipation. But this was possibly a malicious misrepresentation of his very human curiosity and sympathy in the matter of the customs of the savages; which to the ordinary prejudice was indistinguishable from a white man going *fantee*. Anyhow, travelling about alone with nothing but a big Bible, he had learned to study it minutely, first for oracles and commandments, and afterwards for errors and contradictions; for the Bible-smasher is only the Bible-worshipper turned upside down. He pursued the not very arduous task of proving that David and Saul did not on all occasions merit the Divine favour; and always concluded by roundly declaring that he preferred the Philistines. Boon and his Philistines were already a byword of some levity among the young men who, at that moment, were arguing and joking around him.

At that moment Sir Owen Cram was playfully presiding over a dispute between two or three of his young friends about science and poetry. Sir Owen was a little restless man, with a large head, a bristly grey moustache, and a grey fan of hair like the crest of a cockatoo. There was something sprawling and splayfooted about his continuous movement which was compared by thoughtless youth to that of a crab; and it corresponded to a certain universal eagerness which was really ready to turn in all directions. He was a typical amateur, taking up hobby after hobby with equal inconsistency and intensity. He had impetuously left all his money to a museum of natural history, only to become immediately swallowed up in the single pursuit of landscape painting; and the groups around him largely represented the stages of his varied career. At the moment a young painter, who was also by way of being a poet, was defending some highly poetical notions against the smiling resistance of a rising doctor, whose hobby was biology. The data of agreement would have been difficult to find, and few save Sir Owen could have claimed any common basis of sympathy; but the important matter just then was the curious effect of the young men's controversy upon Mr Boon.

'The subject of flowers is hackneyed, but the flowers are not,' the poet was insisting. 'Tennyson was right about the flower in the crannied wall; but most people don't look at flowers in a wall, but only in a wallpaper. If you generalise them, they are dull, but if you simply see them they are always startling. If there's a special providence in a falling star, there's more in a rising star; and a live star at that.'

'Well, I can't see it,' said the man of science, good-humouredly; he was a red-haired, keen-faced youth in pince-nez, by the name of Wilkes. 'I'm afraid we fellows grow out of the way of seeing it like that. You see, a flower is only a growth like any other, with organs and all that; and its inside isn't any prettier or uglier than an animal's. An insect is much the same pattern of rings and radiations. I'm interested in it as I am in an octopus or any sea-beast you would think a monster.'

'But why should you put it that way round?' retorted the poet. 'Why isn't it quite as logical the other way round? Why not say the octopus is as wonderful as the flower, instead of the flower as ordinary as the octopus? Why not say that crackens and cuttles and all the sea-monsters are themselves flowers; fearful and wonderful flowers in that terrible twilight garden of God. I do not doubt that God can be as fond of a shark as I am of a buttercup.'

'As to God, my dear Gale,' began the other quietly, and then he seemed to change his form of words. 'Well, I am only a man . . . nay, only a scientific man, which you may think lower than a sea-beast. And the only interest I have in a shark is to cut him up; always on the preliminary supposition that I have prevented him from cutting me up.'

'Have you ever met a shark?' asked Amos Boon, intervening suddenly.

'Not in society,' replied the poet with a certain polite discomposure, looking round with something like a flush under his fair hair; he was a long, loose-limbed man named Gabriel Gale, whose pictures were more widely known than his poems.

'You've seen them in the tanks, I suppose,' said Boon; 'but I've seen them in the sea. I've seen them where they are lords of the sea, and worshipped by the people as great gods. I'd as soon worship those gods as any other.'

Gale the poet was silent, for his mind always moved in a sort of sympathy with merely imaginative pictures; and he instantly saw, as in a vision, boiling purple seas and plunging monsters. But another young man standing near him, who had hitherto been rather primly silent, cut in quietly; a theological student, named Simon, the deposit of some epoch of faith in Sir Owen's stratified past. He was a slim man with sleek, dark hair and darting, mobile eyes, in spite of his compressed lips. Whether in caution or contempt, he had left the attack on medical materialism to the poet, who was always ready to plunge into an endless argument with anybody. Now he intervened merely to say: 'Do they only worship a shark? It seems rather a limited sort of religion.'

'Religion!' repeated Amos Boon, rudely; 'what do you people know about religion? You pass the plate round, and when Sir Owen puts a penny in it, you put up a shed where a curate can talk to a congregation of maiden-aunts. These people have got something like a religion. They sacrifice things to it – their beasts, their babies, their lives. I reckon you'd turn green with fear if you'd ever so much as caught a glimpse of Religion. Oh, it's not just a fish in the sea; rather it's the sea round a fish. The sea is the blue cloud he moves in, or the green veil or curtain hung about him, the skirts of which trail with thunder.'

All faces were turned towards him, for there was something about him beyond his speech. Twilight was spreading over the garden, which lay near the edge of a chalk cliff above the shore, but the last light of sunset still lay on a part of the lawn, painting it yellow rather than green, and glowing almost like gold against the last line of the sea, which was a sombre indigo and violet, changing nearer land to a lurid, pale green. A long cloud of a jagged shape happened to be trailing across the sun; and the broad-hatted, hairy man from the South Seas suddenly pointed at it.

'I know where the shape of that cloud would be called the shadow of the shark,' he cried, 'and a thousand men would fall on their faces ready to fast or fight, or die. Don't you see the great black dorsal fin, like the peak of a moving mountain? And then you lads discuss him as if he were a stroke at golf; and one of you says he would cut him up like birthday cake; and the other says your Jewish Jehovah would condescend to pat him like a pet rabbit.'

'Come, come,' said Sir Owen, with a rather nervous waggishness, 'we mustn't have any of your broad-minded blasphemies.'

Boon turned on him a baneful eye; literally an eye, for one of his eyes grew larger till it glowed like the eye of the Cyclops. His figure was black against the fiery turf, and they could almost hear his beard bristling.

'Blasphemy!' he cried in a new voice, with a crack in it. 'Take care it is not you who blaspheme.'

And then, before anyone could move, the black figure against the patch of gold had swung round and was walking away from the house, so impetuously that they had a momentary fear that he would walk over the cliff. However, he found the little wooden gate that led to a flight of wooden steps; and they heard him stumbling down the path to the fishing village below.

Sir Owen seemed suddenly to shake off a paralysis like a fit of slumber. 'My old friend is a little eccentric,' he said. 'Don't go, gentlemen; don't let him break up the party. It is early yet.'

But growing darkness and a certain social discomfort had already begun to dissolve the group on the lawn; and the host was soon left with a few of the most intimate of his guests. Simon and Gale, and his late antagonist, Dr Wilkes, were staying to dinner; the darkness drove them indoors, and eventually found them sitting round a flask of green Chartreuse on the table; for Sir Owen had his expensive conventions as well as his expensive eccentricities. The talkative poet, however, had fallen silent, and was staring at the green liquid in his glass as if it were the green depth of the sea. His host attacked with animation the other ordinary topics of the day.

'I bet I'm the most industrious of the lot of you,' he said. 'I've been at my easel on the beach all day, trying to paint this blessed cliff, and make it look like chalk and not cheese.'

'I saw you, but I didn't like to disturb you,' said Wilkes. 'I generally try to put in an hour or so looking for specimens at high tide: I suppose most people think I'm shrimping or only paddling and doing it for my health. But I've got a pretty good nucleus of that museum we were talking about, or at least the aquarium part of it. I put in most of the rest of the time arranging the exhibits; so I deny the implication of idleness. Gale was on the seashore, too. He was doing nothing as usual; and now he's saying nothing, which is much more uncommon.'

'I have been writing letters,' said Simon, in his precise way, 'but letters are not always trivial. Sometimes they are rather tremendous.'

Sir Owen glanced at him for a moment, and a silence followed, which was broken by a thud and a rattle of glasses as Gale brought his fist down on the table like a man who had thought of something suddenly.

'Dagon!' he cried, in a sort of ecstasy.

Most of the company seemed but little enlightened; perhaps they thought that saying 'Dagon' was his poetical and professional fashion of saying 'Damn'. But the dark eyes of Simon brightened, and he nodded quickly.

'Why, of course you're right,' he said. 'That must be why Mr Boon is so fond of the Philistines.'

In answer to a general stare of enquiry, he said smoothly: 'The Philistines were a people from Crete, probably of Hellenic origin, who settled on the coast of Palestine, carrying with them a worship which may very well have been that of Poseidon, but which their enemies, the Israelites, described as that of Dagon. The relevant matter here is that the carved or painted symbol of the god seems always to have been a fish.'

The mention of the new matter seemed to reawaken the tendency of the talk to turn into a wrangle between the poet and the professional scientist.

'From my point of view,' said the latter, 'I must confess myself somewhat disappointed with your friend Mr Boon. He represented himself as a rationalist like myself, and seemed to have made some scientific studies of folklore in the South Seas. But he seemed a little unbalanced; and surely he made a curious fuss about some sort of a fetish, considering it was only a fish.'

'No, no, no!' cried Gale, almost with passion. 'Better make a fetish of the fish. Better sacrifice yourself and everybody else on the horrible huge altar of the fish. Better do anything than utter the star-blasting blasphemy of saying it is *only* a fish. It's as bad as saying the other thing is only a flower.'

'All the same, it *is* only a flower,' answered Wilkes, 'and the advantage of looking at these things in a cool and rational way from the outside is that you can . . .'

He stopped a moment and remained quite still, as if he were watching something. Some even fancied that his pale, aquiline face looked paler as well as sharper.

'What was that at the window?' he asked. 'Is anybody outside this house?'

'What's the matter? What did you see?' asked his host, in abrupt agitation.

'Only a face,' replied the doctor, 'but it was not . . . it was not like a man's face. Let's get outside and look into this.'

Gabriel Gale was only a moment behind the doctor, who had impetuously dashed out of the room. Despite his lounging demeanour, the poet had already leapt to his feet with his hand on the back of the chair, when he stiffened where he stood; for he had seen it. The faces of the others showed that they had seen it too.

Pressed against the dark window-pane, but only wanly luminous as it protruded out of the darkness, was a large face looking at first rather like a green goblin mask in a pantomime. Yet it was in no sense human; its eyes were set in large circles, rather in the fashion of an owl. But the glimmering covering that faintly showed on it was not of feathers, but of scales.

The next moment it had vanished. The mind of the poet, which made images as rapidly as a cinema, even in a crisis of action, had already imagined a string of fancies about the sort of creature he saw it to be. He had thought involuntarily of some great flying fish winging its way across the foam, and the flat sand and the spire and roofs of the fishing village. He had half-imagined the moist sea air thickening in some strange way to a greener and more liquid atmosphere in which the marine monsters could swim about in the streets. He had entertained the fancy that the house itself stood in the depths of the sea, and that the great goblin-headed fishes were nosing round it, as round the cabin windows of a wreck.

At that moment a loud voice was heard outside crying in distinct accents: 'The fish has legs.'

For that instant, it seemed to give the last touch to the monstrosity. But the meaning of it came back to them, a returning reality, with the laughing face of Dr Wilkes as he reappeared in the doorway, panting.

'Our fish had two legs, and used them,' he said. 'He ran like a hare when he saw me coming; but I could see plainly enough it was a man playing you a trick of some sort. So much for that psychic phenomenon.'

He paused and looked at Sir Owen Cram with a smile that was keen and almost suspicious.

'One thing is very clear to me,' he said. 'You have an enemy.'

The mystery of the human fish, however, did not long remain even a primary topic of conversation in a social group that had so many topics of conversation. They continued to pursue their hobbies and pelt each other with their opinions; even the smooth and silent Simon being gradually drawn into the discussions, in which he showed a dry and somewhat cynical dexterity. Sir Owen continued to paint with all the passion of an amateur. Gale continued to neglect to paint, with all the nonchalance of a painter. Mr Boon was presumably still as busy with his wicked Bible and his good Philistines as Dr Wilkes with his museum and his microscopic marine animals, when the little seaside town was shaken as by an earthquake with the incomprehensible calamity which spread its name over all the newspapers of the country.

* * *

Gabriel Gale was scaling the splendid swell of turf that terminated in the great chalk cliff above the shore, in a mood consonant to the sunrise that was storming the skies above him. Clouds haloed with sunshine were already sailing over his head as if sent flying from a flaming wheel; and when he came to the brow of the cliff he saw one of those rare revelations when the sun does not seem to be merely the most luminous object in a luminous landscape, but itself the solitary focus and streaming fountain of all light. The tide was at the ebb, and the sea was only a strip of delicate turquoise over which rose the tremendous irradiation. Next to the strip of turquoise was a strip of orange sand, still wet, and nearer the sand was a desert of a more dead yellow or brown, growing paler in the increasing light. And as he looked down from the precipice upon that plain of pale gold, he saw two black objects lying in the middle of it. One was a small easel, still standing, with a camp-stool fallen beside it; the other was the flat and sprawling figure of a man.

The figure did not move, but as he stared he became conscious that another human figure was moving, was walking over the flat sands towards it from under the shadow of the cliff. Looking at it steadily, he saw that it was the man called Simon; and in an instant he seemed to realise that the motionless figure was that of Sir Owen Cram. He hastened to the stairway down the cliff and so to the sands; and soon stood face to face with Simon; for they both looked at each other for a moment before they both looked down at the body. The conviction was already cold in his heart that it was a dead body. Nevertheless, he said sharply: 'We must have a doctor; where is Dr Wilkes?'

'It is no good, I fear,' said Simon, looking away at the sea.

'Wilkes may only confirm our fears that he is dead,' said Gale, 'but he may have something to say about how he died.'

'True,' said the other, 'I will go for him myself.' And he walked back rapidly towards the cliff in the track of his own footprints.

Indeed, it was at the footprints that Gale was gazing in a bemused fashion at that moment. The tracks of his own coming were clear enough, and the tracks of Simon's coming and going; and the third rather more rambling track of the unmistakable boots of the unfortunate Sir Owen, leading up to the spot where his easel was planted. And that was all. The sand was soft, so that the lightest foot would disturb it; it was well above the tides; and there was not the faintest trace of any other human being having been near the body. Yet the body had a deep wound under the angle of the jaw; and there was no sign of any weapon of suicide.

Gabriel Gale was a believer in commonsense, in theory if not always in practice. He told himself repeatedly that these things were the practical clues in such a case; the wound, the weapon or absence of weapon, the footprints or absence of footprints. But there was also a part of his mind which was always escaping from his control and playing tricks; fixing on his memory meaningless things as if they were symbols, and then haunting him with them as mysteries. He made no point of it; it was rather subconscious than self-conscious; but the parts of any living picture that he saw were seldom those that others saw, or that it seemed sensible to see. And there were one or two details in the tragedy before him that haunted him then and long afterwards. Cram had fallen backwards in a rather twisted fashion, with his feet towards the shore; and a few inches from the left foot lay a starfish. He could not say whether it was merely the bright orange colour of the creature that irrationally riveted his eye, or merely some obscure fancy of repetition, in that the human figure was itself spread and sprawling flat like a starfish, with four limbs instead of five. Nor did he attempt to analyse this aesthetic antic of his psychology; it was a suppressed part of his mind which still repeated that the mystery of the untrodden sands would turn out to be something quite simple; but that the starfish possessed the secret.

He looked up to see Simon returning with the doctor, indeed with two doctors; for there was more than one medical representative in the mob of Sir Owen's varied interests. The other was a Dr Garth, a little man with an angular and humorous face; he was an old friend of Gale's but the poet's greeting was rather *distrait*. Garth and his colleague, however, got to work on a preliminary examination, which made further talk needless. It could not be a full examination till the arrival of the police, but it was sufficient to extinguish any hope of life, if any such had lingered. Garth, who was bent over the body in a crouching posture, spoke to his fellow physician without raising his head.

'There seems to be something rather odd about this wound. It goes almost straight upwards, as if it was struck from below. But Sir Owen was a very small man; and it seems queer that he should be stabbed by somebody smaller still.'

Gale's sub-consciousness exploded with a strange note of harsh mockery.

'What,' he cried, 'you don't think the starfish jumped up and killed him?'

'No, of course not,' said Garth, with his gruff good humour. 'What on earth is the matter with you?'

'Lunacy, I think,' said the poet, and began to walk slowly towards the shore.

As time went on he almost felt disposed to fancy that he had correctly diagnosed his own complaint. The image began to figure even in his dreams, but not merely as a natural nightmare about the body on the seashore. The significant sea creature seemed more vivid even than the body. As he had originally seen the corpse from above, spread flat out beneath him, he saw it in his visions as something standing, as if propped against a wall or even merely drawn or graven on a wall. Sometimes the sandy ground had become a ground of old gold in some decoration of the Dark Ages, with the figure in the stiff agonies of a martyr, but the red star always showed like a lamp by his feet. Sometimes it was a hieroglyphic of a more Eastern sort, as of some stone god rigidly dancing; but the five-pointed star was always in the same place below. Sometimes it seemed a rude, red-sandstone sort of drawing; yet more archaic; but the star was always the reddest spot in it. Now and again, while the human figure was as dry and dark as a mummy, the star would seem to be literally alive, waving its flaming fingers as if it were trying to tell him something. Now and then even the whole figure was upside down, as if to restore the star to its proper place in the skies.

'I told Wilkes that a flower was a living star,' he said to himself. 'A starfish is more literally a living star. But this is like going crazy. And if there is one thing I strongly object to, it is going crazy. What use should I be to all my brother lunatics, if I once really lost my balance on the tightrope over the abyss?'

He sat staring into vacancy for some time, trying to fit in this small and stubborn fancy with a much steadier stream of much deeper thoughts that were already driving in a certain direction. At last, the light of a possibility began to dawn in his eyes; and it was evidently something very simple when it was realised; something which he felt he ought to have thought of before; for he laughed shortly and scornfully at himself as he rose to his feet.

'If Boon goes about everywhere introducing his shark and I go into society always attended by my starfish,' he murmured to himself, 'we shall turn the world into an aquarium bigger and better than Dr Wilkes is fixing up. I'm going down to make some enquiries in the village.'

Returning thence across the sands at evening, after several conversations with skippers and fishermen, he wore a more satisfied expression.

'I always did believe,' he reflected, 'that the footprint business would be the simplest thing in the affair. But there are some things in it that are by no means simple.'

Then he looked up, and saw far off on the sands, lonely and dark against the level evening light, the strange hat and stumpy figure of Amos Boon.

He seemed to consider for a moment the advisability of a meeting; then he turned away and moved towards the stairway up the cliff. Mr Boon was apparently occupied in idly drawing lines on the sand with his shabby umbrella; like one drawing plans for a child's sand-castle, but apparently without any such intelligent object or excuse. Gale had often seen the man mooning about with equally meaningless and automatic gestures; but as the poet mounted the rocky steps, climbing higher and higher, he had a return of the irrational feeling of a visionary vertigo. He told himself again, as if in warning, that it was his whole duty in life to walk on a tightrope above a void in which many imaginative men were swallowed up. Then he looked down again at the drop of the dizzy cliffs to the flats that seemed to be swimming below him like a sea. And he saw the long, loose lines drawn in the sand unified into a shape, as flat as a picture on a wall. He had often seen a child, in the same fashion, draw on the sand a pig as large as a house. But in this case he could not shake off his former feeling of something archaic, like a palaeolithic drawing, about the scratching of the brown sand. And Mr Boon had not drawn a pig, but a shark; conspicuous with its jagged teeth and fin like a horn exalted.

But he was not the only person overlooking this singular decorative scheme. When he came to the short railings along the brow of the cliff in which the stairway terminated, he found three figures leaning on it and looking down; and instantly realised how the case was closing in. For even in their outlines against the sky he had recognised the two doctors and an inspector of police.

'Hullo, Gale,' observed Wilkes, 'may I present you to Inspector Davies; a very active and successful officer.'

Garth nodded. 'I understand the inspector will soon make an arrest,' he said.

'The inspector must be getting back to his work and not talking about it,' said that official good-humouredly. 'I'm going down to the village. Anybody coming my way?'

Dr Wilkes assented and followed him, but Dr Garth stopped a moment, being detained by the poet, who caught hold of his sleeve with unusual earnestness.

'Garth,' he said, 'I want to apologise. I'm afraid I was wool gathering when we met the other day, and didn't hail you as I ought to hail an old friend. You and I have been in one or two queer affairs together, and I want to talk to you about this one. Shall we sit down on that seat over there?'

They seated themselves on an iron seat set up on the picturesque headland; and Gale added, 'I wish you could tell me roughly how you got as far as you seem to have got.'

Garth gazed silently out to sea, and said at last: 'Do you know that man Simon?'

'Yes,' replied the poet, 'that's the way it works is it?'

'Well, the investigation soon began to show that Simon knew rather more than he said. He was on the spot before you; and for some time he wouldn't admit what it was he saw before you turned up. We guessed it was because he was afraid to tell the truth; and in one sense he was.'

'Simon doesn't talk enough,' said Gale thoughtfully. 'He doesn't talk about himself enough; so he thinks about himself too much. A man like that always gets secretive; not necessarily in the sense of being criminal, or even of being malicious, but merely of being morbid. He is the sort that is ill-treated at school and never says so. As long as a thing terrified him, he couldn't talk about it.'

'I don't know how you guessed it,' said Garth, 'but that is something like the line of discoveries. At first they thought that Simon's silence was guilt, but it was only a fear of something more than guilt; of some diabolic destiny and entanglement. The truth is, that when he went up before you to the cliff-head at daybreak, he saw something that hag-rode his morbid spirit ever since. He saw the figure of this man Boon poised on the brink of the precipice, black against the dawn, and waving his arms in some unearthly fashion as if he were going to fly. Simon thought the man was talking to himself, and perhaps even singing. Then the strange creature passed on towards the village and was lost in the twilight; but when Simon came to the edge of the cliff he saw Sir Owen lying dead far out on the sands below, beside his easel.'

'And ever since, I suppose,' observed Gale, 'Simon has seen sharks everywhere.'

'You are right again,' said the doctor. 'He has admitted since that a shadow on the blind or a cloud on the moon would have the unmistakable shape of the fish with the fin erect. But, in fact, it is a very mistakable shape;

anything with a triangular top to it would suggest it to a man in his state of nerves. But the truth is that so long as he thought Boon had dealt death from a distance by some sort of curse or spell, we could get nothing out of him. Our only chance was to show him that Boon might have done it even by natural means. And we did show it, after all.'

'What is your theory, then?' asked the other.

'It is too general to be called a theory yet,' replied the doctor; 'but, honestly, I do not think it at all impossible that Boon might have killed a man on the sands from the top of a cliff, without falling back on any supernatural stuff. You've got to consider it like this: Boon has been very deep in the secrets of savages, especially in that litter of islands that lie away towards Australia. Now, we know that such savages, for all they are called ignorant, have developed many dexterities and many unique tools. They have blowpipes that kill at a considerable distance; they harpoon and lasso things, and draw them in on a line. Above all, the Australian savages have discovered the boomerang that actually returns to the hand. Is it quite so inconceivable that Boon might know some way of sending a penetrating projectile from a distance, and even possibly of recovering it in some way? Dr Wilkes and I, on examining the wound, found it a very curious one: it was made by some tapering, pointed tool, with a slight curve; and it not only curved upwards, but even slightly outwards, as if the curve were returning on itself. Does not that suggest to you some outlandish weapon of a strange shape, and possibly with strange properties? And always remember that such an explanation would explain something else as well, which is generally regarded as the riddle. It would explain why the murderer left no footprints round the body.'

Gale gazed out to sea in silence, as if considering; then he said simply: 'An extremely shrewd argument. But I know why he left no footprints. It is a much simpler explanation than that.'

Garth stared at him for a few moments; and then observed gravely: 'May I then ask, in return, what is your theory?'

'My theory will seem a maze of theories, and nothing else,' said Gale. 'It is, as many would say, of such stuff as dreams are made of. Most modern people have a curious contradiction; they abound in theories, yet they never see the part that theories play in practical life. They are always talking about temperament and circumstances and accident; but most men are what their theories make them; most men go in for murder or marriage, or mere lounging because of some theory of life, asserted or assumed. So I can never manage to begin my explanations in that brisk, pointed, practical way that you doctors and detectives do. I see a man's mind first, sometimes almost without any particular man attached to it. I could only begin this business by describing a mental state . . . which can't be described. Our murderer or maniac, or whatever you call him, is certainly affected by some of the elements attributed to him. His view has reached an insane degree of simplicity, and in that sense of savagery. But I doubt whether he would necessarily transfer the savagery from the end to the means. In one sense, indeed, his view might be compared to the barbaric. He saw every creature and even every object naked. He did not understand that what clothes a thing is sometimes the most real part of it. Have you ever noticed how true is that old phrase, "clothed and in his right mind"? Man is not in his right mind when he is not clothed with the symbols of his social dignity. Humanity is not even human when it is naked. But in a lower sense it is so of lesser things, even of lifeless things. A lot of nonsense is talked about auras; but this is the truth behind it. Everything has a halo. Everything has a sort of atmosphere of what it signifies, which makes it sacred. Even the little creatures he studied had each of them its halo; but he would not see it.'

'But what little creatures did Boon study?' asked Garth in some wonder. 'Do you mean the cannibals?'

'I was not thinking about Boon,' replied Gabriel Gale.

'What do you mean?' cried the other, in sudden excitement. 'Why, Boon is almost in the hands of the police.'

'Boon is a good man,' said Gale, calmly; 'he is very stupid; that is why he is an atheist. There are intelligent atheists, as we shall see presently; but that stunted, stupid, sort is much commoner, and much nicer. But he is a good man; his motive is good; he originally talked all that tosh of the superiority of the savage because he thought he was the underdog. He may be a trifle cracked, by now, about sharks and other things; but that's only because his travels have been too much for his intellect. They say travel broadens the mind; but you must have the mind. He had a mind for a suburban chapel, and there passed before it all the panorama of gilded nature-worship and purple sacrifice. He doesn't know if he's on his head or his heels, any more than a good many others. But I shouldn't wonder if heaven is largely populated with atheists of that sort, scratching their heads and wondering where they are.

'But Boon is a parenthesis; that is all he is. The man I am talking about is very much the point, and a sharp one at that. He dealt in something very different from muddled mysticism about human sacrifice. Human sacrifice is quite a human weakness. He dealt in assassination; direct, secret, straight from a head as inhuman as hell. And I knew it when I first talked to him over the tea-cups and he said he saw nothing pretty in a flower.'

'My dear fellow!' remonstrated Dr Garth.

'I don't mean that a man merely dissecting a daisy must be on the road to the gallows,' conceded the poet, magnanimously, 'but I do say that to mean it as he meant it is to be on a straight road of logic that leads there if he chooses to follow it. God is inside everything. But this man wanted to be outside everything; to see everything hung in a vacuum, simply its own dead self. It's not only not the same, it's almost the opposite of scepticism in the sense of Boon or the Book of Job. That's a man overwhelmed by the mysteries; but this man denies that there are any mysteries. It's not, in the ordinary sense, a matter of theology, but psychology. Most good pagans and pantheists might talk of the miracles of nature; but this man denies that there are any miracles, even in the sense of marvels. Don't you see that dreadful dry light shed on things must at last wither up the moral mysteries as illusions, respect for age, respect for property, and that the sanctity of life will be a superstition? The men in the street are only organisms, with their organs more or less displayed. For such a one there is no longer any terror in the touch of human flesh, nor does he see God watching him out of the eyes of a man.'

'He may not believe in miracles, but he seems to work them,' remarked the doctor. 'What else was he doing, when he struck a man down on the sand without leaving a mark to show where he stood?'

'He was paddling,' answered Gale.

'As high up on the shore as that?' enquired the other.

Gale nodded. 'That was what puzzled me; till something I saw on the sand started a train of thought that led to my asking the seafaring people about the tides. It's very simple; the night before we found the body was a flood-tide, and the sea came up higher than usual; not quite to where Cram was sitting, but pretty near. So that was the way that the real human fish came out of the sea. That was the way the divine shark really devoured the sacrifice. The man came paddling in the foam, like a child on a holiday.'

'Who came?' asked Garth; but he shuddered.

'Who did go dredging for sea-beasts with a sort of shrimping-net along the shore every evening? Who did inherit the money of the old man for his ambitious museum and his scientific career? Who did tell me in the garden that a cowslip was only a growth like a cancer?'

'I am compelled to understand you,' said the doctor gloomily. 'You mean that very able young man named Wilkes?'

'To understand Wilkes you must understand a good deal,' continued his friend. 'You must reconstruct the crime, as they say. Look out over that long line of darkening sea and sand, where the last light runs red as blood; that is where he came dredging every day, in the same bloodshot dusk, looking for big beasts and small; and in a true sense everything was fish that came to his net. He was constructing his museum as a sort of cosmos; with everything traced from the fossil to the flying fish. He had spent enormous sums on it, and had got quite disinterestedly into debt; for instance he had had magnificent models made, in wax or papier maché, of small fish magnified, or extinct fish restored; things that South Kensington cannot afford, and certainly Wilkes could not afford. But he had persuaded Cram to leave his money to the museum, as you know; and for him Cram was simply a silly old fool, who painted pictures he couldn't paint, and talked of sciences he didn't understand; and whose only natural function was to die and save the museum. Well, when every morning Wilkes had done polishing the glass cases of his masks and models, he came round by the cliff and took a turn at the fossils in the chalk with his geological hammer; then he put it back in that great canvas bag of his, and unslung his long shrimping-net and began to wade. This is where I want you to look at that dark red sand and see the picture; one never understands anything till one sees the picture. He went for miles along the shallows of that desolate shore, long inured to seeing one queer creature or another stranded on the sand; here a sea-hedgehog, and there a starfish, and then a crab, and then another creature. I have told you he had reached a stage when he would have looked at an angel with the eye of an ornithologist. What would he think of a man, and a man looking like that? Don't you see that poor Cram must have looked like a crab or a sea-urchin; his dwarfed, hunched figure seen from behind, with his fan of bristling whiskers, his straggling bow legs and restless twisting feet all tangled up with the three legs of his stool; making him look as if he had five limbs like a starfish? Don't you see he looked like a Common Object of the Seashore? And Wilkes had only to collect this specimen, and all his other specimens were safe. Everything was fish that came to his net, and . . .

'He stretched out the long pole in his hand to its full extent, and drew the net over the old man's head as if he were catching a great grey moth. He plucked him backwards off his stool so that he lay kicking on his back on the sand; and doubtless looking more like a large insect than ever. Then the murderer bent forward, propped by one hand upon his pole, and the other armed with his geological hammer. With the pick at the back of that instrument he struck in what he well knew to be a vital spot. The curve you noticed in the wound is due to that sharp side of the hammer being shaped like a pickaxe. But the unusual position of it, and the puzzle of how such a blow could be struck upwards, was due to the queer posture of the two figures. The murderer struck at a head that was upside down. It could only occur as a rule if the victim were standing on his head, a posture in which few persons await the assassin. But with the flourish and sweep of the great net, I fancy a starfish caught in it fell out of it, just beyond the dead man's foot. At any rate, it was that starfish and the accident of its flying so high on the shore, that set my mind drifting in the general direction of tides; and the possibility of the murderer having been moving about in the water. If he made any prints the breakers washed them out; and I should never have begun to think of it but for that red five-fingered little monster.'

'Then do you mean to tell me,' demanded Garth, 'that all this business about the shadow of the shark had nothing to do with it?'

'The shadow of the shark had everything to do with it,' replied Gale. 'The murderer hid in the shadow of the shark, and struck from under the shadow of the shark. I doubt if he would have struck at all, if he had not had the shadow of that fantastic fin in which to hide. And the proof is that he himself took the trouble to emphasise and exaggerate the legend of poor Boon dancing before Dagon. Do you remember that queer incident of the fish's face at the window? How did anybody merely playing a practical joke get hold of a fish's face? It was very lifelike; for it was one of the masks modelled for the Wilkes museum; and Wilkes had left it in the hall in his great canvas bag. It seems simple, doesn't it, for a man to raise an alarm inside a house, walk out to see, and instantly put on a mask and look in at a window? That's all he did; and you can see his idea, from the fact that he proceeded to warn Sir Owen of an enemy. He wanted all this idolatrous and mystical murder business worked for all it was worth, that his own highly reasonable murder might not be noticed. And you see he has succeeded. You tell me that Boon is in the hands of the police.'

Garth sprang to his feet. 'What is to be done?' he said.

'You will know what to do,' said the poet. 'You are a good and just man, and a practical man, too. I am not a practical man.' He rose with a certain air of apology. 'You see, you want an unpractical man for finding out this sort of thing.'

And once more he gazed down from the precipice into the abysses below.

4

The Crime of Gabriel Gale

Dr Butterworth, the famous London physician, was sitting in his summerhouse in his shirt sleeves, for it was a hot day and he had been playing tennis on the sunny lawns outside. He had a solid face and figure and carried everywhere an atmosphere of bodily health and good humour which helped him not a little in his profession; but he was not serious or self-conscious about it. He was not one of those in whom health has degenerated into hygiene. He played tennis when he felt inclined and left off when he felt inclined; as on the present occasion, when he had retired to smoke a pipe in the shade. He enjoyed a game as he enjoyed a joke; which was interpreted by some as meaning that he would never be a player, and by himself as meaning that he would always be able to play. And he enjoyed a joke very much, even the most minute and trivial joke that his roving eye encountered; and at this moment it encountered a quaint detail, which was something of a quaint contrast, in the glowing garden outside. Framed in the dark doorway of the summerhouse, like a lighted scene on the stage, was the perspective of a garden path, bordered with very gay and flamboyant beds of tulips, having something of the gorgeous formality of the borders of a Persian illumination. And down the centre of the central path was advancing a figure that looked by comparison almost completely black, with black top-hat, black clothes and black umbrella; it might have been the mythical Black Tulip come to life and a walking parody of the tall, top-heavy garden flowers. The next moment all such fancies had faded from the doctor's daydream; for he had recognised a familiar face under the top-hat; he knew that the contrast was not merely grotesque; and was shocked with the gravity of the visitor's eyes.

'Hullo, Garth,' he said in a hearty manner, 'sit down and tell us all about yourself. You look as if you were going to a funeral.'

'So I am,' replied Dr Garth, putting his black hat on a chair; he was a small, red-haired, shrewd-faced man and he looked pale and harassed.

'I am so sorry,' said Butterworth quickly, 'if I spoke without thinking. I'm afraid you're really rather cut up.'

'I am going to a queer sort of funeral,' said Dr Garth grimly; 'the sort of funeral where we take special precautions to ensure premature burial.'

'What in the world do you mean?' asked his colleague, staring.

'I mean I've got to bury a man alive,' said Garth with a ghastly calm. 'But it's the sort of burial that requires two doctors' certificates instead of one.'

Butterworth stared at the patch of sunlight and sucked in his cheeks with a soundless whistle. 'Oh . . . I see,' he said.

Then he added abruptly: 'Of course it's always a sad business; but I'm afraid it's rather personal for you. A friend of yours?'

'One of my best friends, I think, barring yourself,' replied Garth; 'and one of the best and brightest young men of our time as well. I was afraid something of the sort might happen; but I hoped it wouldn't be so bad as this.' He stopped for an instant and then said almost explosively: 'It's poor old Gale; and he's done it once too often.'

'Done what?' asked Dr Butterworth.

'It's rather difficult to explain, unless you know him,' said Garth. 'Gabriel Gale is a poet, also a painter and other wild things of that sort; but he has also a wild theory of his own about how to cure lunatics. In short, the amateur set up as a mad doctor and now the doctor is really mad. It's a horrid tragedy; but really he was asking for it.'

'I don't yet understand what it's all about,' said the other doctor patiently.

'I tell you he had a theory,' said Garth. 'He thought he could cure cracked people by what he called sympathy. But it didn't mean what you would mean by sympathy; he meant following their thoughts and going halfway with them, or all the way with them if he could. I used to joke with him, poor fellow, and say that if a lunatic thought he was made of glass, Gale would try hard to feel a little transparent. Anyhow, that was his notion, that he could really look at things to some extent from the lunatic's point of view; and talk to him in his own language. He admitted himself that it was a risky business, to walk on the edge of the precipice like that; and now, as I say, he's done it once too often. I always distrusted it myself.'

'I should think so,' said Dr Butterworth, all his solid sanity stiffening against the suggestion. 'He might as well say that a doctor ought to limp all the way to cure a lame man, or shut his eyes in order to help the blind.'

'If the blind lead the blind,' assented the other gloomily. 'Well, he's fallen into the ditch this time.'

'Why especially this time?' asked Butterworth.

'Well, if he doesn't go to an asylum, he'll go to jail,' said Garth grimly. 'That's why I'm in such a hurry to have him certified; God knows I don't like doing that. But he's broken out this time in a way he never did before. He was always fanciful and eccentric, of course; but I'm bound to say he had a very sane streak in him somewhere. It's exactly because he's never done anything like this before that I'm sure the end has really come. For one thing, he's committed a perfectly crazy assault and apparently tried to murder a man with a pitchfork. But what hits me much harder, who knew him, is that he tried to murder a perfectly mild and shy and inoffensive person; in fact a rather gauche youth from Cambridge, half developed into a curate. Now that's quite unlike Gabriel, even at his maddest. The men with whom he wrestled in spirit, if not in body, were intellectual bullies or mesmerists, the sort of men who wanted somebody to stand up to them; like that thin-lipped Dr Wilkes, or that Russian professor. I can no more see him savaging somebody like poor young Saunders than I can see him kicking a crippled child. And yet I *did* see him do it. The only explanation is that he wasn't himself.

'There was another thing which made me sure he wasn't himself. The weather had been very trying for everybody for some time; hot and stormy and electric; but it was the first time I've ever known him upset by such storms. I've known him to do the silliest things; I've known him stand on his head in the garden; but that was only showing that he was *not* affected by the storm. But this time I'm sure these queer semi-tropical tempests have been too much for him; so that even the very subject of the storm upset him in some way. For this tragedy arose out of the most trivial sort of triviality. The whole terrible unnatural business began with talking about the weather.

'Lady Flamborough said to a guest at her rather damp garden-party, "You brought bad weather with you." Anybody might say that to anybody; but she did say it to young Herbert Saunders, who is awfully awkward and shy, one of those long, loose boys with large feet, who seem to have outgrown their clothes and their wits; the last sort of person who would want to be singled out by any remark, however trifling. So Saunders only gaped and gurgled or was dumb, but somehow the lady's remark seemed to get on Gale's nerves from the first. A little while afterwards Gale met Lady Flamborough again, at another reception where it was raining, and he suddenly pointed, like some comic conspirator, at the tall ungainly figure of Saunders in the distance and said: "He still brings bad weather." Then happened one of those coincidences that are quite natural but seem to drive madmen really mad. The next time all that set happened to get together was on a really beautiful afternoon at Mrs Blakeney's; with a clear blue sky without a cloud in it, so that old Blakeney went pottering round and showed all the first comers his gardens and glasshouses. But after that they all went in to tea, which was served in the great peacock-green drawing-room in the middle of the house; and so it happened that Saunders came late and there was a good deal of laughter as he sat down, much to his embarrassment; because the weather joke had been repeated and people were quite pleased to see it falsified for once. Then they all went out into the rooms nearer the entrance; and Gabriel Gale was walking towards the doorway. Between two pillars he caught sight of one of the outer windows and stood rooted to the spot, rigidly pointing with one arm. That gesture alone warned me that something was really rather wrong with him; but when I looked I could hardly help sharing his shock of surprise. For the windows that had been painted blue with summer sky were painted black with rain. On every side of the house the rain dripped and pattered as dismally as if it had been raining for a hundred years. And ten minutes before the whole garden had seemed a garden of gold like the Hesperides. Gale stood staring at this flying storm from nowhere, that had so suddenly struck the house; then he turned slowly and looked, with an expression not to be forgotten, at the man who was standing a few yards away. It was Herbert Saunders.

'You can imagine it's not much in my line to believe in witchcraft or magicians who control the elements; but there did really seem something funny about that cloudless day having so rapidly overclouded, with the coming of the one man whose name was already associated with it, if only by a jest. It was a mere coincidence, of course; but what worried me was the possible effect on my friend's already rather rickety psychology. He and Saunders were both standing and staring out of the same wide window, looking at the deluge-darkened garden and the swaying and tormented trees; but Saunders's simple face seemed to express only amiable bewilderment; indeed, he was smiling vaguely and shyly, as he did when he received a compliment. For he was one of those whose face after a compliment always looks as if it has received a buffet. He obviously saw nothing in it but a repetition of the joke; perhaps he thought that the English climate was keeping up the joke. And, compared with his face, the face of Gabriel was like the face of a fiend. So it seemed at least, as it sprang white out of the growing dark to meet the first white burst of the lightning; then there followed only thunder and the noise of the roaring rain; but I knew that he stood there rocking with that inexplicable excitement. Through the thunder I heard his voice saying, "It makes one feel like God."

'Immediately under the windows a little path ran on the edge of some meadow land attached to the garden, where the Blakeneys had been getting in their hay; and a moderately large mound of hay looked almost mountainously dark against that low and lowering sky; a two-pronged pitchfork lying across it had certainly something grim about its black outline, which may have captured poor Gale's fancy; for he was always prone to be taken by odd sights as if they were signals. Anyhow at that moment the host and hostess and other guests came hurrying by; the old man lamenting over the ruin of his hay; but the lady of the house apparently much more concerned about the fate of some highly ornamental garden-chairs, which had apparently been left out on the lawn just adjoining the meadow, under the large apple tree whose boughs were now tossing and twisting in the storm.

'Gabriel Gale, when in his right mind, is the most chivalrous of men, and would have regained the lady's chairs at a bound. But now he could do nothing but glare at the unfortunate Saunders; who awoke trembling to his social duties, in that agony of self-consciousness in which a man is afraid to do the right thing and afraid not to do it. At length, however, he jerked himself forward, fumbled with the door, flung it open and ran out into the reverberating rain. Then Gale followed him to the open door and shouted something after him. For most of the company, I think, it was lost in the din; but even if they had heard it, they certainly could not have understood it. I heard it; and I thought I understood it only too well. For what Gale shouted through the storm was, "Why don't you call the chairs and they'll come to you."

'A second or so afterwards he added, as if it were an afterthought, "You might as well tell the tree to come here as well." Naturally there was no answer; and indeed Saunders, partly by his natural clumsiness and partly in the distraction of the driving elements, seemed for the moment to have lost his way and was staggering up the steeper path of the meadow some way to the left of the tree. I could just see his long figure and angular awkward elbows traced against the sky. Then followed the sudden, violent and utterly unintelligible incident. A rope happened to lie half round one of the swathes in the foreground; and Gale, leaping out of the door, caught it up and seemed to be knotting it in a sort of savage haste. The next moment there swept across the sky the great swirling curves of a noose thrown in the manner of a lasso. And I could see the wavering figure on the dark ridge alter its attitude and rear up as against an invisible obstacle, as the rope tightened and tugged it back.

'I looked round for assistance; and was surprised and somewhat alarmed to find I was alone. The host and hostess, and the others, having despatched the obliging Saunders after the chairs, had rushed off to summon the servants or secure other doors and windows, or look after other fittings threatened by the weather; and there was no one but myself to watch the unmeaning and apparently imbecile tragedy outside. I saw Gale drag Saunders like a sack at the end of a rope along the whole length of windows and disappear round a corner of the house. But I turned cold with a new fear when, even as he rushed past, he snatched the hayfork from the mound and seemed to disappear brandishing it, like the fabulous fork of a demon. I rushed after them, but slipping on the wet stones, hurt my foot and had to limp; the raving storm seemed to have swallowed up that lunatic and all his antics; and it was not until some time afterwards that men found how that dance had ended. Herbert Saunders was found tied to a tree, still alive and even unwounded, but presenting the appearance of having barely missed a murderous attack; for the prongs of the pitchfork were driven by sheer fury into the tree on each side of his neck, holding him pinned there as by an iron ring. Gabriel Gale was not found for nearly a day, until after the storm was spent and the sunshine had returned; and he was loitering about in an adjoining meadow blowing the clocks off dandelions. I have seldom known him so serene.'

There was a short silence. 'How is the other fellow . . . Saunders?' asked Butterworth, after a pause of frowning consideration. 'Was he much hurt?'

'Had a shock and is still shaky, of course,' answered Garth. 'Had to go for a rest-cure or something; but I believe he's all right now. Only you can hardly expect a harmless person who's been half murdered in a raving attack like that to feel very friendly or forgiving. So I'm afraid they will make it a case of attempted murder unless we can get our friend off on medical grounds. As a matter of fact, I have him waiting outside in the car.'

'Very well,' said the London doctor, rising with abrupt composure and buttoning up his coat. 'We had better go along to see him now and get it over.'

* * *

The interview between Gale and the two doctors, at an adjacent hotel, was so short and so extraordinary that they went away with their very level heads turning like windmills. For Gale displayed nothing even of the merely childish innocence of levity attributed to him in the tale of the dandelions. He listened with patience, and a humorous and benevolent mildness which made the two doctors, who were considerably his seniors, feel as if they were being treated as juniors. When Garth began to break it to him gently that some sort of rest-cure was required in his own interests, he laughed heartily and anticipated all such periphrases.

'Don't be nervous, old man,' he said, 'you mean I ought to be in a madhouse; and I'm sure you mean well.'

'You know I am your friend,' said Garth earnestly; 'and all your friends would say what I say.'

'Indeed,' said Gale, smiling. 'Well, if that is the opinion of my friends, perhaps it would be better to get the opinion of my enemies.'

'What do you mean,' demanded the other. 'Of your enemies?'

'Shall we say of my enemy?' continued Gale in level tones. 'Of the man to whom I have done this perfectly outrageous thing. Well, really, that is all I ask; that before you lock me up for this outrage, you ask Herbert Saunders himself what he thinks about it.'

'Do you mean,' broke in Butterworth rather impatiently, 'that we are to ask him whether he liked being half-throttled and impaled on a pitchfork?'

'Yes,' said Gale nodding, 'I want you to ask him whether he liked being half throttled and impaled on a pitchfork.'

He slightly knitted his brows as if considering a new and merely practical point and then added: 'I should send him a telegram now . . . say anything . . . "How do you like being lassoed?" or, "What price pitchforks?" or something playful of that sort.'

'We could telephone, if it comes to that,' said Garth.

The poet shook his head. 'No,' he said, 'that sort of man feels much more free in writing. He will only stammer on the telephone. He won't stammer anything like what you imagine, even then; but he will stammer. But writing with his head in one of those little cubicles at the telegraph office, he will feel as free as in a confessional box.'

The two doctors, when they parted in some bewilderment, but tacitly accepting this suggestion of a respite, lost no time in fulfilling the condition required. They sent off a carefully worded telegram to Saunders, who had now returned home to his mother's house, asking him what were his impressions and views about the extraordinary conduct of Gabriel Gale. The reply came back with remarkable promptitude; and Garth came to Butterworth with the open telegram in his hand and a rather dazed expression on his face. For the exact terms of the message were: 'Can never be sufficiently grateful to Gale for his great kindness which more than saved my life.'

The two doctors looked at each other in silence; and in almost as complete a silence got into a car and drove across the hills once more to the Blakeneys' house, where Gale was still staying.

They drove across the hilly country and descended into the wide and shallow valley where stood the house which sheltered that dangerous character, Mr Gabriel Gale. Garth could recall, and Butterworth could imagine, all the irony suggested to the imagination by such a story about such a scene. The house of the Blakeneys stood high and plain just beyond the river; it was one of those houses that strike the eye as old-fashioned and yet not old. Certainly it was not old enough to be beautiful; but it had everything that recalls, to those that faintly remember them, the last traditions of Early Victorian lingering into Mid-Victorian times. The tall pillars looked so very pallid; the long plain windows looked in dismally upon high-ceilinged rooms; the curtains that hung parallel with the pillars were strips of dull red; and even from that distance the humorous Butterworth was certain that they had heavy and quite useless tassels. It was a strange house to have been the scene of an incredible crime or lunacy. It was an even stranger house to have been, as was alleged, the scene of a yet more incredible or mysterious mercy. All about it lay its ordered gardens and its mown or unmown meadows; its plantations of trees and deep alleys and shrubberies; all the things which on that wild night had been given over to the withering splendour of the lightning and the wind. Now the whole landscape was laid bare in a golden calm of summer; and the blue heavens above it were so deep and still that the sound of a humming fly hung there and was heard as far away as the skylark. Thus glittered in the sun, all solid and objective, the stage properties of that hideous farce. Garth saw all the blank and staring windows which he had last beheld streaming with rain and swept by the wind and the wild dance of the lunatic and his victim. He saw the forked tree to which the victim had been bound, still with the two black holes in it where the fork had pierced it, looking like the hollow eyes of a skull, and making the whole seem like some horned goblin. There was the heaped up hay, still to some extent disordered and scattered as by the dizzy dance of a small cyclone; and beyond it rose the high green wall of the unmown and standing grass of the next meadow. From the very thick of this mild jungle or miniature forest, a long thin line of smoke was drawn up into the sky; as if from a very small fire of weeds. Nothing else human or alive was visible in the sultry summer landscape; but Garth seemed to know and recognise the significance of the smoke. He sent a far halloo across the fields, calling out, 'Is that you, Gale?'

Two feet pointed skyward and two long legs upside down rose vertically out of the tall grass, just beyond the smoke; and waved to them like arms, as if according to a preconcerted science of signalling. Then the legs seemed to give a leap and dive and the owner of the legs came the right side up and rose or surged slowly out of the depths of green, gazing across at them with a misty and benevolent expression. He was smoking a long thin cigar: the fire behind the smoke.

He received them and their news with no air of triumph, still less of surprise. Abandoning his grassy nest, he sat down with them on the garden-chairs which had also played their part in the mystery; and only smiled a little as he handed back the telegram.

'Well,' he said; 'do you still think I am mad?'

'Well,' said Butterworth, 'I can't help wondering whether he is.'

Gale leaned across, showing his first eagerness, and said, 'He isn't. But he jolly nearly was.'

Then he leaned slowly back again and stared abstractedly at a daisy on the lawn, almost as if he had forgotten their presence. When he spoke again it was in a clear but rather colourless tone, like a lecturer: 'A very large number of young men nearly go mad. But nearly all of them only nearly do it; and normally they recover the normal. You might almost say it's normal to have an abnormal period. It comes when there's a lack of adjustment in the scale of things outside and within. Lots of those boys, those big healthy schoolboys you hear about, who care for nothing but cricket or the tuckshop, are bursting with a secret and swelling morbidity. But in this young man it was rather symbolically expressed even in the look of him. It was like his growing out of his clothes, or being too big for his boots. The inside gets too big for the outside. He doesn't know how to relate the two things; and generally he doesn't relate them at all. In one way his own mind and self seem to be colossal and cosmic and everything outside them small or distant. In another way the world is much too big for him; and his thoughts are fragile things to be hidden away. There are any number of cases of that disproportionate secretiveness. You know how silent boys have been about incredible abuses in bad schools. Whether or no it's false to say a girl can't keep a secret, it's often really the ruin of a boy that he can keep a secret.

'Now in that dangerous time, there's a dreadfully dangerous moment; when the first connection is made between the subjective and objective: the first real bridge between the brain and real things. It all depends what it is; because, while it confirms his self-consciousness, it may happen to confirm his self-deception. That young man had never really been noticed by anybody until Lady Flamborough happened to tell him that he had brought the bad weather. It came just at the moment when his whole sense of proportions and possibilities had gone wild. I think the first thing that made me suspect he was . . . By the way,' added Gale abruptly, 'what was it that made you first suspect *me* of being mad?'

'I think,' said Garth slowly, 'it was when you were staring out of the window at the storm.'

'The storm? Was there a storm?' asked Gale vaguely. 'Oh yes, now I come to think of it, there was.'

'But, hang it all,' replied the doctor, 'what else could you have been staring out of the window at, except the storm?'

'I wasn't staring out of the window,' answered Gale.

'Really, my dear fellow,' remonstrated Dr Garth.

'I was staring at the window,' said the poet. 'I often stare at windows. So few people ever look at windows, unless they are stained-glass windows. But glass is a very beautiful thing, like diamonds; and transparency is a sort of transcendental colour. Besides, in this case there was something else; and something far more awful and thrilling than a thunderstorm.'

'Well, what *were* you looking at, that was more awful than a thunderstorm?'

'I was looking at two raindrops running down the pane,' said Gale. 'And so was Saunders.'

Seeing the others staring at him he continued: 'Oh yes, it's quite true; as the poet says,' and he recited with great and unusual gravity:

' "Little drops of water,
Little grains of sand,
Make the soul to stagger
Till the stars can hardly stand."

'Haven't I told you a thousand times,' he continued with increasing earnestness and animation, 'that I always find myself looking at some little thing, a stone or a starfish or what not, and that's the only way I can ever learn anything? But when I looked at Saunders, I saw his eyes were fixed on the same spot on the window-pane; and I shuddered from head to foot, for I knew I had guessed right. He was wearing a certain kind of unobtrusive smile.

'You know that incurable gamblers sometimes bet on a race between two raindrops. But there is this specially about the sport; that it is abstract and equal and gives one a sense of impartiality. If you bet on a dog-fight, you may find you really sympathise with a Scotch terrier against an Irish terrier, or vice versa; you may like the look of a billiard player or even the colours of a jockey. Therefore the event may go *against* your sympathies; and you will realise your limitations. But in the case of those two crystal spheres hung in a void of transparency, there is something like the equal scales of an abstract justice; you feel that whichever wins might be the one you had chosen. You may easily, in a certain secret megalomania, persuade yourself it is the one you have chosen. It is easy to imagine oneself controlling things hung so evenly. That was when I said to him, to test whether I was following his train of thought, "It makes you feel like God." Did you think I was talking about the storm? Storm! Pooh! Why should a storm make a man think he's God? If he'd got any sense it might make him feel he wasn't. But I knew that Saunders was just at the delicate crisis, where he was half trying to believe he was. He was half trying to think he had really changed the weather and might change everything; and a game like that of the raindrops was just the thing to encourage him. He really felt as if he were Omnipotence looking at two falling stars: and he was the special providence in them.

'Remember that there is always something double about morbidity; the sound old popular phrase said the madman was "beside himself". There is a part of him encouraging itself to go mad; and a part that still doesn't quite believe in the mania. He would delight in easy self deceptions, as in the raindrops. He would also subconsciously *avoid* tests too decisive. He would avoid *wanting* to want something incredible; as that a tree should dance. He would avoid it; partly for fear it should and partly for fear it shouldn't. And I was suddenly and furiously certain, with every cell of my brain, that he must stop himself instantly, violently, by telling the tree to dance; and finding it wouldn't.

'That was when I shouted to him to tell the chairs and the tree to move. I was certain that unless he learnt his human limitations sharply and instantly, something illimitable and inhuman would take hold of him in that very hour. He took no notice; he rushed out into the garden; he forgot all about the chairs; he ran up that steep meadow with a leap like that of a wild goat; and I knew he had broken loose from reality and was out of the world. He would go careering through waste places, with the storm within and without; and when he returned from that country walk he would never be the same again. He would leap and dance on that lonely road; he would be horribly happy; nothing would stop him. I was already resolved that something must stop him. It must be something abrupt, arresting, revealing the limit of real things; the throttling shock with which a thing comes to the end of its tether. Then I saw the rope and threw it, catching him back like a wild horse. Somehow there rose in my imagination the image of the pagan Centaur rearing backwards, bridled, and rampant against heaven: for the Centaur, like all paganism, is at once natural and unnatural; a part of nature-worship and yet a monster.

'I went through with the whole wild business; and I was sure I was right; as he himself is now sure I was right. Nobody knew but I how far he had already gone along that road; and I knew that there was nothing for it but acute, practical, painful discovery that he could not control matter or the elements; that he could not move trees or remove pitchforks; that he could struggle for two hours with a rope and a pair of prongs and still be bound.

'It was certainly rather a desperate remedy; there is really nothing to be said for it except that it was a remedy. And I believe profoundly that there was no other remedy. Anything in the nature of soothing or quieting him would only have made him yet more secretive and yet more swollen-headed. As for humouring him, it's the very worst thing to do with people who are losing their sense of humour. No; there was something he was beginning to believe about himself; and it was still possible to prove that it wasn't true.'

'Do you think,' asked Dr Butterworth, frowning, 'that there was really anything in that theological imagery in the matter? Do you suppose *he* put it in the form that he could bring the rain and thunder because he was God Almighty? Of course there are cases of religious mania that are rather like that.'

'You must remember,' said Gale, 'that he was a theological student and was going to be a clergyman; and he may have brooded upon doubt and inspiration and prophecy till they began to work the wrong way. The worst is always very near the best; there is something much worse than atheism which is Satanism; otherwise known as Being God. But as a matter of mere philosophy, apart from theology, the thing is much nearer to the nerve of all thinking than you might think. That's why it was so insinuating and so difficult to see or to stop. That's what I mean when I say I had a sympathy with the young lunatic. After all, it was a very natural mistake.'

'My dear Gale,' protested his friend Garth. 'You are getting a little too fond of paradox. A young tadpole of a curate thinks he can control the skies and uproot trees and call up the thunder and you call it a natural mistake.'

'Have you ever lain on your back in a field and stared at the sky and kicked your heels in the air?' asked the poet.

'Not in a public or professional way,' answered the doctor. 'It's not generally considered the best bedside manner. But suppose I did?'

'If you think like that, and go back to primitive things,' said Gale, 'you will find yourself wondering why you can control some things and not others. After all, your legs look a long way off when you wave them in the sky. You can wave legs about, but you can't wave trees about. I'm not sure it's so unnatural, in the abstract, for a man to fancy the whole material universe is his own body; since it all seems equally, in one sense, to be outside his own mind. But when he is in hell is when he fancies it is inside his own mind.'

'I'm afraid I don't bother much about all this metaphysical business,' said Butterworth. 'I suppose I really don't understand it. I know what I mean by a man being outside his mind in the sense of being out of his mind; and I suppose you're right in saying that Saunders was morbid enough to be nearly out of his mind. And as for being outside his body, I know what it means in the sense of his blowing his brains out or his body being left for dead. And really, to be candid, you seem to have come precious near to knocking him out of his body to cure him of being out of his mind. It certainly was an exceedingly desperate remedy; and though it may have been defensible, I shouldn't much like to have to go into a law-court as an expert witness to defend it. I can only go by results, and he certainly seems to be all the better for it. But when it comes to all your mystical explanations, about how it is hell to have everything inside your mind, frankly I give up trying to follow. I'm afraid I'm rather a materialist.'

'Afraid!' cried Gale, as if with indignation; '*afraid* you are a materialist! You haven't got much notion of what there really is to be afraid of! Materialists are all right; they are at least near enough to heaven to accept the earth and not imagine they made it. The dreadful doubts are not the doubts of the materialist. The dreadful doubts, the deadly and damnable doubts, are the doubts of the idealist.'

'I always imagined you were an idealist,' said Garth.

'I use the word idealist in its philosophical sense. I mean the real sceptic who doubts matter and the minds of others and everything except his own ego. I have been through it myself; as I have been through nearly every form of infernal idiocy. That is the only use I am in the world; having been every kind of idiot. But believe me, the worst and most miserable sort of idiot is he who seems to create and contain all things. Man is a creature; all his happiness consists in being a creature; or, as the Great Voice commanded us, in becoming a child. All his fun is in having a gift or present; which the child, with profound understanding, values because it is "a surprise". But surprise implies that a thing comes from outside ourselves; and gratitude that it comes from someone other than ourselves. It is thrust through the letter-box; it is thrown in at the window; it is thrown over the wall. Those limits are the lines of the very plan of human pleasure.

'I also dreamed that I had dreamed of the whole creation. I had given myself the stars for a gift; I had handed myself the sun and moon. I had been behind and at the beginning of all things; and without me nothing was made that was made. Anybody who has been in that centre of the cosmos knows that it is to be in hell. And there is only one cure for it. Oh, I know that people have written all kinds of cant and false comfort about the cause of evil; and of why there is pain in the world. God forbid that we should add ourselves to such a chattering monkey-house of moralists. But for all that, this truth is true; objectively and experimentally true. There is no cure for that nightmare of omnipotence except pain; because that is the thing a man *knows* he would not tolerate if he could really control it. A man must be in some place from which he would certainly escape if he could, if he is really to realise that all things do not come from within. That is the meaning of that mad parable or mystery play you have seen acted here like an allegory. I doubt whether any of our action is really anything but an allegory. I doubt whether any truth can be told except in a parable. There was a man who saw himself sitting in the sky; and his servants the angels went to and fro in coloured garments of cloud and flame and the pageant of the seasons; but he was over all and his face seemed to fill the heavens. And, God forgive me for blasphemy, but I nailed him to a tree.'

He had risen to his feet in a suppressed and very unusual excitement; and his face was pale in the sunlight. For he spoke indeed in parables; and the things of which he was thinking were far away from that garden or even from that tale. There swelled up darkly and mountainously in his memory the slopes of another garden against another storm. The skeleton arch of a ruined abbey stood gaunt against the ghastly light, and beyond the racing river was the low and desolate inn among the reeds; and all that grey landscape was to him one purple patch of Paradise – and of Paradise Lost.

'It is the only way,' he kept repeating; 'it is the only answer to the heresy of the mystic; which is to fancy that mind is all. It is to break your heart. Thank God for hard stones; thank God for hard facts; thank God for thorns and rocks and deserts and long years. At least I know now that I am not the best or strongest thing in the world. At least I know now that I have not dreamed of everything.'

'You look very strange,' said his friend Garth.

'I know it now,' said Gale. 'For there is one who would be here, if dreaming could do it.'

There was again an utter stillness in which the fly could be heard buzzing in the blue; and when he spoke again, though in the same brooding vein, they had an indescribable intuition that a door in his mind had stood open for an instant and had now again closed finally with a clang. He said after the long silence: 'We are all tied to trees and pinned with pitchforks. And as long as these are solid we know the stars will stand and the hills will not melt at our word. Can't you imagine the huge tide of healthy relief and thanks, like a hymn of praise from all nature, that went up from that captive nailed to the tree, when he had wrestled till the dawn and received at last the great glorious news; the news that he was only a man?'

Dr Butterworth was looking across the table with a restrained but somewhat amused expression; for the poet's eyes were shining like lamps and he was speaking on a note not often heard in any man speaking prose.

'If I hadn't got a good deal of special knowledge and experience,' he said, rising, 'I should think there was a bit of a doubt about you after all.'

Gabriel Gale looked sharply over his shoulder and the note of his voice changed once more.

'Don't say that,' he said rather curtly. 'That's the only sort of danger I really run.'

'I don't understand,' said Butterworth. 'Do you mean the danger of being certified?'

'Certify me till all is blue,' said Gale contemptuously. 'Do you suppose I should particularly mind if you did? Do you suppose I couldn't be reasonably happy in a lunatic asylum, so long as there was dust in a sunbeam or shadows on a wall – so long as I could look at ordinary things and think how extraordinary they are? Do you suppose I couldn't praise God with tolerable piety for the shape of my keeper's nose or anything else calculated to give pleasure to a thoughtful mind? I should imagine that a madhouse would be an excellent place to be sane in. I'd a long sight rather live in a nice quiet secluded madhouse than in intellectual clubs full of unintellectual people, all chattering nonsense about the newest book of philosophy; or in some of those earnest, elbowing sort of Movements that want you to go in for Service and help to take away somebody else's toys. I don't much mind to what place I may wander to think in, before I die; so long as the thoughts do not wander too much; or wander down the wrong road. And what you said just now does touch the real danger. It does touch the danger that Garth was really thinking about, when he suggested that I had reclaimed lunatics and might myself become a castaway. If people tell me they really do not understand what I mean – if they say they cannot see so simple a truth as that it is best for a man to be a man, that it is dangerous to give oneself divine honours – if they say they do not see *that* for themselves, but imagine it to be some sort of mysticism out of my own head, *then* I am myself again in peril. I am in peril of thinking something that may be wilder and worse than thinking I am God Almighty.'

'And still I don't understand,' said the smiling physician.

'I shall think I am the only sane man,' said Gabriel Gale.

* * *

There was a sort of sequel which came to Garth's ears long afterwards; an epilogue to the crazy comedy of the pitchfork and the apple tree. Garth differed from Gale in having a more obvious turn for the rational, or at least the rationalistic; and he often found himself debating with the sceptics of various scientific clubs and groups; finding them a very worthy race, often genuinely hard-headed and sometimes tending rather to be wooden-headed. In a particular country place, the name of which is not material, the post of village atheist had become vacant, so to speak, by the regrettable perversity of the cobbler in being a Congregationalist. His official functions were performed by a more prosperous person named Pond, a worthy hatter who was rather more famous as a cricketer. On the cricket field he was often pitted against another excellent cricketer, who was vicar of the parish; indeed they contended more frequently on the field of cricket than on the field of spiritual speculation. For the clergyman was one of the type that is uproariously popular and successful chiefly by his proficiency in such sports. He was the sort of parson whom people praise by saying he is not a bit like a parson. He was a big, beefy, jolly man, red-faced and resolute of manner; still young but the father of a boisterous family of boys, and in most ways very like a boy himself. Nevertheless, as was natural, certain passages of chaff, that could hardly be called controversy, occasionally passed between the parson and the village atheist. There was no need to commiserate the clergyman upon the pinpricks of the scientific materialist; for a pin has no effect on a pachyderm. The parson was the sort of man who seems to be rolled in layers within layers of solid substance resisting anything outside his own cheery and sensible mode of life. But one curious episode had clung to the memory of Pond, and he recounted it to Garth, in something of the puzzled tone in which a materialist tells a ghost story. The rival cricketers had been chipping each other in the usual friendly fashion, which did not go very much below the surface. The vicar was doubtless a sincere Christian, though chiefly what used to be called a muscular Christian. But it is not unfair to him to say that he was more deeply moved in saying that some action was not Cricket than in saying it was not Christianity. On this and other occasions, however, he relied chiefly on ragging his opponent with rather obvious jokes; such as the oft-repeated enquiry as to how often the hatter might be expected to do the hat-trick. Perhaps the repetition of this epigram eventually annoyed the worthy freethinker; or perhaps there was something in the deeper and more positive tones with which the parson dealt with more serious matters, that had the same effect. It was with more than his usual breeziness that the reverend gentleman on this occasion affirmed the philosophy of his life. 'God wants you to play the game,' he said. 'That's all that God wants; people who will play the game.'

'How do you know?' asked Mr Pond rather snappishly and in unusual irritation. 'How do you know what God wants? You never were God, were you?'

There was a silence; and the atheist was seen to be staring at the red face of the parson in a somewhat unusual fashion.

'Yes,' said the clergyman in a queer quiet voice. 'I was God once; for about fourteen hours. But I gave it up. I found it was too much of a strain.'

With these words the Revd Herbert Saunders went back to the cricket tent, where he mingled with Boy Scouts and village girls with all his usual heartiness and hilarity. But Mr Pond the atheist sat for some time staring, like one who has seen a miracle. And he afterwards confided to Garth that for a moment the eyes of Saunders had looked out of his red, good-humoured face as out of a mask; with an instantaneous memory of something awful and appalling, and at the same time empty; something the other man could only figure to himself in vague thoughts of some flat stark building with blank windows in a blind alley; and peering out of one of the windows the pale face of an idiot.

5

The Finger of Stone

Three young men on a walking tour came to a halt outside the little town of Carillon, in the south of France; which is doubtless described in the guide books as famous for its fine old Byzantine monastery, now the seat of a university; and for having been the scene of the labours of Boyg. At that name, at least, the reader will be reasonably thrilled; for he must have seen it in any number of newspapers and novels. Boyg and the Bible are periodically reconciled at religious conferences; Boyg broadens and slightly bewilders the minds of numberless heroes of long psychological stories, which begin in the nursery and nearly end in the madhouse. The journalist, writing rapidly his recurrent reference to the treatment meted out to pioneers like Galileo, pauses in the effort to think of another example, and always rounds off the sentence either with Bruno or with Boyg. But the mildly orthodox are equally fascinated, and feel a glow of agnosticism while they continue to say that, since the discoveries of Boyg, the doctrine of the Homoousian or of the human conscience does not stand where it did; wherever that was. It is needless to say that Boyg was a great discoverer, for the public has long regarded him with the warmest reverence and gratitude on that ground. It is also unnecessary to say what he discovered; for the public will never display the faintest curiosity about that. It is vaguely understood that it was something about fossils, or the long period required for petrifaction; and that it generally implied those anarchic or anonymous forces of evolution supposed to be hostile to religion. But certainly none of the discoveries he made while he was alive was so sensational, in the newspaper sense, as the discovery that was made about him when he was dead. And this, the more private and personal matter, is what concerns us here.

The three tourists had just agreed to separate for an hour, and meet again for luncheon at the little café opposite; and the different ways in which they occupied their time and indulged their tastes will serve for a sufficient working summary of their personalities. Arthur Armitage was a dark and grave young man, with a great deal of money, which he spent on a conscientious and continuous course of self-culture, especially in the matter of art and architecture; and his earnest aquiline profile was already set towards the Byzantine monastery, for the exhaustive examination of which he had already prepared himself, as if he were going to pass an examination rather than to make one. The man next him, though himself an artist, betrayed no such artistic ardour. He was a painter who wasted most of his time as a poet; but Armitage, who was always picking up geniuses, had become in some sense his patron in both departments. His name was Gabriel Gale; a long, loose, rather listless man with yellow hair; but a man not easy for any patron to patronise.

He generally did as he liked in an abstracted fashion; and what he very often liked to do was nothing. On this occasion he showed a lamentable disposition to drift towards the café first; and having drunk a glass or two of wine, he drifted not into the town but out of it, roaming about the steep bare slope above, with a rolling eye on the rolling clouds; and talking to himself until he found somebody else to talk to, which happened when he put his foot through the glass roof of a studio just below him on the steep incline. As it was an artist's studio, however, their quarrel fortunately ended in an argument about the future of realistic art; and when he turned up to lunch, that was the extent of his acquaintance with the quaint and historic town of Carillon.

The name of the third man was Garth; he was shorter and uglier and somewhat older than the others, but with a much livelier eye in his hatchet face; he stepped much more briskly, and in the matter of a knowledge of the world, the other two were babies under his charge. He was a very able medical practitioner, with a hobby of more fundamental scientific enquiry; and for him the whole town, university and studio, monastery and café, was only the temple of the presiding genius of Boyg. But in this case the practical instinct of Dr Garth would seem to have guided him rightly; for he discovered things considerably more startling than anything the antiquarian found in the Romanesque arches or the poet in the rolling clouds. And it is his adventures, in that single hour before lunch, upon which this tale must turn.

The café tables stood on the pavement under a row of trees opposite the old round gate in the wall, through which could be seen the white gleam of the road up which they had just been walking. But the steep hills were so high round the town that they rose clear above the wall, in a more enormous wall of smooth and slanting rock, bare except for occasional clumps of cactus. There was no crack in that sloping wilderness of stone except the rather shallow and stony bed of a little stream. Lower down, where the stream reached the level of the valley, rose the dark domes of the basilica of the old monastery; and from this a curious stairway of rude stones ran some way up the hill beside the watercourse, and stopped at a small and solitary building looking little more than a shed made of stones. Some little way higher the gleam of the glass roof of the studio, with which Gale had collided in his unconscious wanderings, marked the last spot of human habitation in all those rocky wastes that rose about the little town.

Armitage and Gale were already seated at the table when Dr Garth walked up briskly and sat down some what abruptly.

'Have you fellows heard the news?' he asked.

He spoke somewhat sharply, for he was faintly annoyed by the attitudes of the antiquarian and the artist, who were deep in their own dreamier and less practical tastes and topics. Armitage was saying at the moment: 'Yes, I suppose I've seen today some of the very oldest sculpture of the veritable Dark Ages. And it's not stiff like some Byzantine work; there's a touch of the true grotesque you generally get in Gothic.'

'Well, I've seen today some of the newest sculpture of the Modern Ages,' replied Gale, 'and I fancy they are the veritable Dark Ages. Quite enough of the true grotesque up in that studio, I can tell you.'

'Have you heard the news, I say?' rapped out the doctor. 'Boyg is dead.'

Gale stopped in a sentence about Gothic architecture, and said seriously, with a sort of hazy reverence: '*Requiescat in pace*. Who was Boyg?'

'Well, really,' replied the doctor, 'I did think every baby had heard of Boyg.'

'Well, I dare say you've never heard of Paradou,' answered Gale. 'Each of us lives in his little cosmos with its classes and degrees. Probably you haven't heard of the most advanced sculptor, or perhaps of the latest lacrosse expert or champion chess player.'

It was characteristic of the two men that while Gale went on talking in the air about an abstract subject, till he had finished his own train of thought, Armitage had a sufficient proper sense of the presence of something more urgent to relapse into silence. Nevertheless, he unconsciously looked down at his notes; at the name of the advanced sculptor he looked up.

'Who is Paradou?' he asked.

'Why, the man I've been talking to this morning,' replied Gale. 'His sculpture's advanced enough for anybody. He's no end of a chap; talks more than I do, and talks very well. Thinks too; I should think he could do everything except sculpt. There his theories get in his way. As I told him, this notion of the new realism – '

'Perhaps we might drop realism and attend to reality,' said Dr Garth grimly. 'I tell you Boyg is dead. And that's not the worst either.'

Armitage looked up from his notes with something of the vagueness of his friend the poet. 'If I remember right,' he said, 'Professor Boyg's discovery was concerned with fossils.'

'Professor Boyg's discovery involved the extension of the period required for petrifaction as distinct from fossilisation,' replied the doctor stiffly, 'and thereby relegated biological origins to a period which permits the chronology necessary to the hypothesis of natural selection. It may affect you as humorous to interject the observation "loud cheers", but I assure you the scientific world, which happens to be competent to judge, was really moved with amazement as well as admiration.'

'In fact it was petrified to hear it couldn't be petrified,' suggested the poet.

'I have really no time for your flippancy,' said Garth. 'I am up against a great ugly fact.'

Armitage interposed in the benevolent manner of a chairman. 'We must really let Garth speak; come, doctor, what is it all about? Begin at the beginning.'

'Very well,' said the doctor, in his staccato way. 'I'll begin at the beginning. I came to this town with a letter of introduction to Boyg himself; and as I particularly wanted to visit the geological museum, which his own munificence provided for this town, I went there first. I found all the windows of the Boyg Museum were broken; and the stones thrown by the rioters were actually lying about the room within a foot or two of the glass cases, one of which was smashed.'

'Donations to the geological museum, no doubt,' remarked Gale. 'A munificent patron happens to pass by, and just heaves in a valuable exhibit through the window. I don't see why that shouldn't be done in what you call the world of science; I'm sure it's done all right in the world of art. Old Paradou's busts, and bas-reliefs are just great rocks chucked at the public and – '

'Paradou may go to – Paradise, shall we say?' said Garth, with pardonable impatience. 'Will nothing make you understand that something has really happened that isn't any of your ideas and isms? It wasn't only the geological museum; it was the same everywhere. I passed by the house Boyg first lived in, where they very properly put up a medallion; and the medallion was all splashed with mud. I crossed the marketplace, where they put up a statue to him just recently. It was still hung with wreaths of laurel by his pupils and the party that appreciates him; but they were half torn away, as if there had been a struggle, and stones had evidently been thrown, for a piece of the hand was chipped off.'

'Paradou's statue, no doubt,' observed Gale. 'No wonder they threw things at it.'

'I think not,' replied the doctor, in the same hard voice. 'It wasn't because it was Paradou's statue, but because it was Boyg's statue. It was the same business as the museum and the medallion. No, there's been something like a French Revolution here on the subject; the French are like that. You remember the riot in the Breton village where Renan was born, against having a statue of him. You know, I suppose, that Boyg was a Norwegian by birth, and only settled here because the geological formation, and the supposed mineral properties of that stream there, offered the best field for his investigations. Well, besides the fits the parsons were in at his theories in general, it seems he bumped into some barbarous local superstition as well; about it being a sacred stream that froze snakes into ammonites at a wink; a common myth, of course, for the same was told about St Hilda at Whitby. But there are peculiar conditions that made it pretty hot in this place. The theological students fight with the medical students, one for Rome and the other for Reason; and they say there's a sort of raving lunatic of a Peter the Hermit, who lives in that hermitage on the hill over there, and every now and then comes out waving his arms and setting the place on fire.'

'I heard something about that,' remarked Armitage. 'The priest who showed me over the monastery; I think he was the head man there – anyhow, he was a most learned and eloquent gentleman – told me about a holy man on the hill who was almost canonised already.'

'One is tempted to wish he were martyred already; but the martyrdom, if any, was not his,' said Garth darkly. 'Allow me to continue my story in order. I had crossed the marketplace to find Professor Boyg's private house, which stood at the corner of it. I found the shutters up and the house apparently empty, except for one old servant, who refused at first to tell me anything; indeed, I found a good deal of rustic reluctance on both sides to tell a foreigner anything. But when I had managed to make the nature of my introduction quite plain to him, he finally broke down; and told me his master was dead.'

There was a pause, and then Gale, who seemed for the first time somewhat impressed, asked abstractedly: 'Where is his tomb? Your tale is really rather strange and dramatic, and obviously it must go on to his tomb. Your pilgrimage ought to end in finding a magnificent monument of marble and gold, like the tomb of Napoleon, and then finding that even the grave had been desecrated.'

'He has no tomb,' replied Garth sternly, 'though he will have many monuments. I hope to see the day when he will have a statue in every town, he whose statue is now insulted in his own town. But he will have no tomb.'

'And why not?' asked the staring Armitage.

'His body cannot be found,' answered the doctor; 'no trace of him can be found anywhere.'

'Then how do you know he is dead?' asked the other.

There was an instant of silence, and then the doctor spoke out in a voice fuller and stronger than before: 'Why, as to that,' he said, 'I think he is dead because I am sure he is murdered.'

Armitage shut his note book, but continued to look down steadily at the table. 'Go on with your story,' he said.

'Boyg's old servant,' resumed the doctor, 'who is a queer, silent, yellow-faced old card, was at last induced to tell me of the existence of Boyg's assistant, of whom I think he was rather jealous. The professor's scientific helper and right-hand man is a man of the name of Bertrand, and a very able man, too, eminently worthy of the great man's confidence, and intensely devoted to his cause. He is carrying on Boyg's work so far as it can be carried on; and about Boyg's death or disappearance he knows the little that can be known. It was when I finally ran him to earth in a little house full of Boyg's books and instruments, at the bottom of the hill just beyond the town, that I first began to realise the nature of this sinister and mysterious business. Bertrand is a quiet man, though he has a little of the pardonable vanity which is not uncommon in assistants. One would sometimes fancy the great discovery was almost as much his as his master's; but that does no harm, since it only makes him fight for his master's fame almost as if it were his. But in fact he is not only concerned about the discovery; or rather, he is not only concerned about that discovery. I had not looked for long at the dark bright eyes and keen face of that quiet young man before I realised that there was something else that he is trying to discover. As a matter of fact, he is no longer merely a scientific assistant, or even a scientific student. Unless I am much mistaken, he is playing the part of an amateur detective.

'Your artistic training, my friends, may be an excellent thing for discovering a poet, or even a sculptor; but you will forgive me for thinking a scientific training rather better for discovering a murderer. Bertrand has gone to work in a very workmanlike way, I consider, and I can tell you in outline what he has discovered so far. Boyg was last seen by Bertrand descending the hillside by the watercourse, having just come away from the studio of Gale's friend the sculptor, where he was sitting for an hour every morning. I may say here, rather for the sake of logical method than because it is needed by the logical argument, that the sculptor at any rate had no quarrel with Boyg, but was, on the contrary, an ardent admirer of him as an advanced and revolutionary character.'

'I know,' said Gale, seeming to take his head suddenly out of the clouds. 'Paradou says realistic art must be founded on the modern energy of science; but the fallacy of that – '

'Let me finish with the facts first before you retire into your theories,' said the doctor firmly. 'Bertrand saw Boyg sit down on the bare hillside for a smoke; and you can see from here how bare a hillside it is; a man walking for hours on it would still be as visible as a fly crawling on a ceiling. Bertrand says he was called away to the crisis of an experiment in the laboratory; when he looked again he could not see his master, and he has never seen him from that day to this.

'At the foot of the hill, and at the bottom of the flight of steps which runs up to the hermitage, is the entrance to the great monastic buildings on the very edge of the town. The very first thing you come to on that side is the great quadrangle, which is enclosed by cloisters, and by the rooms or cells of the clerical or semi-clerical students. I need not trouble you with the tale of the political compromise by which this part of the institution has remained clerical, while the scientific and other schools beyond it are now entirely secular. But it is important to fix in your mind the fact itself: that the monastic part is on the very edge of the town, and the other part bars its way, so to speak, to the inside of the town. Boyg could not possibly have gone past that secular barrier, dead or alive, without being under the eyes of crowds who were more excited about him than about anything else in the world. For the whole place was in a fuss, and even a riot for him as well as against him. Something happened to him on the hillside, or anyhow before he came to the internal barrier. My friend the amateur detective set to work to examine the hillside, or all of it that could seriously count; an enormous undertaking, but he did it as if with a microscope. Well, he found that rocky field, when examined closely, very much what it looks even from here. There are no caves or even holes, there are no chasms or even cracks in that surface of blank stone for miles and miles. A rat could not be hidden in those few tufts of prickly pear. He could not find a hiding-place; but for all that, he found a hint. The hint was nothing more than a faded scrap of paper, damp and draggled from the shallow bed of the brook, but faintly decipherable on it were words in the writing of the Master. They were but part of a sentence, but they included the words, "will call on you tomorrow to tell you something you ought to know".

'My friend Bertrand sat down and thought it out. The letter had been in the water, so it had not been thrown away in the town, for the highly scientific reason that the river does not flow uphill. There only remained on the higher ground the sculptor's studio and the hermitage. But Boyg would not write to the sculptor to warn him that he was going to call, since he went to his studio every morning. Presumably the person he was going to call on was the hermit; and a guess might well be made about the nature of what he had to say. Bertrand knew better than anybody that Boyg had just brought his great discovery to a crushing completeness, with fresh facts and ratifications; and it seems likely enough that he went to announce it to his most fanatical opponent, to warn him to give up the struggle.'

Gale, who was gazing up into the sky with his eye on a bird, again abruptly intervened.

'In these attacks on Boyg,' he said, 'were there any attacks on his private character?'

'Even these madmen couldn't attack that,' replied Garth with some heat. 'He was the best sort of Scandinavian, as simple as a child, and I really believe as innocent. But they hated him for all that; and you can see for yourself that their hatred begins to appear on the horizon of our enquiry. He went to tell the truth in the hour of triumph; and he never reappeared to the light of the sun.'

Armitage's faraway gaze was fixed on the solitary cell halfway up the hill.

'You don't mean seriously,' he said, 'that the man they talk about as a saint, the friend of my friend the abbot, or whatever he is, is neither more nor less than an assassin?'

'You talked to your friend the abbot about Romanesque sculpture,' replied Garth. 'If you had talked to him about fossils, you might have seen another side of his character. These Latin priests are often polished enough, but you bet they're pointed as well. As for the other man on the hill, he's allowed by his superiors to live what they call the eremitical life; but he's jolly well allowed to do other things, too. On great occasions he's allowed to come down here and preach, and I can tell you there is Bedlam let loose when he does. I might be ready to excuse the man as a sort of a maniac; but I haven't the slightest difficulty in believing that he is a homicidal maniac.'

'Did your friend Bertrand take any legal steps on his suspicions?' asked Armitage, after a pause.

'Ah, that's where the mystery begins,' replied the doctor.

After a moment of frowning silence, he resumed. 'Yes, he did make a formal charge to the police, and the Juge d'Instruction examined a good many people and so on, and said the charge had broken down. It broke down over the difficulty of disposing of the body; the chief difficulty in most murders. Now the hermit, who is called Hyacinth, I believe, was summoned in due course; but he had no difficulty in showing that his hermitage was as bare and as hard as the hill-side. It seemed as if nobody could possibly have concealed a corpse in those stone walls, or dug a grave in that rocky floor. Then it was the turn of the abbot, as you call him, Father Bernard of the Catholic College. And he managed to convince the magistrate that the same was true of the cells surrounding the college quadrangle, and all the other rooms under his control. They were all like empty boxes, with barely a stick or two of furniture; less than usual, in fact, for some of the sticks had been broken up for the bonfire demonstration I told you of. Anyhow, that was the line of defence, and I dare say it was well conducted, for Bernard is a very able man, and knows about many other things besides Romanesque architecture; and Hyacinth, fanatic as he is, is famous as a persuasive orator. Anyhow, it was successful, the case broke down; but I am sure my friend Bertrand is only biding his time, and means to bring it up again. These difficulties about the concealment of a corpse . . . Hullo! why here he is in person.'

He broke off in surprise as a young man walking rapidly down the street paused a moment, and then approached the café table at which they sat. He was dressed with all the funereal French respectability: his black stovepipe hat, his high and stiff black neckcloth resembling a stock, and the curious corners of dark beard at the edges of his chin, gave him an antiquated air like a character out of Gaboriau. But if he was out of Gaboriau, he was nobody less than Lecocq; the dark eyes in his pale face might indeed be called the eyes of a born detective. At this moment, the pale face was paler than usual with excitement, and as he stopped a moment behind the doctor's chair, he said to him in a low voice: 'I have found out.'

Dr Garth sprang to his feet, his eyes brilliant with curiosity; then, recovering his conventional manner, he presented M. Bertrand to his friends, saying to the former, 'You may speak freely with us, I think; we have no interest except an interest in the truth.'

'I have found the truth,' said the Frenchman, with compressed lips. 'I know now what these murderous monks have done with the body of Boyg.'

'Are we to be allowed to hear it?' asked Armitage gravely.

'Everyone will hear it in three days' time,' replied the pale Frenchman. 'As the authorities refuse to reopen the question, we are holding a public meeting in the marketplace to demand that they do so. The assassins will be there, doubtless, and I shall not only denounce but convict them to their faces. Be there yourself, monsieur, on Thursday at half-past two, and you will learn how one of the world's greatest men was done to death by his enemies. For the moment I will only say one word. As the great Edgar Poe said in your own language, "Truth is not always in a well." I believe it is sometimes too obvious to be seen.'

Gabriel Gale, who had rather the appearance of having gone to sleep, seemed to rouse himself with an unusual animation.

'That's true,' he said, 'and that's the truth about the whole business.'

Armitage turned to him with an expression of quiet amusement.

'Surely you're not playing the detective, Gale,' he said. 'I never pictured such a thing as your coming out of fairyland to assist Scotland Yard.'

'Perhaps Gale thinks he can find the body,' suggested Dr Garth laughing.

Gale lifted himself slowly and loosely from his seat, and answered in his dazed fashion: 'Why, yes, in a way,' he said; 'in fact, I'm pretty sure I can find the body. In fact, in a manner of speaking, I've found it.'

* * *

Those with any intimations of the personality of Mr Arthur Armitage will not need to be told that he kept a diary; and endeavoured to note down his impressions of foreign travel with atmospheric sympathy and the *mot juste*. But the pen dropped from his hand, so to speak, or at least wandered over the page in a mazy desperation, in the attempt to describe the great mob meeting, or rather the meeting of two mobs, which took place in the picturesque marketplace in which he had wandered alone a few days before, criticising the style of the statue, or admiring the skyline of the basilica. He had read and written about democracy all his life; and when first he met it, it swallowed him like an earthquake. One actual and appalling difference divided this French mob in a provincial market from all the English mobs he had ever seen in Hyde Park or Trafalgar Square. These Frenchmen had not come there to get rid of their feelings, but to get rid of their enemies. Something would be done as a result of this sort of public meeting; it might be murder, but it would be something.

And although, or rather because, it had this militant ferocity, it had also a sort of military discipline. The clusters of men voluntarily deployed into cordons, and in some rough fashion followed the command of leaders. Father Bernard was there, with a face of bronze, like the mask of a Roman emperor, eagerly obeyed by his crowd of crusading devotees, and beside him the wild preacher, Hyacinth, who looked himself like a dead man brought out of the grave, with a face built out of bones, and cavernous eye-sockets deep and dark enough to hide the eyes. On the other side were the grim pallor of Bertrand and the ratlike activity of the red-haired Dr Garth; their own anti-clerical mob was roaring behind them, and their eyes were alight with triumph. Before Armitage could collect himself sufficiently to make proper notes of any of these things, Bertrand had sprung upon a chair placed near the pedestal of the statue, and announced almost without words, by one dramatic gesture, that he had come to avenge the dead.

Then the words came, and they came thick and fast, telling and terrible; but Armitage heard them as in a dream till they reached the point for which he was waiting; the point that would awaken any dreamer. He heard the prose poems of laudation, the hymn to Boyg the hero, the tale of his tragedy so far as he knew it already. He heard the official decision about the impossibility of the clerics concealing the corpse, as he had heard it already. And then he and the whole crowd leapt together at something they did not know before; or rather, as in all such riddles, something they did know and did not understand.

'They plead that their cells are bare and their lives simple,' Bertrand was saying, 'and it is true that these slaves of superstition are cut off from the natural joys of men. But they have their joys; oh, believe me, they have their festivities. If they cannot rejoice in love, they can rejoice in hatred. And everybody seems to have forgotten that on the very day the Master vanished, the theological students in their own quadrangle burnt him in effigy. In effigy.'

A thrill that was hardly a whisper, but was wilder than a cry, went through the whole crowd; and men had taken in the whole meaning before they could keep pace with the words that followed.

'Did they burn Bruno in effigy? Did they burn Dolet in effigy?' Bertrand was saying, with a white, fanatical face. 'Those martyrs of the truth were burned alive for the good of their Church and for the glory of their God. Oh, yes, progress has improved them; and they did not burn Boyg alive.

But they burned him dead; and that is how they obliterated the traces of the way they had done him to death. I have said that truth is not always hidden in a well, but rather high on a tower. And while I have searched every crevice and cactus bush for the bones of my master, it was in truth in public, under the open sky, before a roaring crowd in the quadrangle, that his body vanished from the sight of men.'

When the last cheer and howl of a whole hell of such noises had died away, Father Bernard succeeded in making his voice heard.

'It is enough to say in answer to this maniac charge that the atheists who bring it against us cannot induce their own atheistic Government to support them. But as the charge is against Father Hyacinth rather than against me, I will ask him to reply to it.'

There was another tornado of conflicting noises when the eremitical preacher opened his mouth; but his very tones had a certain power of piercing, and quelling it. There was something strange in such a voice coming out of such a skull-and-cross-bones of a countenance; for it was unmistakably the musical and moving voice that had stirred so many congregations and pilgrimages. Only in this crisis it had an awful accent of reality, which was beyond any arts of oratory. But before the tumult had yet died away Armitage, moved by some odd nervous instinct, had turned abruptly to Garth and said, 'What's become of Gale? He said he was going to be here. Didn't he talk some nonsense about bringing the body himself?'

Dr Garth shrugged his shoulders. 'I imagine he's talking some other nonsense at the top of the hill somewhere else. You mustn't ask poets to remember all the nonsense they talk.'

'My friends,' Father Hyacinth was saying, in quiet but penetrating tones. 'I have no answer to give to this charge. I have no proofs with which to refute it. If a man can be sent to the guillotine on such evidence, to the guillotine I will go. Do you fancy I do not know that innocent men have been guillotined? M. Bertrand spoke of the burning of Bruno, as if it is only the enemies of the Church that have been burned. Does any Frenchman forget that Joan of Arc was burned; and was she guilty? The first Christians were tortured for being cannibals, a charge as probable as the charge against me. Do you imagine because you kill men now by modern machinery and modern law, that we do not know that you are as likely to kill unjustly as Herod or Heliogabalus? Do you think we do not know that the powers of the world are what they always were, that your lawyers who oppress the poor for hire will shed innocent blood for gold? If I were here to bandy such lawyer's talk, I could use it against you more reasonably than you against me. For what reason am I supposed to have imperilled my soul by such a monstrous crime? For a theory about a theory; for a hypothesis about a hypothesis, for some thin fantastic notion that a discovery about fossils threatened the everlasting truth.

I could point to others who had better reasons for murder than that. I could point to a man who by the death of Boyg has inherited the whole power and position of Boyg. I could point to one who is truly the heir and the man whom the crime benefits; who is known to claim much of the discovery as his own; who has been not so much the assistant as the rival of the dead. He alone has given evidence that Boyg was seen on the hill at all on that fatal day. He alone inherits by the death anything solid, from the largest ambitions in the scientific world, to the smallest magnifying glass in his collection. The man lives, and I could stretch out my hand and touch him.'

Hundreds of faces were turned upon Bertrand with a frightful expression of inhuman eagerness; the turn of the debate had been too dramatic to raise a cry. Bertrand's very lips were pale, but they smiled as they formed the words: 'And what did I do with the body?'

'God grant you did nothing with it, dead or alive,' answered the other. 'I do not charge you; but if ever you are charged as I am unjustly, you may need a God on that day. Though I were ten times guillotined, God could testify to my innocence; if it were by bidding me walk these streets, like St Denis, with my head in my hand. I have no other proof. I can call no other witness. He can deliver me if He will.'

There was a sudden silence, which was somehow stronger than a pause; and in it Armitage could be heard saying sharply, and almost querulously: 'Why, here's Gale again, after all. Have you dropped from the sky?'

Gale was indeed sauntering in a clear space round the corner of the statue with all the appearance of having just arrived at a crowded At Home; and Bertrand was quick to seize the chance of an anti-climax to the hermit's oratory.

'This,' he cried, 'is a gentleman who thinks he can find the body himself. Have you brought it with you, monsieur?'

The joke about the poet as detective had already been passed round among many people, and the suggestion received a new kind of applause. Somebody called out in a high, piping voice, 'He's got it in his pocket'; and another, in deep sepulchral tones, 'His waistcoat pocket.'

Mr Gale certainly had his hands in his pockets, whether or no he had anything else in them; and it was with great nonchalance that he replied: 'Well, in that sense, I suppose I haven't got it. But you have.'

The next moment he had astonished his friends, who were not used to seeing him so alert, by leaping on the chair, and himself addressing the crowd in clear tones, and in excellent French: 'Well, my friends,' he said, 'the first thing I have to do is to associate myself with everything said by my honourable friend, if he will allow me to call him so, about the merits and high moral qualities of the late Professor Boyg. Boyg, at any rate, is in every way worthy of all the honour you can pay to him. Whatever else is doubtful, whatever else we differ about, we can all salute in him that search for truth which is the most disinterested of all our duties to God. I agree with my friend Dr Garth that he deserves to have a statue, not only in his own town, but in every town in the world.'

The anti-clericals began to cheer warmly, while their opponents watched in silence, wondering where this last eccentric development might lead. The poet seemed to realise their mystification, and smiled as he continued: 'Perhaps you wonder why I should say that so emphatically. Well, I suppose you all have your own reasons for recognising this genuine love of truth in the late professor. But I say it because I happen to know something that perhaps you don't know, which makes me specially certain about his honesty.'

'And what is that?' asked Father Bernard, in the pause that followed.

'Because,' said Gale, 'he was going to see Father Hyacinth to own himself wrong.'

Bertrand made a swift movement forward that seemed almost to threaten an assault: but Garth arrested it, and Gale went on, without noticing it.

'Professor Boyg had discovered that his theory was wrong after all. That was the sensational discovery he had made in those last days and with those last experiments. I suspected it when I compared the current tale with his reputation as a simple and kindly man. I did not believe he would have gone merely to triumph over his worst enemy; it was far more probable that he thought it a point of honour to acknowledge his mistake. For, without professing to know much about these things, I am sure it was a mistake. Things do not, after all, need all those thousand years to petrify in that particular fashion. Under certain conditions, which chemists could explain better than I, they do not need more than one year, or even one day. Something in the properties of the local water, applied or intensified by special methods, can really in a few hours turn an animal organism into a fossil. The scientific experiment has been made; and the proof is before you.'

He made a gesture with his hand, and went on, with something more like excitement: 'M. Bertrand is right in saying that truth is not in a well, but on a tower. It is on a pedestal. You have looked at it every day. There is the body of Boyg!'

And he pointed to the statue in the middle of the marketplace, wreathed with laurel and defaced with stones, as it had stood so long in that quiet square, and looked down at so many casual passers-by.

'Somebody suggested just now,' he went on, glancing over a sea of gaping faces, 'that I carried the statue in my waistcoat pocket. Well, I don't carry all of it, of course, but this is a part of it,' and he took out a small object like a stick of grey chalk; 'this is a finger of it knocked off by a stone. I picked it up by the pedestal. If anybody who understands these things likes to look at it, he will agree that the consistency is precisely the same as the admitted fossils in the geological museum.'

He held it out to them, but the whole mob stood still as if it also was a mob of men turned to stone.

'Perhaps you think I'm mad,' he said pleasantly. 'Well, I'm not exactly mad, but I have an odd sort of sympathy with madmen. I can manage them better than most people can, because I can fancy somehow the wild way their minds will work. I understand the man who did this. I know he did, because I talked to him for half the morning; and it's exactly the sort of thing he would do. And when first I heard talk of fossil shells and petrified insects and so on, I did the same thing that such men always do. I exaggerated it into a sort of extravagant vision, a vision of fossil forests, and fossil cattle, and fossil elephants and camels; and so, naturally, to another thought: a coincidence that somehow turned me cold. A Fossil Man.

'It was then that I looked up at the statue; and knew it was not a statue. It was a corpse petrified by the curious chemistry of your strange mountain-stream. I call it a fossil as a loose popular term; of course I know enough geology to know it is not the correct term. But I was not exactly concerned with a problem of geology. I was concerned with what some prefer to call criminology and I prefer to call crime. If that extraordinary erection was the corpse, who and where was the criminal? Who was the assassin who had set up the dead man to be at once obvious and invisible; and had, so to speak, hidden him in the broad daylight? Well, you have all heard the arguments about the stream and the scrap of paper, and up to a point I have entirely followed them. Everyone agreed that the secret was somewhere hidden on that bare hill where there was nothing but the glass-roofed studio and the lonely hermitage; and suspicion centred entirely upon the hermitage. For the man in the studio was a fervent friend of the man who was murdered, and one of those rejoicing most heartily at what he had discovered. But perhaps you have rather forgotten what he really had discovered. His real discovery was of the sort that infuriates friends and not foes. The man who has the courage to say he is wrong has to face the worst hatred; the hatred of those who think he is right. Boyg's final discovery, like our final discovery, rather reverses the relations of those two little houses on the hill. Even if Father Hyacinth had been a fiend instead of a saint, he had no possible motive to prevent his enemy from offering him a public apology. It was a believer in Boygism who struck down Boyg. It was his follower who became his pursuer and persecutor; who at last turned in unreasonable fury upon him. It was Paradou the sculptor who snatched up a chisel and struck his philosophical teacher, at the end of some furious argument about the theory which the artist had valued only as a wild inspiration, being quite indifferent to the tame question of its truth. I don't think he meant to kill Boyg; I doubt whether anybody could possibly prove he did; and even if he did, I rather doubt whether he can be held responsible for that or for anything else. But though Paradou may be a lunatic, he is also a logician; and there is one more interesting logical step in this story.

'I met Paradou myself this morning; owing to my good luck in putting my leg through his skylight. He also has his theories and controversies; and this morning he was very controversial. As I say, I had a long argument with him, all about realism in sculpture. I know many people will tell you that nothing has ever come out of arguments; and I tell you that everything has always come out of arguments; and anyhow, if you want to know what has come out of this, you've got to understand this argument. Everybody was always jeering at poor old Paradou as a sculptor and saying he turned men into monsters; that his figures had flat heads like snakes, or sagging knees like elephants, or humps like human camels. And he was always shouting back at them, "Yes, and eyes like blindworms when it comes to seeing your own hideous selves! This is what you *do* look like, you ugly brutes! These are the crooked, clownish, lumpish attitudes in which you really do stand; only a lot of lying fashionable portrait-painters have persuaded you that you look like Graces and Greek gods." He was at it hammer and tongs with me this morning; and I dare say I was lucky he didn't finish that argument with a chisel. But anyhow the argument wasn't started then. It all came upon him with a rush, when he had committed his real though probably unintentional killing. As he stood staring at the corpse, there arose out of the very abyss of his disappointment the vision of a strange vengeance or reparation. He began to see the vast outlines of a joke as gigantic as the Great Pyramid. He would set up that grim granite jest in the marketplace, to grin for ever at his critics and detractors. The dead man himself had just been explaining to him the process by which the water of that place would rapidly petrify organic substances. The notes and documents of his proof lay scattered about the studio where he had fallen. His own proof should be applied to his own body, for a purpose of which he had never dreamed. If the sculptor simply lifted the body in the ungainly attitude in which it had actually fallen, if he froze or fixed it in the stream, or set it upon the public pedestal, it would be the very thing about which he had so bitterly debated; a real man, in a real posture, held up to the scorn of men.

'That insane genius promised himself a lonely laughter, and a secret superiority to all his enemies, in hearing the critics discuss it as the crazy creation of a crank sculptor. He looked forward to the groups that would stand before the statue, and prove the anatomy to be wrong, and clearly demonstrate the posture to be impossible. And he would listen, and laugh inwardly like a true lunatic, knowing that they were proving the utter unreality of a real man. That being his dream, he had no difficulty in carrying it out. He had no need to hide the body; he had it brought down from his studio, not secretly but publicly and even pompously, the finished work of a great sculptor escorted by the devotees of a great discoverer. But indeed, Boyg was something more than a man who made a discovery; and there is, in comparison, a sort of cant even in the talk of a man having the courage to discover it. What other man would have had the courage to undiscover it? That monument that hides a strange sin, hides a much stranger and much rarer virtue. Yes, you do well to hail it as a true scientific trophy. That is the statue of Boyg the Undiscoverer. That cold chimera of the rock is not only the abortion born of some horrible chemical change; it is the outcome of a nobler experiment, which attests for ever the honour and probity of science. You may well praise him as a man of science; for he, at least, in an affair of science, acted like a man. You may well set up statues to him as a hero of science; for he was more of a hero in being wrong than he could ever have been in being right. And though the stars have seen rise, from the soils and substance of our native star, no such monstrosity as that man of stone, heaven may look down with more wonder at the man than at the monster. And we of all schools and of all philosophies can pass it like a funeral procession taking leave of an illustrious grave and, like soldiers, salute it as we pass.'

6

The House of the Peacock

It happened that some years ago, down a sunny and empty street of suburban gardens and villas, a young man was walking; a young man in rather outlandish clothes and almost prehistoric hat; for he was newly come to London from a very remote and sleepy small town in the West Country. There was nothing else especially remarkable about him, except what happened to him; which was certainly remarkable, not to say regrettable. There cannonaded into him an elderly gentleman running down the street, breathless, bare-headed, and in festive evening dress, who immediately caught him by the lapels of his antiquated coat and asked him to dinner. It would be truer to say that he implored him to come to dinner. As the bewildered provincial did not know him, or anybody else for miles round, the situation seemed singular; but the provincial, vaguely supposing it to be a hospitable ceremony peculiar to London town, where the streets were paved with gold, finally consented. He went to the hospitable mansion, which was only a few doors down the road; and he was never seen again in the land of the living.

None of the ordinary explanations would seem to have fitted the case. The men were total strangers. The man from the country carried no papers or valuables or money worth mentioning; and certainly did not look in the least as if he were likely to carry them. And, on the other hand, his host had the outward marks of almost offensive prosperity; a gleam of satin in the linings of his clothes, a glitter of opalescent stones in his studs and cuff-links, a cigar that seemed to perfume the street. The guest could hardly have been decoyed with the ordinary motive of robbery, or of any form of fraud. And indeed the motive with which he really was decoyed was one of the queerest in the world; so queer that a man might have a hundred guesses before he hit on it.

It is doubtful whether anyone ever would have hit on it, but for the extra touch of eccentricity which happened to distinguish another young man, who happened to be walking down the same street an hour or two afterwards on the same sunny afternoon. It must not be supposed that he brought to the problem any of the dexterities of a detective; least of all of the usual detective of romance, who solves problems by the closest attention to everything and the promptest presence of mind. It would be truer to say of this man that he sometimes solved them by absence of mind. Some solitary object he was staring at would become fixed in his mind like a talisman, and he stared at it till it began to speak to him like an oracle. On other occasions a stone, a starfish, or a canary had thus riveted his eye and seemed to reply to his questions. On the present occasion his text was less trivial from an ordinary standpoint; but it was some time before his own standpoint could be ordinary. He had drifted along the sunny suburban road, drinking in a certain drowsy pleasure in seeing where the laburnum made lines of gold in the green, or patches of white or red thorn glowed in the growing shadows; for the sunshine was taking on the tinge of sunset. But for the most part he was contented to see the green semicircles of lawn repeat themselves like a pattern of green moons; for he was not one to whom repetition was merely monotony. Only in looking over a particular gate at a particular lawn, he became pleasantly conscious, or half-conscious, of a new note of colour in the greenness; a much bluer green, which seemed to change to vivid blue, as the object at which he was gazing moved sharply, turning a small head on a long neck. It was a peacock. But he had thought of a thousand things before he thought of the obvious thing. The burning blue of the plumage on the neck had reminded him of blue fire, and blue fire had reminded him of some dark fantasy about blue devils, before he had fully realised even that it was a peacock he was staring at. And the tail, that trailing tapestry of eyes, had led his wandering wits away to those dark but divine monsters of the Apocalypse whose eyes were multiplied like their wings, before he had remembered that a peacock, even in a more practical sense, was an odd thing to see in so ordinary a setting.

For Gabriel Gale, as the young man was called, was a minor poet, but something of a major painter; and, in his capacity of celebrity and lover of landscape, he had been invited often enough into those larger landscape gardens of the landed aristocracy, where peacocks as pets are not uncommon. The very thought of such country seats brought back to him the memory of one of them, decayed and neglected indeed compared with most, but having for him the almost unbearable beauty of a lost paradise. He saw standing for a moment in such glimmering grass a figure statelier than any peacock, the colours of whose dress burned blue with a vivid sadness that might indeed be symbolised by a blue devil. But when intellectual fancies and emotional regrets had alike rolled away, there remained a more rational perplexity. After all, a peacock was an unusual thing to see in the front garden of a small suburban villa. It seemed somehow too big for the place, as if it would knock down the little trees when it spread its tail. It was like visiting a maiden lady in lodgings, who might be expected to keep a bird, and finding that she kept an ostrich.

These more practical reflections in their turn had passed through his mind before he came to the most practical reflection of all – that for the last five minutes he had been leaning on somebody else's front gate with all the air of repose and finality of a rustic leaning on his own stile. Comment might have been aroused if anybody had come out; but nobody came out. On the contrary, somebody went in. As the peacock again turned its tiny crown and trailed away towards the house, the poet calmly opened the garden gate and stepped across the grass, following in the track of the bird. The darkening twilight of that garden was enriched by masses of red may, and altogether the villa had the look of being cruder and more cockney than the grounds in which it stood. Indeed, it was either actually unfinished or undergoing some new alterations and repairs, for a ladder leaned against the wall apparently to allow workmen to reach an upper storey and, moreover, there were marks of bushes having been cut or cleared away, perhaps for some new plan of building. Red bunches thus gathered from the bushes were stacked on the window-sill of the upper storey, and a few petals seemed to have dropped on the ladder, indicating that they had been carried up by that route. All these things the gaze of Gale gradually took in, as he stood with a rather bewildered air at the foot of the ladder. He felt the contrast between the unfinished house with the ladder and the rich garden with the peacock. It was almost as if the aristocratic birds and bushes had been there before the bourgeois bricks and mortar.

He had a curious innocence which often appeared as impudence. Like other human beings, he was quite capable of doing wrong knowingly and being ashamed of it. But so long as he meant no wrong, it never even occurred to him that there could be anything to be ashamed of. For him burglary meant stealing; and he might have strolled, so to speak, down the chimney into a king's bed-chamber, so long as he had no intent to steal. The invitation of the leaning ladder and the open window was something almost too obvious even to be called an adventure. He began to mount the ladder as if he were going up the front steps of an hotel. But when he came to the upper rungs he seemed to stop a moment, frowned at something; and, accelerating his ascent, slipped quickly over the window-sill into the room.

The twilight of the room seemed like darkness after the golden glare of the evening sunlight, and it was a second or two before the glimmer of light reflected from a round mirror opposite enabled him to make out the main features of the interior. The room itself seemed dusty and even defaced; the dark blue-green hangings, of a peacock pattern, as if carrying out the same scheme as the living decoration of the garden, were themselves, nevertheless, a background of dead colours; and, peering into the dusty mirror, he saw it was cracked. Nevertheless, the neglected room was evidently partly redecorated for a new festivity, for a long table was elaborately laid out for a dinner-party. By every plate was a group of quaint and varied glasses for the wines of every course; and the blue vases on the table and the mantelpiece were filled with the same red and white blooms from the garden which he had seen on the window-sill. Nevertheless, there were odd things about the dinner-table, and his first thought was that it had already been the scene of some struggle or stampede, in which the salt-cellar had been knocked over and, for all he knew, the looking-glass broken. Then he looked at the knives on the table, and a light was beginning to dawn in his eyes, when the door opened and a sturdy, grey-haired man came rapidly into the room.

And at that he came back to common sense like a man flung from a flying ship into the cold shock of the sea. He remembered suddenly where he was and how he had got there. It was characteristic of him that, though he saw a practical point belatedly – and, perhaps, too late – when he did see it he saw it lucidly in all its logical ramifications. Nobody would believe in any legitimate reason for entering a strange house by the window instead of knocking at the door. Also, as it happened, he had no legitimate reason – or none that he could explain without a lecture on poetry and philosophy. He even realised the ugly detail that he was at that very moment fidgeting with the knives on the table, and that a large number of them were silver. After an instant of hesitation, he put down the knife and politely removed his hat.

'Well,' he said at last, with inconsequent irony, 'I shouldn't shoot if I were you; but I suppose you'll send for the police.'

The newcomer, who was apparently the householder, was also fixed for the moment in a somewhat baffling attitude. When first he opened the door he had given a convulsive start, had opened his mouth as if to shout, and shut it again grimly, as if he was not even going to speak. He was a man with a strong, shrewd face, spoilt by painfully prominent eyes which gave him a look of perpetual protest. But by some accident it was not at these accusing eyes that the sleepy blue eyes of the poetical burglar were directed. The trick by which his rambling eye was so often riveted by some trivial object led him to look no higher at the moment than the stud in the old gentleman's shirt-front, which was an unusually large and luminous opal. Having uttered his highly perverse and even suicidal remark, the poet smiled as if in relief, and waited for the other to speak.

'Are you a burglar?' asked the owner of the house at last.

'To make a clean breast of it, I'm not,' answered Gale. 'But if you ask me what else I am, I really don't know.'

The other man came rapidly round the table towards him, and made a motion as if offering his hand, or even both his hands.

'Of course you're a burglar,' he said; 'but it doesn't matter. Won't you stay to dinner?'

Then, after a sort of agitated pause, he repeated: 'Come, you really must stay to dinner; there's a place laid for you.'

Gale looked gravely along the table and counted the number of places laid for dinner. The number disposed of any final doubts he might have had about the meaning of this string of eccentricities. He knew why the host wore opals, and why the mirror had been deliberately broken and why the salt was spilt, and why the knives shone on the table in a pattern of crosses, and why the eccentric householder brought may into the house, and why he decorated it with peacocks' feathers, and even had a peacock in the garden. He realised that the ladder did not stand where it did to permit people to climb by it to the window, but merely that they might pass under it on entering the door. And he realised that he was the thirteenth man to sit down at that banquet.

'Dinner is just coming in,' said the man with the opals with eager amiability. 'I'm just going down to fetch the other fellows up. You'll find them very interesting company, I assure you; no nonsense about them; shrewd, sharp fellows out against all this superstitious nonsense. My name is Crundle. Humphrey Crundle, and I'm pretty well known in the business world. I suppose I must introduce myself in order to introduce you to the others.'

Gale was vaguely conscious that his absent-minded eye had often rested on the name of Crundle, associated with some soap or lozenge or fountain-pen; and, little as he knew of such things, he could imagine that such an advertiser, though he lived in a little villa, could afford peacocks and five different kinds of wine. But other thoughts were already oppressing his imagination, and he looked in a somewhat sombre fashion out on to the garden of the peacock, where the sunset light was dying on the lawn.

The members of the Thirteen Club, as they came trooping up the stairs and settled into their seats, seemed for the most part to be at least quite ready for their dinner. Most of them had a rather rollicking attitude, which in some took the more vivid form of vulgarity. A few who were quite young, clerks and possibly dependants, had foolish and nervous faces, as if they were doing something a little too daring. Two of them stood out from the company by the singularity of being obviously gentlemen. One of these was a little dried-up old gentleman, with a face that was a labyrinth of wrinkles, on the top of which was perched a very obvious chestnut wig. He was introduced as Sir Daniel Creed, and was apparently a barrister of note in his day, though the day seemed a little distant. The other, who was merely presented as Mr Noel, was more interesting: a tall, stalwart man of dubious age but indubitable intelligence, even in the first glance of his eyes. His features were handsome in a large and craggy fashion; but the hollows of the temples and the sunken framework of the eyes gave him a look of fatigue that was mental and not physical. The poet's impalpable intuitions told him that the appearance was not misleading – that the man who had thus come into this odd society had been in many odd societies, probably seeking for something more odd than he had ever found.

It was some time, however, before any of these guests could show anything of their quality, owing to the abounding liveliness and loquacity of their host. Mr Crundle may, perhaps, have thought it appropriate in a President of a Thirteen Club to talk thirteen to the dozen. Anyhow, for some time he talked for the whole company, rolling about in his chair in radiant satisfaction, like a man who has at last realised his wildest vision of happiness. Indeed, there was something almost abnormal about the gaiety and vivacity of this grey-haired merchant; it seemed to be fed from a fountain within him that owed nothing to the circumstances of festivity. The remarks with which he pelted everybody were often rather random, but always uproariously entertaining to himself. Gale could only dimly speculate on what he would be like when he had emptied all the five glasses in front of him. But, indeed, he was destined to show himself in more than one strange aspect before those glasses were emptied.

It was after one of his repeated assertions that these stories about bad luck were all the same sort of damned nonsense that the keen though quavering voice of old Creed got a word in edgeways.

'There, my dear Crundle, I would make a distinction,' he said in a legal manner. 'They are all damned nonsense, but they are not all the same sort of damned nonsense. As a point of historical research, they seem to me to differ in rather a singular fashion. The origin of some is obvious, of others highly obscure. The fancies about Friday and thirteen have probably a religious basis; but what, for instance, can be the basis of objecting to peacocks' feathers?'

Crundle was replying with a joyful roar that it was some infernal rubbish or other, when Gale, who had quickly slipped into a seat beside the man called Noel, interposed in a conversational manner.

'I fancy I can throw a little light on that. I believe I found a trace of it in looking at some old illuminated manuscripts of the ninth or tenth century. There is a very curious design, in a stiff Byzantine style, representing the two armies preparing for the war in heaven. But St Michael is handing out spears to the good angels; while Satan is elaborately arming the rebel angels with peacocks' feathers.'

Noel turned his hollow eyes sharply in the direction of the speaker. 'That is really interesting,' he said; 'you mean it was all that old theological notion of the wickedness of pride?'

'Well, there's a whole peacock in the garden for you to pluck,' cried Crundle in his boisterous manner, 'if any of you want to go out fighting angels.'

'They are not very effective weapons,' said Gale gravely, 'and I fancy that is what the artist in the Dark Ages must have meant. There seems to me to be something that rather hits the wrong imperialism in the right place, about the contrast in the weapon; the fact that the right side was arming for a real and therefore doubtful battle, while the wrong side was already, so to speak, handing out the palms of victory. You cannot fight anybody with the palms of victory.'

Crundle showed a curious restlessness as this conversation proceeded; and a much less radiant restlessness than before. His prominent eyes shot questions at the speakers, his mouth worked, and his fingers began to drum on the table. At last he broke out: 'What's all this mean, eh? One would think you were half on the side of all the stuff and nonsense – all of you talking about it with those long faces.'

'Pardon me,' interposed the old lawyer, with a relish for repeating the logical point, 'my suggestion was very simple, I spoke of causes, not of justifications. I say the cause of the peacock legend is less apparent than that of the bad luck of Friday.'

'Do you think Friday unlucky?' demanded Crundle, like one at bay, turning his starting eyes on the poet.

'No, I think Friday lucky,' answered Gale. 'All Christian people, whatever their lighter superstitions, have always thought Friday lucky. Otherwise they would have talked about Bad Friday instead of Good Friday.'

'Oh, Christians be – ' began Mr Crundle with sudden violence; but he was stopped by something in the voice of Noel that seemed to make his violence a vain splutter.

'I'm not a Christian,' said Noel in a voice like stone. 'It is useless now to wonder whether I wish I were. But it seems to me that Mr Gale's point is a perfectly fair one; that such a religion might well actually contradict such a superstition. And it seems to me also that the truth might be applied yet further. If I believed in God, I should not believe in a God who made happiness depend on knocking over a salt-cellar or seeing a peacock's feather. Whatever Christianity teaches, I presume it does not teach that the Creator is crazy.'

Gale nodded thoughtfully, as if in partial assent, and answered rather as if he were addressing Noel alone, in the middle of a wilderness.

'In that sense of course you are right,' he said. 'But I think there is a little more to be said on the matter. I think most people, as I say, have really taken these superstitions rather lightly, perhaps more lightly than you do. And I think they mostly referred to lighter evils, in that world of rough-and-tumble circumstance which they thought of rather as connected with elves than with angels. But, after all, Christians admit more than one kind even of angels; and some of them are fallen angels – like the people with the peacocks' feathers. Now I have a feeling that *they* might really have to do with peacocks' feathers. Just as lower spirits play low tricks with tables and tambourines, they might play low tricks with knives and salt-cellars.

Certainly our souls do not depend on a broken mirror; but there's nothing an unclean spirit would like better than to make us think so. Whether he succeeds depends on the spirit in which we break it. And I can imagine that breaking the mirror in a certain moral spirit – as, for instance, a spirit of scorn and inhumanity – might bring one in touch with lower influences. I can imagine that a cloud might rest on the house where such a thing was done, and evil spirits cluster about it.'

There was a rather singular silence, a silence that seemed to the speaker to brood and settle even upon the gardens and streets beyond; no one spoke; the silence was punctuated at last by the thin and piercing cry of a peacock.

Then it was that Humphrey Crundle startled them all with his first outbreak. He had been staring at the speaker with bursting eyeballs; at length, when he found his voice, it was so thick and hoarse that the first note of it was hardly more human than the bird's. He stuttered and stammered with rage, and it was only towards the end of the first sentence that he was even intelligible. '. . . Coming here and jabbering blasted drivel and drinking my burgundy like a lord; talking rubbish against our whole . . . against the very first . . . why don't you pull our noses as well? Why the hell don't you pull our noses?'

'Come, come,' cut in Noel in his trenchant tones, 'you are getting unreasonable, Crundle; I understand that this gentleman came here at your own invitation, to take the place of one of our friends.'

'I understood Arthur Bailey sent a wire that he was detained,' observed the more precise lawyer, 'and that Mr Gale had kindly taken his place.'

'Yes,' snapped Crundle, 'I asked him to sit down as thirteenth man, and that alone smashes your superstition; for considering how he came in, he's jolly lucky to get a good dinner.'

Noel again interposed with a remonstrance; but Gale had already risen to his feet. He did not seem annoyed, but rather distrait; and he addressed himself to Creed and Noel, neglecting his excitable host.

'I am much obliged to you gentlemen,' he said, 'but I think I shall be going. It is quite true that I was invited to the dinner, but hardly to the house – well, I can't help having a curious notion about it.'

He played for a moment with the crossed knives on the table; then he said, looking out into the garden: 'The truth is I'm not sure the thirteenth man has been so lucky after all.'

'What do you mean?' cried his host sharply. 'Dare you say you haven't had a good dinner? You're not going to pretend you've been poisoned.'

Gale was still looking out of the window; and he said without moving: 'I am the fourteenth man, and I did not pass under the ladder.'

It was characteristic of old Creed that he could only follow the logical argument in a literal fashion, and missed the symbol and the spiritual atmosphere which the subtler Noel had already understood. For the first time the old lawyer in the red wig really looked a little senile. He blinked at Gale and said querulously: 'You don't mean to say you'd bother to keep all those rules about ladders and things?'

'I'm not sure I should bother to keep them,' replied Gale, 'but I am sure I shouldn't bother to break them. One seems to break so many other things when one begins to break them. There are many things that are almost as easy to break as a looking-glass.' He paused a moment, and added as if in apology: 'There are the Ten Commandments, you know.'

There was another abrupt accidental silence, and Noel found himself listening with irrational rigidity for the ugly voice of the beautiful bird outside. But it did not speak. He had the subconscious and still more meaningless fancy that it had been strangled in the dark.

Then the poet for the first time turned his face to Humphrey Crundle, and looked straight into the goggling eyes as he spoke.

'Peacocks may not be unlucky; but pride is unlucky. And it was in insolence and contempt that you set yourself to trample on the traditions or the follies of humbler men; so that you have come to trample on a holier thing at last. Cracked mirrors may not be unlucky; but cracked brains are unlucky; and you have gone mad on reason and common sense till you are a criminal lunatic this day. And red may need not be unlucky; but there is something that is more red and much more unlucky; and there are spots of it on the window-sill and on the steps of the ladder. I took it for the red petals myself.'

For the first time in his restless hour of hospitality the man at the head of the table sat perfectly still. Something in his sudden and stony immobility seemed to startle all the rest into life, and they all sprang to their feet with a confused clamour of protest and question. Noel alone seemed to keep his head under the shock.

'Mr Gale,' he said firmly, 'you have said too much or too little. A good many people would say you were talking a lot of lurid nonsense, but I have a notion that what you talk is not always such nonsense as it sounds. But if you leave it as it is, it will be simply unsupported slander. In plain words you say there has been a crime here. Whom do you accuse; or are we all to accuse each other?'

'I do not accuse you,' answered Gale, 'and the proof is that if it must be verified, you had better verify it yourself. Sir Daniel Creed is a lawyer, and may very properly accompany you. Go and look yourselves at the marks on the ladder. You will find some more in the grass round the foot of the ladder, leading away in the direction of that big dustbin in the corner of the garden. I think it would be as well if you looked in the dustbin. It may be the end of your search.'

Old Crundle continued to sit like a graven image; and something told them that his goggle eyes were now, as it were, turned inward. He was revolving some enigma of his own which seemed to baffle and blind him, so that the whole disordered scene broke about him unnoticed. Creed and Noel left the room and could be heard running down the stairs and talking in low voices under the window. Then their voices died away in the direction of the dustbin; and still the old man sat with the opal on his breast, as still as an Eastern idol with its sacred gem. Then he seemed suddenly to dilate and glow as if a monstrous lamp had been lit within him. He sprang to his feet, brandished his goblet as if for a toast, and brought it down again on the table so that the glass was shattered and the wine spilt in a blood-red star.

'I've got it; I was right,' he cried in a sort of exaltation. 'I was right; I was right after all. Don't you see, all of you? Don't you see? That man out there isn't the thirteenth man. He's really the fourteenth man, and the fellow here is the fifteenth. Arthur Bailey's the real thirteenth man, and he's all right, isn't he? He didn't actually come to the house, but why should that matter? Why the devil should that matter? He's the thirteenth member of the club, isn't he? There can't be any more thirteenth men afterwards, can there? I don't care a curse about all the rest; I don't care what you call me or what you do to me. I say all this fool's poetical stuff goes to pot, because the man in the dustbin isn't number thirteen at all, and I challenge anybody . . . '

Noel and Creed were standing in the room with very grim faces as the man at the head of the table gabbled on with a frightful volubility. When he gasped and choked for a moment with the rush of his own words, Noel said in a voice of steel: 'I am sorry to say that you were right.'

'Most horrible thing I ever saw in my life,' said old Creed, and sat down suddenly, lifting a liqueur glass of cognac with a shaking hand.

'The body of an unfortunate man with his throat cut has been concealed in the dustbin,' went on Noel in a lifeless voice. 'By the mark on his clothes, which are curiously old-fashioned for a comparatively young man, he seems to have come from Stoke-under-Ham.'

'What was he like?' asked Gale with sudden animation.

Noel looked at him curiously. 'He was very long and lank, with hair like tow,' he replied. 'What do you mean?'

'I guessed he must have looked a little like me,' answered the poet.

Crundle had collapsed in his chair again after his last and strangest outbreak, and made no attempt at explanation or escape. His mouth was still moving, but he was talking to himself; proving with ever-increasing lucidity and repetition that the man he had murdered had no right to the number thirteen. Sir Daniel Creed seemed for the moment almost as stricken and silent a figure; but it was he who broke the silence. Lifting his bowed head with its grotesque wig, he said suddenly: 'This blood cries for justice. I am an old man, but I would avenge it on my own brother.'

'I am just going to telephone for the police,' said Noel quietly. 'I can see no cause for hesitation.' His large figure and features looked notably less languid, and his hollow eyes had a glow in them.

A big florid man named Bull, of the commercial traveller type, who had been very noisy and convivial at the other end of the table, now began to take the stage like the foreman of a jury. It was rather typical of him that he waited for more educated people to lead, and then proceeded to lead them.

'No cause for hesitation. No case for sentimentalism,' he trumpeted as healthily as an elephant. 'Painful business, of course; old member of the club and all that. But I say I'm no sentimentalist; and whoever did this deserves hanging. Well, there's no doubt of who did it. We heard him practically confess a minute ago, when these gentlemen were out of the room.'

'Always thought he was a bad lot,' said one of the clerks; possibly a clerk with an old score of his own.

'I am all for acting at once,' said Noel. 'Where is the telephone?'

Gabriel Gale stepped in front of the collapsed figure in the chair, and turned his face to the advancing crowd.

'Stop,' he cried, 'let me say a word.'

'Well, what is it?' asked Noel steadily.

'I do not like boasting,' said the poet, 'but unfortunately the argument can only take that form. I am a sentimentalist, as Mr Bull would say; I am by trade a sentimentalist; a mere scribbler of sentimental songs. You are all very hard-headed, rational, sensible people who laugh at superstitions; you are practical men, and men of common sense. But your common sense didn't discover the dead body. You would have smoked your practical cigars and drunk your practical grog and gone home all over smiles, leaving it to rot in the dustbin. *You* never found out where your rational sceptical road can lead a man, as it has led that poor gibbering idiot in the chair. A sentimentalist, a dabbler in moonshine, found out that for you; perhaps because he was a sentimentalist. For I really have a streak in me of the moonshine that leads such men astray; that is why I can follow them. And now the lucky sentimentalist must say a word for the unlucky one.'

'Do you mean for the criminal?' asked Creed in his sharp but shaky voice.

'Yes,' replied Gale. 'I discovered him and I defend him.'

'So you defend murderers, do you?' demanded Bull.

'Some murderers,' answered Gale calmly. 'This one was a rather unique sort of murderer. In fact, I am far from certain that he was a murderer at all. It may have been an accident. It may have been a sort of mechanical action, almost like an automaton.'

The light of long-lost cross-examinations gleamed in Creed's aged eyes, and his sharp voice no longer shook.

'You mean to say,' he said, 'that Crundle read a telegram from Bailey, realised there was a vacant place, went out into the street and talked to a total stranger, brought him in here, went somewhere to fetch a razor or a carving knife, cut his guest's throat, carried the corpse down the ladder, and carefully covered it with the lid of the dustbin. And he did all that by accident, or by an automatic gesture.'

'Very well put, Sir Daniel,' answered Gale; 'and now let me put you a question, in the same logical style. In your legal language, what about motive? You say he could not assassinate a total stranger by accident; but why should he assassinate a total stranger on purpose? On what purpose? It not only served no end he had in view; it actually ruined everything he had in view. Why in the world should he want to make a gap in his Thirteen Club dinner? Why in the name of wonder should *he* want to make the thirteenth man a monument of disaster? His own crime was at the expense of his own creed, or cranky doubt, denial, or whatever you call it.'

'That is true,' assented Noel, 'and what is the meaning of it all?'

'I do believe,' replied Gale, 'that nobody can tell you but myself; and I will tell you why. Do you realise how full life is of awkward attitudes? You get them in snapshots; I suppose the new ugly schools of art are trying to snap them; figures leaning stiffly, standing on one leg, resting unconscious hands on incongruous objects. This is a tragedy of awkward positions. I can understand it because I myself, this very afternoon, was in the devil of an awkward position.

'I had climbed in through that window simply out of silly curiosity, and I was standing at the table like a fool, picking up the knives and putting them straight. I still had my hat on, but when Crundle came in I made a movement to take it off with the knife still in my hand; then I corrected myself and put the knife down first. You know those tiny confused movements one sometimes has. Now Crundle, when he first saw me, and before he saw me close, staggered as if I had been God Almighty or the hangman waiting in his dining-room; and I think I know why. I am awkward and tall and tow-haired, too; and I was standing there dark against the daylight where the other had stood. It must have seemed as if the corpse had lifted the dustbin lid and crawled back up the ladder, and taken up his station like a ghost. But meanwhile my own little irresolute gesture with the half-lifted knife had told me something. It had told me what really happened.

'When that poor rustic from Somerset strayed into this room he was what perhaps none of us can be, he was shocked. He came of some old rural type that really did believe in such omens. He hastily picked up one of the crossed knives and was putting it straight when he caught sight of the heap of spilt salt. Possibly he thought his own gesture had spilt it. At that crucial instant Crundle entered the room, adding to the confusion of his guest and hastening his hurried attempt at doing two things at once. The unhappy guest, with fingers still clutched round the knife-handle, made a grab at the salt and tried to toss some of it over his shoulder. In the same flash the fanatic in the doorway had leapt upon him like a panther and was tugging at the lifted wrist.

'For all Crundle's crazy universe was rocking in that instant. You, who talk of superstitions, have you realised that this house is a house of spells? Don't you know it is chock full of charms and magic rites, only they are all done backwards, as the witches said the Lord's Prayer? Can you imagine how a witch would feel if two words of the prayer came right by accident? Crundle saw that this clown from the country was reversing all the spells of his own black art. If salt was once thrown over the shoulder, all the great work might yet be undone. With all the strength he could call from hell he hung on to the hand with the knife, caring only to prevent a few grains of silver dust from drifting to the floor.

'God alone knows if it was an accident. I do not say it as an idle phrase. That single split second, and all that was really hidden in it, lies open before God as large and luminous as an eternity. But I am a man and he is a man; and I will not give a man to the gallows, if I can help it, for what may have been accidental or automatic or even a sort of self-defence. But if any of you will take a knife and a pinch of salt and put yourself in the poor fellow's position, you will see exactly what happened. All I say is this; that at no time and in no way, perhaps, could things have been precisely in that posture, and the edge of a knife been so near to a man's throat without intention on either side, except by this one particular tangle of trivialities that has led up to this one particular tragedy. It is strange to think of that poor yokel setting out from his far-off Somerset village, with his little handful of local legends, and this brooding eccentric and scoffer rushing out of this villa full of rage of his hobby, and their ending locked in this one unique and ungainly grapple, a wrestle between two superstitions.'

The figure at the head of the table had been almost forgotten like a piece of furniture; but Noel turned his eyes slowly towards it, and said with a cold patience as if to an exasperating child: 'Is all this true?'

Crundle sprang unsteadily to his feet, his mouth still working, and they saw at the edge of it a touch of foam.

'What I want to know,' he began in a resonant voice; and then the voice seemed to dry up in his throat and he swayed twice and pitched forward on the table amid the wreck of his own wine and crystal.

'I don't know about a policeman,' said Noel; 'but we shall have to send for a doctor.'

'You will want two doctors for what will have to be done to him,' said Gale; and walked towards the window by which he had come in.

* * *

Noel walked with him to the garden gate, past the peacock and the green lawn, that looked almost as blue as the peacock under a strong moonlight. When the poet was outside the gate, he turned and said a last word.

'You are Norman Noel, the great traveller, I think. You interest me more than that unfortunate monomaniac did; and I want to ask you a question. Forgive me if I imagine things for you, so to speak; it is a way I have. You have studied superstitions all over the world, and you have seen things compared with which all that talk of salt and table-knives is like a child's game of consequences. You have been in the dark forests over which the vampire seems to pass more vast than a dragon; or in the mountains of the werewolf, where men say a man can see in the face of his friend or his wife the eyes of a wild beast. You have known people who had real superstitions; black, towering, terrific superstitions; you have lived with those people; and I want to ask you a question about them.'

'You seem to know something about them yourself,' answered Noel; 'but I will answer any question you like.'

'Were they not happier men than you?'

Gale paused a moment as he put the question, and then went on. 'Did they not in fact sing more songs, and dance more dances, and drink wine with more real merriment? That was because they believed in evil. In evil spells, perhaps, in evil luck, in evil under all sorts of stupid and ignorant symbols; but still in something to be fought. They at least read things in black and white, and saw life as the battlefield it is. But you are unhappy because you disbelieve in evil, and think it philosophical to see everything in the same light of grey. And I speak to you thus tonight; because tonight you have had an awakening. You saw something worthy of hate and you were happy. A mere murder might not have done it. If it had been some old man about town, or even some young man about town, it might never have touched the nerve. But I know what you felt; there was something shameful beyond speech in the death of that poor clumsy country cousin.'

Noel nodded. 'I think it was the shape of his coat-tails,' he said.

'I thought so,' answered Gale. 'Well, that is the road to reality. Good-night.'

And he continued his walk along the suburban road, unconsciously taking in the new tint of the lawns by moonlight. But he did not see any more peacocks; and it may be accounted probable that he did not want to see any.

7
The Purple Jewel

Gabriel Gale was a painter and poet; he was the last person to pretend to be even a very private detective. It happened that he had solved several mysteries; but most of them were the sort of mysteries more attractive to a mystic. Nevertheless, it also happened once or twice that he had to step out of the clouds of mysticism into the more brisk and bracing atmosphere of murder. Sometimes he succeeded in showing that a murder was a suicide, sometimes that a suicide was a murder; sometimes he was even involved in the study of lighter occupations like forgery and fraud. But the connection was generally a coincidence; it concerned some point at which his imaginative interest in men's strange motives and moods happened to lead him, or at any rate them, across the borderline of legality. And in most cases, as he himself pointed out, the motives of murderers and thieves are perfectly sane and even conventional.

'I am no good at such a sensible job,' he would say. 'The police could easily make me look a fool in any practical matter such as they discuss in detective stories. What is the good of asking me to measure the marks made by somebody's feet all over the ground, to show why he was walking about, or where he was going? If you will show me the marks of somebody's hands all over the ground, I will tell you why he was walking upside down. But I shall find it out in the only way I ever do find out anything. And that is simply because I am mad, too, and often do it myself.'

A similar brotherhood in folly probably led him into the very baffling mystery of the disappearance of Phineas Salt, the famous author and dramatist. Some of the parties involved may have accepted the parallel of setting a thief to catch a thief, when they set a poet to find a poet. For the problem did involve, in all probability, some of the purely poetical motives of a poet. And even practical people admitted that these might possibly be more familiar to a poet than to a policeman.

Phineas Salt was the sort of man whose private life was rather a public life; like that of Byron or D'Annunzio. He was a remarkable man, and perhaps rather remarkable than respectable. But there was much to be really admired in him; and there were of course any number of people who admired even what was not so admirable. The pessimistic critics claimed him as a great pessimist; and this was widely quoted in support of the theory that his disappearance was in fact a suicide. But the optimistic critics had always obstinately maintained that he was a True Optimist (whatever that may be) and these in their natural rosy rapture of optimism, dwelt rather on the idea that he had been murdered. So lurid and romantic had his whole career been made in the eyes of all Europe, that very few people kept their heads enough to reflect, or summoned their courage to suggest, that there is no particular principle in the nature of things to prevent a great poet falling down a well or being attacked by cramp while swimming at Felixstowe. Most of his admirers, and all those who were by profession journalists, preferred more sublime solutions.

He left no family, of the regular sort, except a brother in a small commercial way in the Midlands, with whom he had had very little to do; but he left a number of other people who stood to him in conspicuous spiritual or economic relations. He left a publisher, whose emotions were of mingled grief and hope in the cessation of his production of books and the high-class advertisement given to those already produced. The publisher was himself a man of considerable social distinction, as such distinctions go today; a certain Sir Walter Drummond, the head of a famous and well-established firm; and a type of a certain kind of successful Scotchman who contradicts the common tradition by combining being businesslike with being extremely radiant and benevolent. He left a theatrical manager in the very act of launching his great poetical play about Alexander and the Persians; this was an artistic but adaptable Jew, named Isidore Marx, who was similarly balanced between the advantages and disadvantages of an inevitable silence following the cry of 'Author'. He left a beautiful but exceedingly bad-tempered leading actress, who was about to gain fresh glory in the part of the Persian Princess; and who was one of the persons, not indeed few, with whom (as the quaint phrase goes) his name had been connected. He left a number of literary friends; some at least of whom were really literary and a few of whom had really been friendly. But his career had been itself so much like a sensational drama on the stage that it was surprising, when it came to real calculations about his probable conduct, how little anybody seemed to know about the essentials of his real character. And without any such clue, the circumstances seemed to make the poet's absence as disturbing and revolutionary as his presence.

Gabriel Gale, who also moved in the best literary circles, knew all this side of Phineas Salt well enough. He also had been in literary negotiations with Sir Walter Drummond. He also had been approached for poetical plays by Mr Isidore Marx. He had managed to avoid having 'his name connected' with Miss Hertha Hathaway, the great Shakespearean actress; but he knew her well enough, in a world where everybody knows everybody. But being somewhat carelessly familiar with these noisy outer courts of the fame of Phineas, it gave him a mild shock of irony to pass into the more private and prosaic interior. He owed his connection with the case, not to this general knowledge he shared with the world of letters, but to the accident that his friend, Dr Garth, had been the family physician of the Salts. And he could not but be amused, when he attended a sort of family council of the matter, to discover how very domestic and even undistinguished the family council was; and how different from the atmosphere of large rumour and loose reputation that roared like a great wind without. He had to remind himself that it is only natural, after all, that anybody's private affairs should be private. It was absurd to expect that a wild poet would have a wild solicitor or a strange and fantastic doctor or dentist. But Dr Garth, in the very professional black suit he always wore, looked such a very family physician. The solicitor looked such a very family solicitor. He was a square-faced, silver-haired gentleman named Gunter; it seemed impossible that his tidy legal files and strongboxes could contain such material as the prolonged scandal of Phineas Salt. Joseph Salt, the brother of Phineas Salt, come up specially from the provinces, seemed so very provincial. It was hard to believe that this silent, sandy-haired, big, embarrassed tradesman, in his awkward clothes, was the one other remaining representative of such a name. The party was completed by Salt's secretary, who also seemed disconcertingly secretarial to be closely connected with such an incalculable character. Again Gale had to remind himself that even poets can only go mad on condition that a good many people connected with them remain sane. He reflected, with a faint and dawning interest, that Byron probably had a butler; and possibly even a good butler. The disconnected fancy crossed his mind that even Shelley may have gone to the dentist. He also reflected that Shelley's dentist was probably rather like any other dentist.

Nevertheless, he did not lose the sense of contrast in stepping into this inner chamber of immediate and practical responsibilities. He felt rather out of place in it; for he had no illusions about himself as a business adviser, or one to settle things with the private secretary and the family lawyer. Garth had asked him to come, and he sat patiently looking at Garth; while Gunter, the solicitor, laid the general state of things before the informal committee.

'Mr Hatt has been telling us,' said the lawyer, glancing for a moment at the secretary who sat opposite, 'that he last saw Mr Phineas Salt at his own flat two hours after lunch on Friday last. Until about an hour ago, I should have said that this interview (which was apparently very short) was the last occasion on which the missing man had been seen. Rather more than an hour ago, however, I was rung up by a person, a complete stranger to me, who declared that he had been with Phineas Salt for the six or seven hours following on that meeting at the flat and that he was coming round to this office as soon as possible, to lay all the facts before us. This evidence, if we find it in any way worthy of credit, will at least carry the story a considerable stage further and perhaps provide us with some important hint about Mr Salt's whereabouts or fate. I do not think we can say much more about it until he comes.'

'I rather fancy he has come,' said Dr Garth. 'I heard somebody answering the door; and that sounds like boots scaling these steep legal stairs'; for they had met in the solicitor's office in Lincoln's Inn.

The next moment a slim, middle-aged man slipped rather than stepped into the room; there was indeed something smooth and unobtrusive about the very look of his quiet grey suit, at once shabby and shiny and yet carrying something like the last glimmer of satin and elegance. The only other seizable thing about him was that he not only had rather long dark hair parted down the middle, but his long olive face was fringed with a narrow dark beard, which was also parted in the middle, drooping in two separated strands. But as he entered he laid on a chair a soft black hat with a very large brim and a very low crown; which somehow called up instantly to the fancy the cafés and the coloured lights of Paris.

'My name is James Florence,' he said in a cultivated accent. 'I was a very old friend of Phineas Salt; and in our younger days I have often travelled about Europe with him. I have every reason to believe that I travelled with him on his last journey.'

'His last journey,' repeated the lawyer, looking at him with frowning attention; 'are you prepared to say that Mr Salt is dead, or are you saying this for sensationalism?'

'Well, he is either dead or something still more sensational,' said Mr James Florence.

'What do you mean?' asked the other sharply. 'What could be more sensational than his death?'

The stranger looked at him with a fixed and very grave expression and then said simply: 'I cannot imagine.'

Then, when the lawyer made an angry movement, as if suspecting a joke, the man added equally gravely: 'I am still trying to imagine.'

'Well,' said Gunter, after a pause, 'perhaps you had better tell your story and we will put the conversation on a regular footing. As you probably know, I am Mr Salt's legal adviser; this is his brother, Mr Joseph Salt, whom I am advising also; this is Dr Garth, his medical adviser. This is Mr Gabriel Gale.'

The stranger bowed to the company and took a seat with quiet confidence.

'I called on my old friend Salt last Friday afternoon about five o'clock. I think I saw this gentleman leaving the flat as I came in.' He looked across at the secretary, Mr Hatt, a hard-faced and reticent man, who concealed with characteristic discretion, the American name of Hiram; but could not quite conceal a certain American keenness about the look of his long chin and his spectacles. He regarded the newcomer with a face of wood, and said nothing as usual.

'When I entered the flat, I found Phineas in a very disordered and even violent condition, even for him. In fact somebody seemed to have been breaking the furniture – a statuette was knocked off its pedestal and a bowl of irises upset; and he was striding up and down the room like a roaring lion with his red mane rampant and his beard a bonfire. I thought it might be merely an artistic mood, a fine shade of poetical feeling; but he told me he had been entertaining a lady. Miss Hertha Hathaway, the actress, had only just left.'

'Here, wait a minute,' interposed the solicitor. 'It would appear that Mr Hatt, the secretary, had also only just left. But I don't think you said anything about a lady, Mr Hatt.'

'It's a pretty safe rule,' said the impenetrable Hiram. 'You never asked me about any lady. I've got my own work to do and I told you how I left when I'd done it.'

'This is rather important, though,' said Gunter doubtfully. 'If Salt and the actress threw bowls and statues at each other . . . well, I suppose we may cautiously conclude there was some slight difference of opinion.'

'There was a final smash-up,' said Florence frankly. 'Phineas told me he was through with all that sort of thing and, as far as I could make out, with everything else as well. He was in a pretty wild state; I think he had been drinking a little already; then he routed out a dusty old bottle of absinthe and said that he and I must drink it again in memory of old days in Paris; for it was the last time, or the last day, or some expression of that sort. Well, I hadn't drunk it myself for a long time; but I knew enough about it to know that he was drinking a great deal too much, and it's not a thing like ordinary wine or brandy; the state it can get you into is quite extraordinary; more like the clear madness that comes from hashish. And he finally rushed out of the house with that green fire in his brain and began to get out his car; starting it quite correctly and even driving it well, for there is a lucidity in such intoxication; but driving it faster and faster down the dreary vistas of the Old Kent Road and out into the country towards the south-east. He had dragged me with him with the same sort of hypnotic energy and uncanny conviviality; but I confess I felt pretty uncomfortable spinning out along the country roads with twilight turning to dark. We were nearly killed several times; but I don't think he was trying to be killed . . . at least not there on the road by an ordinary motor accident. For he kept on crying out that he wanted the high and perilous places of the earth; peaks and precipices and towers; that he would like to take his last leap from some such pinnacle and either fly like an eagle or fall like a stone. And all that seemed the more blind and grotesque because we were driving further and further into some of the flattest country in England, where he certainly would never find any mountains such as towered and toppled in his dream. And then, after I don't know how many hours, he gave a new sort of cry; and I saw, against the last grey strip of the gloaming and all the flat land towards the east, the towers of Canterbury.'

'I wonder,' said Gabriel Gale suddenly, like a man coming out of a dream, 'how they did upset the statuette. Surely the woman threw it, if anybody did. He'd hardly have done a thing like that, even if he was drunk.'

Then he turned his head slowly and stared rather blankly at the equally blank face of Mr Hatt; but he said no more and, after a slightly impatient silence, the man called Florence went on with his narrative.

'Of course I knew that the moment he saw the great Gothic towers of the cathedral they would mingle with his waking nightmare and in a way fulfil and crown it. I cannot say whether he had taken that road in order to reach the cathedral; or whether it was merely a coincidence; but there was naturally nothing else in all that landscape that could so fit in with his mood about steep places and dizzy heights. And so of course he took up his crazy parable again and talked about riding upon gargoyles, as upon demon horses, or hunting with hell-hounds above the winds of heaven. It was very late before we reached the cathedral; and though it stands more deeply embedded in the town than is common in cathedral cities, it so happened that the houses nearest to us were all barred and silent and we stood in a deep angle of the building, which had something of seclusion and was covered with the vast shadow of the tower. For a strong moon was already brightening behind the cathedral and I remember the light of it made a sort of ring in Salt's ragged red hair like a dull crimson fire. It seemed a rather unholy halo; and it is a detail I remember the more, because he himself was declaiming in praise of moonshine and especially of the effect of stained-glass windows seen against the moon rather than the sun, as in the famous lines in Keats. He was wild to get inside the building and see the coloured glass, which he swore was the only really successful thing religion ever did; and when he found the cathedral was locked up (as was not unusual at that hour) he had a grand final reaction of rage and scorn and began to curse the dean and chapter and everyone else. Then a blast of boyish historical reminiscence seemed to sweep through his changing mind; and he caught up a great ragged stone from the border of the turf and struck thunderous blows on the door with it, as with a hammer, and shouted aloud, "King's men! King's men! Where is the traitor? We have come to kill the archbishop." Then he laughed groggily and said, "Fancy killing Dr Randall Davidson. . . . But Becket was really worth killing. He had lived, by God! He had really made the best of both worlds, in a bigger sense than they use the phrase for. Not both at once and both tamely, as the snobs do. But one at a time and both wildly and to the limit. He went clad in crimson and gold and gained laurels and overthrew great knights in tournaments; and then suddenly became a saint, giving his goods to the poor, fasting, dying a martyr. Ah, that is the right way to do it! The right way to live a Double Life! No wonder miracles were worked at his tomb." Then he hurled the heavy flint from him; and suddenly all the laughter and historical rant seemed to die out of his face and to leave it rather sad and sober; and as stony as one of the stone faces carved above the Gothic doors. "I shall work a miracle tonight," he said stolidly, "after I have died."

'I asked him what in the world he meant; and he made no answer. But he began abruptly to talk to me in quite a quiet and friendly and even affectionate way; thanking me for my companionship on this and many occasions; and saying that we must part; for his time was come. But when I asked him where he was going, he only pointed a finger upwards; and I could not make out at all whether he meant metaphorically that he was going to heaven or materially that he was going to scale the high tower. Anyhow, the only stairway for scaling it was inside and I could not imagine how he could reach it. I tried to question him and he answered, "I shall ascend . . . ; I shall be lifted up . . . but no miracles will be worked at my tomb. For my body will never be found."

'And then, before I could move, and without a gesture of warning, he leapt up and caught a stone bracket by the gateway; in another second he was astride it; in a third standing on it; and in a fourth vanished utterly in the vast shadow of the wall above. Once again I heard his voice much higher up and even far away, crying, "I shall ascend." Then all was silence and solitude. I cannot undertake to say whether he did ascend. I can only say with tolerable certainty that he did not descend.'

'You mean,' said Gunter gravely, 'that you have never seen him since.'

'I mean,' answered James Florence equally gravely, 'that I doubt whether anybody on earth has seen him since.'

'Did you make enquiries on the spot?' pursued the lawyer.

The man called Florence laughed in a rather embarrassed fashion. 'The truth is,' he said, 'that I knocked up the neighbours and even questioned the police; and I couldn't get anybody to believe me. They said I had had something to drink, which was true enough; and I think they fancied I had seen myself double, and was trying to chase my own shadow over the cathedral roofs. I dare say they know better now there has been a hue and cry in the newspapers. As for me, I took the last train back to London.'

'What about the car?' asked Garth, sharply; and a light of wonder or consternation came over the stranger's face.

'Why, hang it all!' he cried. 'I forgot all about poor Salt's car! We left it backed into a crack between two old houses just by the cathedral. I never thought of it again till this minute.'

Gunter got up from his desk and went into the inner room in which he was heard obscurely telephoning. When he came back, Mr Florence had already picked up his round black hat in his usual unembarrassed manner and suggested that he had better be going; for he had told all that he knew about the affair. Gunter watched him walking away with an interested expression; as if he were not quite so certain of the last assertion as he would like to be. Then he turned to the rest of the company and said: 'A curious yarn. A very curious yarn. But there's another curious thing you ought to know, that may or may not be connected with it.' For the first time he seemed to take notice of the worthy Joseph Salt, who was present as the nearest surviving relative of the deceased or disappearing person. 'Do you happen to know, Mr Salt, what was your brother's exact financial position?'

'I don't,' said the provincial shopkeeper shortly, and contrived to convey an infinite degree of distance and distaste. 'Of course you understand, gentlemen, that I'm here to do anything I can for the credit of the family. I wish I could feel quite certain that finding poor Phineas will be for the credit of the family. He and I hadn't much in common, as you may imagine; and to tell the truth, all these newspaper stories don't do a man like me very much good. Men may admire a poet for drinking green fire or trying to fly from a church tower; but they don't order their lunch from a pastry-cook's shop kept by his brother; they get a fancy there might be a little too much green fire in the ginger-ale. And I've only just opened my shop in Croydon; that is, I've bought a new business there. Also,' and he looked down at the table with an embarrassment rather rustic but not unmanly, 'I'm engaged to be married; and the young lady is very active in church work.'

Garth could not suppress a smile at the incongruous lives of the two brothers; but he saw that there was, after all, a good deal of common sense in the more obscure brother's attitude.

'Yes,' he said, 'I quite see that; but you can hardly expect the public not to be interested.'

'The question I wanted to ask,' said the solicitor, 'has a direct bearing on something I have just discovered. Have you any notion, even a vague one, of what Phineas Salt's income was, or if he had any capital?'

'Well,' said Joseph Salt reflectively, 'I don't think he really had much capital; he may have had the five thousand we each of us got from the old dad's business. In fact, I think he had; but I think he lived up to the edge of his income and a bit beyond. He sometimes made big scoops on a successful play or so; but you know the sort of fellow he was; and the big scoop went in a big splash. I should guess he had two or three thousand in the bank when he disappeared.'

'Quite so,' said the solicitor gravely. 'He had two thousand five hundred in the bank on the day he disappeared. And he drew it all out on the day he disappeared. And it entirely disappeared on the day he disappeared.'

'Do you think he's bolted to foreign climes or something?' asked the brother.

'Ah,' answered the lawyer, 'he may have done so. Or he may have intended to do so and not done so.'

'Then how did the money disappear?' asked Garth.

'It may have disappeared,' replied Gunter, 'while Phineas was drunk and talking nonsense to a rather shady Bohemian acquaintance, with a remarkable gift of narration.'

Garth and Gale both glanced sharply across at the speaker; and both, observant in such different ways, realised that the lawyer's face was a shade too grim to be called merely cynical.

'Ah,' cried the doctor with something like a catch in his breath. 'And you mean something worse than theft.'

'I have no right to assert even theft,' said the lawyer, without relaxing his sombre expression; 'but I have a right to suspect things that go rather deep. To begin with, there is some evidence for the start of Mr Florence's story, but none for its conclusion. Mr Florence met Mr Hatt; I take it, from the absence of contradiction, that Mr Hatt also met Mr Florence.'

On the poker face of Mr Hatt there was still an absence of contradiction; that might presumably be taken for confirmation.

'Indeed, I have found some evidence corroborating the story of Salt starting with Florence in the car. There is no evidence corroborating all that wild moonlight antic on the roads of Kent; and if you ask me, I think it very likely that this particular joy-ride ended in some criminal den in the Old Kent Road. I telephoned a moment ago to ask about the car left in Canterbury; and they cannot at present find traces of any such car. Above all, there is the damning fact that this fellow Florence forgot all about his imaginary car, and contradicted himself by saying that he went back by train. That alone makes me think his story is false.'

'Does it?' asked Gale, looking at him with childlike wonder. 'Why, that alone makes me think his story is true.'

'How do you mean?' asked Gunter; 'that alone?'

'Yes,' said Gale; 'that one detail is so true that I could almost believe the truth of all the rest, if he'd described Phineas as flying from the tower on a stone dragon.'

He sat frowning and blinking for a moment and then said rather testily: 'Don't you see it's just the sort of mistake that would be made by that sort of man? A shabby, impecunious man, a man who never travels far except in trains, is caught up for one wild ride in a rich friend's car, drugged into a sort of dream of absinthe, dragged into a topsy-turvy mystery like a nightmare, wakes up to find his friend caught up into the sky and everybody, in broad daylight, denying that the thing had ever happened. In that sort of chilly, empty awakening, a poor man talking to contemptuous policemen, he would no more have remembered any responsibility for the car than if it had been a fairy chariot drawn by griffins. It was part of the dream. He would automatically fall back on his ordinary way of life and take a third-class ticket home. But he would never make such a blunder in a story he had entirely made up for himself. The instant I heard him make that howler, I knew he was telling the truth.'

The others were gazing at the speaker in some mild surprise, when the telephone bell, strident and prolonged, rang in the adjoining office. Gunter got hastily to his feet and went to answer it, and for a few moments there was no sound but the faint buzz of his questions and replies. Then he came back into the room, his strong face graven with a restrained stupefaction.

'This is a most remarkable coincidence,' he said; 'and, I must admit, a confirmation of what you say. The police down there have found the marks of a car, with tyres and general proportions like Phineas Salt's, evidently having stood exactly where James Florence professed to have left it standing. But what is even more odd, it has gone; the tracks show it was driven off down the road to the south-east by somebody. Presumably by Phineas Salt.'

'To the south-east,' cried Gale, and sprang to his feet. 'I thought so!'

He took a few strides up and down the room and then said: 'But we mustn't go too fast. There are several things. To begin with, any fool can see that Phineas would drive to the east; it was nearly daybreak when he disappeared. Of course, in that state, he would drive straight into the sunrise. What else could one do? Then, if he was really full of that craze for crags or towers, he would find himself leaving the last towers behind and driving into flatter and flatter places; for that road leads down into Thanet. What would he do? He must make for the chalk cliffs that look down at least on sea and sand; but I fancy he would want to look down on people, too; just as he might have looked down on the people of Canterbury from the cathedral tower . . . I know that south-eastern road . . . '

Then he faced them solemnly and, like one uttering a sacred mystery, said, 'Margate.'

'And why?' asked the staring Garth.

'A form of suicide, I suppose,' said the solicitor dryly. 'What could a man of that sort want to do at Margate except commit suicide?'

'What could any man want at Margate except suicide?' asked Dr Garth, who had a prejudice against such social resorts.

'A good many millions of God's images go there simply for fun,' said Gale; 'but it remains to be shown why one of them should be Phineas Salt . . . there are possibilities . . . those black crawling masses seen from the white cliffs might be a sort of vision for a pessimist; possibly a dreadful destructive vision of shutting the gates in the cliffs and inundating them all in the ancient awful sea . . . or could he have some cranky notion of making Margate glorious by his creative or destructive acts; changing the very sound of the name, making it heroic or tragic for ever? There have been such notions in such men . . . but wherever this wild road leads I am sure it ends in Margate.'

The worthy tradesman of Croydon was the first to get to his feet after Gale had risen, and he fingered the lapels of his outlandish coat with all his native embarrassment. 'I'm afraid all this is beyond me, gentlemen,' he said, 'gargoyles and dragons and pessimists and such are not in my line. But it does seem that the police have got a clue that points down the Margate road; and if you ask me, I think we'd better discuss this matter again when the police have investigated a little more.'

'Mr Salt is perfectly right,' said the lawyer heartily. 'See what it is to have a business man to bring us back to business. I will go and make some more enquiries; and soon, perhaps, I may have a little more to tell you.'

If Gabriel Gale was, and felt himself to be, an incongruous figure in the severe framework of leather and parchment, of law and commerce, represented by the office of Mr Gunter, it might well have been supposed that he would feel even more of a fish out of water in the scene of the second family council. For it was held at the new headquarters of the family, or all that remained of the family; the little shop in Croydon over which the lost poet's very prosaic brother was presiding with a mixture of the bustle of a new business and the last lingering formalities of a funeral. Mr J. Salt's suburban shop was a very suburban shop. It was a shop for selling confectionery and sweetmeats and similar things; with a sort of sideshow of very mild refreshments, served on little round shiny tables and apparently chiefly consisting of pale green lemonade. The cakes and sweets were arranged in decorative patterns in the window, to attract the eye of Croydon youth, and as the building consisted chiefly of windows, it seemed full of a sort of cold and discolouring light. A parlour behind, full of neat but illogical knicknacks and mementoes, was not without a sampler, a testimonial from a Provident Society and a portrait of George V. But it was never easy to predict in what place or circumstances Mr Gale would find a certain intellectual interest. He generally looked at objects, not objectively in the sense of seeing them as themselves, but in connection with some curious trains of thought of his own; and, for some reason or other, he seemed to take quite a friendly interest in Mr Salt's suburban shop. Indeed, he seemed to take more interest in this novel scene than in the older and more serious problem which he had come there to solve. He gazed entranced at the china dogs and pink pincushions on the parlour mantelpiece; he was with difficulty drawn away from a rapt contemplation of the diamond pattern of lemon-drops and raspberry-drops which decorated the window; and he looked even at the lemonade as if it were as important as that pale green wine of wormwood, which had apparently played a real part in the tragedy of Phineas Salt.

He had been indeed unusually cheerful all the morning, possibly because it was a beautiful day, possibly for more personal reasons; and had drawn near to the rendezvous through the trim suburban avenues with a step of unusual animation. He saw the worthy confectioner himself, stepping out of a villa of a social shade faintly superior to his own; a young woman with a crown of braided brown hair, and a good grave face, came with him down the garden path. Gale had little difficulty in identifying the young lady interested in church work. The poet gazed at the pale squares of lawn and the few thin and dwarfish trees with quite a sentimental interest, almost as if it were a romance of his own; nor did his universal good humour fail him even when he encountered, a few lamp posts further down the road, the saturnine and somewhat unsympathetic countenance of Mr Hiram Hatt. The lover was still lingering at the garden gate, after the fashion of his kind, and Hatt and Gale walked more briskly ahead of him towards his home. To Hatt the poet made the somewhat irrelevant remark: 'Do you understand that desire to be one of the lovers of Cleopatra?'

Mr Hatt, the secretary, indicated that, had he nourished such a desire, his appearance on the historical scene would have lacked something of true American hustle and punctuality.

'Oh, there are plenty of Cleopatras still,' answered Gale; 'and plenty of people who have that strange notion of being the hundredth husband of an Egyptian cat. What could have made a man of real intellect, like that fellow's brother, break himself all up for a woman like Hertha Hathaway?'

'Well, I'm all with you there,' said Hatt. 'I didn't say anything about the woman, because it wasn't my business; but I tell you, sir, she was just blue ruin and vitriol. Only the fact that I didn't mention her seems to have set your friend the solicitor off on another dance of dark suspicions. I swear he fancies she and I were mixed up in something; and probably had to do with the disappearance of Phineas Salt.'

Gale looked hard at the man's hard face for a moment and then said irrelevantly: 'Would it surprise you to find him at Margate?'

'No; nor anywhere else,' replied Hatt. 'He was restless just then and drifted about into the commonest crowds. He did no work lately; sometimes sat and stared at a blank sheet of paper as if he had no ideas.'

'Or as if he had too many,' said Gabriel Gale.

With that they turned in at the confectioner's door: and found Dr Garth already in the outer shop, having only that moment arrived. But when they penetrated to the parlour, they came on a figure that gave them, indescribably, a cold shock of sobriety. The lawyer was already seated in that gimcrack room, resolutely and rather rudely, with his top-hat on his head, like a bailiff in possession; but they all sensed something more sinister, as of the bearer of the bowstring.

'Where is Mr Joseph Salt?' he asked. 'He said he would be home at eleven.'

Gale smiled faintly and began to fiddle with the funny little ornaments on the mantelpiece. 'He is saying farewell,' he said. 'Sometimes it is rather a long word to say.'

'We must begin without him,' said Gunter. 'Perhaps it is just as well.'

'You mean you have bad news for him?' asked the doctor, lowering his voice. 'Have you the last news of his brother?'

'I believe it may fairly be called the last news,' answered the lawyer dryly. 'In the light of the latest discoveries . . . Mr Gale, I should be much obliged if you would leave off fidgeting with those ornaments and sit down. There is something that somebody has got to explain.'

'Yes,' replied Gale rather hazily. 'Isn't *this* what he has got to explain?'

He picked up something from the mantelpiece and put it on the central table. It was a very absurd object to be stared at thus, as an exhibit in a grim museum of suicide or crime. It was a cheap, childish, pink and white mug, inscribed in large purple letters, 'A Present from Margate'.

'There is a date inside,' said Gale, looking down dreamily into the depths of this remarkable receptacle. 'This year. And we're still at the beginning of the year, you know.'

'Well, it may be one of the things,' said the solicitor. 'But I have got some other Presents from Margate.'

He took a sheaf of papers from his breast-pocket and laid them out thoughtfully on the table before he spoke.

'Understand, to begin with, that there really is a riddle and the man really has vanished. Don't imagine a man can easily melt into a modern crowd; the police have traced his car on the road and could have traced him, if he had left it. Don't imagine anybody can simply drive down country roads throwing corpses out of cars. There are always a lot of fussy people about, who notice a little thing like that. Whatever he did, sooner or later the explanation would probably be found; and we have found it.'

Gale put down the mug abruptly and stared across, still open-mouthed, but as it were more dry-throated, coughing and stammering now with a real eagerness.

'Have you really found out?' he asked. 'Do you know all about the Purple Jewel?'

'Look here!' cried the doctor, as if with a generous indignation; 'this is getting too thick. I don't mind being in a mystery, but it needn't be a melodrama. Don't say that we are after the Rajah's Ruby. Don't say, oh, don't say, that it is in the eye of the god Vishnu.'

'No,' replied the poet. 'It is in the eye of the Beholder.'

'And who's he?' asked Gunter. 'I don't know exactly what you're talking about, but there may have been a theft involved. Anyhow, there was more than a theft.'

He sorted out from his papers two or three photographs of the sort that are taken casually with hand-cameras in a holiday crowd. As he did so he said: 'Our investigations at Margate have not been fruitless; in fact they have been rather fruitful. We have found a witness, a photographer on Margate beach, who testifies to having seen a man corresponding to Phineas Salt, burly and with a big red beard and long hair, who stood for some time on an isolated crag of white chalk, which stands out from the cliff, and looked down at the crowds below. Then he descended by a rude stairway cut in the chalk and, crossing a crowded part of the beach, spoke to another man who seemed to be an ordinary clerk or commonplace holidaymaker; and, after a little talk, they went up to the row of bathing-sheds, apparently for the purpose of having a dip in the sea. My informant thinks they did go into the sea; but cannot be quite so certain. What he is quite certain of is that he never saw the red-bearded man again, though he did see the commonplace clean-shaven man, both when he returned in his bathing-suit and when he resumed his ordinary, his very ordinary, clothes. He not only saw him, but he actually took a snapshot of him, and there he is.'

He handed the photograph to Garth, who gazed at it with slowly rising eyebrows. The photograph represented a sturdy man with a bulldog jaw but rather blank eyes, with his head lifted, apparently staring out to sea. He wore very light holiday clothes, but of a clumsy, unfashionable cut; and, so far as he could be seen under the abrupt shadow and rather too jaunty angle of his stiff straw hat, his hair was of some light colour. Only, as it happened, the doctor had no need to wait for the development of colour photography. For he knew exactly what colour it was. He knew it was a sort of sandy red; he had often seen it, not in the photograph, but on the head where it grew. For the man in the stiff straw hat was most unmistakably Mr Joseph Salt, the worthy confectioner and new social ornament to the suburb of Croydon.

'So Phineas went down to Margate to meet his brother,' said Garth. 'After all, that's natural enough in one way. Margate is exactly the sort of place his brother would go to.'

'Yes; Joseph went there on one of those motor-charabanc expeditions, with a whole crowd of other trippers, and he seems to have returned the same night on the same vehicle. But nobody knows when, where or *if* his brother Phineas returned.'

'I rather gather from your tone,' said Garth very gravely, 'that you think his brother Phineas never did return.'

'I think his brother never will return,' said the lawyer, 'unless it happens (by a curious coincidence) that he was drowned while bathing and his body is someday washed up on the shore. But there's a strong current running just there that would carry it far away.'

'The plot thickens, certainly,' said the doctor. 'All this bathing business seems to complicate things rather.'

'I am afraid,' said the lawyer, 'that it simplifies them very much.'

'What,' asked Garth sharply. 'Simplifies?'

'Yes,' said the other, gripping the arms of his chair and rising abruptly to his feet. 'I think this story is as simple as the story of Cain and Abel. And rather like it.'

There was a shocked silence, which was at length broken by Gale, who was peering into the Present from Margate, crying or almost crowing, in the manner of a child.

'Isn't it a funny little mug! He must have bought it before he came back in the charabanc. Such a jolly thing to buy, when you have just murdered your own brother.'

'It does seem a queer business,' said Dr Garth frowning. 'I suppose one might work out some explanation of how he did it. I suppose a man might drown another man while they were bathing, even off a crowded beach like that. But I'm damned if I can understand why he did it. Have you discovered a motive as well as a murder?'

'The motive is old enough and I think obvious enough,' answered Gunter. 'We have in this case all the necessary elements of a hatred, of that slow and corroding sort that is founded on jealousy. Here you had two brothers, sons of the same insignificant Midland tradesman; having the same education, environment, opportunities; very nearly of an age, very much of one type, even of one physical type, rugged, red-haired, rather plain and heavy, until Phineas made himself a spectacle with that big Bolshevist beard and bush of hair; not so different in youth but that they must have had ordinary rivalries and quarrels on fairly equal terms. And then see the sequel. One of them fills the world with his name, wears a laurel like the crown of Petrach, dines with kings and emperors and is worshipped by women like a hero on the films. The other . . . isn't it enough to say that the other has had to go on slaving all his life in a room like this?'

'Don't you like the room?' enquired Gale with the same simple eagerness. 'Why, I think some of the ornaments are so nice!'

'It is not yet quite clear,' went on Gunter, ignoring him, 'how the pastry-cook lured the poet down to Margate and a dip in the sea. But the poet was admittedly rather random in his movements just then, and too restless to work; and we have no reason to suppose that he knew of the fraternal hatred or that he in any way reciprocated it. I don't think there would be much difficulty in swimming with a man beyond the crowd of bathers and holding him under water, till you could send his body adrift on a current flowing away from the shore. Then he went back and dressed and calmly took his place in the charabanc.'

'Don't forget the dear little mug,' said Gale softly. 'He stopped to buy that and then went home. Well, it's a very able and thorough explanation and reconstruction of the crime, my dear Gunter, and I congratulate you. Even the best achievements have some little flaw; and there's only one trifling mistake in yours. You've got it the wrong way round.'

'What do you mean?' asked the other quickly.

'Quite a small correction,' explained Gale. 'You think that Joseph was jealous of Phineas. As a matter of fact, Phineas was jealous of Joseph.'

'My dear Gale, you are simply playing the goat,' said the doctor very sharply and impatiently. 'And let me tell you I don't think it's a decent occasion for doing it. I know all about your jokes and fancies and paradoxes, but we're all in a damned hard position, sitting here in the man's own house, and knowing we're in the house of a murderer.'

'I know . . . it's simply infernal,' said Gunter, his stiffness shaken for the first time; and he looked up with a shrinking jerk, as if he half expected to see the rope hanging from that dull and dusty ceiling.

At the same moment the door was thrown open and the man they had convicted of murder stood in the room. His eyes were bright like a child's over a new toy, his face was flushed to the roots of his fiery hair, his broad shoulders were squared backwards like a soldier's; and in the lapel of his coat was a large purple flower, of a colour that Gale remembered in the garden-beds of the house down the road. Gale had no difficulty in guessing the reason of this triumphant entry.

Then the man with the buttonhole saw the tragic faces on the other side of the table and stopped, staring.

'Well,' he said at last, in a rather curious tone. 'What about your search?'

The lawyer was about to open his locked lips with some question as was once asked of Cain by the voice out of the cloud, when Gale interrupted him by flinging himself backwards in a chair and emitting a short but cheery laugh.

'I've given up the search,' said Gale gaily. 'No need to bother myself about that any more.'

'Because you know you will never find Phineas Salt,' said the tradesman steadily.

'Because I have found him,' said Gabriel Gale.

Dr Garth got to his feet quickly and remained staring at them with bright eyes.

'Yes,' said Gale, 'because I am talking to him.' And he smiled across at his host, as if he had just been introduced.

Then he said rather more gravely: 'Will you tell us all about it, Mr Phineas Salt? Or must I guess it for you all the way through?'

There was a heavy silence.

'You tell the story,' said the shopkeeper at last. 'I am quite sure you know all about it.'

'I only know about it,' answered Gale gently, 'because I think I should have done the same thing myself. It's what some call having a sympathy with lunatics . . . including literary men.'

'Hold on for a moment,' interposed the staring Mr Gunter. 'Before you get too literary, am I to understand that this gentleman who owns this shop, actually is the poet, Phineas Salt? In that case, where is his brother?'

'Making the Grand Tour, I imagine,' said Gale. 'Gone abroad for a holiday, anyhow; a holiday which will be not the less enjoyable for the two thousand five hundred pounds that his brother gave him to enjoy himself with. His slipping away was easy enough; he only swam a little bit further along the shore to where they had left another suit of clothes. Meanwhile our friend here went back and shaved off his beard and effected the change of appearance in the bathing-tent. He was quite sufficiently like his brother to go back with a crowd of strangers. And then, you will doubtless note, he opened a new shop in an entirely new neighbourhood.'

'But *why*?' cried Garth in a sort of exasperation. 'In the name of all the saints and angels, why? That's what I can't make any sense of.'

'I will tell you why,' said Gabriel Gale, 'but you won't make any sense of it.'

He stared at the mug on the table for a moment and then said: 'This is what you would call a nonsense story; and you can only understand it by understanding nonsense; or, as some politely call it, poetry. The poet Phineas Salt was a man who had made himself master of everything, in a sort of frenzy of freedom and omnipotence. He had tried to feel everything, experience everything, imagine everything that could be or could not be. And he found, as all such men have found, that that illimitable liberty is itself a limit. It is like the circle, which is at once an eternity and a prison. He not only wanted to do everything. He wanted to be everybody. To the Pantheist God is everybody: to the Christian He is also Somebody. But this sort of Pantheist will not narrow himself by a choice. To want everything is to will nothing. Mr Hatt here told me that Phineas would sit staring at a blank sheet of paper; and I told him it was not because he had nothing to write about, but because he could write about anything. When he stood on that cliff and looked down on that mazy crowd, so common and yet so complex, he felt he could write ten thousand tales and then that he could write none; because there was no reason to choose one more than another.

'Well, what is the step beyond that? What comes next? I tell you there are only two steps possible after that. One is the step over the cliff; to cease to be. The other is to *be* somebody, instead of writing about everybody. It is to become incarnate as one real human being in that crowd; to begin all over again as a real person. Unless a man be born again . . .

'He tried it and found that this was what he wanted; the things he had not known since childhood; the silly little lower middle-class things; to have to do with lollipops and ginger-beer; to fall in love with a girl round the corner and feel awkward about it; to be young. That was the only paradise still left virgin and unspoilt enough, in the imagination of a man who has turned the seven heavens upside down. That is what he tried as his last experiment, and I think we can say it has been a success.'

'Yes,' said the confectioner with a stony satisfaction, 'it has been a great success.'

Mr Gunter, the solicitor, rose also with a sort of gesture of despair. 'Well, I don't think I understand it any better for knowing all about it,' he said; 'but I suppose it must be as you say. But how in the world did you know it yourself?'

'I think it was those coloured sweets in the window that set me off,' said Gale. 'I couldn't take my eyes off them. They were so pretty. Sweets are better than jewellery: the children are right. For they have the fun of eating rubies and emeralds. I felt sure they were speaking to me in some way. And then I realised what they were saying. Those violet or purple raspberry drops were as vivid and glowing as amethysts, when you saw them from *inside* the shop; but from outside, with the light on them, they would look quite dingy and dark. Meanwhile, there were plenty of other things, gilded or painted with opaque colours, that would have looked much more gay in the shop-window, to the customer looking in at it. Then I remembered the man who said he must break into the cathedral to see the coloured windows from inside, and I knew it in an instant. The man who had arranged that shop-window was not a shopkeeper. He was not thinking of how things looked from the street, but of how they looked to his own artistic eye from inside. From there he saw purple jewels. And then, thinking of the cathedral, of course I remembered something else. I remembered what the poet had said about the Double Life of St Thomas of Canterbury; and how when he had all the earthly glory, he had to have the exact opposite. St Phineas of Croydon is also living a Double Life.'

'Well,' broke out Gunter, heaving with a sort of heavy gasp, 'with all respect to him, if he has done all this, I can only say that he must have gone mad.'

'No,' said Gale, 'a good many of my friends have gone mad and I am by no means without sympathy with them. But you can call this the story of "The Man Who Went Sane".'

8

The Asylum of Adventure

A very small funeral procession passed through a very small churchyard on the rocky coast of Cornwall; carrying a coffin to its grave under the low and windy wall. The coffin was quite formal and unobtrusive; but the knot of fishermen and labourers eyed it with the slanted eyes of superstition; almost as if it had been the misshapen coffin of legend that was said to contain a monster. For it contained the body of a near neighbour, who had long lived a stone's throw from them, and whom they had never seen.

The figure following the coffin, the chief and only mourner, they had seen fairly often. He had a habit of disappearing into his late friend's house and being invisible for long periods, but he came and went openly. No one knew when the dead man had first come, but he probably came in the night; and he went out in the coffin. The figure following it was a tall figure in black, bare headed, with the sea-blast whistling through his wisps of yellow hair as through the pale sea grasses. He was still young and none could have said that his mourning suit sat ill upon him; but some who knew him would have seen it with involuntary surprise and felt that it showed him in a new phase. When he was dressed, as he generally was, in the negligent tweeds and stockings of the pedestrian landscape-painter, he looked merely amiable and absent-minded; but the black brought out something more angular and fixed about his face. With his black garb and yellow hair he might have been the traditional Hamlet; and indeed the look in his eyes was visionary and vague; but the traditional Hamlet would hardly have had so long and straight a chin as that which rested unconsciously on his black cravat. After the ceremony, he left the village church and walked towards the village post office, gradually lengthening and lightening his stride, like a man who, with all care for decency, can hardly conceal that he is rid of a duty.

'It's a horrible thing to say,' he said to himself, 'but I feel like a happy widower.'

He then went in to the post office and sent off a telegram addressed to a Lady Diana Westermaine, Westermaine Abbey: a telegram that said: 'I am coming tomorrow to keep my promise and tell you the story of a strange friendship.'

Then he went out of the little shop again and walked eastwards out of the village, with undisguised briskness, till he had left the houses far behind, and his funeral hat and habit were an almost incongruous black spot upon great green uplands and the motley forests of autumn. He had walked for about half a day, lunched on bread and cheese and ale at a little public-house, and resumed his march with unabated cheerfulness, when the first event of that strange day befell him. He was threading his way by a river that ran in a hollow of the green hills; and at one point his path narrowed and ran under a high stone wall. The wall was built of very large flat stones of ragged outline, and a row of them ran along the top like the teeth of a giant. He would not normally have taken so much notice of the structure of the wall; indeed he did not take any notice of it at all until after something had happened. Until (in fact) there was a great gap in the row of craggy teeth, and one of the crags lay flat at his feet, shaking up dust like the smoke of an explosion. It had just brushed one of his long wisps of light hair as it fell.

Looking up, a shade bewildered by the shock of his hairbreadth escape, he saw for an instant in the dark gap left in the stonework a face, peering and malignant. He called out promptly: 'I see you; I could send you to jail for that!'

'No you can't,' retorted the stranger, and vanished into the twilight of trees as swiftly as a squirrel.

The gentleman in black, whose name was Gabriel Gale, looked up thoughtfully at the wall, which was rather too high and smooth to scale; besides, the fugitive had already far too much of a start. Mr Gale finally said aloud, in a reflective fashion: 'Now I wonder why he did that!' Then he frowned with an entirely new sort of gravity, and after a moment or two of grim silence he added: 'But after all it's much more odd and mysterious that he should *say* that.'

In truth, though the three words uttered by the unknown person seemed trivial enough, they sufficed to lead Gale's memories backwards to the beginning of the whole business that ended in the little Cornish churchyard; and as he went briskly on his way he rehearsed all the details of that old story, which he was to tell to the lady at his journey's end.

* * *

Nearly fourteen years before, Gabriel Gale had come of age and inherited the moderate debts and the small freehold of a rather unsuccessful gentleman farmer. But though he grew up with the traditions of a sort of small squire, he was not the sort of person, especially at that age, to have no opinions except those traditions. In early youth his politics were the very reverse of squires' politics; he was very much of a revolutionary and locally rather a firebrand. He intervened on behalf of poachers and gypsies: he wrote letters to the local papers which the editors thought too eloquent to be printed. He denounced the county magistracy in controversies that had to be impartially adjudged by the county magistrates. Finding, curiously enough, that all these authorities were against him, and seemed to be in legal control of all his methods of self-expression, he invented a method of his own which gave him great amusement and the authorities great annoyance. He fell, in fact, to employing a talent for drawing and painting which he was conscious of possessing, along with another talent for guessing people's thoughts and getting a rapid grasp of their characters, which he was less conscious of possessing, but which he certainly possessed. It is a talent very valuable to a portrait-painter: in this case, however, he became a rather peculiar sort of portrait-painter. It was not exactly what is generally called a fashionable portrait-painter. Gale's small estate contained several outhouses with white-washed walls or palings abutting on the high road; and whenever a magnate or magistrate did anything that Gale disapproved of, Gale was in the habit of painting his portrait in public and on a large scale. His pictures were hardly in the ordinary sense caricatures, but they were portraits of souls. There was nothing crude about the picture of the great merchant prince now honoured with a peerage; the eyes looking up from under lowered brows, the sleek hair parted low on the forehead, were hardly exaggerated; but the smiling lips were certainly saying: 'And the next article?' One even knew that it was not really a very superior article. The picture of the formidable Colonel Ferrars did justice to the distinction of the face, with its frosty eyebrows and moustaches; but it also very distinctly discovered that it was the face of a fool, and of one subconsciously frightened of being found to be a fool.

With these coloured proclamations did Mr Gale beautify the countryside and make himself beloved among his equals. They could not do very much in the matter; it was not libel, for nothing was said; it was not nuisance or damage, for it was done on his own property, though in sight of the whole world. Among those who gathered every day to watch the painter at work, was a sturdy, red-faced, bushy-whiskered farmer, named Banks, seemingly one of those people who delight in any event and are more or less impenetrable by any opinion. He never could be got to bother his head about the sociological symbolism of Gale's caricatures; but he regarded the incident with exuberant interest as one of the great stories calculated to be the glory of the country, like a calf born with five legs or some pleasant ghost story about the old gallows on the moor. Though so little of a theorist he was far from being a fool, and had a whole tangle of tales both humorous and tragic, to show how rich a humanity was packed within the four corners of his countryside. Thus it happened that he and his revolutionary neighbour had many talks over the cakes and ale, and went on many expeditions together to fascinating graves or historic public-houses. And thus it happened that on one of these expeditions Banks fell in with two of his other cronies, who made a party of four, making discoveries not altogether without interest.

The first of the farmer's friends, introduced to Gale under the name of

Starkey, was a lively little man with a short stubbly beard and sharp eyes, which he was in the habit however of screwing up with a quizzical smile during the greater part of a conversation. Both he and his friend Banks were eagerly interested in the story of Gale's political protests, if they regarded them only too much as practical jokes. And they were both particularly anxious to introduce a friend of theirs named Wolfe, always referred to as Sim, who had a hobby, it would seem, in such matters, and might have suggestions to make. With a sort of sleepy curiosity which was typical of him, Gale found himself trailed along in an expedition for the discovery of Sim; and Sim was discovered at a little obscure hostelry called the Grapes a mile or so up the river. The three men had taken a boat, with the small Starkey for coxswain; it was a glorious autumn morning but the river was almost hidden under high banks and overhanging woods, intersected with great gaps of glowing sunlight, in one of which the lawns of the little riverside hotel sloped down to the river. And on the bank overhanging the river a man stood waiting for them; a remarkable-looking man with a fine sallow face rather like an actor's and very curly grizzled hair. He welcomed them with a pleasant smile, and then turned towards the house with something of a habit of command or at least of direction. 'I've ordered something for you,' he said. 'If we go in now it will be ready.'

As Gabriel Gale brought up the rear of the single file of four men going up the straight paved path to the inn door, his roaming eye took in the rest of the garden, and something stirred in his spirit, which was also prone to roaming, and even in a light sense to a sort of rebellion. The steep path was lined with little trees, looking like the plan of a sampler. He did not see why he should walk straight up so very straight a path, and many things in the garden took his wandering fancy. He would much rather have had lunch at one of the little weather-stained tables standing about on the lawn. He would have been delighted to grope in the dark and tumbledown arbour in the corner, of which he could dimly see the circular table and semicircular seat in the shadow of its curtain of creepers. He was even more attracted by the accident by which an old children's swing, with its posts and ropes and hanging seat, stood close up to the bushes of the river bank. In fact, the last infantile temptation was irresistible; and calling out, 'I'm going over here,' he ran across the garden towards the arbour, taking the swing with a sort of leap on his way. He landed in the wooden seat and swung twice back and forth, leaving it again with another flying leap. Just as he did so, however, the rope broke at its upper attachment, and he fell all askew, kicking his legs in the air. He was on his feet again immediately, and found himself confronted by his three companions who had followed in doubt or remonstrance. But the smiling Starkey was foremost, and his screwed-up eyes expressed good humour and even sympathy.

'Rotten sort of swing of yours,' he said. 'These things are all falling to pieces,' and he gave the other rope a twitch, bringing that down also. Then he added: 'Want to feast in the arbour, do you? Very well; you go in first and break the cobwebs. When you've collected all the spiders, I'll follow you.'

Gale dived laughing into the dark corner in question and sat down in the centre of the crescent-shaped seat. The practical Mr Banks had apparently entirely refused to carouse in this leafy cavern; but the figures of the two other men soon darkened the entrance and they sat down, one at each horn of the crescent.

'I suppose that was a sudden impulse of yours,' said the man named Wolfe, smiling. 'You poets often have sudden impulses, don't you?'

'It's not for me to say it was a poet's impulse,' replied Gale; 'but I'm sure it would need a poet to describe it. Perhaps I'm not one; anyhow I never could describe those impulses. The only way to do it would be to write a poem about the swing and a poem about the arbour, and put them both into a longer poem about the garden. And poems aren't produced quite so quickly as all that, though I've always had a notion that a real poet would never talk prose. He would talk about the weather in rolling stanzas like the storm-clouds, or ask you to pass the potatoes in an impromptu lyric as beautiful as the blue flower of the potato.'

'Make it a prose poem, then,' said the man whose name was Simeon Wolfe, 'and tell us how you felt about the garden and the garden-swing.'

Gabriel Gale was both sociable and talkative; he talked a great deal about himself because he was not an egoist. He talked a great deal about himself on the present occasion. He was pleased to find these two intelligent men interested and attentive; and he tried to put into words the impalpable impulses to which he was always provoked by particular shapes or colours or corners of the straggling road of life. He tried to analyse the attraction of a swing, with its rudiments of aviation; and how it made a man feel more like a boy, because it made a boy feel more like a bird. He explained that the arbour was fascinating precisely because it was a den. He told them at some length of the psychological truth; that dismal and decayed objects raise a man's spirits higher, if they really are already high. His two companions talked in turn; and as luncheon progressed and passed they turned over between them many strange strata of personal experience, and Gale began to understand their personalities and their point of view. Wolfe had travelled a great deal, especially in the East; Starkey's experiences had been more local but equally curious, and they both had known many psychological cases and problems about which to compare notes. They both agreed that Gale's mental processes in the matter, though unusual, were not unique.

'In fact,' observed Wolfe, 'I think your mind belongs to a particular class, and one of which I have had some experience. Don't you think so, Starkey?'

'I quite agree,' said the other man, nodding.

It was at that moment that Gale looked out dreamily at the light upon the lawn, and in the stillness of his inmost mind a light broke on him like lightning; one of the terrible intuitions of his life.

Against the silver light on the river the dark frame of the forsaken swing stood up like a gallows. There was no trace of the seat or the ropes, not merely in their proper place, but even on the ground where they had fallen. Sweeping his eye slowly and searchingly round the scene, he saw them at last, huddled and hidden in a heap behind the bench where Starkey was sitting. In an instant he understood everything. He knew the profession of the two men on each side of him. He knew why they were asking him to describe the processes of his mind. Soon they would be taking out a document and signing it. He would not leave that arbour a free man.

'So you are both doctors,' he observed cheerfully, 'and you both think I am mad.'

'The word is really very unscientific,' said Simeon Wolfe in a soothing fashion. 'You are of a certain type which friends and admirers will be wise to treat in a certain way, but it need in no sense be an unfriendly or uncomfortable way. You are an artist with that form of the artistic temperament which is necessarily a mode of modified megalomania, and which expresses itself in the form of exaggeration. You cannot see a large blank wall without having an uncontrollable appetite for covering it with large pictures. You cannot see a swing hung in the air without thinking of flying ships careering through the air. I will venture to guess that you never see a cat without thinking of a tiger or a lizard without thinking of a dragon.'

'That is perfectly correct,' said Gale gravely; 'I never do.'

Then his mouth twisted a little, as if a whimsical idea had come into his mind. 'Psychology is certainly very valuable,' he said. 'It seems to teach us how to see into each other's minds. You, for instance, have a mind which is very interesting: you have reached a condition which I think I recognise. You are in that particular attitude in which the subject, when he thinks of anything, never thinks of the centre of anything. You see only edges eaten away. Your malady is the opposite to mine, to what you call making a tiger out of a cat, or what some call making a mountain out of a molehill. You do not go on and make a cat more of a cat; you are always trying to work back and prove that it is less than a cat; that it is a defective cat or a mentally deficient cat. But a cat is a cat; that is the supreme sanity which is so thickly clouded in your mind. After all, a molehill is a hill and a mountain is a hill. But you have got into the state of the mad queen, who said she knew hills compared with which this was a valley. You can't grasp the thing called a thing. Nothing for you has a central stalk of sanity. There is no core to your cosmos. Your trouble began with being an atheist.'

'I have not confessed to being an atheist,' said Wolfe staring.

'I have not confessed to being an artist,' replied Gale, 'or to have uncontrolled artistic appetites or any of that stuff. But I will tell you one thing: I can only exaggerate things the way they are going. But I'm not often wrong about the way they are going. You may be as sleek as a cat but I knew you were evolving into a tiger. And I guessed this little lizard could be turned by black magic into a dragon.'

As he spoke he was looking grimly at Starkey and out under the dark arch of the arbour, as out of a closing prison, with these two ghouls sitting on each side of the gate. Beyond was the gaunt shape like a gallows and beyond that the green and silver of the garden and the stream shone like a lost paradise of liberty. But it was characteristic of him that even when he was practically hopeless, he liked being logically triumphant; he liked turning the tables on his critics even when, so to speak, they were as abstract as multiplication tables.

'Why, my learned friends,' he went on contemptuously, 'do you really suppose you are any fitter to write a report on my mind than I am on yours? You can't see any further into me than I can into you. Not half so far. Didn't you know a portrait-painter has to value people at sight as much as a doctor? And I do it better than you; I have a knack that way. That's why I can paint those pictures on the wall; and I could paint your pictures as big as a house. I know what is at the back of your mind, Doctor Simeon Wolfe; and it's a chaos of exceptions with no rule. You could find anything abnormal, because you have no normal. You could find anybody mad; and as for why you specially want to find me mad – why that is another disadvantage of being an atheist. You do not think anything will smite you for the vile treachery you have sold yourself to do today.'

'There is no doubt about your condition now,' said Dr Wolfe with a sneer.

'You look like an actor, but you are not a very good actor,' answered Gale calmly. 'I can see that my guess was correct. These rack-renters and usurers who oppress the poor, in my own native valley, could not find any pettifogging law to prevent me from painting the colours of their souls in hell. So they have bribed you and another cheap doctor to certify me for a madhouse. I know the sort of man you are. I know this is not the first dirty trick you have done to help the rich out of a hole. You would do anything for your paymasters. Possibly the murder of the unborn.'

Wolfe's face was still wrinkled with its Semitic sneer, but his olive tint had turned to a sort of loathsome yellow. Starkey called out with sudden shrillness, as abrupt as the bark of a dog.

'Speak more respectfully!'

'There is Dr Starkey, too,' continued the poet lazily. 'Let us turn our medical attention to the mental state of Dr Starkey.'

As he rolled his eyes with ostentatious languor in the new direction, he was arrested by a change in the scene without. A strange man was standing under the frame of the swing, looking up at it with his head on one side like a bird's. He was a small, sturdy figure, quite conventionally clad; and Gale could only suppose he was a stray guest of the hotel. His presence did not help very much; for the law was probably on the side of the doctors; and Gale continued his address to them.

'The mental deficiency of Dr Starkey,' he said, 'consists in having forgotten the truth. You, Starkey, have no sceptical philosophy like your friend. You are a practical man, my dear Starkey; but you have told lies so incessantly and from so early an age that you never see anything as it is, but only as it could be made to look. Beside each thing stands the unreal thing that is its shadow; and you see the shadow first. You are very quick in seeing it; you go direct to the deceptive potentialities of anything; you see at once if anything could be used as anything else. You are the original man who went straight down the crooked lane. I could see how quickly you saw that the swing would provide ropes to tie me up if I were violent; and that going first into this arbour, I should be cornered, with you on each side of me. Yet the swing and the arbour were my own idea; and that again is typical of you. You're not a scientific thinker like the other scoundrel; you have always picked up other men's ideas, but you pick as swiftly as a pickpocket. In fact, when you see an idea sticking out of a pocket you can hardly help picking it. That's where you're mad; you can't resist being clever, or rather borrowing cleverness. Which means you have sometimes been too clever to be lucky. You are a shabbier sort of scamp; and I rather fancy you have been in prison.'

Starkey sprang to his feet, snatching up the ropes and throwing them on the table.

'Tie him up and gag him,' he cried; 'he is raving.'

'There again,' observed Gale, 'I enter with sympathy into your thoughts. You mean that I must be gagged at once; for if I were free for half a day, or perhaps half an hour, I could find out the facts about you and tear your reputation to rags.'

As he spoke he again followed with an interested eye the movements of the strange man outside. The man had recrossed the garden, calmly picking up a chair from one of the little tables, and returned carrying it lightly in the direction of the arbour. To the surprise of all, he set it down at the round table in the very entrance of that retreat, and sat down on it with his hands in his pockets, staring at Gabriel Gale. With his face in shadow, his square head, short hair and bulk of shoulders took on a new touch of mystery.

'Hope I don't interrupt,' he said. 'Perhaps it would be more honest to say I hope I do interrupt. Because I want to interrupt. Honestly, I think you medical gentlemen would be very unwise to gag your friend here, or try to carry him off.'

'And why?' asked Starkey sharply.

'Only because I should kill you if you did,' replied the stranger.

They all stared at him; and Wolfe sneered again as he said: 'You might find it awkward to kill us both at once.'

The stranger took his hands out of his pockets; and with the very gesture there was a double flash of metal. For the hands held two revolvers which pointed at them, fixed them like two large fingers of steel.

'I shall only kill you if you run or call out,' said the strange gentleman pleasantly.

'If you do you'll be hanged,' cried Wolfe violently.

'Oh, no, I shan't,' said the stranger; 'not unless two dead men can get up and hang me on that nursery gallows in the garden. I'm allowed to kill people. There's a special Act of Parliament permitting me to go about killing anybody I like. I'm never punished, whatever I do. In fact, to tell you the truth, I'm the King of England, and the Constitution says I can do no wrong.'

'What are you talking about?' demanded the doctor. 'You must be mad.'

The stranger uttered a sudden shout of laughter that shook the shed and the nerves of all three hearers.

'You've hit it first shot,' he cried. 'He said you were quick, didn't he? Yes, I'm mad all right; I've just escaped from the same sanatorium next door, where you want to take your friend to. I escaped in a way of my own; through the chief doctor's private apartments; and he's kind enough to keep two pistols in his drawer. I may be recaptured; but I shan't be hanged. I may be recaptured; but I particularly don't want your young friend to be captured at all. He's got his life before him; I don't choose he should suffer as I've suffered. I like the look of him; I like the way he turned all your medical tomfoolery upside down. So you'll understand I am at present wielding the power of a perfectly irresponsible sultan. I shall merely be rounding off a very pleasant holiday by blowing both your brains out, unless you will sit quite still and allow your young friend to tie you up with the ropes. That will give us a good start for our escape.'

How he passed through the topsy-turvy transformation scene that followed Gale could afterwards barely remember; it seemed like a sort of dream pantomime, but its results were solid enough. Ten minutes later he and his strange deliverer were walking free in the woods beyond the last hedge of the garden, leaving the two medical gentlemen behind them in the arbour, tied up like two sacks of potatoes.

For Gabriel Gale the wood in which he walked was a new world of wonders. Every tree was a Christmas tree bearing gifts; and every gap in the woods was like a glimpse through the curtain for a child with a toy theatre. For a few moments before all these things had nearly disappeared in the darkness of something worse than death; till heaven had sent him a guardian angel in the shape of an escaped lunatic.

Gale was very young and his youth had not then found its vent and vocation by falling in love. There was in him something of those young Crusaders who made wild vows not to cut their hair till they found the Holy City. His liberty was looking and longing for something to bind itself; and at this moment he could think of but one thing in the world.

Two hundred yards along the path by the river he halted and spoke to his companion: 'It is you who have given me all this,' he said. 'Under God, and so far as my life goes, it is you who have created heaven and earth. You set up along my triumphal way these trees like seven-branched candlesticks with their grey branches silver in the sun. You spread before my feet these red leaves that are better than roses. You shaped clouds. You invented birds. Do you think I could enjoy all these things when I knew you were back again in the hell that you hate? I should feel I had tricked you out of everything you have given me. I should feel like a thief who had stolen the stars. You shan't go back there if I can help it; you saved me and I am going to save you. I owe you my life and I give it you; I vow I will share anything you suffer; God do so to me and more also, if aught but death part thee and me.'

Thus were spoken in that wild place the wild words that determined the life of Gabriel Gale for so many years afterwards; and the walk that began in that wood turned into a wandering over the whole country by those two fantastic outlaws. As a matter of fact a sort of armed truce fell between them and their enemies, for each had something to fear from the other. Gale did not use all he discovered against the two doctors lest they should press the pursuit of his friend; and they did not press it lest he should retaliate with his own revelations. Thus the two came to roam practically unmolested until the day of that adventure, already described in the beginning of all these things, when he fell in love, and his crazy companion fell into a paroxysm which went very near to murder.

In every sense that dreadful day had changed all. That murderous outbreak had at last convinced a sadder and wiser Gabriel that he had other responsibilities besides those of his chivalric vow to his companion-in-arms; and he concluded that their companionship could only be rightly continued in some safe and more secluded form. Then it was that he put his friend into the comfortable and secret house in Cornwall, and spent most of his own time there, leaving a trustworthy servant on guard during his brief absences. His companion, whose name was James Hurrel, had been a business man of great ability and even audacity, until his schemes grew a little too big for his brain; and he lived happily enough in Cornwall, covering the tables with prospectuses and the walls with posters relative to various financial enterprises of the most promising kind. There he died, to all appearance equally happily; and Gale walked back from his funeral a free man.

* * *

Next morning, after a few hours' walking a rise and change in the rolling and wooded country told him that he was on the borders of his enchanted ground. He remembered something in the grouping of the trees, and how they seemed to huddle and stand on tiptoe with their backs to him, looking into the happy valley. He came to where the road curved over the hill, as he had come with his friend in former times; and saw below him the meadows falling steeply as thatched roofs and flattening out till they reached the wide and shallow river, and the ford and the dark inn called the Rising Sun.

The gloomy innkeeper of old days was gone, having found it less gloomy to take service in some stables in the neighbourhood; and a brisker individual with the look of a groom was the recipient of Gale's expansive praises of the beauty of the scene. Gale was good enough to inform the innkeeper of the beauty of the skies in the neighbourhood of his own inn, telling how he, Gale, had once seen a sunset in that valley quite peculiar to it and unequalled anywhere in the world; and how even the storm that had followed the sunset had been something very sublime in that style. His generalisations however were somewhat checked and diverted by a note which the innkeeper put into his hand, a note from the great house across the river. It was without any formal opening, as if the writer had hesitated about a form of address; and it ran: 'I want to hear the story and hope you will come over tomorrow (Thursday). I fear I shall be out today, as I have to go to see a Dr Wilson in Wimbledon about some work I have a chance of doing. I suppose you know we are pretty hard up in these days. D.W.'

The whole landscape seemed to him to darken for an instant as he read the letter, but he did not lose his brisk demeanour and breezy mode of speech.

'I find I made a mistake,' he said, putting the note in his pocket, 'and I must leave here almost at once. I have to visit another spot, if possible more picturesque and poetical than this one. It is Wimbledon that has skies of a strange and unique character at the present time. The sunsets of Wimbledon are famous throughout the world. A storm in Wimbledon would be an apocalypse. But I hope I shall come back here again sooner or later. Goodbye.'

The proceedings of Mr Gale after this were rather more calculated and peculiar. First he sat on a stile and frowned heavily as if thinking hard. Then he sent off a telegram to a certain Dr Garth, who was a friend of his, and one or two other telegrams to persons in rather responsible positions. When he got to London he went into the offices of the vulgarest and most sensational newspaper he knew, and looked up the back files for the details of forgotten crimes. When he got to Wimbledon he had a long interview with a local house agent and ended up towards evening, outside a high garden wall with a green door, in a wide but empty and silent suburban road. He went quietly up to the door and barely touched it with his finger, as if seeing if the paint were wet. But the door, which was barred across with bands of decorative metal work and had every appearance of being shut, immediately fell ajar, showing the patchy colours of garden beds within. 'I thought so,' said Gale to himself and slipped into the garden, leaving the door ajar behind him.

The suburban family which he was presumably visiting, and with which the impoverished Diana Westermaine was presumably to take some post as governess or secretary, was evidently the sort who combined a new neatness with a certain early Victorian comfort and indifference to cost. The conservatories were of antiquated pattern, but full of rich and exotic things; there were things still more old-fashioned, such as a grey and rather featureless classical statue in the centre. Within a few yards of it were things so Victorian as croquet hoops and croquet mallets, as if a game had been in progress, and beyond it under the tree was a table set out with tea things, for people for whom tea was not a trifle. All these human things, unused at the moment by human beings, seemed to emphasise the emptiness of the garden. Or rather, so far as he was concerned, they emphasised the fact that it was almost empty, save for the one thing that could so strangely fill it with life. For far away down one of the paths pointing towards the kitchen garden he saw a figure moving as yet unconsciously towards him. It came out under an arch crowned with creepers and there, after so many years, they met. There seemed something symbolical of seriousness and crisis in the accident that they were both in black.

He had always been able to call up the memory of her dark vivid eyebrows and the high-tinted distinction of her face in connection with corners of the blue dress she had worn; but when he saw her again he wondered that the face had not always annihilated all its lesser associations. She looked at him for a moment with bright motionless eyes and then said: 'Well, really. You seem to be a rather impatient person.'

'Possibly,' he replied; 'and yet I have waited four years.'

'They are coming out to tea in a moment,' she said somewhat awkwardly. 'I suppose I must introduce you to them. I only accepted the post this morning; but they asked me to stay. I was going to wire to you.'

'Thank God I followed you,' he answered. 'I doubt if the wire would have reached me . . . from this house.'

'What do you mean?' she asked, 'and how did you follow?'

'I did not like your Wimbledon address,' he said: and with that, strange figures began to fill the garden, and she walked across to the tea-table. Her face was somewhat paler and more severe than it used to be, but in her grey eyes there was a light not altogether extinguished, curiosity still shot with defiance. By the time they reached the table two or three people had collected round it; and the somewhat irregular visitor had saluted them in a regular and even punctilious fashion.

The host or hostess had apparently not yet become visible; there were only three gentlemen, presumably guests and perhaps members of a house-party. One was introduced as Mr Wolmer, a young man with a fair moustache and a tall fine figure that made his head look small; with a fine bridged nose that ought to have been like a hawk's if the prominence of the eyes and some deficiency of the chin had not somehow made it more like a parrot's. The second was a Major Bruce, a very short man with a very long head streaked with iron grey hair, and an expression which suggested, truly enough, that he very seldom opened his mouth. The third was an elderly person with a black skullcap on his bald head and a fringe or fan of red beard or whiskers; he was evidently a person of some importance and known as Professor Patterson.

Gale partook of tea and indulged in polite conversation in quite an animated fashion, wondering all the time who it was who ought to have been at the head of the table, where Diana Westermaine was pouring out the tea. The demeanour of the man named Wolmer was rather restless; and in a little while he stood up and began, as if from the necessity of doing something, to knock the croquet balls about on the lawn. Gale, who was watching him with some interest, followed suit by picking up a mallet and trying some particular trick of putting two balls through a hoop. It was a trick which needed a test of some minuteness, for he went down on his hands and knees to examine the position more closely.

'Going to put your head through the hoop?' asked Wolmer rudely; for he had been growing more and more impatient, almost as if he had taken a mysterious dislike to the newcomer.

'Not quite,' answered Gale good-humouredly as he rolled the balls away. 'Uncomfortable position, I should think. Like being guillotined.'

Wolmer was glaring balefully at the hoop and said something in a thick voice that sounded like 'Serve you right.' Then he suddenly whirled his mallet above his head like a battle-axe and brought it down with a crash on the hoop, driving it deep into the turf. There was something indescribably shocking about the pantomime, following instantly on the image that had just been suggested of a human head in the hoop. They felt as if an act of decapitation had been done before their very eyes.

'Better put down that mallet now,' said the professor in a soothing voice, putting a rather shaky hand on the other's arm.

'Oh, I'll put it down then,' said Wolmer, and slung it away over his shoulder like a man putting the hammer at the Highland Sports. It flew through the air like a thunderbolt, striking the forlorn plaster statue in the centre and breaking it off short at the top. Mr Wolmer laughed in a rather uncontrolled fashion; and then strode away into the house.

The girl had been watching these things with her dark brows bent and her pallor growing somewhat more marked. There was an unpleasant silence, and then Major Bruce spoke for the first time.

'It's the atmosphere of this place,' he said. 'It is not very wholesome.'

The atmosphere of the suburban garden as a matter of fact was very clear, sunny and pleasant, and Diana looked round with a growing and even creeping mystification at the gay flowerpots and the lawns golden in the evening light.

'Perhaps it is my own misfortune,' resumed the major reflectively. 'The truth is there is something serious the matter with me. I have a malady which makes this particular place rather awful.'

'What do you mean?' she asked quickly.

There was a short silence and then he answered stolidly.

'I am sane.'

Then she looked once more at the warm sunshiny garden and began to shudder as if with cold. A thousand things came back to her out of the last few hours. She knew why she had dimly distrusted her new home. She knew now that there is only one place in the world where men say that they are sane.

As the little man with the long head walked away as stiffly as a wooden automaton, she looked round for Gale and found he had vanished. An appalling emptiness, a vast vacuum of terror, opened around her on every side. In that moment she had admitted many things to herself that had been but half conscious: and no one on earth mattered but the man who had vanished into a void. For the moment she balanced the possibility that she was really mad against the possibility that nobody else was sane; when she caught sight, through the gap of a hedge, of figures moving at the other end of the garden. The old professor in the skullcap was moving rapidly but with trepidation, as if running on tiptoe, his long lean hands flapping like fins and his red chin-beard wagging in the wind. And behind him following, equally softly and swiftly, at the distance of a few yards, was the long grey figure of Gabriel Gale. She could fit together no fancy about what it all meant; she could only continue to stare across the flower-beds at the glasshouses full of monstrous flowers and be vaguely conscious of a sort of symbol in the headless statue in the centre; the god of that garden of unreason.

The next moment she saw Gale reappear at the other extremity of the long hedge and come towards her smiling in the sunshine. He stopped when he saw her white face.

'Do you know what this place is?' she whispered. 'It is a madhouse.'

'It's a very easy one to escape from,' said Gale in a serene manner. 'I've just seen the professor escape from it. He escapes regularly; probably on Wednesdays and Saturdays.'

'This is no time for your jokes,' she cried. 'I tell you we've been trapped inside a madhouse.'

'And I tell you we shall soon be outside the madhouse,' he replied firmly. 'And under those circumstances, I don't mind telling you that I regret to say it is not a madhouse.'

'What do you mean?'

'It is something worse,' replied Gale.

'Tell me what you mean,' she repeated. 'Tell me what you know about this horrible place.'

'For me it will always be a holy place,' he said. 'Was it not under that arch there that you appeared out of the abyss of memory? And after all, it's a beautiful garden and I'm almost sorry to leave it. The house, too, makes a romantic background; and really we might be very comfortable here . . . if only it were a madhouse.' And he sighed with regret.

Then after a pause he added, 'I might say all I want to say to you in a nice, friendly, comfortable lunatic asylum . . . but not in a place like this. There are practical things to be done now; and here come the people who will do them!'

She was never able to fit together again the fragments of that bad dream and its wilder way of breaking up. To her astonishment she beheld a new group advancing up the garden path; in front was a red-haired man in a top-hat, whose shrewd and good-humoured features were faintly familiar to her; behind were two stalwart figures, obviously in 'plain clothes', and between them the unexpected apparition of Professor Patterson in handcuffs.

'Caught him setting fire to a house,' said the red-haired man briefly. 'Valuable documents.'

Later in that bewildering stretch of hours, the friends seated themselves on a garden seat for explanations. 'You remember Dr Garth, I think,' said Gale to the lady. 'He has been helping me to clear up this queer business. The truth is, the police have suspected the nature of this Wimbledon retreat for some time. No; it is not a lunatic asylum; it is a den of very accomplished professional criminals. They have hit on the ingenious idea of being certified as irresponsible by a medical confederate; so that the worst that can happen is that he may be censured for laxity in letting them escape. Look up the records, and you will find them responsible, or irresponsible, for quite a long catalogue of crimes. I happened to follow the notion up, because I happened to guess where the notion came from. By the way, I suppose this is the gentleman who engaged you as a typist.'

As he spoke a small alert figure strode out of the house and across the lawns; his short beard thrust forward with something of the gesture of a terrier.

'Yes, that is Dr Wilson; I made arrangements with him only this morning,' answered Diana, still staring.

The doctor came to a halt in front of them, turning his head right and left in the terrier fashion, and looking at them with wrinkled brows and lids.

'So this is Dr Wilson,' said Gale politely. 'Good-day, Dr Starkey.'

Then as the plain-clothes men shifted and closed round the doctor, Gale added reflectively: 'I knew you would never fail to take a hint.'

* * *

A street or two away from the strange madhouse there was a sort of toy park, not much bigger than a back garden, but laid out in ornamental paths and planted with flowering shrubs, as an oasis for nomadic nurses trailing about the babies of that suburb. It was also ornamented with long seats with curly backs, and one of these seats in its turn was ornamented by a couple clad in black and endeavouring, with some bewilderment, to appear respectable. Wild as were the events of that afternoon, they had moved very rapidly and it was barely evening. The sunset was settling down about the corners of the sky and of the quaint little public garden, and there was little noise except the shrill but faint calling of some children lingering over some long-drawn-out game.

It was here that he told her the whole story of the rash vow and all that happened between the rescue in the riverside garden and the funeral in the Cornish churchyard.

'The only thing I don't understand,' she said at last, 'is why you thought they had got me to that place; or why you thought there was any such place.'

'Why, because,' he said looking at the gravel path with a slight embarrassment, 'because I really was not bragging when I told Starkey at the beginning that I understood the sort of mind he had, and could exaggerate it in the way it was going. Starkey never missed a chance of applying or misapplying an idea, especially anybody else's idea. When poor Jimmy Hurrel boasted of being free from punishment because he was an escaped lunatic, I was sure that a seed had been sown in Starkey's mind that would sprout. I was sure he would follow it up and use it, as he used my fancy for the swing or the arbour. While Jim was alive he knew I had a motive for silence; but the moment Jim died he struck. He was very quick; his mind is like a flash of lightning; quick but crooked. He sent one of his chartered maniacs to brain me with a stone on my way to you. He intercepted my telegram, and lured you away before you could be told the whole story. But what I want to know is what you think of the whole story.'

'The vow was certainly rash enough,' she said. 'All that time you might have been painting pictures and doing all sorts of good. It doesn't seem right that a genius should be tied to a lunatic by a few words.'

He sat up very suddenly. 'For God's sake don't say that!' he cried. 'Don't say one oughtn't to tie oneself to a lunatic by a few words! Don't say that's wrong, I implore you, whatever else you say! A shocking thought! A perfectly foul idea!'

'What do you mean?' she asked. 'Why not?'

'Because,' he said, 'I want you to make a rash vow. I want you to tie yourself with a few words to a lunatic.'

There was a silence, at the end of which she smiled suddenly and put her hand on his arm.

'No,' she said, 'only a silly . . . I always liked you, even when I thought you really were a lunatic; that day when you stood on your head. But now I don't think my vow will be so very rash . . . What on earth are you doing now? . . . Oh, I say – for heaven's sake . . . '

'What else should I do,' he answered calmly, 'after what you have just said? I'm going to stand on my head again.'

The children in the corner of the little garden gazed with interest at a gentleman in funeral full-dress behaving in a somewhat unusual manner.

THE SCANDAL OF FATHER BROWN

The Scandal of Father Brown

Contents

The Scandal of Father Brown

It would not be fair to record the adventures of Father Brown, without admitting that he was once involved in a grave scandal. There still are persons, perhaps even of his own community, who would say that there was a sort of blot upon his name. It happened in a picturesque Mexican road-house of rather loose repute, as appeared later; and to some it seemed that for once the priest had allowed a romantic streak in him, and his sympathy for human weakness, to lead him into loose and unorthodox action. The story in itself was a simple one; and perhaps the whole surprise of it consisted in its simplicity.

Burning Troy began with Helen; this disgraceful story began with the beauty of Hypatia Potter. Americans have a great power, which Europeans do not always appreciate, of creating institutions from below; that is by popular initiative. Like every other good thing, it has its lighter aspects; one of which, as has been remarked by Mr Wells and others, is that a person may become a public institution without becoming an official institution. A girl of great beauty or brilliancy will be a sort of uncrowned queen, even if she is not a Film Star or the original of a Gibson Girl. Among those who had the fortune, or misfortune, to exist beautifully in public in this manner, was a certain Hypatia Hard, who had passed through the preliminary stage of receiving florid compliments in society paragraphs of the local press, to the position of one who is actually interviewed by real pressmen. On War and Peace and Patriotism and Prohibition and Evolution and the Bible she had made her pronouncements with a charming smile; and if none of them seemed very near to the real grounds of her own reputation, it was almost equally hard to say what the grounds of her reputation really were. Beauty, and being the daughter of a rich man, are things not rare in her country; but to these she added whatever it is that attracts the wandering eye of journalism. Next to none of her admirers had even seen her, or even hoped to do so; and none of them could possibly derive any sordid benefit from her father's wealth. It was simply a sort of popular romance, the modern substitute for mythology; and it laid the first foundations of the more turgid and tempestuous sort of romance in which she was to figure later on; and in which many held that the reputation of Father Brown, as well as of others, had been blown to rags.

It was accepted, sometimes romantically, sometimes resignedly, by those whom American satire has named the Sob Sisters, that she had already married a very worthy and respectable business man of the name of Potter.

It was even possible to regard her for a moment as Mrs Potter, on the universal understanding that her husband was only the husband of Mrs Potter.

Then came the Great Scandal, by which her friends and enemies were horrified beyond their wildest hopes. Her name was coupled (as the queer phrase goes) with a literary man living in Mexico; in status an American, but in spirit a very Spanish American. Unfortunately his vices resembled her virtues, in being good copy. He was no less a person than the famous or infamous Rudel Romanes; the poet whose works had been so universally popularised by being vetoed by libraries or prosecuted by the police. Anyhow, her pure and placid star was seen in conjunction with this comet. He was of the sort to be compared to a comet, being hairy and hot; the first in his portraits, the second in his poetry. He was also destructive; the comet's tail was a trail of divorces, which some called his success as a lover and some his prolonged failure as a husband. It was hard on Hypatia; there are disadvantages in conducting the perfect private life in public; like a domestic interior in a shop-window. Interviewers reported doubtful utterances about Love's Larger Law of Supreme Self-Realisation. The Pagans applauded. The Sob Sisterhood permitted themselves a note of romantic regret; some having even the hardened audacity to quote from the poem of Maud Mueller, to the effect that of all the words of tongue or pen, the saddest are 'It might have been'. And Mr Agar P. Rock, who hated the Sob Sisterhood with a holy and righteous hatred, said that in this case he thoroughly agreed with Bret Harte's emendation of the poem: 'More sad are those we daily see; it is, but it hadn't ought to be.'

For Mr Rock was very firmly and rightly convinced that a very large number of things hadn't ought to be. He was a slashing and savage critic of national degeneration, on the *Minneapolis Meteor*, and a bold and honest man. He had perhaps come to specialise too much in the spirit of indignation, but it had had a healthy enough origin in his reaction against sloppy attempts to confuse right and wrong in modern journalism and gossip. He expressed it first in the form of a protest against an unholy halo of romance being thrown round the gunman and the gangster. Perhaps he was rather too much inclined to assume, in robust impatience, that all gangsters were Dagos and that all Dagos were gangsters. But his prejudices, even when they were a little provincial, were rather refreshing after a certain sort of maudlin and unmanly hero-worship, which was ready to regard a professional murderer as a leader of fashion, so long as the pressmen reported that his smile was irresistible or his tuxedo was all right. Anyhow, the prejudices did not boil the less in the bosom of Mr Rock, because he was actually in the land of the Dagos when this story opens; striding furiously up a hill beyond the Mexican border, to the white hotel, fringed with ornamental palms, in which it was supposed that the Potters were staying and that the mysterious Hypatia now held her court. Agar Rock was a good specimen of a Puritan, even to look at; he might even have been a virile Puritan of the seventeenth century, rather than the softer and more sophisticated Puritan of the twentieth. If you had told him that his antiquated black hat and habitual black frown, and fine flinty features, cast a gloom over the sunny land of palms and vines, he would have been very much gratified. He looked to right and left with eyes bright with universal suspicions. And, as he did so, he saw two figures on the ridge above him, outlined against the clear sub-tropical sunset; figures in a momentary posture which might have made even a less suspicious man suspect something.

One of the figures was rather remarkable in itself. It was poised at the exact angle of the turning road above the valley, as if by an instinct for the site as well as the attitude of statuary. It was wrapped in a great black cloak, in the Byronic manner, and the head that rose above it in swarthy beauty was remarkably like Byron's. This man had the same curling hair and curling nostrils; and he seemed to be snorting something of the same scorn and indignation against the world. He grasped in his hand a rather long cane or walking-stick, which having a spike of the sort used for mountaineering, carried at the moment a fanciful suggestion of a spear. It was rendered all the more fanciful by something comically contradictory in the figure of the other man, who carried an umbrella. It was indeed a new and neatly rolled umbrella, very different, for instance, from Father Brown's umbrella: and he was neatly clad like a clerk in light holiday clothes; a stumpy stoutish bearded man; but the prosaic umbrella was raised and even brandished at an acute angle of attack. The taller man thrust back at him, but in a hasty defensive manner; and then the scene rather collapsed into comedy; for the umbrella opened of itself and its owner almost seemed to sink behind it, while the other man had the air of pushing his spear through a great grotesque shield. But the other man did not push it, or the quarrel, very far; he plucked out the point, turned away impatiently and strode down the road; while the other, rising and carefully refolding his umbrella, turned in the opposite direction towards the hotel. Rock had not heard any of the words of the quarrel, which must have immediately preceded this brief and rather absurd bodily conflict; but as he went up the road in the track of the short man with the beard, he revolved many things. And the romantic cloak and rather operatic good looks of the one man, combined with the sturdy self-assertion of the other, fitted in with the whole story which he had come to seek; and he knew that he could have fixed those two strange figures with their names: Romanes and Potter.

His view was in every way confirmed when he entered the pillared porch; and heard the voice of the bearded man raised high in altercation or command. He was evidently speaking to the manager or staff of the hotel, and Rock heard enough to know that he was warning them of a wild and dangerous character in the neighbourhood.

'If he's really been to the hotel already,' the little man was saying, in answer to some murmur, 'all I can say is that you'd better not let him in again. Your police ought to be looking after a fellow of that sort, but anyhow, I won't have the lady pestered with him.'

Rock listened in grim silence and growing conviction; then he slid across the vestibule to an alcove where he saw the hotel register and turning to the last page, saw 'the fellow' had indeed been to the hotel already. There appeared the name of 'Rudel Romanes', that romantic public character, in very large and florid foreign lettering; and after a space under it, rather close together, the names of Hypatia Potter and Ellis T. Potter, in a correct and quite American handwriting.

Agar Rock looked moodily about him, and saw in the surroundings and even the small decorations of the hotel everything that he hated most. It is perhaps unreasonable to complain of oranges growing on orange trees, even in small tubs; still more of their only growing on threadbare curtains or faded wallpapers as a formal scheme of ornament. But to him those red and golden moons, decoratively alternated with silver moons, were in a queer way the quintessence of all moonshine. He saw in them all that sentimental deterioration which his principles deplored in modern manners, and which his prejudices vaguely connected with the warmth and softness of the South. It annoyed him even to catch sight of a patch of dark canvas, half-showing a Watteau shepherd with a guitar, or a blue tile with a commonplace design of a Cupid on a dolphin. His common sense would have told him that he might have seen these things in a shop-window on Fifth Avenue; but where they were, they seemed like a taunting siren voice of the Paganism of the Mediterranean. And then suddenly, the look of all these things seemed to alter, as a still mirror will flicker when a figure has flashed past it for a moment; and he knew the whole room was full of a challenging presence. He turned almost stiffly, and with a sort of resistance, and knew that he was facing the famous Hypatia, of whom he had read and heard for so many years.

Hypatia Potter, *née* Hard, was one of those people to whom the word 'radiant' really does apply definitely and derivatively. That is, she allowed what the papers called her Personality to go out from her in rays. She would have been equally beautiful, and to some tastes more attractive, if she had been self-contained; but she had always been taught to believe that self-containment was only selfishness. She would have said that she had lost Self in Service; it would perhaps be truer to say that she had asserted Self in Service; but she was quite in good faith about the service. Therefore her outstanding starry blue eyes really struck outwards, as in the old metaphor that made eyes like Cupid's darts, killing at a distance; but with an abstract conception of conquest beyond any mere coquetry. Her pale fair hair, though arranged in a saintly halo, had a look of almost electric radiation. And when she understood that the stranger before her was Mr Agar Rock, of the *Minneapolis Meteor*, her eyes took on themselves the range of long searchlights, sweeping the horizon of the States.

But in this the lady was mistaken; as she sometimes was. For Agar Rock was not Agar Rock of the *Minneapolis Meteor*. He was at that moment merely Agar Rock; there had surged up in him a great and sincere moral impulsion, beyond the coarse courage of the interviewer. A feeling profoundly mixed of a chivalrous and national sensibility to beauty, with an instant itch for moral action of some definite sort, which was also national, nerved him to face a great scene; and to deliver a noble insult. He remembered the original Hypatia, the beautiful Neo-Platonist, and how he had been thrilled as a boy by Kingsley's romance in which the young monk denounces her for harlotries and idolatries. He confronted her with an iron gravity and said: 'If you'll pardon me. Madam, I should like to have a word with you in private.'

'Well,' she said, sweeping the room with her splendid gaze, 'I don't know whether you consider this place private.'

Rock also gazed round the room and could see no sign of life less vegetable than the orange trees, except what looked like a large black mushroom, which he recognised as the hat of some native priest or other, stolidly smoking a black local cigar, and otherwise as stagnant as any vegetable. He looked for a moment at the heavy, expressionless features, noting the rudeness of that peasant type from which priests so often come, in Latin and especially Latin-American countries; and lowered his voice a little as he laughed.

'I don't imagine that Mexican padre knows our language,' he said. 'Catch those lumps of laziness learning any language but their own. Oh, I can't swear he's a Mexican; he might be anything; mongrel Indian or nigger, I suppose. But I'll answer for it he's not an American. Our ministries don't produce that debased type.'

'As a matter of fact,' said the debased type, removing his black cigar, 'I'm English and my name is Brown. But pray let me leave you if you wish to be private.'

'If you're English,' said Rock warmly, 'you ought to have some normal Nordic instinct for protesting against all this nonsense. Well, it's enough to say now that I'm in a position to testify that there's a pretty dangerous fellow hanging round this place; a tall fellow in a cloak, like those old pictures of crazy poets.'

'Well, you can't go much by that,' said the priest mildly; 'a lot of people round here use those cloaks, because the chill strikes very suddenly after sunset.'

Rock darted a dark and doubtful glance at him; as if suspecting some evasion in the interests of all that was symbolised to him by mushroom hats and moonshine. 'It wasn't only the cloak,' he growled, 'though it was partly the way he wore it. The whole look of the fellow was theatrical, down to his damned theatrical good looks. And if you'll forgive me, Madam, I strongly advise you to have nothing to do with him, if he comes bothering here. Your husband has already told the hotel people to keep him out – '

Hypatia sprang to her feet and, with a very unusual gesture, covered her face, thrusting her fingers into her hair. She seemed to be shaken, possibly with sobs, but by the time she had recovered they had turned into a sort of wild laughter.

'Oh, you are all too funny,' she said, and, in a way very unusual with her, ducked and darted to the door and disappeared.

'Bit hysterical when they laugh like that,' said Rock uncomfortably; then, rather at a loss, and turning to the little priest: 'As I say, if you're English, you ought really to be on my side against these Dagos, anyhow. Oh, I'm not one of those who talk tosh about Anglo-Saxons; but there is such a thing as history. You can always claim that America got her civilisation from England.'

'Also, to temper our pride,' said Father Brown, 'we must always admit that England got her civilisation from Dagos.'

Again there glowed in the other's mind the exasperated sense that his interlocutor was fencing with him, and fencing on the wrong side, in some secret and evasive way; and he curtly professed a failure to comprehend.

'Well, there was a Dago, or possibly a Wop, called Julius Caesar,' said Father Brown; 'he was afterwards killed in a stabbing match; you know these Dagos always use knives. And there was another one called Augustine, who brought Christianity to our little island; and really, I don't think we should have had much civilisation without those two.'

'Anyhow, that's all ancient history,' said the somewhat irritated journalist, 'and I'm very much interested in modern history. What I see is that these scoundrels are bringing Paganism to our country, and destroying all the Christianity there is. Also destroying all the common sense there is. All settled habits, all solid social order, all the way in which the farmers who were our fathers and grandfathers did manage to live in the world, melted into a hot mush by sensations and sensualities about film stars who divorced every month or so, and make every silly girl think that marriage is only a way of getting divorced.'

'You are quite right,' said Father Brown. 'Of course I quite agree with you there. But you must make some allowances. Perhaps these Southern people are a little prone to that sort of fault. You must remember that Northern people have other kinds of faults. Perhaps these surroundings do encourage people to give too rich an importance to mere romance . . . '

The whole integral indignation of Agar Rock's life rose up within him at the word.

'I hate Romance,' he said, hitting the little table before him. 'I've fought the papers I worked for for forty years about the infernal trash. Every blackguard bolting with a barmaid is called a romantic elopement or something; and now our own Hypatia Hard, a daughter of a decent people, may get dragged into some rotten romantic divorce case, that will be trumpeted to the whole world as happily as a royal wedding. This mad poet Romanes is hanging round her; and you bet the spotlight will follow him, as if he were any rotten little Dago who is called the Great Lover on the films. I saw him outside; and he's got the regular spotlight face. Now my sympathies are with decency and common sense. My sympathies are with poor Potter, a plain straightforward broker from Pittsburgh, who thinks he has a right to his own home. And he's making a fight for it, too. I heard him hollering at the management, telling them to keep that rascal out; and quite right too. The people here seem a sly and slinky lot; but I rather fancy he's put the fear of God into them already.'

'As a matter of fact,' said Father Brown, 'I rather agree with you about the manager and the men in this hotel; but you mustn't judge all Mexicans by them. Also I fancy the gentleman you speak of has not only hollered, but handed round dollars enough to get the whole staff on his side. I saw them locking doors and whispering most excitedly. By the way, your plain straightforward friend seems to have a lot of money.'

'I've no doubt his business does well,' said Rock. 'He's quite the best type of sound business man. What do you mean?'

'I fancied it might suggest another thought to you,' said Father Brown; and, rising with rather heavy civility, he left the room.

Rock watched the Potters very carefully that evening at dinner; and gained some new impressions, though none that disturbed his deep sense of the wrong that probably threatened the peace of the Potter home. Potter himself proved worthy of somewhat closer study; though the journalist had at first accepted him as prosaic and unpretentious, there was a pleasure in recognising finer lines in what he considered the hero or victim of a tragedy. Potter had really rather a thoughtful and distinguished face, though worried and occasionally petulant. Rock got an impression that the man was recovering from an illness; his faded hair was thin but rather long, as if it had been lately neglected, and his rather unusual beard gave the onlooker the same notion. Certainly he spoke once or twice to his wife in a rather sharp and acid manner, fussing about tablets or some detail of digestive science; but his real worry was doubtless concerned with the danger from without. His wife played up to him in the splendid if somewhat condescending manner of a Patient Griselda; but her eyes also roamed continually to the doors and shutters, as if in half-hearted fear of an invasion. Rock had only too good reason to dread, after her curious outbreak, the fact that her fear might turn out to be only half-hearted.

It was in the middle of the night that the extraordinary event occurred. Rock, imagining himself to be the last to go up to bed, was surprised to find Father Brown still tucked obscurely under an orange tree in the hall, and placidly reading a book. He returned the other's farewell without further words, and the journalist had his foot on the lowest step of the stair, when suddenly the outer door sprang on its hinges and shook and rattled under the shock of blows planted from without; and a great voice louder than the blows was heard violently demanding admission. Somehow the journalist was certain that the blows had been struck with a pointed stick like an alpenstock. He looked back at the darkened lower floor, and saw the servants of the hotel sliding here and there to see that the doors were locked; and not unlocking them. Then he slowly mounted to his room, and sat down furiously to write his report.

He described the siege of the hotel; the evil atmosphere; the shabby luxury of the place; the shifty evasions of the priest; above all, that terrible voice crying without, like a wolf prowling round the house. Then, as he wrote, he heard a new sound and sat up suddenly. It was a long repeated whistle, and in his mood he hated it doubly, because it was like the signal of a conspirator and like the love-call of a bird. There followed an utter silence, in which he sat rigid; then he rose abruptly; for he had heard yet another noise. It was a faint swish followed by a sharp rap or rattle; and he was almost certain that somebody was throwing something at the window. He walked stiffly downstairs, to the floor which was now dark and deserted; or nearly deserted. For the little priest was still sitting under the orange shrub, lit by a low lamp; and still reading his book.

'You seem to be sitting up late,' he said harshly.

'Quite a dissipated character,' said Father Brown, looking up with a broad smile, 'reading *Economics of Usury* at all wild hours of the night.'

'The place is locked up,' said Rock.

'Very thoroughly locked up,' replied the other. 'Your friend with the beard seems to have taken every precaution. By the way, your friend with the beard is a little rattled; I thought he was rather cross at dinner.'

'Natural enough,' growled the other, 'if he thinks savages in this savage place are out to wreck his home life.'

'Wouldn't it be better,' said Father Brown, 'if a man tried to make his home life nice inside, while he was protecting it from the things outside.'

'Oh, I know you will work up all the casuistical excuses,' said the other; 'perhaps he was rather snappy with his wife; but he's got the right on his side. Look here, you seem to me to be rather a deep dog. I believe you know more about this than you say. What the devil is going on in this infernal place? Why are you sitting up all night to see it through?'

'Well,' said Father Brown patiently, 'I rather thought my bedroom might be wanted.'

'Wanted by whom?'

'As a matter of fact, Mrs Potter wanted another room,' explained Father Brown with limpid clearness. 'I gave her mine, because I could open the window. Go and see, if you like.'

'I'll see to something else first,' said Rock grinding his teeth. 'You can play your monkey tricks in this Spanish monkey-house, but I'm still in touch with civilisation.' He strode into the telephone-booth and rang up his paper; pouring out the whole tale of the wicked priest who helped the wicked poet. Then he ran upstairs into the priest's room, in which the priest had just lit a short candle, showing the windows beyond wide open.

He was just in time to see a sort of rude rope-ladder unhooked from the window-sill and rolled up by a laughing gentleman on the lawn below. The laughing gentleman was a tall and swarthy gentleman, and was accompanied by a blonde but equally laughing lady. This time, Mr Rock could not even comfort himself by calling her laughter hysterical. It was too horribly genuine; and rang down the rambling garden-paths as she and her troubadour disappeared into the dark thickets.

Agar Rock turned on his companion a face of final and awful justice; like the Day of Judgement.

'Well, all America is going to hear of this,' he said. 'In plain words, you helped her to bolt with that curly-haired lover.'

'Yes,' said Father Brown, 'I helped her to bolt with that curly-haired lover.'

'You call yourself a minister of Jesus Christ,' cried Rock, 'and you boast of a crime.'

'I have been mixed up with several crimes,' said the priest gently. 'Happily for once this is a story without a crime. This is a simple fireside idyll; that ends with a glow of domesticity.'

'And ends with a rope-ladder instead of a rope,' said Rock. 'Isn't she a married woman?'

'Oh, yes,' said Father Brown.

'Well, oughtn't she to be with her husband?' demanded Rock.

'She is with her husband,' said Father Brown.

The other was startled into anger. 'You lie,' he said. 'The poor little man is still snoring in bed.'

'You seem to know a lot about his private affairs,' said Father Brown plaintively. 'You could almost write a life of the Man with a Beard. The only thing you don't seem ever to have found out about him is his name.'

'Nonsense,' said Rock. 'His name is in the hotel book.'

'I know it is,' answered the priest, nodding gravely, 'in very large letters; the name of Rudel Romanes. Hypatia Potter, who met him here, put her name boldly under his, when she meant to elope with him; and her husband put his name under that, when he pursued them to this place. He put it very close under hers, by way of protest. The Romanes (who has pots of money, as a popular misanthrope despising men) bribed the brutes in this hotel to bar and bolt it and keep the lawful husband out. And I, as you truly say, helped him to get in.'

When a man is told something that turns things upside-down; that the tail wags the dog; that the fish has caught the fisherman; that the earth goes round the moon; he takes some little time before he even asks seriously if it is true. He is still content with the consciousness that it is the opposite of the obvious truth. Rock said at last: 'You don't mean that little fellow is the romantic Rudel we're always reading about; and that curly-haired fellow is Mr Potter of Pittsburgh.'

'Yes,' said Father Brown. 'I knew it the moment I clapped eyes on both of them. But I verified it afterwards.'

Rock ruminated for a time and said at last: 'I suppose it's barely possible you're right. But how did you come to have such a notion, in the face of the facts?'

Father Brown looked rather abashed; subsided into a chair, and stared into vacancy, until a faint smile began to dawn on his round and rather foolish face.

'Well,' he said, 'you see – the truth is, I'm not romantic.'

'I don't know what the devil you are,' said Rock roughly.

'Now *you* are romantic,' said Father Brown helpfully. 'For instance, you see somebody looking poetical, and you assume he is a poet. Do you know what the majority of poets look like? What a wild confusion was created by that coincidence of three good-looking aristocrats at the beginning of the nineteenth century: Byron and Goethe and Shelley! Believe me, in the common way, a man may write: "Beauty has laid her flaming lips on mine," or whatever that chap wrote, without being himself particularly beautiful. Besides, do you realise how old a man generally is by the time his fame has filled the world? Watts painted Swinburne with a halo of hair; but Swinburne was bald before most of his last American or Australian admirers had heard of his hyacinthine locks. So was D'Annunzio. As a fact, Romanes still has rather a fine head, as you will see if you look at it closely; he looks like an intellectual man; and he is. Unfortunately, like a good many other intellectual men, he's a fool. He's let himself go to seed with selfishness and fussing about his digestion. So that the ambitious American lady, who thought it would be like soaring to Olympus with the Nine Muses to elope with a poet, found that a day or so of it was about enough for her. So that when her husband came after her, and stormed the place, she was delighted to go back to him.'

'But her husband?' queried Rock. 'I am still rather puzzled about her husband.'

'Ah, you've been reading too many of your erotic modern novels,' said Father Brown; and partly closed his eyes in answer to the protesting glare of the other. 'I know a lot of stories start with a wildly beautiful woman wedded to some elderly swine in the stock market. But why? In that, as in most things, modern novels are the very reverse of modern. I don't say it never happens; but it hardly ever happens now except by her own fault. Girls nowadays marry whom they like; especially spoilt girls like Hypatia. And whom do they marry? A beautiful wealthy girl like that would have a ring of admirers; and whom would she choose? The chances are a hundred to one that she'd marry very young and choose the handsomest man she met at a dance or a tennis-party. Well, ordinary business men are sometimes handsome. A young god appeared (called Potter) and she wouldn't care if he was a broker or a burglar. But, given the environment, you will admit it's more likely he would be a broker; also, it's quite likely that he'd be called Potter. You see, you are so incurably romantic that your whole case was founded on the idea that a man looking like a young god couldn't be called Potter. Believe me, names are not so appropriately distributed.'

'Well,' said the other, after a short pause, 'and what do you suppose happened after that?'

Father Brown got up rather abruptly from the seat in which he had collapsed; the candle-light threw the shadow of his short figure across the wall and ceiling, giving an odd impression that the balance of the room had been altered.

'Ah,' he muttered, 'that's the devil of it. That's the real devil. Much worse than the old Indian demons in this jungle. You thought I was only making out a case for the loose ways of these Latin Americans – well, the queer thing about you' – and he blinked owlishly at the other through his spectacles – 'the queerest thing about you is that in a way you're right.

'You say down with romance. I say I'd take my chance in fighting the genuine romances – all the more because they are precious few, outside the first fiery days of youth. I say – take away the Intellectual Friendships; take away the Platonic Unions; take away the Higher Laws of Self-Fulfilment and the rest, and I'll risk the normal dangers of the job. Take away the love that isn't love, but only pride and vainglory and publicity and making a splash; and we'll take our chance of fighting the love that is love, when it has to be fought, as well as the love that is lust and lechery. Priests know young people will have passions, as doctors know they will have measles. But

Hypatia Potter is forty if she is a day, and she cares no more for that little poet than if he were her publisher or her publicity man. That's just the point – he was her publicity man. It's your newspapers that have ruined her; it's living in the limelight; it's wanting to see herself in the headlines, even in a scandal if it were only sufficiently psychic and superior. It's wanting to be George Sand, her name immortally linked with Alfred de Musset. When her real romance of youth was over, it was the sin of middle age that got hold of her; the sin of intellectual ambition. She hasn't got any intellect to speak of; but you don't need any intellect to be an intellectual.'

'I should say she was pretty brainy in one sense,' observed Rock reflectively.

'Yes, in one sense,' said Father Brown. 'In only one sense. In a business sense. Not in any sense that has anything to do with these poor lounging Dagos down here. You curse the Film Stars and tell me you hate romance. Do you suppose the Film Star, who is married for the fifth time, is misled by any romance? Such people are very practical; more practical than you are. You say you admire the simple solid Business Man. Do you suppose that Rudel Romanes isn't a Business Man? Can't you see he knew, quite as well as she did, the advertising advantages of this grand affair with a famous beauty. He also knew very well that his hold on it was pretty insecure; hence his fussing about and bribing servants to lock doors. But what I mean to say, first and last, is that there'd be a lot less scandal if people didn't idealise sin and pose as sinners. These poor Mexicans may seem sometimes to live like beasts, or rather sin like men; but they don't go in for Ideals. You must at least give them credit for that.'

He sat down again, as abruptly as he had risen, and laughed apologetically. 'Well, Mr Rock,' he said, 'that is my complete confession; the whole horrible story of how I helped a romantic elopement. You can do what you like with it.'

'In that case,' said Rock, rising, 'I will go to my room and make a few alterations in my report. But, first of all, I must ring up my paper and tell them I've been telling them a pack of lies.'

* * *

Not much more than half an hour had passed, between the time when Rock had telephoned to say the priest was helping the poet to run away with the lady, and the time when he telephoned to say that the priest had prevented the poet from doing precisely the same thing. But in that short interval of time was born and enlarged and scattered upon the winds the Scandal of Father Brown. The truth is still half an hour behind the slander; and nobody can be certain when or where it will catch up with it. The garrulity of pressmen and the eagerness of enemies had spread the first story through the city, even before it appeared in the first printed version. It was instantly corrected and contradicted by Rock himself, in a second message stating how the story had really ended; but it was by no means certain that the first story was killed. A positively incredible number of people seemed to have read the first issue of the paper and not the second. Again and again, in every corner of the world, like a flame bursting from blackened ashes, there would appear the old tale of the Brown Scandal, or Priest Ruins Potter Home. Tireless apologists of the priest's party watched for it, and patiently tagged after it with contradictions and exposures and letters of protest. Sometimes the letters were published in the papers; and sometimes they were not. But still nobody knew how many people had heard the story without hearing the contradiction. It was possible to find whole blocks of blameless and innocent people who thought the Mexican Scandal was an ordinary recorded historical incident like the Gunpowder Plot. Then somebody would enlighten these simple people, only to discover that the old story had started afresh among a few quite educated people, who would seem the last people on earth to be duped by it. And so the two Father Browns chase each other round the world for ever; the first a shameless criminal fleeing from justice; the second a martyr broken by slander, in a halo of rehabilitation. But neither of them is very like the real Father Brown, who is not broken at all; but goes stumping with his stout umbrella through life, liking most of the people in it; accepting the world as his companion, but never as his judge.

The Quick One

The strange story of the incongruous strangers is still remembered along that strip of the Sussex coast, where the large and quiet hotel called the Maypole and Garland looks across its own gardens to the sea. Two quaintly assorted figures did, indeed, enter that quiet hotel on that sunny afternoon; one being conspicuous in the sunlight, and visible over the whole shore, by the fact of wearing a lustrous green turban, surrounding a brown face and a black beard; the other would have seemed to some even more wild and weird, by reason of his wearing a soft black clergyman's hat with a yellow moustache and yellow hair of leonine length. He at least had often been seen preaching on the sands or conducting Band of Hope services with a little wooden spade; only he had certainly never been seen going into the bar of an hotel. The arrival of these quaint companions was the climax of the story, but not the beginning of it; and, in order to make a rather mysterious story as clear as possible, it is better to begin at the beginning.

Half an hour before those two conspicuous figures entered the hotel, and were noticed by everybody, two other very inconspicuous figures had also entered it, and been noticed by nobody. One was a large man, and handsome in a heavy style, but he had a knack of taking up very little room, like a background; only an almost morbidly suspicious examination of his boots would have told anybody that he was an Inspector of Police in plain clothes; in very plain clothes. The other was a drab and insignificant little man, also in plain clothes, only that they happened to be clerical clothes; but nobody had ever seen *him* preaching on the sands.

These travellers also found themselves in a sort of large smoking-room with a bar, for a reason which determined all the events of that tragic afternoon. The truth is that the respectable hotel called the Maypole and Garland was being 'done-up'. Those who had liked it in the past were moved to say that it was being done down; or possibly done in. This was the opinion of the local grumbler, Mr Raggley, the eccentric old gentleman who drank cherry brandy in a corner and cursed. Anyhow, it was being carefully stripped of all the stray indications that it had once been an English inn; and being busily turned, yard by yard and room by room, into something resembling the sham palace of a Levantine usurer in an American film. It was, in short, being 'decorated'; but the only part where the decoration was complete, and where customers could yet be made comfortable, was this large room leading out of the hall. It had once been honourably known as a Bar Parlour and was now mysteriously known as a Saloon Lounge, and was newly 'decorated', in the manner of an Asiatic Divan. For Oriental ornament pervaded the new scheme; and where there had once been a gun hung on hooks, and sporting prints and a stuffed fish in a glass case, there were now festoons of Eastern drapery and trophies of scimitars, tulwars and yataghans, as if in unconscious preparation for the coming of the gentleman with the turban. The practical point was, however, that the few guests who did arrive had to be shepherded into this lounge, now swept and garnished, because all the more regular and refined parts of the hotel were still in a state of transition. Perhaps that was also the reason why even those few guests were somewhat neglected, the manager and others being occupied with explanations or exhortations elsewhere. Anyhow, the first two travellers who arrived had to kick their heels for some time unattended. The bar was at the moment entirely empty, and the Inspector rang and rapped impatiently on the counter; but the little clergyman had already dropped into a lounge seat and seemed in no hurry for anything. Indeed his friend the policeman, turning his head, saw that the round face of the little cleric had gone quite blank, as it had a way of doing sometimes; he seemed to be staring through his moonlike spectacles at the newly decorated wall.

'I may as well offer you a penny for your thoughts,' said Inspector Greenwood, turning from the counter with a sigh, 'as nobody seems to want my pennies for anything else. This seems to be the only room in the house that isn't full of ladders and whitewash; and this is so empty that there isn't even a potboy to give me a pot of beer.'

'Oh . . . my thoughts are not worth a penny, let alone a pot of beer,' answered the cleric, wiping his spectacles, 'I don't know why . . . but I was thinking how easy it would be to commit a murder here.'

'It's all very well for you, Father Brown,' said the Inspector good-humouredly. 'You've had a lot more murders than your fair share; and we poor policemen sit starving all our lives, even for a little one. But why should you say . . . Oh I see, you're looking at all those Turkish daggers on the wall. There are plenty of things to commit a murder *with*, if that's what you mean. But not more than there are in any ordinary kitchen: carving knives or pokers or what not. That isn't where the snag of a murder comes in.'

Father Brown seemed to recall his rambling thoughts in some bewilderment; and said that he supposed so.

'Murder is always easy,' said Inspector Greenwood. 'There can't possibly be anything more easy than murder. I could murder you at this minute – more easily than I can get a drink in this damned bar. The only difficulty is committing a murder without committing oneself as a murderer. It's this shyness about owning up to a murder; it's this silly modesty of murderers about their own masterpieces, that makes the trouble. They will stick to this extraordinary fixed idea of killing people without being found out; and that's what restrains them, even in a room full of daggers. Otherwise every cutler's shop would be piled with corpses. And that, by the way, explains the one kind of murder that really *can't* be prevented. Which is why, of course, we poor bobbies are always blamed for not preventing it. When a madman murders a King or a President, it can't be prevented. You can't make a King live in a coal-cellar, or carry about a President in a steel box. Anybody can murder him who does not mind being a murderer. That is where the madman is like the martyr – sort of beyond this world. A real fanatic can always kill anybody he likes.'

Before the priest could reply, a joyous band of bagmen rolled into the room like a shoal of porpoises; and the magnificent bellow of a big, beaming man, with an equally big and beaming tie-pin, brought the eager and obsequious manager running like a dog to the whistle, with a rapidity which the police in plain clothes had failed to inspire.

'I'm sure I'm very sorry, Mr Jukes,' said the manager, who wore a rather agitated smile and a wave or curl of very varnished hair across his forehead. 'We're rather understaffed at present; and I had to attend to something in the hotel, Mr Jukes.'

Mr Jukes was magnanimous, but in a noisy way; and ordered drinks all round, conceding one even to the almost cringing manager. Mr Jukes was a traveller for a very famous and fashionable wine and spirits firm; and may have conceived himself as lawfully the leader in such a place. Anyhow, he began a boisterous monologue, rather tending to tell the manager how to manage his hotel; and the others seemed to accept him as an authority. The policeman and the priest had retired to a low bench and small table in the background, from which they watched events, up to that rather remarkable moment when the policeman had very decisively to intervene.

For the next thing that happened, as already narrated, was the astonishing apparition of a brown Asiatic in a green turban, accompanied by the (if possible) more astonishing apparition of a Noncomformist minister; omens such as appear before a doom. In this case there was no doubt about evidence for the portent. A taciturn but observant boy cleaning the steps for the last hour (being a leisurely worker), the dark, fat, bulky bar-attendant, even the diplomatic but distracted manager, all bore witness to the miracle.

The apparitions, as the sceptics say, were due to perfectly natural causes. The man with the mane of yellow hair and the semi-clerical clothes was not only familiar as a preacher on the sands, but as a propagandist throughout the modern world. He was no less a person than the Revd David Pryce-Jones, whose far-resounding slogan was Prohibition and Purification for Our Land and the Britains Overseas. He as an excellent public speaker and organiser; and an idea had occurred to him that ought to have occurred to Prohibitionists long ago. It was the simple idea that, if Prohibition is right, some honour is due to the Prophet who was perhaps the first Prohibitionist. He had corresponded with the leaders of Muhammadan religious thought, and had finally induced a distinguished Muslim (one of whose names was Akbar and the rest an untranslatable ululation of Allah with attributes) to come and lecture in England on the ancient Muslim veto on wine. Neither of them certainly had been in a public-house bar before; but they had come there by the process already described; driven from the genteel tea-rooms, shepherded into the newly decorated saloon. Probably all would have been well, if the great Prohibitionist, in his innocence, had not advanced to the counter and asked for a glass of milk.

The commercial travellers, though a kindly race, emitted involuntary noises of pain; a murmur of suppressed jests was heard, as 'Shun the bowl', or 'Better bring out the cow'. But the magnificent Mr Jukes, feeling it due to his wealth and tie-pin to produce more refined humour, fanned himself as one about to faint, and said pathetically: 'They know they can knock me down with a feather. They know a breath will blow me away. They know my doctor says I'm not to have these shocks. And they come and drink cold milk in cold blood, before my very eyes.'

The Revd David Pryce-Jones, accustomed to deal with hecklers at public meetings, was so unwise as to venture on remonstrance and recrimination, in this very different and much more popular atmosphere. The Oriental total abstainer abstained from speech as well as spirits; and certainly gained in dignity by doing so. In fact, so far as he was concerned, the Muslim culture certainly scored a silent victory; he was obviously so much more of a gentleman than the commercial gentlemen, that a faint irritation began to arise against his aristocratic aloofness; and when Mr Pryce-Jones began to refer in argument to something of the kind, the tension became very acute indeed.

'I ask you, friends,' said Mr Pryce-Jones, with expansive platform gestures, 'why does our friend here set an example to us Christians in truly Christian self-control and brotherhood? Why does he stand here as a model of true Christianity, of real refinement, of genuine gentlemanly behaviour, amid all the quarrels and riots of such places as these? Because, whatever the doctrinal differences between us, at least in his soil the evil plant, the accursed hop or vine, has never – '

At this crucial moment of the controversy it was that John Raggley, the stormy petrel of a hundred storms of controversy, red-faced, white-haired, his antiquated top hat on the back of his head, his stick swinging like a club, entered the house like an invading army.

John Raggley was generally regarded as a crank. He was the sort of man who writes letters to the newspaper, which generally do not appear in the newspaper; but which do appear afterwards as pamphlets, printed (or misprinted) at his own expense; and circulated to a hundred waste-paper baskets. He had quarrelled alike with the Tory squires and the Radical County Councils; he hated Jews; and he distrusted nearly everything that is sold in shops, or even in hotels. But there was a backing of facts behind his fads; he knew the county in every corner and curious detail; and he was a sharp observer. Even the manager, a Mr Wills, had a shadowy respect for Mr Raggley, having a nose for the sort of lunacy allowed in the gentry; not indeed the prostrate reverence which he had for the jovial magnificence of Mr Jukes, who was really good for trade, but a least a disposition to avoid quarrelling with the old grumbler, partly perhaps out of fear of the old grumbler's tongue.

'And you will have your usual, Sir,' said Mr Wills, leaning and leering across the counter.

'It's the only decent stuff you've still got,' snorted Mr Raggley, slapping down his queer and antiquated hat. 'Damn it, I sometimes think the only English thing left in England is cherry brandy. Cherry brandy does taste of cherries. Can you find me any beer that tastes of hops, or any cider that tastes of apples, or any wine that has the remotest indication of being made out of grapes? There's an infernal swindle going on now in every inn in the country, that would have raised a revolution in any other country. I've found out a thing or two about it, I can tell you. You wait till I can get it printed, and people will sit up. If I could stop our people being poisoned with all this bad drink – '

Here again the Revd David Pryce-Jones showed a certain failure in tact; though it was a virtue he almost worshipped. He was so unwise as to attempt to establish an alliance with Mr Raggley, by a fine confusion between the idea of bad drink and the idea that drink is bad. Once more he endeavoured to drag his stiff and stately Eastern friend into the argument, as a refined foreigner superior to our rough English ways. He was even so foolish as to talk of a broad theological outlook; and ultimately to mention the name of Mahomet, which was echoed in a sort of explosion.

'God damn your soul!' roared Mr Raggley, with a less broad theological outlook. 'Do you mean that Englishmen mustn't drink English beer, because wine was forbidden in a damned desert by that dirty old humbug Mahomet?'

In an instant the Inspector of Police had reached the middle of the room with a stride. For, the instant before that, a remarkable change had taken place in the demeanour of the Oriental gentleman, who had hitherto stood perfectly still, with steady and shining eyes. He now proceeded, as his friend had said, to set an example in truly Christian self-control and brotherhood by reaching the wall with the bound of a tiger, tearing down one of the heavy knives hanging there and sending it smack like a stone from a sling, so that it stuck quivering in the wall exactly half an inch above Mr Raggley's ear. It would undoubtedly have stuck quivering in Mr Raggley, if Inspector Greenwood had not been just in time to jerk the arm and deflect the aim. Father Brown continued in his seat, watching the scene with screwed-up eyes and a screw of something almost like a smile at the corners of his mouth, as if he saw something beyond the mere momentary violence of the quarrel.

And then the quarrel took a curious turn; which may not be understood by everybody, until men like Mr John Raggley are better understood than they are. For the red-faced old fanatic was standing up and laughing uproariously as if it were the best joke he had ever heard. All his snapping vituperation and bitterness seemed to have gone out of him; and he regarded the other fanatic, who had just tried to murder him, with a sort of boisterous benevolence.

'Blast your eyes,' he said, 'you're the first man I've met in twenty years!'

'Do you charge this man, Sir?' said the Inspector, looking doubtful.

'Charge him, of course not,' said Raggley. 'I'd stand him a drink if he were allowed any drinks. I hadn't any business to insult his religion; and I wish to God all you skunks had the guts to kill a man, I won't say for insulting your religion, because you haven't got any, but for insulting anything – even your beer.'

'Now he's called us all skunks,' said Father Brown to Greenwood, 'peace and harmony seem to be restored. I wish that teetotal lecturer could get himself impaled on his friend's knife; it was he who made all the mischief.'

As he spoke, the odd groups in the room were already beginning to break up; it had been found possible to clear the commercial room for the commercial travellers, and they adjourned to it, the potboy carrying a new round of drinks after them on a tray. Father Brown stood for a moment gazing at the glasses left on the counter; recognising at once the ill-omened glass of milk, and another which smelt of whisky; and then turned just in time to see the parting between those two quaint figures, fanatics of the East and West. Raggley was still ferociously genial; there was still something a little darkling and sinister about the Muslim, which was perhaps natural; but he bowed himself out with grave gestures of dignified reconciliation; and there was every indication that the trouble was really over.

Some importance, however, continued attached, in the mind of Father Brown at least, to the memory and interpretation of those last courteous salutes between the combatants. Because, curiously enough, when Father Brown came down very early next morning, to perform his religious duties in the neighbourhood, he found the long saloon bar, with its fantastic Asiatic decoration, filled with a dead white light of daybreak in which every detail was distinct; and one of the details was the dead body of John Raggley bent and crushed into a corner of the room, with the heavy-hilted crooked dagger rammed through his heart.

Father Brown went very softly upstairs again and summoned his friend the Inspector; and the two stood beside the corpse, in a house in which no one else was as yet stirring. 'We mustn't either assume or avoid the obvious,' said Greenwood after a silence, 'but it is well to remember, I think, what I was saying to you yesterday afternoon. It's rather odd, by the way, that I should have said it – yesterday afternoon.'

'I know,' said the priest, nodding with an owlish stare.

'I said,' observed Greenwood, 'that the one sort of murder we can't stop is murder by somebody like a religious fanatic. That brown fellow probably thinks that if he's hanged, he'll go straight to Paradise for defending the honour of the Prophet.'

'There is that, of course,' said Father Brown. 'It would be very reasonable, so to speak, of our Muslim friend to have stabbed him. And you may say we don't know of anybody else yet, who could at all reasonably have stabbed him. But. . . but I was thinking . . . ' And his round face suddenly went blank again and all speech died on his lips.

'What's the matter now?' asked the other.

'Well, I know it sounds funny,' said Father Brown in a forlorn voice. 'But I was thinking . . . I was thinking, in a way, it doesn't much matter who stabbed him.'

'Is this the New Morality?' asked his friend. 'Or the old Casuistry, perhaps. Are the Jesuits really going in for murder?'

'I didn't say it didn't matter who murdered him,' said Father Brown. 'Of course the man who stabbed him might possibly be the man who murdered him. But it might be quite a different man. Anyhow, it was done at quite a different time. I suppose you'll want to work on the hilt for fingerprints; but don't take too much notice of them. I can imagine other reasons for other people sticking this knife in the poor old boy. Not very edifying reasons, of course, but quite distinct from the murder. You'll have to put some more knives into him, before you find out about that.'

'You mean – ' began the other, watching him keenly.

'I mean the autopsy,' said the priest, 'to find the real cause of death.'

'You're quite right, I believe,' said the Inspector, 'about the stabbing, anyhow. We must wait for the doctor; but I'm pretty sure he'll say you're right. There isn't blood enough. This knife was stuck in the corpse when it had been cold for hours. But why?'

'Possibly to put the blame on the Muhammadan,' answered Father Brown. 'Pretty mean, I admit, but not necessarily murder. I fancy there are people in this place trying to keep secrets, who are not necessarily murderers.'

'I haven't speculated on that line yet,' said Greenwood. 'What makes you think so?'

'What I said yesterday, when we first came into this horrible room. I said it would be easy to commit a murder here. But I wasn't thinking about all those stupid weapons, though you thought I was. About something quite different.'

For the next few hours the Inspector and his friend conducted a close and thorough investigation into the goings and comings of everybody for the last twenty-four hours, the way the drinks had been distributed, the glasses that were washed or unwashed, and every detail about every individual involved, or apparently not involved. One might have supposed they thought that thirty people had been poisoned, as well as one.

It seemed certain that nobody had entered the building except by the big entrance that adjoined the bar; all the others were blocked in one way or another by the repairs. A boy had been cleaning the steps outside this entrance; but he had nothing very clear to report. Until the amazing entry of the Turk in the Turban, with his teetotal lecturer, there did not seem to have been much custom of any kind, except for the commercial travellers who came in to take what they called 'quick ones'; and they seemed to have moved together, like Wordsworth's Cloud; there was a slight difference of opinion between the boy outside and the men inside about whether one of them had not been abnormally quick in obtaining a quick one, and come out on the doorstep by himself; but the manager and the barman had no memory of any such independent individual. The manager and the barman knew all the travellers quite well, and there was no doubt about their movements as a whole. They had stood at the bar chaffing and drinking; they had been involved, through their lordly leader, Mr Jukes, in a not very serious altercation with Mr Pryce-Jones; and they had witnessed the sudden and very serious altercation between Mr Akbar and Mr Raggley. Then they were told they could adjourn to the Commercial Room and did so, their drinks being borne after them like a trophy.

'There's precious little to go on,' said Inspector Greenwood. 'Of course a lot of officious servants must do their duty as usual, and wash out all the glasses; including old Raggley's glass. If it weren't for everybody else's efficiency, we detectives might be quite efficient.'

'I know,' said Father Brown, and his mouth took on again the twisted smile. 'I sometimes think criminals invented hygiene. Or perhaps hygienic reformers invented crime; they look like it, some of them. Everybody talks about foul dens and filthy slums in which crime can run riot; but it's just the other way. They are called foul, not because crimes are committed, but because crimes are discovered. It's in the neat, spotless, clean and tidy places that crime can run riot; no mud to make footprints; no dregs to contain poison; kind servants washing out all traces of the murder; and the murderer killing and cremating six wives and all for want of a little Christian dirt. Perhaps I express myself with too much warmth – but look here. As it happens, I do remember one glass, which has doubtless been cleaned since, but I should like to know more about it.'

'Do you mean Raggley's glass?' asked Greenwood.

'No; I mean Nobody's glass,' replied the priest. 'It stood near that glass of milk and it still held an inch or two of whisky. Well, you and I had no whisky. I happen to remember that the manager, when treated by the jovial Jukes, had "a drop of gin". I hope you don't suggest that our Muslim was a whisky-drinker disguised in a green turban; or that the Revd David Pryce-Jones managed to drink whisky and milk together, without noticing it.'

'Most of the commercial travellers took whisky,' said the Inspector. 'They generally do.'

'Yes; and they generally see they get it too,' answered Father Brown. 'In this case, they had it all carefully carted after them to their own room. But this glass was left behind.'

'An accident, I suppose,' said Greenwood doubtfully. 'The man could easily get another in the Commercial Room afterwards.'

Father Brown shook his head. 'You've got to see people as they are. Now these sort of men – well, some call them vulgar and some common; but that's all likes and dislikes. I'd be content to say that they are mostly simple men. Lots of them very good men, very glad to go back to the missus and the kids; some of them might be blackguards; might have had several missuses; or even murdered several missuses. But most of them are simple men; and, mark you, just the least tiny bit drunk. Not much; there's many a duke or don at Oxford drunker; but when that sort of man is at that stage of conviviality, he simply can't help noticing things, and noticing them very loud. Don't you observe that the least little incident jerks them into speech; if the beer froths over, they froth over with it, and have to say, "Whoa, Emma," or "Doing me proud, aren't you?" Now I should say it's flatly impossible for five of these festive beings to sit round a table in the Commercial Room, and have only four glasses set before them, the fifth man being left out, without making a shout about it. Probably they would all make a shout about it. Certainly *he* would make a shout about it. He wouldn't wait, like an Englishman of another class, till he could get a drink quietly later. The air would resound with things like, "And what about little me?" or, "Here, George, have I joined the Band of Hope?" or, "Do you see any green in my turban, George?" But the barman heard no such complaints. I take it as certain that the glass of whisky left behind had been nearly emptied by somebody else; somebody we haven't thought about yet.'

'But can you think of any such person?' ask the other.

'It's because the manager and the barman won't hear of any such person, that you dismiss the one really independent piece of evidence; the evidence of that boy outside cleaning the steps. He says that a man, who well may have been a bagman, but who did not, in fact, stick to the other bagmen, went in and came out again almost immediately. The manager and the barman never saw him; or say they never saw him. But he got a glass of whisky from the bar somehow. Let us call him, for the sake of argument, The Quick One. Now you know I don't often interfere with your business, which I know you do better than I should do it, or should want to do it. I've never had anything to do with setting police machinery at work, or running down criminals, or anything like that. But, for the first time in my life, I want to do it now. I want you to find The Quick One; to follow The Quick One to the ends of the earth; to set the whole infernal official machinery at work like a drag-net across the nations, and jolly well recapture The Quick One. Because he is the man we want.'

Greenwood made a despairing gesture. 'Has he face or form or any visible quality except quickness?' he enquired.

'He was wearing a sort of Inverness cape,' said Father Brown, 'and he told the boy outside he must reach Edinburgh by next morning. That's all the boy outside remembers. But I know your organisation has got on to people with less clue than that.'

'You seem very keen on this,' said the Inspector, a little puzzled.

The priest looked puzzled also, as if at his own thoughts; he sat with knotted brow and then said abruptly: 'You see, it's so easy to be misunderstood. All men matter. You matter. I matter. It's the hardest thing in theology to believe.'

The Inspector stared at him without comprehension; but he proceeded.

'We matter to God – God only knows why. But that's the only possible justification of the existence of policemen.' The policeman did not seem enlightened as to his own cosmic justification. 'Don't you see, the law really is right in a way, after all. If all men matter, all murders matter. That which He has so mysteriously created, we must not suffer to be mysteriously destroyed. But –'

He said the last word sharply, like one taking a new step in decision.

'*But*, when once I step off that mystical level of equality, I don't see that most of your important murders are particularly important. You are always telling me that this case and that is important. As a plain, practical man of the world, I must realise that it is the Prime Minister who has been murdered. As a plain, practical man of the world, I don't think that the Prime Minister matters at all. As a mere matter of human importance, I should say he hardly exists at all. Do you suppose if he and the other public men were shot dead tomorrow, there wouldn't be other people to stand up and say that every avenue was being explored, or that the Government had the matter under the gravest consideration? The masters of the modern world don't matter. Even the real masters don't matter much. Hardly anybody you ever read about in a newspaper matters at all.'

He stood up, giving the table a small rap: one of his rare gestures; and his voice changed again. 'But Raggley did matter. He was one of a great line of some half a dozen men who might have saved England. They stand up stark and dark like disregarded signposts, down all that smooth descending road which has ended in this swamp of merely commercial collapse. Dean Swift and Dr Johnson and old William Cobbett; they had all without exception the name of being surly or savage, and they were all loved by their friends, and they all deserved to be. Didn't you see how that old man, with the heart of a lion, stood up and forgave his enemy as only fighters can forgive? He jolly well *did* do what that temperance lecturer talked about; he set an example to us Christians and was a model of Christianity. And when there is foul and secret murder of a man like that – then I do think it matters, matters so much that even the modern machinery of police will be a thing that any respectable person may make use of . . . Oh, don't mention it. And so, for once in a way, I really do want to make use of you.'

And so, for some stretch of those strange days and nights, we might almost say that the little figure of Father Brown drove before him into action all the armies and engines of the police forces of the Crown, as the little figure of Napoleon drove the batteries and the battle-lines of the vast strategy that covered Europe. Police stations and post offices worked all night; traffic was stopped, correspondence was intercepted, enquiries were made in a hundred places, in order to track the flying trail of that ghostly figure, without face or name, with an Inverness cape and an Edinburgh ticket.

Meanwhile, of course, the other lines of investigation were not neglected. The full report of the post-mortem had not yet come in; but everybody seemed certain that it was a case of poisoning. This naturally threw the primary suspicion upon the cherry brandy; and this again naturally threw the primary suspicion on the hotel.

'Most probably on the manager of the hotel,' said Greenwood gruffly. 'He looks a nasty little worm to me. Of course it might be something to do with some servant, like the barman; he seems rather a sulky specimen, and Raggley might have cursed him a bit, having a flaming temper, though he was generally generous enough afterwards. But, after all, as I say, the primary responsibility, and therefore the primary suspicion, rests on the manager.'

'Oh, I knew the primary suspicion would rest on the manager,' said Father Brown. 'That was why I didn't suspect him. You see, I rather fancied somebody else must have known that the primary suspicion would rest on the manager; or the servants of the hotel. That is why I said it would be easy to kill anybody in the hotel . . . But you'd better go and have it out with him, I suppose.'

The Inspector went; but came back again after a surprisingly short interview, and found his clerical friend turning over some papers that seemed to be a sort of dossier of the stormy career of John Raggley.

'This is a rum go,' said the Inspector. 'I thought I should spend hours cross-examining that slippery little toad there, for we haven't legally got a thing against him. And instead of that, he went to pieces all at once, and I really think he's told me all he knows in sheer funk.'

'I know,' said Father Brown. 'That's the way he went to pieces when he found Raggley's corpse apparently poisoned in his hotel. That's why he lost his head enough to do such a clumsy thing as decorate the corpse with a Turkish knife, to put the blame on the nigger, as he would say. There never is anything the matter with him but funk; he's the very last man that ever would really stick a knife into a live person. I bet he had to nerve himself to stick it into a dead one. But he's the very first person to be frightened of being charged with what he didn't do; and to make a fool of himself, as he did.'

'I suppose I must see the barman too,' observed Greenwood.

'I suppose so,' answered the other. 'I don't believe myself it was any of the hotel people – well, because it was made to look as if it must be the hotel people . . . But look here, have you seen any of this stuff they've got together about Raggley? He had a jolly interesting life; I wonder whether anyone will write his biography.'

'I took a note of everything likely to affect an affair like this,' answered the official. 'He was a widower; but he did once have a row with a man about his wife; a Scotch land-agent then in these parts; and Raggley seems to have been pretty violent. They say he hated Scotchmen; perhaps that's the reason . . . Oh, I know what you are smiling grimly about. A Scotchman . . . Perhaps an Edinburgh man.'

'Perhaps,' said Father Brown. 'It's quite likely, though, that he did dislike Scotchmen, apart from private reasons. It's an odd thing, but all that tribe of Tory Radicals, or whatever you call them, who resisted the Whig mercantile movement, all of them did dislike Scotchmen. Cobbett did; Dr Johnson did; Swift described their accent in one of his deadliest passages; even Shakespeare has been accused of the prejudice. But the prejudices of great men generally have something to do with principles. And there was a reason, I fancy. The Scot came from a poor agricultural land, that became a rich industrial land. He was able and active; he thought he was bringing industrial civilisation from the north; he simply didn't know that there had been for centuries a rural civilisation in the south. His own grandfather's land was highly rural but not civilised . . . Well, well, I suppose we can only wait for more news.'

'I hardly think you'll get the latest news out of Shakespeare and Dr Johnson,' grinned the police officer. 'What Shakespeare thought of Scotchmen isn't exactly evidence.'

Father Brown cocked an eyebrow, as if a new thought had surprised him. 'Why, now I come to think of it,' he said, 'there might be better evidence, even out of Shakespeare. He doesn't often mention Scotchmen. But he was rather fond of making fun of Welshmen.'

The Inspector was searching his friend's face; for he fancied he recognised an alertness behind its demure expression. 'By Jove,' he said. 'Nobody thought of turning the suspicions *that* way, anyhow.'

'Well,' said Father Brown, with broad-minded calm, 'you started by talking about fanatics; and how a fanatic could do anything. Well, I suppose we had the honour of entertaining, in this bar-parlour yesterday, about the biggest and loudest and most fat-headed fanatic in the modern world. If being a pig-headed idiot with one idea is the way to murder, I put in a claim for my reverend brother Pryce-Jones, the Prohibitionist, in preference to all the fakirs in Asia, and it's perfectly true, as I told you, that his horrible glass of milk was standing side by side on the counter with the mysterious glass of whisky.'

'Which you think was mixed up with the murder,' said Greenwood, staring. 'Look here, I don't know whether you're really serious or not.'

Even as he was looking steadily in his friend's face, finding something still inscrutable in its expression, the telephone rang stridently behind the bar. Lifting the flap in the counter Inspector Greenwood passed rapidly inside, unhooked the receiver, listened for an instant, and then uttered a shout; not addressed to his interlocutor, but to the universe in general. Then he listened still more attentively and said explosively at intervals, 'Yes, yes . . . Come round at once; bring him round if possible . . . Good piece of work . . . Congratulate you.'

Then Inspector Greenwood came back into the outer lounge, like a man who has renewed his youth, sat down squarely on his seat, with his hands planted on his knees, stared at his friend, and said: 'Father Brown, I don't know how you do it. You seem to have known he was a murderer before anybody else knew he was a man. He was nobody; he was nothing; he was a slight confusion in the evidence; nobody in the hotel saw him; the boy on the steps could hardly swear to him; he was just a fine shade of doubt founded on an extra dirty glass. But we've got him, and he's the man we want.'

Father Brown had risen with the sense of the crisis, mechanically clutching the papers destined to be so valuable to the biographer of Mr Raggley; and stood staring at his friend. Perhaps this gesture jerked his friend's mind to fresh confirmations.

'Yes, we've got The Quick One. And very quick he was, like quicksilver, in making his get-away; we only just stopped him – off on a fishing trip to Orkney, he said. But he's the man, all right; he's the Scotch land-agent who made love to Raggley's wife; he's the man who drank Scotch whisky in this bar and then took a train to Edinburgh. And nobody would have known it but for you.'

'Well, what I meant,' began Father Brown, in a rather dazed tone; and at that instant there was a rattle and rumble of heavy vehicles outside the hotel; and two or three other and subordinate policemen blocked the bar with their presence. One of them, invited by his superior to sit down, did so in an expansive manner, like one at once happy and fatigued; and he also regarded Father Brown with admiring eyes.

'Got the murderer, Sir, oh yes,' he said; 'I know he's a murderer, 'cause he bally nearly murdered me. I've captured some tough characters before now; but never one like this – hit me in the stomach like the kick of a horse and nearly got away from five men. Oh, you've got a real killer this time, Inspector.'

'Where is he?' asked Father Brown, staring.

'Outside in the van, in handcuffs,' replied the policeman, 'and, if you're wise, you'll leave him there – for the present.'

Father Brown sank into a chair in a sort of soft collapse; and the papers he had been nervously clutching were shed around him, shooting and sliding about the floor like sheets of breaking snow. Not only his face, but his whole body, conveyed the impression of a punctured balloon.

'Oh . . . Oh,' he repeated, as if any further oath would be inadequate. 'Oh . . . I've done it again.'

'If you mean you've caught the criminal again,' began Greenwood. But his friend stopped him with a feeble explosion, like that of expiring soda-water.

'I mean,' said Father Brown, 'that it's always happening; and really, I don't know why. I always try to say what I mean. But everybody else means such a lot by what I say.'

'What in the world is the matter now?' cried Greenwood, suddenly exasperated.

'Well, I say things,' said Father Brown in a weak voice, which could alone convey the weakness of the words. 'I say things, but everybody seems to know they mean more than they say. Once I saw a broken mirror and said "Something has happened" and they all answered, "Yes, yes, as you truly say, two men wrestled and one ran into the garden," and so on. I don't understand it, "Something happened," and "Two men wrestled," don't seem to me at all the same; but I dare say I read old books of logic. Well, it's like that here. You seem to be all certain this man is a murderer. But I never said he was a murderer. I said he was the man we wanted. He is. I want him very much. I want him frightfully. I want him as the one thing we haven't got in the whole of this horrible case – a witness!'

They all stared at him, but in a frowning fashion, like men trying to follow a sharp new turn of the argument; and it was he who resumed the argument.

'From the first minute I entered that big empty bar or saloon, I knew that what was the matter with all this business was emptiness; solitude; too many chances for anybody to be alone. In a word, the absence of witnesses. All we knew was that when we came in, the manager and the barman were not in the bar. But when *were* they in the bar? What chance was there of making any sort of timetable of when anybody was anywhere? The whole thing was blank for want of witnesses. I rather fancy the barman or somebody was in the bar just before we came; and that's how the Scotchman got his Scotch whisky. He certainly didn't get it after we came. But we can't begin to enquire whether anybody in the hotel poisoned poor Raggley's cherry brandy, till we really know who was in the bar and when. Now I want you to do me another favour, in spite of this stupid muddle, which is probably all my fault. I want you to collect all the people involved in this room – I think they're all still available, unless the Asiatic has gone back to Asia – and then take the poor Scotchman out of his handcuffs, and bring him in here, and let him tell us who did serve him with whisky, and who was in the bar, and who else was in the room, and all the rest. He's the only man whose evidence can cover just that period when the crime was done. I don't see the slightest reason for doubting his word.'

'But look here,' said Greenwood. 'This brings it all back to the hotel authorities; and I thought you agreed that the manager isn't the murderer. Is it the barman, or what?'

'I don't know,' said the priest blankly. 'I don't know for certain even about the manager. I don't know anything about the barman. I fancy the manager might be a bit of a conspirator, even if he wasn't a murderer. But I do know there's one solitary witness on earth who may have seen something; and that's why I set all your police dogs on his trail to the ends of the earth.'

The mysterious Scotchman, when he finally appeared before the company thus assembled, was certainly a formidable figure; tall, with a hulking stride and a long sardonic hatchet face, with tufts of red hair; and wearing not only an Inverness cape but a Glengarry bonnet, he might well be excused for a somewhat acrid attitude; but anybody could see he was of the sort to resist arrest, even with violence. It was not surprising that he had come to blows with a fighting fellow like Raggley. It was not even surprising that the police had been convinced, by the mere details of capture, that he was a tough and a typical killer. But he claimed to be a perfectly respectable farmer, in Aberdeenshire, his name being James Grant; and somehow not only Father Brown, but Inspector Greenwood, a shrewd man with a great deal of experience, was pretty soon convinced that the Scot's ferocity was the fury of innocence rather than guilt.

'Now what we want from you, Mr Grant,' said the Inspector gravely, dropping without further parley into tones of courtesy, 'is simply your evidence on one very important fact. I am greatly grieved at the misunderstanding by which you have suffered, but I am sure you wish to serve the ends of justice. I believe you came into this bar just after it opened, at half-past five, and were served with a glass of whisky. We are not certain what servant of the hotel, whether the barman or the manager or some subordinate, was in the bar at the time. Will you look round the room, and tell me whether the bar-attendant who served you is present here.'

'Aye, he's present,' said Mr Grant, grimly smiling, having swept the group with a shrewd glance. 'I'd know him anywhere; and ye'll agree he's big enough to be seen. Do ye have all your inn-servants as grand as yon?'

The Inspector's eye remained hard and steady, and his voice colourless and continuous; the face of Father Brown was a blank; but on many other faces there was a cloud; the barman was not particularly big and not at all grand; and the manager was decidedly small.

'We only want the barman identified,' said the Inspector calmly. 'Of course we know him; but we should like you to verify it independently. You mean . . .?' And he stopped suddenly.

'Weel, there he is plain enough,' said the Scotchman wearily; and made a gesture, and with that gesture the gigantic Jukes, the prince of commercial travellers, rose like a trumpeting elephant; and in a flash had three policemen fastened on him like hounds on a wild beast.

'Well, all that was simple enough,' said Father Brown to his friend afterwards. 'As I told you, the instant I entered the empty bar-room, my first thought was that, if the barman left the bar unguarded like that, there was nothing in the world to stop you or me or anybody else lifting the flap and walking in, and putting poison in any of the bottles standing waiting for customers. Of course, a practical poisoner would probably do it as Jukes did, by substituting a poisoned bottle for the ordinary bottle; that could be done in a flash. It was easy enough for him, as he travelled in bottles, to carry a flask of cherry brandy prepared and of the same pattern. Of course, it requires one condition; but it's a fairly common condition. It would hardly do to start poisoning the beer or whisky that scores of people drink; it would cause a massacre. But when a man is well known as drinking only one special thing, like cherry brandy, that isn't very widely drunk, it's just like poisoning him in his own home. Only it's a jolly sight safer. For practically the whole suspicion instantly falls on the hotel, or somebody to do with the hotel; and there's no earthly argument to show that it was done by anyone out of a hundred customers that might come into the bar: even if people realised that a customer could do it. It was about as absolutely anonymous and irresponsible a murder as a man could commit.'

'And why exactly did the murderer commit it?' asked his friend.

Father Brown rose and gravely gathered the papers which he had previously scattered in a moment of distraction.

'May I recall your attention,' he said smiling, 'to the materials of the forthcoming Life and Letters of the Late John Raggley? Or, for that matter, his own spoken words? He said in this very bar that he was going to expose a scandal about the management of hotels; and the scandal was the pretty common one of a corrupt agreement between hotel proprietors and a salesman who took and gave secret commissions, so that his business had a monopoly of all the drink sold in the place. It wasn't even an open slavery like an ordinary tied house; it was a swindle at the expense of everybody the manager was supposed to serve. It was a legal offence. So the ingenious Jukes, taking the first moment when the bar was empty, as it often was, stepped inside and made the exchange of bottles; unfortunately at that very moment a Scotchman in an Inverness cape came in harshly demanding whisky. Jukes saw his only chance was to pretend to be the barman and serve the customer. He was very much relieved that the customer was a Quick One.'

'I think you're rather a Quick One yourself,' observed Greenwood; 'if you say you smelt something at the start, in the mere air of an empty room. Did you suspect Jukes at all at the start?'

'Well, he sounded rather rich somehow,' answered Father Brown vaguely. 'You know when a man has a rich voice. And I did sort of ask myself why he should have such a disgustingly rich voice, when all those honest fellows were fairly poor. But I think I knew he was a sham when I saw that big shining breast-pin.'

'You mean because it was sham?' asked Greenwood doubtfully.

'Oh, no; because it was genuine,' said Father Brown.

The Blast of the Book

Professor Openshaw always lost his temper, with a loud bang, if anybody called him a Spiritualist; or a believer in Spiritualism. This, however, did not exhaust his explosive elements; for he also lost his temper if anybody called him a disbeliever in Spiritualism. It was his pride to have given his whole life to investigating Psychic Phenomena; it was also his pride never to have given a hint of whether he thought they were really psychic or merely phenomenal. He enjoyed nothing so much as to sit in a circle of devout Spiritualists and give devastating descriptions of how he had exposed medium after medium and detected fraud after fraud; for indeed he was a man of much detective talent and insight, when once he had fixed his eye on an object, and he always fixed his eye on a medium, as a highly suspicious object. There was a story of his having spotted the same Spiritualist mountebank under three different disguises: dressed as a woman, a white-bearded old man, and a Brahmin of a rich chocolate brown. These recitals made the true believers rather restless, as indeed they were intended to do; but they could hardly complain, for no Spiritualist denies the existence of fraudulent mediums; only the Professor's flowing narrative might well seem to indicate that all mediums were fraudulent.

But woe to the simple-minded and innocent Materialist (and Materialists as a race are rather innocent and simple-minded) who, presuming on this narrative tendency, should advance the thesis that ghosts were against the laws of nature, or that such things were only old superstitions; or that it was all tosh, or, alternatively, bunk. Him would the Professor, suddenly reversing all his scientific batteries, sweep from the field with a cannonade of unquestionable cases and unexplained phenomena, of which the wretched rationalist had never heard in his life, giving all the dates and details, stating all the attempted and abandoned natural explanations; stating everything, indeed, except whether he, John Oliver Openshaw, did or did not believe in Spirits; and that neither Spiritualist nor Materialist could ever boast of finding out.

Professor Openshaw, a lean figure with pale leonine hair and hypnotic blue eyes, stood exchanging a few words with Father Brown, who was a friend of his, on the steps outside the hotel where both had been breakfasting that morning and sleeping the night before. The Professor had come back rather late from one of this grand experiments, in general exasperation, and was still tingling with the fight that he always waged alone and against both sides.

'Oh, I don't mind you,' he said laughing. 'You don't believe in it even if it's true. But all these people are perpetually asking me what I'm trying to prove. They don't seem to understand that I'm a man of science. A man of science isn't trying to prove anything. He's trying to find out what will prove itself.'

'But he hasn't found out yet,' said Father Brown.

'Well, I have some little notions of my own, that are not quite so negative as most people think,' answered the Professor, after an instant of frowning silence; 'anyhow, I've begun to fancy that if there is something to be found, they're looking for it along the wrong line. It's all too theatrical; it's showing off, all their shiny ectoplasm and trumpets and voices and the rest; all on the model of old melodramas and mouldy historical novels about the Family Ghost. If they'd go to history instead of historical novels, I'm beginning to think they'd really find something. But not Apparitions.'

'After all,' said Father Brown, 'Apparitions are only Appearances. I suppose you'd say the Family Ghost is only keeping up appearances.'

The Professor's gaze, which had commonly a fine abstracted character, suddenly fixed and focused itself as it did on a dubious medium. It had rather the air of a man screwing a strong magnifying-glass into his eye. Not that he thought the priest was in the least like a dubious medium; but he was startled into attention by his friend's thought following so closely on his own.

'Appearances!' he muttered, 'crikey, but it's odd you should say that just now. The more I learn, the more I fancy they lose by merely looking for appearances. Now if they'd look a little into Disappearances – '

'Yes,' said Father Brown, 'after all, the real fairy legends weren't so very much about the appearance of famous fairies; calling up Titania or exhibiting Oberon by moonlight. But there were no end of legends about people *disappearing*, because they were stolen by the fairies. Are you on the track of Kilmeny or Thomas the Rhymer?'

'I'm on the track of ordinary modern people you've read of in the newspapers,' answered Openshaw. 'You may well stare; but that's my game just now; and I've been on it for a long time. Frankly, I think a lot of psychic appearances could be explained away. It's the disappearances I can't explain, unless they're psychic. These people in the newspaper who vanish and are never found – if you knew the details as I do . . . and now only this morning I got confirmation; an extraordinary letter from an old missionary, quite a respectable old boy. He's coming to see me at my office this morning. Perhaps you'd lunch with me or something; and I'd tell the results – in confidence.'

'Thanks; I will – unless,' said Father Brown modestly, 'the fairies have stolen me by then.'

With that they parted and Openshaw walked round the corner to a small office he rented in the neighbourhood; chiefly for the publication of a small periodical, of psychical and psychological notes of the driest and most agnostic sort. He had only one clerk, who sat at a desk in the outer office, totting up figures and facts for the purposes of the printed report; and the Professor paused to ask if Mr Pringle had called. The clerk answered mechanically in the negative and went on mechanically adding up figures; and the Professor turned towards the inner room that was his study. 'Oh, by the way, Berridge,' he added, without turning round, 'if Mr Pringle comes, send him straight in to me. You needn't interrupt your work; I rather want those notes finished tonight if possible. You might leave them on my desk tomorrow, if I am late.'

And he went into his private office, still brooding on the problem which the name of Pringle had raised; or rather, perhaps, had ratified and confirmed in his mind. Even the most perfectly balanced of agnostics is partially human; and it is possible that the missionary's letter seemed to have greater weight as promising to support his private and still tentative hypothesis. He sat down in his large and comfortable chair, opposite the engraving of Montaigne; and read once more the short letter from the Revd Luke Pringle, making the appointment for that morning. No man knew better than Professor Openshaw the marks of the letter of the crank; the crowded details; the spidery handwriting; the unnecessary length and repetition. There were none of these things in this case; but a brief and businesslike typewritten statement that the writer had encountered some curious cases of Disappearance, which seemed to fall within the province of the Professor as a student of psychic problems. The Professor was favourably impressed; nor had he any unfavourable impression, in spite of a slight movement of surprise, when he looked up and saw that the Revd Luke Pringle was already in the room.

'Your clerk told me to come straight in,' said Mr Pringle apologetically, but with a broad and rather agreeable grin. The grin was partly masked by masses of reddish-grey beard and whiskers; a perfect jungle of a beard, such as is sometimes grown by white men living in the jungles; but the eyes above the snub nose had nothing about them in the least wild or outlandish. Openshaw had instantly turned on them that concentrated spotlight or burning-glass of sceptical scrutiny which he turned on many men to see if they were mountebanks or maniacs; and, in this case, he had a rather unusual sense of reassurance. The wild beard might have belonged to a crank, but the eyes completely contradicted the beard; they were full of that quite frank and friendly laughter which is never found in the faces of those who are serious frauds or serious lunatics. He would have expected a man with those eyes to be a Philistine, a jolly sceptic, a man who shouted out shallow but hearty contempt of ghosts and spirits; but anyhow, no professional humbug could afford to look as frivolous as that. The man was buttoned up to the throat in a shabby old cape, and only his broad limp hat suggested the cleric; but missionaries from wild places do not always bother to dress like clerics.

'You probably think all this another hoax, Professor,' said Mr Pringle, with a sort of abstract enjoyment, 'and I hope you will forgive my laughing at your very natural air of disapproval. All the same, I've got to tell my story to somebody who knows, because it's true. And, all joking apart, it's tragic as well as true. Well, to cut it short, I was missionary in Nya-Nya, a station in West Africa, in the thick of the forests, where almost the only other white man was the officer in command of the district, Captain Wales; and he and I grew rather thick. Not that he liked missions; he was, if I may say so, thick in many ways; one of those square-headed, square-shouldered men of action who hardly need to think, let alone believe. That's what makes it all the queerer. One day he came back to his tent in the forest, after a short leave, and said he had gone through a jolly rum experience, and didn't know what to do about it. He was holding a rusty old book in a leather binding, and he put it down on a table beside his revolver and an old Arab sword he kept, probably as a curiosity. He said this book had belonged to a man on the boat he had just come off; and the man swore that nobody must open the book, or look inside it; or else they would be carried off by the devil, or disappear, or something. Wales said this was all nonsense, of course; and they had a quarrel; and the upshot seems to have been that this man, taunted with cowardice or superstition, actually did look into the book; and instantly dropped it; walked to the side of the boat – '

'One moment,' said the Professor, who had made one or two notes. 'Before you tell me anything else. Did this man tell Wales where he had got the book, or who it originally belonged to?'

'Yes,' replied Pringle, now entirely grave. 'It seems he said he was bringing it back to Dr Hankey, the Oriental traveller now in England, to whom it originally belonged, and who had warned him of its strange properties. Well, Hankey is an able man and a rather crabbed and sneering sort of man; which makes it queerer still. But the point of Wales's story is much simpler. It is that the man who had looked into the book walked straight over the side of the ship, and was never seen again.'

'Do you believe it yourself?' asked Openshaw after a pause.

'Well, I do,' replied Pringle. 'I believe it for two reasons. First, that Wales was an entirely unimaginative man; and he added one touch that only an imaginative man could have added. He said that the man walked straight over the side on a still and calm day; but there was no splash.'

The Professor looked at his notes for some seconds in silence; and then said: 'And your other reason for believing it?'

'My other reason,' answered the Revd Luke Pringle, 'is what I saw myself.'

There was another silence; until he continued in the same matter-of-fact way. Whatever he had, he had nothing of the eagerness with which the crank, or even the believer, tried to convince others.

'I told you that Wales put down the book on the table beside the sword. There was only one entrance to the tent; and it happened that I was standing in it, looking out into the forest, with my back to my companion. He was standing by the table grumbling and growling about the whole business; saying it was tomfoolery in the twentieth century to be frightened of opening a book; asking why the devil he shouldn't open it himself. Then some instinct stirred in me and I said he had better not do that, it had better be returned to Dr Hankey. "What harm could it do?" he said restlessly. "What harm did it do?" I answered obstinately. "What happened to your friend on the boat?" He didn't answer, indeed I didn't know what he could answer; but I pressed my logical advantage in mere vanity. "If it comes to that," I said, "what is your version of what really happened on the boat?" Still he didn't answer; and I looked round and saw that he wasn't there.

'The tent was empty. The book was lying on the table; open, but on its face, as if he had turned it downwards. But the sword was lying on the ground near the other side of the tent; and the canvas of the tent showed a great slash, as if somebody had hacked his way out with the sword. The gash in the tent gaped at me; but showed only the dark glimmer of the forest outside. And when I went across and looked through the rent I could not be certain whether the tangle of the tall plants and the undergrowth had been bent or broken; at least not farther than a few feet. I have never seen or heard of Captain Wales from that day.

'I wrapped the book up in brown paper, taking good care not to look at it; and I brought it back to England, intending at first to return it to Dr Hankey. Then I saw some notes in your paper suggesting a hypothesis about such things; and I decided to stop on the way and put the matter before you; as you have a name for being balanced and having an open mind.'

Professor Openshaw laid down his pen and looked steadily at the man on the other side of the table; concentrating in that single stare all his long experience of many entirely different types of humbug, and even some eccentric and extraordinary types of honest men. In the ordinary way, he would have begun with the healthy hypothesis that the story was a pack of lies. On the whole he did incline to assume that it was a pack of lies. And yet he could not fit the man into his story; if it were only that he could not see that sort of liar telling that sort of lie. The man was not trying to look honest on the surface, as most quacks and impostors do; somehow, it seemed all the other way; as if the man *was* honest, in spite of something else that was merely on the surface. He thought of a good man with one innocent delusion; but again the symptoms were not the same; there was even a sort of virile indifference; as if the man did not care much about his delusion, if it was a delusion.

'Mr Pringle,' he said sharply, like a barrister making a witness jump, 'where is this book of yours now?'

The grin reappeared on the bearded face which had grown grave during the recital. 'I left it outside,' said Mr Pringle. 'I mean in the outer office. It was a risk, perhaps; but the less risk of the two.'

'What do you mean?' demanded the Professor. 'Why didn't you bring it straight in here?'

'Because,' answered the missionary, 'I knew that as soon as you saw it, you'd open it – before you had heard the story. I thought it possible you might think twice about opening it – after you'd heard the story.'

Then after a silence he added: 'There was nobody out there but your clerk; and he looked a stolid steady-going specimen, immersed in business calculations.'

Openshaw laughed unaffectedly. 'Oh, Babbage,' he cried, 'your magic tomes are safe enough with him, I assure you. His name's Berridge – but I often call him Babbage; because he's so exactly like a Calculating Machine. No human being, if you can call him a human being, would be less likely to open other people's brown-paper parcels. Well, we may as well go and bring it in now; though I assure you I will consider seriously the course to be taken with it. Indeed, I tell you frankly,' and he stared at the man again, 'that I'm not quite sure whether we ought to open it here and now, or send it to this Dr Hankey.'

The two had passed together out of the inner into the outer office; and even as they did so, Mr Pringle gave a cry and ran forward towards the clerk's desk. For the clerk's desk was there; but not the clerk. On the clerk's desk lay a faded old leather book, torn out of its brown-paper wrappings, and lying closed, but as if it had just been opened. The clerk's desk stood against the wide window that looked out into the street; and the window was shattered with a huge ragged hole in the glass; as if a human body had been shot through it into the world without. There was no other trace of Mr Berridge.

Both the two men left in the office stood as still as statues; and then it was the Professor who slowly came to life. He looked even more judicial than he had ever looked in his life, as he slowly turned and held out his hand to the missionary.

'Mr Pringle,' he said, 'I beg your pardon. I beg your pardon only for thoughts that I have had; and half-thoughts at that. But nobody could call himself a scientific man and not face a fact like this.'

'I suppose,' said Pringle doubtfully, 'that we ought to make some enquiries. Can you ring up his house and find out if he has gone home?'

'I don't know that he's on the telephone,' answered Openshaw, rather absently; 'he lives somewhere up Hampstead way, I think. But I suppose somebody will enquire here, if his friends or family miss him.'

'Could we furnish a description,' asked the other, 'if the police want it?'

'The police!' said the Professor, starting from his reverie. 'A description . . . Well, he looked awfully like everybody else, I'm afraid, except for goggles. One of those clean-shaven chaps. But the police . . . look here, what *are* we to do about this mad business?'

'I know what I ought to do,' said the Revd Mr Pringle firmly, 'I am going to take this book straight to the only original Dr Hankey, and ask him what the devil it's all about. He lives not very far from here, and I'll come straight back and tell you what he says.'

'Oh, very well,' said the Professor at last, as he sat down rather wearily; perhaps relieved for the moment to be rid of the responsibility. But long after the brisk and ringing footsteps of the little missionary had died away down the street, the Professor sat in the same posture, staring into vacancy like a man in a trance.

He was still in the same seat and almost in the same attitude, when the same brisk footsteps were heard on the pavement without and the missionary entered, this time, as a glance assured him, with empty hands.

'Dr Hankey,' said Pringle gravely, 'wants to keep the book for an hour and consider the point. Then he asks us both to call, and he will give us his decision. He specially desired, Professor, that you should accompany me on the second visit.'

Openshaw continued to stare in silence; then he said, suddenly: 'Who the devil is Dr Hankey?'

'You sound rather as if you meant he was the devil,' said Pringle, smiling, 'and I fancy some people have thought so. He had quite a reputation in your own line; but he gained it mostly in India, studying local magic and so on, so perhaps he's not so well known here. He is a yellow skinny little devil with a lame leg, and a doubtful temper; but he seems to have set up in an ordinary respectable practice in these parts, and I don't know anything definitely wrong about him – unless it's wrong to be the only person who can possibly know anything about all this crazy affair.'

Professor Openshaw rose heavily and went to the telephone; he rang up Father Brown, changing the luncheon engagement to a dinner, that he might hold himself free for the expedition to the house of the Anglo-Indian doctor; after that he sat down again, lit a cigar and sank once more into his own unfathomable thoughts.

* * *

Father Brown went round to the restaurant appointed for dinner, and kicked his heels for some time in a vestibule full of mirrors and palms in pots; he had been informed of Openshaw's afternoon engagement, and, as the evening closed-in dark and stormy round the glass and the green plants, guessed that it had produced something unexpected and unduly prolonged. He even wondered for a moment whether the Professor would turn up at all; but when the Professor eventually did, it was clear that his own more general guesses had been justified. For it was a very wild-eyed and even wild-haired Professor who eventually drove back with Mr Pringle from the expedition to the North of London, where suburbs are still fringed with heathy wastes and scraps of common, looking more sombre under the rather thunderstorm sunset. Nevertheless, they had apparently found the house, standing a little apart though within hail of other houses; they had verified the brass-plate duly engraved: 'J. I. Hankey, MC, MRCS'. Only they did not find J. I. Hankey, MC, MRCS. They found only what a nightmare whisper had already subconsciously prepared them to find: a commonplace parlour with the accursed volume lying on the table, as if it had just been read; and beyond, a back door burst open and a faint trail of footsteps that ran a little way up so steep a garden-path that it seemed that no lame man could have run up so lightly. But it was a lame man who had run; for in those few steps there was the misshapen unequal mark of some sort of surgical boot; then two marks of that boot alone (as if the creature had hopped) and then nothing. There was nothing further to be learnt from Dr J. I. Hankey, except that he had made his decision. He had read the oracle and received the doom.

When the two came into the entrance under the palms, Pringle put the book down suddenly on a small table, as if it burned his fingers. The priest glanced at it curiously; there was only some rude lettering on the front with a couplet:

They that looked into this book
Them the Flying Terror took;

and underneath, as he afterwards discovered, similar warnings in Greek, Latin and French. The other two had turned away with a natural impulsion towards drinks, after their exhaustion and bewilderment; and Openshaw had called to the waiter, who brought cocktails on a tray.

'You will dine with us, I hope,' said the Professor to the missionary; but Mr Pringle amiably shook his head.

'If you'll forgive me,' he said, 'I'm going off to wrestle with this book and this business by myself somewhere. I suppose I couldn't use your office for an hour or so?'

'I suppose – I'm afraid it's locked,' said Openshaw in some surprise.

'You forget there's a hole in the window.' The Revd Luke Pringle gave the very broadest of all broad grins and vanished into the darkness without.

'A rather odd fellow, that, after all,' said the Professor, frowning.

He was rather surprised to find Father Brown talking to the waiter who had brought the cocktails, apparently about the waiter's most private affairs; for there was some mention of a baby who was now out of danger. He commented on the fact with some surprise, wondering how the priest came to know the man; but the former only said, 'Oh, I dine here every two or three months, and I've talked to him now and then.'

The Professor, who himself dined there about five times a week, was conscious that he had never thought of talking to the man; but his thoughts were interrupted by a strident ringing and a summons to the telephone. The voice on the telephone said it was Pringle, it was rather a muffled voice, but it might well be muffled in all those bushes of beard and whisker. Its message was enough to establish identity.

'Professor,' said the voice, 'I can't stand it any longer. I'm going to look for myself. I'm speaking from your office and the book is in front of me. If anything happens to me, this is to say goodbye. No – it's no good trying to stop me. You wouldn't be in time anyhow. I'm opening the book now. I . . . '

Openshaw thought he heard something like a sort of thrilling or shivering yet almost soundless crash; then he shouted the name of Pringle again and again; but he heard no more. He hung up the receiver, and, restored to a superb academic calm, rather like the calm of despair, went back and quietly took his seat at the dinner-table. Then, as coolly as if he were describing the failure of some small silly trick at a séance, he told the priest every detail of this monstrous mystery.

'Five men have now vanished in this impossible way,' he said. 'Every one is extraordinary; and yet the one case I simply can't get over is my clerk, Berridge. It's just because he was the quietest creature that he's the queerest case.'

'Yes,' replied Father Brown, 'it was a queer thing for Berridge to do, anyway. He was awfully conscientious. He was also so jolly careful to keep all the office business separate from any fun of his own. Why, hardly anybody knew he was quite a humorist at home and – '

'Berridge!' cried the Professor. 'What on earth are you talking about? Did you know him?'

'Oh no,' said Father Brown carelessly, 'only as you say I know the waiter. I've often had to wait in your office, till you turned up; and of course I passed the time of day with poor Berridge. He was rather a card. I remember he once said he would like to collect valueless things, as collectors did the silly things they thought valuable. You know the old story about the woman who collected valueless things.'

'I'm not sure I know what you're talking about,' said Openshaw. 'But even if my clerk was eccentric (and I never knew a man I should have thought less so), it wouldn't explain what happened to him; and it certainly wouldn't explain the others.'

'What others?' asked the priest.

The Professor stared at him and spoke distinctly, as if to a child: 'My dear Father Brown, Five Men have disappeared.'

'My dear Professor Openshaw, no men have disappeared.'

Father Brown gazed back at his host with equal steadiness and spoke with equal distinctness. Nevertheless, the Professor required the words repeated, and they were repeated as distinctly. 'I say that no men have disappeared.'

After a moment's silence, he added, 'I suppose the hardest thing is to convince anybody that 0 + 0 + 0 = 0. Men believe the oddest things if they are in a series; that is why Macbeth believed the three words of the three witches; though the first was something he knew himself; and the last something he could only bring about himself. But in your case the middle term is the weakest of all.'

'What do you mean?'

'You saw nobody vanish. You did not see the man vanish from the boat. You did not see the man vanish from the tent. All that rests on the word of Mr Pringle, which I will not discuss just now. But you'll admit this; you would never have taken his word yourself, *unless* you had seen it confirmed by your clerk's disappearance; just as Macbeth would never have believed he would be king, if he had not been confirmed in believing he would be Cawdor.'

'That may be true,' said the Professor, nodding slowly. 'But *when* it was confirmed, I knew it was the truth. You say I saw nothing myself. But I did; I saw my own clerk disappear. Berridge did disappear.'

'Berridge did not disappear,' said Father Brown. 'On the contrary.'

'What the devil do you mean by "on the contrary"?'

'I mean,' said Father Brown, 'that he never disappeared. He appeared.'

Openshaw stared across at his friend, but the eyes had already altered in his head, as they did when they concentrated on a new presentation of a problem. The priest went on: 'He appeared in your study, disguised in a bushy red beard and buttoned up in a clumsy cape, and announced himself as the Revd Luke Pringle. And you had never noticed your own clerk enough to know him again, when he was in so rough-and-ready a disguise.'

'But surely,' began the Professor.

'Could you describe him for the police?' asked Father Brown. 'Not you. You probably knew he was clean-shaven and wore tinted glasses; and merely taking off those glasses was a better disguise than putting on anything else. You had never seen his eyes any more than his soul; jolly laughing eyes. He had planted his absurd book and all the properties; then he calmly smashed the window, put on the beard and cape and walked into your study; knowing that you had never looked at him in your life.'

'But why should he play me such an insane trick?' demanded Openshaw.

'Why, *because* you had never looked at him in your life,' said Father Brown; and his hand slightly curled and clinched, as if he might have struck the table, if he had been given to gesture. 'You called him the Calculating Machine, because that was all you ever used him for. You never found out even what a stranger strolling into your office could find out, in five minutes' chat: that he was a character; that he was full of antics; that he had all sorts of views on you and your theories and your reputation for "spotting" people. Can't you understand his itching to prove that you couldn't spot your own clerk? He has nonsense notions of all sorts. About collecting useless things, for instance. Don't you know the story of the woman who bought the two most useless things: an old doctor's brass-plate and a wooden leg? With those your ingenious clerk created the character of the remarkable Dr Hankey; as easily as the visionary Captain Wales. Planting them in his own house – '

'Do you mean that place we visited beyond Hampstead was Berridge's own house?' asked Openshaw.

'Did *you* know his house – or even his address?' retorted the priest. 'Look here, don't think I'm speaking disrespectfully of you or your work. You are a great servant of truth and you know I could never be disrespectful to that. You've seen through a lot of liars, when you put your mind to it. But don't *only* look at liars. Do, just occasionally, look at honest men – like the waiter.'

'Where is Berridge now?' asked the Professor, after a long silence.

'I haven't the least doubt,' said Father Brown, 'that he is back in your office. In fact, he came back into your office at the exact moment when the Revd Luke Pringle read the awful volume and faded into the void.'

There was another long silence and then Professor Openshaw laughed; with the laugh of a great man who is great enough to look small. Then he said abruptly: 'I suppose I do deserve it; for not noticing the nearest helpers I have. But you must admit the accumulation of incidents was rather formidable. Did you *never* feel just a momentary awe of the awful volume?'

'Oh, that,' said Father Brown. 'I opened it as soon as I saw it lying there. It's all blank pages. You see, I am not superstitious.'

The Green Man

A young man in knickerbockers, with an eager sanguine profile, was playing golf against himself on the links that lay parallel to the sand and sea, which were all growing grey with twilight. He was not carelessly knocking a ball about, but rather practising particular strokes with a sort of microscopic fury; like a neat and tidy whirlwind. He had learned many games quickly, but he had a disposition to learn them a little more quickly than they can be learnt. He was rather prone to be a victim of those remarkable invitations by which a man may learn the Violin in Six Lessons – or acquire a perfect French accent by a Correspondence Course. He lived in the breezy atmosphere of such hopeful advertisement and adventure. He was at present the private secretary of Admiral Sir Michael Craven, who owned the big house behind the park abutting on the links. He was ambitious, and had no intention of continuing indefinitely to be private secretary to anybody. But he was also reasonable; and he knew that the best way of ceasing to be a secretary was to be a good secretary. Consequently he was a very good secretary; dealing with the ever-accumulating arrears of the Admiral's correspondence with the same swift centripetal concentration with which he addressed the golf-ball. He had to struggle with the correspondence alone and at his own discretion at present; for the Admiral had been with his ship for the last six months, and, though now returning, was not expected for hours, or possibly days.

With an athletic stride, the young man, whose name was Harold Harker, crested the rise of turf that was the rampart of the links and, looking out across the sands to the sea, saw a strange sight. He did not see it very clearly; for the dusk was darkening every minute under stormy clouds; but it seemed to him, by a sort of momentary illusion, like a dream of days long past or a drama played by ghosts, out of another age in history.

The last of the sunset lay in long bars of copper and gold above the last dark strip of sea that seemed rather black than blue. But blacker still against this gleam in the west, there passed in sharp outline, like figures in a shadow pantomime, two men with three-cornered cocked hats and swords; as if they had just landed from one of the wooden ships of Nelson. It was not at all the sort of hallucination that would have come natural to Mr Harker, had he been prone to hallucinations. He was of the type that is at once sanguine and scientific; and would be more likely to fancy the flying ships of the future than the fighting ships of the past. He therefore very sensibly came to the conclusion that even a futurist can believe his eyes.

His illusion did not last more than a moment. On the second glance, what he saw was unusual but not incredible. The two men who were striding in single file across the sands, one some fifteen yards behind the other, were ordinary modern naval officers; but naval officers wearing that almost extravagant full-dress uniform which naval officers never do wear if they can possibly help it; only on great ceremonial occasions such as the visits of Royalty. In the man walking in front, who seemed more or less unconscious of the man walking behind, Harker recognised at once the high-bridged nose and spike-shaped beard of his own employer the Admiral. The other man following in his tracks he did not know. But he did know something about the circumstances connected with the ceremonial occasion. He knew that when the Admiral's ship put in at the adjacent port, it was to be formally visited by a Great Personage; which was enough, in that sense, to explain the officers being in full dress. But he did also know the officers; or at any rate the Admiral. And what could have possessed the Admiral to come on shore in that rig-out, when one could swear he would seize five minutes to change into mufti or at least into undress uniform, was more than his secretary could conceive. It seemed somehow to be the very last thing he would do. It was indeed to remain for many weeks one of the chief mysteries of this mysterious business. As it was, the outline of these fantastic court uniforms against the empty scenery, striped with dark sea and sand, had something suggestive of comic opera; and reminded the spectator of *Pinafore*.

The second figure was much more singular; somewhat singular in appearance, despite his correct lieutenant's uniform, and still more extraordinary in behaviour. He walked in a strangely irregular and uneasy manner; sometimes quickly and sometimes slowly; as if he could not make up his mind whether to overtake the Admiral or not. The Admiral was rather deaf and certainly heard no footsteps behind him on the yielding sand; but the footsteps behind him, if traced in the detective manner, would have given rise to twenty conjectures from a limp to a dance. The man's face was swarthy as well as darkened with shadow, and every now and then the eyes in it shifted and shone, as if to accent his agitation. Once he began to run and then abruptly relapsed into a swaggering slowness and carelessness. Then he did something which Mr Harker could never have conceived any normal naval officer in His Britannic Majesty's Service doing, even in a lunatic asylum. He drew his sword.

It was at this bursting-point of the prodigy that the two passing figures disappeared behind a headland on the shore. The staring secretary had just time to notice the swarthy stranger, with a resumption of carelessness, knock off a head of sea-holly with his glittering blade. He seemed then to have abandoned all idea of catching the other man up. But Mr Harold Harker's face became very thoughtful indeed; and he stood there ruminating for some time before he gravely took himself inland, towards the road that ran past the gates of the great house and so by a long curve down to the sea.

It was up this curving road from the coast that the Admiral might be expected to come, considering the direction in which he had been walking, and making the natural assumption that he was bound for his own door. The path along the sands, under the links, turned inland just beyond the headland and solidifying itself into a road, returned towards Craven House. It was down this road, therefore, that the secretary darted, with characteristic impetuosity, to meet his patron returning home. But the patron was apparently not returning home. What was still more peculiar, the secretary was not returning home either; at least until many hours later; a delay quite long enough to arouse alarm and mystification at Craven House.

Behind the pillars and palms of that rather too palatial country house, indeed, there was expectancy gradually changing to uneasiness. Gryce the butler, a big bilious man abnormally silent below as well as above stairs, showed a certain restlessness as he moved about the main front-hall and occasionally looked out of the side windows of the porch, on the white road that swept towards the sea. The Admiral's sister Marion, who kept house for him, had her brother's high nose with a more sniffy expression; she was voluble, rather rambling, not without humour, and capable of sudden emphasis as shrill as a cockatoo. The Admiral's daughter Olive was dark, dreamy, and as a rule abstractedly silent, perhaps melancholy; so that her aunt generally conducted most of the conversation, and that without reluctance. But the girl also had a gift of sudden laughter that was very engaging.

'I can't think why they're not here already,' said the elder lady. 'The postman distinctly told me he'd seen the Admiral coming along the beach; along with that dreadful creature Rook. Why in the world they call him Lieutenant Rook – '

'Perhaps,' suggested the melancholy young lady, with a momentary brightness, 'perhaps they call him Lieutenant because he is a Lieutenant.'

'I can't think why the Admiral keeps him,' snorted her aunt, as if she were talking of a housemaid. She was very proud of her brother and always called him the Admiral; but her notions of a commission in the Senior Service were inexact.

'Well, Roger Rook is sulky and unsociable and all that,' replied Olive, 'but of course that wouldn't prevent him being a capable sailor.'

'Sailor!' cried her aunt with one of her rather startling cockatoo notes, 'he isn't my notion of a sailor. The Lass that Loved a Sailor, as they used to sing when I was young . . . Just think of it! He's not gay and free and whats-its-name. He doesn't sing chanties or dance a hornpipe.'

'Well,' observed her niece with gravity. 'The Admiral doesn't very often dance a hornpipe.'

'Oh, you know what I mean – he isn't bright or breezy or anything,' replied the old lady. 'Why, that secretary fellow could do better than that.'

Olive's rather tragic face was transfigured by one of her good and rejuvenating waves of laughter.

'I'm sure Mr Harker would dance a hornpipe for you,' she said, 'and say he had learnt it in half an hour from the book of instructions. He's always learning things of that sort.'

She stopped laughing suddenly and looked at her aunt's rather strained face.

'I can't think why Mr Harker doesn't come,' she added.

'I don't care about Mr Harker,' replied the aunt, and rose and looked out of the window.

The evening light had long turned from yellow to grey and was now turning almost to white under the widening moonlight, over the large flat landscape by the coast; unbroken by any features save a clump of sea-twisted trees round a pool and beyond, rather gaunt and dark against the horizon, the shabby fishermen's tavern on the shore that bore the name of the Green Man. And all that road and landscape was empty of any living thing. Nobody had seen the figure in the cocked hat that had been observed, earlier in the evening, walking by the sea; or the other and stranger figure that had been seen trailing after him. Nobody had even seen the secretary who saw them.

It was after midnight when the secretary at last burst in and aroused the household; and his face, white as a ghost, looked all the paler against the background of the stolid face and figure of a big Inspector of Police. Somehow that red, heavy, indifferent face looked, even more than the white and harassed one, like a mask of doom. The news was broken to the two women with such consideration or concealments as were possible. But the news was that the body of Admiral Craven had been eventually fished out of the foul weeds and scum of the pool under the trees; and that he was drowned and dead.

* * *

Anybody acquainted with Mr Harold Harker, secretary, will realise that, whatever his agitation, he was by morning in a mood to be tremendously on the spot. He hustled the Inspector, whom he had met the night before on the road down by the Green Man, into another room for private and practical consultation. He questioned the Inspector rather as the Inspector might have questioned a yokel. But Inspector Burns was a stolid character; and was either too stupid or too clever to resent such trifles. It soon began to look as if he were by no means so stupid as he looked; for he disposed of Harker's eager questions in a manner that was slow but methodical and rational.

'Well,' said Harker (his head full of many manuals with titles like 'Be a Detective in Ten Days'). 'Well, it's the old triangle, I suppose. Accident, Suicide or Murder.'

'I don't see how it could be accident,' answered the policeman. 'It wasn't even dark yet and the pool's fifty yards from the straight road that he knew like his own doorstep. He'd no more have got into that pond than he'd go and carefully lie down in a puddle in the street. As for suicide, it's rather a responsibility to suggest it, and rather improbable too. The Admiral was a pretty spry and successful man and frightfully rich, nearly a millionaire in fact; though of course that doesn't prove anything. He seemed to be pretty normal and comfortable in his private life too; he's the last man I should suspect of drowning himself.'

'So that we come,' said the secretary, lowering his voice with the thrill, 'I suppose we come to the third possibility.'

'We won't be in too much of a hurry about that,' said the Inspector to the annoyance of Harker, who was in a hurry about everything. 'But naturally there are one or two things one would like to know. One would like to know about his property, for instance. Do you know who's likely to come in for it? You're his private secretary; do you know anything about his will?'

'I'm not so private a secretary as all that,' answered the young man. 'His solicitors are Messrs Willis, Hardman and Dyke, over in Suttford High Street; and I believe the will is in their custody.'

'Well, I'd better get round and see them pretty soon,' said the Inspector.

'Let's get round and see them at once,' said the impatient secretary.

He took a turn or two restlessly up and down the room and then exploded in a fresh place.

'What have you done about the body, Inspector?' he asked.

'Dr Straker is examining it now at the police station. His report ought to be ready in an hour or so.'

'It can't be ready too soon,' said Harker. 'It would save time if we could meet him at the lawyer's.' Then he stopped and his impetuous tone changed abruptly to one of some embarrassment.

'Look here,' he said, 'I want . . . we want to consider the young lady, the poor Admiral's daughter, as much as possible just now. She's got a notion that may be all nonsense; but I wouldn't like to disappoint her. There's some friend of hers she wants to consult, staying in the town at present. Man of the name of Brown; priest or parson of some sort – she's given me his address. I don't take much stock in priests or parsons, but – '

The Inspector nodded. 'I don't take any stock in priests or parsons; but I take a lot of stock in Father Brown,' he said. 'I happened to have to do with him in a queer sort of society jewel case. He ought to have been a policeman instead of a parson.'

'Oh, all right,' said the breathless secretary as he vanished from the room. 'Let him come to the lawyer's too.'

Thus it happened that, when they hurried across to the neighbouring town to meet Dr Straker at the solicitor's office, they found Father Brown already seated there, with his hands folded on his heavy umbrella, chatting pleasantly to the only available member of the firm. Dr Straker also had arrived, but apparently only at that moment, as he was carefully placing his gloves in his top hat and his top hat on a side-table. And the mild and beaming expression of the priest's moonlike face and spectacles, together with the silent chuckles of the jolly old grizzled lawyer, to whom he was talking, were enough to show that the doctor had not yet opened his mouth to bring the news of death.

'A beautiful morning after all,' Father Brown was saying. 'That storm seems to have passed over us. There were some big black clouds, but I notice that not a drop of rain fell.'

'Not a drop,' agreed the solicitor toying with a pen; he was the third partner, Mr Dyke; 'there's not a cloud in the sky now. It's the sort of day for a holiday.' Then he realised the newcomers and looked up, laying down the pen and rising. 'Ah, Mr Harker, how are you? I hear the Admiral is expected home soon.' Then Harker spoke, and his voice rang hollow in the room.

'I am sorry to say we are the bearers of bad news. Admiral Craven was drowned before reaching home.'

There was a change in the very air of the still office, though not in the attitudes of the motionless figures; both were staring at the speaker as if a joke had been frozen on their lips. Both repeated the word 'drowned' and looked at each other, and then again at their informant. Then there was a small hubbub of questions.

'When did this happen?' asked the priest.

'Where was he found?' asked the lawyer.

'He was found,' said the Inspector, 'in that pool by the coast, not far from the Green Man, and dragged out all covered with green scum and weeds so as to be almost unrecognisable. But Dr Straker here has – What is the matter, Father Brown? Are you ill?'

'The Green Man,' said Father Brown with a shudder. 'I'm so sorry . . . I beg your pardon for being upset.'

'Upset by what?' asked the staring officer.

'By his being covered with green scum, I suppose,' said the priest, with a rather shaky laugh. Then he added rather more firmly, 'I thought it might have been seaweed.'

By this time everybody was looking at the priest, with a not unnatural suspicion that he was mad; and yet the next crucial surprise was not to come from him. After a dead silence, it was the doctor who spoke.

Dr Straker was a remarkable man, even to look at. He was very tall and angular, formal and professional in his dress; yet retaining a fashion that has hardly been known since Mid-Victorian times. Though comparatively young, he wore his brown beard very long and spreading over his waistcoat; in contrast with it, his features, which were both harsh and handsome, looked singularly pale. His good looks were also diminished by something in his deep eyes that was not squinting, but like the shadow of a squint. Everybody noticed these things about him, because the moment he spoke, he gave forth an indescribable air of authority. But all he said was: 'There is one more thing to be said, if you come to details, about Admiral Craven being drowned.' Then he added reflectively, 'Admiral Craven was not drowned.'

The Inspector turned with quite a new promptitude and shot a question at him.

'I have just examined the body,' said Dr Straker; 'the cause of death was a stab through the heart with some pointed blade like a stiletto. It was after death, and even some little time after, that the body was hidden in the pool.'

Father Brown was regarding Dr Straker with a very lively eye, such as he seldom turned upon anybody; and when the group in the office began to break up, he managed to attach himself to the medical man for a little further conversation, as they went back down the street. There had not been very much else to detain them except the rather formal question of the will. The impatience of the young secretary had been somewhat tried by the professional etiquette of the old lawyer. But the latter was ultimately induced, rather by the tact of the priest than the authority of the policeman, to refrain from making a mystery where there was no mystery at all. Mr Dyke admitted, with a smile, that the Admiral's will was a very normal and ordinary document, leaving everything to his only child Olive; and that there really was no particular reason for concealing the fact.

The doctor and the priest walked slowly down the street that struck out of the town in the direction of Craven House. Harker had plunged on ahead of him with all his native eagerness to get somewhere; but the two behind seemed more interested in their discussion than their direction. It was in rather an enigmatic tone that the tall doctor said to the short cleric beside him: 'Well, Father Brown, what do you think of a thing like this?'

Father Brown looked at him rather intently for an instant, and then said: 'Well, I've begun to think of one or two things; but my chief difficulty is that I only knew the Admiral slightly; though I've seen something of his daughter.'

'The Admiral,' said the doctor with a grim immobility of feature, 'was the sort of man of whom it is said that he had not an enemy in the world.'

'I suppose you mean,' answered the priest, 'that there's something else that will not be said.'

'Oh, it's no affair of mine,' said Straker hastily but rather harshly. 'He had his moods, I suppose. He once threatened me with a legal action about an operation; but I think he thought better of it. I can imagine his being rather rough with a subordinate.'

Father Brown's eyes were fixed on the figure of the secretary striding far ahead; and as he gazed he realised the special cause of his hurry. Some fifty yards farther ahead the Admiral's daughter was dawdling along the road towards the Admiral's house. The secretary soon came abreast of her; and for the remainder of the time Father Brown watched the silent drama of two human backs as they diminished into the distance. The secretary was evidently very much excited about something; but if the priest guessed what it was, he kept it to himself. When he came to the corner leading to the doctor's house, he only said briefly: 'I don't know if you have anything more to tell us.'

'Why should I?' answered the doctor very abruptly; and striding off, left it uncertain whether he was asking why he should have anything to tell, or why he should tell it.

Father Brown went stumping on alone, in the track of the two young people; but when he came to the entrance and avenues of the Admiral's park, he was arrested by the action of the girl, who turned suddenly and came straight towards him; her face unusually pale and her eyes bright with some new and as yet nameless emotion.

'Father Brown,' she said in a low voice, 'I must talk to you as soon as possible. You must listen to me, I can't see any other way out.'

'Why certainly,' he replied, as coolly as if a gutter-boy had asked him the time. 'Where shall we go and talk?'

The girl led him at random to one of the rather tumbledown arbours in the grounds; and they sat down behind a screen of large ragged leaves. She began instantly, as if she must relieve her feelings or faint.

'Harold Harker,' she said, 'has been talking to me about things. Terrible things.'

The priest nodded and the girl went on hastily. 'About Roger Rook. Do you know about Roger?'

'I've been told,' he answered, 'that his fellow-seamen call him the Jolly Roger, because he is never jolly; and looks like the pirate's skull and cross-bones.'

'He was not always like that,' said Olive in a low voice. 'Something very queer must have happened to him. I knew him well when we were children; we used to play over there on the sands. He was harum-scarum and always talking about being a pirate; I dare say he was the sort they say might take to crime through reading shockers; but there was something poetical in his way of being piratical. He really was a Jolly Roger then. I suppose he was the last boy who kept up the old legend of really running away to sea; and at last his family had to agree to his joining the Navy. Well . . .'

'Yes,' said Father Brown patiently.

'Well,' she admitted, caught in one of her rare moments of mirth, 'I suppose poor Roger found it disappointing. Naval officers so seldom carry knives in their teeth or wave bloody cutlasses and black flags. But that doesn't explain the change in him. He just stiffened; grew dull and dumb, like a dead man walking about. He always avoids me; but that doesn't matter. I supposed some great grief that's no business of mine had broken him up. And now – well, if what Harold says is true, the grief is neither more nor less than going mad; or being possessed of a devil.'

'And what does Harold say?' asked the priest.

'It's so awful I can hardly say it,' she answered. 'He swears he saw Roger creeping behind my father that night; hesitating and then drawing his sword . . . and the doctor says father was stabbed with a steel point . . . I can't believe Roger Rook had anything to do with it. His sulks and my father's temper sometimes led to quarrels; but what are quarrels? I can't exactly say I'm standing up for an old friend; because he isn't even friendly. But you can't help feeling sure of some things, even about an old acquaintance. And yet Harold swears that he –'

'Harold seems to swear a great deal,' said Father Brown.

There was a sudden silence; after which she said in a different tone: 'Well, he does swear other things too. Harold Harker proposed to me just now.'

'Am I to congratulate you, or rather him?' enquired her companion.

'I told him he must wait. He isn't good at waiting.' She was caught again in a ripple of her incongruous sense of the comic: 'He said I was his ideal and his ambition and so on. He has lived in the States; but somehow I never remember it when he is talking about dollars; only when he is talking about ideals.'

'And I suppose,' said Father Brown very softy, 'that it is because you have to decide about Harold that you want to know the truth about Roger.'

She stiffened and frowned, and then equally abruptly smiled, saying: 'Oh, you know too much.'

'I know very little, especially in this affair,' said the priest gravely. 'I only know who murdered your father.' She started up and stood staring down at him stricken white. Father Brown made a wry face as he went on: 'I made a fool of myself when I first realised it; when they'd just been asking where he was found, and went on talking about green scum and the Green Man.'

Then he also rose; clutching his clumsy umbrella with a new resolution, he addressed the girl with a new gravity.

'There is something else that I know, which is the key to all these riddles of yours; but I won't tell you yet. I suppose it's bad news; but it's nothing like so bad as the things you have been fancying.' He buttoned up his coat and turned towards the gate. 'I'm going to see this Mr Rook of yours. In a shed by the shore, near where Mr Harker saw him walking. I rather think he lives there.' And he went bustling off in the direction of the beach.

Olive was an imaginative person; perhaps too imaginative to be safely left to brood over such hints as her friend had thrown out; but he was in rather a hurry to find the best relief for her broodings. The mysterious connection between Father Brown's first shock of enlightenment and the chance language about the pool and the inn, hag-rode her fancy in a hundred forms of ugly symbolism. The Green Man became a ghost trailing loathsome weeds and walking the countryside under the moon; the sign of the Green Man became a human figure hanging as from a gibbet; and the tarn itself became a tavern, a dark subaqueous tavern for the dead sailors. And yet he had taken the most rapid method to overthrow all such nightmares, with a burst of blinding daylight which seemed more mysterious than the night.

For before the sun had set, something had come back into her life that turned her whole world topsy-turvy once more; something she had hardly known that she desired until it was abruptly granted; something that was, like a dream, old and familiar, and yet remained incomprehensible and incredible. For Roger Rook had come striding across the sands, and even when he was a dot in the distance, she knew he was transfigured; and as he came nearer and nearer, she saw that his dark face was alive with laughter and exultation. He came straight towards her, as if they had never parted, and seized her shoulders saying: 'Now I can look after you, thank God.'

She hardly knew what she answered; but she heard herself questioning rather wildly why he seemed so changed and so happy.

'Because I am happy,' he answered. 'I have heard the bad news.'

* * *

All parties concerned, including some who seemed rather unconcerned, found themselves assembled on the garden-path leading to Craven House, to hear the formality, now truly formal, of the lawyer's reading of the will; and the probable, and more practical sequel of the lawyer's advice upon the crisis. Besides the grey-haired solicitor himself, armed with the testamentary document, there was the Inspector armed with more direct authority touching the crime, and Lieutenant Rook in undisguised attendance on the lady; some were rather mystified on seeing the tall figure of the doctor, some smiled a little on seeing the dumpy figure of the priest. Mr Harker, that Flying Mercury, had shot down to the lodge-gates to meet them, led them back on to the lawn, and then dashed ahead of them again to prepare their reception. He said he would be back in a jiffy; and anyone observing his piston-rod of energy could well believe it; but, for the moment, they were left rather stranded on the lawn outside the house.

'Reminds me of somebody making runs at cricket,' said the Lieutenant.

'That young man,' said the lawyer, 'is rather annoyed that the law cannot move quite so quickly as he does. Fortunately Miss Craven understands our professional difficulties and delays. She has kindly assured me that she still has confidence in my slowness.'

'I wish,' said the doctor, suddenly, 'that I had as much confidence in his quickness.'

'Why, what do you mean?' asked Rook, knitting his brows; 'do you mean that Harker is too quick?'

'Too quick and too slow,' said Dr Straker, in his rather cryptic fashion. 'I know one occasion at least when he was not so very quick. Why was he hanging about half the night by the pond and the Green Man, before the Inspector came down and found the body? Why did he meet the Inspector? Why should he expect to meet the Inspector outside the Green Man?'

'I don't understand you,' said Rook. 'Do you mean that Harker wasn't telling the truth?'

Dr Straker was silent. The grizzled lawyer laughed with grim good humour. 'I have nothing more serious to say against the young man,' he said, 'than that he made a prompt and praiseworthy attempt to teach me my own business.'

'For that matter, he made an attempt to teach me mine,' said the Inspector, who had just joined the group in front. 'But that doesn't matter. If Dr Straker means anything by his hints, they do matter. I must ask you to speak plainly, doctor. It may be my duty to question him at once.'

'Well, here he comes,' said Rook, as the alert figure of the secretary appeared once more in the doorway.

At this point Father Brown, who had remained silent and inconspicuous at the tail of the procession, astonished everybody very much; perhaps especially those who knew him. He not only walked rapidly to the front, but turned facing the whole group with an arresting and almost threatening expression, like a sergeant bringing soldiers to the halt.

'Stop!' he said almost sternly. 'I apologise to everybody; but it's absolutely necessary that I should see Mr Harker first. I've got to tell him something I know; and I don't think anybody else knows; something he's got to hear. It may save a very tragic misunderstanding with somebody later on.'

'What on earth do you mean?' asked old Dyke the lawyer.

'I mean the bad news,' said Father Brown.

'Here, I say,' began the Inspector indignantly; and then suddenly caught the priest's eye and remembered strange things he had seen in other days. 'Well, if it were anyone in the world but you I should say of all the infernal cheek – '

But Father Brown was already out of hearing, and a moment afterwards was plunged in talk with Harker in the porch. They walked to and fro together for a few paces and then disappeared into the dark interior. It was about twelve minutes afterwards that Father Brown came out alone.

To their surprise he showed no disposition to re-enter the house, now that the whole company were at last about to enter it. He threw himself down on the rather rickety seat in the leafy arbour, and as the procession disappeared through the doorway, lit a pipe and proceeded to stare vacantly at the long ragged leaves about his head and to listen to the birds. There was no man who had a more hearty and enduring appetite for doing nothing.

He was, apparently, in a cloud of smoke and a dream of abstraction, when the front doors were once more flung open and two or three figures came out helter-skelter, running towards him, the daughter of the house and her young admirer Mr Rook being easily winners in the race. Their faces were alight with astonishment; and the face of Inspector Burns, who advanced more heavily behind them, like an elephant shaking the garden, was inflamed with some indignation as well.

'What *can* all this mean?' cried Olive, as she came panting to a halt. 'He's gone!'

'Bolted!' said the Lieutenant explosively. 'Harker's just managed to pack a suitcase and bolted! Gone clean out of the back door and over the garden-wall to God knows where. What *did* you say to him?'

'Don't be silly!' said Olive, with a more worried expression. 'Of course you told him you'd found him out, and now he's gone. I never could have believed he was wicked like that!'

'Well!' gasped the Inspector, bursting into their midst. 'What have you done now? What have you let me down like this for?'

'Well,' repeated Father Brown, 'what have I done?'

'You have let a murderer escape,' cried Burns, with a decision that was like a thunderclap in the quiet garden; 'you have *helped* a murderer to escape. Like a fool I let you warn him; and now he is miles away.'

'I have helped a few murderers in my time, it is true,' said Father Brown; then he added, in careful distinction, 'not, you will understand, helped them to commit the murder.'

'But you knew all the time,' insisted Olive. 'You guessed from the first that it must be he. That's what you meant about being upset by the business of finding the body. That's what the doctor meant by saying my father might be disliked by a subordinate.'

'That's what I complain of,' said the official indignantly. 'You knew even then that he was the – '

'You knew even then,' insisted Olive, 'that the murderer was – '

Father Brown nodded gravely. 'Yes,' he said. 'I knew even then that the murderer was old Dyke.'

'Was *who*?' repeated the Inspector and stopped amid a dead silence; punctuated only by the occasional pipe of birds.

'I mean Mr Dyke, the solicitor,' explained Father Brown, like one explaining something elementary to an infant class. 'That gentleman with grey hair who's supposed to be going to read the will.'

They all stood like statues staring at him, as he carefully filled his pipe again and struck a match. At last Burns rallied his vocal powers to break the strangling silence with an effort resembling violence.

'But, in the name of heaven, *why*?'

'Ah, why?' said the priest and rose thoughtfully, puffing at his pipe. 'As to why he did it . . . Well, I suppose the time has come to tell you, or those of you who don't know, the fact that is the key of all this business. It's a great calamity; and it's a great crime; but it's not the murder of Admiral Craven.'

He looked Olive full in the face and said very seriously: 'I tell you the bad news bluntly and in few words; because I think you are brave enough, and perhaps happy enough, to take it well. You have the chance, and I think the power, to be something like a great woman. You are not a great heiress.'

Amid the silence that followed it was he who resumed his explanation.

'Most of your father's money, I am sorry to say, has gone. It went by the financial dexterity of the grey-haired gentleman named Dyke, who is (I grieve to say) a swindler. Admiral Craven was murdered to silence him about the way in which he was swindled. The fact that he was ruined and you were disinherited is the single simple clue, not only to the murder, but to all the other mysteries in this business.' He took a puff or two and then continued.

'I told Mr Rook you were disinherited and he rushed back to help you. Mr Rook is a rather remarkable person.'

'Oh, chuck it,' said Mr Rook with a hostile air.

'Mr Rook is a monster,' said Father Brown with scientific calm. 'He is an anachronism, an atavism, a brute survival of the Stone Age. If there was one barbarous superstition we all supposed to be utterly extinct and dead in these days, it was that notion about honour and independence. But then I get mixed up with so many dead superstitions. Mr Rook is an extinct animal. He is a plesiosaurus. He did not want to live on his wife or have a wife who could call him a fortune-hunter. Therefore he sulked in a grotesque manner and only came to life again when I brought him the good news that you were ruined. He wanted to work for his wife and not be kept by her. Disgusting, isn't it? Let us turn to the brighter topic of Mr Harker.

'I told Mr Harker you were disinherited and he rushed away in a sort of panic. Do not be too hard on Mr Harker. He really had better as well as worse enthusiasms; but he had them all mixed up. There is no harm in having ambitions; but he had ambitions and called them ideals. The old sense of honour taught men to suspect success; to say, "This is a benefit; it may be a bribe." The new nine-times-accursed nonsense about Making Good teaches men to identify being good with making money. That was all that was the matter with him; in every other way he was a thoroughly good fellow, and there are thousands like him. Gazing at the stars and rising in the world were all Uplift. Marrying a good wife and marring a rich wife were all Making Good. But he was not a cynical scoundrel; or he would simply have come back and jilted or cut you as the case might be. He could not face you; while you were there, half of his broken ideal was left.

'I did not tell the Admiral; but somebody did. Word came to him somehow, during the last grand parade on board, that his friend the family lawyer had betrayed him. He was in such a towering passion that he did what he could never have done in his senses; came straight on shore in his cocked hat and gold lace to catch the criminal; he wired to the police station, and that was why the Inspector was wandering round the Green Man. Lieutenant Rook followed him on shore because he suspected some family trouble and had half a hope he might help and put himself right. Hence his hesitating behaviour. As for his drawing his sword when he dropped behind and thought he was alone, well that's a matter of imagination. He was a romantic person who had dreamed of swords and run away to sea; and found himself in a service where he wasn't even allowed to wear a sword except about once in three years. He thought he was quite alone on the sands where he played as a boy. If you don't understand what he did, I can only say, like Stevenson, "you will never be a pirate". Also you will never be a poet; and you have never been a boy.'

'I never have,' answered Olive gravely, 'and yet I think I understand.'

'Almost every man,' continued the priest musing, 'will play with anything shaped like a sword or dagger, even if it is a paper-knife. That is why I thought it so odd when the lawyer didn't.'

'What do you mean?' asked Burns, 'didn't what?'

'Why, didn't you notice,' answered Brown, 'at that first meeting in the office, the lawyer played with a pen and not with a paper-knife; though he had a beautiful bright steel paper-knife in the pattern of a stiletto? The pens were dusty and splashed with ink; but the knife had just been cleaned. But he did not play with it. There are limits to the irony of assassins.'

After a silence the Inspector said, like one waking from a dream: 'Look here . . . I don't know whether I'm on my head or my heels; I don't know whether you think you've got to the end; but I haven't got to the beginning. Where do you get all this lawyer stuff from? What started you out on that trail?'

Father Brown laughed curtly and without mirth.

'The murderer made a slip at the start,' he said, 'and I can't think why nobody else noticed it. When you brought the first news of the death to the solicitor's office, nobody was supposed to know anything there, except that the Admiral was expected home. When you said he was drowned, I asked when it happened and Mr Dyke asked where the corpse was found.'

He paused a moment to knock out his pipe and resumed reflectively: 'Now when you are simply told of a seaman, returning from the sea, that he has been drowned, it is natural to assume that he has been drowned at sea. At any rate, to allow that he may have been drowned at sea. If he had been washed overboard, or gone down with his ship, or had his body committed to the deep, there would be no reason to expect his body to be found at all. The moment that man asked where it was found, I was sure he knew where it was found. Because he had put it there. Nobody but the murderer need have thought of anything so unlikely as a seaman being drowned in a landlocked pool a few hundred yards from the sea. That is why I suddenly felt sick and turned green, I dare say; as green as the Green Man. I never *can* get used to finding myself suddenly sitting beside a murderer. So I had to turn it off by talking in parables; but the parable meant something, after all. I said that the body was covered with green scum, but it might just as well have been seaweed.'

* * *

It is fortunate that tragedy can never kill comedy and that the two can run side by side; and that while the only acting partner of the business of Messrs Willis, Hardman and Dyke blew his brains out when the Inspector entered the house to arrest him, Olive and Roger were calling to each other across the sands at evening, as they did when they were children together.

The Pursuit of Mr Blue

Along a seaside parade on a sunny afternoon, a person with the depressing name of Muggleton was moving with suitable gloom. There was a horseshoe of worry in his forehead, and the numerous groups and strings of entertainers stretched along the beach below looked up to him in vain for applause. Pierrots turned up their pale moon faces, like the white bellies of dead fish, without improving his spirits; niggers with faces entirely grey with a sort of grimy soot were equally unsuccessful in filling his fancy with brighter things. He was a sad and disappointed man. His other features, besides the bald brow with its furrow, were retiring and almost sunken; and a certain dingy refinement about them made more incongruous the one aggressive ornament of his face. It was an outstanding and bristling military moustache; and it looked suspiciously like a false moustache. It is possible, indeed, that it was a false moustache. It is possible, on the other hand, that even if it was not false it was forced. He might almost have grown it in a hurry, by a mere act of will; so much was it a part of his job rather than his personality.

For the truth is that Mr Muggleton was a private detective in a small way, and the cloud on his brow was due to a big blunder in his professional career; anyhow it was connected with something darker than the mere possession of such a surname. He might almost, in an obscure sort of way, have been proud of his surname; for he came of poor but decent Nonconformist people who claimed some connection with the founder of the Muggletonians; the only man who had hitherto had the courage to appear with that name in human history.

The more legitimate cause of his annoyance (at least as he himself explained it) was that he had just been present at the bloody murder of a world-famous millionaire, and had failed to prevent it, though he had been engaged at a salary of five pounds a week to do so. Thus we may explain the fact that even the languorous singing of the song entitled, 'Won't You be My Loodah Doodah Day?' failed to fill him with the joy of life.

For that matter, there were others on the beach, who might have had more sympathy with his murderous theme and Muggletonian tradition. Seaside resorts are the chosen pitches, not only of pierrots appealing to the amorous emotions, but also of preachers who often seem to specialise in a correspondingly sombre and sulphurous style of preaching. There was one aged ranter whom he could hardly help noticing, so piercing were the cries, not to say shrieks of religious prophecy that rang above all the banjos and castanets. This was a long, loose, shambling old man, dressed in something like a fisherman's jersey; but inappropriately equipped with a pair of those very long and drooping whiskers which have never been seen since the disappearance of certain sportive Mid-Victorian dandies. As it was the custom for all mountebanks on the beach to display something, as if they were selling it, the old man displayed a rather rotten-looking fisherman's net, which he generally spread out invitingly on the sands, as if it were a carpet for queens; but occasionally whirled wildly round his head with a gesture almost as terrific as that of the Roman Retiarius, ready to impale people on a trident. Indeed, he might really have impaled people, if he had had a trident. His words were always pointed towards punishment; his hearers heard nothing except threats to the body or the soul; he was so far in the same mood as Mr Muggleton, that he might almost have been a mad hangman addressing a crowd of murderers. The boys called him Old Brimstone; but he had other eccentricities besides the purely theological. One of his eccentricities was to climb up into the nest of iron girders under the pier and trail his net in the water, declaring that he got his living by fishing; though it is doubtful whether anybody had ever seen him catching fish. Worldly trippers, however, would sometimes start at a voice in their ear, threatening judgement as from a thundercloud, but really coming from the perch under the iron roof where the old monomaniac sat glaring, his fantastic whiskers hanging like grey seaweed.

The detective, however, could have put up with Old Brimstone much better than with the other parson he was destined to meet. To explain this second and more momentous meeting, it must be pointed out that Muggleton, after his remarkable experience in the matter of the murder, had very properly put all his cards on the table. He told his story to the police and to the only available representative of Braham Bruce, the dead millionaire; that is, to his very dapper secretary, a Mr Anthony Taylor. The Inspector was more sympathetic than the secretary; but the sequel of his sympathy was the last thing Muggleton would normally have associated with police advice. The Inspector, after some reflection, very much surprised Mr Muggleton by advising him to consult an able amateur whom he knew to be staying in the town. Mr Muggleton had read reports and romances about the Great Criminologist, who sits in his library like an intellectual spider, and throws out theoretical filaments of a web as large as the world. He was prepared to be led to the lonely château where the expert wore a purple dressing-gown, to the attic where he lived on opium and acrostics, to the vast laboratory or the lonely tower. To his astonishment he was led to the very edge of the crowded beach by the pier to meet a dumpy little clergyman, with a broad hat and a broad grin, who was at that moment hopping about on the sands with a crowd of poor children; and excitedly waving a very little wooden spade.

When the criminologist clergyman, whose name appeared to be Brown, had at last been detached from the children, though not from the spade, he seemed to Muggleton to grow more and more unsatisfactory. He hung about helplessly among the idiotic side-shows of the seashore, talking about random topics and particularly attaching himself to those rows of automatic machines which are set up in such places; solemnly spending penny after penny in order to play vicarious games of golf, football, cricket, conducted by clockwork figures; and finally contenting himself with the miniature exhibition of a race, in which one metal doll appeared merely to run and jump after the other. And yet all the time he was listening very carefully to the story which the defeated detective poured out to him. Only his way of not letting his right hand know what his left hand was doing, with pennies, got very much on the detective's nerves.

'Can't we go and sit down somewhere,' said Muggleton impatiently. 'I've got a letter you ought to see, if you're to know anything at all of this business.'

Father Brown turned away with a sigh from the jumping dolls, and went and sat down with his companion on an iron seat on the shore; his companion had already unfolded the letter and handed it silently to him.

It was an abrupt and queer sort of letter, Father Brown thought. He knew that millionaires did not always specialise in manners, especially in dealing with dependants like detectives; but there seemed to be something more in the letter than mere brusquerie.

> DEAR MUGGLETON – I never thought I should come down to wanting help of this sort; but I'm about through with things. It's been getting more and more intolerable for the last two years. I guess all you need to know about the story is this. There is a dirty rascal who is a cousin of mine, I'm ashamed to say. He's been a tout, a tramp, a quack doctor, an actor, and all that; even has the brass to act under our name and call himself Bertrand Bruce. I believe he's either got some potty job at the theatre here, or is looking for one. But you may take it from me that the job isn't his real job. His real job is running me down and knocking me out for good, if he can. It's an old story and no business of anybody's; there was a time when we started neck and neck and ran a race of ambition – and what they call love as well. Was it my fault that he was a rotter and I was a man who succeeds in things? But the dirty devil swears he'll succeed yet; shoot me and run off with my – never mind. I suppose he's a sort of madman, but he'll jolly soon try to be some sort of murderer.
>
> I'll give you £5 a week if you'll meet me at the lodge at the end of the pier, just after the pier closes tonight – and take on my job. It's the only safe place to meet – if anything is safe by this time.
>
> J. BRAHAM BRUCE

'Dear me,' said Father Brown mildly. 'Dear me. A rather hurried letter.'

Muggleton nodded; and after a pause began his own story; in an oddly refined voice contrasting with his clumsy appearance. The priest knew well the hobbies of concealed culture hidden in many dingy lower and middle-class men; but even he was startled by the excellent choice of words only a shade too pedantic; the man talked like a book.

'I arrived at the little round-house at the end of the pier before there was any sign of my distinguished client. I opened the door and went inside, feeling that he might prefer me, as well as himself, to be as inconspicuous as possible. Not that it mattered very much; for the pier was too long for anybody to have seen us from the beach or the parade, and, on glancing at my watch, I saw by the time that the pier entrance must have already closed. It was flattering, after a fashion, that he should thus ensure that we should be alone together at the rendezvous, as showing that he did really rely on my assistance or protection. Anyhow, it was his idea that we should meet on the pier after closing time, so I fell in with it readily enough. There were two chairs inside the little round pavilion, or whatever you call it; so I simply took one of them and waited. I did not have to wait long. He was famous for his punctuality, and sure enough, as I looked up at the one little round window opposite me I saw him pass slowly, as if making a preliminary circuit of the place.

'I had only seen portraits of him, and that was a long time ago; and naturally he was rather older than the portraits, but there was no mistaking the likeness. The profile that passed the window was of the sort called aquiline, after the beak of the eagle; but he rather suggested a grey and venerable eagle; an eagle in repose; an eagle that has long folded its wings. There was no mistaking, however, that look of authority, or silent pride in the habit of command, that has always marked men who, like him, have organised great systems and been obeyed. He was quietly dressed, what I could see of him; especially as compared with the crowd of seaside trippers which had filled so much of my day; but I fancied his overcoat was of that extra elegant sort that is cut to follow the line of the figure, and it had a strip of astrakhan lining showing on the lapels. All this, of course, I took in at a glance, for I had already got to my feet and gone to the door. I put out my hand and received the first shock of that terrible evening. The door was locked. Somebody had locked me in.

'For a moment I stood stunned, and still staring at the round window, from which, of course, the moving profile had already passed; and then I suddenly saw the explanation. Another profile, pointed like that of a pursuing hound, flashed into the circle of vision, as into a round mirror. The moment I saw it, I knew who it was. It was the Avenger; the murderer or would-be murderer, who had trailed the old millionaire for so long across land and sea, and had now tracked him to this blind-alley of an iron pier that hung between sea and land. And I knew, of course, that it was the murderer who had locked the door.

'The man I saw first had been tall, but his pursuer was even taller; an effect that was only lessened by his carrying his shoulders hunched very high and his neck and head thrust forward like a true beast of the chase. The effect of the combination gave him rather the look of a gigantic hunchback. But something of the blood relationship that connected this ruffian with his famous kinsman showed in the two profiles as they passed across the circle of glass. The pursuer also had a nose rather like the beak of a bird; though his general air of ragged degradation suggested the vulture rather than the eagle. He was unshaven to the point of being bearded, and the humped look of his shoulders was increased by the coils of a coarse woollen scarf. All these are trivialities, and can give no impression of the ugly energy of that outline, or the sense of avenging doom in that stooping and striding figure. Have you ever seen William Blake's design, sometimes called with some levity, "The Ghost of a Flea", but also called, with somewhat greater lucidity, "A Vision of Blood Guilt", or something of that kind? That is just such a nightmare of a stealthy giant, with high shoulders, carrying a knife and bowl. This man carried neither, but as he passed the window the second time, I saw with my own eyes that he loosened a revolver from the folds of the scarf and held it gripped and poised in his hand. The eyes in his head shifted and shone in the moonlight, and that in a very creepy way; they shot forward and back with lightning leaps; almost as if he could shoot them out like luminous horns, as do certain reptiles.

'Three times the pursued and the pursuer passed in succession outside the window, treading their narrow circle, before I fully awoke to the need of some action, however desperate. I shook the door with rattling violence; when next I saw the face of the unconscious victim I beat furiously on the window; then I tried to break the window. But it was a double window of exceptionally thick glass, and so deep was the embrasure that I doubted if I could properly reach the outer window at all. Anyhow, my dignified client took no notice of my noise or signals; and the revolving shadow-pantomime of those two masks of doom continued to turn round and round me, till I felt almost dizzy as well as sick. Then they suddenly ceased to reappear. I waited; and I knew that they would not come again. I knew that the crisis had come.

'I need not tell you more. You can almost imagine the rest, even as I sat there helpless, trying to imagine it; or trying not to imagine it. It is enough to say that in that awful silence, in which all sounds of footsteps had died away, there were only two other noises besides the rumbling undertones of the sea. The first was the loud noise of a shot and the second the duller noise of a splash.

'My client had been murdered within a few yards of me, and I could make no sign. I will not trouble you with what I felt about that. But even if I could recover from the murder, I am still confronted with the mystery.'

'Yes,' said Father Brown very gently, 'which mystery?'

'The mystery of how the murderer got away,' answered the other. 'The instant people were admitted to the pier next morning, I was released from my prison and went racing back to the entrance gates, to enquire who had left the pier since they were opened. Without bothering you with details, I may explain that they were, by a rather unusual arrangement, real full-size iron doors that would keep anybody out (or in) until they were opened. The officials there had seen nobody in the least resembling the assassin returning that way. And he was a rather unmistakable person. Even if he had disguised himself somehow, he could hardly have disguised his extraordinary height or got rid of the family nose. It is extraordinarily unlikely that he tried to swim ashore, for the sea was very rough; and there are certainly no traces of any landing. And, somehow, having seen the face of that fiend even once, let alone about six times, something gives me an overwhelming conviction that he did not simply drown himself in the hour of triumph.'

'I quite understand what you mean by that,' replied Father Brown. 'Besides, it would be very inconsistent with the tone of his original threatening letter, in which he promised himself all sorts of benefits after the crime . . . there's another point it might be well to verify. What about the structure of the pier underneath? Piers are very often made with a whole network of iron supports, which a man might climb through as a monkey climbs through a forest.'

'Yes, I thought of that,' replied the private investigator; 'but unfortunately this pier is oddly constructed in more ways than one. It's quite unusually long, and there are iron columns with all that tangle of iron girders; only they're very far apart and I can't see any way a man could climb from one to the other.'

'I only mentioned it,' said Father Brown thoughtfully, 'because that queer fish with the long whiskers, the old man who preaches on the sand, often climbs up on to the nearest girder. I believe he sits there fishing when the tide comes up. And he's a very queer fish to go fishing.'

'Why, what do you mean?'

'Well,' said Father Brown very slowly, twiddling with a button and gazing abstractedly out to the great green waters glittering in the last evening light after the sunset. 'Well . . . I tried to talk to him in a friendly sort of way – friendly and not too funny, if you understand, about his combining the ancient trades of fishing and preaching; I think I made the obvious reference; the text that refers to fishing for living souls. And he said quite queerly and harshly, as he jumped back on to his iron perch, "Well, at least I fish for dead bodies." '

'Good God!' exclaimed the detective, staring at him.

'Yes,' said the priest. 'It seemed to me an odd remark to make in a chatty way, to a stranger playing with children on the sands.'

After another staring silence his companion eventually ejaculated: 'You don't mean you think he had anything to do with the death.'

'I think,' answered Father Brown, 'that he might throw some light on it.'

'Well, it's beyond me now,' said the detective. 'It's beyond me to believe that anybody can throw any light on it. It's like a welter of wild waters in the pitch dark; the sort of waters that he . . . that he fell into. It's simply stark staring unreason; a big man vanishing like a bubble; nobody could possibly . . . Look here!' He stopped suddenly, staring at the priest, who had not moved, but was still twiddling with the button and staring at the breakers. 'What do you mean? What are you looking like that for? You don't mean to say that you . . . that you can make any sense of it?'

'It would be much better if it remained nonsense,' said Father Brown in a low voice. 'Well, if you ask me right out – yes, I think I can make some sense of it.'

There was a long silence, and then the enquiry agent said with a rather singular abruptness: 'Oh, here comes the old man's secretary from the hotel. I must be off. I think I'll go and talk to that mad fisherman of yours.'

'*Post hoc propter hoc?*' asked the priest with a smile.

'Well,' said the other, with jerky candour, 'the secretary don't like me and I don't think I like him. He's been poking around with a lot of questions that didn't seem to me to get us any further, except towards a quarrel. Perhaps he's jealous because the old man called in somebody else, and wasn't content with his elegant secretary's advice. See you later.'

And he turned away, ploughing through the sand to the place where the eccentric preacher had already mounted his marine nest; and looked in the green gloaming rather like some huge polyp or stinging jellyfish trailing his poisonous filaments in the phosphorescent sea.

Meanwhile the priest was serenely watching the serene approach of the secretary; conspicuous even from afar, in that popular crowd, by the clerical neatness and sobriety of his top hat and tail-coat. Without feeling disposed to take part in any feuds between the secretary and the enquiry agent, Father Brown had a faint feeling of irrational sympathy with the prejudices of the latter. Mr Anthony Taylor, the secretary, was an extremely presentable young man, in countenance, as well as costume; and the countenance was firm and intellectual as well as merely good-looking. He was pale, with dark hair coming down on the sides of his head, as if pointing towards possible whiskers; he kept his lips compressed more tightly than most people. The only thing that Father Brown's fancy could tell itself in justification sounded queerer than it really looked. He had a notion that the man talked with his nostrils. Anyhow, the strong compression of his mouth brought out something abnormally sensitive and flexible in these movements at the sides of his nose, so that he seemed to be communicating and conducting life by snuffling and smelling, with his head up, as does a dog. It somehow fitted in with the other features that, when he did speak, it was with a sudden rattling rapidity like a gatling-gun, which sounded almost ugly from so smooth and polished a figure.

For once he opened the conversation, by saying: 'No bodies washed ashore, I imagine.'

'None have been announced, certainly,' said Father Brown.

'No gigantic body of the murderer with the woollen scarf,' said Mr Taylor.

'No,' said Father Brown.

Mr Taylor's mouth did not move any more for the moment; but his nostrils spoke for him with such quick and quivering scorn, that they might almost have been called talkative.

When he did speak again, after some polite commonplaces from the priest, it was to say curtly: 'Here comes the Inspector; I suppose they've been scouring England for the scarf.'

Inspector Grinstead, a brown-faced man with a grey pointed beard, addressed Father Brown rather more respectfully than the secretary had done.

'I thought you would like to know, sir,' he said, 'that there is absolutely no trace of the man described as having escaped from the pier.'

'Or rather not described as having escaped from the pier,' said Taylor. 'The pier officials, the only people who could have described him, have never seen anybody to describe.'

'Well,' said the Inspector, 'we've telephoned all the stations and watched all the roads, and it will be almost impossible for him to escape from England. It really seems to me as if he couldn't have got out that way. He doesn't seem to be anywhere.'

'He never was anywhere,' said the secretary, with an abrupt grating voice, that sounded like a gun going off on that lonely shore.

The Inspector looked blank; but a light dawned gradually on the face of the priest, who said at last with almost ostentatious unconcern: 'Do you mean that the man was a myth? Or possibly a lie?'

'Ah,' said the secretary, inhaling through his haughty nostrils, 'you've thought of that at last.'

'I thought of that at first,' said Father Brown. 'It's the first thing anybody would think of, isn't it, hearing an unsupported story from a stranger about a strange murderer on a lonely pier. In plain words, you mean that little Muggleton never heard anybody murdering the millionaire. Possibly you mean that little Muggleton murdered him himself.'

'Well,' said the secretary, 'Muggleton looks a dingy down-and-out sort of cove to me. There's no story but his about what happened on the pier, and his story consists of a giant who vanished; quite a fairy tale. It isn't a very creditable tale, even as he tells it. By his own account, he bungled his case and let his patron be killed a few yards away. He's a pretty rotten fool and failure, on his own confession.'

'Yes,' said Father Brown. 'I'm rather fond of people who are fools and failures on their own confession.'

'I don't know what you mean,' snapped the other.

'Perhaps,' said Father Brown, wistfully, 'it's because so many people are fools and failures without any confession.'

Then, after a pause, he went on: 'But even if he is a fool and a failure, that doesn't prove he is a liar and a murderer. And you've forgotten that there is one piece of external evidence that does really support his story. I mean the letter from the millionaire, telling the whole tale of his cousin and his vendetta. Unless you can prove that the document itself is actually a forgery, you have to admit there was some probability of Bruce being pursued by somebody who had a real motive. Or rather, I should say, the one actually admitted and recorded motive.'

'I'm not quite sure that I understand you,' said the Inspector, 'about the motive.'

'My dear fellow,' said Father Brown, for the first time stung by impatience into familiarity, 'everybody's got a motive in a way. Considering the way that Bruce made his money, considering the way that most millionaires make their money, almost anybody in the world might have done such a perfectly natural thing as throw him into the sea. In many, one might almost fancy, it would be almost automatic. To almost all it must have occurred at some time or other. Mr Taylor might have done it.'

'What's that?' snapped Mr Taylor, and his nostrils swelled visibly.

'I might have done it,' went on Father Brown, '*nisi me constringeret ecclesiae auctoritas*. Anybody, but for the one true morality, might be tempted to accept so obvious, so simple a social solution. I might have done it; you might have done it; the Mayor or the muffin-man might have done it. The only person on this earth I can think of, who probably would not have done it, is the private enquiry agent whom Bruce had just engaged at five pounds a week, and who hadn't yet had any of his money.'

The secretary was silent for a moment; then he snorted and said: 'If that's the offer in the letter, we'd certainly better see whether it's a forgery. For really, we don't know that the whole tale isn't as false as a forgery. The fellow admits himself that the disappearance of his hunchbacked giant is utterly incredible and inexplicable.'

'Yes,' said Father Brown; 'that's what I like about Muggleton. He admits things.'

'All the same,' insisted Taylor, his nostrils vibrant with excitement. 'All the same, the long and the short of it is that he can't prove that his tall man in the scarf ever existed or does exist; and every single fact found by the police and the witnesses proves that he does not exist. No, Father Brown. There is only one way in which you can justify this little scallywag you seem to be so fond of. And that is by producing his Imaginary Man. And that is exactly what you can't do.'

'By the way,' said the priest, absent-mindedly, 'I suppose you come from the hotel where Bruce has rooms, Mr Taylor?'

Taylor looked a little taken aback, and seemed almost to stammer. 'Well, he always did have those rooms; and they're practically his. I haven't actually seen him there this time.'

'I suppose you motored down with him,' observed Brown; 'or did you both come by train?'

'I came by train and brought the luggage,' said the secretary impatiently. 'Something kept him, I suppose. I haven't actually seen him since he left Yorkshire on his own a week or two ago.'

'So it seems,' said the priest very softly, 'that if Muggleton wasn't the last to see Bruce by the wild sea-waves, you were the last to see him, on the equally wild Yorkshire moors.'

Taylor had turned quite white, but he forced his grating voice to composure: 'I never said Muggleton didn't see *Bruce* on the pier.'

'No; and why didn't you?' asked Father Brown. 'If he made up one man on the pier, why shouldn't he make up two men on the pier? Of course we do know that Bruce did exist; but we don't seem to know what has happened to him for several weeks. Perhaps he was left behind in Yorkshire.'

The rather strident voice of the secretary rose almost to a scream. All his veneer of society suavity seemed to have vanished.

'You're simply shuffling! You're simply shirking! You're trying to drag in mad insinuations about me, simply because you can't answer my question.'

'Let me see,' said Father Brown reminiscently. 'What was your question?'

'You know well enough what it was; and you know you're damned well stumped by it. Where is the man with the scarf? Who has seen him? Whoever heard of him or spoke of him, except that little liar of yours? If you want to convince us, you must produce him. If he ever existed, he may be hiding in the Hebrides or off to Callao. But you've got to produce him, though I know he doesn't exist. Well then! Where is he?'

'I rather think he is over there,' said Father Brown, peering and blinking towards the nearer waves that washed round the iron pillars of the pier; where the two figures of the agent and the old fisher and preacher were still dark against the green glow of the water. 'I mean in that sort of net thing that's tossing about in the sea.'

With whatever bewilderment, Inspector Grinstead took the upper hand again with a flash, and strode down the beach.

'Do you mean to say,' he cried, 'that the murderer's body is in the old boy's net?'

Father Brown nodded as he followed down the shingly slope; and, even as they moved, little Muggleton the agent turned and began to climb the same shore, his mere dark outline a pantomime of amazement and discovery.

'It's true, for all we said,' he gasped. 'The murderer did try to swim ashore and was drowned, of course, in that weather. Or else he did really commit suicide. Anyhow, he drifted dead into Old Brimstone's fishing-net, and that's what the old maniac meant when he said he fished for dead men.'

The Inspector ran down the shore with an agility that outstripped them all, and was heard shouting out orders. In a few moments the fishermen and a few bystanders, assisted by the policemen, had hauled the net into shore, and rolled it with its burden on to the wet sands that still reflected the sunset. The secretary looked at what lay on the sands and the words died on his lips. For what lay on the sands was indeed the body of a gigantic man in rags, with the huge shoulders somewhat humped and bony eagle face; and a great red ragged woollen scarf or comforter, sprawled along the sunset sands like a great stain of blood. But Taylor was staring not at the gory scarf or the fabulous stature, but at the face; and his own face was a conflict of incredulity and suspicion.

The Inspector instantly turned to Muggleton with a new air of civility.

'This certainly confirms your story,' he said. And until he heard the tone of those words, Muggleton had never guessed how almost universally his story had been disbelieved. Nobody had believed him. Nobody but Father Brown.

Therefore, seeing Father Brown edging away from the group, he made a movement to depart in his company; but even then he was brought up rather short by the discovery that the priest was once more being drawn away by the deadly attractions of the funny little automatic machines. He even saw the reverend gentleman fumbling for a penny. He stopped, however, with the penny poised in his finger and thumb, as the secretary spoke for the last time in his loud discordant voice.

'And I suppose we may add,' he said, 'that the monstrous and imbecile charges against me are also at an end.'

'My dear sir,' said the priest, 'I never made any charges against you. I'm not such a fool as to suppose you were likely to murder your master in Yorkshire and then come down here to fool about with his luggage. All I said was that I could make out a better case against you than you were making out so vigorously against poor Mr Muggleton. All the same, if you really want to learn the truth about this business (and I assure you the truth isn't generally grasped yet), I can give you a hint even from your own affairs. It *is* rather a rum and significant thing that Mr Bruce the millionaire had been unknown to all his usual haunts and habits for weeks before he was really killed. As you seem to be a promising amateur detective, I advise you to work on that line.'

'What do you mean?' asked Taylor sharply.

But he got no answer out of Father Brown, who was once more completely concentrated on jiggling the little handle of the machine, that made one doll jump out and then another doll jump after it.

'Father Brown,' said Muggleton, his old annoyance faintly reviving: 'Will you tell me why you like that fool thing so much?'

'For one reason,' replied the priest, peering closely into the glass puppet-show. 'Because it contains the secret of this tragedy.'

Then he suddenly straightened himself; and looked quite seriously at his companion.

'I knew all along,' he said, 'that you were telling the truth and the opposite of the truth.'

Muggleton could only stare at a return of all the riddles.

'It's quite simple,' added the priest, lowering his voice. 'That corpse with the scarlet scarf over there is the corpse of Braham Bruce the millionaire. There won't be any other.'

'But the two men – ' began Muggleton, and his mouth fell open.

'Your description of the two men was quite admirably vivid,' said Father Brown. 'I assure you I'm not at all likely to forget it. If I may say so, you have a literary talent; perhaps journalism would give you more scope than detection. I believe I remember practically each point about each person. Only, you see, queerly enough, each point affected you in one way and me in exactly the opposite way. Let's begin with the first you mentioned. You said that the first man you saw had an indescribable air of authority and dignity. And you said to yourself, "That's the Trust Magnate, the great merchant prince, the ruler of markets." But when I heard about the air of dignity and authority, I said to myself, "That's the actor; everything about this is the actor." You don't get that look by being President of the Chain Store Amalgamation Company. You get that look by being Hamlet's Father's Ghost, or Julius Caesar, or King Lear, and you never altogether lose it. You couldn't see enough of his clothes to tell whether they were really seedy, but you saw a strip of fur and a sort of faintly fashionable cut; and I said to myself again, "The actor."

'Next, before we go into details about the other man, notice one thing about him evidently absent from the first man. You said the second man was not only ragged but unshaven to the point of being bearded. Now we have all seen shabby actors, dirty actors, drunken actors, utterly disreputable actors. But such a thing as a scrub-bearded actor, in a job or even looking round for a job, has scarcely been seen in this world. On the other hand, shaving is often almost the first thing to go, with a gentleman or a wealthy eccentric who is really letting himself go to pieces. Now we have every reason to believe that your friend the millionaire was letting himself go to pieces. His letter was the letter of a man who had already gone to pieces. But it wasn't only negligence that made him look poor and shabby. Don't you understand that the man was practically in hiding? That was why he didn't go to his hotel; and his own secretary hadn't seen him for weeks. He was a millionaire; but his whole object was to be a completely disguised millionaire. Have you ever read "The Woman in White"? Don't you remember that the fashionable and luxurious Count Fosco, fleeing for his life before a secret society, was found stabbed in the blue blouse of a common French workman? Then let us go back for a moment to the demeanour of these men. You saw the first man calm and collected and you said to yourself, "That's the innocent victim"; though the innocent victim's own letter wasn't at all calm and collected. I heard he was calm and collected; and I said to myself, "That's the murderer." Why should he be anything else but calm and collected? He knew what he was going to do. He had made up his mind to do it for a long time; if he had ever had any hesitation or remorse he had hardened himself against them before he came on the scene – in his case, we might say, on the stage. He wasn't likely to have any particular stage-fright. He didn't pull out his pistol and wave it about; why should he? He kept it in his pocket till he wanted it; very likely he fired from his pocket. The other man fidgeted with his pistol because he was nervous as a cat, and very probably had never had a pistol before. He did it for the same reason that he rolled his eyes; and I remember that, even in your own unconscious evidence, it is particularly stated that he rolled them *backwards*. In fact, he was looking behind him. In fact, he was not the pursuer but the pursued. But because you happened to see the first man first, you couldn't help thinking of the other man as coming up behind him. In mere mathematics and mechanics, each of them was running after the other – just like the others.'

'What others?' enquired the dazed detective.

'Why, these,' cried Father Brown, striking the automatic machine with the little wooden spade, which had incongruously remained in his hand throughout these murderous mysteries. 'These little clockwork dolls that chase each other round and round for ever. Let us call them Mr Blue and Mr Red, after the colour of their coats. I happened to start off with Mr Blue, and so the children said that Mr Red was running after him; but it would have looked exactly the contrary if I had started with Mr Red.'

'Yes, I begin to see,' said Muggleton; 'and I suppose all the rest fits in. The family likeness, of course, cuts both ways, and they never saw the murderer leaving the pier – '

'They never looked for the murderer leaving the pier,' said the other. 'Nobody told them to look for a quiet clean-shaven gentleman in an astrakhan coat. All the mystery of his vanishing revolved on your description of a hulking fellow in a red neckcloth. But the simple truth was that the actor in the astrakhan coat murdered the millionaire with the red rag, and there is the poor fellow's body. It's just like the red and blue dolls; only, because you saw one first, you guessed wrong about which was red with vengeance and which was blue with funk.'

At this point two or three children began to straggle across the sands, and the priest waved them to him with the wooden spade, theatrically tapping the automatic machine. Muggleton guessed that it was mainly to prevent their straying towards the horrible heap on the shore.

'One more penny left in the world,' said Father Brown, 'and then we must go home to tea. Do you know, Doris, I rather like those revolving games, that just go round and round like the Mulberry Bush. After all, God made all the suns and stars to play Mulberry Bush. But those other games, where one must catch up with another, where runners are rivals and run neck and neck and outstrip each other; well – much nastier things seem to happen. I like to think of Mr Red and Mr Blue always jumping with undiminished spirits; all free and equal; and never hurting each other. 'Fond lover, never, never, wilt thou kiss – or kill.' Happy, happy Mr Red!

> 'He cannot change; though thou hast not thy bliss,
> For ever will thou jump; and he be Blue.'

Reciting this remarkable quotation from Keats, with some emotion, Father Brown tucked the little spade under one arm, and giving a hand to two of the children, stumped solemnly up the beach to tea.

The Crime of the Communist

Three men came out from under the low-browed Tudor arch in the mellow façade of Mandeville College, into the strong evening sunlight of a summer day which seemed as if it would never end; and in that sunlight they saw something that blasted like lightning; well-fitted to be the shock of their lives.

Even before they had realised anything in the way of a catastrophe, they were conscious of a contrast. They themselves, in a curious quiet way, were quite harmonious with their surroundings. Though the Tudor arches that ran like a cloister round the College gardens had been built four hundred years ago, at that moment when the Gothic fell from heaven and bowed, or almost crouched, over the cosier chambers of Humanism and the Revival of Learning – though they themselves were in modern clothes (that is in clothes whose ugliness would have amazed any of the four centuries) yet something in the spirit of the place made them all at one. The gardens had been tended so carefully as to achieve the final triumph of looking careless; the very flowers seemed beautiful by accident, like elegant weeds; and the modern costumes had at least any picturesqueness that can be produced by being untidy. The first of the three, a tall, bald, bearded maypole of a man, was a familiar figure in the Quad in cap and gown; the gown slipped off one of his sloping shoulders. The second was very square-shouldered, short and compact, with a rather jolly grin, commonly clad in a jacket, with his gown over his arm. The third was even shorter and much shabbier, in black clerical clothes. But they all seemed suitable to Mandeville College; and the indescribable atmosphere of the two ancient and unique Universities of England. They fitted into it and they faded into it; which is there regarded as most fitting.

The two men seated on garden chairs by a little table were a sort of brilliant blot on this grey-green landscape. They were clad mostly in black and yet they glittered from head to heel, from their burnished top hats to their perfectly polished boots. It was dimly felt as an outrage that anybody should be so well-dressed in the well-bred freedom of Mandeville College. The only excuse was that they were foreigners. One was an American, a millionaire named Hake, dressed in the spotlessly and sparklingly gentlemanly manner known only to the rich of New York. The other, who added to all these things the outrage of an astrakhan overcoat (to say nothing of a pair of florid whiskers), was a German Count of great wealth, the shortest part of whose name was Von Zimmern. The mystery of this story, however, is not the mystery of why they were there. They were there for the reason that commonly explains the meeting of incongruous things; they proposed to give the College some money. They had come in support of a plan supported by several financiers and magnates of many countries, for founding a new Chair of Economics at Mandeville College. They had inspected the College with that tireless conscientious sightseeing of which no sons of Eve are capable except the American and the German. And now they were resting from their labours and looking solemnly at the College gardens. So far so good.

The three other men, who had already met them, passed with a vague salutation; but one of them stopped; the smallest of the three, in the black clerical clothes.

'I say,' he said, with rather the air of a frightened rabbit, 'I don't like the look of those men.'

'Good God! Who could?' ejaculated the tall man, who happened to be the Master of Mandeville. 'At least we have some rich men who don't go about dressed up like tailors' dummies.'

'Yes,' hissed the little cleric, 'that's what I mean. Like tailors' dummies.'

'Why, what do you mean?' asked the shorter of the other men, sharply.

'I mean they're like horrible waxworks,' said the cleric in a faint voice. 'I mean they don't move. Why don't they move?'

Suddenly starting out of his dim retirement, he darted across the garden and touched the German Baron on the elbow. The German Baron fell over, chair and all, and the trousered legs that stuck up in the air were as stiff as the legs of the chair.

Mr Gideon P. Hake continued to gaze at the College gardens with glassy eyes; but the parallel of a waxwork confirmed the impression that they were like eyes made of glass. Somehow the rich sunlight and the coloured garden increased the creepy impression of a stiffly dressed doll; a marionette on an Italian stage. The small man in black, who was a priest named Brown, tentatively touched the millionaire on the shoulder, and the millionaire fell sideways, but horribly all of a piece, like something carved in wood.

'*Rigor mortis*,' said Father Brown, 'and so soon. But it does vary a good deal.'

The reason the first three men had joined the other two men so late (not to say too late) will best be understood by noting what had happened just inside the building, behind the Tudor archway, but a short time before they came out. They had all dined together in Hall, at the High Table; but the two foreign philanthropists, slaves of duty in the matter of seeing everything, had solemnly gone back to the chapel, of which one cloister and a staircase remained unexamined; promising to rejoin the rest in the garden, to examine as earnestly the College cigars. The rest, in a more reverent and right-minded spirit, had adjourned as usual to the long narrow oak table, round which the after-dinner wine had circulated, for all anybody knew, ever since the College had been founded in the Middle Ages by Sir John Mandeville, for the encouragement of telling stories. The Master, with the big fair beard and bald brow, took the head of the table, and the squat man in the square jacket sat on his left; for he was the Bursar or business man of the College. Next to him, on that side of the table, sat a queer-looking man with what could only be called a crooked face; for its dark tufts of moustache and eyebrow, slanting at contrary angles, made a sort of zig-zag, as if half his face were puckered or paralysed. His name was Byles; he was the lecturer in Roman History, and his political opinions were founded on those of Coriolanus, not to mention Tarquinius Superbus. This tart Toryism, and rabidly reactionary view of all current problems, was not altogether unknown among the more old-fashioned sort of dons; but in the case of Byles there was a suggestion that it was a result rather than a cause of his acerbity. More than one sharp observer had received the impression that there was something really wrong with Byles; that some secret or some great misfortune had embittered him; as if that half-withered face had really been blasted like a storm-stricken tree. Beyond him again sat Father Brown and at the end of the table a Professor of Chemistry, large and blond and bland, with eyes that were sleepy and perhaps a little sly. It was well known that this natural philosopher regarded the other philosophers, of a more classical tradition, very much as old fogies. On the other side of the table, opposite Father Brown, was a very swarthy and silent young man, with a black pointed beard, introduced because somebody had insisted on having a Chair of Persian; opposite the sinister Byles was a very mild-looking little Chaplain, with a head like an egg. Opposite the Bursar and at the right hand of the Master, was an empty chair; and there were many there who were glad to see it empty.

'I don't know whether Craken is coming,' said the Master, not without a nervous glance at the chair, which contrasted with the usual languid freedom of his demeanour. 'I believe in giving people a lot of rope myself; but I confess I've reached the point of being glad when he is here, merely because he isn't anywhere else.'

'Never know what he'll be up to next,' said the Bursar, cheerfully, 'especially when he's instructing the young.'

'A brilliant fellow, but fiery of course,' said the Master, with a rather abrupt relapse into reserve.

'Fireworks are fiery, and also brilliant,' growled old Byles, 'but I don't want to be burned in my bed so that Craken can figure as a real Guy Fawkes.'

'Do you really *think* he would join a physical force revolution, if there were one,' asked the Bursar smiling.

'Well, *he* thinks he would,' said Byles sharply. 'Told a whole hall full of undergraduates the other day that nothing now could avert the Class War turning into a real war, with killing in the streets of the town; and it didn't matter, so long as it ended in Communism and the victory of the working-class.'

'The Class War,' mused the Master, with a sort of distaste mellowed by distance; for he had known William Morris long ago and been familiar enough with the more artistic and leisurely Socialists. 'I never can understand all this about the Class War. When I was young, Socialism was supposed to mean saying that there are no classes.'

' 'Nother way of saying that Socialists are no class,' said Byles with sour relish.

'Of course, you'd be more against them than I should,' said the Master thoughtfully, 'but I suppose my Socialism is almost as old-fashioned as your Toryism. Wonder what our young friends really think. What do you think, Baker?' he said abruptly to the Bursar on his left.

'Oh, I don't think, as the vulgar saying is,' said the Bursar laughing. 'You must remember I'm a very vulgar person. I'm not a thinker. I'm only a business man; and as a business man I think it's all bosh. You can't make men equal and it's damned bad business to pay them equal; especially a lot of them not worth paying for at all. Whatever it is, you've got to take the practical way out, because it's the only way out. It's not our fault if nature made everything a scramble.'

'I agree with you there,' said the Professor of Chemistry, speaking with a lisp that seemed childish in so large a man. 'Communism pretends to be oh so modern; but it is not. Throwback to the superstitions of monks and primitive tribes. A scientific government, with a really ethical responsibility to posterity, would be always looking for the line of promise and progress; not levelling and flattening it all back into the mud again. Socialism is sentimentalism; and more dangerous than a pestilence, for in that at least the fittest would survive.'

The Master smiled a little sadly. 'You know you and I will never feel quite the same about differences of opinion. Didn't somebody say up here, about walking with a friend by the river, "Not differing much, except in opinion". Isn't that the motto of a university? To have hundreds of opinions and not be opinionated. If people fall here, it's by what they are, not what they think. Perhaps I'm a relic of the eighteenth century; but I incline to the old sentimental heresy, "For forms of faith let graceless zealots fight; he can't be wrong whose life is in the right." What do you think about that, Father Brown?'

He glanced a little mischievously across at the priest and was mildly startled. For he had always found the priest very cheerful and amiable and easy to get on with; and his round face was mostly solid with good humour. But for some reason the priest's face at this moment was knotted with a frown much more sombre than any the company had ever seen on it; so that for an instant that commonplace countenance actually looked darker and more ominous than the haggard face of Byles. An instant later the cloud seemed to have passed; but Father Brown still spoke with a certain sobriety and firmness.

'I don't believe in that, anyhow,' he said shortly. 'How can his life be in the right, if his whole view of life is wrong? That's a modern muddle that arose because people didn't know how much views of life can differ. Baptists and Methodists knew they didn't differ very much in morality; but then they didn't differ very much in religion or philosophy. It's quite different when you pass from the Baptists to the Anabaptists; or from the Theosophists to the Thugs. Heresy always does affect morality, if it's heretical enough. I suppose a man may honestly believe that thieving isn't wrong. But what's the good of saying that he honestly believes in dishonesty?'

'Damned good,' said Byles with a ferocious contortion of feature, believed by many to be meant for a friendly smile. 'And that's why I object to having a Chair of Theoretical Thieving in this College.'

'Well, you're all very down on Communism, of course,' said the Master, with a sigh. 'But do you really think there's so much of it to be down on? Are any of your heresies really big enough to be dangerous?'

'I think they have grown so big,' said Father Brown gravely, 'that in some circles they are already taken for granted. They are actually unconscious. That is, without conscience.'

'And the end of it,' said Byles, 'will be the ruin of this country.'

'The end will be something worse,' said Father Brown.

A shadow shot or slid rapidly along the panelled wall opposite, as swiftly followed by the figure that had flung it; a tall but stooping figure with a vague outline like a bird of prey; accentuated by the fact that its sudden appearance and swift passage were like those of a bird startled and flying from a bush. It was only the figure of a long-limbed, high-shouldered man with long drooping moustaches, in fact, familiar enough to them all; but something in the twilight and candle-light and the flying and streaking shadow connected it strangely with the priest's unconscious words of omen; for all the world, as if those words had indeed been an augury, in the old Roman sense; and the sign of it the flight of a bird. Perhaps Mr Byles might have given a lecture on such Roman augury; and especially on that bird of ill-omen.

The tall man shot along the wall like his own shadow until he sank into the empty chair on the Master's right, and looked across at the Bursar and the rest with hollow and cavernous eyes. His hanging hair and moustache were quite fair, but his eyes were so deep-set that they might have been black.

Everyone knew, or could guess, who the newcomer was; but an incident instantly followed that sufficiently illuminated the situation. The Professor of Roman History rose stiffly to his feet and stalked out of the room, indicating with little finesse his feelings about sitting at the same table with the Professor of Theoretical Thieving, otherwise the Communist, Mr Craken.

The Master of Mandeville covered the awkward situation with nervous grace. 'I was defending you, or some aspects of you, my dear Craken,' he said smiling, 'though I am sure you would find me quite indefensible. After all, I can't forget that the old Socialist friends of my youth had a very fine ideal of fraternity and comradeship. William Morris put it all in a sentence, "Fellowship is heaven; and lack of fellowship is hell." '

'Dons as Democrats; see headline,' said Mr Craken rather disagreeably. 'And is Hard-Case Hake going to dedicate the new Commercial Chair to the memory of William Morris?'

'Well,' said the Master, still maintaining a desperate geniality, 'I hope we may say, in a sense, that all our Chairs are Chairs of good-fellowship.'

'Yes; that's the academic version of the Morris maxim,' growled Craken. ' "A Fellowship is heaven; and lack of a Fellowship is hell." '

'Don't be so cross, Craken,' interposed the Bursar briskly. 'Take some port. Tenby, pass the port to Mr Craken.'

'Oh well, I'll have a glass,' said the Communist Professor a little less ungraciously. 'I really came down here to have a smoke in the garden. Then I looked out of the window and saw your two precious millionaires were actually blooming in the garden; fresh, innocent buds. After all, it might be worth while to give them a bit of my mind.'

The Master had risen under cover of his last conventional cordiality, and was only too glad to leave the Bursar to do his best with the Wild Man. Others had risen, and the groups at the table had begun to break up; and the Bursar and Mr Craken were left more or less alone at the end of the long table. Only Father Brown continued to sit staring into vacancy with a rather cloudy expression.

'Oh, as to that,' said the Bursar. 'I'm pretty tired of them myself, to tell the truth; I've been with them the best part of a day going into facts and figures and all the business of this new Professorship. But look here, Craken,' and he leaned across the table and spoke with a sort of soft emphasis, 'you really needn't cut up so rough about this new Professorship. It doesn't really interfere with your subject. You're the only Professor of Political Economy at Mandeville and, though I don't pretend to agree with your notions, everybody knows you've got a European reputation. This is a special subject they call Applied Economics. Well, even today, as I told you, I've had a hell of a lot of Applied Economics. In other words, I've had to talk business with two business men. Would you particularly want to do that? Would you envy it? Would you stand it? Isn't that evidence enough that there is a separate subject and may well be a separate Chair?'

'Good God,' cried Craken with the intense invocation of the atheist. 'Do you think I don't want to apply Economics? Only, when we apply it, you call it red ruin and anarchy; and when you apply it, I take the liberty of calling it exploitation. If only you fellows would apply Economics, it's just possible that people might get something to eat. We are the practical people; and that's why you're afraid of us. That's why you have to get two greasy Capitalists to start another Lectureship; just because I've let the cat out of the bag.'

'Rather a wild cat, wasn't it?' said the Bursar smiling, 'that you let out of the bag?'

'And rather a gold-bag, wasn't it,' said Craken, 'that you are tying the cat up in again?'

'Well, I don't suppose we shall ever agree about all that,' said the other. 'But those fellows have come out of their chapel into the garden; and if you want to have your smoke there, you'd better come.' He watched with some amusement his companion fumbling in all his pockets till he produced a pipe, and then, gazing at it with an abstracted air, Craken rose to his feet, but even in doing so, seemed to be feeling all over himself again. Mr Baker the Bursar ended the controversy with a happy laugh of reconciliation. 'You are the practical people, and you will blow up the town with dynamite. Only you'll probably forget the dynamite, as I bet you've forgotten the tobacco. Never mind, take a fill of mine. Matches?' He threw a tobacco-pouch and its accessories across the table; to be caught by Mr Craken with that dexterity never forgotten by a cricketer, even when he adopts opinions generally regarded as not cricket. The two men rose together; but Baker could not forbear remarking, 'Are you really the only practical people? Isn't there anything to be said for the Applied Economics, that remembers to carry a tobacco-pouch as well as a pipe?'

Craken looked at him with smouldering eyes; and said at last, after slowly draining the last of his wine: 'Let's say there's another sort of practicality. I dare say I do forget details and so on. What I want you to understand is this' – he automatically returned the pouch; but his eyes were far away and jet-burning, almost terrible – 'because the inside of our intellect has changed, because we really have a new idea of right, we shall do things you think really wrong. And they will be very practical.'

'Yes,' said Father Brown, suddenly coming out of his trance. 'That's exactly what I said.'

He looked across at Craken with a glassy and rather ghastly smile, saying: 'Mr Craken and I are in complete agreement.'

'Well,' said Baker, 'Craken is going out to smoke a pipe with the plutocrats; but I doubt whether it will be a pipe of peace.'

He turned rather abruptly and called to an aged attendant in the background. Mandeville was one of the last of the very old-fashioned Colleges; and even Craken was one of the first of the Communists; before the Bolshevism of today. 'That reminds me,' the Bursar was saying, 'as you won't hand round your peace pipe, we must send out the cigars to our distinguished guests. If they're smokers they must be longing for a smoke; for they've been nosing about in the chapel since feeding-time.'

Craken exploded with a savage and jarring laugh. 'Oh, I'll take them their cigars,' he said. 'I'm only a proletarian.'

Baker and Brown and the attendant were all witnesses to the fact that the Communist strode furiously into the garden to confront the millionaires; but nothing more was seen or heard of them until, as is already recorded, Father Brown found them dead in their chairs.

It was agreed that the Master and the priest should remain to guard the scene of tragedy, while the Bursar, younger and more rapid in his movements, ran off to fetch doctors and policemen. Father Brown approached the table on which one of the cigars had burned itself away all but an inch or two; the other had dropped from the hand and been dashed out into dying sparks on the crazy-pavement. The Master of Mandeville sat down rather shakily on a sufficiently distant seat and buried his bald brow in his hands. Then he looked up at first rather wearily; and then he looked very startled indeed and broke the stillness of the garden with a word like a small explosion of horror.

There was a certain quality about Father Brown which might sometimes be called blood-curdling. He always thought about what he was doing and never about whether it was done; he would do the most ugly or horrible or undignified or dirty things as calmly as a surgeon. There was a certain blank, in his simple mind, of all those things commonly associated with being superstitious or sentimental. He sat down on the chair from which the corpse had fallen, picked up the cigar the corpse had partially smoked, carefully detached the ash, examined the butt-end and then stuck it in his mouth and lit it. It looked like some obscene and grotesque antic in derision of the dead; and it seemed to him to be the most ordinary common sense. A cloud floated upwards like the smoke of some savage sacrifice and idolatry; but to Father Brown it appeared a perfectly self-evident fact that the only way to find out what a cigar is like is to smoke it. Nor did it lessen the horror for his old friend, the Master of Mandeville, to have a dim but shrewd guess that Father Brown was, upon the possibilities of the case, risking his own life.

'No; I think that's all right,' said the priest, putting the stump down again. 'Jolly good cigars. Your cigars. Not American or German. I don't think there's anything odd about the cigar itself; but they'd better take care of the ashes. These men were poisoned somehow with the sort of stuff that stiffens the body quickly . . . By the way, there goes somebody who knows more about it than we do.'

The Master sat up with a curiously uncomfortable jolt; for indeed the large shadow which had fallen across the pathway preceded a figure which, however heavy, was almost as soft-footed as a shadow. Professor Wadham, eminent occupant of the Chair of Chemistry, always moved very quietly in spite of his size, and there was nothing odd about his strolling in the garden; yet there seemed something unnaturally neat in his appearing at the exact moment when chemistry was mentioned.

Professor Wadham prided himself on his quietude; some would say his insensibility. He did not turn a hair on his flattened flaxen head, but stood looking down at the dead men with a shade of something like indifference on his large froglike face. Only when he looked at the cigar-ash, which the priest had preserved, he touched it with one finger; then he seemed to stand even stiller than before; but in the shadow of his face his eyes for an instant seemed to shoot out telescopically like one of his own microscopes. He had certainly realised or recognised something; but he said nothing.

'I don't know where anyone is to begin in this business,' said the Master.

'I should begin,' said Father Brown, 'by asking where these unfortunate men had been most of the time today.'

'They were messing about in my laboratory for a good time,' said Wadham, speaking for the first time. 'Baker often comes up to have a chat, and this time he brought his two patrons to inspect my department. But I think they went everywhere; real tourists. I know they went to the chapel and even into the tunnel under the crypt, where you have to light candles; instead of digesting their food like sane men. Baker seems to have taken them everywhere.'

'Were they interested in anything particular in your department?' asked the priest. 'What were you doing there just then?'

The Professor of Chemistry murmured a chemical formula beginning with 'sulphate', and ending with something that sounded like 'silenium'; unintelligible to both his hearers. He then wandered wearily away and sat on a remote bench in the sun, closing his eyes, but turning up his large face with heavy forbearance.

At his point, by a sharp contrast, the lawns were crossed by a brisk figure travelling as rapidly and as straight as a bullet; and Father Brown recognised the neat black clothes and shrewd doglike face of a police-surgeon whom he had met in the poorer parts of town. He was the first to arrive of the official contingent.

'Look here,' said the Master to the priest, before the doctor was within earshot. 'I must know something. Did you mean what you said about Communism being a real danger and leading to crime?'

'Yes,' said Father Brown smiling rather grimly, 'I have really noticed the spread of some Communist ways and influences; and, in one sense, this is a Communist crime.'

'Thank you,' said the Master. 'Then I must go off and see to something at once. Tell the authorities I'll be back in ten minutes.'

The Master had vanished into one of the Tudor archways at just about the moment when the police-doctor had reached the table and cheerfully recognised Father Brown. On the latter's suggestion that they should sit down at the tragic table, Dr Blake threw one sharp and doubtful glance at the big, bland and seemingly somnolent chemist, who occupied a more remote seat. He was duly informed of the Professor's identity, and what had so far been gathered of the Professor's evidence; and listened to it silently while conducting a preliminary examination of the dead bodies. Naturally, he seemed more concentrated on the actual corpses than on the hearsay evidence, until one detail suddenly distracted him entirely from the science of anatomy.

'What did the Professor say he was working at?' he enquired.

Father Brown patiently repeated the chemical formula he did not understand.

'*What?*' snapped Dr Blake, like a pistol-shot. 'Gosh! This is pretty frightful!'

'Because it's poison?' enquired Father Brown.

'Because it's piffle,' replied Dr Blake. 'It's simply nonsense. The Professor is quite a famous chemist. Why is a famous chemist deliberately talking nonsense?'

'Well, I think I know that one,' answered Father Brown mildly. 'He is talking nonsense, because he is telling lies. He is concealing something; and he wanted specially to conceal it from these two men and their representatives.'

The doctor lifted his eyes from the two men and looked across at the almost unnaturally immobile figure of the great chemist. He might almost have been asleep; a garden butterfly had settled upon him and seemed to turn his stillness into that of a stone idol. The large folds of his froglike face reminded the doctor of the hanging skins of a rhinoceros.

'Yes,' said Father Brown, in a very low voice. 'He is a wicked man.'

'God damn it all!' cried the doctor, suddenly moved to his very depths. 'Do you mean that a great scientific man like that deals in murder?'

'Fastidious critics would have complained of his dealing in murder,' said the priest dispassionately. 'I don't say I'm very fond of people dealing in murder in that way myself. But what's much more to the point – I'm sure that *these* poor fellows were among his fastidious critics.'

'You mean they found his secret and he silenced them?' said Blake frowning. 'But what in hell was his secret? How could a man murder on a large scale in a place like this?'

'I have told you his secret,' said the priest. 'It is a secret of the soul. He is a bad man. For heaven's sake don't fancy I say that because he and I are of opposite schools or traditions. I have a crowd of scientific friends; and most of them are heroically disinterested. Even of the most sceptical, I would only say they are rather irrationally disinterested. But now and then you do get a man who is a materialist, in the sense of a beast. I repeat he's a bad man. Much worse than – ' And Father Brown seemed to hesitate for a word.

'You mean much worse than the Communist?' suggested the other.

'No; I mean much worse than the murderer,' said Father Brown.

He got to his feet in an abstracted manner; and hardly realised that his companion was staring at him.

'But didn't you mean,' asked Blake at last, 'that this Wadham is the murderer?'

'Oh, no,' said Father Brown more cheerfully. 'The murderer is a much more sympathetic and understandable person. He at least was desperate; and had the excuses of sudden rage and despair.'

'Why,' cried the doctor, 'do you mean it was the Communist after all?'

It was at this very moment, appropriately enough, that the police officials appeared with an announcement that seemed to conclude the case in a most decisive and satisfactory manner. They had been somewhat delayed in reaching the scene of the crime, by the simple fact that they had already captured the criminal. Indeed, they had captured him almost at the gates of their own official residence. They had already had reason to suspect the activities of Craken the Communist during various disorders in the town; when they heard of the outrage they felt it safe to arrest him; and found the arrest thoroughly justified. For, as Inspector Cook radiantly explained to dons and doctors on the lawn of Mandeville garden, no sooner was the notorious Communist searched, than it was found that he was actually carrying a box of poisoned matches.

The moment Father Brown heard the word 'matches', he jumped from his seat as if a match had been lighted under him.

'Ah,' he cried, with a sort of universal radiance, 'and now it's all clear.'

'What do you mean by all clear?' demanded the Master of Mandeville, who had returned in all the pomp of his own officialism to match the pomp of the police officials now occupying the College like a victorious army. 'Do you mean you are convinced now that the case against Craken is clear?'

'I mean that Craken is cleared,' said Father Brown firmly, 'and the case against Craken is cleared away. Do you really believe Craken is the kind of man who would go about poisoning people with matches?'

'That's all very well,' replied the Master, with the troubled expression he had never lost since the first sensation occurred. 'But it was you yourself who said that fanatics with false principles may do wicked things. For that matter, it was you yourself who said that Communism is creeping up everywhere and Communistic habits spreading.'

Father Brown laughed in a rather shamefaced manner.

'As to the last point,' he said, 'I suppose I owe you all an apology. I seem to be always making a mess of things with my silly little jokes.'

'Jokes!' repeated the Master, staring rather indignantly.

'Well,' explained the priest, rubbing his head. 'When I talked about a Communist habit spreading, I only meant a habit I happen to have noticed about two or three times even today. It is a Communist habit by no means confined to Communists. It is the extraordinary habit of so many men, especially Englishmen, of putting other people's matchboxes in their pockets without remembering to return them. Of course, it seems an awfully silly little trifle to talk about. But it does happen to be the way the crime was committed.'

'It sounds to me quite crazy,' said the doctor.

'Well, if almost any man may forget to return matches, you can bet your boots that Craken would forget to return them. So the poisoner who had prepared the matches got rid of them on to Craken, by the simple process of lending them and not getting them back. A really admirable way of shedding responsibility; because Craken himself would be perfectly unable to imagine where he had got them from. But when he used them quite innocently to light the cigars he offered to our two visitors, he was caught in an obvious trap; one of those too obvious traps. He was the bold bad Revolutionist murdering two millionaires.'

'Well, who else would want to murder them?' growled the doctor.

'Ah, who indeed?' replied the priest; and his voice changed to much greater gravity. 'There we come to the other thing I told you; and that, let me tell you, was not a joke. I told you that heresies and false doctrines had become common and conversational; that everybody was used to them; that nobody really noticed them. Did you think I meant *Communism* when I said that? Why, it was just the other way. You were all as nervous as cats about Communism; and you watched Craken like a wolf. Of course, Communism is a heresy; but it isn't a heresy that you people take for granted. It is Capitalism you take for granted; or rather the vices of Capitalism disguised as a dead Darwinism. Do you recall what you were all saying in the Common Room, about life being only a scramble, and nature demanding the survival of the fittest, and how it doesn't matter whether the poor are paid justly or not? Why, *that* is the heresy that you have grown accustomed to, my friends; and it's every bit as much a heresy as Communism. That's the anti-Christian morality or immorality that you take quite naturally. And that's the immorality that has made a man a murderer today.'

'What man?' cried the Master, and his voice cracked with a sudden weakness.

'Let me approach it another way,' said the priest placidly. 'You all talk as if Craken ran away; but he didn't. When the two men toppled over, he ran down the street, summoned the doctor merely by shouting through the window, and shortly afterwards was trying to summon the police. That was how he was arrested. But doesn't it strike you, now one comes to think of it, that Mr Baker the Bursar is rather a long time looking for the police?'

'What is he doing then?' asked the Master sharply.

'I fancy he's destroying papers; or perhaps ransacking these men's rooms to see they haven't left us a letter. Or it may have something to do with our friend Wadham. Where does he come in? That is really very simple and a sort of joke too. Mr Wadham is experimenting in poisons for the next war; and has something of which a whiff of flame will stiffen a man dead. Of course, he had nothing to do with killing these men; but he did conceal his chemical secret for a very simple reason. One of them was a Puritan Yankee and the other a cosmopolitan Jew; and those two types are often fanatical Pacifists. They would have called it planning murder and probably refused to help the College. But Baker was a friend of Wadham and it was easy for him to dip matches in the new material.'

Another peculiarity of the little priest was that his mind was all of a piece, and he was unconscious of many incongruities; he would change the note of his talk from something quite public to something quite private, without any particular embarrassment. On this occasion, he made most of the company stare with mystification, by beginning to talk to one person when he had just been talking to ten; quite indifferent to the fact that only the one could have any notion of what he was talking about.

'I'm sorry if I misled you, doctor, by that maundering metaphysical digression on the man of sin,' he said apologetically. 'Of course it had nothing to do with the murder; but the truth is I'd forgotten all about the murder for the moment. I'd forgotten everything, you see, but a sort of vision of that fellow, with his vast unhuman face, squatting among the flowers like some blind monster of the Stone Age. And I was thinking that some men are pretty monstrous, like men of stone; but it was all irrelevant. Being bad inside has very little to do with committing crimes outside. The worst criminals have committed no crimes. The practical point is why did the practical criminal commit this crime. Why did Baker the Bursar want to kill these men? That's all that concerns us now. The answer is the answer to the question I've asked twice. Where were these men most of the time, apart from nosing in chapels or laboratories? By the Bursar's own account, they were talking business with the Bursar.

'Now, with all respect to the dead, I do not exactly grovel before the intellect of these two financiers. Their views on economics and ethics were heathen and heartless. Their views on Peace were tosh. Their views on Port were even more deplorable. But one thing they did understand; and that was business. And it took them a remarkably short time to discover that the business man in charge of the funds of this College was a swindler. Or shall I say, a true follower of the doctrine of the unlimited struggle for life and the survival of the fittest.'

'You mean they were going to expose him and he killed them before they could speak,' said the doctor frowning. 'There are a lot of details I don't understand.'

'There are some details I'm not sure of myself,' said the priest frankly. 'I suspect all that business of candles underground had something to do with abstracting the millionaires' own matches, or perhaps making sure they had no matches. But I'm sure of the main gesture, the gay and careless gesture of Baker tossing his matches to the careless Craken. That gesture was the murderous blow.'

'There's one thing I don't understand,' said the Inspector. 'How did Baker know that Craken wouldn't light up himself then and there at the table and become an unwanted corpse?'

The face of Father Brown became almost heavy with reproach; and his voice had a sort of mournful yet generous warmth in it.

'Well, hang it all,' he said, 'he was only an atheist.'

'I'm afraid I don't know what you mean,' said the Inspector, politely.

'He only wanted to abolish God,' explained Father Brown in a temperate and reasonable tone. 'He only wanted to destroy the Ten Commandments and root up all the religion and civilisation that had made him, and wash out all the common sense of ownership and honesty; and let his culture and his country be flattened out by savages from the ends of the earth. That's all he wanted. You have no right to accuse him of anything beyond that. Hang it all, everybody draws the line somewhere! And you come here and calmly suggest that a Mandeville Man of the old generation (for Craken was of the old generation, whatever his views) would have begun to smoke, or even strike a match, while he was still drinking the College Port, of the vintage of '08 – no, no; men are not so utterly without laws and limits as all that! I was there; I saw him; he had not finished his wine, and you ask me why he did not *smoke*! No such anarchic question has ever shaken the arches of Mandeville College . . . Funny place, Mandeville College. Funny place, Oxford. Funny place, England.'

'But you haven't anything particular to do with Oxford?' asked the doctor curiously.

'I have to do with England,' said Father Brown. 'I come from there. And the funniest thing of all is that even if you love it and belong to it, you still can't make head or tail of it.'

The Point of a Pin

Father Brown always declared that he solved this problem in his sleep. And this was true, though in rather an odd fashion; because it occurred at a time when his sleep was rather disturbed. It was disturbed very early in the morning by the hammering that began in the huge building, or half-building, that was in process of erection opposite to his rooms; a colossal pile of flats still mostly covered with scaffolding and with boards announcing Messrs Swindon & Sand as the builders and owners. The hammering was renewed at regular intervals and was easily recognisable: because Messrs Swindon & Sand specialised in some new American system of cement flooring which, in spite of its subsequent smoothness, solidity, impenetrability and permanent comfort (as described in the advertisements), had to be clamped down at certain points with heavy tools. Father Brown endeavoured, however, to extract exiguous comfort from it; saying that it always woke him up in time for the very earliest Mass, and was therefore something almost in the nature of a carillon. After all, he said, it was almost as poetic that Christians should be awakened by hammers as by bells. As a fact, however, the building operations were a little on his nerves, for another reason. For there was hanging like a cloud over the half-built skyscraper the possibility of a Labour crisis, which the newspapers doggedly insisted on describing as a Strike. As a matter of fact, if it ever happened, it would be a Lock-out. But he worried a good deal about whether it would happen. And it might be questioned whether hammering is more of a strain on the attention because it may go on for ever, or because it may stop at any minute.

'As a mere matter of taste and fancy,' said Father Brown, staring up at the edifice with his owlish spectacles, 'I rather wish it would stop. I wish all houses would stop while they still have the scaffolding up. It seems almost a pity that houses are ever finished. They look so fresh and hopeful with all that fairy filigree of white wood, all light and bright in the sun; and a man so often only finishes a house by turning it into a tomb.'

As he turned away from the object of his scrutiny, he nearly ran into a man who had just darted across the road towards him. It was a man whom he knew slightly, but sufficiently to regard him (in the circumstances) as something of a bird of ill-omen. Mr Mastyk was a squat man with a square head that looked hardly European, dressed with a heavy dandyism that seemed rather too consciously Europeanised. But Brown had seen him lately talking to young Sand of the building firm; and he did not like it. This man Mastyk was the head of an organisation rather new in English industrial politics; produced by extremes at both ends; a definite army of non-Union and largely alien labour hired out in gangs to various firms; and he was obviously hovering about in the hope of hiring it out to this one. In short, he might negotiate some way of outmanoeuvring the Trade Union and flooding the works with blacklegs. Father Brown had been drawn into some of the debates, being in some sense called in on both sides. And as the Capitalists all reported that, to their positive knowledge, he was a Bolshevist; and as the Bolshevists all testified that he was a reactionary rigidly attached to bourgeois ideologies, it may be inferred that he talked a certain amount of sense without any appreciable effect on anybody. The news brought by Mr Mastyk, however, was calculated to jerk everybody out of the ordinary rut of the dispute.

'They want you to go over there at once,' said Mr Mastyk, in awkwardly accented English. 'There is a threat to murder.'

Father Brown followed his guide in silence up several stairways and ladders to a platform of the unfinished building, on which were grouped the more or less familiar figures of the heads of the building business. They included even what had once been the head of it; though the head had been for some time rather a head in the clouds. It was at least a head in a coronet, that hid it from human sight like a cloud. Lord Stanes, in other words, had not only retired from the business but been caught up into the House of Lords and disappeared. His rare reappearances were languid and somewhat dreary; but this one, in conjunction with that of Mastyk, seemed none the less menacing. Lord Stanes was a lean, long-headed, hollow-eyed man with very faint fair hair fading into baldness; and he was the most evasive person the priest had ever met. He was unrivalled in the true Oxford talent of saying, 'No doubt you're right,' so as to sound like, 'No doubt you think you're right,' or of merely remarking, 'You think so?' so as to imply the acid addition, 'You would.' But Father Brown fancied that the man was not merely bored but faintly embittered, though whether at being called down from Olympus to control such trade squabbles, or merely at not being really any longer in control of them, it was difficult to guess.

On the whole, Father Brown rather preferred the more bourgeois group of partners, Sir Hubert Sand and his nephew Henry; though he doubted privately whether they really had very many ideologies. True, Sir Hubert Sand had obtained considerable celebrity in the newspapers; both as a patron of sport and as a patriot in many crises during and after the Great War. He had won notable distinction in France, for a man of his years, and had afterwards been featured as a triumphant captain of industry overcoming difficulties among the munition-workers. He had been called a Strong Man; but that was not his fault. He was in fact a heavy, hearty

Englishman; a great swimmer; a good squire; an admirable amateur colonel. Indeed, something that can only be called a military make-up pervaded his appearance. He was growing stout, but he kept his shoulders set back; his curly hair and moustache were still brown while the colours of his face were already somewhat withered and faded. His nephew was a burly youth of the pushing, or rather shouldering, sort with a relatively small head thrust out on a thick neck, as if he went at things with his head down; a gesture somehow rendered rather quaint and boyish by the pince-nez that were balanced on his pugnacious pug-nose.

Father Brown had looked at all these things before; and at that moment everybody was looking at something entirely new. In the centre of the woodwork there was nailed up a large loose flapping piece of paper on which something was scrawled in crude and almost crazy capital letters, as if the writer were either almost illiterate or were affecting or parodying illiteracy. The words actually ran: 'The Council of the Workers warns Hubert Sand that he will lower wages and lock out workmen at his peril. If the notices go out tomorrow, he will be dead by the justice of the people.'

Lord Stanes was just stepping back from his examination of the paper, and, looking across at his partner, he said with rather a curious intonation: 'Well, it's you they want to murder. Evidently I'm not considered worth murdering.'

One of those still electric shocks of fancy that sometimes thrilled Father Brown's mind in an almost meaningless way shot through him at that particular instant. He had a queer notion that the man who was speaking could not now be murdered, because he was already dead. It was, he cheerfully admitted, a perfectly senseless idea. But there was something that always gave him the creeps about the cold disenchanted detachment of the noble senior partner; about his cadaverous colour and inhospitable eyes. 'The fellow,' he thought in the same perverse mood, 'has green eyes and looks as if he had green blood.'

Anyhow, it was certain that Sir Hubert Sand had not got green blood. His blood, which was red enough in every sense, was creeping up into his withered or weather-beaten cheeks with all the warm fullness of life that belongs to the natural and innocent indignation of the good-natured.

'In all my life,' he said, in a strong voice and yet shakily, 'I have never had such a thing said or done about me. I may have differed – '

'We can none of us differ about this,' struck in his nephew impetuously. 'I've tried to get on with them, but this is a bit too thick.'

'You don't really think,' began Father Brown, 'that your workmen – '

'I say we may have differed,' said old Sand, still a little tremulously, 'God knows I never like the idea of threatening English workmen with cheaper labour – '

'We none of us liked it,' said the young man, 'but if I know you, uncle, this has about settled it.'

Then after a pause he added, 'I suppose, as you say, we did disagree about details; but as to real policy – '

'My dear fellow,' said his uncle, comfortably, 'I hoped there would never be any real disagreement.' From which anybody who understands the English nation may rightly infer that there had been very considerable disagreement. Indeed the uncle and nephew differed almost as much as an Englishman and an American. The uncle had the English ideal of getting outside the business, and setting up a sort of an alibi as a country gentleman. The nephew had the American ideal of getting inside the business; of getting inside the very mechanism like a mechanic. And, indeed, he had worked with most of the mechanics and was familiar with most of the processes and tricks of the trade. And he was American again, in the fact that he did this partly as an employer to keep his men up to the mark, but in some vague way also as an equal, or at least with a pride in showing himself also as a worker. For this reason he had often appeared almost as a representative of the workers, on technical points which were a hundred miles away from his uncle's popular eminence in politics or sport. The memory of those many occasions, when young Henry had practically come out of the workshop in his shirt sleeves, to demand some concession about the conditions of the work, lent a peculiar force and even violence to his present reaction the other way.

'Well, they've damned-well locked themselves out this time,' he cried. 'After a threat like that there's simply nothing left but to defy them. There's nothing left but to sack them all now; instanter; on the spot. Otherwise we'll be the laughing-stock of the world.'

Old Sand frowned with equal indignation, but began slowly: 'I shall be very much criticised – '

'Criticised!' cried the young man shrilly. 'Criticised if you defy a threat of murder! Have you any notion how you'll be criticised if you don't defy it? Won't you enjoy the headlines? "Great Capitalist Terrorised" – "Employer Yields to Murder Threat".

'Particularly,' said Lord Stanes, with something faintly unpleasant in his tone. 'Particularly when he has been in so many headlines already as "The Strong Man of Steel-Building".'

Sand had gone very red again and his voice came thickly from under his thick moustache. 'Of course you're right there. If these brutes think I'm afraid – '

At this point there was an interruption in the conversation of the group; and a slim young man came towards them swiftly. The first notable thing about him was that he was one of those whom men, and women too, think are just a little too nice-looking to look nice. He had beautiful dark curly hair and a silken moustache and he spoke like a gentleman, but with almost too refined and exactly modulated an accent. Father Brown knew him at once as Rupert Rae, the secretary of Sir Hubert, whom he had often seen pottering about in Sir Hubert's house; but never with such impatience in his movements or such a wrinkle on his brow.

'I'm sorry, sir,' he said to his employer, 'but there's a man been hanging about over there. I've done my best to get rid of him. He's only got a letter, but he swears he must give it to you personally.'

'You mean he went first to my house?' said Sand, glancing swiftly at his secretary. 'I suppose you've been there all the morning.'

'Yes, sir,' said Mr Rupert Rae.

There was a short silence; and then Sir Hubert Sand curtly intimated that the man had better be brought along; and the man duly appeared.

Nobody, not even the least fastidious lady, would have said that the newcomer was too nice-looking. He had very large ears and a face like a frog, and he stared before him with an almost ghastly fixity, which Father Brown attributed to his having a glass eye. In fact, his fancy was tempted to equip the man with two glass eyes; with so glassy a stare did he contemplate the company. But the priest's experience, as distinct from his fancy, was able to suggest several natural causes for that unnatural waxwork glare; one of them being an abuse of the divine gift of fermented liquor. The man was short and shabby and carried a large bowler hat in one hand and a large sealed letter in the other.

Sir Hubert Sand looked at him; and then said quietly enough, but in a voice that somehow seemed curiously small, coming out of the fullness of his bodily presence: 'Oh – it's you.'

He held out his hand for the letter; and then looked around apologetically, with poised finger, before ripping it open and reading it. When he had read it, he stuffed it into his inside pocket and said hastily and a little harshly: 'Well, I suppose all this business is over, as you say. No more negotiations possible now; we couldn't pay the wages they want anyhow. But I shall want to see you again, Henry, about – about winding things up generally.'

'All right,' said Henry, a little sulkily perhaps, as if he would have preferred to wind them up by himself. 'I shall be up in number 188 after lunch; got to know how far they've got up there.'

The man with the glass eye, if it was a glass eye, stumped stiffly away; and the eye of Father Brown (which was by no means a glass eye) followed him thoughtfully as he threaded his way through the ladders and disappeared into the street.

* * *

It was on the following morning that Father Brown had the unusual experience of oversleeping himself; or at least of starting from sleep with a subjective conviction that he must be late. This was partly due to his remembering, as a man may remember a dream, the fact of having been half-awakened at a more regular hour and fallen asleep again; a common enough occurrence with most of us, but a very uncommon occurrence with Father Brown. And he was afterwards oddly convinced, with that mystic side of him which was normally turned away from the world, that in that detached dark islet of dreamland, between the two wakings, there lay like buried treasure the truth of this tale.

As it was, he jumped up with great promptitude, plunged into his clothes, seized his big knobby umbrella and bustled out into the street, where the bleak white morning was breaking like splintered ice about the huge black building facing him. He was surprised to find that the streets shone almost empty in the cold crystalline light; the very look of it told him it could hardly be so late as he had feared. Then suddenly the stillness was cloven by the arrowlike swiftness of a long grey car which halted before the big deserted flats. Lord Stanes unfolded himself from within and approached the door, carrying (rather languidly) two large suitcases. At the same moment the door opened, and somebody seemed to step back instead of stepping out into the street. Stanes called twice to the man within, before that person seemed to complete his original gesture by coming out on to the doorstep; then the two held a brief colloquy, ending in the nobleman carrying his suitcases upstairs, and the other coming out into full daylight and revealing the heavy shoulders and peering head of young Henry Sand.

Father Brown made no more of this rather odd meeting, until two days later the young man drove up in his own car, and implored the priest to enter it. 'Something awful has happened,' he said, 'and I'd rather talk to you than Stanes. You know Stanes arrived the other day with some mad idea of camping in one of the flats that's just finished. That's why I had to go there early and open the door to him. But all that will keep. I want you to come up to my uncle's place at once.'

'Is he ill?' enquired the priest quickly.

'I think he's dead,' answered the nephew.

'What do you mean by saying you think he's dead?' asked Father Brown a little briskly. 'Have you got a doctor?'

'No,' answered the other. 'I haven't got a doctor or a patient either . . . It's no good calling in doctors to examine the body; because the body has run away. But I'm afraid I know where it has run to . . . the truth is – we kept it dark for two days; but he's disappeared.'

'Wouldn't it be better,' said Father Brown mildly, 'if you told me what has really happened from the beginning?'

'I know,' answered Henry Sand; 'it's an infernal shame to talk flippantly like this about the poor old boy; but people get like that when they're rattled. I'm not much good at hiding things; the long and the short of it is – well, I won't tell you the long of it now. It's what some people would call rather a long shot; shooting suspicions at random and so on. But the short of it is that my unfortunate uncle has committed suicide.'

They were by this time skimming along in the car through the last fringes of the town and the first fringes of the forest and park beyond it; the lodge gates of Sir Hubert Sand's small estate were about half a mile farther on amid the thickening throng of the beeches. The estate consisted chiefly of a small park and a large ornamental garden, which descended in terraces of a certain classical pomp to the very edge of the chief river of the district. As soon as they arrived at the house, Henry took the priest somewhat hastily through the old Georgian rooms and out upon the other side; where they silently descended the slope, a rather steep slope embanked with flowers, from which they could see the pale river spread out before them almost as flat as in a bird's-eye view. They were just turning the corner of the path under an enormous classical urn crowned with a somewhat incongruous garland of geraniums, when Father Brown saw a movement in the bushes and thin trees just below him, that seemed as swift as a movement of startled birds.

In the tangle of thin trees by the river two figures seemed to divide or scatter; one of them glided swiftly into the shadows and the other came forward to face them; bringing them to a halt and an abrupt and rather unaccountable silence. Then Henry Sand said in his heavy way: 'I think you know Father Brown . . . Lady Sand.'

Father Brown did know her; but at that moment he might almost have said that he did not know her. The pallor and constriction of her face was like a mask of tragedy; she was much younger than her husband, but at that moment she looked somehow older than everything in that old house and garden. And the priest remembered, with a subconscious thrill, that she was indeed older in type and lineage and was the true possessor of the place. For her own family had owned it as impoverished aristocrats, before she had restored its fortunes by marrying a successful business man. As she stood there, she might have been a family picture, or even a family ghost. Her pale face was of that pointed yet oval type seen in some old pictures of Mary Queen of Scots; and its expression seemed almost to go beyond the natural unnaturalness of a situation, in which her husband had vanished under suspicion of suicide. Father Brown, with the same subconscious movement of the mind, wondered who it was with whom she had been talking among the trees.

'I suppose you know all this dreadful news,' she said, with a comfortless composure. 'Poor Hubert must have broken down under all this revolutionary persecution, and been just maddened into taking his own life. I don't know whether you can do anything; or whether these horrible Bolsheviks can be made responsible for hounding him to death.'

'I am terribly distressed, Lady Sand,' said Father Brown. 'And still, I must own, a little bewildered. You speak of persecution; do you think that anybody could hound him to death merely by pinning up that paper on the wall?'

'I fancy,' answered the lady, with a darkening brow, 'that there were other persecutions besides the paper.'

'It shows what mistakes one may make,' said the priest sadly. 'I never should have thought he would be so illogical as to die in order to avoid death.'

'I know,' she answered, gazing at him gravely. 'I should never have believed it, if it hadn't been written with his own hand.'

'What?' cried Father Brown, with a little jump like a rabbit that has been shot at.

'Yes,' said Lady Sand calmly. 'He left a confession of suicide; so I fear there is no doubt about it.' And she passed on up the slope alone, with all the inviolable isolation of the family ghost.

The spectacles of Father Brown were turned in mute enquiry to the eyeglasses of Mr Henry Sand. And the latter gentleman, after an instant's hesitation, spoke again in his rather blind and plunging fashion: 'Yes, you see, it seems pretty clear now what he did. He was always a great swimmer and used to come down in his dressing-gown every morning for a dip in the river. Well, he came down as usual, and left his dressing-gown on the bank; it's lying there still. But he also left a message saying he was going for his last swim and then death, or something like that.'

'Where did he leave the message?' asked Father Brown.

'He scrawled it on that tree there, overhanging the water, I suppose the last thing he took hold of; just below where the dressing-gown's lying. Come and see for yourself.'

Father Brown ran down the last short slope to the shore and peered under the hanging tree, whose plumes were almost dipping in the stream. Sure enough, he saw on the smooth bark the words scratched conspicuously and unmistakably: 'One more swim and then drowning. Goodbye. Hubert Sand.' Father Brown's gaze travelled slowly up the bank till it rested on a gorgeous rag of raiment, all red and yellow with gilded tassels. It was the dressing-gown and the priest picked it up and began to turn it over. Almost as he did so he was conscious that a figure had flashed across his field of vision; a tall dark figure that slipped from one clump of trees to another, as if following the trail of the vanishing lady. He had little doubt that it was the companion from whom she had lately parted. He had still less doubt that it was the dead man's secretary, Mr Rupert Rae.

'Of course, it might be a final afterthought to leave the message,' said Father Brown, without looking up, his eye riveted on the red and gold garment. 'We've all heard of love-messages written on trees; and I suppose there might be death-messages written on trees too.'

'Well, he wouldn't have anything in the pockets of his dressing-gown, I suppose,' said young Sand. 'And a man might naturally scratch his message on a tree if he had no pens, ink or paper.'

'Sounds like French exercises,' said the priest dismally. 'But I wasn't thinking of that.' Then, after a silence, he said in a rather altered voice: 'To tell the truth, I was thinking whether a man might not naturally scratch his message on a tree, even if he had stacks of pens, and quarts of ink, and reams of paper.'

Henry was looking at him with a rather startled air, his eyeglasses crooked on his pug-nose. 'And what do you mean by that?' he asked sharply.

'Well,' said Father Brown slowly, 'I don't exactly mean that postmen will carry letters in the form of logs, or that you will ever drop a line to a friend by putting a postage stamp on a pine tree. It would have to be a particular sort of position – in fact, it would have to be a particular sort of person, who really preferred this sort of arboreal correspondence. But, given the position and the person, I repeat what I said. He would still write on a tree, as the song says, if all the world were paper and all the sea were ink; if that river flowed with everlasting ink or all these woods were a forest of quills and fountain-pens.'

It was evident that Sand felt something creepy about the priest's fanciful imagery; whether because he found it incomprehensible or because he was beginning to comprehend.

'You see,' said Father Brown, turning the dressing-gown over slowly as he spoke, 'a man isn't expected to write his very best handwriting when he chips it on a tree. And if the man were not the man, if I make myself clear – Hullo!'

He was looking down at the red dressing-gown, and it seemed for the moment as if some of the red had come off on his finger; but both the faces turned towards it were already a shade paler.

'Blood!' said Father Brown; and for the instant there was a deadly stillness save for the melodious noises of the river.

Henry Sand cleared his throat and nose with noises that were by no means melodious. Then he said rather hoarsely: 'Whose blood?'

'Oh, mine,' said Father Brown; but he did not smile.

A moment after he said: 'There was a pin in this thing and I pricked myself. But I don't think you quite appreciate the point . . . the point of the pin, I do'; and he sucked his finger like a child.

'You see,' he said after another silence, 'the gown was folded up and pinned together; nobody could have unfolded it – at least without scratching himself. In plain words, Hubert Sand never *wore* this dressing-gown. Any more than Hubert Sand ever wrote on that tree. Or drowned himself in that river.'

The pince-nez tilted on Henry's enquiring nose fell off with a click; but he was otherwise motionless, as if rigid with surprise.

'Which brings us back,' went on Father Brown cheerfully, 'to somebody's taste for writing his private correspondence on trees, like Hiawatha and his picture-writing. Sand had all the time there was, before drowning himself. Why didn't he leave a note for his wife like a sane man? Or, shall we say . . . Why didn't the Other Man leave a note for the wife like a sane man? Because he would have had to forge the husband's handwriting; always a tricky thing now that experts are so nosey about it. But nobody can be expected to imitate even his own handwriting, let alone somebody else's, when he carves capital letters in the bark of a tree. This is not a suicide, Mr Sand. If it's anything at all, it's a murder.'

The bracken and bushes of the undergrowth snapped and crackled as the big young man rose out of them like a leviathan, and stood lowering, with his thick neck thrust forward.

'I'm no good at hiding things,' he said, 'and I half-suspected something like this – expected it, you might say, for a long time. To tell the truth, I could hardly be civil to the fellow – to either of them, for that matter.'

'What exactly do you mean?' asked the priest, looking him gravely full in the face.

'I mean,' said Henry Sand, 'that you have shown me the murder and I think I could show you the murderers.'

Father Brown was silent and the other went on rather jerkily.

'You said people sometimes wrote love-messages on trees. Well, as a fact, there are some of them on that tree; there are two sort of monograms twisted together up there under the leaves – I suppose you know that Lady Sand was the heiress of this place long before she married; and she knew that damned dandy of a secretary even in those days. I guess they used to meet here and write their vows upon the trysting tree. They seem to have used the trysting tree for another purpose later on. Sentiment, no doubt, or economy.'

'They must be very horrible people,' said Father Brown.

'Haven't there been any horrible people in history or the police-news?' demanded Sand with some excitement. 'Haven't there been lovers who made love seem more horrible than hate? Don't you know about Bothwell and all the bloody legends of such lovers?'

'I know the legend of Bothwell,' answered the priest. 'I also know it to be quite legendary. But of course it's true that husbands have been sometimes put away like that. By the way, where was he put away? I mean, where did they hide the body?'

'I suppose they drowned him, or threw him in the water when he was dead,' snorted the young man impatiently.

Father Brown blinked thoughtfully and then said: 'A river is a good place to hide an imaginary body. It's a rotten bad place to hide a real one. I mean, it's easy to say you've thrown it in, because it might be washed away to sea. But if you really did throw it in, it's about a hundred to one it wouldn't; the chances of it going ashore somewhere are enormous. I think they must have had a better scheme for hiding the body than that – or the body would have been found by now. And if there were any marks of violence – '

'Oh, bother hiding the body,' said Henry, with some irritation; 'haven't we witness enough in the writing on their own devilish tree?'

'The body is the chief witness in every murder,' answered the other. 'The hiding of the body, nine times out of ten, is the practical problem to be solved.'

There was a silence; and Father Brown continued to turn over the red dressing-gown and spread it out on the shining grass of the sunny shore; he did not look up. But, for some time past he had been conscious that the whole landscape had been changed for him by the presence of a third party; standing as still as a statue in the garden.

'By the way,' he said, lowering his voice, 'how do you explain that little guy with the glass eye, who brought your poor uncle a letter yesterday? It seemed to me he was entirely altered by reading it; that's why I wasn't surprised at the suicide, when I thought it was a suicide. That chap was a rather low-down private detective, or I'm much mistaken.'

'Why,' said Henry in a hesitating manner, 'why, he might have been – husbands do sometimes put on detectives in domestic tragedies like this, don't they? I suppose he'd got the proofs of their intrigue; and so they – '

'I shouldn't talk too loud,' said Father Brown, 'because your detective is detecting us at this moment, from about a yard beyond those bushes.'

They looked up, and sure enough the goblin with the glass eye was fixing them with that disagreeable optic, looking all the more grotesque for standing among the white and waxen blooms of the classical garden.

Henry Sand scrambled to his feet again with a rapidity that seemed breathless for one of his bulk, and asked the man very angrily and abruptly what he was doing, at the same time telling him to clear out at once.

'Lord Stanes,' said the goblin of the garden, 'would be much obliged if Father Brown would come up to the house and speak to him.'

Henry Sand turned away furiously; but the priest put down his fury to the dislike that was known to exist between him and the nobleman in question. As they mounted the slope, Father Brown paused a moment as if tracing patterns on the smooth tree-trunk, glanced upwards once at the darker and more hidden hieroglyph said to be a record of romance; and then stared at the wider and more sprawling letters of the confession, or supposed confession of suicide.

'Do those letters remind you of anything?' he asked. And when his sulky companion shook his head, he added: 'They remind me of the writing on that placard that threatened him with the vengeance of the strikers.'

* * *

'This is the hardest riddle and the queerest tale I have ever tackled,' said Father Brown, a month later, as he sat opposite Lord Stanes in the recently furnished apartment of No. 188, the end flat which was the last to be finished before the interregnum of the industrial dispute and the transfer of work from the Trade Union. It was comfortably furnished; and Lord Stanes was presiding over grog and cigars, when the priest made his confession with a grimace. Lord Stanes had become rather surprisingly friendly, in a cool and casual way.

'I know that is saying a good deal, with your record,' said Stanes, 'but certainly the detectives, including our seductive friend with the glass eye, don't seem at all able to see the solution.'

Father Brown laid down his cigar and said carefully: 'It isn't that they can't see the solution. It is that they can't see the problem.'

'Indeed,' said the other, 'perhaps I can't see the problem either.'

'The problem is unlike all other problems, for this reason,' said Father Brown. 'It seems as if the criminal deliberately did two different things, either of which might have been successful; but which, when done together, could only defeat each other. I am assuming, what I firmly believe, that the same murderer pinned up the proclamation threatening a sort of Bolshevik murder, and also wrote on the tree confessing to an ordinary suicide. Now you may say it is after all possible that the proclamation was a proletarian proclamation; that some extremist workmen wanted to kill their employer, and killed him. Even if that were true, it would still stick at the mystery of why they left, or why anybody left, a contrary trail of private self-destruction. But it certainly isn't true. None of these workmen, however bitter, would have done a thing like that. I know them pretty well; I know their leaders quite well. To suppose that people like Tom Bruce or Hogan would assassinate somebody they could go for in the newspapers, and damage in all sorts of different ways, is the sort of psychology that sensible people call lunacy. No; there was somebody, who was not an indignant workman, who first played the part of an indignant workman, and then played the part of a suicidal employer. But, in the name of wonder, why? If he thought he could pass it off smoothly as a suicide, why did he first spoil it all by publishing a threat of murder? You might say it was an afterthought to fix up the suicide story, as less provocative than the murder story. But it wasn't less provocative *after* the murder story. He must have known he had already turned our thoughts towards murder, when it should have been his whole object to keep our thoughts away from it. If it was an afterthought, it was the afterthought of a very thoughtless person. And I have a notion that this assassin is a very thoughtful person. Can you make anything of it?'

'No; but I see what you mean,' said Stanes, 'by saying that I didn't even see the problem. It isn't merely who killed Sand; it's why anybody should accuse somebody else of killing Sand and then accuse Sand of killing himself.'

Father Brown's face was knotted and the cigar was clenched in his teeth; the end of it glowed and darkened rhythmically like the signal of some burning pulse of the brain. Then he spoke as if to himself: 'We've got to follow very closely and very clearly. It's like separating threads of thought from each other; something like this. Because the murder charge really rather spoilt the suicide charge, he wouldn't normally have made the murder charge. But he did make it; so he had some other reason for making it. It was so strong a reason that perhaps it reconciled him even to weakening his other line of defence: that it was a suicide. In other words, the murder charge wasn't really a murder charge. I mean he wasn't using it as a murder charge; he wasn't doing it so as to shift to somebody else the guilt of murder; he was doing it for some other extraordinary reason of his own. His plan had to contain a proclamation that Sand would be murdered; whether it threw suspicion on other people or not. Somehow or other the mere proclamation itself was necessary. But why?'

He smoked and smouldered away with the same volcanic concentration for five minutes before he spoke again. 'What could a murderous proclamation do, besides suggesting that the strikers were the murderers? What *did* it do? One thing is obvious; it inevitably did the opposite of what it said. It told Sand not to lock out his men; and it was perhaps the only thing in the world that would really have made him do it. You've got to think of the sort of man and the sort of reputation. When a man has been called a Strong Man in our silly sensational newspapers, when he is fondly regarded as a Sportsman by all the most distinguished asses in England, he simply can't back down because he is threatened with a pistol. It would be like walking about at Ascot with a white feather stuck in his absurd white hat. It would break that inner idol or ideal of oneself, which every man not a downright dastard does really prefer to life. And Sand wasn't a dastard; he was courageous; he was also impulsive. It acted instantly like a charm: his nephew, who had been more or less mixed up with the workmen, cried out instantly that the threat must be absolutely and instantly defied.'

'Yes,' said Lord Stanes, 'I noticed that.' They looked at each other for an instant, and then Stanes added carelessly: 'So you think the thing the criminal wanted was – '

'The Lock-out!' cried the priest energetically. 'The Strike or whatever you call it; the cessation of work, anyhow. He wanted the work to stop at once; perhaps the blacklegs to come in at once; certainly the Trade Unionists to go out at once. That is what he really wanted; God knows why. And he brought that off, I think, really without bothering much about its other implication of the existence of Bolshevist assassins. But then . . . then I think something went wrong. I'm only guessing and groping very slowly here; but the only explanation I can think of is that something began to draw attention to the real seat of the trouble; to the reason, whatever it was, of his wanting to bring the building to a halt. And then belatedly, desperately, and rather inconsistently, he tried to lay the other trail that led to the river, simply and solely because it led away from the flats.'

He looked up through his moonlike spectacles, absorbing all the quality of the background and furniture; the restrained luxury of a quiet man of the world; and contrasting it with the two suitcases with which its occupant had arrived so recently in a newly finished and unfurnished flat. Then he said rather abruptly: 'In short, the murderer was frightened of something or somebody in the flats. By the way, why did *you* come to live in the flats? . . . Also by the way, young Henry told me you made an early appointment with him when you moved in. Is that true?'

'Not in the least,' said Stanes. 'I got the key from his uncle the night before. I've no notion why Henry came here that morning.'

'Ah,' said Father Brown, 'then I think I have some notion of why he came . . . I *thought* you startled him by coming in just when he was coming out.'

'And yet,' said Stanes, looking across with a glitter in his grey-green eyes, 'you do rather think that I also am a mystery.'

'I think you are two mysteries,' said Father Brown. 'The first is why you originally retired from Sand's business. The second is why you have since come back to live in Sand's buildings.'

Stanes smoked reflectively, knocked out his ash, and rang a bell on the table before him. 'If you'll excuse me,' he said, 'I will summon two more to the council. Jackson, the little detective you know of, will answer the bell; and I've asked Henry Sand to come in a little later.'

Father Brown rose from his seat, walked across the room and looked down frowning into the fireplace.

'Meanwhile,' continued Stanes, 'I don't mind answering both your questions. I left the Sand business because I was sure there was some hanky-panky in it and somebody was pinching all the money. I came back to it, and took this flat, because I wanted to watch for the real truth about old Sand's death – on the spot.'

Father Brown faced round as the detective entered the room; he stood staring at the hearthrug and repeated: 'On the spot.'

'Mr Jackson will tell you,' said Stanes, 'that Sir Hubert commissioned him to find out who was the thief robbing the firm; and he brought a note of his discoveries the day before old Hubert disappeared.'

'Yes,' said Father Brown, 'and I know now where he disappeared to. I know where the body is.'

'Do you mean – ?' began his host hastily.

'It is here,' said Father Brown, and stamped on the hearthrug. 'Here, under the elegant Persian rug in this cosy and comfortable room.'

'Where in the world did you find that?'

'I've just remembered,' said Father Brown, 'that I found it in my sleep.'

He closed his eyes as if trying to picture a dream, and went on dreamily: 'This is a murder story turning on the problem of How to Hide the Body; and I found it in my sleep. I was always woken up every morning by hammering from this building. On that morning I half-woke up, went to sleep again and woke once more, expecting to find it late; but it wasn't. Why? Because there *had* been hammering that morning, though all the usual work had stopped; short, hurried hammering in the small hours before dawn. Automatically a man sleeping stirs at such a familiar sound. But he goes to sleep again, because the usual sound is not at the usual hour. Now why did a certain secret criminal want all the work to cease suddenly; and only new workers come in? Because, if the old workers had come in next day, they would have found a new piece of work done in the night. The old workers would have known where they left off; and they would have found the whole flooring of this room already nailed down. Nailed down by a man who knew how to do it; having mixed a good deal with the workmen and learned their ways.'

As he spoke, the door was pushed open and a head poked in with a thrusting motion; a small head at the end of a thick neck and a face that blinked at them through glasses.

'Henry Sand said,' observed Father Brown, staring at the ceiling, 'that he was no good at hiding things. But I think he did himself an injustice.'

Henry Sand turned and moved swiftly away down the corridor.

'He not only hid his thefts from the firm quite successfully for years,' went on the priest with an air of abstraction, 'but when his uncle discovered them, he hid his uncle's corpse in an entirely new and original manner.'

At the same instant Stanes again rang a bell, with a long strident steady ringing; and the little man with the glass eye was propelled or shot along the corridor after the fugitive, with something of the rotatory motion of a mechanical figure in a zoetrope. At the same moment, Father Brown looked out of the window, leaning over a small balcony, and saw five or six men start from behind bushes and railings in the street below and spread out equally mechanically like a fan or net; opening out after the fugitive who had shot like a bullet out of the front door. Father Brown saw only the pattern of the story; which had never strayed from that room; where Henry had strangled Hubert and hid his body under impenetrable flooring, stopping the whole work on the building to do it. A pin-prick had started his own suspicions; but only to tell him he had been led down the long loop of a lie. The point of the pin was that it was pointless.

He fancied he understood Stanes at last, and he liked to collect queer people who were difficult to understand. He realised that this tired gentleman, whom he had once accused of having green blood, had indeed a sort of cold green flame of conscientiousness or conventional honour, that had made him first shift out of a shady business, and then feel ashamed of having shifted it on to others; and come back as a bored laborious detective; pitching his camp on the very spot where the corpse had been buried; so that the murderer, finding him sniffing so near the corpse, had wildly staged the alternative drama of the dressing-gown and the drowned man. All that was plain enough, but, before he withdrew his head from the night air and the stars, Father Brown threw one glance upwards at the vast black bulk of the cyclopean building heaved far up into the night, and remembered Egypt and Babylon, and all that is at once eternal and ephemeral in the work of man.

'I was right in what I said first of all,' he said. 'It reminds one of Coppée's poem about the Pharaoh and the Pyramid. This house is supposed to be a hundred houses; and yet the whole mountain of building is only one man's tomb.'

The Insoluble Problem

This queer incident, in some ways perhaps the queerest of the many that came his way, happened to Father Brown at the time when his French friend Flambeau had retired from the profession of crime and had entered with great energy and success on the profession of crime investigator. It happened that both as a thief and a thief-taker, Flambeau had rather specialised in the matter of jewel thefts, on which he was admitted to be an expert, both in the matter of identifying jewels and the equally practical matter of identifying jewel-thieves. And it was in connection with his special knowledge of this subject, and a special commission which it had won for him, that he rang up his friend the priest on the particular morning on which this story begins.

Father Brown was delighted to hear the voice of his old friend, even on the telephone; but in a general way, and especially at that particular moment, Father Brown was not very fond of the telephone. He was one who preferred to watch people's faces and feel social atmospheres, and he knew well that without these things, verbal messages are apt to be very misleading, especially from total strangers. And it seemed as if, on that particular morning, a swarm of total strangers had been buzzing in his ear with more or less unenlightening verbal messages; the telephone seemed to be possessed of a demon of triviality. Perhaps the most distinctive voice was one which asked him whether he did not issue regular permits for murder and theft upon the payment of a regular tariff hung up in his church; and as the stranger, on being informed that this was not the case, concluded the colloquy with a hollow laugh, it may be presumed that he remained unconvinced. Then an agitated, rather inconsequent female voice rang up requesting him to come round at once to a certain hotel he had heard of some forty-five miles on the road to a neighbouring cathedral town; the request being immediately followed by a contradiction in the same voice, more agitated and yet more inconsequent, telling him that it did not matter and that he was not wanted after all. Then came an interlude of a Press agency asking him if he had anything to say on what a Film Actress had said about Moustaches for Men; and finally yet a third return of the agitated and inconsequent lady at the hotel, saying that he was wanted, after all. He vaguely supposed that this marked some of the hesitations and panics not unknown among those who are vaguely veering in the direction of Instruction, but he confessed to a considerable relief when the voice of Flambeau wound up the series with a hearty threat of immediately turning up for breakfast.

Father Brown very much preferred to talk to a friend sitting comfortably over a pipe, but it soon appeared that his visitor was on the war-path and full of energy, having every intention of carrying off the little priest captive on some important expedition of his own. It was true that there was a special circumstance involved which might be supposed to claim the priest's attention. Flambeau had figured several times of late as successfully thwarting a theft of famous precious stones; he had torn the tiara of the Duchess of Dulwich out of the very hand of the bandit as he bolted through the garden. He laid so ingenious a trap for the criminal who planned to carry off the celebrated Sapphire Necklace that the artist in question actually carried off the copy which he had himself planned to leave as a substitute.

Such were doubtless the reasons that had led to his being specially summoned to guard the delivery of a rather different sort of treasure; perhaps even more valuable in its mere materials, but possessing also another sort of value. A world-famous reliquary, supposed to contain a relic of St Dorothy the martyr, was to be delivered at the Catholic monastery in a cathedral town; and one of the most famous of international jewel-thieves was supposed to have an eye on it; or rather presumably on the gold and rubies of its setting, rather than its purely hagiological importance. Perhaps there was something in this association of ideas which made Flambeau feel that the priest would be a particularly appropriate companion in his adventure; but anyhow, he descended on him, breathing fire and ambition and very voluble about his plans for preventing the theft.

Flambeau indeed bestrode the priest's hearth gigantically and in the old swaggering musketeer attitude, twirling his great moustaches.

'You can't,' he cried, referring to the sixty-mile road to Casterbury. 'You can't allow a profane robbery like that to happen under your very nose.'

The relic was not to reach the monastery till the evening; and there was no need for its defenders to arrive earlier; for indeed a motor-journey would take them the greater part of the day. Moreover, Father Brown casually remarked that there was an inn on the road, at which he would prefer to lunch, as he had been already asked to look in there as soon as was convenient.

As they drove along through a densely wooded but sparsely inhabited landscape, in which inns and all other buildings seemed to grow rarer and rarer, the daylight began to take on the character of a stormy twilight even in the heat of noon; and dark purple clouds gathered over dark grey forests. As is common under the lurid quietude of that kind of light, what colour there was in the landscape gained a sort of secretive glow which is not found in objects under the full sunlight; and ragged red leaves or golden or orange fungi seemed to burn with a dark fire of their own. Under such a half-light they came to a break in the woods like a great rent in a grey wall, and saw beyond, standing above the gap, the tall and rather outlandish-looking inn that bore the name of the Green Dragon.

The two old companions had often arrived together at inns and other human habitations, and found a somewhat singular state of things there; but the signs of singularity had seldom manifested themselves so early. For while their car was still some hundreds of yards from the dark green door, which matched the dark green shutters of the high and narrow building, the door was thrown open with violence and a woman with a wild mop of red hair rushed to meet them, as if she were ready to board the car in full career. Flambeau brought the car to a standstill, but almost before he had done so, she thrust her white and tragic face into the window, crying: 'Are you Father Brown?' and then almost in the same breath; 'who is this man?'

'This gentleman's name is Flambeau,' said Father Brown in a tranquil manner, 'and what can I do for you?'

'Come into the inn,' she said, with extraordinary abruptness even under the circumstances. 'There's been a murder done.'

They got out of the car in silence and followed her to the dark green door which opened inwards on a sort of dark green alley, formed of stakes and wooden pillars, wreathed with vine and ivy, showing square leaves of black and red and many sombre colours. This again led through an inner door into a sort of large parlour hung with rusty trophies of Cavalier arms, of which the furniture seemed to be antiquated and also in great confusion, like the inside of a lumber-room. They were quite startled for the moment; for it seemed as if one large piece of lumber rose and moved towards them; so dusty and shabby and ungainly was the man who thus abandoned what seemed like a state of permanent immobility.

Strangely enough, the man seemed to have a certain agility of politeness, when once he did move; even if it suggested the wooden joints of a courtly step-ladder or an obsequious towel-horse. Both Flambeau and Father Brown felt that they had hardly ever clapped eyes on a man who was so difficult to place. He was not what is called a gentleman; yet he had something of the dusty refinement of a scholar; there was something faintly disreputable or *déclassé* about him; and yet the smell of him was rather bookish than Bohemian. He was thin and pale, with a pointed nose and a dark pointed beard; his brow was bald, but his hair behind long and lank and stringy; and the expression of his eyes was almost entirely masked by a pair of blue spectacles. Father Brown felt that he had met something of the sort somewhere, and a long time ago; but he could no longer put a name to it. The lumber he sat among was largely literary lumber; especially bundles of seventeenth-century pamphlets.

'Do I understand the lady to say,' asked Flambeau gravely, 'that there is a murder here?'

The lady nodded her red ragged head rather impatiently; except for those flaming elf-locks she had lost some of her look of wildness; her dark dress was of a certain dignity and neatness; her features were strong and handsome; and there was something about her suggesting that double strength of body and mind which makes women powerful, particularly in contrast with men like the man in blue spectacles. Nevertheless, it was he who gave the only articulate answer, intervening with a certain antic gallantry.

'It is true that my unfortunate sister-in-law,' he explained, 'has almost this moment suffered a most appalling shock which we should all have desired to spare her. I only wish that I myself had made the discovery and suffered only the further distress of bringing the terrible news. Unfortunately it was Mrs Flood herself who found her aged grandfather, long sick and bedridden in this hotel, actually dead in the garden; in circumstances which point only too plainly to violence and assault. Curious circumstances, I may say, very curious circumstances indeed.' And he coughed slightly, as if apologising for them.

Flambeau bowed to the lady and expressed his sincere sympathies; then he said to the man: 'I think you said, sir, that you are Mrs Flood's brother-in-law.'

'I am Dr Oscar Flood,' replied the other. 'My brother, this lady's husband, is at present away on the Continent on business, and she is running the hotel. Her grandfather was partially paralysed and very far advanced in years. He was never known to leave his bedroom; so that really these extraordinary circumstances . . .'

'Have you sent for a doctor or the police?' asked Flambeau.

'Yes,' replied Dr Flood, 'we rang up after making the dreadful discovery; but they can hardly be here for some hours. This roadhouse stands so very remote. It is only used by people going to Casterbury or even beyond. So we thought we might ask for your valuable assistance until – '

'If we are to be of any assistance,' said Father Brown, interrupting in too abstracted a manner to seem uncivil, 'I should say we had better go and look at the circumstances at once.'

He stepped almost mechanically towards the door; and almost ran into a man who was shouldering his way in; a big, heavy young man with dark hair unbrushed and untidy, who would nevertheless have been rather handsome save for a slight disfigurement of one eye, which gave him rather a sinister appearance.

'What the devil are you doing?' he blurted out, 'telling every Tom, Dick and Harry – at least you ought to wait for the police.'

'I will be answerable to the police,' said Flambeau with a certain magnificence, and a sudden air of having taken command of everything. He advanced to the doorway, and as he was much bigger than the big young man, and his moustaches were as formidable as the horns of a Spanish bull, the big young man backed before him and had an inconsequent air of being thrown out and left behind, as the group swept out into the garden and up the flagged path towards the mulberry plantation. Only Flambeau heard the little priest say to the doctor: 'He doesn't seem to love us really, does he? By the way, who is he?'

'His name is Dunn,' said the doctor, with a certain restraint of manner. 'My sister-in-law gave him the job of managing the garden, because he lost an eye in the War.'

As they went through the mulberry bushes, the landscape of the garden presented that rich yet ominous effect which is found when the land is actually brighter than the sky. In the broken sunlight from behind, the tree-tops in front of them stood up like pale green flames against a sky steadily blackening with storm, through every shade of purple and violet. The same light struck strips of the lawn and garden beds; and whatever it illuminated seemed more mysteriously sombre and secret for the light. The garden bed was dotted with tulips that looked like drops of dark blood, and some of which one might have sworn were truly black; and the line ended appropriately with a tulip tree; which Father Brown was disposed, if partly by some confused memory, to identify with what is commonly called the Judas tree. What assisted the association was the fact that there was hanging from one of the branches, like a dried fruit, the dry, thin body of an old man, with a long beard that wagged grotesquely in the wind.

There lay on it something more than the horror of darkness, the horror of sunlight; for the fitful sun painted tree and man in gay colours like a stage property; the tree was in flower and the corpse was hung with a faded peacock-green dressing-gown, and wore on its wagging head a scarlet smoking-cap. Also it had red bedroom-slippers, one of which had fallen off and lay on the grass like a blot of blood.

But neither Flambeau or Father Brown was looking at these things as yet. They were both staring at a strange object that seemed to stick out of the middle of the dead man's shrunken figure; and which they gradually perceived to be the black but rather rusty iron hilt of a seventeenth-century sword, which had completely transfixed the body. They both remained almost motionless as they gazed at it; until the restless Dr Flood seemed to grow quite impatient with their stolidity.

'What puzzles me most,' he said, nervously snapping his fingers, 'is the actual state of the body. And yet it has given me an idea already.'

Flambeau had stepped up to the tree and was studying the sword-hilt through an eyeglass. But for some odd reason, it was at that very instant that the priest in sheer perversity spun round like a teetotum, turned his back on the corpse, and looked peeringly in the very opposite direction. He was just in time to see the red head of Mrs Flood at the remote end of the garden, turned towards a dark young man, too dim with distance to be identified, who was at that moment mounting a motor-bicycle; who vanished, leaving behind him only the dying din of that vehicle. Then the woman turned and began to walk towards them across the garden, just as Father Brown turned also and began a careful inspection of the sword-hilt and the hanging corpse.

'I understand you only found him about half an hour ago,' said Flambeau. 'Was there anybody about here just before that? I mean anybody in his bedroom, or that part of the house, or this part of the garden – say for an hour beforehand?'

'No,' said the doctor with precision. 'That is the very tragic accident. My sister-in-law was in the pantry, which is a sort of outhouse on the other side; this man Dunn was in the kitchen-garden, which is also in that direction; and I myself was poking about among the books, in a room just behind the one you found me in. There are two female servants, but one had gone to the post and the other was in the attic.'

'And were any of these people,' asked Flambeau, very quietly, 'I say any of these people, at all on bad terms with the poor old gentleman?'

'He was the object of almost universal affection,' replied the doctor solemnly. 'If there were any misunderstandings, they were mild and of a sort common in modern times. The old man was attached to the old religious habits; and perhaps his daughter and son-in-law had rather wider views. All that can have had nothing to do with a ghastly and fantastic assassination like this.'

'It depends on how wide the modern views were,' said Father Brown, 'or how narrow.'

At this moment they heard Mrs Flood hallooing across the garden as she came, and calling her brother-in-law to her with a certain impatience. He hurried towards her and was soon out of earshot; but as he went he waved his hand apologetically and then pointed with a long finger to the ground.

'You will find the footprints very intriguing,' he said; with the same strange air, as of a funereal showman.

The two amateur detectives looked across at each other. 'I find several other things intriguing,' said Flambeau.

'Oh, yes,' said the priest, staring rather foolishly at the grass.

'I was wondering,' said Flambeau, 'why they should hang a man by the neck till he was dead, and then take the trouble to stick him with a sword.'

'And I was wondering,' said Father Brown, 'why they should kill a man with a sword thrust through his heart, and then take the trouble to hang him by the neck.'

'Oh, you are simply being contrary,' protested his friend. 'I can see at a glance that they didn't stab him alive. The body would have bled more and the wound wouldn't have closed like that.'

'And I could see at a glance,' said Father Brown, peering up very awkwardly, with his short stature and short sight, 'that they didn't hang him alive. If you'll look at the knot in the noose, you will see it's tied so clumsily that a twist of rope holds it away from the neck, so that it couldn't throttle a man at all. He was dead before they put the rope on him; and he was dead before they put the sword in him. And how was he really killed?'

'I think,' remarked the other, 'that we'd better go back to the house and have a look at his bedroom – and other things.'

'So we will,' said Father Brown. 'But among other things perhaps we had better have a look at these footprints. Better begin at the other end, I think, by his window. Well, there are no footprints on the paved path, as there might be; but then again there mightn't be. Well, here is the lawn just under his bedroom window. And here are his footprints plain enough.'

He blinked ominously at the footprints; and then began carefully retracing his path towards the tree, every now and then ducking in an undignified manner to look at something on the ground. Eventually he returned to Flambeau and said in a chatty manner: 'Well, do you know the story that is written there very plainly? Though it's not exactly a plain story.'

'I wouldn't be content to call it plain,' said Flambeau. 'I should call it quite ugly – '

'Well,' said Father Brown, 'the story that is stamped quite plainly on the earth, with exact moulds of the old man's slippers, is this. The aged paralytic leapt from the window and ran down the beds parallel to the path, quite eager for all the fun of being strangled and stabbed; so eager that he hopped on one leg out of sheer light-heartedness; and even occasionally turned cartwheels – '

'Stop!' cried Flambeau, angrily. 'What the hell is all this hellish pantomime?'

Father Brown merely raised his eyebrows and gestured mildly towards the hieroglyphs in the dust. 'About half the way there's only the mark of one slipper; and in some places the mark of a hand planted all by itself.'

'Couldn't he have limped and then fallen?' asked Flambeau.

Father Brown shook his head. 'At least he'd have tried to use his hands and feet, or knees and elbows, in getting up. There are no other marks there of any kind. Of course the flagged path is quite near, and there are no marks on that; though there might be on the soil between the cracks; it's a crazy pavement.'

'By God, it's a crazy pavement; and a crazy garden; and a crazy story!' And Flambeau looked gloomily across the gloomy and storm-stricken garden, across which the crooked patchwork paths did indeed give a queer aptness to the quaint old English adjective.

'And now,' said Father Brown, 'let us go up and look at his room.' They went in by a door not far from the bedroom window; and the priest paused a moment to look at an ordinary garden broomstick, for sweeping up leaves, that was leaning against the wall. 'Do you see that?'

'It's a broomstick,' said Flambeau, with solid irony.

'It's a blunder,' said Father Brown; 'the first blunder that I've seen in this curious plot.'

They mounted the stairs and entered the old man's bedroom; and a glance at it made fairly clear the main facts, both about the foundation and disunion of the family. Father Brown had felt from the first that he was in what was, or had been, a Catholic household; but was, at least partly, inhabited by lapsed or very loose Catholics. The pictures and images in the grandfather's room made it clear that what positive piety remained had been practically confined to him; and that his kindred had, for some reason or other, gone Pagan. But he agreed that this was a hopelessly inadequate explanation even of an ordinary murder; let alone such a very extraordinary murder as this. 'Hang it all,' he muttered, 'the murder is really the least extraordinary part of it.' And even as he used the chance phrase, a slow light began to dawn upon his face.

Flambeau had seated himself on a chair by the little table which stood beside the dead man's bed. He was frowning thoughtfully at three or four white pills or pellets that lay in a small tray beside a bottle of water.

'The murderer or murderess,' said Flambeau, 'had some incomprehensible reason or other for wanting us to think the dead man was strangled or stabbed or both. He was not strangled or stabbed or anything of the kind. Why did they want to suggest it? The most logical explanation is that he died in some particular way which would, in itself, suggest a connection with some particular person. Suppose, for instance, he was poisoned. And suppose somebody is involved who would naturally look more like a poisoner than anybody else.'

'After all,' said Father Brown softly, 'our friend in the blue spectacles is a doctor.'

'I'm going to examine these pills pretty carefully,' went on Flambeau. 'I don't want to lose them, though. They look as if they were soluble in water.'

'It may take you some time to do anything scientific with them,' said the priest, 'and the police-doctor may be here before that. So I should certainly advise you not to lose them. That is, if you are going to wait for the police-doctor.'

'I am going to stay here till I have solved this problem,' said Flambeau.

'Then you will stay here for ever,' said Father Brown, looking calmly out of the window. 'I don't think I shall stay in this room, anyhow.'

'Do you mean that I shan't solve the problem?' asked his friend. 'Why shouldn't I solve the problem?'

'Because it isn't soluble in water. No, nor in blood,' said the priest; and he went down the dark stairs into the darkening garden. There he saw again what he had already seen from the window.

The heat and weight and obscurity of the thunderous sky seemed to be pressing yet more closely on the landscape; the clouds had conquered the sun which, above, in a narrowing clearance, stood up paler than the moon. There was a thrill of thunder in the air, but now no more stirring of wind or breeze; and even the colours of the garden seemed only like richer shades of darkness. But one colour still glowed with a certain dusky vividness; and that was the red hair of the woman of that house, who was standing with a sort of rigidity, staring, with her hands thrust up into her hair. That scene of eclipse, with something deeper in his own doubts about its significance, brought to the surface the memory of haunting and mystical lines; and he found himself murmuring: 'A secret spot, as savage and enchanted as e'er beneath a waning moon was haunted by woman wailing for her demon lover.' His muttering became more agitated. 'Holy Mary, Mother of God, pray for us sinners . . . that's what it is; that's terribly like what it is; *woman wailing for her demon lover*.'

He was hesitant and almost shaky as he approached the woman; but he spoke with his common composure. He was gazing at her very steadily, as he told her earnestly that she must not be morbid because of the mere accidental accessories of the tragedy, with all their mad ugliness. 'The pictures in your grandfather's room were truer to him than that ugly picture that we saw,' he said gravely. 'Something tells me he was a good man; and it does not matter what his murderers did with his body.'

'Oh, I am sick of his holy pictures and statues!' she said, turning her head away. 'Why don't they defend themselves, if they are what you say they are? But rioters can knock off the Blessed Virgin's head and nothing happens to them. Oh, what's the good? You can't blame us, you daren't blame us, if we've found out that Man is stronger than God.'

'Surely,' said Father Brown very gently, 'it is not generous to make even God's patience with us a point against Him.'

'God may be patient and Man impatient,' she answered, 'and suppose we like the impatience better. You call it sacrilege; but you can't stop it.'

Father Brown gave a curious little jump. 'Sacrilege!' he said; and suddenly turned back to the doorway with a new brisk air of decision. At the same moment Flambeau appeared in the doorway, pale with excitement, with a screw of paper in his hands. Father Brown had already opened his mouth to speak, but his impetuous friend spoke before him.

'I'm on the track at last!' cried Flambeau. 'These pills look the same, but they're really different. And do you know that, at the very moment I spotted them, that one-eyed brute of a gardener thrust his white face into the room;

and he was carrying a horse-pistol. I knocked it out of his hand and threw him down the stairs, but I begin to understand everything. If I stay here another hour or two, I shall finish my job.'

'Then you will not finish it,' said the priest, with a ring in his voice very rare in him indeed. 'We shall not stay here another hour. We shall not stay here another minute. We must leave this place at once!'

'What!' cried the astounded Flambeau. 'Just when we are getting near the truth! Why, you can tell that we're getting near the truth because they are afraid of us.'

Father Brown looked at him with a stony and inscrutable face, and said: 'They are not afraid of us when we are here. They will only be afraid of us when we are not here.'

They had both become conscious that the rather fidgety figure of Dr Flood was hovering in the lurid haze; now it precipitated itself forward with the wildest gestures.

'Stop! Listen!' cried the agitated doctor. 'I have discovered the truth!'

'Then you can explain it to your own police,' said Father Brown, briefly. 'They ought to be coming soon. But we must be going.'

The doctor seemed thrown into a whirlpool of emotions, eventually rising to the surface again with a despairing cry. He spread out his arms like a cross, barring their way.

'Be it so!' he cried. 'I will not deceive you now, by saying I have discovered the truth. I will only confess the truth.'

'Then you can confess it to your own priest,' said Father Brown, and strode towards the garden gate, followed by his staring friend. Before he reached the gate, another figure had rushed athwart him like the wind; and Dunn the gardener was shouting at him some unintelligible derision at detectives who were running away from their job. Then the priest ducked just in time to dodge a blow from the horse-pistol, wielded like a club. But Dunn was just not in time to dodge a blow from the fist of Flambeau, which was like the club of Hercules. The two left Mr Dunn spread flat behind them on the path, and, passing out of the gate, went out and got into their car in silence. Flambeau only asked one brief question and Father Brown only answered: 'Casterbury.'

At last, after a long silence, the priest observed: 'I could almost believe the storm belonged only to that garden, and came out of a storm in the soul.'

'My friend,' said Flambeau. 'I have known you a long time, and when you show certain signs of certainty, I follow your lead. But I hope you are not going to tell me that you took me away from that fascinating job, because you did not like the atmosphere.'

'Well, it was certainly a terrible atmosphere,' replied Father Brown, calmly. 'Dreadful and passionate and oppressive. And the most dreadful thing about it was this – that there was no hate in it at all.'

'Somebody,' suggested Flambeau, 'seems to have had a slight dislike of grandpapa.'

'Nobody had any dislike of anybody,' said Father Brown with a groan. 'That was the dreadful thing in that darkness. It was love.'

'Curious way of expressing love – to strangle somebody and stick him with a sword,' observed the other.

'It was love,' repeated the priest, 'and it filled the house with terror.'

'Don't tell me,' protested Flambeau, 'that that beautiful woman is in love with that spider in spectacles.'

'No,' said Father Brown and groaned again. 'She is in love with her husband. It is ghastly.'

'It is a state of things that I have often heard you recommend,' replied Flambeau. 'You cannot call that lawless love.'

'Not lawless in that sense,' answered Father Brown; then he turned sharply on his elbow and spoke with a new warmth: 'Do you think I don't know that the love of a man and a woman was the first command of God and is glorious for ever? Are you one of those idiots who think we don't admire love and marriage? Do I need to be told of the Garden of Eden or the wine of Cana? It is just because the strength in the thing was the strength of God, that it rages with that awful energy even when it breaks loose from God. When the Garden becomes a jungle, but still a glorious jungle; when the second fermentation turns the wine of Cana into the vinegar of Calvary. Do you think I don't know all that?'

'I'm sure you do,' said Flambeau, 'but I don't yet know much about my problem of the murder.'

'The murder cannot be solved,' said Father Brown.

'And why not?' demanded his friend.

'Because there is no murder to solve,' said Father Brown.

Flambeau was silent with sheer surprise; and it was his friend who resumed in a quiet tone: 'I'll tell you a curious thing. I talked with that woman when she was wild with grief; but she never said anything about the murder. She never mentioned murder, or even alluded to murder. What she did mention repeatedly was sacrilege.' Then, with another jerk of verbal disconnection, he added: 'Have you ever heard of Tiger Tyrone?'

'Haven't I!' cried Flambeau. 'Why, that's the very man who's supposed to be after the reliquary, and whom I've been commissioned specially to circumvent. He's the most violent and daring gangster who ever visited this country; Irish, of course, but the sort that goes quite crazily anticlerical. Perhaps he's dabbled in a little diabolism in these secret societies; anyhow, he has a macabre taste for playing all sorts of wild tricks that look wickeder than they are. Otherwise he's not the wickedest; he seldom kills, and never for cruelty; but he loves doing anything to shock people, especially his own people; robbing churches or digging up skeletons or what not.'

'Yes,' said Father Brown, 'it all fits in. I ought to have seen it all long before.'

'I don't see how we could have seen anything, after only an hour's investigation,' said the detective defensively.

'I ought to have seen it before there was anything to investigate,' said the priest. 'I ought to have known it before you arrived this morning.'

'What on earth do you mean?'

'It only shows how wrong voices sound on the telephone,' said Father Brown reflectively. 'I heard all three stages of the thing this morning; and I thought they were trifles. First, a woman rang me up and asked me to go to that inn as soon as possible. What did that mean? Of course it meant that the old grandfather was dying. Then she rang up to say that I needn't go, after all. What did that mean? Of course it meant that the old grandfather was dead. He had died quite peaceably in his bed; probably heart failure from sheer old age. And then she rang up a third time and said I was to go, after all. What did that mean? Ah, that is rather more interesting!'

He went on after a moment's pause: 'Tiger Tyrone, whose wife worships him, took hold of one of his mad ideas, and yet it was a crafty idea, too. He had just heard that you were tracking him down, that you knew him and his methods and were coming to save the reliquary; he may have heard that I have sometimes been of some assistance. He wanted to stop us on the road; and his trick for doing it was to stage a murder. It was a pretty horrible thing to do; but it wasn't a murder. Probably he bullied his wife with an air of brutal common sense, saying he could only escape penal servitude by using a dead body that couldn't suffer anything from such use. Anyhow, his wife would do anything for him; but she felt all the unnatural hideousness of that hanging masquerade; and that's why she talked about sacrilege. She was thinking of the desecration of the relic; but also of the desecration of the deathbed. The brother's one of those shoddy – scientific – rebels who tinker with dud bombs; an idealist run to seed. But he's devoted to Tiger; and so is the gardener. Perhaps it's a point in his favour that so many people seem devoted to him.

'There was one little point that set me guessing very early. Among the old books the doctor was turning over, was a bundle of seventeenth-century pamphlets; and I caught one title: *True Declaration of the Trial and Execution of My Lord Stafford*. Now Stafford was executed in the Popish Plot business, which began with one of history's detective stories; the death of Sir Edmund Berry Godfrey. Godfrey was found dead in a ditch, and part of the mystery was that he had marks of strangulation, but was also transfixed with his own sword. I thought at once that somebody in the house might have got the idea from here. But he couldn't have wanted it as a way of committing a murder.

He can only have wanted it as a way of creating a mystery. Then I saw that this applied to all the other outrageous details. They were devilish enough; but it wasn't mere devilry; there was a rag of excuse; because they had to make the mystery as contradictory and complicated as possible, to make sure that we should be a long time solving it – or rather seeing through it. So they dragged the poor old man off his deathbed and made the corpse hop and turn cartwheels and do everything that it *couldn't* have done. They had to give us an Insoluble Problem. They swept their own tracks off the path, leaving the broom. Fortunately we did see through it in time.'

'You saw through it in time,' said Flambeau. 'I might have lingered a little longer over the second trail they left, sprinkled with assorted pills.'

'Well, anyhow, we got away,' said Father Brown, comfortably.

'And that, I presume,' said Flambeau, 'is the reason I am driving at this rate along the road to Casterbury.'

* * *

That night in the monastery and church at Casterbury there were events calculated to stagger monastic seclusion. The reliquary of St Dorothy, in a casket gorgeous with gold and rubies, was temporarily placed in a side room near the chapel of the monastery, to be brought in with a procession for a special service at the end of Benediction. It was guarded for the moment by one monk, who watched it in a tense and vigilant manner; for he and his brethren knew all about the shadow of peril from the prowling of Tiger Tyrone. Thus it was that the monk was on his feet in a flash, when he saw one of the low-latticed windows beginning to open and a dark object crawling like a black serpent through the crack. Rushing across, he gripped it and found it was the arm and sleeve of a man, terminating with a handsome cuff and a smart dark-grey glove. Laying hold of it, he shouted for help, and even as he did so, a man darted into the room through the door behind his back and snatched the casket he had left behind him on the table. Almost at the same instant, the arm wedged in the window came away in his hand, and he stood holding the stuffed limb of a dummy.

Tiger Tyrone had played that trick before, but to the monk it was a novelty. Fortunately, there was at least one person to whom the Tiger's tricks were not a novelty; and that person appeared with militant moustaches, gigantically framed in the doorway, at the very moment when the Tiger turned to escape by it. Flambeau and Tiger Tyrone looked at each other with steady eyes and exchanged something that was almost like a military salute.

* * *

Meanwhile Father Brown had slipped into the chapel, to say a prayer for several persons involved in these unseemly events. But he was rather smiling than otherwise, and, to tell the truth, he was not by any means hopeless about Mr Tyrone and his deplorable family; but rather more hopeful than he was for many more respectable people. Then his thoughts widened with the grander perspectives of the place and the occasion. Against black and green marbles at the end of the rather rococo chapel, the dark-red vestments of the festival of a martyr were in their turn a background for a fierier red; a red like red-hot coals; the rubies of the reliquary; the roses of St Dorothy. And he had again a thought to throw back to the strange events of that day, and the woman who had shuddered at the sacrilege she had helped. After all, he thought, St Dorothy also had a Pagan lover; but he had not dominated her or destroyed her faith. She had died free and for the truth; and then had sent him roses from Paradise.

He raised his eyes and saw through the veil of incense smoke and of twinkling lights that Benediction was drawing to its end while the procession waited. The sense of accumulated riches of time and tradition pressed past him like a crowd moving in rank after rank, through unending centuries; and high above them all, like a garland of unfading flames, like the sun of our mortal midnight, the great monstrance blazed against the darkness of the vaulted shadows, as it blazed against the black enigma of the universe. For some are convinced that this enigma also is an Insoluble Problem. And others have equal certitude that it has but one solution.

The Vampire of the Village

At the twist of a path in the hills, where two poplars stood up like pyramids dwarfing the tiny village of Potter's Pond, a mere huddle of houses, there once walked a man in a costume of a very conspicuous cut and colour, wearing a vivid magenta coat and a white hat tilted upon black ambrosial curls, which ended with a sort of Byronic flourish of whisker.

The riddle of why he was wearing clothes of such fantastic antiquity, yet wearing them with an air of fashion and even swagger, was but one of the many riddles that were eventually solved in solving the mystery of his fate. The point here is that when he had passed the poplars he seemed to have vanished; as if he had faded into the wan and widening dawn or been blown away upon the wind of morning.

It was only about a week afterwards that his body was found a quarter of a mile away, broken upon the steep rockeries of a terraced garden leading up to a gaunt and shuttered house called the Grange. Just before he had vanished, he had been accidentally overheard apparently quarrelling with some bystanders, and especially abusing their village as 'a wretched little hamlet'; and it was supposed that he had aroused some extreme passions of local patriotism and eventually been their victim. At least the local doctor testified that the skull had suffered a crushing blow that might have caused death, through probably only inflicted with some sort of club or cudgel. This fitted in well enough with the notion of an attack by rather savage yokels. But nobody ever found any means of tracing any particular yokel; and the inquest returned a verdict of murder by some persons unknown.

A year or two afterwards the question was reopened in a curious way; a series of events which led a certain Dr Mulborough, called by his intimates Mulberry in apt allusion to something rich and fruity about his dark rotundity and rather empurpled visage, travelling by train down to Potter's Pond, with a friend whom he had often consulted upon problems of the kind. In spite of the somewhat port-winy and ponderous exterior of the doctor, he had a shrewd eye and was really a man of very remarkable sense; which he considered that he showed in consulting a little priest named Brown, whose acquaintance he had made over a poisoning case long ago. The little priest was sitting opposite to him, with the air of a patient baby absorbing instruction; and the doctor was explaining at length the real reasons for the journey.

'I cannot agree with the gentleman in the magenta coat that Potter's Pond is only a wretched little hamlet. But it is certainly a very remote and secluded village; so that it seems quite outlandish, like a village of a hundred years ago. The spinsters are really spinsters – damn it, you could almost imagine you saw them spin. The ladies are not just ladies. They are gentlewomen; and their chemist is not a chemist, but an apothecary; pronounced potecary. They do just admit the existence of an ordinary doctor like myself to assist the apothecary. But I am considered rather a juvenile innovation, because I am only fifty-seven years old and have only been in the county for twenty-eight years. The solicitor looks as if he had known it for twenty-eight thousand years. Then there is the old Admiral, who is just like a Dickens illustration; with a house full of cutlasses and cuttle-fish and equipped with a telescope.'

'I suppose,' said Father Brown, 'there are always a certain number of Admirals washed up on the shore. But I never understood why they get stranded so far inland.'

'Certainly no dead-alive place in the depths of the country is complete without one of these little creatures,' said the doctor. 'And then, of course, there is the proper sort of clergyman; Tory and High Church in a dusty fashion dating from Archbishop Laud; more of an old woman than any of the old women. He's a white-haired studious old bird, more easily shocked than the spinsters. Indeed, the gentlewomen, though Puritan in their principles, are sometimes pretty plain in their speech; as the real Puritans were. Once or twice I have known old Miss Carstairs-Carew use expressions as lively as anything in the Bible. The dear old clergyman is assiduous in reading the Bible; but I almost fancy he shuts his eyes when he comes to those words. Well, you know I'm not particularly modern. I don't enjoy this jazzing and joy-riding of the Bright Young Things – '

'The Bright Young Things don't enjoy it,' said Father Brown. 'That is the real tragedy.'

'But I am naturally rather more in touch with the world than the people in this prehistoric village,' pursued the doctor. 'And I had reached a point when I almost welcomed the Great Scandal.'

'Don't say the Bright Young Things have found Potter's Pond after all,' observed the priest, smiling.

'Oh, even our scandal is on old-established melodramatic lines. Need I say that the clergyman's son promises to be our problem? It would be almost irregular, if the clergyman's son were quite regular. So far as I can see, he is very mildly and almost feebly irregular. He was first seen drinking ale outside the Blue Lion. Only it seems he is a poet, which in those parts is next door to being a poacher.'

'Surely,' said Father Brown, 'even in Potter's Pond that cannot be the Great Scandal.'

'No,' replied the doctor gravely. 'The Great Scandal began thus. In the house called the Grange, situated at the extreme end of the Grove, there lives a lady. A Lonely Lady. She calls herself Mrs Maltravers (that is how we put it); but she only came a year or two ago and nobody knows anything about her. "I can't think why she wants to live here," said Miss Carstairs-Carew; "we do not visit her." '

'Perhaps that's why she wants to live there,' said Father Brown.

'Well, her seclusion is considered suspicious. She annoys them by being good-looking and even what is called good style. And all the young men are warned against her as a vamp.'

'People who lose all their charity generally lose all their logic,' remarked Father Brown. 'It's rather ridiculous to complain that she keeps to herself; and then accuse her of vamping the whole male population.'

'That is true,' said the doctor. 'And yet she is really rather a puzzling person. I saw her and found her intriguing; one of those brown women, long and elegant and beautifully ugly, if you know what I mean. She is rather witty, and though young enough certainly gives me an impression of what they call – well, experience. What the old ladies call a Past.'

'All the old ladies having been born this very minute,' observed Father Brown. 'I think I can assume she is supposed to have vamped the parson's son.'

'Yes, and it seems to be a very awful problem to the poor old parson. She is supposed to be a widow.'

Father Brown's face had a flash and spasm of his rare irritation. 'She is supposed to be a widow, as the parson's son is supposed to be the parson's son, and the solicitor is supposed to be a solicitor and you are supposed to be a doctor. Why in thunder shouldn't she be a widow? Have they one speck of *prima facie* evidence for doubting that she is what she says she is?'

Dr Mulborough abruptly squared his broad shoulders and sat up. 'Of course you're right again,' he said. 'But we haven't come to the scandal yet. Well, the scandal is that she is a widow.'

'Oh,' said Father Brown; and his face altered and he said something soft and faint, that might almost have been 'My God!'

'First of all,' said the doctor, 'they have made one discovery about Mrs Maltravers. She is an actress.'

'I fancied so,' said Father Brown. 'Never mind why. I had another fancy about her, that would seem even more irrelevant.'

'Well, at that instant it was scandal enough that she was an actress. The dear old clergyman of course is heartbroken, to think that his white hairs should be brought in sorrow to the grave by an actress and adventuress. The spinsters shriek in chorus. The Admiral admits he has sometimes been to a theatre in town; but objects to such things in what he calls "our midst". Well, of course I've no particular objections of that kind. This actress is certainly a lady, if a bit of a Dark Lady, in the manner of the Sonnets; the young man is very much in love with her; and I am no doubt a sentimental old fool in having a sneaking sympathy with the misguided youth who is sneaking round the Moated Grange; and I was getting into quite a pastoral frame of mind about this idyll, when suddenly the thunderbolt fell. And I, who am the only person who ever had any sympathy with these people, am sent down to be the messenger of doom.'

'Yes,' said Father Brown, 'and why *were* you sent down?'

The doctor answered with a sort of groan: 'Mrs Maltravers is not only a widow, but she is the widow of Mr Maltravers.'

'It sounds like a shocking revelation, as you state it,' acknowledged the priest seriously.

'And Mr Maltravers,' continued his medical friend, 'was the man who was apparently murdered in this very village a year or two ago; supposed to have been bashed on the head by one of the simple villagers.'

'I remember you told me,' said Father Brown. 'The doctor, or some doctor, said he had probably died of being clubbed on the head with a cudgel.'

Dr Mulborough was silent for a moment in frowning embarrassment, and then said curtly: 'Dog doesn't eat dog, and doctors don't bite doctors, not even when they are mad doctors. I shouldn't care to cast any reflection on my eminent predecessor in Potter's Pond, if I could avoid it; but I know you are really safe for secrets. And, speaking in confidence, my eminent predecessor at Potter's Pond was a blasted fool; a drunken old humbug and absolutely incompetent. I was asked, originally by the Chief Constable of the County (for I've lived a long time in the county, though only recently in the village), to look into the whole business; the depositions and reports of the inquest and so on. And there simply isn't any question about it. Maltravers may have been hit on the head; he was a strolling actor passing through the place; and Potter's Pond probably thinks it is all in the natural order that such people should be hit on the head. But whoever hit him on the head did not kill him; it is simply impossible for the injury, as described, to do more than knock him out for a few hours. But lately I have managed to turn up some other facts bearing on the matter; and the result of it is pretty grim.'

He sat louring at the landscape as it slid past the window, and then said more curtly: 'I am coming down here, and asking your help, because there's going to be an exhumation. There is very strong suspicion of poison.'

'And here we are at the station,' said Father Brown cheerfully. 'I suppose your idea is that poisoning the poor man would naturally fall among the household duties of his wife.'

'Well, there never seems to have been anyone else here who had any particular connection with him,' replied Mulborough, as they alighted from the train. 'At least there is one queer old crony of his, a broken-down actor, hanging around; but the police and the local solicitor seem convinced he is an unbalanced busybody; with some *idée fixe* about a quarrel with an actor who was his enemy; but who certainly wasn't Maltravers. A wandering accident, I should say, and certainly nothing to do with the problem of the poison.'

Father Brown had heard the story. But he knew that he never knew a story until he knew the characters in the story. He spent the next two or three days in going the rounds, on one polite excuse or another, to visit the chief actors of the drama. His first interview with the mysterious widow was brief but bright. He brought away from it at least two facts; one that Mrs Maltravers sometimes talked in a way which the Victorian village would call cynical; and, second, that like not a few actresses, she happened to belong to his own religious communion.

He was not so illogical (nor so unorthodox) as to infer from this alone that she was innocent of the alleged crime. He was well aware that his old religious communion could boast of several distinguished poisoners. But he had no difficulty in understanding its connection, in this sort of case, with a certain intellectual liberty which these Puritans would call laxity; and which would certainly seem to this parochial patch of an older England to be almost cosmopolitan. Anyhow, he was sure she could count for a great deal, whether for good or evil. Her brown eyes were brave to the point of battle, and her enigmatic mouth, humorous and rather large, suggested that her purposes touching the parson's poetical son, whatever they might be, were planted pretty deep.

The parson's poetical son himself, interviewed amid vast village scandal on a bench outside the Blue Lion, gave an impression of pure sulks. Hurrel Horner, a son of the Revd Samuel Horner, was a square-built young man in a pale grey suit with a touch of something arty in a pale green tie, otherwise mainly notable for a mane of auburn hair and a permanent scowl. But Father Brown had a way with him in getting people to explain at considerable length why they refused to say a single word. About the general scandal-mongering in the village, the young man began to curse freely. He even added a little scandalmongering of his own. He referred bitterly to alleged past flirtations between the Puritan Miss Carstairs-Carew and Mr Carver the solicitor. He even accused that legal character of having attempted to force himself upon the acquaintance of Mrs Maltravers. But when he came to speak of his own father, whether out of an acid decency or piety, or because his anger was too deep for speech, he snapped out only a few words.

'Well, there it is. He denounces her day and night as a painted adventuress; a sort of barmaid with gilt hair. I tell him she's not; you've met her yourself, and you know she's not. But he won't even meet her. He won't even see her in the street or look at her out of a window. An actress would pollute his house and even his holy presence. If he is called a Puritan he says he's proud to be a Puritan.'

'Your father,' said Father Brown, 'is entitled to have his views respected, whatever they are; they are not views I understand very well myself. But I agree he is not entitled to lay down the law about a lady he has never seen and then refuse even to look at her, to see if he is right. That is illogical.'

'That's his very stiffest point,' replied the youth. 'Not even one momentary meeting. Of course, he thunders against my other theatrical tastes as well.'

Father Brown swiftly followed up the new opening, and learnt much that he wanted to know. The alleged poetry, which was such a blot on the young man's character, was almost entirely dramatic poetry. He had written tragedies in verse which had been admired by good judges. He was no mere stage-struck fool; indeed he was no fool of any kind. He had some really original ideas about acting Shakespeare; it was easy to understand his having been dazzled and delighted by finding the brilliant lady at the Grange. And even the priest's intellectual sympathy so far mellowed the rebel of Potter's Pond that at their parting he actually smiled.

It was that smile which suddenly revealed to Father Brown that the young man was really miserable. So long as he frowned, it might well have been only sulks; but when he smiled it was somehow a more real revelation of sorrow.

Something continued to haunt the priest about that interview with the poet. An inner instinct certified that the sturdy young man was eaten from within, by some grief greater even than the conventional story of conventional parents being obstacles to the course of true love. It was all the more so, because there were not any obvious alternative causes. The boy was already rather a literary and dramatic success; his books might be said to be booming. Nor did he drink or dissipate his well-earned wealth. His notorious revels at the Blue Lion reduced themselves to one glass of light ale; and he seemed to be rather careful with his money. Father Brown thought of another possible complication in connection with Hurrel's large resources and small expenditure; and his brow darkened.

The conversation of Miss Carstairs-Carew, on whom he called next, was certainly calculated to paint the parson's son in the darkest colours. But as it was devoted to blasting him with all the special vices which Father Brown was quite certain the young man did not exhibit, he put it down to a common combination of Puritanism and gossip. The lady, though lofty, was quite gracious, however, and offered the visitor a small glass of port-wine and a slice of seed-cake, in the manner of everybody's most ancient great-aunts, before he managed to escape from a sermon on the general decay of morals and manners.

His next port of call was very much of a contrast; for he disappeared down a dark and dirty alley, where Miss Carstairs-Carew would have refused to follow him even in thought; and then into a narrow tenement made noisier by a high and declamatory voice in an attic . . . From this he re-emerged, with a rather dazed expression, pursued on to the pavement by a very excited man with a blue chin and a black frock-coat faded to bottle-green, who was shouting argumentatively: 'He did not disappear! Maltravers never disappeared! He appeared: he appeared dead and I've appeared alive. But where's all the rest of the company? Where's that man, that monster, who deliberately stole my lines, crabbed my best scenes and ruined my career? I was the finest Tubal that ever trod the boards. He acted Shylock – he didn't need to act much for that! And so with the greatest opportunity of my whole career. I could show you press-cuttings on my renderings of Fortinbras – '

'I'm quite sure they were splendid and very well-deserved,' gasped the little priest. 'I understood the company had left the village before Maltravers died. But it's all right. It's quite all right.' And he began to hurry down the street again.

'He was to act Polonius,' continued the unquenchable orator behind him. Father Brown suddenly stopped dead.

'Oh,' he said very slowly, 'he was to act Polonius.'

'That villain Hankin!' shrieked the actor. 'Follow his trail. Follow him to the ends of the earth! Of course he'd left the village; trust him for that. Follow him – find him; and may the curses – ' But the priest was again hurrying away down the street.

Two much more prosaic and perhaps more practical interviews followed this melodramatic scene. First the priest went into the bank, where he was closeted for ten minutes with the manager; and then paid a very proper call on the aged and amiable clergyman. Here again all seemed very much as described, unaltered and seemingly unalterable; a touch or two of devotion from more austere traditions, in the narrow crucifix on the wall, the big Bible on the bookstand and the old gentleman's opening lament over the increasing disregard of Sunday; but all with a flavour of gentility that was not without its little refinements and faded luxuries.

The clergyman also gave his guest a glass of port; but accompanied by an ancient British biscuit instead of seed-cake. The priest had again the weird feeling that everything was almost too perfect, and that he was living a century before his time. Only on one point the amiable old parson refused to melt into any further amiability; he meekly but firmly maintained that his conscience would not allow him to meet a stage player. However, Father Brown put down his glass of port with expressions of appreciation and thanks; and went off to meet his friend the doctor by appointment at the corner of the street; whence they were to go together to the offices of Mr Carver, the solicitor.

'I suppose you've gone the dreary round,' began the doctor, 'and found it a very dull village.'

Father Brown's reply was sharp and almost shrill. 'Don't call your village dull. I assure you it's a very extraordinary village indeed.'

'I've been dealing with the only extraordinary thing that ever happened here, I should think,' observed Dr Mulborough. 'And even that happened to somebody from outside. I may tell you they managed the exhumation quietly last night; and I did the autopsy this morning. In plain words we've been digging up a corpse that's simply stuffed with poison.'

'A corpse stuffed with poison,' repeated Father Brown rather absently. 'Believe me, your village contains something much more extraordinary than that.'

There was abrupt silence, followed by the equally abrupt pulling of the antiquated bell-pull in the porch of the solicitor's house; and they were soon brought into the presence of that legal gentleman, who presented them in turn to a white-haired, yellow-faced gentleman with a scar, who appeared to be the Admiral.

By this time the atmosphere of the village had sunk almost into the subconsciousness of the little priest; but he was conscious that the lawyer was indeed the sort of lawyer to be the adviser of people like Miss Carstairs-Carew. But though he was an archaic old bird, he seemed something more than a fossil. Perhaps it was the uniformity of the background; but the priest had again the curious feeling that he himself was transplanted back into the early nineteenth century, rather than that the solicitor had survived into the early twentieth. His collar and cravat contrived to look almost like a stock as he settled his long chin into them; but they were clean as well as clean-cut; and there was even something about him of a very dry old dandy. In short, he was what is called well preserved, even if partly by being petrified.

The lawyer and the Admiral, and even the doctor, showed some surprise on finding that Father Brown was rather disposed to defend the parson's son against the local lamentations on behalf of the parson.

'I thought our young friend rather attractive, myself,' he said. 'He's a good talker and I should guess a good poet; and Mrs Maltravers, who is serious about that at least, says he's quite a good actor.'

'Indeed,' said the lawyer. 'Potter's Pond, outside Mrs Maltravers, is rather more inclined to ask if he is a good son.'

'He is a good son,' said Father Brown. 'That's the extraordinary thing.'

'Damn it all,' said the Admiral. 'Do you mean he's really fond of his father?'

The priest hesitated. Then he said, 'I'm not quite so sure about that. That's the other extraordinary thing.'

'What the devil do you mean?' demanded the sailor with nautical profanity.

'I mean,' said Father Brown, 'that the son still speaks of his father in a hard unforgiving way; but he seems after all to have done more than his duty by him. I had a talk with the bank manager, and as we were enquiring in confidence into a serious crime, under authority from the police, he told me the facts. The old clergyman has retired from parish work; indeed, this was never actually his parish. Such of the populace, which is pretty pagan, as goes to church at all, goes to Dutton-Abbot, not a mile away. The old man has no private means, but his son is earning good money; and the old man is well looked after. He gave me some port of absolutely first-class vintage; I saw rows of dusty old bottles of it; and I left him sitting down to a little lunch quite *recherché* in an old-fashioned style. It must be done on the young man's money.'

'Quite a model son,' said Carver with a slight sneer.

Father Brown nodded, frowning, as if revolving a riddle of his own; and then said: 'A model son. But rather a mechanical model.'

At this moment a clerk brought in an unstamped letter for the lawyer; a letter which the lawyer tore impatiently across after a single glance. As it fell apart, the priest saw a spidery, crazy crowded sort of handwriting and the signature of 'Phoenix Fitzgerald'; and made a guess which the other curtly confirmed.

'It's that melodramatic actor that's always pestering us,' he said. 'He's got some fixed feud with some dead and gone fellow mummer of his, which can't have anything to do with the case. We all refuse to see him, except the doctor, who did see him; and the doctor says he's mad.'

'Yes,' said Father Brown, pursing his lips thoughtfully. 'I should say he's mad. But of course there can't be any doubt that he's right.'

'Right?' cried Carver sharply. 'Right about what?'

'About this being connected with the old theatrical company,' said Father Brown. 'Do you know the first thing that stumped me about this story? It was that notion that Maltravers was killed by villagers because he insulted their village. It's extraordinary what coroners can get jurymen to believe; and journalists, of course, are quite incredibly credulous. They can't know much about English rustics. I'm an English rustic myself; at least I was grown, with other turnips, in Essex. Can you imagine an English agricultural labourer idealising and personifying his village, like the citizen of an old Greek city state; drawing the sword for its sacred banner, like a man in the tiny medieval republic of an Italian town? Can you hear a jolly old gaffer saying, "Blood alone can wipe out one spot on the escutcheon of Potter's Pond"? By St George and the Dragon, I only wish they would! But, as a matter of fact, I have a more practical argument for the other notion.'

He paused for a moment, as if collecting his thoughts, and then went on:

'They misunderstood the meaning of those few last words poor Maltravers was heard to say. He wasn't telling the villagers that the village was only a hamlet. He was talking to an actor; they were going to put on a performance in which Fitzgerald was to be Fortinbras, the unknown Hankin to be Polonius, and Maltravers, no doubt, the Prince of Denmark. Perhaps somebody else wanted the part or had views on the part; and Maltravers said angrily, "You'd be a miserable little Hamlet"; that's all.'

Dr Mulborough was staring; he seemed to be digesting the suggestion slowly but without difficulty. At last he said, before the others could speak: 'And what do you suggest that we should do now?'

Father Brown arose rather abruptly; but he spoke civilly enough. 'If these gentlemen will excuse us for a moment, I propose that you and I, doctor, should go round at once to the Horners. I know the parson and his son will both be there just now. And what I want to do, doctor, is this. Nobody in the village knows yet, I think, about your autopsy and its result. I want you simply to tell both the clergyman and his son, while they are there together, the exact fact of the case; that Maltravers died by poison and not by a blow.'

Dr Mulborough had reason to reconsider his incredulity when told that it was an extraordinary village. The scene which ensued, when he actually carried out the priest's programme, was certainly of the sort in which a man, as the saying is, can hardly believe his eyes.

The Revd Samuel Horner was standing in his black cassock, which threw up the silver of his venerable head; his hand rested at the moment on the lectern at which he often stood to study the Scripture, now possibly by accident only; but it gave him a greater look of authority. And opposite to him his mutinous son was sitting asprawl in a chair, smoking a cheap cigarette with an exceptionally heavy scowl; a lively picture of youthful impiety.

The old man courteously waved Father Brown to a seat, which he took and sat there silent, staring blandly at the ceiling. But something made Mulborough feel that he could deliver his important news more impressively standing up.

'I feel,' he said, 'that you ought to be informed, as in some sense the spiritual father of this community, that one terrible tragedy in its record has taken on a new significance; possibly even more terrible. You will recall the sad business of the death of Maltravers; who was adjudged to have been killed with the blow of a stick, probably wielded by some rustic enemy.'

The clergyman made a gesture with a wavering hand. 'God forbid,' he said, 'that I should say anything that might seem to palliate murderous violence in any case. But when an actor brings his wickedness into this innocent village, he is challenging the judgement of God.'

'Perhaps,' said the doctor gravely. 'But anyhow it was not so that the judgement fell. I have just been commissioned to conduct a post-mortem on the body; and I can assure you, first, that the blow on the head could not conceivably have caused the death; and, second, that the body was full of poison, which undoubtedly caused death.'

Young Hurrel Horner sent his cigarette flying and was on his feet with the lightness and swiftness of a cat. His leap landed him within a yard of the reading-desk.

'Are you certain of this?' he gasped. 'Are you absolutely certain that that blow could not cause death?'

'Absolutely certain,' said the doctor.

'Well,' said Hurrel, 'I almost wish this one could.'

In a flash, before anyone could move a finger, he had struck the parson a stunning crack on the mouth, dashing him backwards like a disjointed black doll against the door.

'What are you doing?' cried Mulborough, shaken from head to foot with the shock and mere sound of the blow. 'Father Brown, what is this madman doing?'

But Father Brown had not stirred; he was still staring serenely at the ceiling.

'I was waiting for him to do that,' said the priest placidly. 'I rather wonder he hasn't done it before.'

'Good God,' cried the doctor. 'I know we thought he was wronged in some ways; but to strike his father; to strike a clergyman and a non-combatant – '

'He has not struck his father; and he has not struck a clergyman,' said Father Brown. 'He has struck a blackmailing blackguard of an actor dressed up as a clergyman, who has lived on him like a leech for years. Now he knows he is free of the blackmail, he lets fly; and I can't say I blame him much. More especially as I have very strong suspicions that the blackmailer is a poisoner as well. I think, Mulborough, you had better ring up the police.'

They passed out of the room uninterrupted by the two others, the one dazed and staggered, the other still blind and snorting and panting with passions of relief and rage. But as they passed, Father Brown once turned his face to the young man; and the young man was one of the very few human beings who have seen that face implacable.

'He was right there,' said Father Brown. 'When an actor brings his wickedness into this innocent village, he challenges the judgement of God.'

* * *

'Well,' said Father Brown, as he and the doctor again settled themselves in a railway carriage standing in the station of Potter's Pond. 'As you say, it's a strange story; but I don't think it's any longer a mystery story. Anyhow, the story seems to me to have been roughly this. Maltravers came here, with part of his touring company; some of them went straight to Dutton-Abbot, where they were all presenting some melodrama about the early nineteenth century; he himself happened to be hanging about in his stage dress, the very distinctive dress of a dandy of that time. Another character was an old-fashioned parson, whose dark dress was less distinctive and might pass as being merely old-fashioned. This part was taken by a man who mostly acted old men; had acted Shylock and was afterwards going to act Polonius.

'A third figure in the drama was our dramatic poet, who was also a dramatic performer, and quarrelled with Maltravers about how to present *Hamlet*, but more about personal things, too. I think it likely that he was in love with Mrs Maltravers even then; I don't believe there was anything wrong with them; and I hope it may now be all right with them. But he may very well have resented Maltravers in his conjugal capacity; for Maltravers was a bully and likely to raise rows. In some such row they fought with sticks, and the poet hit Maltravers very hard on the head, and, in the light of the inquest, had every reason to suppose he had killed him.

'A third person was present or privy to the incident, the man acting the old parson; and he proceeded to blackmail the alleged murderer, forcing from him the cost of his upkeep in some luxury as a retired clergyman. It was the obvious masquerade for such a man in such a place, simply to go on wearing his stage clothes as a retired clergyman. But he had his own reason for being a very retired clergyman. For the true story of Maltravers's death was that he rolled into a deep undergrowth of bracken, gradually recovered, tried to walk towards a house, and was eventually overcome, not by the blow, but by the fact that the benevolent clergyman had given him poison an hour before, probably in a glass of port. I was beginning to think so, when I drank a glass of the parson's port. It made me a little nervous. The police are working on that theory now; but whether they will be able to prove that part of the story, I don't know. They will have to find the exact motive; but it's obvious that this bunch of actors was buzzing with quarrels and Maltravers was very much hated.'

'The police may prove something now they have got the suspicion,' said Dr Mulborough. 'What I don't understand is why you ever began to suspect. Why in the world should you suspect that very blameless black-coated gentleman?'

Father Brown smiled faintly. 'I suppose in one sense,' he said, 'it was a matter of special knowledge; almost a professional matter, but in a peculiar sense. You know our controversialists often complain that there is a great deal of ignorance about what our religion is really like. But it is really more curious than that. It is true, and it is not at all unnatural, that England does not know much about the Church of Rome. But England does not know much about the Church of England. Not even as much as I do. You would be astonished at how little the average public grasps about the Anglican controversies; lots of them don't really know what is meant by a High Churchman or a Low Churchman, even on the particular points of practice, let alone the two theories of history and philosophy behind them. You can see this ignorance in any newspaper; in any merely popular novel or play.

'Now the first thing that struck me was that this venerable cleric had got the whole thing incredibly mixed up. No Anglican parson could be so wrong about every Anglican problem. He was supposed to be an old Tory High Churchman; and then he boasted of being a Puritan. A man like that might personally be rather Puritanical; but he would never call it being a Puritan. He professed a horror of the stage; he didn't know that High Churchmen generally don't have that special horror, though Low Churchmen do. He talked like a Puritan about the Sabbath; and then he had a crucifix in his room. He evidently had no notion of what a very pious parson ought to be, except that he ought to be very solemn and venerable and frown upon the pleasures of the world.

'All this time there was a subconscious notion running in my head; something I couldn't fix in my memory; and then it came to me suddenly. This is a Stage Parson. That is exactly the vague venerable old fool who would be the nearest notion a popular playwright or play-actor of the old school had of anything so odd as a religious man.'

'To say nothing of a physician of the old school,' said Mulborough good-humouredly, 'who does not set up to know much about being a religious man.'

'As a matter of fact,' went on Father Brown, 'there was a plainer and more glaring cause for suspicion. It concerned the Dark Lady of the Grange, who was supposed to be the Vampire of the Village. I very early formed the impression that this black blot was rather the bright spot of the village. She was treated as a mystery; but there was really nothing mysterious about her. She had come down here quite recently, quite openly, under her own name, to help the new enquiries to be made about her own husband. He hadn't treated her too well; but she had principles, suggesting that something was due to her married name and to common justice. For the same reason, she went to live in the house outside which her husband had been found dead. The other innocent and straightforward case, besides the Vampire of the Village, was the Scandal of the Village, the parson's profligate son. He also made no disguise of his profession or past connection with the acting world. That's why I didn't suspect him as I did the parson. But you'll already have guessed a real and relevant reason for suspecting the parson.'

'Yes, I think I see,' said the doctor, 'that's why you bring in the name of the actress.'

'Yes, I mean his fanatical fixity about not seeing the actress,' remarked the priest. 'But he didn't really object to seeing her. He objected to her seeing him.'

'Yes, I see that,' assented the other. 'If she had seen the Revd Samuel Horner, she would instantly have recognised the very unreverend actor Hankin, disguised as a sham parson with a pretty bad character behind the disguise. Well, that is the whole of this simple village idyll, I think. But you will admit I kept my promise; I have shown you something in the village considerably more creepy than a corpse; even a corpse stuffed with poison. The black coat of a parson stuffed with a blackmailer is at least worth noticing and my live man is much deadlier than your dead one.'

'Yes,' said the doctor, settling himself back comfortably in the cushions. 'If it comes to a little cosy company on a railway journey, I should prefer the corpse.'

The Donnington Affair

The following statement of the Donnington affair has been written from the original notes by the priest-in-charge of the Parish of Borrow-in-the-Vale.

John Barrington Cope came to Sussex from King's College, Cambridge, at a time when the aged vicar could no longer undertake single-handed even the pleasant duties of that rural charge.

He had been nearly two years at Borrow when the tragedy occurred. A man of considerable scholastic attainment, he appears immediately to have realised the magnitude of the mystery and to have set down, without loss of time, an orderly statement of the facts as they presented themselves to him.

The accepted lover of Evelyn Donnington's sister Harriet, he enjoyed the liberties of Borrow Close, and was almost daily at the house. It was at his suggestion that 'another' was summoned from London to investigate a case which promised at an early moment to baffle alike the vigilance of the police and the curiosity of the public.

Mr Cope's notes were written primarily for Father Brown's perusal. An amplification of them seems to be the swiftest method of putting the reading public in possession of the salient features of this amazing occurrence.

I

My name is John Barrington Cope, and I had been priest-in-charge of the parish of Borrow-in-the-Vale for twenty-one months.

I last saw Evelyn Donnington alive on Sunday evening at a quarter past ten o'clock. I had supped at Borrow Close as it has been my privilege to do almost every Sunday evening since I came to the parish. The fact that my fiancée, Harriet Donnington, was and is at Bath made no difference.

Sir Borrow Donnington has few friends. He is not a man who loves the society of other men, nor, for that matter, of women. It may be that I understand him a little better than his fellows. I am welcome at Borrow Close, and there is no other house which has a prior claim upon me.

I saw Evelyn Donnington alive and well at a quarter past ten on the evening of Sunday last, the 24th day of July. She came to the porch with me to tell me of a letter she had received from Harriet on the previous day, and there I said 'good-night' to her.

The rectory stands perhaps a third part of a mile across the park, and is best reached by a bridle-path through what is known as Adam's Thicket.

The way is dark and shut in by the magnificent beeches for which Borrow is famous. I saw no living thing as I returned to the rectory, nor heard any sound that was ominous.

Two hours later a footman from the Close awakened me to say that Evelyn was dead. 'Murdered, sir!' he gasped, and without another word he ran on headlong towards the doctor's house.

I had fallen into a light sleep when this man's ring awakened me. There had been much trouble at Borrow Close since I came to the parish. The world is well acquainted with the nature of this, and knows much of the shame which has overtaken the Donnington family. Whatever sympathy it may have withheld from Sir Borrow Donnington himself, it has lavished freely upon his daughters.

To me Evelyn was already as a sister. I was to have married Harriet in September, though God knows what may be in store for us now.

Men deride omens, though often they are but the mind's logic waging a war upon our optimism. Though the affair of Southby Donnington would appear to have been settled by his conviction and imprisonment, I dreaded from the first that such could not be the end of it; and it was of Southby Donnington, Sir Borrow's only son, that I had been dreaming in my sleep when the footman awakened me.

What a sardonic chapter in the history of human nature! An only son – a wealthy father! Upon the one side a profligacy almost without parallel, upon the other side a parsimony stupendous in its ironic selfishness.

Southby Donnington was sent to Eton and to Trinity (Cambridge) as an Army candidate. A disgraceful affair at a gambling den in London, with a subsequent appearance at a police-court, finished his university career in his first term. He could not even pass the trivial examination now demanded for Sandhurst. He would suggest no other vocation. The man became a derelict in the dangerous seas of London's underworld. In vain his sisters pleaded with Sir Borrow. The baronet had finished with his son. A man of iron resolution which nothing could bend, he swore that Southby should never enter his house again. There followed the cataclysm.

We heard of the boy's arrest in London upon a charge of forgery. He was committed for trial, defended with what money his sisters could supply him, sent to the Old Bailey, convicted. The sentence was one of three years' penal servitude. We learned that he had been taken to Wormwood Scrubs, and nine months later that he was at Parkhurst.

It is no place here to dwell upon the secrets of the stricken house or of the aftermath of this terrible downfall.

Borrow Close is an old mansion lying between Ashdown Forest and Crowborough. It has always been remote from men and affairs, and there is no domain in the south of England so wonderful in its solitudes.

All about it is the forest. The very park is primeval woodland; here abounding in undergrowth so thick that the foot of man might never have been set therein; there characterised by marshy pools and groves where noonday is but a shimmer of reluctant light. Few were admitted to the house even in the days when Lady Donnington was its mistress. Since her death it has become medieval in its isolation. The old baronet had nothing in common with his neighbours; his daughters were always afraid of him, and they go through life as it were on tiptoe, fearing that if they speak above a whisper they will awake the curiosity of the world beyond their gates.

It is true that Southby flouted the sanctities of this retreat, despite the baronet's displeasure. Parties of wild undergraduates made the 'welkin ring' during the vacations; the story of Evelyn and Harriet's beauty was not unknown in the courts at Cambridge. Few of the boys, however, had the courage to persist, and I think that even Southby himself was astonished when Captain Willy Kennington appeared suddenly upon the scene as a suitor for Evelyn's hand, and was not to be repulsed even by Sir Borrow's savage discouragement.

Captain Kennington had met Evelyn at her aunt's house in Kensington some three months before the downfall. Her womanly gifts should have made an appeal to any man who became well acquainted with them, and I do not wonder that the young soldier surrendered to the spell.

Very simple in all her ideas, not a little afraid of the world, yet gifted with an imagination which years of solitary reading had stimulated, she seemed to be at once the woman and the child; wise above her years, yet afflicted by those ideals for which woman often pays so dearly. Fear of her father forbade that immediate acceptance of the soldier's advances which her heart dictated. She returned to Borrow Close, and was followed there shortly by the captain himself.

What was my astonishment to hear a few days later that Sir Borrow had refused all discussion of the matter, and in one of those violent paroxysms of temper, with which neither God nor man could reason, had ordered the captain from his house.

To give him his due, Southby played a man's part in this affair. He interceded warmly for his sister, returning from South Africa for that purpose. The scene between father and son is remembered at the Close as the culminating episode of an estrangement as discreditable to one as to the other. Passion dominated it, and set finality upon it. No word was spoken between these two men until the end.

Three months later Southby was a convict, and I remained the one man who visited the baronet in the days of his shame.

2

These are the events of sixteen months ago. I have already disclaimed any intention of dwelling upon the intimate days of sorrow which followed after. 'The evil that men do lives after them,' and while for the world the tragedy was but a nine days' wonder, it lay heavy upon the house of Borrow. No longer did the old baronet receive the visits of the few friends hitherto admitted to the Close. He shut the doors alike upon the old world and the new. His daughters saw no one but the servants and myself. In their turn, his neighbours shrank from him. Men had come to say that lust of gold drove Southby to the crime, and to believe that the boy was less guilty than the father.

The one man who stood by the stricken family was Captain Kennington, who owed so little to the baronet. Now, in the darkest hour, he came forward to demand Evelyn's hand anew. It went without saying that she would not accept him. A rare type of womanhood, the very fact that she loved was the barrier between them. Nothing, she felt, could ever blot out the shame of this happening, or minimise its consequences. The harvest of sin was not gathered in Parkhurst Prison, but here in the ancient house, where women reaped with sickles of tears.

My own relations to Harriet were, God be praised, but superficially affected by Southby's downfall. We had learned to know each other so well before the trouble came that it but set a seal upon our mutual sense of help and sacrifice, and although I knew that she would not marry me immediately, I left the future to lead us as it might. Sir Donnington himself now seemed to find in my society the sole consolation of his declining years. He did not go to church, but I visited them for worship early every Sunday morning, and was always at the Close to supper when in residence at the rectory.

So the months rolled on, and time, the healer, came to our aid. The bitterness of fear and doubt had passed down and given place to a brave attempt to face the future. We made many plans for Southby upon his release, and were determined to start him in a farm in South Africa if we could. Kennington went so far as to visit the prison and see the convict. His own father was one of the visiting inspectors, as it chanced, and so an advantage was permitted him.

He told us that he found Southby quite resigned to his fate, and he spoke of him as a man who was convinced that he had not committed a crime, but had been the victim of those who had betrayed him when they discovered that nothing was to be extorted from the baronet.

Parkhurst, it seems, is the gentleman's prison, and Southby was in aristocratic company there. I confess that the intimation was not without its saving humour, and permitted some reflection upon the permanence of those social aspirations which could afflict men even in a prison. Better, it appeared, to pick oakum with a lord than to earn an honest living among plebeians.

Kennington spoke of cheerfulness and of content, but I remembered afterwards one phrase in his letter which should have struck me as significant. Prison makes strange bedfellows, and so far as man may have a confidant in captivity, Southby had found one in a man by the name of Mester.

'This fellow,' said Kennington, 'is the cheeriest soul possible. He has been well educated in France, where he fell upon evil times. Then, he became chauffeur to an Austrian baron, entered a motor car factory at Suresnes, turned his attention to flying at Issy, and finally was accused of a savage assault and an attempt to rob an old lady at Dover who was about to establish him in a motor car business there.'

Mester declared to the end that the crime was the work of others. He protested that he was the victim of circumstances, and that the clues upon which the police convicted him were false. Nevertheless, he was found guilty and sentenced to four years' penal servitude upon the day following Southby's conviction.

Between these men a strange friendship took root. Each believed himself wrongfully convicted; each could sympathise with the other. And just as Mester declared that he would bring the old baronet to his senses when he got out, so could Southby interest himself in Mester's story, and implore certain old colleagues on the Press to investigate it.

As we know, one great novelist has already busied himself with the affair, and is convinced of the man's innocence. Admittedly a person of no stable character and unquestionably the associate of thieves, there would yet seem to be a doubt whether the graver crime were committed, and quite a reasonable supposition that the police may have been in error.

Mester himself did not hesitate to affirm that if he were free for a month he would establish his innocence beyond all question. So convinced was he of this that he appears to have told Southby quite plainly that he would escape from Parkhurst if the opportunity presented itself.

I thought nothing of the matter at the time, and, indeed, the threat must be one often made by prisoners to whom crime has not become a habit and the cell a refuge. But I confess that astonishment was no word for it when, a few weeks later, upon opening my morning paper, I read that two men had escaped from Parkhurst, and, despite the efforts of the police, were still at large.

'Southby and Mester,' I said to myself. I was not wrong, as you shall presently hear.

3

Here was an upset if you will, and one to send me running to the Close with the tidings. Sir Borrow himself I would not tell, dreading the effect of the news upon a mind so deranged; but Evelyn and Harriet heard me eagerly, and the former I began to suspect was already in possession of the story. This fact did not in the beginning impress me as it should have done. Some letter, I thought, must have come from Southby himself, and yet had I reflected upon it I would have perceived that such a thing was hardly possible under the circumstances.

The man had escaped but yesterday, and even had a letter been posted from the Isle of Wight or the mainland on the previous evening, it would not have reached Borrow Close at nine o'clock. Later on I discovered, quite accidentally, that Captain Kennington hinted at some such possibility in a letter received on the previous day, and whatever thoughts the discovery suggested, I kept them strictly to myself. The immediate thing was the excitement the news occasioned at the Close, and the momentous events which must follow upon it.

For my own part, I was early of the opinion that the fugitive would swiftly be overtaken, and that that would be the end of the matter. Their escape, briefly narrated in the newspapers, had been admirably contrived. It appears that they scaled a high wall at a moment when a heavy mist drifted across the island from the mainland, that they then crossed an enclosure in which other prisoners were at work, climbed a second wall by the aid of a silk ladder, which they left behind them, and so made their way to the sea.

Authority believed that their flight was there cut short, and that they had not succeeded in reaching the mainland; but another account spoke of a mysterious motorboat which had been seen recently off St Catherine's Point, and, remembering Mester's acquaintance with the motor fraternity and its less desirable characters, the writer of the report seemed to be of the opinion that this might have some connection with the matter. The latter, I must confess, occurred to me as a plausible deduction. These flying people are unusually clever. They possess a daring which is proved, and their resources are many. I detected now the meaning of Southby's friendship for this undesirable mechanic, and I saw that the men were pledged to make the attempt together. For the moment it looked as though they had succeeded.

It was a little before nine o'clock when I arrived at the Close, and not until after lunch that I left. As usual, Sir Borrow spent the morning about his gardens, and kept me some while with him speaking of this plant or that with which I was always familiar, but never naming the son who would succeed to this splendid inheritance. When he retired to his study at twelve o'clock, I took the girls aside and resumed a conversation so full of meaning for us all. Naturally, we asked each other many questions which we were unable to answer. Where would Southby go if he reached the mainland? Could he get money? Would he return to Borrow?

'If he comes here,' said I, 'he is lost! It will be the first place the police will watch!'

Harriet agreed with me in this. Yet where else could he go with any prospect of getting money, by which alone ultimate success could be assured?

We thought of many places, but of one with conviction. Sir Borrow's sister, the aged Lady Rosmar, then lived at Bath. She had been staunch to the boy as far as her means permitted, and might be still a friend to him in such an emergency as this. We decided that Harriet should go to Bath without loss of time, in case she could be of any assistance there. Evelyn and I, meanwhile, would watch and wait at Borrow. God knows what we hoped to do if the boy came there, yet I think we both prayed for his coming.

It seemed such an impossible thing that he could evade the hue and cry which must attend his flight. Yet if he did evade it, might not we take up his burden and start him in that new life wherein so much might be achieved if the lesson had been truly learned? Foolish the hope may have been, yet it came natural to those who had suffered so much, and over whom the prison gate was ever the emblem of a terrible sorrow. We believed that Southby would come, and in ten days' time our faith was justified. He was there at Borrow Close, the police upon his heels, his own father ignorant that the house harboured him. Of such dire things have I now to tell in the story that comes after.

4

I have said that we supposed the house would be watched by the police, and in this we were not mistaken.

Frequently, in the few days immediately prior to Southby's return, I had seen strange men in the park, and more than once I had been stopped upon an idle pretence and questioned concerning Sir Borrow and his affairs. Such a subterfuge would have deceived no one, and, fortunately, I was able to deal with the men quite frankly.

'You are a police officer,' I said to one of them.

And he did not deny it.

'The lad's sure to come here, sir,' was his answer, 'and, if he does, we shall take him. There isn't a road within ten miles we are not watching.'

We fell to other talk, and chiefly of the escape. Officially the police thought there had been some connivance on the part of the warders, but of this I naturally knew nothing.

'The young men had a lot of friends between them,' the detective said, 'and as for Lionel Mester, he knows half the crooks in Europe!'

I replied that in such a case the friends in question might be expected to shelter their comrades.

'And,' said I, 'it is idle to look for your men here. Surely you know of the relations between Sir Borrow and his son?'

He was much interested in this, and questioned me closely – a proceeding I did not resent under the circumstances. A few days later I was stopped in the park by an American lady and her daughter, who pretended to be much interested in the old place, and asked me if it were not possible to get permission to visit it. In these I recognised also the agents of the police, and I put them off with what excuses I could; not that it would have mattered at such a time, for Southby had not then returned. He was to come three days afterwards, at dead of night, and the two who were to know of his coming would have stopped at nothing for his sake. They were his sister Evelyn and Wellman, the butler, who had loved Southby as his own son.

It was from Wellman himself that I had the news at nine o'clock on the following morning. He came carrying a pretended letter from Sir Borrow, and not until we were alone in my study, and the door shut behind us, did he dare to speak freely.

'Mr Southby's home, sir,' he said in a whisper. 'He's in the priest's room.'

I feared to speak for a moment. Instantly I had visions of the hunted lad, fleeing from thicket to thicket of the forest he knew so well, and finally gaining that deep glen wherein is the subterranean entrance to the Close. That he had thought of it when none of us remembered! Of course, the police would know nothing of that. The very servants, save Wellman alone, are in ignorance of the existence of the passage, and locally it is believed that it perished long ago. Sir Borrow let them think so.

It was one of his humours to have the place opened up by the engineers who came from London to sink his artesian well. He liked to go to and fro as he pleased, to catch his servants when they least expected him. And so he used the priest's room for the purpose, or did use it until the tragedy happened. Nothing afterwards interested him. The secret chamber remained unopened after Southby was convicted. The rest of us, I think, had almost forgotten its existence.

The chamber lies at the western end of the long gallery. There is an octagon tower there, with an ancient stone staircase cunningly built within its walls. To this you gain access from the gallery by opening a panel upon the right-hand side of the smaller chimney. The room lies at the foot of one flight of stairs, and is lighted from two narrow windows giving upon the battlements. These are filled by stained glass of the fourteenth century, and show former abbots of Borrow in alb and chasuble. The room itself is large and commodious, and has a fireplace and an alcove for the bed. Those who desire to go from it to the forest descend the staircase until they find themselves in the old crypt which dates from Saxon times. The subterranean passage leads from that to Adam's Thicket, where it enters an ancient well, long dried up, and now but a pit of grass and bramble. I did not doubt that Southby had gained the forest by a devious route and had made his way by one of those paths which no stranger would discover. And so he had gone straight to the priest's chamber, and thence to Evelyn's bedroom.

'He waked her about one this morning,' said Wellman, who still appeared to be trembling with the excitement of the news. 'They wouldn't let you know sooner, sir, for fear of the police. Miss Evelyn is dreadfully afraid that the squire will find out, and so I came to you at once. Lucky for us, it was only yesterday afternoon that Superintendent Matthews searched the Close from garret to cellar. He must have had wind that Mr Southby was on the road.'

I was astonished to hear this.

'Superintendent Matthews – yesterday!' I exclaimed. 'Is it really possible, and Miss Evelyn told me nothing of it? But, of course, it may have been difficult to send. Does he know anything of the priest's hole, Wellman? Surely you don't fear that?'

He shook his head, being a man of uncommon caution.

'They know a great deal too much nowadays, sir – more's the pity. The question is, what are we to do with the young master, since Miss Evelyn is at her wits' end? She would be pleased to see you at the Close, indeed and she would. It's a hard task for a young lady, as you can well imagine, sir.'

I agreed, and, putting on my hat, went over with him immediately. Our way lay through Adam's Thicket, and I confess that I suffered some alarm when a stranger appeared upon our path not a hundred paces from the ancient basin by which the passage is reached. He was a short, thick-set man, wearing a serge suit with black leather leggings and a peaked cap, and when he saw us he stopped abruptly for a moment, then turned his back upon us and pretended to light a cigarette while we passed.

'He is no policeman,' I said to Wellman, when the stranger was out of hearing. The old servant agreed with me.

'But he might be an inquiry agent, sir. I've heard tell in London of the tricks they play with their clothes. Don't trust him too far.'

'I am not going to trust him at all,' said I. 'The fellow looked to me as though he were a chauffeur.'

'A bad lot, believe me, sir. There's been few honest men upon wheels since they robbed us of our horses. A man wants the nose of a setter to keep track of such as him. I wouldn't trust one of them with a silver-plated soup-ladle, upon my word I wouldn't.'

I told him he was a *laudator temporis acti*, but as that conveyed nothing to him we pushed on, and found Evelyn in the boudoir.

She was dreadfully agitated, but Sir Borrow being there, no word of the affair might pass between us. The baronet plainly thought that his daughter had become hysterical, and when I was alone with him he hinted that she must have had some news from that d—d scoundrel.

'Whatever it is,' he added, 'I don't want to hear of it or of him. It would be a great day for me if the fellow were six feet under ground, and I hope to God he soon will be. That's the truth, Cope, and none of your philosophy can change it. I no longer have a son; I am trying to forget that I ever had one.'

I shrank from his anger, knowing well how little such a man would suffer a rebuke. Happily, he set out to drive into the town almost immediately, and Evelyn and I went at once to the priest's hole and interviewed Southby. He was in a sorry plight, I must say, his face and hands torn by the brambles of the thickets, his clothes splashed with mud, his beard unshaved, and his eyes bloodshot. I thought also a little delirious from want of food and exposure, and he talked incoherently of ships and the sea, of men who had betrayed him, and of others who were his friends. By-and-by, when he became calmer, he told me that the ignominy of prison affected him to such an extent that he would have gone mad if he had remained at Parkhurst.

'I couldn't have done it, Cope, by God I couldn't,' he said. 'You don't know what it means to a man who has lived as I have. I had to go or it would have been all up with me. If they take me I will shoot myself. That's an oath and I'll keep it.'

'But,' cried I, 'whatever will you do, Southby? You must know that we cannot long protect you here.'

He laughed defiantly, pushing the black hair from his forehead quite in the old way.

'Lionel will do it,' he said. 'I trust Lionel. He got me out; he'll see I don't get in again. You must know Lionel. He's a white man all through, and the prison that can hold him has yet to be made. Why, it was his idea about the motorboat – who else would have thought of it? – his and his friend at Hendon. They picked us up in the cover at high tide, and we were landed at Hayling Island before morning. I knew we should get through when Lionel undertook it.'

'Then,' exclaimed I, quite at hazard, 'Captain Kennington knew nothing of it?'

His brow darkened at this. He looked at Evelyn curiously, and appeared afraid to speak out.

'No, I don't trust Kennington – not much. Mind what you're doing in that quarter, Evelyn. Kennington isn't thirty cents – you remember it.'

She flashed out at this, a girl of spirit and a good heart.

'Do not say a word against Captain Kennington!' she cried. 'He is the only friend you ever had who remained staunch to you. You should be grateful to him.'

He still persisted, though with a weakening resolution.

'That may or may not be. It's my opinion he tried to give us away, and I shall stick to it. Now, get me a drink for heaven's sake. I am as dry as a camel.'

She fetched him a brandy-and-soda, and he drank it eagerly. It was already a danger to pass to and from the long gallery, and I began to perceive the peril of the situation. Let the servants know and sooner or later the news would go to the village, and thence to the police. When we discussed it frankly between ourselves there seemed but one solution. Evelyn must be ill, and Harriet must be recalled from Bath to wait upon her. Meanwhile, Wellman must have a confidante, and none seemed better suited to the purpose than Turner, the head housemaid. Sooner or later this woman would discover us. We determined that it should be sooner, and, calling her to the conference, we put our fortunes into her hands. Good woman, she had a brother of her own, and Evelyn was beloved by them all.

We made our plans, and for the moment they were successful.

Harriet, unfortunately, could not return from Bath, her aunt being taken seriously ill and really requiring her assistance. Evelyn, however, feigned an indisposition very cleverly, and although it put me to some conscientious difficulty, I suffered myself to think of the greater good of that unhappy family and to acquiesce. Nevertheless, I understood that it was but a brief respite. The perils of the situation were manifest. Any day, any hour might discover us, and we began to go as those who feared their own shadows.

Perhaps my fears may have been responsible for a delusion, but there were moments when I thought that Sir Borrow suspected us. His manner became suddenly aggressive, and he questioned me more closely than he had done for a long time. Had I heard from that 'd—d' son of his? Was Evelyn worrying about 'the worthless scoundrel'? To all of which I responded with what wit I could, though God knows my position was difficult. Later on I discovered him in Evelyn's bedroom, and that very night, after dinner, he spoke of Kennington. Oddly enough, his opinion of that gallant soldier was exactly that of his son. He did not trust him, doubted his record, and stigmatised him most unjustly as a penniless adventurer. As to my knowledge the captain is in possession of an income of eight hundred pounds a year, I resented the slander, and did not fear to speak my mind. The result was a sharp quarrel, and the expression upon his part of a shabby apology, with which in any other circumstances I would have been far from satisfied. As it was, I had to bear with him, and to listen while he told me that, whatever happened, he would not have Kennington in the house again. Then he went off to his study, I to the priest's room to tell them of my suspicions.

Southby had always been afraid of his father. My news alarmed him, and he did not hesitate to affirm that the old man would deliver him up to the police should he be discovered at the Close. Evelyn herself appeared to be of the same opinion, and when we were alone she confessed the terror of her situation.

'Captain Kennington is coming here at the weekend,' she said.

I told her what Sir Borrow had said, and it did but alarm her the more.

'Sometimes I wish I were dead,' she declared.

And I, who knew how much that gentle soul had suffered, prayed to God that strength might be granted her.

The following night I was to meet Lionel Mester in the thicket, and to experience an apprehension more acute than any I had yet suffered in this woeful affair.

It was the Sabbath eve, and I was returning from the Close to the choir practice in our beautiful old parish church. A hundred yards from the well's head, where the secret entrance lies, I met again the short, thick-set man whom Wellman had declared to be a detective. This time he stopped, and begging me to step aside into the thicket, he introduced himself immediately.

'You'll have heard of me, sir – Lionel Mester, Mr Southby's pal.'

'Yes,' I said, 'I have heard of you. Why do you come to this dangerous place?'

'Because there's something Southby must know, and it can't come any other way. You see him every day, and can take this letter to him. I've been hanging about nearly a week trying to get it delivered. Usually I don't trust devil dodgers – not much. But you've got a decent mug on you, and I'm going to trust you. Take him this letter, and tell him, if he acts on it, it's all right and the wheels go round. Otherwise I do a double watch, and be d—d to it! Lord, I've been sleeping on stinging nettles for a week, and that's about enough of it! Tell Southby so, and you'll see no more of me.'

He thrust a bulky letter into my hand, and was about to say more when we heard a sound of footsteps, and instantly he plunged into the undergrowth with the agility of a wildcat. He was shod, I saw, in rubber-soled shoes, and carried a formidable stick; but the quickness of his movements was the surprising thing, and uttering but one word, 'police', he disappeared from my view. For my part, I thrust the letter into the inner pocket of my coat and at once regained the path. Fifty paces further on I passed Superintendent Matthews, and exchanged a good-night with him. He appeared to be in a hurry, and was going towards the Hall. But he did not stop to gossip with me, as he usually does, and for that I was grateful.

It will be understood that this unexpected turn perplexed me very much. I had expected that Lionel Mester would come to Borrow sooner or later, but now that he had come I perceived how considerable a danger he must be to us all. It was not to be hidden from me that I myself might be the victim of this unhappy family, and must answer to the law for the part that I had played. So much I was willing to do for a woman's sake, but now that discovery trod upon our heels, and all the shame and suffering of exposure hovered in the shadows about that ancient house, I confess that my courage almost failed me. The letter seemed a damning document which would convict me in any court. Yet I determined to deliver it, and that very night, about ten o'clock, I went up to the Hall and put it into Evelyn's hands. Upon my return an unknown man followed me through the thicket, and watched me enter the rectory. I believe that he was a police officer, though whether he were so or not mattered little since the letter was delivered.

That night I slept but ill, fearing so many things, dreading the peril of a situation which had become almost intolerable. The next day was the Sabbath, given almost entirely to the schools and the church, and it was not until we sat down to supper at the Close that I got the news of Evelyn. She had given out that she was a little better, and would sit down with us. The few words we exchanged in the porch when I said 'good-night' to her were of some moment, though not unexpected.

'Southby is going tonight,' she said.

I answered, 'Thank God,' for I knew that none of us could stand the strain of it much longer.

And so we parted, and I was never to see her alive again. So brave, so gentle she was, blessed among women truly, an offering to man's sin, a martyr for whom men's tears should fall. They heard a loud cry in the house a little before midnight. Sir Borrow was awake, and first upon the scene. They found her lying at the foot of the circular staircase which leads down from the long gallery to the secret room.

Evidently there had been a struggle. A jagged bar of iron lay upon the stairs at her feet. The lamp she had carried was shattered; the very window in the angle of the octagon was broken, and the glass littered about. What was not a little remarkable was the discovery of nine pounds in gold wrapped in a yellow kid glove, the very shape and colour of the gloves always worn by Captain Kennington.

She was dressed in a long bedgown, I should tell you, and wore a dressing-gown over it. The door of the secret chamber stood open, but no one was to be discerned within. Southby had fled the house. Sir Borrow and Wellman alone stooped to the assistance of the stricken woman.

She was quite dead, a terrible wound in the throat having deprived her of life almost instantaneously. Naturally the police were called upon the instant, and not a moment was lost by them. Beaters began to search every thicket of the forest round about; there were motors abroad upon every road. Yet nothing was discovered, not a shadow of a clue to be found. Even Captain Kennington could offer no suggestion. I discovered to my surprise that he had come to Borrow on Saturday evening as he promised, but hearing Evelyn's story had gone to the town to sleep. The hue and cry waked him – to such a morn as few men are called upon to live.

And so here is this terrible crime committed, and no man to be brought to justice for it. God send us enlightenment that the guilty may be punished!